Voice of the Heart

Remember

_____

Barbara Taylor Bradford

Diamond Books
An Imprint of HarperCollins*Publishers*,
77–85 Fulham Palace Road,
Hammersmith, London W6 8JB

This Diamond Books Omnibus Edition first published 1993
9 8 7 6 5 4 3 2 1

Voice of the Heart © Barbara Taylor Bradford 1983
Remember © Barbara Taylor Bradford 1991

ISBN 1 85813 288 6 (UK)
ISBN Diamond Books 0 261 66169 8 (international edition)

Typeset by Hewer Text Composition Services, Edinburgh
Printed in France by Maury-Eurolivres

Contents

Voice of the Heart

Contents

For my husband Robert Bradford
with love

'*That voice of the heart, which, Lamartine says,*
"alone reaches the heart".'

MARCEL PROUST

Overture
1978

'How like the prodigal doth she return.'

William Shakespeare

CHAPTER ONE

I came back because I wanted to, of my own free will. No one forced me to return. But now that I am here I want to take flight, to hide again in obscurity, to put this vast ocean between myself and this place. It bodes me no good.

As these thoughts finally took shape, assumed troubling proportions and jostled for prominence in her mind, the woman's fine hands, lying inertly in her lap, came together in a clench so forceful that the knuckles protruded sharply through the transparent skin. But there was no other outward display of emotion. She sat as rigid as stone on the seat. Her face, pale and somewhat drawn in the murky morning light, was impassive as a mask and her gaze was fixed with unwavering intensity on the Pacific.

The sea was implacable and the colour of chalcedony on this bleak and sunless day, one that was unnaturally chilly for Southern California, even though it was December when the weather was so often inclement. The woman shivered. The dampness was beginning to seep through her trenchcoat into her bones. She felt icy, and yet there was a light film of moisture on her forehead and neck and between her breasts. On an impulse she rose from the seat, her movements abrupt, and with her head bent against the wind and her hands pushed deep into her pockets she walked the length of the Santa Monica pier, which was now so entirely deserted it looked desolate, even forbidding, in its emptiness.

When she arrived at the farthermost tip where the turbulent waves lashed at the exposed underpinnings, she paused and leaned against the railing. Once again her eyes were riveted on the ocean curling out towards the dim horizon. There, on that far indistinct rim, where sea and sky merged in a smudge of limitless grey, a great liner bobbed along like a child's toy, had been turned into an object of insignificance by the vastness of nature.

We are all like that ship, the woman said inwardly, so fragile, so inconsequential in the overall scheme of things. Although do any of us truly believe that, blinded as we are by our self-importance? In our arrogance we all think we are unique, invincible, immune to mortality and above the law of nature. But we are not, and that *is* the only law, inexorable and unchanging.

She blinked, as if to rid herself of these thoughts. The winter sky, curdled and ominous, was littered with ragged ashy clouds which were slowly turning black and extinguishing the meagre light trickling along their outer edges. A storm was imminent. She ought to return to the waiting limousine and make her way back to the Bel-Air Hotel, before the rain started. But to her amazement she discovered she was unable to move. She did not want to move, for it seemed to her that only out here on this lonely pier was she able to think with a degree of clarity, to pull together her scattered and disturbing thoughts, to make sense out of the chaos in her mind.

The woman sighed with weariness and frustration. She had known, even when she had first made her decision, that to return was foolhardy, maybe even dangerous. She was exposing herself in a manner she had never done before. But at the time – was it only a few weeks ago? – it had seemed to be the only solution, in spite of the obvious hazards it entailed. And so she had made her plans, executed them efficiently and embarked for America with confidence.

I took a voyage towards the unknown. Was it the unknown which was the source of her distress? But the unknown had always tempted and beckoned her, had been the spur because of its inherent excitement and the challenge it invariably offered. But that was in the past, she told herself, and thought: I am a different person now.

Panic rose in her like a swift tide, dragging her into its undertow, and she gripped the railing tighter and drew in her breath harshly as another truth struck at her. *If she stayed she would be risking so much. She would be endangering all that she had gained in the past few years.* Far better, perhaps, to go, and if she was going it must be immediately. Today. Before she changed her mind again. In reality it was so easy. All she had to do was make a plane reservation to anywhere in the world that took her fancy, and then go there. Her eyes sought out the liner, so far away now it was a mere speck. Where was it bound for? Yokohama, Sydney, Hong Kong, Casablanca? Where would *she* go? It did not matter and no one would care; and if she left today, whilst it was still safe, no one would be any the wiser, no harm would have been done, least of all to her.

The idea of disappearing into oblivion, as if she had never set foot in the country, suddenly appealed to some deep-rooted instinct in her, to her innate sense of drama, and yet . . . Is it not juvenile to run away? she asked herself. For most assuredly that was exactly what she would be doing. *You* will know you lost your nerve and *you* will live to regret it, a small voice at the back of her mind insisted.

She closed her eyes. Her thoughts raced, as she considered all the possibilities open to her and weighed the consequences of her actions, whatever they would ultimately be. Thunder rattled behind the blackening clouds, which rolled with gathering speed before the force of the gale blowing up. But she was so immersed in her inner conflict, so rapt in her concentration as she strived to reach a final decision, she was oblivious to the hour, the weather, her surroundings. Eventually she came to grips with herself and recognized one fundamental: she could no longer afford to procrastinate. Time was of the essence. Suddenly she made up her mind. She would stay, despite her misgivings and her sense of apprehension. She must, no matter what the cost to herself.

Large drops of rain began to fall, splashing onto her face and her hands. She opened her eyes and glanced down at her fingers still gripping the railing, watching the water trickling over them. Like my tears, she said to herself, and then, quite involuntarily, she laughed out loud, and it was a rich amused laugh. There would be no more tears. She had done all the mourning she was going to do. You're such a fool, Cait, she murmured softly to herself, remembering Nick's old nickname for her, borrowed from the Welsh Caitlin because he had said she had a Celtic soul, all poetry and mystery and fire.

She pulled herself up straight and threw back her head with a proud and defiant gesture, and her extraordinary eyes, not blue, not green, but a curious unique turquoise, were no longer opaque and clouded with uncertainty and fear. They sparkled brightly with new determination. Soon, in a few days, when her courage had been completely reinforced, and she had gathered it around her like a protective mantle, she would go to Ravenswood.

That would be her first step into the unknown. The beginning of her new life. And perhaps, finally, the beginning of peace.

In the Wings
1979

'And even then, I dare not let it languish,
Dare not indulge in Memory's rapturous pain;
Once drinking deep in that divinest anguish,
How could I seek the empty world again?'

Emily Brontë

CHAPTER TWO

Francesca Avery had long ago ceased to regret her actions, having years before reached the conclusion that since regrets could not undo what had been done, they were generally unproductive.

But as she inserted the key into the front door of her apartment and stepped into the silent and shadowy hall, she experienced such an overwhelming sense of regret at having returned to New York without her husband that she was momentarily startled. The heavy door slammed shut behind her, but she hesitated before moving forward into the apartment, thrown off-balance by this unfamiliar feeling, and one so unprecedented in her that she found it disconcerting. Harrison had not wanted her to leave Virginia ahead of him, and she had done so only out of a sense of duty to the charity committee of which she had recently become chairwoman. Ten days earlier, the secretary of the committee had telephoned her in Virginia, to say that an urgent provisional meeting had been called, because of unforeseen difficulties with their plans for the summer concert to be held at Avery Fischer Hall. Only *she* had the power and connections to get the benefit back on the track, the secretary had gone on to point out, adding that no one else could rally the support that was necessary. In short, her presence was imperative.

Francesca knew Harrison thought otherwise, although he had not actually come out and said so. Years in the Foreign Service had refined his innate ability to get his point across by subtle implication, in his usual diplomat's manner. He had gently intimated that he thought the committee members were panicking unnecessarily, and had made a quiet reference to the fact that the telephone service was as efficient in Virginia as it was in Manhattan. Francesca tended to agree that anxiety was prompting the committee to act prematurely, and she was about to decline, but then the matter of the interview had come up and she felt obliged to comply with both of their requests.

Francesca sighed. Duty had been inculcated in her since childhood and to shirk it would be unthinkable, even shoddy, and quite alien to her nature. Nevertheless, she wished she was back at the rambling old house with Harry and his boisterous and unruly grand-daughters, surrounded by the spontaneous love and camaraderie of that special, if somewhat unpredictable and unorthodox, clan. Resolutely she quenched the rising impulse to turn around and go back to La Guardia Airport to catch the next shuttle for Washington.

Francesca groped for the light switch and snapped it down impatiently. She blinked in the sudden brightness. The immense antique French chandelier, with its cascading slivers of crystal prisms and blades and elongated teardrops, flooded the black-and-white marble hall with a blinding blaze. It threw into bold relief the Gobelin tapestry soaring high on the staircase wall, the Rodin busts and Sèvres palace vases in their respective niches and the Louis XV commode, once owned by Madame de Pompadour, upon which reposed a Ming Dynasty vase containing a lovely arrangement of yellow roses, their sweet scent bringing the nostalgic fragrance of a summer garden to the wintry stillness.

Once again her eyes swept over the splendid hall with its priceless objects of art, a setting which never failed to impress with its perfection and timeless beauty, and then, quite involuntarily, she shivered despite the warmth of the hall. Somebody walked over my grave, she thought. How silly she was being, yet there was no denying the fact that she felt curiously alone and lost without Harrison. She was baffled by her reaction. She often came to New York on her own. There was nothing unusual about that, but today she felt decidedly odd, vulnerable, and exposed in the most peculiar way. Oh, it's just the aftermath of Christmas and I'm tired, she decided.

She walked in determined, measured steps across the hall to the library, the high heels of her boots resounding with a sharp metallic ring against the cold marble, the echo disturbing the silence. She stopped in her tracks abruptly. Perhaps that was it – the quietness after the bustling activity of the house in Virginia, with the continual comings and goings of the servants, Harry's grandchildren and guests. The apartment seemed so still, so deserted and devoid of life. Of course, that was undoubtedly the explanation. She was simply missing the girls, their whoops of joy and excitement, their running feet and constant laughter. She would call Harrison later and suggest they all come to the city for a few days. This thought gladdened her heart, and her face brightened as she pushed open the door and went into the library. Although this room was, in many respects, just as imposing as the entrance hall, it was much less intimidating. It appeared welcoming and intimate with its ash-panelled walls, English antiques and comfortable sofas and chairs covered in a cheerful floral chintz. A fire burned brightly in the grate and several lamps had been turned on; and the combination of this warming light cast a lovely glow throughout, one that was both cheerful and reassuring.

Francesca sat down at the English Regency desk and read the note from her housekeeper, Val, who had apparently gone shopping and would return within the hour. She glanced at a number of telephone messages received that morning and then turned her attention to the mail, quickly flipping through it, discarding unopened several invitations, her bank statement and bills. The last envelope had a Harrogate postmark and she recognized her brother's handwriting. Picking up the gold and malachite opener, she slit the envelope and leaned back in the chair, reading Kim's letter eagerly. It was mainly about his children and their Christmas activities, along with bits of news of their mutual friends. There were a few complaints about the burdens of running the estate, but she knew these to be justified. By nature Kim was not a whiner and, God knows, managing the ancestral Langley lands and making them pay was no mean feat these days. He ended the letter with a reminder that he was expecting to see her now that all the seasonal festivities were out of the way. There was a postscript. *Happy New Year, darling. And let's hope 1979 is going to be better for both of us.*

A strand of her blonde hair fell across her face and Francesca pushed it aside quickly, looping it over one ear in her habitual way. Thoughtfully, she perused the letter again, endeavouring to read between the lines, to truly assess Kim's mood and disposition. She detected a certain wistfulness there – no, it was sadness really – and it bespoke his unhappiness, despite the cheerful tone he had adopted in an obviously conscious effort to reassure her. Francesca put down the letter, which troubled her, and stared into space, frowning deeply. Her hazel eyes, soft and transparent, were suddenly reflective, and they betrayed her concern.

Kim was two years older than she, yet she always thought of him as her baby brother, for she had looked after him and shielded him all through their childhood and youth, after their mother's death when they were small. These days she was more protective of him than ever, anxious about his well-being and state of mind. He had simply not been the same since Pandora had left him, and Francesca understood the reasons why. She, too, had been completely astounded by Pandora's extraordinary behaviour, for it had been the perfect marriage, and outwardly the happiest union she had ever encountered. Kim's stunned shock, his heartbreak and profound hurt had been hers, for she had felt them just as acutely.

Will he never recover from that blow? Francesca asked herself, and she did not like the resounding 'no' that reverberated in her head. A proud young woman, and infinitely more pragmatic than her brother, Francesca had long since come to believe that broken hearts were the stuff of romantic dreams and bore no relationship to the true reality of everyday life. You picked up the pieces, glued them together, and went on living as best you could, until the pain receded. That was exactly what she had done years before, and she was fully convinced that no one was irreplaceable. Despite these beliefs, and because she was blessed with considerable intelligence and insight, she realized Kim was different, knew intuitively that he would mourn Pandora, not replace her, as most other men would have done.

She shook her head sadly. He was so isolated in Yorkshire, and lonely with his two elder children away at boarding school. She wished he would spend more time in London with his friends, but then had to admit this was not always feasible. His responsibilities kept him tied to Langley for most of the year. On the other hand, if she were in England she might conceivably be able to exercise some influence over him, persuade him to lead a more active social life than was his custom.

Francesca decided she must go home to England at the end of the month. Harrison would not object, she was certain of that, and perhaps he would accompany her if he was not overburdened with work in Washington. Since his retirement from the Foreign Service a year ago, her husband seemed to be busier than he ever was as an ambassador. He was the country's foremost elder statesman, and consequently he was constantly being sought out by senators and political bigwigs and members of the cabinet; and then again, his role as an adviser to the President on Foreign Affairs was time-consuming and exceedingly tiring. Although he had fully recovered from his two heart attacks and was enjoying good health, Francesca watched over him like a hawk, for ever stricturing him to slow down and take things at a gentler pace. Harrison always readily concurred, and then did exactly as he pleased, caught up in the complex machinations of politics and thoroughly enjoying every exciting minute of it. A trip to England would be a tonic for Harry, as well as an enforced rest, and she resolved to take him with her, was determined to brook no argument from him.

Francesca took out her engagement book and opened it. The meeting of the charity committee had been arranged for one o'clock, and then at four she had the interview with Estelle Morgan of *Now Magazine*. She grimaced as she contemplated this. There were so many other more important obligations to be dealt with, but Estelle had pressed hard for it, and Francesca remembered from past experience the woman's unflagging persistence. It had been far easier on the nerves, and more expedient, to agree immediately.

Also Francesca had wisely acknowledged, when she took on the charity, that she would have to submit to a certain number of interviews. She did not delude herself into thinking the charity needed her solely for her practical turn of mind and her organizing ability. They also wanted her because they felt she had a certain cachet and glamour – how she hated that word – and was, in their minds, the ideal candidate for their publicity purposes. She was dedicated to the charity and took her responsibilities seriously, and refusing to see Estelle would have appeared churlish and even mean-spirited to the committee. Well, it was in a good cause and she *had* made the date. The simplest thing would be to deal with Estelle quickly, and with the best possible grace. Her thoughts shifted to her engagements for the remainder of the week. She glanced at her book to refresh her memory. Francesca walked across the room to the window, thinking again of her brother. She parted the curtains and looked out across Fifth Avenue to Central Park, an absent-minded expression on her delicately-etched face.

It was a very cold, very January day. Portions of the window had iced up and the frost made funny little patterns composed of diamonds and stars and circles on the surface, so that the glass was opaque in parts, and her view of the park was faintly blurred. The patterns and the opaqueness produced a strange optical illusion, one of dreamlike diffusion. It had apparently snowed hard for the past few days, and huge banks drifted over seats and railings and rambling paths, obscuring the familiar landscape with an unbroken sweep of glistening white, like an ocean of rising waves, their crests frozen into rigid immobility; and the skeletal black trees were festooned with crystalline flakes that transformed the branches into fragile feathered plumes.

Behind them, the skyscrapers on the West Side merged to form an indistinguishable grey mass of granite that rose up like a rugged mountain range into a vaulted sky. Images ran together in her head . . . the snow-scape of the city became the soaring pristine mountains above Königssee . . . changed into the high-flung Yorkshire fells which overshadowed her childhood home . . . those were the familiar places that took shape as she stared through the frosty tracery of the glass. She squinted through half-closed lids, and saw in her mind's eye the famous oil by Monet, which he had painted on a trip to Norway around 1895. It was called 'Mount Kolsaas', and she knew it well, for Harrison had always wanted it. But it was owned by another collector and unlikely ever to be his. This fact did not stop him hankering after it. That which is beyond our reach is always the more desirable because of its very unattainability, she thought. Just as Pandora is out of Kim's yearning reach.

Francesca touched the icy window with a polished pink fingernail and abstract-edly scratched at it, her thoughts returning to her brother. She had not been able to suggest a cure, at the very least an antidote for what ailed him.

20

Perhaps one doesn't exist for Kim, she reflected forlornly, unless, quite simply, it *is* time. The passing of time had worked miracles for her, but she was uncertain of the effect it would have on him. It struck her then that her going to England was hardly a solution to Kim's problems. Might it not be infinitely better if he came to New York? The more she thought about this, the more Francesca was convinced it was the most effective and practical solution. She would remove him from his normal environment and propel him into a round of social activities on this side of the Atlantic. Francesca was nothing if not decisive and she hurried to the desk, picked up the telephone and dialled her home in Virginia.

'Hello, Harrison. It's me,' she said when her husband answered.

'Ah, darling, so there you are. I was just going to call you. Why didn't you awaken me before you left? You know I like to say goodbye. Creeping off like that was grossly unfair of you. Ruined my day, I don't mind telling you.'

As he was speaking Francesca was, as always, conscious of the rich timbre of his voice, and touched by the warmth and love it exuded. He was such a dear man. How lucky she was. She smiled into the telephone. 'You were sleeping so soundly, my darling, I didn't have the heart to disturb you.'

'Did you have a nice trip? How are things at the apartment?' he asked.

'Smooth trip, and everything is fine here.'

'I forgot to tell you last night, I'd like you to stop by at the gallery and chivy Leclerc about the Utrillo, if you don't mind. I'd really appreciate it, and I think a personal visit would be more effective than a 'phone call. Any time this week will do, whenever you can fit it in.'

'Of course, darling. Actually, Harry, I called you for a couple of reasons, apart from wanting to say hello. I wondered if you'd like to come up for a couple of days? Perhaps on Wednesday. You could bring the girls. They would enjoy it, and so would I, and we can all fly back to Virginia together, on Friday.'

'I'd love to, Francesca, but I can't. I have some special meetings in Washington, which I must attend, and a Democratic dinner. So sorry. Next week maybe. If you're going to New York again,' he said, regret echoing in his voice.

'Fine,' she said, suppressing her own disappointment. 'There's another matter I must discuss with you, Harry dear. I've received a rather disturbing letter from Kim.' She went on to tell him about its contents and her dismay about Kim's depressed mood.

'So I thought it might be a good idea to invite him here to New York, Harry. And then I thought we might all go to the estate in Barbados for a week or so. That would be more beneficial to you than going to England. After all, you'd only get embroiled with your political cronies in the British government, and it wouldn't be a rest at all.'

Harrison Avery chuckled. How well she knew him. 'You're correct there, my sweet girl. And Barbados does appeal to me. Can't say I fancy London in winter. Too damned cold and damp for these old bones. And I agree with you wholeheartedly about Kim. I think you should invite him here immediately, Francesca. I've been a little concerned about him myself. Why don't you give him a call right now?' he proposed.

'It's so easy to refuse on the telephone, Harry, and he might just do that, without giving it any real thought. I'd prefer to write to him and then

21

telephone him next week when he's had the letter. To persuade him, if necessary.'

'You know best, of course, darling. But I hope he comes over at once, if he can get away from Langley. You know I've always had a soft spot for that brother of yours, and I think he needs us both right now.'

'Yes, he does. Thank you for being so understanding and supportive, Harry dear. I'd better go. I must write the letter, and I've got rather a busy day. I'll speak to you later in the week.'

'Fine, darling. Goodbye.'

Since the plans for Kim's trip were uppermost in her mind at this moment, that sense of regret Francesca had experienced on entering the apartment earlier was entirely forgotten. Yet only a few weeks later she was to remember it, and with a sudden surge of clarity, wondering if it had been some kind of premonition of impending disaster, and not regret at all. Ridiculous as it was, she even entertained the notion that events would have progressed differently, the consequences been averted, if she had followed her original impulse and returned to Virginia. But hindsight was meaningless. By then it was already too late. Her life and the lives of others had been changed irrevocably, and so profoundly they would never be the same again.

Now, this morning, preoccupied as she was with her brother's well-being, her speculation about the future revolved solely around him. She picked up her pen and began the letter. When it was finished she sealed it quickly, addressed the envelope and found an airmail stamp in the desk drawer. There, it was done! She leaned back in the chair and regarded the letter propped up against a malachite bookend. It was articulate and persuasive and so lovingly couched, Kim would be unable to reject her invitation, of that she was absolutely convinced. She thought then of the postscript at the end of *his* letter, and she made a solemn vow to herself: 1979 was going to be a better year for him, no matter what was entailed or what she had to do to ensure this outcome.

Francesca pushed back the chair, filled with a sense of purpose and renewed energy. She smiled happily to herself as she hurried upstairs to change her clothes and refresh her make-up, in readiness for the day's appointments. Kim would come to New York and she would help him to recover from his hurt and pain and melancholy. She would help to make him whole again. Everything was going to be all right.

CHAPTER THREE

Estelle Morgan was too early for her appointment with Francesca Avery, and as the taxi sped up Madison Avenue she decided to alight a few blocks away from the apartment, and walk the rest of the way. She paid off the cab at Seventy-Fourth

Street and Madison and stepped out into the crisp afternoon air. It had stopped snowing at lunch time, and a watery sun was trying to penetrate the bloated etiolated clouds with scant success.

As she turned onto Fifth Avenue and approached the palatial and imposing building where the Averys lived, a self-congratulatory smile slipped onto her face, giving her a smug look. How right she had been to wear her mink coat.

The doormen of these apartment buildings where the very rich lived were invariably snootier than their privileged inhabitants, and she wasn't going to have even one of them look *her* over with disdain and treat her dismissively.

Estelle had hesitated about the coat at first, because it was snowing hard at eight o'clock and she did not want to get it wet. But it looked far better than her raincoat, and so she decided to take a cab to the office. It had been a worthwhile investment. The coat made her feel chic and bolstered her self-confidence. It was her pride and joy really. To complete the outfit Estelle had chosen a red dress, black patent knee-high boots and a large black patent shoulder bag, a copy of a famous Italian design. Earlier that morning as she had surveyed herself in the mirror, she had nodded at her reflection with complete gratification. She thought she was the epitome of a glamorous, successful international journalist. Sadly, Estelle Morgan did not think very deeply about anything, and so it never occurred to her that an outfit could not transform her into all the things she believed herself to be.

She glanced at her watch as she waited for the traffic lights to change at Seventy-Ninth Street. It was a few seconds to four, but she was almost there and would arrive exactly on time. Punctuality was not one of her strong suits, but she recalled that Francesca Avery, the cold bitch, was a stickler about time and, not wanting to start off on the wrong foot, she had made a concerted effort not to be late. After giving her name and being announced, she was permitted to enter the grandiose building at Eighty-First Street.

She was greeted at the Avery apartment by a middle-aged woman in black, undoubtedly the housekeeper, who asked for her coat, laid it carefully over a chair, and then ushered her across the hall. Estelle had been to many elegant homes during the course of her career, but she had never seen anything quite as impressive as the Avery entrance hall, particularly in New York City. Jesus, it looks as if it's been transported lock, stock and barrel from Versailles, she thought as she followed the housekeeper in silence, her eyes popping.

After she had shown Estelle into the library, the housekeeper gave her a small cool smile and said, 'I'll tell her Ladyship you're here.' Estelle murmured her thanks as the housekeeper departed.

She crossed the room to the fire, her boots sinking into the deep silken pile of the antique Chinese carpet. Her eyes flicked around yet again, curiosity glittering in them. They took in the antiques, and moved on to regard the paintings gracing the panelled walls. She was not particularly well informed about art, but Estelle had acquired a smattering of borrowed knowledge about innumerable subjects. And so she was able to recognize at once that these were not merely good copies, nor hardly likely to be in *this* apartment. They were originals and quite famous enough to identify, masterpieces from the Post-Impressionist period. That's undoubtedly a Van Gogh on the far wall, she decided, hurrying over to examine it, delighted with

23

her accurate guesswork when she saw the signature. She scrutinized the others with lightning speed. A Seurat. A Cézanne. A Gauguin.

A moment later the door swung open and Francesca Avery was standing there, her eyes sparkling with vitality, a smile on her tranquil face. 'Estelle!' she exclaimed, moving forward with grace and elegance, swaying slightly on the precariously high heels that drew attention to her fine ankles and long slender legs.

As she approached the fireplace, Estelle noted that the English-rose complexion was still quite flawless and the burnished amber-blonde hair as silky and luxuriant as it had ever been. Why, she hasn't changed at all, Estelle commented to herself in astonishment, and with a stab of annoyance.

'Do forgive me for keeping you waiting,' Francesca apologized. 'But here I am. And it's so nice to see you again.' She stretched out her hand.

The journalist arranged a pleasant smile on her face and grabbed Francesca's long cool fingers clumsily. 'I've only been here a few minutes, my dear. I didn't mind waiting at all. And especially in this lovely room. What marvellous taste you have.'

Francesca extracted her hand, wincing inside. Estelle had always been something of a sycophant and time had apparently not tempered her obsequiousness. Although this was nauseating, she supposed it was harmless enough. Francesca moved away from the fireplace and murmured, 'How kind of you to say so. Now I think we might be more comfortable over there.' She indicated the sofa and chairs grouped against the back wall underneath the Gauguin painting of a Tahitian girl. Estelle followed her hostess's suggestion and bounced over to the seating arrangement. She took her time settling comfortably and then she looked at Francesca, smiled with a fraudulent sweetness and said, 'And I must say, my dear, it's lovely to see you too, after such a long time. It seems like centuries.'

'Not quite that,' Francesca responded with a dry laugh. 'About five years. I think the last time we ran into each other was in Monte Carlo, wasn't it?'

'Yes, at Grace's benefit. She's such a lovely person, and Rainier is quite the charmer. I'm so fond of them both,' she gushed.

Francesca was astounded at this blatant boasting of friendship with the Grimaldis, knowing it to be utterly false. Estelle was no more on intimate terms with the Prince and Princess of Monaco than *she* was with the Queen of England. Reluctant to embark on a conversation that could only prove embarrassing to Estelle, she refrained from passing comment, and asked in a brisk tone, 'Can I offer you something? Tea, coffee or a drink perhaps?'

Disappointment flooded through Estelle, was quickly replaced by aggravation. But she caught herself in time. 'Tea would be very nice, thank you.' And then in an effort to conceal her annoyance at being deprived of an opportunity to show off, she went on, 'With lemon please, and a sweetener if you have it. Must keep my figure, you know.'

'Of course,' said Francesca. 'I'll go and ask Val to make it, and then we can catch up, and get on with the interview. Please excuse me.' She hurried to the door, wondering with dismay how she would cope with Estelle for the next hour.

Estelle's narrowed gaze followed Francesca as she glided out. Why is it she always seems to float not walk? she wondered sourly. And how has she kept her looks? She's got to be at least forty-two, yet she looks ten years younger.

24

Francesca returned almost immediately, interrupting Estelle's thoughts. 'Val already had the kettle boiling,' she explained, placing the Georgian silver tray, with its matching tea service, on the coffee table. She sat down on the chair opposite, poured the tea and went on: 'The last time I saw you I believe you were working for one of the newspapers. How long have you been writing for *Now Magazine?*'

'Oh, about three years and I'm the Features Editor actually.'

'Why that's marvellous, Estelle. It must be a very important job, although I should imagine it's rather hectic as well.'

'It is. But it's exciting. I lead a very interesting life, you know, jetting all over the world, staying in the best hotels, or with the best people, doing my in-depth interviews with famous personalities.' Puffing up with self-importance, she continued, 'I also have quite a large staff working for me. But I make sure I get the best interviews for myself, especially those abroad.'

Francesca thought: Well, at least she's honest, and said, 'How very smart of you.'

'Just one of the many tricks of the trade,' Estelle said and reached for her handbag. She took out a small tape recorder and placed it on the butler's tray table between them. 'You don't mind if I use this, do you?'

'No, whatever you prefer. I'd like to tell you something about the charity. I assume you're going to mention it, since you went through my committee to arrange our meeting, and they're expecting it, you know. Now –'

'We'll get to that later,' Estelle interjected so brusquely Francesca was taken aback. The journalist hurried on without pause, 'First I want you to talk about *you*, your life style, your personal life, your career, that kind of thing. After all, you're the subject of my interview, not the charity. My readers are interested in personalities, and how they live, not organizations or institutions.' She threw Francesca a look that seemed somehow challenging.

'Oh. I see,' Francesca replied softly, wondering what she had so foolishly let herself in for, albeit with the best of intentions. She also found the sharp rebuff rather discourteous and then dismissed it as insensitivity, or perhaps simply enthusiasm for the job. Estelle had always been a graceless person and never intentionally meant to give offence.

Francesca leaned forward and reached for a cigarette in the onyx and gold box on the table. She lit it and sat back in the chair, waiting patiently as Estelle fiddled with the machine, experiencing acute embarrassment for her. Estelle had obviously dressed in a manner she thought appropriate for the occasion, and even smart, but the red wool frock, although expensive, was a most unbecoming choice. The colour was disastrous with her florid complexion and flaming red hair. Francesca was aware this was the natural colour, but Estelle seemed to be resorting to the bottle these days. It was several shades too bright, and harsh.

Drawing on her cigarette, Francesca glanced away quickly, chastising herself for her lack of generosity, and suddenly, being compassionate, she was touched by pity for Estelle. They had first met years ago in London when they were in their twenties, but the intervening years had not been kind to the woman sitting opposite her. Francesca was unexpectedly saddened. Poor Estelle. Her life was probably not half as glamorous as she pretended. It might even be a terrible struggle in so many

25

different ways. Yet Estelle was a clever writer, and had been full of talent and promise in those early years. What had happened to her dreams of becoming a novelist? Quite clearly they had gone by the wayside. And then she thought: But who am I to criticize Estelle? Everyone did what they could in life, and hoped for the best. She had a particular distaste for those who constantly wanted to play God and passed judgment on their peers. She had always chosen not to indulge in that gratuitous pastime.

'There, I'm all set,' Estelle exclaimed and settled back comfortably.

And so the interview began. Where did she get her clothes? Did she prefer French or American designers? What kind of entertaining did she like best? Did she give large or small dinner parties? Or cocktail parties? How did she cope with homes in New York, Virginia and Barbados? How many servants did she have? Did she decorate her own homes? Did she have any hobbies? What was it like being the wife of an ambassador? Did Harrison enjoy his new role as a presidential adviser? What was his state of health? Did she go to the White House frequently? Who were the people she entertained? Did she enjoy a good relationship with Harrison's grandchildren? Did she prefer living in America to England, or other countries? And why? Did Harrison have any hobbies? How did they relax? What were their leisure activities?

It seemed to Francesca that the questions were interminable. She answered honestly and with cordiality, pausing from time to time to freshen their tea or light a cigarette. But as Estelle probed and probed she grew steadily weary and a trifle impatient with this cross-examination of her life, began to see it as an intrusion into her privacy, and certainly not exactly what she had bargained for when she had agreed to the meeting. Furthermore, to Francesca's growing unease, Estelle had not mentioned the charity once. She was just about to tactfully introduce this subject when the questions changed in character.

'Do you think Teddy Kennedy will run for the Presidency in 1980?'

Surprise flickered in Francesca's eyes. 'I never discuss politics. I leave that to Harrison.'

'But you must have an opinion, and I'm interviewing you, not your husband. Come on, Francesca, you're a bright, liberated woman. What do you think? Will he try to run?'

'You really must respect my wishes, Estelle. I don't want to discuss politics on any level.'

'Well then, on to other subjects. Let's touch on your career. You haven't written a book lately. Is that because the one about Edward IV and the Wars of the Roses didn't do very well? I really *felt* for you when I read the reviews. Personally, *I* didn't think it was dull, long-winded or verbose.'

Francesca stifled a gasp. Estelle's expression was smoothly bland, revealing nothing. Maybe she doesn't know she is being inflammatory, Francesca thought, and then laughed inwardly at her own *naïveté*. This was the new style of journalism. Being provocative to elicit angry or unthinking responses inevitably made for a better story. She was not going to fall into that trap. Conscious that journalists always had the last word when they sat down at their typewriters, she refused to take offence or to be chivied into losing her composure.

'The reviews weren't all bad. In fact, I had some excellent ones,' she said.

26

'And contrary to your impression, Estelle, the book did sell, both in hardcover and paperback. Of course, you're right in one sense, in that it wasn't a runaway best seller like my books on Chinese Gordon or Richard III.' She shrugged nonchalantly. 'You win a few and lose a few, I suppose. Anyway, to answer your question, the real reason I haven't written another book in the past few years is simply because I haven't found the right historical figure to focus on, but I expect I will come up with something eventually.'

'I love your historical biographies, and I happen to think you're equal to Antonia Fraser any time, even though she is a much bigger name. You know, in my opinion, you really are rather a good writer, my dear.'

Although this was uttered with pleasantness there was a patronizing undertone to the words, which Francesca could not fail to miss. And she thought, with sudden acuity: Hostility is implicit in this woman. *She* may not be conscious of it, but *I* know she does not like me at all. Her guard went up.

Estelle, who was so self-involved she was fundamentally oblivious to other people's feelings, went on unperturbedly, 'Oh dear, I see the tape's run out. I'll have to change it.' Obviously the session was far from over in Estelle's mind. It was almost six and it had grown dark outside, and the concert had not yet been broached. Francesca's good manners were bred in the bone, and to be impolite or inhospitable to a guest in her home would go against the grain. Nevertheless, she felt disinclined to extend herself any further. She tightened her lips in aggravation and admitted she would have to endure Estelle's presence until she had talked about the charity, otherwise the whole afternoon would have been a disgraceful waste of time.

Against her better judgment, Francesca now felt obliged to ask: 'Would you care for a drink, Estelle? I thought I might have a glass of white wine, but there's plenty to choose from, if you'd prefer something else.' She waved her hand in the direction of the console table in the far corner. This held a large array of bottles, decanters and crystal glasses.

'Oooh! What a lovely idea, my dear. I'll have white wine too, please.'

Francesca nodded, retrieved the tea tray and escaped to the kitchen. Within minutes she was back, carrying a silver bucket containing a bottle of white wine. She took this over to the console, poured two glasses and rejoined Estelle. She felt as though she was on the verge of screaming.

'*Santé*,' Estelle said. 'I do appreciate good wines. After all my trotting back and forth to France I guess I'm spoiled. What is this? It's delicious.'

'Pouilly Fuissé,' Francesca replied with a thin smile, marvelling at her considerable patience. But it was dwindling fast.

In the kitchen Francesca had finally resolved to seize control of the situation and bring the interview to its conclusion as rapidly and as diplomatically as possible. Adopting a businesslike tone, she plunged in: 'I must talk to you about the charity, Estelle. It's getting late and I have a dinner engagement. I'm sure your time is precious too.'

'But I have more questions about –'

'Please, Estelle, let's be fair,' Francesca interrupted firmly. 'I have given you two hours already. I only agreed to this interview because I felt your story would be beneficial to a good cause, and help us with the concert, and this was made

27

quite clear to you at the time. Normally I don't give interviews of this type. I loathe personal publicity.'

Estelle had her glass halfway to her mouth. She put it down and gaped at Francesca. 'Don't like publicity! You're *always* in the columns.'

'I can't help it if I'm constantly being mentioned in the newspapers. It's none of my doing, I can assure you of that. But don't let's digress.' Francesca glanced pointedly at her watch. 'I'll have to bring our visit to a close very shortly, I'm afraid.'

'Oh sure, that's all right,' Estelle responded affably. 'Please go ahead, Francesca dear. I'd just *love* to hear about your charity.'

Relieved that she had turned the discussion around to her advantage, Francesca launched into all the salient details of the elaborate star-studded concert she and the committee were planning. She spoke quickly, but articulately, for about fifteen minutes. Finally she concluded, 'That's about it. What can I add, but to say again that it *is* for a truly worthy cause, and naturally we'd appreciate any mention you can give.'

'There's no problem. I'll give the charity a nice fat plug, right up front in the story.' Estelle cleared her throat and added quickly, 'I'd like to have a photographer come up next week and take a few candids of you, whenever it's convenient. Can you give me a date and time, please?'

'Oh dear!' Francesca stopped, and began to finger her pearls. 'I hadn't realized you'd want to take special photographs,' she said with a degree of hesitance. 'Would next Wednesday at two o'clock be suitable? It's really the only time I have free.' She was not especially enamoured of this new development, but she knew herself to be trapped.

'That's fine. I'll book our very *best* photographer.' Estelle leaned forward and snapped off the tape recorder.

Sitting back in the chair, Francesca permitted herself to relax. She felt exhausted and longed to be alone, but it seemed that Estelle was determined to finish her drink, and at her own leisure.

'I have something to tell you,' Estelle began, lifting her glass and regarding Francesca closely over the rim. There was a small pause before she said, 'Katharine's coming back to New York.'

Francesca sat up swiftly and threw her an astonished glance, frowning. 'Katharine?' she echoed.

'Yes. Katharine Tempest. The one and only Katharine,' Estelle smiled. 'Don't tell me you didn't know who I meant!'

'Naturally I knew. I was a little surprised, that's all. Actually, I'd lost track of her. Why are you telling me anyway? It's of no interest to me.'

'Katharine wants to see you.'

Francesca tensed. She felt her face stiffening and her eyes, opening very widely, brimmed with shock. She did not believe Estelle, but as she studied the other woman's face in silence she knew from her gloating expression that it was indeed true. She was momentarily speechless. She managed to say, 'Whatever for? Why would she want to see me?'

'I can't imagine,' Estelle replied sardonically. 'But she wanted me to request a meeting. Lunch, dinner, tea, drinks, whichever you prefer. Just give me a date.

She'll be arriving in about a week or ten days, and she expects me to have arranged it by then. When can you see her?'

Anger was fulminating in Francesca. And she, who was never rude, said with unusual vehemence, her voice rising, 'I cannot see her! I will not see her! I think you have –'

'I know you two became drawn enemies,' Estelle exclaimed peremptorily. 'That's why I can't understand Katharine. She's being very foolish, in my opinion. I don't –'

'I was about to say, when you interrupted me, that I think you have behaved in the most despicable manner!' Francesca cried. 'How *dare* you wangle your way into my home, on the pretext of doing an interview, when it's patently obvious the real reason you're here is to carry messages for Katharine Tempest.' Francesca's anger now spiralled into cold fury. 'How devious and underhanded of you! You're a disgrace to your profession. But then I suppose I shouldn't have expected better behaviour from you, Estelle. You always were *her* lackey. I think you had better leave.'

Estelle did not budge. She was enjoying Francesca's discomfort. She gave her a slow derisive smile, and triumph flicked into the small brown eyes. 'My, my, I never thought I'd see the day when *you* would display so much emotion.'

Dismay had lodged like a stone in the pit of Francesca's stomach, but she took firm control of herself. Recovering some of her self-possession, she said, in a steadier voice, 'You may tell Katharine Tempest I have no wish to see her. Ever again. I have nothing to say to her.'

'It's no skin off my nose either way, and although I don't understand Katharine's motives, I did agree to help.' Estelle crossed her legs and lolled back in the chair, regarding Francesca with quizzical eyes. She shook her head wonderingly. 'I'm surprised at you, Francesca. Why don't you give a little, for once in your life, and get down off your pedestal. Let bygones be bygones. We're all a bit older and more mature. I think Katharine expected you, of all people, to be more understanding.'

'More understanding!' Francesca gasped. 'After what she did to me! You must be as demented as she apparently is. I absolutely refuse to continue this ridiculous discussion. I would appreciate it if you would leave my house. I think you have not only outstayed your welcome, but abused my hospitality.'

Estelle lifted her shoulders in a gesture of resignation, picked up the tape recorder and dropped it into her handbag. She could not resist a final attempt at effecting a reconciliation. 'She only wants to be friends again. With everyone. That's why she asked me to contact all of you. Come on, be generous, change your mind.'

'I will not. *Never*. The others can do as they wish, but *I* will not see her.' Francesca's face had paled and her eyes blazed. 'I don't want anything to do with her. There's nothing to be gained by a . . . a . . . reunion.' Francesca drew a quick intake of breath. 'And *I'm* surprised at *you*, Estelle. Why do you permit her to use you in this way?'

'Use me! Good God, that's a laugh. If ever she's used anyone, it's been you!' Estelle regretted this remark the instant it left her mouth. Katharine had warned her not to let her antagonism towards Francesca get in the way, and she had done just that in the heat of the moment.

A bone-chilling coldness had settled over Francesca. She nodded her head slowly and with deliberation. 'You are quite correct, Estelle. And I do not propose to be used again. *Ever*,' she intoned with such icy finality that the journalist shrank back in her chair.

'I will show you out,' Francesca continued in the same glacial voice. She rose and, without giving Estelle another glance, walked to the door. She opened it and stood aside. 'Please leave.'

Estelle cleared her throat. 'I'll see you next Wednesday then, with the photographer.'

'I hardly think the photographs will be necessary, since you are not going to write the story. You might as well admit it, Estelle, the interview was just a ruse to see me,' she snapped in an accusatory tone. 'You could have told me this on the telephone, instead of wasting hours of my time doing a bogus interview.'

Estelle's florid face filled with darker colour. 'I *am* going to write the story, so you see, I will need the photographs.'

'Obviously I must refuse.'

Even a woman as intrinsically obtuse as Estelle could not fail to understand that she had destroyed herself irrevocably in Francesca's eyes and, knowing she had nothing to lose, she now exclaimed heatedly, 'Seemingly your precious charity is not that important to you after all.' She pushed herself out into the hall, grabbed her coat from the chair and flung it over her arm. She then swung around to face Francesca, who was watching her from the doorway of the library, a look of distaste flickering in her eyes.

The jealousy and envy at the root of Estelle's antipathy for Francesca surfaced. Self-control and all rationality left her. 'You always were a stuck-up, rotten snob!' she almost screamed. 'Whatever Katharine did to you is not half as bad as the things you did to her, and when she needed you the most. It's because of you she has been isolated from everyone all this time. You've added to her suffering. The least you could do is see her. You cold unfeeling bitch!'

The mask of affability had been ripped off to reveal a face that was malevolent with hatred. Estelle headed for the front door. When she reached it she flung herself around and laughed an inane laugh. 'I do believe you are *afraid* to see Katharine!'

With this final strident statement Estelle flounced out and slammed the door so ferociously behind her, Francesca flinched. She leaned against the door and closed her eyes. Her head was swimming and a sick feeling of dismay lingered. Vaguely she heard Val's step in the corridor and with some effort she pulled herself together, moving towards the staircase.

'My goodness, whatever was that?' Val asked.

'Miss Morgan. Leaving in a huff,' said Francesca, turning around on the stairs.

'I thought the roof was falling in,' Val exclaimed, glancing about, suspecting damage to the more fragile art treasures. She shook her head, and her tightened lips signalled her immense disapproval of such undignified goings on. 'Dear, dear, all that yelling and screaming like a fishwife. So common, M'lady.' Val, who was the youngest sister of Melly, Francesca's old nanny, and had known her since she was a child, was motherly and protective. Now she peered closely at Francesca and said, 'I hope she hasn't upset you unduly, M'lady. You look a bit peaked.'

'No, Val, she hasn't. I'm all right, really I am. I'm also late for Mr Nelson's dinner party.' She smiled weakly. 'I'd better go upstairs and get ready.'

'I'll come and help you, M'lady.'

'No, you don't have to, Val,' Francesca murmured, desperately wanting to be by herself. 'Thank you, but I can manage.' She smiled again and retreated up the stairs.

CHAPTER FOUR

The bedroom of the Avery duplex overlooked Fifth Avenue and the park. It was large, airy and light, an oasis of pale green highlighted with white. Cool and restful, the room was accented with touches of yellow, pink and blue, all fresh bright colours that might have been plucked from a bouquet of English flowers.

Apple-green watered silk covered the walls, and framed the two windows with long tied-back draperies and handsome matching valances. There were several Louis XVI *bergères* and a small Louis XVI sofa grouped in a semi-circle in front of the white marble fireplace.

It was a cheerful, happy room, one that reflected Francesca's naturally sunny, outgoing personality and her serene disposition, as well as her good taste. But her demeanour was less tranquil than normal as she closed the door firmly behind her and hurried across the floor. She sank gratefully into one of the chairs near the fireplace and leaned back, waiting for the trembling of her limbs to subside. She was unaccustomed to such flagrant displays of emotion, whether by herself or others, had an abhorrence of turbulent scenes, which she found uncivilized and distressing. She was not only horrified by Estelle's duplicity and her virulent tirade, but aghast at her own loss of control, finding this to be immature, and also demeaning. She closed her eyes, attempting to gather her disordered senses, to restore her equilibrium and calm herself in readiness for the evening. No sooner had she begun to relax when the telephone on the bedside table began to ring, making her start. Reluctantly, she roused herself from her reverie, and went to answer it. 'Hello?'

'Francesca darling, Nelson here. It's a very bad night. Snowing like the devil. I've sent a car for you. Dayson just left.'

'Oh, Nelson, that's so thoughtful of you.' Her hand flew to her pearls and she played with them nervously. 'I'm afraid I'm running terribly late. I haven't changed yet. I was awfully delayed by an appointment. I'm so sorry. I'll be as quick as I can –'

'What's wrong, Francesca?' he interrupted. They had been friends for a number of years before she had married his elder brother, and he knew and understood her with a precision and insight that was rare.

'Nothing. Truly, Nelson. Just a rather troublesome afternoon with a difficult

31

journalist who came to interview me.' She sat down on the bed and kicked off her shoes, flexing her toes.

'Oh! From which publication?'

'*Now Magazine*. She was a little hostile, but I'm sure there is nothing to worry about. Honestly, it's all right.'

'That's owned by Everett Communications. Tommy Everett is one of my oldest friends. Spent all of our summers together in Bar Harbor when we were boys. Tommy is also a client of the bank. And it just so happens I'm a major stockholder of Everett Communications.' He chuckled and, taking control in his usual masterful manner, continued: 'So you see, there's no problem. I'll talk to Tommy right now. Call him at home, in fact. I'll have the story killed and the journalist fired immediately. I'm not going to have you hounded by that particular magazine and disturbed in this way. It's perfectly outrageous. What's the name of the journalist?'

Francesca hesitated and, ignoring the question, said, 'No, don't do anything, Nelson. Please. At least not at the moment. I'm not really worried about the story. I'll discuss it with you this evening, and then we can decide.'

Nelson sighed, knowing better than to press the point with her. 'Just as you wish, darling. But I don't like you to be so perturbed. And don't deny it either, because I can tell from your voice that you are.'

'Nelson, there's something else –' She took a deep breath and said, 'Katharine Tempest wants to see me.' As she spoke Francesca acknowledged to herself that this was the real reason for her distress.

A prolonged silence at the other end of the telephone. And then, 'I knew she would turn up again one day, like the damned bad penny she is. She's a troublemaker, Francesca. I sincerely hope you are not going to see her.'

'No, I'm not.'

'The right decision, darling. Now, if you hurry, you'll arrive before the other guests and we can have a quiet chat about all this. Dayson should be there in about twenty minutes to half an hour, depending on the traffic. It was bad earlier, when I came up from Wall Street. See you shortly.' As an afterthought, he added quietly, 'And don't dwell on Katharine Tempest. She's not worth it. Dismiss her from your mind.'

'Yes, I will. Thank you, Nelson.'

There was no time to waste if she was to be ready when the car arrived and Francesca did as Nelson suggested, turning her thoughts away from Katharine Tempest as she went into her dressing room. She undressed quickly, slipped into a towelling robe and sat down at the dressing table to attend to her face and hair, working with concentration on her appearance.

At one moment she did pause to think about Estelle, and discovered, much to her amazement, that her anger had abated considerably. Her mind strayed back to the interview, and she ruminated on the outcome. Estelle had protested her innocence of any deviousness, arguing that she fully intended to write the story. But Francesca was not entirely convinced of the veracity of this statement, still believing the journalist had connived, and had entered her home under false pretences. On the other hand, she might be genuinely sincere about doing the piece. It struck Francesca then, and with an uneasy jolt, that it would be relatively easy for Estelle to do a vicious hatchet job on her, simply by making her appear to be the spoiled, pampered and indolent wife of a very rich and powerful man, who took up charities out of perpetual boredom. Estelle could make her look ridiculous, and there was no more devastating weapon than ridicule, especially in print. All those questions about her clothes, her home, her servants and her life in general, apparently so meaningless on the surface, now gained greater significance.

Worry clouded Francesca's eyes. Undoubtedly Estelle was not very bright in certain areas, and she was obviously living in a world of fantasy. Yet she was also a clever journalist with a flair for words, and there was no denying her fervid hostility. She might be motivated by sheer maliciousness to dip her pen in venom, and that could prove to be embarrassing to Harrison, not to mention the charity. She bit her lip, attempting to outguess Estelle, and then gave up, knowing it to be a fruitless task. And, of course, there was always Nelson, ready to interfere.

Over the years Francesca had acquired a sense of irony about life, and now she thought: Poor pathetic Estelle, playing out of her league again. How little she knows about the power brokers in this town, the most influential of whom is Nelson. Not only in New York, but from coast to coast. He could demolish Estelle with one telephone call. But Francesca was too big a woman to be vindictive, and she had no wish to deprive anyone of a livelihood, particularly an unfortunate creature like Estelle. And so, for these reasons, she now decided she must exercise prudence, speak with the utmost caution to Nelson when he questioned her about the interview later. Otherwise he would act with lightning speed, out of fierce protection and love for her, wielding his immense power to Estelle's detriment. Perhaps she was being foolish and soft-hearted in view of Estelle's reprehensible behaviour, but for the moment she thought it wiser to keep her own counsel. She wanted to analyse the situation before making any moves and enlisting Nelson's help. And if she did resort to the latter, it would be with the understanding that the only action to be taken was the suppression of the story.

Francesca brought her gaze back to the selection of cosmetics in front of her. She picked up a pot of silver eyeshadow and smoothed the merest trace of it on her lids, added several layers of brown mascara to her lashes, and then outlined her mouth with soft peach lipstick. She sat back, looking in the mirror with a critical eye and decided Val was right; she did seem peaked. Rectifying her pallor with a light stroking of rouge on her high cheekbones, she then lifted the silver-backed brush and ran it through her hair several times, and finally completed her toilet with a few sprays of Joy perfume. As she rose the intercom buzzed. It was Val, announcing the arrival of the car.

'Thank you, Val. Tell Dayson I'll be down shortly. I'm not quite ready.'

Having selected her clothes for the evening earlier in the day, Francesca was dressed within seconds, and she added the two strands of opera-length pearls she invariably wore, along with the other jewellery she had taken out of the safe that morning. As with the necklace, none of these pieces was ostentatious or elaborate, just plain pearl studs for her ears, a simple pearl bracelet with a coral clasp, and a coral-and-pearl ring she slipped on next to her platinum wedding band. A peach silk evening bag, identically matched to her high-heeled silk pumps, lay on the dressing table. She put in her keys and a few items she required for the evening, picked it up and moved towards the door.

On an impulse she turned, and walked back to the far end of the dressing room. Here it widened into a more spacious area and became a deep, relatively large alcove. This was lined with closets running from the floor to the ceiling on all three walls, and they were entirely sheathed with mirrors that created a glittering cocoon of shimmering light and reflections, this effect intensified by hidden spots in the ceiling.

Francesca paused in the centre of the alcove to view herself full length. After a moment's consideration she frowned and shook her head, suddenly dissatisfied with the way she looked, although she was not quite certain why. Unless it was the dress which was new and had never been worn before. Like all her clothes this was understated and simple, a rippling column of peach-coloured panné velvet, cut like a Roman tunic and falling to the floor in straight fluid lines. The long wide sleeves helped to soften its basic severity, the square-shaped neckline beautifully emphasized her slender stem-like neck, and the off-centre slit in the skirt revealed enough of her right leg to lend a dash of sophistication. There was no question in her mind that the dress was elegant, and perfectly suitable for Nelson's intimate dinner party. And yet there was something she was not sure about, something which troubled her, and she wondered whether to change into another gown, even though she was running late.

She turned from side to side, looking at herself appraisingly from all angles, and finally made a long slow turn. It was then that Francesca saw her reflection doubled, tripled and quadrupled. An infinity of images in an infinity of mirrors assaulted her eyes, and she was confronted by a dizzying number of Francescas encased in a sliver of supple peach velvet. Peach from head to toe. *Peach*. She caught her breath and drew closer to the central mirror, staring intently, and a look of surprise mixed with dawning comprehension spread across her face. It was not the style of the dress that disturbed her, but the *colour*. Of course that was it. She had not worn peach for years, over twenty years to be exact.

And as she continued to gaze at herself, mesmerized by the peach dress, up from the inner recesses of her mind there was dredged a memory, a memory so carefully, so deliberately and so deeply buried it had lain dormant for years.

A scene enacted two decades before leapt out of her mind, was projected onto the mirror with such blinding accuracy and clarity that Francesca was propelled instantly backwards into the past. And she saw herself from a long distance, as she had once been.

A night sky. Smooth. Still. Flashed with brilliant stars. A perfect Mediterranean sky. A balmy breeze. The brinish smell of the sea mingling with the scent of honeysuckle and night-blooming jasmine and eucalyptus. Candlelight glowing. Francesca sitting on the long white marble terrace of the Villa Zamir, on the promontory at Cap Martin. Francesca weeping. Katharine hovering solicitously. Katharine apologizing over and over again for being clumsy. Katharine doing nothing to help, but hovering, always hovering. Francesca barely listening. Francesca gazing in stupefied horror at the wine Katharine had spilled on her. Watching the stain seep down from the bodice on to the skirt, a red and violent stain, like fresh blood on the peach organza evening frock. A floating, romantic, dreamlike frock her father could scarcely afford. Ruined before the dance had even begun. Kim, handsome in his dinner jacket, hurrying to her with salt and soda water. And Nick Latimer arriving. Nicky mopping up Francesca's tears, trying to be jocular and making a bad joke about tragic heroines. Her father. Sweet, consoling, concerned, but quite helpless. Doris Asternan. Her face cold with anger. Doris camouflaging the damage with a trailing spray of honeysuckle entwined with roses quickly picked from the garden. The flowers. Hardly covering the stain and wilting too soon. Francesca's tears. Dripping on to the dress to mingle with the stain. Francesca weeping inconsolably because she had wanted to be beautiful for Victor. Francesca waiting. Waiting for Vic, who did not come. Francesca's heart breaking . . .

Francesca snapped her eyes tightly shut to block out the scene, not wanting to remember any more about the past. The past was irrelevant, it no longer mattered to her. An instant later she opened her eyes and stepped swiftly away from the mirror, and she saw again a woman of forty-two, the woman she had become in the intervening years. Attractive, elegant and coolly poised. And infinitely wiser than she had been then.

She turned on her heel and left for Nelson's dinner party.

Sleep eluded her.

Since her return from Nelson's house several hours ago she had restlessly tossed around in the bed, unable to find repose, her eyes wide open and staring into the filtered greyness of the room. Finally, in exasperation, she sat up, turned on the light and got out of bed. Slipping into her robe, she went downstairs to the kitchen. She made herself a cup of hot milk and carried it back upstairs to the bedroom, where she sat drinking it, huddled in a chair near the fireplace, enveloped in introspection, unaware of the time or the chill in the air.

Slowly, and with some deliberation, Francesca reviewed the events of the afternoon, carefully weighing and analysing all that had happened, all that had been said. And inevitably her mind came to rest on Katharine Tempest, for she had begun to realize, during these long dawn hours, that she had over-reacted to the news of the woman's impending return to New York and request for a meeting.

She did not want anything to disrupt or threaten her orderly and contented life. The life she had so painstakingly created with Harrison and his family. A life she enjoyed, and was comfortable living, and one she was determined to protect at all cost. Nelson was correct in his assessment of her former friend. Wherever Katharine Tempest went she dragged trouble in her wake. No, Katharine could not be permitted to enter her life again.

A sigh of deep sadness broke the heavy silence in the shadow-filled room. She and Katharine had been so very close once, inseparable for years, until that ugly denouement when everything had erupted so explosively and the loving friendship had ended abruptly, and with acrimony. They had not seen each other since that day, over ten years ago, and during this time Francesca had schooled herself not to think of Katharine, and eventually, as the years passed, she had succeeded in achieving her goal. And she had forgiven Katharine long ago, forgiven her for so many things, in the wisdom of her own growing maturity. But seemingly she had not forgotten. She understood that now.

Memories began to assail her. Memories of other times, other places, other people. She endeavoured to push them aside, clearly recognizing that memories were ineluctably treacherous. Particularly memories of Katharine, for they were shrouded in a web of turbulent emotions and raw feelings, and they evoked pain, the pain of Katharine's own treachery and betrayal of her. But Katharine had not always been like that. Not in the beginning. She had been different then. They had all been different at that point in time.

At that point in time. Francesca repeated the phrase to herself, and she thought: There is no past, no present, no future. Time is not circumscribed. Albert Einstein proved that time is a dimension. The fourth dimension. Therefore all time exists *now.*

The decades dissolved. It was a gradual dissolve, like a film running in slow motion before her eyes, and everyone was in perfect focus, and brilliantly captured on the film of her memory – the way they were then. And the year 1956 was as real to Francesca as it had been twenty-three years ago.

It was now.

Act One
Downstage Right
1956

'The most decisive actions of our life ...
are most often unconsidered actions.'

André Gide

CHAPTER FIVE

'Don't be an old stick-in-the-mud,' Kim said with a genial smile, lolling nonchalantly against the door frame. 'You just said you don't have a date this evening. Come on, Francesca, be a good sport.'

Francesca was seated behind the large cluttered desk in the upstairs study of their father's London house. She put down the pen she was holding and leaned back in the chair, regarding her brother with affection. She was amazed to discover that for once in her life she did not feel like being a good sport, not even for her adored Kim. She had been working all day, and now, in the late afternoon, she was exhausted yet determined to finish what she had set out to do that morning. Her brother's unexpected arrival had surprised her, so absorbed was she in her papers.

Conscious he was waiting for a response, she shook her head, and said in a weary voice that was also surprisingly firm, 'I'd like to help you, Kim, but I simply can't. I have to finish this research. I really do. I'm sorry.'

'You and your mouldy old books!' Kim exclaimed in goodnatured exasperation. 'Whenever I see you these days you're peering into them as if your life depended on it. Who cares about Chinese Gordon anyway? If the old geezer hadn't been dead for hundreds of years I'd say you had some sort of girlish crush on him. I don't see the point – '

'Gordon hasn't been dead for hundreds of years,' Francesca interrupted mildly enough, but her eyes were intense. 'Seventy-one years, to be precise,' she went on, 'and anyway, you know very well I am going to write a biography about him one day.'

'You're wasting your time, my girl. Nobody will buy it.'

'Yes they will!' Francesca retorted fiercely, her weariness instantly dissipating. 'There are a lot of people who are interested in British history, and a great soldier and hero like Chinese Gordon. I intend to take a fresh approach, to delve into the psychology of the man. It will be a modern study, and I'm going to write it in such a way it will make very popular reading. Father agrees with me. He thinks it will work, and that it might even be commercial. So there, Kim Cunningham! *Shoo*! Go away and leave me in peace.'

Kim was taken aback by her vehemence, and he realized, for the first time, that she was in earnest about the book, a project she had talked about for some months. Inwardly he reproached himself for his remark, which had been made in an off-hand manner, and thoughtlessly so. He had not only given offence, but hurt her, and that was the last thing he wanted to do. Apart from being his sister and very dear to him, Francesca was his best friend and confidante, and they had always been inseparable.

He tried to be conciliatory. 'I'm sorry, Francesca darling. I didn't mean to be dismissive. Father is undoubtedly right.' He flashed her a wide smile tinged with self-mockery. 'What do I know about books? I'm not blessed with intellectual capacities, like you and the old man. You've got all the brains in the family, my love. What's a dull farmer like me to do?' He grimaced and went on, 'My only excuse is that I didn't quite understand how serious you were about the book. I will be supportive, I promise. Truce?'

Francesca managed a watery smile and a nod, not trusting herself to speak. She buried her head in the papers, so that he would not see her incipient tears.

Aware of her discomfiture, Kim wisely remained silent. He positioned himself in front of the fireplace, warming his back, his long legs spread wide apart, his hands thrust into the pockets of his tweed jacket. Made of fine cloth and tailored in the best Savile Row tradition, this had long since seen better days, was worn and out of shape. But Kim had such an air of distinction about him, wore the jacket with such panache, its shabbiness was hardly noticeable.

Adrian Charles 'Kim' Cunningham, the 14th Viscount Ingleton, who would one day become the 12th Earl of Langley, was not handsome in the given sense of that word; however, a number of unusual qualities combined to lift him out of the ordinary. He was a pleasant-looking young man, with a fair complexion, light brown hair that was soft and straight, and a sensitively-wrought face whose chief characteristic was one of gentleness. His personality was most apparent in his generous mouth, always touched with laughter, and in his liquid grey eyes, which were, for the most part, illuminated by kindness, humour and goodwill. They rarely flashed with anger or temperament, for Kim was easy-going and placid by nature.

He had inherited the tall, lean build of his ancestors, but his slender-looking frame was deceptive. Blessed with a grace and elegance unusual in a man, he carried himself with extraordinary self-assurance that bespoke his breeding and his centuries-old lineage. All in all, at twenty-one, he was so prepossessing, so sincere, and so good natured, everyone, and most especially young women, found him to be an engaging friend and companion.

As he stood reflectively gazing at the tips of his shoes, waiting for his sister to compose herself, Kim was thinking of one young woman in particular, and wondering how to persuade Francesca to agree to his plans for that evening. After a moment he said, 'Well, if you feel you must work, I suppose you must. But it is Saturday night, and to tell you the truth, I thought it would be fun for you to meet this girl. You're always telling me that you love cooking and find it relaxing.'

Francesca, who had been making a show of sifting through the papers scattered across the desk, lifted her head quickly. 'You mean you want me to cook dinner, as well as act as your hostess for drinks! Gosh, you do have a cheek,' she spluttered, her eyes widening. 'And what would I cook? We're on a tight budget this month! I only bought enough groceries for the two of us for the weekend, and I skimped at that. I thought you had accepted Aunt Mabel's invitation to go to Gloucestershire tonight, and were not coming back until after lunch tomorrow. I'd counted on it, in fact. That's why I was so surprised when you strolled in like the lord of the manor and made your announcement.'

Kim groaned and rolled his eyes upwards, 'I don't know who gave you that idea. About Gloucestershire, I mean. Not I. Dotty old Aunt Mabel *indeed*. No, I am staying in town, my sweet.' He smiled at her affectionately. 'Come on, please say yes. It's ages since you've had any fun. It'll do you good, Frankie.'

'Don't think you can worm your way into my good graces by calling me Frankie. I don't like that nickname anymore.'

'That's a sudden change of heart. You used to insist I call you Frankie.'

'When I was small and wanted to be a boy like you. Because I worshipped you, misguided child that I was. It may interest you to know I don't worship you in the way I used to, and certainly *not* today.'

Kim grinned. 'Oh yes you do. Just as I adore you and always will.' He strode over to the desk and perched on the edge, looking down at her, tenderness flooding his eyes. It occurred to him that Francesca appeared more delicate than ever, and her classical English face, with its finely-drawn features, seemed smaller and slightly pinched and pale. After studying her for a few seconds he decided it was the bulky navy blue fisherman's sweater she was wearing and her hair style that gave her such an air of attenuated fragility. She had swept her blonde tresses on top of her head and fastened them with antique tortoiseshell combs into a loose kind of pompadour, and this seemed far too heavy for her slender column of a neck. It was an old-fashioned hairdo, harking back to the Victorian era, yet it was oddly becoming on her. A strand of hair had fallen over one of her eyes and he leaned forward and gently tucked it into place.

'There, that's better,' he said and kissed her cheek. 'You've also got ink on your neck.' He tweaked her ear fondly, and continued, 'I wonder, how can I bribe you, Frankie?'

'You can't,' she answered, adopting a brisk tone. She picked up her pen purposefully. 'I must finish this research today, Kim, and I am absolutely not going to do any cooking. So stop being a perfect pest.'

Kim decided he must persevere. 'Look here, Francesca, if this girl weren't so special I wouldn't ask you to do this, honestly I wouldn't. But she is a super girl. You will love her. So will Father – I hope. I'm going to take her to Yorkshire soon. That's one of the reasons I wanted you to meet her first. Tonight.'

Francesca was startled by this statement and her face changed. She gazed at her brother with interest, her eyes searching his. This was the first time he had ever suggested taking one of his innumerable girl friends to Langley. Such an exception to his own rigid rule changed everything. 'Are you trying to tell me you're serious about her?' she asked, trying to keep the surprise out of her voice.

'I'm not sure that's the right word,' Kim said, returning her unblinking stare. He rubbed his chin, reflecting, and finished, 'But I am keen. Very keen, in fact, and I think I could get serious about her, yes.'

In these few seconds Kim had succeeded in gaining his sister's undivided attention. Being overly-protective of him, she was about to pronounce him too young to be serious about any girl, and quickly changed her mind. It might alienate him, or even worse, push him farther into the girl's arms. Kim had a tendency to be impetuous at times, and she did not want to unwittingly trigger a situation that might easily get out of hand. Instead she asked, 'Who is she? What's her name?'

A beatific smile settled on Kim's bright young face, and he coloured slightly. 'Katharine. Katharine Tempest,' he said, and waited expectantly. When he observed Francesca's blank expression, he added with a knowing look, '*The Katharine Tempest.*'

Francesca frowned. 'Sorry, Kim, but I'm afraid I don't know her. You sound as if I should. Oh, wait a tick, is she related to the Tempest Stewarts? I used to go to dancing class with Lady Anne. You know, the school in Eaton Square with the crazy Russian ballet mistress.'

Kim threw back his head and laughed. 'No, she isn't related to Lord Londonderry. Far from it. I don't suppose I should expect you to know who she is. You've always got your face pushed into a history book, living in the past. God, what am I going to do with you, Frankie?' he asked. 'Katharine Tempest is a fabulous young actress who is literally wowing them every night in one of the biggest hits in the West End. She is young, beautiful, talented, charming, intelligent, warm and witty. In short, she is absolutely – '

'Too good to be true, by the sound of it,' Francesca suggested dryly, smothering a small amused smile.

Kim grinned at her in a sheepish fashion. 'I know I sound like a babbling idiot, but if only you would meet her, you'd find out for yourself. She really is very special.'

'I believe you. But I'm not so sure Father will welcome her with open arms. An *actress*. Gosh! You know how stuffy he can be at times – ' Her voice trailed off and she thought for a minute. 'Perhaps you *had* better pass her off as a Tempest Stewart, at least in the beginning, until the ice is broken. But let's get back to the point. If she is starring in a play, how can you invite her to dinner?'

'She'll come after the play.'

'That means we'll be having dinner at eleven o'clock, or even later! Oh, Kim, you are incorrigible.'

'When we go to the theatre with the old man we always dine afterwards. There's nothing strange about that.'

Francesca groaned. 'Look, I'm very tired. I don't think I could make the effort tonight. But I'll compromise, since I *would* like to meet her. I'll make something light for you, and have a drink with you when she arrives. Then I'll disappear to my room. You would enjoy that much better anyway. You can have a lovely romantic supper *à deux*.'

'It'll be a romantic supper *à trois*, I'm afraid,' Kim responded glumly. 'She's bringing some chap with her. That's another reason I wanted you to join us, to make it a foursome.'

'How can I rustle up dinner for four! I've only got enough for one. *Me*,' Francesca wailed. 'And anyway, who's the spare bod she wants to drag along? Who am *I* supposed to charm in the early hours of the morning? And why does she have to bring him at all?'

'Because he doesn't know many people in London, and she's kind of taken him under her wing.' Kim gave her a careful look, and then smiled. 'And when I tell you who he is, I don't want you to faint. Promise,' he demanded, his eyes twinkling.

'Oh, don't be so ridiculous.' Francesca airily dismissed such a preposterous idea. 'And why should I faint, for heaven's sake?'

'Most women would. The spare bod, as you call him, is Victor Mason. And I know that even *you* know who *he* is.'

Francesca was not unduly impressed. 'Of course I do. The whole world knows him, or rather, of him. I must say, this is a bit of a departure for you, isn't it, an actress and a film star from – ' Francesca stopped abruptly and stared at Kim as another thought occurred to her. 'You haven't invited them already, have you?'

'I'm afraid I have.'

'Oh Kim!' She considered the meagre supplies in the kitchen with dismay.

Kim put his arms around her and hugged her to him. 'Hey, come on, you silly goose. Don't get upset. It's not that important. I just didn't stop to think, that's all. I asked Katharine to dinner tonight because I wanted you to meet her very badly. She suggested inviting Victor, not only because he's at a loose end, but to even it out. We both thought you'd like to meet him, and it seemed like a good idea at the time. Now I can see it was a mistake. We'll do it another evening. Look, I'll put them off.'

'You can't do that. It's so rude, and especially at this hour.' Francesca pulled away gently, and sat back in her chair. 'I'm sorry to sound like a spoil-sport, Kim dear. I know I must get on your nerves, always nagging about money. But everything is so, so . . . well, such a struggle at times. Daddy doesn't have a clue about anything except Langley. The amount he allocates for running this house is next to nothing. I usually have to use the bit of money from Mummy's Trust for food and some of the bills, and that's still not – '

'You're not supposed to do that!' Kim interjected fiercely. 'The Trust money is for your personal use. Pin money. And I realize it's just a pittance. Does the old man know what you're doing?'

'No, and you mustn't tell him! He has enough to worry about, what with running the estate and everything. And if he knew he might just close up the house here for economical reasons. Then I'd have to move to Langley with you and Daddy. It's not that I don't love you both,' she went on rapidly, 'I do. But I don't want to be buried in the wilds of Yorkshire all year round, and besides, I have to be near the British Museum for my research. Anyway, I don't mind using my money, really I don't. I only mentioned it to you so you would understand the situation.'

'I do understand. And as far as the dinner is concerned, well, let's forget it.' He shrugged. 'Maybe I'll take them to a restaurant. We could go to Le Matelot in Elizabeth Street.'

'Even that would be far too expensive. Let me think a minute.'

Kim walked over to the sofa and flopped down on it, all the gaiety washed off his face. 'So much for the bloody British aristocracy,' he said disconsolately. 'At least the impoverished side of it.' He ran his hand through his hair, and muttered, 'It's a hell of a thing when a chap can't afford to take a couple of chums to dinner.' And then his face instantly brightened. 'Perhaps with a bit of luck Victor Mason will pick up the bill.'

'Kim, that's positively *awful*. We may be impoverished, but we're not spongers. Remember, you invited them.'

'I have the money I was saving for a pair of new riding boots.' He smiled ruefully. 'I could blow that.'

'I won't let you! You know, I could make a rather splendid breakfast. After all, we are going to be eating late. I could prepare *omlettes fines herbes*, or maybe a kedgeree. How does that sound to you? Do you fancy either?'

43

Kim pulled a face and Francesca nodded in agreement. 'You're right. That's out then.'

'Do you think Father would object if I nipped out to Fortnum's and charged a few goodies to his account?'

'*He* might not, but I certainly would, especially when the bill came in.' Quite unexpectedly, a broad smile spread across her face and she straightened up in the chair. 'I've just thought of something!' She jumped up, rushed out of the room and plunged down the staircase at breakneck speed.

'What is it? You sound as if you've had a brainstorm,' Kim called, racing after her. Francesca halted at the bottom of the stairs and turned to look up at him. 'I have indeed. Follow me, Macbeth, down into the dark, dark dungeons. And thank God for Doris!' She beckoned histrionically and disappeared. Still mystified, Kim followed her into the cellars underneath the house. He found her in the large pantry next to the wine cellar, rummaging through a wicker hamper.

'What have you got there, Frankie?'

Francesca went on rummaging. 'A Fortnum and Mason hamper. You just jogged my memory about it. Doris sent it to us at Christmas. Don't you remember? There are still a few things left. Father gave it to me to bring back here after the holidays. I also raided the larder at Langley and put in some of Melly's bottled fruits. I'd forgotten all about it.'

'Good old Doris. *She* never does anything by halves.'

'Look what I've found,' Francesca cried excitedly, her eyes shining. '*Caviar*! Only a small pot, I'm afraid, but it is Beluga. There's a tin of *pâté de foie gras Strasbourg*, a crock of aged Stilton cheese with port, and three tins of turtle soup.' She examined the label. 'I say, quite a posh brand too. It's got sherry in it.' Francesca flipped down the lid of the hamper and patted it possessively. 'I'm taking this up to the kitchen. It's certainly part of the dinner. Why don't you poke around in the wine cellar. I'm sure there are some bottles of champagne left from your twenty-first, and it would be nice to have it with the caviar.'

A few minutes later Kim joined her in the kitchen, a smile of triumph on his face, a bottle of champagne in each hand. 'You were right. Moët & Chandon.' He displayed them gleefully and then sat down at the table and eyed the items Francesca had removed from the hamper and arranged in front of her. 'Is there going to be enough, do you think?' he asked doubtfully.

'It's a beginning at least. I thought we could have the champagne before supper. I can stretch the caviar with chopped eggs and chopped onions, and lots of Melba toast, and serve the pâté as well. The turtle soup will do very well for starters, and I can make a green salad to go with the Stilton. We can finish with the bottled fruit and cream.'

'And what do we eat after the soup and before the pudding?' Kim teased. 'You've forgotten the main course. Or is that all you intend to serve?'

'No, of course it isn't, silly,' Francesca said with a smile. 'I have some minced beef in the refrigerator. I was going to make a cottage pie with it, for my supper tonight. If I buy some more beef I can make a larger pie for all of us. Do you think Victor Mason ever had so lowly a dish as cottage pie?' She grinned at her brother. 'I suppose there's always a first time for everything. He'll probably think it quaint and very English.'

'I'm sure Victor Mason will be more impressed with the cottage pie than with the caviar. Isn't that what movie stars eat for breakfast every day? Tell you what though, I'll bring up some really good wine later. The Ninth might have been a spendthrift, but he did leave us one of the best cellars in London. What about a Mouton Rothschild?'

'That will be lovely, Kim. In the meantime, would you mind going to Shepherd Market for me, before the shops close?'

'Of course not, and I'll pay for whatever we need. I have a few quid.' Observing her expression he laughed and shook his head. 'No, it's not from the riding boots money.'

Francesca busied herself with a shopping list and Kim's gaze returned to the items spread on the table, his eyes reflective. He lit a cigarette and smoked in silence for a few minutes. Suddenly he said, 'Has Father mentioned Doris to you lately?'

'No, why do you ask?' Francesca spoke without looking up.

'She's been noticeably absent from Langley of late. I wondered if they'd had a row, or even a parting of the ways.'

His sister raised her head, her brows drawing together. 'Not that I know of; in fact, I spoke to Doris only last week. She's gone to the South of France.'

'Good God, in February. Whatever for?'

'To look for a villa for the summer. She wants to rent a large one, she told me, so that we can all go and stay with her. So I'm quite certain everything is perfectly all right.'

'I wonder if Father will marry her?'

Francesca did not respond immediately. She herself had ruminated on this possibility from time to time, for it seemed to her that Doris Asternan had become a permanent fixture in her father's life. Her mind turned to Doris, the nice American widow whom she and Kim liked so much. She wondered if Doris did have expectations, and then smiled to herself at such an old-fashioned word. It was more than likely. Her father was attractive, charming and good natured like Kim, and the title was tempting to most women, but particularly so to an American. He was quite a catch really. And what of her father? He had grieved for their mother for a number of years after her death, and then quite suddenly there had been a steady flow of women, whom he seemed to quickly lose interest in – until Doris. She wondered.

'What do you think, Frankie? Will the old man make a trip down the aisle with Doris?' Kim pressed.

Francesca shrugged. 'I honestly don't know. Daddy hasn't made me his confidante, and neither has Doris, for that matter.'

'She's certainly preferable to some of the others he's had in tow. And at least Doris has pots and pots of money. Millions of lovely dollars.'

Francesca could not help laughing. 'As if that would influence *our* father. He's too romantic by far. He's looking for true love.'

'Christ! At his age! Well, I suppose there's life in the old dog yet.'

'Kim, he's only forty-seven. You make him sound ancient.' She thrust the shopping list at him. 'Come on, you lazy old thing. Do the shopping for me, and leave Doris to Daddy. I have better fish to fry than to sit here gossiping with you.'

She glanced at the battered alarm clock on top of the refrigerator. 'It's almost five. The butcher will be closed if you don't hurry. And I'd better prepare the dining room table and start on some chores. Now that you've so cleverly managed to manoeuvre me into giving this dinner, I might as well push the boat out for you.'

Kim stuffed the shopping list into his pocket and stood up. 'Thanks for going to all this trouble for me, Frankie. I really appreciate it.' He headed for the door. When he reached it he turned around and grinned at her. 'And you know, with Doris's goodies and a few bottles of the Ninth's vintage wine, we're not going to seem so poverty-stricken after all.'

The house in Chesterfield Street, where Francesca lived most of the year, had been the London residence of the Earls of Langley for some sixty-six years, having been purchased in 1890 by Francesca's great-grandfather, the Ninth Earl. It was a typical Mayfair town house, situated in a row of almost identical houses, tall and narrow with a relatively simple architectural façade. The exterior appearance belied the interior: graceful charming rooms, considerably larger and more generously proportioned than the narrowness of the house suggested. In particular, the reception rooms on the main floor were singularly elegant, with high ceilings, wide windows and handsome Adam fireplaces of carved oak or marble. The rooms on the second, third and fourth floors grew increasingly smaller the closer they came to the roof, but even these had a special charm of their own.

The spacious drawing room, a handsome book-lined library, and the dining room opened off a small square entrance hall, where a lovely old staircase with a carved oak banister rose to the upper floors. Beyond the dining room there was a large family kitchen, somewhat old-fashioned in design, but relatively efficient since Francesca had partially modernized it with a new Aga stove and a refrigerator. 'They look a bit incongruous. Out of place, wouldn't you say,' her father had ventured cautiously on first viewing the shiny new objects. Francesca had glanced proudly at her innovations, raised an eyebrow and pronounced, 'But they *work*, Daddy.' Recognizing that her tone discouraged further discussion, the Earl had murmured, 'Quite so, my dear,' and retreated to the safety of the library. He had fled, the next day, to Yorkshire. The additions to the kitchen were only part of the refurbishing of the house, which Francesca had plunged into, flouting her father's wishes. He was, for the most part, opposed to her plans, considering them far too elaborate, and far too costly.

For all of his adult life, Francesca's father, David Cunningham, the Eleventh Earl of Langley, had been striving to make ends meet. At an early age he had wisely come to the conclusion that he could not recoup the considerable fortune his grandfather, the Ninth Earl, had frittered away on mistresses and merrymaking and the high-stepping living that was obligatory for that charmed circle who were members of the Marlborough House Set of the Edwardian era. Keeping pace with, and in step with, Edward Albert, the Prince of Wales, had brought ruin to more than one noble house of England. If the Ninth Earl had not exactly ruined the Langley family with his extravagant living, he had certainly made considerable inroads into their immense wealth, before he had died at the age of fifty-five in the delectable arms of his twenty-year-old mistress, literally in *flagrante delicto*.

The task of replenishing the almost-denuded family coffers was one that David's father, the Tenth Earl, had undertaken with enormous relish and only a fair amount of success. Whilst he had not decreased their worth, neither had he made them newly prosperous. He had merely plugged the dam, so to speak. And then, towards the end of his life, he had plunged into a financial venture, one highly speculative in nature, which he was convinced would enable him to restore the fortune his own father had so carelessly squandered. The failure of the scheme brought him up short and doused his enthusiasm for any type of further business activity that might endanger his family's future. He had enjoined David, the present Earl, not to follow his example. 'Preserve what we have,' he had implored. His son, who had never harboured any desire to indulge in the tricky game of financial wheeling and dealing, considering it too risky by far, had willingly acquiesced at once, since he was simply adhering to the decision of his youth.

Death duties, the running of the vast estate in Yorkshire, the education of Kim and Francesca, and maintaining the style of living his position dictated continually stretched his resources to the limit. However, although David Cunningham was cash poor, he was land rich. The Yorkshire estate covered hundreds of miles of fertile farming acres, forests and parklands. In more than one sense the situation was ludicrous, but even if he had wanted to, David could not have sold off any of the land. Or, for that matter, any of the family's other properties, comprised of Langley Castle, the Home Farm, the tenant farms, or the valuable antique furniture, Georgian silver and paintings, many by some of the great English masters. Although the Langley Collection included bucolic landscapes by Constable and Turner, that unsurpassed water-colourist being also represented by several of his marine paintings, the collection was most especially renowned for its superb examples of the work of such inimitable and celebrated portraitists as Sir Peter Lely, Sir Joshua Reynolds, Thomas Gainsborough and George Romney. In the main these were full length, life-size depictions of the Langley ancestors, presented with grace and charm in all of their elegance and finery. However, the Langley Collection, other properties and possessions and the land were either entailed or in trust. Furthermore, the Earl's own natural instincts and inclinations would have prevented him from plundering the estate; also, he took his promise to his father seriously and he wanted to keep the holdings intact for new generations of Cunninghams.

In consequence, from an early age, Kim and Francesca had been brought up to understand and accept their responsibilities to their great family name and their ancient heritage. Scrimping, saving and making do whenever possible had become a way of life; thrift was the byword of their youth; and keeping up the proper front on virtually next to nothing was so ingrained in them it was now second nature.

The maintenance of the Yorkshire estate, the castle, the Home Farm and the tenant farms were the first priorities, took precedence before anything else. There was rarely, if ever, any spare money available for luxuries, and one luxury the Earl deemed totally unnecessary was the redecoration of the Chesterfield Street house, despite Francesca's arguments to the contrary: arguments which had increased as she had become ever more conscious of such things. And so the house had deteriorated into shabbiness over the years, and by 1955 it was in such a sorry state it was almost beyond redemption.

Early in January of that year, three months before Kim's twenty-first birthday, their father had announced he planned to give a birthday party for Kim at Langley Castle in March. He also explained that he fully intended to do more entertaining in London than was his usual habit, during this important and significant year when his only son and heir came of age. In essence, the Earl made it perfectly clear, he was determined to launch Kim into London society in the manner only fitting for a man of his standing. Francesca had once again viewed the London house with concern, worried about its dilapidated condition and disreputable appearance, in view of her father's plans for Kim. She had immediately launched another highly voluble campaign for its refurbishing, but to her surprise her father had been coldly adamant in his refusal to accede to her wishes. She had told him angrily, and in no uncertain terms, that he was not only being cavalier in his attitude, but downright unfair to Kim. He had shrugged, uninterested in her opinion and unmoved by her words, and he told her, with unusual firmness, never to broach the subject again. It was then she decided to take the matter into her own hands, and risk the consequences of her father's disapproval.

Francesca owned a diamond ring, an heirloom passed down through generations of women on the maternal side of the family. She had inherited it upon her mother's death, and for years it had reposed in their bank vault in London, along with other pieces of jewellery and a seventeenth-century diamond tiara which had been worn by successive Countesses of Langley on State occasions in Westminster Abbey, all part of the family trust. Francesca had taken her ring to a leading dealer in antique jewellery, who had promptly offered to purchase it for a thousand pounds.

When he heard about this decisive and unprecedented action on the part of his daughter, who was then only eighteen, the Earl had been outraged. However, since the ring belonged to Francesca, and was not part of the Langley Trust, he could merely voice his objections not act upon them. Finally, Francesca's logical reasoning and persuasiveness, not inconsiderable, had brought him round, if only to a degree. Realizing she had engaged in an enterprise that threatened his authority, and knowing she had acted presumptuously, Francesca had been astute enough to ask her father's permission to use the money for the redecoration of the house, it being his property.

The Earl had given his blessing, albeit reluctantly, believing it to be a ridiculous extravagance. Later he did confess he thought her gesture was admirable and touching. Kim had been overwhelmed by her unselfishness, but, understanding her obstinate nature, he had not wasted time protesting, and by then it was already too late. He had thanked her profusely and then shown his appreciation by plunging into the transformation of the house as energetically and enthusiastically as she.

There was barely enough money to do everything required, and Francesca portioned it out in the most practical way, stretching the thousand pounds as far as she could. She had the roof and the exterior walls repaired, the interior walls replastered wherever this was necessary, and she put in new pipes and electrical wiring. The remainder of the money from the ring was used for what she termed 'my cosmetic job', and it was exactly that. The scuffed parquet floors in the dining room, the library and the drawing room were refinished and polished; the wall-to-wall carpets in the bedrooms and the upstairs study were shampooed; and the draperies and slipcovers still in good repair were dry-cleaned. Francesca threw away the worn Oriental carpet which had lain on the dining room floor since 'spendthrift Teddy's' day, and the slipcovers on the furniture in the drawing room quickly followed suit. The Aubusson carpet in this room was sent to a restorer of old tapestries and rugs, where it was hand-cleaned and painstakingly repaired. To Francesca's delight it came back looking like the lovely museum piece it was. The Hepplewhite and Sheraton furniture in the two reception rooms, family heirlooms and valuable, were also repaired and refinished to their original beauty.

To save money, Francesca and Kim undertook the painting themselves. Wearing old clothes, surrounded by ladders and buckets, and amidst peals of laughter, the two of them happily set about the task, splashing as much paint on each other as on the walls. But they succeeded in doing a relatively professional job, working down from the upper floors to the drawing and dining rooms. Francesca selected fir green for the dining room, repeating the colour of the leather upholstery on the Hepplewhite chairs, and used pristine white paint for the doors, chair rail, and mouldings to offset the dark green walls. The drawing room, which she and Kim had always thought looked barren and cold, acquired a wholly new appearance when the grubby ivory walls were washed with a dark coral paint that was almost terra cotta in tone. Her only purchases, other than the paint, were yards and yards of moss green velvet for new curtains and slipcovers in the drawing room, white damask for the dining room curtains, various pieces of coloured silk for cushions, and new shades for the lamps.

Francesca's father had a great sense of fair play, and when he at last viewed the finished results he was quick to congratulate her on the miracle she had performed, and his pride in her knew no bounds. The family heirlooms were shown to advantage for the first time in years, and he also had to admit that her improvements had given the house a new graciousness, whilst enhancing its actual value as well. The Earl conceded it was more valuable than ever before, and could readily be turned into cash, being neither entailed nor part of the trust. It struck him that Francesca had shown great foresight, and he determined to repay the thousand pounds as soon as possible. That May, on her nineteenth birthday, he presented her with the gold filigree and topaz necklace which had been made for the Sixth Countess of Langley in 1760. However, this was only on loan to her until his death, when it would pass to Kim, since it was part of the trust.

Now, as she stood in the doorway of the drawing room on this Saturday evening in February, a year later, Francesca smiled with pleasure. The room looked truly beautiful. Kim had lighted the fire an hour earlier and the logs were crackling brightly in the huge carved oak fireplace, the sparks flying merrily up the chimney. He had also drawn the curtains to shut out the depressing drizzle and dampness of the cold evening, and turned on the leaf-green Chinese jade lamps shaded in cream silk.

The atmosphere was inviting and the lovely old furniture gleamed in the refracted light. The coral-tinted walls made the perfect backdrop for the classical Hepplewhite Pembroke tables, a large Sheraton bookcase with glass doors, made of mahogany inlaid with fruitwoods, and for those bucolic English landscapes brushstroked in variegated greens and blues. These were now most effectively set off by their newly-gilded wood frames, enterprisingly touched up by Kim with a pot of gold-leaf paint. Rafts of the new moss-green velvet rippled at the three stately windows, and covered two large sofas and four armchairs, and this verdant colour added to the richness of the scheme. The green sofas were enlivened with cream, coral and blue cushions, which Francesca had made from the remnants of silk, whilst her great-grandmother's collection of Meissen and Wedgwood ornaments introduced additional fragile colour accents on the wood surfaces.

After another admiring glance, Francesca moved briskly across the Aubusson carpet, heaped more logs on the fire, plumped up the cushions, checked the cigarette boxes and then hurried back to the dining room to finish the table she had started earlier that evening. She took four white linen napkins from the Hepplewhite sideboard and placed one at each setting, put out several silver ashtrays and a silver condiment set, and added wine and water glasses, moving rapidly around the long oval table. When she stood back to regard her handiwork she suddenly wished she had some flowers for a centrepiece. But they were so expensive at this time of year and quickly died, and the two four-arm silver candelabra were certainly elegant with their tall white candles. She decided the table looked quite beautiful as it was and did not need any further embellishment.

Francesca turned to go into the kitchen just as Kim walked in, humming under his breath. He stopped, let out a long low whistle of surprise, grabbed her hand and twirled her around, continuing to whistle in a wolfish tone.

'You look positively ravishing, old thing,' he said, stepping away from her, his eyes bright with approval.

'Thank you. But are you sure I'm not a bit too dressy?' she asked anxiously.

He shook his head. 'No, you're not, and I'm certain Katharine will be dressed up.' He scrutinized her, his head on one side, an appraising expression on his face.

Francesca smiled at him tentatively and twirled around again on her elegantly shod feet. She was wearing her favourite shoes, a pair of black silk evening pumps, in the smartest new Italian style, with the thinnest, highest heels and extremely pointed toes. Doris had bought them in Rome for her as a Christmas present, and Francesca knew they were exactly right with the outfit she had chosen – a long-sleeved grey wool top with a boat neckline and a silvery-grey taffeta skirt she had sewn herself. The skirt puffed out like a bell flower over the buckram-and-tulle crinoline petticoat Melly had made for her, another Christmas gift. This type of stiff petticoat was all the rage, and Francesca loved the bouffant effect it created because it was flattering to her legs, which she considered to be too thin.

Coming to a standstill after a final twirl, Francesca peered at her brother. 'You're frowning, Kim. Is there something you don't like about my outfit after all?'

'It's fine, and you do look lovely, but you know, with your hair piled up in that pompadour thing your neck seems longer than ever. Don't you have some beads, or something?'

Her hand went to her neck. 'Not really. At least, not anything suitable. Unless I wear the antique necklace. What do you think?'

'That's a super idea. I'm sure it'll do the trick.' He looked at his watch. 'Gosh, I'd better be going for Katharine.'

They went out into the hall together, where Kim grabbed his old raincoat from the cupboard and strode to the front door. He opened it and then slammed it shut immediately. 'It's raining cats and dogs all of a sudden. I was going to walk to the theatre, but I'd better take the car. And a brolly.' He lifted an umbrella out of the stand, gave her a quick kiss, grinned and left, whistling jauntily between his teeth.

Francesca ran upstairs to her bedroom, unlocked the bottom drawer of her dressing table and took out the worn and rubbed black leather case containing her great-great-great-great-grandmother's necklace. It was fragile and she lifted it out carefully, gazing at it with admiration. The intricate web of slender gold chains was inset with topazes that gleamed with mellow colour and threw off myriads of golden prisms in the lamp-light. How beautiful it was. But to her it was so much more than a lovely piece of jewellery. It represented an unbroken line of generations of Cunninghams and her own heritage, and as always she was assailed by an almost awesome sense of history. After fastening it around her neck she glanced in the mirror. Kim had been correct. The necklace did do the trick, adding the perfect finishing touch to her outfit. She tucked a stray curl into place and hurried back to the kitchen to finish her chores.

At one moment Francesca paused in her tasks, staring out of the small window, trying to visualize Katharine Tempest without success. Knowing her brother as well as one could ever truly know another person, Francesca was convinced Kim was already deeply involved with Katharine, perhaps more than he himself comprehended. She thought of their father, and her heart sank. Although he could be vague and absentminded, and was easy-going and good-natured, he was, at all times, conscious of class, background and breeding. He had always made it absolutely clear that he expected Kim to marry a girl who was properly endowed with all of the suitable qualities required in the future 12th Countess of Langley. Although her father was not a snob *per se*, he did believe Kim should select a wife from their echelon of society, one who had a similar family background and upbringing, who understood her duties and responsibilities as keenly as Kim did. Francesca sighed. An actress hardly seemed a likely candidate for this particular real-life role, and she knew instinctively that her father would be disapproving. If Kim was indeed as serious about the girl as she felt he was, then he was exposing himself to a great deal of heartache, not to mention their father's anger. Again she wondered what Katharine Tempest was like, riddled with curiosity about her, and concerned for Kim. She found she could not even hazard a guess.

CHAPTER SIX

The curtain came down on the kind of applause every actor hopes and prays for and is ineluctably sustained and nourished by. Thunderous. Slowly, it rose again and the performers returned to the stage one by one, the bit players first, then the character actors, the second male lead, and the leading man. The clapping spiralled markedly upwards for him, but became a tumultuous crescendo that was deafening when finally Katharine Tempest swept on to join the two male stars in the centre of the stage. The entire cast linked hands and bowed and smiled and bowed again.

As the heavy gold-trimmed red velvet curtain fell and rose for a second time, Katharine stepped forward to ringing cheers, and 'Bravo! Bravo! Bravo!' reverberated throughout the proscenium. Her face was radiant, wreathed in smiles and she bowed low and blew kisses from her fingertips and mouthed, 'Thank you. Thank you.'

Against the backdrop of the giant-sized scenery, depicting ancient Greece in all its glory, she seemed such a small, frail figure as she stood alone before the audience at the edge of the stage, graciously accepting their adulation. Yet she did not feel alone or lonely but, rather, more like the favourite member of a large and adoring family. Her family. Her only family. She belonged to them, and they to her, and nothing could ever change this fact.

Katharine's heart crested with joy, and euphoria swarmed through her as she felt the waves of love washing over her from beyond the glittering footlights. And mingled with the joy was a marvellous sense of fulfilment, and the reaffirmation of her talent. And then it came, as it always did, the surge of relief that she had succeeded yet again. All of the dedication and discipline, hard work and straining for perfection was worth it just for this intoxicating and uplifting feeling. It was the ultimate reward.

She longed to stand there indefinitely, savouring the triumph of her victory, basking in the fervour of their approbation, but Katharine was conscious of her stage manners, and considerate of the rest of the cast, and she knew she had to give way, to permit the other stars of the play to take their individual bows. To receive their hard-won dues.

With a grand theatrical flourish she proffered a last handful of heartfelt kisses to the audience and bestowed a final luminous smile on them, before she turned to Terrence Ogden, her leading man, and stretched out her hand. He took it and moved closer to her, bowing first to Katharine and next to the audience, who were wildly ecstatic. Katharine half turned once more, this time to her left, and John Layton, the second male lead, came forward to complete the magnetic trio, who seemingly this night had surpassed themselves. There were four more rousing curtain calls before the red velvet finally rose and fell for the last time, and the cast slowly dispersed.

Katharine hurried off stage without exchanging a few words with her fellow actors as she usually did, anxious to return to her dressing room without delay. She felt uncomfortably hot, her costume was soaked and clinging to her clammy body, and the flowing red wig was heavier and more constricting than ever; it had begun to make her head itch to such an extent that it was an unbearable irritation.

In the last act she had perspired profusely and somewhat unnaturally for her, and she wondered dismally if she was coming down with a cold. Certainly her throat ached and felt scratchy, but she was fully aware she had overworked it, both at the matinee and this last performance. The effort to project her voice effectively into the cavernous depths of the St James's Theatre had apparently taken its toll for once. This bothered her not a little, and she resolved to increase her lessons with Sonia Modelle, London's foremost vocal coach. She would also make a point of doing her breathing exercises more regularly and diligently, since breathing correctly was the key to a good voice, as Sonia had instilled in her. For the past four years Katharine had worked extremely hard in the cultivation of voice technique. Through assiduousness and single-minded concentration she had developed tone, pitch, pace, range and rhythm to a remarkable degree, and had most effectively obliterated the American Midwest inflection so easily distinguishable in her speech patterns when she had first arrived in England. Sonia was amazed and gratified by her exceptional progress, and although the respected coach was usually scant with her praise, she had told Katharine only a few weeks before that there was now a peerless musicality to her voice, a quality few actresses ever attained. Nonetheless, Katharine recognized she must continue to work on her voice to strengthen it. Only absolute perfection would satisfy her.

Terry Ogden caught up with her in the wings. 'Hey, Puss, you're in a tearing hurry tonight, aren't you?'

Katharine paused and swung around quickly. She half smiled, half grimaced. 'I feel pretty done in, Terry. Giving two entirely different performances in one day doesn't usually disturb me at all, but for some reason I'm exhausted this evening.'

Terry nodded sympathetically. 'I know exactly what you mean. But they *were* great performances, darling,' he exlaimed. 'And you do adjust to the mood of the audience quite instinctively, and quicker and more expertly than anyone I know. That's a rare talent indeed, Puss, and especially in one so young.'

'Why thank you, kind sir,' Katharine said. 'You're also very adept yourself.' She looked up at him and smiled.

It was a smile of such genuine sweetness, and her eyes reflected such wonderment and innocence, Terry felt his heart clenching. He always experienced this feeling when she regarded him in this particular way, for the gaze held an indefinable quality unique to her. There was also a curious vulnerability about Katharine that touched him, a frailty mixed in with the tenacity he suspected lurked beneath the surface, and he often found himself wanting to shield and protect her, as one would a defenceless child.

Becoming aware of her eyes concentrated on his face, he said, 'I'm pretty agile most of the time, Puss, but I was certainly a bit off my mark tonight. Thanks for coming to my rescue. I can't believe I almost fluffed that line in the second act. And such a crucial line!'

Neither could Katharine. Terrence Ogden was one of England's greatest stage actors, comparable only to Laurence Olivier in his youth, according to the critics, who judged Terry to be an impressive and gifted performer. Matchless in declamation, he had immense depth and range, these qualities strengthened by enormous intelligence and insight. Another prince among players, he was an idol to the public, being blessed with a boyish charm and rather striking blond good looks; and his singular flair for romantic entanglements of a decidedly flamboyant nature had done nothing to diminish his professional reputation. If anything, this penchant had enhanced it to a formidable degree, endowing him with the image of the great lover. His private life aside, everyone predicted that one day he, too, would be knighted by the Queen, as Olivier had been. In essence, he was the heir apparent to the reigning king of the English-speaking theatre, and Larry himself fondly regarded him as such, was his mentor, benefactor and close friend. At the age of thirty, Terrence Ogden, the coal miner's son from Sheffield, was, as he liked to pronounce in his native North Country dialect, 'Cock of t'heap, by gum!' having relentlessly nudged aside most of his rivals, the famed Richard Burton included.

Katharine leaned against a piece of scenery and her eyes narrowed, rested on him thoughtfully as she remembered how he had unaccountably dried up on stage, and had flashed her a look that bespoke his horror and his panic. 'What did happen?' she asked at last. 'It's not like you, Terry.'

He frowned and shook his head and his irritation with himself flared, brought an irate gleam to his eyes. 'I'm damned if I know, Puss darling. It's not occurred since I was a kid in rep, and I can assure you it will never happen again. Anyway, you saved the old bacon with that swift and inspired prompt. I shall be eternally grateful. I must tell you, Katharine my love, you're one of the most unselfish actresses it's ever been my pleasure to work with. Really, I mean that.'

Katharine glowed and murmured her thanks, but nevertheless she began to edge slowly towards the fire door that led off stage. They were standing in an awkward spot, were being jostled by the other actors leaving the stage and straggling back to their dressing rooms, and by the numerous stage hands who were milling around, busily shifting scenery and joking amongst themselves. The noise, the bustle and the heat were enervating, and that peculiar fusty smell, so indigenous to every back stage, seemed suddenly malodorous and suffocating. It was a strange odour compounded of dry dust and damp, the resinous vapours emanating from the varnished sets, the grease paint, the hair spray, the mingled stale perfumes and the effluvium of the actors and the stage hands. Usually it sent a thrill tingling through Katharine's veins, as it always had since the first day she had stepped on to a stage as a child. But at this precise moment she was filled with an immense aversion to it. And then, quite unexpectedly, she started to cough.

Terry, who was now talking about one of the other actresses in the play, stopped in the middle of his sentence. He looked down at her in alarm as she spluttered and choked and covered her mouth with her hand. 'Hey, Puss, are you all right?' he asked worriedly.

Katharine was quite unable to utter a word. The coughing and the gasping for breath continued. She shook her head, motioned to the fire door and moved with swiftness out of the wings. Terry helped her down the stone steps to the corridor where the dressing rooms were located. When they reached his, which was one of the first, he flung open the door unceremoniously and called to his dresser, 'Quick, Norman, get a glass of water for Katharine, please.' The dresser ran to the basin with a glass, and Terry pressed Katharine down on to the sofa, worry and concern flooding his face. The paroxysms eventually subsided and she leaned back and gratefully took the water, sipping it slowly, breathing deeply between sips. Terry handed her a tissue to wipe her watering eyes.

Continuing to regard her with anxiety, he said, 'My God, I thought you were choking, Puss. Whatever brought that on? Are you sure you're all right now?'

'Yes, I'm fine, thank you, Terry. And I don't know what happened. Perhaps it was the dust, and my throat was very dry. The combination of the two might explain it, but it was strange.' Katharine stood up purposefully. 'I know I'll feel much better when I get out of my costume, and this rotten wig.'

He nodded, and stared hard at her, as if to satisfy himself she was completely recovered, and then said, 'What are you doing tonight? I've invited a few chums to the Buxton Club for supper. Care to join us, Puss?'

Katharine declined, choosing her words with care, not wanting to offend him. An invitation from Terry was rare, and was something in the nature of a royal command when it *was* extended. 'But it's sweet of you to include me,' she added. 'Unfortunately, I have a long-standing supper date with Kim Cunningham and his sister.'

'And Victor Mason perhaps?' The look he focused on her was full of speculation.

Although she was rather taken aback by this comment, Katharine chose not to show it. She merely nodded. 'Yes, Victor's coming along. But why do you assume he would be? I don't know him all that well.'

Terry shrugged and half turned away. 'I heard he was paying court. You know what this business is like. You can't keep anything quiet.'

Katharine's eyebrows shot up. 'There's nothing to keep quiet. We're just friends, that's all,' she said lightly. She moved nearer to the door and smiled at Terry's dresser. 'Thanks for helping the maiden in distress, love.'

'Any time, Katharine.' Norman grinned, and picked up Terry's towelling robe. 'Sorry it was only London corporation champagne, and not the genuine thing.'

Terry said, 'Well, have a good time tonight.' He sat down on the sofa, adjusted the short Grecian tunic over his knees and started to remove his sandals. His tone had been coolly dismissive and now Katharine thought he appeared to be angry for some reason, although she could not imagine why. 'Thanks. You too, Terry,' she replied in a low voice, and slipped out.

It was with a great sense of relief that Katharine entered her own dressing room and closed the door firmly behind her. She exhaled deeply and rested against the closed door for a moment. Unlike the cluttered and untidy quarters she had just left, here absolute order reigned supreme. Everything was meticulously in its given place. The costumes hung side by side on a metal clothes rack Katharine herself had purchased, considering the regulation wardrobe to be undersized. The collection of sandals was lined up neatly on the floor underneath it, the red wigs reposed on their wig stands on a small card table, and the theatrical make-up and creams and lotions, powders and a variety of other toilet articles were arranged with a military-like precision on the dressing table.

There was a paucity of clutter in the room: indeed it was sterile in appearance, being devoid of the usual theatrical mementos and memorabilia. Even the mandatory congratulatory telegrams, notes and cards from family and friends, which were always taped to a performer's mirror in fluttering profusion, were noticeably missing. Actually, Katharine had received only three telegrams on opening night, from Terry, Sonia and her agent. She had no one else to wish her luck.

The dressing room not only reflected Katharine's neat, spruce little flat in Lennox Gardens, but was yet another manifestation of her personal fastidiousness. This excessive neatness was becoming a fetish. Her drawers at the theatre, and at the flat, were laden with piles of beautiful underwear, and without exception she changed her under garments at least three times a day during her working week. One set was donned in the morning, was replaced by another for the performance, and this was discarded for a third, fresh set to wear after the theatre. On matinee days she used up four sets, much to the continued amazement of her dresser, Maggie. Other drawers, both at home and at the theatre, contained innumerable pairs of newly laundered stockings, folded and stacked in neat piles alongside clean handkerchiefs, dozens of pairs of white kid gloves of varying lengths, and a staggering selection of silk and chiffon scarves as pristine as the day they left the store. Every pair of shoes she owned boasted shoe trees; her hats were kept on the proper stands; her handbags were stuffed with tissue paper; sweaters were folded into plastic bags; and almost every garment in her wardrobe, from day dresses to evening frocks, hung in a dust-proof bag. Every time an outfit had been worn it was given to Maggie to be sponged and pressed, or was sent out to the dry cleaners.

Katharine was equally immaculate about herself, and was heavily addicted to perfumes and deodorants as if she was afraid that her own very natural and feminine body odours might possibly give offence, and she used breath sprays, mouth wash and toothpaste lavishly. Not surprisingly, she had an enormous distaste for anyone or any place that was dirty, grubby or unkempt.

The tranquillity, orderliness and coolness of the dressing room was like a balm to Katharine after the intensity of the lights and the heat of the stage, and particularly so tonight. Maggie had asked to leave an hour earlier than usual to attend a special family gathering, and Katharine had agreed at once. Maggie's absence was welcome, and she was glad to be alone to collect herself. She struggled out of the Grecian costume, laid it on the small sofa.

Seating herself at the dressing table Katharine removed the tiresome wig. As she did she experienced a lovely sense of freedom. She unpinned her own hair and shook it loose. After brushing it vigorously until it gleamed, she tied it back with a white cotton bandana, and then creamed off the heavy stage make-up until there was not the merest trace of it left. A folding screen camouflaged a wash basin in the corner of the room, and now Katharine stepped behind this, where she gave herself a thorough body sponging. She then washed her face, cleaned her teeth, gargled, dusted herself with talcum powder, sprayed on deodorant, perfumed herself with Ma Griffe scent and so finished her evening toilette, which was invariably something of a ritual with her.

Whilst she dressed Katharine contemplated the evening ahead and suddenly

56

she wished she had arranged the supper for tomorrow night instead. The two performances had vitiated her energy, and she, who was normally so full of vigour at this hour, felt ready to curl up and go to sleep. But she knew she had to pull herself together, strike a pose of sparkling gaiety and be entertaining for a few more hours. Certainly it was impossibly late to cancel the evening, and undoubtedly Kim was already patiently waiting at the stage door as arranged. And of course there was Victor, who was going directly to the house in Chesterfield Street. She sighed. Having paid punctilious attention to every detail and carefully contrived this entire situation, she was now hoist by her own petard. If only my throat weren't so sore, she said to herself, sliding the pure-silk-and-lace slip over her head. God, I hope I'm not really getting a chest cold.

This thought was so alarming it propelled her across the room to the dressing table. She pulled open a drawer and took out the bottle of cough medicine she kept there. She was sparing with the mixture because it had a high alcohol content, and on several occasions it had made her a trifle whoozy. She gulped down the medicine and grimaced.

Lowering herself into the chair, Katharine leaned forward and examined her face in the mirror. At least she looked in perfect health, and she recognized she must do everything in her power to ensure this state of well being. Under no circumstances could she permit herself to become sick. The next few weeks were going to be the most important weeks of her life. Nothing could be allowed to interfere with her plans, so diligently and painstakingly formulated. Nothing and nobody.

How hard she had strived to arrange everything to her advantage, to manipulate events, to make her dreams come true. They had to come true. *They just had to!* Her face, so tender and young, tightened with intensity and her heart raced as she envisioned her triumph if she succeeded in all that she planned. Not *if* but *when*, she chastised herself firmly. She was not even going to acknowledge the possibility of failure.

Still preoccupied with her rapidly moving thoughts, Katharine brushed out her hair, carelessly stuck two combs at each side, pulling it away from her face, and filled in her mouth with lipstick. Without even a cursory second glance at herself she rose and went to the wardrobe. She slipped on the black dress, stepped into the black suede pumps and added the turquoise silk scarf at her neck before pulling on the black wool coat. She took a pair of white gloves from the drawer, picked up the black suede handbag and glided to the door.

For a moment her hand rested on the knob. She let her body go slack, and took several deep breaths, inhaling and exhaling for a few seconds. And then drawing on all of her inner resources and every ounce of energy she could muster, she straightened up, stiffened her back and threw back her head. Consummate actress that she was, Katharine was able to summon any facial expression and mood at will, and she assumed a demeanour that was carefree and vital before stepping out into the corridor. And her step was remarkably determined as she mounted the stone stairs.

Kim, who was hovering near the stage door chatting to Charlie, the doorman, excused himself and rushed forward when he saw her approaching. 'Katharine darling, you look absolutely ravishing!' he exclaimed, his eyes lighting up. He bent down and kissed her on the cheek.

'Thank you,' Katharine said, giving him a glowing smile. She squeezed his arm affectionately and looked up at him through sparkling eyes. 'Sorry I kept you waiting.'

'Don't give it another thought,' Kim replied quickly. 'And at least it's stopped raining. It was coming down in torrents when I arrived.'

'Good night, Charlie,' Katharine called as Kim bustled her out of the door.

''Night, Miss. And 'ave a nice evening.' Charlie nodded in Kim's direction. 'And you too, yer lordship.'

'Good night, Charlie. And thanks so much for entertaining me.'

The door slammed behind them and Kim took hold of Katharine's arm, hurrying her down the narrow alley adjoining the theatre. 'Let's get to the car before it starts pouring again.'

'Tell me, Kim, how was old Charlie managing to entertain you?'

Kim chuckled. 'He was regaling me with marvellous stories about the "stage-door Johnnies" he has known in his time. He was frightfully funny, and even a bit risqué.'

'Oh, and does he think you're one?' Katharine asked. 'Are you his idea of a modern "stage-door Johnny"?'

'Most probably!' He glanced down at her. 'I must say, old Charlie is very devoted to you, Katharine.' He hesitated before adding. 'And so is Terrence Ogden. He stopped to exchange a few words with me when he was leaving, and he positively raved about you. He also seemed a bit curious about this evening and our plans. He said he had wanted us to join him at the Buxton, that he had invited us.'

Katharine experienced a small jab of astonishment, and thought: invited *us* indeed. She said slowly, 'Yes, he's having a few chums to supper.'

'Well, you do agree, don't you?'

'Agree about what, Kim?'

'That Terry is devoted to you.' Kim coughed behind his hand, and his voice was gruff as he ventured, 'Actually, I think he has a crush on you.'

Laughter bubbled up in Katharine at the absurdity of this idea, and she was unable to suppress it. She looked up at Kim, her eyes crinkling with merriment. In the faint light from the street lamp she noticed the look of gloomy consternation on his face, and knew she must reassure him instantly.

'Of course he doesn't! He was only raving about me tonight because I helped him out in the second act. He almost blew his lines. And as for the invitation, well, he was just trying to be sociable, that's all.' Katharine was not sure she believed her own words. Perhaps Kim was correct in his assumption. If so it would explain Terry's churlish attitude after she had refused the invitation, and his comment about Victor also. But she had no intention of confirming Kim's suspicions. Rather, she had to allay them, and immediately. 'Anyway, Terry is in love with Alexa Garrett. They are having a wild and highly-publicized romance, don't you know?'

'I see,' Kim said, sounding less than convinced, even though he knew she was being truthful. He had seen items about Terry and Alexa in the newspapers. On the other hand, Terry had spoken very possessively about Katharine, and in a manner which disturbed Kim. 'Why does he always call you Puss?' Kim asked, striving for an off-handed tone without much success. 'It seems awfully familiar to me.'

This comment momentarily floored Katharine, and she was about to point out that the theatre, by its very nature, bred familiarity, but changed her mind. She was aware of Kim's tenseness, and sensing the question sprang from a spark of jealousy rather than any oblique criticism of her, she explained, 'Because when I was a student at RADA, Terry saw me play Cleopatra in *Caesar and Cleopatra*. He thought I was decidedly feline, and has called me Puss ever since.'

'Oh,' Kim murmured, at a loss for words. He looked at her through the corner of his eye and said, 'I didn't know you had been friends with Terry for *that* long. I thought you met him for the first time when you went into the play.'

'I'm not sure what you mean by *that* long, Kim. I've only been out of the Royal Academy a couple of years. Anybody would think I'm a decrepit old woman, the way you talk,' she laughed.

They had arrived at the car. Kim released her arm and went to unlock it. He returned and helped her in, then slid into his seat, and he was oddly silent as he drove up the Haymarket and into Piccadilly, heading in the direction of Mayfair. After a while Katharine touched his arm lightly and there was a soft expression on her face. 'Terry's not interested in me, at least not romantically, Kim. Honestly.'

'If you say so,' Kim replied grudgingly. It was not Katharine's fault that Ogden had behaved like an ass earlier, and here he was being surly with her.

The last thing Katharine wanted was for Kim to be in a jealous frame of mind this evening because of its extreme importance to her. She needed his goodwill; furthermore she did not want him to be prickly or difficult with Victor present. She said carefully, 'Even if he were attracted to me in that way, it wouldn't matter to me. For the simple reason that I'm not interested in Terrence Ogden. Not the least little bit.' She laughed disdainfully. 'I know too much about actors and their monumental egos to get entangled with them, my love. Besides, you know I'm not fickle. How could I possibly care for Terry when I'm so involved with you.'

Kim visibly relaxed, and his wide smile virtually illuminated the little car. 'I'm glad to hear that, Katharine darling,' was about all he could manage at this moment. Kim knew that he had been leading Katharine along until she made some sort of verbal commitment to him. This was the strongest statement he had heard in the few months he had known her, but for the time being it sufficed. Within seconds his warm, easygoing manner was completely restored, and he eventually launched into a long story about the planting of new trees at Langley. Katharine settled back to listen, although this was only with half an ear.

She was engrossed in her own thoughts. Victor Mason was most prominent in them. She wondered if he had been to the play tonight, but more importantly, whether he had kept his promise to her. Quite unexpectedly, Katharine's heart missed a beat and she caught her breath. For the first time she was struck by the precarious nature of her immediate plans. They hinged on one man – Victor Mason. If Victor let her down then she had wasted weeks of precious time, and everything would have been in vain. My God, if she had misjudged him the setback would be enormous. She clasped her handbag more tightly, and admitted, with a sinking feeling, that despite her meticulous planning, she had not allowed for one vital contingency: the possibility that Victor Mason might change his mind.

Katharine was a peculiar amalgam of *naïveté* and sophistication. Whilst she was inexperienced in some aspects of life, she nonetheless had an innate shrewdness and was perceptive about people, often displaying amazing insight. Her understanding of human nature was astonishing in one so young, and she rarely made mistakes in her judgment. She took solace in this now, deciding she had no alternative but to trust her instincts. They confirmed her original assessment of Victor as being wholly correct. She relaxed her grip on the handbag, absolutely convinced he had kept the promise he had made to her several weeks ago. Perhaps not out of friendship, or generosity of spirit towards her, but for one other very simple reason, and it was the most compelling reason of all. Self-interest. Victor Mason needed her, and she had astutely recognized this the first time she had met him.

Cynical as this thought was, it did happen to be the truth, and recalling that Katharine cheered up. Also, to her relief, she discovered she was feeling much better physically. The exhaustion which had been so debilitating at the end of the evening performance had miraculously disappeared. The quick walk from the theatre to the car had been invigorating, and the fresh air, damp though it was, had filled her lungs with oxygen.

'Anyway, those trees do make all the difference at the far end of the Long Pasture, and Father is really pleased I thought of starting the small copse. It's going to be invaluable in years to come,' Kim was saying.

'That's wonderful. I'm glad it worked out so well,'

Katharine answered automatically. Kim was given to waxing eloquent about the land, and even though she had heard it all before, more or less, she always endeavoured to show real interest. She had come to understand, very early in their relationship, that Kim's love of the land reached deep into his soul. He was a dedicated farmer, and would be for the rest of his life. Langley, and all it encompassed, *was* his life.

'Well, here we are,' Kim announced briskly, bringing the car to a standstill in Chesterfield Street.

Katharine said, 'You know, you haven't told me much about your sister, except that she's pretty, Kim. Don't you think – '

'And I haven't told her much about you either,' Kim interrupted laughingly. 'It's better that way. Neither of you has any preconceived ideas about the other.'

'But she must know I'm an actress.'

'She does.'

'Does she work? Does she do anything special?' Although Katharine was neither nervous nor apprehensive about meeting Kim's sister, she did harbour a few reservations, even doubts, about the chances of their becoming close friends. Lady Francesca Cunningham, titled in her own right as the daughter of an earl, might easily be one of those cold, snobbish debutantes so typical of the British aristocracy. The fact that Kim was the exception to the rule in this class-conscious society did not guarantee that his sister was cut from the same cloth. And if this was the case they would have little in common, and there would be no real basis upon which to build a friendship. Of course it wasn't absolutely necessary for them to become bosom chums, Katharine acknowledged. As long as there was a cordiality between them everything would work out, and certainly it would make the situation much easier to control.

'From your silence, I gather she's a lady of leisure,' Katharine went on lightly. Her fingers curled around the door handle and she made to alight.

Kim reached out and restrained her gently. 'She doesn't go to work but she does work hard,' he explained. 'She's a writer. At the moment she's doing research for an historical biography. She's always poking around in history books and she's practically moved into the British Museum. Anyway, she's kind of artistic, so I know you'll have lots in common. Don't worry.'

'Oh, I'm not in the least bit worried,' Katharine assured him with a bright self-confident smile, and she meant every word, for few things ever fazed her.

CHAPTER SEVEN

The moment Katharine Tempest entered the drawing room Francesca's eyes were riveted on her. She found herself staring in astonishment and she thought: This girl is too improbable to be real. Everything about her is improbable. Only Francesca's good manners prevented her from displaying her startled reaction as she rose from the chair near the fireplace to welcome her guest.

The girl who walked with an easy swinging grace across the floor was obviously in her early twenties, perhaps twenty-one or twenty-two. She wore an extremely sophisticated dress, and in consequence, to Francesca, she looked like a little girl dressed up in mother's clothes. Made of fine black wool crepe, the dress was of mid-calf length, with a draped neckline, a straight skirt and dolman sleeves, and it was unrelieved by any touches of accent colour or jewellery. It struck Francesca that it was the perfect foil for the girl's looks, and she decided it was exactly right on her after all.

Kim followed closely on Katharine's heels, smiling broadly, and when they neared the fireplace he stepped forward to introduce the two girls to each other.

As Francesca stretched out her hand she found herself looking into the most extraordinary face she had ever seen. Katharine Tempest was lovely, and breathtakingly so. Her eyes, not blue, not green, but a unique turquoise, made the initial impact, and they were startling in their vividness of colour. They were large and set wide apart, fringed with silky black lashes, and they appeared to swamp her face with radiance.

Francesca thought the girl's features could not have been more exquisite if they had been chiselled by a sculptor. They were harmoniously distributed in an oval face that was perfectly balanced: a smooth brow, a small straight nose, high cheekbones above hollow cheeks, and a rounded chin. The symmetrical brows matched the rich dark-chestnut hair. This was parted in the centre and cascaded in glossy waves to her shoulders. Her white skin, which was exceptionally fine, was totally devoid of colour, which was why her full mouth, painted with the brightest of red lipstick, seemed all the more striking. Yet it was a child-like mouth, and now, as she smiled, it turned up at the corners to give her a look of innocence. There was also an unusual sweetness in her face that was both poignant and touching. In those first few moments, Francesca could only stand and stare speechlessly at this slender young woman who was accompanying her brother.

It was Katharine who broke the silence.

'Thank you for inviting me.' She spoke softly and her gaze was open and friendly as she regarded Francesca with not inconsiderable interest. Aware though she was of her own startling beauty and the impact it made, vanity was not one of Katharine's chief characteristics. In some ways she was even self-effacing at times, and she strove always to find something special in others, especially those she wanted to like. She said to herself: Kim didn't do his sister justice. She's really lovely. The perfect English rose.

'And I'm so glad you could come,' Francesca said, returning the smile. 'Please make yourself comfortable, Katharine. And Kim, why don't you open the champagne. It's over there on the chest.'

'Splendid idea,' Kim said. He beamed at them both and hurried across the room, rattling the bottle in the silver bucket as he attacked the cork. 'I think I need a cloth to grip this better,' he said and went out to the kitchen.

Apart from her physical beauty and unquestionable talent, Katharine possessed that most essential and desirable of all human ingredients, the quality of natural charm, and it was a charm so powerful it was at once dangerous and devastating in its potency. Seating herself on the sofa, Katharine looked across at Francesca and the full force of that charm was now levelled with great concentration in her direction. Katharine smiled. It was her most dazzling smile, guaranteed to disarm, ensnare and enchant.

She said: 'It's very nice of you to make supper for us, especially at this late hour. That's the only problem with being an actress, my world is topsy turvy, and my social life begins when everyone is going to bed.' She laughed her spiralling laugh. 'It's a terrible imposition on my nontheatrical friends, I'm afraid, having to entertain me in the wee small hours. If they want to see me, that is. Sometimes they don't, and I can't say I blame them. Not everyone wants to be carousing at midnight, sometimes even later than that!'

'Oh, I don't mind, really I don't,' Francesca was quick to say. 'And at least it's Sunday tomorrow. We can all sleep late.'

Katharine turned and glanced around the room. She was conscious of the beauty of the setting, with its gleaming antiques, the objects of art and the fine paintings. The coral walls gave it a roseate cast, this ambience further enhanced by the lamplight and the fire glowing in the grate. Katharine thought of her little birdcage of a flat, in comparison so sparse and utilitarian. But there was not a shred of envy in her. She was reminded instead of another room, from the happy time of her childhood, before her mother had fallen ill, when her life had been joyous, filled with love and tenderness. It was so very long ago now it might have been a lovely dream, yet Katharine knew otherwise. And it seemed to her that this elegant drawing room in London was just as safe as that other room had been, for it gave her a similar sense of permanence and security. She felt protected from the harsh world that existed beyond these walls. Unexpectedly, she experienced a feeling of longing she did not fully comprehend.

'How beautiful this room is, Francesca. It's so gracious, and I love a fire on a nasty wintry night.' A wistful expression flickered briefly on her face, and there was a small silence before she added quietly, 'It's so friendly and inviting.'

'And comforting too,' Francesca suggested in a tone that was full of understanding.

Their eyes met and inwardly they assessed each other. Neither Katharine nor Francesca knew it but something very special was beginning between them. A bond was being forged, and it would prove to be a bond so strong and enduring it would resist all outside forces and influences for well over a decade. And when it was finally broken, both of them would be devastated.

But now, this night, they simply knew they liked each other, although they did not, as yet, reveal this. The prolonged silence continued to drift between them, but there were no feelings of awkwardness and they went on appraising each other quite overtly.

Finally a sweet smile floated on to Katharine's face. 'And do you know something, Francesca? I even like a fire in summer,' she began. 'It's –'

'Absolutely necessary in this bloody awful climate,' cried Kim, as he strode into the room. 'And especially at Langley. No wonder the ancestors trudged around in that ghastly armour. It was undoubtedly the only way they could keep warm.'

The mood of quiet introspection was broken, and Francesca and Katharine glanced at each other in amusement. Then Katharine said, 'By the way, it's very good of you to include Victor Mason, Francesca. I'm sure you'll like him. He's not a bit like one would expect. He's . . . he's . . .' She stopped, sought the appropriate word and finished, 'Well, he's certainly very different.'

'I've never met a film star before, so I don't know what to expect,' Francesca admitted with a shy smile. 'To tell you the truth, I haven't seen many of his films. Maybe two or three at the most, and certainly nothing lately. How terrible. I do feel at such a disadvantage.'

'Oh, heavens, you don't have to worry about that!' Katharine exclaimed. 'I think Victor is relieved when he doesn't have to discuss his movies or his career. And he's one of the few actors I know who doesn't want to talk about himself endlessly. Thank goodness he's not having a love affair with himself, like some performers I know. We can be a pretty boring narcissistic breed at times.' She twisted the gold signet ring on her little finger absently, wondering what had happened to Victor. He should have been here by now.

'Have you known him long?' Francesca asked.

Katharine crossed her legs and smoothed her dress. 'No, only a few months. Sometimes I think he's rather a lonely man.' Her face became still and contemplative and she stared into the blazing fire, lost for a moment in her wandering thoughts.

Francesca could not help noticing this change and it disturbed her. At some time in her life she has been touched by a terrible sadness, she thought. It runs deep in her. This notion at once seemed so ridiculous, so farfetched, Francesca immediately pushed it away. But she did consider Katharine's remark about Victor Mason rather odd, in view of his fame. She was wondering how best to respond to it, when Kim saved her the trouble.

'Champagne!' he proclaimed, handing them each a crystal flute. He retrieved his own glass from the chest, proposed a toast and hovered over Katharine. His eyes hardly left her face, and Francesca well knew the reason why. She was finding it difficult to tear her own gaze away, was in danger of staring as rudely as she had done initially. Suddenly more than conscious of this, she focused her attention on Kim, who was now standing behind the sofa, intent on Katharine.

Meeting his sister's direct look, he said, 'I've decided to stay in town next week. I can drive back to Langley with the old man at the weekend. I'll leave you the Mini, old thing.'

'Is Father coming up to London? He didn't mention it to me, when we spoke yesterday. How odd,' Francesca said.

Kim chortled. 'You know how vague he is. It wouldn't surprise me if he's forgotten about it himself. But he has to come up to see Marcus, something about the trust, I believe. Anyway, he's supposed to arrive late tomorrow evening.'

'In that case you'd better ring him up first thing in the morning and remind him,' Francesca instructed. 'And thanks for offering the Mini. I can use it.' She shook her head in mock bewilderment, and looked at Katharine. 'Kim saying Daddy is vague is like the pot calling the kettle black. He's equally bad at times. He's been here since Thursday and he didn't even bother to tell me of Daddy's plans. Men are so thoughtless.'

'It's congenital,' Katharine declared. She had been listening carefully and, never one to miss an opportunity which would work to her advantage, she seized the one which had just presented itself. She leaned forward eagerly, her face lighting up, her wistfulness completely dispelled. 'I would love you to come to the play with your father, while he's in town, Francesca. In fact, I'd like you all to be my guests.' She glanced over her shoulder at Kim. 'I'll get house seats for you. Oh, do come! Please! I'm sure you'll enjoy it. Kim told me you're interested in history.'

'Why, yes, I am. And how very generous of you to invite us,' said Francesca, touched by Katharine's thoughtfulness. 'I would adore to see it.' Her eyes shone with warmth, but a note of caution crept into her voice as she added, 'I'm sure Daddy would too. I'll certainly ask him.' She halted, contemplating her father's reaction to Katharine. He could not fail to like her. She had a natural sweetness and lovely manners, and was so obviously a properly brought up young woman, as well as being such a beauty. But liking her did not necessarily guarantee his full approbation, or his acceptance of her as a wife for Kim. Daddy is out of date, Francesca thought with a spurt of exasperation. Katharine might very well be perfect for Kim, just what he needs. She became aware of Katharine's eyes focused on her, and she remarked quickly, 'I've always found Greek mythology fascinating. The play's about Helen and Paris and the Trojan War, isn't it?'

'That's right.' Katharine's face filled with animation, and she explained, with a kind of shining earnestness, 'It's very dramatic and moving, really wonderful entertainment. We're playing to a packed house every night, standing room only. And we're sold out for weeks in advance. Naturally we're all happy about that. Knowing we're going to be working for some time is very reassuring, apart from the stunning reception the play is getting.'

Kim interjected, 'The critics raved about Katharine. Actually, they were ecstatic. As well they should be. She gives a super performance, and steals everybody's thunder.'

'How thrilling for you to have such a big hit!' Francesca exclaimed. As she spoke she decided Katharine made the perfect Helen of Troy. The face that launched a thousand ships. How very apt. 'You must be a very talented actress to have this kind of success in your first West End play. Gosh, to have become a star overnight is simply marvellous. What an extraordinary achievement at your age.'

Had this breathless exultation of her success been uttered by anyone else, it might have sounded gushing, even meretricious to Katharine. But she knew Francesca meant every word. Not unnaturally, Katharine was filled with delight at the obviously genuine accolades. 'Yes, it is exciting. And thank you, Francesca,' she said. 'Having a smash hit is gratifying to all of the cast. We worked hard in rehearsals and wanted the play to succeed.' A smile played around her mouth. 'But obviously that doesn't ensure anything. There are a lot of other elements involved, so many other considerations, and there's always a kind of nervous uncertainty until we're actually playing to the public. We need the feedback, the reactions of the audience.'

'I'm sure you must,' Francesca remarked, somewhat diffidently. 'Most people think being an actress is so easy, and the theatrical life very glamorous as well. But I suspect acting must be a particularly difficult art to master.'

She became more confident. 'Interpreting the playwright's intentions, and expressing emotions and thoughts and feelings must be highly complex. I'm sure it requires a great deal of intelligence and insight to handle everything.' She grimaced. 'I know I couldn't do it. Not in a thousand years.'

Katharine gave Kim's sister a seraphic smile. 'How beautifully you express it! And you're absolutely right. In reality there is very little glamour or glitter to the theatre, despite what everyone thinks. The public see only the most obvious things, the outer trappings. Acting is the most gruelling work, the salt mines really. It's demanding, exhausting, frustrating, nerve-racking and challenging. But I find it very satisfying. And of course I don't deny that it does have its moments of excitement.' There was a sparkle about her, a lovely glow. The last remnants of her tiredness evaporated in the friendly atmosphere, induced by Francesca's warmth and sympathetic demeanour. 'But heavens, we're boring poor Kim with our chatter.'

'No, you're not,' Kim said. He was relieved that Francesca and Katharine had taken to each other and with such spontaneity. His expression was loving as he added, 'It's very entertaining. Actually, I'm glad I've hardly been able to get a word in edgewise. Imagine how ghastly I would have felt if you two hadn't had anything to say to each other.' He lit a cigarette and thought: this augurs well for the meeting with Father. Francesca will help to smooth the way.

Katharine herself was patently aware of Francesca's readiness to be friends, and she smiled inwardly, remembering her faint misgivings. How wrong she had been. Francesca was a delight, and she felt completely relaxed in her company, conscious as she was of the other girl's approval. And approval, above all else, was essential to Katharine Tempest.

'Why don't you come to the theatre on Monday evening?' Katharine asked, wanting to pin Francesca down, her mind teeming with elaborate plans for dinner afterwards. 'We're always in good form after our weekend break, and it's generally a great performance.' She broke into laughter. 'Having made that sweeping statement, it's bound to be the worst show of the week!'

Francesca said, 'I know it will be quite wonderful, and I would like to come on Monday evening, providing Father can make it. What about you, Kim?'

'I'm definitely on! I'd love to see it again. Now, how about another glass of champagne, girls?'

'Thank you.' Katharine handed him her empty glass.

Francesca declined. 'I'm all right for the moment, and I don't want to get tiddly. I have the supper to serve, you know.' She turned back to Katharine. 'It must be an extraordinary experience working with Terrence Ogden. I've always thought he was a brilliant actor. He's also quite the ladies' man, isn't he? All my girl friends have a crush on him. Is he really as divine as he looks?'

Katharine groaned to herself. She did not want to embark on a discussion of Terry's merits as a great lover, in view of Kim's jealous display earlier. But there was a look of such eager expectancy on Francesca's face she did not want to disappoint or offend her by brushing the question aside in a peremptory manner. She drew nearer and dropped her voice. 'I suppose he does have a bit of a reputation, but it's rather exaggerated. Terry himself encourages that though. He seems to think it's good publicity, being linked with lots of lovely ladies in the press, although I'm not so sure myself. Actually, he is very dedicated to his work. I enjoy acting with him. He's very generous as a performer, and I've learned a lot from him.'

If Francesca found Katharine's answer unrewarding, she did not show it. Her eyes rested briefly but thoughtfully on Kim, who was standing by the chest pouring the champagne, and then shifted to Katharine again. She nodded her head, as if she intuitively understood it was unwise to pursue this line of conversation. 'Kim told me you're an American, Katharine. Have you lived in England for a long time?'

Francesca had changed the subject, much to Katharine's considerable relief. 'A few years.' There was an almost imperceptible hesitation before she volunteered, 'I went to the Royal Academy of Dramatic Art for a couple of years, before doing repertory in the provinces.'

Kim handed Katharine her glass. She looked up at him and those glorious eyes were full of tenderness as they met his. She patted the sofa. 'Sit down, Kim darling, and let's talk about something else. I feel as if I've been dominating the conversation, and I'm also getting bored with all this chit-chat about the theatre, even if you're not.'

'Listening to your lovely voice is music to my ears, my sweet. You could read Debrett's Peerage to me, and I would still be entranced,' he teased, seating himself next to her.

'Oh phooey!' Katharine winked at Francesca, who simply smiled with benevolence, understanding perfectly Kim's infatuation. She knew that she herself was also rapidly falling under the girl's spell. Let's hope that Father will too, she mused, and discovered she wanted him to approve of Katharine just as much as Kim wanted it.

Katharine, who was intrigued by Francesca, now focused her complete attention on her. 'I hear you're doing research for a book, that you're a writer. Now *that* is fascinating and I'm sure it's just as difficult as being an actress, if not more so.'

66

Surprise flicked on to Francesca's face and she shot a questioning look at Kim, who simply grinned like a Cheshire cat and then shrugged off-handedly. After a moment's hesitation she said, 'Yes, I'm researching, and I hope to write my book on Chinese Gordon one day, but I wouldn't call myself a writer. At least not yet. Ernest Hemingway said a person is not a writer until he or she has readers. So I feel I can't possibly make that claim until I'm actually a published author.' She took a small sip of her champagne. Wishing to avert a discussion about herself, for she was both reticent and modest about her talents, she said casually, 'Do you think Victor Mason is still coming?'

Kim, who had entirely forgotten about Victor, immediately straightened up on the sofa and frowned. 'I telephoned him earlier this evening to confirm, before I went to pick up Katharine. He said he would be arriving when we did.' He stared at the ornate ormolu clock on the mantel-piece and shook his head in disbelief. 'But we've been here almost an hour already. Perhaps I had better give him another buzz at the hotel.'

'I don't think you need bother. I'm afraid he's notorious for being late,' Katharine fibbed. 'I know he'll be here any minute.' This last remark was said with a degree of assurance Katharine did not truly feel. Victor's absence had been weighing heavily for some time, and she had been hoping it was merely tardiness on his part. Now she was no longer sure this was the case. She would be mortified if he did not come to supper; this could only have one meaning: He was unable to face her because he had not kept his promise to her.

She felt her throat tightening as the tension took hold of her, and although she rarely smoked, she reached for a cigarette in the silver box on the table in front of her.

Kim gave her a light and took a cigarette himself. He blew a smoke ring, peered at his sister, and said, 'I say, I hope you haven't got anything spoiling in the kitchen.'

'No, I haven't. Everything is under control, Kim. Don't fuss so. All I have to do is light the oven when Victor gets here. Are you getting hungry, Katharine?'

'Not really. Thank you, anyway. It always takes me a while to unwind after the performance. Shedding the part.'

'But I'm ravenous,' Kim announced. 'I wouldn't mind sampling some of that caviar, and the pâté, which you have so conveniently forgotten, Francesca.'

Laughing, Francesca rose. She, who was so beautifully mannered, had indeed forgotten the food she had intended to serve with the drinks. It was a rare lapse. She had been so fascinated by Katharine and engrossed with her, everything else had been swept out of her mind. 'How awful of me. Please excuse me. I won't be a minute.' She flew out of the drawing room, her taffeta skirt crackling as she moved.

The minute they were alone, Katharine turned to Kim and, quenching her rising anxiety about Victor, she said, 'I think your sister is really lovely.'

'She likes you, too, I'm sure,' Kim murmured. He moved closer to Katharine and put his arms around her, kissing her neck and her hair. 'And that goes for me too,' he whispered. He felt the warmth of her enveloping him, the delicate perfume of her silky skin intoxicating him, and as always when he held her like this his excitement surged in him.

'Oh, Katharine, Katharine, I do adore you so,' and he buried his face against her neck.

Katharine stroked the back of his fair head and returned his embrace, but she said nothing. At this moment Victor filled her mind and one thought turned endlessly against itself: *How could he have let her down?* She never broke *her* promises. Men. They were all the same. Untrustworthy. Just like her father, the bastard. She squeezed her eyes tightly shut, endeavouring to obliterate the image of *him*.

After a moment, Kim drew away from her; as he looked down at her nestled in his arms he was overcome by his longing for her. He slowly lowered his mouth to hers, wanting to devour those warm lips. Katharine pushed him back, but with gentleness.

Somehow she managed to find her voice. 'Please, Kim darling, don't start this now. Francesca will be back any moment, and how would it look if she catches us necking on the sofa.' She extracted herself from his tight embrace and stood up, tugging at her skirt and smoothing her hair. 'I'm surprised at you,' she pronounced sternly, but the tone was soft.

Kim fell back against the cushions helplessly, groaning out loud. 'It's all your fault. You're a temptress, don't you know. And the most maddening it's ever been my great good luck to encounter. What am I going to do with you?'

'Nothing at the moment,' she said. 'But you can get me another glass of champagne.'

He grinned at her good naturedly, pushed himself up off the sofa and brought the bottle. He filled the Waterford flutes, and then eyed the empty bottle, shaking it. 'Well, this one's a dead soldier. I'd better put another one on ice. We'll need it when Victor gets here.' As he reached the door, he swung around and said, 'If he ever turns up, that is, which I seriously doubt now. Back in a jiffy, my sweet one.'

Katharine nodded, not trusting herself to respond coherently. Kim had voiced the one fear nagging at her. She turned and rested her hand on the mantelpiece and gazed down into the fire miserably. She had been in control of her own destiny since the age of twelve. She had never relied on anyone for anything, for mistrust was paramount in her nature, and especially so when it came to men. Yet she had broken her own stringent rule and trusted Victor Mason. Damn, damn, damn, she muttered under her breath.

Francesca came in carrying a large silver tray. 'I hope you'll try a little of this, Katharine,' she said. 'I think I will.'

'I'm not really hungry, thank you,' Katharine answered and returned to her place on the sofa.

Francesca seated herself in the chair, and picked up a pearl-handled silver knife. She plunged it into the mound of sturgeon's roe, so glistening and moist in the crystal dish, spread a portion on a piece of Melba toast and squeezed lemon over it. Smiling, she offered it to Katharine, who shook her head, and then handed it to Kim, who had joined them again.

'I say, this is superb!' Kim exclaimed, after devouring it. 'You don't have to bother with the cottage pie. This will do just nicely for me.'

Francesca said, 'Try the pâté too. It's –' The shrilling of the door bell caused her to stop. She glanced from Kim to Katharine, arching her blonde brows. 'Could that be our missing guest at long last?'

Katharine rose with unusual swiftness. 'Perhaps I'd better answer the door, Kim. After all, you've never met Victor.'

CHAPTER EIGHT

'Where the hell have you been?' Katharine hissed, her eyes blazing as she confronted Victor Mason on the door step.

'Charming welcome,' he said, adding with a huge grin, 'am I allowed in, or shall I be on my merry way?'

'Of course you're allowed in,' Katharine cried, and fearing he was about to depart she quickly snatched at the sleeve of the trenchcoat thrown casually over his shoulders, and drew him towards her possessively.

Victor turned to his driver, who hovered on the step next to him, holding a large black umbrella over them both. 'I guess I'll be a couple of hours or so, Gus. That is if I don't get thrown out on my rear end before then. You can mosey off for a while. I'll see you later. Have fun.' His mouth twitched. 'But don't do anything I wouldn't do.'

'Right you are, Mr Mason,' Gus responded, and retreated to the car as Victor stepped inside the house.

'Well, at least he's stopped calling you Guv, thank heavens,' Katharine remarked.

Victor threw her a swift, amused look, chuckled softly and said, 'Only in front of people. When we're alone he still calls me Guvnor. I don't mind. In fact, I like it.' He thrust a package at her, winked theatrically and declared 'Beware of Italians bearing dubious gifts.'

Katharine accepted the package in grudging silence. She was not so easily placated and the tension was still flaring within her. In consequence, she was a little on edge and her patience had worn thin. There was a cold silence, during which she continued to glare at him, and then she said, 'I thought you weren't coming. You're very late. Abominably late. You've heard of the telephone haven't you? It's a small instrument that enables you to communicate between two points –'

He cut in with a throaty laugh, 'Save me the sarcasm, honey.' Shrugging off the trenchcoat he glanced around. 'Where shall I put this?'

Katharine nodded in the direction of the hall cupboard. 'In there.' She looked down at the package she was holding. 'What is this, anyway?'

'A peace offering. Champagne. Pink champagne.'

'Pink! Now I know what you mean by dubious,' she retorted.

'My, my, we are being gracious tonight,' Victor said. But he did not seem in the least put out by her scathing words or her frosty manner. In fact, he appeared sanguine, and his voice was even as he said, 'Look, honey, I'm sorry, I really am. The delay was unavoidable. I had to wait for a call from the Coast. An important business call. Come on, Katharine, give a guy a break.'

His smile was so sincere, and he sounded so genuinely apologetic that Katharine found herself smiling back at him. She was also shrewdly aware that it would be foolish to antagonize Victor, and by so doing put her assiduously-made plans into certain jeopardy. Need her he well might, but his goodwill was absolutely crucial to her, and since he had finally made an appearance her troubling doubts about him were subsiding, were replaced by the optimistic belief that he had not reneged on his promise to her. And so she softened her manner and her chameleon-like ability to present a different visage went into immediate play. The smile became infinitely more luminous and beguiling and the turquoise eyes were instantaneously veiled with affectionate lights.

'I'm sorry too,' she told him. 'I didn't mean to sound so sharp, but the English are very peculiar about time and the proper form and all that, as I've mentioned to you before.' She returned the package to him. 'And it was very sweet of you to bring this. Truly. But I think it would be more appropriate if you gave it to your hostess. I know she'll appreciate your thoughtfulness. Now, come on, my darling, we're wasting time. Let's go in.'

Victor tucked the bottle under his arm with a jaunty flourish, glanced at himself in the Georgian mirror, adjusted his tie, and said, 'I'm all yours, honey. Lead the way.'

Kim and Francesca stopped talking when Victor and Katharine walked into the drawing room, and Victor saw two pairs of eyes focused on him intently and with enormous interest. Considering he was a world-famous film star, and had been for a number of years, he was not unaccustomed to this kind of fixed and curious scrutiny, for everyone had their own vision of him, which was not always compatible with the man he truly was.

But what brought him up short and filled him with amazement was his consciousness of the girl in grey, seated near the fireplace, who was now slowly rising. Like a brilliant lodestar she drew him magnetically towards her, and he felt a need, indeed a compulsion, to rush over to her, was filled with an urgency not only to meet her, but to know every facet of her. He had no desire to appear foolish, even immature, and he realized, too, that this kind of behaviour would be incorrect and a rank display of that 'bad form' the British, and Katharine, were always muttering about. Nor did he have any intention of giving Katharine the opportunity to lecture him about his manners. Before he could take another step, the young man next to her, obviously Katharine's boyfriend, Kim, was hurrying forward, smiling broadly.

Kim grasped Victor's hand. 'I'm Kim Cunningham. Delighted you could come.'

'So am I,' Victor replied, shaking Kim's hand vigorously. And he apologized and again explained his reason for being late.

'Oh, please don't give it another thought,' Kim exclaimed. He grinned. 'We've been very cosy here, guzzling champagne and chatting. Now, do come and meet my sister, and then I'll get you a drink. What do you prefer? Champagne, or something else, perhaps?'

'I'd like Scotch-on-the-rocks with a splash of soda, please.'

Kim took hold of Victor's arm and propelled him across the room to the fireplace. 'This is Francesca,' he said, and, after bestowing a bright smile on them, he disappeared in the direction of the drinks chest to pour a Scotch for Victor.

'How nice to meet you, Mr Mason,' Francesca said.

Their hands met and held and their eyes locked, and simultaneously they exchanged a startled glance. Looking down into the delicate face upturned to him, Victor saw the shining amber-flecked eyes widen and fill with the astonishment he himself was feeling. A tremulous smile touched her mouth briefly, and was gone. I've never met her before, but I recognize her, he thought with incredulity. I know her. I've always known her, somewhere deep in my heart and soul. This strange and surprising knowledge shook him, and momentarily he was thrown off balance.

Being adroit, he swiftly pulled himself together. 'I'm pleased to meet you too, Lady Francesca,' he said with a slow lazy smile, but his black eyes were serious and searching, and his gaze remained unswervingly on her face.

'Oh please, do call me Francesca.' Two faint spots of colour stained her ivory cheeks.

'I'll be glad to, if you'll call me Victor.'

She nodded and gently extracted her hand, which he was still holding tightly, and stepping back, she lowered herself into the chair. Victor remembered the package under his arm, bent forward and handed it to her, instantly wishing it were something more personal, more appropriate like – like an armful of fragile white May lilac, fragrant after a drenching of spring rain. Yes, lilac was the ideal flower for her. It suited her delicacy and freshness. He said, 'I almost forgot. This is for you.'

Francesca looked up at him, surprised. 'Why thank you. How very kind.' She began to unwrap it, her head bent, her fingers moving slowly, and she wondered why she was suddenly trembling internally, not recognizing the dynamic chemistry interacting between them. However, Victor, who was wise in the ways of the world and of men and women, knew it. At least, he knew *she* had affected him strongly, and that he had responded to her on a variety of levels, not the least of which was sexual. He looked at her sharply, a keenness in his eyes. She appeared serene and unperturbed. Cool as a cucumber, he thought. He remembered that look of astonishment they had shared a moment ago, the startled glance exchanged. Had he imagined them? He was not sure. Perhaps the attraction had not been mutual, but merely one-sided. His side. He smiled faintly to himself.

Victor had no way of knowing that Francesca had a natural poise that belied her years, and a great measure of that special self-confidence so endemic to the English aristocracy. She rarely lost her composure. And so, despite her equally strong reaction to Victor, one she found extraordinary and baffling, she let no emotion show on her face. But she *was* disturbed, and understandably so. To begin with, she had had little or no experience of men, and certainly she had never encountered one of Victor Mason's ilk. Then again, her boyfriends had been, for the most part, chums of Kim's and the same age, and she had never taken any of them seriously. At nineteen she was sexually inexperienced, and, in comparison to her girl friends, who were much more worldly, unusually innocent for a young woman who mixed in smart London society.

In all truth, Victor Mason had unnerved Francesca. Gradually this realization began to formulate in her mind. How absurd she was being, allowing herself to become rattled by this man. Yet, she had to admit he was devastatingly attractive; she thought: If Katharine Tempest seems improbable, with her stunning beauty and allure and vivacious personality, then he is undoubtedly larger than life. And very disconcerting.

Abruptly, Victor left his position in front of the fire, and without glancing at her or addressing another word to her, he moved over to the chest. He stood talking to Kim as if they were old friends, and not total strangers from worlds so wide apart it was debatable whether they had any common ground upon which to meet. Francesca observed him through the corner of her eye, her head still bent in concentration on the package. It struck her that he looked unconcerned, as if she no longer existed, as if he had not given her those fierce stares. It was then that she wondered whether he always behaved in this manner, when first meeting women, in view of who and what he was, believing, perhaps, that it was expected of him. Although she was not the typical film fan, she was sufficiently well-informed to know that Victor Mason was idolized by women all over the world. Few men had ever been the recipients of the kind of female adulation which was showered on him. There was no doubt in her mind that he could pick and choose at will from a galaxy of women infinitely more beautiful and interesting than her, and so she concluded she had not been singled out for any special treatment. And why should she be?

Francesca swung her eyes away from Victor when Katharine's clear laughter echoed across the room; then she could not resist focusing her attention on the three of them. Victor turned slightly, also laughing, and leaned towards Katharine, teasing her. Katharine looked up at him as she returned his banter.

Clutching the crumpled wrapping paper and the bottle of Pommery and Greno, Francesca got up and went to the door. Without looking at Victor, she exclaimed, 'Thank you for the champagne. It's lovely. Look, Katharine. Kim. Victor brought this.' She held out the bottle and went on, 'I'll go and put it in the refrigerator. And turn the oven on, otherwise we'll never get supper tonight.' She went out, closing the door quietly behind her.

When Francesca returned a few minutes later, she was surprised to see Victor standing at the far end of the drawing room, quite obviously admiring the paintings that graced the walls. He and Katharine were listening attentively to Kim, who was giving them a long dissertation on the Constables and Turners in the room. Francesca chose not to join them. She went to the fireplace, picked up the brass fire tongs, plopped a couple of logs on the diminished embers, sat down in the chair and picked up her glass. She peered at Victor over the rim. A faint image of him from his films had apparently lingered at the back of her mind, for it surfaced suddenly. It was the image of an excessively handsome man, glossy and too sleek, who looked as if he had been patted and pummelled and polished, and then varnished into smooth and characterless perfection. She sneaked another look at him, and saw how utterly false this image now proved to be.

He was handsome, there was no quarrelling with that, yet in reality he was rough-hewn and rugged. His face was more craggy and raw-boned than she had remembered and, far from lacking character, it had a virility and strength, and was webbed around the eyes with those faint tell-tale lines of experience which are the real evidence of a life well-lived, and to the fullest. His skin had a leathery, almost weather-beaten texture, and she knew that his deep sunburn was the type acquired only by a man who is always out of doors. His features were more sharply defined than she had recalled, from the strong Roman nose and the prominent black brows above those black and forceful eyes, to the wide humorous mouth and the large white teeth. Even the thick black hair, brushed smoothly back from the furrowed brow, seemed to have a vitality and life of its own. He was powerfully built, broad-shouldered and massive across the chest and back.

In all truthfulness, the only sleek things about Victor Mason were his clothes. They were of the finest quality and appeared to have been assembled with unerring precision. And they're just a little too perfect, Francesca thought. She noted the excellent cut of the black cashmere jacket, the grey flannel slacks with their knife-edge creases, the pale blue cotton-voile shirt, the darker blue silk tie, the grey silk handkerchief in the breast pocket of the jacket, the velvet-soft brown suede loafers on his feet. He lifted his hand at this moment and put a cigarette in his mouth and lit it, and she caught the gleam of sapphires in the French cuff, the flash of gold on the wrist. Poor Kim, he looks positively shabby in comparison, she said to herself, even though he is wearing his new suit. Unaccountably, this had a crumpled and well-lived-in appearance. Francesca had to smile. Victor Mason's clothes would never look crumpled, of that she was quite positive.

Watching them, or more precisely, watching Victor, Francesca was struck by a sudden and unsettling thought. There was something about Victor which disturbed her, something she could not put her finger on. It came to her. She felt curiously threatened by him. But why? She did not have to do much analysing to define the reasons. Because he is extraordinarily good looking, a famous celebrity, and very, very rich, she said to herself. And all of these so-called assets add up to one thing – power. Yes, he had immense power, albeit of a somewhat special nature, and powerful men, whatever the roots of their power, were eminently dangerous to know. He is also arrogant and so ... so ... sure of himself, and filled with a conceit that is quite insufferable. She shivered involuntarily and goose-flesh ran up her arms. He also frightens me, she thought, and she resolved, at once, to be on her guard with him.

Francesca Cunningham was not really afraid of Victor Mason. She was afraid of herself in relationship to him. And her judgment of Victor was flawed. She was accurate in her assumption that he was a man who wielded power, and a great deal of it, but mistaken in her belief that he was arrogant and conceited. He was neither. What he did possess, though, was great presence, that rare and curious combination of authority and *savoir-faire*, mingled with a vital charisma. In essence, these ingredients created in him an animal magnetism that was quite magical, and it was this which came across on the screen with such force. It had made him one of the biggest box-office names in the world. Victor was the first to admit this, since he did not believe himself to be a great actor in the grand tradition of the theatre. In this he did himself something of an injustice, for he was a well-rounded, well-seasoned and disciplined performer, a real professional whom few of his peers in Hollywood ever underestimated. Especially those who had worked with him. Having seen him on the set, they were aware of how brilliantly and skilfully he

73

used the camera to his own enormous advantage, thereby diminishing any other actor or actress who happened to be on the screen with him at the same time.

Victor was also a man of sensitivity and understanding. Now he was very much aware of Francesca seated at the opposite end of the room, and he knew she had carefully and minutely appraised him from head to toe. Although he could not see her face, intuitively he sensed that somehow he had not fared well in her estimation, that he had received bad marks, and this made him smile. He stood and sipped his Scotch, chatting to Kim and Katharine about art for a few seconds longer, and then he excused himself and headed back to the fireplace.

When she saw him approaching, Francesca leapt up. 'Please don't think I'm being rude, but I do have to attend to the food. Excuse me for a few minutes.'

He did not miss the crisp tone. He seated himself in the chair she had vacated, stretched out his long legs and crossed them at the ankles. Settling back, he smiled and with a vast and secret amusement, although he was not truly certain who amused him the most – himself or Francesca. She had just bolted like a frightened filly, obviously to avoid him. On the other hand, he had behaved like a dumbstruck schoolboy on first meeting her. And now that the initial impact had dissipated, he was damned if he knew why. Francesca was lovely in a fresh, girlish way, but not exactly his type. And in any event, beautiful women were the norm of his life, not the exception and, as his friend Nicky Latimer was always saying, were a dime a dozen for a man of his calibre and looks and unquestionable fame. *And money*. He sighed. Two new wives and countless other less legal liaisons in the past few years had left him immune to beauty, and these days he felt jaded and weary of the emotional turmoil women invariably created in his life, once they became entangled with him. He had sworn off '*les girls*', as he laughingly called them, six months ago, and when he had come to England he had determined to concentrate on his career. He had no intention of breaking this rule. Not even for Francesca Cunningham. Victor was not given to self-delusion, and he was always brutally honest with himself, and so he readily admitted the attraction had been powerful, that he had momentarily been bowled over by her. But apparently she had not responded in the same way. He shrugged. He was not in the mood to pursue.

Another thought struck him and he nearly laughed out loud. He was thirty-nine years old, almost forty, and Francesca could not be more than eighteen. A baby. Was it possible he had suddenly become susceptible to young girls? Was he afflicted with the nymphet syndrome? Not long ago, dear old Nicky, the soothsayer, had told him he was suffering from a terminal Don Juan complex. This had made him roar with laughter, considering the lustful mouth from which this caustic little comment had issued forth, even though it was based in truth. After his first wife's tragic death Victor had gone haywire with grief. And then, in the intervening years, he had become something of a womanizer, and he didn't mind who knew it. Conversely, he did not relish the idea of being dubbed a dirty old man.

Katharine sat down on the sofa, struck an elegant pose and said, 'What are you doing on Monday night?'

Victor threw her a questioning look. 'Nothing. You should know that, considering you've completely taken charge of my social life. Do I ever make a move without you? But why do you ask?'

'Because I've invited Francesca, Kim and their father to be my guests at the play. I'm sure you don't want to see it again, but I thought it would be nice if you took us all to dinner afterwards, to reciprocate this evening.'

'Sure, why not,' he said amiably. He took out a packet of mentholated cigarettes and lit one, drawing on it deeply.

Kim, who had seated himself next to Katharine, looked at her askance. 'Oh, I say, darling, that's not necessary. Victor doesn't have to reciprocate,' he exclaimed. 'He doesn't want to be saddled with our tribe –'

'Sure I do,' Victor interrupted. 'I think it's a terrific idea. I'd love to take you all to dinner. Now, where do you want to go, Katharine? Ziegi's Club, the Caprice, Les Ambassadeurs, the Casanova or the River Club?'

'Why, Victor, I wasn't thinking of such ritzy places,' cried Katharine, who had indeed had one of them in mind, considering it essential for her career to be seen in smart restaurants. She looked across at him, her eyes wide with innocence, and smiled winningly. 'But since you did ask *my* preference, I think it would be super if you took us to Les A. I haven't been there for ages, and it's one of my favourite places. Wouldn't that be lovely, Kim?'

Kim, who had never set foot in Les Ambassadeurs, but frequently read about it in the columns, nodded slowly. 'It's most awfully kind of you, Victor,' he said. He lifted his glass, wondering what his father would think, whether he would approve of such goings-on with show-business folk in a fancy supper club. But then, why not? After all, the old man was squiring Doris around, and she was a leading light in international café society. It also struck him that Victor's presence might make the evening less tense. This cheered him up and helped to dispel his mild irritation with Katharine for placing Victor in such an awkward position. Perhaps she, too, had considered this point.

Katharine said, 'Should I get a ticket for you, Victor darling?'

'No. Thanks anyway, honey. I'm afraid I have to do some work on Monday night. I have a number of calls to make to the Coast and New York, and because of the time differences I can't really start until five or six o'clock. I'll make a reservation for around eleven and meet you there.'

Francesca poked her head around the door. 'Supper's ready, if you'd like to come in,' she said.

Katharine joined Francesca, and the two girls crossed the hall to the dining room. In a confiding voice she told Francesca about the newly-made plans. 'I do hope your father is going to be free. I just know we'll have lots of fun.'

Francesca drew in her breath sharply. After a short pause, she said, 'I'm sure he will be.' And then, hearing the echo of Victor's voice behind her, she hoped her father had another engagement. She had been looking forward to seeing Katharine in the play, but unexpectedly the whole idea of the evening had now lost its appeal.

CHAPTER NINE

The dining room was impressive, both in its dimensions and its decoration. Tonight the room was dimly lit, but attractively so. Tall white candles flickered in the heavy, chased-silver candelabra placed at each end of the sideboard and in the centre of the dining table. In this warm and golden light the mahogany table gleamed with dark, ripe colour, and its highly polished surface had the glassy sheen of mirror. Reflected against it was the glitter of Georgian silver and hand-cut lead crystal wine goblets, the sparkle of white bone china plates, rimmed in gold and bearing the Langley family crest, also in gold.

The fir green walls, as cool and dark as a bosky forest, gave the room its restful tranquillity, made a superb muted backdrop for the incomparable oil paintings. Each one was mounted in an ornately carved and gilded-wood frame, and effectively illuminated by a small picture light attached to the top of the frame. The fluttering candles and the picture lights, the only illumination in the room, infused the ambience with a mellowness that was quite lovely, gave it an intimacy that was at once both charming and inviting.

Francesca showed Katharine and Victor to their places, and then went to the sideboard to serve the turtle soup, spooning it into green-and-gold Royal Worcester bowls from a large silver tureen. Victor observed her closely, struck by her elegance. His eyes roved around the room, and with interest. He admired its beauty and style. *Background* was the message it telegraphed to him, and that, he thought, is something no amount of money can buy. As he absorbed his surroundings his attention was caught by the painting on the end wall. It was a full-length, life-size portrait of a woman in an elaborate blue taffeta gown. Her pale blonde hair was piled high in an intricate pompadour surmounted by several plumes of blue feathers. Topaz earrings gleamed at her ears, and a topaz necklace fell down from her slender neck to fill out the *décolletage*. Of course, it was Francesca, and it was an exquisite portrait, beautifully executed and with explicit attention to every minute detail. Victor had the feeling that if he reached out and touched the dress his fingers would encounter silk, so realistically was the texture of the fabric depicted by the peerless brushstrokes.

After distributing the bowls of soup, Francesca sat down at the foot of the table, opposite Kim, who was seated at the head. Victor turned to her immediately, and said with some admiration, 'That's a remarkable portrait of you. And it's very beautiful.'

She stared at him uncomprehending for a second, and then followed his gaze. 'Oh, that one. But it's not of me,' she said, and picked up her soup spoon. 'It's of my great-great-great-great-grandmother, the Sixth Countess of Langley. Traditional and classical portraits of that nature are not in vogue any more. Furthermore, they are rarely painted these days, except by Annigoni occasionally. He did the Queen, you know.'

'Oh,' Victor said. Rebuffed, he dropped his eyes. She's certainly put you in your place, he thought. Only the English have the knack of making everyone else look stupid and ignorant in an insidious way, and without really appearing to be rude. As he reached for his spoon he repressed a smile. It was a long time since he had been slapped in the face, figuratively speaking, by a woman. If it was a bit demeaning, it was also something of a novelty.

Katharine, who missed nothing, was dismayed at Francesca's tone and non-plussed by the snub to Victor. She exclaimed swiftly, 'Well, Francesca, it does bear a striking resemblance to you. It would have fooled me. Who painted it?'

'Thomas Gainsborough,' Kim volunteered. 'Around 1770. And I agree with both of you. It does look like Francesca. There is another portrait of the Sixth, as we call her, at Langley. By George Romney. The likeness is most apparent in that one, too.' He paused, and on the spur of the moment, said, 'I hope you will both come to Langley soon, for a weekend, and then you'll see it for yourselves. We must make plans for a visit. I know Father would enjoy having you. Wouldn't he, Francesca?'

Stiffening, Francesca straightened up in the chair. 'Yes,' she said, her tone low, and she did not elaborate. She was flabbergasted. Kim was incorrigible, issuing an invitation like that. He presumed too much. If their father didn't like Katharine, the invitation would have to be rescinded. Then Katharine would be hurt, and with good reason.

'Kim, that would be wonderful!' Katharine cried with genuine delight. Her face fell. 'But, gosh, I don't know how I could manage it, with the two Saturday performances. Unless – ' Her face lit up again, and she looked across the table at Victor. 'Unless Gus drove us to Yorkshire late one Saturday night, after the play, and brought us back on Monday afternoon. That would work. Could we do it one weekend, Victor? Please.'

Victor nodded, and concentrated on his soup, not wishing to make another *faux pas*. Although Francesca's disdainful attitude had amused him somewhat, he was experiencing a sense of discomfort. Since these feelings were unparalleled in him they were therefore all the more confusing and troubling. He tried to shake them off, and then he thought: But I've got to hand it to Katharine. She's got guts, and a cool assurance, that is enviable. And she certainly seems in her natural element whenever she mixes in this upper echelon of English society. He wondered again about her background, as he had so often in the three months he had known her. Funny how she never mentioned it. The only facts he had been able to pry out of her told him virtually nothing. She had been born in Chicago. She had lived in England for almost six years. And she was an orphan. Well, she acquired her inimitable style somewhere, he commented dryly to himself. She's to the manner born, to be sure.

It was true that Katharine was perfectly at ease. Victor's presence had alleviated her anxiety; and his ready acceptance of her suggestion about dinner on Monday had further dispelled the notion that he was untrustworthy. There *was* a residue of tension lingering in her, but this was most skilfully veiled by the smiling façade she presented, the irrepressible gaiety which so readily materialized to delight and enchant them.

And as the dinner progressed Katharine took over. She was the true star. And she gave a stunning performance. She glittered. She dazzled. She captivated. She entertained. Without really seeming to do so, she dominated the conversation, discussing everything from the theatre and the movie business, to British politics and blood sports, and she did so with charm, *élan*, grace and intelligence. She also managed to successfully bridge the brief but acute sense of awkwardness which had prevailed at the outset of the meal, and she created an atmosphere that was light yet stimulating.

Slowly Victor found himself being drawn into the conversation quite naturally. He sipped the excellent Mouton Rothschild Kim had poured, savouring its smooth velvety texture, and he began to relax again. He discovered in Kim an unusual warmth and empathy, and a genuinely sympathetic and interested listener. Almost against his own volition, he opened up and spoke about his ranch in Southern California, his horses and his land, and the latter proved to be of common interest to the two men. Yet, withal, he was conscious of Francesca's thoughtful manner, her silences, unbroken except when she served the various dishes and attended to their needs. She did not even bother to participate in the general small talk, and he thought this decidedly odd.

Francesca knew that she was being remiss as a hostess, that the burden of the conversation had fallen on Katharine. She had not purposely set out to behave this way, nor was her coolness and reticence specifically directed at Victor. Very simply, she felt she had nothing of importance to contribute, and she had withdrawn into herself. Also, serving the meal had preoccupied her. Yet whilst she had not been rude, neither had she been very gracious, and she chided herself for this lapse in etiquette. It was inexcusable.

With an effort she turned to Victor and said, 'Are you going to be making a film here?'

He was so startled to hear her voice he temporarily lost his own. He cleared his throat and said, 'Why, yes, I am.' She was regarding him with keen interest and her expression was friendly, and so he was encouraged to continue. 'I'm not only starring in it, but producing it as well. It's my first time out in charge, so to speak, and I'm looking forward to it. Obviously it's quite a challenge.'

Katharine, whose eyes had flown to his face when he started to speak, held her breath, not daring to say a word, waiting for him to go on. Her heart was hammering hard in her chest.

Francesca spoke again. 'Can you tell us about it? Or is it a big secret?'

'Why sure I can. I'm about to remake the greatest love story ever written in the English language. And I hope it will be as good as the original, which has become something of a classic. I'm doing a remake of *Wuthering Heights*. We start shooting in two months.' Victor relaxed in his chair. Now that he was on his own ground he felt more comfortable.

'Love story!' Francesca spluttered, staring at Victor in astonishment. 'But *Wuthering Heights* isn't a *love* story, for God's sake! It's a death-obsessed novel about hatred, revenge, brutality and violence. But mostly it's about revenge. How on earth can you think it's a love story? That's the most ridiculous thing I've ever heard!' Francesca had spoken with such extraordinary vehemence everyone was startled. Kim looked discomfited. Victor seemed stunned. Katharine's face had turned the colour of bleached-out bone, and she was seething. Victor might easily be influenced by these comments, especially since they emanated from Francesca. Like so many Americans, he thought anything English was classy and superior, even a little intimidating. And Francesca had sounded so authoritative. Supposing he decided to abandon the project? Damn, she thought, and not trusting herself to utter a civil word, she stared at her plate – and prayed.

Kim found his voice first. 'Really, Francesca, you're being a bit strong, aren't you? And frightfully rude, if you ask me!' Whenever she had occasion to speak about English literature, her pet subject, she became impossibly opinionated, almost overbearing, as he and his father knew only too well. Kim glared at her, hoping to convey his annoyance.

Francesca swung to face Victor. 'I do apologize. I really didn't mean to be rude. Truly I didn't,' she said, but a faint hint of defiance flickered in her eyes. 'However, I'm afraid I can't apologize for my opinions, particularly since I believe my concept of the book to be correct. And by the way, it is a concept shared by many scholars of English literature, and a number of well-known critics. Of course, there is no denying it is a book of great genius, but nevertheless, it is a paean to death. Emily Brontë was obsessed with death all her life, you know. Anyway, if you don't want to take my word for it, I will be happy to lend you some books about Emily Brontë and her work, and also some critical studies of *Wuthering Heights*. Then perhaps you'll understand it's not a love story after all. Honestly, it really isn't. You see, I read English literature, and did a thesis on the Brontë sisters, so I do know what I'm talking about.'

Katharine could not believe her ears, and she desperately wished Francesca would shut up. She could cheerfully strangle her. Didn't the girl know she was being tactless and inflammatory? For once in her life Katharine was speechless. Her agile, inventive mind raced as she sought a way to smooth the situation over again, to break the deafening silence at the table. Yet unaccountably, she remained at a loss to know what to do or say, and so she picked up her glass and sipped the wine, staring fixedly at the wall opposite, her face stony. Kim fiddled with his fork, poking at the fruit on his plate. Victor continued to frown, musing thoughtfully, and only Francesca appeared tranquil, apparently oblivious to the impact she had made.

However, although Victor was frowning, he was not angry or upset. Oh, the terrible arrogance of the young, he thought. They are so sure. So *absolute*. So certain they have the answers to everything. He was astute enough to recognize Francesca had not intended to be rude, or to offend. Quite simply, she was too straightforward and too honest a girl not to speak her mind about a subject seemingly of great importance to her. She had been in earnest and had meant every word in all sincerity, without realizing she was being provocative. And she *was* so very young. 'You don't have to apologize to me, and I respect your opinion. In fact, you could be right about the book. But the original movie of *Wuthering Heights* was made as a love story, and that is the way I aim to film it. I would be foolish not to do so. I just hope I can make as good a picture as Sam Goldwyn did in 1939. He spoke with an assurance that absolutely forbade argument.

'Oh, I'm sure you will,' Francesca said hurriedly. In the last few seconds she had noticed Katharine's stricken face, the panic in her eyes, and Kim's glowering expression had also registered, and most forcefully. Somehow, and quite unintentionally, she had upset them both, although she was not sure why. Curiously enough, Victor seemed unconcerned.

Francesca lifted her glass. 'I'd like to make amends for my hasty comments by proposing a toast.' She smiled weakly at Katharine and Kim, who lifted their glasses silently, still put out with her. 'To the remaking of *Wuthering Heights*, and to your success, Victor.'

'Thank you,' Victor said and touched his glass to hers.

Wishing to be even more friendly Francesca rushed on, 'And who is going to play Catherine Earnshaw to your Heathcliff, Victor?'

'The role hasn't been cast yet. Naturally every actress worth her salt wants it. But – ' He stopped mid-sentence and chuckled. 'I'm hoping it's going to be the young lady sitting right here.' His eyes rested fondly on Katharine. 'I've arranged a screen test for you. And in colour. You're getting the whole enchilada, honey. And if it's good I know my partners will go along with me, and give you the part.'

Katharine was not sure whether she was going to laugh or burst out crying. For a split second she was unable to say anything. She felt the prick of tears behind her eyes. She pushed them back, said in a quavering voice, 'Oh, Victor! Thank you! Thank you!' Radiance flooded her face and those matchless eyes shone with excitement. She was thrilled, almost beside herself with happiness. 'How can I ever repay you?'

'By making a terrific test, honey.'

Francesca, who was now beginning to understand everything, was again dismayed by her thoughtless remarks. Poor Katharine. No wonder she had been so distressed. She said, 'You'll be marvellous in the part, Katharine! You're absolutely perfect for it. Why it's made for you, isn't it, Kim?'

'Indeed it is.' Kim's face was wreathed in smiles. 'Congratulations!'

Katharine thought she would explode from sheer excitement, and her laughter filled the dining room. 'Don't congratulate me yet. I've got to do the test first, before I even have a chance of getting the part.'

'You'll be perfectly bloody marvellous!' Kim's eyes shone with pride in her. 'This news calls for a toast. Let's go into the drawing room and have some brandy with our coffee. Come on all of you!' He pushed back his chair purposefully, stood up and ushered everyone out.

Walking across the hall, Katharine thought: Victor kept his promise after all. *He did it.* As only he could do it. No one else would have been able to arrange a screen test for me so easily. She was filled with a feeling of great buoyancy, a buoyancy not only of the spirit but of the body as well. She felt as light as a feather, as though she was floating three feet above the ground on balmy air, and the anxiousness and worry which had burdened her for the past few weeks had been vanquished. She paused to wait for Victor at the door of the drawing room. They walked in together, and she took hold of his arm and squeezed it, gazing up at him. 'I meant it, Victor. I don't know how I can ever repay you.'

He returned her gaze unflickeringly. The humorous smile still played around his mouth, but his black eyes were alert and the look he gave her pierced through her. 'You know how, Katharine,' he said, *sotto voce.*

There was a silence. 'Yes.' Her tone was as soft as his, and her heart missed a beat.

'It was nice of you to stay and help me with the dishes,' Francesca said, swirling the water over the last remaining glasses in the sink. 'You really didn't have to, you know. I could have managed.'

'It was the only way I could get Katharine to go home. She was so insistent about helping you,' Victor replied. 'But I saw she was bone tired and falling apart. Two performances in one day are taxing. She suddenly looked done in to me.'

'Yes, I noticed, and it *is* very late.' Francesca handed him another wine goblet to dry. 'Still, I doubt that she'll sleep. She's too worked up about the screen test.'

'That's true, and I hope it goes well, that none of us is in for a big disappointment when we see the footage.'

'What do you mean? Why shouldn't it go well? After all, Katharine is so beautiful, and from what I understand she is a good actress.'

'You're right on both counts. But – ' Victor hesitated. He was sorry he had made the remark. He had spoken without thinking, had left himself wide open to innumerable questions, none of which he felt like answering. He also wondered, suddenly, what the hell he was doing standing in this kitchen in London, in the early hours of the morning, washing dishes with a teenager. Well, she was hardly that. 'Please tell me what you meant,' Francesca persisted stubbornly. 'You sounded so pessimistic.'

Victor sighed. 'Look, forget I said it, okay? I'm sure she'll make a terrific test. Was that the last of the glasses?' Francesca nodded. He rolled down his shirtsleeves and slowly fastened the sapphire cufflinks. 'I'd better be shoving off,' he added, and went out of the kitchen.

Francesca followed him slowly, frowning. 'I don't mean to be a pest, but I wish you'd explain. It was a strange remark to make. Why are you testing her, and considering her for the part, if you think she won't be any good?'

Victor halted in the hall and spun around to face Francesca. 'I didn't say that!' he snapped. 'And I'm not going to embark on a long discussion about movie acting with you, particularly at this hour. It's far too late, and I'm not sure you'd understand what I'm talking about anyway.'

Concern had settled on her face and her eyes held a plea. He felt a stab of remorse for his brusqueness and impatience. 'Oh, what the hell! Come on, give me one for the road, and I'll try to explain as best as I can, in simple terms.'

'And I'll endeavour to understand,' Francesca retorted. She walked ahead into the drawing room, bristling with irritation. Earlier, over coffee and liqueurs, her reservations about him had started to crumble, and she had even begun to like him. He had been warm and understanding, and a marvellous raconteur, keeping them entertained with hilarious anecdotes, and had shown a lovely sense of humour. But once again he had brushed her the wrong way. Her back was up.

Victor poured Remy Martin into two large brandy snifters and carried them over to the fireplace, where Francesca had seated herself, her body rigid in the chair. Her face was closed and her pretty mouth had narrowed into a thin slit of obduracy.

Victor's glance swept over her and unexpectedly a corner of his mouth twitched, but he swallowed his amusement and handed her a snifter silently. He sat down opposite her, picked up his brandy and contemplated for a few moments. Then, without looking at her, he started slowly, 'Katharine Tempest knows more about acting in her little finger than I do in my whole body, and I've been at this game much longer. She's instinctive, the consummate actress. She's quite brilliant, in fact. *On a stage.* But great stage actresses don't always make great movie stars.'

'Why not?' He had fully captured Francesca's interest and she leaned forward, her irritation forgotten.

'Because on a stage everything is more pronounced, slightly exaggerated. By that I mean mannerisms, movements, voice projection. It must be just the opposite on film. Understated. Underplayed, if you like. It's the camera, of course. A movie camera is lethal.' He laid great emphasis on the last word. 'Really lethal. And for one very simple reason. The movie camera photographs your thoughts, and sometimes it even appears to photograph your very soul. You see, movie acting has to do with *thinking* and *intelligence*, much more than histrionics and an expression of excessive emotion. And actors who have been trained for the stage don't always grasp that properly.'

He took another swallow of the brandy, and continued, 'Let me give you an example. Clarence Brown was a wonderful director who made many of Garbo's pictures, including *Anna Karenina*. When he was making that particular film, he kept thinking she wasn't giving him what he wanted, and he would shoot a scene over and over again. But later, when he saw the takes of the scene on the screen, he realized she had had what he was after all the time, from the very first take. You see, Garbo did something not visible to the human eye, but very visible to the camera's eye. She projected her innermost thoughts to it, and yes, her soul, and all this was beautifully captured on film. When that happens, it's extraordinary, and quite magical. Another director, Fred Zinnemann, always says, "The camera's got to love you." And he's absolutely right. If it doesn't, if that chemistry isn't there, then you're dead. Do you follow me?'

'Yes, you explain it very well. What you're saying is that you're not sure Katharine will have this . . . this chemistry with the camera.'

'Exactly. Oh, I know she has talent, great ability, a wonderful speaking voice, and that she'll photograph magnificently in colour, but there's a lot more to it than that. Acting in front of a camera is a very special technique. I'm lucky, in that I have always had great rapport with the camera, and yet I'm not so sure I would be as good as Katharine on a stage. I might fail miserably, as many other movie stars have in that medium. It's funny, but you simply can't lie to the camera. If you do, the lies are there on film.'

'But surely Katharine must understand about this special technique. She *is* a professional – '

'I don't know whether she does or not. To be honest I've never discussed movie acting with her. I should have done, I suppose, but I wanted to fix the test for her first.'

'But you will help her, talk to her, won't you?'

'Sure. I plan to do it some time next week. I can give her a few hints, and the director I've chosen to make the test will take her through her paces first.'

82

'I should jolly well hope so!'

Victor looked at her with some amusement. 'And tell me, Francesca, why are you so interested in Katharine's career?'

'Because I like her, and I know how tremendously important the test is to her. It was easy to see that, after the way she reacted at the dinner table. That's why I feel so ghastly about the awful things I said. About the book, I mean. It was none of my business, and you didn't ask my opinion. I'm not a bit surprised she was so upset. And I'm sure you wanted to kill me, too.'

'Not at all.' He smiled crookedly. 'But I'll have to keep you away from my screenwriter. I don't want you planting any radical ideas in *his* head.'

'Gosh, I wouldn't dream of doing anything like that!'

'I'm kidding. Knowing Nicky, I'm sure he's more than well acquainted with the intrinsic truths in the novel.'

'Nicky?'

'Nicholas Latimer.'

'Do you mean the novelist?'

'That's right. America's boy wonder of literature. I can see, by the look on your face, that you're wondering why I'm using an American to adapt an English classic for the screen. And that you disapprove.'

'No, I don't,' Francesca protested.

He grinned. 'Nick Latimer does happen to be a Rhodes Scholar, as well as a hell of a fine writer.'

'I'm a great admirer of his.'

'Then you have good taste.' Victor tossed down the last of his cognac, and rose. 'Well, now that I've enlightened you a bit about movie acting, I'm going to let you go to bed.' He picked up his jacket and put it on, and together the two of them went out into the hall.

Victor took his trenchcoat from the cupboard and threw it over his arm. He turned to say goodnight, and as he looked at Francesca he experienced that same curious shock of recognition which had so startled him at the beginning of the evening. She hovered near the drawing room door, shrouded in shadows. In the diffused light her face was partially obscured, the pristine features blurred, and she seemed, at that moment, terribly familiar to him, although he knew tonight was the first time he had ever set eyes on her. And yet . . . an evanescent memory stirred in some remote corner of his mind, and was gone before he could grasp it. He stepped closer to her, in order to see her more clearly, and an unanticipated surge of desire rushed through him; he had the spontaneous urge to take her in his arms and crush her to him. For one awful moment he thought he was going to be stupid enough to do so.

Instead, he found himself saying, somewhat hoarsely, 'How old are you, Francesca?'

She lifted her face and looked up at him, her eyes wide and luminous. 'Nineteen,' she said.

'I thought as much.' He thrust out his hand. 'Thanks for a swell evening. Good night.'

'Good night, Victor.'

He turned and left. She stared at the door for several seconds, frowning, and then she went to switch off the lights. As she moved from room to room, she wondered why she felt strangely let down and disappointed.

CHAPTER TEN

Victor Mason sat at the desk in the sitting room of his suite at Claridge's Hotel, studying the budget for his intended remake of *Wuthering Heights*.

With his usual punctiliousness, he examined the columns of figures, analysed each projected expenditure with objectivity, endeavouring to ascertain whether, and how, it could be trimmed. Painstakingly, he began to make headway, jotting notes on a yellow legal pad as he found ways to reduce the costs, and eventually at the end of two hours, through scrupulous cutting, he had saved four hundred thousand dollars.

He put down his pen and stared at the figures, and a smile of satisfaction settled on his face. It still wasn't enough, but it *was* a start. The last thing he wanted to do was diminish the quality of the production, but he had always felt the budget was far too high, and when Jake Watson, his line producer, had called from Hollywood last night his qualms had been confirmed. Jake had pointed out, and in rather colourful language, that the estimated budget of three million dollars was simply not feasible for a film of this nature.

'I've always felt it wouldn't fly,' Victor had told him, 'even though it was prepared by one of the top production guys in Hollywood, as you know. Maybe that's the essence of the problem. Since the picture is being made entirely in England, there are probably many ways I can save, which he didn't consider, perhaps wasn't even aware of, to be really fair. I'll try and find a way to bring it in at two million five.'

Jake, whom Victor had just signed for the project, had retorted gloomily, 'That's still too high. Try to cut as much of the fat off as you can. I'll work on it over the weekend. By Tuesday I should have some new figures.'

Jake is right, of course, Victor commented to himself. Two million *is* nearer the mark. But how do I cut another six hundred thousand dollars? He reached for the telephone to call Jerry Massingham, the English production manager he had engaged last week, and then his hand fell away. Why disturb the man on Sunday. They were scheduled to meet tomorrow and could discuss all the relevant details at that time. There was no real emergency for the next couple of days, and between Jake, Jerry and himself, they ought to be able to pull together a more realistic set of figures. Victor wanted every detail of the project settled and as quickly as possible. With all the facts and figures at his fingertips he could move ahead at once, and negotiate from strength.

Victor took off his horn-rimmed glasses and rubbed his eyes, and then stood up and walked across the room, stretching his legs. He had been at the desk for three hours already and although his progress had been slow, the decisions both trying and difficult, the effort had been worth it. But now he wanted a break. He suddenly wished he was back in Southern California and could take a canter around his ranch. Being essentially a physical man, accustomed to spending a great deal of time outdoors, he always found desk work constraining, despite the fact that budgets and figures intrigued him.

Oddly enough, and unlike most other actors, Victor Mason had acquired a trenchant understanding of the financial and business side of picture making, was aware of its countless ramifications, conversant with the myriad complexities not always comprehended by other artists. He had started his movie career as an extra in Hollywood at the age of twenty, and as he had embarked on the gruelling, rung-by-rung climb up the steep and slippery ladder to stardom, he had diligently made it a point to learn every aspect of movie making. This was for his own protection, with an eye to the future as well as his present work. If there ever came a time when he no longer wanted to be an actor, he would have a second career as a producer to fall back on.

Victor was not stupid. On the contrary, he had a keen intelligence, the ability to assess people and situations accurately, and he was a tough negotiator. Apart from being shrewd and calculating, he was ambitious and driven, and he was the complete realist with his eyes perpetually scanning the profit line. Most importantly, he was blessed with an unusual amount of foresight.

Long before any of his colleagues had seen it coming, he had predicted a radical change in the motion picture industry. He had proved to be right. Just as he had envisaged late in 1949, the old studio system had begun to disintegrate rapidly and was still plunging on its downward journey into total extinction. More and more stars were breaking free of the restrictions imposed upon them by the long-term contracts that tied them to such studios as Warner Brothers, Metro-Goldwyn-Mayer, Twentieth Century-Fox and Columbia. Not only the stars but all the other talent as well, such as producers, directors and writers, wanted their independence, control of their own careers and total approval of the projects they were involved with. And as far as the stars were concerned, a bigger chunk of the money, a percentage of the profits, to which they were undoubtedly entitled.

Victor had been one of the first to buck the studio system, and he had left the studio which had built him into a big name as soon as his long-term contract had expired. When the president had wanted to sign him up for another seven years he had demurred, and in 1952 he had started his own production company. Until now he had always engaged an outside independent producer to make the films he starred in, and which his company, Bellissima Productions, partially financed. With this remake of the old classic he would not only be on the screen but at the helm.

My first real freedom, he thought. But freedom does bring its own responsibilities.

The telephone rang. He turned around and stared at it in irritation, realizing he had forgotten to ask the hotel switchboard operator to monitor his calls. It shrilled again, insistently, and cursing himself for being so remiss earlier, he went to answer it.

'Hello,' he said in a gravely, muffled tone, attempting to disguise his voice.

'You sound as if you were out on the tiles again last night, you old reprobate. I hope I'm not disturbing you, that this is not an inopportune moment. You sound half asleep for God's sake. Disgusting at this hour. Are you not alone, perchance?'

Victor chuckled, recognizing Nicholas Latimer's voice. This was standard dialogue between them, an old joke. They were both early risers, no matter what time they had gone to bed, or with whom. 'Nicky, you son-of-a-gun, it's great to hear from you. And of course I'm alone. What else. How's Paris? How's it going?'

'Paris! You must be kidding. All I've seen of Paris are the walls of a hotel suite. And it's not going badly. Quite the opposite, I'd say.'

'That's swell. When are you coming in?'

'Soon,' Nick replied laconically.

'What the hell does that mean? Come on, give me a date, Nicky. I want to see you, to talk to you. It's not the same when you're not around. I miss my sparring partner.'

Nick said, 'You all right? I detect a hint of – dejection maybe?'

'I'm fine, not a bit dejected,' Victor answered. 'When can I expect you?'

'I told you. Soon. When I've finished the second draft. It's rolling pretty well. I've licked all the problems, and I think you'll like the changes. Minor ones, really, but I believe they bring additional drama and effectiveness to the last few scenes.'

'I'm certain I'll like the new draft, Nick. There wasn't much wrong with the first one, as far as I'm concerned.'

'I know you were fairly well satisfied, Vic, but I felt it didn't move quickly enough, that the pace was slow at the end. Anyway, I've sharpened it up in parts, and I'm pretty sure I'm on the right track now. Incidentally, have you heard from Mike Lazarus?'

Victor caught the subtle change in Nick's tone, the worried intonation. 'No, not for a few days. Why?' he asked, instinctively alerted.

'No real reason. I just wondered, that's all. He's a difficult bastard, and I know he's been on your back for the second draft.'

'Don't worry about Lazarus, Nicky. I'm not. I can deal with him. And take all the time you need with the screenplay. We can't start shooting for at least two months, you know.'

'Points well taken, Victor. Listen, I've got to run, I have an appointment. It was nice talking to you, and I'll be seeing you soon. Sooner than you think, kid.'

'I can't wait,' Victor replied with a laugh, and they both hung up. He immediately lifted the receiver, told the operator to screen his calls and asked for room service. He ordered coffee, and then turned his attention to the production sheets again, wanting to make a final check of the new figures in readiness for the meeting with the production manager the next day. But his concentration had fled. He found himself thinking instead of Nicholas Latimer, and with not a little affection. He missed Nick and would be glad when he returned from Paris, where he had insisted on going, 'To hole up and do the rewrite in peace and quiet, with no distractions,' Nick had explained. Victor missed the younger man, for he had come to rely on his friendship, his companionship, his sharp wit and his incisive mind.

They had first met six years ago, when the writer, then only twenty-three, was being acclaimed as the bright new star on the American literary scene, after publication of his first novel. They had been at a chic party in Bel Air, and had taken to each other immediately. Discovering their mutual boredom with

86

the other guests and the banal movie industry chit-chat, they had made their escape to a bar in Malibu, where they had quickly exchanged confidences and laughed a lot, slowly and diligently getting roaring drunk in the process. Within the space of the next few days, most of which were spent roistering and drinking, they had become firm friends. There were some of their intimates who thought the relationship between the glamorous macho Hollywood movie star and the East Coast intellectual novelist a trifle improbable, even ludicrous, in view of the many diversities in their personalities and backgrounds. Victor and Nicky cocked a snook at these gratuitous opinions.

They knew the reason for their friendship, the foundation for their growing closeness. Quite simply, they understood each other on a fundamental level, and they recognized, too, that this closeness actually sprang from those very disparities in their characters, backgrounds, upbringing and careers. 'And let's face it, we do share one common denominator. Neither of us is a wasp. But then *I* happen to think a wop and a yid make an unbeatable team,' Nick had said sardonically at the time. Victor had roared. Nicky's irreverence and his ability to laugh at himself were traits the actor appreciated. Nicholas Latimer and Victor Mason might have been tipped out from the same mould, for both were mavericks at heart.

Nick had rapidly become a permanent fixture in Victor's life. He was a constant visitor at the ranch near Santa Barbara, he often travelled with Victor to the foreign locations of his movies, and he wrote two original screenplays for him, one of which turned out to be a smashing critical and commercial hit, and earned the two men an Oscar each. Nick also advised Victor on which movie properties to buy, and became a partner in Bellissima Productions. When they were not working, they took trips together. They went up to Oregon, to shoot duck, or fish for salmon at the mouth of the Rogue River; they went skiing in Klosters; they drank and womanized their way from Paris down to the French Riviera and on to Rome, leaving behind a trail of empty champagne bottles and a string of broken hearts. They had fun, they laughed a lot, and, in short, they became inseparable. As the years had passed they had grown to care for each other deeply, in that special way two completely heterosexual men can.

Nick is the best friend I've ever had, Victor said to himself, as he sat reflecting. The only real friend I've ever had. He instantly corrected himself. Except for Ellie. Yes, Ellie had been his truest and dearest friend, as well as his devoted wife, and he still missed her after all these years.

The numbing ache, which had dwelt in him since her death, flared savagely, and he squeezed his eyes tightly shut. Would he never be free of that terrible sense of loss, this perpetual ache in his gut? He doubted it. Ellie had been the one real miracle of his life, the one thing of true value, and she had possessed that rarest of all human qualities – absolute goodness. There never would be another woman like Ellie, not for him at least. No man was ever fortunate enough to have two such perfect relationships in a lifetime. It just wasn't in the cards.

Ellie was the only one who deserved to share his fame, the comfort and privilege which came with his wealth, for she had worked like a dog to help him achieve it. But she had not lived to see him make it into the big time, to enjoy her well-earned rewards. There were times when it seemed to him that his fame was hollow without her beside him. In a sense, he thought of his success as an anomaly. Once the initial euphoria wore off, it had little real meaning, because there was no one to enjoy it with him, no one special who had been there at the beginning, who truly knew the heartache, the sacrifice, the struggle and the immense work it had taken to grasp it. And later, the effort expanded to hold onto it firmly with tenacious hands. That was perhaps the hardest part of all – holding onto the success. In reality it was so ephemeral. And it was lonely at the top. Hellish lonely.

Years ago, when he had been Victor Massonetti, construction worker, the simple Italian-American kid from Cincinnati, Ohio, he had laughed disbelievingly when he had heard someone mouth that cliché. Now he knew it to be true.

Victor realized for the thousandth time how empty his life was without Ellie, and in so many different ways. His other two wives did not count at all, except for the aggravation they had managed to cause him, and neither had ever been able to expunge the memory of his lovely Ellie, or even remotely take her place. But, at least he had the twins. He thought of Jamie and Steve, back home in the States, and instantly the pain lessened, as it always did. And wherever Ellie was now, if there was such a thing as an afterlife, then she knew their boys were loved and safe and protected, and would be for all the days of *his* life. His mind lingered on his sons and then he made an effort to rouse himself, attempting to push aside the despondent mood which had descended on him so inexplicably.

After a while he felt more composed, and he started to check the figures in front of him, but he had no sooner begun on the second column than a loud knocking on the door disrupted the silence. Surprised, he looked up and frowned. That's the fastest room service I've ever had in this hotel, he thought, striding to the door. He jerked it open, and his jaw dropped.

Nicholas Latimer was standing there, propped up against the door frame, grinning from ear to ear.

'Sooner than I think indeed!' Victor exclaimed huffily, glaring at Nick. But his mouth began to twitch with laughter.

'I know, don't say it! I'm a bastard and a childish one at that, pulling this assinine trick on you,' Nick declared. They grasped hands and embraced roughly, and Victor said, 'Well, don't stand there, you clown. Come on in.'

'I took the first plane from Paris this morning. I just checked in a while ago,' Nick said, his wide grin intact. 'When I called you I was already in the suite down the hall, as you've probably guessed. Couldn't resist it, kid.' He ambled into the sitting room and glanced around. 'Mmmm. Not bad. I like this better than the other suite you had, it's more your style.' Nick lowered his long, lanky frame into the nearest chair, slumped down into it, and threw a manilla envelope onto the coffee table with casual grace. 'I tried to call you last night, but you were out. So – ' He shrugged. 'Well, I decided to fly in. I thought I'd surprise you.'

'You succeeded. And I'm glad you're here. I just ordered coffee. Do you want some? How about breakfast?'

'Just coffee. Thanks, Vic.'

Victor went to the telephone and Nick stood up and took off his sports jacket. He draped it over the back of a chair and sat down again. His icy-blue eyes, usually twinkling and full of mischief, were contemplative, and the grin that gave his boyish face a puckish quality, was missing. He looked across at Victor, and his face softened with fondness. He had been right to pack up in Paris and come to

London. This was too important to discuss on the telephone. And two heads are infinitely better than one in this kind of situation, he thought. He lit a cigarette and stared at the burning tip, wondering how Victor would receive the news he was about to impart. With equanimity? Or would his Latin temperament get the better of him, as it sometimes did when he was thwarted. Of course, Victor would be angry, and with good reason, but he had a reservoir of self-control and the ability to sheath his emotions when he so wished. Nick decided it could go either way.

Victor sat down opposite Nick, his eyes focused on the envelope. 'Is that the second draft of the screenplay?' he asked.

'It sure is, kid. It's more or less finished. I have a few changes to make on the last six pages, but I can do that tomorrow. In the meantime, it's all yours. You can read it later.' He fell silent, drawing on his cigarette. 'I came in a couple of days earlier than I'd planned because I wanted to talk to you,' he said finally.

Recalling Katharine's words on the previous evening, Victor said, 'You've heard of the telephone, haven't you?' He smiled at Nick. 'Don't answer that. Obviously you have something important to say, or you wouldn't be here. Not with Natalie stashed in Paris. Or did you bring her with you?'

'No. She's not in Paris either. She had to go back to the Coast to start her new picture. She left in the middle of this past week.' Nick eyed the rolling cart holding bottles of liquor and soft drinks. 'I don't think I want coffee after all. I'd prefer a drink. How about you?'

Victor peered at his watch. 'Why not. The pubs are now officially open, so I might as well start pouring. What do you want? Scotch or vodka?'

'Vodka with some tomato juice. And fix yourself a stiff drink. I believe you're going to need it.'

Victor, who was half-way to the bar, swivelled, staring hard at Nick. He said carefully, 'Oh. *Why?*'

'I've given you the good news about the screenplay.' Nick attempted a smile, but it faltered instantly. 'But we've got a problem. A really serious problem.'

'Let's have it.' Victor picked up the bottle of vodka and proceeded to make Nick's drink.

'Mike Lazarus is in Paris – '

'Lazarus! But I spoke to him only last Wednesday and he was in New York,' Victor cried. He carried the drinks back to the seating arrangement in front of the fireplace, and sat down.

'Maybe so. But right now he's well ensconced in the Plaza-Athénée.' Noting the surprise registering on Victor's face, Nick exclaimed heatedly: 'You should know what he's like by now, Vic! When you're the president of a multinational corporation, as he is, you're ubiquitous. And he thinks nothing of hopping onto that private plane of his and hitting the sky as casually as though he's driving down the Los Angeles freeway.' He lifted his glass. 'Cheers.'

'Down the hatch.' Victor fixed his eyes tightly on Nick. 'I have the oddest feeling you're about to tell me Lazarus is on the war-path. About the picture. So what? I'm ready for him. And I've told you before, I can deal with him. Believe me, I really can.'

Nick raised his hand. 'Wait, Vic. Just hear me out, please. You're right. Lazarus is on a rampage. He's also heading for London – '

'How come you're so well informed about Lazarus? And what he's up to? How do you know so much?'

Nick said slowly, choosing his words with care, 'You know, life is full of surprises, and it can be awfully ironic. Do you remember Hélène Vernaud, the Dior model I used to date?'

'Sure. The tall brunette with the stunning figure and the great legs.'

Nick could not resist laughing. Trust Victor to remember a beautiful girl. 'Let's forget about her figure. She happens to be a graduate of the Sorbonne and the London School of Economics, and she is extremely astute. In fact, she's a hell of a lot smarter than most people I know. Anyway, as you know, we remained friends after we split up, and I called her when I got to Paris three weeks ago. We had lunch, a few laughs remembering old times, and all that jazz. Halfway through lunch she asked me what I was writing. I told her I was doing the screenplay of *Wuthering Heights*. For you. She immediately became tense and strained, even a little agitated, much to my amazement. She then blurted out that she knew something about the picture because she was involved with its main backer, Mike Lazarus. To tell you the truth, I was floored. But, not to digress. Hélène begged me not to mention our lunch. Apparently Lazarus is very jealous and keeps her on a tight rein.' Nick stood up. 'I need another Bloody Mary. Can I fix you a Scotch?'

Victor declined, then asked, 'What's a beautiful, bright, high-class girl like Hélène doing with that slimy snake-in-the-grass Lazarus?'

'God knows.' Nick returned to his chair. 'In any event, I promised her she could rely on my absolute discretion, should I have the misfortune to be in Mike Lazarus's company in the near future. We finished lunch in a more relaxed manner, and that was that. Natalie flew in from Hollywood for a few days, and I forgot all about Hélène and her involvement with Lazarus. Until yesterday morning. She called me from her mother's apartment, sounding very secretive and nervous, and asked me to meet her there within the hour. I didn't know what it was all about. Obviously. But I think enough of Hélène to trust her judgment. I'm glad I do. Last Friday she was having dinner with Lazarus in his suite at the Plaza-Athénée, when he received a call. It was either from New York, or the Coast, Hélène wasn't sure – '

'And she heard something of importance about the picture, is that it?' Victor interrupted.

'Yep.'

'Look, I don't want to throw aspersions on Hélène's veracity, or whatever, but I hardly think a man like Mike Lazarus is going to discuss important business in front of a girl friend. He's secretive and paranoid, among other things.'

'I agree with you. And perhaps someone less bright than Hélène would not have been able to put two and two together and make six. It was all pretty cryptic. However, a number of things he said led her to believe he was referring to us, and our picture, although he didn't actually mention any names.'

'Then how can she be so sure?' Victor demanded, giving Nick a doubtful stare, one brow lifting.

'Because he had some scathing things to say about a screenplay by an esoteric novelist who is also a Rhodes Scholar, to quote Hélène quoting him. He was also extremely disparaging about a movie star who thought he was a producer, who was suffering from *la folie des grandeurs*. Again, that's a direct quote. It *has* to be us, Vic.'

Straightening up in the chair, Victor said, 'O.K. I'll grant you that. Now shoot. Give it to me straight.'

Nick took a deep breath. 'He wants a new script by another writer. He won't approve of an unknown actress playing the female lead. He thinks the budget is astronomically high. He discussed that at great length, by the way, with whoever was on the other end of the line. Hélène distinctly heard him say he thought it was padded, that three million dollars couldn't be justified, couldn't possibly show up on the screen. He seemed to think, from the tenor of his conversation, that he was about to be bled dry and robbed blind. Finally, he said he was going to remove the producer if he didn't toe the line, and make him do what he did best. *Acting*.'

'The son of a bitch!' Victor exclaimed quietly, and his black eyes flashed dangerously. 'What makes him think he can take over *my* film without so much as a by your leave! A project I've worked on for almost a year!'

Nick said evenly, 'Because he has unmitigated *chutzpah* and also because he's holding the cheque book. That's why he thinks he can take over. And you know it.'

Victor gazed at Nick silently. Then he nodded, and after a long moment, he said, 'Lazarus is correct about the budget, Nicky. It *is* too high. Mind you, it's not padded. Merely erroneous.' He glanced at the desk. 'I've been sitting there all morning, cutting production costs.' He related the conversation he had had with Jake Watson the previous evening, and went on, 'I'm trying to bring the picture in at two million dollars.'

'That ought to more than satisfy Lazarus,' Nick said. 'But there's still the question of the script, and your position as producer – '

Cutting in, Victor said, with unusual sharpness, 'Lazarus knows he cannot, and I repeat *cannot*, remove me as producer under any circumstances, however much screaming he does. He's obviously trying to pull one on. And as the producer I have the final word on the script, and Lazarus knows that too.'

'Even so, I honestly think he'll give you trouble about casting an unknown in the Catherine Earnshaw role.' Nick stopped, wondering uncertainly whether or not he should go on, and then he plunged in: 'Listen, Vic, perhaps that is a bad idea. I know you can carry the picture yourself, that you don't need any other big-name stars backing you up, but maybe Lazarus does have a point. Why even bother to test Katharine Tempest? Why don't you give the part to an established movie actress, and save yourself additional problems with Lazarus?'

Victor shook his head. 'No, Nicky. I'm testing Katharine.'

Nick observed him closely, and noting the adamant set of his jawline, he refrained from comment. He wondered to himself if Victor and Katharine were romantically involved, and quickly dismissed the idea as highly unlikely. But even if they were, the days of the casting couch were long since gone. Besides which, Victor was too shrewd, too tough and too much of the businessman to fall into that dangerous trap. He wouldn't take any chances with his career, or his money, for a quick fling with a passing fancy. Notwithstanding, Nick was curious. 'Why are you so keen on testing her?'

'Because I gave her my promise, and because in a way she has earned it. Of course, there's another reason, the most important reason of all. I just happen to believe she would be perfect in the part. There's a kind of wildness in her, a fire, that reminds me very much of Cathy in *Wuthering Heights*. I think she would be as good as Merle Oberon in the role, perhaps even better. It strikes me Katharine Tempest has a lot more vivacity and spirit. If she tests the way I hope she will, I'm going to put her in the picture, and to hell with my backers, whoever they are.' Victor's mood changed abruptly, and he gave Nick a smile that hinted at his satisfaction. 'I'm also going to sign her to a contract with Bellissima Productions. You see, I have a sneaking feeling Katharine Tempest is going to be a big star one day, although I wouldn't say that to anyone else but you until after I've seen the test. Look, trust me. I know what I'm doing. From the very first moment I met Katharine I have felt that she has that – that indescribable thing, that IT. Charisma. Star quality. Whatever you want to call it. If she can project this quality to the camera, and I hope she can, then she's home free. She'll be very, very big. If she can't – ' He pursed his lips regretfully. 'Well, she'll go on being a brilliant actress. On the stage.' Now he chuckled, his eyes merry. 'I don't know why you haven't spotted this quality in her yourself.'

'As a matter of fact, I have. But – ' Nick's voice trailed off and he lifted his shoulders in a weary gesture. 'Look, Vic, I have to repeat that Lazarus will never go for the idea of an unknown actress in this role, however good she is. He seems hell bent on getting a big female movie star to play opposite you. You know something else? I have a strong suspicion he's going to arrive in London before you can blink. I wouldn't be a bit surprised if he's here already.'

Victor rose and poured himself another Scotch. 'I might as well tell you, I've been seriously thinking of dumping Lazarus.' This was uttered with casualness, indifference even, and he looked unconcerned. 'In fact, the thought's been hovering at the back of my mind for a couple of weeks. He's an autocratic, interfering bastard. A megalomaniac. And just because he runs a giant multinational corporation doesn't mean he knows how to produce a movie, although he undoubtedly believes he does. But he's a rank amateur in our business. It has struck me innumerable times lately, and quite forcibly, that I'm letting myself in for a lot of headaches if I take him into Bellissima Productions. Or rather, let him invest in the picture. I'm sorry I ever got involved with him, to tell you the truth. And what I've just heard from you makes me more wary than ever. I think I have to lose him, and quickly.'

'Jesus, Vic! That would be great. But how are you going to get rid of him? I thought you had a contract.'

'A contract was drawn between Bellissima Productions and Lazarus, but I haven't signed it yet. There were a couple of clauses in it that bothered me, and I sent it over to my solicitor here. A copy has also gone to my lawyer in Beverly Hills. I'm waiting for their opinions before I sign. So you see, I can dump him any time I want, without fear of repercussions. As yet, Mike Lazarus hasn't invested a nickel, you know. So basically, he has no claims whatsoever. I'm still in the driver's seat.' He settled back, looking smug.

'But how will you finance the picture without him?' Nick asked worriedly.

'Ah, and therein lies the rub, to quote good old Will Shakespeare. To be honest, I don't know right now. I hadn't wanted to go to one of the majors for financing as well as distribution, but I might have to in the end.

Anything is better than Lazarus. Metro might be interested. What do you think?'

Nick frowned. 'I honestly don't know. They might not be too excited by a remark of *Wuthering Heights*. Did you see that story in *Variety* a couple of weeks back? The exhibitors were sounding off about remakes, and in very strong terms. They think they are box office poison, that people aren't interested in them.'

'Oh come on, sport, forget it, and let me worry about the timeliness of the picture, the money, and all that jazz. I think Hélène's information about Lazarus has spooked you a bit. For God's sake, don't let's get depressed about that joker. I'll find a way to pull the deal together. Now, why don't we get out of here? I'd like some fresh air and a brisk walk. Shall we mosey on up to the Connaught Hotel for lunch? It's the whole enchilada on Sunday.'

'That's a great idea,' Nick said, trying to sound cheerful.

'Give me five minutes to get dressed. And help yourself to another drink while you're waiting.'

'Thanks, I will.' Nick stood up and walked over to the bar cart, deep in thought. He turned. 'I say, Vic, can I ask you something?'

'Sure.' Victor paused at the bedroom door, his hand resting on the knob, conscious of the gravity in Nick's tone.

Nick's face was unusually solemn. 'Assuming you definitely decide *not* to go ahead with Mike Lazarus as your main backer, what will you do if you can't get financing from one of the majors, such as Metro, Twentieth or Warners?'

A thoughtful look drifted across Victor's face, and he cleared his throat. 'I'll have to abort the production. Cancel the picture. I'll have no alternative,' he said with some deliberation, having already confronted this possibility and made his decision. 'The pre-production money will go down the drain unfortunately, but there's not much I can do about that. And thank God it won't cripple Bellissima Productions. It can be written off as a tax loss.' He sighed lightly. '*C'est la guerre*, old buddy.' He gave Nick a lopsided grin and went through into the bedroom.

Cancel the picture, Nick thought, staring after him, staggered, disbelieving. After all the hard work they had put into it. Jesus Christ! Not only the pre-production money would go down the drain, but a year of their lives as well. Yet Nick knew Victor meant every word. Things were always carefully evaluated and well thought out before he made a judgment. His decisions were nothing if not judicious and pragmatic.

Nick felt his own sharp disappointment as he considered the screenplay he had laboured on so diligently and with such love these past endless months. He knew it to be one of his best pieces of writing, and he suddenly felt sick at heart at the idea of its never seeing the light of day.

You're being selfish. You're only thinking about yourself, he muttered, carrying his drink over to the window. He parted the curtains and looked out, but saw nothing except a dim blur of grimy buildings washed in wintry sunlight. But a lot of other people will be disappointed too, thought Nick sadly, not the least Victor, who had dreamed of making *Wuthering Heights* for the longest time, was aching to play Heathcliff for the sheer challenge the role offered to him. Nick knew Victor wanted to stretch his talent, was weary of being thought of simply as an immense presence on the screen.

He and Victor would recover from their disappointment relatively quickly, as would the production team, and move on to other projects. Victor had several offers for future films lined up, and he himself had a new novel fermenting in his head, and was anxious to start working on it as soon as possible. Yes, he and Victor were lucky in that respect. They would cut their losses, lick their wounds and walk away reasonably unscarred. But what of Katharine Tempest? She was staking everything on the screen test and the role in the film. It was a rare chance for her to catapult herself into the big time with unusual speed. Without Victor and this film it could be years before she was offered another such incredible break. If ever. Undoubtedly Katharine had put all her chips on this roll of the dice. She could win big. Or lose hard. And if she lost she would be devastated. Nick knew all of this although he had never been the recipient of any confidences from her. He simply knew it through intuition.

Nick let his thoughts dwell on Katharine. He understood why Victor saw great potential in her as a movie actress. Nick was not blind to Katharine's attributes, which were manifold. However, conversely, his personal reaction to her was quite different from everyone else's. Her extraordinary beauty had not beguiled him, nor had her enormous charm captivated him. In essence, she had failed to touch him as a man, and very simply he was not sure of her as a woman. Nick had detected an inherent coldness in her personality. It was a frigidity really, and, to him, this seemed all the more peculiar in view of her apparent sensuality. Except that instinctively he felt this was a façade she presented to the world, was bound up with her looks and had nothing to do with her true nature. The sensuality was on the surface. It did not run deep in her. On the few occasions he had been in her company, he had become increasingly aware of other traits which disturbed him. It struck him, unexpectedly, that there was a dichotomy in Katharine's makeup. There was no denying her warmth and gaiety. Yet at other times she appeared strangely removed, to him, as if she had the ability to stand away from herself, as though she viewed everthing with cool indifference. No, immense detachment. He thought now: She is isolated and uninvolved with anyone on a human level.

He shook his head in bewilderment. Oh, Christ, I'm being over imaginative, he decided. There's nothing wrong with the girl really. She's excessively ambitious perhaps, but then who isn't in this business. With a small shock Nick admitted he did not particularly like her, and this revelation astonished him. There was no real basis for his active dislike, and yet dislike her he did.

As he stood, sipping his drink and staring out of the window, striving to analyse his feelings, Nicholas Latimer did not know that it would take him years to fully comprehend his complex emotions in regard to Katharine Tempest.

CHAPTER ELEVEN

Katharine stood in the tiny kitchen of her flat in Lennox Gardens, waiting for the kettle to boil for her morning tea. She put a piece of bread in the toaster, and then, standing on tiptoe, she reached up into the cupboard, taking out a cup and saucer, and a plate. She opened the refrigerator door, removed the butter dish and a stone jar of Dundee marmalade, and placed them on a tray with the other china, her movements swift yet graceful.

The kitchen was so small that there was only enough space for one person in it, but because it was so sparklingly fresh and neat and free of the unnecessary clutter Katharine detested, it seemed much less claustrophobic than it actually was. When Katharine had taken the flat two years earlier, she had had the walls and the cabinets painted a pale duck-egg blue, and this delicate colour helped to open up the confined dimensions, as did the matching marbleized linoleum on the floor. Blue cotton curtains, gauzy and weightless, framed the small window, and on the windowsill itself there was a selection of red geraniums in clay pots, and these introduced a spark of vivid colour and springlike greenery.

Katharine stepped to the window and glanced out. The flat was on the top floor and had once been the attics of the house, before it had been converted into flats. Consequently, she had a charming bird's eye view from her little eyrie, and one which faced onto the enclosed gardens situated in the centre of the semi-circular terrace of imposing Victorian mansions. In the summer months she looked down onto great leafy domes and cupolas shimmering with iridescent green light as the sunshine filtered through the lacy texture of the interwoven branches weighted with verdant leaves. On this February morning, the gardens were bereft, the trees stripped of beauty and life. But their black and bony branches did reach up into the prettiest sky she had seen in a long time. The dark and tumescent clouds which had shrouded London in perpetual greyness for weeks had miraculously been blown away. For once it was not raining.

It's almost like an April morning, Katharine thought with a happy smile, and she decided there and then that she would walk to the restaurant for her luncheon appointment at one o'clock. She debated what to wear and settled on the new outfit her dressmaker had delivered last week. She was mentally reviewing the accessories which would best go with it, when the kettle's piercing whistle cut into her musings, and she turned off the gas, filled the teapot, put the toast on the plate and carried the breakfast tray into the living room.

Despite the sunlight flooding in through the windows, this room had an air of overwhelming coldness. Essentially, this was induced by the colour scheme and the overall style of the decoration, which was austere. Everything in the room was of the purest white. Gleaming white-lacquered walls flowed down to meet a thick white carpet covering the entire floor. White silk draperies rippled icily at the windows, and white wool sheathed the long sofa and several armchairs. The latter were sleek and modern in design, as was all of the furniture in the room, including two end tables flanking the sofa, a large square coffee table and an *étagère* set against one wall. These pieces were made of chrome and glass, and they introduced a hard and glittering aspect that further emphasized an atmosphere excessively glacial in its overtones.

There were few accent colours in this setting, so evocative of a frozen landscape, and these were dark and muted tones of steel grey and black, and did little to counteract the chilly monotony that prevailed. Tall pewter lamps on the glass end tables were topped with steel grey linen shades, and the same metallic grey was repeated in the velvet cushions on the sofa and chairs. Black and white etchings of knights in armour, framed in chrome, marched along one wall, while a huge cylindrical glass vase containing spidery black branches stood sentinel in one corner. The *étagère* displayed a pair of black-lacquered candlesticks sprouting white candles and a black-lacquered Japanese bowl. There were no photographs of family or friends, none of the usual intimate objects that provide evidence of past, treasured memories, or a personal life. The room, in all truth, had the sterility of a nun's barren and virginal cell, and it echoed the adjoining bedroom, also washed completely in pure white and unrelieved by any contrasting colours whatsoever. Katharine had furnished and decorated the flat herself, and if anyone had told her it was icy and lifeless and intimidating, she would have gaped at them askance. She loved the pristine effect she had so carefully created, considered it to be elegant and sophisticated, saw only beauty in its purity and cleanliness, elements so necessary to her well being.

Hurrying across the room, she put the tray on the coffee table and sat down on the sofa. There was a dreamy faraway expression on her face, and as she sipped her tea she allowed herself to drift with her meandering thoughts. Katharine was feeling marvellous. Euphoria and excitement had carried her through the week and now, on this Thursday morning, it seemed to her that every day that had passed since Saturday night had been a huge success.

Both Francesca and the Earl had loved her performance as Helen of Troy, and the dinner at Les Ambassadeurs, with Victor acting as the host, had been memorable. Most important to Katharine, the Earl had taken to her immediately, and she knew he had been charmed, and therefore she did not envision him creating any problems or interfering in her relationship with Kim.

Katharine was not wrong in her belief that the Earl of Langley had liked her. In fact, they had been impressed with each other, the conservative English peer of the realm and the young American beauty, and their easy accord had created a warm and friendly atmosphere, had made for a relaxed evening. Everyone had enjoyed themselves to such a degree that Victor had extended the party into the early hours, and had taken them upstairs to the Milroy to dance to Paul Adams and his orchestra. Katharine, the actress incarnate, had surpassed herself, intuitively striking the perfect balance between reticence and gaiety.

The following day, Victor had taken her to lunch at Claridge's, the sole purpose being to discuss more fully the screen test, and to enumerate the many differences between acting on a stage and before a camera. He had held forth at great length, offering her many helpful and instructive guidelines. Katharine had been touched by this thoughtfulness on his part, and grateful to him for his sound advice. He had arranged to meet with her again, for another session before the test itself, which had been confirmed for Friday of the coming week, eight days away. Tomorrow evening the Earl was taking her to dinner with Kim and Francesca, before returning to Yorkshire with Kim at the weekend.

Katharine smiled to herself, and it was a smile of self congratulation and jubilance. Events were moving with the precision of clockwork; all the plans she had so painstakingly made were coming to fruition. She would marry Kim and become Viscountess Ingleton, and she would be a big international movie star. She settled back contentedly, cuddling down into her woollen dressing gown, hugging herself with joy. Her dreams would soon be realized. There would be no more pain and heartache and grief. Her life was going to be wonderful from now on.

As she sat daydreaming on the sofa, it never occurred to Katharine Tempest that things might be just a little too good to be true, or that something beyond her control might happen to mar these halcyon days. And if such a thought had crossed her mind she would have dismissed it at once, and with a degree of scorn. For unfortunately, Katharine was afflicted with a character flaw that was almost Hellenic in its proportions. She was crippled by hubris, that defect the Greeks defined as the temerity to tempt the Gods, in essence, an excess of overweening pride and the unwavering conviction of personal invulnerability. Being blindly unaware of this blemish in herself, she had no qualms about anything she did, and so she was also quite confident about the result of the screen test. She would be marvellous and Victor would give her the part in the film.

Victor Mason had told Katharine he intended to start principal photography in April, and this starting date suited Katharine admirably. Her contract with the theatrical producers of *Trojan Interlude* had an 'out-of-the-play' clause, and this came into effect after she had been in the play for one year. The year would be up at the end of March and so she could invoke the clause and leave the production to do the film. The shooting schedule was for twelve weeks, with exteriors to be shot in Yorkshire, interiors at one of the major studios in London. Victor had also told Katharine that he planned to have the footage edited quickly, since he wanted the answer print by September. From this master print he intended to strike two more prints, he had gone on to explain. The film could thus be shown in cinemas in New York and Los Angeles, for one week before the end of the year, thereby making the picture eligible, under the rules, for the Academy Awards of 1956. Although Victor would not be putting the film into general distribution until the spring of 1957, he had confided he did not want to miss a chance at the Oscar nominations.

What if *she* won an Oscar! This prospect was at once so stunning, so electrifying, so dazzling, Katharine felt momentarily dizzy. And because she had that most unique of all talents, the talent for believing in herself, the idea that she had a chance of winning was not at all beyond the realms of possibility in her mind. But even if she did not win an Oscar, Katharine did not doubt that she would be a star when the picture was released. And her success would not only bring her fame on a grand scale, but money, lots of money, a very special kind of power.

A faint white shadow glanced across Katharine's face, tinging it with unfamiliar bitterness and dislodging the joy which had previously rested there.

Soon, very soon, she would be able to make her moves, put her final plan into operation, and execute it with the sure knowledge that she would be triumphant. A tiny fluttering sigh escaped Katharine's lips. It was too late to save her mother, but not too late to save her brother, Ryan. Her dearest Ryan. Lost to her for so long. This desire had been one of the prime motivations behind many of Katharine's actions for the past few years, and just as she was unremittingly driven to succeed in her career, so too was she driven to rescue Ryan from their father's domination, from his contaminating influence. Sometimes, when she thought of Ryan, panic moved through Katharine and she quivered with fear for him. Ryan was nearly nineteen, and she often wondered to what degree his soul had been poisoned by that man. Had Ryan inevitably become their father's creature, partially if not wholly? This idea was so repugnant to her, so unacceptable, and so terrifying, she pushed it away fiercely, denying it with silent vehemence; but her resolution to get her brother away from Chicago and to keep him with her wherever she was living, was reinforced more strongly than ever.

Katharine thought about Ryan, and the daunting expression slowly lifted from her face; her features grew soft, the hardness tempered by love and tenderness. But as always when she contemplated him, other images intruded. Her hands tightened in her lap and she sat staring into space fixedly, without moving, her body as immobile as a statue. Surrounding Ryan like a fateful nimbus was that brooding grotesque house where they had grown up, and where Ryan still lived, that awful mausoleum of a place, that dubious tribute to her father's wealth and position and his terrible power. She had always loathed that house with its dusky hallways and winding staircases and dolorous rooms stuffed to overflowing with expensive ugly antiques, all manner of bric-a-brac and undistinguished paintings. It was a master-piece of ostentation, reeking of bad taste, new money and suffocating unhappiness. To Katharine it was also a house of deprivation. Oh, they had had expensive clothes and the best food and cars and servants, for their father was a millionaire many times over. But it was, to Katharine, still a deprived house, for there had been so little genuine love in it. She shuddered involuntarily. She had not set foot in that house for six years, and on the day she had left it she had vowed she would never darken its doors again.

Katharine's thoughts rushed to her father, and although she consistently obliterated his image in her mind's eye, today she did not even attempt to extinguish it. She saw him quite vividly, as if he stood before her, Patrick Michael Sean O'Rourke, with his handsome saturnine face and ebony-black hair, eyes as blue as sapphires and as hard as that stone they so closely resembled. He was a dreadful man, and she realized suddenly that she had always understood this, even when she had been a very small child. She had simply not known the words to properly describe him then. Today she had them at the tip of her tongue. He was exigent, rapacious and ruthless, a venal man who had made money his mistress and power his God. The world did not know Patrick Michael Sean O'Rourke as she knew him. He was a monumental anachronism: the charming, laughing, entertaining, silver-tongued Irishman in public, the stern, glowering and dictatorial tyrant in his own home. Katharine hated him. Just as he hated her. Gooseflesh speckled her arms and she pulled her robe closer around her. She recalled, with the most sharp and awful clarity, the day she had first recognized her father's virulent hatred for her. It had been in August 1947. She had been twelve years old.

On that day, nearly nine years ago, Katharine had been her happiest in many months, this state engendered by her mother's unexpected presence at lunch. Rosalie O'Rourke was feeling so much better she had decided to join her children at their noonday meal. Katharine had been singularly overjoyed to see her mother looking practically like her old self; and if Rosalie was not brimming with the vitality which had once been such an essential and natural part of her personality, she seemed lighthearted, almost carefree. Her eyes, widely set and a clear tourmaline green, sparkled with laughter, and her abundant red hair, crackling with life, was a burnished bronze helmet above her heart-shaped face, which was free of pain today, and had lost some of its waxen pallor. She was wearing a pale green silk-shantung dress with long sleeves and a full skirt, and its style disguised her thin body, so tragically wasted by illness. A choker of lustrous pearls encircled her neck, and there were matching pearl studs in her ears; her tapering fingers glittered with beautiful rings set with diamonds and emeralds.

Mrs O'Rourke had instructed Annie, the housekeeper, to serve luncheon in the breakfast room, one of the few cheerful spots in the dim and shadowy house, and which Rosalie herself had personally decorated. It had a lovely aura of airy lightness, was brushstroked throughout in a pretty *mélange* of crisp white and sharp lemon yellow, rafts of these refreshing colours appearing everywhere. It was furnished, in the main, with white wicker furniture, unusual handsome pieces from the Victorian era, and there were colourful prints of exotic birds and rare orchids on the walls and an abundance of tall green plants. Decorated in the same charming manner as Rosalie's suite of rooms on the second floor, it was refined and gracious, yet without being at all stylized in appearance.

As she had sat gazing adoringly at her mother across the table, Katharine had thought how distinguished and elegant she looked, perfectly groomed and smelling faintly of lilies of the valley as she invariably did. To Katharine her mother was, and always would be, the epitome of beauty and feminine grace, and she idolized her. Katharine, at this moment, was filled with renewed hope for her mother, who seemed to be on the way to recovering from the mysterious illness which had afflicted her for the past two years, an illness no one really discussed, except in whispers.

Since it was a weekday, Patrick O'Rourke had not been present, and in consequence, the tension which generally accompanied their meals was fortunately missing. Ryan had chattered like a magpie, had kept them entertained, and they had laughed a lot and enjoyed themselves. Katharine had felt secure, basking in her mother's love. It was a love given unstintingly and with all of Rosalie's tender and caring heart.

Only one thing marred this joyful occasion for Katharine, and this was her mother's poor appetite, and she had watched with growing dismay as Rosalie had picked at her food desultorily, leaving untouched most of the delicious and tempting dishes their housekeeper Annie had prepared. After lunch, Ryan had disappeared, intent on some boyish escapade. When her mother had asked Katharine to spend another hour with her, she had delightedly accepted. Nothing pleased the twelve-year-old girl more than to be alone with her mother in the cool secluded suite she occupied. Katharine loved the comfortable rooms with their pastel colour schemes and delicate fabrics, French Provincial furniture and lovely paintings, so unlike the rest of the house which bore her father's vulgar stamp. The sitting room, in particular, was Katharine's favourite, and most especially on cold days. Then the fire blazed and crackled in the hearth and they sat before its roaring flames in that special twilight hour, toasting their toes and chatting cosily about books and music and the theatre, or relaxing in silence, always in perfect harmony, for there was a deep understanding and abiding love between them. That afternoon they had seated themselves by the window overlooking Lake Michigan, not talking very much, content to be sharing this time. It had been a long while since they had had an opportunity to spend an afternoon with each other because of Rosalie's precarious health.

At thirty-two Rosalie O'Rourke had made her peace with herself and her God, and this new-found tranquillity showed in her face, which, despite her illness, was still lovely. Today it had an ethereal quality lightly overshadowed by a faint wistfulness, and her eyes were soft and filled with the tenderest of lights as she sat gazing out over the lake, endeavouring to gather her strength. The lunch had vitiated her energies, but she did not wish this to show, wanted Katharine to be reassured about her condition. Rosalie had not experienced much joy in her life after her marriage, except through her children, mostly Katharine, whom she adored. She had quickly discovered she was no match for Patrick, with his rampant virility and quick Irish temper, his lust for life in all its aspects, and his hunger for money and power, which was insatiable. Her refinement and delicacy, her fragility and artistic nature had inevitably isolated her from her husband, and her gentle soul continually shrank from his blatant masculinity and voracious appetites. Despite her love for him, curiously undiminished, she had come to regret the union, recognizing the unsuitability of their temperaments. Few knew the real Patrick, for he was adept at concealment, cloaking his true nature behind an austere and dignified façade; and he was a past master at the art of dissimulation, adroit, and persuasive of tongue.

'That one's kissed the Blarney stone, by God he has, and not once but many times over,' her father had said to her early in the whirlwind courtship. Her father had continued to be ambivalent about Patrick long after their marriage, never truly sure the relationship would work. In certain ways it had been successful, in others it had not, and there had been times when Rosalie had contemplated leaving Patrick. But divorce was unthinkable. She was a Catholic, as was he, and there were the children, whom she knew he would never relinquish. And she still had deep feelings for him, regardless of his faults.

Although Rosalie hardly ever acknowledged it as a fact, or dwelt upon it morbidly, she knew that she was dying. The spurts of vigour and renewed energy and remissions were quite meaningless, and they were growing increasingly infrequent. Now, as she sat with her daughter, she thought sadly: I have so little time left on this good earth, so little time to give to Katharine and Ryan, God help them.

Every day Rosalie, who was devout, gave thankful prayers to the Almighty that her daughter and her son were more like her in their basic characters, and had not inherited many of their father's dismaying traits, at least so far as she could ascertain. She glanced at Katharine, sitting sedately in the chair, obedient and

100

well mannered, and she marvelled at her yet again. The child looked so young and demure in her yellow cotton dress and white socks and black patent-leather strap shoes. And yet there was something oddly grownup in her demeanour, as though she had seen much of life, had encountered its pain and pitfalls and was wise and knowing. Rosalie realized this was an idiotic idea, since the girl was over-protected, had never been exposed to anything but luxury and the safety of her family and her home. But one thing which could not be denied was Katharine's extraordinary physical appearance. She was a great beauty, even at this tender age, with her lovely features and rich chestnut hair and those liquid eyes with their curious turquoise hue. Katharine had a sweet and loving personality which echoed the sweetness in her face, but Rosalie knew this disguised a streak of wilful stubbornness. She also suspected that her daughter might have a touch of Patrick's ruthlessness in her as well, but perhaps this was all to the good. Rosalie instinctively felt Katharine was capable of looking after herself, protecting herself against Patrick and the world at large, for she had the spirit of a fighter, and she would survive against all odds. And for this Rosalie was suddenly thankful.

Of her two children, it was Ryan whom she worried about the most. He was far too timid to effectively defend himself against Patrick, who doted on him in the most alarming way, seeing in Ryan the heir apparent who would glorify the name O'Rourke, and who was the malleable tool for Patrick's own terrifying ambition. How Pat had longed for this son; how disappointed he had been when he had first set eyes on Katharine, a mere girl. Ryan's birth had been perhaps the single most important occasion in Patrick's life, and he had had his plans worked out for the boy that very day. Possibly they had been formulated years before, those high-flown grandiose plans that sickened Rosalie. Her efforts to dissuade her husband had been futile, her entreaties had fallen on stony ground, and to the sound of laughter and angry, condemning words. She was helpless. She could not prevent Patrick from putting those plans into eventual motion. She would not be alive when that day finally arrived. She could only pray that Ryan would have the strength and the willpower to stand up to his father, the inner resources to walk away from Patrick, with his integrity intact, when the time came. If he did do this, Patrick would immediately disinherit and disown him, of that she had no doubt. Ryan would be penniless. A poor young man. But he would be safe, and ultimately rich in that he would be free of his father's domination and control. He would be his own man, not a puppet manipulated by Patrick O'Rourke.

Rosalie sighed, thinking of Patrick, and she wondered why she still had such overpowering emotions for him, when she knew him to be quite monstrous. How strange and perverse women are, she thought.

'Is anything wrong, Mother?' Katharine asked in a small worried voice, cutting into Rosalie's thoughts.

Rosalie managed to force a smile onto her face, and she replied quickly, lightly, 'No, darling, of course not. I was just thinking how neglectful I've been of you lately, but you know I haven't had much strength or energy. I wish we could spend more time together, especially now that you have school vacation.'

'Oh, so do I, Mother,' Katharine exclaimed. 'But you mustn't worry about me. All I want is for you to get better.' Katharine jumped down off the chair and joined Rosalie on the sofa. She took hold of her mother's fine hand and gazed up into

101

her face, and unexpectedly she saw something in the green eyes that frightened her. She was not sure what it was. A look of immense sadness perhaps. Or was it resignation? The girl was unable to pinpoint it accurately, but her heart clenched and her own eyes filled with sudden bright tears. 'You *will* get better, won't you, Momma?' Katharine hesitated and her lip quivered as she whispered, 'You're not going to die, are you?'

Rosalie laughed and shook her burnished copper curls. 'Of course not, you silly child! I'm going to be fine, and very soon I'll be my old self.' The smile widened and she continued bravely, 'After all, I have to be around when you star in your first play. I have to see your name in lights on the marquee, and be there on opening night. You do still want to be an actress, don't you, honey?'

Rosalie spoke with such assurance, Katharine's fears were allayed. She blinked back her tears and instantly brightened. 'Oh, yes, I do, Momma. I really do.' Although her smile was watery, there was extraordinary determination in her child's voice. Then she asked, 'You don't think *he'll* object, do you?'

A frown touched Rosalie's pale face and was gone. 'Your father? I'm sure he won't. And why should he?' Rosalie shifted slightly on the sofa and eased herself back against the cushions, experiencing a twinge of pain. 'You know what fathers are like. They don't pay much attention to such things. They think their daughters should get married the moment they leave college, and then have lots of babies. I suppose he'll simply think it's a nice way for you to pass your time until you do get married.'

'But I've no intention of getting married,' said Katharine with unprecedented fierceness, and her eyes flared with the sharpest of blue flame. 'I want to be a famous actress like Sarah Bernhardt and Eleanora Duse and Katharine Cornell. I intend to devote my *life* to the theatre. I won't have any time for a foolishness like marriage,' she scoffed.

Rosalie bit back a smile of amusement. 'Well, darling, you might change your mind one day, especially when you fall in love.'

'Oh, I know I won't!'

Rosalie made no comment to this last remark, but continued to smile lovingly at her daughter. Eventually she said, 'I'm sorry we couldn't go for our usual summer visit to Aunt Lucy's in Barrington. It would have been such a pleasant change from Chicago. It's so hot here right now. But your father thought the trip would overtire me. You don't mind being in the city too much, do you, Katharine?'

'No, Momma. I like going to Barrington, but not without you. I just want to stay here and keep you company.'

'That's sweet of you.' Rosalie pondered for a moment and then asked softly, 'You do like your aunt, don't you, dear?'

Katharine was surprised by this question. ''Course I do, Momma. I love Aunt Lucy.'

Rosalie squeezed Katharine's small hand. 'She has been a great source of strength for me as long as I can remember, and my dearest friend, as well as my sister.' Rosalie stopped. There was something else which she needed to say, but she did not want to alarm Katharine, and so she sought her words with great care. 'Aunt Lucy loves you dearly, Katharine. You're like the daughter she never had. And she will always be there for you, my darling. Don't ever forget that, will you?'

102

Straightening up on the sofa, Katharine drew away from her mother and stared at her, her wide eyes searching that gentle face intently. But it was peaceful and her mother appeared to be untroubled. Nevertheless, Katharine murmured tensely, 'What a funny thing to say, Momma. Why should I ever need Aunt Lucy, when I have you?'

'We all need friends, my darling. That's all I meant. Now, would you like to read to me for a while. A little poetry. I think something by Elizabeth Barrett Browning would be nice.'

Katharine took out the leather-bound book of poetry and seated herself in the chair; she turned the pages to the sonnets, and scanned them carefully until she came across the one she liked the most, and which she knew her mother preferred to all of them.

Her voice, as light and as clear as a crystal bell, rang out in the quiet room:

'How do I love thee? Let me count the ways.
I love thee to the depth and breadth and height
My soul can reach, when feeling out of sight
For the end of Being and ideal Grace.
I love thee to the level of every day's
Most quiet need, by sun and candlelight.
I love thee freely, as men strive for Right;
I love thee purely, as they turn from Praise.
I love thee with the passion put to use
In my old griefs, and with my childhood's faith.
I love thee with a love I seemed to lose
With my lost saints, – I love thee with the breath,
Smiles, tears, of all my life! – and if God choose,
I shall but love thee better after death.'

Katharine lifted her head and looked at her mother for approval, a smile on her face. But it slipped, and she put the book down instantly, and flew to the sofa. Tears shimmered on Rosalie's translucent cheeks and the hand that was lifted to wipe them away shook.

'Momma, Momma, what is it?' Katharine cried, embracing her mother. 'Why are you crying? I didn't mean to pick a sonnet that was sad or would upset you. I thought you loved that particular one.'

'I do, darling,' Rosalie said, thinking sorrowfully of Patrick, but smiling through her tears. 'I'm not sad, really I'm not. The sonnet is beautiful, and I was very moved by your voice, and the way you read it with so much meaning and emotion, Katharine. I know you're going to be a marvellous actress.'

Katherine kissed her mother's cheek. 'Shall I read you another one? Something more cheerful?'

Rosalie shook her head. 'I think I'm going to lie down for a while, Katharine. I'm feeling a little tired after all.' She leaned closer and touched Katharine's cheek lightly with the tip of her finger. 'You're very special, my beautiful Katharine. And I do love you so very much.'

'I love you too, Momma.'

Rosalie stood up, holding onto the arm of the sofa to steady herself, making a tremendous effort to hide the sudden trembling which had seized her from her daughter. 'Will you come and see me later, dear?'

'Yes, Momma,' Katharine said.

Rosalie nodded, too exhausted to respond, and moved towards the bedroom.

Katharine went in search of Ryan, scouring the house for him. As she mounted the stairs to the third floor she noticed it had grown stifling hot. The air was heavy with humidity, and the house was airless and more suffocating than usual. She had grown hot on her long climb up to her old nursery, and by the time she reached the door her cotton frock was damp and clinging to her body.

She found Ryan sitting at the table, just as she had expected, and as usual he was painting. His head, with its mop of reddish-golden curls, was bent in concentration. He looked up when she came in. He was smiling.

'Can I see?' Katharine asked, crossing the floor to join him.

Ryan nodded. 'Sure. I've just finished it. Don't pick it up though. It's still a bit damp.'

Katharine had been astonished by the watercolour. It was not merely good but outstanding, a landscape awash with tender spring greens and ashy pinks, faded chrome yellow and melting blues, and the misty colours and exquisite configurations gave it a dreamlike quality that was perfectly magical. It was the best painting he had ever done, and Katharine was awed, recognizing what an extraordinary talent he had. It did not seem possible that a boy of only ten years had painted this piece of art.

'Did you copy it from a book?' she asked, peering over his shoulder.

'No, I didn't!' Ryan cried indignantly. His deep green eyes, so like their mother's, flickered with hurt, and then he grinned. 'Don't you recognize it, Dopey?'

Katharine shook her head. Ryan searched around the table and produced a snapshot. 'See. It's Aunt Lucy's garden at Barrington,' he announced, pushing the photograph under her nose. 'But you've made it look so much more beautiful,' Katharine exclaimed, further impressed with his astonishing ability. 'Why, Ryan, you're a true artist. You'll be famous one day, I bet, and I'll be so proud of you.'

He grinned again, the freckles dancing around like a sprinkling of brown sugar across the bridge of his nose and cheeks. 'Do you really think I'll be a real artist one day, Katie? Tell me the truth and say honest injun.'

'Honest injun, Ryan, and cross my heart and hope to die,' she smiled.

At this moment the door flew open with such swiftness and force, both children jumped and stared at each other with startled eyes. Patrick O'Rourke was standing on the threshold. It was an unexpected and unprecedented appearance, especially at this hour of the day, and he entered the room like a hurricane. 'So here you both are! What the hell are you doing up here, when I've built a perfectly good playroom downstairs? Have I wasted my money?'

Katharine felt Ryan's thin shoulders tensing under her hand resting on them. She said slowly, 'No, Father, you haven't wasted your money.' There was a slight pause. 'We use the playroom most of the time,' she lied quickly.

'I'm glad to hear it,' Patrick said, and seated himself in the rocking chair. He was a tall, well-built man, and the chair was a fraction too small for him, but he did not seem to notice, or care about this. He regarded them both thoughtfully for a moment, his blue eyes acute. Finally, he fixed his narrowed gaze on Ryan. 'Have you had a nice day, son?'

'Yes, Da,' Ryan said softly, as always intimidated by his father's presence.

'Good. Good.' Patrick settled back and began to rock gently, musing to himself. Suddenly he lifted his dark leonine head and said, 'Were your ears burning today, Ryan?'

'No, Da.' Ryan appeared baffled by this question and he wrinkled his nose nervously, looking confused.

'Well, they should have been, my boy. I was talking about you, and at great length, with some of my political friends at lunch today. Ward bosses. I was downtown to make my usual, and considerable, contribution to the Democratic Party. We have the best damn political machine in the country, you know. Magnificent.' He beamed at Ryan. 'And the Irish control it, I might add. Don't you ever let that slip your mind, my boy. Anyway, I told my friends that my son is going to be the greatest politician Chicago has ever seen. Yes, I told them how you're going to be a congressman and then a senator, and I was delighted by their reactions.'

Patrick was quite oblivious to the dismay washing across Ryan's little face, and the look of astonishment quickening on Katharine's, as he went on: 'I also made them a promise, and it's a promise I fully intend to keep. I – ' Patrick bit off the rest of his sentence abruptly, and he paused dramatically as if to give additional weight and importance to his next statement.

He took a deep breath, stared hard at his children, and said with immense conviction and pride, 'I promised them that my son is going to be the first Irish Catholic President of the United States!' Patrick folded his hands across his vast chest, well pleased with himself, and he leaned back in the rocking chair, scrutinizing both of them, waiting.

When neither spoke, Patrick said, 'Well, Ryan, don't gape at me like a ninny! Haven't you anything to say for yourself? How do you like the idea of being a politician? And then the President of this great country of ours, the greatest country in the world?'

'I don't know,' Ryan whispered at last, his voice quavering. His face was as white as death, and the freckles stood out like disfiguring stains.

Patrick chuckled. 'I don't blame you, my boy. It's all a bit overwhelming to comprehend immediately, I'll grant you that. But I have great ambitions for you, son. Great ambitions. And what's wrong with having ambitions?' He did not wait for a response but hurried on compulsively, 'If I hadn't had ambitions, I wouldn't be the multi-millionaire I am today. With a son who is going to be the first Irish Catholic President of America. And there's nothing for you to worry your head about, Ryan. Nothing at all. I'll do your thinking for you at all times. I'll mastermind your career, and my money and my clout and my friends will propel you right into the Oval Office of the White House, you wait and see. You'll make *my* dreams come true, Ryan, I have no doubts. And I'm going to make *you* the most powerful politician this century has known and will ever know. Just you leave it all to me, son.'

Ryan gulped and opened his mouth but no words came. He glanced up at Katharine, his eyes filled with mute appeal.

Katharine was flabbergasted at her father's words. If they had been uttered by anyone else she would have dismissed them as boastful idle talk, and to be taken with a grain of salt. But she knew her father meant every word, and she trembled inwardly for Ryan. Her brother was terrified, and with good reason; she tightened her embrace, drew the boy closer to her.

She said, 'But Ryan doesn't want to be a politician, Father.' She could never bring herself to call him the more affectionate Da, as Ryan did.

Patrick glowered. 'What?' he demanded in a low tone that was ominous, even threatening. 'What did you say?'

'Ryan doesn't want to be a politician. He wants to be a painter,' Katharine replied in a quiet but resolute voice. Her father might strike terror in Ryan's heart, but not in hers: She was not one bit afraid of him.

'How dare you tell *me* what my *son* wants, Katie Mary O'Rourke!' Patrick shouted, leaping to his feet. His face was brimming with dark colour and there was a dangerous glint in his steely blue eyes.

'But Ryan is so gifted. Look at this watercolour,' she cried, undeterred by his displeasure.

'I don't want to look at it! I'll have no more of this sissy stuff in my house. You and his mother! Filling his head with artistic nonsense. It's going to stop, and right now.' He strode to the table, struggling with his anger, and snatched up the watercolour. Without glancing at it, he tore it in half, and threw it to the floor.

Ryan stifled a tiny cry, like a small animal in pain, and brought his fist up to his trembling lips. Katharine flinched, and gazed at their father in fascinated horror. With one furious gesture of his large hand, Patrick swept the paint box, the brushes, the jar of water and the sketching pad off the table. He stamped on them, crushing them under his heavy feet. Katharine's face reflected her disgust, and she thought: He's a dreadful man. Vulgar and uncouth. He thinks he's a gentleman with his custom-tailored gabardine suits and hand-made shoes and soft silk shirts, but he's not. He'll never be anything but an ignorant peasant. Shanty Irish.

Patrick pointed a long bony finger at Ryan and exclaimed excitedly, 'Now listen to me, son. There's going to be no more of this painting. I forbid it, do you hear me. It's not for a great lad like you. It's not masculine enough. You're going to be a politician, Ryan O'Rourke, even if it kills me in the process. And the President of these United States one day. Furthermore, you're going to start training for it immediately, with dedication and discipline and single-mindedness of purpose. Just like a boxer trains. Do you understand me, son? Have I made myself clear?'

'Yes, Da,' said Ryan meekly, still quivering with a mixture of fear and shock, and swamped with unhappiness.

Patrick turned to face Katharine, glaring at her. 'As for you, young lady, I want no more interference. I've had quite enough of you lately. You're a real troublemaker, not to mention a little liar, Katie Mary O'Rourke. Don't think I've forgotten the unspeakable things you said about your Uncle George. Scurrilous. Disgusting. I never thought a daughter of mine would have such filth in her mind!'

Katharine felt as if the blood was draining out of her, and her legs wobbled. For a moment she thought she was going to be sick, and her large eyes became larger in her face. Beads of sweat popped out on her forehead, and she had to clench her fists to control herself. How could her father be so cruel and mean, embarrassing her by saying such frightful things in front of little Ryan. She took a deep breath to control herself and said, in a voice that was surprisingly steady, 'George Gregson is not my uncle. He's only your business partner. *And I didn't tell you any lies!*'

'Go to your room immediately!' Patrick thundered, harshness and fury bringing a rasp to his voice. 'How dare you answer me back. You're impertinent as well as a liar, it seems. And don't venture downstairs for dinner, my girl. I don't want to look at your face tonight. Annie will bring a tray to your room later.'

Katharine was rooted to the spot, and automatically, with a sense of protectiveness, she tightened her hand on Ryan's shoulders. Her father observed this gesture, and commanded imperiously, 'Stand away from your brother! Stand away! You're always slobbering over him. It strikes me as you're turning him into a girl like yourself. Now, go to your room.'

'I will,' Katharine retorted with some spirit, walking rapidly across the floor. 'But not before I've looked in on Mother, to see if she wants anything.'

Patrick seemed about to explode, but he said nothing. When she reached the door of the nursery, Katharine stopped and turned her head. She looked directly at her father, and said with cold deliberation, 'I took a message for you earlier. It's on the desk in the library. It's from a Miss McGready. She said you can call her at the usual restaurant. In the Loop.'

Patrick's jaw went slack and he stared at her, momentarily stupefied. His mouth tightened into a slit and his eyes hardened, and it was then that she saw the naked hatred on his face. Katharine recoiled, aghast. But she recovered herself at once and stared back at him defiantly, her eyes challenging, and she knew that he knew that she knew exactly what kind of man he was. Something rose up in Katharine like bile, gagging her, and with the child's wisdom that springs from instinct and blind perception she understood that she was confronting evil. Her blood ran cold, and it was then that the first seeds of bitter purpose were sown in her. She vowed to herself that she would fight her father for Ryan, and for Ryan's soul, if it took all the days of her life. She did not know that her own hatred blazed out from her young face with such intensity and force that Patrick was staggered by it.

That night Katharine lay in her bed, listening to Ryan's sobs through the wall. They had started almost immediately, when he had returned from dinner, and they had continued unabated. Her heart ached for him and she longed to go and comfort him. The only thing which prevented her from doing so was the thought of her father's wrath if he caught her. It was not that she was afraid for herself, for, in all truth, she was not afraid of anything. Her concern was for Ryan. Instinctively, she knew that if she attempted to protect her little brother, her father would take drastic measures, would remove him from her care. With a prescience rare in a girl of her age she understood that things would never be the same in this house ever again. She would have to watch her step, for Ryan's sake.

But in the end she could not bear to listen to the racking sobs any longer, and she got out of bed and crept to the door, opening it quietly. She peered out. The corridor was dark and silent, and no light filtered out from her father's room, to her enormous relief. He was either downstairs or he had gone out. To meet Miss McGready perhaps. Holding her breath, she ventured forth into Ryan's room and tiptoed over to the bed. 'It's me,' she whispered, sitting down on the edge. She took him in her arms, and stroked his hair and made gentle hushing sounds. Eventually he calmed a little, and nestled against her, his small arms clamped tightly around her neck.

'I'm scared, Katie,' he whispered in the darkness, his body still heaving with dry sobs. 'I don't want to be a politician. I want to be an artist. What will I do? I'm so scared of Da.'

'Hush, honey, don't get upset again. We'll think of something.'

'Why did Da tear up my beautiful painting? I was going to give it to Momma.'

'I don't know. Well, perhaps he was angry with *me*. But you'll do another for Momma, Ryan, real soon.'

'No, I won't,' he wailed. 'Da has forbidden it. I'll never be able to paint again, Katie.'

'Please, honey, don't talk so loud,' Katharine cautioned, and went on with some assurance, 'And you *will* paint, we'll find a way, I promise. Everything is going to be all right.'

'Are you sure, Katie?'

'Yes, trust me, honey. Now try to sleep.' She loosened his arms gently, and made him nestle down in the bed, tucking him in. She sat stroking his hair for a while, murmuring softly to him, until he began to doze. As she stood up, he suddenly roused himself, and clutched her arm, 'Katie, what did Da mean when he said you'd told him lies about Uncle George?'

'Shush, honey,' Katharine whispered, 'it's nothing. Now go to sleep.'

'Yes, Katie,' he said with his usual obedience. He closed his eyes and curled up into a small ball, and Katharine slipped out.

Long after she had returned to her own room, Katharine was still wide awake, her mind filled with the hateful memory of that day when George Gregson had come to the house. It had been a Sunday. All the servants were off, except for Annie, the housekeeper, who was taking her afternoon nap. Ryan was out with Aunt Lucy, her father was playing golf, and her mother was in the hospital. She had been alone in the house, except for the sleeping woman upstairs. Katharine tried to block out the disgusting details, but they came flooding back, were relentless and distressing, and she lay, mute and shaking, covered in a cold sweat. She saw his ugly congested face. It was drawing closer to hers. She felt his hand on her small breast and the other one sliding up her dress, probing and pinching between her legs.

Katharine now experienced the same revulsion which engulfed her when George Gregson had unbuttoned his trousers and pushed her face down into his lap. She leapt out of bed and flew to the bathroom, staggering to the washbasin, filled with nausea. She leaned over it retching, and she threw up again and again, just as she had vomited on that terrible Sunday, all over George Gregson's trousers.

Katharine had not told anyone Gregson had molested her, for she was too ashamed and embarrassed, and also curiously afraid. But when he had attempted to waylay her on several succeeding occasions, she had endeavoured to communicate some of her mounting fears to her father. She could not confide in her mother, who was far too sick. Haltingly, choosing her words carefully, Katharine had informed her father about the incident as delicately as possible. To the girl's amazement, and immense shock and distress, her father had not believed her.

He had called her a damned liar. As he had done that very afternoon in the nursery.

Katharine shuddered, wiped her face and drank a glass of water. She ran a bath, pouring in great quantities of the bubble bath her Aunt Lucy had given her. She lay in the water for a long time, and afterwards, when she had dried herself, she covered her entire body with talcum powder and cleaned her teeth three times. Only after this long ritual of cleansing was she able to return to her bed, and finally, as dawn was breaking, she fell into an exhausted sleep.

Contrary to what Katharine had expected, her father made no reference to their altercation at breakfast the next day. Nor did he bring it up in the days which followed. Slowly, things drifted back to normal, and although Ryan was not given new paints, the two children were allowed to spend their days together, and Katharine found herself breathing a little easier. But at the end of the summer vacation their father moved with efficiency and speed, and, to Katharine, with an awful finality. Ryan was packed off to a military academy on the East Coast, and she herself was enrolled as a boarder in the convent where she had previously been a day pupil. One year later Rosalie was dead and buried. Katharine was devastated by grief, and inconsolable; there were times when she so yearned and fretted for her mother that she made herself violently ill physically. It was her Aunt Lucy who eventually brought the thirteen-year-old girl a measure of peace and a semblance of security, through her understanding, compassion and love. The two drew closer together as the next few years passed, and when Katharine was sixteen it was Lucy who prevailed upon Patrick to send the girl to school in England, as Katharine wished. Patrick had readily agreed, as Katharine had known he would. She was well aware that he could not stand the sight of her, or bear her silent accusations, or face her condemning gaze.

After Katharine left the English boarding school, she had gone to study at the Royal Academy of Dramatic Art, again through Lucy's intervention with Patrick. In all this time she had rarely heard from her father, or from Ryan. She attributed her brother's silence to fear of reprisals from their father if he communicated with her, convinced that he was under Patrick O'Rourke's thumb. But her Aunt Lucy was a diligent and regular correspondent, and kept her well informed about their activities, and a cheque from her father arrived promptly every month.

Katharine blinked, and straightened up on the white sofa. It was patently obvious her father was paying her to stay away from Chicago. He was glad to be rid of her. Apart from the fact that she knew too much, he was afraid of her influence over Ryan. He would not let anything, or anyone, obstruct his schemes for Ryan, schemes which she had never once been foolish enough to discount, even when she was a child. Her father fully intended to carry them through no matter what the cost, for he craved power, and he believed that Ryan was the key to the greatest power in the land, the Presidency of the United States.

Katharine's mouth twisted contemptuously. Well, she thought grimly, I'll show him yet. And when I'm a star and have enough money of my own to support Ryan, I'll send him to study art in Paris, or wherever he wants to go. This thought galvanized her. She had much to accomplish before that day came, and she could not afford to waste a single moment dwelling on Patrick Michael Sean O'Rourke. The bastard. As far as she was concerned, the die had been cast years before. And she herself had been set upon a course from which she could never deviate, even if she so wished. Saving Ryan and thwarting her father had been intricately interwoven into the fabric of her destiny, had become integral threads in her excessive ambition for herself.

Katharine now picked up the breakfast tray and took it into the kitchen. Automatically, her thoughts turned to the impending screen test, upon which so much depended, and for which she had one week to prepare. She was not especially worried about her performance. What concerned her more was the material she would use. She knew exactly what this should be, but it must be adapted and written out as dialogue, and for this task she needed a professional writer. Her mind began to work with its usual avidity and an illuminating smile spread itself across her face. Why, she could surely solve that little problem over lunch. Providing she was persuasive enough.

CHAPTER TWELVE

At the other side of London, on this same lovely February morning, David Cunningham, the Earl of Langley, sat at his desk in the library of his Mayfair town house, drinking a cup of tea. *The Times*, and various other daily newspapers, lay unopened, since he had neither the inclination nor interest to peruse any of them. A variety of matters occupied his mind, not the least of which was the large and ominous-looking pile of bills stacked on the leather-bound blotter.

Hell, he thought, I might as well tackle these blasted things first. I certainly can't deal with any of my other problems just now. Sighing, he began to sort through the pile, pulling out the most critical and pressing. He wrote a number of cheques, made a few calculations and returned the remainder of the bills to the drawer. Most of these were also urgent, but he felt they could safely wait until next month. They would have to wait. 'I'm always robbing Peter to pay Paul,' he muttered out loud. A gloomy expression dulled his fine intelligent eyes, and there was an unfamiliar droop to his mouth.

David Cunningham scrimped and scraped and economized in every conceivable way, and yet he was always beset by the most acute financial worries. Income from the estate and farming, as well as other holdings, was continually swallowed up by general overheads, maintenance of the castle and the estate and new farming equipment. He was gradually replacing the old and outdated machinery with more modern pieces, but this was a slow and increasingly costly process. Certainly the new equipment had introduced greater efficiency and improved his farming methods; even so, his latest projections indicated he would not be out of the red and into the black for almost another two years. Until then the cash flow would continue to be an excruciating problem, and what he sorely needed was a little ready cash to put everything on an even keel, but there was scant possibility of getting it. Unless

. . . He could sell the two prize heifers to Giles Martin, a neighbouring farmer who had been pressing him to let them go for almost a year. He had been somewhat reluctant to resort to this measure, since he did not want to deplete the herd, and yet the sale would partially ease his current burdens. Perhaps it was the easiest solution, and one he should not be so ready to dismiss.

David made the decision he had been baulking at for the longest time. By God, he would sell the heifers, and the moment he returned to Yorkshire. In fact, he would telephone Giles later in the day and so inform him. David smiled to himself. And he had better make that call, before he changed his mind again.

He immediately felt a sense of relief, and the heavy constricting feeling in his chest, which he had been experiencing for several hours, now lifted. In general, the Earl was a relaxed, even-tempered man, who had a positive outlook on life, a rare good humour and was unaffected by his daily worries.

He flipped through the morning mail. Not very interesting, except for a letter from Doris Asternan, who was still in Monte Carlo. He read it eagerly. Doris had written to tell him that she was returning to London early next week, having finally found an appropriate, and apparently beautiful, villa on the promontory at Cap Martin. It was near Roquebrune, on the way to the Italian border, and according to the preponderance of adjectives she had used to describe it, the house was nothing short of a palace, set in spacious and exquisite grounds which she said were out of this world. It overlooked the Mediterranean, had its own private beach, a swimming pool and a tennis court. She had already signed the lease and was staying on to interview the present staff, who were available if she wished to engage them for the summer. Doris had rented the villa from a French industrialist for four months, from June through September, and she ended the letter with a reiteration of the generous invitation she had extended previously to himself and his children. They were welcome to spend as much of the summer at the villa as they wished.

David put the letter down and stood up, walking over to the fireplace in long, easy strides. Tall, ramrod straight and elegant, he was proud of his bearing and, at forty-seven, was amazingly youthful looking. His features, typically Anglo-Saxon, were sensitive and refined, his grey eyes eloquent, his complexion fair, as was his hair. He was a handsome man, and he held great appeal for women, who thought his appearance not only romantic but dashing as well. Consequently, he was in constant demand socially, and had he been less moral and discriminating he could easily have been a Lothario of no mean proportions. As it was, his fastidious nature prevented him from taking advantage of the opportunities which were for ever presenting themselves, and he never indulged in random love affairs.

He stood in front of the fireplace, absently staring at the wall of books opposite, thinking about Doris. She had wrought many changes in his life, all for the better, as he was the first to acknowledge. She had given him a rare type of companionship he had not experienced with any other woman since his wife's death, and a great deal of understanding, devotion, love, and physical pleasure as well. He had come to rely on her constant presence. In fact, he had to admit Doris was now quite indispensable to him. He was not naïve enough to think this circumstance had developed by accident, knowing perfectly well that Doris had diligently set out to make herself wanted and needed. But he did not consider it devious. Every woman

111

strove to weave a web around the man she loved, in an effort to bind him to her irrevocably.

David knew he should marry Doris. He would be a fool not to, and, in fact, he wanted to marry her. Yet he continued to procrastinate, and he was not exactly certain why he did so. She had all the right qualities, at least those *he* thought were important in a woman, and she would make a superb wife for him. His own feelings aside, his children approved and had a genuine fondness for her. And, of course, there was her money, which would solve his financial difficulties once and for all. Doris, the thirty-five-year-old widow of an American meat-packing tycoon, was childless, and she made it abundantly clear to him that her immense fortune would be at his disposal if they married. But David Cunningham was not the kind of man who could be influenced by money when it came to the serious business of marriage. In his lexicon this was the least of all considerations. Love and compatibility took precedence with him. Well, he *did* love Doris, and they *were* inordinately compatible. But . . .

The door of the book-lined library was open, and David heard Francesca's quick light step in the hall. He hurried to the door and looked out. 'Good morning, my dear.' There was a lilt in his voice and his eyes instantly brightened.

'Good morning, Daddy darling,' she responded and, smiling, reached up to kiss his cheek.

The Earl hugged her to him, and then he stood back. 'Feeling patriotic today, are you, Frankie?'

Francesca looked at her father nonplussed. He was regarding her with fondness, his eyes twinkling. 'What do you mean?' she asked with a slight frown.

'The colour scheme you've adopted this morning.' His glance swept over her again. 'Borrowed from the Union Jack, wouldn't you say?'

Francesca laughed, and swinging around she looked at herself in the mirror, her head on one side. She was wearing a new white cotton shirt, her best navy-blue Jaeger skirt and a navy-blue melton-cloth reefer jacket. 'I think that's a bit of an exaggeration,' she retorted mildly, but nevertheless she unfastened the red-white-and-blue silk scarf tied around her neck and pushed it into her jacket pocket. She turned back to her father. 'Is that better?' she asked. Her father's taste in women's clothes ran to the subdued, even the dowdy at times, and she knew it was the vivid scarf to which he objected. 'I just thought the dash of colour would cheer up my outfit,' she said.

'You don't need anything to cheer up your clothes. Your face inevitably does that.' His smile was tender as he went on, 'And where are you off to at this hour?'

'The British Museum.'

'Ah, yes indeed. Gordon beckons, I've no doubt.' The Earl half turned and stepped into the library. He said, 'I'd like to talk to you, Frankie, if you can spare me a few minutes.'

'Why yes, of course I can, Daddy.'

'Then come in and close the door behind you. I think a little privacy is in order.'

Francesca did as he asked, her gaze resting on him, her face sobering. The seriousness of his tone alarmed her, and she thought: Oh God, there's trouble brewing. Being extremely close to her father and attuned to his moods, she invariably anticipated him, and she was positive he could only want to talk to her about one of two things: Kim or money. Probably the latter, she said to herself, eyeing the bills and the chequebook on the desk. Suddenly she felt selfish and guilty. Here she was, probably wasting her time researching a book that might never get written, when she could be earning money. Maybe she ought to get a job to help out. But deciding this was not the time to suggest it, she said, 'You seem awfully worried, Daddy. Is there something wrong? Is it money?'

'That's always a problem, my dear. But somehow we always seem to manage, don't we?' He did not wait for her response. 'However, I didn't bring you in here to talk about the monthly accounts. Actually, I wanted to discuss this new development with you.'

Francesca tensed and her eyes were watchful. 'New development?' she echoed. 'I'm not sure I know what you mean.'

'Come, come, Frankie, don't hedge. You're talking to *me*. You know perfectly well I'm referring to Kim and Katharine.'

She accepted the gentle reprimand in silence, playing for time. The silence grew, hung between them. The Earl studied his daughter keenly. Finally, he said, 'I presume your lack of response is an acknowledgement of the facts. I also presume you know Kim is very serious about this girl.'

Realizing she could not remain mute indefinitely, Francesca thought the safest thing would be to repeat Kim's words to her. 'Well, Daddy, I'm not sure *serious* is the right word, but I do think he's quite keen.'

The Earl laughed knowingly. 'That's undoubtedly the understatement of the year! Your brother is madly in love. Even a blind man would know that.' He leaned forward over the desk. His cool grey eyes, which had narrowed perceptibly, were fixed unblinkingly on his daughter. He asked quietly, 'And what is your opinion of Katharine, Frankie?'

Francesca's face lit up at once. 'I like her enormously! In fact, I took to her the instant I met her. I think she's a super girl. And to tell you the truth, I thought you did, Daddy. On Monday evening you seemed . . . well, enchanted, if you don't mind me saying so.' Her words held a challenge, as did her gaze.

'You're absolutely correct, I was,' the Earl conceded evenly. 'Katharine has a variety of assets, all of them most apparent, so I won't waste time enumerating them. And she is quite the lady – '

'Well, then,' Francesca interrupted swiftly, her brows lifting expressively, 'why are you so perturbed?'

David ignored this pointed question by saying, 'What do you actually know about her, my dear?'

Francesca was startled. 'Haven't you talked to Kim about Katharine? I think it's his place to tell you about his new girl friend, not mine, don't you?'

'Indeed I do, darling. And I have spoken to him. Unfortunately he was extremely vague, even a little evasive. To be frank, I decided not to press him for the time being. I felt it would be wiser not to make too much of a fuss, since that would only give the matter tremendous importance in his mind. On the other hand, because I believe he has serious intentions, I do think I should know more about the girl he is apparently thinking of marrying. I intend to have a heart-to-heart talk with Kim when we get back to Langley, but, in the meantime, I thought you might be able to give me a few more facts.' He waited, and then observing the expression on her face, he added gently, 'You think I'm putting you in an awkward position, I know, but I'm not really. It was I who brought you up to have a sense of honour, to be loyal, so I would certainly never ask you to betray a confidence. Still, under the circumstances, I don't think it would be disloyal to Kim if you repeat what he's told you, or what Katharine has said about herself. I'm hardly asking you to divulge state secrets,' he finished with a soft chuckle.

Francesca stared down at her hands. Everything her father said made sense. Surely there was no harm in telling him what she knew. It was then she realized, and with a little stab of dismay, that there was hardly anything to repeat. 'Kim hasn't confided in me, and neither has Katharine,' she answered. 'To tell you the truth, now that I think about it, she hasn't said much about her life. Here or in America.'

'I see,' said David, masking his surprise. He looked at her clear and lovely face, the candid gaze, and he knew she was being her usual truthful self. Until this moment he had been convinced his daughter would be able to enlighten him. She and Kim were extremely close. Obviously she had been kept in the dark. Very curious indeed. Then he wondered why.

Francesca volunteered, 'I understand from Kim that Katharine comes from Chicago, and that she's an orphan, poor girl.'

'Yes, he told me that too. He also mentioned she went to school here and afterwards attended RADA.' The Earl shook his head in bemusement. 'Not much to go on, is it?'

'No,' Francesca agreed. It struck her how foolish Kim had been. He should have adopted a more direct approach with their father, instead of being close-mouthed, secretive. His posture, so silly and unnecessary, had precipitated an unfortunate situation, one which could only end up being troublesome.

'Do you think she has any family at all?' the Earl asked.

'I don't think so – ' Francesca bit off her sentence and shook her head. 'I shouldn't say that, because actually I don't really know,' she corrected herself.

David Cunningham stared across the room, his eyes focused on an antique hunting print, a preoccupied expression on his face. After a few seconds, he swung his head to face Francesca. 'Look here, dear, I'm not passing any judgments on Katharine, nor am I out to create undue problems for Kim. God knows, I have his well being and happiness at heart. And believe me, as of this moment, I don't have strong objections to the girl. I'm sure she is most admirable, and she might be ideal for him. But, as Kim's father, I feel I am entitled to some information about Katharine's background. It's not much to ask, is it?'

'No, Daddy,' Francesca said, understanding his concern. He was being much more reasonable than she had originally anticipated. Voicing the one thing which had chiefly worried her, she ventured tentatively, 'Then you don't mind that she's an actress?'

'I'm not that old fashioned, my dear,' David exclaimed with a faint chuckle. 'And times have changed. Naturally, I would have preferred Kim to have fallen in love with a girl from his own world, but I can't control his emotions, now can I?'

'No, I don't suppose you can.'

'And anyway, if she and Kim do marry, she would automatically give up her acting career. She would have to, and I hope Kim has made that clear to her.' David rested his elbows on the desk and brought the tips of his fingers together to form a steeple. He peered over them, and asked, 'Do you think Tempest is Katharine's real name, or one she adopted for the stage? I must say, it struck me as being rather theatrical.'

'Theatrical! How can you say that, Dad? What about your old friend, Lord Londonderry? His family name is Tempest. Well, anyway, Tempest Stewart.'

'Hmmm. Quite so. However, you haven't answered my question. Do you think it's her real name?'

'I've no way of knowing. Why?'

'Doris comes from Chicago – '

'I thought she came from Oklahoma.'

'She does, but after her marriage to Edgar Asternan she moved to Chicago, his home town, and lived there for many years. If Katharine's family was a prominent one, I'm sure Doris would have been acquainted with them. Certainly she would have heard of them, since she was very social and involved in numerous civic activities. It occurred to me she might be able to give me a few salient facts.'

'Yes, she might.' Francesca stood up and walked to the window. She glanced out, her mind on Kim. He really was impossible at times. And so thoughtless. Her father had enough worries without this problem to add to his burdens. Poor Dad, he really is troubled, she thought. She turned and said impulsively, 'Perhaps you ought to 'phone Doris right now. You never know, Daddy, she might be able to put your mind at rest immediately. After all, it *is* a small world.'

'No, darling, I don't think I will. I'll wait until Doris gets back next week, and discuss it with her then. I don't believe there's that much of a panic.'

'You know best, Dad. And please don't worry. I'm sure Doris can check out Katharine for you, just like that.' She snapped her fingers, and her smile was reassuring.

'Good Lord, Frankie, I don't want to check the girl out, as you seem to infer! Turn her inside out and upside down! That would be perfectly reprehensible.' The Earl was genuinely shocked at the suggestion, and went on, 'As I said, I merely want to know more about her, and her family. Background. That sort of thing. Just the usual sort of information a father likes to have, before he sanctions a serious relationship. Actually, I'm willing to give them my blessing, you know, providing I'm satisfied Katharine is everything she appears to be.'

Francesca went to her father. Impulsively, she threw her arms around him, and said, her cheek against his, 'Kim and I are lucky to have you as a father.'

'And I'm lucky to have the two of you,' David said warmly. 'Certainly neither of you has ever caused me any trouble.' He looked up at her and grinned boyishly. 'But then I haven't given you any either. I've never curtailed your activities or poked around in your lives. In fact, I think I've always given you a lot of rope. Because I trust you both implicitly. That's why I can't understand Kim's attitude at all.' He half-smiled at Francesca. 'I've brought you and Kim up to take people at face value, to accept them for their worth on a human level, and not to be influenced by money or power or more worldly things, and I know I was right to do that. At the same time, I expect you both to have common sense, exercise judgment and discretion, and select friends who are at least appropriate – '

'Don't you think Katharine is appropriate?' Francesca interrupted, her eyes clouding over.

'How can I possibly know that, Frankie? On the surface, yes, I would say she appears to be appropriate. But no adult ever comes to us like a newborn babe, without a history, a past. And since I have no knowledge of Katharine's upbringing, I can hardly make a proper assessment of her, decide whether or not she is suitable for Kim. As a wife that is. I don't have to remind you of his responsibilities, I know that. On the other hand, have you thought of what Katharine's life would be like if she married Kim? She would be buried in the country most of the year; a *farmer's* wife, albeit a farmer's wife with a title, and country living is hardly the most exciting existence, my darling, as well you know. It's never been *your* cup of tea. And then again, there are all the duties and responsibilities she would have to take on, with the estate workers, the villagers, the Women's Voluntary Service, not to mention our rather demanding vicar. Think of the church activities alone – garden fêtes, bazaars, jumble sales, the Harvest Festival, the Christmas festivities, and so many more endless tasks. More importantly, perhaps, does *Katharine* know what marriage to Kim *really* entails?' David shook his head and did not wait for her reply. 'I doubt it. I'm sure Kim hasn't bothered to explain the ramifications of his life, just as he hasn't sought to find out more about her. Personally, I think he's so damned infatuated he hasn't given a passing thought to these things. Probably thinks they're irrelevant and far too mundane. But they're not. They're an integral part of his life, as my son and heir. They're his *duty*,' he concluded with a sigh. As an after-thought, he added, 'You know, he's been bowled over by Katharine's looks, and his head is in the clouds. You saw how he behaved at Les Ambassadeurs the other night. He's quite hypnotized by her. You do agree with that, at least, don't you, Frankie dear?'

'I . . . I . . . suppose you're right.'

David adopted a milder tone. 'I had hoped we were close enough, that you and Kim both trusted me enough, to be open with me, to seek my guidance on important matters in your lives. I thought you knew I would always be fair, and certainly most understanding.'

'I do know that, Daddy, and so does Kim. Really and truly we do!' she protested.

David looked at his daughter closely. 'I don't want you to misunderstand me, Frankie. I'm not trying to play God in your lives. It's hardly a role I relish, and it invariably creates havoc. However, although I'm not infallible, I have had some experience of life, and I want you both to have the benefit of the bit of wisdom I've acquired, for what it's worth.' He paused. 'I'll tell you something else. Years ago I vowed I would never make the same mistake my father did.'

Francesca's eyes strayed to the photograph of her father's older sister. 'You're thinking of Aunt Arabella, aren't you, Dad?'

David followed her gaze, directed at the photograph of his sister, taken when she had been presented at court. He nodded. 'Yes, I am. As you know, your grandfather objected to Kurt von Wittingen most strongly, even though he was a prince and wealthy, because he was a German. Yet Arabella married him anyway. Father lived to regret his decision, even though he never came out and actually said so. I believe it broke his heart, never seeing her again.' Yes, it truly did, he added to himself.

If only the old man had been less obdurate, more reasonable, I know she would not have acted so rashly. That's a family trait, rashness in the face of opposition, he thought. And Kim's inherited Arabella's impetuousness. 'I'm sorry, Frankie, I missed what you just said. Wool gathering, I'm afraid,' he apologized.

'I said it was a very tragic story . . . Arabella's and Kurt's. But still, because of them we do have Diana and Christian, don't we?'

'We certainly do, my darling. And that reminds me, I had a letter from Diana just last week. From Königssee. Christian and she want to come over and spend a few weeks with us this summer. I hope you'll make it a point to be at Langley when they're there.'

'Gosh, Daddy, you know I wouldn't miss their visit for anything,' she cried. Francesca had always been especially close to her German cousins, who made frequent trips to England and spent many holidays at Langley. She squeezed her father's arm affectionately. 'It will be lovely to see them.' Her face became intent. 'I know I haven't really been very helpful about Katharine. But I'm absolutely certain everything's going to be fine. I know it is.'

'I hope so, my dear.'

Francesca looked at her watch. 'Oh, it's getting late. I must get to the Museum. You don't mind if I scoot off, do you?'

'No, my dear, you run along. Incidentally, any instructions for Mrs Moggs?'

Francesca laughed at his pained expression. 'No, I left a note for her in the kitchen. I'm sorry you have to cope with her this morning. She's a holy terror, but she does mean well. If I were you, I'd do a disappearing act as soon as you can, then she won't be able to boss you around.' Francesca leaned forward and kissed him. 'Have a nice day, and I'll see you tonight for dinner.'

'I'm looking forward to it, darling.'

After Francesca had left for the British Museum, David sat debating with himself about the best course of action to take. Being a man of integrity and decency, he was reluctant to make pointed inquiries about Katharine Tempest. It was abhorrent to him. It smacked of prying, the worst type of spying and infringement of personal privacy. It also showed lack of trust in Kim's judgment, and anyway, he would much prefer to hear the facts about Katharine from his son, and not indirectly. And yet . . . David shook his head in aggravation. It was precisely Kim's behaviour which was causing him to view the situation with a degree of alarm. Until his talk with Francesca, he had believed Kim's vagueness to be evasiveness, a defence mechanism induced by the resentment he felt because he thought he was being treated like a child. Sadly, David now acknowledged, Kim had been vague because he knew next to nothing about the girl with whom he was so infatuated. It was most apparent to David that Kim had no information because the girl herself had not been forthcoming.

People in love invariably confided in each other, and talked about their past, didn't they? Unless . . . Unless they had something to hide. Did Katharine have something to hide? He told himself this was a stupid, even insane, idea, and hardly worthy of protracted consideration. After all, he *had* been impressed with Katharine. He understood the reasons for his son's enthralment, and so he had not given much thought to her background until last night, after his frustrating talk with Kim. The boy had been unable to answer the simplest and most innocent of questions, to David's utter amazement. Since then he had been looking for flaws in her. The trouble was he had found none. Katharine Tempest seemed to be perfect in every way.

Unexpectedly, as he was pondering her attributes, a thought hit him. That was it. She was far *too* perfect. Obviously the girl could not help her staggering beauty, that was nature's doing, and her undeniable talent for acting was another of God's generous gifts. But what about her personality, her immense charm and her exquisite manners? Had they perhaps been consciously distilled over the years? he wondered. Another disturbing thought crept into his mind: Katharine was uncommonly smooth for her age. She had none of the rough edges of youth. His own children had pleasant personalities, self-confidence and lovely manners, but occasionally they displayed a *naïveté*, and yes, even a certain gaucheness at times, traits quite natural in view of their youth. She *is* awfully smooth, he decided, and also a shade too mysterious.

Damnation! he cursed inwardly. I wish there was someone I could talk to about this, someone a little more mature than my darling Frankie, who's obviously prejudiced about Katharine anyhow. Doris. Of course, Doris. There was no one better equipped to listen than she, and she was sincere and wise and down-to-earth, amongst other things. David picked up the telephone. He dialled the operator, gave her the number of the Hôtel de Paris in Monte Carlo, and waited.

'*Madame Asternan, s'il vous plaît,*' he said, when the hotel finally answered.

A moment later Doris's sleepy voice was murmuring hello.

'Good morning, Doris. It's David. I hope I didn't awaken you, my dear.'

'Yes, you did,' she laughed. 'But that's all right. I can't think of a nicer way to be awakened. How are you, darling?'

'I'm fine. I had your letter this morning, and I'm delighted about the house.'

'Oh David, the Villa Zamir is perfectly divine! You're going to love it, and so are Francesca and Kim.'

'I'm sure we will.' He smiled to himself. Doris might be a millionairess, but she was the least jaded person he knew. Her enthusiasm and gaiety and zest for life invariably lifted his spirits. 'I can't wait to see it. In the meantime, I also called to ask you something, so I'll get straight to the point. Have you heard of a family in Chicago called Tempest?'

'No, no, I don't think I have,' Doris said hesitantly. After a brief pause, whilst she obviously pondered on it, she said more positively, 'I'm sure I haven't. I would have remembered the name. It's quite unusual. Anyway, why do you want to know, darling?'

'Apparently Kim has been seeing a girl for a number of months. She's from Chicago and her name is Tempest.' He then proceeded to tell her about his concern, and the reasons for it.

Doris listened carefully. When he had finished, she asked, 'Do you really believe Kim wants to marry her, David?' her tone alert.

'Yes, I do. And since he's almost twenty-two he doesn't need my permission. Whilst I don't want to play the heavy Victorian father, I don't want him to make a mistake either. A mistake he'll regret.' He sighed heavily. 'Maybe I'm wrong, but I find it damned peculiar he knows so little about the girl and – '

'So do I,' Doris broke in. 'You knew my entire life story within a week of meeting me.'

'Yes, and you knew mine,' he answered, gratified that she confirmed his own opinion.

'Listen, I have an idea. Why don't you talk to the girl herself?' Doris suggested. 'Ask her to fill you in about her background.'

David drew in his breath sharply. 'Oh, I couldn't do that, Doris. At least not yet. I've only just met her. It would be frightfully bad form, poor taste, and besides – '

'Good heavens, David, you English never cease to astound me. Here you are worried to death, or at least you sound as if you are, and you talk to me about *bad form*. To hell with bad form! If the girl is intelligent she'll understand your reasons.'

'Yes, there's some truth in what you say, but to be honest, I don't want to precipitate anything at this moment, and I certainly don't want to give the relationship too much importance in their eyes.'

'But, David darling, it's obviously important in your mind.'

'Well, yes it is. But I don't want Kim to know I take the relationship seriously. Oh, hell, Doris, I'm not making any sense at all, am I?'

'Yes, you are. To me at any rate. You think that by simply ignoring the romance it might easily fizzle out. Whereas if you start asking too many questions, giving it credence, they'll start to view it in a different light themselves. That's what you mean, isn't it, darling?'

'Yes, Doris. As usual, you're right on target. Parental interference and pressure often cause two people to draw closer together than they otherwise might. Fighting the world, so to speak.' He rubbed his chin and exclaimed impatiently, 'Oh, Christ, Doris, maybe I'm blowing this whole thing out of proportion!'

'Yes, you could be, darling,' she said. 'And you know what young people are like. They're madly in love one day, and can't stand the sight of each other the next. They blow hot and cold with comparative ease. I realize you believe Kim has serious intentions, but he hasn't actually announced them to you, has he?'

'No,' David admitted. But he's going to, he thought.

'Then in my opinion I think you should play it cool. Ignore the whole thing for the time being. Let it run its course. Kim might change his mind. Or the girl might,' Doris soothed. Then she asked curiously, 'By the way, what's she like, the mysterious young lady from Chicago.'

'Rather lovely, to be truthful. It's easy to see why the boy's smitten. Francesca also seems very sold on her, and I was quite impressed with Katharine myself. She's certainly an unusual girl, I'll say that.'

There was a silence at the other end of the telephone and then Doris said slowly, 'Wait a minute, David, you're not talking about Katharine Tempest, the young actress, are you? The girl in the Greek play in the West End?'

'Yes, I am. I say, do you know her after all, Doris?' His hopes soared.

'No, afraid not, darling. But she was pointed out to me in the Mirabelle last summer. Stunning girl, I must agree with you there. I didn't know she was an American, and from Chicago no less . . .' Doris hesitated, and then said, with a laugh, 'I can tell you one thing, darling, she's as Irish as Paddy's pig.'

'What on earth do you mean?'

119

'The dark hair, the white skin, the bluer-than-blue eyes. She's very Irish looking, David. I remember thinking that last summer in the restaurant.'

'How can you be so certain?'

'I've met enough of the Irish in Chicago to recognize that look of theirs. The women in particular are often extraordinary beauties.' She chuckled. 'The men aren't that bad either.'

'Then she's probably a Roman Catholic.'

'Does that matter, David?' There was a startled echo in her voice.

'No, I don't suppose it does, although we've always been a Protestant family – ' His voice trailed off lamely. He regretted the comment. He found religious and racial prejudice intolerable in others. He hoped Doris did not misunderstand him.

Before he got a chance to clarify himself, Doris exclaimed, 'Look here, cheer up, darling. I'll be back in a couple of days and we can discuss this further. In the meantime – ' She stopped and, after a moment, went on carefully, 'I almost hesitate to suggest this, because I know prying is not your style, but if you want me to, I'll make a couple of calls to Chicago. I might be able to find out something about the Tempest family. Discreetly of course, without mentioning your name, or involving you.'

'No, I don't think that's necessary, Doris. Thanks anyway. If Kim ever discovered we'd done such a thing, he'd be hurt and furious, and understandably so. And you're right, it's not to my taste at all. However I will take your advice and let sleeping dogs lie for the time being. Kim and I will be at Langley together for several weeks, and I'm sure I'll get an opportunity to go over this with him.' He paused to light a cigarette, then dashed on, 'Actually, if anyone asks any questions about the Tempest family, it should be Kim. And of Katharine, don't you think?'

'Yes, I do, darling, and please don't worry so much.'

'No, I won't. I feel better now that I've talked to you. Thanks for listening, Doris.' His voice dropped, became more intimate and tender. 'Incidentally, for what it's worth, I've missed you, my darling.'

'That's worth a lot to me, you silly man!'

They talked for a few minutes longer, said fond goodbyes, and hung up. The smile she had brought to his eyes lingered there for a moment. Doris had the marvellous ability to allay his anxieties, whatever they might be. Perhaps she was right, too, about Kim and Katharine. Maybe it was merely a youthful infatuation which would soon cool off. Not only that, he was taking Katharine and the children to dinner tomorrow evening. With a bit of luck he might glean more information, especially if he formulated his questions skilfully.

'Good morning, your grace.'

David looked up quickly, startled to see Mrs Moggs, their daily, hovering in the doorway. He had not heard her come into the house. 'Good morning, Mrs Moggs,' he said wondering where on earth she had found her extraordinary hat. It was an exotic creation trimmed with poppies and cornflowers. He then remembered it had been a Christmas present from Francesca, one of her more exuberant flights of fancy into millinery design. He had made unflattering remarks about it at the time, but apparently Mrs Moggs adored it.

'Now, your grace, 'ow about a nice steaming 'ot pot of tea?' Mrs Moggs suggested, still loitering in the doorway.

'No, thank you. I've had my morning tea, Mrs Moggs.' He cleared his throat. 'Er . . . er . . . Mrs Moggs, I hope you don't mind me mentioning this again, but one only addresses a *duke as your grace*.'

'Dukes, earls, viscounts, marquesses, lords, barons, they're all the same to me, your grace, if you don't mind me saying so,' she beamed. 'Fair makes your blinking head swim, it does, having to call 'em all by different things, as I was saying to my Albert the other day. An' my Albert says – '

'Quite so, Mrs Moggs,' David murmured hurriedly. 'If you'll excuse me, I have some paperwork to finish.'

She beamed at him again, hitched her shopping bag onto her arm, and then did a little pirouette and disappeared. He shook his head in exasperation, but nevertheless a smile of amusement flew across his face. Mrs Moggs was impossible, and an infernal nuisance, always 'popping in' as she called it, when he was deep in work. But Francesca thought she was marvellous and continually refused to get rid of her. How fortunate he was in having Francesca. She had turned out very well, that girl, and he had no doubts about her.

He pulled his address book towards him, found Giles Martin's number in Yorkshire and dialled it, ready to start haggling about the price of the two prize heifers.

CHAPTER THIRTEEN

Wherever she went Katharine Tempest invariably created a flurry of excitement, for there was a magical quality about her, one that evoked the most romantic of images. It was compounded of a variety of ingredients: the spectacular looks that startled with their impact; the innate sense of personal style; the instinctive flair for selecting and wearing with great panache the most eye-catching of clothes, and finally, but by no means the least, the dignity in her bearing. All of these added up to the kind of magnetism that was spellbinding, and so, not unnaturally, attention was centred on her when she entered the Arlington Club. And, as always, she eclipsed everyone present, especially the women, who all paled in comparison.

Katharine did not slavishly follow current fashion trends, except for skirt lengths, and all her clothes reflected a very personal and individualistic taste; they were made by a dressmaker, mostly from Katharine's own designs. Her choices might have looked *outré*, even ridiculous, if worn by others, but on her they simply added to the ravishing looks and underscored her appeal. Today she cut quite a swathe in her newest outfit, and more than a few women in the club envied her ability to carry it off with such aplomb. She was wearing a full flared cape, cut like a highwayman's cloak, and made of the softest wool in the brightest of scarlets. Underneath the cape was a matching skirt, full and gathered at the waist and cinched by a wide black suede belt. Her sweater, made of the finest, silkiest cashmere, was also black, and against this gleamed a heavy gold chain holding a large gold Maltese cross. Black suede boots and a matching bag, plus her white kid gloves, completed the outfit, which was elegant yet youthful and dashing and a dramatic counterpoint to her altogether dramatic looks.

Her thick, dark-chestnut hair, pulled back severely from her face and held firmly in place by a red-velvet hair band, fell almost to her shoulders in a soft page-boy style. After her brisk walk to the club, her usually pale complexion had a tinge of natural colour across the high cheekbones, and the luminous eyes were set off by a touch of turquoise eye shadow so that they looked even larger and more compelling than ever.

Katharine was early for her luncheon date and so she swept up to the small bar adjoining the restaurant and slid onto a stool. Joe, the bartender, raised a hand in greeting and waved from the other end of the bar, where he was serving a customer. Katherine proffered him one of her most dazzling smiles, as always the glittering and vivacious actress in public. Years before she had made her stage debut in the West End in 1955, she had begun to mentally perfect the image she would project when she was a star. This image sprang from her own inner vision of herself, along with her idealized conception of how a star should look and behave. In essence, this was based on the Hollywood screen goddesses of the late 'thirties and early 'forties, those legendary ladies who were the embodiment of glamour and allure, with their gorgeous clothes, exquisite grooming and ineffable charm. Although not particularly vain personally, Katharine, nonetheless, consciously set out to create that identical aura of glamour for herself. She did so very simply because she thought it was an essential element in the persona of a star, and therefore professionally desirable, if not, indeed, an imperative.

'Hello, Joe,' she said gaily, as the bartender positioned himself in front of her.

'Top of the morning to you, Miss Tempest.' After giving her an appreciative glance, he asked, 'And what's your pleasure today?'

Katharine wrinkled her nose. 'I think I'd like one of your special concoctions, Joe, please.'

'What about a mimosa, Miss Tempest? It seems to me it's just the thing on this lovely day.'

'That sounds delicious. Thank you, Joe.'

Joe moved off to mix the drink and Katharine looked around, pulling off her gloves in the process. She nodded to a couple of Fleet Street journalists she knew, who were propping up the bar, and then tucked her gloves in her bag to keep them clean, as she always did. She was glad she had chosen the Arlington Club, commonly known as 'Joe's' after the bartender, who was something of a character and had a large following. It was an intimate and congenial spot, patronized by well-known newspapermen, writers and film people. Also, being located in Arlington Street, directly opposite the Caprice, it was a popular watering hole for stars, directors and producers, who dropped in for a drink either before or after lunch at the Caprice. For all these reasons, Katharine thought it was an excellent place to be seen, and also to observe.

'Here you are, Miss Tempest,' said Joe, placing the mimosa before her.

'And thanks again for the tickets. I loved you in the play. You were right smashing.'

'Why thank you, Joe. I'm glad you enjoyed it,' Katharine said.

Joe went to take orders from two new arrivals, whom Katharine knew to be the editor of the *Sunday Express* and the paper's show business columnist, John Logan. The latter had interviewed her and written a glowing story, and he was something of a fan, both professionally and personally. She returned their friendly waves and smiles, and then shifted her position slightly on the stool and took a sip of her drink. She reached into her handbag for a cigarette and immediately changed her mind, thinking of her throat.

Katharine worried a great deal about her health, since she had a somewhat delicate constitution, and was particularly prone to chest colds and bronchial attacks. Her throat was no longer sore, but she did not want the condition to recur, especially with the screen test imminent; smoking was hardly conducive to the crystal-clear tones she had perfected so assiduously.

At the age of twenty-one Katharine was already a highly complex young woman, and there was a curious duality in her personality, as Nicholas Latimer suspected. Talented to a point of true brilliance, she nonetheless strove endlessly to perfect her craft in ways not always necessary, and despite her immense belief in herself there were times when she was in need of reassurance about her acting ability. Sweet of nature, she had an understanding heart and great generosity of spirit, and would go to extraordinary lengths to help a friend or colleague. She was loyal, devoted and considerate almost to a fault, and nothing was ever too much trouble for her. Yet cold calculation, self-interest, and a ruthless determination to get her own way at all costs, stamped the reverse side of this otherwise glittering medallion, and she had no qualms about using anyone to suit her own ends.

And now, as she sat at the bar, toying with her drink, her mind turned once again to the material she would use for the test, the words she would say. She knew she had to compel and convince in a way she never had before. Everything depended on that. Damn, she thought, if only Nicholas Latimer hadn't been so difficult and indifferent, I wouldn't be facing this problem today. She was wondering what stratagem to use, to get the material adapted, when a voice behind her said, 'You're Katharine Tempest, aren't you?'

Katharine swung her head swiftly, and found herself staring at a heavy-set girl with a florid complexion and the brightest of carrot-red hair. She was a vision, if a somewhat eccentric one, in a suit of violent purple and a small emerald felt hat with a long purple feather. What a strange outfit, Katharine thought, but said, 'Why, yes, I am.' A crease puckered her brow. For a moment she was at a loss, and unable to identify the girl. Then she exclaimed. 'And of course, you're Estelle Morgan! How are you?' Katharine extended her hand, smiling warmly. Adept at self-promotion, she was never one to slight a journalist. Even those she considered to be insignificant were treated to a very large and compelling dose of the inimitable Tempest charm, since they might be important one day and therefore useful.

The carrot-haired girl took hold of Katharine's hand and squeezed it tightly, grinning with delight. 'I'm feeling pretty dandy. And how lovely of you to remember me, a famous actress like you.'

How could anyone possibly forget you, Katharine thought to herself. But

123

she wisely bit this back, and murmured sweetly, 'You're very striking, you know.'

Estelle positively glowed. 'Didn't we meet at Lady Winner's bash, or was it at the Duke's? Bedford, that is.'

Katharine laughed, inwardly tickled at the unabashed name-dropping, and shook her head, still laughing, 'No, as a matter of fact, I think we were introduced at the party John Standish gave for Terry Ogden a few months ago.'

'That's right! And you looked absolutely ravishing in a little black number and lots of pearls. In fact, I said so to Hilary Pierce, and she agreed you were the chicest, most beautiful woman there. I like Hilary, she's a lovely girl, although I thought she was behaving in a dippy way that night, didn't you?'

Katharine's eyes widened, and she stared back at Estelle, a blank expression on her face. 'No, I can't say I did.'

Estelle volunteered, with considerable glee, 'Oh, but I saw it all! Why, Hilary spent the entire evening drooling over Terry. Mind you, I can't say I blame her. He's something to drool over. But I thought, at the time, it was a good thing Mark was off shooting a film somewhere in darkest Africa or India. I think he would have been pretty jealous if he'd witnessed their performance.'

Katharine's ears had pricked up at the mention of Hilary Pierce in connection with Terry Ogden. An unlikely combination, she said to herself. She was riddled with curiosity about the incident, but she thought it wiser to curb her inquisitiveness and not probe Estelle for further details. Instead she tucked the information away at the back of her mind, for future reference, and said, 'I'm afraid I misssed that particular scene. Still, I do remember one thing. If I'm correct, you're a columnist for an American magazine, aren't you?'

'What a fabulous memory you *do* have! Yes I write for several American magazines. I'm the roving European correspondent for them, on a freelance basis. I'm mainly covering café society, the *beau monde*, you know, and show business as well.'

It had become apparent to Katharine that Estelle Morgan was intent on hovering and not about to budge, and so she said pleasantly, 'Would you care for a drink?'

'Oooh! How super-duper of you. Yes, thanks.' She heaved herself on to the next stool and, pointing an emerald-gloved hand at Katharine's drink, cried, 'What's that?'

Katharine winced inside at her gaucherie, and said, 'It's a mimosa. Mainly champagne and orange juice. Why don't you try it. It's delicious.'

'That's a fab idea. I think I will.'

Katharine motioned to Joe for two more of the same, and then she focused all her attention on Estelle, radiating charm. She gave her the benefit of that most glittering of smiles, and said, 'Your job must be lots of fun. Do you find plenty to write about in London?'

'Sure. But although this is my base for the moment, I do a lot of flitting around.' She giggled. 'Gay Paree. Monte. Biarritz. Rome. Venice. I hit all the high spots, in the appropriate season of course. Chasing the *beau monde*, Katharine.' She emitted another high-pitched giggle, and asked, 'I *can* call you Katharine, can't I?'

'Naturally, *Estelle*,' Katharine replied quickly, deciding it would be smart to cater to the journalist's most patent desire to be chummy.

'I thought you were divine in *Trojan Interlude*. Absolutely divine!' Estelle exclaimed. Her manner was fawning, and she kept giving Katharine admiring glances. 'I expect you're going to have a long run in the play, but I must tell you, when I saw you on stage it occurred to me you ought to be in pictures.' She peered myopically at Katharine, and asked, 'Any films coming up in the near future?'

'No, I don't think so. But then one never knows in this business, does one?' Katharine murmured. Inwardly she cautioned herself to be cagey with Estelle.

'No, one doesn't.' And unexpectedly Estelle winked in a conspiratorial fashion. 'I saw you dining with Victor Mason at the River Club a few weeks ago. I wondered at the time if you might be going to make a picture with *him*. Are you his next co-star? Or is this relationship strictly personal?'

Katharine stiffened slightly, irritated by this last remark, but she kept her voice pleasant and neutral. 'We're just good friends,' she answered with a small off-handed smile.

'That's the stock remark everyone makes,' Estelle chortled. 'I can't help being nosey, I'm afraid. Occupational hazard. However, I don't work for *Confidential*, so you don't have to worry about little old me.'

'I'm not,' Katharine replied, a frosty note edging into her voice. 'And Victor and I really are only good friends, that's all. Oh, thanks, Joe,' she added as the drinks materialized in front of them.

Joe moved away, and Estelle picked up her mimosa. 'Skol!'

Katharine said, 'Cheers, Estelle.' She took a small swallow and gave the journalist a long look that was quizzical. After a short pause, she asked cautiously, 'What made you mention *Confidential*? That's an awful magazine, devoted to exposés of movie stars and celebrities. There's nothing to expose about me. Or Victor for that matter. Or the two of us together, I might add.' The second this last sentence left her mouth, Katharine silently chastised herself. I've said too much, she thought.

Estelle had detected a mixture of concern and genuine puzzlement in Katharine's manner, and she said in a confiding whisper, 'I guess you didn't know, but Arlene Mason is suing Victor for a divorce. I understand she's the bitch of all time. Anyway, she seems out to make trouble and is demanding a fortune. And I mean a fortune. Under California law she might just get it too. Community property and all that. It seems she has a lot of juicy things to say about Victor's extra-marital love affairs with a number of delectable ladies, and I do mean juicy! She's babbling away to all and sundry who will listen, particularly journalists. As I said, most of us think she's a bitch on wheels, and that she's out to embarrass Victor by creating a public scandal. But he does happen to have a lot of loyal friends in the press, so she won't get to first base. But you might warn him that *Confidential* seems to be paying attention to her. In fact, I heard on the grapevine that they're looking for a journalist to do a piece on him and his romantic activities in merry old England.'

Although Katharine knew Victor was having trouble with his divorce, she was both taken aback and troubled by this additional information. However, uncertain of Estelle's motives, she concealed her reaction behind a bland façade, and said, after a slight hesitation, 'I knew about his divorce, but not the details. And I must say, it's very nice of you to pass on the information about the magazine. I *will* warn Victor. I'm sure he'll be most appreciative.'

125

'My pleasure,' Estelle said, lifting her drink and glancing about, looking star struck, as indeed she was.

There was a soft disarming smile on Katharine's lovely face as she regarded Estelle, but her mind was working with icy precision. She was considering the journalist with great objectivity at this moment. Was Estelle sincere in wanting to warn Victor? Or was she dissembling to cover her own tracks? Estelle might very well be working for *Confidential* herself. Suddenly, instinct and her well-honed perception, told Katharine otherwise. She had already discerned that Estelle was a flatterer, and unctuous, and, very transparently, a sycophant who preferred to make the famous her friends rather than her enemies. She was also a bit dim. Without deliberating further, Katharine made a snap judgment and decided to take a chance on Estelle. It also struck her that if possible she ought to find a way to totally neutralize her, whilst making use of her if she could. Girls like Estelle, who fed off their associations with the famous, were often invaluable, and they never really minded being used. The flatterers feel flattered, Katharine thought sardonically. It appeals to their diminished egos. Makes them feel important.

Shifting her position on the bar stool, and crossing her legs, Katharine drew closer, pinning the other girl with her hypnotic gaze. She said, in a voice as sweet as honey, 'You know, Estelle, I've been thinking about the things you've just told me, and perhaps you ought to talk to Victor yourself.' She paused, and improvising quickly, went on, 'He's giving a small supper this coming Sunday. I know he would be delighted if you came with me. Also, you might meet some interesting people you can write about.' Katharine did not know who these would be, since she had only just thought up the idea of the supper, but she would worry about the guest list later.

Estelle positively glowed. 'I say, that's really great of you, Katharine. I'd love it.' Her dark and avid little eyes glittered like chips of jet. 'Actually, I think I should write a story about *you*. I heard somewhere that you're an American. Is that true? You don't sound as if you are.'

'Oh, but I am,' Katharine assured her. 'It's nice of you to want to write about me, but I have a lot of other commitments just now. Perhaps in a few weeks.' Seeing the crushed look on Estelle's face and deeming it necessary to appease, she suggested hurriedly, 'But listen, why don't you interview Victor? He's about to remake *Wuthering Heights*. I could arrange an exclusive for you, if you want, Estelle. Since Victor hasn't made any announcements about the film as yet, it could be quite a *coup* for you. A scoop,' she finished with a gay laugh.

'Hey, that's a terrific idea!' Estelle fished around in her bag and brought out a card. 'Here's my number. Do let me know about the dinner party. What time is it, and where, and all the other details – ' She stopped, staring at the entrance to the club, and then said, 'I think your lunch date has just arrived. At least, the girl standing over there is looking this way.'

Katharine turned and spotted Francesca near the door. She waved, slipped off the stool and went to meet her. Francesca stepped forward, smiling broadly.

'There you are, Francesca dear!' Katharine cried, her face lighting up with pleasure. They clasped hands warmly.

Francesca said, 'Hello, Katharine. I'm sorry I'm late.' She was out of breath and flushed.

126

'Oh, that doesn't matter. I've not been here very long anyway. Now do come and meet Estelle Morgan, a very dear journalist friend of mine. Estelle, this is Lady Francesca Cunningham.'

Estelle, who was preening at being termed a dear friend, grabbed hold of Francesca's outstretched hand and pumped it. 'Delighted to meet you,' she purred. 'Well, I see my own date has arrived at long last, so I'll be on my way. Thanks for the drink, Katharine. See you Sunday.'

Katharine guided Francesca to the stool Estelle had vacated. 'I'm having a mimosa. It's very refreshing. Would you like one?'

Francesca said, 'Yes, thank you. It sounds very festive and just what I need.' She perched on the stool and looked across at Katharine, smiling, and then she caught her breath, startled yet again by Katharine's extraordinary loveliness. She thought: Hers is exactly the kind of unforgettable beauty that has inspired great poets and artists for centuries. It's romantic and mysterious and heartstopping in its poignancy. No one could remain unmoved by it for very long, she decided. And once again Francesca found herself entirely captivated by her new friend.

After Katharine had ordered from Joe, she touched Francesca's arm lightly, affectionately, and her face was happy and radiant as she told her, 'I'm so glad you could make lunch today. I was dying to see you again, and talk to you.'

'Yes, so was I,' Francesca responded with warmth and the same eager enthusiasm. Now her eyes roamed around the club, taking in the elegant décor. She grinned and said, 'This looks like a rather nice place. I usually go to a grotty greasy spoon for a revolting sandwich when I'm at the BM. Obviously it's hardly as smart as this.'

Katharine asked with some curiosity, 'What's the BM?'

'The British Museum. My home away from home, as Kim calls it.'

'Oh yes, of course. Were you there this morning?'

'Yes. I was doing some digging into the background of Gordon's siege at Khartoum this morning, when I suddenly bogged down in the worst way.' She sighed. 'The more research I do the more I realize what a monumental task I have ahead of me. Hundreds of documents to sift through and read, masses of material to analyse and evaluate.'

'But Kim told me you have been researching for almost eight months already, and every day!' Katharine exclaimed, an eyebrow lifting in amazement.

'Yes, I have.' Francesca grimaced. 'And I still have a long way to go before I'm finished. Sometimes I think the book will never get written,' she wailed. She retreated into silence as Joe arrived with the drinks. Actually she was surprised she had so readily voiced this troubling thought, one that had nagged at her for days, and which she had diligently pushed away in an effort to deny it.

'Of course you'll write it!' Katharine said emphatically, and moved the glass towards Francesca. 'Try your mimosa. It'll do you good. Cheers.'

'Cheers.' Francesca attempted a smile without much success and picked up her glass.

Katharine looked at her closely, wondering how to cheer her up. She was about to say something suitably encouraging when the *maître d'hôtel* hurried over, apologized for interrupting and handed Katharine a note. She thanked him, gave Francesca a puzzled smile and opened it. She saw at once that it was from Estelle.

It was brief and to the point. Quickly she read: '*I have some important info. about that magazine and V.M. During lunch go to the ladies room and I'll follow you to give you the dope. E.*'

Alarm stabbed at Katharine but she repressed it, screwed the note into a ball and pushed it into the pocket of her skirt. She explained, with a dismissive laugh, 'Estelle wants me to arrange an interview with Victor. She would like to write a feature about him for one of the American magazines she represents here.'

'Oh, I see,' Francesca mumured with the most obvious lack of interest.

Katharine was quiet for a few minutes, a stillness settling over her. She sipped her drink thoughtfully, her mind focused on Victor. All at once she pigeon-holed her worry about him, deciding she must concentrate on Francesca for the moment. She said in a voice full of understanding, 'I know you're disturbed about the book, Francesca. Do you want to talk about it?'

'I'm not sure,' Francesca replied, uncertainty apparent in her tone and manner. But in point of fact, Francesca did feel like unburdening herself. Kim's derogatory remark about the book not selling, whilst jocular in intent, had unfortunately had an adverse effect on her, one which had intensified rather than diminished since Saturday. She was filled with grave doubts about its ultimate success, and, in all truth, she had not only become intimidated by the massive job ahead of her, but unsure of her ability to write the biography. These factors, plus her increasing worry about earning money to help out at home, had combined to dampen her original enthusiasm. She had thought of talking to her father about her work, but he was far too preoccupied at the moment, and she knew none of her girl friends would be interested. The majority of them whiled away the days doing nothing, or worked in inconsequential jobs, marking time until they found the right young man to marry. What she needed was an intelligent person who would listen with a sympathetic ear. And Katharine seemed the most appropriate candidate. Apart from the fact that she seemed genuinely interested, and caring, she was also a creative artist and had a proper career. Katharine would therefore comprehend her predicament and her feelings far better than anyone else.

Taking a deep breath, Francesca now found herself confiding, 'To tell you the truth, Katharine, I was thinking of abandoning the book this morning. I really am disheartened, and for two pins I *would* chuck it in.'

'But you can't do that!' Katharine cried with unusual sharpness. She stared at Francesca aghast, and then she leaned forward and adopted her most solicitous manner and convincing tone. 'Look, you mustn't lose heart. You've got to keep going, you really do.'

Francesca shook her head, the miserable expression intensifying on her young face. 'I don't even know if it will ever get published. What if I can't sell it? Then I'll have wasted my time. Years probably.'

'I know you'll sell it!' Katharine pronounced airily and asserted with great certainty, 'I bet there'll be dozens of publishers beating your door down. Fighting to get the book.'

'I doubt that,' Francesca laughed, but there was no humour in the laughter. 'Actually, I think I'm deluding myself in believing I can have a career as a writer. It would be much more practical if I got myself a job in a shop, selling undies or something. At least I'd be earning some money and helping out at home.'

128

This remark so startled Katharine, she gaped at her. She was about to ask Francesca what she meant, but she checked herself and said, 'Kim told me you have a natural talent for writing, and – '

'He's just being loyal,' Francesca retorted.

Katharine squeezed Francesca's arm, wanting to both reassure and comfort her. 'I'll concede that, up to a point. Still, he's no fool, and I value his opinion. He also told me that you'd sold several magazine articles, so that must prove something to you.' When Francesca did not answer, she added spiritedly, 'Well, it does to *me*. As far as I'm concerned, you're a professional writer.'

'Not really, Katharine,' Francesca murmured in a negative voice. 'Magazine articles don't mean that much, and anyway a book is an entirely different kettle of fish, especially an historical biography of this nature. I know it's going to take me years, and I'm not sure it's worth all the time and effort I'll have to put into it.' Her frustration rose to the surface, and she finished, 'I'm awfully down in the mouth about it today, and perhaps I shouldn't be boring you with it, after all. It's not very fair, dumping my depression on you.'

'Don't be silly, I want to help,' Katharine said. 'I think we should discuss it a bit more, and then perhaps we'll get to the root of the problem. Come on, Francesca, try and tell me.'

Francesca forced a smile onto her face, and she laughed thinly. 'That's just it, I don't know what I feel. Ambivalent, I suppose, about the book's chance of getting published and of it being a success if it ever does. And uncertain of myself, my capabilities as a writer . . .' She faltered, seemed on the verge of tears.

Katharine identified with Francesca's problems and empathized. There was a brief silence, and then she hazarded slowly, 'I think I know what's wrong with you.' She waited a moment before continuing, and her tone was gentle as she added, 'You're suddenly afraid. You've lost your nerve. But you mustn't lose it, Francesca. I *know* you can write the book. I also feel sure it will be a great success. A smash hit. I'm not sure how I know, but I do. Truly.' Katharine cleared her throat, and volunteered, 'Don't think I don't understand what you're going through, because I've been exactly where you are at different times. Unsure of myself in a role, worried I might fail, even crippled by stage fright. I suppose it's a kind of self-doubt, but if you keep going it passes, truly it does.'

Katharine saw that the other girl was plunged into despair. Francesca's golden-amber eyes had darkened, she bit her lip nervously, and fiddled with the stem of the glass, her face slightly averted. After a few seconds Katharine decided to take another approach. 'You know, Francesca, I think it's important for us all to try and master something we're afraid of, for that great sense of accomplishment we feel when we've actually done it. Of course, it takes a lot of strength and determination. And courage. But it's worth it in the end. You mustn't give up now, Francesca darling.' Being single-minded of purpose, dedicated, disciplined and ambitious, Katharine was always a little puzzled when she sensed these essential drives were missing in others. Now she wanted to fire Francesca on, to imbue in her that same intense desire to succeed which had so motivated her own career as an actress. To Katharine, personal gratification, as well as fame and money, was the spur that goaded her on.

She scrutinized Francesca and exclaimed with enormous conviction, 'You must pursue your dreams, because without our dreams we have nothing. And then life isn't worth living.'

Francesca, who had been listening closely, shook her head dismally. 'I know what you're trying to say, Katharine, but perhaps I just don't believe in myself enough.' Her mouth tightened. 'And it's a bit arrogant, isn't it, thinking I can tackle an historical biography of this magnitude, and get it published to boot?'

'No, it isn't!' Katharine declared. 'You have talent and you're very intelligent, and hard working and – ' She left her sentence dangling in mid-air and broke into laughter. 'I suppose a lot of people thought I was arrogant, believing I could get the part of Helen in *Trojan Interlude*. But whatever they thought, and even said to me, I ignored them. And I did get it.' Her manner became more persuasive than ever. 'Listen to me, Francesca! If you abandon this project now you'll regret it for the rest of your life. You'll never have the nerve or the self-confidence to attempt another book. And you'll be wasting your talent, just throwing it down the drain, and that would be a terrible crime. You'll end up feeling bitter about the "might-have-beens" and all you've missed. And think of the research you've already done. All those months will have been wasted too.'

'Yes, I suppose you're right,' Francesca agreed. She was surprised at the extent of Katharine's concern, her supportiveness and her genuine desire to be helpful. She was also grateful, and she admitted finally, 'And I believe you hit the nail on the head. I think I *have* lost my nerve. And the immensity of the work I still have to do frightens me. I keep thinking I've bitten off more than I can chew.'

'And you mustn't be negative.' Katharine's smile was consoling. 'You know, you're probably just a bit tired and out-faced by it all. I think you ought to step away from the book, and take a few days off. Spend your time doing something totally removed from the biography. You'll feel refreshed and raring to go again after a rest.' Another thought occurred to Katharine. She said quickly, 'Look, is there anything I can do to help you? Maybe some research. I'd be glad to, honestly I would, if it would make things easier.'

Francesca straightened up on the bar stool and stared at Katharine. She was temporarily at a loss. Unexpectedly, her father's concern, which he had voiced earlier that morning, popped into her mind. But he had no reason to worry. She was convinced of that now. Katharine was everything she appeared to be, and so much more besides. She was sweet and loving and so unselfish. All the troubling thoughts Francesca herself had had were immediately dispelled, and she was tremendously relieved she had not asked Katharine those leading questions about her life in Chicago, as she had planned to do. Questions she had even rehearsed on the bus on the way from the British Museum. How rude and suspicious and unkind I would have seemed, Francesca thought to herself. Out loud she said, 'That's so sweet of you, Katharine. But I'm afraid I'm the only one who can do the research, because I'm the only one who knows what I'm looking for.' The laughter flickering on her mouth was real as she said, as an afterthought, 'At least I *think* I know. Thank you, anyway, for offering. It was a super gesture.'

'Just give me a yell, if you do need some help,' Katharine responded with a jaunty grin. 'Promise me you won't abandon the book, and that if you do get down in the dumps again you'll talk to me about it. *Promise*!'

'I promise.'

'I'll hold you to that. Now perhaps we'd better go in for lunch.'

After they were comfortably seated, Katharine gave the menu a cursory glance, and asked, 'What would you like?'

'I don't really know,' Francesca answered, her eyes scanning the list of delicious dishes. She was horrified at the prices, and decided to take her cue from Katharine. 'What are you having?'

'I'll most probably have the grilled Dover sole and a green salad.'

Francesca nodded. 'I think I'll have that too. It sounds good.'

'Would you like some wine?'

'Gosh no! It makes me sleepy during the day.'

Katharine laughed her spiralling girlish laugh. 'Me too. I'd better refrain as well, otherwise my performance might be off tonight.' The waiter came to their table and Katharine ordered, and then she turned to Francesca and said, 'Will you excuse me for a minute, I've got to go to the powder room.'

'Of course.'

Katharine pushed back her chair, stood up and floated through the restaurant, her eyes focused on the arched doorway ahead, quite oblivious of the admiring glances and heads that turned as she weaved through the maze of tables. When she reached the powder room she took a lipstick out of her bag and redid her mouth. She had only been there a few seconds, standing in front of the mirror, when the door burst open and Estelle flew in, looking as if she could hardly contain herself.

Katharine swung around to face her, but before she could open her mouth, Estelle cried excitedly, 'Katharine, guess what! I've stumbled on something terribly important. Pay dirt. The man I'm lunching with told me there is definitely a writer in London who is filing material back to *Confidential*.'

'My God!' Katharine stared at Estelle. 'Is he sure?'

'Yes, he's pretty certain.'

'How does he know?'

'Peter, that's the guy I'm with, runs the London office of a top Hollywood publicity company, who handle a number of big stars and some of the top movies. His Los Angeles office alerted him about the *Confidential* reporter. Right now some of his company's biggest clients are filming here in London, or in Europe, and Peter's been told to warn them to watch their step, and keep their feet dry.' Estelle giggled and rolled her eyes upwards, then proceeded, 'He's also been instructed to scrupulously check out every freelance journalist who requests an interview, just to be sure they're really accredited to the publications they claim they represent.'

'Are you trying to say he doesn't actually *know* who the reporter is from *Confidential*?'

'You don't think writers who work for that magazine would be foolish enough to announce it, do you? Every door would be slammed in their faces! And anyway, they usually use a phony by-line, so they are hard to check out properly.'

'Yes, I see what you mean,' Katharine acknowledged quietly. Then she asked, 'Does your friend know whether it's a man or a woman?'

'He thinks it's a man. Peter's been racking his brains to narrow it down, but he's not been able to pinpoint anyone. Actually, that's why he mentioned it to me. He thought I might have heard who it was on the grapevine, but I haven't. I didn't even know they had someone based in London. Anyway, I think you'd better mention it to Victor immediately. Put him on his guard. It's more than likely he's one of the current targets, because of his bitchy wife's big mouth.'

'I will. Thank you, Estelle. You've been really terrific, alerting me to all this. I won't forget it, and neither will Victor. Look, I've got to get back to the table. I'll call you tomorrow, and let you know about Sunday. Thanks again, Estelle darling.'

'Any time, Katharine,' Estelle beamed, suffused with self-satisfaction about the way she was so cleverly cementing the relationship. 'I'm only too glad to help if I can.'

When she returned to the table, Katharine sat down and said with an apologetic laugh, 'Sorry I was so long, but I ran slap-bang into Estelle, and I'm afraid she can be awfully garrulous at times. But she's quite a good sport, and I didn't want to offend her.'

'Oh, that's perfectly all right,' Francesca replied. 'I do understand. Thank you for listening, Katharine. And for the marvellous pep talk. You helped me a lot, and I'm going to take your advice. I've decided to take a few days off, and make a new start on the book next week.'

Katharine was delighted. 'I'm so glad, Francesca. And listen, any time you need a sounding board, I'm here. Incidentally, when I was in the ladies room it struck me you ought to have a literary agent. I assume you don't have one. Or do you?'

'No. And to be honest I wouldn't know where to get one either. Anyway, I don't have a manuscript to show at this moment.'

'I realize that. On the other hand, it might be a good idea to talk to a few agents, and see what they say. Later, when you've finished the book, you'd be better off using a literary agent, rather than trying to sell it yourself. At least I know that much.' She paused and then excitement animated her. 'I know what we can do. We can ask Victor to get you one.'

'No!' Francesca cried, and flushed with embarrassment, realizing she had snapped at Katharine, and without good reason.

Katharine gave her a peculiar look, but merely shrugged. 'Then I suppose I could ask Nicholas Latimer. He'd never do anything for me, but I'm sure he wouldn't mind helping you.'

'Why wouldn't he do anything for you?' Francesca asked with a confused frown. 'He was very charming at Les Ambassadeurs on Monday night. I thought he liked you enormously. He certainly behaved as if he did.'

'Oh but he doesn't,' Katharine said with a cool and knowing smile. 'He is pleasant, and he teases me a lot, and behaves as if he's my best buddy. But haven't you noticed his flat blues when he's talking to me?'

'Flat blues? What do you mean?'

'His eyes. Flat and blue and hard. His mouth might be smiling, but his eyes drip ice. I know he hates my guts.'

Francesca was flabbergasted. 'Oh but surely you're wrong, Katharine! I would have noticed. Anyway, I can't imagine anyone hating *your* guts,' she pronounced with certainty. 'And please don't ask him for any favours for me. I don't want you putting yourself in an awkward position. And as I said, I don't need an agent at the moment.'

'No, I suppose you don't,' Katharine answered. 'Anyway, we can always hold Nicholas Latimer in reserve, I guess. Incidentally, talking of favours, I was going to ask one of you – '

'Would you like the fish off the bone, madame?' the waiter interrupted, displaying the sole with a splendid flourish.

'Yes, thank you very much. Would you, Francesca?'

Francesca nodded, and when the waiter was out of earshot, she said eagerly, 'What kind of favour, Katharine?'

Katharine leaned across the table and explained. 'I need someone to write the material I want to use for the screen test, and I was wondering if you would do it for me.'

Francesca looked at her in amazement. 'Gosh, Katharine, I wouldn't know how! I mean, dialogue and that kind of thing is way beyond me. Good Lord, I wouldn't know where to begin!'

Katharine said, 'Oh,' in a very small voice. Crushed, she dropped her eyes and stared at the tablecloth.

'It's not that I don't want to help you,' Francesca exclaimed anxiously, her voice rising. 'I'd do anything for you, Katharine, I really would. I just don't know how to write something like that. Honestly, I don't,' she persisted, feeling downright mean for refusing. Then she was filled with chagrin. Katharine had shown her extraordinary understanding, and kindness, had been so patient and encouraging. She felt she was somehow letting her new friend down by refusing to accede to this request. She said, 'Please don't be upset. I couldn't bear it. Let's talk about it at least.'

Katharine lifted her head sharply and smiled beguilingly. 'I *know* you can do it! I really do, especially since it's a long passage from *Wuthering Heights*. You said on Saturday that you knew the book extremely well.'

'Yes, that's true, I do . . .' Francesca's brows went up in a quirk. 'But why do you need me to write something for you? I thought Victor Mason had a finished screenplay.'

'When I asked Victor for the particular pages I need, he said that I could have them. At first. Later he called me back and told me that Nicholas Latimer was rewriting that whole section of the script, and therefore I couldn't have them after all.' Katharine bent her head closer to Francesca's, and lowered her voice. 'But I don't believe Nick *is* rewriting. Don't misunderstand me. It's not Victor being difficult. It's Nick. I don't think he wants me to have those pages.'

'How rotten of him! But surely Victor can – '

'Nicholas Latimer has a great deal of influence over Victor. It seems to me that anything Nick says goes. They're as thick as thieves. If I didn't know better, I'd swear to God they were a couple of fags.' She burst out laughing when she saw Francesca's face. 'Don't look so shocked. Anyway, they're *not*. As I was going to say, their reputations as studs precede them. Nick, in particular, thinks every woman he meets is going to fall flat on her back for him.' She laughed again, and went on, 'In any event, Nick probably lied to Victor when he told him he was working on the screenplay, and did it just to thwart me. Victor suggested I do something from *Trojan Interlude*.' Katharine shrugged. 'What could I say. When I told him I preferred to use something that was fresher to me, he said I could select anything I wanted that ran about thirty minutes. I went through *Wuthering Heights* again, and I really studied the scene I like. And to be honest, it wouldn't be difficult to adapt.'

'Which scene is it?' Francesca asked, her interest aroused.

'It's the one where – ' Katharine stopped when the waiter approached the table with the food, and then said, 'I'll tell you about it later.'

Once lunch had been served, Katharine took a few mouthfuls and then put down her knife and fork, suddenly unable to eat. 'You know something, Francesca, every time I think about that scene I get excited. I know it's exactly right for the screen test. And I do want Victor to see me playing Cathy, not Helen of Troy. It's that very moving and dramatic scene, where Cathy comes back from Thrushcross Grange and tells Nelly Dean that Edgar Linton wants to marry her. They get into a long discussion about her feelings for Linton, as opposed to her feelings for Heathcliff. Nelly tries to stop Cathy, who is being very outspoken. She knows Heathcliff is listening outside the door. But Cathy presses on, and says something about how it would degrade her to marry Heathcliff, because her brother has brought him so low – '

'And then Cathy starts talking about her love for Heathcliff,' Francesca cut in, her face alive with excitement, her eyes shining. 'And there are those marvellous lines about their souls. I can almost quote it to you verbatim. Cathy says, "*He shall never know how I love him; and that, not because he's handsome, Nelly, but because he's more myself than I am. Whatever our souls are made of, his and mine are the same; and Linton's is as different as moonbeam from lightning, as frost from fire.*" Of course I know it, and very well, Katharine. And you're right. It is dramatic and emotional.'

Katharine had observed Francesca's enthusiasm, her growing interest, and now she seized the moment. She said, 'If you look at that particular chapter in the book again, and study it, you'll see there's enough dialogue between Nelly and Cathy to create a good thirty-minute scene, which is all I need for the screen test. Listen, Francesca, I *know* you can do it, and in a very short time. I also thought it would be a change of pace for you, and would get you away from your research for a day or two. Oh please, do say yes,' she cajoled. She gazed at Francesca, her expression pleading, then finished, 'I need you, I really do. Please, won't you give it a stab? The test is so important to me.' Katharine's eyes did not leave Francesca's face.

Francesca bit her lip, unsure of herself. But she did want to help Katharine, to please her, and so she swallowed her uncertainty. 'Well, all right,' she said. 'If *you* think I can do it, then I'll give it a try.'

'Oh, thank you, Francesca darling! Thank you. I'm so grateful,' Katharine cried.

'It might not be right, you know, not exactly what you want, but I promise I'll do my very best. And you'll have to tell me how many pages you need, where I should begin and end the scene. I will need a little guidance.'

'I'll help you. In fact, I can explain some things over lunch. You won't find it difficult, because it is all there in the book,' Katharine assured her.

Francesca nodded and stared at her plate. When she lifted her head she looked slightly perplexed. 'You seem to have a lot of confidence in me, Katharine. Why?'

Katharine thought for a second, and then she smiled. 'Instinct,' she replied.

CHAPTER FOURTEEN

As Katharine approached the St James's Theatre, she felt a quickening inside, and her heart beat a little faster, excitement tingling through her in short sharp waves. She always experienced these feelings when she went to work, and never once had they diminished or lessened. The thrill, the anticipation and the expectation mingled to bring a spring to her step, a blithe smile of eagerness to her face, and she increased her pace, hurrying down the alley to the stage door.

For as long as she could remember, the theatre for her had been a place of refuge and her happiest moments had been spent on a stage. When she was ten years old she had appeared in a nativity play at the convent in Chicago, and ever since that time she had known she would become an actress, for her destiny had been truly sealed that day. It was the only life she could bear to live, the only one which had any real meaning, and purpose, to her. In a sense, the magical unreality of the stage was her only reality. She found escape in her roles, bringing to them such belief and intensity, she literally became the characters she played. And it was this extraordinary commitment, total and unwavering, that gave her portrayals the absolute ring of dramatic truth, and was perhaps one of her greatest strengths as an actress. She never failed to touch, to move, and perhaps, more importantly, to convince. Even as a student, her interpretations of classical parts, in particular Shakespearean heroines, were innovative and individualistic, and she brought to them wholly new dimensions which staggered with their brilliance.

Charlie, the stage-door attendant, gave her a cheery greeting, and after exchanging a few friendly words with him, she went down the stone staircase to her dressing room. She sighed with relief as she closed the door and snapped on the light. She was home again. Safe and secure. Here nothing could harm her.

Katharine always went to the threatre several hours before first curtain call. She needed this time to relax, to empty her head of extraneous matters, to repose, to concentrate and to psyche herself into the part of Helen of Troy. This afternoon she was earlier than usual, but she welcomed the chance to be alone, to think and plan her strategy for the next few days. She still had a lot to achieve before the screen test. After her lunch with Francesca, she had debated whether to go back to her flat, and then decided against it, realizing it was a waste of energy to return to Lennox Gardens for only an hour at the most. Instead, she had strolled down Piccadilly, stopped at Hatchards to buy several books, and then made her way to the Haymarket. She had attempted to call Victor Mason from a telephone booth, to give him Estelle's information about *Confidential*. To her frustration he was not at the hotel, and so she had left a cryptic message, adding that she would call again later.

Now, as she took off her cape, her skirt and her sweater, she concentrated on the supper she had dreamed up on the spur of the moment at the Arlington Club. She was quite positive Victor would not object, since he relied on her for much of his social life, and he had already intimated he wanted to take her to dinner with Francesca on Sunday night. So he'll give a small party instead, she thought, slipping into her towelling robe and sitting down on the couch to pull off her boots. After she had carefully put all her clothes away in the wardrobe, she found a small note pad and pencil, and moved to the dressing table to make a tentative guest list. There would be Victor. And Nicholas Latimer. Naturally, she thought with a small caustic smile. And Francesca, Estelle and herself. She needed at least three more people, perhaps even five, to make up an entertaining group. Well, Kim and the Earl were out, as they were returning to Yorkshire on Sunday afternoon. She paused, the pencil poised in mid-air, considering various friends who would be suitable to include. The Shand-Elliots were possibilities if . . .

There was a light tapping on the dressing room door, and she looked at it in surprise. 'Who is it?' she called.

'It's me, Katharine. Norman,' Terry's dresser said.

'Oh, come in, love,' she exclaimed, smiling broadly as Norman's head appeared around the door. But the smile fled when she saw his face. Norman, usually breezy, jovial and as bright-eyed as a chirpy Cockney sparrow, wore a dour expression and distress was mirrored in his light brown eyes. Katharine saw immediately that he was agitated. He entered the dressing room with unusual swiftness and closed the door almost furtively. He leaned against it, his body taut, his nervousness spilling out of him.

'Norman, whatever's wrong?' Katharine cried, straightening up in the chair, her eyes fixed on him. 'You look terribly upset.'

He nodded, his movements jerky. 'I am. And thank God I've found you. I've been 'phoning your flat for ages. I even ran over there and pushed a note through your letter box. Then I decided to come to the theatre, just on the offchance you might be here.'

'But Norman, tell me what's wrong!' Katharine demanded impatiently, her voice more high pitched than usual. She tensed, and unexpectedly felt a rush of real fear as she observed his anxiety increasing.

'Sssh! Not so loud,' Norman warned. 'It's Terry. He's in real trouble, and I need your help, Katharine. Now.'

'Trouble,' Katharine repeated, keeping her voice low. 'What kind of trouble?' Her eyes were wide with apprehension, for Norman's acute distress was being transmitted more forcibly than ever.

'Well, for one thing, he's dead bloody drunk. Three sheets to the wind,' he told her in a voice that was practically inaudible. 'Can you get dressed and come with me to Albany? I'll fill you in on the way there.'

'Yes, love,' Katharine said, rising at once. She wrenched her clothes out of the wardrobe, dashed behind the screen and was dressed within a few seconds. She emerged and said, 'I just have to get my boots, then I'm ready.' Seating herself on the couch she began to pull them on.

Looking up, her eyes questioning, she stated: 'Terry's insisting on going on tonight, isn't he?'

'Yes. The bloody fool,' Norman responded with a tight grimace. 'And he mustn't. At least not in his present condition.' He glanced at his watch. 'It's almost four o'clock. We've got three hours to sober him up. If we can't, then I'll have to try and restrain him somehow, and his understudy will have to play tonight.' Norman's eyes remained on her face and he regarded her carefully. After a second, he said with a worried frown, 'If Terry does go on, it'll be quite a burden for you, Katharine. I'm afraid the whole play will be on your shoulders. And Terry's going to need every bit of help you can give him. You'll have to cue him, lead him, cover up for him, and literally carry him through his performance.' He smiled faintly. 'It won't be easy, Katharine. It's going to take all your strength and ability and ingenuity to camouflage his disabilities from the audience.'

Katharine's heart sank but she returned Norman's steady gaze with one equally level. Although her face was grave, the tone she adopted was light and cheerful. 'Yes, I understand what you're saying, Norman. But we'll think about that eventuality later. Come on,' she cried. 'Let's go!'

CHAPTER FIFTEEN

Nicholas Latimer, being the consummate novelist, often elected to play the spectator. He sat back, enveloped in silence, and listened and watched and stored everything away in the computer that was his mind, for future reference and use in his work. Once, a few years ago, a female acquaintance had said she hated having writers as friends, because, as she stringently pointed out, 'They steal everything about you, and recycle it in their books.' He had exploded with laughter at the time, but now he suddenly recalled her comments, and he said to himself: she was right.

At this moment he was once again the spectator, and he knew he was going to revel in the scene which was on the verge of being enacted before him. And naturally he would hoard it away, and push it into the typewriter when he needed it. The protagonists were fascinating opposites, which added to the drama – Victor Mason and Mike Lazarus. And they were poised like gladiators about to do battle, to fight to the death. Nick smiled at his own rather melodramatic analogy. On the other hand, much was at stake, and if the daggers were not exactly drawn, they were sheathed and waiting, figuratively speaking, of course.

Instinctively, he knew Victor would emerge the . . . victor. He smiled again at his childish game but he couldn't help himself. Words were his drug, and old habits were hard to break. Victor had had the upper hand before they had met Lazarus. Not that Lazarus realized this, being ignorant of the meeting with Hélène Vernaud and thus unaware that she had passed on a certain amount of crucial information. Lazarus most probably thought he had the upper hand, especially since it was the hand which held the chequebook.

Nick had been taken aback when Victor had told him they were meeting Lazarus in the lounge of the Ritz Hotel. For tea. Good God, for tea! When he had questioned Victor about this somewhat weird location, Victor had laughed dryly and remarked: 'Wasn't it Napoleon who said that when he was about to do battle with the enemy, *he* liked to select the location and the time for his preference? He believed it gave him the advantage. So do *I*.'

Nick had nodded, constantly amazed at Victor's esoteric knowledge, and said, 'Yes, it was Napoleon. But why a public place, kid?' Another dry chuckle from Victor, who had gone on to explain, 'When we reach an impasse, as we undoubtedly will, I don't want to have to kick him out of my hotel suite, or have him eject me from his offices. Also, on neutral territory, such as the Ritz, he'll have to curb his temper. He's hardly likely to throw one of his famous tantrums in the middle of the hotel.' Nicholas had nodded and said nothing, but he had thought: Well, you're wrong there, because he just might. Lazarus is unpredictable, according to what I've heard.

So here they were, the three of them, at four o'clock in the afternoon, sitting in a secluded corner of the Ritz, amidst gilded period furniture, potted palms and elegant, behatted ladies. All very genteel and civilized, Nick commented to himself, and swallowed a laugh of wry amusement. There was nothing very genteel or civilized about Mike Lazarus, despite his impeccable linen and well-tailored suit and his façade of genial containment. Nick had never met Lazarus before, but he knew of him by reputation. It was common knowledge that he would go for the jugular at the least provocation, if it suited his purposes to do so. He was cold and ruthless.

As Nick observed them both, his best friend and his best friend's adversary, he had to admit there was something unusual about Lazarus. For a moment he was not quite sure what this was. He was stocky and muscular, had angular features and dark hair slightly tinged with grey. Nondescript was perhaps the best word to describe him. As he studied Mike Lazarus Nick suddenly reversed this opinion. Lazarus was not really nondescript at all, he just seemed curiously diminished in comparison to Victor. But then what man isn't, Nick said to himself. Victor's immense presence was as potent off the screen as on it, probably even more so.

Nick moved his head slightly, and his cool blue eyes swept over Victor, regarded him objectively, took in the dark grey pin-striped suit, the stark white shirt, the silver grey silk tie. Elegant. Immaculate. Conservative. In contrast, the handsome face and dark arresting looks and raw masculinity acquired a greater vibrancy, stunned with their startling impact. And there was a very special aura surrounding Victor, one that set him apart from other men. Success, fame, wealth, Nick thought. Yet it was more elemental than that. Is it his sexuality? Nick wondered. Partially, he answered himself. It's also his adventurous spirit. Soldier of fortune. Buccaneer. Riverboat gambler, he characterized, and then smiled inwardly and said to himself: Maybe I've seen too many of his movies.

Nick's eyes rested briefly on Mike Lazarus now, and he was conscious yet again of a quality in the other man. It was something not immediately definable, or initially apparent, yet it grew on one, slowly and most forcefully. Suddenly, like a bolt of lightning striking, Nick knew what it was. Mike Lazarus had the *effluvium* of power. Enormous power. He exuded it, reeked of it, and it was distinguishable in the way he held himself in the chair, his body tautly controlled like a panther ready to spring, and in his very pale blue eyes, as cold as a dead fish's, yet strangely magnetic and compelling. They seemed to penetrate with their keen intelligence, and Nick unexpectedly had the unpleasant feeling that those eyes were like lasers, beaming into his brain to pierce his thoughts. He looked away quickly, and reached for a cigarette, filled with discomfort.

From all the things he had read and heard about Lazarus, he knew the man had an austere discipline, an abrasive energy and a restless ambition. Nick, who on his Rhodes Scholarship to Oxford University had read history, was addicted to the sixteenth-century period. He thought: If Lazarus had lived at the time of Catherine de Medici he would undoubtedly have been a Prince of the Blood, one of those dark and sinister figures stalking across the complex and elaborate tapestry that was France in the 1500s. A Bourbon Prince, such as a Condé, perhaps. Or possibly a *duc* from the notorious House of Guise. Yes, the latter most assuredly, for there was something decidedly Guisardian about Lazarus, with his scheming Machiavellian mind, his stealth, his penchant for plotting, his unquestionable aptitude for dissimulation, his avarice, and his absolute fearlessness. But he wasn't French. Nick had read somewhere that Lazarus was of German-Jewish extraction, like himself. Or had his family been Russian-Jewish émigrés? Now he was not sure. Notwithstanding, the man was brilliant. He had to be, to have created a multinational conglomerate of the magnitude of Global-Centurion, whose claws were embedded in the surface of the entire world. More or less. And he was only forty-five or thereabouts. Funny, Nick mused, despite the millions of words written about him, I've never read much about his personal life, or his early beginnings. They are shrouded in mystery. He wondered, absently, how much Hélène Vernaud knew about Lazarus's past. He must ask her some time.

The two men facing each other across the small tea table had not begun to skirmish yet, but were skirting each other warily, and with great adeptness, using verbal thrusts and parries, testing each other. He smelled the tension between them. It hung in the air like a curtain of gauze. He knew that Victor detested Lazarus. But it was difficult to ascertain Lazarus's feelings for Victor. The man had adopted a posture of geniality. A constant benign smile played around his mouth. But the eyes were alert and watchful and chilling in their deadliness.

The two men droned on about the stock market, and Nick turned away, stifling a yawn.

Lazarus made a remark about trouble brewing in the Middle East, and spoke for a few minutes about oil, and the attitude of the Arab states eventually changing; and then unexpectedly, and abruptly, he switched from this topic.

Suddenly, Lazarus said, 'Well, Victor, you've procrastinated for days about this meeting, presumably because you were having the contract dissected by your battery of lawyers. Since you're sitting here, I assume all is in order. And I trust you brought the contract with you. *Signed*. I can't delay my return to New York any longer. I'm leaving tomorrow, and I want to wind things up with you before doing so.'

'Yes, I've brought it,' Victor responded in a pleasant, easy tone. He moved in his chair, crossed his long and elegant legs, and leaned back, on the surface relaxed. Observing him quietly, Nick knew he was as taut as Lazarus.

'Ah. Good,' Lazarus said. 'Seemingly we are making progress at last. I'd like to give you my ideas, and my conditions, now that we're partners. Or at least about to be, after I've signed the contract. First of all, I cannot sanction the budget of this movie. It's excessive. Three million dollars is, in my estimation, exactly one million dollars too much.'

'Agreed,' Victor said with a small cool smile.

If Lazarus was surprised at this ready acquiescence, he did not display it. Not an eyelash flickered. 'How do you propose to cut production costs, might I ask?' There was a sarcastic edge to his voice but he was seething inside. Victor Mason wasn't very much different from the rest, in spite of his reputation for honesty. They were all trying to steal from him, in one way or another, when they came with their elaborate schemes and questionable deals. But none of them were a match for him. Inevitably he outsmarted them all.

'There are ways and means to do it,' Victor replied, sounding and looking enigmatic.

'I see.' Lazarus remained motionless in the chair, holding his annoyance in check. Mason was such a fool, being evasive, and wasting his valuable time. The man would have to reveal his plans eventually. But Lazarus decided not to press. Instead, he drawled softly, 'How much can you save?'

'About a million dollars.'

Lazarus regarded Victor closely, with those keen and assessing eyes. A cynical smile touched his mouth fleetingly. 'Then I feel justified in my assumption that the budget was padded. That's the trouble with the motion picture industry. Too much waste, too much fat. An inefficient business in my opinion.'

'You're wrong. About the budget. It wasn't padded, merely erroneous,' Victor shot back sharply, sheathing his irritation. 'An easy mistake for a production man to make when he's sitting in Hollywood.'

'Obviously you picked the wrong production man, Victor. A shame.' He made the last word sound ominous, even though his voice was soft. Lazarus sighed lightly and took a sip of his tea. 'A good production man doesn't make mistakes, Victor, wherever he's sitting. Poor judgment on your part. I hope it will be less flawed when it comes to other areas of our project. I also sincerely pray we're not going to have the pleasure of *his* company here in England, when we start shooting.' Lazarus laughed thinly. 'Otherwise, we might find the budget escalating to four million dollars. Perhaps even five. And why not!'

'He was not hired on a permanent basis,' Victor answered, ignoring the sarcastic jibes. 'As a matter of fact, the entire production team will be English.' He lit a cigarette, furious with himself for even bothering to justify his actions to Lazarus. But Lazarus had a way of putting everyone on the defensive.

'Well, that's a step in the right direction,' Lazarus responded, his tone patronizing. 'Let's talk about casting. I've been doing a lot of thinking, analysing, and I've decided on the female lead. Ava Gardner. She would be marvellous as Catherine Earnshaw, and I –'

'No.' Victor's voice was even but emphatic. 'I'm testing Katharine Tempest. And if she tests the way I believe she will, then she gets the part.'

Lazarus stared at Victor, and his lip lifted slowly, disdainfully. 'And who in hell is Katharine Tempest? If I've never heard of her, then you can bet your last dime the American public hasn't either. I don't want an unknown in my picture. I want an established movie star, who is an international name. I want a few box office guarantees, my friend.'

I'm not your friend, Victor thought, bristling. But he contained himself, and he chose not to remind Lazarus that he was one of the biggest box office names in the world. If not *the* biggest. Aloud he remarked, 'Katharine Tempest is a brilliant young actress who's starring in the West End play, *Trojan Interlude*, at the moment. And she is the perfect Cathy. You have to agree, she certainly looks right for the part.'

'I told you, I don't know who she is,' Lazarus responded, coldly impatient.

The lazy smile eased onto Victor's mouth. 'You couldn't take your eyes off her on Monday evening. At Les Ambassadeurs,' he rejoined swiftly. 'Much to the annoyance of your female companion. If looks could've killed, you'd be dead, *my friend*.'

Nick's eyes swivelled between them alertly. He didn't remember seeing Lazarus on Monday evening. But then he had arrived late, when Victor and his other guests had already moved into the restaurant. Mike Lazarus had leaned forward slightly, and Nick detected a faint flicker of sudden interest in those inscrutable eyes. Lazarus was silent for a split second, regarding Victor unblinkingly, and then he said slowly, 'You must be talking about the very dark girl with those extraordinary eyes.' Remembering the girl's beauty, he felt a flare of internal excitement, but took care to conceal this behind a façade that was expressionless, adding, 'I can't imagine you are referring to that insipid blonde, the debutante type, who was with you.'

'Dead right,' Victor answered. He was angered by the disparaging reference to Francesca, but instantly clamped down on it. 'Katharine has quite a face, hasn't she? She's as beautiful as Ava Gardner.'

There was no response for a moment. Lazarus seemed thoughtful, and then he said, 'I'll reserve my judgment until after I've seen the test. And even if the test is good, I'm still not sure we can use an unknown. I'll have to consider it carefully. Yes, very carefully. Now, I'd like to discuss the script with you. Frankly, it has to go. It's far too arty for my liking. Not commercial enough by any stretch of the imagination. We'd better get a new screenwriter on the job. Immediately. We've no time to waste.'

There was an awkward silence. Nick, who had flinched, thought: The lousy son of a bitch. He's behaving as if I'm not here. I guess I'm not, as far as he's concerned. He was on the point of exploding from frustration. He wanted to defend himself, and his work, and even jab Lazarus a swift right hook. But Victor had asked him to keep silent, whatever ensued, and so he kept his clenched fist pressed into the side of the chair, and waited.

Victor, whose face was stony and closed, said with quiet authority, 'It's a damned great script, Mike. Not just good, but *great*. Furthermore, it's the script I have every intention of shooting. And let me tell you something else. Nick is not going to be replaced by any other screenwriter. Not today. Not next week. Not ever, *my friend*.'

'Now, look here, Victor, nobody's going to tell me how to make my own picture, the picture I'm bankrolling to the tune of two million dollars. I must say, I thi –'

'Oh, shut up,' Victor murmured.

141

Lazarus was so startled that he did exactly that. He sat staring at Victor, an expression of disbelief washing over his face.

It took all Nick's self-control to suppress the laughter rising in his throat. Mike Lazarus looks as if he's just been hit in the face with a wet fish, he thought, and glanced away, biting his lip.

Lazarus recovered himself immediately. 'We'd better get something straight, my friend. And right now. Nobody, but *nobody*, ever tells me to shut up!'

'I just did,' Victor said. He leaned forward and lifted his briefcase onto his lap. He opened it. 'Here's the contract.' He handed Lazarus a manilla envelope, snapped down the lid and locked his briefcase.

In spite of the fury boiling within him, Mike Lazarus could not resist opening the envelope. The contract was in two halves, had been ripped across the middle. His eyes were riveted on the two pieces he was holding. For a moment he appeared to be mesmerized. Never in the whole of his life had he been so humiliated, so insulted. A slow flush rose from his neck, filled his face with deep colour. When he lifted his head, his eyes were like steel blades, and condemning.

Before he could utter a word, Victor, swift on the draw, said, 'That's what I think about your contract. And I'm sure you know what you can do with it. As hard as this might be for you to believe, I don't want your money, and I most certainly don't want you involved in *my* picture.' Victor retrieved his briefcase and stood up. 'I'll be seeing you, Mike,' he finished with a mirthless little smile. His black eyes were as cold and as hard as marble.

Nick had also risen and Lazarus regarded them both furiously for a prolonged moment. The bright colour had drained from his face. He was chalk white, and his voice, although as soft as always, was deadly as he said, 'You'll live to regret this, Victor. Truly, truly regret it. I'll make damned sure of that.'

Victor did not bother to respond. He took hold of Nick's arm and said, 'Come on, sport, let's get out of here. I do believe I'm in need of a bit of fresh air.'

Victor was striding rapidly towards the lobby. Nick kept in step, and when there was enough distance between themselves and Lazarus, he said, 'Jesus, Vic, you really –'

'Let's wait until we're in the street, Nicky.' They collected their coats from the men's cloakroom in silence. Victor shrugged into his camel-coloured cashmere overcoat and looked at Nicholas out of the corner of his eye. He winked theatrically, murmured, 'That was short and sweet. Very sweet,' and headed for the revolving door that opened onto Piccadilly.

Nick was so elated he could hardly contain himself. He had been a champion boxer at Princeton, and once they were outside he could not resist executing a few nimble, ballet-like steps. He feinted, and then delivered a light punch on Victor's shoulder, exclaiming, 'You really shoved it to him! Gave him the whole enchilada!'

'I'm lucky I was able to do so,' Victor said with a grin. 'Thank God I really don't need him, or his lousy money.'

'So you've made a deal with a major? For financing?' Nick questioned, his bright blue eyes probing.

Victor shook his head negatively. 'No, not yet. But it's in the works. Metro's considering it, and very seriously. But even if they turn it down, I'm not going to

142

abort the production after all. I've decided to go ahead. Too much sweat, yours and mine, has gone into this project for me to let it go that easily.'

Relief flooded through Nick. 'Hey, that's great, kid. But can Bellissima finance the picture completely?'

'Just about. *If* I defer my salary, and *if* I can find other ways to cut production costs, which Jerry Massingham seems to think we can do. But I'm pretty sure Metro's going to roll with us. They want me for another picture of theirs, so they're willing to play ball with me on this one.'

'Will you do their picture, after *Wuthering Heights?*'

'Most likely. I've more or less said yes, in principle. Subject to reading the script of course.'

Nick chuckled and jabbed Victor's arm again. 'Did you see Lazarus's face, when he realized that you'd torn up the contract? I thought he was going to have apoplexy. I wish he had, the slimy bastard. I almost punched him in the nose when he was raving on about the script as if I wasn't there.'

Victor laughed. 'I thought you might myself. That's why I didn't dare look at you. Thanks for restraining yourself, old sport. We could have all ended up on the front page of the *Daily Mirror* if you hadn't.'

'Well, despite the insulting way in which he treated me, I wouldn't have missed being there for anything. I bet it's the first time anybody's turned down his money. He was staggered.'

Victor nodded in agreement. 'You're probably right. That's part of his problem. He's had too much power for too long, running that fiefdom of his. He thinks he can push everybody around. I suppose I could have been more above board with him, and told him days ago that I wasn't prepared to go ahead with the deal. But I'm afraid the actor in me overrode my scruples. I couldn't resist playing the scene out to the bitter end. And I have to admit, Nicky, it gave me a lot of satisfaction, dumping him exactly the way I did.'

'Me too. But I didn't like his parting shot though. About your regretting it. He's got a nasty reputation . . . for being vindictive. And there is something inimical about him. He might just try to get back at you, Vic.' Nick's voice vibrated with nervousness. 'I think he's creepy. Sinister. To be honest, he kind of scares me. Doesn't he scare you?'

'Not at all.' Victor looked at Nick quickly, his eyes narrowing. 'And I don't think he scares you either, sport. As for being sinister, I think that's your writer's imagination working overtime. You know you enjoy playing casting director and visualizing people in various roles. The whores and the ladies, the good guys and the heavies. Goodness versus evil, and all that jazz.'

'I suppose I do,' Nick agreed. 'Nonetheless, I think he's bloody unscrupulous. And you said yourself he's paranoid. Jesus, I feel sorry for Hélène. I don't relish the idea of her being involved with a guy like him –'

'I know what you mean,' Victor interrupted. 'But she's a big girl. I think she's capable of taking care of herself when it comes to men. Don't you?'

'I guess. Incidentally, did you notice that flicker of interest when you explained who Katharine was?'

'Sure, and I saw that same look, only much more pronounced, on Monday night in the bar at Les A. Lazarus came in with this well-stacked, stately redhead, dripping jewellery from every pore, and clinging to him like an octopus. And from the moment he noticed Katharine, she might as well have not been there. And don't think she wasn't aware of his attention straying. It was all very pointed. They left after one drink, just before you arrived.'

'Who was the redhead?'

'I've no idea,' Victor responded. 'But I can tell you one thing, Nick. I think Mike Lazarus is a womanizer in his own quiet but rather predatory way. Something I hadn't realized before.'

'That's what I meant, about his being unscrupulous. I bet he's a real bastard where women are concerned. And it's apparent to me he keeps a girl in every port. Hélène in Paris. The redhead here in London. God knows *who* he's got stashed *where*.' He sighed. 'Poor Hélène. She doesn't deserve him. But then I guess that's her problem, not mine.'

Victor was striding out quickly, suddenly preoccupied. After a moment he said, 'Do you mind if we take a long walk, Nicky? I don't feel like going back to Claridge's just yet. I'm restless, and I need the exercise.'

'That's fine with me, kid.'

Victor and Nick kept up a brisk pace, not talking, but perfectly at ease with each other, as they had been since their first meeting. They were so well attuned to each other's moods. Both were immersed in their own thoughts as they walked along Piccadilly, past Green Park, heading towards Hyde Park Corner.

Victor was pondering the current negotiations now under way with MGM, structuring the deal in his head, endeavouring to formulate all the elements which would make it even more tempting to them than it already was. His presence in the film gave them the box office guarantee they required, and they were not challenging him about casting an unknown actress in the female lead. But if he could offer them a prize package of superior talent, then the deal would really fly, and fly high. There was no question in his mind that he needed a back-up of good, solid British actors who were names, most especially Terry Ogden for the important role of Edgar Linton. And the right director was an imperative. Mark Pierce. Unfortunately Mark had already turned the picture down, because he did not want to direct a remake. Or so he said. Victor knew he had to have him, must get him at any price. But he didn't really have to worry about either Mark Pierce or Terry. That problem was in other capable hands, would imminently be solved. Now if he could get Ossie Edwards then he was in clover. He was the best damned cinematographer in England, and he was already establishing an international reputation. There was also the matter of a completion guarantee. He might have to get that from one of the financial guys in New York, but Jake Watson would advise him. Jake was due to arrive early next week, and was itching to start shooting. Yes, everything was starting to roll along smoothly, now that he had made a few crucial decisions.

As they pushed ahead, Nick looked at Victor from time to time, but said nothing, not wishing to intrude. His own thoughts had stayed with Mike Lazarus. Despite what Victor said about his writer's imagination, nothing could dissuade him from the belief that the man was somehow dangerous. His parting words had sounded ominous, even threatening. But what could Mike Lazarus do to harm Victor? He did not carry any weight in the motion picture industry, and besides Vic was a big star, a superstar in fact, who was also part of the old Hollywood Establishment, that cliquish upper echelon that was almost a private club. Jesus, you are stupid! Nick suddenly exclaimed to himself. Men with the kind of power Lazarus wielded invariably, and inevitably, had influence with somebody or other in every business where big money was involved. He turned the matter over in his mind several times, analysing and worrying, as was his custom. Finally he gave up, recognizing that worrying would not solve anything. Victor seemed calm enough, and was confidently going ahead with the film. Best not to borrow trouble, Nick decided. If Lazarus comes at Vic, he'll just have to meet the bastard head on. And I'll be right there with him in the fray.

Nick shivered and hunched further into his trenchcoat, suddenly feeling the nip in the air, and the bite of the wind which had blown up. They were on Park Lane now, approaching the Dorchester Hotel, and beyond he could see the top of Marble Arch silhouetted against the sky. He lifted his head quickly, squinting. It was no longer the spring sky it had been earlier in the day, golden and glorious and shimmering with blue luminosity, like the glaze on antique Chinese porcelain. The sun was fugitive, and the blueness had been obliterated by daubs of darker and more sombre hues, a range of greys, ombréd from pearl to opal to cinereous, and leaking into lividity at the outer edges. There, on the rim of the horizon, splinters of light suddenly poked out like shards of broken crystal, and pierced the darkening cloud mass with spears of glittering brilliance. In an instant it had become an unearthly sky, the kind that presaged, or followed, a thunderstorm, and to Nick it was perfectly beautiful.

He did not mind the rain and fog and greyness of London in the midst of winter. Unlike Victor, who missed the sunshine and balmy breezes of Southern California, Nick loved England's inclement weather and changing seasons. Perhaps because it reminded him of New York and his childhood, and also of his years at Oxford University. Salad days. A wave of nostalgia swept over him. For no reason at all, his thoughts turned to Francesca Cunningham. Now *she* was really something else. There's a lot more to that one than meets the eye, he thought.

Nick tapped Victor's shoulder and said, with a soft laugh, 'Lazarus was a bit hard on Francesca, wasn't he? I'd hardly call her insipid. I think she's quite a dazzler!'

'I'll say she is!' Victor exclaimed, glancing at him. 'I got the distinct impression Lazarus was attempting to be inflammatory when he made the comment.'

Nick peered at him, his brow furrowed. 'Did you, now?' He studied Victor reflectively, and then went on, 'But why would *he* think that a derogatory remark about Francesca would inflame *you*? Does he know something I don't? Come on, Vic, 'fess up. What gives?'

Victor laughed. 'I guess you could call that a Freudian slip on my part. No, he doesn't know anything. There isn't anything to know. But he might have noticed I was paying special attention to Francesca in the bar for a while, trying to make her feel comfortable. Mind you, I was really only being my usual charming and gallant self.'

'Hey, come on, kid! You can't get out of it that easily. I know you too well. And what did you mean by Freudian slip? Explain.'

'If you must know, I *was* rather taken with her, when I first met her. And, well

. . . Well, I guess she has been dancing around in my head a bit. But that doesn't mean a thing. She's a mere child, Nicholas. A baby.'

'San Quentin quail, eh?' Nick grinned, his eyes twinkling with considerable amusement.

'Hardly that. She *is* nineteen.'

'She's too young for you, maestro.'

'You're damned right she's too young,' Victor shot back sharply. 'Twenty years too young.'

Nick gave Victor a sceptical look, trying to recall his behaviour on Monday evening. If he remembered correctly, Vic had been extremely proper and hadn't paid undue attention to Francesca, or even spoken to her much. But that's meaningless with him, Nick muttered under his breath. He's a dark horse. 'Are you trying to tell me you're not going to do anything about her?' Nick asked.

'Of course I'm not going to do anything about her. She's off limits. But regardless of that, I don't think she's interested in me anyway. So this discussion is pointless.'

Nick threw back his head and roared. 'What do you bet, old buddy? What do you bet? I'll give you a hundred to one she is more than interested.'

'If she is, I'll never know, because I'm not even going to try to find out. I told you, she's far too young, and naïve, and we're from different worlds anyway. It would be a bad mix. Trouble I don't need.'

'That's true. By the way, talking of trouble, have you heard anything from Arlene The Bitch?'

Victor frowned. 'Not a peep out of her, or her fancy lawyers, who are no doubt still figuring out ways to take me to the goddamn cleaners. Listen, don't even mention her name, you're spoiling my day.'

'Sorry, Vic,' Nick answered, and went on, 'I got the impression Francesca is terrified of you.'

Victor gave him a baffled look and said, 'Terrified of me! You gotta be kidding, *kid*. What the hell do you mean?'

'Oh, I don't think she's afraid of you the way most women are, you know, of your fatal charm. Far from it. I think she's quite a cool customer, very self-possessed. But when we were talking the other night, she said she came from Yorkshire. I asked her what she thought of *Wuthering Heights*, and she told me you had forbidden her to discuss it with me. Then she closed up like a clam and didn't open her mouth for ages.' He gave him a quizzical look and asked, '*Did* you forbid her to talk to me about it?'

Victor couldn't help laughing. 'No, of course not. I made some joking remark about keeping her away from you. Because she has strong opinions, Lady Francesca does. She told me, and in no uncertain terms, that it wasn't a love story at all, but a novel about revenge.'

'She's right.'

'She is?' Vic said, sounding a bit doubtful.

'Sure. But it *is* a love story as well, and a rather touching and heart-breaking one at that.' Nick grinned. 'Intelligent as well, eh? Lethal combination, as far as you're concerned. You'd better watch yourself there, old sport.'

'Go to hell,' Victor exclaimed, and then laughed. 'I'm too preoccupied with the picture to start any romantic relationships, particularly with a teenager who has stardust in her eyes.'

Nick made no comment and the two of them walked on in silence, pushing through the shoppers milling around Oxford Street. They cut back, down North Audley Street, to escape the flood of humanity and roaring traffic on the main thoroughfare, and approached the more gracious and tranquil streets of Mayfair with relief. Nick glanced about, his eyes scanning the charming old houses and elegant edifices that dated back to another century. He thought fondly of his father, who had first brought him and his sister Marcia to London when they were children, and had lovingly imparted so much of his own considerable knowledge about the history of this city. He and his father had been inseparable then. He now wondered how he had ever lived through the terrible years of his father's monumental anger with him, after he had announced he wanted to be a writer, did not want to join him in the bank. He had not enjoyed being on the receiving end of his father's thunderous silence. They were on better terms of late, and for that Nicky was thankful. He had always loved his father. The terrible things parents do to their children, he thought with a stab of sadness. And children are equally bad.

Victor suddenly stopped in his tracks, staring ahead. They were drawing close to a construction site where a high building was rising slowly, its skeletal frame soaring into the sky like the fleshless bones of some gargantuan prehistoric monster.

'What's up, Vic?'

'Nothing.' Victor took a step backwards and raised his head, craning to see the highest point of the towering steel girders, where two solitary workmen were perched like ants, finishing up at the end of the day. Memories flooded through him. He brought his gaze to meet Nick's puzzled eyes.

A pained smile played around Victor's mouth. 'You don't know what fear is, sport, until you've dangled up there in the sky, with nothing between you and the ground but a narrow edge of metal and lots of yawning air. And then seen one of your friends slip and go plunging down, crumpling like a rag doll on the way. If you're ever going to freeze, that's when you freeze, when you know you can't go up, can't hit the sky ever again. The freeze, when you get it, is paralysing. Later come the shakes. Shakes like a dypsomaniac never knew existed.'

Nick was silent, observing the grimness on Victor's face, the anguish in his eyes. But the expression passed, and Nick asked gently, 'Did that happen to you, Vic?'

'Sure as hell it did. But the funny thing was, I didn't get the freeze when Jack actually fell. I was too concerned about him that day, I guess. It hit me forty-eight hours later.' He shook his head. 'Every construction worker dreads the freeze, because, for ever after, your days on the job are numbered. Of course you try to conceal it, bury it, because you need the work, but it gets to you in the end. The fear becomes impossible to live with, and there is no way of faking, because as the building goes up, you've got to go up. And up and up and up. If you don't, you get thrown off the job. And pronto. Anyway, your buddies always smell it on you . . . the fear.'

'Is that when you got out?'

'Yes, after a few weeks. Ellie smelled the fear on me, Nick. Her father and her brothers were construction workers. That's how I met her, through Jack. He was her youngest brother. Just a kid when he fell. Hell, she knew, Nicky, really *knew*.

From past experience . . . with them. And she begged me to quit. I wouldn't at first. *I* had to be different. Naturally. *I* had to conquer the fear. And I did. A week after Jack had slipped, another young kid got stuck on the girders at the top of a sixty-storey building. It had started to rain and a wind had blown up. A terrific gale. The kid remembered Jack's accident, and he froze. He was unable to come down. I went up and got him. About a week later I left the construction business for good, much to Ellie's relief. That's when we packed up and left Ohio for California. The twins weren't even a year old. We bought an old pick-up and drove it across the country. The four of us and the luggage, what little there was of it, packed in like sardines. But I'll tell you something, Nicky, they were the good days. I had Ellie and the boys, and that's all that mattered to me.' Victor chuckled. 'Jesus, and I wasn't even twenty.'

'And Ellie's brother Jack? Was he killed when he fell?'

'No, he was paralysed. He's been in a wheel chair ever since. Thank God I eventually made it, and have been able to look after him properly over the years.'

Nick was unable to speak for a moment, a lump constricting his throat. He thought: There's nobody in this world quite like Vic. At least that I know of. That makes eight people he supports, to my knowledge, quite apart from the friends he helps out all the time. He's got a heart the size of a goddamn mountain.

Victor had thrown back his head and was surveying the soaring girders for a second time, his lips compressed, his expression unreadable. When he lowered his head he half smiled at Nick. And then he said slowly, and with great care, 'So you see, I know what *real* fear is, Nicky. And I've conquered it. Believe me, I ain't afraid of Mike Lazarus.'

'I believe you, Vic.'

CHAPTER SIXTEEN

Norman Rook, Terry's dresser, was walking so rapidly he was almost running, and Katharine was finding it hard to keep pace. Finally, when they neared the top of the Haymarket, she caught up with him and tugged him to a standstill.

Breathlessly, she said, 'Please, Norman, can't you slow down a bit? I'm really puffed.'

'Oh, sorry, ducks,' he muttered apologetically. 'I'm anxious to get back to Albany as quickly as possible.' He set off walking again, and if his steps were not exactly leisurely, at least they were more measured. Katharine was now able to keep abreast of him, and several times she stole a look at his face, conscious he was plunged in gloom. But fortunately, now that they were away from the theatre, his agitation seemed to have lessened. When Norman had appeared in her dressing room fifteen minutes earlier, his distress had alarmed her to such a considerable degree that she had responded to the urgency in his manner with swiftness, and without really thinking, anxious to be of help.

The brisk walk had given Katharine time to sort things out in her mind, and she found one fact singularly troubling, and so perplexing. This was Norman's reaction to Terry's drunken state. In her view, it was not only rather extreme, but unwarranted in many ways. Every actor, herself included, hated to miss a performance, but sometimes it was unavoidable, usually for health reasons. Terry had only been out once, since the play opened, and that was nothing short of fantastic. A record. She herself had missed three shows because of a cold, and John Layton, the second male lead, had been absent for two weeks with a dislocated knee cap. It won't be the end of the world if Terry doesn't appear tonight, so why is Norman so frantic? she questioned herself.

Katharine clutched the dresser's arm so forcefully, and her grip was so tenacious, that he had no alternative but to stop again. 'I don't understand you, Norman! Why are you so worked up about Terry missing tonight's show?'

Norman stared back blankly. 'I'm not!' he protested. He took a deep breath. 'Hell, I wish he wouldn't even attempt it, I think he's bloody bonkers! Terry knows I'd lie in my teeth for him. I could easily say he has laryngitis. But he won't listen. I don't know how I'm going to stop him going to the theatre tonight. That's what worries me, duckie. Restraining him.' He gave her a sickly smile. 'Terry's twice my size.'

Katharine was satisfied with the explanation and recognized the truth in it. 'Yes, I know he makes two of you. But look, why can't you simply lock him in the flat, Norman?'

'Don't think I haven't thought of that! But . . . Well, Terry can be bloody difficult when he's boozed up. Belligerent, for starters.'

That sense of dismay Katharine had experienced in the dressing room, reactivated, and it struck her that Terry must be far worse than she had imagined. She wondered what had motivated him to behave so irresponsibly. Still, there was nothing to be gained by dwelling on that. Action was the imperative.

'Maybe we could find somebody to help us,' she suggested. 'I could ask Victor Mason to run over! He's as big as Terry, a lot bigger in fact and more powerfully built. I bet he could handle Terry easily.'

Norman gawked at her. 'Don't be daft, ducks, we can't drag other people into this mess.' Not bloody likely, he thought to himself. And without another word he swung around and rushed on, obviously propelled by the urgent need to get to Albany, and Terry, as speedily as possible. Katharine stared at his retreating figure, filled with exasperation, and then she set off after him.

The dresser, small and spry, was bounding ahead like a wiry terrier, his raincoat flapping out behind him as he dodged between pedestrians. My God, he's behaving like a maniac, she thought, her exasperation flaring into real annoyance. It occurred to her then that perhaps Norman was afraid Terry had managed somehow to get out, and was already staggering drunkenly to the theatre. Yes, that's obviously the explanation, she decided, and instantly changed her mind. She knew John Standish's flat, where Terry was presently staying. Apart from having a strong oak door, there were also three locks, because of John's valuable antiques, paintings and other objects of art. He made sure it was difficult to break into – or out of, for

149

that matter. She increased her speed in an effort to catch up with Norman. When she drew level with the Piccadilly Hotel, she saw, to her surprise and immense relief, that Norman had finally stopped and was actually waiting for her.

'You are being unfair,' she gasped, positioning herself determinedly in front of him. 'You promised to fill me in and you haven't. Not only that, you're behaving so strangely I'm beginning to think you're hiding something. What's wrong, Norman? You haven't told me everything, have you?'

Norman gulped several times, striving for control. Finally, he said, 'No, I haven't, love.' He shook his head sadly, and his shoulders sagged with weariness. 'I was going to tell you everything when we got a little closer to Albany. Honest, I was. I wasn't going to let you walk into that . . . that shambles unprepared. I just didn't want to tell you in the middle of the street . . .' He took her hand in his and said slowly, in a lower tone, 'Terry's not just sloshed, Katharine. He's been . . . Terry's been stabbed.'

For a moment his words did not seem to penetrate. Katharine gaped at him, uncomprehending, and then a look of horror washed over her face as his words finally registered. 'Stabbed,' she repeated, her voice quavering. She leaned against the wall, trembling from shock, and her heart suddenly began to pound. 'Is he all right?' she asked.

'Yes, yes, he's all right,' Norman quickly assured her. 'Sorry for blurting it out like that. I didn't mean to upset you. He has a flesh wound on his upper arm. Not too deep, thank God. My wife's there. She used to be a nurse, and she managed to stop the bleeding earlier.' Norman sucked in his breath, rushed on. 'The doctor isn't there. I didn't send for one.'

When Norman saw the flash of anger and panic on Katharine's chalky face, he cried hurriedly, 'I couldn't, Katharine! The doctor would have had to report the stabbing to the police, and there would be an investigation and lots of lousy publicity. You know what the papers are like when they get hold of something like this!'

'But are you sure he's going to be all right?' Katharine persisted. 'Really sure?' she demanded, clutching Norman's arm, her eyes searching his.

'Yes, I am. Honest to God, ducks. And so is Penny. I told you, she stopped the flow of blood and was bandaging him when I left. The wound isn't all that serious. Luckily. By now I hope she's managed to sober him up a bit.'

For a moment Katharine did not trust herself to speak, as she acknowledged the gravity of the situation, and also grappled with a variety of emotions. Uppermost was her enormous horror. Intrepid though she was, she nevertheless had an overwhelming abhorrence of violence, whether verbal or physical, and when confronted with it she was rendered helpless. Now she felt nauseous, and her head had started to ache. But conscious of Norman's beseeching eyes, she somehow caught hold of herself. She said slowly, 'He really can't go on tonight, Norman, even if he is sobering up. He'd never get through the show.'

Norman agreed. 'I'm hoping you'll be able to talk some sense into Terry. He'll listen to you. That's the main reason why I came to get you. You will give it a try, won't you, love?'

'You know I'll do anything to help.' She hesitated, reluctant to ask the next question. But she screwed up her nerve. 'Norman, who do you think . . . stabbed Terry?'

Norman grimaced and shook his head. 'I couldn't make head or tail out of what Terry was saying.'

'You don't think it was Alexa Garrett do you?' Katharine's voice was hushed.

'No. No, I'm sure it wasn't,' Norman asserted, but to Katharine he sounded unconvincing, and he looked away, unable to meet her gaze, which was shrewdly assessing.

'Then who?' she pressed.

'I . . . I . . . Honestly, I'm not sure.' Norman thought for a second and volunteered grimly, 'There was some sort of altercation though. A lot of bloody stuff was broken. John's going to be in a hell of a rage when he finds out. He lent Terry his flat, out of the goodness of his heart, and now half of his valuables have been damaged, and he's only been gone for a few weeks.'

'You don't mean some of those jade pieces and the porcelain things in the drawing room, do you, Norman?' Katharine asked, incredulity spreading across her face.

He nodded, unable to respond.

Katharine exclaimed, 'That's just awful, Norman. Terrible. John spent years collecting those lovely things, and he was so proud of them. Terry will have to replace everything, that's all there is to it,' she concluded firmly.

'Yes,' Norman replied. But with what? he thought. Terry's dead broke and up to his eyes in debt. Not to mention a lot of other rotten lousy problems. Norman was about to confide some of his crushing worries about Terry, but instantly changed his mind. Terry would have his guts for garters if he betrayed any secrets, and besides, Terry's present condition was the most vital priority just now. Norman said quickly, 'Come on then, me old love. Let's shake a leg. The bloomin' sand is running out. Don't be too shocked when you see the boy, Katharine. He's a bit under the weather.'

'No, I won't.' She took his arm and hurried him down Piccadilly, as anxious as he was to get to the flat.

They were only a short distance from Albany. The entrance was just a stone's throw away from the Burlington Arcade, and adjacent to the Royal Academy, the famed art gallery. Albany House, built by Lord Melbourne in 1770, had been turned into gentlemen's chambers at a later date, *pied-à-terre* in the heart of Piccadilly for members of the English aristocracy and men of letters. The chambers, generally referred to as 'rooms' rather than flats, had become exclusive and desirable places of residence over the ensuing centuries, and those who lived there considered it a privilege to do so.

Norman ushered Katharine across the courtyard and up the steps to the glass doors which opened into the building. She sneaked a look at him, and saw at once that he seemed calmer now that they had finally arrived. They went in, and were greeted by an ancient uniformed porter, who looked as if he had been left over from the Battle of Balaclava. The stone-flagged hall was shadowy and silent, and their footsteps echoed hollowly as they crossed to a second set of doors at the other end. These led out to the Rope Walk, a covered walkway traversing the entire interior area of the building which was designed in the style of an atrium.

151

When they reached the door of John's flat, Norman inserted the key and they went inside together. They were greeted quietly by Norman's wife, Penny, who was standing in the hall near the drawing room, and it was most apparent she was relieved to see them. Penny, a petite and dainty blonde with pretty features, was pale and her face was tight with worry, but she was coolly controlled.

'How is he holding up?' Norman asked.

'Not too good. He's very shaky. But fortunately his arm hasn't started to bleed again,' Penny responded, summoning a cheerful tone. She nodded in the direction of the drawing room. 'Let's pop in there for a tick, before you see him, and I'll fill you in.'

Walking into the drawing room, Katharine saw at once that Norman had not exaggerated in the least when he said the place was in a shambles. If anything, he had underplayed the result of the altercation. More like a bar brawl, Katharine commented to herself, compressing her lips. The room, which she had always admired for its beauty and elegance, was in great disarray. Two large Chinese porcelain lamps had been smashed and, with their dented silk shades, had been placed in a corner out of the way; and several small antique tables with broken legs were laid on their sides next to the lamps. A large and extraordinarily lovely Venetian mirror, hanging above the white-marble fireplace, was cracked and splintered down the middle, and John's collection of prized pink and green Chinese jade ornaments had been reduced to dozens of small pieces. They lay on a newspaper on top of a circular Georgian rent table, looking like a rare jigsaw puzzle about to be reassembled. The pale blue carpet had several cigarette burns and dark splotches where red wine had been spilled, and the same ugly wine stains splattered across the cushions on the pale blue velvet sofa, also streaked down the blue silk draperies at the window.

Katharine was appalled. It was apparent to her that either Penny, or Norman earlier, had endeavoured to clean up and restore a semblance of order, but even so the considerable damage was only too visible. Her eyes swept around the room again, and her face reflected her distress. 'How could Terry let this happen?' she cried, turning to Norman who was close behind her.

'I don't know,' Norman murmured miserably. 'I've also been wondering how he could let himself get stabbed.'

Katharine flushed deeply. 'Oh, sorry,' she said. She hadn't meant to sound so callous, or dismissive of Terry's injury, certainly more important than broken furnishings. She looked at Penny. 'You said Terry was shaky. What do *you* think about his appearing tonight?'

Penny shook her head. 'I think it would be disastrous, Katharine. I've tried to sober him up, and certainly he's a lot better than he was, but a real hangover's settling in.'

Norman groaned. 'I'm at my bloody wits' end! It's up to you now, Katharine. Perhaps you'll be able to persuade him to stay put for twenty-four hours. What he needs is a good kip.'

'I'll give it a try,' she replied. 'Shall we go in and see him?' Katharine followed Norman and Penny out of the drawing room. Norman suddenly halted at the bedroom door at the other end of the entrance hall. 'Perhaps I'd better warn him. Tell him you're here, Katharine. He didn't know I'd gone to fetch you.' He hurried into the bedroom and Penny and Katharine hovered outside the door, which stood open a few inches.

They could hear Norman talking in a low tone, and then Terry's voice reverberating loudly, as he shouted, 'Jesus bloody Christ! What did you have to go and do that for? You silly sod!' There was low murmuring, as Norman attempted to calm Terry down, and then he poked his head around the door and motioned for them to come into the bedroom.

Katharine hesitated imperceptibly before moving forward, realizing that Terry was most probably discomfited because she was seeing him in a disreputable condition: The great lover as the rake.

Penny gave her a little push and she was forced to take a few more steps, and suddenly Terry was in her line of vision. Her heart dropped when she saw him, but she was able to keep her face expressionless, her shock concealed, and her smile barely faltered.

Terry was lying on top of the bedcover, propped up against a pile of snowy white pillows, wearing only black silk pyjama bottoms. His wounded left arm was almost completely covered in bandages, and she noticed that he had sustained other injuries. His right shoulder and arm were black and blue with angry bruises, and there were ragged vivid scratches on his neck. And apart from his battered body, his appearance was so much worse than she had envisioned, she was further alarmed. Terry looked ghastly. His unshaven face was puffy and swollen and without a drop of colour, and his blue eyes were bloodshot and red-rimmed with faint mauve smudges underneath them. He seemed slightly dazed, his eyes glazed, and he had trouble focusing on Katharine. There was an aura of such terrible dissipation about him, Katharine was sickened and yet curiously sad for him.

A pressing question dangled on the tip of her tongue: Who did this to you, Terry darling? But she was unable to utter the words, fearful of exciting him or causing him more pain at this moment. Instinctively she knew, too, that he would not tell her.

'Hello, Puss,' Terry said, his voice weak and hoarse, as if his loud shouting of a few seconds before had drained him. 'Fine pickle I'm in, eh?'

'Yes, love, it is,' Katharine answered, producing a radiant smile, one that was also loving. Her voice was softly comforting, as she continued, 'But it could be worse, you know. You'll feel better after a good night's sleep. Why, Norman just said to me all you need is a good kip.' She smiled again, and remarked in a matter-of-fact tone, 'You'll be back on stage tomorrow night.'

Gathering the remainder of his diminished strength, Terry pushed himself up on the pillows and positively glared at her. '*Tonight*! I'm not missing a performance. Not because of this piddling little scratch. Not bloody likely, Puss.'

Somewhat to Katharine's surprise, Terry did not sound at all slurred. Quite the contrary, he was enunciating clearly; on the other hand, there was no question in her mind that he was incapacitated. He would not be able to meet the fierce demands placed on him by his taxing role. His hands resting on top of the bed trembled slightly, and it was very clear to her that the quantity of alcohol he had drunk, lack of sleep, the knife wound and the fight in the drawing room had all taken their considerable toll.

Katharine approached the bed and stood at the foot. She said, in her most commanding voice, 'You can't possibly go on, Terry dear. It would be insane to do so. Honestly, you won't get through the first act, never mind the whole play. Now be sensible.'

'I'm going on, I told you!' Terry half screamed, his voice surprisingly vibrant again. 'I appreciate your concern, Puss, and it was sweet of you to come over,' he continued, speaking now in a softer key. 'But I'd be grateful if you ladies would buzz off, so that Norman can help me to get ready. I'm not a blasted zoo tea, you know.' He fell back against the pillows and reached for the glass of water on the bedside table. His hand shook so much he slopped half of the water on the table before getting the glass finally to his parched lips.

'Just look at you,' Katharine cried with fierceness, her eyes blazing. 'You're trembling like a leaf. You'll never make it.'

Terry smiled at her grimly and his tone was sardonic. 'Oh yes I will. I've had a hell of a lot more stage experience than you, my pet. Once I've done my make-up and get into my costume, I'll hit the footlights with my usual aplomb. And I'll be perfectly bloody fine. I'm an old trouper, didn't you know?' He laughed wildly.

'Now listen to me,' Katharine said. 'I'm not even going to permit you to go to the *theatre*, never mind hit the footlights. Over my dead body, Terrence Ogden. You're out of your mind thinking you can try it.' She paused and the look she gave him was deadly serious. 'You have a responsibility to the audience! And a responsibility to the rest of the cast. It's not fair to burden them, and me, with your problems. You know we'd all have to carry you. *I* don't mind doing that, but I'm sure the others would resent it. And just think how mortified you'd feel later, for giving a lousy performance. You love acting too much to give less than your best. I know for a fact that you could never live with yourself, if you behaved disgracefully on a stage. You couldn't stand the humiliation, for one thing.' She glared at him, her defiant eyes dared him to contradict her.

Terry laughed even more hysterically than before, and cried out dramatically, 'Ah, my sweet Kate, you're so young, so idealistic, so filled with noble thoughts ...' He broke off and reached for the glass of water. '"Tempt not a desperate man." *Romeo and Juliet*. Act ... I forget which act, but never mind, my sweet, sweet Kate.' He flung out his arm, making a grand gesture, and the water splashed out of the glass on to the sheet. He looked down at the wet patch and shook his head, smiling to himself. 'Tears. Ah, yes, tears.' He lay supine on the pillows and murmured, '"To weep is to make less the depth of grief." *Henry VI*. The Bard always got to the heart of the matter, did he not, my sweet Kate.' He closed his eyes wearily. The eyelids fluttered and then were still.

Katharine's troubled face now met Norman's, and he shrugged, helpless and resigned.

Penny said, 'I think Terry's falling asleep. Perhaps we should let him rest for a while.'

'Oh no, I'm not, Penelope. The wise and wonderful Penn – ell – ohpee,' Terry cried, opening one bloodshot blue eye and leering wickedly at them.

Katharine turned to Norman and said carefully, 'I agree with Penny. Terry'll feel better in about half an hour, then you can get him ready.' Aware that Norman was about to protest, she signalled him to be silent with her expressive eyes, and rushed on, 'Maybe you should run a bath in the meantime.' Her cool blue glance rested on

154

Terry and she remarked casually, 'When you're ready, Norman and I will take you to the theatre. Come on Norman, Penny.' She swung around and walked across the room, her steps purposeful.

'Thanks, Puss. I knew I could rely on your understanding,' Terry muttered, raising himself on his right arm. Instantly he collapsed on the mound of pillows, looking more exhausted than ever.

Norman threw Katharine a questioning look once they were outside, and Penny began crossly, 'What kind of idea is –'

'Hush,' Katharine whispered, and pulled Penny after her into the drawing room. Norman followed and closed the door firmly behind him. He leaned against it and said, 'If you've come up with a plan, it'd better be a flaming good one, ducks.'

Katharine sat down on an easy chair, and smiled faintly. 'It's not a plan exactly, only a little common sense. Look, Norman, as long as we argue with Terry about going on tonight, he'll continue to fight us until we're blue in the face. So . . . I think we ought to go through the motions of getting him bathed and dressed. Didn't you see how docile he became when I suggested that you get him ready?'

They nodded in unison, and Katharine proceeded, 'It's pretty apparent to me that Terry is wiped out physically, and he's still a bit drunk, you know. That's why I don't think he'll have any juice left in him by the time you've got him shaved, bathed and in his clothes. He's going to be awfully drowsy after a bath, particularly if you make it a hot one. I have a feeling he'll simply fall apart, and then we can get him to bed without any arguments, or a struggle.'

Norman smiled for the first time that day. 'Katharine, you're a little genius. Of course it's the only solution. Hell, I wish we had some knockout drops as well.'

'I have some sleeping pills on me . . .' Penny began hesitantly, and stopped when she saw Norman's glowering expression.

'Why the bloody hell didn't you say so before,' Norman snapped, staring at his wife in irritation.

'Well, actually, I haven't had a chance, have I?' she retorted reprovingly, with a small glare. 'There's no need to be so snippy, Norman. Anyway, when you rang me up to tell me about Terry, I threw a lot of things in a shopping bag. A first-aid kit, bandages, aspirin and sleeping pills. I was reluctant to suggest giving him one of those though, because he's been drinking.'

'Christ, I didn't think of that,' Norman answered, looking shamefaced. 'But *one* wouldn't hurt, would it?'

'I don't think so.' Penny went to her shopping bag and pulled out the bottle. She popped it in the pocket of her cardigan and said, 'We'll never get him to take it voluntarily, Norman. I'll have to crush it and put it in a glass of hot milk. He won't taste it, if I add a bit of sugar.'

'Good idea, love.' He gave Penny a fond look, and added, 'And I'm sorry. I didn't mean to snap.' He jumped up. 'I think I'd better go and run a bath for him. Back in two shakes of a lamb's tail.'

The moment Norman left the room, Katharine turned to Penny and said, 'This is pretty awful, isn't it? What's it all about, Penny darling?'

Penny bit her lip. 'I've absolutely no idea,' she murmured.

Katharine gave her a hard stare. 'Did Norman tell you anything?'

'No,' Penny responded, returning the stare with one equally as hard.

'How did Norman find out about the stabbing?'

'Terry had asked him to pick up a suit from his tailor's and deliver it here. Norman brought it over this afternoon. He found Terry lying on the bed in a pool of blood, drunk as a skunk. He 'phoned me and told me to get over here as fast as I could, and then I believe he tried to question Terry. But he didn't find out anything. Terry was much worse earlier, unintelligible, from what Norman told me. That's about it . . .'

'It's a good thing Norman had reason to come over here today,' Katharine said with a small shiver, imagining the consequences if Norman had not arrived on the scene at the right time. She looked down at her hands, and when she lifted her head her eyes held a quizzical look. 'I asked Norman if he thought Alexa Garrett had done it, and he said no. But he didn't really convince me. I think Norman suspects her, don't you?'

'I'm not sure,' Penny responded uncertainly. 'But *I* suspect her. I think she's a bit of a Tartar, that one. I wouldn't put anything past *her*. Terry's had nothing but bad luck since she's been around. Jinxed him, that she has. I never liked her, stuck-up little piece of nothing. She's led Terry into bad ways, Katharine. Very bad ways indeed, I don't mind telling you. But then, Terry never did have much taste in women. Always going for the dolly birds. Except for Hilary Rayne. He should have married Hilary, instead of that last wife of his – Megan. I never liked her either, another stuck-up article, if ever I saw one. Exactly like Alexa. Two peas in a pod, if you ask me, and rotten bloody peas at that.'

Katharine was taken aback at this second reference to Hilary in one day, and intrigued and inquisitive, remembering Estelle's comments about the party. She said, 'Yes, I agree with you, about Hilary. She's a lovely person. But she's married to Mark Pierce now, so she's hardly available for Terry.'

Penny was startled. 'Oh, I didn't know *you* knew Hilary. Known her long, have you?'

'Not very long, but she's –' Katharine cut off her sentence as Norman rushed in. He seemed elated and he grinned at them both and made Winston Churchill's V for Victory sign with two fingers. 'I think it's going to work. I had to wake Terry to get him into the bathroom. Right now he's sitting in a tub of hot water, looking as weak as a kitten and sounding very groggy. He didn't even want me to shave him. Why don't you go and boil the milk, Penny love, and then I'll try to get him to drink it. After that, it'll be never-never-land time.'

Penny hurried out, and Norman peered at his watch. 'It's just turning five-thirty, Katharine. Do you want to get off to the theatre?'

'No, I'll wait for you, Norman. Just to be sure everything is all right. We can go together,' she said.

Norman stood in the wings of the St James's Theatre, watching the last scene of the last act of *Trojan Interlude*. And silently he applauded Katharine. She was superb. She had carried the entire play with ease and brilliance and immense flair, radiating her own extraordinary magic, a magic quite unique to her. Peter Mallory, Terry's understudy, was good, but he lacked Terry's fire and declamatory ability, and although his performance was sound it was without inspiration.

If the audience felt a little cheated because of his lack-lustre performance, they had been more than compensated by Katharine's stunning protrayal of Helen of Troy. She had given them everything she had, with every fibre of her being, and Norman decided it was probably her most outstanding rendition to date. She had surpassed herself, had held them in the palm of her hand all night long, and now, as the play drew to its finale, they were her entranced and willing captives, breathless in their seats, hanging on every word. He suspected there wouldn't be a dry eye in the house when the curtain fell in a few minutes.

Norman turned and meandered out of the wings, making his way slowly down the stone stairs to the dressing rooms. He had had to come to the theatre tonight, to dress Terry's understudy, who didn't have one of his own. In many ways he had been glad to get away from the flat. It had enabled him to clear his head. Terry had dropped off to sleep before he and Katharine left, and Penny had assured him she was capable of coping with any emergency which might arise. Norman had telephoned his wife several times during the course of the play, and to his great relief she had told him Terry was still out like a light, and probably wouldn't awaken until the next morning. But as a precaution, he and Penny had elected to stay the night there, just in case Terry needed anything.

And tomorrow he would have a serious talk with Master Terrence. It was long overdue. Norman now chastised himself for not having done so before. He was devoted to Terry, and protective of him, and in the six years he had been his dresser they had drawn extremely close and intimate, were like brothers. Norman, failed and frustrated actor that he was, guarded Terry's career as he would the Holy Grail, and he was prepared to go out on a limb for him at any time, to ensure his position and standing in the English theatre. Talent such as Terry possessed was rare and precious, and it had to be cherished and nurtured. To Norman it was a national treasure that belonged to the people, to be preserved for them.

Norman hovered outside Terry's dressing room, waiting for Katharine to come off stage. He had done a great deal of thinking in the past few hours and had at last resolved to confide in her. She was the only person he dare trust with Terry's secrets. Norman sighed under his breath. Terry's troubles were becoming too weighty and complex for him to carry alone, and after the nightmarish day he had spent, he knew he must unburden himself, seek objective advice. And quickly, if he was to avert further disaster. He was not sure she *could* properly advise him, but sometimes it was simply enough to voice fears. Communicating them to someone else helped to clarify them and often produced solutions which otherwise might have remained elusive. And at least Katharine might be able to make Terry see sense.

He heard her laughter as she tripped lightly down the steps, and he went along the corridor to meet her, smiling broadly. He grabbed her, somewhat roughly, but with genuine affection, and hugged her to him. 'You were smashing, love,' he exclaimed. 'Staggering. You pulled out all the stops.'

'Thanks, Norman.' She exhaled several times. 'I did it for Terry,' she said softly, and with the sweetest of smiles. 'I acted for both of us tonight. But it was rough going at times. Look at me. I'm soaked to my skin.'

'You'd better get out of your damp costume immediately,' Norman ordered in a fatherly manner, bundling her towards her dressing room door. 'By the way, can I buy you a drink later, love?'

157

'That's so sweet of you, Norman, but I have a date.'

'Just one. Ten minutes of your time. It's important, Katharine.'

She noted the anxiety in Norman's voice, and she thought, Oh God, Terry's taken a turn for the worse. She said swiftly, and with a degree of nervousness, 'Is he all right? There's nothing wrong is there?'

'No, he's fast asleep. Actually, I need a bit of advice . . . About Ter . . . our boy . . .' Norman's voice trailed off. He gave her a pointed look. 'Understand what I mean?'

'Yes, I do.' She did not have the heart to refuse him. Also, she was worried about Terry herself, and riddled with curiosity about these recent events, and her inquisitiveness now got the better of her. She said, 'Kim Cunningham's bringing a picnic over to my flat later. We're going to have a midnight supper.' She wrinkled her nose. 'He's very romantic. Anyway, we can have a drink there, Norman. We have plenty of time to talk before he arrives.'

Norman was hesitant, shrinking away from this suggestion. He always felt faintly ill-at-ease when he was with the nobs. Being the son of a man who had spent forty years of his life in service to one of the premier dukes of England, he had been brought up to know his place. And his place was certainly not at any social gathering, particularly one of this intimate nature. 'Oh well, if his lordship's coming courting, perhaps we'd better leave it.'

'Don't be *silly*, Norman. I want you to come. And I certainly want to help you and Terry if I can.'

'Okay. And thanks, Katharine, you're a real brick,' Norman beamed. 'I'm going to pop along and help Peter, but I won't be long. Knock on the door when you're ready to leave.'

'I'll hurry. About fifteen minutes,' she said, disappearing into her dressing room.

CHAPTER SEVENTEEN

'I'd like a pink gin, please,' Norman said, lighting a cigarette as he sat back on the white sofa in Katharine's flat.

'Oh dear, I don't have any angostura bitters,' she answered with a frown. 'But I do have gin. Would you like a splash of tonic water with it?'

'Thanks, love, that'll be fine.'

Katharine smiled, returning to the kitchen. Norman glanced around with considerable interest. Very posh, he thought. And expensive. But not to my taste at all. The room was too cold, too sterile and too . . . hygienic. All this white. It reminded him of a hospital. The only thing missing was the smell of disinfectant and that peculiar medicinal odour which always permeated the wards. The décor was so frigid and icy it was oddly depressing, and despite the warmth emanating from the large electric fire in the fireplace, Norman felt chilled. He had trouble reconciling the room with Katharine and what he knew of her. Earlier, at the theatre, when she had invited him to her flat, he had imagined a setting quite different from this one. She was such a cheerful, open and vivacious girl, with a warm personality and a sweet disposition, and this place where she lived was somehow alien in its austerity and, yes, its lifelessness.

White. It struck an odd chord in his memory. White was the mourning colour in India, wasn't it? He shivered again and his thoughts swept to Terry. We might have been mourning him, he said inwardly, except for the slip of the knife. The right slip, in this instance. Norman's chest tightened, and he felt a spurt of intense rage. Deep inside he was furious with Terry for constantly putting himself in such precarious situations, for jeopardizing his career. His brilliant career. And, today, his safety as well.

Katharine arrived with the drinks. She handed the gin and tonic to Norman and seated herself on the chair facing him.

'Cheers,' she said with a friendly smile, and took a sip of her vodka on the rocks.

'Cheers,' Norman responded. 'I really appreciate this, Katharine.' He looked away, wondering where to begin, how to launch into the story and enumerate the terrible worries which plagued him, which could no longer be shoved under the rug. The trouble was, there was so much to tell.

Katharine waited patiently, regarding Terry's dresser with not a little curiosity, wondering how much he was going to divulge about the stabbing. For undoubtedly that was what he wanted to discuss with her. She had half expected him to say something on their way from the theatre, but he had mostly raved about her performance, not touching on his troubles.

As if he had read her mind, Norman now cleared his throat and blurted out, 'Terry's on a path to self-destruction! I don't know how to stop him, Katharine. I'm out of my mind with worry. Honest to God, I don't know what to do any more!'

Katharine sat up straight. 'What do you mean . . . self-destruction?'

'The way he's been behaving, the situations he gets himself into, and with increasing frequency. He's not very stable.' He immediately saw the challenge in her large turquoise eyes, the disbelief washing across her lovely young face, and he said with great firmness, 'I'm *not* exaggerating! Believe me I'm not! I've thought for a long time that he'd come a cropper one day, but it was sooner than I expected. And much worse. Christ Almighty, don't you realize he could have been killed today! It was a fluke he wasn't!'

'Yes, I know.' Katharine shifted in her chair and leaned forward slightly. 'Why don't you tell me about the stabbing, Norman dear. You'll feel much better if you get it off your chest.'

Norman half laughed bleakly. 'There's not much to tell about *that* incident. I've been trying to piece things together as best I could from Terry's incoherent mumblings, and I've come up with one theory at least. I wish I'd talked to you before, and then perhaps this bloody mess might have been avoided. But to be honest, I didn't want to discuss Terry's troubles. I . . . I . . . felt it would be terribly disloyal.' Norman took a cigarette, lit it and continued, 'I know I can trust

159

you though. I mean, I know you understand that what I'm going to tell you about Terry is absolutely confidential – '

'I would never repeat anything you told me to anyone,' Katharine interrupted. 'I promise you, Norman.'

'Thanks, love.' His eyes rested on her, searching, as he began slowly, diffidently, 'I know you suspect Alexa, and so does Penny, but I don't think she was involved. Terry told me the other day that she was going to Zurich to see her father, and as far as I know she did. I think she's still there. Actually, I'm sure it was a man,' he rushed on, his voice gaining in strength and conviction. 'But listen, love, I don't want my theory repeated. You've got to promise me you won't say a word to a soul about this matter either.'

Katharine moved to the edge of the sofa, absorbing his words. She said, 'Of course I won't. I realize you can't go around accusing people of attempted murder.'

'Have you ever seen Terry with a young, good-looking bod? Dark haired, very well dressed, almost foppish?'

'Yes, I think so,' Katharine said, her brows puckering. 'Does he have a yellow Jag that he parks in the Haymarket?'

'That's the bloke!' Norman cried. He took a long swallow of the gin and tonic, and said flatly, in a cold voice, 'I think it was him that did it.'

'Norman, are you sure?' Katharine asked nervously.

'Of course I can't be sure. I wasn't there,' he replied snappishly. In a more even tone he added, 'But from what Terry said to me, and because of the things I know myself, everything points to him.'

'But who is he, Norman?' Katharine demanded.

'He calls himself Rupert Reynolds.'

'*Calls* himself! Isn't that his real name?'

'No, it's not. Actually, he's the son of a very prominent man.'

Katharine looked at Norman sharply. 'How do you know, if he uses a false name? Did Terry tell you?'

'No, he didn't. In fact, Terry had no idea who the hell he was until I filled him in. You see, this bod was getting to be a bit of a nuisance to Terry, so I made a few inquiries about him.' Norman laughed grimly. 'He's the black sheep of a prominent family, and not on good terms with his old man. Anyway, I believe he was having lunch with Terry at the flat today, when they had a row. And then Rupert slashed him with the knife.' Norman's head moved up and down a few times jerkily, as though he was confirming his suspicions to himself.

'But why?' Katharine asked, horrified that anyone would want to harm Terry.

'Jealousy,' he pronounced.

Taken aback though she was, she refrained from commenting. Finally, she said, 'Don't tell me Terry pinched one of his girl friends.'

'Well, yes, and then, no. It's a shade more convoluted than that . . .' Norman ran his hand through his thinning hair, blinking rapidly, obviously distressed. 'I'll try and make the story as simple as possible. About six months ago this Rupert chap met Terry at a party. He claimed to be a playwright. Anyway, he attached himself to Terry. Like a bloody leech, I don't mind telling you. I warned Terry he was a sponger, a hanger-on of the worst kind, but Terry simply laughed at me.

He seemed to be impressed with the bloke, God knows why. He thought Rupert was entertaining. Rupert was trying to shove a play down Terry's throat, one he'd written. He wanted Terry to help him get it staged, and to star in it. Bloody cheek, if you ask me. And a load of codswallop, it was. Drivel. At least Terry had the sense to say no to that little project, but still, he wasn't able to shake Rupert. Terry was beginning to get fed up with him, and they had some sort of a barney. Rupert made himself scarce for a few weeks. Suddenly, out of the blue, he was back on the scene with Alexa Garrett in tow. He introduced her as his girl friend, and, I must say, they did seem very chummy. Stone the crows, the next thing I know she and Terry are shacking up together and madly in love. Talking of marriage. Bloody hell, you could have knocked me down with a bloomin' feather.'

'And so that's why Rupert stabbed Terry? Because he was jealous of him?'

'No, I don't think so . . .' Norman gave Katharine the most careful of looks, and his voice was muffled as he told her, 'I think the bugger was jealous of Alexa. I think . . . well, to be honest, Katharine, he's a bit decadent in my opinion. You know, swings either way on a windy day. AC-DC.'

Katharine was staring at Norman, momentarily nonplussed. Eventually, she asked incredulously, in a surprised voice, 'Are you trying to tell me this Rupert what's-his-name has a *thing* about Terry?'

Norman nodded. 'I bloody well am! But hey, Katharine, it's not mutual! Terry's as straight as a die. Nothing in the least bit bent about our boy. He loves the ladies too much to tango with the gents, as you well know. And *I* know for a fact he hasn't encouraged the chap, other than being friendly with him. Terry can be generous to a fault.'

'But didn't Terry realize that this Rupert was . . .'

'Queer as a coot?' Norman interjected and laughed sarcastically. 'No, not initially. Rupert Reynolds is a deceptive kind of bloke. He always had a lot of dolly birds hanging around, and was for ever boring us, boasting about his conquests. But I began to get an inkling about his predilections a couple of months ago, when he started acting possessive with Terry. I remarked about it, but Terry just laughed again and brushed it off. 'Course, I'd alerted him. Then Alexa confirmed my suspicions and Terry had to listen to *her*, now didn't he? You can imagine Terry's reaction. He dropped Rupert like a hot spud. Yes, Master Reynolds was suddenly *persona non* bloody *grata* around the old homestead. We haven't seen hide nor hair of him for weeks.'

'Until today,' Katharine volunteered.

'That's right. When I got to the flat and found Terry bleeding on the bed, he muttered something about Rupert being bonkers, and repeated it several times too. I couldn't make out everything he was saying, but blimey, Katharine, it don't take much to put two and two together, does it?'

'Oh Norman, it's so little to go on, really it – '

'I found this,' Norman interrupted peremptorily, and reached into his pocket, producing a gold cufflink. He handed it to Katharine, who took it and studied it, turning it over in her hand.

'It has some sort of crest on it.' She looked at Norman questioningly.

'That's correct. A family crest, and it's Rupert's all right. I've seen it before. No two ways about it, ducks, and I found it right in the middle of the living room floor. Listen, the ashtrays were full of the cigs he smokes. Some foul-smelling Frog brand.'

Katharine said curiously, 'Is that why you wanted my advice? I mean about this Rupert fellow?'

'No, as a matter of fact, it isn't – '

'But somebody like that could still be dangerous,' Katharine cried. 'Aren't you afraid he'll try and hurt Terry again? You know what they say, hell hath no fury like a – '

'Good God, no.' Norman laughed, and she caught the edge of grimness in his laughter. 'I'm sure he's already scarpered across the Channel by now, and if he hasn't, you can bet your bottom dollar he's packing at this very moment, intent on doing a moonlight bloody flit to foreign parts. I doubt he relishes the idea of being in the dock at the Old Bailey, up on a murder charge. Or rather, attempted murder. No, we won't be hearing a peep from that nasty bit of work again, don't you fret, duckie. And if he should be stupid enough to show his mug, I'll threaten to go to his father. That'll scare the living daylights out of him.'

'Well, I suppose you know best, Norman,' Katharine murmured, sounding both hesitant and doubtful. She was perplexed and asked pointedly, 'So what was it you actually wanted my advice about?'

Norman said, 'How to get Terry out of the trouble he's in right now, and as quickly as possible.'

'What kind of trouble?' Katharine cried anxiously. What else could Norman possibly have up his sleeve?

'All kinds of problems . . . I suppose the best thing is to just plunge in at the deep end, so to speak, and tell you about them. So, here goes. First of all, Terry is up to his eyes in debt. And I really mean up to his eyes – drowning. He's paying alimony and child support to Glenda, his first wife, and he'll also have to fork out alimony to Megan, once they're divorced. *She* ain't about to let him off the bloody hook, I can tell you that! So, you see, two ex-wives are going to prove very expensive, unless they both remarry, and pretty sharpish. Then again, take Terry himself. He lives like a bloomin' pasha. The best Savile Row suits, shirts from Turnbull's, shoes from Maxwell's. He's always in chic restaurants, and nothing short of the best will do for our Terrence. And he entertains very expansively, and expensively. Now there's the damage at John's flat. That's not going to be cheap to put right. Not on your nelly. I've been doing a bit of arithmetic, and right now Terry needs at least forty or fifty thousand pounds to square everything away. And don't ask me where he's going to get it, 'cos I don't have any ideas. I'm stymied.'

Katharine had been listening attentively, and she realized Norman was not exaggerating. Everything he said was true; she knew herself that Terry lived high, although she had never given it much thought until this moment. 'Couldn't he go to the bank and get an overdraft?' she suggested.

'Not bloody likely! He has one already.' A tired sigh escaped Norman's lips, and he said, 'Jesus, Katharine, Terry spends money like a drunken sailor when the fleet's in, and there's just no end to it. But his financial worries aside, there's also Alexa. I agree with Penny that she's been a bad influence on him, and he'd be a lot better off without her in his life. And don't think he isn't influenced by his women,' he muttered almost to himself. After a pause he went on, 'For one thing,

162

he's been boozing heavily since he met her. Oh, I don't mean he has a real drinking problem . . . at least, not yet. Terry's always been able to knock a few back, but he's tippling more than usual. If he weren't, I doubt the incident with Reynolds would have erupted and ended the way it did today. To be honest with you, I wish I could get Terry out of London, away from Alexa and that fast crowd of hers he's running with. I think he'd straighten out very quickly. One possibility has come up. He's been invited by the Shakespeare Memorial Company to go to Australia on a long tour, as the leading actor, the star attraction. I've been wondering how to persuade him to sign the contract. It would solve a lot of things. What do you think? I'd really like your advice.'

Katharine pondered, but only for a moment. She exclaimed authoritatively, 'But they pay so little, much less than he's earning now in the play. It would hardly solve his money problems. And I don't think it would do much for his career. I realize Larry and Viv used to do those tours, but, well, they were international stars already. No, I think Australia would be a real mistake, Norman.'

'I expect you're right,' Norman mumbled glumly, and fell silent.

Katharine sat back on the sofa, reflecting on everything Norman had said. Once again, she knew he was absolutely correct in his assessment of the situation. She knew, too, that he was motivated strictly out of concern for Terry. Norman was the most selfless person she had met in a long time, and Terry was exceptionally fortunate to have such a dedicated dresser and loyal and devoted friend. Katharine's mind was like a well-oiled Swiss watch, finely tuned and precise, and now it turned with amazing swiftness.

Quite suddenly she saw everything with such vivid clarity she almost jumped off the sofa in her excitement.

She held herself in check, but she was unable to disguise the jubilant smile spreading across her face. 'Norman, I have it! The *only* solution, and to every one of Terry's problems.' She sat up, as straight as an arrow, her hands tightly clenched in her lap and her smile turned into one of immense confidence.

Norman gave her a long and questioning look. '*All* of them?' he asked, his doubtfulness apparent.

Katharine's radiant smile widened. 'Yes. Yes, I know how to turn Terry's life around, and almost immediately.'

'If you do, it's nothing short of a bloody miracle, that's all I can say,' Norman said grudgingly, still doubting. 'Let's have it then.'

'Do you remember my talking to Terry a few weeks ago? About his playing the role of Edgar Linton in Victor Mason's remake of *Wuthering Heights*?'

Norman, who was giving her his total concentration, inclined his head without comment, uncertain of what was on her mind.

Katharine continued spiritedly, 'As you know, Terry turned it down. At the time I thought he was being foolish. Now I realize just how foolish. Terry has an out-of-the-play clause in his contract, so he could leave *Trojan* to do the film without any difficulty. I know, too, that Victor would pay him well, because he really and truly wants Terry in the picture, is ever so anxious to get him. Perhaps Victor would pay as much as seventy thousand pounds, maybe even more – '

'Christ!' Norman cut in excitedly, 'as much as that!' He was overwhelmed at the thought and quickly lit a cigarette. A surge of hope shot through him, and he picked

163

up his gin and tonic and took a long swallow, his eyes glued on Katharine. 'Go on,' he said, 'I'm all ears.'

'So, Norman, don't you see, if Terry made the film he would be able to solve his terrible financial problems practically immediately, and for only a few months' work. He'd even have some money to spare. Now, listen, Norman, there's more to it . . . the film's going to be made mostly in Yorkshire, which means Terry would be out of London for a number of weeks. Far away from Alexa and her cronies, and in turn, that might help to solve his drinking pr – '

'You don't know Alexa, ducks,' he exclaimed with a hollow laugh. 'She'd be tearing after him with the speed of a fox fleeing the bloody hounds.'

'I'm sure there are ways to cope with her, Norman. For instance, I could talk to Victor, say she was a troublemaker, and get him to ban her from location. He listens to me.'

'That'd be a bit difficult, love.' Norman gave her a small wry smile. 'It's still a free country here, you know. This ain't the USSR. You can't stop somebody going to Yorkshire, even if you can keep them off a set. Besides, that one's as tough as Old Nick, and she has a skin like an alligator. She'd be hard to control; you mark my words, Katharine, I know what I'm talking about. She's led Terry a merry dance ever since he's known her, the little bitch. Alexa does what she wants, when and how she wants, and nobody stops her.'

'Don't be so sure of that, Norman. I think she's the least of our problems actually. It seems to me money is the most pressing . . .' Katharine's sentence dangled in mid-air. She stared hard at the dresser as another idea streaked through her active brain. 'Norman . . .' she began, 'what if Terry was . . . was under someone else's influence, you know, someone he really respected . . .'

'Like who?'

'Hilary.'

Norman shot bolt upright on the sofa and gawked at her in stupefaction, 'Hilary! Stone the crows, Katharine, you're out of your tiny mind. She's married to Mark Pierce now.'

'I'm well aware of that,' Katharine responded in a cool voice, which sounded slightly superior. 'But Victor is hoping to sign Mark to direct the picture. Hilary's bound to go on location with him, and if she does, she can easily keep an eye on Terry. I've always thought Hilary was a stable, down-to-earth girl.' She gave Norman a knowing smile, and then, stabbing in the dark, she fibbed, 'You see, Norman dear, I happen to know that Hilary is still very fond of Terry, and vice versa, so don't deny it.'

Where the hell does she get her information? Norman asked himself, baffled.

'Well, it's true, isn't it?' Katharine persisted.

'In certain ways, yes,' Norman admitted a trifle reluctantly. 'But only on a fraternal basis,' he hastened to add. 'Still, Hilary might not go on location with Mark. She doesn't always.'

'There's a way around that,' Katharine remarked, again with such self-confidence Norman had no alternative but to listen and give her the benefit of any doubts.

'Victor is looking for a really talented costume designer, and Hilary's as good as any in London. If *I* recommend her, I know he'll sign her for the picture too,'

Katharine finished on a triumphant note, inwardly congratulating herself. She knew this to be inspired, and she wished she'd thought of it before. She couldn't wait to suggest it to Victor.

Norman was not only filled with astonishment but a considerable amount of admiration as well. This girl really was staggering. 'Blimey, Katharine, you've certainly thought of everything.' He grinned at her, feeling as if an enormous weight had been lifted, and then his face fell. 'But Hilary's away. I'm not sure when she's coming back to town. You see, I tried . . . tried reaching her today.'

'I understand, Norman. To help with Terry. Of course. But surely we can easily find out when she's returning, can't we?'

'I'll try. And Terry does listen to her,' he found himself confiding. 'Takes notice of her, always has. And, as I said, they have a good relationship these days, the sort of brother-and-sister type. And Mark doesn't seem to object to their friendship. It's platonic now, of course,' he felt bound to reiterate.

'I have Hilary's number. I can call the house, if you like,' Katharine suggested. 'Personally, I think she'd jump at the idea of designing the costumes for *Wuthering Heights*. After all, it's going to be a major film, and the credits would be marvellous for her. Not only that, she'd be working with her husband. She likes to collaborate with him, I know. She'd also be working with Terry.' Katharine gave Norman a coy glance from underneath her dark sweeping lashes and smiled wickedly. 'Her favourite actor, no doubt.'

Norman had to laugh. He rubbed his hand over his chin, thinking hard, and then he laughed more heartily than before, immensely tickled at the mere thought of thwarting Alexa Garrett, of extracting Terry from her clutches. 'This here combination of yours is highly complex,' he ventured. 'Bloody dicey, in fact. But it just might work. Christ, it just might! If we're lucky,' he added as an afterthought.

Katharine sat back, inwardly hugging herself with delight, a smile ringing her mouth. 'So you'll help me to talk Terry into doing the picture?'

'You're on, duckie,' Norman exclaimed, coming to a decision.

Stretching out her hand, she said, 'Then let's shake on it, Norman.' They clasped hands tightly, both grinning broadly, happy to be conspirators, albeit loving and well-intentioned ones determined to save Terrence Ogden from Alexa Garrett and also from himself. Katharine went on, 'I think we should have another drink. To . . . seal the deal?'

'Good idea, love. Make mine a light one though. I've got to be off in a tick. Penny's waiting for me at John's flat.'

Katharine picked up their glasses and rose. Halfway to the door she paused and spun around. 'That reminds me, there's another thing I can help you with. I *think*. I'd like you to stay a few minutes when Kim arrives. It just occurred to me, he might be able to help you sort out the damage at John's place. Suggest how you can get the furniture, carpet and curtains fixed, and also tell us where to find replacements for the broken items. Without the whole thing costing the earth. He knows a lot about antiques and art treasures, Norman.'

'Okay,' was Norman's laconic response. 'But wait a tick! How are you going to explain the damage in the first place?'

'Oh, don't worry about that,' Katharine said, airily dismissive. 'We'll tell him Terry had a party, and that two of the more boisterous guests got into a

165

fight. Kim doesn't have to know the gory details. And actually, he's not likely to ask.'

'Right you are,' Norman said. He leaned back, and he relaxed for the first time that day. And he prayed that Katharine's scheme would work. There were too many *ifs* involved to permit Norman absolute peace of mind. On the other hand, her suggestions did have a degree of plausibility, and she sounded so confident and so sure of herself, perhaps she would be able to pull them off successfully. Apart from that, *he* didn't have any better or brighter ideas himself, so they might as well put hers into operation. What did they have to lose? Nothing, he decided. Then Norman superstitiously crossed his fingers, closed his eyes and said three sincere Hail Marys under his breath.

CHAPTER EIGHTEEN

Kim Cunningham, who had a chicken leg halfway to his mouth, put it down, staring at Katharine. 'What's so funny?' he asked, wiping his fingers on a napkin. He picked up his glass of Montrachet and took a sip.

Katharine giggled again, unable to suppress her amusement, her expression merry, her demeanour lighthearted. 'I was just thinking of your face when you walked in and saw Norman Rook sitting here. You looked as if you'd caught me with my hand in the cookie jar.'

'What do you mean?' Kim's grey eyes flickered with perplexity and a frown creased his brow.

'As if I was doing something I shouldn't. Two-timing you perhaps.' This thought caused her more amusement; her laughter echoed in the stillness of the room and her eyes danced. Katharine's gaiety was not assumed. It had been engendered by a number of things, chiefly her relief that Terry's injury was not serious and her gratification that she and Norman had everything under control. Norman was her ally now, would help her to put her plans into effect, and ultimately she would be enabled to keep her commitment to Victor. Hilary was the key, of course.

Conscious of Kim's eyes on her, Katharine tore her mind away from the film and her involved schemes, and flashed him a smile. She was sitting on a pile of cushions on the floor in front of the glass coffee table, and she tucked her bare feet under her and leaned back on one elbow, emanating insouciance. Then she glanced at Kim, who was seated opposite on the sofa, and reaffirmed with another laugh, 'Don't worry, Norman's no competition for you.'

'I didn't think he was,' Kim responded in his usual goodnatured way, laughing with her, fully aware that she was teasing him. 'He's hardly Terrence Ogden, my sweet. Actually, I was surprised, that's all. I just wondered if we'd ever be alone.'

'Norman's far too polite to overstay his welcome,' Katharine murmured and picked up her glass of wine. 'He was fretting so much, earlier at the theatre, about the damage those idiots did to John's flat, I couldn't help taking pity on him. I just had to invite him over to meet you, Kim. I was certain you'd be able to give him a few tips. Thanks for being so helpful.'

'Oh, it was no trouble,' Kim answered genially. 'I told him to give me a buzz tomorrow, and I'll pass on the names of some dealers in Chinese antiques where I hope Terry will be able to replace those porcelain lamps and some of the other items. The jade pieces are going to be expensive though, I can tell you that right now.'

Katharine nodded. 'I guessed they would be. Still, Terry does feel he has to make everything right at the flat.'

'Yes. Yes, I understand,' Kim remarked. He picked up the chicken leg, bit into it and munched. Between bites, he asked her, 'Don't you like the things I brought for our midnight feast? You're not eating.'

'Of course I do! I've had some chicken, and half a scotch egg. I always have problems eating after the show, you should know that by now. It takes me ages to wind down, and especially tonight.' She lifted her wine glass again. 'Terry being out with a sore throat made it doubly tough for me this evening, Kim. Peter Mallory is a bit wooden as an actor. In fact, I more or less had to carry the play.'

'Yes, so Norman told me, when you were in the bedroom changing. He also mentioned how marvellous your performance was.' Kim's admiring eyes swept over her. 'I must admit, you do look delectable, my pet.'

'Thank you, kind sir,' she smiled prettily.

Earlier, after she had introduced Kim and Norman, Katharine had excused herself and left them to talk, hurrying into the bedroom, where she had quickly changed out of her black cashmere sweater and red skirt. She had chosen a long house robe, cut something in the style of the Chinese cheongsam, except that it was much looser and flowing, with long sleeves, wide at the cuffs. Made of brocade, in a clear turquoise embroidered with tiny gold leaves, the shade perfectly matched the colour of her eyes, seemed to emphasize their depth and brilliance and intensity.

Kim thought, as he gazed at her lovingly, that he had never seen her looking more beautiful than she did at this moment. Her exquisite face, with its sculptured features, had a vulnerability, the texture almost translucent, like the most fragile of transparent bone china, and there was a delicate sheen to her skin. Her chestnut hair was hanging loosely around her face in waves and curls and there were tendrils at the temples. Katharine had complained several times of feeling tired, and perhaps she did, but as he carefully scrutinized her Kim could see no trace of weariness in that remarkable face, the most perfect face he had ever beheld.

Kim pulled his eyes away, aware that he was staring at her rudely, and made a show of finishing the chicken leg, although he no longer felt hungry. He drank his wine, poured another glass, and then lit a cigarette, leaning back on the sofa. He *had* been surprised to see Norman, and even a bit put out at first, miffed really, believing Katharine had invited him to join them for supper. She had quickly made it clear this was not the case and Kim had been able to relax, realizing they would eventually be by themselves. Now he sighed. It seemed to him that they had not had much time alone together lately, and he was not only dismayed about this situation but unusually irritated. There were so many things he wanted to talk to her about . . . most especially their feelings for each other and the future. He also supposed he ought to discuss her attitude to her career and ask her about her family, certain points Francesca had made to him earlier that evening, albeit in a veiled way, but nonetheless he had received the message loud and clear. Francesca had not wanted to admit it, but he was absolutely convinced their father had been asking probing questions. Somehow I never get the opportunity to talk to Katharine seriously, he said to himself. Perhaps tonight he would.

Katharine broke the silence and his train of thought. 'If you don't want anything else to eat, I think I'll take these dishes away, Kim darling.' She sat up abruptly as she spoke, and made a move to rise.

'No. No, I'll do it,' Kim cried, stubbing out his cigarette and leaping to his feet. 'You stay here and take it easy. It won't take me a minute; I'm a dab hand at this. Francesca's expert drilling over the years.' Before she could protest he had gently pushed her against the mound of pillows and was collecting some of the plates of food.

Katharine did as he said, lying back and closing her eyes, endeavouring to relax. But she was finding it difficult to do so, as she had since leaving the theatre. Her brain was far too busy. Deep down in her heart of hearts, she was truly fond of Kim, and cared for him more than she had ever cared for any other man, but at this precise moment she wished he would leave. She knew there was little chance of his doing so, since he seemed intent on dragging out the evening into the early hours. A few seconds before, when she had glanced at the clock on the mantelshelf, she had been startled to see it was turned one-thirty. Oh hell, she thought dismally, he'll stay for another hour at least, if I know him. She wondered how to get rid of Kim, with tact, and gave up. Whatever she said, he would hang on until the bitter end, as he always did, until she bustled him out firmly, claiming total exhaustion.

Katharine had not had to feign tiredness tonight. She really did feel weary; her back and legs ached, and there was an acute tightness across her shoulders which reached up into the back of her neck. But her mind was alert, as it sifted through the events of the past twelve hours. What an extraordinary day it had been, starting with her curious encounter with Estelle Morgan and finishing with Norman and the problems with Terry. Oh how she wanted to be alone, to concentrate her energies on her next moves, all of which she knew must be foolproof and properly implemented if they were to succeed. Her priority was talking to Victor. In the bedroom, after she had changed into her robe, she had tried to reach him at Claridge's. There had been no reply from his suite. She had left another message, saying she would 'phone the following morning, realizing it would be extremely awkward speaking in front of Kim, should Victor return her call that night. What she had to convey was confidential. She smiled to herself. Victor was going to be delighted with her. Norman had voiced the opinion that her schemes were too complex and, therefore, dicey. She did not agree.

'There! I'm all finished,' Kim exclaimed, bounding back into the living room for the third time. 'I put the food in the fridge, and stacked the dirty plates in the sink.'

Katharine opened her eyes languorously. 'Thanks, Kim. That was so sweet of you.'

'Now, darling, how about a cup of coffee?'

'No. No thanks. Really.'

'Then I won't have any either. We'll just finish the wine and relax. Shall I put a record on?' he continued, full of *joie de vivre*. He headed in the direction of the small built-in cupboard next to the fireplace which housed the record player. 'I wouldn't mind a bit of romantic music – '

'Please, Kim, I'm awfully tired,' Katharine exclaimed. 'I can do without music, if you don't mind.'

'Oh, sorry,' he apologized. 'Well then, let's sit and talk for a while. It's ages since I've had you to myself.'

Before Katharine had a chance to suggest it was time for him to leave, Kim was lowering himself next to her on the floor. He smiled as he gazed down at her. There was something emphatically feline about her just now, in the way her eyes slanted as they regarded him almost warily, under the long silky black lashes, in the graceful pose she had struck, reclining elegantly on the pillows, her head tilted to one side ever so slightly. All of the niggling questions he had been on the point of asking her immediately fled. His mind went blank as he continued to observe that tantalizing and seductive face. And he was entranced with her, mesmerized.

Kim touched her cheek with his index finger. 'My dearest, sweetest Katharine,' he murmured so softly she scarcely heard him, and then, leaning forward, he took her in his arms and kissed her swiftly, catching her offguard. It was a light and tender kiss initially, and Katharine did not struggle, even though she was far too preoccupied for his kisses.

Slowly the pressure of Kim's mouth increased. He pressed her down into the pillows, his tongue feverishly seeking hers, one hand stroking her neck. A moment later, his other hand was on her breast, warm and gentle as it caressed, and then it strayed down, following the curve of her hip on to her thigh, moving in longer firmer strokes. Kim shifted his body slightly, so that it was partially covering hers, and she felt his hardness through his trousers and the thin silk of her robe and was suddenly aware of the rapid pounding of his heart, his laboured breathing as he paused briefly between his kisses. And those kisses began to increase and intensify in their voluptuousness and force and fervency, his ardour running unchecked.

A mixture of panic and fear assaulted Katharine, and she held her breath, squeezing her eyes tightly shut, seeking a way to make him stop without offending him. She did not want him to continue his lovemaking, and a tremor rippled through her, and then again, and again and again.

Kim, overwhelmed by his strong and deeply-felt emotions, mistook her trembling, believing it to be an echo of his own urgent need . . . the overwhelming need to possess her fully, to become one with her, to join his body with hers . . . irrevocably. He had wanted her for so long now, all these endless months, and apparently so had she. Even though she had not really shown it before. Not exactly. Not responsively like this.

His heart, thundering in his chest, was bursting with the purest joy, and he thought: Oh my love my sweet darling love my Katharine my only love. He was burning up with excitement, and he lifted his body so that he was lying on top of her completely. She was so soft and melting under him, and he moulded himself to her legs and her lovely breasts and her stomach. How perfectly she fitted under him and with him. He found her mouth with his own, so hungry and yearning, and crushed his lips to hers. And he thought he was going to explode.

169

Katharine was trapped unbearably under his weight, unable to move and terrified. I don't want this. I don't want it, a voice in her head screamed. I've got to make him stop. Oh my God what am I going to do? Now, to her immense horror, that warm and loving hand was touching her bare calf, stroking gently, and rising slowly to her knee under the robe. His hand lingered on her knee and progressed up her leg and then trailed across the inside of her upper thigh, where it lingered again, the tips of his fingers expertly tracing circles on her flesh, almost imperceptibly, so delicate was their touch. Katharine turned her head, trying to breathe, and then she strangled a cry of protest in her throat and she went cold all over. Kim's hand was drifting across her stomach and moving down, ever so slowly down and she stiffened, holding her body taut.

Although she did not push him away from her, Katharine's sudden and enormous coldness communicated itself to Kim. He was conscious of the unusual rigidity of her body, no longer pliable and yielding under his, nor quivering under his touch. He pulled his hand away hurriedly, as if he had been scalded, and after a moment he raised himself on one elbow. His eyes were baffled and questioning and he stared into her face, and his own was covered with hurt and confusion.

It took him a short while to recover his equilibrium, to throw off the shock of her emotional withdrawal and physical frigidity. At last he mumbled, his voice choked, 'What's wrong?' And then he flushed deeply. 'Don't you want me to kiss you? To touch you? Are you off me?'

'No. No, it's not that,' Katharine began and halted, alarmed by the anger trickling into his eyes. 'I told you, I'm very tired, Kim, and anyway, I'm not a te – '

'You don't have to mention your tiredness again, for God's sake! You've been rubbing it in all evening!' Kim was beset by a terrible shaking and he jumped up, charged with rage. He reached for the packet of cigarettes on the coffee table, lit one swiftly and then strode over to the fireplace. He turned to face her, and said with unfamiliar coldness, 'I don't understand you any more, Katharine. You blow hot and cold at the drop of a hat. And it's damned unnerving, to say the least!'

'No, I don't,' Katharine said defensively, returning his icy stare. She got to her feet with swiftness, smoothed down her robe and positioned herself on the sofa.

'Oh yes, you do,' Kim retorted, his anger unabated. 'When we're with other people you're sweet and loving and flirtatious and encouraging. But when we're alone you're as distant as Mount Everest and just as bloody chilly. Tonight I thought you were going to be different. A grave error! My God, you let me kiss you and fondle you, and you didn't stop me. In fact, you returned my kisses, and, mistakenly it seems, I thought you returned my feelings as well. It certainly appeared so. Then inexplicably you turn into a block of ice,' he finished furiously, the deep colour darkening on his face. 'You're not very fair, Katharine.'

She drew herself up on the sofa with some dignity, and adopted an injured air. 'I started to say, a moment before, that I'm not a tease – '

'But you are!' Kim cut in with a hard laugh. 'The way you dress and get yourself up, oh so alluringly, and then set out to entice. I'd say you're a hell of a tease, my dear.'

Katharine glared at him, truly taken aback and also annoyed. 'In that case, you can say all women are teases, simply because they're women! What I meant was

170

that I didn't want to encourage you any more tonight, to get you . . . well, get you worked up and then leave you frustrated – '

'But you did exactly that!' he cried with indignation, interrupting her again. 'Good Lord, Katharine, I'm not made of iron. I'm a man. How much do you think I can take of this heavy petting . . . without . . . fulfilment?'

Katharine leaned forward, a patient expression firmly in place, and said placatingly, with reasonableness, 'Kim, that's why I've been so very, very careful with you. You just said I'm not fair, but I believe I've been exceedingly fair, simply by not allowing our petting *ever* to go as far as it did tonight. Not ever in the past.'

'Then why did you permit it this evening?' he demanded. He was still furious with her, but the shaking had stopped, much to his relief.

This was the first time Kim had been angry or spoken one harsh word to her, and Katharine decided it would be far wiser to smooth his ruffled feathers rather than plunge into a long and complicated discussion about sex. Her eyes and her mouth smiled at him gently. 'I didn't *really* allow it. It just sort of . . . well . . . happened, and before I could stop it. I let things get out of hand, I suppose. Perhaps because I am so terribly tired. Not thinking clearly. And despite what you believe, these past few weeks have been difficult for me. I take the screen test very seriously,' she continued, adopting a different tack to divert him. 'It *has* put extra pressures on me. And frankly, today in particular has been quite rough. I had an important lunch, and then Norman dropped the bombshell, about Terry being sick. Also, there was the strain of tonight's performance, and Norman's – '

'It strikes me you're only tired and feeling the strain when you're with me. Alone with me. And that's another thing. Inviting Norman over here to talk about blasted antiques, when you knew we had this very special date! I could have given the same information to you to pass on to him or Terry quite easily, you know. And whilst we're on the subject of other people, what's so important about lunch with my sister?'

'Didn't Francesca tell you she's going to adapt a scene from *Wuthering Heights*? For my screen test?' she asked, ignoring the comment about Norman and making her voice sweet and melting, hoping to mollify him. She could hardly tell him the real reason for Norman's presence in the flat, not without breaking a confidence and her promise. And that she would never do.

'Yes, she did,' Kim said edgily.

'It was important to me, even if you don't see it that way. I'm very grateful for Francesca's help. And look, I'm sorry I upset you. I am, honestly.'

Kim was silent. He lit another cigarette, and then poured himself a glass of wine, stepping away from the coffee table and Katharine quickly. He positioned himself in front of the fireplace as before, his face set, a small pulse beating in his temple. He was still seething inside. His feelings of hurt, anger and frustration sprang, not unnaturally, from his disappointment, and the belief that she had wilfully led him on, only to finally reject him. Kim Cunningham was not accustomed to being rejected.

On the contrary, until he had met Katharine Tempest, he had been the pursued rather than the pursuer, for like his father, he was irresistibly attractive to women from all walks of life. For a young man not yet twenty-two he was remarkably experienced sexually and had a voracious appetite. Before the advent of Katharine

171

in his life, he had had one involved love affair and a number of liaisons of lesser significance. His only involved relationship, until Katharine, had been with the German princess he had met on a skiing holiday in Königssee, when visiting his cousins Diana and Christian. Astrid, the lady in question, had been seven years his senior, twenty-six at the time, and married. It was the latter reason which had led the Earl to intervene, but only at the request of the irate husband. The prince had not taken too kindly to his younger wife's dalliance with a nineteen-year-old 'pup', as he disparagingly termed Kim. Although the Earl had immediately articulated his annoyance to Kim and insisted the affair end, he had been amused. He was also patently aware it was merely a passing fancy on the part of the princess, who had married a fortune she had no intention of forgoing, and therefore in no way represented a threat to his son.

Kim thought of Astrid now. She had been so warm and loving and passionate, and it was she who had awakened his latent sensuality, the voluptuousness that lay hidden behind his contained and reserved façade. It was Astrid who had imparted her own expertise to him, which in turn had been so appreciated by all of those other young women who had followed in her footsteps. For reasons unknown to himself, and despite his now well-developed needs, Kim had never pressed Katharine into succumbing to his advances, or been sexually aggressive with her. In fact, he had always been extraordinarily restrained. He wondered about this as he continued to ruminate in front of the fire, sipping his drink, and he came to the conclusion that he had been behaving in a way that was quite foreign to his nature. Was that because she herself was always so restrained? No, *controlled* was a much better word. He was not sure, and he was also puzzled. Why had he invariably handled her with kid gloves?

Watching him intently, Katharine now recognized and with a sense of dismay, that Kim's anger was not going to dissipate as rapidly as she had anticipated. He had never acted in this manner before, when she had adroitly side-stepped him, slithering out of his embraces, laughing lightly, reproving him, but sweetly so, making plausible excuses. She asked herself if Kim was going to become a problem in the way the others had been a problem, and her heart dropped. She did not relish the idea of having to fight him off physically, which inevitably became ugly and unpleasant. In the past she had always been able to deal with him without affronting him. In her own way Katharine loved Kim, and she had set her heart on marrying him. She was fully aware that she could not afford to hurt him again, not like this, and perhaps lose him in the process, simply because she baulked at lovemaking.

Her eyes rested on him. He looked so handsome in his Anglo-Saxon way, with his pleasant, open and sensitive face and fine eyes and fair hair. Perhaps it was his very Englishness, as well as his refinement and his aristocratic bearing, that was so appealing.

'Kim . . .' she began in her silkiest voice.

'Yes?' he responded frostily.

She ignored the tone and gave him a look guaranteed to warm the hardest of hearts. 'We have tomorrow, darling. I'll be feeling better by then and – '

'We don't have tomorrow,' he told her peremptorily. 'I haven't had a chance to tell you, but I'm afraid my father has cancelled the dinner.'

172

Surprise registered in Katharine's eyes and she stared at him. 'Oh!' she said after a pause, and then, most carefully, 'Might I ask the reason why?' She had not considered the Earl to be an obstacle and this announcement momentarily threw her off balance.

'The old man had a call from the bailiff at Langley, earlier this evening. Some pipes have burst and ruined parts of the panelling in the Widow's Gallery where a lot of the family portraits by Gainsborough, Lely and Romney hang. Fortunately, none of the paintings has been damaged, but my father is worried the leak might have spread to other areas underneath the panelling. Areas not visible. We have to get to Langley as quickly as possible. We're leaving for Yorkshire at the crack of dawn.'

'Oh Kim, I am sorry! Really and truly,' Katharine said with absolute sincerity. 'It must be awfully worrying for your father . . . and you, too, of course. How awful.' Disappointed though she was, she forced a smile on to her face. And then she admitted the truth, as she said, 'I thought perhaps your father didn't like me, didn't approve of me.' Her voice, low and quiet, sounded so plaintive and she was gazing at Kim with such a woebegone expression in her eyes, he was suddenly unable to sustain his anger. His rage fell away as swiftly as it had attacked him.

'Don't be a silly goose. He thinks you're smashing. And so do I. I suppose that's the root of the problem.' Kim gave her a gentle smile, quickly replaced by a shamefaced look, and there was an echo of contriteness as he added, 'Sorry I was so cross. It's well . . . as I said, I do adore you, and you've kept me at arm's length for ages.' He attempted a cheery laugh, not very successfully. 'Come to think of it, you were much more . . . responsive, shall we say, when we first met. I expect that's why I became so furious tonight. You are very baffling, you know.'

Katharine did not answer immediately. She sought a way to appease him further, make amends and bind him to her. Why not tell him the truth. Instantly she changed her mind. Partial truths were infinitely more appropriate, so much easier to deal with, and by everyone. She patted the sofa. 'Please, Kim, come here. I'd like to explain about tonight. At least try.'

He sat down beside her, and she took his hand in hers, stroking it, playing with his strong fingers absently. 'I adore you too, you know, as I've tried to tell you in different ways lately. And because I care about you, I can't play games with you. Lead you on, tease you, get you all excited and then turn you down. I think that would be cruel and provocative. That's why I've kept you at a distance.' She draped her arms around his neck, lightly, loosely, and stared deeply into his eyes. Then she kissed him on the lips, a long slow kiss that was equally as passionate as any he had given her. She drew away and touched his cheek. 'But despite my strong feelings, I do want to be sure about us and our deepest emotions before taking that last step. I'm not promiscuous, Kim.'

'Oh, gosh, Katharine, I never thought you were!' he protested fiercely.

'My being chaste with you is as difficult for me as it is for you, Kim,' she told him, bending the truth. 'When you became so angry a little while ago I couldn't stand it. I . . . I . . .' Katharine broke off dramatically and dropped her head, and when she raised it tears were welling in her eyes and glistening on her black lashes. 'I couldn't bear to lose you, darling. It would break my heart.' She took a deep breath. The tears spilled over and trickled down her cheeks in little rivulets. 'So if you still want to . . . now . . . I mean . . .' She moved closer to him, pressing her body invitingly against his and kissed him deeply, her hands playing with the tendrils of hair on the back of his neck.

Kim was astonished at her sudden reversal, but before he could sort things out in his head, he felt himself being carried along with her, staggered yet again by the extraordinary sexual power she had over him. His heart was hammering, blood rushed up into his face and he was aroused and losing control. And then, just as he was about to sweep her up in his arms and carry her into the bedroom, some deep-rooted instinct told him to resist this impulse.

Gently, and with a great deal of effort, he extracted himself. He held her away from him, his hands firm on her arms. 'No,' he said, his voice gruff. 'You're only trying to please me. I want it the way you want it. When it's exactly right for you. When you feel ready. It has to be perfect between us, Katharine . . .' He looked down into her face, upturned to his and awash with sweetness and innocence, and his heart tightened. He said impetuously, 'And that will only be when we're married.' He had surprised himself. He had not intended to propose just yet, but now that he had, he was glad. It struck him then that Katharine had always been different from the other women he had known, because she was extra special and important to him. Undoubtedly this was the real reason why he had always treated her so . . . so . . . reverently.

Katharine's heart seemed to soar at his words. For a moment she was speechless, and she simply stared into his eyes, her own still sparkling with tears.

Kim lifted his hand and wiped her cheeks with the tips of his fingers, first one and then the other. 'There, I've said it. Now you know how much I care.' He smiled a little lopsidedly. 'I'm in love with you, Katharine.' His eyes remained on her face. And he waited.

'I love you, too,' she whispered finally.

'And you will marry me, won't you, darling?' he asked anxiously, taking her hands in his.

'Yes,' Katharine murmured, her eyes sparkling. 'I want to very much, Kim.' She bit her lip and said hesitantly, 'But I also want us to be very sure about each other.'

'I am sure! Aren't you?' he cried nervously.

She nodded, her face radiant. 'Oh yes, I'm pretty sure I'm sure.'

Kim relaxed. 'I'll have to speak to the old man, before we get engaged.'

'Don't! At least, not yet.'

'Whyever not? You said you'd marry me, and I think he ought to be told of my very serious intentions, our intentions!' he exclaimed excitedly.

'Yes, he should,' she agreed, adding in that same beguiling voice, 'However, perhaps it's wiser not to spring it on him for the moment. I feel he ought to get better acquainted with me, just as we should get to know each other a bit more intimately – '

'Splendid idea!' he cut in, laughing, and breaking the tension between them.

Katharine laughed too. 'I didn't mean it that way, you wolf! Look, Kim, we've only been dating a few months and a lot of that time you've been in Yorkshire. Let's wait a while before we announce our engagement. Let's keep our feelings a secret for the moment. Our secret. Promise?'

'Can't I tell Francesca?'

Katharine shook her head.

'All right, I promise.' He sounded reluctant.

'How long will you be in Yorkshire this time?' she asked, adopting her plaintive little girl's voice and widening her eyes prettily.

'A few weeks. Which reminds me, getting back to the cancelled dinner. Father is going to 'phone you tomorrow, some time late morning, to apologize, and also to invite you to Langley for a weekend. You will come, won't you? I think you should see where you're going to live, and in the not too distant future if I get my way.'

'Oh yes, Kim! Of course. I'd love it. When does he want me to come for the visit?'

'Oh any time in the next month. Actually, he's going to invite Victor and Nicholas Latimer to join us at the same time. He rather liked them, Victor especially. Doris Asternan will be there, and the old man wants to make it a nice, jolly weekend house party. Gus will be able to drive you up together on a Saturday night after the play. Just as you suggested to Victor, if you remember.'

'Yes,' Katharine replied in a subdued tone. 'How kind of your father.'

'Then it's settled.' Kim took her in his arms and held her close to him, stroking her hair. He lifted her face and kissed her, but pulled away after one kiss, suddenly brimming with laughter. 'I think you'd better throw me out, before I forget I'm a gentleman, and take you up on that tempting offer you made me a few minutes ago.'

Perhaps any other young woman would have agreed at once to become engaged to Kim. He was young, attractive and intrinsically a kind and loving person. He had position, a title in his own right, and was heir to one of the oldest earldoms in England. In short, he was enormously eligible.

But not Katharine. She was far too intelligent and clever and calculating to rush into the engagement without being assured of the Earl's blessing. She knew instinctively that, whatever Kim's feelings, the Earl's total acceptance of her was crucial. Without his approval, consent, and co-operation, there would be no wedding, of that there was no doubt in her mind. Her shrewdness had prompted the suggestion that the Earl become better acquainted with her. She was confident she could charm him, win him over to her side with the greatest of ease, and in the shortest possible time. However, she was also aware that the engagement of the Earl's only son and heir would be an occasion for celebration and thus entail all manner of social obligations. Distractions of this nature she could not afford at this time. First she must make the film. That was her most vital priority. And so she had demurred, but she did not believe she was taking a gamble. Katharine was eminently sure of herself, and doubly sure of her place in Kim's affections.

Now, as she sat relaxing in the bath, she smiled. She had not even considered it a gamble when she had offered herself to him a short while ago. She had enough psychological insight into Kim to understand that his sense of honour and decency would ultimately prevent him from accepting her proposition. Very simply put, his conscience would not permit him to take advantage of a virginal girl. The way she had presented it, with tears and hesitancy, had ensured the outcome. She would never have made the offer if she had believed otherwise.

She lifted a shapely leg and rested her foot on the tap, regarding the pink-painted toenail reflectively. It *is* better to wait a while before announcing our engagement, and later on I'll convince Kim that I should continue my acting career. Even if he objects at first, I'll manage to persuade him. Kim will do anything I want, he loves me so much. She smiled again, filled with happiness, and slipped farther down into the water, so that it lapped around her aching neck and shoulders. She made her body go limp, relaxing completely, and closed her eyes, and the wheels turned endlessly in her head.

It had been an incredible day. Even memorable in one sense, because of Kim's proposal of marriage. Quite involuntarily she thought of her father. How would he react when he discovered she had married an Englishman and a titled one at that? He hated her, so he wouldn't care. Inwardly she laughed cynically. But he hated the Sassenachs more, and so he would be furious. How he ranted and raved about the English and what they had done to Ireland. She had grown sick and tired of hearing about the 'ould sod' during her childhood, the Potato Famine and the cruelty and the injustices. As if he knew anything about the Potato Famine. It had been long before his time, and anyway he had been born in Chicago. Yes, her father would be irate on principle. The thought of his anger pleased her for she was not without spite where he was concerned.

Well, her life was going to be very different soon, with her success and her fame and her money and her title. And Kim of course. A wonderful life. What a terrible mess Terry has made of *his* life, she thought with a rush of sadness. But she was going to save him. She would soon straighten him out and get his life organized. He would agree to make the film. He had no option really, because of his terrible financial problems.

Hilary. She was the crux of the matter, not only with Terry but with Mark as well. If she agreed to design the costumes, and there was no reason why she shouldn't jump at the chance, she could undoubtedly be persuaded to exercise her influence over Mark, to prevail upon him to direct *Wuthering Heights.* Katharine wished she had thought of Hilary Pierce before. If she had, Mark might have been signed up already, and she would have avoided all those sleepless nights worrying about the right approach to make to him. He adored his wife, who was twenty-two years his junior, and would do anything for her. In turn, Hilary would do anything for Terry.

But would she?

This last possibility had not previously occurred to Katharine and she sat up in the bath with a start. Essentially, her schemes revolved around the assumption that Hilary still cared for Terry. But did she really? Estelle had said Hilary had drooled over Terry all night at the Standish party several months ago. Naturally she still cares, Katharine reassured herself. What woman could resist the opportunity to help a former lover save his career and extricate himself from the clutches of another female, in this instance Alexa Garrett, who was very beautiful and consequently a threat to most women. It was too tempting by far. But I'll have to have a very serious talk with Hilary, explain everything to her, so that she understands all the ramifications, Katharine added to herself. Understands that Mark is the vital factor, that he must agree to be the director, otherwise Victor might not sign her as the costume designer.

Katharine considered Victor Mason now. A bargain had been struck between them. Although it had not been couched in so many words, Katharine knew, nevertheless, that it was a deal. A deal Victor would hold her to, no matter what. His offer had been irresistible. Her screen test in return for Terrence Ogden and Mark Pierce. Delivered to him on a plate. Victor had failed to persuade them to do the film. She had been given the task of doing it for him. He hadn't even guaranteed her the part. Only the test. And everything hinged on her success with these two. Until Norman had unwittingly presented her with exactly the right tools, she had been frantically seeking ways to make them change their minds.

A smile of triumph flickered on Katharine's face as she stepped out of the bath and towelled herself dry. 'They're both in the bag!' she said out loud, still thinking of Terry and Mark. She slipped into her nightgown and padded through into the bedroom, where she sat down at the dressing table. She began to brush her hair, briskly at first and then more slowly. Terry was going to be so grateful to her for arranging everything so beautifully for him, and certainly the film would be a boost to his career. He had nothing to worry about any more, not even the damage to the flat. She would handle all that with Kim's help. And Hilary would be thrilled to work with a world-famous movie star like Victor Mason. What a marvellous credit for her. It would certainly give her the stamp of approval, and lead to other major pictures. Come to think of it, Mark would be delighted too. His last movie had not been all that well received. Even though he might not at first realize it, he actually needed *Wuthering Heights*. It was going to be an artistic triumph for him. Why, he might even win an Oscar, just as she herself might. As she continued to gaze at herself in the mirror a beatific expression crossed her face and settled there, and she was filled with such enormous self-gratification it bordered on smugness. This new emotion, so suddenly induced, sprang from the genuine conviction that she was being a wonderful friend, loyal and loving and concerned. A Good Samaritan to Terry, a benefactor to Hilary and Mark Pierce. In her eyes, her actions were so unselfish that they were all the more commendable, and would earn her friends' undying gratitude.

Katharine Tempest had always had the curious knack of justifying everything she did, especially when other people were involved. She usually managed to convince herself, somewhat misguidedly, that she was motivated out of the sheer goodness of her heart and by the selfless desire to help everyone solve their insurmountable problems. She did not seem to comprehend that she was driven chiefly by self-interest and the need to gain her private ends. And so, with blithe indifference to the consequences, and prodded along by her egotism, she constantly meddled in others' lives. A most dangerous game.

By the time she climbed into bed and snapped out the light, Katharine had become the heroine of the hour, and holding this thought she contentedly fell fast asleep.

CHAPTER NINETEEN

In a few minutes the lights would dim in the private screening room and Victor Mason would run the test of Katharine Tempest playing Catherine Earnshaw in a scene from *Wuthering Heights*.

Francesca sat in the next seat to Katharine, filled with a complex mixture of excitement and anticipation underscored by apprehension, and as the seconds ticked by her apprehension accelerated. Her anxiety was not for herself, nor was it in any way linked to the scene she had written for Katharine.

In all truth, Francesca did not feel she had contributed very much to the test, for there was little or no conceit in her. As far as she was concerned, she had simply taken some of those immortal words from Emily Brontë's monumental masterpiece and arranged them as straight dialogue, without adding or subtracting anything. In consequence, her ego was not on the line. She was not about to be judged. But Katharine was, and therein lay the root of her fear, and her concern was solely for her friend. The points Victor had made to her about the technique of acting in front of a camera now echoed ominously in her ears, and she prayed that Katharine had not been tempted to over-act or be histrionic; or that she had not swung in the other direction and been too low key to make the proper impact; that Katharine had, in fact, hit just the right note and given a balanced performance.

In the past few weeks Francesca and Katharine had become the closest and most intimate of friends. There was a shared trust and empathy and understanding between them, all of which had developed without benefit of time. It had been thus since that first meeting, when they had instinctively reached out in silent communication, striking chords in each other to which they had both responded from their innermost hearts.

And so, not unnaturally, the success of the screen test meant as much to Francesca as it did to Katharine, and she had lived through every single moment of it with her new friend, was living it now, on tenterhooks. Moving her head slightly to one side, Francesca stole a look at the other girl. That beautiful profile appeared more spectacular than ever. But Katharine sat straight-backed and rigid on the seat, and Francesca detected her tension, her extreme nervousness, controlled though it was. Impulsively she reached out and touched Katharine's hand. It lay immobile in her lap, and it was icy.

Katharine looked at Francesca swiftly, gave her a small weak smile and shrugged.

'It's going to be all right. I know it is. Don't worry,' said Francesca quietly, her smile confident and full of love. She squeezed Katharine's hand again and held on to it tightly, wanting to warm those icy fingers, to reassure, to alleviate the other girl's anxiousness if she possibly could.

Katharine nodded and turned back to stare at the darkened screen. She was mute with nerves. All the worries she wanted to voice to Francesca were strangled in her throat. She had been supremely self-confident since making the test, filled with absolute certainty about the final result. She knew she had done a superlative job, and Bruce Nottley, the director hired for the test, had been wonderful to work with. He had been patient and kind, understanding her initial nervousness of the camera, encouraging and complimentary afterwards. But in the last few days that overriding self-confidence had ebbed away, leaving her riddled with the most awful self-doubt, and mounting disquiet.

Katharine was well aware that Victor had induced these feelings in her. He had already seen the test, yet when she had questioned him about it, he had been noncommittal, even vague, and this worried her. Surely, if it was good he would have been excited and would have hired her at once. On the other hand, she reasoned, if it was bad, why had he bothered to invite half a dozen other people to view it with him today? Unless, of course, he was uncertain and wanted other opinions. Victor's attitude puzzled Katharine, and so much so she no longer knew what to make of the situation. She sighed wearily. In desperation and misery, she broke her recently-made rule about not smoking during the day, and took a cigarette from her handbag and lit it.

Francesca was glancing around the room with interest. This was the first time she had ever been to a private screening, and she was fascinated. In fact, she had discovered that many areas of film-making intrigued her, and she had gained a wealth of knowledge in the past few weeks. Victor and Nicholas Latimer were seated in the row behind them, several places along, and both of them were talking to the man Victor had introduced as Jake Watson, the line producer, who had flown in from Hollywood recently. Francesca had not understood the meaning of the title *line producer*, and had asked Nicky for clarification. He had told her it meant the working producer, the person who was on the set at all times, 'On the line, so to speak, making sure everything works, that nothing goes wrong with the production on a day-to-day basis.' He had further explained that Victor was the executive producer, 'Who's not so much concerned with the daily details but more with the overall aspects of the project. Financing, casting, script, director, and distribution. But making a film is teamwork essentially, and it's up to the executive producer to put the best team together,' he had finished, adding with a sly grin, 'And let's hope the kid has done so.'

A few rows in front, Jerry Massingham, the English production manager, was slumped down in his seat, biting on an unlit briar pipe, and nodding from time to time to his assistant. Jerry, a rumpled-looking man, heavyset and with shaggy red hair, invariably spoke in statistics, or so it seemed to Francesca.

Francesca shifted in her seat, making herself more comfortable, and stared at the lifeless screen, momentarily drifting with her thoughts. She had been thrilled when Katharine had announced that Victor had given his permission for her to come along this morning, and had accepted immediately. She was only sorry Kim was not present. Katharine had wanted him to attend as well, but he was in Yorkshire, running the Home Farm and also coping with the problems of the burst pipes at Langley Castle. There had been several more leaks at the concave end of the Widow's Gallery this past week. Fortunately these had been caught in time, and the Turner and Constable landscapes on display there were safe, but additional sections of the centuries-old panelling had been completely ruined. The damaged panelling was currently being replaced, slowly and painstakingly. According to Kim, their father was still plunged in gloom because the repairs and the new panelling were going to cost a fortune. Her father had deemed it necessary to engage a master cabinetmaker, a craftsman from the old school, since he insisted that the reproduction panelling be a facsimile of the original, and authentic down to the last detail. Apart from carefully treating the new wood so that it looked aged, the craftsman was going to use the old-fashioned method of pegging the panelling into position, a process that was slow, not to mention difficult.

Poor Daddy, Francesca thought, remembering his distress on the day they had received the upsetting news. But at least Kim is there to give him moral support, and the money he's received from Giles Martin for the prize heifers will more or less cover the cost of the panelling and the new plumbing being installed.

The disaster at the castle had precipitated yet another discussion about money that particular Thursday evening, after Kim had gone off to meet Katharine at her flat, armed with the Fortnum's hamper laden with the food Francesca had prepared for them. She had finally plucked up her courage and suggested to her father that she look for a job, perhaps in a reputable Mayfair gallery dealing in antiques or art, in order to help with their heavy expenses. He had refused to countenance the idea and had been horrified at first, later somewhat amused. Laughingly, he had pointed out that she couldn't possibly earn more than a pittance, which would hardly solve their grave problems. But the Earl had been touched by Francesca's generous offer, especially unselfish in view of her dedication to her writing. Subsequently she had poured all of her energies into the book on Chinese Gordon. But she continued to fret about the situation in general, and one night, when Katharine came to supper at the Chesterfield Street house, she had confided her worries about money. Carefully, Francesca had enumerated some of the facts, endeavouring to explain in the simplest terms such things as entailment and trusts, and her great-grandfather's curious will. This had actually been dictated by her great-grandmother, in much the same way that this redoubtable lady had conceived, structured and dictated the various family trusts. The Ninth Countess of Langley, aware of 'Spendthrift Teddy's' proclivity for extravagant living and young mistresses, had been determined to protect her children, her grandchildren and their progeny from any foolishness on his part. To this end she had bullied her husband into acceding to her wishes, and the family's solicitors had been obliged to create a number of iron-clad trusts which could not be invaded or broken. Everything was neatly and very tightly sewn up for ever, making it virtually impossible to sell anything. Whilst successfully tying her husband's hands, the Ninth Countess had also hamstrung future generations. 'We're rich in land, paintings, and possessions, but cash poor,' Francesca had pointed out gloomily, adding, with a surge of youthful optimism, 'At least until the Home Farm starts making a profit, which won't be long, now that Daddy has modernized the operation. It'll soon be on a paying basis.'

Katharine had been understanding, but she had categorically taken the Earl's side. She had advised Francesca, rather vociferously, to double her efforts on the biography, in the hope that it would be a commercial success and earn her a bushel of money. Katharine had continued to be supportive, and a receptive and patient listener whenever Francesca wanted to discuss the book, for which Francesca was grateful.

Suddenly Francesca felt a light tap on her shoulder, and she swung her head to face Nicholas Latimer, who was leaning forward. It was almost as if he had been plugged into her mind like an amp, for he said, 'Did you take my advice about bridging and spanning time, the early years of Gordon's life?'

She smiled. 'Yes, I did, Nicky. Thanks so much.'

'Keep at it, kid. You'll write that last page one day.'

'I hope so. Incidentally, what's this delay about?'

Nick grinned. 'We're waiting for God. We can't possibly begin until he arrives.'

'God?'

'Yes. The guy from Monarch Pictures. He now holds our fate in his hands, since they're going to be distributing *Wuthering Heights* and, more importantly, financing it. Mind you, they're not making a problem about who plays the female lead. All they're really interested in is getting one of Victor's pictures. It'll give them the prestige they need, and it's quite a coup that he signed with them. Metro really wanted the film too. Anyway, Vic thought Hilly Street ought to see Katharine's test. A courtesy gesture.'

'*Hilly Street*? That's not really his name, is it?' Francesca giggled, eyeing Nick doubtfully, aware of his penchant for teasing her unmercifully. 'I don't believe you. I think you just invented it.'

Nick laughed. 'Sure I did. But years ago. And the nickname stuck.'

'But why such a peculiar nickname?'

'It's appropriate. Doing business with him is like riding a bike up a very hilly street. Excessively bumpy. His real name's Hillard Steed, which prompted my play on words, I guess, and he's not such a bad guy. Congenitally late though.'

Victor, who had overheard their conversation, straightened up and glanced at Nick. 'I'll give Hilly about ten more minutes and then I'll tell the projectionist to roll it.' He looked at his watch. 'It's almost eleven. As usual, Hilly's going to be half an hour late. I told him ten-thirty.' Victor stood up, dwarfing them with his great bulk. 'I'm going into the projection room, Nick. Excuse me.' He nodded rather curtly to Francesca, who managed a bleak little smile in return before he disappeared.

A knowing glint flicked into Nick's eyes as he observed this cool and perfunctory exchange. Francesca had become something of a permanent fixture in their lives, and Vic's behaviour when she was around was causing Nick considerable amusement. Ever since meeting Victor, Katharine Tempest had spent a great deal of her free time with him, especially when Kim was in Yorkshire, introducing him into the smartest social circles and to the *crème de la crème* of London society. This had not changed, except that now she had her new bosom chum trailing along in her wake. Wherever Katharine went Francesca's presence was sure to follow, like the proverbial little lamb. Nick felt Francesca's presence as acutely as Victor did. She was astonishingly bright and gay, articulate to the point of being rather outspoken at times, unusually self-assured for her age, and yes, enormously pretty. Quite beautiful, really, in that understated English way that was dewdrop fresh and reminiscent of a spring garden. No, it wasn't easy to ignore the Lady Francesca, as Nick had quickly come to understand.

Victor always seemed delighted at the prospect of their company, until the girls arrived, and then his demeanour instantly changed, and radically, in relation to Francesca. He was either remote and vague and retreated into protracted silences, or became excessively jolly and avuncular, alien postures which did not sit well on him. To Nick, Vic appeared curiously transparent and out of sync when Francesca was in the same room. For a quintessential actor he was doing a pretty lousy job of concealing his feelings. In fact, his abnormal behaviour only confirmed his immense attraction to Francesca more forcibly than ever. For her part, she was completely natural, her comportment relaxed and pleasant, and she was apparently oblivious to Victor's indisputable interest in her. Maybe I'm the only one who's aware of it, because I know him so well, Nick thought, and another possibility quickly insinuated itself into his mind. Could it be that Victor did not comprehend his feelings for the girl? Hardly likely, Nick answered himself. Still, Vic might have buried his emotions so deep he was able to ignore them, and therefore did not have to confront or deal with them. If that's the case, he's being very foolish, Nick decided.

Nicholas Latimer was the first to admit he was very taken with Francesca. In the short time he had known her he had grown extremely fond of her in a brotherly fashion, and in some respects she reminded him of his sister Marcia. She took his banter exceptionally well, in the spirit it was given. Francesca was a good sport. Unlike Katharine, he commented inwardly, and smiled with acerbity. His wit and irreverent joshing fell on stony ground when directed at her. Oh she smiled, even laughed occasionally, but the eyes were so glacial he thought he would get frostbite from them one day. Because of her impeccable manners, Katharine was always civil to him, even cordial, but this could be so excessive it bordered on parody, in Nick's view, at any rate. *Frigid* was the only word he could ever find to properly characterize her to himself.

In contrast, he thought of Francesca as warm and loving and sunny of nature. An uncomplicated young woman who was lots of fun, and had a terrific sense of humour. In particular, Nicky liked her smart mind. She was also keen and incisive and he admired her vast knowledge of history.

On that tedious Sunday evening, a couple of weeks earlier, when Victor had been inveigled by Katharine into giving a supper party in his suite, Francesca had started to look as bored as he was feeling. She had drifted over to join him during cocktails, and had remained resolutely glued to his side thereafter. Nick had been delighted to have her company. He had sensed rather than observed her irritation with Estelle Morgan's ridiculous affectations and inanities. In fact, Francesca's distant manner was a reflection of his own attitude, and his growing impatience with the journalist, whom Nick mentally categorized as a pushy New York broad of the worst kind.

That evening he and Francesca had spent several hours discussing the historical figures who most intrigued them. She had talked about Richard Neville, the Earl of Warwick, known as the Kingmaker, that glittering figure who, in the fifteenth century, had placed Edward Plantagenet on the shaky throne of England after the Wars of the Roses. Nick had listened to her in astonishment, discovering she had an amazing ability to make both the man and the events surrounding him come vividly alive in the manner of a born storyteller. He had been encouraging her efforts to write ever since, had volunteered to help her in any way he could, and had already spoken to his English publisher about her book.

Now, as he reflected, Nick could not remember enjoying an evening so much in a long time. Yes, there was something unique about Francesca Cunningham. His only regret was that she was so very young. Otherwise she would have been perfect for Victor. Exactly the kind of woman he needed in his life. Too damned bad, Nick muttered under his breath, and then he frowned. Who had decided she was too young? Victor, of course. But I did tease him about her age, Nick thought, regretting this now, wondering if he had sounded disapproving. I'd better correct that impression, he resolved.

Again, Nick found himself focusing on Katharine Tempest, contemplating the test he was about to see. Was it really any good? Victor had been close-mouthed, even cagey, about it and for once Nick had been unable to read his best friend. When Nick had pestered him, Vic had merely said, 'I think you'd better see it for yourself. I don't want to influence you in advance. And listen, old buddy, I want an honest opinion from *you*.'

Nick strictured himself to be unbiased, to keep an open mind. He must not let his dislike of Katharine as a woman becloud his judgment of her as an actress. Nick merely tolerated her company out of deference to Victor, who was oddly attached to her. Sometimes he wondered about that attachment.

Hillard Steed finally arrived. He and Victor were chatting in the doorway, and Nick sauntered over, greeting Hilly with amiability. Victor interrupted sharply, with, 'Okay boys, let's get this show on the road. You can talk later.' Nick winked at Hilly, gave Victor a smart military salute and edged along the row. A second later, Victor lowered himself into the next seat, swung his head, and indicated to the projectionist peering out of the booth window that he wanted to start.

Francesca gave Katharine's hand a quick squeeze without looking at her. Her eyes were glued to the screen and she sat perfectly still. Katharine herself was suddenly petrified and she wanted to flee, but that would be cowardly and she prided herself on her courage. Her nervousness increased and she felt as if her heart was in her mouth. Outwardly she remained contained and unruffled, but she was glad Francesca was there to lend her support. Katharine closed her eyes, and she, who was not particularly religious, found herself saying a small silent prayer: *Please God, let me be good. So much depends on this. My future and Ryan's too.* Her eyes opened and she settled back against the seat, willing herself to relax.

The overhead lights were doused, and there was a flickering on the screen, but it went black and a collective groan rose and echoed around the screening room. Almost immediately the reel started and the titles on a clap-board read: SCREEN TEST: MISS KATHARINE TEMPEST: WUTHERING HEIGHTS.

And so the scene began.

Ann Patterson, the actress playing Nelly Dean, sat in the kitchen of Wuthering Heights, the Earnshaw farm, singing a lullaby to the baby Hareton, actually a doll wrapped in a shawl. In the Brontë novel, Heathcliff had been present, talking to Nelly a moment before she had lifted the child from its crib. Then he had walked across the room and flung himself down on a bench against the wall, hidden from view by a large settle. He had remained in the kitchen.

Francesca had included this in her version, since she believed it was Heathcliff's hidden presence that helped to give the chapter a great deal of its dramatic impetus, in that Heathcliff overhears the unflattering things Cathy has to say about him, as opposed to Edgar Linton, and the recitation of her feelings for them both.

However, Victor had limited Bruce Nottley to only one other actor to play opposite Katharine, to keep the costs of the test down to a minimum. And so the first few pages of Francesca's relatively short, twenty-eight-minute script had been dropped by the director, eliminating the need for an actor to play the role of Heathcliff. Katharine had been concerned that this tampering with the script, minor though it was, would diminish the values in the scene. But Bruce had managed to reassure her, explaining that Ann could easily indicate to the viewer that there was an eavesdropper present, simply through worried glances directed to the far end of the kitchen, her vain attempts to silence Cathy increasing Nelly's nervousness. Katharine had no choice but to acquiesce, since Bruce, as the director of the test, had the last word.

The elderly actress continued to croon softly to the child, and the screening room was now completely hushed, the silence broken only by the gentle whirring of the projector. The tension and expectancy were high, seemed to vibrate like waves in the air. Everyone was keyed up and waiting, wondering if they were about to witness a disastrous failure or the birth of a new star. Only Victor knew the answer and he had given none of them the vaguest clue.

The kitchen door flew open and Katharine Tempest was on the screen. Her first lines, spoken in a whisper, were, 'Are you alone, Nelly?' All eyes were focused on her as she floated forward to join Nelly Dean by the hearth, in the foreground of the shot. She looked like a dream in a white muslin frock sprigged with tiny cornflowers. Her thick chestnut hair was parted in the centre and held back at each side with small blue-velvet bows, and it fell softly to her shoulders in loose waves. The camera dollied in for a close-up and there were several quite audible gasps as it lingered there to reveal the perfect features, the purity and innocence in those matchless eyes.

Katharine seemed to leap out from the screen, blazingly alive, larger than life. Her acting was superb, but the force she projected had little to do with this, or her grace of movement, her facial expressions, the mellifluous ring to her voice, although, indeed, all were in great evidence. It was something far beyond these attributes which came across so powerfully and magnetically, which stunned with its impact. It was sheer force of personality. Katharine had incredible presence, and glamour, and charisma personified, and all spelled STAR in no uncertain terms. And the camera truly loved her.

As the scene unfolded, Katharine ran the gamut of emotions. Her initial quiet anxiety on entering was quickly replaced by lighthearted gaiety tinged with skittishness, which in turn moved on to indignation and a hint of imperiousness. She was also defiant, cajoling, sweetly endearing and, finally, was held in the grip of a passion so intensely, so eloquently expressed it was heart-stopping in its pathos and realism. Francesca was mesmerized and on the edge of her seat, clasping her hands tightly together. Gooseflesh ran up her arms when Katharine began Cathy Earnshaw's famous declaration of her all-consuming love for Heathcliff. She was unusually familiar with the words, had heard them said many times before; but it seemed to her that Katharine was giving them new life and meaning and with a depth of feeling that was remarkable. She was touched and moved in a way she had never been before in her young life, and she knew she was watching genius. Katharine Tempest was spellbinding.

On the screen Katharine was at Nelly's feet, one hand on her knee, and, as she looked up at her, those huge turquoise eyes beseeched, were flooded with mingled suffering and ecstasy and final acceptance of her overpowering love. Slowly she said:

"'My love for Linton is like the foliage in the woods: time will change it, I'm well aware, as winter changes the trees. My love for Heathcliff resembles the eternal rocks beneath: a source of little visible delight, but necessary.'" Katharine paused for a beat and in that dramatic, split-second pause the tears seeped out of her eyes and trickled unchecked down her cheeks. And then she declared: "'Nelly, I *am* Heathcliff! He's always, always in my mind: not as a pleasure, any more than I am always a pleasure to myself, but as my own being. So don't talk of our separation again: it is impracticable – '"

Katharine buried her head in the folds of Nelly's skirt, racked with sobs, and there was a slow fade-out as the camera pulled back for a final long shot of the two women. The screen went black, and the scene, which had run for exactly twenty-four and a half minutes, came to an end.

The test was electrifying.

There was total silence in the screening room. Not a single person stirred until the overhead lights finally went on, and then a hubbub broke out, and everyone was excitedly talking at once. Francesca, wiping a tear, caught a glimpse of Hillard Steed surreptitiously doing the same, looking sheepish.

Francesca quickly turned to Katharine, her eyes watery, and threw her arms around her, hugging her friend tightly. 'Oh, Katharine, Katharine, you were absolutely marvellous!'

Katharine blinked several times, feeling curiously numb, and before she could fully take hold of herself they were suddenly crowding around her. Slowly she stood up, still looking slightly startled, smiling with uncertainty, overcome by shyness. They began to congratulate her in the most lavish terms, and the accolades were flying so fast and furious around her she could hardly take them all in. Victor hovered at the edge of the group, beaming, and exuding an air of quiet pleasure and much pride, and a hint of possessiveness besides.

Only Nicholas Latimer remained seated. Being decent and fair, and very much the professional, he was not one to begrudge credit where it was due, especially to a creative artist who excelled at what she did. And he fully intended to offer Katharine congratulations once he had recovered his equanimity.

He was still considerably shaken by her performance. Nick had known, within the first few minutes of the test, that she was pure magic. She would be a star. Not a run-of-the-mill star either, but big, very big. Probably the biggest of them all. She was unadulterated box-office material, for she had the extraordinary ability to project the stuff of romantic dreams, and that was what mass audience motion pictures were all about. Her staggering looks, her sexuality mingled with a touch of innocence, her incredible brilliance as an actress were more than enough to guarantee her the most glittering place in the Hollywood firmament of stars. And she would go to Hollywood. There was no doubt in his mind about her eventual destination.

He replayed the test in his head. She had astounded him with her sense of timing. It was perfect. She had paused dramatically when he had not anticipated it, and increased her speed when he had expected her to adopt a slower pace. But she had been correct. Her instinct is infallible, he said to himself, and that's something you can't teach an actor. It was there, or it wasn't. Besides timing, she had been gripping, exciting, and so convincing, that when she had said, 'Nelly, I *am* Heathcliff!' he had thought instantly: And she *is* Cathy. She's not acting this, she's living it, and with every fibre of her being. It will always be the same with her, whatever role she's playing. She's a natural, just as Vic is a natural, and like him she has that same mysterious communication with the camera. To Nick, it was almost as if Katharine had had a love affair with the lens, and it had captured so many things about her he had not realized she possessed: vulnerability, a poignancy that tugged at the heart, a restless tempestuousness, and hidden fire.

He remembered some of the lines he himself had adapted for the actual screenplay, of Heathcliff crying out, in the anguish of his love: 'My wild sweet Cathy! My wild heart!' How appropriate those words had become in the space of twenty-five minutes. They not only so aptly described Catherine Earnshaw but Katharine Tempest, who truly was the embodiment of them.

Finally, Nick rose and edged his way into the aisle, and approached Katharine who was surrounded by Jake, Jerry and Hilly, with Francesca and Victor standing on the sidelines. She was laughing gaily, enjoying this moment of triumph, but when she saw him the laughter broke off, and her face turned stony and hostile. The gaze she levelled at him was one of icy blue disdain, and he saw challenge mirrored there as well.

Nick experienced a sharp tightening across his chest and he shivered, feeling suddenly cold and drained. And he did not understand himself at all. He drew to a standstill in front of Katharine, staring down at her; it struck him how small and fragile she appeared, and he wondered why he'd never really noticed this before.

Growing conscious of the prolonged silence, of all eyes on him, he said softly, '*You are Cathy*. I'll never believe anyone else in the part now. Not after seeing you. To use Vic's favourite expression, you're the whole enchilada.'

Stunned by this unfamiliar and unexpected approbation from Nicholas Latimer, Katharine returned his stare, not sure whether or not she had heard him correctly. Immediately she was suspicious and wary, steeled herself for the barbed line, the snide remark that inevitably fell from his mouth. But to her growing astonishment he remained silent, and he was looking at her with such warmth she was unnerved. And very slowly the frostiness in her eyes dissolved.

Katharine smiled back at Nick, and it was the only sincere smile she had given him since their first meeting. Aware that he was impervious to her, she had never bothered to exercise her devastating charm on him in the past, believing it would be a waste of time.

Hesitantly, she said, 'Do you mean you actually thought I was good?'

'Not good, Katharine. Brilliant.'

There was another silence, in reality a sudden stillness between them, and then she asked, 'Are you sure, Nick? Really really sure?'

'Yes, I am, Katharine,' he replied in a voice that was low and serious. But as he turned to Francesca, his wicked grin flashed. 'And you did a pretty damned good job with the scene, kid. I'd better watch myself, or I'm going to be out of a job. Christ, the amateurs are getting to be real professionals around here. And some of them are still in diapers.'

Delighted, Francesca burst out laughing, and she clutched his arm. 'I was wondering what you'd say, and coming from a writer like you, those are words of praise indeed. Thank you.' Nick took this opportunity to lead Francesca away from the group, out of the limelight, all the while trying to define the cause of his discomfort, diagnose the reason for the chill in his bones. It *had* to be the flu.

Katharine's gaze followed them, and lingered briefly on Nicholas Latimer. If this man who so hated her said she was brilliant, then it must be true. Know thine enemy, she thought, and unexpectedly remembered something her father had said years ago – that it was often wiser to seek the truth from an enemy rather than a friend. Now she could not help thinking of her brother Ryan, picturing his face when he saw her on the screen, when he understood she was a famous star. Or about to be one. She wished her brother had been here today. To witness the beginning of it all. And it was the beginning, just the way she had planned it.

Katharine's young heart quickened, and that driving ambition, that fierce and relentless determination to succeed were intensified within her as never before, and yet again she silently reiterated her resolution to rescue Ryan and destroy her father's hold on him. It won't be long now, she promised herself, not long at all . . .

'I'm sure it goes without saying that you've got the part,' Victor exclaimed.

Startled, Katharine looked across at him, her eyes scanning his face. After a moment she said, 'I hope so. Thank you, Victor.' She laughed. 'I'm definitely hired?'

'You are. I've prepared the contract for your agent to look over. He'll be getting it later today.'

'Thanks . . .' She stopped, frowning, and then pronounced in a careful tone, 'I'd like to ask you something. Why were you so noncommittal, so vague with me about the test? I don't unders – '

'That's right, you bastard,' Nick interjected with a broad grin. Adopting an exaggerated English accent, he went on, 'Awfully bad show, old boy, keeping us in the dark. Not very sporting of you, wot?'

A smile swept across Victor's face. 'I had a good reason for playing it cool, and close to the chest. Very simply, I wanted to be absolutely sure I would get honest reactions from everyone. I was worried I might set you up, influence you, if I let my own excitement show, and I almost did several times. That's why it was easier for me to keep quiet. When I first ran the test I could hardly contain myself. Then I ran it again, and again, looking for flaws, but there weren't any. Actually, I've seen it four times altogether,' he admitted, 'and in my opinion it gets better every time. I knew I couldn't be wrong in my assessment, but I wanted to see if you were all going to be swept off your feet, like I had been.'

'We certainly were,' Francesca exclaimed, and then blushed furiously. There were nods of agreement, and Hillard Steed volunteered, 'I think Monarch would be interested in signing a contract with Katharine.' He swung his eyes away from Victor and let them rest appraisingly on Katharine, finishing, a trifle pompously, 'How do you feel about that, young lady?'

Before she could open her mouth, Victor cried, 'Hold your horses, Hilly! Not so fast. Bellissima Productions has a verbal commitment from Katharine, and the contract is right here in my pocket.' He patted the front of his jacket and, noting Hilly's disbelief, he immediately pulled out an envelope. 'Do you want to see it, Hilly?'

Hilly shook his head, his disappointment apparent. 'No, I believe you, Vic. And I don't blame you. Congratulations to you too. You've got yourself a major new star on your hands.' Another thought struck him, and he said quickly, 'Would you be interested in a loan out? That is, if you don't have another picture in mind for Katharine after *Wuthering Heights*? I'd like to talk about that possibility with you, even start negotiations.'

Victor looked interested. 'Do you have a particular property in mind, Hilly?' he asked, knowing he undoubtedly did, otherwise he wouldn't have made the proposal. Not Hilly Street, who was a veteran film maker.

'Sure do, Victor.' Hilly's eyes narrowed, and he waited, purposely holding back, anticipating a string of pertinent questions from Victor, wanting his announcement to have the maximum effect.

But Victor, also percipient, merely smiled, well versed in Hilly's ploys and tactics, and not about to take the bait too swiftly. He lit a cigarette, out-waiting Hilly, and turning to Nick, he said, 'Incidentally, talking of properties, did you read the script by Frank Lomax? The one the Morris office sent. Now that would be a great vehicle for Katharine.'

Nick, understanding immediately Victor's strategy, jumped in with, 'It's terrific. I think we should grab it, and Bellissima can produce it – '

'Don't be too hasty,' Hilly interrupted sharply. 'Not until you've heard me out.' He cleared his throat. 'I want Katharine for . . . the new Beau Stanton picture.' He let his words sink in, and went on rapidly, 'We're all set to go, except for the female lead. Naturally, we've a few top stars in mind, but personally I think Katharine would play off marvellously against Beau. They'd make a great team. Script by Henry Romaine. The best in the business, as you know, Vic. Willy Adler directing. Morton Lane producing. Costumes by Edith Head. We start shooting in October. In Hollywood. Locations in San Francisco and New York. Twelve weeks shooting schedule.'

Victor swallowed. This he had not expected, and he was tremendously impressed by the prestigious names attached to the film, all adding up to a quality production, and not the least was the male star. Richard Stanton, commonly known as Beau in the industry, was a big box-office name and had been for the past twenty years or so. An English actor who had first made it big in the Hollywood of the thirties, Beau was one of the longest-lasting perennials, handsome, debonair, suave, and ageless. He was a leading man of faultless grace, inimitable style, great elegance, and had an easy charm that wholly captivated women. His penchant for light, glossy, sophisticated comedy had become his forte, and his films were always highly commercial successes. If Katharine went into a picture with Beau immediately after starring opposite Vic himself, then her career in the movies was not merely launched but would be jet-propelled. Meteoric. She would be established as an international name instantaneously.

Jesus! Vic thought. Concealing his excitement, he said evenly, with cool thoughtfulness, 'Obviously I have to talk to Katharine first, explain about loan outs. And I would want to see the script before I make a final decision. But I'm not negative, Hilly, not at all. I think we'd better sit down and talk this out later in the week. In the meantime, shall we go to lunch? A celebration lunch. I've booked a table at Les Ambassadeurs. It's champagne and the whole – '

'Enchilada,' Katharine finished for him. Her face, calm and inscrutable, revealed nothing. But her heart was pounding, her mind was racing and she could hardly breathe. She smiled a small secretive smile as she linked her arm through Victor's and guided him towards the door.

Nick took hold of Francesca's hand and hurried her up the aisle after them. *It's all going too fast. Far too fast*, he thought, shafted by dismay. *There's going to be trouble. Nothing but trouble.* And suddenly he had an awful sense of foreboding, one so real to him he faltered momentarily. As they stepped into the lift Nick's uneasiness increased, and then he laughed inwardly and told himself he was being over imaginative, even ridiculous. And he laughed again, trying to shake the feeling off. But he could not dispel it, and it was to linger in him for the rest of that day, and for many months to come.

CHAPTER TWENTY

'And don't worry about the old man; he's going to be all right,' Kim said, heaving Francesca's suitcase up onto the luggage rack. He glanced down at her, and continued: 'After all, he's got Doris hovering like a ministering angel, pampering him like a baby, and he loves it. She seems to be enjoying the role too.' Kim grinned and his eyes danced with mischief. 'A latter-day Florence Nightingale, got up in Christian Dior and diamonds.'

Francesca laughed, despite her concern for her father. 'Yes, I know exactly what you mean. I think there's definitely something afoot there, don't you?'

'I do indeed.' Kim sat down on the edge of the seat opposite her, and searched around in the pocket of his suede and sheepskin jacket for his cigarettes. He brought out the packet, lit one, and added, 'Wedding bells about to ring maybe?' A brow shot up.

'I'm not sure,' Francesca responded. 'Neither of them is very confiding. But Doris does have a decided sparkle in her eyes, and she's adopted a rather proprietary attitude with Daddy. Not only that, she seems to have taken charge at Langley, and she's never done that before. I don't mind about Doris marrying Daddy, do you, Kim?'

He shook his head. 'No. Actually, I'm really rather glad about their relationship, and the new turn it's taken. I hope they *do* get married. I think Doris is a good egg, and ideal for Father. He needs someone who's fun loving and vivacious and kind. And very devoted, I might add. Besides, she's got pots and pots of money –'

'God, you are awful!' Francesca exclaimed. 'I've told you before, that wouldn't influence Daddy one iota. How can you think such a dreadful thing!' She shot him a disapproving glare.

'Oh, I realize the old man isn't interested in her money, Frankie. But all of those lovely dollars won't do him any harm. Quite the contrary, I would say.' Kim drew on his cigarette and blew out a smoke ring, watching it curl into the air, his grey eyes reflective. After a moment he said, 'But getting back to Father's health, do put the accident out of your mind.'

'I'll try to,' Francesca promised, her good humour with him restored. 'But I can't help feeling it was all my fault –'

'Stuff and nonsense! These things have a way of happening. *You* weren't responsible.'

'Still, if he hadn't been on the step-ladder in the library, looking for that book for me, he would never have fallen.'

Kim groaned mildly. 'But he did fall, Frankie dear, and worrying about it, after the fact, won't accomplish anything.' Noting her glum expression, he tried to cheer her up. 'Look, darling, Dr Fuller said he's going to be fine, providing he stays on his back for a week or two, and Fuller is giving him medication to kill the pain. A fractured pelvic bone is a damnable thing, because it's impossible to set, but as long as he rests it will mend properly.'

'Yes, I know. It must be awfully uncomfortable though.'

'I expect it is, but at least Father is rather bright at the moment, what with good old Doris hanging around. And also because of that marvellous little windfall, courtesy of you and Katharine.'

'Thanks to Katharine, you mean. I really didn't have anything to do with it,' Francesca stated. Her face lit up and her smoky, amber-hazel eyes glowed with affection. 'She's a marvellous girl, isn't she, Kim?'

'She's absolutely the tops. Super!' he declared, his own face wreathed in smiles. 'And don't forget to give her my love, will you? 'Phone her the moment you get in.'

'How could I possibly forget. You've repeated yourself half a dozen times in the last hour,' she laughed. The sound of carriage doors slamming and the guard's whistle caught her attention, and she glanced out of the window. 'You'd better be going, Kim, otherwise you'll get whisked off to London with me.'

'I wouldn't mind that at all,' Kim asserted, thinking longingly of Katharine. He groaned and pulled a face. 'Unfortunately, duty calls, and I'm needed at Langley more than ever right now.' He stood up, bent over to kiss her on the cheek, and squeezed her shoulder lovingly. 'Have a nice journey, Frankie, and do take care of that awful cold.' He moved to the carriage door, then swung around and reassured, 'Dad's in good hands, so please try to relax. Remember, I'm at Langley and I'll make sure he follows doctor's orders.'

'I know you will. 'Bye, darling.'

''Bye,' he smiled, and jumped swiftly onto the platform, slamming the carriage door shut as the train started to roll slowly along the tracks, pulling out of Harrogate railway station and heading on its long journey south.

Francesca sat back, settling herself in the corner, burrowing deeper into her heather-toned tweed top coat, shivering slightly even though she was wearing a

190

matching heavy tweed skirt and a woollen twinset under the coat, as well as a cashmere scarf and boots. But it was chilly in the carriage, the steam heat slow in circulating. Also, she had caught a cold earlier in the week and had been unable to shake it off. Melly, their old nanny who lived in retirement in an estate cottage at Langley, had poured all manner of old-fashioned concoctions down her, but even these tried and tested remedies of her childhood had been to no avail. She had the cold, and, if anything, it was much worse.

Francesca opened her handbag and took out the packet of throat lozenges Melly had pressed into her hand yesterday, smiling to herself, filled with fond thoughts of Melly, who had raised her. The lozenges were called Fisherman's Friend, and, according to Melly, had been specially formulated for the Fleetwood deep sea fishermen working in the Icelandic frost and fog conditions. She and Kim had been force-fed them as children, and they were so strong they almost blew the head off, but Melly swore by them, and they were effective in helping to ease a raspy throat. Francesca popped one into her mouth and sucked on it, gazing out of the window, watching the landscape flying past as the train hurtled through the Dales towards Leeds. The fields were black and barren, covered with a fine coating of hoary frost, and the stark unadorned trees were like proud and solitary sentinels, rising up against a fading sky that was daunting in its coldness. Spring would be late this year, and there were none of the usual signs of gentling greenness, baby lambs gambolling or early daffodils billowing in the breeze, even though it was already the first week of March. A telegraph pole came into her line of vision a short way ahead, sprouting up between the trembling hills to ruin the beauty of the graceful rolling vista. To Francesca it was a sharp reminder of the problems she had encountered in the past week, when she had been guiding Jerry Massingham and his assistant Ginny around Yorkshire, helping them to scout locations for the film.

In many respects, the first few days had been trying, even difficult. Jerry had grown increasingly irritated and his frustration had spiralled as they had toured the county, the largest in England. Every time they came across a place suitable for exterior shooting some kind of ugly man-made tribute to the twentieth-century technology had rudely intruded, rendering it inappropriate for a film which was supposed to be set in the nineteenth century. Telegraph poles, pylons and water towers had hardly been part of the scenery in Victorian England.

Finally, in desperation, Francesca had decided to lead them much farther afield than she had originally planned. She had driven them up beyond Ripon, Middleham and Leyburn, into Swaledale, Wensleydale and Coverdale, where endless uninhabited moors were balanced by deep valleys and intersected by tumbling, fast-flowing little becks and cascading waterfalls which shimmered in the northern light. They had stopped at Wain Wath Force, Gunnerside and Healaugh, breathtaking spots unmarred by modern inventions. At the highest point on Bellerby Moor, high-flung above the picturesque village of Grinton, Jerry had heaved a sigh of relief as he had viewed the surrounding landscape. And he had been stunned, disbelief washing over his face, as he had scanned the unbroken expanse of undulating moorland, so bleak, so desolate, iced with vagrant patches of lingering winter snow, yet curiously beautiful, even awesome in its very austerity. Here there was an untamed wildness and immense solitude, and grandeur in the soaring fells pitched up at precarious leaning angles into the brooding cloud-laden sky. And on the valley floor, far below, there was a contrasting softness in the neat and orderly patchwork of fields, with the River Swale curving gently down to Richmond, a narrow, twisting ribbon of silver, sparkling brightly in the crystalline sunshine that occasionally broke through the cumulus mass. Jerry had not only been captivated by what he saw, but held utterly spellbound, and he had approvingly pronounced the area perfect from every point of view, and unbelievably photogenic. They were able to quickly select a number of places in which to film, mapping out the logistics as they went along.

Francesca had enjoyed her week working with the production manager and his charming assistant, and she had felt rather dishonest accepting the cheque for two hundred pounds, since she believed she had done so little to earn it. But Jerry had been adamant about the amount, and in much the same way he had been insistent that her father accept a five-thousand-pound fee for use of certain rooms in the castle, in which some of the important interior scenes were eventually to be filmed. Her father had been astounded by the amount, just as she herself had been startled when the idea had originally been presented to her.

It had all come about quite by accident, on the day of the private screening of Katharine's test, and it was to Katharine herself that the Cunninghams owed this sudden bit of good fortune. At Victor's lunch at Les Ambassadeurs, after many celebratory toasts and endless bottles of Dom Pérignon, the conversation had turned to the various aspects of the production. Jerry, concerned as usual with the budget, had begun to grumble about the costs entailed in building a set for the elegant ball scene at Thrushcross Grange, a key sequence in *Wuthering Heights*, especially the film version. Katharine, listening attentively, had suddenly interrupted Jerry's flow of words. 'But why don't you use a hall or a ballroom that already exists, in a country house or stately home?' she had suggested. 'Langley Castle, for instance. I've seen a photograph of the ballroom there, and I think it would be perfect.'

There had been a small silence at the table, and it seemed to Francesca now, as she remembered, that all eyes had been suddenly focused on her intently, expressions curious, expectant and questioning. Victor had cleared his throat, and asked, 'What do you think, Francesca? If the ballroom *is* suitable, would your father give us his permission to film there?'

'Yes . . . I think so,' she had said slowly, wondering if her father would acquiesce, and not really certain of the answer.

'I bet it would be much cheaper than building an elaborate set,' Katharine had quickly pointed out. 'I'm sure the Earl would not ask an exorbitant fee.'

Flabbergasted by this last comment, Francesca had started to demur. 'Gosh, Daddy wouldn't want to be pa –' She had bitten off the rest of her sentence as Katharine had given her a swift kick on the ankle, and she had blushed, feeling self-conscious and uncertain of what she ought to say next.

Victor had saved her the trouble. 'Of course the film company would pay your father a fee for the use of parts of the castle,' he had exclaimed in a businesslike voice. 'I wouldn't have it any other way.'

Katharine had chuckled, her eyes shining, and it was then she had apparently had yet another brainwave. She had voiced the opinion, and in a most authoritative manner, that Francesca should be hired to scout locations with Jerry, who had announced earlier that he was planning a trip to Yorkshire for this express purpose. 'With all due respect to you, Jerry, I'm sure Francesca knows the area much better, since she grew up there,' Katharine had said. 'Just think of the time you'll save, having a guide like her. Not only that, I'm sure Francesca will be able to take you to any number of beauty spots off the beaten track which you might not otherwise find by yourself.'

Victor and Jerry had exchanged looks, obviously seeing the perfect sense in this idea, and they had seized upon it at once. Francesca had found herself being swept along by their immense enthusiasm, flattered by their keenness to have her work with them, and their concerted efforts in persuasiveness had scarcely been necessary. She had agreed almost immediately, not wishing to be the only outsider, wanting, instead, to be part of it all, to participate in their exciting world, and also hoping to help Jerry solve his production problems.

Help Victor, be part of *his* world, you mean, Francesca now murmured under her breath. Her critical perceptions of him had long since been laid to waste, her reservations and her initial fear buried beneath layers of new and burgeoning emotions of a type she had not experienced before. In the week she had been in Yorkshire she had discovered, somewhat to her surprise, that she missed him, and he had rarely been out of her thoughts. Last night, in the quietness of her room at Langley, she had sat for hours by the fire, examining her feelings, trying to be as analytical as she possibly could. Distance and separation had given her fresh objectivity, and finally she had had to accept a single stark reality: she was infatuated with Victor Mason. Frightened by the waves of panic mingled with confusion and internal turmoil that had swamped over her, she had resolutely shied away from the word *love*, wanting to believe her involvement with him was a passing thing and, therefore, not to be taken seriously.

Now she wondered about that. She sighed and closed her eyes, and leaned her head against the seat, considering the situation once more. It was hopeless, really. Dismay trickled through her at this realization. Victor only accepted her because of Katharine, and she knew there would never be anything but friendship between them, if even that. He treated her like a little girl, albeit tolerantly and pleasantly, but nevertheless she knew she was still a child in his eyes. Yet despite this knowledge, and her awareness of his lack of interest in her as a woman, Francesca suddenly realized it would be hard, if not indeed impossible, for her to extinguish her feelings for him. She understood, too, that up until this moment it had been enough to be in the same room with him. But what of the future? Could she bear to be near him and yet, in all truth, so far removed, knowing how she actually felt? She was doubtful. It would be agonizing.

Long after she had gone to bed last night, she had continued to think of him, unable to sleep, her mind and her heart and her body wanting him. And more than ever she had become conscious of the dangerous physical stirrings within her, of unfamiliar needs and desires and longings that inflamed her with their urgency, and made her feel like a stranger to herself, her own body suddenly alien and mysterious. She had wrapped her arms around the pillow, clutching it tightly to her, endeavouring to control her wild and vivid imaginings, to curb her fantasies about Victor and of making love with him, of giving herself up to him completely and without restraint. Sexually inexperienced though she was, she had discovered in those restless dawn hours, that her mind was an extraordinary erogenous zone, her thoughts of Victor excessively erotic and sensual, and so uninhibited she was shocked at herself and almost blushed in the dark.

That morning, when she had awakened, her arms were still holding the pillow, and she was clinging to it fiercely, as if it was Victor she so passionately embraced. If only it was him, she had thought, and slowly the tears had begun to fall, trickling down her cheeks until she was sobbing with despair, filled with the pain of unrequited love. She cried for a long time. Later, when she had calmed herself, she made the decision not to see him ever again. Somehow she must extract herself from his tight-knit little group, although she was not exactly certain what excuses she would make to Katharine, who had no inkling of her feelings.

But now, as the train rattled on towards London, she was filled with ambivalence, fluctuating between depression and euphoria, torn between her cool and reasoning head and her eager heart. Her superior intelligence told her to stay away from him, out of self-protectiveness; but her emotions propelled her inexorably to him. And being young, and unscarred by life and its inevitable disappointments, hope was intact within her, and she could still dream. Perhaps he would change his mind about her, fall in love with her, as she had with him.

Francesca felt a twinge of panic. I'm not in love with him, she told herself. I'm not! I'm really not! I'm just infatuated . . . it's only a silly crush.

The carriage door sliding open caused her to turn her head sharply. The Pullman car attendant was standing there, smiling warmly. His name was Beaver and he had been on the Edinburgh to London run for years. She had known him since she was a small child, travelling up to town twice a year with her father and Kim and Melly.

''Morning, your ladyship,' he said.

'Good morning, Beaver. How are you?'

'Doing nicely, thank you. And you? And his lordship, and the young viscount?'

'We're all fine, thank you.'

He nodded and smiled again. 'We'll be serving breakfast in a few minutes, your ladyship, if you'd like to go into the dining car. Train's pretty packed this morning, so we'll be filling up quickly, especially after Leeds.'

'Thank you, Beaver, I'll pop along now.' She picked up her handbag and Nick's book from the seat, and rose. Beaver stepped aside to let her pass, closed the carriage door behind her, and continued along the swaying corridor of the train, in the opposite direction.

Francesca found a table in the dining car and sat down. She glanced at the breakfast menu and discovered she was not hungry, but she was longing for a hot drink. She ordered a pot of tea and toast, and then opened Nick's book. It was one of his early novels and he had given it to her as a present, fondly inscribed. She had already read it several times, loving every page, struck as always by his extraordinary command of language, his brilliant use of words that came so vividly alive. She re-read a particular passage she liked, and then put the book down as the tea and toast materialized.

Her thoughts stayed with Nick. They had become such good friends, and there was a special kind of understanding between them. She valued his opinions and listened carefully to the advice he gave about writing, and so generously,

194

appreciating his interest in her. Ten days ago she had asked him to read some of the first pages of her book on Chinese Gordon.

Nick's words reverberated in her head again. 'The pages are terrific. Keep going. And don't look back,' he had told her. And then, more thoughtfully, he had added: 'Listen, kid, you've got talent. But talent isn't enough. You've also got to have dedication, discipline, determination and drive. You've got to be obsessed with a book. Without that obsession it won't work. And there's another D. D for desire. That must be there too. You've got to want to write more than you want to do anything else, and you've got to be prepared to make sacrifices to do it.' He had grinned in his impish way. 'There's a sixth D, and this one is vital. D for distraction, the enemy of every writer. You've got to build an imaginary wall around yourself so that nothing, no one intrudes. Understand me, kid?'

Nick often called her kid, just as he called Victor kid, and she had come to understand that in his vocabulary it was a special meaningful term, one of endearment, and used selectively. Francesca smiled to herself, sipping her hot tea, filled with enormous affection for Nick. It struck her then that she had never heard him call Katharine *kid*; he always addressed her rather formally as *Katharine*. But perhaps that was because he was in awe of her great beauty and talent as an actress. Certainly Francesca did not believe Nicky hated her friend, whatever *she* did. Neither did Kim. They both thought Katharine was seeing something which did not exist. Pondering this, Francesca recalled that Nick treated Katharine in much the same way he treated her, with cordiality and a sort of tongue-in-cheek amusement. But now she had to admit that at times he did appear to be a little constrained, as if holding back. Even at the celebration lunch, after his lovely compliments about the screen test, he had retreated behind a mask, curiously isolated from the jolly proceedings. On the other hand, during lunch he had confided that he thought he was coming down with the 'flu, and his face *had* looked drawn, pinched and white around the mouth. Perhaps this explained his behaviour that particular day. She hoped he was all right, that he was not as ill as she was beginning to feel.

After breakfast, Francesca made her way back to the carriage, relieved to see that she continued to be its only occupant. She huddled in her coat in the corner of the seat, and attempted to sleep. She did doze intermittently, but for most of the journey she was coughing and blowing her nose, and by the time the train arrived at King's Cross she was feverish, her eyes were watering and she was running a temperature.

She alighted from the train into drenching rain, and flew down the grimy, smoke-filled platform, heading for the ticket barrier, clutching her suitcase, praying that the queue for taxis would be short. Fortunately she was one of the first passengers to arrive at the taxi stand and she managed to get a cab relatively quickly. Within minutes the cabbie was manoeuvring through the congested traffic towards Marylebone and across town, heading in the direction of the West End and Mayfair. The rain was falling in torrents, as if there had been a cloudburst, and several times Francesca caught the flash of lightning streaking across a sky that was sombre and growing darker, and there was the cracking of distant thunder as the storm swept over London.

Francesca's physical discomfort increased during the cab ride to the house in

Chesterfield Street, and she could hardly wait to get home. She was beginning to feel miserable. Every bone in her body ached, she was shivering so much she could hardly keep a limb still, and several times she was seized by coughing and sneezing. It was with some relief that she paid the cabbie, went up the steps to the house and let herself in quickly. As she closed the door behind her, Mrs Moggs sallied forth from the dining room, a feather duster in one hand, a broad smile on her face, worn but cheery underneath the outrageous hat bedecked with flowers. Francesca wondered if she ever took it off.

'There you are, your ladyship,' Mrs Moggs cried, and nodded her head so hard in greeting the poppies shook. 'Best get out of your wet fings, and have a barf. I've got a nice pan of 'ot soup bubbling. You can drink a cup in bed,' she instructed in a commanding tone. 'Got to watch these colds, that we have, M'lady.'

'Hello, Mrs Moggs,' Francesca managed to get in at last, smiling weakly. She put down her case, took off her damp coat and hung it in the hall cupboard. Turning, she stared at Mrs Moggs, puzzlement registered on her face. 'And how did you know I had a cold?'

'Mrs Asternan! That's 'ow!' Mrs Moggs announced, bursting with importance. 'She rung me up 'ere this morning to tell me. To give me instructions. She said to make you some 'ot soup and get you to bed immediately. What a nice lady she is. Yes, an' she told me His Grace 'ad 'ad a 'orrible accident.' Mrs Moggs clucked sympathetically, and breezed on, 'Blimey, what a shame! But them stepladders is ever so dicey, as I'm always telling my Albert when 'e's cleaning me winders. Still, it ain't so bad really, if you stop to think. His Grace might 'ave broken 'is bloomin' neck.' She nodded to herself. 'That 'e might, your ladyship.'

Francesca shivered, conscious of chilliness in the small hall, and picked up her suitcase, stepping out towards the stairs. But she stopped and swung around, as Mrs Moggs exclaimed: 'Oooh, I almost forgot. That there Miss Temple rung up as well. About an hour ago.'

'Miss Tempest,' Francesca corrected quietly. 'Did she leave a message, Mrs Moggs?'

'Yes, your ladyship. Miss Temple wanted to remind you about dinner. And I told 'er that you was bloomin' poorly, and wouldn't be up to 'aving no dinner. I told 'er Mrs Asternan 'ad rung me up, and I passed on the bad news about His Grace's 'orrible accident. She was ever so upset, Miss Temple was. Anyways, she said she'd 'phone you later, 'cos she was orf to luncheon. In a 'urry, she was. She told me to tell you not to worry about tonight. She's calling the dinner orf, your ladyship. And a good fing, if you don't mind me saying so.'

'Honestly, Mrs Moggs!' Francesca began crossly, on the verge of reprimanding her for being an interfering busybody. But instantly she bit back the words. Mrs Moggs was a well-intentioned old dear, and she was only being her usual bossy self. 'I suppose you're right, Mrs Moggs. I think I had better stay in bed for the next twenty-four hours. I do feel pretty ghastly, and it's a perfectly awful day. I think I'll go and have that bath. It might warm me.' Climbing the stairs to her room Francesca realized with a tiny spurt of disappointment, that she would not be seeing Victor Mason tonight after all. It was he who had arranged the dinner, and now Katharine had cancelled it. Damnation, she muttered to herself, and then grimaced wryly, baffled by her many inconsistencies.

CHAPTER TWENTY-ONE

Victor Mason gave Jerry Massingham a long, hard stare and said in his briskest tone, 'You'd better make sure we take out plenty of insurance on Langley Castle itself, apart from our overall insurance for the film. And I do mean *plenty*, Jerry. I sure as hell don't want problems, should there be any accidents or damage to their valuables. In fact, I'd prefer to think we were over-insured.'

'I've already spoken to Jake about it, so don't worry,' Jerry answered him quickly, wondering if Victor thought he was a dimwit. Certainly for the past hour he had sounded as if he was trying to teach him how to suck eggs. But then Jake Watson had also been at the receiving end of similar treatment. Jerry grinned to himself, fully aware that Victor was simply in one of his businesslike, take-charge moods this morning: the executive producer rather than the star, well-versed in every facet of the production and shrewdly assessing the minutest detail. And letting us know it, Jerry added silently.

Suddenly conscious of Victor's dark eyes resting on him, Jerry felt obliged to add, 'I also intend to remove most of the lamps, vases and ornaments in the rooms we'll be shooting in, and I'll be replacing them with reproductions, to be on the safe side –'

'Yes, you'd better,' Victor cut in. He leaned back in his chair, flicked a speck of dust off the sleeve of his dark blue jacket and remarked, 'I imagine the place is full of expensive carpets, isn't it?'

'Yes. The Earl pointed out an Aubusson, several Savonneries and a couple of antique Orientals. Seemed a bit worried about them, but I explained we'll be using transparent plastic sheets underneath the cameras and the other equipment, whether there are carpets down or not. And we'll take up the rare carpets I've just mentioned. Actually, Victor, the castle is jam-packed with the most incredible treasures, priceless objects of art, so we can't take any chances.' He shook his head wonderingly. 'It's an amazing old place and extraordinarily beautiful. And the paintings!' He whistled in admiration, shaking his head again. 'My God, they've got to be worth a small fortune. But look, don't worry, I've got everything well in hand. I don't miss a trick.'

'I know you're a stickler for detail, but then so am I, Jerry. I like to be doubly sure, and surprises don't sit well on me. Particularly nasty surprises.' Victor threw Jerry a brief smile, and turned his attention to the many black and white photographs Jerry had taken in Yorkshire the previous week. He spread them out on the table, studying them closely and with keen and expert eyes.

Jerry sat back, tensely waiting for judgment to be passed, as he knew it would be. Victor could be relied upon to speak his mind, and with a candour that sometimes startled in its bluntness.

Victor was concentrating on the photographs. 'When will the colour shots be ready?' he asked without raising his head.

'Later this week. And you'll be stunned. Yorkshire is quite a magical place. I hadn't realized that before. Actually, the scenery took my breath away.'

'Yes, I can see from the black and whites exactly why it did. You hit on some truly great photogenic spots.' Victor looked up, nodding approvingly, impressed. A wry smile touched his mouth. 'Better than the back lot any time, eh, Jerry?'

'Not half,' said Jerry, happy to hear this unexpected approbation. 'And I do think we found some superb locations, I really do. 'Course that was no accident. It was entirely due to Francesca. Lovely girl. Surprisingly diligent, and very sweet. Not a bit toffee-nosed, like the usual deb.'

Victor's ears pricked up at the mention of Francesca's name, and innumerable questions flew to his tongue. He muffled these, and adopted a cautious tone as he asked, 'She worked out okay then? You thought it was worth having her along?'

'God, yes! I'd have been lost without her. She saved us a lot of time, not to mention aggravation.'

'I'm glad to hear that,' Victor murmured, wondering whether or not she was back in London. He was about to question Jerry, but instantly changed his mind, considering it wiser to remain discreetly silent. 'How did you get on with the Earl?' he asked, draining his coffee cup.

'Very well. He's a nice chap. Rather down-to-earth, I thought, and most obliging. Made us feel very much at home. He seemed tickled we want to film at the castle, looking forward to all the excitement probably. A farmer's life is pretty dull, I suppose, and that's what he is really. A gentleman farmer. And I must say, he was startled when I told him the fee. I don't believe he expected so much. If anything at all.' Jerry paused and drew on his cigarette, meditating. After a moment, he voiced the thought which had nagged at him all weekend, when he stated, with a touch of dourness, 'Maybe you've been over generous, old chap. You could have paid him much less, and he'd still be ecstatic.'

'Come on, Jerry, don't be such a tight wad!' Victor reproved, although his voice was tinged with laughter. 'We're well within the budget, and I understand from Katharine Tempest that the Earl's pretty short on walking around money.' Noting the baffled look on Jerry's face, he grinned and explained, 'Ready cash.' He reached for the second set of photographs, fanned them out, and commented, 'These rooms look exactly right for the interiors of Thrushcross Grange. We'll be saving ourselves a fortune on sets. So I'm glad to help the family if I can. Listen, it's cheap at the price.'

'I suppose so,' Jerry agreed grudgingly, and then on a more defensive note, he continued, 'And be happy I *am* a tight wad. I'm keeping the budget under control, aren't I?'

'Yes, and for that I'm very grateful, Jerry. So is Jake Watson. You're making life a lot easier, I can tell you. And speaking of our brilliant line producer, where in hell is he?'

'When I went out to get us coffee, he was interviewing Harry Pendergast. The set designer. He's damned good by the way.'

'Damned expensive too,' Victor pointed out. 'Oh, by the way, I was talking to Jake over the weekend, and we both came to the conclusion we might need an auxiliary generator for the kliegs. Did you think to check that out?'

'I did. I spoke to the Earl on Friday, just before I left for London. He seemed a bit vague about the capacity of the generator at the castle, and Francesca promised to follow it through for me.' He jumped to his feet. 'Glad you brought it up, old chap. She stayed on to spend the weekend with her father, but she was due back this morning. I think I'll give her a tinkle right now. Get the matter settled. Excuse me a minute, Victor. I'll just pop back to the production office to make the call. I left some of my notes there.'

Victor rose and crossed to a small table at the far end of the conference room. He poured himself another cup of coffee, dropped in a spoonful of sugar, stirring absent-mindedly, thinking of Francesca. So she had returned to London after all. She had sounded vague about her plans before leaving, had been uncertain about joining them for dinner tonight. *Tonight*. He smiled, feeling a little surge of elation at the thought of seeing her. There was no point in lying to himself. He *had* noticed her absence.

Whistling merrily, he carried the cup of coffee back to the table, sat down and picked up Jerry's photographs of the ballroom at Langley Castle. Jerry had taken a number of different angles, and he could see that the dimensions were exactly right. But it looked to him as if it needed a paint job, and a bit of sprucing up. Beautiful crystal chandelier and candelabra though, he commented to himself. He turned to the rough sketch of the room on which were indicated the possible areas for setting up the cameras, the klieg lights and other mandatory movie equipment. There was obviously plenty of space in which to shoot a superb ballroom scene, a brilliant and glittering scene, with beautifully attired guests waltzing to a small orchestra. Jake agreed with him that this touch of real glamour, Hollywood style, was vital. He sifted through the other views of various interiors, which Jerry had selected for potential scenes, carefully following the action in Nick's screenplay. There was a period bedroom, a handsomely-appointed drawing room and a book-lined library, and the Earl had been most accommodating in agreeing to make all of them available if they were required.

So this is where she was born and raised, he mused, eyeing the photographs again, and from an entirely different point of view, no longer seeing them as possible locations for his film, but as rooms in someone's home. *Her home.* He picked up a coloured picture post card Jerry had purchased in the village of Langley. It was an exterior of the castle itself, a long shot taken from a distance. It showed a portion of a lovely crystal lake, partially bordered by trees, and a verdant, grass-covered hillock sweeping up from the water's edge to the castle. This was poised on the crest of the hill, under a wide and iridescent sky that was china blue and cloudless. The castle was ancient and proud, with its crenellated walls and high-flung towers, the bleakness of the time-worn grey stones softened by rafts of dark-green ivy rippling over much of their surface. To one side of the castle were several grand, stately old oaks and plump clumps of rhododendron bushes abloom with delicate mauve and pink flowers. Victor could see that the shot had been taken in early summer, and there was a pastoral beauty to the scene, a quiet timelessness which was essentially and indigenously English.

He was struck by the imposing beauty of the castle, conscious of all that it stood

199

for, mindful of the things it represented. The evidence leapt out at him, could not be denied; it was an integral part of the ancient history of this country, the symbol of an impressive lineage and of a family name that was centuries old. It hit him more forcibly than ever that Francesca was a true aristocrat of great breeding and background.

Victor wondered, curiously, what it had been like to grow up in a place like this. He had an instant mental picture of that crowded kitchen in the small house in Cincinnati . . . redolent with the delicious aromas of spicy Italian food cooking . . . the walls reverberating with the sounds of laughter raised in raucous competition with the phonograph . . . and above the perpetual ear-splitting din, his mother's strong and loving voice shouting . . . 'Vittorio, Armando, Gina, stopya horsing around. I'ma listening to the greata Caruso!' He smiled, remembering, and a bitter-sweet nostalgia overtook him. What a funny kid he had been. Smart-assed, sassy, street-wise, always fighting, nose always bloodied, experienced too young in the ways of exigent men and a cold, uncaring, indifferent world. And yet despite his clenched fists, eternally raised to do battle, his contentious attitude and his tough, combative approach to life, he had been oddly addicted to the most unlikely things: books, an avid if secretive reader; music; the theatre; and movies. All had been his means of escape, and they had helped to fire his imagination, had, in a sense, helped to shape his life and led him inevitably to where he was today.

I bet *she* had a wholly different childhood, he reflected. Undoubtedly hers must have been a privileged, protected and excessively strictured childhood. He contemplated Francesca, endeavouring to envision her as she must have been then, his mind forming images of a small, angelic, fair-haired little girl, playing hide-and-seek in that great castle, romping with puppies, riding a pony, flying through the air on a garden swing, being taught by a governess. She must have been the most adorable child imaginable.

What the hell, she is still a child! This thought brought him up sharply in the chair. Victor lit a cigarette, glowering. He had better take himself in hand immediately. Thoughts of her had intruded far too frequently of late. But Francesca Cunningham was off limits. Absolutely off limits. He had made that decision weeks ago and nothing and no one could induce him to reverse it. He agreed with Nick's assessment of Francesca. Anyone in their right mind would. She *was* lovely, and charming and bright, and she was a pleasant companion. But he now refused to acknowledge she was anything more than that, and, like Katharine, merely an antidote to boredom and loneliness. The situation would remain exactly the way it was, and under his tight control. He could not afford distractions, or God forbid, any entanglements, particularly with a girl like *her*. The circumstances were all wrong. At this moment, he thought, the cards are stacked against me. Well, so be it. And in the meantime, I have work to do.

Resolutely, Victor began making rapid notes on a yellow pad, listing a number of additional points to take up with Jerry and Jake. After ten minutes, he took off his horn-rimmed glasses and sat back in the chair, glancing around Monarch's conference room, and with distaste. He found the ambience oddly depressing. The dark wood-panelled walls, the heavy mahogany furniture and the expensive wine-coloured carpet were ponderous and ugly, created a cheerless, dismal effect that reminded him of a funeral parlour. Somebody, most likely Hilly,

200

Victor guessed, had felt obliged to hang a number of ornately-framed blow-ups of Monarch's former contract stars on the walls, and this flashy gallery of retouched glossies, now considerably outdated, looked somehow ridiculous and incongruous in the setting which was decidedly Victorian in its overtones.

His thoughts settled on Hillard Steed. Although Hilly was an inveterate and endless memo-writer, and a fearsome perfectionist who tended to nit-pick in the most exasperating way, Victor was happy he had made the deal with Monarch. He had almost been on the verge of signing with Metro when, quite by accident, he had discovered that Mike Lazarus held a large quantity of Metro stock. Whilst this in itself did not mean Lazarus could interfere in any current productions, since he was not on Metro's board, it did give Victor reason to pause, to evaluate and to reassess with caution. He came to the conclusion that Lazarus, being a megalomaniac, was more than likely to be entrenched with the top echelon at the studio. Remembering Nick's anxiety about Lazarus, his terse warnings after the meeting at the Ritz, he had adroitly switched the deal to Monarch, who were poised, and eagerly so, on the sidelines. And in the final analysis, I made a far more advantageous deal, Victor told himself. *Wuthering Heights* aside, he and Hilly had already begun discussions about a number of possible properties they could co-produce, and both of them were thinking in terms of a long association between Monarch and Bellissima. The future looked decidedly rosy. And if Hillard Steed was something of a bugbear, he was, nevertheless, a weight that Victor Mason believed rested lightly on his broad shoulders. There were many other production heads who were much worse, if not downright tyrannical.

Feeling restless, Victor stood up and strolled across the room to the window. He parted the curtains and looked down into South Audley Street. It was still pouring with rain. As usual, he thought, and with resignation, cursing the English weather, wishing he was in Southern California, not necessarily at the ranch, just anywhere the sun was shining. He swung around as Jerry came back into the room, with Jake Watson following closely behind.

Both men looked unusually serious, and Victor at once suspected trouble, which he always did, trouble being endemic to any production. 'What's the problem now, boys? Don't tell me the Earl reneged?'

'No, no. Nothing quite as bad as that, old chap,' Jerry instantly assured him. 'We're all set there. Everything's perfectly okay. Although, speaking of the Earl, he's had an accident. Oh yes, and Francesca's ill,' he mentioned as an afterthought. He rushed on, without drawing breath, 'We *are* going to need the auxiliary generator. Francesca spoke to the bailiff, and the generator at the castle is sound, but he doesn't think it's completely safe to throw the whole load on to it. Jake and I agree. Those kliegs are hellish powerful. Incidentally, she came up with an idea that will help the budget no end –'

'Jesus, Jerry! What's got into you!' Victor exploded, infuriated by his apparent callousness. 'What do you mean, Francesca's sick and the Earl's had an accident? I'd like to know about my friends. Jesus Christ!' He shook his head in disbelief, glowered with ferocity at Jerry, and then swung his irate gaze on Jake. The latter was now grinning, but his face sobered at once.

'Oh, sorry, Victor, old chap,' Jerry apologized nervously, looking abashed. 'I'm afraid I am inclined to get carried away with my budget, aren't I? Yes. Well. Er . . .

201

er . . . nothing to worry about really. The Earl had a fall and fractured a pelvic bone. No problem, he'll be up and about in a couple of weeks. Francesca, poor thing, has a rotten cold. At worst, just a touch of the 'flu.'

Victor sat down at the conference table, surprised at his sense of relief. 'I'm glad to hear neither of them are at death's door,' he remarked, the sarcastic bite in his voice underlining his continuing irritation. 'So . . .' He leaned back in the chair, steepled his fingers and gazed at his two associates over them, his eyes cold. 'Since everything is hunky-dory, why were you both looking as if we had a major crisis?'

Jake said swiftly, 'A *minor* crisis. Hilly Street to be exact. We ran into him in the corridor, and he informed us we can only have two more offices for the production staff. He says he can't release any more space to Bellissima, so we're short of one office.'

'Is that all!' Victor's face was a picture of disgust. 'Let's hope most of our problems are as serious. If they are, we'll breeze through the picture. And there's a very simple solution to this one, Jake. Tell Hilly that Bellissima are taking a suite at Claridge's for the rest of the production staff, and that we're charging it to Monarch. Believe me, Jake, he'll find you that extra office within the next hour, even if he has to turf out one of his executives.'

Jake chuckled. 'It'll be my pleasure. I'll go and see him right now.'

The minute they were alone, Jerry flopped down into a chair. He said softly, 'Hell, Victor, I didn't mean to sound so cold-blooded and heartless . . .' He fidgeted in his seat and ran his hand through his unruly red hair. 'It's not that I'm oblivious to people or their problems,' he explained, selecting his words with care. 'I'm just preoccupied with the film, and I'm afraid this does cloud my judgment . . . But still, I know that's no excuse.' His voice petered out lamely. He was at a loss for words, understanding he had blundered.

Sensing the other man's acute discomfort and embarrassment, Victor smiled, his charming manner restored. 'Relax Jerry. Forget it. I know you didn't mean any harm, and your dedication to the film is commendable. I've no quarrel with you there. And I didn't mean to come down on you so hard.' He laughed self-deprecatingly. 'I guess I'm a bit sensitive in certain areas. I took a bad fall once, on location, and before I could open my eyes, pick myself up and shake the dust off me, I heard the line producer voice the opinion that I'd just screwed up the budget by getting myself killed. He was actually annoyed at my carelessness, and was still exclaiming about all the wasted footage when I threw him a right hook.' Victor roared. 'The bastard hadn't anticipated getting slugged, least of all by a supposed corpse.' He continued to chuckle, recalling the incident and its repercussions.

Jerry joined in, but his laughter was stilted. I sounded downright cavalier, he thought regretfully, and then he cautioned himself yet again to watch his step around Victor Mason, who was obviously an original, and quite unlike the Hollywood stars with whom he had worked in the past. For the most part they had been egomaniacs, and insensitive bastards to boot. Mason continued to surprise him, and in the most unexpected and unpredictable ways. He might be a stern and demanding task master, a tough executive producer who had his eyes smartly peeled and was ten jumps ahead of everyone else, but it was clear he was a superior human being. It appeared he was decent and caring. Nor was he bizarre in an industry in which to be bizarre was more often than not quite normal.

202

As yet, he had not once played the star; he had made no peculiar demands; and he treated everyone as an equal. I've got to hand it to him, he's got immense style, Jerry thought.

Conscious of the growing silence, and in an effort to dispel Jerry's lingering uneasiness, Victor's tone relaxed. 'Anyway, onward and upward. What did you start to say about Francesca having an idea?'

Relieved that the awkwardness between them had evaporated, Jerry said, 'Ah yes, Francesca. Apparently the attics of the castle are stuffed with old furniture, lamps, bric-a-brac, lots of stuff, in fact. And according to Francesca, it's not particularly valuable. She thinks we might be able to use some of it for the film. I'd told her about replacing certain items in the rooms where we'll be shooting. She suggested we sort through the junk – her word, not mine – and select anything we think we can utilize.'

'That's very bright of her,' Victor pronounced, suppressing a small amused smile, inwardly applauding her shrewdness. 'It *will* save us money, providing the stuff is appropriate. Once we've decided on a set designer, let's get him to Langley Castle to make a few choices.' He picked up his gold lighter and toyed with it, and said guardedly, 'What about Francesca? Is she very sick? I feel a bit guilty, Jerry; after all, she obviously caught the cold when she was working for us.'

'She says she sounds much worse than she feels, but personally I think she's down with a bad bout of the 'flu.'

'She is back in London, though? You reached her at the house here?'

'Yes, and not to worry, old chap. I'm sure she's being properly looked after. By the daily cleaning woman. A Mrs Moggs. It was she who answered the 'phone. Very reluctant to get Francesca out of bed. Sounded motherly and capable.' Jerry rubbed his hand across his chin thoughtfully. 'Poor kid, I'm sure she did get a chill up on those moors. Very bleak, and the weather was raw. Maybe I should send her a basket of fruit from Bellissima Productions. That would be a nice gesture, don't you think?'

'Good thought, Jer. Get one of those fancy, super-de luxe jobs from Harte's in Knightsbridge. Now, did Jake tell you about the meeting this afternoon? I'd like you to be there, incidentally.'

Jerry was flattered by this invitation and he smiled broadly and exclaimed, 'He told me about the meeting, but not that you wanted me to come along. Delighted to do so, old chap. I was going out to the studios, but there's no urgency about that trip. And incidentally, Victor, congratulations on signing Mark Pierce. To be honest, I never thought you'd get him. He's a difficult bugger. In fact, I told Jake a few weeks ago that, in my opinion, you were barking up the wrong tree. Just goes to show, you never know in life.' Jerry stared hard at Victor, his eyes narrowed, inquisitiveness flicking into them. 'How the hell *did* you get him?'

Victor smiled lazily. 'I charmed him,' he answered cryptically. How could he properly explain all the ramifications, and Hilary Pierce's willing complicity in Katharine's convoluted schemes and manipulations. And there was no question in Victor's mind that Katharine *had* been extremely manipulative. However, she had achieved the desired results and he was disinclined to probe her *modus operandi*. Besides, she herself had been vague, even uncommunicative, except for saying that Hilary was the key, insisting that he sign Mark's wife to do the clothes. Since

203

Hilary Pierce was undeniably talented and enjoyed a fine reputation in the field of theatrical costume design, he had readily agreed. However, this long *histoire* would sound decidedly peculiar to an unimaginative and prosaic guy like Jerry Massingham, who was evidently more at ease dealing with columns of figures and budgets than people. Victor cleared his throat. 'Sorry, Jerry, I missed that. What did you say?'

'I was just wondering out loud what the meeting was about, and who's coming.'

'You, of course. Jake, Mark, and the casting director. We must make our final decisions today . . . about the overall casting,' Victor said. 'I've also asked Nicholas Latimer to sit in, since Mark might have some script questions. I want to get everything buttoned up today. You do know I've signed Terrence Ogden to play Edgar Linton?'

'So Jake said, before you arrived. Terry'll be good. I've always said he had real film potential. It's a pity he's only made one before, and that it was a flop. Perhaps that's why he's been less than eager to attempt another.'

Both men turned their heads and glanced at the door, as Jake Watson, grinning hugely, hurried in, closing the door swiftly. He leaned against it, and it was obvious he could hardly contain himself. 'I thought Hilly was going to keel over when I told him about getting a suite at Claridge's, Victor. He's scurrying around right now, trying to produce an additional office for us.'

Victor's mouth twitched. 'Let's hope it's large enough.'

Jake gaped at him. 'Oh no, Victor! You wouldn't!' He began to laugh. 'You wouldn't dare refuse it, say it was too small, insist on the suite . . . Would you?' Jake knew the answer almost before the question had left his mouth. He had worked with Victor on five pictures, and they were old friends. He was therefore more than acquainted with his sense of humour, his mischievous penchant for making the top brass squirm, especially those who were arbitrary and pompous, as Hilly was pre-disposed to be.

'I just might,' Victor's black eyes were twinkling with mirth. 'Give him a run for his money. He begged, literally *begged* for *WH* and he hasn't stopped griping about the costs ever since. It would behove him to put his own house in order. Jesus, the waste here is unbelievable.' Faintly, at the back of his mind, Victor heard an echo of Mike Lazarus's words. That son of a bitch was right in many respects, he told himself, recalling the critical comments Lazarus had made about the motion picture industry. Victor looked at Jake. 'But running the London offices of the Monarch Picture Corporation of America is Hilly's problem not ours. Right?' He glanced at his watch. 'I made a few notes when you were both out. I'd like to review a number of things with you before I leave.'

For the next half an hour the three men discussed a variety of matters pertaining to the production and were able to come to several decisions, some only tentative, because Mark Pierce, as the director, would have to be consulted. Along with Victor, he would have the final word on major points. But they were able to cover most of the details regarding the second unit; review the credentials of various other set designers, as well as Harry Pendergast, whom they all agreed sounded the best; touch on appropriate composers for the musical score; also arrive at possible dates for the start of principal photography.

As the discussion drew to its conclusion, Victor said, 'Well, that's about it. I think we're pretty well prepared for this afternoon. Also, by then I'm hoping we'll have a decision from Ossie Edwards. Mark has talked to him several times, and I think he'll come with us. He's the perfect cameraman for the picture, in my opinion.' He stood up, stretching.

Jerry said, 'Yes, I agree. And he'll be in his element in Yorkshire. He's got a painter's eye for landscapes.'

'And beautiful women,' Victor retorted.

'Well, I'm going back to the hotel. I've a few things to take care of States-side.' He paced across the room, paused to pick up his trenchcoat, flung it over his arm. 'Claridge's. At three. See ya, boys.' He gave them a jaunty grin and left.

When Victor stepped into the street, he saw, much to his relief, that it had finally stopped raining. He looked up and down, and spotted Gus leaning against the car, which was parked a short distance away. Gus straightened up when he saw Victor, rushed to open the door and asked, 'Where to now, Guv?'

'Back to Claridge's. Thanks, Gus.' Victor had one foot inside the car when he changed his mind. 'No, on second thoughts, I think I'm going to walk back. I'd like some fresh air. I won't be needing you until this evening, Gus. Why don't you check in around four o'clock though, so I can tell you my plans.'

'Right you are, Guvnor.'

Victor stepped back, and as Gus pulled out and drove off he gazed admiringly at his new Bentley Continental drophead coupé, a recent purchase. It had been expensive, he had to admit, but it was worth it, a gorgeous piece of machinery with its glazed claret finish, pale buff-coloured hood and white-wall tyres. And it was a dream to drive with its automatic gear shift and fluid fly wheel. Victor prided himself on two things: his impeccable taste in automobiles and his keen and discerning eye for thoroughbred horses. He preferred his cars and his horseflesh to be graceful, sleek and fast, and as smooth as velvet.

Reaching Curzon Street, Victor turned left and headed towards Berkeley Square, intending to do a full circle around Mayfair before returning to the hotel. But he drew to a sharp halt when he passed the end of Chesterfield Street. Impulsively, he thought: Maybe I should drop in on Francesca, to check that she really is all right. No harm in that, surely. He turned smartly, retraced his steps and walked leisurely up the street, but as he approached the house he found himself increasing his pace. It had suddenly occurred to him that if he did stop by to see her, she would be annoyed, would regard it as an intrusion, a breach of etiquette. The English were so damned peculiar about certain things. He remembered Katharine's constant mutterings about good form and bad form. To arrive on Francesca's doorstep unannounced would most certainly be considered bad form. He glanced swiftly at the door and with quickening interest, but curbed himself, and strode on determinedly, without stopping. He pushed up into Chesterfield Hill, then veered to the right and continued down Charles Street, aiming for Berkeley Square.

The first thing he noticed when he entered the square were the windows of Moyses Stevens, the renowned florist. They were awash with water, and he paused to look. Mechanical things had always intrigued him and he was constantly tinkering with the machinery at the ranch, although never with cars. As Nick said, costly cars were *verboten* to amateur mechanics like himself.

Water streamed down the glass like a fine, undulating curtain. It was probably being released from hidden ducts or some kind of similar system in the ceiling, then recycled back through intricate piping. He watched it for a moment, fascinated, before pressing closer to the glass, peering through this constantly-moving, liquid curtain, his eyes resting on banks of the most beautiful flowers he had seen for a long time. Colour flamed vividly in a profusion of variegated reds and oranges intermingled with magenta and purple, paled to soft fading yellows and crisp white; and interspersed amongst these brilliant hues and the more fragile tints were innumerable dark and light greens, leaves so luxuriant and shiny they looked as if they had been individually polished to a glossy sheen. A smile touched Victor's lips and his spirits lifted. The array of flowers and plants were like a breath of spring, evoked images of sharp clear sunlight on green meadows, trees newly bursting with tender young leaves, and blue and radiant skies. Such a contrast to this dreary rain-sodden March day, he thought. And if the flowers made him feel light-hearted, then certainly they would bring a smile of pleasure to Francesca's face.

This time there was no hesitation on Victor's part. Decisively, he pushed open the door of the florist's shop and went inside. Instantly his nostrils were assaulted by all manner of mingled scents and the fresh and pungent smell of damp earth and growing greenery. He selected a huge armful of mimosa, brilliant yellow and sweetly fragrant, flown in that morning from Nice, he was informed. He added three dozen scarlet-tipped white tulips from Holland, and several bunches of pale and fragile narcissi from the Scilly Isles. He also bought a china *cachepot* which had been planted with hyacinths, tall, waxy, and a light hazy-blue in colour, but chosen mainly because he could not resist their heady perfume. He knew he had gone overboard with the flowers, especially since Jerry was sending the basket of fruit. But what the hell, he muttered under his breath; everyone expects a movie star to make the grand and extravagant gesture.

The sales lady showed him the tray of cards, so that he could write a message, before she went off to wrap his purchases. Victor took a card and stared at it for several seconds, frowning, wondering what to say. He did not want Francesca to misunderstand the gift of flowers, to misinterpret their meaning, read something into them which did not exist. In the end, after several false starts and wasted cards he penned a bland line, wishing her well, and signed it simply, 'From Nicky and Victor.' He slipped the card in the envelope, sealed it and addressed it clearly. When the sales lady returned with his bill he handed her the card and the money, and asked when the flowers would be delivered. 'Within the hour, Mr Mason,' she said with a polite, rather shy smile. 'You are Victor Mason, aren't you?'

'Yes,' he smiled back, radiating charm.

Glowing, she gave him his change, and went on, in a confiding though deferential manner. 'I just wanted to say that I really enjoy your films, Mr Mason. I go to see all of them. In fact, I'm quite a fan of yours.'

'Why, thank you,' he responded. 'Thanks very much. It's nice to hear.'

'Do come in again, Mr Mason,' she called as he went through the door. He swung his head, waved and told her he would.

That's what I like about the English, he thought, stepping out into the street. They're so courteous. And so absolutely bloody civilized, he added in mental mimicry of Kim's upper-class English voice. He stepped out briskly, heading in the direction of Claridge's, and several times he smiled to himself, although he was not sure why he did so. Nor did he understand the reason for his sudden sense of quiet happiness, a feeling of genuine tranquillity the nature of which he had not experienced for a number of years.

There was a pile of mail and a number of telephone messages waiting for Victor at the hotel. He asked the operator for Nick's suite and sat down. There was no reply. Putting on his glasses, he began to peruse the mail.

Three letters from Beverly Hills gained his attention first. They were from his business manager, his agent and his lawyer. He opened the one from his lawyer with some trepidation, fully expecting it to contain distasteful and distressing news about Arlene and their impending divorce. To his surprise it did not, although it did concern his second wife, Lillianne. Apparently she wanted to sell the Dali, and had asked Ben Challis, his lawyer, to find out if he would be interested in purchasing it from her. He laughed out loud. The painting had been part of *their* divorce settlement. I've got to hand it to her, she's got nerve, he thought, his mouth twitching with amusement. She actually wants me to buy back something which was mine in the first place! I'll be damned. He shook his head, still laughing as he put the letter down. But why not? He did not own much good art and he *had* been attached to the Dali. She must be in desperate need of cash to sell it. As usual. Vaguely he wondered what Lillianne did with money. He had been very generous with her when they had separated. According to Ben, she was constantly in strained financial circumstances, and he had come to her rescue more than once in the past few years.

His second marriage, like his third, had not been particularly happy, but Lillianne was not a bitch, which was more than he could say for the tempestuous and vituperative Arlene, who was currently on a rampage and hell bent on creating a scandal. He sighed, and asked himself why he had had no luck with women since Ellie's death. He continually made dreadful mistakes in his private life, which was in constant upheaval, and yet, funnily enough, he never made the same mistake twice in his profession or in his business dealings. But now I've turned over a new leaf, he muttered, and brushed away these speculations about wives and women, which were not only a waste of time, but irritating. He glanced at the other two letters from Beverly Hills, which were of no great importance, and reached eagerly for the envelope from the travel agency in Bond Street. He opened it quickly and pulled out two first-class airline tickets for Zurich, and his face lit up.

Next week he and Nick were going to Klosters, via Zurich, on a five-day skiing trip, and they were both like excited schoolboys about to sally forth on their first adventurous spree. Victor, being an intensely physical man and accustomed to the most strenuous of outdoor activities, felt increasingly constrained in London, hemmed in and restless as his sedentary existence began to create mounting tension in him. Apart from this, he knew he was out of condition, and gruelling exercise and a thorough workout had become imperative. In a sense, he considered the trip to be a medical necessity, since it would be therapeutic in a number of ways.

Jake had tried to dissuade him from going, being fearful he would break a leg or an arm and consequently throw the picture off schedule. But he had managed to convince the line producer that he was going solely for health reasons, and not riotous fun or distractions of a feminine nature. Finally, he had had to solemnly promise not to take any chances on the slopes, swearing he would stick to the gentler ski runs.

We'll see about that, he thought, smiling with pleasure at the prospect of a few days in the Alps. He and Nick had discovered Klosters two years before, actually through Harry Kurnitz, a writer friend of Nick's, who was an habitué of the place. It was also the favourite gathering ground for a small group of other Americans, all skiing aficionados, in particular the novelists Irwin Shaw and Peter Viertel, and the movie director Bob Parrish.

Victor contemplated the trip with longing. He could hardly wait to leave, remembering how marvellously fit he felt in the mountains, with the cold bracing air stinging his face and the wind at his back as he sped at breakneck speed down the glistening white mountain sides. Apart from wanting the physical exertion which so refreshed and rejuvenated him, and craving the exhilaration and sheer thrill of skiing, he also looked forward to the relaxed evenings of camaraderie. After a day of hard skiing the group gathered in the local tavern, feasted on a few delicious local dishes and then sat around the roaring fire, exchanging exaggerated stories about their prowess in all fields, and drinking cherry-flavoured *Kirschwasser* until dawn broke or they ran out of tall tales.

Thoughts of his favourite Swiss dishes made his mouth water, and he suddenly realized he was hungry. Once again he tried Nick's suite, wanting to tell him the trip was all set, and to ask him what he wanted for lunch, but to his sharp disappointment there was still no answer. He stared at the telephone, trying to recall whether they had made a definite date for a snack before the meeting. He could have sworn they had. Perhaps Nick had misunderstood or forgotten. He called room service and ordered a club sandwich and a cold beer, reminding the waiter who took his order that the kitchen had his precise written instructions for preparing the club sandwich exactly the way he liked it. He walked across to the small portable bar and poured himself a Scotch and soda and, returning to the desk, he leafed through the telephone messages, tossing most of them to one side. He re-read the one from Katharine, asking him to call her at the Caprice Restaurant, where she would be until three o'clock. He did so.

'Hello, Victor,' she said when she came onto the line.

He laughed. 'How could you be sure it was me?'

'No one else knows I'm having lunch here. Victor, about tonight. Francesca's sick and –'

'Yes, I know, honey. Jerry told me.'

'Do you still want to have dinner after the play, as we planned?'

The thought of eating at midnight suddenly palled on him. 'Would you mind if I backed out tonight? I think I ought to concentrate on my lines. But hey, honey, I don't want to leave you high and dry. Listen, I'll talk to Nicky. Why don't the two of you have dinner together?'

'Oh no! I couldn't. I really couldn't.' This was said so emphatically he was surprised. There was an imperceptible hesitation at the other end of the telephone before she explained, in a softer tone, 'I mean, I wouldn't want to impose on him. Let's forget it. I don't mind, honestly, and I should do the same as you, and study my part.'

'Yes, maybe you should, and listen, honey, thanks for being so understanding. I owe you one. Who're you lunching with?' he asked, although more out of a desire to be friendly than any curiosity on his part.

'Hilary Pierce and Terry Ogden. It's a celebration lunch, because we'll all be working on *Wuthering Heights*.'

'Another one! Well, have fun, and I'll talk to you later in the week. We'll fix a date for supper.' They hung up, and Victor sipped his drink, his mind revolving around Katharine. She was the most indefatigable young woman he had ever met. Always busy with her lunches, her parties and her dinners. For ever running and doing. For ever in the biggest hurry. By the same token, her social obligations never seemed to interfere in any way with her work. She was a real professional and supremely dedicated to her craft. Victor also suspected that her social life, which she took very seriously, was totally bound up with her ambition, for he had come to understand that she *was* excessively ambitious and driven and tireless when it came to her career. She seemed to live and breathe it with extraordinary intensity. But there's no harm in that, he reflected, and she's a great girl. The best. A fond smile lingered on his face. He had an extremely soft spot for Katharine, and now their lives were going to be entwined to an even greater extent. She had signed the personal contract with Bellissima, and in so doing had placed herself entirely in his hands; for the next few years he would be guiding her career, all aspects of it. He had strongly advised her to do the Beau Stanton picture, following completion of *Wuthering Heights*, and after listening to him attentively, and reading the script, she had agreed at once to be loaned out to Monarch.

Some of her questions had been so intelligent, so well formulated, so incisive, he had been taken aback for a moment. He had discovered she had an astute head for business, at least in relation to herself and her career. This had not displeased him, rather she had risen in his estimation. Unlike many other young actresses, Katharine was nobody's fool when it came to money, and she had shrewdly put a high value on herself and her services. Yes, he said inwardly, the little lady knows exactly where she's heading. To the top and as rapidly as possible. More power to her, he thought. This was the roughest, toughest business in the world, as he knew from experience, populated with the best and the worst. Hollywood had spawned more than its fair share of opportunistic, ruthless, exigent and venal characters, along with its talented, gifted and dedicated men. Katharine was smart to have her wits about her, even though she would have the benefit of his protection and patronage so long as she was under contract to Bellissima.

Now he made a mental note to talk to Hilly about the loan-out contract with Monarch when he next saw him. There were several special clauses he wanted included. Victor did not envision any problems with Monarch, since they were delighted that the arrangement had been made with comparative ease, as was Beau Stanton. A week ago, Hilly Steed had flown a print of Katharine's screen test to the Coast, and Beau had been bowled over by Katharine's looks and her talent. Who isn't, Victor thought, and pursed his lips, aware that there was at least one person who was not exactly crazy about Katharine Tempest. The waiter appeared with the club sandwich, correctly prepared, he was glad to see, and the beer was really cold, something of a miracle in England. After Victor had consumed both, he returned all his local calls, spoke briefly to his stockbroker in New York, and finally reached his manager at the ranch near Santa Barbara. They talked for a good fifteen minutes, settled a couple of small problems and then, satisfied that everything was under control at Rancho Che Sarà Sarà, Victor said goodbye. He hurried through into the bathroom to freshen up for the impending meeting, relieved he had been able to attend to most of his urgent business for the entire week in one day.

Jerry and Jake were the first to arrive. Ted Reddish, the casting director, followed closely behind, and Mark Pierce knocked on the door at precisely three o'clock. They sat around chatting amiably, waiting for Nick to join them. At twenty minutes past three, growing increasingly exasperated, Victor excused himself and went into the bedroom. He tried Nick's suite again. This time the line was busy. Damn! Victor hurried back into the sitting room.

He said, to the room at large, 'I have a feeling I might not have made it clear to Nick that I needed him at the meeting. He's on the 'phone. I'll just run along and bang on his door. In the meantime, why don't you go over the ground we covered this morning, Jake. And Jerry, let Mark take a look at the location pictures. I'll be right back.'

CHAPTER TWENTY-TWO

The key was in the door. Victor knocked and opened it, called, 'It's me, Nicky,' and walked in without waiting to be invited.

Nick was standing in the sitting room with his back to the door, talking on the telephone. 'All right. Do your best. Thanks. Goodbye.' He hung up.

'Did you forget the meeting? Everyone else has arrived and we've been waiting for –' Victor began, and stopped as Nick swung around. Nick's face was haggard and, despite his tan, there was a greyish cast to his complexion.

'What is it, Nicky?' Victor asked, frowning. He searched his friend's face. The pain in Nick's eyes leapt out at him.

Nick shook his head, lifted his hands in a gesture of futility and sat down on the sofa without answering. He looked as if he was about to say something, but then his mouth drooped and he remained silent. He took a cigarette and lit it shakily, and there was an air of bleakness about him.

'Jesus Christ, Nick, what's happened?'

After a moment, Nick lifted his head and sighed. Finally, in a constricted voice he said: 'I was sitting here. Minding my own business. Working on the new novel. Feeling great. Just sitting here. Working. And then . . . and then the call came through –' He was not able to continue and his bright blue eyes darkened. He brushed his hand across them and looked away. He took a long breath. 'It's

Marcia, Vic. She –' Once more he paused, the rest of the sentence stuck in his throat.

Victor's eyes had not left Nick's face. 'What about your sister Marcia, Nicky? Is something wrong with her?'

Nick moved his head from side to side as if he was trying to deny an awful fact, one he found unacceptable. There was another silence before he replied, in a shaken voice, 'She's dead, Vic. Marcia's dead.'

'Oh my God! No!' Victor stared at Nick stupefied. Speechlessly he sat down heavily in the chair opposite, and a numbing coldness washed over him. Very slowly, he said, 'I don't understand . . . we spoke to her the other day.' He coughed, clearing his throat. 'What happened?' He faltered, was incapable, at this moment, of saying another word.

Nick said dully, 'A freak accident. Marcia was walking down Park Avenue on Sunday afternoon. Yesterday. Going to my mother's. A stinking lousy car went out of control. Mounted the sidewalk. It slammed into Marcia at full force. They got her to the hospital at once. She was still alive. But the internal injuries . . .' He shook his head. 'She died at five o'clock this morning.'

Victor's face reflected his shock. 'Oh Nick, Nick, I'm so sorry. So very sorry. What a tragic, senseless thing to happen.'

'Why her, Vic?' Nicky demanded, anger spilling out of him. 'In God's name, *why?*' His tone rose. 'She was only twenty-two. Twenty-two, for Christ's sake! Her life was just beginning. She was only a baby, and she was so full of life, and good, and loving, and generous in every conceivable way. And she never hurt anybody in her life. It's not fair, Vic!'

'I know, Nick, I know.' Victor's voice was gentle and understanding. He bent towards Nick. 'What can I do for you? How can I help you to –'

Nick seemed not to hear these words. He cried 'God damn it! God damn it to hell!' Grief and rage took hold of him and he began to pound the back of the sofa with his clenched fist, and his face was ringed with a wrenching hurt.

Watching him, Victor flinched, and he wondered desperately how to assuage Nick's suffering, but he knew he could do nothing. His heart went out to his friend, and then it clenched with sorrow and he was besieged by a terrible helplessness.

'I can't believe it,' Nick cried. 'I just can't. I keep telling myself it's some awful mistake.' He leapt to his feet, staring directly at Victor, 'My baby sister. She's . . . she's gone.' He half ran across the floor in the direction of the bedroom.

Victor followed him, propelled by a need to help Nick, seeking words of consolation. But words were meaningless, utterly worthless. He shivered involuntarily, remembering. Remembering Ellie.

Nick was in the bathroom, standing with his head pressed against the tiled wall, his shoulders hunched over, his narrow shoulder blades protruding through the thin blue cotton shirt. He looked so vulnerable, young and defenceless, and Victor wanted to take Nick in his arms and comfort him as one would a small child in distress. But he did not move. He knew Nick was struggling to contain his emotions, wishing to be strong, fighting back his tears, believing tears were unmanly. But Victor knew the ability to weep was rooted in immense strength, had nothing to do with weakness at all.

'Let it out, Nicky,' he finally said from the doorway. 'Let it out. Don't hold the

211

grief back like this. It won't do you any good. Please, Nicky.' He walked in and put his hand on Nick's shoulder.

There was a muffled gasp and Nick leaned closer to the wall, hiding his face, and then unexpectedly he spun around to face Victor, his expression baffled, beseeching. A sob rose up in him and he brought his hands to his face. Victor stepped closer and put his arm around Nick, and again there was nothing he could say except, 'I'm here, Nicky, I'm here, old buddy.'

After a while, Nick regained some of his self-possession. 'I'll be all right, Vic,' he muttered, forcing the words out. 'I'll be all right.' He moved away from Victor and grabbed a towel, pressing it to his face. His voice was low as he said, 'Let me be for a while, Vic.'

'Sure, Nicky.' Victor went back into the sitting room and flung himself into the nearest chair disconsolately. Automatically he lit a cigarette and sat smoking. He was filled with deep sadness. He understood why Nick found his sister's death hard to believe. He was having a problem comprehending it fully himself. Death was always unacceptable to those left behind to grieve, but in this instance it was the unexpectedness of it, the senselessness of the accident, which so appalled.

Marcia, that tall, lovely girl, sunny and outgoing in disposition, the replica of Nick, with the same blonde hair and his clear blue, mischievous eyes. To Victor, Marcia had always been a golden girl, bubbling with irrepressible laughter and optimism about life. He had grown extremely attached to Marcia over the years, and they had become great buddies when she had come out to the ranch to spend part of her summer vacations with Nick and him. His sons, Steve and Jamie, had also been smitten with her, following her around like devoted puppy dogs, and she had reciprocated their youthful adoration with a tenderness that had been infinitely touching to him. He had spoken to her only on Saturday. Saturday night for God's sake, and from this very suite. It did not seem possible that she was lying in some hospital morgue in New York. He closed his aching eyes, recoiling from the horror of it.

Nicoletta, named for Nick, had been one year old on Saturday, and the family had gathered at Marcia's apartment for the child's first birthday party. Nick, the baby's godfather, had telephoned New York, wanting to be part of the celebration even from long distance, anxious to speak to his beloved Marcia, and to make certain the gifts for his little niece had arrived in time. What a happy occasion it had been, and who could have known it presaged such sorrow. Victor thought of the child, motherless now, and of Hunter, Marcia's young husband, and of Nick and Marcia's parents. He stubbed out the cigarette and dropped his head in his hands, endeavouring to marshal his troubled thoughts.

Victor jumped up, shaking himself, making a supreme effort to quell the despondency which had descended on him, and with great deliberation he walked around the room, turning on all the lamps. He forced his mind to work on practicalities. Apart from being grief-stricken, Nick was suffering from shock, and it was obvious that someone had to set the wheels in motion to get him back to the States immediately. He would have to do Nick's thinking for him. Victor ran the priorities through his head: plane reservation. Packing. Gus to take them to the airport. Car at Idlewild when Nick arrived.

Oh God, the production meeting. Victor grimaced. They were all waiting for him back in his suite. He had better speak to Jake at once. He moved forward to the desk, intending to call Jake, when Nick walked into the sitting room.

Nick's eyes were red-rimmed, but they were dry, and on the surface he appeared to be calmer and in control of himself. 'Sorry I broke down like that, Victor. I'd been pushing the grief back ever since I heard. You unplugged the dam.'

Victor nodded, understanding. 'Perhaps it's for the best, Nicky,' he said. He went over to the sideboard, poured Scotch into two glasses and carried them over to the coffee table. 'Come and sit down, and drink this. Then we'd better get you organized, and quickly. When are you planning to leave for New York? Have you made a plane reservation yet?'

'That's the problem,' Nick replied. 'I went to all the airlines at lunch time. I'm having trouble getting out of here tonight. I was talking to PAN AM when you arrived. They're fully booked. So are TWA and BOAC. I'm on standby with those three.' He picked up the Scotch and drank most of it in one gulp.

Victor said, 'I'd better get Jerry to handle the reservation, and I'll tell Jake to go ahead with the meeting.'

'Oh hell, Vic, the meeting went right out of my mind. I'm sorry –'

'Forget it,' Victor interrupted. He reached for the 'phone and asked for his suite. Jake answered. Victor said, 'You'll have to have the production meeting without me, Jake. Nick's had very tragic news. His sister has been killed in a car accident. I'm going to stay with him until he leaves.' There was a silence as Victor listened, and then he murmured, 'Yes, yes, Jake. Thank you. I'll tell him. Now, let me speak to Jerry a minute, please.

'Hello, Jerry,' Victor said. 'Jake told you about Nick's sister? Yes, thank you. Look, Nick's having problems getting a plane to New York tonight. He's on standby with PAN AM, TWA and BOAC. Can you pull any strings? Rustle up a seat?' Victor waited, nodding to himself. 'Great. Great. Get to it right away. Call me back as soon as you know something. Oh and Jerry, Gus will be checking in imminently. Tell him to come over to the hotel and wait. I'll want him to take us to the airport later, but he'd better be on hand in case there are any errands to do.' He hung up, his hand resting on the receiver.

Nick said, 'Please, Vic, go back to the meeting. I'll be fine.'

'Are you crazy? I'm staying with you until you step onto that plane. I wouldn't let you be alone. Jerry said to tell you how sorry he is, Nick, as you probably gathered.' Victor did not wait for a response, but hurried on. 'He says he's got a terrific contact at BOAC, and he's calling him right now. We'll get you out, don't worry. Now, have you eaten anything at all today?' he asked, his tone brisk.

'No.' Nick made a face. 'I don't think I can get anything down.'

'You ought to try. This might be the last chance you have to eat for a number of hours. How about some soup at least. You should put something inside you.'

'Okay.' Nick could not be bothered to argue, and he also knew Victor was right. It would be an interminable flight and when he arrived in New York there would be his parents and Hunter to comfort and sustain. And the ritual of death, of mourning, would begin. He closed his eyes.

Victor observed him in silence, and with concern, and then he picked up the 'phone. When room service finally responded he ordered hot consommé, two soft-boiled eggs, toast and coffee. He put down the receiver, poured another Scotch for Nick, and took it over to him.

'Here, drink this, old buddy. It'll do you good,' Victor said in the softest of voices, handing him the glass. 'Would you like me to fly to New York with you?'

'God no, Vic! Thanks anyway, and it's wonderful of you to offer, but I'll cope.' There was a faint darkening in Nick's face, and then it became very still. He said slowly, 'Does it ever get any easier to bear?'

'Yes. Eventually. You bear it because there's no alternative.' Victor's eyes rested briefly on Nick, were gentle in their wisdom and compassion. He looked towards the window, plunged for a moment in his thoughts, and then he went on, 'Death is the absolute loss, Nick. And so you come to accept it, hard as that is to do. It's not like a lost love or a broken friendship, which perhaps can be regained in the future. Death is final.' He clenched his hands together in his lap, and the look he gave Nick was full of love and friendship and sympathy. 'I went crazy with grief after Ellie died, as I've told you before. There wasn't a day I didn't think about her, for years, and I still think about her now, and very often. In a way she lives on in me, and in the boys. I've derived a degree of comfort from that, although perhaps you're not able to understand what I mean at this moment. Your grief is too raw, and perhaps I shouldn't even bring it up now . . . it's cold comfort really . . .' His voice trailed off, and he sat back, wondering if he had said far too much, and far too soon.

Nick did not speak, and sat back, staring abstractedly at the wall, brooding to himself, a vacant look in his eyes. He took a sip of the drink eventually, and pulling himself together, he said, 'I'm grateful you told me to get some of my grief out, Vic, because I'm going to have to clamp down on it for a while. My parents, Hunter, they're devastated. They're going to need my courage. I'm going to have to be strong for them, to help them get through this.'

'Yes,' Victor said, 'yes, I know.'

Nick stood up. 'I think I'd better attempt to pack.' He went through into the bedroom and opened the wardrobe door, looking over his clothes, seeking a dark suit. For the funeral. *Marcia's funeral.* His hand trembled as he reached for the hanger. He blinked back the sudden rush of tears and wished then that the memories of Marcia would go away. But they kept flooding back relentlessly – things he had not realized had been important to him until now. It was curious how the trivial could mean so much, could be so significant and also so crippling in the crushing pain it caused.

They did not talk much on the way to London airport. Occasionally Victor stole a surreptitious look at Nick, but said nothing, not wishing to disturb him, preferring instead to leave him to his own ruminations.

Nick's expression was tight and sombre, and a deadly calm had settled over him. He was exercising an iron-clad control, preparing himself for the ordeal awaiting him in New York. He had been able to subdue his own grief temporarily and was drawing on all his inner resources for courage and in order to give consolation and support to his parents and Hunter.

All of a sudden, just before they reached the airport, Nick said, in a dim, yet oddly contained tone, 'Religion is ridiculous, isn't it?'

214

Startled from his own reverie, Victor looked across at him with interest. 'What do you mean?'

Nick said, 'What I really meant was, religious prejudice is ridiculous. I was thinking of my father and how he objected to Hunter because he wasn't Jewish. He didn't think Marcia should marry him. In fact, he fought their relationship right up to the day of the wedding. But in the end, Hunter Davidson III, a goy and therefore not appropriate as a husband for my sister, turned out to be a better son to my father than I ever was –'

'I wouldn't say that,' Victor interrupted swiftly.

'Well, Hunt went into the bank, which is more than I did, and he abides by all the traditions my father holds dear, leads a very proper and conservative life, is totally dedicated to his work, is devoted to my parents. He not only turned out to be a marvellous husband, but he also gave my father a grandchild, which is another thing I haven't done.'

'But your father is very proud of you, Nick, and of your achievements.'

'Yes, I suppose he is now, but he would have been much *happier* if I'd followed in his footsteps, if I'd conformed. After my brother Ralph was killed at Okinawa, I inherited his mantle. Dad set his heart on my becoming a banker, carrying on the family tradition and one day heading the family bank, leading a very upright life. He expected me to marry a nice Jewish girl, have a couple of beautiful kids, join all the right clubs –' He stopped and shrugged. 'I think I disappointed him in so many respects.'

Victor said, 'But you chose to go your own way, Nicky, and dwelling on all this now serves no good purpose. Parents do have enormous expectations of their children, but usually they are expectations which cannot be met under any circumstance. Not only that, parents can't live their children's lives for them. Even thinking that this is possible is unrealistic, leads to nothing but resentment, bitterness and eventual heartache. Maybe your father was disappointed initially, but he's too wise not to understand that permitting you to do what you wanted to do has brought *you* happiness and fulfilment. And basically, all most parents ever want is for their children to be happy.'

'I guess you're right.' Nick leaned forward and glanced out of the car window. 'We're almost at the airport,' he said. 'I don't know when I'll be back, Vic. We have to sit *shivah* for at least three days after the funeral, and I think I should stay on in New York for a few weeks. To be with my father and mother.'

'Yes, you must, Nick. And please don't worry about the film. Mark Pierce loved the script, and if there are any changes they'll only be minor.'

'You can always call me, should there be any problems, and I'll dictate the revisions. I can –' Nick inhaled quickly. 'Oh God, Vic, I've just remembered our trip to Klosters. I'm sorry. You were really looking forward to it.'

'Hey come on, Nick, that's not important. We'll do it another time. Don't worry about me. You've enough to contend with right now. And remember, if you need anything, just pick up a 'phone. Are you sure I can't arrange a limousine to meet you at Idlewild?'

'Positive. Thanks for offering though. When I spoke to Hunt, to let him know my arrival time, he said he'd send my father's car and driver.'

'Okay.'

As the Bentley slid noiselessly to a standstill at the terminal entrance, Nick turned to face Victor. 'Don't come in. You'll be surrounded. You know what it's like when you show that ugly mug of yours.' He grabbed Victor's hand. 'Thanks, Vic, thanks for everything.'

Victor grasped Nick by the shoulders and hugged him affectionately. 'So long, Nicky.'

On the drive back to London Victor Mason sat immersed in his thoughts, which mostly centred on Nick Latimer. He thought of the long and lonely journey he was about to embark on, of the tragic reason for his unexpected return to the States, of the sorrowful period of time ahead of his friend. Victor was still having trouble reconciling himself to Marcia's death. It was inconceivable that she was gone. How unpredictable life was, how precarious, and there were no guarantees about anything. Except for that ultimate guarantee. Death. We're all so vulnerable, so fragile. We're here one moment, gone the next. He thought of the hours he wasted on inconsequential things, hours which once frittered away could never be regained nor relived, and he was filled with regret about the precious time he had so carelessly squandered in the past.

It was then he made a solemn promise to himself: From now on every hour of his life would count, and he would live every day to the fullest, for who knew about tomorrow, and what it would bring. Indeed, who knew how many tomorrows there would be.

CHAPTER TWENTY-THREE

Francesca pushed open the kitchen door cautiously and was assailed by the waves of heat and steam that billowed out. She recoiled, stepping back for a split second, and then edged inside, peering through the vaporous haze. She said, 'I wish you'd let me do something to help.'

Victor, who was poised in concentration over the Aga stove, swung around at the sound of her voice. She saw at once that his face was flushed and that he was the picture of domesticity in the kitchen, where all manner of foodstuffs lay scattered on the table and the counter top near the sink. He had taken off his tie, his sleeves were rolled up, and he wore one of her dainty cotton aprons tied around his waist. She hid a smile, and ventured, 'Can I at least stir one of the pots for you?'

He shook his head slowly, giving her his lazy smile. 'Negative. There's a line about too many cooks spoiling the broth that happens to be the truth. Besides, you don't think I'd let an *English* girl tamper with my specialities, do you?' he teased. 'I told you earlier only a *paesano* knows how to cook a real Italian dinner. So go away, and let me get back to my culinary creations.' He grinned at her and put down the wooden spoon he was holding. 'There is one thing you can do though.' He strode to the refrigerator and opened the door, handing her a bottle of pink champagne.

'Stick this in the ice bucket, over there on the table. And please go back to the drawing room. I'll join you in a few minutes. It's far too steamy in here, and I don't want you catching another cold after I've just cured the last one.'

Francesca shivered as she went through the adjoining dining room, acknowledging to herself that Victor had been right. Earlier in the evening, when he had first arrived, he had pronounced the dining room chilly and hardly the ideal spot for her after a bout of influenza and several days lying prostrate in bed. He had suggested they should have supper in the drawing room, and after she had produced a folding card table, he had covered it with a red gingham cloth, which he had found in the kitchen cupboard, and brought two chairs from the dining room.

Francesca eyed the table now as she walked in with the champagne. He had placed it to one side of the fireplace and set it himself, refusing to let her help, had even added a silver candlestick with a red candle and a tulip in a bud vase, charming touches she had not anticipated from a man, least of all him. Once this task had been accomplished, Victor had disappeared into the kitchen to unpack the bags of groceries he had bought in Soho, and to start preparing the meal. She had trailed after him, volunteering to help, but he had resolutely shooed her away and literally closed the door in her face. Francesca had shrugged helplessly. She had come to understand that Victor Mason could be very assertive, and just a mite overpowering. At the beginning of the week she had felt debilitated and had been unable to maintain her wails of protest, had allowed him to take charge in his masterful way. Tonight she was feeling far too happy to fight him, enjoying the attention he was showering on her.

She examined the cork in the bottle, decided to let Victor struggle with it, and moved in the direction of the fireplace. Seating herself in the wing chair, she smoothed down her skirt, adjusted the collar on her sweater and sat back, propping her feet on the fender, waiting for him to emerge from the kitchen. The heat from the blazing logs in the hearth had brought out the varied scents of the flowers and, to Francesca, the drawing room smelled and looked like a garden bower in mid-summer, the profusion of lovely blooms enhancing the inherent beauty of the charming room, so mellow and tranquil in the firelight. Several great Chinese porcelain vases spilled with masses of the scarlet-tipped white tulips, the pale and fragile narcissi flourished in a number of smaller china bowls, whilst the Limoges *cachepot* planted with hyacinths stood in the centre of the coffee table. The mimosa had also been beautiful, and delicately fragrant, but the blossoms had faded and dried out quickly, as they always did, and reluctantly she had thrown them away on Thursday.

Francesca leaned forward and breathed deeply over the hyacinths, inhaling their exquisite scent. It struck her that there was something infinitely luxurious about the fresh flowers at this time of the year, particularly since it still seemed like winter to her, with the perpetual thunder-storms and gales and dark overcast skies that had not lifted all week. She touched the smooth waxy petals of the hyacinths, recalling her excitement when the delivery van had arrived from Moyses Stevens on Monday afternoon. She had held her breath as she tore open the envelope and pulled out the card, believing it to be from Victor, for only he would have been so lavish and sent a veritable truckload of flowers. Her face had dropped when she read the signatures, and severe disappointment had followed sharply on the heels of expectation, crushing her joy. She was quite certain Nick had been the initiator of the gesture, that they were actually his gift, and only his, and that he had simply included Victor's name as a matter of course, or perhaps as a form of courtesy.

Now Francesca's expression changed, became pensive, her mind fastening on Nicholas Latimer. Her thoughts were sad as she envisioned his grief, knowing how anguished she would feel if her beloved Kim had been so tragically killed. When Victor had told her about Marcia's accident, she had asked him for Nicky's address in New York. She had immediately written a short but expressive letter, offering her sympathy and condolences, filled with genuine affection and concern for Nick, who had become such a dear friend. Victor had posted the letter for her the next day. It seemed to Francesca that Victor had been doing so many things for her this past week, and certainly she owed her rapid recovery to his devoted ministrations. She smiled. He had clucked over her and coddled her, and was continuing to do so, and she wished with all of her young heart that it would never end. But of course it would. That was an inevitability, since her health was practically restored to normal.

Francesca sat back in the chair and closed her eyes, contemplating Victor Mason, whom she now recognized was a most remarkable man, her mind dwelling on his many kindnesses to her.

Victor had made his presence more potently felt than ever several days ago, on Tuesday. That morning he had telephoned Francesca to ask how she was feeling. She had said she was a bit better, but it had not taken much insight on his part to realize that she was resorting to a white lie. Francesca had sounded dreadful with her raw, raspy throat and nagging cough. A string of pertinent questions, and a great deal of persistence from him, had left her no option but to confess she had not been visited by a doctor and that there was no one to take care of her. Under his fierce pressure, she had admitted that Mrs Moggs, who only came twice a week to clean the house, would not be returning until Friday. Imperiously brushing aside her warnings about germs and the possibility of his catching the 'flu, Victor had announced he was coming over to see her. A short while later he had arrived, armed with antibiotics and cough mixture from the doctor used by Monarch Pictures, lemons, oranges and two large glass jars of chicken soup from Les Ambassadeurs.

Francesca had been self-conscious and embarrassed when first greeting him in the hall, aware that she was looking ghastly. Here she was, confronting the only man for whom she wanted to be beautiful, and he was seeing her at her very worst. Her face had been pale and drawn, her nose red, her eyes watering, her hair rumpled and unkempt. Victor had not seemed to notice her appearance, which, now that she thought about it, was quite normal behaviour for him. He had always been oblivious to the way she looked, had never once paid her a compliment.

Taking a cursory glance at her as they stood in the hall, Victor had bundled her back to bed without delay, waiting until she was comfortably settled before hurrying downstairs. He had left her bedroom door ajar, and faintly, in the distance, she had heard him rattling around in the kitchen. Not long after, he had returned, marching into her room unceremoniously, carrying a large tray laden with a jug of freshly squeezed orange juice, a Thermos flask of hot tea spiced with lemon and honey, and the various medicines. With great firmness, he had ordered her to take the antibiotics three times a day, drink plenty of the orange juice and the hot tea, and, as he had left, he had told her the chicken soup was in a pot on the stove, ready to be reheated that evening.

To Francesca's surprise, Victor had visited her every day thereafter, and he had never once arrived empty handed, usually bringing something special which had been prepared in the kitchens of Les Ambassadeurs. She knew that John Mills, the owner of the private club, was a friend of Victor's, and apparently he was most obliging when it came to supplying nourishing dishes for a sick girl. Although Victor was inclined to be somewhat domineering with her, he was also gentle at times, and very kind, concerned about her well being. He had also adopted a rather matter-of-fact manner whilst tending to her needs, and this had enabled Francesca to ignore her unattractive appearance, to forget it really. And anyway, she was feeling so awful those first few days, she no longer cared what he actually thought, since she knew he had no interest in her as a woman.

Katharine had been equally sweet and devoted. She had telephoned every day, but unlike Victor, she had listened to reason and had not insisted on visiting Francesca, for she was worried as always about her health, and fearful of getting sick in view of her career commitments. Katharine's first call had been early on Monday evening, just before she had gone on stage, and she had been delighted when Francesca had told her about the basket of fruit from Jerry and Bellissima Productions, and the flowers from Nick. The next day Katharine had sent a selection of the latest books from Hatchards, with a charming and amusing note which had made Francesca smile with affection for her friend. That same afternoon, when she had 'phoned to see how Francesca was, Katharine had wanted to bring soup and other food to the Chesterfield Street house.

'I'll leave everything on the doorstep and run away, so you don't have to worry about infecting me with your germs,' Katharine had said, laughing. 'Please let me do this for you, darling, I'm so anxious about you.'

'Thank you, Katharine, but I'm all right, honestly I am,' Francesca had responded swiftly. 'And I don't need anything. Victor was here earlier today, and he brought fresh oranges and chicken soup and medicines.'

There had been a sudden silence before Katharine had exclaimed, 'That's the least he could do! After all, you caught that cold when you were working for him. In my opinion, he should have arranged for someone to be there looking after you. He knows you're all alone.'

Francesca had been startled by this comment, considering it quite extraordinary. 'But he doesn't have to do anything at all,' she had said slowly. 'I'm not his responsibility. And it really isn't his fault that I got ill when I was scouting locations in Yorkshire. Gracious, Katharine, I could have caught 'flu before I left London, for all I know.'

Katharine had murmured something about not agreeing, but then they had quickly gone on to talk about Kim, her father's accident, and a number of other matters.

After they had hung up, Francesca had felt unusually depressed and more miserable than ever, and she could not help dwelling on Katharine's words. Of course she was right in what she had said. Victor was simply being a considerate employer, and that was all. Francesca's hopes that his feelings towards her had somehow radically changed were instantly dashed to the ground. For the rest of the week she steeled herself to his presence, curbing her vivid imagination, and exercising as much control over her emotions as she could muster. This had not been an easy task, since Francesca was enormously attracted to him physically, and infatuated with him to such an extent that he totally occupied her thoughts, and in consequence she was vulnerable to him in every way. It was for these reasons that she assiduously avoided mentioning his name to Katharine again, not wishing to hear her friend's pragmatic reasons for Victor's attentiveness, which would have been like pouring vinegar into the wound. She preferred instead to believe that, if nothing else, he came to see her out of friendship.

Francesca did have one consolation. Victor had unexpectedly dropped his jolly, fatherly posture, and he was also much less distant with her; and if he treated her rather like a chum, this was infinitely more acceptable than being cast in the role of a child. By Friday she had begun to realize that a new easiness existed between them, that there had been a lifting of certain barriers. It soon occurred to her that it would have been abnormal if it had been otherwise. After all, there was nothing more intimate than taking care of someone who was sick, which, out of necessity, bred a certain kind of familiarity and closeness. Francesca had been extremely touched by his thoughtfulness, his solicitousness, and she had begun to count on his visits, even though he kept these to the point, and relatively short. Until yesterday.

When he arrived on Friday, just after lunch, he had been delighted to see her up and dressed, and looking more like her old self. Mrs Moggs, full of oohs and ahs about meeting a famous film star, had made coffee for them, and they had sat chatting together in the drawing room for almost two hours. He had told her about the progress of the film, recounting his hectic week in the greatest detail, and with an enthusiasm that was almost boyish in its eagerness. A few minutes before he had taken his leave, he had pronounced her fit enough to enjoy a splendid Italian dinner, which, he explained, he intended to make for her on Saturday night, informing her he was not only a terrific cook but an inspired one at that. Francesca had laughed gaily, and graciously acquiesced to his idea, sheathing her excitement at the prospect of spending an evening alone with him. She had thought of nothing else since then, wishing the hours away, filled with a breathless, nervous anticipation.

You've been an absolute idiot, living in a fool's paradise, Francesca unexpectedly thought, and this brought her up sharply in the chair. She gazed wistfully into the fire, her amber eyes bright and beautiful, despite the sadness now flickering in them. Tonight is the beginning of the end of our new relationship, she said to herself with dim resignation, suddenly confronting reality, preparing herself to face the pain this inevitably brought. They would drink the pink champagne, eat the Italian specialities he was so carefully preparing, consume quantities of the Soave he had brought, and he would be charming and kind, as he had been for the entire week. And then he would leave and things would never be the same again. It would be over – their newfound intimacy and easiness with each other. He would undoubtedly assume his remote and avuncular posture, and she would be . . . what would she be in his eyes? Solely an appendage to Katharine, and the little girl, not to be taken seriously.

But I'm a woman, she sighed. If only *he* could see that. Francesca stood up and crossed to the mirror hanging on the wall between the two soaring windows. She peered at herself closely, immediately admiring the new sweater she was wearing. At least she looked smart. The sweater was chic and expensive, and it had arrived that morning from Harte's department store in Knightsbridge, a gift from the ever-generous Katharine. 'My way of saying thank you for your help with the screen test,' the note had read. It was made of scarlet cashmere, soft and silky, with loose, three-quarter-length sleeves and a draped cowl neckline that fell prettily around her long neck. Francesca had fastened an antique gold pin on the collar, and she wore gilt hoop earrings that matched the gilt-metal chain belt around the waist of her black felt skirt, bouffant over the stiff buckram petticoat. She tilted her head slightly, regarding her reflection critically. A little makeup, adroitly applied, had done wonders for her, and that afternoon she had washed her hair and towelled it dry in front of the drawing room fire. It fell to her shoulders, smooth and straight and unstyled, and now she wished she had attempted to set it or had piled it up in the more sophisticated pompadour she sometimes favoured. She looked so *young* with it hanging in simple folds around her face. On the other hand, it *was* clean and shone golden-bright in the muted light from the lamps. If only I were beautiful like Katharine, she thought, staring hard at herself, dissatisfied with the face that stared back. It was pale and attenuated. She rubbed her cheeks, wanting to bring a touch of colour to their pallor, regretting she had not been more generous with the rouge, and then she smoothed her hair back away from her face.

'You look very lovely.'

Francesca started and turned quickly. Victor was standing in the doorway, his hands resting on the door jamb, regarding her thoughtfully. Mortified to have been caught preening and primping in front of the mirror, she felt the sudden heat flooding into her face.

'Thank you,' she finally said in a tiny voice, and looked away, moving closer to the drinks chest under the ornate gilded mirror. 'I was about to open the champagne,' she explained, and started to untwist the wire on the cork, averting her flushed face.

'Here, let me do that,' he said, striding into the room. In an instant he was beside her, his hands over hers on the bottle. His touch was like an electric shock, and for a moment her fingers remained immobile under his. She gazed down at his hands, tanned and large, and at his strong sunburned arms lightly speckled with dark hairs, and her throat tightened with desire. She felt the heat rush into her face again, and, not daring to look at him, she extracted her hands gently and went to the fireplace, suddenly conscious of a trembling in her legs. I'll never get through the evening, she told herself shakily, gratefully sinking into the chair. You stupid fool, she inwardly chastised herself and, swallowing hard, she took a firm grip on her emotions. And then she thought: Enjoy this evening for what it is. Don't dwell on what it might be. That will be self-defeating, ruinous.

He was standing over her then, offering her the glass of champagne, smiling affably, his dark eyes warm. She looked up at him timorously and smiled back, taking the glass, relieved that her equilibrium was partially restored, that her hand was steady, her eyes no longer moist.

They said 'cheers' in unison, and Victor sat down on the sofa, lit a cigarette and remarked, 'I forgot to ask you how your father is doing? Is he on the mend?'

'Yes, he's much better, thank you, and being the model patient –'

'Like father, like daughter,' he interjected with a lopsided grin.

'Yes, I suppose so,' she murmured softly, and went on, 'I haven't really thanked you properly for looking after me, Victor. You've been super. So thoughtful and kind. I know I owe my speedy recovery entirely to you, and your . . . your coddling.'

'I was glad to do what I could.'

Francesca rose, glanced at him, flashed him a fleeting smile. 'I have something for you. A small gift.'

'Hey, that's not necessary,' he began. She stopped at the Sheraton bookcase and opened the glass doors. Admiration flicked onto his face. She's got the greatest legs in the world. She's *verboten*, he reminded himself. Watch it, Mason. He dragged his eyes away.

She was back in a moment and handed him a small package, wrapped in decorative floral paper and tied with a silver ribbon. 'I hope you like it, Victor.'

'You didn't have to do this, you know,' he muttered, nevertheless looking pleased as he began to unwrap the gift, filled with curiosity. He found himself holding a copy of *Wuthering Heights*, and he saw at once that it was very old. The wine Moroccan-leather binding was faded, and the pages, as he turned them slowly, crackled dryly, were yellowed at the edges by the passing of time, and fragile. He lifted his eyes and looked across at Francesca and shook his head. 'I can't accept this. It's obviously an antique and rare, and most probably very valuable –'

'It's a first edition, and it is quite rare. If you look at the frontispiece, you'll see the date, 1847. And you must take it. I want you to have it. I'll be insulted if you refuse.'

'But it must be worth a great deal of money. What about your father? I mean, won't he object? What will he say?'

Francesca stiffened, irritated by his inference that she could not act without parental consent. He's treating me like a child again, she thought angrily, but said, as mildly as possible, 'It has nothing to do with my father. The book belongs to me. It's from a collection of first edition classics my mother left me, which was handed down from her grandfather, Lord Drummond, to her father, and so on. That happens to be my mother's family crest on the cover, not Daddy's. And so you see, I can give it away if I wish. I want you to have it as a memento of the film.'

Victor sat back, gripping the book, unaccountably at a loss for words, infinitely moved by the gift, and not the least because it was something so very personal, part of her history, a cherished heirloom that had been passed down in her family over the years. He leafed through the pages again, his expression introspective, and for a reason he did not comprehend, a lump came into his throat. After a long moment, he said, 'Thank you. I shall treasure it always, Francesca. It's one of the nicest and most meaningful presents anyone has ever given me.'

'I'm so glad,' she said, her eyes shining with pleasure at *his* most obvious pleasure. Rising, she took their glasses and refilled them. 'I'm sorry we've had to cancel the weekend visit to Langley, because of Daddy's accident.' She refrained from mentioning that her father had fallen off the stepladder in the library when

222

he had been searching for this particular book for her. She went on, 'He's terribly disappointed, and so is Doris. They were really looking forward to it, I know Katharine was too. But perhaps it's just as well. It wouldn't be the same without Nicky, would it?' she asked, placing the drink on the table in front of him, returning to the chair.

'No, it wouldn't,' he responded in the quietest of voices, wondering about her most apparent interest in Nick. To his amazement, and considerable annoyance, he experienced a spurt of jealousy. Good God, he thought, startled at himself, and pushed this unfamiliar emotion aside, recognizing it was unworthy of him, and also patently ridiculous. Conscious of the sudden silence, he cleared his throat a shade too noisily. 'I haven't heard a peep out of Nick, but I guess it's a bit too soon. No doubt he'll surface next week. And he'll be all right. He's pretty resilient,' he finished, almost to himself.

'Yes, don't worry, he'll be fine.' Francesca watched him closely, detecting the concern in his voice. In an effort to divert the subject away from Nicky, she exclaimed, with a show of cheerfulness, 'When I spoke to Doris this afternoon, she suggested we arrange the weekend house party to coincide with the start of exterior shooting in Yorkshire, or alternatively, when you film at the castle. It would be rather fun to do it then, don't you think?'

'Yes, it's a terrific idea,' he answered, brightening. 'Who's Doris, by the way? You've mentioned her several times in the past few days.'

'Of course, you don't know about Doris Asternan. She's my father's girl friend, and a jolly nice person. Really super. I'm all for her, and so is Kim. We both wish Daddy would stop procrastinating and pop the question, then we could all relax, especially Doris.'

Victor chuckled, highly amused. 'You seem anxious to have a stepmother, but more to the point, does your father really want a wife? That's the key question, isn't it?'

'Of course he does!' This was said with such youthful confidence, Victor was further entertained. Before he could comment, she swept on, 'Well, let me put it this way, he needs *Doris* as his wife. She's perfect for him.'

'Is she now!' His glance was keen, and he saw from her expression that she was being utterly sincere. But then she knew no other way to be. He found himself warming to her, admiring her. 'Doris is damned lucky to have you as a champion, Francesca. Damned lucky. Most daughters wouldn't react as you're reacting, and with such openmindedness, such generosity.'

'Oh, children can be pretty selfish. They usually think only of themselves, and they don't give a hoot about the single parent, or his or her problems,' she remarked, becoming serious. 'They don't take into consideration the need for companionship, not to mention love and friendship and a shared life. I suppose they simply dismiss loneliness, believe it's of no consequence. But people can die of loneliness.' She waited, and waited, and when no response was forthcoming, she insisted. 'Well, they can, can't they?'

'Yes,' he said, taken aback by the maturity and understanding inherent in these words. 'Living life alone is, very often, a kind of death,' he murmured and clamped his mouth shut, realizing this was a most revealing remark. Feeling self-conscious, he jumped up. 'How about another glass of bubbly?'

'Thank you.' Francesca sat back, staring after him as he went over to the chest near the windows. He's well acquainted with loneliness, she thought with a flash of perception, intuitively understanding that nothing was ever the way it seemed on the surface. No wonder he has such a need for Nick's friendship, she added to herself, and her tender heart filled with sympathy. He was a strong, vigorous, handsome man in the prime of his life, world famous and rich, the idol of millions, and yet there was something so . . . so very vulnerable about him. This had never occurred to her before, and she was surprised at the thought and stiffened in the chair. She swung her head away as he turned around, not wanting him to see the adoration and longing written on her face.

Victor brought the ice bucket back to the coffee table, poured champagne and then loped over to the sofa in strides. He stretched himself over most of it, casually draped one arm on the back and crossed his long legs. 'Tell me more about Doris,' he encouraged with one of his elliptical smiles. 'What's this paragon really like?'

'Oh she's not a paragon!' Francesca cried. 'Far from it. I suppose that's one of the reasons I like her so much. She's very human and full of the most lovely imperfections, which I think help to make her a marvellous woman. She's also a great sense of humour and she's lots of fun, not a bit stuffy. She's enthusiastic about everything, but at the same time she's rather down-to-earth and sensible.' Francesca crinkled her eyes, thinking hard. 'Let me see, what else can I tell you? Well, she's tall and rather pretty, with short curly red hair and the brightest green eyes you've ever seen. Outgoing. Effervescent. Doris really and truly cares about Daddy, and that's the most important thing to me.'

'Mmmm. Quite a picture you've painted of her. Glowing. No wonder you want her for a stepmother,' Victor said, amusement lingering on his face. 'Have they been dating long?'

'A couple of years.' Francesca picked up her glass and took a sip, her eyes focused on him over the rim. 'Oh and she's an American. From Oklahoma.'

'I'll be damned,' he said with a flicker of astonishment, immediately recalling the Earl's inbred elegance, trying to visualize him with a hick from the Midwest. But if David Cunningham was enamoured of the lady, then she was hardly likely to be a hick. Victor's brows drew together as another thought struck him. 'Did you say her name was Asternan?'

'Yes, that's right. Doris is the widow of Edgar Asternan. He was a meat-packing tycoon. It's Doris's company now.' Francesca paused to stare at him. 'You're looking even more surprised, Victor. Have you met Doris? Do you know her?'

'No, I don't. But I know of the Asternan company. It's a household name in the States, and big, like Armour, and Swift, who're also based in Chicago because of the stockyards.' Victor whistled. 'That's quite a company she's inherited, and a hell of a fortune.'

'Seemingly so.' Francesca was reflective and after a moment she found herself confiding, 'Daddy is so strange at times, and I have an awful feeling her money is getting in the way –' She faltered and glanced down at her hands.

Victor said, his voice gentle, 'That's understandable, Francesca. He has his pride.' He looked at her carefully and added, 'But don't worry your pretty little head about them. They'll work it out, if they've a mind to do so. And whatever happens will be for the best. Life has a way of taking care of itself.' He got up.

'Now, I think I'd better get back to the kitchen before everything is burned to a cinder.'

She half rose. 'I'll come and help you.'

'No,' he said from the doorway. 'You can light the candle, but that's all you can do. And I hope you've worked up an appetite, because you're about to eat one of the greatest Italian meals that's ever been cooked. Superb!' He kissed his bunched fingertips and rolled his eyes theatrically. 'I've outdone myself tonight, believe me I have. This dinner's the whole enchilada!'

Francesca laughed. 'If the chef is satisfied, then I'm certain I will be too. Incidentally, I've been meaning to ask you for ages, what does that expression mean?'

'The whole enchilada? *The whole works*. It's a very Californian saying, and I'll explain the derivation later. In the meantime, my hot stove beckons.' He winked and went out.

Francesca went to the mirror, taking a quick peek at herself. The warmth of the room and the champagne had brought a hint of shell pink to her high cheekbones and her eyes were unusually bright. From the champagne or Victor? Victor, without question. She hurried back to the table and slid onto the chair, not wishing to be caught primping a second time. Francesca hugged herself with joy, thinking about his compliments, and of the way the evening was progressing. It was a success thus far, and so much so she felt like pinching herself, just to make sure she was not dreaming. She had half expected him to be stiff and distant, and also, being conscious of him on all levels, had been nervous about conducting herself with aplomb. But he was relaxed and natural and, more importantly, he seemed to be accepting her for herself. In turn, this had made her feel at ease and comfortable with him.

'First course coming up,' Victor announced, and walked in carrying two plates of food, a basket filled with breadsticks and the butter dish wedged in between them, as well as a bottle of chilled Soave.

He had put on his powder-blue silk tie and his pale grey cashmere sports jacket, and as he came towards her Francesca was yet again struck by his elegance, the costliness of his beautiful clothes, the aura of success and glamour he emanated. He had seemed so homely in his shirtsleeves. Now he looked like the famous movie star again, and this unexpectedly unsettled her; she was acutely aware of her own lack of sophistication, her simple appearance, her inexpensive, homemade felt skirt. But at least the new sweater was nice, and anyway she had been brought up to understand that clothes did not make the man, nor the woman for that matter. Nonetheless, recognizing the intrinsic truth in this did not prevent her from wishing she was wearing a gorgeous dress, the kind Katharine owned.

She looked up at him and said brightly, 'That's the best balancing act I've ever seen.'

'It sure is, but then I've had lotsa practice. I used to be a waiter. Don't look so doubtful, it's true.' He grinned, tickled by her astonishment, and set down the Soave, then the bread basket, and finally the plates. He lifted the butter dish out of the basket, and explained, 'When I first went to Hollywood I had to find a way to support my wife and the boys, in between my jobs as an extra at the studios. So I became a waiter. And a damned good one, even if I say so myself.'

225

'Oh,' she said, her eyes widening, believing him. And then she thought: There's so much I don't know about him . . . his whole life really.

'I hope you like prosciutto,' Victor remarked casually, seating himself opposite her, pouring the wine, taking a breadstick and breaking it in half.

'Actually, I've never had it before.'

'It's smoked Italian ham, sliced paper-thin, and it's usually served with melon, but I often use other fruit for a change of pace.'

'So I see. Where on earth did you find fresh figs at this time of year?' She eyed the tender green fruit which he had split in half to expose the luscious pink pulpy centre.

'Harte's. Where else? I'm really hung up on their food department. I could spend hours just browsing.'

'I know. It's my favourite shop.'

'*Buono appetito.*'

'*Bon appétit.*' Francesca tasted the ham, told him it was delicious and, between mouthfuls, went on, 'The woman who owns Harte's is a friend of ours, well, of my father's and she's quite incredible. The most remarkable woman I've ever met.' As she ate, Francesca recited everything she could remember hearing about the legendary Emma Harte, whom she greatly admired.

Victor was fascinated, and he listened attentively and with growing interest, thinking that Nick had been correct when he said Francesca had a talent for telling a good story, and telling it well. 'I like the sound of your Emma Harte,' he said, when she had finished. 'I've always been partial to strong, independent and determined women. I can't stand clinging violets.' He winked. 'They'll never cling to me.'

Francesca's eyes were watchful. 'Most men feel threatened by a strong woman.'

'Not this man.'

She said nothing, smiled enigmatically, and tucked this bit of information away to add to her store of knowledge about him.

After they had finished the prosciutto and figs, Victor cleared the plates, and before Francesca had time to blink he returned, pushing the trolley into the room in front of him. The cart was stacked with an array of silver serving dishes, and she said, 'Goodness, it looks as if you've made enough to feed an army!'

Victor nodded, laughter rippling across his wide mouth. 'Yes, I know, and I always do, I'm afraid. I'm sure the tendency springs from once being very poor. I'm overcompensating now, I guess. But, Jeez, I can't stand empty cupboards or an empty refrigerator either. They've got to be stacked to overflowing to satisfy mc, to make me feel good.' He hovered over the trolley, removed various lids with a flourish, beamed at her and went on, 'Fettuccine Alfredo, exactly the way they make it at Alfredo's in Rome. His recipe by the way, and he gave it to me as a special favour.' Victor served the pasta expertly, handed her the plate, took another larger one, and explained, 'And it's accompanied by a veal chop, pink and succulent and tender. I hope. There you are.' He put the veal chop in front of her. 'How does that look to you?'

'Everything looks absolutely marvellous, Victor. Thank you.'

'I've also made a salad of basil leaves, tomatoes and mozzarella cheese, but let's tackle this first.' He served himself, sat down and lifted his glass of white wine.

Francesca followed suit and they clinked glasses, and before he could propose a toast, she exclaimed, 'To the chef!'

'*Grazie.*' He tasted the Soave. 'Mmmm. Not bad, not bad at all,' he said, savouring it. He touched her glass with his again. 'And here's to my beautiful patient. Fortunately fully recovered.'

Francesca inclined her head. 'Why thank you, Victor.' She was relieved she could accept this compliment without blushing.

As the meal progressed Francesca realized he had not exaggerated about his talents in the kitchen, and she was impressed. The food, which he had prepared so painstakingly, and apparently so lovingly, was delicious. The pasta was cooked to perfection, the sauce creamy without being over rich, whilst the veal chop was as tender as he had hoped and her knife slid through it as though cutting butter.

'I'm really staggered,' she told him at one moment. 'Where did you learn to cook like this?'

'The best place, the only place. At my mother's knee.' He drank some of his wine, and told her, 'I love cooking. It helps me to unwind, and there's nothing I like better than pottering around in the kitchen at the ranch. And I want you to know I'm pretty versatile.' His black and brilliant eyes danced. 'I can rustle up terrific steaks on the barbecue, and I make the best chicken and dumplings you've ever tasted. They're out of this world.'

'I don't doubt it,' she laughed, enjoying him, revelling in his company. In the past they had never once been alone, had always been accompanied by Nick and Katharine, and surrounded by a tribe of other people as well. She was delighted to have him to herself, to see a wholly different side of him.

Victor talked a lot during dinner, and about a variety of things, but mostly he talked about his ranch near Santa Barbara, his love of horses and the outdoor life, the quiet and essentially private existence he led when he was not working in a picture. But he did touch on the professional side of his life several times, regaling her with funny anecdotes about his early years in Hollywood and stories about some of the crazy characters who were his friends. He was witty and amusing and he kept her laughing and vastly entertained.

For his part Victor was enjoying himself as much as Francesca. She was an avid listener, the best captive audience he had ever had, and when she did ask questions these were intelligent or pointed, and usually pertinent. Her comments ran from acerbic to the hilarious. He began to realize he had not had such a good time for months, maybe even years.

Victor Mason was very much the domesticated male animal who had always preferred to relax in the luxury and privacy of his own home, rather than gallivanting in public. It suddenly occurred to him that this type of intimate evening was the one thing he had missed with his last two wives. Both had been perpetual and tireless party-goers, social butterflies of the most relentless kind, and they had wearied him to a point of suffocating boredom, as had the endless parties to which they had dragged him, invariably protesting.

But mostly, he knew, it was Francesca's presence which was making the evening so pleasurable for him. She was companionable, and lots of fun, and tranquil to be with. Victor discovered he was drawn to her more than ever and for a variety of reasons. Prominent amongst these were her sweet disposition and her natural manner, coupled with her ingenuousness and straightforward honesty. He could not abide women who were crafty or coy or coquettish, who played oblique sexual games, and it was a relief to him to be with someone who was so utterly without guile, who was not out to set a trap for him. Because of her intelligence, her intellectual promise, her many lightning perceptions and her unusual self-confidence, Victor was beginning to forget about her extreme youth, that singular and most disconcerting fact which had continually nagged at him for weeks. And in so doing he set a trap, albeit unwittingly, for himself.

After dinner they seated themselves in front of the blazing fire, sipping coffee and chatting desultorily. Victor was ensconced in the wing chair, nursing a cognac and smoking one of the Earl's best cigars, both of which Francesca had brought to him, once he had finished clearing away the dishes and the remnants of their meal. She sat opposite him, curled up in one of the large easy chairs, her feet tucked under her.

A silence had fallen between them, yet it was a compatible silence. Victor eased back in the chair and stretched out his long legs, crossing them at the ankles. He puffed on the cigar contentedly, regarding her through the haze of the smoke.

She smiled at him. 'When do you actually start shooting in Yorkshire?'

'Some time in May or June. We must be certain of good weather. But we start principal photography at Shepperton Studios the first week of April. That's a firm date, and we'll get as much footage in the can as possible, before going on location. Why do you ask?'

'I'd like to give my father a tentative date for the weekend house party.'

'I'll check it out with Jake Watson on Monday, and let you know before I leave. I'm going away next week.'

Francesca felt the muscles in her face tighten. 'Oh,' she said. 'I . . . I didn't know.' She fiddled with the fastening on her chain belt and ventured quietly, 'Are you going back to Hollywood?'

'Nope. I'm going to Switzerland. To Klosters. It was a trip I'd planned to take with Nicky, and since he's no longer available, I was going to cancel it. But then I decided I might as well go off by myself. I need a few days' break before plunging into the picture. I'm leaving this coming Wednesday, for about five days. It's the last chance I'll have before I'm firmly battened down by Jake.'

'How lovely. I'm sure you'll have a wonderful time,' she said with as much enthusiasm as she could manage.

Victor took a mouthful of the brandy, and then stared deeply into the glass, asking himself whether he would enjoy the trip without Nick. He never travelled unless Nick was able to accompany him and, unexpectedly, the prospect of five days alone, even in Klosters, did not seem appealing.

He put the brandy on the table and leaned forward. 'Listen, Francesca, I've just had a terrific idea. Why don't you come with me?' He sat back, not sure he had heard himself correctly. That he had taken her by surprise was evident. Jesus, he'd surprised himself.

Francesca was thunderstruck. She was unable to answer, and sat gaping at him, her lips parted, her eyes conveying her amazement.

Victor's expression mirrored hers. He had spoken on the spur of the moment, without thinking things out clearly, and a number of snags flew into his mind. On the other hand, having extended the invitation he could hardly rescind it without appearing foolish. Besides, it *is* a good idea, and for a variety of reasons, he decided. 'Well, what do you say?'

Astounded though she was, Francesca was thrilled and excited. She was on the point of accepting when she saw the impossibility of the situation. Her excitement ebbed away.

She swallowed. 'I'm afraid I can't,' she began, and said no more. She bit her lip, knowing she had no alternative but to explain her refusal, lest he be offended. This was the last thing she wanted.

'You see it would be very difficult to go away without telling my father, and he'd be . . . well . . . er . . . er . . . *You know*. I mean, he might think it a bit funny.' She could not go on, and she looked at Victor helplessly, embarrassed by her admission that she was still obliged to inform her father about her movements, that she needed his approval.

Victor stared at her aghast. She had misunderstood him, and his motives. Jesus Christ! Seduction was the last thing on his mind. He must clarify that, set her straight before the discussion went any further. 'I hope you don't think I'm trying to proposition you!' he exclaimed fiercely. 'Because I'm n – '

'Of course I don't!' Francesca cried with the same vehemence, sharply cutting him off. 'It never entered my head.' Her gaze was cool and her manner haughty. 'Nor would my father think such a thing. He brought me up to have a sense of right and wrong, and he trusts me implicitly. It's just that, well, I've never been away with a – ' She cleared her throat. 'What I'm trying to say is that Daddy is rather old-fashioned, and he would think it quite improper for me to take a holiday alone with you.'

'I can't say I blame him,' Victor replied, adopting the lightest, most dismissive tone he could. He lolled back in the chair, and his smile was rueful as he went on, 'I guess it wasn't such a good idea after all.' He shrugged, attempted nonchalance. 'No harm done, I sincerely hope.' Then he felt a need to explain himself further. 'And again, I hope *you* didn't misinterpret the invitation, take it the wrong way. It simply struck me, suddenly, that the mountain air would do you good, since you've been so sick, and, to be honest, you would've been great company for me. I hate travelling by myself. I get pretty lonely. And we have become close buddies this past week.' When she was unresponsive, he pressed, 'Well, we have, haven't we?'

'Yes,' she murmured, crushed and let down. I'm just a surrogate Nicholas Latimer, she thought miserably. A bloody chum. How could I have possibly imagined otherwise?

'Hey, don't look so glum.' Victor was laughing, visibly relaxing. 'It's not the end of the world. And I understand why your father would be against it. After all, you're only nineteen, Francesca. I keep forgetting that. Mind if I help myself to another cognac?'

'Please do.' Bridling at his reference to her age, she continued, 'I'd like one too, please.'

'Sure.'

Francesca put her elbows on her knees and dropped her chin into her hands. Her face was thoughtful, brooding. So badly did she want to be part of Victor's life, to spend time with him on a one-to-one basis, she was now prepared to accept the relationship on any terms. More precisely, his uncompromising terms. She would settle for a platonic friendship. If they could only be buddies, as he phrased it, then so be it. She focused on the trip to Klosters. I'm going with him next week, come hell or high water, she made up her mind. I must, to cement our friendship. But how to accomplish this without dissembling? She was incapable of lying to anyone, particularly her father. I don't have to lie, she thought, I can simply go, without telling him. But this would be deceitful. It was another form of lying in a way, and if he 'phoned the house and she was not there he would be concerned, if not, indeed, disturbed. Francesca knew she could not inflict this kind of worry on her father. He had enough to contend with. Somehow Daddy must be circumvented, she told herself.

Victor handed her a brandy snifter, interrupting her thoughts with, 'Here you are.'

'Oh, thanks. Cheers,' she said abstractedly, and took a large swallow.

'Hey, you're meant to sip that, otherwise you'll get loaded,' he warned mildly.

'No I won't. I've got a hollow leg.'

'That makes two of us.' He chuckled and so did she. Yet there was a flatness to her laughter and he caught the shadow in her eyes. He studied her. Was she embarrassed because she had been forced to refuse his invitation? A hundred to one she is, old buddy, he answered himself.

'Look here, Francesca, I hope you're not worrying about Klosters. I'm not offended. Let's forget it. I want to do some hard skiing, and that wouldn't be much fun for you, even if you're a crack skier. I start at dawn, finish at dusk, and you'd probably hardly have the stamina to keep up with – '

'*Skiing,*' she repeated, not permitting him to finish.

'Sure. Why do you think I'm going to Klosters?'

Francesca sat very still. An extraordinary idea took hold. It filled her with a joyful optimism, since it might be the solution she had been seeking. Be cool, be casual, be sophisticated, she cautioned herself. Don't rush in like a silly schoolgirl. She had no wish to sound forward, or presumptuous, and so she began to structure her next sentence with immense care. Aware that he was waiting for a response, she toyed with her glass, took a sip of the cognac, gaining time. She ignored his question, and asked, 'Would you really be lonely going to Klosters on your own?' She was pleased her voice was controlled.

'Sure I would. I told you, I'm used to travelling tandem with Nicky. Besides, I've discovered I never have much fun by myself. I like to share places, the scenery, good food and wine, experiences in general.' He eyed her with curiosity, wondering why she had been prompted to ask the question. Hadn't he made himself clear initially?

'So what you actually want is a replacement for Nicky?'

'If you want to put it that way, yes, I guess I do,' he admitted. 'But naturally it would have to be the right person . . . Listen, I wouldn't just pick anybody . . . at random. That'd be asking for trouble.' He was filled with wariness, alarmed she might have someone in mind. Her brother for instance. He was not open to suggestions about travelling companions. He said quickly, 'That's why I invited *you*. We're compatible, we get along, we understand each other.'

She said, with a faint smile, 'Oh I know we do, Victor.' She cleared her throat.

230

'Unless I'm wrong, what you're saying is that the person you go with is as important to you as the place, perhaps even more so and – '

'You've got it.' He looked at her oddly. 'I'm puzzled. What's all this leading up to, Francesca?'

'Bavaria.'

'Bavaria?' he echoed with a puzzled frown. 'You've lost me.'

Francesca shifted in the chair. A calm smile dimpled her mouth. 'If you changed your plans and went to a place called Königssee I *could* go with you. Unless there's someone else you'd like to invite to Klosters, instead of me. And if there is, I do understand, really I do.'

'There isn't anyone I'd even consider, let alone ask,' he assured her truthfully. 'But I don't get it, Francesca. If you can go to Königsee with me, why can't you go to Klosters?'

'Very simply because I don't need my father's approval to go to Bavaria. My cousins Diana and Christian live there, and I have an open invitation to visit them any time I wish. The skiing is superb, well into spring, and there're some marvellous ski runs, as well as a number of fine old inns. Diana would know the best, and she could book you a suite at one of them. Naturally, I'd have to stay with my cousins. But don't you see, my father couldn't possibly object. I'd be . . . I'd be very well chaperoned, wouldn't I?'

Victor gave her a long look, his eyes merry. 'That's true,' he agreed, smiling to himself.

'So what do you think?'

'It sounds great. But – ' Now there was a sudden hesitancy in his manner, a pulling back. 'Look, are you sure you want to go? Could you stand being alone with me for five or six days without getting bored?'

She met his questioning stare with a steady, level gaze, even though her heart was fluttering wildly at the thought of having him entirely to herself. 'Don't be silly, Victor. Of course I wouldn't be bored and, as you said yourself, we do get along like a house on fire.'

'I had to ask. It strikes me we've only talked about your father's attitude in relation to the trip, not how you felt. You haven't said you'd like to go.'

'I would, I really would. Anyway, I think you're right about the mountain air doing me good,' she volunteered in a matter-of-fact tone, endeavouring to conceal the excitement growing inside her. Noticing the uncertainty lingering on his face, she could not resist adding hurriedly, 'I wouldn't have suggested you change your plans if I'd had any qualms about making the trip with you. Now would I?'

'I guess not. It's settled then.' He beamed. 'I'll talk to the travel agency on Monday morning, and switch the air tickets to Königssee. I've never been to Germany, so I'll find it interesting.' His face sobered as he recalled the snags that had occurred to him at the outset of the conversation. After ruminating a second, he remarked cautiously, 'There are a couple of problems though. Hell, I shouldn't call them problems. Let's say there are several points I've got to get straightened out with you.'

He stood up, dropped a log onto the fire, returned to the chair, and said, 'Would you mind flying alone on Tuesday?'

231

Francesca was startled. 'No,' she said. 'But why can't I go with you on Wednesday?'

'You *can* go on Wednesday, if you wish, but I'd prefer you to take an earlier flight than I do. I don't think we should be on the same plane.'

'Whyever not?'

'People might misunderstand, if they saw us travelling together. It would be much more discreet for us to make our way separately.' When he saw she was thrown by these remarks, he said, 'Hasn't Katharine told you about my divorce, and *Confidential Magazine*?'

'She mentioned you were in the middle of a difficult divorce, but she hasn't said anything about *Confidential*. I'm probably being very stupid, but I don't understand the connection.' Her face was filling with confusion.

Victor leaned forward, his hands clasped together, his mouth settling into a severe line. Without mincing words, he gave her a rapid and succinct run-down on the magazine and the kind of sensational and damaging stories which appeared in its pages. He repeated Estelle Morgan's warnings to Katharine and himself, added a quick profile of his estranged wife, Arlene, and elucidated in detail her predilection for causing trouble, plus her tendency to talk rather revealingly to the press.

'Don't you see, from the things Estelle has told me, I'm convinced I'm a target, and that *Confidential* is trying to work up a scurrilous piece about me. They'll seize on anything, whether it's the truth or not, and they're not above inventing what they don't know. Personally, I don't give a damn about myself. I've got a broad back, and a skin like a rhinoceros after living in the public eye for so long. Headlines have never intimidated me, but I mustn't expose *you* in any way whatsoever. I can't allow you to be dragged into a scandal, especially since you're an innocent bystander. And though the trip is above board, it could very easily be presented in entirely the wrong light. I don't think your father would appreciate that. And *I* certainly wouldn't, Francesca.'

'My God, how awful! But don't people have any redress: can't they sue for libel?'

'Some stars and other celebrities have already done so. But most of my friends who've been dragged through the mud by them decided to turn a blind eye, believing it smarter to ignore the bad publicity, to rise above it. Still, it's pretty lousy stuff to live with.'

She nodded her understanding. 'I can imagine. Obviously I'll go on Tuesday, and perhaps it's a good idea anyway. I can check the hotel Diana books for you, make sure you have the best suite. I'll give her a ring tomorrow, to tell her we're coming.'

'Good girl. And let's not alert the locals to my impending arrival. Can you ask her to book the suite in her name?'

'Yes, that's no problem.'

'There's one more thing, Francesca,' he began tentatively, seeking the right words, knowing he must exercise great tact. 'Are you going to tell your father I'll be in Bavaria too, when you're visiting your cousins?'

'I was going to, yes. Don't you want me to mention it, Victor?'

'No, I don't think you should. I know how straightforward you are, but leaving something unsaid is not actually lying – '

232

'It's lying by omission, isn't it?' she suggested, raising an eyebrow.

'Yes, I reckon it is,' he answered, reminding himself how scrupulous of nature she was. He got up and stood with his back to the fire, gazing out into the room, reflecting, and then he looked down at her. 'I do have my reasons for asking you not to say anything,' he began slowly. 'Very good reasons.' He wanted to both convince and reassure her, and he said, 'Look, Francesca, if your father knows I'm in Königssee, Kim will know, and in turn he'll tell Katharine. Very honestly, I'd prefer her to be in the dark. I want her to think I'm in Klosters. I want everyone to think the same. Except Jake Watson. He has to know where I am, in case he needs to reach me about the picture. But I'm not worried about Jake. He'll keep his mouth buttoned.'

Francesca was dismayed. 'Why on earth don't you want Katharine to know?' she cried. 'She's my very best friend, and a close friend of yours! She would never breathe a word! Not to anyone. After all, she knows about *Confidential*, so I would think she'd really be on her guard. In fact, I'm positive she would. Honestly, Victor, I trust her completely.'

'Hell, so do I, Francesca,' Victor said, sounding emphatic. In all truth, he was not distrustful of Katharine, but being a man of the world he knew how easily a careless slip of the tongue could create untold misery. Also, although he detested covertness, he was genuine in his desire to protect Francesca, and so he considered secrecy imperative.

He explained this carefully, and she listened, obviously digesting his words. Feeling compelled to dispel any false impression he might have given about Katharine's integrity, he then proceeded, 'I know as well as you do that Katharine is exceptionally loyal, and that she wouldn't intentionally hurt either one of us. But hell, you know how she gets around in London society, and with the show business crowd. Journalists are always on the fringes, or in the midst, of these groups. She might say something accidentally – and to the wrong person. Imagine your father's distress if that lousy magazine did run some sort of suggestive, disgusting story about us, or if there was gossip among your friends.'

His eyes rested on her, and he finished gently, 'I know you want to be open with your father. On the other hand, I think we should be as circumspect as possible, don't you?' When she was quiet, he went on, 'Later, when you're back in London, you can tell him we ran into each other in the Alps, also say that I spent some time with you and your cousins.'

Francesca nodded her head slowly, recognizing the soundness of his suggestion. Also, she was no fool, and she understood that if she did not agree he would revert to his original plan. He would go to Klosters. Alone. Her yearning to be with Victor was so forceful it was overcoming her few remaining qualms about her father.

Victor was watching her, waiting, and wondering, suddenly, why he had invited her to go with him in the first place. Now it seemed like a big mistake.

As if he had read her mind, he bent towards her and said, 'Look, I don't want you to go against your principles. Perhaps we'd better forget the whole idea. I'll go to Klosters by myself, as I originally intended.'

Francesca laughed lightly, and exclaimed, 'I was just about to say you're absolutely correct. My father would be dreadfully upset if our name was besmirched, so we should be careful.' She did not give him a chance to answer, and rushed on,

'I like your suggestion about telling Daddy I ran into you when I get back. It really is the ideal solution. And he won't be at all surprised I'm going off to see Diana and Christian for a few days. I usually go over once a year. So . . .' She took a deep breath. 'So, I'm on, if you are.'

'Okay!' he exclaimed. 'It's a deal.' His misgivings of a moment ago dissipated instantly, and he grinned at her. 'We'll have a great time, kid.'

She looked at him quickly. It was the first time he had used any term of endearment when addressing her. *Kid* was hardly that, but coming from him, it did denote affection. Unless he looks at me and sees Nicky, she thought; but nevertheless, she was pleased. Another thought occurred to Francesca, and she said, 'I'm going to have to explain the situation to Diana, to be on the safe side. Is that all right?'

'I guess you'll have to fill her in, so go ahead, but make sure she understand . . . understands we're just friends.'

'Naturally,' Francesca said sweetly, glancing at him through the most innocent of eyes. 'I wouldn't want her to get the wrong impression either.' God forbid, she added to herself, and swallowed a laugh. Victor was as old-fashioned as her father, and equally stuffy, it seemed.

Victor said, 'I'll have your tickct to Königssee by Monday afternoon at the latest. Gus will bring it over, and he'll drive you out to the airport on Tuesday.'

'Thank you very much. But there isn't an airport in Königssee. We have to fly to Salzburg and drive across the Austrian border into Germany. But it's not a long trip, only about an hour.'

'Salzburg it is then. By the way, I'm curious. How come you have cousins living in Germany? When did they move there?'

'They didn't, they were born there. My father's elder sister, Arabella, married a German in the late 1920s. It is she who is their mother. Diana and Christian are very English in many ways, and they're bilingual, so you don't have to worry about language barriers.'

'That's a relief,' he said. 'And what about your aunt and uncle? Do they live in Königssee too? And will I be meeting them?' he asked.

There was a tiny silence before she said in a low voice, 'No, I don't think so.'

Victor was not certain, but he thought he saw the merest trace of sadness trickle into her eyes. He looked at her again, and more closely. The expression had disappeared, if it had been there at all. He told himself he had imagined it, and went on, 'So give me the dope on your cousins. How old are they? What do they do?'

'I know you'll like them,' she said, and thought of Diana and Christian, and then of the tragic events which had engulfed their lives. But she only ever mentioned positives when speaking of her cousins, and she said brightly, 'Christian is thirty, and he's very involved with music. He plays the violin beautifully and he's an expert on Mozart. Diana is twenty-six. She has a boutique in Königssee, and another one in Munich. She surprised us all when she went into business, and her German grandmother was awfully put out. But, credit where it's due, she's been ever so successful. Also, Diana's a great skier, and she'll be able to show you the best runs.'

'Terrific. I assume Christian also skis.'

'Oh no,' Francesca said quickly. 'No, he doesn't.'

'And what about you? Am I going to have the pleasure of your company at the top of the mountain?'

Francesca pulled a face, and then she giggled. 'Not at the top. The bottom, I'm afraid. I've never graduated from the nursery slopes, and I seem to spend most of my time slithering around on my backside. I'm very clumsy.'

'I find that hard to believe,' Victor chuckled. 'So it looks as if I'm stuck with Diana, or vice versa.'

'That's right. And I bet she gives you a run for your money.'

CHAPTER TWENTY-FOUR

Salzburg airport was relatively quiet on Wednesday morning. Victor Mason walked out of Customs into Arrivals, followed by a porter with his luggage, and quickly scanned the few people waiting for passengers. Francesca was not amongst them, and although he was momentarily surprised he was not perturbed. He knew she would appear within minutes, and he headed towards the main entrance, preferring to wait outside in the fresh air.

The porter deposited his two suitcases next to him, propped the skis in their custom-made leather bag against the wall, and asked him if he needed a taxi. Victor shook his head, thanked him, gave him a generous tip, and then glanced around, his eyes eagerly absorbing the surroundings.

It was a shimmering sunlit morning. The air was dry and crisp, and for Victor the glorious weather was the most uplifting change after the dreary dankness of London. He took several deep and satisfying breaths, felt a rush of exhilaration, and lifted his head to regard the scenery. In the distance, imposing greyish-purple mountains with white-glazed plateaux and icy, crystal peaks leapt up into a sky that was the clear sharp blue of alpine gentians and without a solitary cloud. It seemed to Victor that everything around him sparkled – the landscape, the sky, the very air itself.

A tingle of excitement ran through him. He could not wait to get up on the slopes. It was perfect skiing weather. Ambivalent though he had been at various times over the weekend, the last vestiges of doubt now disintegrated, and he knew that despite a few earlier misgivings the trip was going to be a success. He discovered he was in a festive mood and the right frame of mind for a five-day vacation away from the burdens, and problems of the picture.

The fierce sunlight stabbed at his eyes. He blinked, took out his dark glasses and put them on. He was about to light a cigarette when he heard a horn tooting merrily and repetitively.

Victor swung his head alertly and spotted a bright red Volkswagen skimming around the corner. It slewed to a standstill and Francesca jumped out, laughing as she flew towards him across the snow, her fresh young face as sparkling and as sunny as the morning. She looked like a vivid bird escaped from its exotic jungle habitat, a flash of brilliance against the snowscape, in a canary-yellow sweater and a matching woollen cap. Both the sweater and the pert little concoction on her head were trimmed with scarlet pom-poms, and she wore yellow ski pants tucked into short leather boots also of bright scarlet.

The sight of her in the colourful outfit brought a smile of pleasure to his face. 'Hi, kid,' he cried, moving forward. He caught her in his arms roughly and hugged her several times.

This display of spontaneous affection on his part delighted Francesca. He seemed more handsome than ever, and her heart was pounding rapidly from his close embrace. She took hold of herself and said, 'Sorry we're late. We hit a bad patch of ice on the mountain, and it slowed us down.'

'I've only been waiting five minutes at the most,' he said, releasing his grip on her arms. Playfully he flicked the pom-poms, strung on lengths of wool and dangling from the shoulder of her sweater. 'You look exactly the way I feel.'

'And how's that?' she asked.

'Gay. Lighthearted. And I'll tell you something else, kid. I think I'm getting high on this fabulous air. It beats Dom Pérignon any time.'

She laughed. 'Yes, it is marvellous, isn't it. And I'm glad you're in a carefree mood, because we are too. Oh look, here's Diana.'

Victor turned. He was not quite sure what he had expected Francesca's cousin to be like, certainly not as stunning and stylish as the girl approaching them. Taken aback though he was, he camouflaged his startled reaction behind an affable smile.

Diana was dressed entirely in white, even to the leather boots that rose above her ski pants. The latter were beautifully tailored and fitted her like a second skin, and with them she wore a loose sweater-tunic of fluffy angora wool, belted with a white silk rope which was tasselled at the ends. Her hair was the most astonishing thing about her. It was the colour of silver gilt and it rippled, long and straight, halfway down her back, parted in the centre above a wide brow. As she drew closer he saw that her face was small and delicate, and patrician like Francesca's, but they bore little physical resemblance to each other apart from this one distinction. Their features were markedly different, and in contrast to Francesca, who was tall and willowy, Diana was small-boned, diminutive, elfin.

She came to a standstill, her eyes sweeping over him with unabashed interest and curiosity. If the face upturned to his was not exactly beautiful, it was arresting, and he was instantly struck by the extraordinary peacefulness that dwelt there. And then she smiled, and he could not help thinking: The Gioconda Smile. The face of a madonna indeed. Her silver-grey eyes, fringed with thick lashes the same silver gilt as her hair, were large, and intelligence and merriment shone out from them. Her complexion had been tanned to a soft golden bronze, and it was patently obvious to Victor that she was a natural, outdoor girl who did not need to resort to the artifice of cosmetics for her appeal. The only make-up she wore was a touch of coral lipstick.

Francesca said, 'Diana, this is Victor Mason. Victor, this is my cousin, Diana von Wittingen.'

'How do you do, Mr Mason.' Diana stretched out her hand. 'I'm pleased to meet you.'

'So am I,' he said, shaking her hand. 'And please let's drop the formalities. Call me Victor. Can I call you Diana?'

'Yes, of course,' she said, the Mona Lisa smile flickering. 'If you'll excuse me for a moment, I must go into the airport to 'phone the house. I'm sure Cheska told you there's ice on the driveway. I want someone to put down sand and cinders; otherwise there'll be an accident. Whilst I'm 'phoning, perhaps you'd help Cheska stow your luggage. You'll have to put the skis in the back of the Volks, and manoeuvre them around a bit. They'll fit, if you stick them through one of the windows.'

'I hope you're right.' He looked at the tiny car doubtfully as Diana disappeared into the airport. He glanced after her and said to Francesca, 'What a great-looking girl!'

'Yes, she is. Bavaria is scattered with broken-hearted swains, dying of love for her.' Continuing in a brisker tone, Francesca said, 'Now, let's get the cases into the car. One will fit in the boot, the other will have to be wedged on the back seat, along with the skis. And me.' Francesca picked up the ski bag and walked to the Volkswagen.

Victor followed with his cases. 'You two are being over optimistic. Maybe I should get a taxi and have it follow us,' he suggested. 'You're going to be damned uncomfortable, surrounded with all my stuff.'

'Oh, I'll be all right, don't worry. We managed with my two bags yesterday. Mind you, I didn't have skis.'

Victor took off his cashmere overcoat and flung it on the front seat, then tackled the luggage. It was a tight squeeze, but everything was tucked away in the Volkswagen when Diana returned. She burst into gales of laughter when she saw Francesca squashed in the back, firmly anchored into position by the huge case on one side and the skis which stretched diagonally in front of her and jutted out of the back window.

'Poor darling!' Diana exclaimed, getting in and slamming the door. 'It's a good thing you're not a fat girl, and that it's not a long trip.'

'I'm perfectly fine,' Francesca replied. 'Come on, Dibs, let's get off. We're wasting time.'

Diana turned on the ignition and pulled out with rapidity, whizzing through the airport at such a speed Victor cringed. She slowed down as they turned onto the main road, and remarked, 'I hope you won't be disappointed, Victor, but I'm going to skirt around Salzburg today, so that I can take the fastest route to Königssee. If you want to see the town, we can always come back later in the week. Salzburg is quite beautiful, and the Baroque and Gothic architecture is unique.'

'Yes, later perhaps,' Victor said, thinking of the skiing he had planned to do, and which he had no wish to forgo for a round of sightseeing, visiting monuments, museums and churches.

Diana caught his reluctance, and said casually, 'We don't have to make a decision about that now.' Without turning around, she said over her shoulder to Francesca, 'Are you going to tell Victor, or shall I?'

'Tell me what?'

'I will, Dibs.' Francesca smiled faintly at Victor, who had swivelled in his seat. 'There's been a slight change of plan. Diana hasn't booked you into a hotel. She's had second thoughts about it, and she thinks you should stay with us. She'd like you to be her house guest.'

Victor's black brows shot up. 'That's really swell of you, and I appreciate your kindness, Diana, but I think it would be more circumspect if I stayed at a hotel, as planned.'

Diana looked at him through the corners of her eyes, and a smile played around her mouth. 'I'm not sure it would be circumspect. Cheska has explained everything to me, and I think you'd be far too conspicuous in a hotel. You're so well known, you'd be recognized immediately. There are journalists in Germany too, you know. Our house is halfway up a mountain, rather isolated from town, and also very private. If you stay with us, no one need know you're even in Bavaria. We don't have to go into the town at all, and in your skiing gear and goggles you'll be faceless on the slopes.'

'Points well taken,' Victor said. He was thoughtful, mulling the idea over, realizing she made sense. 'Maybe it *is* the wisest thing to do. Still, I don't want Francesca to feel awkward about it. I guess I've got to toss the ball back to her. What do *you* want me to do, kid?'

Francesca leaned forward, her hands resting on the skis, her smile wide with happiness. 'I'd like you to stay at Wittingenhof with us,' she said, having resolved earlier to be honest with him, to let her feelings show, regardless of the consequences. She waited, became aware of his indecisiveness, and rushed on, 'Diana took me down to the hotel in Königssee late yesterday afternoon, and although it's the best, it's not what you're used to, and they didn't have a suite available. Only a rather grotty room. So apart from anything else, you'd be much more comfortable at the house.'

Victor looked at her carefully. This is one hell of a switch on her part, he thought. He said, 'Won't it create problems for you later, if I do? Won't you have to explain to yo – '

She cut him short. 'Of course not!' she exclaimed, smiling reassuringly. 'I don't think we should worry about that now.' Her voice was smooth, unconcerned.

Momentarily nonplussed, in view of their long discussion about her father on Saturday night, Victor intensified his scrutiny. He could see that her mood of gaiety and enthusiasm was undiminished, and he was suddenly convinced she knew what she was doing. Yet he had difficulty in acquiescing. He was not sure why. 'Well, I'm still – '

'Excuse me for interrupting, Victor,' Diana said. 'But I'd like to make something clear. The Schloss is large. You would have your own suite of rooms and your privacy. We won't intrude on you in any way, and you can come and go as you like.' She laughed lightly, threw him a quick glance. 'I never restrict my guests.'

'Hey, Diana, that's not why I'm hesitating. I know you'd make me welcome and comfortable.' He swung his head to face Francesca, noted the expectancy in her eyes, made a snap decision. 'Okay,' he said. 'I'll stay at the house. Providing *you're* sure it's all right, Francesca.'

'Absolutely,' she cried, unable to disguise her excitement. 'Oh good. It's settled. On to Wittingenhof, Dibs darling.'

Victor chuckled. If Francesca could accept the situation with such apparent insouciance and pleasure, who was he to argue. He settled back in the seat, relaxing, and took out a packet of cigarettes. He lit one, smoking in silence for a few minutes, and then he said, 'I hope this doesn't mean a lot of extra work for you, Diana.'

'Not at all, we have excellent help. And actually, your suite is already prepared and waiting for you. Christian insisted on that. Ah, we're almost at the Austrian border. Do you have your passport handy, Victor?'

'Sure do.' He reached into the inside pocket of his Harris tweed sports jacket and pulled it out.

'*You* have mine,' Francesca said, tapping Diana lightly on the shoulder.

Diana nodded. 'Yes, I do. They may not be needed, but it's best to have them ready.' She braked as the border guards came forward to meet the car. When they saw Diana, who was leaning out of the window, they smiled and nodded and waved her on. Within a few minutes she was sliding to a stop at the German frontier. Once again the border patrol seemed to know her and they chatted cordially, glanced indifferently at the passports, and signalled her to pass through the barrier which had just been raised.

When they were over the border, and speeding down the road again, Victor said, 'They didn't seem particularly interested in us. Is that normal procedure?'

'Not really, but I'm backwards and forwards to Salzburg all the time, and the guards at the German side live in and around the area. They've known me for many years,' Diana explained. She slackened her speed. 'Victor, do look around. Isn't Bavaria beautiful?'

He peered out of the windows with interest. Forests of pine rose majestically on either side of the road, the stately firs of a green so dark they were almost black, their branches weighted with frostings of snow that glistened in the brilliant sunshine. The wooded landscape stretched as far as the eye could see, its impressive sweep unbroken by any form of habitation or signs of civilization. And towering above these great coniferous forests were the glacial Alps, awesome in their grandeur and solitary beauty under a sky of dazzling azure.

'It's breathtaking,' Victor pronounced. 'I can't wait to hit those slopes.' He indicated the range of mountains on the far horizon.

'I know what you mean,' Diana said. 'Francesca tells me you're a champion skier.'

'She said the same about you!'

'Oh, I'm not too bad,' Diana answered off-handedly. 'And since you're obviously an experienced skier, I've decided to take you up on the Jenner tomorrow. Then if you want a longer run, we can tackle the Rossfeld on Friday. The snow has been good this year. It's lasted well. Conditions are ideal. You'll get some good skiing, Victor.'

'I hope so. I've been looking forward to this break for weeks on end.'

Francesca said, 'I don't think I'll be joining the two of you. At least not on the Jenner or the Rossfeld. They're too difficult. To tell you the truth, even the nursery slopes seem a bit frightening to me this year. Perhaps I should skip the skiing entirely.'

'That might be best. You'd better not tax yourself,' Victor cautioned. 'You've

239

been sick, remember. I think it's wiser and safer to do something less dangerous.'

'I'll potter around the Schloss and keep Christian company.'

'Oh that *will* please him, Cheska,' Diana smiled, affection ringing in her voice. She said to Victor, 'I hear you usually go to Klosters. The skiing is certainly comparable here.' She sighed lightly and shook her head. 'When you're up above six thousand feet everything down below seems so very petty, utterly sham, wherever the mountain is located. Up there, surrounded by such incredible beauty and purity, you feel closer to God, nearer to the truth, and you suddenly get a totally different perspective on the world, see it with clearer eyes. Isn't that so, Victor?'

Before he had the opportunity to respond, her laughter echoed around the small car. 'Oh dear, I'm sounding much too serious and philosophical. The wrong mood entirely.' Her eyes flicked to Victor and she smiled, brought her gaze back to the road. 'Cheska and I decided last night that these next few days are going to be carefree, and lots of fun.'

'That suits me,' Victor said. 'And I hope you're going to let me take you all out to dinner one night . . .' He stopped, remembering Diana had said he was conspicuous, and added, with a quirky smile, 'I guess I'll have to go incognito, wearing my skiing gear and goggles.'

The girls laughed, and Diana said, 'That's an interesting thought. And thank you for your lovely invitation. As a matter of fact, there are some charming old taverns in the area, and also in Salzburg, which I know you'd enjoy. But . . . well, we'll see,' she finished on a noncommittal note.

Francesca reached out and touched Victor's shoulder. 'It's Diana's birthday later this week. There's going to be a small dinner party on Thursday evening. It was planned before she and Christian knew we were coming. You don't mind meeting a few of their friends, do you?'

'I'm entirely in your hands, kid. And the party sounds great.' He made a mental note to talk to Francesca about a birthday present for her cousin, wondering absently if there were any good shops in the town.

Diana and Francesca launched into a discussion about clothes and the outfits they would wear for the party, and Victor lit another cigarette, listening to them with half an ear, amused by their feminine chatter, as well as by the turn of events. You never know in life, old buddy, you just never know, he said to himself.

Victor sank into his own thoughts for a few moments. Francesca's cousin was unusually mature and sophisticated in the best sense of that word. Young as she was, she had undoubtedly experienced her own heartache. There had been a ring of conviction and truth and knowledge in her voice when she had mentioned the worthless, the petty, and the sham. The whole world was sham, wasn't it? The question hung there and he pondered it, and found himself thinking about Francesca. There was nothing sham or shoddy about her. She was pure gold, and very real. The genuine thing, and then some. She's also *verboten*, he reminded himself with a start. Unexpectedly, Victor was no longer able to push aside his feelings for her, nor ignore the attraction she held for him. And he was filled with disquiet, contemplating the five days ahead of him, and of living under the same roof with her. Oh Christ, he thought, what have I done?

*　　*　　*

240

Victor glanced at his watch. They had been on the road for almost an hour now, and he was about to ask how much farther it was to Wittingenhof, when Diana announced, 'Here we are, Victor.'

She dropped her speed and came to a standstill, waiting for another car to pass, and then she drove across the highway and began to climb a dirt road, patched with ice in places and recently layered with cinders. It was narrow and twisting, and rose steeply through a dense wood of giant Scotch pines and drifting banks of frozen snow. They continued to climb for a good twenty minutes. The road began to widen and gradually it levelled off, became a wide flat plateau where the forest thinned out.

Victor was staring ahead. He could see a stone gatehouse, its white-washed façade intersected with dark wood beams, small windows with wooden shutters and brass carriage lamps on either side of a great stone arch. This cut through the centre of the gatehouse like a tunnel, and from it swung massive black iron gates hanging wide open. Victor lifted his eyes as the Volkswagen rumbled over the cobblestones under the archway. He read the name, Schloss Wittingenhof, and the date, 1833, carved in the stonework above the entrance leading into an estate of some considerable size.

Diana swung left and stopped in front of a complex of buildings adjoining the gatehouse, obviously stables and garages, and pulled on the brake. She jumped out of the car, calling to Victor, 'Let's release poor Cheska, shall we?' and began tugging at the skis.

'I'll do that,' he cried, also alighting, but she had already removed them when he came round to the other side of the Volkswagen. Francesca clambered out, stretched herself, and pulled a face. 'God, I was just about ready to scream. I'm terribly cramped and stiff.'

'Don't blame me. I offered to get a taxi for the luggage,' he reminded her. 'Listen, swing your arms and touch your toes. That'll work out the kinks.' She did as he suggested, and he made a motion to lift his bag off the back seat.

Diana hoisted his skis onto her shoulder. She said, 'Don't bother with your luggage, Victor. Manfred will bring it in later.' She set off down a patch cut through a wide expanse of clean snow, her silver-gilt hair gleaming in the sunlight as she walked in the direction of the house.

Victor retrieved his overcoat from the front seat and hurried after Francesca, who was gaily skipping along behind Diana, for all the world like a little yellow bird let out of her cage. He smiled at his comparison, his eyes fastening on her. And it was true, Francesca did seem different to him, freer and less constrained than she was in London. Perhaps her present demeanour had something to do with being in a foreign country, far away from the strictures of her everyday life and all that this entailed; it could be induced by the holiday spirit they all shared; it might even be Diana's influence at work. But whatever had wrought the change was irrelevant, as far as he was concerned. He liked her joyful, unfettered mood, for it suited her and, furthermore, it made him feel more relaxed.

Victor pulled his eyes away from Francesca and directed them sharply to the end of the path. Here stood Schloss Wittingenhof in all its ancient glory. Although Diana had said it was large, he had not envisioned a house quite this size, nor one so impressive, for in essence it was a grand manor house of some distinction. It was of excellent proportions, long and relatively low and rambling, with various wings protruding from the central structure. These wings, perfectly balanced to the main building, helped to create a flowing and harmonious effect. Roofs of blue-grey slate pitched gently down to touch stone walls the colour of eggshell, a soft off-white that had a hint of beige. The many windows were flanked by black and white shutters, whilst the double front door, with a lintel of stone, was painted white and decorated with black nail heads and black iron hinges. A series of dormer windows were cut into the roofs, which, in turn, were topped by fat squat chimneys, and all added to the charm of the picturesque architecture.

Wittingenhof nestled against a backdrop of splendid fir trees. These swept upwards over the slopes of the mountain, which continued its soaring ascent immediately behind the Schloss. The mountain, for all its immensity of size and spread and height, did not diminish the house. Rather, it threw Wittingenhof into bold relief, the grandeur of the natural setting underscoring its intrinsic beauty. The plateau upon which the house was built was on high ground, and the atmosphere was clear, bracing, and the intense glare from the crystalline snow converged with the lucency of the sky to create a light of supernatural brilliance, a light that blinded with its clarity. Victor blinked, shielded his eyes with his hand, and caught up with Francesca. 'The Schloss looks a sensational place,' he said.

'Yes, it's lovely, and wait 'til you see inside. Diana has done a marvellous job with it.'

'Is the architecture typical of the area?' he asked, falling into step.

'Yes, to a certain extent. It's very much in the Bavarian tradition, but modified, less Hansel and Gretelish. I forget who designed it, someone quite famous in his time though. Wittingenhof is considered an architectural classic, and it's well over a hundred years old.'

'Yes, I noticed the date on the entrance when we drove in, I guess it was built for the family, wasn't it?'

Francesca nodded. 'One of Diana's ancestors owned this mountain and the surrounding land, and I understand that he built the Schloss for his young wife, who was frail in health and needed the air at this altitude. She must have had lung problems. After she died, the house fell into disuse. The family only occupied it occasionally in the summer months, for holidays. It was Diana who actually decided to open it up for full-time use, and she and Christian have made it their permanent home for a number of years now. It's just as beautiful in the summer. These . . .' She pointed to the snowy areas in front of the house, 'are all lawns and there are meadows at the back, and a lovely lake. Oh look, Victor . . . you've got a welcoming committee!' she cried tugging at his arm.

He followed the movement of her head and his face lit up. A gaggle of geese, sleek, plump and immaculate, were marching across the snow, comical in their sedateness. Victor looked down at Francesca, his eyes laughing. 'They couldn't have staged this better in Hollywood. Tell me, kid, how do the geese know how to march out on cue?'

'I've no idea,' Francesca grinned. 'But they always make an appearance around this time. Feeding hour, I suppose. Come on, Diana's waiting.'

Diana stood in the doorway, leaning on the skis. 'I'd like to add *my* welcome,' she said. 'I hope you enjoy your stay at Wittingenhof, Victor. You must consider it your home too.'

'Thanks, Diana. You're being very kind.'

Turning she said to Francesca, 'Why don't you take Victor down to the cloakroom, and I'll go and tell Christian we've arrived.' She handed the skis to Victor. 'Would you mind carrying these, please? Francesca will show you where we store them.'

'Sure,' he said, taking the bag from her.

The two girls walked across the entrance foyer and Victor followed in their wake, looking around with quickening interest. The entrance was small and square, with a beamed ceiling, white stucco walls and a floor composed of terracotta tiles, glazed to a burnished hue by the sunlight shafting through the windows. A massive mirror, framed in intricately-chased silver, hung above a carved pine chest, and in its glassy depths trembled reflections of the entire area. Next to it stood a silver urn bursting with branches of red berries. At the opposite end the small foyer splayed out on either side to become an impressive great hall, with many doors opening off it and a spectacular curving staircase floating gracefully up to other floors. It was sparsely furnished, the only pieces being an armoire, several carved wooden chairs, and a desk near the stairwell, all in a rustic country style and made of oak.

This hall had baronial overtones, with a high-flung ceiling and walls painted the same soft eggshell as the exterior of the house. An immense and eye-catching tapestry, depicting a medieval hunting scene, was suspended on the rise above the staircase, a wrought-iron chandelier dropped on long chains from the centre of the ceiling, and the floor of dark wood, polished to a high gloss, was entirely bare.

Diana veered to the right, waving to them as she went into one of the rooms. Francesca guided Victor to the left, along a corridor and down a short flight of stone steps. These stopped in another hallway, on the lower level, where French windows opened onto a paved loggia and beyond, in the distance, was a view of the frozen lake and a copse of trees, their spidery black branches dripping icicles.

Marvellous aromas of food cooking floated on the warm air. Victor sniffed. 'I guess we're near the kitchen,' he said, eyeing Francesca.

'Yes, it's down there.' She nodded to the end of the hallway.

'I just realized how starved I am. Ravenous. I was up at the crack of dawn to get the plane.'

'Manfred will bring something up to the sitting room shortly. A little snack with our drinks, before lunch. Come on, put your skis in here.' She opened a cupboard, moved on, and turned the iron handle on another door. 'And this is the cloakroom.'

Victor propped his bag next to several pairs of skis lined up in the cupboard, closed it, and followed her. The cloakroom was a *mélange* of blue and white, these colours appearing in the tiles on the floor and in a faded floral paper on the walls and ceiling. Francesca stuck her yellow woollen cap on one of the pegs attached to the wall, where an assortment of anoraks, Loden jackets and capes already hung. 'You can put your coat here, and the bathroom's through that door, if you want to freshen up.'

'Thanks.'

She turned to the mirror standing on the pine chest, ran a comb through her hair, then shook it free casually. 'I'll be in the drawing room, upstairs.'

'I don't think I'll get lost, kid,' he said.

CHAPTER TWENTY-FIVE

Francesca bounded up the stone stairs, humming under her breath. She was in a happy mood, engendered by Victor's presence in the house. Although she was not foolish enough to think this particular circumstance would bring about a change in him, or cause him to suddenly reciprocate her feelings, she did believe their friendship had a better chance of flowering here at Wittingenhof than in London. Furthermore, and most importantly, she had him entirely to herself, did not have to compete with Nicky or Katharine, and the rest of his entourage, for his attention, and this in itself was most gratifying to her.

She swung down the Deer Hall, walking swiftly, still humming, but as she passed the library her steps faltered. The door was firmly closed, and it was thick; nonetheless, she heard Diana exclaiming, 'Oh, for God's sake!' and with such impatience Francesca was startled. Again, Diana's voice rang out, now in a staccato burst of rapid German which Francesca did not understand; however, it was quite apparent her cousin was irritated. She did not wish to hear any more, and so she hurried on in the direction of the gallery, frowning to herself. It was unusual for Diana to sound cross, and especially so with her brother, with whom she was invariably gentle and mild. She wondered what had ruffled Diana, and instantly dropped the thought. It was none of her business, and she preferred not to delve too deeply into certain matters in *this* household.

When she entered the sitting room, Francesca went immediately to the cabinet where the records were stored, found a classical piece she liked and put it on the record player. Then she crossed to the high stone hearth and sat down on it, warming her hands in front of the fire.

A dreamy expression suffused her face, and she leaned back, her thoughts caught up with Victor and the five days stretching ahead of them. Last night, after she had explained the situation to Diana, told her of the need for secrecy in view of Victor's complicated life, his impending divorce, and his worry about *Confidential Magazine*, she had confided in her cousin. But the confidences had only been partial ones, for as always Francesca held back her innermost feelings. Being essentially an exceedingly private person, she deemed these to be too intimate to impart to anyone, even someone close to her. This was chiefly the reason she had not said anything about Victor to Katharine, although fear of appearing foolish and juvenile had also induced reticence, along with a reluctance to give Katharine an opportunity to fill her ears with tid-bits about Victor's many love affairs, as she was prone to do. Francesca was wise enough to understand this knowledge would only underscore her anxiety and undermine her self-confidence.

After Francesca had finished her carefully-edited recital about her attraction to Victor, Diana had been thoughtful for a while. Eventually she had said, 'I think you must ignore his attitude towards you, otherwise you'll be miserable the entire time you're here, darling. I also think you should be completely natural with him, even let him see you're attracted to him, like him as much as you do.' Diana had stopped, her laughter breaking loose, her eyes merry. 'Don't look like *that*, Cheska! You can make him aware of your interest in him without being flagrant, or throwing yourself at him.'

Diana had leaned forward and squeezed Francesca's arm. 'Listen to me, darling. Men can be very peculiar, quite odd. And they're as afraid of rejection as we are, you know. So sometimes they need a little gentle encouragement to make them feel more at ease. And there's another thing. If I were you I'd forget my age, forget his age, and also forget who he is. He might be a famous movie star, but he's a man like any other man. That's how you should view him. Apart from anything else, you'll feel more relaxed if you do. And who knows, he might pick up on that, and relax himself.'

The cousins had continued to talk along these lines for some while longer, and when Francesca had gone to bed she had felt positive and optimistic, and had decided to take Diana's advice. What do I have to lose? she asked herself now. Nothing, she concluded. I might even have a lot to gain.

So preoccupied was she at this moment, she was unaware that Diana was standing in the arched doorway to the sitting room. Diana was regarding Francesca closely, but lovingly so, filled with the tenderest of feelings for her cousin. She was suddenly glad Francesca was visiting them at this time, for her presence was comforting, reassuring even. That's because she's so down-to-earth, and so very steady, Diana thought. She has a normalizing effect on us all.

Diana now took a deep breath, trying to still the troubling thoughts that continued to nudge at the back of her mind in the most maddening way. She was a little upset, she had to admit. Upset with Dieter Mueller, currently ensconced in the library with Christian; upset with herself, too, for allowing her irritation with Dieter to show so blatantly.

Francesca lifted her head, saw her cousin and smiled. Diana moved forward, heading for the fireplace. She sat down heavily on the hearth next to Francesca, and said in a low tone 'Cheska . . . Mummy's in Munich.'

Francesca tried to keep her expression bland, but she knew it reflected the concern swamping her. 'Is she coming here?' she asked, her voice equally subdued.

Diana shook her head. 'No. But she's in Bavaria because of my birthday. She came specially to see me, so I'm meeting her on Friday. For the day.' Her voice trembled slightly, as she added, 'I'm dreading it, I really am.'

'I'll go with you,' Francesca volunteered at once. 'Perhaps I can be of some help.' She genuinely meant this; nevertheless, the prospect of making the trip filled her with dismay, and her heart dropped.

Diana was silent, considering, and then she said, 'No, it's not necessary, and there's no point. You father saw her last summer, when he was here with Doris, and it didn't do a bit of good . . .' Her voice trailed away, and her eyes filled up. 'I adore Mummy, Cheska, you know that, so it's unbearably painful for me to see her like this – so troubled and distracted.' She blinked, brushed her eyes with her hand, swallowed hard. 'I feel utterly at a loss. I don't know what to do to help her any more . . . so frustrating . . .'

'Oh Dibs darling, don't tear yourself apart, please, please don't. Your *love* helps her. It truly does, and in so many different ways.' Francesca took Diana's hand in hers, held onto it tightly, wanting so much to comfort and reassure. 'And your immense courage gives her such a lot of strength. Don't forget, you and Christian keep her going, and there's not much more you can do than that. Unless you can persuade her to take Daddy's advice to go home to England, to live on the estate at Langley. That would be the best solution I'm su – '

'You know she'll never leave Berlin! *Never.*'

'I suppose not.' Francesca bit her lip and shook her head resignedly, knowing Diana was right in this assumption. She asked, 'Is Christian going with you to Munich?'

'Yes, of course. Try to keep him away. He's in the same boat as I am, as far as Mummy is concerned. He adores her, worries about her, and is constantly seeking a way to make her lead a more normal life. Anyway, we're leaving very early on Friday morning, around six o'clock, and we'll get back in time to have supper with you'

'That's such a short visit. Look, why don't you stay longer?'

'I would like to spend the weekend with her, but when she 'phoned this morning she told Christian she's going back to Berlin on Saturday. She never stays away from there very long . . .'

'Perhaps that's understandable in a way, Dibs. Her memories are in Berlin. And so many hopes.'

Diana looked past Francesca, her face washed with sadness as she stared into the distance. Finally, she said, 'False hopes, Cheska. Futile hopes.'

'You and Daddy, and I too, believe they're futile, but she doesn't and she never will. Aunt Arabella is very stubborn. Kim takes after her in that respect, and perhaps I do too.'

'Yes, it seems to be a family trait.' Diana sighed. Suddenly she looked at Francesca quickly. 'Incidentally, what are we going to do about Victor on Friday? It just occurred to me, there's no one to take him skiing unless you want to brave it, and I really don't think you should,' she finished, aware of Francesca's ineptitude on skis and her fear of high slopes.

'Dibs, you don't have to worry about Victor. He can go by himself. He won't mind. Anyway, surely Manfred can drive him to the Rossfeld, or perhaps you can dig up one of your friends to go along. Don't give it another thought. He'll understand.'

A watery smile flickered on Diana's face. 'I trust your judgment on that one, and look, I'm sorry I got all weepy just then. I didn't mean to upset you, or burden you with my problems. You know I'm usually more controlled. But Dieter Mueller is with Christian right now, and I suppose he brought a number of things into focus. And he annoyed me more than usual, made me feel nervous. He means well, yet he only seems to create additional problems. Also, I wasn't expecting Mummy to arrive for my birthday, and it's thrown me a bit. Don't misunderstand me, Cheska, I'm glad she's here, and it'll be lovely to see her.

246

It's just, well, to be honest, the thing I dread about visiting her is having to witness her awful pain.'

'I realize that, darling.' Francesca put her arms around Diana and hugged her. 'I'm here, if you need me, and you know I'll always do whatever I can.'

'You're a great comfort to me, darling. Anyway, I'm not going to think about Friday until Friday comes.' Diana's face visibly cheered and her smile became more certain. 'I said we were going to make your vacation a happy one, and we are. Enough of all this. I'll cope, in much the same way I've been coping for the past two years, simply by taking every day as it comes, one day at a time.' Diana stood up. 'I'd better go and telephone Mummy. I won't be long, and then we'll have that drink before lunch. In the meantime, when Victor comes up, why don't you show him his suite?'

'Oh, there's no great hurry, Dibs. We'll sit here and wait for you and Christian. Victor can see his suite after lunch.'

'Fine, whatever you want.' Diana touched Francesca's shoulder lightly. 'Thanks for being lovely, lovely you, Cheska.' She turned abruptly and went through the door leading to the west wing of the Schloss.

Gazing after her, Francesca thought: She's pretty amazing. She's so tiny, so fragile, yet she has more strength than anyone I know, and her heart's as big as a paving stone. Instantly her thoughts flew to her aunt. *She* is beyond our help really, Francesca said inwardly. How Diana handled this difficult and troubling situation so well, and usually with such equanimity, was sometimes beyond her comprehension. But Francesca had come to realize that her cousin was dauntless. There was a well-spring of courage within her which she could continually draw upon; in much the same way, she had the rock of her unshakable faith to cling to. Last year, when Diana had been staying at Langley, they had had a most unusual talk, one which had taken Francesca by surprise, and it had been most revealing.

On a sunny July afternoon, after a shopping trip to Harrogate and lunch at a local pub, they had strolled through the gardens at Langley. Diana had spoken at length about her mother and the latter's state of mind, and then, she had expressed the opinion that there was a grand design to life itself, a pattern that existed everywhere, and for everyone.

'Things can happen to us, terrible things which we cannot understand when they're actually occurring. They seem so cruel and unjust and incomprehensible at the time,' Diana had said. 'But they are simply meant to be ... they are part of the pattern. And I'm certain that one day the pattern becomes clear to us all, takes on a definite shape, so that finally we see its true meaning.'

After several long moments of silence, she had murmured, and so softly Francesca had had to strain to hear, 'God has His reasons for everything. And there will come a time in all our lives when we do understand His purpose, His divine pattern.'

Francesca had listened carefully, and though she had found her cousin's words as extraordinary as they were unexpected, she knew Diana had meant everything she had said. Perhaps it was this spiritual knowledge and this inner sureness that underpinned Diana's natural fortitude.

And remembering those words now, Francesca was again convinced that Diana believed the tragedies which had befallen her parents had been God's will, and thus were unalterable. She saw them as a fragment of that divine pattern, and consequently they were her own destiny too. This is what sustains her, enables her to shoulder her burdens so stoically, to carry on with the business of life and of living in such a positive way, Francesca whispered to herself. And that's not such a bad thing, when you think about it.

As Victor made his way through the Deer Hall he understood at once the reason for its name. A collection of antlers and stags' heads were mounted above the archway leading into the gallery and on the walls on either side of the arch. Close by was a glass-fronted gun cabinet.

Being a hunter, and a gun collector himself, he approached this eagerly. The cabinet was locked, and he cupped his hands around his eyes, peering through the glass at a fine collection of hunting rifles and other firearms displayed there. All were in first-rate condition, and some were rare antique specimens. He would ask Diana if he could examine them later. He also made up his mind to pay that visit to Purdey's when he was back in London, as he had long intended, to pick out a couple of new hunting rifles for himself and Nicky.

Victor moved away from the cabinet and strolled down the gallery, his feet clattering loudly against the parquet floor, and this made him conscious of the lack of rugs and carpets in the Schloss. Were the von Wittingens as strapped as the Earl? It didn't seem likely. Diana was beautifully turned out, and the house was elegant and well kept. But anything's possible, he muttered, thinking of Francesca, who was always smartly if simply dressed. He was well aware the aristocracy had a clever knack for keeping up the proper front no matter what. It's all a question of pride, he said to himself, thinking of his own, smiling wryly as he continued on down the gallery.

A number of sombre oil paintings hung on the walls, otherwise it was unfurnished except for an odd-looking cart in the centre of the floor. As he drew closer he realized this was actually a marvellous old-fashioned sleigh, a charming relic from the past. The sleigh had a colourful painted base, brass ornamentation and polished old leather that gleamed dully in the dim light filtering through several stained glass windows. It had been stacked with greenery, flowering plants, and nosegays of dried flowers tied with moss-green velvet ribbons. He guessed the sleigh was Diana's artistic handiwork, for it seemed to echo the spirit of the girl, whom he had taken to immediately. He found her an interesting study, a combination of gaiety and gravity which was most appealing.

The gallery led directly into the sitting room, and as Victor meandered in he stopped short, all his senses coming into play. His first impression was visual and it was an impression of that lucent light so peculiar to the mountains. It streamed in glittering cataracts through the many shining windows, glanced off reflective surfaces and objects, washed over creamy colours and delicate jewel tones. Instantaneously he became aware of sounds ... the hiss and crackle of the fire, the haunting, bittersweet strains of a piano concerto rising and falling in waves, and wafting to him on the still air was a mingling of the most evocative smells ... the pungency of pine needles and wooded hills, the perfume of tuberoses, the aroma of ripening fruit.

Francesca was standing at the far end of the long, low-ceilinged room, a flash of yellow against the stone fireplace, one so high and wide it dwarfed her. He went into the room, returning her smile, his feet sinking into velvety pile, and he was aware of sudden warmth, understated luxury, a setting of extraordinary loveliness.

He saw, at a glance, antique chests and tables, cream walls, a cream carpet of Persian design, its graceful configurations running from ruby, rose quartz and amethyst to aquamarine and sapphire. Cushions in some of these tints sparked the two huge sofas, covered in cream velvet, which were grouped in front of the fireplace, and there were vases of fresh flowers and plants in profusion, many candles, and a plethora of objects of art that added the glitter of silver and crystal, the sharp clear hues of Meissen porcelain.

'Diana had to make a quick 'phone call to Munich,' Francesca explained, coming to meet him. She took his arm with the utmost naturalness, no longer self-conscious, nor intimidated by him, and steered him to the fire. 'She'll be back in a few minutes, and Christian will join us in a moment. Apparently he had an unexpected visitor, and he's just saying goodbye. As soon as they're both here we're going to have a drink and a snack.'

'That sounds terrific.' He stood with his back to the fire, reached into his pocket for his cigarettes and lit one. 'You were right about the house. Jeez, it's just beautiful, Francesca.' His eyes swept over the sitting room appreciatively. 'I could sit here and dream the days away, forget about everything. In an odd way, it reminds me of the ranch, although it's different, of course, as far as the furniture goes. But there's the same stillness, that sense of peace.'

'I'm glad you like it,' Francesca said, filling with pleasure. 'I was pretty certain you would. Still, I must admit, I was a bit worried you might find it far too isolated, and that you'd be bored, stuck up here on the top of a mountain with only us three for company.'

'The world well lost, I'd say,' he murmured, glancing down at her. 'This music is lovely. What is it?'

'Rachmaninov's Piano Concerto No. 2 in C minor.' At this moment the record came to an end, and she moved swiftly to the cabinet adjacent to the fireplace. 'Would you like to hear the rest of it?'

'Sure, I'd love it.'

Francesca turned the record over, started the player, and rejoined him. 'Diana didn't think you'd want to ski today, after the plane trip. So we're going to have a leisurely lunch, and take it easy. But we can go for a walk later, if you like. The woods are perfectly beautiful. Come to the window and see the view from – '

She broke off as an oak door on the far wall opened and a grey-haired, middle-aged man appeared. He was dressed in green Loden trousers and a matching high-necked Bavarian jacket. '*Gnädige Frau* . . .' He waited respectfully.

'Oh Manfred, do come in, please. Victor, this is Manfred, who looks after us so well. Manfred, this is Herr Mason.' She spoke slowly, enunciating her words with care.

'Herr Mason'. Manfred smiled, inclined his head deferentially. 'Velcom. Luggage iss in your suite. *Ja.*' He nodded his head, still smiling. 'I vill haff

Clara unpack, iff you vill, Herr Mason. *Ja?*' His English was halting, accented, but easily understandable.

'Sure. Thanks a lot, Manfred. That's great, terrific. Thanks again.'

Manfred inclined his head once more, his expression courteous. His kindly blue eyes settled on Francesca. '*Die Prinzessin hat mir aufgetragen, den Champagner zu servieren.*'

'*Danke schön*, Manfred.' He retreated, and Francesca said to Victor, 'Diana's obviously still on the 'phone, and she's told Manfred to serve the champagne now.'

'I sort of gathered as much. I also caught the word *Prinzessin*.' He looked at her sharply. 'Is she? Is Diana a princess?'

'Yes. Oh gosh, didn't I tell you?'

Victor laughed good-naturedly. 'No, you didn't, and it's not the only thing you forgot, kid. What about her birthday? I wish you'd mentioned it, then I could've brought a gift with me from London.'

'I feel awful about that myself. I remembered on the plane when it was too late.' Her expression was chagrined, and she rushed on, 'I would've chosen some American records. She loves those, especially anything by Frank Sinatra. I'll make a trip into town tomorrow, whilst you're off skiing, to buy something from us both. I think perfume is probably the best thing to get her.'

'Aren't there any shops where you can get the records she likes?'

Francesca shook her head, grimaced. 'There is one shop in town, but I don't think there'd be much choice. Anyway, I'm sure Diana's already bought up their entire collection.'

'Then I guess it'll have to be perfume. Listen, about the dinner party tomorrow night. I didn't bring a dinner jacket. I hope it isn't formal.'

'Oh dear, I'm sure it will be, but I'll explain to Diana, and perhaps she can ask her friends to dress appropriately, so you won't be embarrassed. Victor, there's something I want to tell you. It's about Christian – ' Francesca got no further. Manfred returned, carrying a tray of crystal flutes and a bottle of champagne. He was accompanied by a young woman holding a silver chafing dish. She was dressed in a dirndl of Loden cloth and a sweater of the same muted green under a large white apron. They walked, one after the other, across the floor to a console table, and Manfred addressed Francesca. '*Gnädige Frau*, I open, *ja?*'

'Please, Manfred.' Francesca glanced up at Victor. 'This is Clara, Manfred's daughter. Clara, Herr Mason.'

The girl returned Victor's friendly greeting rather shyly, half smiled, excused herself and slipped out. Francesca stepped to the console, lifted the chafing dish lid and looked inside. '*Wunderbar!*' She turned to Manfred, who was opening the champagne, and began to speak to him in uncertain German.

Victor searched for an ashtray, found one on a long library table behind a sofa, and stubbed out his cigarette. The table held a selection of photographs in silver frames, and he scanned them quickly, his eyes settling on one of a lovely fair-haired young woman wearing an evening gown and a diamond tiara. It had obviously been taken in the nineteen twenties or thereabouts, and he guessed it was of Francesca's aunt, for he was instantly struck by the family resemblance. The young woman had a look of the Earl around the eyes, the same refined and chiselled features. Victor's attention strayed to the other photographs, several snapshots of two beautiful children, apparently Diana and her brother when they were young. Placed a little apart from them was another somewhat formally posed portrait, similar to that of the young woman, this time of a darkly handsome man in a rather dated dinner jacket. Their father?

Leaning forward, Victor intensified his scrutiny. The man was exceptional looking, and there was dignity, even regality, in his bearing. However, it was not these characteristics which held his interest so completely. There was a unique quality in the face, a quality of purity, of goodness, but it was the eyes which so stunned in their impact. They were dark, expressive. Powerful, piercing eyes that compelled with their intensity and fervour. Victor stared hard at the photograph, hypnotized by the face. And he, who was only too familiar with the power of the lens and the truth it invariably revealed, thought, with a flash of perception: I am seeing the soul of this man. And it is the soul of a saint . . .

'Hello!' a strong masculine voice rang out.

Victor straightened up and swung around on his heels, and he was jolted. 'Hello,' he responded immediately, hoping his surprise did not show on his face. He forced a wide smile onto his mouth.

The young man who had just greeted Victor sat in a wheelchair. It was not so much the chair that startled Victor, but rather its occupant. He was the living embodiment of the man in the photograph. They might be one and the same person, except that Victor knew otherwise, knew this could not be so. Caught on film was the image of the father. Here in the flesh was the son, of that he was quite certain, and if the face he was now regarding was not the face of a saint, certainly it was one of nobility and unusual gentleness.

The young man smiled, and before Victor could make a move towards him he was propelling himself down the long stretch of Persian carpet. He did so rapidly, and surely, displaying the expertise and ease of one long acquainted with this chair.

'Christian,' Francesca cried and flew across to the fireplace, positioning herself next to Victor. 'I just asked Manfred to come and find you. This is Victor.'

'Of course it is!' Christian said, laughing. He thrust out his hand as he came to a stop in front of Victor. 'Welcome to Wittingenhof.'

Francesca said, 'Victor, this is my cousin, His Highness Prince Christian Michael Alexander von Wittingen und Habst.'

'Really, Francesca,' Christian said quietly, 'we don't need the whole mouthful.' He shook his head, as if reproving her, but his smile was fond.

'I'm delighted to meet you,' Victor said, also smiling, knowing her recital of the string of names and the title were solely for his benefit, after his mild chastising of a few minutes ago. He added, 'Thanks so much for inviting me to stay with you.'

'It's our pleasure, believe me,' Christian said, his English as natural and as faultless as that of his sister. 'And do forgive me for not being here to greet you, when you first arrived. I had a surprise visit from . . . an old friend . . . of my father's, and he stayed much longer than I expected.'

'Please don't apologize. Francesca looked after me very well, and I've been enjoying this room. It's lovely.'

251

'Thank you. Now, how about a glass of champagne? Francesca, will you do the honours, my dear?'

'Of course.' She hurried to the console, poured the champagne and brought the tray of flutes over to the low, glass and brass coffee table situated between the sofas. She passed the glasses around and sat down. Victor joined her on the sofa, and they all raised their glasses as Christian said, '*Prosit*.'

'*Prosit!*' Victor and Francesca reiterated in unison.

'I'm sorry Diana is delayed. Some problem with her boutique in Munich,' Christian remarked, resorting to a white lie in order to avoid a long explanation about his mother. He took a sip of champagne, smiled broadly and continued, 'But she's pretty good at sorting things out, and I don't suppose she'll be very long. You must be hungry after your trip. Bertha made some Swedish meatballs. They're delicious. Please, do help yourself.'

'I think I will.' Victor half rose.

'I'll serve you,' Francesca said, and was across the room in a flash. 'Can I get some for you too, Christian?' she asked as she spooned meatballs onto a glass plate.

'Not at the moment, thank you.' He pushed his chair closer to the coffee table, bent forward and took a cigarette from the silver box. After lighting it, he said to Victor, 'It's simply marvellous for us to have guests at this time of year. It's generally very quiet. After the onslaught at Christmas, we don't have many friends visiting us again until the summer. They like to come for the Salzburg Festival. The music's the attraction, of course.'

'Yes, so I've heard,' said Victor. 'And I understand the festival's the whole enchilada.'

Christian looked at Victor in puzzlement. 'The whole enchilada?'

Francesca, returning with the plate of food, grinned and said, 'That's Victor's favourite expression. It's very Californian, and it means the whole works, Christian.' She put the plate in front of Victor, glanced at him under her lashes, and remarked, 'You promised to explain its derivation, and you never did.'

'Sorry. An enchilada's a corn tortilla, a Mexican flat bread, something like a pancake. It's filled with a variety of things, chopped beef, cheese, vegetables, then rolled and served with any one of a number of sauces. It's sort of . . .'

He stopped, grinned back at her, and finished, 'Well, it's the whole works.'

'Also rather colourful,' Christian pronounced, obviously amused. 'I think I might adopt it myself.'

'Adopt what?' Diana asked from the doorway.

Christian swung his head, and repeated everything Victor had said whilst she poured herself a glass of champagne. Munching on a meatball, Victor scrutinized them, very much intrigued by this brother and sister. Not unnaturally he was riddled with curiosity, and it was a curiosity that ran on a variety of levels. Innumerable questions about the von Wittingens, those both present and absent, floated around in his head. Perhaps Francesca would enlighten him later. Apparently she had been on the verge of explaining Christian's disability when Manfred had arrived with the champagne, cutting her short. He glanced at the young prince surreptitiously. Christian looked extremely healthy, despite his confinement to the chair, and there was a certain vitality about him. Victor recognized immediately that this was not so

252

much physical as mental, had more to do with his state of mind and his personality than his bodily well being. Victor detected a forcefulness in him, just below the level of the gentleness.

Diana joined them, seated herself on the hearth, looked across at Victor and said, 'Can one use that expression, the whole enchilada, to describe people, or houses, for instance? I mean could one say that Wittingenhof was the whole enchilada?'

There was a hint of laughter in her voice and a mischievous glint in her eyes, and Victor was not sure if she was teasing him or not, but he decided to treat her question seriously. 'Surely you could. And incidentally, it *is*, at least what I've seen of it so far.'

'Why thank you, Victor. That's nice of you. We love it. We've been very happy here, haven't we, Christian?'

'Yes, we have, darling.'

'Francesca told me the house wasn't used for many years. I can't imagine anyone wanting to close this place up. Not permanently. Didn't your parents even bring you here when you were children?' Victor asked Diana.

She did not respond. Like Christian, she was reluctant to open up areas of conversation that were complex, often painful, and which also required long explanations. She had learned it was far better to avoid them when she could, without appearing rude.

Always attuned to others, Victor instantly sensed an awkwardness, and he wondered why his innocent remarks had caused this strange silence. He looked at Diana sharply, saw a faint flicker of distress cross her face, and then quite suddenly she smiled and shook her head.

Lighting a cigarette, she remarked, 'No, they didn't bring us here. Ever. In fact, they never came themselves. My father wasn't very keen on Bavaria.' There was a slight hesitation in Diana. She had surprised herself by saying as much as she had. It was Victor of course. There was something in him that made her feel relaxed, a trait in his personality that encouraged confidences. His eyes held hers, and she saw the questions, the bafflement on his face. Almost against her own volition, she found herself volunteering, 'Bavaria was a hotbed of politics in the twenties and thirties. The wrong politics as far as my father was concerned – ' She halted when Christian coughed, not sure she ought to continue, looking at him uncertainly, wondering if he disapproved.

Apparently he did not, for he spoke up himself. 'Our father was an anti-Fascist, Victor, and he had many adversaries here. Hitler's nasty little band of gangsters was pretty well entrenched in Munich, you know.' Christian leaned forward, his face quickening, his dark eyes darkening to coal black and becoming intent. 'Then again, lots of other Right Wing organizations had made their headquarters here, fanatics incensed about the Versailles Treaty, and God knows what else. There were also the Bavarian monarchists champing at the bit, wanting to have an independent state and their own king back, if you can believe that one! In any event, the whole area was dangerous for a man like my father. You see, he did not merely pay lip service to his beliefs, but was an active opponent of all those who were determined to destroy the Republic. He wanted democracy for Germany, not dictatorship, and he committed his energy, his time and his fortune to fight the destructive forces tearing the country apart.'

Christian shifted slightly in the wheelchair, and proceeded: 'Naturally, it was better if he stayed away from here, safer for him in Berlin, or at our other Schloss, just outside Berlin. That's why Wittingenhof remained closed, you see, was unoccupied for years, except for the caretakers.'

'Very valid reasons, too,' Victor said. He had not been mistaken about that remarkable face in the dated photograph. What he had spotted in those burning eyes was the fervour of the dedicated idealist. He could not help adding, 'And what does a house mean, when your life is at stake. Your father sounds like an extraordinary man, Christian, a man of great integrity and honour. I hope I get the opportunity to meet him one – ' Francesca caught Victor's eye and the look now washing over her face prevented him from saying another word. Instinctively he knew he was on dangerous ground, that he had somehow blundered. There was an uncomfortable hush.

It was broken by Christian, who said calmly, 'There are few men in this world like my father, Victor, men who recognize evil where others do not, who fight it all their lives and with every fibre of their being.' He smiled gently. 'But perhaps now is the wrong time to get involved in this particular kind of discussion.' The smile became dismissive, but it was also friendly. 'To continue the story of the house. After the war, we decided to move back to Bavaria, mainly because we had nowhere else to go. Our house in Berlin was flattened to the ground, and the area outside the city, where the Schloss was located, had suddenly become part of the East Zone controlled by the Russians. Our grandmother had inherited a house in Munich from her brother, and she knew the only solution to the family's predicament was to open it up. We lived with her for several years or so, and then Diana came to the conclusion that Wittingenhof would be wonderful for my health – the mountain air and all that.' He gave Victor a sly grin, chuckled. 'We also wanted to escape Grandmama, I must admit, who is marvellous, but a bit of an old dragon.'

'I'll say she is!' Francesca exclaimed, relieved Christian had so adroitly diverted the conversation. 'Oops! Sorry, Christian, I didn't mean to sound rude or disrespectful about Princess Hetti.'

Diana and Christian smiled at her affectionately. The air miraculously cleared, and Victor looked at Francesca, who nodded imperceptibly, as if she was saying everything was now all right. Diana got up and brought the bottle of champagne, refilling their glasses. 'But it does happen to be the truth, Cheska.' She glanced at Victor. 'You should have heard how Grandmother carried on when I opened my first boutique here. "Going into *trade*!" she kept repeating over and over again, making trade sound like a life of ill repute.'

There was more laughter and Christian said, 'Poor old thing, living in the past, I'm afraid, but she has a certain sweetness, even if she is a bit dictatorial, and she loves us dearly, wants only the best for us.'

Victor nodded. 'Naturally she does.' He directed his attention to Diana and went on, 'Francesca tells me you've been very successful with your business venture. Congratulations.'

'Thank you.' She smiled at him, liking him, hoping to communicate this with her eyes, wanting him to feel comfortable and at ease with them again.

The warmth flowing out of her registered with Victor, and he returned her smile.

254

'You've also done a fantastic job on this house. There's something quite magical about it, and the tranquillity is just out of this world.'

'I'm glad you feel that way,' she responded with quickness. 'And when you go for a walk with Francesca later, you'll be even more conscious of the peacefulness here, and the views from the mountain are quite spectacular.'

Manfred came in, announced quietly that lunch was ready to be served, and disappeared. Diana led the way into the dining room.

This adjoined the sitting room and was long and narrow in shape, with a stone fireplace on one wall, and a large window at the opposite end overlooking the snow-covered sloping lawns, and a panoramic vista of distant mountains. The room, with its white stucco walls, bare polished floor and dark wood furniture in Bavarian style, was somewhat masculine in overtone. But the basic austerity that prevailed was softened by a number of lovely floral arrangements in huge copper jugs, a collecting of green plants grouped in one corner, and a series of striking wood figures, intricately carved and painted in bright colours. These graced the tops of two long chests and the mantelpieces above the roaring log fire.

Christian propelled himself to the head of the refectory table that stretched down the centre of the floor, and said, 'Sit wherever you want, old chap, no formality here.'

'Thanks,' Victor said, sliding into the chair opposite Francesca. Diana took a seat at the other end of the table. 'I hope you like the first course, Victor,' she remarked, indicating the small covered bowl in front of him. She lifted the lid off her own, and went on, 'It's lentil soup, a local speciality, and very tasty.'

'I love any kind of soup,' he answered. 'And I don't mind telling you, I've worked up quite an appetite by now.'

'Good. Bertha, Manfred's wife, is a superb cook, and she's prepared a typical Bavarian lunch for us today. Well, for *you* really.'

'That's nice,' he said, picking up his spoon. 'You must make a point of introducing me to her later, so that I can thank her personally.'

'She'll be thrilled.'

Whilst they were eating their soup, Manfred and Clara came in carrying huge platters of steaming sauerkraut, red cabbage, boiled potatoes, and a large serving plate of *Bratwurst*, thick veal sausages browned to perfection and topped with rich gravy. They placed the dishes on the sideboard, and then Manfred hurried to the table, where he poured local white wine, chilled and sparkling, into long-stemmed, green crystal glasses.

Christian said, 'Lunch is always buffet style, Victor,' and swung his chair over to the adjacent sideboard. 'Come along, help yourself.'

Victor and Francesca rose together and followed him. As they filled their plates, Victor leaned forward and murmured in her ear, 'It smells as good as my Italian dinner, doesn't it, kid?'

She looked up at him carefully, smiling a knowing smile and said nothing. But her eyes did not leave his face and eventually she said, in a low voice of unmistakable intimacy, 'There'll never be a meal comparable to that one, at least not for me. It was especially *delicious*, and in more ways than one.'

The look she now gave him was lingering, appraising, and of such intensity Victor was momentarily dazzled by it, found he was unable to tear his gaze away from those topaz eyes. He felt a sudden tightness in his throat as he thought: She's flirting with me. By God, she really is. I'll be damned.

When they had returned to the table and were eating lunch and chatting, Victor remembered a comment Nick Latimer had made to him weeks ago, something about there being more to Francesca than met the eye. Perhaps Nicky, the soothsayer, had been right. This thought stayed with him throughout the meal, during which he spent a great deal of time studying her, was most attentive to every word she uttered, whether to himself or her cousins. He was totally tuned-in to her, conscious of every nuance in her voice, her every gesture. At one moment he asked her an innocuous question, and her reply was casually couched and utterly proper, but her expression was inviting, her eyes reflecting a hidden sexuality he had not seen there before. That's a come-hither look, if ever I've seen one, he thought, amused. But a surge of excitement ran through him, one so forceful he was unable to ignore it. Unexpectedly, he was hot under the collar *and* below the belt, an unprecedented reaction for him across a dining table, at least these days. Well, well, well, so much for the little lady, he commented inwardly. She's full of surprises.

Later, when they were back in the sitting room, drinking coffee and sipping *Obstler*, Victor had completely readjusted his thinking about Francesca, and he saw her in an entirely different light. Earlier in the day, on the car ride from the airport, he had finally admitted his attraction to her. Now there was no question in his mind that she felt exactly the same way as he did. But was he prepared to do anything about it? Probably not, under the circumstances. Don't kid yourself, old buddy, he reproved silently, coming to grips with his emotions. You know damn well she's under your skin, and has been since the first moment you met her.

Diana walked abreast of Christian, who was slowly wheeling himself down the gallery. She was thoughtful, her eyes subdued, her expression serious. She said quietly, 'I do wish Dieter Mueller hadn't come today.'

Christian brought the chair to a stop and swung his head. His eyes searched her face, and he reached out and touched her hand. 'Yes, in a way so do I. He upset you very much, and I hate to see that.'

'His information is so sketchy, I can't take him seriously. Actually, I haven't been able to for a long time. Personally, I think he's merely clutching at straws. He believes every little rumour, every little story, because he wants to believe them.'

'Perhaps.'

'Did he say anything else, after I left you alone?'

'Not very much. He did suggest we put the pressure on again. In Bonn.'

'Oh God, Christian, that won't do much good. It hasn't in the past. Why should it now?'

'There's always the chance that something might give on the other side. It might be worth a stab . . . just one more time. I told him I'd think about it.'

'You're not going to mention anything to Mummy, are you?' she asked worriedly.

'No, of course I'm not. There's no point. It would only agitate her more than ever. Please relax, Diana, and forget about Dieter.'

'Yes, I will. Life must go on, as I've been saying for the past few years, and as normally as possible. I don't know why I let him get to me today. Stupid really.' She shook her head, and a smile sprang easily to her lips. 'Dieter Mueller is already forgotten, my darling, I promise you.'

Christian's eyes filled with tenderness. He was so sure of her, trusted her, believed her. She always said what she meant, did what she promised. He wondered what he would do without her. Her courage gave him courage, and her determination to make their life normal gave him the strength to do the same. He said now, 'About the dinner party tomorrow . . . did you invite Giorgio?'

'No. Actually, I've decided not to see him any more.'

'Oh!' he exclaimed, surprised.

'I discovered the other day, quite by accident, that he's lied to me. Christian, he's never been separated from his wife. Not ever. Apart from the fact that I can't stand duplicity, I'm furious that he's wasted my time. You know my feelings about married men – strictly no future.'

'Who told you about Giorgio?'

'Astrid. Who else?'

'Ah! . . . I see. Then it must be true. She's many things, our little Astrid, but not a liar. Nor a troublemaker. I'm sorry, Diana. I hope you're not hurting too much.'

'On the contrary, I think I'm rather relieved,' she laughed. 'The Latin lover is a myth, in my opinion. Looking back, I'm beginning to realize Giorgio was more in love with himself than with me; and to be honest with you, his silly games were starting to tire me.'

'As long as you're not sad or unhappy, darling. Incidentally, whilst we're on the subject of romance, does Francesca know Astrid is coming?'

'Yes. She doesn't care. Anyway, she's always liked Astrid. I think the affair with Kim caused her a great deal of amusement. Certainly she doesn't blame Astrid in any way whatsoever. I don't suppose Kim does either. He's a big boy.'

'Too true,' Christian said, chuckling. 'I think if anyone was upset it was poor Astrid. I know she didn't want that liaison to come to an end, at least not when it did.'

Diana smiled. 'Yes, she was a bit dramatic at the time. But she soon found consolation elsewhere.'

They paused at the door of the library, and Christian said, 'I'm going to try to finish my Mozart piece for the *Sunday Times*. I want to get it off to London tomorrow. What are you going to do this afternoon?'

'Finalize the details for the dinner.'

'I'll see you later then,' he said as he wheeled himself into the library and closed the door.

Turning, Diana saw Francesca running down the main staircase. She waved and went to meet her. 'Where's Victor?'

'In his suite, which he loves by the way. He's making a call to Jake Watson in London. That's the line producer on the film. Then he'll change his clothes and we'll go for a walk. Do you want to come with us?'

'Heavens no, darling. I wouldn't dream of intruding,' Diana laughed. She linked her arm through Francesca's and they walked down the hall together in the direction of Diana's den.

Francesca looked at her cousin. 'Dibs, I think Victor's finally beginning to notice me. I mean me as a woman.' She was unable to hide the joy she was feeling.

'I *know* he is, I caught the look he gave you, when you were getting your food, and he didn't take his eyes off you all through lunch. Frankly, I thought he was going to eat you up right there and then.'

Francesca glowed. 'You do like him, don't you, Dibs?'

'Yes. He's the most gorgeous thing I've ever seen. But more importantly, he's terribly nice and intelligent and kind. Yes, of course I like him. He's very special, and this may sound like an odd thing to say, but I trust him. I don't mean on a man to woman basis necessarily. Rather, I mean I trust him in the *broadest* sense of that word – you know, on a human level. I think he is loyal, that he'd be a really good friend, and that one could count on him in a pinch. Am I making sense?'

'Yes you are. As a matter of fact, Daddy liked him too, the night we all had dinner together. Afterwards, he told me he thought Victor was a good human being. Quite a compliment coming from Daddy, wouldn't you say?'

'Yes indeed.' Diana opened the door of her den, which also served as an office. 'Enjoy yourself. Tea in the sitting room around four-thirty, four-forty-five.'

'That'll be lovely, Dibs.' Francesca leaned over and kissed Diana on the cheek.

Diana was halfway through the door, when she stopped and glanced over her shoulder at Francesca. 'By the way, darling, we've simply got to break him of that bad habit.'

'Which bad habit?' Francesca frowned.

'Calling you *kid* all the time. Most unromantic.'

'We can't! I mean, that's affectionate, coming from him!'

Diana gave her cousin a look of mock horror and then disappeared through the door, smiling to herself.

CHAPTER TWENTY-SIX

They were high on the mountain, nowhere near the top, but well above the Schloss nestling far below in the pines, a doll's house now, its size and grandeur lessened by the immensity of the surrounding landscape.

Victor and Francesca had been walking for a good half hour, taking the upward-winding road at a steady pace. They had not talked very much since leaving the house, caught up as they were in their private thoughts. But there was a tension building between them, and this sprang from their awareness of each other. Knowing she had finally elicited a response from him filled her with excitement; for his part, he fully understood, at long last, that she was vulnerable to him.

What the hell, I'm also vulnerable to her, he said to himself. Well, for the moment anyway. He stole a sidelong glance at her, took in the proud tilt of the shapely head, the honey-coloured hair turned to a deep golden hue by the late afternoon light. His eyes dwelt on her. The Loden cape she was wearing was far too large, more than likely Christian's, but its bulkiness only served to emphasize her fragility and delicacy, and she seemed defenceless and feminine, more so than ever.

When she had taken him up to see his suite after lunch, he had been filled with her, had had to stifle the urge to take her in his arms, to make love to her without preamble. The scent of her had lingered with him long after she had left, and her image had danced before his eyes for the entire twenty minutes he had talked to Jake in London. During the course of their business discussion, Jake mentioned that Nick had been trying to reach him from New York. Nothing important, it seemed. Nick had merely wanted to touch base; he had told Jake to pass on the message that he would call again next week.

Now, as he trudged along, Victor's mind strayed to Nicky and he was momentarily saddened himself. Poor bastard. I don't envy him. I bet he's been through the wringer half a dozen times by now. Victor sighed and glanced again at his companion, this lovely, willowy girl, striding out next to him through the snow. She was so vibrant, so full of life. All at once his sadness lifted, and he experienced such a surge of joyousness, he was startled, and he began to reflect on the reason for his abrupt swing in mood. Don't analyse, just accept it, he said under his breath.

They continued in silence for some time, following the steep path into the heart of the forest. Here the stately ancient firs were massive, interlocking overhead to shut out the sky, and all was green darkness, infinite stillness, and gentle peace in this soaring cathedral wrought from nature. But as the trees began to thin out, rays of light, faint, fading, intermittent, were penetrating the cool darkness here and there, creating a delicate pattern-play of shifting shadows on the pale ground. A shaft of brilliant sunshine broke through, glazing the windswept snowdrifts with a silvery sheen, turning the icicles bedecking the trees into shreds of shimmering crystal. Everything was bathed in this iridescent light, the scene ethereal and breathtaking in its silent beauty. Victor thought: *Oh God, it's so good to be alive.* And it was then that he remembered his vow not to fritter away his time, made on the day he had learned of Marcia's untimely death. Seize the moment, live for the day, taking everything it offers. Dangerous? Perhaps. But then what was life without an element of danger? Hardly worth living, surely . . .

'How is Jake?' Francesca asked, turning to him.

Victor cleared his throat, and said, 'Hunky-dory. No problems at the moment, thank God. We're still on the same schedule, and start principal photography the first week of April, as planned. Jake also told me Mark Pierce has found the perfect actor to play the young Heathcliff. He met with him this morning, and it looks as if we're all set there.'

'I hadn't realized you'd definitely decided to go with that idea.'

'Yep. We tossed it around a lot, finally came to the conclusion it would be wiser to cast someone else to portray Heathcliff in the early years. Nicky tried to call me today. He's going to be staying in New York for some time. He wants to be with his folks.'

'But he *is* all right, isn't he?'

'Yes,' he said laconically. He was thoughtful. After a second, he remarked in the most guarded of voices, 'You like Nicky a lot, don't you?'

'Yes, I do.' Francesca had caught something curious in his tone, and she had the merest flicker of a thought: Was he jealous because he believed she had a crush on Nick? She said evenly, 'He *is* one of the nicest people I've ever met, and he's been awfully kind to me, very encouraging about my writing, most helpful actually. I like to think he'll be my very good *friend* always.'

'He will, kid,' Victor replied, his voice a shade lighter. 'When Nicky takes to somebody, the way he's taken to you, he's devoted. Nothing fair weather about him either.'

Francesca said, 'I sensed that. Don't you think it odd that he and Katharine are so antagonistic towards each other?'

'That's pretty smart of you, picking up on the undercurrents between those two. I didn't realize anyone else had noticed their carefully-veiled dislike, and it is a bit puzzling, yes. On the other hand, you never know about people. We all bring out different things in each other, present different sides of ourselves.' A short pause, another swift glance at her, and then, 'You and Katharine seem to be closer than ever. Unusual really, for two such pretty girls to be inseparable. Women are generally very competitive, in my experience anyway. You two are the exception to the rule, I guess.'

Francesca nodded emphatically. 'Yes, that's true I think. And she is quite marvellous, and so good for Kim. If she *is* going to become my sister-in-law, I know I couldn't ask for a better one.'

Victor was dumbfounded. 'Are you trying to tell me those two are serious?'

She regarded him in surprise. 'I thought you'd realized how involved they are. Yes, I think they're very serious, although, to be honest, they haven't confided in me.'

'I'll be damned,' he muttered half to himself, and wondered how Katharine Tempest, rising star, intended to manage her career in Hollywood, where she was destined to go, and marriage with a member of the English aristocracy. A farmer no less, based in the wilds of Yorkshire, and one who was entirely involved with his heritage. Christ, he thought, she'll have to do a lot of expert juggling. A smile touched his eyes. No one was more adept at that little trick than Katharine, as he had recently come to understand. Sweet and thoughtful though she was, there was a manipulative side to her character, and it was so deeply ingrained it was second nature. 'And how does your father feel about having a movie star in the family?' he asked. 'That must really thrill him.'

Francesca picked up the edge of his sarcasm and gave him an odd look. 'I haven't discussed it with him lately, but he does like Katharine very much. Why wouldn't he? In fact, I'd say he's enchanted by her.' Not wishing to become further embroiled in this conversation, she added, 'There's the gazebo Diana was telling you about at lunch.' She pointed towards a small stone structure, just visible on the crest of the hill ahead of them, a little beyond the edge of the forest. It was circular, with a domed roof and four side columns, built in the manner of a pavilion, and it was obviously very old. 'From there we'll be able to see for miles and miles around, right across the valley.'

'I'll race you,' he cried, and charged forward before she could respond, leaving her well behind as he sped through the few remaining trees, across the snow and up the slope. Francesca began to run after him and when she finally reached the stone steps leading into the pavilion she was panting.

Victor was already standing inside and he leaned forward to give her his hand. 'Watch the steps,' he cautioned. 'They're a bit icy.' He steadied her with his free hand and helped her up. Francesca, who was familiar with the spot, led him to the far side of the structure, which faced out towards a range of mountains punctuating the horizon above the floor of the deep wide valley below.

'Diana was right!' he exclaimed. 'The views are magnificent.' He put his arm around Francesca's shoulder in a companionable way, and brought her close to his side. They stood for a long time like that, not speaking, regarding the awesome beauty of the glacial snowscape stretching endlessly before them, engulfed by the infinite white silence and the crystalline light pouring out of a sky of the clearest blue.

Francesca, conscious of Victor's proximity, could hardly breathe. She was shaking inside and her heart was pounding, filled as she was with a mixture of joy and anticipation. And the longer he held her next to him, the sharper his desire became, and he was finding it increasingly difficult to release his hold on her.

Then, as though they had read each other's thoughts, they turned slowly. Their eyes met and each one saw the longing and desire so clearly revealed on the other's face they were momentarily staggered. Francesca's lips parted slightly and she wanted to say his name, but it choked in her throat and she could only continue to stare up at him speechlessly. Her adoration of him blazed on her face, and to Victor it was heartstopping in its depth and sincerity, and he was spellbound by her. He felt a rush of intense emotion. His eyes bored into her, devoured her, and she returned his gaze unwaveringly, baring her innermost feelings, and in her expression he recognized irrevocable commitment to him. For the longest moment they were unable to look away. They were entranced, breathless, bound up in their infatuation with each other, and they both knew there was no going back.

Victor finally discarded the tight rein he had had on himself for weeks. He leaned forward and pulled her into his arms roughly, and his mouth was on hers, and he kissed her passionately and for a long time, as if slaking a consuming thirst. And she responded so ardently, meeting his passion head on, without restraint, and this sent thrill upon thrill shooting through him, and he wanted to take her without delay. But he knew he could not. Not now. Not here. And yet he was unable to quell his urgent need for her, and he tightened his embrace, lavishing her face and her neck and her hair with kisses, his heart racing, the blood pounding in his temples.

At last he held himself away from her, and guided her into the shelter of the gazebo, out of the wind, his hand gripping her arm forcefully. He leaned her against one of the stone columns and stood in front of her, looking down into her face, brimming with expectancy and paler now. His gabardine parka was fur-lined and cumbersome, a barrier between them, and he unzipped it, throwing it open, and then he took her hands in his and pulled off her woollen mittens. With his own he tossed them onto the floor.

She was in his arms again, their mouths meeting as if for the first time, their tongues entwining, their bodies cleaving together, straining to be joined. Victor's kisses were slow, prolonged. He ran his hands through her silky hair and grasped the nape of her neck, his fingers biting into her skin; and she reached up to touch his face, stroking it languorously, and she thought she was about to dissolve in his arms. His control was slipping, slipping away from him completely, and he felt his hardness growing as she returned the pressure of his body with her own. He was on a dangerous explosive edge, wild with longing, and suddenly he thrust himself up against her savagely, pinning her against the stone column; his mouth grew more demanding, was unrelenting on hers. He wanted to draw all of her into him, to know every part of her body intimately, to make her truly his.

The rage to possess her drove him on, and his hand went under her cape and he cupped her breast and fondled it lovingly. He felt her nipple harden through the wool, and he slid his hand around her back and up under the sweater. His fingers plucked impatiently, and expertly, on her bra strap, freeing her, and at last he was caressing her bare flesh, gently, tenderly, and then with growing urgency and fervour. He heard a faint moan of pleasure from her throat, and he brought his mouth down to her breast and kissed it with sensuality, savouring the warm silken flesh, drinking in the delicate perfume of her body, so yielding and so obviously craving his.

It seemed to Francesca that his mouth was ravaging her, an exquisite tingling sensation spreading up from her thighs through her whole being. She was intoxicated with him. Her legs weakened and she swayed against him, aching for total domination, wanting to give herself to him. And the erotic fantasies she had harboured about him in the past few weeks converged and exploded in her head. Her fingers embedded themselves in his thick black hair, and she called his name, saying it over and over again, and she quivered under his touch, every one of her senses clamouring for him.

Consumed with his passion for her though he was, Victor knew dimly, at the back of his mind, that to continue like this out here in the open was foolish and unfair to them both. He must bring their lovemaking to an end, and immediately, get a grip on himself, and on her, for there was no way she would even attempt to stop him. She wanted this as much as he did, was his willing ally. Excruciating as it was for Victor to curtail their loving, he finally did so. He lifted his face from her breast, pulled down her sweater and wrapped the huge cape around her body. Then he enfolded her in his arms, protecting her with his parka. He stroked the crown of her head slowly, pressing her face against his chest, endeavouring to calm her. She cried suddenly, 'Oh, Victor! Victor!' and he heard the yearning, the disappointment echoing.

He said hoarsely, 'I know, baby. I know. Later. I promise you, baby. All of me later.'

They stood clinging to each other until they had both regained a measure of composure. Eventually they drew apart and stared wonderingly into each other's eyes. Victor's heart clenched, and he experienced that same shock of recognition he had felt when first meeting her, and the elusive memory stirred again but evaporated before he could pinpoint it accurately. Her upturned face, still faintly glazed over with a residue of desire for him, was exquisite. He brought his hand up to touch her cheek, and his gaze was steadfast, their silent communication more explicit than words could ever be. Victor nodded his head slowly, but with great deliberation, as though confirming his recent promise to her, confirming the mutuality of their feelings. He brought her out of the stone gazebo without speaking.

Together they went down the hill, hand in hand, each shaken by the intensity of their desire for each other and by the fierce sexuality which had been aroused and unleashed between them. And they were a little benumbed as they headed back to the narrow path which plunged precariously through the pines to Wittingenhof and the estate far below on the plateau. Glancing up at the sky, Victor realized how long they had been on the mountain. The sun had long since set, the light was swiftly fading and there was a biting chill in the air. As they entered the forest, darker now than ever, he squeezed her hand reassuringly, and hurried her on, anxious to get her back to the warmth of the house. At one moment, he said, with a sheepish laugh, '*My* timing leaves a lot to be desired! I certainly picked one hell of a place to make love to you, didn't I?'

Her laughter echoed his in the silent air. 'Yes, you did. And that's the perfect way for us both to catch our deaths.'

'Ah, but watta way to go, kid.'

A mist had materialized and it was rolling down the mountainside to swirl around them as they pushed ahead. It was a light fog really, dank and cold and pervasive, and it was shrouding the forest with gossamer layers of pearl grey that obscured visibility. At Victor's insistence, they increased their pace, were almost running as they took the last stretch of pathway through the wood. When they finally came out of the trees onto the flat ground, twilight was already descending, the sky drained of its icy blueness and darkening to sombre pewter. Still clasping hands, they continued to run across the long meadow to the Schloss, and its lights, twinkling brightly in the distance, were a welcome sight. 'I think we just made it in time,' Victor said, slowing to a trot. 'I'd hate to get caught on that mountain when it's really dark.'

'It can be treacherous. And it's very easy to get lost,' Francesca told him as they went inside, crossed the hall and made their way down the stone stairs to the cloakroom on the lower floor. She hung up her Loden cape, and went on, 'Diana's always warned me about getting back before sunset. She's probably quite worried by now. We'd better hurry, and go up for tea.'

'Sure,' Victor said, struggling out of his parka. He sat down, pulled off his heavy walking boots, and slipped into a pair of black suede loafers. He rose, looked at himself in the mirror, ran a comb through his hair and carefully straightened his black cashmere sweater. He swung around to face Francesca, and unaccountably he began to laugh.

She threw him a startled look. 'What is it?'

Victor shook his head in a bemused way. 'I was just thinking about all the time I've wasted with you. All the opportunities we've had these past weeks . . .' He said no more, merely smiled lopsidedly. 'I guess I've been kind of ambivalent about you.'

'*Why?*'

'The problems with Arlene, with my divorce. Worry about *Confidential*. Preoccupation with the picture. A decision not to get involved with anyone. But I suppose your age did have a lot to do with it.'

'I'll be twenty in May,' she answered, her tone defensive.

'And I'll be forty in June,' he said flatly, suddenly facing this reality. 'I'm far too old for you, Francesca. Twenty years too old. Jesus, I was a married man when

263

I was your age – before you were even born. The boys are older than you, for God's sake. Listen, kid, I've lived a lifetime already. There's nothing I haven't seen, haven't done, haven't experienced. In fact, there's nothing new to me on this earth. I'm pretty goddamn jaded, if you want the truth.' He shook his head a trifle sadly, and his sigh was heavy. With a hint of regret, he finished, 'I'm not being *fair* to you, Francesca. You ought to be with someone nearer your own age, not an old reprobate like me.'

'What a stupid thing to say!' she cried, and her concentrated stare was furious. Her expression changed, became grave, concerned, and a stricken look smudged out the light in her eyes. 'Are you trying to tell me you're sorry then? I mean sorry about what happened between us on the mountain?'

'And that's a particularly stupid question,' he responded swiftly, reaching out for her. He pulled her into his arms and kissed her deeply, wanting to expunge the mingled hurt and panic on her face. A moment ago he *had* experienced a twinge of guilt about the disparity in their ages, and he *had* meant every word he said. But perhaps she was right, maybe age was irrelevant. Surely the way they felt was more important than anything else. He found himself whispering into her hair, 'I'm not sorry about what we did, darling. But I am sorry we had to stop so abruptly.'

'But you did say *later*,' she whispered back, and blushed, surprised at herself.

He did not answer but increased the pressure of his arms around her, before sliding his strong hands over her shoulders and down her back onto her buttocks. He crushed her body into his, moving against her, welding her to him firmly, and finally he found her mouth with his own. His passion spiralled, made him reel. And then he groaned. His erection was enormous again. More inopportune timing, he thought, every part of him screaming for her. He murmured in the softest of voices, 'I also said *all of me*. Do you want that, baby?' He tipped her face up to his with one hand, and his expression was earnest and searching.

Francesca was mesmerized by those black eyes, his undisguised and compelling need. She was only too conscious of his sudden arousal and she shivered involuntarily. For a split second she was weak with her own longing, and her head swam.

'Yes,' she said firmly, without hesitation. 'Yes, I do.'

Victor smiled his slow lazy smile, and he bent down and kissed her forehead with the utmost tenderness, and ran his finger along her cheek and onto her neck. It lingered there for a moment, and at last he said, 'Then let's go and find Diana, and get tea over with as quickly as possible. I can't wait to get you alone. To myself. For myself. *Capisce?*'

'Capish,' she repeated softly. 'What does *that* mean?'

'It means *understand*. You do, don't you, Francesca?'

She nodded, unable to speak.

'Sorry we're late, Diana,' Francesca apologized as she and Victor went into the sitting room a few minutes later.

Diana was sitting in her favourite spot on the hearth, nursing a small white dog, patiently waiting for them. 'No problem, darling,' she said with a cheerful smile. 'When you didn't get back on time, I delayed tea for half an hour. Clara only just brought it up a few minutes ago, so it's still hot. But I have to admit, I was getting

264

a bit anxious about you both out there in the dark. Anyway, do come to the fire and warm yourselves. You looked awfully chilled.'

'A wind was blowing up when we came out of the forest, but otherwise it wasn't too bad,' Francesca told her, and then stopped in her tracks, exclaiming, 'Oh Diana, how pretty Tutzi looks after her bath. Or is it Lutzi? I always get them mixed up, they're so alike.'

'It's Lutzi,' Diana said. Hearing his name, the dog glanced up at her, then leapt off her lap and raced towards Francesca, for all the world like a small woolly lamb as he gambolled across the floor. When the dog reached Francesca, he reared up on his hind legs and danced around her, pawing her affectionately and squeaking in excitement. Francesca bent down to fondle him, her face wreathed in smiles. 'Yes, yes, I know,' she laughed gaily. 'I'm happy to see you too, Lutzi.'

Victor stood watching her in fond amusement. 'What a gorgeous little animal.'

'But we mustn't forget his sister,' Francesca interjected. 'She's just as beautiful as Lutzi. Where is she, Diana?' Her eyes swept around the room. 'They're never far apart, those two.'

Diana nodded in the direction of the sofa. 'She's over there, squashed behind the cushions, observing us with great curiosity, as usual.'

Victor spied the dog, strode across the floor and sat down on the sofa. He picked her up in his large hands, holding her in front of his face. 'Hello, Tutzi,' he said. 'I see you're another fluffy little number. A real powder puff,' he chuckled. The dog began to lick his hand, and Victor grinned at Diana and said, 'I've never seen dogs like these. What's the breed?'

'Bichon Frise.'

Victor frowned, puzzlement on his face. 'Afraid I've never heard of it.' He glanced down at the dog, noting the silky fur, the unusual tail resembling an ostrich feather, the long floppy ears, the black button of a nose, and the huge round eyes, sparkling like black diamonds. 'She *is* a beauty,' he enthused, and placed the dog on his lap. He began to scratch her head, still smiling broadly.

Diana was pleased by Victor's loving reaction to her pets, and she told him, 'They're marvellous little dogs, Victor. Bright, intelligent and gay, with endearing habits. And although they're rather pretty to look at, they're also quite feisty. Like you, I'd never heard of Bichon Frises until Francesca told me about them. They're her favourite dogs. A friend of hers in Yorkshire breeds them, and Lutzi and Tutzi are from the same litter. I got them a couple of years ago when I was staying at Langley Castle. They were just ten weeks old, and so adorable I couldn't resist them.'

'Oh, so they're an English breed,' Victor said, continuing to fondle Tutzi, who had settled down with him contentedly, enjoying the attention.

'No, as a matter of fact, they're not. The Bichon comes from the Mediterranean region, the Spanish mainland to be exact. At least, that's where they apparently originated. And they're an ancient breed, dating back to the time of Cleopatra.'

'No kidding,' Victor exclaimed. 'Tell me more about them. I'm crazy about dogs.'

Diana laughed dismissively. 'I've been known to wax eloquent about them for a full hour, so perhaps you'd better not get me going on the subject now.'

265

'Listen, I meant it. I've never seen such gorgeous dogs in my life. I'm very curious about them, so come on, fill me in,' Victor insisted.

'Well, all right, a potted history, but that's all. It seems that Spanish sailors took the dogs abroad, around the fifteenth century, mainly to the Canary Islands, Tenerife in particular. That's why they were known as the Bichon Tenerife for centuries. Later, the sailors used them for sale or barter at the Italian ports, and they became popular pets with the Italian nobility. In the sixteenth century, after the French invaded Italy, the returning soldiers brought the little Bichon back to France. The dogs were court favourites during the reigns of Francis the First and Henry the Third. Fragonard often depicted them in his portraits of the French aristocracy, and actually, so did Goya, in his paintings of the Infantas of Spain, who also favoured the Bichons. During the reign of Napoleon the Third, in the middle of the eighteen hundreds, they also enjoyed great popularity, but they fell out of fashion in the early part of this century.' Diana paused, lit a cigarette, and continued, 'For a while the Bichon became a sort of little nomad, cavorting through the streets, accompanying the organ grinder and delighting everyone with his merry disposition and friendly personality. As a matter of fact, Bichons became extraordinarily talented trick dogs and performed complicated routines at fairs. They even went into the circus.' Diana laughed. 'Believe it or not, Victor, they *are* very acrobatic, given half a chance.'

'And how!' Francesca reiterated. 'You should see the way Tutzi and Lutzi take flying leaps on and off my bed. And usually late at night, when I'm trying to sleep. Not only that, I can never get rid of them. They'd be happy to frisk around with me until dawn.'

'I can't say I blame them.' Victor winked at her, and his smile was so wickedly suggestive, Francesca flushed. She turned her head, cursing herself for having given him such a marvellous opportunity to tease her.

Diana, who had not missed this small exchange, hid her amusement at them both, and went to join Francesca on the sofa. She said, in a matter-of-fact tone, 'How do you like your tea, Victor? With milk or lemon?'

'Lemon, please. So they became circus dogs. Mmmm. Very interesting.' He ruffled Tutzi's crown of hair. 'No wonder I had such an instantaneous affinity with them. Fellow entertainers, eh?' Diana and Francesca smiled with him, but before either were able to comment, he went on, 'And then what happened?'

Diana poured the tea, and proceeded to explain, 'Just after the First World War they became very popular again as pets, but it wasn't until the early thirties that serious breeding programmes were started and the French Kennel Club admitted the Bichon to its Stud Book –' Diana broke off and gaped at him. 'Oh God, Victor, we got started on the dogs and I forgot all about the 'phone call. For you – from a Mr Watson. Actually, you only just missed him by about fifteen minutes.'

'Thanks,' Victor said, taking the cup from her, asking: 'Does Jake want me to call him back?'

'No. He gave me a message. He asked me to tell you that your suitcase will be here no later than tomorrow afternoon. He's sending it by the film service Monarch use for delivering cans of film.' She handed Francesca her cup, and added, 'It's being brought here directly, by a special courier.'

'You didn't send for your dinner jacket!' Francesca gasped, looking at Victor disbelievingly, yet knowing at once this was exactly what he had done. She was flabbergasted, and it showed in her face. 'Or go to all that dreadful expense just for Diana's birthday party tomorrow. It wasn't *necessary*, really it wasn't'

Victor was taken aback by her quiet vehemence. He wondered why she sounded so put out. 'I also needed a few other things I'd forgotten, as well as my dinner jacket, kid,' he answered, his manner mild. He addressed Diana. 'I hope the guy finds this house okay. Did you give Jake directions?'

'I started to do so, then I realized it would be very difficult for anyone to find this house easily, even a cab driver from Salzburg, who might well know something about the area. So I suggested to Mr Watson that he instruct the courier to take a taxi from the airport to the boutique I own in Königssee. From the shop he can telephone here, and Manfred will go down and pick up your suitcase.'

'Hey, you're terrific Diana. Smart thinking. Thanks a lot.'

'It was rather gallant of you, sending for your dinner jacket for my little celebration. But Cheska's right, it wasn't necessary. I'd intended to ring all of my friends tonight, to tell them not to dress after all.'

'So Francesca explained earlier. But I didn't want to be the one to spoil your elegant evening. After all, you've been planning it for weeks apparently, and part of the fun on these special occasions is getting all gussied up, isn't it?' He smiled wryly. 'If the men don't wear their tuxedos, then you girls won't be able to show off your pretty gowns, now will you?'

'No, we won't, that's true. How sweet of you to be so considerate.' Diana beamed at him, picked up a silver knife and cut a large chocolate layer cake topped with a mountain of thick whipped cream and decorated with cherries. 'Do try this, it's absolutely scrumptious.'

'I'll bet it is,' he said with a grin, and then grimaced. 'And it's undoubtedly very fattening. I've got to stay trim for the picture. But okay, why not. Make it a small piece though, please.' After a short pause, he remarked, 'Can you give me the dope on the Jenner? What kind of a downhill run is it? And what are our skiing plans for tomorrow?'

Diana filled him in about the Jenner in detail, and the two of them were soon embarked on a long discussion about the skiing they would do the following morning. Francesca sat back, sipping her tea, not paying much attention to their conversation. She was regarding Victor from under her lashes, her mind turning things over. How ridiculous and extravagant, she thought. Only a Hollywood film star would do such a crazy thing . . . Imagine, having his dinner jacket flown in just for a party, just for *one* evening. Such a flagrant waste of money, so alien to her nature and her upbringing, appalled her, and unexpectedly she experienced a tiny flash of irritation. But it dissipated almost at once, and she felt mean for having spoken so sharply to him a moment ago. If any other man had made such a grand gesture, she would have pronounced him a show-off and pretentious, but in all honesty she could not pin these labels on Victor. Instinctively she knew he had not given the merest thought to what it would cost, or the impression he would make. He never did, it seemed. He had simply wanted to please . . . please Diana, and perhaps even her. And it *was* gallant, she admitted, thinking of Diana's words.

Francesca moved her position on the sofa, but continued to sneak furtive glances at him. He fascinated her more than ever. There were so many different sides to him. She wondered if she would ever truly know him, this complex and baffling man who resembled a small boy at times. She thought then of the gentleness that he had displayed with the dogs, and this made her smile inside, filled her with additional warmth towards him. She remembered something her father had once said, about gaining insight into a person's character by watching their behaviour with dogs. Her father had gone on, 'Better still, study the dog and the way it reacts towards a human, and you'll get an even better picture of the person. Dogs *know* character.' Yes, they do, she mused. It's instinct, and it never fails.

Now her eyes were glued to Victor, and if he was aware of her intense appraisal, he was not permitting it to show. He was still talking about skiing, with great authority, and Francesca could not help noticing that Diana, a crack skier of championship standards, was hanging onto his every word. Francesca blinked, suddenly seeing Victor Mason through objective eyes, as Diana herself was undoubtedly seeing him at this very moment. He was extraordinarily handsome with his tanned, virile face, black wavy hair and expressive eyes. He exuded vitality and energy and sex appeal, his shoulders massive, his body powerfully built and showing to advantage in the black cashmere sweater. He was dressed entirely in black, and this dramatized his dark good looks. True glamour, she thought, that's what he possesses in such abundance. He was lolling on the sofa, draped across it in his usual fashion, one arm flung along its back, the other wrapped around Tutzi, his long legs crossed, his whole frame relaxed, and he was laughing as he spoke animatedly to Diana. More than ever conscious of him, Francesca shivered, remembering his kisses, his intimate caresses in the gazebo, his promise and its implications. She dropped her eyes, and poured herself another cup of tea, aware that her deepest feelings were bound to be showing in her face. She wasn't very clever about masking what she felt, and most especially with him.

'I do hope there's some tea left.'

Christian's vibrant voice penetrated Francesca's reverie, and she swung her head, smiling at her cousin, who was poised in the doorway. 'Hello, darling,' she cried, relieved to see him. 'And yes, there's masses.'

As Christian wheeled himself up to the fireplace to join them, Victor added, 'Plus a very lethal chocolate cake.' His smile was jovial, but his eyes clouded over. He recognized that he and Francesca were really trapped now. They would not be able to retreat upstairs quite as quickly as he had planned, because of Christian's arrival. Victor lit a cigarette and racked his brains for a way to escape with grace – and speed.

CHAPTER TWENTY-SEVEN

Victor took the stairs two at a time, sped along the corridor and stopped at the door of Francesca's room. He opened it and went inside swiftly. He closed it firmly behind him and leaned against it, staring at her, a look of incredulity on his face. 'Your timing is about as good as mine, kid! I couldn't believe it when you asked Christian to show me the gun collection.'

'Neither could I,' she laughed a little nervously, her embarrassment of earlier returning. She gave him an apologetic grin, and went on, 'It just popped out, before I could stop myself actually, and then you were stuck. And you looked so aghast, and furious with me, I had to flee. Sorry.'

'You should be sorry. Jesus, I spent the last half hour trying to concentrate on what he was telling me about those lousy guns, and my mind was up here with you,' he spluttered, merely feigning exasperation now.

'You're lucky you've escaped so quickly. My dear cousin generally takes an hour, sometimes even two, once he gets going on the history of that particular collection. He's very thorough.'

'I'll say he is,' Victor laughed, realizing she was teasing him, just as he was teasing her. He did not move, but remained near the door, looking at her intently. She was seated on the sofa near the fire, still wearing her yellow ski outfit. The room was filled with dusky shadows, for only one small reading lamp had been turned on, but a fire burned brightly, was casting a warm glow around her, bringing her into focus. In the flickering light from the flames she resembled a delicate statue sculpted from pure gold. Her hair was combed loose, was shot through with dancing lights, and it fell in shimmering swatches around her face. Her skin seemed to have been polished to a golden sheen, was iridescent, and her large hazel eyes were the colour of tawny topazes, clear and bright.

There was the suggestion of a smile on her lips, and in her expression he saw anticipation, and yes, just a hint of apprehension reflected there as well. But both were fleeting emotions instantly overshadowed by the desire which was flooding her eyes. A thrill ran through him as her gaze remained riveted on him, telling him so much, as before expressing everything he was feeling within himself. He wanted her, God, how he wanted her. He was filled with impatience, beside himself in reality, and he turned with suddenness and locked the door.

Victor was across the floor in a few quick strides, opening his arms to her, not speaking, his face tense. She rose from the sofa and flew to him, and they clung together, their hearts racing, their excitement running quick.

Their mouths met, and Victor savoured her sweet lips, her sweet breath, and then he parted those lips and found her tongue. His own lingered on it, and then he drew it into his mouth, possessing it as he wished so desperately to possess her. He tightened the pressure of his arms, and pulled her hard against his body, and he felt her excitement growing, and his own, and he was conscious of the electrical charges running between them. Slipping his hand under her sweater he undid her bra strap. And once more he caressed her breast lovingly until she was trembling and swaying weakly in his arms. He glanced down at her quickly. Her eyes were closed, her face was flushed, and a pulse was beating on her neck. The sight of her arousal sent his own desire soaring, and propelled by its urgency he stepped away from her and plucked impatiently at her sweater, lifting it up over her head. He threw it to one side carelessly, and leaning towards her he gently removed her bra and dropped it to the floor. He stood gazing at her. Francesca began to tremble afresh. He seized her, pulling her to him, running his hands over her smooth rounded shoulders and down her back, thrilling to the touch of her skin, and he said, his voiced choked with passion, 'Take the rest of your clothes off, baby.'

He turned and moved to the far side of the bedroom into the shadows, wanting to give her privacy. He kicked off his loafers, removed his sweater and unzipped his pants, sliding out of them hurriedly. When he was completely undressed he swung around, and he saw, to his surprise, that she was standing exactly where he had left her, was not lying on the bed as he had anticipated she would be. She was regarding him – warily, he decided – and he thought he detected a nervousness in her, an uncertainty. But he dismissed this idea immediately, considering it to be ridiculous, ascribing her seeming awkwardness to shyness. After all she was very young, and hardly likely to be as experienced as he in the game of love.

'Don't be embarrassed, darling,' he murmured softly, reassuringly. His smile conveyed kindness, understanding, but his eyes were bold, roamed over her slender naked body and rested on her for a long time, and he noted the high, firm but unusually full breasts, the gently curving hips, the long beautifully proportioned legs. At last he said, his voice still husky with longing, 'You're lovely, Francesca, really lovely. Don't be self-conscious.'

Francesca was unable to speak and incapable of moving. Her eyes grew huge in her face and her lips parted as she watched him approaching, looming up in front of her to block out the firelight. His chest was lightly covered with black hairs, and so broad it seemed to be more immense naked than it was clothed. But surprisingly, he had a narrow waist and narrow hips above his long legs, and even though the light was dim, she could see, as he drew closer, that his body was as tanned as his face. It was well-muscled, strong and firm, an athlete's body, honed to perfection, and it was dominating in its masculinity.

She held her breath, and tried to still the shaking that had assaulted her again. This was not a manifestation of fear, for she was not afraid, nor was she uncertain or embarrassed as he imagined. Quite simply, she was overpowered by Victor, by the sheer physical beauty of him, his grace, his sexual magnetism which radiated from him so potently, and with such force. He made her feel weak and helpless. Also she was overwhelmed by her own burning desire – overwhelmed by her innermost emotions. That she was in love with him she had known for weeks, deny it though she might have done. But in all truth, she had not understood the extent of her love, its depth and intensity. She knew now that it was immeasurable.

Still misunderstanding her muteness, her extraordinary immobility, Victor wrapped his arms around her when he reached her side. He did so with gentleness, and pushed her hair away from her face, and peered into her eyes. They seemed to him to be far too grave. 'What's bothering you, darling? You're not shy with me, are you?' he asked in a low tone.

She shook her head.

'So what is it, darling? Stage fright?'

Francesca found herself blinking under the force of his direct and concentrated stare, and she did not answer, hypnotized yet again by that stunningly handsome face so close to hers. Unexpectedly her eyes filled with tears. How that face had haunted her . . . haunted her every waking moment and perhaps even her sleep as well. It was indelibly etched on her mind and her heart for all time, the dearest face to her in the world, and it would be for the rest of her life. Oh how she loved him.

Her heart leapt, and began to clatter unreasonably, and she wanted to tell him how she felt, but she dared not articulate her love. Not yet.

Aware that he was watching her closely, waiting for an answer, she said slowly, 'It's just that . . . well, I never thought we'd be together . . . not like this anyway. I think I'm shaken. But that's all. Honestly.'

'But you do want it, don't you? Want to be with me?'

'Oh yes, Victor, *yes*. You must know that.' She buried her face against his bare chest, and her arms went around him, and she held him close as if never to let him go. 'I've been sitting here waiting for you for the last half hour, dreading the thought that you might not come to my room after all, that you'd changed your mind. Actually, I've been waiting for you for weeks and weeks,' she found herself confessing.

And I've been waiting for you for years and years, Francesca. He bit back these words, did not wish to express this curious thought, one that had truly surprised him. Instead, he brushed it aside quickly, and without another word he swung her up into his arms and carried her over to the enormous four-poster bed at the other side of the room. As he strode out, he said in a hoarse voice, 'I think we've wasted enough time already, baby, don't you?'

Francesca sighed and said nothing. She closed her eyes and clung to him, nestling her face against his shoulder. She inhaled the scent of him and kissed his neck and the weakness invaded her again.

Victor placed Francesca on top of the eiderdown and lay down next to her, cradling her in his arms, wrapping his body around hers, kissing her hair, her brow, her ears and finally her lips. He closed his eyes, drinking in the warmth and softness and beauty of her, revelling in her. Soon his mouth roamed down to her throat, and he began to smooth his hands over her body, and he marvelled at the texture of her skin, felt as though he was touching the purest sleekest silk. He had not known skin like hers ever in his life. Moving his head slightly, he kissed the cleft between her breasts, and stroked them, his hands strong but gentle, and with his tongue he touched the tip of each nipple in turn, delicately so that it was hardly perceptible. After a moment, he was kissing her mouth again, grasping her tightly in his arms, drowning in her.

Francesca was quivering under his touch, straining towards him, and she responded as ardently as she had on the mountain, returning his feverish kisses with unrestrained passion, a passion that more than matched his own. Her fingers fluttered over his wide shoulders, down his back and along his spine, and then returned to touch his face and his hair. But despite her willingness to give of herself wholeheartedly, and her most transparent joy in their lovemaking, Victor knew, almost at once, that she had no real expertise in the art of love. Furthermore, somewhat to his amazement, he was beginning to realize she was unusually inexperienced sexually. Yet this knowledge only served to fire him on, imbued in him the wish to give her the kind of happiness she had probably never known with any other man. His hands roved over her boldly, provocatively, fondling, caressing, exploring, arousing, and she blossomed under his touch. And he discovered that her simplicity and innocence were not only endearing but inordinately exciting to him, accustomed as he was to more worldly women. Inflamed in a way he had not been in years, he intensified his loving, lost himself in her.

Other men. There had never been any other men. Victor did not know how he knew this, would never know, but all at once he was absolutely convinced she was a virgin. Sweet Jesus! A virgin. Instantly he recoiled from this idea, and also from her, although he was sensitive enough not to cease his caresses all that abruptly. Finally he could not help himself, and his hands did fall away from her body, as he baulked at continuing, but he brought her into his arms and he held her gently.

'Is something wrong?' she asked after a while, her voice small, muffled against his chest.

'No, baby. But you're exciting me too much. Let's rest a minute.'

Now Victor seriously considered retreating, of dressing and leaving her. But how could he stop their lovemaking at this stage? They were both taut with longing, craving each other desperately. Anyway, if he stopped with suddenness and departed, she would believe he was rejecting her for some reason. That would be cruel and unfair, and it could easily scar her psychologically for years. Discuss it with her? Hardly. To start asking probing personal questions would only create awkwardness, and embarrass her. It would also break the mood which existed between them, one that struck a delicate balance between the most tender feelings and high-voltage excitement of an unusually thrilling nature. He wrestled with the problem, torn by indecision.

As if she had somehow managed to read his thoughts, as if instinctively she understood he had perceived her lack of experience in bed, Francesca now brought her hand up to touch his chest, and lightly she began to finger one of his nipples. Slowly she trailed her fingertips down his chest and onto his stomach. They hovered there, moving across and then up and down, delicate, erotic, tracing patterns. A shiver ran through him, and when her hand slipped down to rest between his legs, tentatively, with uncertainty, he almost leapt out of his skin. Her touch excited him to such an extent he had to bite his inner lip to stop from crying out with pleasure, and he felt his hardness growing even though she had removed her hand.

Victor Mason was entirely undone. He was incapable of leaving her. He pressed Francesca into the pillows and started to devour her mouth so fiercely his teeth grazed hers. Moving his body so that he was lying on top of her, he pushed his hands under her shoulder blades and lifted her up to him, crushing her. And he made up his mind to one thing; since he was the first, and he knew without a shadow of a doubt that he *was*, then he was not going to make a hash of this, spoil it for her as another man might in his selfishness, impatience and lack of knowledge. She was not going to have problems with sex ever in the future, as so many women did, because some dolt had perpetrated a bad, difficult or unrewarding initiation on them. He was going to love her well, and truly, and with every part of himself. He would bring her to the fine edge of rapture and beyond that into ecstasy, before he took her and satisfied himself. Her loss of innocence at his hands was going to be beautiful, radiant, filled with joyousness, and also as painless as he could possibly make it.

For all her inexperience, Victor realized there was a basic sensuality in Francesca, and this thrilled him, for he was sensual himself and needed a woman to respond to him on the same level. Knowing that her sensuality had not been truly awakened, he slowly brought it to full flower, kissing her, caressing her, prolonging this stage of their lovemaking. He carried her to new heights, soothed and gentled her quivering body when she grew over excited, and started all over again when she was calm. In the most subtle of ways, with care and delicacy and sensitivity, he created in her a state of voluptuousness that was making her faint and breathless.

Suddenly he had a need to see her face and he lifted his head and gazed down at her, and caught his breath. Never had he seen a woman looking more beautiful than she did at this moment. Her supine body, spread out before him, was so languid and relaxed it seemed to have a unique kind of fluidity, her long legs stretched out gracefully in a half curve, her superb arms flung above her head. To him she appeared more willowy and supple than ever, a long-stemmed flower, and glorious, with her hair fanning out behind her like skeins of silk, and her matchless skin was dappled to a dusky gold by the blazing firelight. She was exquisite in her fresh young beauty and innocence and purity. He felt a tightening in his loins, a further quickening in his blood, and he raised himself on his elbow, studying her intently, watching her eyelids fluttering as he caressed her shoulder, ran his hand down over her outer thigh.

It was then that Victor experienced a deep yearning in his heart, an unrecognized and unfamiliar yearning he did not truly comprehend at first. But with a swift flash of insight into himself, he thought: Is this more than sexual attraction? Have I fallen in love with her?

Francesca stirred and opened her eyes, and looked up at him, her adoration spilling out from her face. He stared back at her, held in fascination, his eyes impaled on hers. They were searching, questioning, burning with a longing that sprang from the inner recesses of his heart and not his body, and he was moved in a way he had not been moved in years. Momentarily he was thrown off balance by the deep emotions tearing at him. His throat thickened and he felt unaccustomed tears behind his eyes.

Francesca watched the intense feelings washing over his face, swamping his dark and brilliant eyes, and she recognized them immediately, knew at once what they meant, for they mirrored her own. She held her breath, hardly daring to move, and thought: He loves me. I know he loves me. Her heart began to flutter and all the love she felt for him rose up in her, and she knew she must tell him. She opened her mouth to speak, but Victor bent forward and kissed her deeply, silencing her. He held her close and said, 'My darling, oh my darling,' and he enveloped her with his body and found her mouth again. She cleaved to him, returned his wild, impassioned kisses, and stroked the nape of his neck and shoulders, and ran her hands down his back.

Her touch scorched him, sent the heat flaming through him. His blood raced, his heart thundered in his chest and his desire was rampant in him, made his head swim. And he needed to know every part of her, to make every inch of her his, and his alone. He brought his lips to her breasts and kissed her sensuously, and slid his hand down over her stomach until his fingers were entwined in the golden silk between her thighs. Slowly, and with infinite tenderness, he sought the core of her femininity enclosed in its protective velvet petals.

Francesca was quivering and moaning gently under his loving hands, excited in a way she had not imagined possible even in her wildest fantasies about him.

Victor was arousing her to a point of agitation and she was overwrought, and yet she did not want him to stop. She wanted his hands, his lips, his body, wanted all of him, wanting him to prolong the exquisite sensations trickling through her. He was dazing her, blinding her, thrilling her beyond belief. Suddenly she caught her breath, trembling uncontrollably, and a stronger fiercer heat flooded her, and she gave herself up to him. He was learning her intimately, and with thoroughness, and he drove her on and on relentlessly, until she was gasping and caught on the brink of the most rapturous feeling she had ever known.

And Victor, besotted with her, enthralled by her, was being carried along by the onrushing tide of their mutual passion. He brushed his lips across her thigh, and as he caressed the core of her it felt as if a rare exotic flower had suddenly bloomed under his hands, one that was slowly unfolding its sun-drenched buds to him. Tremors rippled along her thighs and he shifted his body, moving lightly on the bed. He brought his head down and kissed her with delicacy, until spasms replaced the tremors and she cried out, 'Oh Vic! Oh Vic!'

He continued to kiss her until the spasms lessened and then he lifted his head and slid up onto her body, and took her to him with great swiftness, plunging into her with such force he felt the impact himself. He hoped this unexpected domination of her at the height of her excitement would dim the pain. But she did stiffen under him, and she stifled a cry with a quick gasp, and held herself tense. He gripped her, his hands under her back, and he moved into her more forcefully, knowing this was the only way to lessen the pain, to sweep her up and away from it to new heights.

Gradually Francesca relaxed as the sharp flaring pain receded, and she felt a different and more marvellous warmth spreading through her as Victor began to thrust deeper and deeper into her. And her heart crested with ecstasy as he took complete possession of her, made her truly his.

She was liquid fire under him and he was being consumed by the heat emanating from her. He took her harder, loving her with a fervour he had long forgotten, with the strength and virility and wildness of his youth. He felt her body arching up to meet his clamorously, and she blended into him, moved with him, found his new rhythm, and he was dimly conscious of instinctive movements from her. Her arms tightened on the small of his back and her legs went around him automatically, so that he could love her more thoroughly and with all of himself. He was trapped now in a velvet vice, the possessor being possessed. He was hot, his body burning up with hers, and then he felt as though he was falling, falling through space, spinning down the slope, taking the long downhill run with the speed of light. Faster, faster, his speed increasing, breathless as he hurtled on into the blinding glare . . . white snow . . . white heat . . . infinity. Oh God, oh God, I love her, he screamed silently to himself. I've always loved her from the very first day . . .

Victor lay on top of Francesca, shudders still rippling through him, his face buried in her neck. She smoothed his shoulders lightly, gentling him as he had gentled her earlier, waiting for a calmness to settle over him. At the very last moment he had moved against her almost violently and had gripped her arms so tightly she had winced in pain. Then the shuddering had started and he had erupted with a frenzied burst of passion, calling her baby again and again, and begging her to take all of him.

274

Francesca kissed the top of his head, and smiled inwardly, loving him more than ever. She *had* taken all of him, just as she had given him all of herself, and he belonged to her now. It did not matter that there had been countless women before her, for her instincts told her that something quite extraordinary had occurred, not only for herself but for Victor too. She also knew he had not taken their lovemaking lightly, was convinced in her heart of hearts that he did love her. She shifted imperceptibly, easing his weight without disturbing him, and she smiled to herself again. Her body ached, but it was a delirious feeling, like having the imprint of him on her. Euphoria pervaded her whole being. She thought she was going to burst with happiness, and her arms went around him and she held him closer and with tenderness.

Victor was drained. He felt as though every ounce of his strength had trickled out of him. He had loved Francesca in a way he had not made love to a woman for years, not merely with physical enthusiasm and vigour, but with all the passion of his heart and mind. Yet despite the exhaustion, he was experiencing an inner exultation coupled with the most wonderful sense of peace, a peace rooted in the kind of contentment that had eluded him for the longest time. He had forgotten what it was like to feel completely fulfilled emotionally as well as physically. His own fault maybe. He was always seeking solace in the wrong arms, and coming up empty in the end. So many women, so many faces, the famous and the unknowns, those faces long since blurred. He sighed. There were far too many for him to remember and, for reasons of good taste, to count. But *she* was different.

He raised himself on one elbow and looked down at her, his emotions still high on the surface. The fire had burned low and the light had dimmed, but he could see her quite clearly. His eyes rested on her reflectively. What was it about her that made her so different from all the others, that affected him so strongly? His answer to himself was instant: It was some indefinable thing that he could not quite grasp.

Francesca's gaze was wide and candid as she searched his face. She lifted her hand and touched his cheek with ineffable gentleness and her eyes grew wide and more brilliant. 'Oh Vic, oh Vic, darling,' she began, and sighed and said no more, and her mouth trembled.

He read the adoration and devotion in her face with the greatest of ease, and he saw her love reflected there, and suddenly his heart missed a beat. It was not only the way she was looking at him, but the use of his diminutive and the particular way she had said it which now struck a chord in his mind. It was *déjà vu* . . . he had seen that look and heard his name pronounced in exactly that same tone before, long long ago . . . And then that evanescent memory which had so nagged at him since their first meeting now took shape, became substance.

Francesca reminded him of Ellie. It was not that she looked like his first wife, for in all truth she did not, rather it was a special quality of personality that was the link between them. Implicit in Francesca's character were honesty, sincerity and goodness, outward manifestations of an extraordinary inner beauty and grace which she possessed in great abundance, as had Ellie. He was unable to speak, but he leaned forward and kissed her brow, and then he ensnared her in his arms. Everything had become quite clear to him.

They lay for a long time, embracing each other, not speaking, drifting with their thoughts, watching the firelight dancing on the walls and the ceiling. At one moment Francesca shivered slightly and Victor pulled the eiderdown over them and drew her closer to him. At last, recovered from his surprise, he said, 'It's funny, the way you suddenly started to call me Vic – '

'I'm sorry,' Francesca said, rousing herself, recalling that he seemed to dislike this abbreviation of his name. She had heard him correct Hilly Steed several times. 'You hate it. I'd forgotten.'

'I don't hate it from you, or Nicky, just as I never minded when Ellie used it. Anyone else, yes, particularly someone I'm not close to, I guess because it smacks of familiarity.' He chuckled softly. 'Also, I was brainwashed by my mother. She never permitted anyone to shorten my name when I was a kid. But it sounds nice when you say it, sort of soft and gentle.' He rested his head on hers, and went on, 'I've heard your father and Kim call you Frankie, and Diana calls you Cheska. Which do you prefer?'

'Cheska, I suppose. Frankie sounds so, well, so boyish.'

'I don't think anyone would mistake you for a boy, baby. Not by a long shot,' he laughed.

'But I don't mind *kid*, or *baby* either,' she asserted, settling back in the crook of his arm contentedly. 'They've become very special, to me at any rate.'

'Have they now.' He smiled and ruminated for a few seconds. Brushing his lips across her shoulder, he went on, in a low voice, 'I *was* the first, wasn't I? The first man in your life, I mean.'

This question did not really startle Francesca, for she had guessed that *he* had guessed, but she remained silent. Finally she whispered, 'Yes.'

'Why didn't you tell me?'

'It never occurred to me. It didn't seem to be of such great importance, certainly not to me. Why, was it important to you, Vic?'

He was thoughtful, and after a beat, he replied carefully, 'Yes, it was in many ways. And I hope I didn't hurt you. I tried to make it as – '

'Sssh,' she murmured, pressing her fingertips to his mouth. 'And you didn't hurt me. Well, not too much.'

She felt him smiling against her shoulder and then he said, 'I didn't shock you, did I? Some of the things I did . . .'

'No.' She felt her cheeks grow hot as she remembered their lovemaking, and then she brushed aside her sudden selfconsciousness, and finished shyly, 'I . . . I . . . liked everything you did.'

He laughed. 'I'm glad to hear it.' He slipped out of bed, padded across the room, threw a couple of logs on the fire, found his cigarettes in one of his trouser pockets, and returned to the four poster. He propped the pillows behind him, settled down next to her and lit a cigarette. He said, 'By the way, what time's dinner?'

'Nine o'clock, but we should go down about half an hour before, for drinks.' Francesca glanced at her small travelling clock on the bedside table. 'It's almost eight already,' she exclaimed in surprise.

'I'll smoke this and then I'd better go back to my room and shower and dress. I guess I have to put on a shirt and tie?'

'Yes, but you don't have to wear a suit, if you don't want to. A sports jacket is perfectly fine.'

'If I'd been smart, I'd have stopped off and picked up my robe before coming in here.' He looked at her sideways. 'But I was anxious to get to you, baby. Now I guess I have to make myself decent to return to my suite. I can't very well flit along the corridor clutching my clothes in my hands.'

'I'll go and get your dressing gown,' Francesca cried, and had swung her legs out of bed before he could stop her.

'Come on, baby, that's not necessary,' he protested as she disappeared into the bathroom. She returned almost at once, struggling into a bathrobe. 'I'll be back in a flash,' she told him and went out.

Victor lay back against the pillows, smoking his cigarette, musing on Francesca. He smiled. They were perfect together. Within seconds voices outside the door disturbed his train of thought, and he straightened up, listening alertly. Francesca had obviously run into her cousin. He heard Diana's light laugh, a few mumbled words exchanged between them, and then Diana said something more clearly, in German, which he did not understand.

The door opened and Francesca came back into the room. Looking across at him, she said, 'I just ran into Diana.'

'Yes, so I heard. She knows then . . . knows I'm in here . . . knows about us?'

'I don't think she *thinks* I'm borrowing your robe,' Francesca laughed, her eyes dancing. 'It's far too large to fit me.'

'What did she say?'

'Nothing.' Francesca's blonde brows shot up. 'It's really none of her business, you know. Besides, apart from being very romantic, she likes you a lot, so I'm sure she approves.'

'No, no, I was referring to the remark she made to you in German.'

Francesca sat down on the end of the bed, still clutching his white silk robe to her. 'Diana said, "*das letzte Hemd hat keine Taschen.*" That means, the last shirt has no pocket. What she was trying to say was that you can't take it – '

'With you,' he finished for her. 'I get the drift. She's a smart one, that lovely cousin of yours. And she's right, life's too short to waste.' Now Victor's curiosity about the von Wittingens surfaced again, and innumerable questions about the parents, and also the reason for Christian's disability, flew to his tongue. But he realized it was the wrong moment to embark on such a discussion, and so he held back, reserving the questions for another time. He stubbed out his cigarette and got out of bed. Francesca handed him his robe. He slipped into it, belted it tightly and stood looking at her, then he pulled her up off the bed and into his arms. Kissing her very tenderly, he murmured into her hair, 'My sweet, sweet baby.' With a swift glance at her, he asked, 'You are mine, aren't you?'

'Yes, Vic. Oh yes, darling, I am,' she replied, and her face was radiant.

They drew together again, reluctant to leave each other, and their kisses became long and passionate. It was Victor who finally broke their clinging embrace. He said, with an irreverent, lopsided grin, 'Listen, lady, I'd better get outta here, otherwise we'll never make dinner tonight.'

CHAPTER TWENTY-EIGHT

'The dress looks divine on you, Cheska,' Diana said.

'Perfect. I'm so glad I remembered I had it in the stock room.'

Smiling, Francesca turned to look at herself again in the cheval mirror. The evening gown Diana had loaned her from the boutique was made of silk velvet in a lovely shade of clear amethyst. The skirt was cut on the cross, flaring to the floor, and the close-fitting bodice had a low scooped-out neckline and long sleeves. It was elegant and its svelte lines made her look more lithesome than ever, whilst the colour was immensely flattering to her fair English-rose complexion and honey-blonde hair.

'Yes, it is nice,' she agreed, swinging back to face her cousin. 'Actually, if it's not too expensive, I think I'd like to buy it. I could do with it, to tell you the truth. Most of my evening clothes are horribly dull.'

'Oh *do* keep it, Cheska. It suits you so well, and naturally you can have it at cost.'

'That's sweet of you, but you sold me the yellow ski outfit for practically nothing – '

'I wouldn't dream of letting you pay the boutique price,' Diana exclaimed. 'Anyway, I feel pretty awful. It was my stupid fault you didn't bring any evening clothes with you. My only excuse is that when you rang to say you were coming to Wittingenhof, I forgot all about the dinner party in my excitement.'

'You mustn't feel badly, Dibs. And you've been a darling about the clothes. I'm very grateful. And I did want to get myself a few things with the money I earned for scouting locations. It's ages since I've had anything new.'

'Then it's settled. Tomorrow, when Victor's off skiing, I want you to go down to the town and pick out anything you want from the shop. In the meantime – ' Diana stopped and looked at Francesca closely, her head on one side, her expression assessing. 'I want you to wear this tonight.' As she spoke she brought her hands from behind her back, took a step forward and handed Francesca a red leather case. 'I think this will add just the right finishing touch.'

Francesca stared at Diana and then at the case. She opened it and caught her breath. 'Oh how beautiful.' Her eyes widened as they focused on the three-strand choker of lustrous creamy pearls nestling on the red velvet.

'Here, let me help you.' Diana lifted the choker out of the case and fastened it around Francesca's neck. 'Turn the clasp to the front,' she suggested. 'Yes, that's right. Let it rest there in the middle of your throat.' Diana smiled. 'I suddenly thought of this because the clasp has an amethyst in the centre. See how it picks up the colour of the dress. Marvellous.'

'Diana, what a gorgeous piece. I've never seen you wear it though. Is it new?'

278

'It was Grandmother's. She gave it to me for Christmas.'

'It's so nice of you to lend it to me. Thank you. But don't you want to wear it yourself tonight?'

'No. My dress has a rather high neckline so the choker wouldn't look right.' She moved towards the door, halted and turned. Her eyes rested on Francesca lovingly, and she said with a rush of genuine feeling, 'I'm so happy for you, Cheska. Really happy. And you see, I was right. I told you everything would work out, didn't I?'

'Yes.' Francesca's mouth curved up in a happy smile and her eyes shone. 'Victor said Wittingenhof was magical, and so it has proved to be. For me. Oh Dibs, he's wonderful.'

'And a pretty cool customer,' Diana laughed.

'What do you mean?' Francesca's face was instantly touched by apprehension.

'Darling, don't get upset. I wasn't being critical. I was referring to his behaviour at dinner last night. He certainly kept a poker face. As a matter of fact, you astonished me too. You were extraordinarily contained yourself.'

'Well, I had to be. Victor thinks we should be discreet. He's afraid of gossip, as I explained before. Naturally he realizes you know about us, but he doesn't think we should flaunt our relationship in front of you and Christian either. He – ' Francesca hesitated and rolled her eyes upwards, then confided, 'Do you know, this afternoon he actually spent a good fifteen minutes explaining how we're going to act towards each other tonight. I couldn't believe my ears.'

Diana burst out laughing. 'You're joking. And how are *you* supposed to behave?'

Francesca also began to laugh. Recovering herself, she said, 'Like a chum, what else?'

'And presumably he'll be cool and faintly distant with you. Am I correct?'

'Of course you are.'

'Well then, so be it,' Diana shrugged. 'After all, it's not so important in view of his true feelings. Now I *must* scoot, otherwise I'll be greeting our guests in this dressing gown.'

Once she was alone Francesca walked to the dressing table and sat down. As she placed the jewel case on it her eyes lighted on the card. She picked it up and read it again. *For you, baby. Because you are. Victor.*

The card had been attached to the package she had found on her bed, when she had gone to her room to freshen up just before they all sat down to a very late lunch, delayed until Diana and Victor had returned from skiing. She had not understood the words until she had ripped off the paper. It was the largest bottle of perfume she had ever seen, and it was Joy by Jean Patou. She had been thrilled by his message, his meaning, as well as by the gift itself. Moreover, she had recognized the writing at once. She had seen it before – only last week, on the card which accompanied the truckload of flowers from Moyses Stevens. Francesca smiled.

Removing the stopper, she dabbed her wrists and the cleft between her breasts with the perfume, loving its scent, which was full-bodied and floral. She had never been able to afford Joy. He's so terribly extravagant, but the most delicious man, she thought, aware of the trouble he had taken to obtain the perfume for her. That afternoon, when they had been together in her room, Victor had explained that Jake Watson had purchased it for him in London, along with a collection of the latest

Frank Sinatra records for Diana. All had been in his suitcase with his dinner jacket, which had arrived in Königssee around noon, also courtesy of Jake.

'Poor old Jake undoubtedly thinks I'm up to no good by now,' Victor had chortled. 'What with romantic records, expensive perfume and my dinner jacket. And he's right,' he had finished gleefully, pushing her back against the pillows and finding her mouth with his.

A door banging in the distance reminded Francesca of the time, and she straightened up in the chair, glanced in the mirror, patted a wave in her already immaculate pompadour, and rose. Hurrying to the armoire, she took out her own gift for Diana and headed to the door, then she stopped and looked down at her feet, frowning worriedly. Since she had only brought day shoes with her, there had been a problem about evening sandals, until Diana had produced the high-heeled black silk mules she was now wearing. The trouble was they were really bedroom slippers and also a size too small. On the other hand, they looked quite passable since Diana had cut off the ostrich feathers, and because they were mules their tightness was at least bearable. I'll just have to manage, she muttered, opened the door and went out.

Christian was the only occupant of the sitting room, looking darkly handsome in his dinner jacket. He sat in the wheelchair, fiddling with the knobs of the record player.

'It looks as if I'm the first, and I thought I was horribly late!' Francesca cried, tripping across the floor to him. She planted a kiss on his cheek, and continued, 'I do hope Dibs likes her gift. I took your advice and went to the little antique shop in town. I found a carved figurine, smaller than the ones she has, but it will fit into her collection.'

'She'll love it,' Christian said, smiling up at her. 'Stand a little farther away, so that I can see you properly.' He nodded his approval. 'You look beautiful, Frankie. But different somehow.' He peered at her more closely, his lips pursed in consideration. 'Older, a little more worldly, shall we say? Perhaps it's the upswept hairstyle that makes you seem so very grown up.' He nodded, as if confirming the fact. 'In any event, I like the new you, my dear. So will all the men tonight. You're suddenly a most intriguing woman.'

'Why thank you, Christian,' Francesca said. 'And it probably *is* my hairdo. It's sophisticated, isn't it? But then so is this dress. You're not used to seeing me looking so elegant.' She stepped to the coffee table and deposited Diana's gift on it, and then wondered suddenly if something showed in her face. Did it reflect her recent experiences and Victor's loving? Were those things detectable? She didn't care. Unlike Victor, who was determined to keep their romance a secret, she wanted to shout it to the whole world.

Diana rushed in and joined them near the fireplace. She was out of breath and unusually flushed. 'Sorry, my darlings. I had a problem with my hair,' she began, and pulled a face. 'It took much longer than I anticipated.'

'But worth waiting for, my dear,' Christian said. 'I predict you and Frankie are going to outshine everyone this evening.'

The girls laughed, and Francesca, eyeing Diana, exclaimed, 'And you do look super, Dibs. How on earth did you manage to create that effect by yourself?'

'I didn't. Clara helped me, and it *was* rather complicated,' Diana explained. 'I saw the idea in French *Vogue* and thought it was different.'

'It certainly is, and it's lovely on you,' Francesca smiled, examining her cousin's hairdo.

Diana's extraordinary silver-gilt hair had been pulled back from her face, parted in the middle and plaited. Wine silk ribbon was threaded through the waist-length plait, along with tiny white artificial flowers and green leaves. The elaborateness of the hair style was balanced by the simplicity of her gown, which was made of wine-coloured silk jersey. It had a high rolled neckline, long sleeves and a gathered skirt which fell in soft folds to the floor. Her jewellery was minimal.

'Gosh, you are inventive and clever, Dibs. I wish I had your flair.'

'I don't know about you two, but I'd like a drink,' Christian announced, wheeling himself over to the console. 'I'll open the champagne.'

'Oh yes, do, darling,' Diana agreed. 'And perhaps I'd better check the dining room, just to be sure everything is in order.'

Christian waved her to a standstill. 'You don't have to bother. I looked in a few minutes ago and Manfred has done a splendid job.'

'That's a relief. I can relax at last. It's been quite a hectic day.' Diana picked up a cushion, put it on the hearth and sat down. She smoothed her skirt, crossed her legs, and said, 'I didn't get an opportunity to say much about our morning on the slopes during lunch. But I must tell you, Victor's a marvellous skier. At first I thought he was going to be a wild skier, you know, the kind we despise, who takes bigger risks than he should. I was wrong. He handled the Jenner perfectly, and we had a superb run. He's – ' Diana broke off, her eyes fastened on the doorway. 'There you are, Victor. I was just talking about you – about your prowess on the slopes.' She proffered him a welcoming smile.

Victor laughed as he came towards them down the long stretch of carpet, white teeth flashing in his sunburned face, black eyes merry. His tuxedo, like all his clothes, had great distinction. It was expensive, faultless, fitted his expansive frame to perfection, and the white dress shirt enhanced his deep tan, made it look that much darker. Black onyx-and-diamond studs punctuated the ruffled front of the shirt, and a red silk handkerchief flared in his breast pocket. He was elegant, and every inch the star.

Francesca had never seen Victor in evening clothes before, and he seemed more glamorous than ever. She felt overpowered by him again, and her stomach fluttered nervously. Weak at the knees and experiencing a sudden tightness across her chest, she sat down on the sofa and attempted to compose herself. She was amazed at the effect he had on her, especially in view of their recent intimacy. Would she never become accustomed to his stunning looks, his extraordinary presence?

Drawing to a stop in front of Diana, Victor embraced her. 'Once again, a very happy birthday.' He handed her the two gifts he was carrying. 'And these are for you, from Francesca and me.'

'Thank you. How exciting. I do love birthdays.'

Victor smiled, turned to greet Francesca. Bracing one hand on the arm of the sofa and the other on its back, he leaned over her, his eyes intent. After a long look, he pressed his mouth to her cheek and gave her a lingering kiss, but as he drew away he winked. He straightened up, glanced down at her and then across at Diana.

281

'I must compliment you, ladies. You both look mighty fetchin', mighty fetchin' indeed, I do declare. Why, you fair take a man's breath away with your not inconsiderable charms,' he said, executing a bull's eye imitation of Clark Gable as Rhett Butler, and bowing to them with an elaborate old-fashioned gallantry.

'Victor, what a splendid mimic you are,' Christian exclaimed.

Victor grinned, and in an instant he was across the room, shaking his host's hand. 'Evening, Christian. Just one of the tools of the trade, I reckon.'

'What would you like to drink, old chap? Champagne?'

'I'd prefer Scotch-on-the-rocks with a splash of water. Thanks.'

Diana said, 'The presents are divine . . . all these fantastic Sinatras, and Arpège as well. Thank you both so much.' She beamed, her eyes swivelling from Francesca to Victor.

'And this is from . . . us,' Francesca said, finding her voice and rising. She gave the gift to Diana and hugged her warmly.

'You're both far too generous.' Diana unwrapped the figurine, her eyes lighting up when she saw it. 'Oh Cheska, Victor, it's charming. Thank you again.' She shook her head, laughing. 'Everyone is spoiling me today.' She held out her arm, displaying her garnet ring and a matching bracelet. 'Christian gave these to me this afternoon.'

'They're beautiful.' Francesca squeezed her shoulders, and went on, 'And you deserve to be spoiled. I know this is going to be a very special and wonderful year for you, Dibs darling.'

They had just finished toasting Diana when Manfred appeared. He told them the cars were arriving at the gatehouse and that some of the guests were already halfway down the path.

'Excuse me,' Diana said, getting up. 'I must go and greet them. Coming, Christian?'

'Naturally.' He promptly put down his drink and followed her to the entrance of the sitting room.

Francesca murmured, 'I'll tidy up,' and began collecting the crumpled wrapping paper. Throwing it into the fire, she then placed the gifts on a side table.

As she passed in front of him, Victor caught her arm, grasping it firmly and pulling her to him. He leaned into her, and said, 'You ought to be arrested for looking the way you do. You'll be the cause of my undoing yet.'

The glances she threw him was reproving but her eyes were flirtatious and teasing. 'Hadn't you better be careful, Mr Mason. Someone might get the wrong impression, if they see you grabbing me so . . . so possessively. I'm supposed to be your chum, not your inamorata. Remember?'

'*Touché*. And I'll deal with you later, madame. In the meantime, stand here and give me the dope on everyone.'

'Do you know, you can be quite bossy at times,' Francesca said, but, nevertheless, she picked up her glass and joined him in front of the fire. 'I'll do my best, but I don't know all the people who've been invited. Ah, that's Astrid hugging Diana now. Princess Astrid von Böler.' She drew closer, dropped her voice and added, with a small laugh, 'A great love of Kim's, until her husband broke up their affaire.'

Victor's brows lifted. 'No kidding! Your brother has good taste. Who's that with her? The husband?'

'No. Some Polish count with an unpronounceable name. Her latest . . . friend, I believe.'

'And the other people?'

'Graf and Gräfin Durmann. He's something to do with banking, I think.'

'What's Graf? A title?'

'Yes, it means count. Anyway, I've met them before, and they're awfully nice. His first name's Heinrich, and hers is Tatiana.'

Within the next few minutes all the guests streamed in, eight couples in all. Francesca endeavoured to acquaint Victor with a few salient details about those she knew, but too quickly they were surrounded by people. Somehow Victor was separated from her. She was stranded near the fireplace with Astrid and the Polish count, along with two other men she had not previously met. They closed in on her, apparently much taken. Yet she was conscious of Victor all the time.

Effortlessly, he was the focus of attention in the room, had taken the centre of the stage and was holding it. Francesca knew this was not only by virtue of his fame, but also because of his startling looks, his physique and bearing, his commanding manner and his natural charm. Since he was six feet three and towered above everyone else, it was easy for Francesca to keep him in her line of vision. Also, every so often, he would seek her out with his eyes, signalling a private message with a particular look, a smile, occasionally a quick, knowing wink.

But as the cocktail hour continued, with Clara, and another maid hired for the evening, serving the drinks and canapés, Francesca abandoned any thought of joining him. Most of the women had formed a phalanx around him, and were vying for his attention. And very adroitly, and somewhat maddeningly, he appeared to be flirting with each and every one of them. Francesca experienced a spurt of jealousy, but doused it, and retaliated in kind in her own quiet way. Günther Rundt, an acquaintance of Kim's, had beaten a swift path to her side. He was being flattering and attentive, lavishly so in fact, and she responded with smiles, a few coquettish glances, and summoned an enthralled expression to her face, hanging onto his every word. Out of the corner of her eye she caught Victor staring at her at one moment, and she stifled a laugh. He looked really miffed. She was delighted.

Eventually Manfred announced that dinner was served and the group slowly drifted towards the dining room. Victor caught up with Francesca and said in a low voice, 'Who's that guy?'

'Which guy do you mean?' she asked innocently, adopting a nonplussed air.

'You know. The one who was practically grinding you into the wall.'

She laughed lightly. 'Oh, that's a friend of Kim's . . . I assume you do mean Günther. He's very sweet.'

'If that's what you call sweet, then I'm angelic,' he countered, falling in step. She did not answer, and as they went into the room, he added, 'I hope we're sitting together, baby.'

'I doubt it. I'm sure you'll be sitting at Diana's right, I at Christian's right. I expect dinner'll be quite formal tonight.'

'Then I'll have to be satisfied with thoughts of what's yet to come . . . later, when we're alone,' he murmured through the side of his mouth. Surreptitiously he ran his fingers down her back before striding ahead to join Diana, who was beckoning him.

The grace and beauty of the Schloss, elements which had struck Victor so forcefully when he had arrived yesterday, were in great evidence tonight. The ambience in the dining room was decidedly romantic, had an almost fairytale quality. This was created in no small measure by the incredible number of white candles, in all manner of holders, which had been massed together in clusters everywhere, stood on the chests, the sideboard, the mantelpiece and the windowsills. A log fire flared in the immense stone hearth and the room was washed in a soft and mellow light. Dozens of votive candles had been used to encircle the small bowls of flowers, six in all, which marched down the centre of the long refectory table, and interspersed between the bowls were Meissen porcelain birds in the most radiant of colours. The table had been set with the finest china, crystal and silver, and was the decorative focal point. There were flowers and flowering plants banked around the perimeter of the room, and these introduced additional life and colour to an already breathtaking setting.

The flickering candlelight was flattering, and everyone looked their best, the women beautiful in their elegant gowns and glittering jewels, the men handsome in their dinner jackets. It was a young group and they were festive. The conversation was brisk, sparkling, entertaining, and Victor was enjoying himself, even though he was seated far away from Francesca. Occasionally he glanced down the table at her and caught her eye, and she would smile obliquely and continue her conversation. She was anchored between Christian and Vladimir, the Polish count, whilst he was next to Diana, as Francesca had said he would be. Astrid was also at his end of the table, and although she was charming, for the most part he concentrated his attention on Diana.

Francesca also discovered she was having a good time. Her gaiety and warmth quickly surfaced, and her naturalness was endearing to everyone. She laughed a lot, since Vladimir was proving to be a stimulating dinner companion, with his agility of wit and incisive repartee, and hilarity was high at their end of the table. However, as the dinner progressed, Francesca began to realize the others were taking it for granted that Victor was Diana's date for the evening. That he was now encouraging this in subtle ways was most apparent, and Francesca smothered a little smile, fully understanding his motivation. She also marvelled at his stamina. For a man who had left her room as dawn broke, after a sleepless night, had skied all morning and then made passionate love to her again in the afternoon, he was in remarkable fettle and showed no outward signs of fatigue whatsoever. Twenty years younger though she might be, she was vaguely conscious of aching limbs and a tiredness induced by their nocturnal activities.

Leaning forward ever so slightly, she looked at Victor, feeling the unique thrill of possession. Whatever anyone present believed, and whomever he flirted with, he nonetheless belonged to her. She, too, now thought of later, of when they would be alone, and a shiver ran through her. How extraordinary life is, she mused. A week ago she had been dying on the vine, miserable with longing for him, and he so seemingly beyond her tender reach; tonight she was more alive than at any other time in her life. And all because of him. He had become the centre of her world. Everyone and everything dimmed in comparison . . .

Vladimir said, 'I understand the Langley Collection is remarkable for its great paintings. Presumably it is open to the public, is it not?'

'Oh yes,' Francesca responded, dragging her mind back to the present proceedings. 'Every day during the summer months, and at weekends in the winter. My father believes great art should be shared. If ever you come to England, you must stop off at Langley to see the collection. You're obviously interested in art.'

'Thank you. How kind. Yes, I would love to visit your home. And I *am* very keen on art, especially old masters.' Vladimir went on, 'It is my dream to go to Russia one day, to view the paintings in the Hermitage. Catherine the Great was an extraordinary woman on many levels, but especially so as a collector of fine paintings. It's amazing, when one considers her resourcefulness in garnering such an incredible number of masterpieces from all over Europe. She built the Hermitage to house them you know . . . a marvellous legacy to leave.' He smiled and added, 'Catherine has always intrigued me, I must admit. An unscrupulous but fascinating woman. She was involved with one of my ancestors when she was in her twenties, and perhaps that's why she has always piqued my interest.'

'That must have been Count Stanislaus Poniatowski, who later became King of Poland. Am I right?'

'You are indeed, Francesca,' Vladimir told her, obviously surprised at this display of historical knowledge. He launched into a long story about his ancestor's love affair with the Empress of all the Russias, and in a most amusing manner. So much so, Francesca was instantly caught up in what he had to say, and the time passed swiftly.

It was suddenly the end of the dinner. Clara carried in a large birthday cake, ablaze with candles. Manfred served champagne, and Diana was the recipient of more toasts and congratulations.

Francesca said, as the toasts came to an end, 'Diana darling, now you must blow out all the candles and make a wish. A secret wish. Don't tell us!'

Victor, surveying the cake, leaned towards Diana and teased, 'Twenty-seven candles. That's pretty brave of you, honey, letting everyone know how old you are today.'

'A woman who can't tell her age doesn't know who she is,' Diana retorted pithily. 'I like to think *I* do.'

It was turned midnight when the last of the guests finally departed. Christian and Diana accompanied them to the front door to say their goodbyes, and Victor and Francesca were left alone in the sitting room.

Victor, nursing a brandy and smoking a cigar, looked across at her seated on the opposite sofa and began to chuckle.

'What is it?' she asked.

He said, his eyes twinkling, 'Do you realize I was the only person present tonight without a title?'

'Then we have to find one for you immediately,' Francesca pronounced, smiling with him. 'I have it! How about King . . . of the Silver Screen?'

Victor shook his head emphatically. 'Not possible, kid. Gable's the King, and he always will be, even after he's gone. Nobody, but nobody, will ever inherit *that* title. I doubt they'd want to. Clark's a very special guy, much loved, and revered, too, these days. No, there'll only be one King of Hollywood in everyone's minds.'

'Will you settle for Prince of the Silver Screen then?' she ventured, leaning back against the sofa, her eyes soft and loving as she regarded him.

He smiled, said nothing, stood up and took her glass from the coffee table. He moved across the room to the console. 'What is this stuff you're drinking, kid?'

'Pear William, please.'

Lifting the bottle he poured a generous measure, then held the bottle up, staring at it. 'How the hell did this pear get in here?' he asked, swinging to face her.

'I'll give you three guesses.'

'Well, let me see. A glass blower formed the bottle around the pear. I can see from the disgusted look on your face that the answer's *no*. Mmmmm. I have it! It's a collapsible pear, like one of those ships on a string that goes into the bottle flat, and is then pulled up straight,' he said, obviously teasing her now.

'Only one more guess, Vic, then you have to pay a penalty.'

'That sounds interesting. What did you have in mind?'

Observing his face as he came back to the fireplace, she started to laugh. She exclaimed, 'Not what you think, you wretch.'

He sat down next to her and handed her the glass. 'Too bad. In that case, I'd better 'fess up that I've known all along that the pear started out very small, and just growed and growed in the bottle. Down the hatch, kid.' He took a sip of his brandy, retrieved his cigar from the ashtray and puffed on it for a few seconds, then he reached out and touched her face with one finger. 'It's nice to have you to myself, Ches. It seems as if I ain't seen you all evening.'

'Yes, I know. But it was fun, wasn't it? You did enjoy the dinner party?'

'Sure did.' He settled back, feeling relaxed and contented and comfortable with her. His eyes roved around the room, and fell on the photographs arranged on the library table behind the sofa facing them. He allowed his gaze to linger, and after a short while, he said, 'I haven't wanted to pry, but I gotta admit I'm riddled with curiosity. Ever since I arrived here, I've sensed a sort of, well, a kind of mystery, I guess. About your aunt and uncle. Where are they?'

He got no further. Francesca had stiffened and he felt her sudden tenseness. He saw that the laughter had fled out of her, and seriousness mingled with sadness had crept onto her face. He waited, uncertain whether he ought to continue.

At last Francesca said, 'My Aunt Arabella lives in West Berlin.'

'And your uncle? Where is he?'

She returned his concentrated look, bit her lip and glanced down at her hands. 'I'd rather not . . . not talk about it, Vic,' she said softly.

'We're not sure where my father is, if indeed he's alive.' Christian's voice rang out clearly as he propelled himself to the fireplace.

Victor went cold and he held himself very still. He shook his head slowly and lifted his hand, as if telling Christian to say no more. He was acutely embarrassed. Clearing his throat, he apologized, 'I'm sorry. I'm blundering in again – into something that's none of my business. Please, let's forget I ever asked the question.'

'No, no, Victor, that's all right. And don't be upset,' Christian replied. 'I couldn't help overhearing. And, as I said, Father's whereabouts are unknown. We don't talk about him very often, especially with friends, because – well, because Diana and I have come to realize it's easier to ignore the situation whenever we can. Naturally, it's always there, at the back of our minds, although we do try not to dwell on it, for our own sanity.'

'He's dead!' Diana's pronouncement startled them all, and three pairs of eyes followed her movements. She entered the room purposefully, her face uncommonly pale. She took up her position in her favourite spot on the hearth, and continued firmly, 'At any rate, *I* believe he's dead. Originally, when the rumours started about two years ago, I thought there was a possibility of his being alive. But now I can't give credence to the stories . . .' Her voice trailed off, and then she said, 'Victor, would you mind getting me another drink, please? White mint over ice.'

'Sure.' He sprang up. 'What about you, Christian?'

'Thanks. I'll have a cognac.'

There was a silence whilst Victor fixed the drinks. Francesca, her hands clasped tightly in her lap, looked apprehensively from Diana to Christian, and wished Victor had not opened this particular Pandora's box. On the other hand, in all fairness to him, his inquisitiveness was only natural. Perhaps it would have been simpler if she had told a white lie a moment ago, and said her uncle also lived in West Berlin. Yet the family were so aware of Kurt von Wittingen's uncertain fate, it was always there in the background, hanging over them like the sword of Damocles.

Victor passed the drinks around without a word, said finally, in a subdued tone, 'Look, let's forget I ever – '

'Just a minute, Victor,' Christian interrupted and turned his gaze on Diana. 'I really think we owe Victor an explanation, darling, don't you?'

'Yes.'

'Good. You'd better make yourself comfortable,' Christian suggested, addressing Victor, all of his attention now focused on him. 'The story I have to tell you is complex, one I have partially pieced together myself over the years, from bits of information from my mother, my grandmother and several of my father's friends.' He sighed faintly under his breath. 'Can I presume you don't know too much about German politics in the years before World War Two?'

'You can,' Victor said.

Christian nodded, took a deep breath. 'I'm not going to bore you with a long dissertation about the rise of Adolf Hitler, but to understand my father's story, you must also understand what was happening in Germany in those days. In the middle of the nineteen twenties the Weimar Republic, which had been created in 1919, was extremely shaky. By 1928 Hitler had re-established his leadership of the Nazi Party, membership in the Party had reached sixty thousand, and the Nazis got two point six per cent of the vote in the Reichstag elections that particular year. In 1933 Hitler was appointed Chancellor by President Hindenburg, and between the burning of the Reichstag a month later, in February, and the elections in March, Hitler had become virtual dictator of Germany. His rise to power had horrified and frightened liberals, my father amongst them. As I told you yesterday, Father was an anti-Fascist who had dedicated his fortune, his energy and his time to fighting Fascism – actively but secretly. There was no way he could come out into the open without exposing himself and the family to extreme danger and arrest. However, for years he had been a leading member of an underground movement in Germany, helping Jews, Catholics, Protestants and so-called "political offenders" of all types who sought to flee Germany.' Christian took a swallow of his cognac, and asked, 'Did you ever read a book by Baroness Orczy called *The Scarlet Pimpernel*, Victor?'

'No. But I saw the movie starring Leslie Howard.'

'Good. Then I know you'll understand what I mean when I say my father was, in many ways, a modern-day Scarlet Pimpernel. Oddly enough, his code name was Blue Gentian, after the alpine flower. You see it was absolutely necessary that my father's identity be kept a secret from the Nazis, from everyone actually, and according to my mother it was Dieter Mueller, another leader in the underground, who invented the name. Dieter was a professor in literature, and I suppose he thought the name suited my father admirably. After all, Father was an aristocrat, a member of a socially prominent family, and seemingly beyond reproach, who had nothing but time and money on his hands to lead a life of leisure and gaiety in elegant circles. Yet at the same time he was actually a clandestine operator risking his life to save the lives of others.'

'But wasn't that kind of pointing a finger at your father?' Victor asked swiftly.

'You mean because of the parallels between the Scarlet Pimpernel and my father, the same use of flowers as code names, of course? But no, not at all. I doubt anyone would have thought of making the analogy, and besides Prince Kurt von Wittingen was above suspicion. Not only that, all the men in the underground movement were known by the names of flowers. Dieter's idea again, who himself had the code name of Edelweiss. But to continue. In the middle of the nineteen twenties my father became a senior consultant to Krupp, the German armaments king. He was travelling all over Europe, handling top-level negotiations, entertaining foreign dignitaries, acting as a kind of roving ambassador, in fact. It was the perfect cover for him. It enabled him to come and go almost as he wished, gave him easy access to all manner of important people, and thus fantastic sources of privileged information. In the spring of 1939, fully aware that the situation in Germany was worsening, Father sent my mother, Diana and me to England, to stay with Uncle David at Langley Castle, ostensibly on a prolonged vacation but really for safety's sake. By June of that year my mother, like most well-informed people, knew that war between England and Germany was inevitable, and, wanting to be with Father, she decided to return to Berlin. He would not hear of it, and rented a small house in Zurich for us, since it was relatively easy for him to visit Switzerland. He was with us from time to time, even after 1939, but generally he was either travelling or in Berlin.'

After another sip of his drink, Christian continued, 'We didn't see him much in 1941, not at all during 1942, but he was with us in Zurich in the early part of 1943, *en route* from Oslo to Berlin. It seems Mother was growing increasingly fearful that Father's clandestine activities would be discovered, and she desperately wanted him to remain with us in Switzerland. He would not. He felt he was needed by the movement, also he was worried about his mother. Father's two sisters, Ursula and Sigrid, had both been killed in Allied air raids over Berlin, and Grandmother was entirely alone, having been widowed years before. So he went back. A disastrous decision, I'm afraid.' Christian's face tightened sharply, and he took a cigarette and lit it.

Victor had been listening closely. He shivered and his hands tightened around the glass. 'And you never saw your father again,' he asserted, his eyes glued on the young prince.

'I did. Mother and Diana were not so fortunate. However, I'm jumping ahead of my story. Over the years my mother had always received messages from Father in various ways, but when he returned to Berlin in 1943 it was as if he suddenly dropped off the face of the earth. Months went by without any word from him. I was almost eighteen, and finally old enough to become my mother's confidant. She told me of her worries, and against her wishes I followed my father to Berlin . . .'

'How the hell did you manage that?' Victor cried.

'With my family's connections I had access to a lot of people. They all helped. Also, the times were confusing and erratic, so it wasn't too difficult to arrange. Mind you, it was very risky in more ways than one, I must admit. I got to our house in Berlin eventually, where I spent twenty-four hours with Grandmother. She told me that she had seen Father a few months earlier, but only briefly. Like us, she had received no word from him since. She had simply assumed he was travelling for the Krupp organization. The next day I was picked up by the Gestapo. Either by deduction, or through traitorous information, they had at last ear-marked my father as one of the leaders of the underground movement. He was on the top of their most wanted list, and they had obviously been watching the house for weeks. I was the guest of those *gentlemen* – ' Christian snapped off the end of his sentence and a grim smile flicked onto his mouth. 'In any event, the Gestapo kept me for over six months, working on me day and night, before they finally released me.' His eyes darkened. He lowered them and looked down at his legs. 'I've not been able to walk properly since then.'

Victor felt a trembling inside, and his hands shook slightly as he lifted the brandy balloon to his mouth and took a long swallow of his drink, which he badly needed. Christian's words, unadorned and spoken gently, were all the more deadly because of their quietness and simplicity. Oh God, oh God, Victor thought, how easily we forget. And yet it's only a handful of years ago that the Nazis were committing all manner of unspeakable atrocities and brutalities, that this young man talking to me so calmly was turned into a permanent cripple by them. When he was only a boy. And who knew what torture had been inflicted on him. Jesus Christ!

No one spoke nor moved, and the only sound was the faint hissing of the logs in the fireplace, the distant ticking of a clock somewhere in the room.

Christian met Victor's gaze with grave eyes, and his voice was controlled and steady as he went on, 'I didn't break, Victor. Still, I have never considered that a great act of courage on my part. You see, I knew so very little of my father's activities, it was simple for me to keep repeating the same thing over and over again. After the Gestapo finally discarded me, Grandmother managed to nurse me back to partial health, though God only knows how, conditions and shortages being what they were then. In 1944, Dieter Mueller got a message to me . . . *the blue gentians are in full bloom*. Since my mother had told me Father's code name, in case I needed to use it after I'd returned to Berlin, I knew immediately what the message meant. Father was safe. It was enough to bolster my courage and keep me going. Then, in the early summer of 1945, not very long before Berlin fell to the Allies, Father miraculously arrived at the house in Berlin. He did not explain where he had been and I knew better than to ask.'

Now Christian sat back in the wheelchair looking drained and exhausted. He finished sombrely, 'Father was with us for two weeks. One morning he left the house, saying he would return later that day. But he didn't come back ... Grandmother and I never saw him again.' Turning to Diana, Christian said, 'Maybe you can finish the story, darling.'

'Yes, of course I will. But are you all right, Christian?' she asked.

'Yes, I'm fine, I really am.'

'You don't have to continue.' Victor sat motionless in the chair, his face serious and reflecting his disquiet, his immense sadness for them both. 'I don't know what to say, how to express my regret for having opened up so many wounds. It was thoughtless of me to pry. I've caused you such unnecessary heartache, making you relive these terrible events.'

'Don't chastise yourself, Victor dear,' Diana murmured. 'And you might as well hear the rest of the story, so that you can truly understand why Christian and I are so reluctant to constantly thrash it over. At first, Christian and Grandmother were not too worried when my father did not return that night. As a matter of fact, they weren't particularly concerned even after several days had elapsed. After all, continually coming and going was Father's normal pattern of behaviour. By this time, Grandmother knew a little about her son's activities as a clandestine member of the underground movement, since Christian had filled her in, albeit in a sketchy way. Also, there seemed to be less reason for them to be alarmed, in that the Third Reich had collapsed, Berlin was in the hands of the Allies – the British, the Americans and the Russians were occupying Berlin. What could possibly happen to the notorious Blue Gentian now? He was amongst friends, wasn't he? However, as the days became weeks, their anxiety increased, and inquiries were made. They turned up nothing. Father had simply disappeared. A few weeks later, another member of the underground movement, who had been wounded during the fighting in Berlin, finally came out of hospital. When he heard that my father was missing, he told Dieter that he had seen Daddy talking to some Russian officers in the part of the city which became the East Zone. That man, Wolfgang Schroeder, had seen Daddy only a few days after he had left Grandmother's house, and they had actually exchanged greetings. Wolfgang said he was convinced my father had been a casualty during the last-ditch fighting in the final battle of Berlin. Dieter seized on this and set to work. Hospitals were searched, people were questioned, the dead were carefully checked. In fact, the whole of Berlin was turned upside down by Dieter and his friends. To no avail.'

Diana closed her eyes for an instant. When she opened them, she said in the lowest of voices, 'Daddy was never found, his body was never found, and in the end we had to assume he had been killed during the last days of the war. Naturally, as things gradually became a little more normal, Mummy wanted to get back to Christian and Grandmother. We eventually packed up in Zurich and returned to Berlin. Slowly, we attempted to pick up our lives, to go on living as best we could, grieving for Daddy but having to accept the fact that he was gone. You more or less know what happened next, how we moved from Berlin to Munich, then to Wittingenhof. Nine years passed. Two years ago, Dieter came to see Mummy. He was excited, jubilant almost. It seemed he had a possible solution to my father's mysterious disappearance, as well as information about his whereabouts.'

'Your father had finally been in touch with Dieter then?' Victor was on the edge of his seat, innumerable questions running through his head.

Diana shook her head. 'No. But by accident he had stumbled on a strange story. Let me explain something. In 1953 and 1954, numerous Germans – civilians actually – who had been arrested for one reason or another by the Russians at the time Berlin surrendered were straggling back. They had been released from Lubyanka Prison in Moscow. Anyway, there was talk amongst them about a mystery prisoner who was kept in solitary confinement most of the time. Apparently he was an *aristocrat*, and a *German*. Furthermore, he had been in Lubyanka since 1945. The man had been seen occasionally by many other prisoners, and his physical description, his age, along with other details, fitted my father like a glove. This tale was told to Dieter by his cousin, whose father-in-law had just returned from the Russian prison. It didn't take Dieter long to come to the obvious conclusion that the man in Lubyanka might conceivably be my father. He spoke to lots of repatriated prisoners and the more he heard, the more certain he became that the mystery prisoner was the Blue Gentian, alias Rudolf Kurt von Wittingen. Armed with this information he came to Mummy, and that's when the trouble really started.'

'What do you mean by trouble?' Victor asked, raising an eyebrow.

'Mummy had been able to lead a reasonable existence up until then, a relatively normal life. Believing her husband to be dead, she had been content to build her life around us, her children. The idea that Daddy was alive after all, and rotting in Lubyanka, changed all that. In the last two years she has become a tormented woman . . . demented by worry, uncertainty and anguish, alternatively buoyed up by hopes . . . futile hopes in my opinion.'

'What a horrendous thing for her to live with, for you all to live with!' Victor stared at Diana aghast. 'Are you saying that you haven't been able to find out if it is your father or not?'

Diana nodded. 'Precisely. Dieter, Mummy, Christian and I all went to Bonn, and through political connections of Dieter's we were able to meet with Chancellor Adenauer. The West German Government took up the case, and they made a formal request to the Russians for confirmation that the prisoner in Lubyanka was Daddy. The Russians categorically denied the existence of any such prisoner, let alone one who was a German prince. In the last twelve months, Christian and I have been to Bonn twice, and more pressure has been exerted. In consequence, our Government made further approaches to the Russians, only to be stonewalled.' She bit her lip, frowned. 'We're at an impasse.'

Victor was silent. He sat back on the sofa, ruminating on the things he had just heard. Finally he glanced from Diana to Christian and said slowly, 'Forgive my ignorance, but why would the Russians arrest your father in 1945 in the first place? What possible reason could they have had to take him prisoner?'

Christian smiled faintly. 'It's not ignorance, Victor. It's a perfectly normal question, and one we all asked each other two years ago. Dieter was able to supply the answer only too readily. He believes my father was taken by the Russians because they thought he was a spy. Specifically, a spy for the Americans, and therefore an enemy of the Soviet Union.' Christian shook his head. 'Don't look so sceptical, Victor. Apparently many Germans were arrested by the Russians at that time because they suspected them of being spies – I'll go further, were convinced they were spies. For the Americans. But whatever the reason, it's irrelevant really, in as much as Mother and Dieter are quite positive my father *is* the man in Lubyanka.'

'And you? What do you think, Christian?' Victor asked, snuffing out his cigar which had been smouldering in the ashtray, forgotten.

After a few minutes, Christian admitted, 'I honestly don't know what to think, old chap. I really don't. I waver between doubt and certainty. One minute I'm agreeing with Mother, and then, unexpectedly, I'm swayed by Diana's conviction that Father is dead. But when Dieter makes an appearance, as he did yesterday, with more rumours, I'm siding with the two of – '

'We don't have enough concrete facts!' Diana cried peremptorily, her voice unusually high-pitched for her. 'The longer I ponder the story the more I come to realize how flimsy it is, in reality. I'm sure Daddy was killed at the end of the war in Berlin, and that his body was one of the many unidentified. I suppose, in a way, I hope he *is* dead.' Her tone was suddenly tremulous and she blinked and looked away. She finished, in a sad little voice, 'Perhaps that's preferable to me, because then he would not be suffering. I can't stand the thought that he's alive in Lubyanka and being subjected to . . . to – ' Diana was unable to continue and her emotions took hold of her.

Francesca instantly jumped up and joined her on the hearth. She put her arms around her cousin and said soothingly, 'Oh Dibs darling, don't cry. It's not much consolation, I know, but Daddy and I agree with you.' As she spoke Francesca glanced at Christian, her eyes full of love and compassion. 'I'm sorry, darling, but we *do* believe that Uncle Kurt died in 1945, as we've told Aunt Arabella many times.'

Christian half inclined his head. 'Yes,' he said, and wheeled himself over to the console. He poured himself a cognac, a thoughtful look in his eyes. Returning to the fireside, he focused on Victor. 'Having heard this extraordinary story, what do *you* think? Is my father dead, or is he in Lubyanka?'

'I can't give an opinion either way,' Victor pursed his lips. Suddenly he changed his mind. 'I guess I'm ambivalent, like you, Christian. I don't know what to think. Jesus, what a goddamn lousy thing to live with on a day-to-day basis. It's a heartrending situation. No wonder you never want to discuss it. It's all my fault everyone's upset. I shouldn't be so nosey. I've only succeeded in ruining a lovely evening.'

'Oh please, Victor, don't be silly,' Christian said. 'There's no need to keep apologizing. And you haven't spoiled the evening, has he, Diana?'

'Hardly. In fact, you've made it extra special and memorable.' She smiled at Victor. 'But would you mind if we drop the subject now? I'd like to concentrate on the present, the next few days to be exact.' She took a deep breath and, adopting a more cheery tone, went on, 'Christian and I are going to Munich tomorrow, to spend the day at Grandmother's, with our mother. I won't be able to take you skiing on the Rossfeld. However, Astrid and Vladimir will go with you. Is that all right?'

'Sure. That'll be great,' Victor said, pulling his mind away from his troubled thoughts, looking at her with admiration. There was something very unusual in this girl, a certain indomitability that took his breath away. 'But what about Francesca? She'll be all alone here.'

'Oh don't worry about me, I've got lots of things to do,' Francesca assured him with a warm smile. 'You will be back for lunch though, won't you?'

Before he could respond, Diana said, 'Astrid wants both of you to have lunch at her house, Cheska. It'll be fun for you, and I know Victor will enjoy seeing the von Böler estate. It's most impressive and puts Wittingenhof to shame.'

'That's nice of her,' Francesca said. 'I wouldn't mind seeing the place myself. Kim told me it's like a miniature Versailles.'

'That's true.' Diana stood up. 'Well, if you'll excuse me, I'm going to tell Manfred to lock up, and then get off to bed. We have to leave very early in the morning.' She kissed Francesca and Christian, and then moved across the floor to Victor. He rose and hugged her to him. 'You're an extraordinary person, Diana,' he said, and kissed her gently on the forehead.

'So are you,' she responded, squeezing his arm, her expression affectionate. She turned and walked to the doorway. 'Good night everyone.'

Shortly afterwards, Christian also took his leave of them. The minute they were by themselves, Victor said, 'I guess you can't take me anywhere, kid. I'm a dumb idiot.'

'Hush!' Francesca exclaimed, and moved over to sit next to him on the sofa. She took his hand in hers, and insisted, 'Please do let's forget all this, Vic. Diana's right, we must put the tragedy of Uncle Kurt out of our minds. Just as she and Christian do most of the time. And honestly, they're not angry or upset with you. Neither am I.'

'That's a helluva relief.' He put his arm around her and pulled her closer. 'Mind if we sit here for a bit?'

'Not at all. Would you like another drink, darling?'

'Sure, why not. One for the road, I guess.' He released his hold and his eyes following her as she walked across the room were filled with tenderness. 'Do me a favour, baby, kill the lights in here, please.'

'All right. Shall I put on a record, one of the Sinatras maybe?'

'Terrific idea ... the Cole Porter selection ... together those two are an unbeatable team, about the greatest.'

Within minutes the room was entirely in darkness, its edges grey and murky, but the fireside was bathed in roseate tints and the logs spurted and flared in the grate so that a pool of isolated golden light surrounded them like a nimbus. They sat for a long time on the sofa, wrapped in each other's arms, listening to the romantic ballads, speaking hardly at all, content to be alone together. At one moment Victor turned his head and glanced out of the windows which intersected the wall opposite. Beyond the glass, an indigo sky, speckled with the brightest stars, was being intermittently streaked with silver radiance as the moon came out from behind black clouds. It clearly illuminated the landscape, breathtaking even at this hour in its white and silent beauty.

It's so peaceful out there, he thought, just as this room is also enveloped in tranquillity. Victor averted his face and stared into the fire, his eyes reflective now. Images of the dinner party danced before him in the flames. It had been perfect down to the last detail. And so civilized. The guests had been charming, cultured, intelligent and well informed, the men elegantly attired, the lovely women exquisitely gowned and bejewelled, and all had been gathered together in the most

293

gracious of settings, partaking of excellent food and vintage wines. Yes, it had been an occasion of gaiety and joyfulness as befitted Diana's birthday.

Coming so quickly after this glittering, happy scene, the story of Kurt von Wittingen had been chilling, had had a curious unreality about it to Victor, as though it were somehow out of sync. Yet this was not the case, and it was only too real, just as Auschwitz, Buchenwald and Dachau had been real, as Christian's ruined legs were real. Victor dwelt on all that had been said in the last hour and his disquiet returned, and he felt a sudden and terrible coldness in the region of his heart. Evil had cast its dark shadow over this night. But evil is always there, lurking, he found himself thinking, as it has lurked since the beginning of time when man first discovered his immense capacity for it. And as long as man walks this earth it will flourish, for it is man's invention not God's. A sigh rippled through him and he closed his eyes.

Francesca shifted her body against his, swivelled her head and looked up into his face. 'What is it? Is something wrong, Vic?'

He opened his eyes and stared at her. He was tempted, for a moment, to voice his thoughts, but changed his mind. 'I'm okay. Nothing's wrong, Ches,' he murmured and lifted his hand and touched the top of her head, and she relaxed and settled back in his arms and a silence fell between them again. It was long after the music had stopped and the fire had burned low to dying embers that Victor finally roused himself. He led her out of the sitting room, down the long gallery and up the great staircase, and not once did he let go of her hand so tightly clasped in his.

CHAPTER TWENTY-NINE

Three months later, Terrence Ogden walked briskly across the ancient Market Place in Ripon, dropped a large manilla envelope in the post box and went into the first tobacconist's shop he saw. He bought a newspaper and a packet of cigarettes, exchanged a friendly word with the girl behind the counter, and swung through the door of the shop, whistling under his breath.

He headed out of the Market Place, past the Town Hall and the Wakeman's House, and down the hill at a rapid pace, returning to the Spa Hotel at the edge of town where the cast and crew of *Wuthering Heights* were staying.

It was a Saturday morning in late June, and the kind of glorious summer day he remembered so vividly from his childhood, but which had been sadly infrequent in the ensuing years. Or so it seemed to him. Terry wondered absently if, in the way that memory can play peculiar tricks, he had simply imagined those golden days of his early boyhood. Perhaps the summers had been as inclement then as they were now. A faintly ironic gleam flashed in his light blue eyes. It was odd how the lovely weather, whether real or a figment of his imagination, was the only pleasant thing he remembered about those poverty-stricken years of growing up in Sheffield. All his other recollections had a desperate, almost Dickensian flavour to them. Empty belly. Patched clothes. Socks so darned they were all darn. Broken-down shoes letting the snow and the rain seep through. Dad on the dole. And when he was working, it was down the pit, filling his lungs full of coal dust. Mam scrubbing and cleaning, washing, ironing, charring for the rich. Old before she was young.

Terry shrugged and blinked and discarded these thoughts. They served no purpose now. Those days were long gone. Times had changed in merry old England and he, thank God, had been able to change his parents' lives. And for the better. He took a deep breath and straightened his shoulders, feeling healthier than he had in years. Terrence Ogden was also a somewhat chastened man after his drunken brawl with Rupert Reynolds earlier in the year. He was fully conscious that he had had a close call, a brush with death, and he had taken himself in hand, with firmness. If he was not exactly abstinent, he had cut down on his drinking considerably, and had thrown all of his energies into his work. Now he wondered vaguely where Reynolds had skipped off to, where he was hiding. Norman had said he was most likely on the Continent. Not far enough away for me, Terry mumbled under his breath.

'Hey, Terry, what's the hurry, me old cock?'

Terry swung around. Jerry Massingham, astride a bicycle, was pedalling down the road as if his life depended on it, his red hair mussed by the light breeze, his coat flapping out behind him. Dressed in an unsuitable heavy tweed suit, a Viyella shirt and a canary-yellow wool tie, Jerry looked like a country doctor on his morning rounds.

'Good God, Jerry, this is one way to make certain you get a heart attack!' Terry said as the production manager slowed to a stop and jumped off the bicycle. 'And what the hell are you doing rushing up and down the country lanes on a bloody bike in the first place?'

'I like riding a bike, it's good exercise,' Jerry informed him, a wide grin creasing his flushed face. He fell into step with Terry, wheeling the bicycle between them. 'I had to get to the post office before it closed, to send an express package to London. There weren't any production cars available an hour ago. The second unit's using them. They're out on the moors, getting some background shots. And what are you doing abroad at this hour? Taking a constitutional?'

'I also went to post a letter, and to buy a paper. Besides, it's turned eleven.' He gave Jerry a swift look, finished caustically, 'I don't normally spend my mornings liggin in bed, contrary to what *you* might think.'

'What does liggin mean?'

'It's Yorkshire dialect for lying – as in lying in bed wasting the day away.'

'Is it now. Humph. No offence intended, laddie. I mean about being out and about at this hour. I was merely surprised to see you, considering how whacked you looked at two this morning. Mind you, the night shooting was gruelling, especially hard on you and Katharine. Come to think of it, the rest of the cast were pretty done in by the time we finished. Or so it appeared. Actually, I haven't seen hide nor hair of a single actor this morning. Usually they're milling around the hotel when we're not filming. Have you run into any of your confrères perchance?'

'No, I haven't perchance,' Terry responded with a chortle. 'I did speak to Katharine earlier, on the 'phone. She sounded full of beans, as usual. She told me half the cast have gone off on a picnic, up to Middleham Castle in Wensleydale. Shades of Richard III, no doubt. He was born there, you know.'

'They must be made of iron.'

'Stamina is an actor's stock in trade, Jerry.'

'True enough. But a picnic. Ugh! Jolly good luck to them! I saw you do Richard III. At Stratford. Memorable, Terry, memorable.'

'Thanks, Jerry. It's a bloody tough role.'

'Mmmm. Funny though, how you make it look so easy.' The production manager glanced at Terry and said, 'We got some damned good footage in the can last night, and providing there are no more mishaps, and the weather holds, we should be able to get out of here next Friday, as planned. That should make you delirious.'

Terry threw Jerry a baffled look. 'I haven't minded being on location, mate. As a matter of fact, I've quite enjoyed it this time around. I was pretty miserable when we were here in May, but then who wasn't, with all that rain. Getting sodden to the skin every day is hardly my idea of a joy ride.'

Jerry laughed at Terry's dour expression, his glum delivery. 'Nor mine. And I wasn't singling you out in any sense,' he remarked. 'We'll *all* be glad to get back to London and the studios. A week of final interiors and then it's a wrap.'

Terry eyed him, a faint smile flickering. 'Still, despite the problems, and the weather, we're on schedule and within the budget. That should make *you* delirious, Jerry.'

'It does.' He leaned across the bicycle, and said, 'You've been a real trouper, Terry, taking so much rotten flak from Mark Pierce as good-naturedly as you have. He's a difficult bugger.'

'But a great director. I simply put it down to the temperament of a genius. And to be fair, he's been hard on the entire cast, as well as on me. They've been troupers too.'

'Yes,' Jerry said quietly. He thought: But Mark's had his knife in you and to the hilt. He had his own ideas about the real cause of the trouble between the actor and the director. Victor was suspicious and had attempted to get to the root of it, without success. Too much tension, too many undercurrents on this film, Jerry said inwardly. I'll be relieved when the last bloody frame has been shot.

'I heard a rumour you're going to be on the Bolding picture, Jerry. True or false?'

'Affirmative, old boy. And I'm looking forward to it. A classy production. Shooting in the South of France later this summer. Good cast too.'

'Congratulations.'

'And you? Anything in the offing?'

'A couple of things,' Terry said cautiously. 'A play in the West End for starters, if I want it.'

'Stick to films from now on, Terry,' the production man advised. 'You can really cut it, and you come off well on the screen. When I saw the rushes I was most impressed. You've brought something very special to the role of Edgar Linton, given it dimension and stature.'

'Thanks. That's nice to hear. Especially from you. Getting it from the horse's mouth, so to speak.'

Jerry smiled but said nothing and the two men walked on in silence. Within a

couple of minutes they reached the entrance to the hotel grounds, and amble
through the gates and up the short driveway. As they drew closer to the front steps
of the Spa Hotel, both of them stopped short and glanced at each other swiftly.

'Our star departs!' Terry said.

'Looks like it.' Jerry's response was gruff and a flash of annoyance replaced
his startled expression as he surveyed the scene ahead. Victor Mason's gleaming
wine-coloured Bentley Continental was parked in front of the door, and Gus was
loading the boot with Victor's expensive luggage.

'I thought he wasn't leaving until next week,' Terry said.

'So did I. Tuesday to be precise.'

At this moment Jake Watson came through the door and hurried down the steps,
his arms laden with cans of film. He carried these to the car and placed them inside
on the back seat. Turning, he saw them and waved. 'Hi, you guys!'

''Morning, Jake,' Jerry said, moving forward quickly, pushing the bicycle.

'Good morning.' Terry returned Jake's wave and grinned. 'Are we losing
our star?'

Jake nodded. 'Yep. Victor's about to leave for London.'

'I wish to hell you'd told me!' Massingham exclaimed heatedly, his face
colouring. 'If I'd known earlier it would have saved me the bother of getting
that package of documents to the post office. Victor could have taken it with him,'
he groused. 'Racing up and down the roads on this bloody thing is all I need this
morning.' He stomped off to park the bicycle, bristling.

'Don't get so hot under the collar, Jer,' Jake soothed, staring after him,
recognizing his nose was out of joint. He probably thought he had been cut out
of some top-level decision-making. 'Victor only decided to beat it an hour ago.
I came looking for you, as soon as I knew about his change in plan, but you'd
already split.'

'When's he coming back? Correction. He's not, if the luggage is anything to go
by,' Jerry muttered, swinging around to face Jake, glaring at him.

'That's right.'

'It was my understanding Mark needed Victor for an extra scene on Monday,'
Terry remarked carefully, his curiosity aroused.

'Mark changed his mind,' Jake said, deciding it would be more discreet to tamper
with the truth than tell it the way it really was. 'He had a breakfast meeting with
Victor this morning, to go over the rest of the shooting schedule, and he decided the
additional scene would be redundant, a waste of film, *and* everybody's time. He's
got far too much footage in the can as it is, he's over-shot like crazy as he always
does, and a lot of it has to end up on the cutting room floor. Victor agreed the scene
wasn't really necessary. It wasn't in the script in the first place. It's the one Mark
added, you know, when Heathcliff is walking on the moors late at night and thinks
he sees Cathy ahead of him . . . well, the ghost of Cathy. The scene would've had
to be shot at night, which they wanted to avoid. Also, they both decided it was a bit
too esoteric,' Jake finished, feeling rather pleased with his censored version of the
stormy breakfast meeting at which Victor had finally put his foot down.

Jerry Massingham's attitude changed, and for the better. He grinned delightedly.
'Well, I'm glad to hear it. A smart decision. I knew all along we didn't need that new
scene. We've got enough mystical bloody mumbo-jumbo in this picture as it is. Not

at I would presume to tell Mark how to make his *bouillabaisse*, of course. Good. ...'ll save us some money in the long run.'

Jake said, 'That's the spirit, Jer. I was pretty damned sure you'd see the practical side. And listen, *bubeleh*, I'm sorry you had to sweat it up to the post office, particularly on that antiquated machine.'

'No harm done, laddie,' Jerry replied with geniality, his good humour completely restored.

'Well, you two, I've got to push off, I'm afraid. See you later,' Terry announced and edged in the direction of the steps.

'Righto, old boy,' Jerry said, and Jake added, 'Take it easy, Terrence.' He put his arm around Massingham's shoulders and went on, 'I need to talk to you about a couple of production matters.'

Terry left them with their heads lowered, huddled together near the car, and bounded up the front steps. Inside the lobby he stopped at the desk to inquire if there were any messages, and then took the lift to the second floor. He peered at his watch as he went down the corridor, saw that he was late. Katharine wouldn't mind, he was sure of that. She had said she was going to study her scenes until he arrived.

He rapped on the door and she opened it almost immediately. 'Hello, Puss,' he said.

'Terry darling!' she exclaimed. Her eyes swept over him. 'Don't you look gorgeous,' she added, opened the door wider and led him into her suite.

'Thanks, and I must return the compliment. Night shooting appears to agree with you, from the way *you* look.'

'*Merci, monsieur,*' Katharine laughed. 'Come and sit here, it's lovely and sunny. I just ordered fresh tea, and this funny peppery sort of cake that I simply adore.'

Terry joined her, glanced at the chunks of moist brown cake on the plate and grinned down at her. 'That's parkin, Katharine. One of my favourite treats when I was a kid. And it's ginger you can taste, you silly girl, not pepper. I think I will have a piece, and milk please, not lemon, in the tea.' He lowered himself into a chair, and announced, 'I just bumped into Jake. And get this! Victor's leaving us today.'

'Yes, I know,' Katharine replied blithely, lifting the milk jug. 'He was here a little while ago – to say goodbye.'

'*Naturally.*' Terry chuckled knowingly, a sardonic gleam in his eyes.

Katharine's dark head flew up and she frowned at him. 'What's that supposed to mean?'

'Teacher's pet ... of course he wouldn't leave without taking his fond farewells.'

'For what it's worth, he also stopped off to take his fond farewell of *you*,' she retorted in an airy tone. 'But you were out. So he told me to give you his best, and you're to "sock it to 'em next week", quote unquote.'

'I see.'

'Oh stop teasing me about Victor, Terry,' Katharine exclaimed, sounding impatient; but there was fondness in her expression and her turquoise eyes danced with merriment. 'Victor doesn't pay much more attention to me than he does to anyone else in the film.' She smiled dismissively.

'Oh come on Katharine!' Terry spluttered. 'How can you say that! You have

lunch with him practically every day, sit next to him on the set, or with him in h
trailer here on location, and he never takes his eagle eyes off you.'

'But I'm under personal contract to him, or rather, to Bellissima Productions,
and anyway I've never made a film before. *You have*. He's only trying to help me,'
she protested. 'Besides, you've had lunch with him a lot too, and you've also been
ensconced in the trailer with hi –'

'Playing poker, Puss.' Terry's look was full of speculation. 'What *do* you two do
in his trailer?' he asked with a suggestive smirk.

'Terry! That's enough! I don't like the implication, particularly since you know
very well I'm dating Kim Cunningham.'

'Don't get your knickers in a twist, Puss. I'm only pulling your leg. How is Kim,
by the way? I thought he looked awfully morose last night.'

'He's all right – I suppose,' Katharine sighed, her face becoming sombre. 'I think
he feels a bit neglected. He's made it very difficult for me in some ways. He thought
we'd be seeing each other every night while we were shooting in Yorkshire, but
that's been impossible. You know what it's like at the end of the day. Frankly,
I'm drained, and I've had my new scenes to concentrate on at night, and my
preparations for the next day. Mark's such a stickler about every single detail, as
we've all found out. And Victor's been on my back about getting lots of rest.' She
made a small moue. 'I haven't had a great deal of spare time for poor Kim, and I
guess he resents it.'

'The work *does* come first with you, doesn't it, love?'

'Yes,' she agreed emphatically, and hesitated. 'But –' Katharine leaned back,
and changing the subject, she said, 'You sounded so mysterious on the 'phone.
I've been dying to know why you wanted to see me this morning. Come on, my
darling, tell me what this is all about.'

He looked at her carefully, a small smile trickling across his mouth. 'It seems as
though I never stop thanking you these days, Puss darling. That's why I'm here.
To thank you again for another good deed.'

'What do you mean –' She stopped abruptly. Her eyes filled with happiness,
and she clapped her hands. 'Oh goody! Hilly Steed! It worked, didn't it, Terry?'
He nodded, excitement bubbling over in him. '*Yes*. And how! He offered me a
three-picture deal with Monarch. The contracts arrived yesterday from my agent.
I signed them this morning and posted them a little while ago. It looks as if we're
going to be in Hollywood together, Katharine. I start my first picture under the
contract in October, when you're starting yours. I've read the script and it's bloody
marvellous. A superb drama. I've got the second male lead, but after the first film
I'll be playing only leading men. So Hilly promised me. He's got great plans, wants
to build me.' Terry reached out and patted her hand. 'Anyway, I owe my good
fortune to you, love. You started the ball rolling with Hillard, and whatever you
said to him obviously made the right impression.'

'Oh how wonderful, darling! I'm so excited for you, and thrilled,' Katharine
cried, her pleasure and sincerity genuine. 'And I didn't do much, Terry. You
did it yourself really. You're marvellous in the picture. Hilly was ecstatic about
the rushes –'

'What *did* you say to him?'

'Do you really want to know?' She did not wait for a reply. 'I was quite clever ally. That day I had lunch with Hilly at Shepperton he was raving about you, and told him Victor felt the same way. Then I said, "In fact, I think Victor's going to sign Terry to a personal contract with Bellissima. He believes Terry is going to be very big after *Wuthering Heights* is released." I let *that* sink in, and I could see Hilly was turning *rather* green with envy. He's very competitive with Victor, as a producer I mean. Then I delivered my punch line. I sighed, a bit sadly, patted Hilly's arm in commiseration and said, "What a pity you didn't think of signing Terrence Ogden first, Hilly. After all, you just missed getting *me* by a hair's breadth. It looks as if Victor is about to steal another march on you. Certainly he's cornering the market on new young talent." Poor Hilly, he couldn't finish his lunch. Awfully upset, poor thing. I do believe I ruined his day,' she laughed. 'I could *see* his mind ticking over. He asked me a few questions, also whether you had actually signed with Victor nor not. Naturally I was suitably vague. I suggested he call you.' Katharine sat back, looking sweetly innocent and gratified with herself.

'You're incorrigible, Katharine.' Terry shook his head.

'Oooh, I know I am.' She smiled at him prettily, for all the world like a mischievous child. 'But sometimes it's fun to be incorrigible. And I did get the desired results, didn't I?'

'Yes. And what if Hillard had spoken to Victor first? Then where would you have been?'

Katharine gave him the benefit of a withering look and said, her tone scathing, 'You don't know Hilly Street very well. He would *never* tip his hand like that. I was *positive* he would approach you immediately, that he would try to cut Victor out, and he was true to form.' She shrugged. 'Elementary psychology, my dear Watson.'

'Quite so, Holmes, quite so,' Terry responded, taking her cue, amusement tugging at his mouth. He lit a cigarette, observing her through slightly narrowed eyes. There were those who might consider that Katharine had been cunning and conniving. *He* preferred to think of her dealings with Hillard Steed in less derogatory terms, attributing them to an inveterate shrewdness rather than any form of deviousness. Although this was not the first occasion she had displayed her inimitable brand of astuteness, again he was startled, as he had been in the past. Perhaps this was because her looks belied her intelligence, which he knew to be considerable, as did her air of childlike *naïveté*, never more pronounced than it was this morning.

Katharine filled the teapot with hot water, and asked, 'Another cup, Terry?'

'Yes, thanks.' He watched her closely, his eyes evaluating. She was wearing a tailored white shirt of fine cotton voile and a navy blue cotton skirt. Both were simple, demure, could only be described as schoolgirl clothes. In point of fact, she did not look much older than sixteen at this moment. A line of Petruchio's flew into his mind: *Yet sweet as springtime flowers*. Yes, that was the impression she made today, with her chestnut hair falling in tumbling waves to her shoulders, her eloquent face sparkling fresh, entirely devoid of makeup except for the bright red lipstick she generally favoured, and her eyes so brilliantly alive. A bonny Kate indeed, the prettiest Kate in Christendom, Kate of Kate Hall, my super-dainty Kate, he thought, borrowing from Shakespeare again. But no shrew was she. Just the opposite, for there was a vulnerability about her, a poignancy in her that always tugged at his heartstrings. Yet he knew she had a will of iron, a terrifying self-sufficiency and great tenacity. Perhaps this duality in her personality was the secret of her extraordinary appeal, for it gave her an elusive quality that was intriguing. Once, months back, he had seriously toyed with the idea of sweeping her off the stage, off her feet – both literally and figuratively – and into his bed smartly. But suddenly he had wavered and ultimately he had changed his mind. He was not sure why he had done so, and the moment had passed and he had never felt the impulse again. It no longer mattered. Hilary, his own true love, had come back to him, bringing him priceless gifts of adoration and understanding and belief, making him a whole and complete man once more. Giving meaning to his life.

'You're looking terribly serious. Is something wrong, Terrence?'

'No, Puss.' A gentle smile, and then, 'Just wool-gathering, that's all.'

Katharine returning his smile, took a sip of her tea, put the cup down and said slowly, 'What about . . . Hilary?'

How much had she guessed? He felt himself stiffening but he asked casually enough, 'What about Hilary?'

'How did she react when she heard about your contract and that you're leaving for California shortly?'

'She was overjoyed. She believes that only by going to Hollywood can one truly become an international movie star. And you know Hilary, she only ever wants the best for her friends.'

'Yes, she's a lovely person.' Katharine shifted in the chair, and glanced out of the window. She had been about to remark that Hilary would miss him, but she swallowed these words. Despite their new closeness, there were still some lines she was afraid to cross. There was an imperiousness in Terry, an aloofness that sprang from his natural reserve, held him apart, forbade familiarity of a certain nature. As an actor he was nonpareil, particularly with his brilliant and stunning interpretations of Shakespearean roles, and she was for ever conscious of his prominence and standing in the English theatre, of the reverence in which he was held by his peers, and not unnaturally these considerations served as a further restraint. After a second, Katharine swung her gaze back to him, and asked, 'And Norman? What did he say?'

'Aha! Good old Norman! He's on top of the world for me, of course. And very excited. I'm taking him with me to California, and Penny too; they're so devoted and loyal, I couldn't leave them behind. They're going to be looking after me in their usual loving way. Apart from continuing to be my dresser, Norman's also agreed to try his hand at being my secretary, and he'll do a bit of driving. I suppose you could say he'll be my major domo, or general factotum, whatever,' Terry grinned. 'Penny will run the house, a sort of unofficial housekeeper. You see, I've decided to rent a place for a couple of years. Hilly thinks Monarch will be able to find something suitable for me, either in Beverly Hills or Bel-Air.' He stubbed out his cigarette and finished, with a lilt in his voice, 'I'm really looking forward to this move across the Atlantic. The timing is exactly right, in more ways than one. Do you know where you'll be camping out, Puss?'

'Originally Victor was thinking of a bungalow at the Beverly Hills Hotel for me. But then he changed his mind. I think I'll be staying at the Bel-Air Hotel. He seems to prefer that. I'm not sure why.' Katharine bent closer. 'Oh darling, it's going to be great fun being there together. We *will* have some fun, won't we?' she cried.

301

'Yes, course we will, love.' Terry was thoughtful for a moment, then he remarked, 'He's awfully deceptive, isn't he?'

'Who is?' she asked with a tiny frown.

'Victor Mason.'

'I'm not sure I know what you mean.'

'On the surface he seems to be very easygoing, but he's not really. Victor runs a tight ship, and he's tough. Bloody hard-headed actually. Lately I've seen him lock horns with Mark Pierce more than once, and it's not always about the spiralling costs, or the budget, even though money does preoccupy him. He wants things done his way. I suspect there's a bit of the tyrant in Victor, in spite of his lazy, effortless charm.'

'You're right,' Katharine said, 'but let's not forget that he's the producer, as well as the star. He's only being professional.'

'I *know* that, love, and I wasn't being critical. I was merely making a few observations, and anyone who underestimates him is a downright fool. Victor's a damn sight smarter than one expects him to be. And I like him; he's been pretty decent to me on the picture. Incidentally, talking about your admirers, how does his lordship feel about your impending departure for distant shores?'

Ignoring the innuendo, Katharine said, 'Kim was a little startled when I first told him, but he's accepted it now, and I'll only be gone a few months.'

'Oh,' Terry said, taken aback. 'I hadn't realized that. I thought Victor would have another film lined up for you, after the Beau Stanton comedy's finished.'

'He hasn't mentioned anything, so I'm sure there's nothing special on the horizon.'

Terry looked at his watch. 'I've got to be leaving, Puss. I have an interview with Estelle Morgan in about ten minutes, and afterwards I'm obliged to take her to lunch. That's another reason I popped in to see you. I'd like you to join us.'

'Oh dear, I don't think I should, Terry. I know Estelle wouldn't like it. I'm sure she'll want to be alone with you.'

'But I don't want to be alone with her,' Terry declared. 'That's the problem. She makes me frightfully nervous. I keep thinking she's going to pounce on me at any moment.' He grimaced and rolled his eyes. 'A very predatory lady, our Estelle. Be a good sport, say yes. *Please*, Puss.'

Katharine's laughter filled the room and she regarded him through merry eyes. 'Don't be such a scaredy cat. She's harmless, and anyway, you're perfectly capable of looking after yourself.' But noting the plea on his face, she capitulated. 'Oh, all right, I'll come and protect you. But I don't want to be there for the interview. Now *that* she *would* regard as an intrusion. She doesn't like an audience when she's interviewing a subject, and I have to respect her point of view. She's right really. Shall we say one o'clock?'

Terry exhaled a sigh of relief. 'Thanks, Puss. And one o'clock's fine. In the bar. That's where we're doing the interview, so I'll –' Terry paused, his eyes swivelling to the shrilling telephone.

Katharine ran to answer it. 'Hello, Norman,' she cried. 'Yes, he's here. Just a minute, love.' She turned to Terry, beckoned to him. He strode over and took the telephone from her, and Katharine returned to her chair. Leaning back, she closed her eyes, listening. Terry had one of the greatest voices on the English stage today,

302

and distinctively his. How many actors had tried to imitate it and failed miserably? Hundreds.

Her lids lifted and she looked more closely at that refined face and at the light blue eyes, so open and guileless. A shiver ran through her and gooseflesh speckled her arms. Terry was such easy prey for the unscrupulous. She was glad Norman and Penny were going with him to Hollywood. They would give him protection. Her gaze pulled back a fraction, and then roved over him swiftly. He was wearing dark grey slacks, a navy blue blazer and a white turtle neck sweater. Tall and lean, he looked casually elegant and debonair. The matinée idol personified, she thought. He would be a sensation in the States, of that there was no doubt in her mind.

Terry said goodbye, dropped the receiver in the cradle, and asked, 'Why the long stares, Puss? Don't I look all right for the interview? Should I change, put on a tie?'

Katharine shook her head. 'Don't be silly, your clothes are perfect. And I'm sorry. I didn't mean to sit here and scrutinize you like an insect under a microscope. Actually, I was thinking of the impact you'll have in Hollywood. You're going to bowl them over with your talent and your looks. As Victor would say, you're the whole enchilada, my darling.'

Terry laughed. 'And as Hamlet would say, "season your admiration for a while". I'm glad *you* like my togs. Hilary thinks I look like a German U-boat commander in them!' He stepped to the door, swung around. 'I'm going to give a small luncheon tomorrow, at the Red Lion in South Stainley, the marvellous old inn I was telling you about. I've invited a few of my close chums in the cast. None of them know about the Monarch contract, but it's bound to leak out in a few days. So, I thought I'd tell them myself, and it's a good excuse for a little celebration. We'll have a real English Sunday lunch, the kind I've been promising you since we've been here. You know, Yorkshire pud, roast beef and horseradish, roast potatoes and brussels sprouts, the lot. And trifle afterwards. Will you come, Puss? With Kim, of course. And look, bring Francesca along if you want.'

'Why, Terry, how lovely. Thanks, we'd love to come, and I'll ask Francesca when she gets here. I'm expecting her in a few minutes.'

'Good. And *I'll* be expecting *you* in about an hour. Don't let me down.' He opened the door and almost collided with Francesca. 'Sorry, love.'

'That's all right, Terry. How are you?' Francesca asked.

'Fine and dandy, but late for an appointment.' He opened the door and let her pass. 'Toodle-oo,' he said, waved, and disappeared down the corridor.

Francesca closed the door and came into the room, a striking picture in buff-colour riding breeches, highly-polished black boots, a pink cotton shirt and red silk cravat. Her blonde hair was pulled back in a pony tail and caught at the nape of her neck with a black bow, and her peaches-and-cream complexion looked more perfect than ever. A shopping basket was slung over one arm and she was carrying a large bunch of flowers.

'Hi, darling,' Katharine exclaimed, her face wreathed in smiles as she came to meet Francesca. She kissed her on the cheek and went on, 'I'm so glad you 'phoned.'

Francesca returned her kiss. 'And hello to you too, stranger,' she laughed

303

gaily. 'These are for you. I picked them in the gardens at Langley this morning.'

'How sweet of you, darling. Thank you so much.' Katharine took the flowers, buried her face in them. 'They smell divine. I'd better put them in water immediately. In the meantime, make yourself comfortable. Do you want coffee, or a drink? I can order something from room service.'

'No, thanks anyway.' Francesca put the shopping basket on the floor and flopped into one of the chairs. 'Since I had to come into Ripon, to get a few things for Melly, I thought I might as well stop by for a few minutes.'

'I'm so glad you did,' Katharine called from the bathroom. She returned to the sitting room a moment later, carrying a vase of water, and stood by a side table, arranging the flowers in it. 'I've missed you, Frankie.'

'I know. I've missed you too, Kath. Gosh, I see more of you in London than I do when you're here on location.'

'Isn't it stupid! But Mark has been working us awfully hard. He likes to rehearse every scene like a play, not wing it.' She stepped back, regarding her handiwork, her head on one side, and then rearranged a few blooms. 'There, that does it.'

'It *is* going well now, though, isn't it?'

'Oh yes, everyone's terribly pleased,' Katharine responded, adopting an off-handed air, not wanting to discuss the film, which had been troubled from the start. She joined Francesca near the windows. 'Kath . . .' Francesca said, 'come and sit down. I have something to tell you.'

'You sound excited.' Katharine gave her a curious look and lowered herself into the chair opposite.

'Well, yes, I am.' Francesca's face was eager with happiness. 'Daddy and Doris have decided to get married.'

Katharine blanched. 'But . . . but . . . How marvellous . . .' She faltered and stared at Francesca blankly, at a loss for words.

Francesca regarded her keenly. 'You sound funny, Katharine, and not very enthusiastic. I thought you'd be pleased.' A frown creased Francesca's smooth brow. She found her friend's reaction slightly odd.

'I'm startled, that's all,' Katharine exclaimed hurriedly, endeavouring to correct her mistake. 'I suppose I hadn't realized it was such a serious relationship. I don't know how I got the impression, but somehow I always thought Doris planned to go back to the States. I mean, she has such vast holdings there, and she is so very American.' Katharine laughed nervously. 'But naturally I'm pleased,' she now had the good sense to add, even though in all truth she was utterly dismayed. Recognizing it was crucial to allay Francesca's doubts about her feelings, she reached out and took hold of her hand, squeezing it warmly. Summoning all of her superlative acting ability, and drawing on her immense charm, she said, with that dazzling smile, 'Oh Frankie, it *is* exciting. And so wonderful for your father. I'm happy for him, really and truly.' She shook her head in a reproving way. 'Kim's rather naughty. Why didn't he tell me last night?'

'He didn't know then, nor does he know now,' Francesca explained. 'Daddy telephoned from the South of France this morning to tell us, but Kim had already left for Skipton. Anyway, there's going to be an engagement party, at Doris's villa,'

304

she hurried on happily. 'Later this summer, probably in August. Doris is planning to give a supper dance, and everybody's invited.'

'What do you mean by everybody?' Katharine asked, striving to keep her voice light. She wished the tight knot in her stomach would go away.

'Kim and I, of course, and you too. Oh Kath darling, do say you'll come. It won't be the same if you're not there.'

Katharine managed another of her sparkling smiles. 'How lovely of Doris to invite me.' She instantly wondered if, indeed, Doris had extended the invitation, or whether it was solely Francesca's idea.

'Doris wouldn't leave *you* out! She knows Kim's potty about you. She also said she'd like you to stay with us at the Villa Zamir at Cap Martin. And for as long as you want. She expects me to spend August there, and I suppose I will. I do hope you can manage a couple of weeks at least, Katharine. It won't interfere with your preparations for your trip to Hollywood, will it?'

'No, I don't think there'll be a problem. And how really kind of Doris,' Katharine murmured, amazed at this apparent, but unexpected, show of friendliness from Madame Asternan. 'When will the wedding take place?'

'Not until the autumn. November, Daddy said. Here in Yorkshire at the church in Langley. Oh gosh, you'll be in California. Damn and blast! I hadn't thought of that. I was hoping we could both be bridesmaids. I was going to suggest it to Doris.'

Katharine began to laugh, picturing, in her mind's eye, Doris's face when she was apprised of this particular idea. *Me* a bridesmaid for Doris. Over Doris's dead body, she thought with some asperity.

Mistaking her laughter for excitement and pleasure, Francesca said, 'Even though you won't be able to be a bridesmaid, I *can* tell Doris you'll come to Cap Martin, can't I?'

'Yes. It'll be nice to have a vacation, a rest, before I start the Beau Stanton picture. Well, this has certainly been *my* morning for unexpected news.'

'Oh, really.'

'Yes, Terry was also here to make an announcement. He came to tell me he had just signed a contract with Monarch. He's off to Hollywood too.' Katharine went on to explain about this, and finished, 'Anyway, he's giving a celebration lunch tomorrow, and he'd like you to join us, Frankie.'

'I'd love to, but I'm afraid I can't, Kath. I'm going up to town this afternoon.'

'To *London*?' Katharine blinked, looking surprised.

'Yes. Have you forgotten? I told you ages ago that my cousin Diana's arriving from Paris tomorrow. She's going to be staying with me for a couple of weeks.'

'Heavens, I did forget. But I've been so preoccupied with my work and with my scenes, everything else has been pushed out of my mind. God, actors are so selfish, so self-involved, it's terrible. And I'm also very stupid! If only I *had* remembered, I could have asked Victor to give you a lift. He only just left for London himself, about an hour ago.'

'Oh,' Francesca said, and glanced down at her shopping basket. She picked it up and placed it on her knee, searching inside for something. Without lifting her head, not daring to look at Katharine, she continued, 'Well, that would have been nice, but, in a way, I really prefer to go on the train. I want

305

o check my notes, draft my next chapter. It's a good opportunity to do a little work.'

'How is the book coming along, darling?' Katharine asked with eagerness, as always genuinely interested in Francesca's writing career.

'Quite well, actually. Better than I expected, to be honest.' Francesca took the package out of the basket. 'This is also for you. I know you've become addicted to parkin, so I asked Val to make some for you.'

'Aren't you a love. Thanks so much.' Katharine placed the package on the coffee table, and threw Francesca a wistful look. 'Then you won't be at Langley for dinner tonight after all,' she stated in a tiny voice.

'No, I won't, Kath. I'm so sorry about that, but I did promise Diana I'd meet her plane tomorrow morning, and I can't let her down.'

'Oh, I know. Still, I was really looking foward to being with you.'

'Don't be silly, Kath dear,' Francesca said softly, seeing the disappointment registering on Katharine's face. 'You'll have Kim entirely to yourself, and that's much more romantic.'

Katharine twisted the gold signet ring on her little finger, a sense of misgiving invading her. She had counted on Francesca's presence at dinner, for apart from enjoying her company, she was worried about the prospect of being alone with Kim. His sister always acted as a buffer between them. In a rush, she confided, 'He's been awfully annoyed with me. I've had to put him off so many times this week. He blames me, when it's really not my fault at all. He seems to forget I'm in Yorkshire to work. That's so unfair of him. Also I've been under enough strain and pressure without having to cope with his jealousy.' She sighed. 'Mark's tyrannical, Victor's dictatorial, and as for Kim, well, he's just plain unreasonable.'

Francesca said nothing. She was on Katharine's side and filled with sympathy for her, patently aware that she spoke the truth. Mark and Victor *were* demanding, a couple of slave drivers, in her opinion, and Kim *had* been exceptionally difficult, impossible really. On the other hand, she did understand her brother's feelings. She was going through much the same thing with Victor, who had been so involved with the picture, and embroiled in its manifold problems, he had had little time for her.

After a moment, Francesca remarked quietly, 'I have a feeling Kim realizes he's been unfair to you, Kath. I had a long talk with him the other day, and told him he was being perfectly boorish, immature, and that he'd better start behaving himself, otherwise he'd lose you. I hope you don't mind me butting in.'

'Of course not,' Katharine said. Her face brightened. 'I'm grateful. I really am, darling. And perhaps you are right about the two of us being alone. It will give us a chance to talk things out properly, clear the air.'

Francesca, still wishing to play the peacemaker, quickly pointed out, 'Remember one thing, Katharine. Kim's in love with you, so it's only natural he wants to be with you as much as possible. As for being jealous . . .' She laughed softly, and continued, 'You are very lovely, and you're surrounded by lots of men on the picture. If he weren't jealous, he'd be abnormal. You can't hold that against him, can you?'

'I suppose not,' Katharine acknowledged, albeit grudgingly. 'However, I don't give him any reasons to be jealous, honestly I don't, Frankie,' she insisted.

Francesca looked at her fondly. 'Men don't always need a reason to behave outrageous ways. Sometimes they just can't help themselves.' Rising, she picke up the basket. 'You'll see, everything'll be fine this evening, and from the way Kim was talking about you yesterday, he'll be all sweetness and light.'

'I hope so,' Katharine replied, getting up from the chair. She linked her arm through Francesca's and walked with her to the door. 'I'll be glad when we get back to London next week. Things'll be easier then.' She hugged Francesca, then stood away from her, gazing at her. Quite unexpectedly she felt a rush of warmth in her throat, was filled with the most tender of feelings. Impulsively, she said, 'You're the sweetest, dearest friend I've ever had in my whole life, Frankie. And the *best*. I don't know what I'd do without you.'

'And you're very special to me too, Kath,' Francesca answered. 'You're like the sister I never had.' Francesca's face became solemn, reflective. 'I don't think that's really quite the right analogy, because not all sisters are as close and as loving as we are. To me you're better than a sister, better than a best friend even.'

Katharine's unique turquoise eyes turned misty, and there was a tremulous quality to her tone as she said, 'What a truly beautiful thing to say, darling. And that's exactly the way I feel about you too, and I always will.'

Francesca's affirmation of her friendship had given Katharine a marvellous sense of security, for approval was essential to her well being. Besides, she genuinely cared for Francesca, and was gratified to know her feelings were reciprocated. And so, after the other girl had left, she was filled with euphoria as she busied herself in the suite, singing gaily whilst she went about various small tasks. Finally she went through into the bedroom to select an outfit to wear to lunch with Terry and Estelle.

Sadly, her happy carefree mood was shortlived. Quite suddenly thoughts of the Earl's impending marriage to Doris Asternan intruded, forcing everything else to the back of her mind. She hung the blue linen suit on the open door of the wardrobe and sat down heavily on the bed, staring at the suit but not really seeing it at all. And she focused her mind on Doris Asternan.

From the first moment they had met, Katharine had understood instinctively that she was confronting a real adversary. Time had only confirmed this. *Doris did not like her at all*. Not that the older woman was exactly blatant in her dislike. She strove always to conceal her antipathy behind girlishly-made confidences, and claims of sistership because they were both American. With her acuity of perception, Katharine knew that Doris's pleasant acceptance of her was entirely counterfeit. The woman did not accept her at all, neither did she approve of her relationship with Kim. Furthermore, much to Katharine's irritation, Doris was excessively possessive of the Cunninghams, seemed to believe she had an exclusive relationship with them, and was also their self-appointed protector. This was particularly in evidence when it came to fellow Americans. Katharine recalled how keenly Doris had scrutinized and questioned Victor when they had both been guests at Langley Castle in May. Just as she herself had been weighed up and down, and so assiduously grilled about her early life in Chicago she had been utterly taken aback. But somehow she had managed to sidestep Doris's probings without it seeming as if she had something to hide.

I don't have anything to hide, Katharine said to herself, and then groaned out loud. How stupid she had been. She had told a silly little white lie when she had first started classes at the Royal Academy – she had pretended to be an orphan. Repetition had propagated the lie to such an extent she was not only stuck with it, but hamstrung by it. How could she possibly tell anyone the truth now? And why in God's name had she ever said such a foolish thing in the first place? The answer eluded her.

A wave of self-pity washed over her, but she squashed it before it had a chance to take root. She must concentrate on her most pressing priority, which was rectifying the lie, and the only way to do that was to tell the truth and in so doing clarify the sitution about her background.

She grimaced, thinking now of Doris. As a girl friend of David Cunningham's she had not seemed to be a threat; but as his wife she would have great influence on him.

'Oh damn,' Katharine exclaimed out loud, worrying about Doris, wondering how to get around her. Katharine, clever and inventive, turned and turned the problem over in her mind, but no solution was forthcoming. Why had Doris invited her to the South of France? Had it been the Earl's idea? Could Francesca have suggested it? Was Doris merely attempting to appear generous of nature solely for the Earl's benefit? Or was Doris setting her up, trying to trap her? This last possibility was so unsettling to Katharine that she brushed it aside swiftly. However, a valid reason for this show of friendliness on Doris's part remained as elusive as a means of circumventing her, and although she concentrated on both for some time, in the end Katharine gave up in exasperation.

Glancing at the clock, she sprang off the bed. Terry was expecting her in the bar in fifteen minutes and she could not waste any more time dwelling on Doris Asternan and the Earl.

I'll think things out more carefully later, she told herself. After all, it's still only June. Slipping out of her skirt and blouse, she put on the blue linen suit, stepped into a pair of bone kid pumps, and then turned to look at herself in the mirror. How pale she looked, and drawn around her eyes. Although she was not over fond of make-up and always used it sparingly, Katharine dipped into several small pots, adding a touch of delicate pink rouge on her high cheekbones, and a film of hazy turquoise eyeshadow on her lids.

Satisfied with the overall effect, she ran a comb through her hair. And she made her mind up to one thing: she must be especially sweet to Kim this evening, and in the weeks to come, conciliatory, charming and adoring. Yes, she must use all her not inconsiderable powers to ensure his complete devotion and abiding love. This was an imperative, and surely it was the key to everything . . . her inevitable triumph over Doris, her future life as Kim's wife, as the Viscountess Ingleton. She repeated the title, liking the sound of it, and a happy smiled expunged the worry in her eyes.

The smile was still intact some ten minutes later when Katharine reached the lobby of the hotel and headed in the direction of the bar. In her usual way, she had convinced herself, somewhat unwisely, that she could bend life to her will; in consequence her problems had evaporated completely. And Doris Asternan had been dismissed from her mind.

CHAPTER THIRTY

The huge soaring oak doors of Langley Castle stood wide open. Bright sun poured in through this ancient portal, gilding everything to pure gold, diminishing the overriding austerity of the immense and high-flung great hall built entirely of grey stone. Dust motes rose up, insect like, in these slanting corridors of trembling light, the only motion in the quiescent air, and there was no sound at all except for the faint whispering of the trees outside.

Francesca stood poised on the staircase looking down, gripped for an instant by that sense of the past which so often invaded her at unexpected moments when she was in her ancestral home. Erected in 1360, by one James Cunningham of Langley, a great magnate and warrior knight who fought at the side of the Black Prince, it had remained relatively unchanged since the fourteenth century. Her eyes swept over the suits of armour glinting in the dappled sunshine, focused on the crossed swords mounted over the doorway, moved on to take in the shields and silken banners of their armorial bearings that spilled lively colour onto the sombre walls, settled finally on the huge bowl of flowers on the long oak table, which she had arranged early that morning. Suddenly a butterfly floated in, hovered over the mixed white blossoms, and then fluttered away, a fleeting flash of intense scarlet on the languorous air. The tranquility and beauty of the scene below her was a palpable thing, and it made her catch her breath with delight. On gleaming summer days such as this the castle was the most perfect spot in the whole world to her, and one she never wanted to leave.

Now a tiny frown marred her joyful face, and she thought wistfully: If only Victor did not insist on this continuing secrecy we would have been able to spend the weekend here, instead of rushing off to London. How lovely that would have been. As it was, he was rip-roaring anxious to be gone, could not wait to escape from the Spa Hotel in Ripon, and the rest of the cast and crew. She knew only too well that he had found the past ten days constricting, and although she had not seen much of him, they had talked every day on the telephone. He had grumbled constantly about his lack of privacy, the loss of his free time, meagre as it was, and the tiresome role of peacemaker which had been thrust upon him by Mark Pierce's curious irrationalities. She exhaled quietly. Victor himself could also be perverse at times, powerful and compelling in his vehement attentions to her when they were alone, detached and coolly indifferent when they were in public. Dismaying though this dichotomy in his behaviour was, most of all she hated the secrecy he was still enforcing. Straightforward of nature, deception did not sit easily on her young shoulders, and she loathed dissembling with Kim and Katharine, especially Katharine in whom she was longing to confide. But she had to abide by his wishes, or perhaps risk losing him if she did not.

The sound of subdued voices penetrated her consciousness. Several visitors were entering the great hall from the Widow's Gallery where most of the famed Langley Collection was housed. They were escorted by Osborne, the castle guide, who conducted the tours and gave a brief history of the Cunninghams of Langley. Reaching the bottom of the wide stone staircase, she smiled and nodded to them, exchanged a quick word with Osborne before going into the private wing of the castle not open to the public. She crossed the anteroom, hurried through the vast book-filled library and out into the circular hall of their private apartments. This was smaller and cosier than the immense stone hall, panelled in dark wood and furnished with graceful Georgian pieces. Various rooms opened off the hall, and a curving staircase of elaborately carved oak led to the upper floors.

Francesca pushed open the door of the kitchen and poked her head around it. Val, the housekeeper, stood in front of a table near the windows preparing a summer pudding of mixed berries and bread. Francesca said, 'I'm about to leave, Val.'

The housekeeper swung around quickly, her face lighting up. 'Righto, M'lady,' she replied. 'Now, are you sure you don't want me to run you into Harrogate to the train?'

'No, thanks, Val. It's sweet of you to offer, but you've enough to do today. I'll catch the bus at the end of Langley Lane. I'll see you next weekend, and don't forget, my cousin will be with me.'

'Yes, I know, M'lady. I'm really looking forward to seeing Princess Diana again, and so is Melly. I'll have everything ready, don't you fret. I know she likes the Lavender Suite, and it'll be prepared for her. By the by, I sent Rosemary out to walk Lada, and to cut some flowers for you to take to London. You'll find her in Frances's Garden. When you leave will you send her up for lunch please, M'lady?'

'Yes, of course. And the flowers were a lovely thought, Val. Thanks. Cheerio.'

'Goodbye, M'lady, and have a pleasant journey.'

Francesca hurried back to the circular hall, glancing at the Victorian grandfather clock in the corner as she did so and realizing she was running late. She picked up her small overnight case and her shoulder bag and went outside, walking rapidly along the paved terrace and down the stone steps at the end of it.

In the distance Francesca could see Rosemary and Lada, the little Bichon Frise puppy Victor had given her in April. Francesca had wanted to call the dog Enchilada, and although Victor had been highly amused, he had said the name wasn't appropriate for such a pretty little girl. And so they had compromised, agreeing finally on the abbreviation Lada. The dog, now almost six months old, had become Francesca's shadow, trotting after her devotedly wherever she went. Both she and Victor had become extremely attached to the white ball of fluff, and he had insisted she bring the puppy with them this weekend.

The sunken garden was centuries old and had been designed and built by the Sixth Countess of Langley, the renowned Frances, whose great beauty had been immortalized by Gainsborough and Romney, and to whom Francesca bore such a striking resemblance. For this reason it was often referred to as Frances's Garden, and today it was ablaze with rafts of intense colour, and aromatic with the scent of June roses, the lavender that grew in profusion along the borders and the delicate mingled fragrances of the perennial summer species now in riotous bloom.

A smile glanced across Francesca's face as she drew closer. Rosemary, Val's ten-year-old daughter, was walking Lada around the paved garden paths on the leash, looking sedate and important, a large bunch of roses and other flowers clasped tightly in her free hand.

'Hello, Rosemary,' Francesca said. Lada immediately went into paroxysms of squeaking, jumping up and down excitedly and pawing at the skirt of Francesca's lime-green cotton frock. 'Goodness gracious me, Lada, anyone would think I'd been gone a whole month instead of only an hour,' Francesca laughed, patting the puppy. She said to Rosemary, 'Thank you for walking the little one, and also for picking such a lovely bouquet.'

Rosemary beamed, handing her the flowers. 'I made sure I got the best for you, Lady Francesca, just like me mam told me, and I wrapped 'em ever so careful like in newspaper, and tied 'em with string.'

'So I see, and you're very efficient. Come along, dear, I'm in a hurry.'

'Yes, Lady Francesca.'

A thick door of aged wood, overlaid with decorative metalwork, was set in the brick wall at the opposite end of the sunken garden, and it was towards this that Francesca and the little girl now walked, with Lada bouncing along between them. When they reached it, Rosemary bent down and hugged the white puppy affectionately. 'Be a good girl, Lada, and come back ever so soon. I'll miss you,' she whispered. She gave the leash to Francesca with obvious reluctance.

Turning the old iron key, Francesca gazed down at Rosemary. 'Lock the door after me, dear, and then go up to the castle. Your mother has lunch ready. And don't dawdle.'

'No, I won't, Lady Francesca. Ta'rar then.'

''Bye, Rosemary.' Francesca tugged the old door open and stepped out into the driveway, waiting until Rosemary had relocked it before striking out in the direction of the imposing wrought-iron gates at the back entrance of the castle grounds. Since this area of Langley Park was strictly private, she was startled to see a man and a youth sitting on the low wall bordering grazing pastures on one side of the driveway. Francesca paused when she drew level with them, noting that they looked unsavoury and scruffy.

'Excuse me,' she said politely, and went on with some firmness, 'this part of Langley Park is not open to the public. You probably don't realize it, but you are trespassing.'

Looking her over swiftly, the man said, with a small snicker, 'Ever so sorry, yer ladyship. We didn't know. We was just about to 'ave our picnic.' He glanced at several large tattered brown paper bags on the wall. 'If yer insists we move on, then I expects we'll 'ave to . . .' He paused, regarding her through watchful eyes.

Francesca frowned, feeling churlish and mean. It was such a glorious summer day and people like this, so obviously from one of the nearby industrial cities, hardly ever got the opportunity to breathe the clean air, enjoy the loveliness of the countryside. She said, in a slightly milder tone, 'I am sorry to have to ask you to leave. However, this is a private area of the estate, and anyway you'd be much more comfortable if you went up to the castle courtyard. There's a

311

small café which serves hot and cold drinks, and ice cream. You can have your picnic there.'

The man shook his head. 'Can't afford nuffin like that, Lady Francesca.' He laughed. 'Brought us own grub and us own tea, that we did. Still, perhaps we'd best shove off then.'

'Oh never mind,' Francesca responded hurriedly, relenting. 'You can stay here this time. If you should come back, please use the public areas of the park.' She smiled at the youth, feeling sorry for him. He seemed so undernourished and sickly, and then her smile faded. He was glowering at her with hostility in his pale cold eyes. Francesca turned away with a small internal shudder, noticing, as she did, the binoculars on the wall, immediately thinking how odd it was that these two should own such an expensive item.

The man, conscious of her close scrutiny, followed the direction of her gaze, and said, 'We're bird watchers, Lady Francesca. My Jimmy won them there opera glasses in a school competition. He's a right born naturalist, my Jimmy is, yer ladyship.'

'How very nice.' Francesca inclined her head. 'Well, enjoy your picnic.'

She hurried off, instinctively tightening her grip on Lada's leash, frowning as she almost ran down the driveway, anxious to get to Victor who would be parked in Langley Lane. She found herself shivering despite the warmth of the radiant sunshine, and admitted she did not like the look of the two men at all. But there was not much she could do about them just now, even if they were poachers as she suspected. There had been a spate of excessive poaching in Langley Park, and on neighbouring estates, in recent months, and her father had pressed several of the villagers into service as temporary wardens to patrol their lands. If Jimmy and his father ran into one of them they would have serious trouble to contend with, not to mention the village bobby, and possibly the West Riding county police.

She wondered how the two disreputable characters had managed to get into this private part of the grounds, and she expected to find the new padlocks on the back gates broken. To her immense relief this was not the case when she reached the entrance. Once outside in Langley Lane she took great care to secure the padlocks again, rattled the gates to make sure they held fast, and dropped the spare key Kim had given her into her shoulder bag. She peered through the wroughtiron railings, focusing on the two men sitting on the wall. They appeared to be eating their lunch with unconcerned nonchalance. Perhaps she had been mistaken after all. They were probably quite harmless. Nevertheless, when she rang Kim from London that evening she would mention the incident, alert him to the possibility of poachers roaming the vast estate.

The Bentley was parked only a few yards down the lane and Victor jumped out of the car grinning from ear to ear. Lada leapt forward when she saw him, emitting little mewls of ecstasy, tugging hard on the leash. It took all of Francesca's strength to control the frisky puppy and manage her suitcase, her handbag and the flowers as well. Laughing joyously, she dropped the case heedlessly and ran pell-mell into his outstretched arms, burying her head against his chest. He held her very tightly, showering her hair and her face with kisses, then he reached down and patted Lada, an expression of fondness ringing his wide mouth. 'Can't leave you out, little one,

312

now can I,' he murmured softly, scratching the tuft of white fluff on her tiny head.

After a moment he straightened up, tilted Francesca's chin and looked down into her face, his black eyes bright with eagerness. He kissed her on the mouth, then said, 'It sure is great to have my girl back. It was getting to be a helluva strain, baby.'

'Yes, I know. I felt as though the whole world was breathing down our necks, Vic.'

'A large portion of it was,' he replied, the boyish, lopsided grin flashing engagingly. 'But that's all finished now. Come on, kid, let's beat it.' Within seconds, Victor was pulling the Bentley out of Langley Lane and turning into Harrogate Road, Lada curled up in a small contented ball between them on the front seat.

Francesca found herself relaxing, as she always did when she was with him, everything else swept out of her head. Suddenly his desire for secrecy, his odd behaviour, no longer seemed of any import. She stole a look at him and caught her breath, her heart clattering wildly. Whenever he came back to her, even after the briefest of separations, she was inevitably shaken by his looks, his overpowering presence. In spite of his back-breaking work, the constant night shooting, and all his other problems with the picture, he looked extraordinarily fit and brimming with health. He was wearing a pale blue cotton shirt and blue slacks. The shirt was expensive, and of such a fine texture it was almost transparent, revealed his tanned skin, his athlete's body. Her eyes rested on his broad back, his well-muscled upper arms. How she longed to have those arms around her. She studied his dark and shapely head, the arresting profile, the large strong hands on the steering wheel, and all of her love for him rose up in her, and she had to quell the urge to reach out and touch him. Oh how she loved him, and with such intensity and depth of feeling it was unendurable being away from him for a single moment.

Francesca turned her head quickly and glanced out of the window, swallowing hard several times. Finally, when she was more composed, she said in as light a tone as possible, 'Did Gus get off to London all right, Vic?'

'Sure. We had an hour to waste in Harrogate, before the train left, since I beat a pretty hasty retreat from the hotel this morning. So I took your advice and we stopped off at the Old Swan Hotel for a coupla drinks. Nice little bar, like you said. Then I threw Gus onto the train looking as happy as a clam and glad to have the weekend off.'

'Oh good. And I hope you haven't been waiting too long for me.'

'About twenty minutes. I studied the script, smoked a cigarette, but mostly I thought about the next few days.' He chuckled, threw her a loving look. 'I've got the whole week off, with nothing much to do until the unit moves back to the studios. A few meetings with Hilly at Monarch, but that's about all. I sincerely hope you're not planning to spend much time at the British Museum, baby.'

The prospect of a whole week alone with him sent her heart soaring, brought a glowing smile to her face. 'No, I'm not. I'm all yours, my darling.'

'You'd better be.'

Oh I am, I am, she thought, but said, 'Incidentally, I've got some exciting news for you, Vic.'

'Shoot, baby.'

'Daddy 'phoned me from Cap Martin this morning, just after I'd spoken to you. He proposed to Doris. Finally. And she accepted. They're getting married in November.'

'Hey, that's terrific. Really great. And knowing your feelings about Doris, I bet you're as delighted as the future bride.' He looked at her through the corner of his eye, and chortled with some hilarity. 'So Diamond Lil pulled it off. Good for her.'

'*Diamond Lil.* Is that your nickname for Doris?' she asked with a small puzzled smile, although she was not particularly amused.

'Not mine, baby, Katherine's. A little bitchy maybe, but dead on target. Doris ain't shy about flaunting her loot. Jesus, she was dripping diamonds from every pore the weekend we spent at the castle. I don't know about you, kid, but I was blinded. Particularly after sunset.'

Francesca had to laugh. 'We all were, but somehow Doris does carry it off rather well, you must admit.' There was a sudden hesitancy in her manner, as she added, 'Funny though, Katharine has never used that nickname with me.'

'Maybe she thought you'd be offended.' He reflected for a split second, and murmured, 'There's no love lost there, Ches.'

'What do you mean?' Francesca asked.

'They don't like each other,' Victor pronounced bluntly. He shrugged and continued, 'Don't ask me why. I haven't the vaguest idea, unless there's a feeling of competition between them. Certainly Katharine seems to be wary of Doris, and she's even been a bit scathing about her at times. As for Doris, she could be jealous of Katharine's looks I suppose.' He grimaced. 'What the hell, who knows about women around other women.' He swivelled his eyes, smiled at her. 'I only know about you. You're sweet with everyone. Anyway, I think Doris is a terrific broad. Your father's damned lucky.'

'Yes, he is. But why do you call Doris a broad? That doesn't sound very complimentary to me.'

'That's the way I meant it though. One of your favourite writers, Mr E. Hemingway no less, said, and I quote, "I love tough broads but I can't stand hard dames." My sentiments exactly, and I wasn't being rude or unkind about Doris. When I use the term *broad* I do so affectionately.'

'Yes, I understand. And I know you and Doris hit it off immediately. But as for Katharine and Doris not liking each other, honestly, you're wrong, Vic.' As these words left her mouth Francesca remembered Katharine's initial reaction to the news of the engagement. Was there perhaps an element of truth in Victor's statement? No, she decided, Katharine was merely surprised, that's all. She said, '*I* certainly haven't seen any indications of dislike, and Doris has invited Kath to stay at the Villa Zamir.'

'Did she accept?' Victor cut in sharply.

'Yes, and she seemed very pleased about the invitation.'

'Then I guess I'm wrong,' he commented in a softer tone, thinking sardonically: This is a helluva *volte face* on Katharine's part. Doris's too, for that matter. Or is it simply the first sign of a truce? Nonetheless, he knew he was accurate about their mutual antipathy for each other. Francesca was an uncomplicated and loving girl who believed the best about everyone. He realized now that her deep affection for both women blinded her to their true natures. 'And how did Kim react?'

'He'd already left for the day when Daddy rang up. He'll get my note when he returns from Skipton later. And I will 'phone him tonight.' Francesca settled back happily, half turned to face Victor, and added excitedly, 'Doris is going to give a really super engagement party, a dance actually. You will come, won't you, Vic?'

'Sure,' he replied, and then asked with a dry laugh, 'Am I invited?'

'You're about to be, and so is Nicky, even though Doris doesn't know him. I happened to mention you'd both be in the South of France around that time, and she seized on it immediately. She very much wants you to come. The trip to Beaulieu-sur-Mer *is* still on, isn't it?'

Francesca had been unable to keep the nervousness and anxiety out of her voice, and Victor picked up on both immediately. 'Sure it is, baby,' he assured her. 'Nick and I will be staying at La Réserve. I've already booked a couple of suites, as I told you I would. We're going to have a terrific time this summer, Ches. Lots of sun and rest, also a little fun, a few parties, side trips up and down the coast. It'll be great, kid,' he enthused, forcing a lightness into his voice he did not feel. He had not anticipated these latest developments, nor Katharine's presence on the Riviera, and he was now experiencing sudden qualms. *Oh Jesus.* More complications in his already complicated life. He suppressed a groan, swiftly cast aside the troublesome thoughts. Anything could happen between now and August. Speculating about the future was a futile occupation. His main interest was in the present, the next few days to be precise. He was not prepared to project beyond that length of time.

Francesca broke into his thoughts, when she said gaily, 'The summer will be super, Vic, I just know it will, darling. It'll be Königssee all over again, in fact.'

No, he thought, it won't. But he said nothing. For a while he concentrated on driving, enjoying the feel of the Bentley, its smoothness, its speed and its power, and also revelling in the isolation and intimacy within the car. Without taking his eyes off the road, he said: 'Listen, Ches, talking of Nick. *I've* got some great news for *you*. He's arriving in London tonight. From New York. I thought we'd have dinner with him tomorrow. Okay, baby?'

'Oh yes, Vic! It'll be lovely to see him after all these weeks,' she cried enthusiastically. 'I can hardly wait. He's been gone far too long.'

Victor chuckled. 'Hey, slow down. Don't get so carried away. You're making me jealous.' He reached for her hand and brought it to his lips, kissing the palm lingeringly. 'I can't begin to tell you how much I've wanted you these last few days, Ches.' He closed her fingers tightly, squeezed her hand, placed it back on her lap. 'I'd better not get started on that particular subject, otherwise I'll have to pull over and ravish you on the side of the road.'

'I wouldn't put anything past *you*,' she joked, happiness and pleasure flowing through her.

'You're right, you shouldn't, kid.'

'You haven't forgotten that Diana arrives tomorrow also, have you? I'll have to go to the airport to meet her, darling.'

'What do you mean *you'll* have to go,' Victor exclaimed. 'We'll *both* go. I'm not letting you out of my sight for the next week. Besides, I'm looking forward to seeing that lovely cousin of yours again. Hey, she'll be able to join us for dinner with Nick.'

The boyish smile struck his mouth, and there was a mischievous note in his voice as he announced, 'Know what? I bet you a hundred to one they take to each other just like that.' He lifted his hand from the wheel, snapped his fingers in the air.

'I wouldn't dream of taking you up on that particular bet, Mr Mason,' Francesca laughed. 'In this instance you're absolutely right.' She lifted Lada onto her lap, edged closer to Victor, reached out to touch his hand on the wheel. 'I've missed you so much, Vic. It's been awful for me, too,' she whispered, her longing for him echoing, her eyes overflowing with her love.

His sideward glance was penetrating and it betrayed his own emotions only too clearly. He took hold of her hand and brought it to his mouth again. He ran his lips over it. 'I know, darling, I know. And it won't be long now . . . we'll soon be together.'

CHAPTER THIRTY-ONE

It was a little after two o'clock when Nick Latimer swung his Aston Martin DB2–4 through the gates of Shepperton Studios on Thursday afternoon in the first week of July. He parked next to Victor's Bentley, turned off the ignition, and jumped out. After locking the door he stood back, gazing at the car admiringly. It had been waiting for him at the David Brown showroom in Piccadilly when he had returned to London ten days ago, an unexpected gift from Victor. He had been flabbergasted, and had exclaimed vehemently to Vic about his unparalleled extravagance.

Victor had reminded him that he had been hankering after this bit of high-powered machinery for the longest time, indecisive about buying it. 'So I got it for you, old buddy,' Victor had gone on. 'Life's too damned short to deprive ourselves of the few things which might give us a bit of pleasure in this tough world. I thought it would cheer you up.' Touched by his friend's thoughtfulness and understanding, Nick had accepted the car graciously, acknowledging that men like Victor Mason were a rare breed.

Nick patted the bonnet of the car appreciatively, and then loped across to the cluster of sound stages in the distance. They always reminded him of aeroplane hangars in appearance. Unpretentious on the outside; cold and utilitarian on the inside. Only there did they differ from aeronautical garages, filled as they were with complex equipment, plus armies of dedicated technicians and gifted artists striving to create a special kind of magic called motion pictures. Glamour factories. But like all factories, singularly unglamorous. Nonetheless, he enjoyed being on the set, derived a feeling of gratification and participation as he stood on the sidelines watching, hearing his words take on meaning when the actors breathed life into them. As he walked, he straightened his tie, wondering how the morning had gone. This was the final day of shooting. At three o'clock Victor would walk out onto the set to do his last scene with Katharine Tempest and Terrence Ogden. It was wrap. God willing, he muttered under his breath.

Since his return from New York, Victor had regaled him with innumerable stories about the shenanigans of the past few months, and he had listened in astonishment and morbid fascination, aware that Vic was not exaggerating when he pronounced it one of the most difficult pictures he had ever worked on. Nick was well aware that trouble went hand in hand with movie making, but it seemed to him that *Wuthering Heights* had had more than its share, had been cursed from its very inception. When he had been out at the studios on Tuesday he had witnessed first hand a few tense little contretemps, and both Jake Watson and Jerry Massingham had confirmed that the explosive atmosphere was nothing if not normal. Also, from what he had heard from the two production executives, everyone would be delighted when the last frame was shot, the missing footage in the can. All would walk away relieved that this particular ensemble was breaking up.

A regrettable ending, Nick thought sadly. To him, perhaps the most marvellous thing about making a movie was the camaraderie that developed between those involved; the sense of an intimate close-knit family, of unselfish collaborative effort and teamwork that generally evolved over a period of time. According to Jake, only Victor's diplomacy, his stupendous efforts to smooth ruffled feathers on a continuing basis, plus his constant words of encouragement and praise, had kept things together and under reasonable control.

'Pip pip! Toot toot! Hi there, Nicholas.'

He recognized the shrill voice at once, and swallowing his dismay he turned around. 'Hello, Estelle,' he said, staring at the approaching figure, trying to conceal his aversion behind a smile that was bland if not particularly friendly. 'How are you?'

'In the pink, thanks much. I'm also footloose and fancy free at the moment. Are you, my darling?' she simpered.

'I'm all tied up right now, Estelle.'

'What a shame, my love. I've always thought we'd make sweet music together. I can almost hear the clickety-click of our twin typewriters.'

Nick winced and retorted, 'People in the same profession should never be foolish enough to get involved. It doesn't work. You know what they say – there's only room for one star in the family.'

'*Touché*,' she giggled, and tucked her arm through his possessively, making eyes at him. He said, in a kinder tone, 'I guess you're here for the wrap party later.'

'Oh yes, I wouldn't have missed it for the world. And I thought I might. I just got back in time – from the Côte d'Azur. I was down there for the wedding.'

'Wedding?'

'Good God, Nick, where have you been? Grace Kelly's wedding, dum-dum, you know, to Prince Rainier of Monaco.'

'Oh sure, I forgot.' He laughed lightly. 'Ah well, another promising career curtailed, just when it was reaching its peak.'

'Grace is going to make more movies, I'm sure of that.'

'I doubt it. And more's the pity. I always thought she had something very special. I like her cool, pristine beauty. My blood type,' he grinned, and instantly saw vivid images of Francesca and Diana, who, each in their different ways, possessed this

317

me quality in appearance. He disentangled his arm from her tight grasp, opened the heavy steel door of Stage Three, ushered her in, and said, with a forced smile, 'See ya, Estelle.'

'You betcha, Nicholas. I haven't given up on you yet,' she giggled. Then she stared hard at him, and her face changed, filled with unfamiliar sincerity. She said, in a gentler tone, 'So very sorry, Nick. About your sister.' She did not wait for a response, but sailed off, waving to Alan Medbury, the unit publicist, who was talking to a camera man, crying, 'Toot toot! Pip pip, Alan!'

Nick looked after her, a mixture of surprise and chagrin seeping into his eyes. He had not expected a show of sympathy from Estelle, and he felt a small twinge of guilt about his sarcastic jab at her a moment ago.

'Over here, Nicky!'

Jake Watson's voice echoed hollowly across the relatively deserted sound stage, currently occupied only by a sprinkling of technicians. Nick swung around, raised his hand in brief salute. He edged between the cameras, klieg lights and sound equipment, carefully stepping over the snaking lengths of cable, making his way to Jake, who was standing in a corner talking to Jerry Massingham. Drawing nearer, Nick saw at once that both men looked gloomy and depressed. This was par for the course with Jerry, who always appeared to be carrying the troubles of the world on his shoulders, but not affable, imperturbable, dapper Jake Watson, film producer *par excellence* and a veteran of many bloody production wars. *He* usually radiated an air of insouciance whatever stress he was under, and so his present mien and dishevelled appearance were somewhat out of character.

Not wishing to become embroiled in their troubles, at least not initially if he could help it, Nick knew the wisest tactic would be to ignore their obvious disgruntlement. He decided to resort to an old game he and Jake had invented out of mutual ennui on picture locations around the world. They structured their dialogue in movie titles, using these to make the salient point, testing their memory and mental agility, and in the process they had had a lot of fun in the past.

And so Nick flung an arm around Jake's shoulder, said with a breezy grin, 'All Quiet on the Western Front, I see.'

Jake responded tersely, 'Momentarily.' Almost immediately his face relaxed, acquired the geniality that was more normal for him. He smiled apologetically. 'I didn't mean to bite your head off. Welcome, friend.' And then he winked, added with swiftness, 'You've just walked into Stalag 17.'

Jerry looked from one to the other in puzzlement, shrugged, and thrust out his hand. 'Afternoon, old boy. And Jake's right, bloody prison camp this is. Can't imagine why you've come back, unless it's to share our misery.'

'Hello, Jerry.' Nick shook the production manager's hand. 'Everything seems peaceful enough to me. Positively tranquil.'

'Yes, you might say there's a lull right now, and I do sincerely hope it's not the proverbial bloody lull before another storm,' Jerry declared, the moroseness on his face intensifying.

'Rough morning?'

'Bad Day at Black Rock,' Jake announced, his tone gone slightly sour. He ran an immaculately-manicured hand through his waving silver hair. 'Pray. Light candles. Genuflect. Face Mecca on your knees. Practise witchcraft. Just do anything you think will get us through this afternoon without another hitch, Nicholas, so that we can fold our tents and quietly steal away. Shooting Mark Pierce might be an idea.'

'Shall I take him out to the parking lot?' Nick asked with a droll smile, his light blue eyes mischievous.

Jake cracked up. 'Jesus, I sure am glad you're back, *bubeleh*. At least I get a few laughs when you're around.'

'I'm glad to hear somebody does. Anyway, where is Little Caesar?' Nick glanced over his shoulder, scanning the set with considerable interest. Other members of the crew were slowly straggling back, and it was gradually filling up with people as zero hour approached.

'Mark? Grinding his heel into Terry, I've no doubt,' Jerry intoned derisively.

'That bad, huh?' Nick shook his head sadly. 'Cheer up, you guys, and take heart from the fact that this is the last day. And Victor? Where's he?'

'In his dressing room,' Jake said.

'Then I guess I'll go in to see him, before you start rolling again.'

'No, don't!' Jake grabbed his arm, restraining him.

'Why not?'

'He's got Katharine in there. They're having a conference. He doesn't want to be disturbed.' Jake shrugged. 'Sorry about that.'

'Oh! But look, he's expecting – ' Nick broke off as the continuity girl hurried up. She handed a sheaf of papers to Jerry, and retreated rapidly without uttering a single word.

Jerry grimaced at Jake. 'Hells bloody bells, *she* looks as if she's got a feather up her bum. I'd better go and find out what in God's name has gone wrong now.' He strode off, muttering under his breath.

Nick and Jake exchanged concerned glances, and Jake said softly, 'Don't worry. Whatever the problem is, Jerry'll handle it. He's a good guy, I don't know what I'd have done without him, to tell you the truth. He's been terrific back-up for me. I'd have him on a picture any time.' Jake sighed, fumbled in his pocket for a cigarette, lit it. 'I must confess, Nicky, it's struck me more than once that Mark sets out to create unnecessary tension – perhaps that's the only climate he can work in.' His shoulders lifted in a gesture of resignation. 'But then I could be wrong. Anyway, what the hell, it's all water under the bridge now.'

'Yes, it is. From what Victor has said, I gather there has been a great deal of free-floating emotion in general.'

'That's true, Nick,' Jake agreed with a brief nod. 'As you well know, when you corral a lot of creative people together, you're also amassing an extraordinary amount of talent, sensitivity and temperament. All these things are bouncing around, interacting between everyone. A few fireworks are not only expected but inevitable. But Jeez, Nicky, on this picture it's been like the Fourth of July almost every day. Still, I've got to hand it to Victor, he's kept his cool pretty damn well. But then he's a real pro.' Jake hesitated, gave Nick a close and piercing look. After a moment he said, in a guarded tone, 'It's only these last few days he's been a bit moody. Sort of brooding. Controlled as always, but more reserved than usual. Uncommunicative in some ways. Know what's bugging him?'

Nick was taken aback, and it showed on his face, 'Nothing. So far as I know,' he said in all truthfulness, baffled by this unexpected revelation. 'He was in good spirits last week, when you were in Yorkshire, and he seemed to be his normal self when I saw him on Tuesday night. I've spoken to him on the 'phone every day, and I didn't detect anything out of the ordinary, either in his voice or conversation.'

Jake was thoughtful, said slowly. 'To tell the truth, it's begun to concern me. He really hasn't seemed like himself. Preoccupied. Worried even. You must have noticed something. Don't hold back on me, Nick. Come on, let's talk *mama-loshen.*'

'I am being straight with you, Jake, honestly, I am. I don't know a thing. I repeat, there's been nothing untoward in his manner or his behaviour.' Nick pondered, his face reflective. At last, he said, 'Look, perhaps the tension finally got to him, affected him these last few days. You've worked on enough pictures with him to know he considers excessive temperament to be juvenile and unprofessional, that he likes a peaceful set. Anything less tends to irritate him.'

'Oh Christ, you're probably right, Nicky. Maybe it's just my imagination doing a job on me, and listen, that wouldn't surprise me. This goddamn movie is making me paranoid.'

'Relax, old sport.' Nick placed his hand on Jake's shoulder affectionately, his eyes knowing, gleaming with confidence. 'And whether the picture is making you paranoid or not, it is *spectacular.* I saw some of the rushes yesterday, and I was knocked for a loop, I really was, Jake!' Nick's excitement was evident in his tone. 'Mark Pierce might be a son of a bitch, but he's a brilliant director. And the wonderful thing is that none of the troubles shows up on the screen.'

Jake nodded, and his weary eyes visibly brightened. 'That's usually the case. The more troubled the picture, the greater it often is in the end. And I agree with you, I think we've got a winner, a sure-fire hit.' Jake leaned closer, said in a confiding tone, 'What do you think of Tempest? It's her picture, of course. She steals it, walks away with it.'

'Almost, but not quite.' Nick's response was so fast, so positive, that Jake looked at him alertly, convinced the writer was being objective. He was all ears.

'She is absolutely sensational, I'll grant you that. I'll even go so far as to say she's sheer genius in the role. But Victor is still the dominating force, as he always is on screen. He's never anything but larger than life, and this time he surpasses himself. He's the Byronic hero incarnate. Tormented suffering, tragic, and more romantic than he's ever been, in my opinion. He sparks all manner of emotions. Know something? He actually moved me to tears in several scenes,' Nick confessed with a self-conscious grin. 'This is the greatest performance he's ever given. It's Oscar-time stuff, Jake. And incidentally, Terry Ogden is extraordinary as Edgar Linton. As a matter of fact, he reminds me of a young Leslie Howard, and I'm not a bit surprised Hilly Street has signed him. Terry's a winner all the way, the real old-fashioned matinée idol, a type that's coming into vogue again.'

'Nicky, you've just made my day. I felt I wasn't wrong about the dailies, but there are times when you sometimes wonder if you're losing your objectivity, because you're too close to the project. As for Terry, Victor and I agree with you, think he's got a helluva career ahead of him in movies.' Jake rubbed his chin, appeared momentarily confounded, as he ventured, 'I can't understand why Mark has been so down on Terry. He's performed brilliantly, but nothing he's done has been good enough for Pierce.'

'So I understand. Victor told me he thought there was some kind of personal animosity there, that this was the only possible explanation.'

'Yes, we discussed that at one point, and Victor pulled Katharine into one of our confabs, convinced she knew more than she was admitting. But she was evasive, then insisted Mark and Terry were good friends.' Jake shifted on his feet restlessly, his expression becoming enigmatic. Bringing his eyes back to Nick, he said, 'She's a smart one, our Little Miss Goody Two Shoes, no question about that. Yes, indeedy, she knows the score, and then some.'

Nicholas could not fail to miss the derisory edge to Jake's tone, and he looked at the producer keenly. He realized, with a sudden spurt of surprise, that here was one other person who had reservations about Katharine Tempest. Seemingly Jake had not been blinded by the lady's dazzle either. 'What are you getting at?'

'Looks as if butter wouldn't melt in her mouth, doesn't she? But she's quite the little operator.' Jake's laughter sounded cynical, and then he went on, 'Listen, don't get me wrong, Nick. Professionally I can't fault her. She's a marvellous actress, inspired in my opinion, and dedicated. She's also a hard worker. However, there's something about her as a person, as a woman, that makes me ponder. Can't quite put my finger on it, but it's there, nevertheless. Perhaps . . . well, I guess she seems too good to be true.'

Nick gaped at Jake, and curiously so. 'I don't know . . .' he began cautiously, and hesitated, reluctant to broadcast his dislike of Katharine, which he had hitherto kept to himself. Settling for a compromise, he said, 'I've thought, at times, that she gives the impression of being untouchable, remote, uninvolved, a little frigid. And God knows, it's patently obvious she's excessively ambitious. But I've never considered her to be a *devious* person. Is that what you're suggesting?'

'That's a strong word. I'm not even prepared to say she's two-faced,' Jake murmured, adding with a sly grin, 'slippery, maybe. And sharp, Nick. Knows how to play all the angles, and to her best advantage. Victor has cosseted her and protected her all through the picture, devoted an enormous amount of time to her. So has Pierce. Oh he's been tough, but she's had a great deal of attention from him. As for Ossie Edwards! Christ, he's so stuck on her he can't see straight. I shouldn't say that. He can certainly see straight when he's looking through the camera at *her*. He's photographed her like a dream, which is not difficult, I realize, since she is beautiful. But he's spent endless hours perfecting her lighting, her camera angles, and he's favoured her in every scene. Naturally, she's playing up to Ossie – in fact she's got a lot of people bamboozled around here except yours truly, so I guess she's not doing too badly, considering it's her first movie.' He nodded his head, finished with dryness, 'It's not surprising to me that she's the focus of a lot of jealousy in this neck of the woods. You'd be surprised at the number of pairs of eyes which have turned a most *unattractive* shade of green in the last twelve weeks.'

Nick was somewhat astonished at Jake's recital. That Katharine was clever he had never doubted; that he had underestimated the extent of her cleverness was now transparent.

Finally, Nick said, 'I suppose I've only seen a certain side of her character, and nobody's one-dimensional, I know that. You've had more exposure to her these

321

last few months than I have. So you probably have a better understanding of her.' He half smiled. 'A working relationship can be revealing, can't it? And it's not surprising that people are jealous of her.' It struck Nick then, and with some force, that Katharine would always be a target. As if thinking aloud, he remarked, 'Let's be honest though, Katharine is too richly endowed to be treated normally by her peers, or *fairly*, for that matter. She's going to be a source of envy in her profession all of her life, and that's a bit unjust. After all, she can't help her natural gifts – those stunning looks, that immense talent.'

Jake offered Nick a cigarette, lit his own, and replied, with a hollow laugh, 'Whoever said there was any justice or fairness in this damn world, Nicholas? Katharine wants stardom in the worst way, and the kind of fame and success she craves doesn't come cheap. There's an old saying, Nicky . . . "Take whatever you want from life but never forget God expects you to pay one day." Katharine will get her lumps, and she'll have to swallow them like everyone else has, and does. Let's hope it's only envy and jealousy she has to cope with in the future. I'll tell you this, too. She is going to be one of the biggest stars we've ever seen. Bar none.'

'I know, Jake.'

A contemplative expression settled on the producer's narrow, angular face. He said, 'This may sound weird, but I believe Katharine would be big whether she wanted to be or not. She's like a force of nature. She exists, therefore she will be. There's just no stopping her now. Mind you, I doubt that she'd be able to stop herself, even if she tried. It's gone beyond her control. In fact, the only way Katharine could avoid stardom would be if she retired from this business and hid herself in a nunnery. That girl was born to be a star. It's an inevitability . . . it's her destiny.'

Although Nick knew at once what Jake was implying, recognized the sincerity behind the words, he could not help exclaiming, 'But you're being inconsistent! Suddenly you're saying her career has been preordained, or some such things, whereas a few minutes ago you told me she was a little operator.'

Jake cried assertively, 'That she is, Nicholas. And a very shrewd one, in my opinion. But don't you *see*, she doesn't really have to be. Katharine Tempest has everything going for her without playing the angles, loading the dice. Jesus, she's a natural. All she has to do is sit still and let it happen. And believe me it will in record time. I'm afraid Katharine wastes far too much energy – unnecessarily. Let's hope she doesn't waste her talent.' He cleared his throat. 'Let's also hope that fame and glory don't go rushing to *her* head.'

'Yes,' Nick murmured. 'It's all pretty potent stuff. But I'm sure she can handle it.' As he spoke he wondered if she could.

'Don't look so serious, Nicholas.' Jake punched him on the arm. 'And after today Katharine Tempest will no longer be any concern of mine. Come October she'll be Monarch's problem.'

'But after that you may find yourself stuck with her again, old sport. You're bound to be the line producer on Victor's next picture for Bellissima, and it would be criminal if he didn't use Katharine. Let's face it, they are magical together.'

'True. Very true, Nicholas. But in the meantime, I'm taking a sabbatical. I fully intend to . . . Leave Her to Heaven.'

'You had to have the last word, didn't you,' Nick laughed. 'Here comes our star.

The conference must be over.' Nick waved to Victor, who was hurrying across the sound stage towards them. He was already dressed for his role as Heathcliff, looking impossibly handsome in an elegantly-cut black Victorian frock coat, narrow pants, matching waistcoat and a white shirt with a ruffled front.

'Hi Jake, Nicky.' He eyed the writer, and asked, 'How long have you been here, kid?'

'About half an hour. You were tied up.'

'Yep. Talking the scene over with Katharine, after Mark's mandatory run-through earlier. It's the one before the death scene. As you know, we shot that in Yorkshire. I wanted her to feel absolutely confident about it, so that she'll be relaxed.' He glanced at Jake, his eyes sharp. 'No problems?'

'Not at the moment. But don't hold your breath. You've been to make-up I see. I guess you're all ready to go.'

'Sure, I'm all set. Katharine's having her hair done, and Terry's almost dressed. The troops are geared up to do battle, any time the big man wants. Where is he, Jake?'

'I haven't seen him for well over an hour. He disappeared after the run-through. Don't worry, he'll show up at five minutes to three, cracking his whip and snarling.'

'For the last time,' Victor retorted.

'I'll say *amen* to that!' Jake exclaimed. 'If you don't need me for anything, Victor, I'd better go and round up All the King's Men.'

Victor gave the producer a swift look. 'So you and Nicky are still playing that old game, are you? Sure, go ahead. And Jake, remember one thing – it may be Battleground today, but tomorrow it'll be Bright Victory.' The lazy grin slid onto his mouth. 'Surprised you, didn't I? But *I* know a few movie titles, too. Give me a yell if you need anything.' Victor grabbed Nick's arm and led him over to a group of canvas directors' chairs arranged to one side of the cameras and facing towards the set to be used for the last scene. 'Here, take my chair, kid,' Victor said.

Nick sat down, remarked, 'Aren't you joining me, Vic?'

'I prefer to stand while we visit. I don't want to crease these trousers. They're as tight as hell.'

'It's a tough world, old sport, Nick laughed.

Victor went on, 'I'm going to see the assembled footage this weekend with Pierce, and next week I'll do the dubbing he needs for my exteriors. Then I thought we'd take off for Paris. Spend a few days there before heading south to Beaulieu. How does that sound to you?'

'Great. You realize I'll be dragging my typewriter along. I must get back to work.'

Victor nodded. 'Sure, I know that. It's the best thing for you, Nicky. You'll be able to write undisturbed at La Réserve and by then the area should be much quieter, less crowded with tourists. I gather there have been more people than ever on the Riviera this summer, because of Grace Kelly's wedding. Oh, incidentally, after Jake's supervised some of the editing with Pierce, and mopped up here in general, he'll be joining us for a week or so. You don't mind do you?'

'Of course I don't.' Nick looked at Victor.

'I suppose it's already crossed your mind that it's going to be like old home week.

Hollywood on the Med. Hilly Street will be floating around, or so I've heard, and so will Jerry. We'll be tripping over a lot of familiar faces.

'Including Beau Stanton, not to mention whomever he's got in tow from the Coast. He was a guest at Grace's wedding, and rented a villa at Cap d'Antibes for the summer. He's in London at the moment, flew in Tuesday night. He came to see Hilly about the comedy.' Victor leaned forward, dropped his voice an octave, 'It's not been announced yet, but Hilly's going to be made head of worldwide production for Monarch, operating out of Los Angeles, starting some time in October. He'll see the Bolding picture on its way in France before handing over to his successor here.'

'Hey, that's terrific news, Vic. It augurs well for Bellissima, doesn't it?'

'Sure. He wants to continue the association. Anyway, getting back to our vacation, as soon as I heard about the Bolding crowd converging on Monte Carlo, I started studying the map, picking out some choice places we could mosey off to for several days at a time.'

Nick listened carefully as Victor went on to outline his ideas and plans for the rest of the summer, observing him acutely, seeking tell-tale signs of the moodiness and worry Jake mentioned earlier. To his relief, Victor seemed untroubled. On the other hand, the actor was just that – an actor, and a consummate one. Deception was part of his professional stock in trade. It even crept into his personal life sometimes. Nick thought then of Vic's secretiveness about his relationship with Francesca. Other than Diana, he was the only person who knew about them. Vic had certainly kept the lid down tight on that situation. Besides, Victor did have a marvellous ability to shelve any personal problems when he was working, in order to concentrate completely on his current role, and so he could easily be covering up. Nick knew it would be both thoughtless and imprudent to start prodding his friend at this most crucial moment before the final scene, and so wisely he held his tongue. If Vic did have worries, he would confide them soon enough.

'I'd toyed with the idea of driving to the south, of taking the Bentley to France, but perhaps we're better off flying,' Victor was saying. 'I'll talk to the travel agency tomorrow about our tickets, a hotel in Paris. I'm wondering if we should stay at the George Cinq, the Ritz or the Raphael . . .' Victor stopped, distracted by a small flurry of noise. He swung his head, glanced towards the door, turned back. 'There's Mark now. This is it. Let's hope we can lock this scene up in less than the usual five or six takes.'

'You will. Go and sock it to 'em, Vic.'

'I'll do my damnedest.' He strode off.

Nick leaned back in the chair and relaxed, his gaze riveted on Mark Pierce, who was conferring with Ossie Edwards, Jake and Jerry. The director was a short, compact, attractive-looking man, with a mild manner in social situations, one that truly belied his fierce temper and tyrannical posturings when he was working. Nick had only met him a couple of times before leaving for New York, and had found him to be erudite and contemplative. However, his attitudes and opinions very much reflected the British Establishment, and Nick had stamped him a snob, and a pompous one at that. He had not particularly liked Pierce.

Ego problems there, Nick thought. Like all extremely small men he adopts a bombastic and dictatorial manner to compensate for his lack of height. Napoleon complex. Nick concentrated his attention on the group with undisguised interest. Victor was gesturing towards the set, and all four men moved over to it in one body, talking amongst themselves. After several seconds of further discussion they dispersed. Mark brought the set decorator and a prop man over to the set, and they began to make some minor adjustments to the furniture arrangement. Victor ambled across to Terry and Katharine, who had walked onto the sound stage accompanied by Ann Patterson, who played Nelly Dean in the film, as she had in Katharine's screen test.

Technicians were materializing as if from thin air; stagehands, sound engineers, the continuity girl, and an assortment of assistants were milling around, and activity accelerated as the crew prepared to start shooting. Ossie Edwards was behind the camera, talking to his assistant, and Pierce positioned himself nearby. And then, before Nick could blink, Jerry Massingham's voice rang out: 'Extinguish all cigarettes, please. Silence. Lights.' A low hubbub continued, and again Jerry bellowed: 'SILENCE!'

Quietness descended immediately. The set, depicting Catherine Earnshaw Linton's bedroom at Thrushcross Grange, was flooded with brilliant illumination from the kliegs. Mark beckoned to Katharine, who floated forward. She was wearing a white summer dress of period design, cut loose and flowing, since she was supposed to be pregnant by Edgar Linton, and there was a lacy wool shawl of sky blue around her shoulders. Her chestnut hair fell in a dark tumble of waves around her face, which was without a spot of colour and made her spectacular turquoise eyes seem more startling than ever. Mark went up and spoke to her. She nodded, stepped onto the set and seated herself in a chair. He waited until Katharine had settled herself comfortably, placed a book on her lap, and laid her hands on it listlessly.

Mark then motioned to Victor and Ann, who disappeared behind the set so that they could enter it through the door built into the backdrop. He then resumed his stance near the camera, and without taking his eyes off Katharine, he raised his hand, called, 'Camera. Action.'

The door opened. Ann led Victor into the room, guiding him towards the chair where Katharine sat.

Nick leaned forward, his elbow resting on the arm of the chair, his chin cupped in his hand, his entire attention focused on the actors. Always prepared to take part in the make-believe of the theatre and of film, his willing suspension of disbelief was, nonetheless, so instantaneous he was surprised. Within a split second he had accepted the two leading performers so completely he was convinced and mesmerized by them. Katharine and Victor were no longer themselves. They *were* Catherine and Heathcliff.

The fatally-ill Catherine, half reclining, half sitting in the chair looked exhausted and weak, her life ebbing out of her. There was a faraway expression in her eyes and her face was dreamy and gentle.

In contrast, Heathcliff exuded power, was filled with vigour and strength and lithe animal grace, this despite his agonized countenance which so revealed his own suffering.

Now he stepped forward boldly, fell into her direct line of vision, and immediately an extraordinary change was wrought in her, was so forceful it leapt out at those watching. There was a straining in her, a breathless expectancy, an eagerness, as if Heathcliff brought with him the very breath of life, her life's blood itself. He was by her side in a few quick strides, emotion spilling out of him. He took her in his arms hungrily, and his anguish and despair were as tangible as her expectancy and hope as he gazed down into her lovely face. And they conveyed the deepest, most intense feelings without uttering one single word to each other. Heathcliff had the first line, and Nick's face prickled with gooseflesh as it was uttered.

'*Oh, Cathy! Oh, my life! How can I bear it?*'

As the scene progressed to its climax, Nick could almost feel the silence around him. It was absolute. He was also aware of the mounting tension on the set, knew that dozens of pairs of eyes were fixed in concentration on these two electrically-charged beings, who were so caught up in a vortex of passion and heartbreak they were oblivious to everything but themselves. They were hypnotic together, held everybody spellbound. Their performance was stunning; it went beyond performing to Nick. He had no words to describe what was happening on the set this afternoon, could only think of it as something quite miraculous.

After another passage of dialogue between Catherine and Heathcliff, during which they had remained virtually motionless, Heathcliff went to stand behind her chair, endeavouring to hide his pain and suffering from her. Then suddenly he was in front of the fireplace, glowering, and turning from her, and Catherine herself had risen, was supporting herself on the arm of the chair, imploring him with her eyes when, finally, his gaze met hers.

Heathcliff swung his head away, brought it back to regard her, the tears streaming down his face, and then – they were in each other's arms again. Heathcliff began to kiss her wildly, whilst rebuking her in quiet anger, his voice finally falling away into black despair.

'You teach me how cruel you've been – cruel and false. *Why* did you despise me? *Why* did you betray your own heart, Cathy? I have not one word of comfort. You deserve this. You have killed yourself. Yes, you may kiss me, and cry, and wring out my kisses and my tears; they'll blight you – they'll damn you! You loved me – then what right did you have to leave me? What right – answer me – for that poor fancy you felt for Linton? Because misery and degradation and death and nothing that God or Satan could inflict would have parted us, *you*, of your own will, did it. I have not broken your heart – *you* have broken it, and in breaking it you have broken *mine*. So much the worse for me, that I am strong. Do I want to live? What kind of living will it be when you – Oh God! Would you like to live with your soul in the grave?'

And Catherine responded tearfully, 'Let me alone. Let me alone. If I've done wrong, I'm dying for it. It is enough! You left me too. But I won't upbraid you! I forgive you. Forgive me!'

Heathcliff cried, 'It is hard to forgive and to look at those eyes, and feel those wasted hands. Kiss me again and don't let me see your eyes. I forgive what you have done to me. I love *my* murderer. But *yours*. How can I!' They clung together, their tears mingling.

Nick lifted his hand up to his eyes and wiped the wetness from his own face, and he saw the flash of white here and there, as others on the sound stage did the same with handkerchiefs. Before he could catch his breath, the scene was moving on with gathering momentum. Nelly Dean had come out of the shadows, was warning them that Linton would be returning from church imminently. Heathcliff starts to explain to Cathy that he must leave, for her sake, promises to wait outside her window in the garden. Catherine, sobbing and distraught, clings to him more desperately than before. She implores him to stay, declares she will die if he goes now. Taken by a more violent paroxysm of weeping, she faints in Heathcliff's arms.

At this moment the door in the backdrop flew open and Terry Ogden stepped into the bedroom.

Nick tensed and clasped his hands tightly together. He wanted Terry to be great, prayed inwardly that he would match the quality of the acting that had gone before. Terry, as Edgar Linton, was the perfect foil for Heathcliff. Nick knew immediately that his Linton *would* be as compelling and as convincing and as believable as Victor's Heathcliff and Katharine's Cathy.

Looking astonished and enraged to find Catherine in Heathcliff's arms, Linton took a step forward as if to strike the hated interloper, his sensitive ascetic face white and stark, his anger blazing. Heathcliff instantly managed to thwart the attack by placing Catherine in Linton's arms, begging him to help her. Without another word Heathcliff slipped out through the door.

Edgar, his gestures gentle and tender, endeavoured to revive his wife, murmuring words of comfort and love to her, as though tending a child. Slowly she came round, and, opening her eyes, she regarded Linton with vagueness. Linton, filled with anxiety and apprehension for her, appeared to have forgotten all about Heathcliff. His face mirrored his joy as he observed a spark of life in Cathy, and he began to kiss her forehead, clasping her to him, his face pressed into her hair.

'Cut. And print,' Mark's voice echoed sharply around the sound stage.

Startled, Nicholas sat bolt upright and blinked rapidly. He glanced about, saw that everyone else was momentarily taken aback, directed his eyes towards the set again. Katharine and Terry, frozen into their positions like statues, were staring out at the sound stage, their eyes seeking Mark expectantly.

Victor, who had exited through the door in the backdrop and walked around the set, was standing to one side of the sound stage. He was the first to break the silence.

'Is that it, Mark? Just *one* take?' he asked, unable to disguise his incredulity. 'You did say cut and *print*, didn't you?' he went on, heading towards Mark poised near the camera.

'Yes, my dear Victor, *yes* to all those questions,' responded Mark, his smile faintly superior. 'It was a perfect master shot. I doubt that any of you will be able to top yourselves. Certainly I'm not even going to have you try. Why tempt providence. So . . . I think we can move along and do the close-ups now. Katharine's first, then yours, Victor, and finally Terrence's. And do let us hope you will all emote as impeccably as you did for the master so that we can make this a wrap today.'

Patronizing bastard, Nick thought, lighting a cigarette and settling back in the chair.

*   *   *

'I'd like to write an original screenplay for you and Katharine,' Nicky said. He was stretched out on the sofa in Victor's dressing room, his hands behind his head, his legs crossed at the ankles, and there was a thoughtful look in his eyes.

Victor, who was hurriedly discarding his costume, glanced across at him. 'I recognize that intense expression of yours, Scribe. You've got an idea on the burner and bubbling already. Am I right?'

'More or less. I have to refine the story line a bit . . . Anyway, what do you think? Do you want to make another picture with the lady?'

'Sure, why not?' Victor had stripped down to his underpants and he reached for his towelling bathrobe. Seating himself at the dressing table, he began to clean off his make-up, and continued, 'I have that old commitment to Fox to fulfil. The screenplay they just sent me is not too bad. I'd like you to read it some time in the next few days, give me your opinion. I'll make my decision based on your feelings about the script. I'd be doing the Fox picture in Texas and Mexico, while Katharine's working on the Beau Stanton comedy. I'm free after that, so it would dovetail very well.'

'What's the Fox picture? Not another Western, for Christ's sake.'

'What else, baby.' Victor looked at Nick in the mirror. 'I've been wondering what to do with Katharine. If *I* don't star in something with her, then I'll have to find a suitable vehicle for her talents, one we can produce under the Bellissima banner. Or I'll have to look for more loan outs. Now, if you come up with a screenplay for the two of us, that'll solve my problems. I'm pretty sure I can make a deal with Monarch. I told you, Hilly's indicated he'd like to continue our relationship.'

Nick sat up and swung his legs to the floor decisively. 'I have a great idea for you and Katharine. A contemporary story. Romantic. Glamorous. Highly dramatic though, not comedic. I'll toss it around for the next few days, develop it further, and if you like the sound of it I'll do a treatment for you.'

'Okay, Nicky, you're on.' Victor stood up, went to the wash basin, rinsed his face and combed his hair. He began to dress in his own clothes, talking about the events of the past few hours, purposely changing the subject, knowing Nick would resist any further questions about his intended screenplay. He was always reluctant to discuss plot until it was entirely clear in his head. 'I'll tell you this, Nicky, you could have knocked me down with a feather when Pierce settled for *one* take on the master shot, and let's face it, he was pretty easy-going about the close-ups.'

'There was no reason for him to be anything else,' Nick said. 'You were all superb, Vic. And despite the headaches you've had, you've got one hell of a picture in the can.'

'Mmmm. Let's hope so.' Slipping his tie under the collar of his pale blue shirt, Victor knotted it carefully, peering into the mirror. 'And as far as this afternoon goes – well, the pleasant working atmosphere certainly sets the right mood for the wrap party.'

Nick regarded the mountain of boxes near the door. He said, 'I see you've been your usual extravagant self. Gifts for the cast and crew?'

'Sure. And they've all earned 'em, kid.'

'What did you select for Pierce? A gun or a bottle of arsenic?' Nick asked, grinning wickedly.

'No, as a matter of fact, I bought him a camera.'

'Christ, you didn't, Vic! That's sort of double-edged, isn't it? Like telling him point blank he ought to go back to being a cameraman.'

'Come on, Nicky, I'm kidding. I must admit I did consider it though. A camera would have been a nice little tongue-in-cheek dig. There were times on location when I was ready to scream from frustration. Mark had Ossie linger over some of the landscape shots for hours. To me, a tree is a tree, a sky is a sky.' Disgust trickled onto Victor's face. 'That's often the trouble with directors who've been cinematographers. They think every shot must be a work of art, a painting, or so it seems.' Victor lifted the jacket of his grey pin-striped suit off the hangr, slipped into it. 'In any event, I bought Mark a pair of gold cufflinks.'

'And Katharine?'

'A diamond bracelet.'

Nick let out a long low whistle, registered amazement. 'Pretty ritzy gift, maestro. I hope Francesca won't be jealous.'

It was Victor's turn to look astonished. 'Why should she be? Ches isn't that kind of girl. Anyway, she knows Katharine's earned it.' He turned to the mirror again, fiddled with the grey silk handkerchief in his breast pocket, remarked, 'Apart from being a true professional and a really disciplined actress, Katharine's made other contributions. I never told you, but it was she who persuaded Terry and Mark to do the picture, when I was having trouble getting them to sign. I think she deserves a special token of my appreciation.'

'I'll be damned,' Nick muttered. 'I mean about her influence with Mark and Terry.' He was surprised, although he knew he ought not to be after the things Jake had said about Katharine. It seemed the producer had been right on target.

Victor said, 'Besides, I gave Francesca the pearl choker she was wearing on Tuesday evening. I'm sure you noticed it. But did I have a problem getting her to accept it!'

'Why?'

'She said her father would disapprove of her taking expensive jewellery from a man, even if it was a birthday present, which it was, of course, for her twentieth birthday.'

A small smile tugged at the corner of Nick's mouth. '*She* would say that. No gold digger, she. And tell me, sport, how *did* you persuade her?'

Victor laughed. 'I also went out and bought gifts for her father and Kim, as an expression of my gratitude for their help on location, the use of the castle. By giving *them* presents at the same time, the pearls seemed impersonal and very legit.'

'The choker suited her. She looked particularly lovely on Tuesday. That girl's got it bad, Vic. She's very serious about you. Very serious indeed.'

'Yeah, yeah,' Victor muttered, scowling, and turned his back on Nick abruptly. He began to shuffle through the papers in his briefcase, obviously disinclined to continue the conversation.

This laconic, even dismissive, response, with its hint of indifference, confused Nick, and he stared at Victor's broad back, a frown crossing his face. Before he could stop himself, he exclaimed, 'Aren't you serious about *her*?'

'How the hell can I be serious about her, Nicky? I'm still married to Arlene!' Victor's voice, rising angrily, sliced through the air like a blade, and he kept his face averted, cursing Nick under his breath for broaching this particular subject.

329

Nick's sharp intake of breath and strangled exclamation caused him to glance over his shoulder. He glowered at the writer, asked tersely, 'Or had you forgotten that impediment? There are also a lot of other major complications, many to do with Francesca herself. Furthermore, I still have plenty of worries about the picture, so romance is hardly on my mind now. *Capisce?*'

Nick was silent. In all truth he was astounded, not only by Victor's actual words and his curt delivery, but by his unusually aggressive manner. After a moment, Nick said, in a low, dismayed voice, 'Yes, I understand, and no, I hadn't forgotten you're married. But you are shaking free of Arlene, and you seem pretty damned hooked on Francesca to me.' Nick's shoulders lifted in a half shrug, and he muttered, 'Sorry I asked, Vic.'

'That's okay,' Victor replied in a milder tone, swinging around and leaning against the wardrobe. His mouth tightened imperceptibly and he sighed, and then his expression softened, and he said slowly, 'I shouldn't have taken it out on you, Nicky, or snarled like that. Sorry, kid, I guess I'm all tensed up this week. End of picture nerves. Let's go down to the sound stage and have a drink. I could use one, and they're probably waiting for me before they can start the wrap party.'

'Sure, Vic.' Nick pushed himself up from the sofa, managing a smile.

The sound stage had acquired a more festive appearance. Long wooden trestle tables had been covered with pristine white cloths. All were laden with bottles of liquor, champagne and soft drinks, and there were plates of assorted cheeses, devilled eggs, game pies, thin sandwiches and a variety of other canapés. A number of waiters and waitresses hovered behind them, ready to start serving, and two bartenders busied themselves polishing glasses. All the cast and crew had assembled, were clustered together in small groups, talking amongst themselves, obviously awaiting the arrival of their star.

Jake said, 'There's an empty table for your gift boxes over there. Why not distribute them after the first drink? I think they're all raring to go, anxious to toast you.'

'Sure,' Victor said.

The chief stagehand broke into the refrain, '*For he's a jolly good fellow*', and everyone joined in as Victor strode into their midst, radiating his immense and charismatic charm. Instantly he was surrounded by his colleagues, who were shaking his hand, slapping him on the back, and generally showing their affection and admiration for him. That he was extremely popular there was little doubt.

Nicholas Latimer hung back, preferring to remain on the sidelines. He was no longer much in the mood for a party, felt put out with Victor. Although they had had their disagreements and arguments in the past, these had never been of a very serious nature, nor long-lasting, and certainly Nick had never had an occasion to think badly of Victor. That he was doing so now filled him with discomfort, made him feel vaguely disloyal. And yet it was impossible to deny he was annoyed with his friend. I'm also disappointed in him, Nick acknowledged. Normally he paid no attention to Vic's philandering, since he himself tended to be equally opportunistic when it came to women. But Francesca – she was different. If *he* understood this, then surely Vic did too. He's being unfair to the girl, Nick muttered under his breath, and his fierce protectiveness of her, which had developed steadily as he had come to know her better, automatically surfaced. He thought suddenly of his sister;

330

Francesca had always reminded him of Marcia, with her sweetness and innocence, her gentle ways, her straightforward nature. Familiar sorrow stabbed at him, and he closed his eyes, holding himself still, waiting for it to pass.

Over the last few months, Nick had come to accept Marcia's death, but there were odd, unexpected moments when he experienced feelings of loss. He knew he would never be quite the same again. Something youthful had gone out of him. He had always had a devil-may-care, irreverent attitude to almost everything in life, the one exception to this rule being his work. But lately his angle of vision had shifted direction, and his natural flippancy was tempered now by a new sobriety.

Opening his eyes, he looked across at Victor, studying the actor with objectivity. It was then he realized he had been slightly shocked by his friend's cold dismissal of Francesca, especially in view of the circumstances. Being gallant, and a trifle close-mouthed about some things, Victor never indulged in locker-room gossip about the women in his life, and so he had confided relatively little about their relationship. But Nicky knew that they were having an affair. Despite his affection for Vic, which bordered on adoration, Nick had to admit that for once he was on the woman's side.

Jake Watson, who was standing near one of the bars, caught his eye and beckoned. Nick strolled over to join him, and Jake said, 'You're looking down in the mouth, *bubeleh*. Come on, have a drink. What would you like?'

'Vodka on the rocks with a twist, please.'

Jake turned, asked for the drink, then handed the vodka to Nick a moment later. They clinked glasses and Jake asked, 'Is something bothering you, Nicholas?'

'No. Why?'

'Apart from looking morose, you're a bit grey around the gills.'

Nick laughed. 'I'm paying for my sins of last night, I'm afraid. Been fighting a hangover all day. But this should fix me up.'

An understanding smile touched Jake's lips and he nodded, as if accepting the explanation. He was not sure that he did. The novelist, loitering on the fringes of the crowd, *had* seemed unduly troubled a minute ago. Jake stole a sidelong glance at him, one which was appraising. The tired expression in Nick's eyes, coupled with the gauntness of his face, extinguished the puckish quality that was so endearing. But then this change had been noticeable on Tuesday, so much so, Victor had commented on it, and they had both attributed the sombre demeanour to his family worries of the last few months. Jake, deciding not to pry further, said, 'I wonder what happened to Hilly? It's going to look lousy if he doesn't show.'

Nick, who had been observing Katharine Tempest talking to Terry Ogden, swung his gaze away from her and said, 'You know he's never on time for anything. And where the hell's Gus? He should have been here by now.'

'I don't blame you for being anxious,' Jake shot back teasingly, with a provocative grin. 'She's a knock out.'

'Who is?' Nick asked in mock innocence, widening his eyes.

'Diana. Who else? I understand you two have fallen madly in love.'

'Keep it a secret,' Nick retorted sharply, and took hold of Jake's arm. 'I think congratulations are in order. Let's wander over and give Terry his due.'

'And Katharine hers.'

'Yes.'

She was wearing an elegant, stylishly-cut black linen dress, with three-quarter-length sleeves and wide revers of starched white cotton, and it was exceedingly becoming to her, emphasized her fragility, the delicacy of her features, made her flawless complexion seem more translucent than ever. Her hair was pulled back from her face, parted in the middle, and the abundant, cascading waves were caught in a black crocheted snood. As they drew closer, Nick saw that she already wore the diamond bracelet, and it sparkled like her brilliant eyes as she lifted the glass of champagne to her bright red lips. She leaned closer to Terry, said something, laughed gaily, and then she caught sight of him, and it seemed to Nick that her eyes frosted over and the smile fled.

Almost against his own volition, and without understanding why he did it, Nick leaned forward and kissed her on the cheek lightly. 'You were superb, Katharine.'

'Why thank you, Nicholas,' she responded coolly, and if she was at all startled by his unprecedented show of affection, small though it was, she did not show it.

'She was bloody marvellous!' Terry proclaimed.

'And so were you. Congratulations,' said Nick, shaking the young actor's hand.

'Thanks, Nicholas. Thanks also for those great words you wrote for me to say.'

'Not mine, I'm afraid. Emily Brontë's.'

'Nevertheless, you did a splendid adaptation.' Terry smiled, and took hold of Jake's elbow. 'Can I have a word with you, old chap?' he asked. 'This'll only take a moment,' he added, and drew the producer to one side.

They were alone. Nick looked down at Katharine and murmured, 'I said it before, and I'll say it again. You *are* Cathy. And you're unforgettable in the role. Know something else? You'll always be Cathy in everyone's minds from now on, just as Vivien Leigh will always be Scarlett O'Hara.'

She returned his long stare, found she was unable to look away, held by the intense blue gaze focused on hers. She parted her lips, but nothing was forthcoming. Blinking, she took a step backwards, noticed the change in his appearance since she had last seen him in early March. He's been through a bad time, she thought, instantly seeking the right words to properly convey her condolences. But she baulked, as always nervous in his presence. And so she, who considered thoughtlessness to be the most cardinal of sins, ignored his recent bereavement.

Instead she considered his last comment and, being leery of him, forever anticipating the caustic jibe, she now reacted adversely. She said huffily, with a light toss of her head, 'What a terrible remark to make to an actress. You're implying I've only got one kind of performance in me, that I can only play one kind of role. Well, it might interest you to know that Victor and Mark think I'm very versatile as an actress!'

'Look, I didn't mean it the way you've taken it.'

She cut him off peremptorily. 'Oh *there's* Ossie Edwards! I must go and thank him for being so wonderful to me on the picture. Do excuse me.' She looked up at him, her turquoise eyes icier than he had ever seen them, but her smile was saccharine sweet – and patently fraudulent. She took several steps in Edwards' direction, brought her head around and said over her shoulder, her voice dripping acid, 'And you, my dear Nicholas, will always be remembered for your *adaptation* of *Wuthering Heights*.'

332

'Ouch,' he muttered, and winced. He watched her walk across the sound stage, looking for all the world like a testy little schoolgirl whose pride was injured because she had had her hair pulled hard by some recalcitrant schoolboy. A faint abashed smile touched his mouth. He realized she had misinterpreted his words in the worst possible way and wished she had not, for whatever he thought of her as a woman, he did admire her as an actress. And then, to his amazement, unanticipated anger washed through him, and his face glazed with coldness. This was the first time he had seen her since Marcia's death, and she had not bothered to offer him one word of sympathy. Even Estelle Morgan had had the decency to do that. Within seconds the anger was nudged aside by a curious sense of hurt. This so vexed and disconcerted him, he gulped down the remainder of his drink, wondering why he expected anything from *her*. His intense dislike of Katharine Tempest was reactivated, and more forcibly than ever. He glanced over at Jake and Terry, who were engaged in deep conversation. Cigarette dangling from lips, drink in hand, he meandered off, looking for Jerry Massingham, or any other friendly face he could find.

'Nick darling! Nicky!'

As he wheeled he caught the gleam of silver-gilt hair, saw the small exquisite face seeking his in the crowd. Diana waved. He waved back, and pushed through the throng to her. She was standing next to one of the cameras with Francesca, looking glamorous in a chic suit of apricot silk and an organza blouse of paler apricot. Her extraordinary hair was plaited and coiled on top of her head like a tiny crown, and this style, combined with her high-heeled pumps, made her look taller than she actually was.

Her smile, eager and bright and loving, warmed his heart and his bellicose humour dissipated entirely as he grasped her hand tightly, bent over and kissed her on the cheek. 'Hello, my love,' he said, drawing back, staring down into that tranquil face which had so captivated him from the first moment he had seen it.

'Hello, Nick. Sorry we're late,' Diana replied, still smiling at him. 'Lots of traffic, I'm afraid.'

'I was getting impatient, but now that you're here everything's all right.' He turned to Francesca, hugged her affectionately and murmured, 'Vic's tied up with the crew and cast, kid.'

'I assumed he would be. Don't worry.' Francesca peered around. 'I don't see Katharine. Where is she?'

'Oh she's somewhere out there . . . in the madding crowd. Last I saw of her she was talking to Ossie Edwards. Now, my beauties, how about a glass of bubbly? Or would you prefer something else?'

'Champagne would be lovely. Thank you, Nick,' Francesca said, and Diana nodded in agreement.

Nick handed Diana his glass, 'Hold this for me, darling. I'll be back in a flash. Don't move. Stay right here, otherwise you'll get swallowed up by that mob.' When he returned with their drinks, he found Jake and Terry talking to the girls. Terry had not met Diana when she had come out to the studios earlier in the week, and Nick saw at once that the actor was being extremely charming and gallant. *He's* putting his best foot forward, Nick thought with a stab of irritation, and discovered he was jealous. He smiled inwardly. *In jealousy there is more self-love than love*, he reminded himself, recalling the line by La Rochefoucauld. He gave the girls their champagne, and as he took his own glass from Diana and met her eyes he was able to relax, even though she half turned and resumed her conversation with Terry. Jake was being attentive to Francesca, inquiring about her father and Kim. Nick positioned himself next to her, listening vaguely, caught up in his own thoughts. He wondered if Jake harboured any suspicions about her and Vic, and decided it was most unlikely, since secretiveness seemed to be Victor's rule of thumb in this situation.

He observed Francesca thoughtfully. How lovely she was in the simple white summer frock overpatterned with tiny blue flowers. His awareness of her youthfulness was most acute. She looked so *tender*, she stabbed at his heart, and suddenly he was afraid for her. Nick blinked and glanced away, his eyes searching out Victor. He spotted him immediately, towering above Katharine, Hilly Steed, Mark and Hilary Pierce, Ginny Darnell and Ossie Edwards. Victor's gaze was directed towards Nick, and he nodded his head imperceptibly. He knows she's arrived, Nick thought. He doesn't miss a trick. *Ever.*

Within the space of a few seconds, Victor finally joined them, all smiles and geniality, and after a few words of welcome, a couple of amusing quips, he swept Diana away to be introduced to everyone. Terry excused himself and ambled off, heading for the Pierces, and Jake took his leave also, murmuring he was going to get a refill.

The minute they were by themselves, Francesca said nervously, 'Was it a difficult afternoon?'

Nick shot her a rapid glance, perceiving the tension in her. He squeezed her arm. 'No, not at all, kid. As a matter of fact, everyone was singularly unruffled, the shooting as smooth as silk.' He began to give her a blow-by-blow description of the last scene, the quality of the acting, the moving performances he had witnessed. He was unable to keep the excitement and enthusiasm out of his voice, even when he spoke about Katharine's portrayal. Then he went on to rave about the picture in general, and spent a good ten minutes expounding his opinions of its overall merits. He was about to ask her how her writing was progressing when he became conscious of her drifting interest, realized that she was entirely absorbed in Victor, who was talking to Katharine Tempest. They stood alone, apart from the crowd surrounding Diana, and Katharine was regarding Victor earnestly, her hand clutching his arm so tightly it denoted possession. For his part, Victor was giving Katharine his undivided attention, his expression indulgent and fond, then he laughed with animation, leaned forward and whispered to her. It struck Nick that there was something rather intimate and suggestive about this little scene, at least it could easily be interpreted that way.

Nick said, 'He's not interested in *her.*'

Francesca spun to Nick, looked at him curiously. Her face was without expression and difficult to read. 'I know that,' she replied, her voice neutral. 'Still, I do keep realizing – '

'Nor is *she* interested in Victor,' Nick broke in, eyeing her for a minute. He noticed that her inscrutable face was in conflict with the anxiety now filling her eyes, and hurried on, 'In point of fact, she's not interested in any man. Katharine Tempest is far too involved with herself to give a damn about *anyone* for that matter. The rest of the world doesn't exist for her. We're all dirt under her feet.'

Francesca was aghast, and she gaped at him. 'What terrible things to say! You misjudge Kath. You're making her out to be awfully selfish, and she's not at all. Anyway, you're absolutely wrong about her being uninterested in men. Why, she's practically engaged to my brother.'

Nick was dumbfounded. He exclaimed, 'I knew they were dating. But marriage! Good God, that's an unlikely match!'

'*I* don't think it is,' Francesca replied, her tone frosty.

Recovering himself promptly, he remarked, with a dry laugh, 'I can't imagine why I'm reacting in such a startled manner. Nothing *she* does would surprise me. Quite the busy little bee, isn't she?'

'Nicky, you're being terribly mean and most uncharitable! I'm surprised at *you*. Kath is truly the most loving human being I know, generous, kind and thoughtful. Furthermore, she is my very dearest, closest friend.'

Ah, but is she yours? he wondered, and said, 'Some sister-in-law you'll be getting. And how do you think she'll fit into your world? The English aristocracy can be pretty snooty. Snobbish, in my experience. Do you really think they'll accept *her*? I doubt it. My God, an actress!'

'Oh don't be so silly. You're living in Dick's days. Those things don't matter any more,' Francesca spluttered. 'Besides, actress or not, Kath is a lady, so stop being disparaging. I don't like this conversation, I really don't, Nick.'

'She acts the lady, plays the role to the hilt, I'll grant you that. Never forget, she is *acting*. On the other hand, you are one, Francesca, born and bred. There's a big difference, so don't delude yourself into thinking otherwise.'

Deciding to ignore this last comment, Francesca replied with firmness, 'What I started to say originally, when I saw Vic and Kath so engrossed and obviously talking about the film, was that I realized, yet again, how apart I am from his professional life. Sometimes I feel like a spare wheel, sort of on the fringes and uninvolved in his world. But frankly it never crossed my mind there was anything between them, other than business. I know Kath only has eyes for Kim, and besides, I trust Victor completely.'

'Does he know how lucky he is, Francesca?'

She smiled, her eyes suddenly clear and untroubled. 'Do you think he is, Nicky?'

'Sure I do. He's been blessed, finding you.'

'But I'm the luckiest of all, having him.' As she spoke her head pivoted on her slender neck. Nick followed her gaze, which had settled on Victor once more. He stood out, larger than life, towering above his worshipful colleagues, one arm flung around Terry's shoulders. He was laughing unrestrainedly, his eyes irreverent, his startling good looks and masculinity overpowering.

Nick said, 'You're on a fast track with a downhill racer, kid.'

She swung her head. Her eyes grew enormous and she frowned. 'What on earth is that supposed to mean?'

He regretted the remark, was furious with himself. Intended flippantly, it had come out sounding ... cautionary. Fuming at his own stupidity, he remained mute.

Francesca searched his face, shook her head. 'You're saying some awfully strange things, Nick, awfully strange indeed . . .' Her face had paled.

'Yes, that I am, kid,' Nick agreed hastily. 'Forget everything I've said in the last half hour. Come on, let's get another drink and find Diana.'

Propelling her across to the bar, he asked himself why he was viewing the world through such jaundiced eyes today. He had no ready answer. But he made his mind up to one thing: he was going to play everything in a lighter vein, a much lighter vein.

With fresh drinks in their hands, Nick and Francesca skirted the perimeters of the sound stage, eventually spotting Diana talking to an exotic-looking girl with raven hair and sloe eyes. She was introduced to Nick as Hilary Rayne Pierce, Mark's wife, and the costume designer on the picture. Apparently they had been discussing fashion, and the conversation continued along these lines for the next few minutes. Nick hovered next to them, sipping his vodka.

Suddenly, Hilary was excusing herself, saying she must find Mark. Nick thrust out his hand to take hers, was amazed at its iciness, curious considering the heat in the studio, which was stifling. He was about to remark on this, then bit back the comment that had sprung to his lips. 'It was nice meeting you too,' he said with a smile.

Diana stared at Hilary, 'What a lovely person, Cheska. So charming, and well informed about fashion. She gave me some helpful tips about buying clothes in London . . . for the boutique.'

'Yes, she is awfully nice, and I'm glad she was helpful. I told you she would be, Dibs.'

'She's Indian, isn't she?' Nick asked Francesca.

'Anglo-Indian. Her mother is the daughter of some maharajah from a minor principality near Rawalpindi. Her father is Sir James Rayne, and seemingly there was quite a fuss when he upped and left his regiment and married the little Indian princess, or maharanee, or whatever she was. But that was over thirty-five years ago, and the dust has long since settled. Times *have* changed. Anyway, everyone adores Lady Rayne, and she's quite a remarkable person. She's still rather beautiful, and Hilary looks a lot like her.'

'You're a walking encyclopedia, kid,' Nick grinned.

'Actually, I'm just naturally nosy,' Francesca said, her equilibrium now fully restored. 'Always asking questions. Consequently I'm a fountain of information, most of it absolutely useless.'

'I wouldn't say that. And maybe you can supply the answer to another more pertinent question: where is our star taking us to dinner tonight?'

'Now *that* I don't know, I'm afraid.'

'You can ask Victor yourself, Nicky darling,' Diana informed him. 'He's making a beeline for us right now.'

Victor said, 'I know you're upset about something, old buddy, so come on, let's have it.' He sat sipping a drink in Nick's suite at Claridge's. 'I know you far too well, Nicky, not to understand something's amiss. You've been very subdued with me for the last five days, ever since the wrap party. Have I offended you in some way?'

'No, of course not,' Nick rejoined hurriedly.

336

Victor grinned. 'You're a poor liar, kid. Anyway, you don't have to spell it out for me. I can guess. It's to do with Francesca, isn't it?'

'Sort of,' Nick found himself admitting.

Victor lit a cigar, sat back, and met Nick's inspection unflinchingly. 'I thought as much. I realize I was pretty dismissive about her the other day in my dressing room, but only because it was the wrong moment for that type of discussion. I told you then that I still had a number of concerns about the picture. What I didn't explain is that I also have a variety of other problems to contend with. Personal problems of a very serious nature.'

Nick sat up and looked at Victor's face. The worry was now clearly revealed, no longer concealed by the actor's mask. He knew without a doubt that Jake had not imagined anything after all. 'You should have told me before,' he began, and stopped when Victor held up his hand.

'The wrap party was about to begin. I didn't want to cast a cloud over the celebration.' Victor leaned forward. 'Sure I'm heavily involved with Francesca. You weren't wrong there, kid. However, until I resolve my difficulties with Arlene, I can't do much about Ches. Look at the facts, Nicky. She's barely twenty, a baby in so many different ways. Her life is just beginning, there's so much ahead of her. She comes from a distinguished background, is therefore highly eligible on the marriage market. And with her looks and brains, I've no doubt her father expects her to make a spectacular match. With a young man from their echelon of society. I don't want to ruin her chances for a good life, should I be unable to unravel my mess. So you see, I must handle the situation with care, extreme caution.' He took a swallow of his Scotch and continued: 'I can just see the Earl's face if his only daughter, not yet twenty-one, is dragged into a sensational and scandalous divorce, because of her involvement with *me*. A movie star, and one who's had three wives, has grown sons *her* age. Jesus, Nicky, I'm almost her father's contemporary, twenty years older than she is, and something of a reprobate. So I don't know that David Cunningham would approve of me, even if I weren't so damned entangled.'

Distressed that he had misjudged Victor, Nick chided himself for his lack of faith. 'So the divorce is going through?' he asked.

'No, not at this moment.' Victor's tone was as gloomy as his expression, and he explained, 'Arlene is being contentious in every conceivable way. And she's just pulled something so outrageous, I'm floored. She and her goddamn fancy lawyers are out to ruin me, skin me alive if they possibly can.'

'Are you talking about the settlement, Vic?'

'Among other things. You know the law in California . . . community property being the key phrase. She's after property all right, everything I own practically. She wants the ranch, and fifty per cent of Bellissima Productions.'

'Holy Christ!' Nick gasped, understanding everything clearly for the first time. No wonder Victor was troubled, angry and hurt. Arlene Mason was stretching out her greedy hands to grasp two of the things he loved most, and which he had worked long and hard to build. 'I'll be a son of a bitch,' Nick cursed. 'But what the hell, Vic, she doesn't stand a chance. No judge would grant her – '

'Don't be too sure,' Victor exclaimed, 'I'm not going to speculate, or attempt to second guess any judge, or a court of law. Anything could happen.'

Nick racked his brains for a possible solution. 'What about offering her a hunk of dough. Surely that – '

'We did,' Victor cut in. 'Last week my lawyers made a counter offer. Three million dollars as a cash settlement, plus ten grand alimony per month, for five years. That comes to another six hundred thousand dollars. And she gets the alimony for the full period, even if she remarries during that time. She turned it down, and I thought I was being *pretty* generous.'

Nick shook his head in dismay. 'What a bitch she is, Vic, and she's being inordinately spiteful. My God, Arlene always hated the ranch, never wanted to spend any time there with you. And as far as the company goes, why the hell would she want to own half of that, except to hurt you.'

'Don't I know it. She says she's going to expose me to the world as a cruel and heartless husband, a sex fiend who flaunted his many love affairs with other women when we were still living together as man and wife, etcetera, etcetera, etcetera. Not strictly accurate, as *you* well know. She's twisting the truth to suit her own ends. Furthermore, she's attempting to use the threat of bad publicity as a weapon, so the spectre of *Confidential* still hovers over my head. Charming, isn't she? Not that I care about myself, Nick, but I do have to protect Ches.'

Nick said swiftly, 'But Arlene doesn't know about Francesca. You've been so careful.' He bit his lip, then asked worriedly, 'You have, haven't you? I mean Arlene couldn't have anything on you, could she?'

'No. I've been scrupulous, and I've never been seen alone in public with Francesca.'

'What about your trip to Königsee?'

'We flew separately, there and back, and we stayed close to the house, never went to restaurants or public places. And when we were on location in Yorkshire, Ches and I hardly saw each other, and when we did, we were always surrounded by other people. I know what you're intimating, Nicky, but even if Arlene is having me tailed by a private eye, or two or three, there's been nothing to spot. I'm safe on that score. And as long as I move in the midst of a group at all times when we're in the South of France, my relationship with Francesca will still be under wraps. But it's tough, sneaking around corners all the time, especially on the little one.'

'Francesca's a smart girl, Vic. I'm sure she understands.'

'More or less.'

'What's your next move, regarding Arlene?'

'Negotiate. That's my only course. Listen, kid, just between *us*, I'm prepared to go up another million on the settlement, and let the alimony stand. I'll even throw in the Bel-Air house. But I can't let her get her hands on Che Sará Sará, or on Bellissima Productions. It's out of the question.'

Nick caught the desperation in his voice. 'And I always thought Arlene was a dumb, redheaded starlet, with nothing but air space between her neck and the top of her head. I'm pretty stupid!' he announced.

'I haven't been much smarter myself. Taken in by a gorgeous face and the greatest legs since Betty Grable's. I think I need a frontal lobotomy,' Victor laughed. 'As for Arlene, she makes Mike Lazurus look like a babe in arms. Jesus, I wish I could dump her as easily as I dumped him.'

'I second that. And let's stay away from actresses from now on. But getting back to you, I'll do anything I can to help, Vic.'

'Thanks, Nicky. Right now all we *can* do is sit back and wait for Arlene's next move. And there's nothing to be gained by dwelling on the problems. Mainly, I wanted to clear the air with you, as well as fill you in.' Victor leaned back, puffed on his cigar, remarked carefully, 'Incidentally, I haven't told Francesca anything about the trouble I'm having with Arlene. I would rather she didn't know. Ches would only worry. So, under the circumstances, the less she knows the better.'

'Sure, Vic, I understand.'

Nick jumped up as the telephone rang, and went to answer it. 'Hello? Hi there. Yes, sure he is. Just a minute.' Nick put the 'phone down, said, 'It's for you, maestro. Your lady.'

Victor covered the floor in three quick strides. 'Hello, darling,' he said, pressing the receiver to his ear. His worried expression was dislodged by a happy smile as he listened to her voice.

Suddenly the scowl reappeared. 'I see. No, I didn't know anything about it, Ches,' he exclaimed. Then his delivery increased in rapidity. 'No. No. I don't want you to do that, baby. Under no circumstances. Too hard on you. Not very safe. Dangerous. Yes, I think it would be dangerous.' There was a small silence as Victor heard her out, then he said, 'Look, let me think about it for a while. And don't call Doris yet. There's plenty of time to tell her. Now please, *relax*, baby. We'll discuss it at dinner tonight.' Another brief pause on Victor's part, before he finished, 'Yes, I will, Francesca. So long, baby.' He replaced the receiver thoughtfully.

Having heard one side of the conversation, and now observing the look of disquiet on Victor's face, Nick asked quickly, 'What could be dangerous, Vic?'

'Francesca driving Doris Asternan's Rolls-Royce to the South of France by herself. It's a long journey as you know, having driven it with me. I can't let her go all that way alone ... through the Loire Valley, and miles and miles of other equally lonely and deserted countryside. There's no way I'm going to sanction that idea.'

Nick nodded. 'I agree with you. But I thought Katharine Tempest was making the trip with her, sharing the driving.'

'Yes, that was the plan, However, Katharine has just backed off. A few minutes ago. She called Ches to tell her she can't leave on schedule this weekend as agreed, that she has to stay in London for a couple of weeks. Because she has important meetings on her new picture. With Hilly Steed. And Beau Stanton.'

'Does she?' Nick asked, his eyes glued on Victor's face.

'This is the first I've heard of it.' Victor picked up his cigar and put it in his mouth, taking a long draw, and he could not help wondering what Katharine's game was now. He had no way of knowing that Nicholas Latimer was posing the identical question to himself.

CHAPTER THIRTY-TWO

Doris Asternan walked along the white marble terrace of the Villa Zamir with graceful precision, veering neither to the right nor the left, placing one foot carefully after the other, as though she were following some chalked-in line.

Doris was thinking; and when she thought she walked. Her mind was ticking over with the same precision as her evenly balanced paces, analysing the information currently stored in her not inconsiderable brain, selecting and evaluating, and some-times discarding, the different approaches she could take. Doris was troubled.

It was late afternoon, early evening almost, that peculiarly hushed and gentle hour which hovers between declining day and impending nightfall when the earth is still and every living thing seems temporarily at rest. The August fireball of a sun had long since dropped down behind the hills above Roquebrune, its last rays fluttering streamers of saffron and gold at the edge of the cobalt sky, and soon the diffused light would prevail. But the breeze was soft, hardly a breeze at all, and the balmy air held the warmth of the sun.

The great white villa slumbered and there was a sense of peacefulness every-where, the atmosphere redolent of honeysuckle and frangipani, roses, heliotrope and carnations. Nothing broke the silence except the click of Doris's gold sandals against the hard marble, the faint swishing of her pale green silk caftan as it swirled around her long legs. The sounds of irrepressible laughter, cheerful young voices, popular music blaring from the record player, the plop-plop of tennis balls, whoops of enthusiasm echoing up from the pool – all were absent for once. The villa was relatively deserted, apart from the servants, and Doris welcomed the solitude. Kim had driven up to Grasse to visit an old school friend and would be gone until tomorrow. Francesca had disappeared at noon, with Diana in tow, murmuring something about a picnic with Nicholas Latimer, who was helping her with her book on Chinese Gordon. David was taking a nap, and Christian had also retired to his room. Both had claimed fatigue after they had returned from a luncheon party at the home of friends in Monte Carlo. A luncheon that had been rather heavy on champagne and light on food, in Doris's opinion.

A slight noise distracted her, and she came to a standstill, peered over her shoulder, Yves, the butler who was head of the staff attached to the villa, had opened the French doors leading from the main salon to the terrace.

'*Bonsoir, Madame,*' he said, nodding politely.

'*Bonsoir, Yves.*'

The butler proceeded to wheel out the large brass and glass trolley that served as an outdoor bar. It was loaded with all kinds of *apéritifs*, liquor, mixes, soft drinks, and crystal glasses that rattled as he trundled the cart to the far corner, near the seating arrangement of terrace furniture. Once he had positioned it to his satisfaction, he asked her if she had finished with the tea tray. Doris told him she had, thanked him; with a brief deferential smile Yves lifted the tray from the glass coffee table and departed.

Doris looked at her watch. Soon the girls would return. David and Christian would appear, the cocktail hour would commence, and she would be submerged in people. Fifteen minutes, she thought, fifteen more minutes to think things out clearly. Decide on my strategy. She moved across the terrace and sat down on the two-seater hammock, sinking against the upholstered yellow cushions, not bothering to stop its motion, letting the sofa swing backwards and forwards. The canopy cast shadows across her face, freckled and bronzed by the sun, and they underscored its brooding aspect as she fell into further contemplation. Excessive ambition, she said inwardly, how it drives people to extremes, causes them to do the most extraordinary, and often unthinkable, things.

Doris herself was ambitious, but not to the point of damaging others, or sacrificing personal happiness on the altar of ambition. She was a giving and loving woman; love was her whole life really. She had married Edgar for the man himself, not his millions; by the same token she was about to marry David Cunningham, the 11th Earl of Langley, for reasons of the heart not the head. Money and titles do hold a certain intrinsic appeal, Doris was honest enough to now acknowledge, but she also knew that neither had been determining factors in her decisions at any time in her life.

Doris Asternan's ambition sprang from the intellect, was rooted in the desire to be associated with people of calibre and superior character, who were educated and civilized. Men and women from whom she could learn – and thus grow. My ambition is abstract in nature, she thought, and *has* been tempered by reason and judgment. Whereas *she* is driven solely by ambition, to the exclusion of all else, and therein lies the danger.

Doris shivered, even though there was not the slightest chill in the air, and glanced around, became conscious of the dimming light. The sky was losing the last of its colour, the blue draining away into pearl and opalescent tints, and the terrace was suddenly murky with shadows, and gloomy. She bent forward, lifted the glass chimney off the lamp, found the box of matches next to it on the table. Cupping her hand around the wick of the stout white candle, she lit it, blew out the match. She sat back quickly, and so forcefully that her movements started the hammock swinging again. As she rocked gently to and fro, fragmented thoughts intruded, decimated her concentration, tore her mind away from her dilemma.

She remembered another hammock, in another place, at another time in her life. On her grandmother's porch of the trim white house in Oklahoma City. The house where she had been raised by a doting mother and equally devoted and adoring grandparents. A house full of love and humour and honesty and solid values, although not a great deal of money. She closed her eyes and saw that porch in minute detail, with its vivid pots of flowering plants, wicker furniture, the old Victrola, the pitcher of lemonade and cookies in a silver dish, set on a white-painted table with a blue checked cloth.

The porch had been *the* gathering spot in the hot summer months and on lovely fall evenings throughout the years of her growing up . . . a place of laughter and good talk, of wisdom and gentleness . . . those were the things it spelled to her, and so much more besides. Grandpa smoking his pipe and rocking as she was rocking now, and reading wondrous stories to her from his many books when she was a small child; her school friends congregating there; and then, in later years, it had become the corner for conspiratorial whispers and stolen kisses when the boy of the moment had dropped her off after the Saturday night dance at the church.

Edgar Asternan had sat on that porch the first day they had met, rocking, talking to her grandfather, calling him Doc as if he had known him all of his life. Two men wholly different yet curiously alike in so many respects, one dedicated to the practice of medicine, the other to big business. Dedication and similar beliefs: perhaps those had been the link. Certainly they had understood each other, instantaneously.

How odd life is, Doris mused, recognizing that she might never have met Edgar Asternan if she had not been downtown, shopping for a new dress; if she had not stepped off the sidewalk at the precise moment she had done so. Edgar had almost run her over. Distraught and apologetic, even though it had not been his fault, he had insisted on driving her home in the Buick convertible that belonged to the manager of his Oklahoma City meat-packing plant.

It had been a Saturday afternoon, sultry, with not a breath of air. Edgar had been pressed into staying for a cool refreshing glass of Grandma's lemonade. When Grandpa had returned from a confinement a short while later, he had shaken his head, replaced the lemonade with good sour mash whiskey and informed them that this was the only *real* drink for a man. The time had passed quickly; it was suddenly supper time. Grandpa, having already established that Edgar had no pressing engagement, would not allow him to leave, nor had Edgar wanted to go. Her grandmother had brought out one of the best lace cloths and their finest china, and they had eaten chicken and dumplings followed by freshly-baked apple pie and homemade ice cream, and the dining room had reverberated with laughter throughout the entire meal. Edgar had stayed until midnight, relaxed and at ease, enjoying the lazy evening with his new friends, interested in everything about them. That night was entrapped in Doris's mind like one of those miniature scenes set in the centre of a glass ball: the two men on the hammock, Gran in the rocking chair. Her mother's bright auburn head bent over the tapestry she was working, her needle flying, and Doris herself curled up on the wicker chaise, chin in hands, listening in fascination to Edgar and Grandpa. Smoke curling up from the men's cigars; the clink of their coffee cups; Sinatra's young emotional voice crooning 'All or nothing at all' on the radio; the low murmur of deeply masculine voices talking of many things, but mainly of the war in Europe. And none of them had realized that only a few short months later America would be plunged into the fray, following the attack on Pearl Harbor.

She had been twenty-one that September, a kindergarten teacher, and extra-ordinarily pretty. Sweet, virginal, and yes, something of a country girl. Edgar had been fifty-seven, widowed and childless, a dynamic, sophisticated, multi-millionaire from Chicago, who was bored with making money inasmuch as he had no one to leave it to or spend it on; a busy man, yet lonely. He had fallen in love with her All-American college girl good looks, her whole-someness, her quick, inquiring mind, her intelligence, and the potential he saw in her. Three months later, on a sunny December afternoon a few days after President Roosevelt had made formal declaration of war on Japan, Doris

Halliday became the second Mrs Edgar Asternan. Her life had never been the same since.

A wooden shutter slamming back against the wall of the villa brought Doris back to the present. She leaned forward, looking down the terrace. Light was spilling out of the windows of the library, which she had converted into a bedroom for Christian. He began to play his violin, and the strains of a classical piece drifted down to her, poignant, melancholy, and beautiful in the silent twilight. Mozart, Doris thought. He always plays Mozart, and with such feeling and brilliance. A deep sadness enveloped her. How her heart ached for Christian, and also Diana. They were both far too young to carry such terrible burdens. She had invited David's sister to join them for the summer, and although Arabella had tentatively accepted, Doris knew she would not come, as did Diana. Neither of them had dared voice this shared opinion to David, who was elated at the prospect of propelling his sister 'back into the land of the living'. But Doris understood – understood the woman's state of mind, her motivation. Princess Arabella von Wittingen, caught in limbo with time suspended, could not bring herself to leave West Berlin for any prolonged period. She was waiting for her husband to return from the dead.

Sighing, Doris lit a cigarette. In the flare of the match her sapphire and diamond ring glittered like sharp blue flame. Doris studied it for a moment. It was her engagement ring from David. He had brought it back to France with him last weekend, when he and Kim had driven the Rolls-Royce down. It was part of the Langley Trust, and normally he was reluctant to take such heirlooms out of the country, in case of loss or theft. But, he had said, he wanted her to wear it immediately. 'It makes our engagement official, and it also says "hands off" to all the stray wolves around here,' he had laughed when giving it to her. She twisted the ring, smiling thoughtfully, knowing it had been worn by his grandmother, his mother, and his late wife, Margot, mother of Francesca and Kim. Doris loved it because of its significance in this family, her family now. Her hand went up to her throat to finger the necklace resting there, a delicate thread of sapphires and diamonds, understated and beautiful, with a matching bracelet and earrings which she was wearing tonight. Edgar had given her the sapphires only a couple of days before he had died four years ago.

Overpowering though her grief had been, time *had* subdued and lessened it. Yet even so, Doris knew that she would never forget that terrible day as long as she lived. How shocked and stunned she had been when Edgar had dropped dead, felled by a heart attack in his Chicago office. She had been inconsolable, her sense of loss so enormous she had been unable to function.

Doris saw Edgar then, as though he were standing before her on this terrace, saw him as he had looked that morning before he had left the mansion on Astor Street. A handsome, vigorous man, full of life and fit as a fiddle at sixty-six. Yes, his death had indeed devastated her, for Edgar Asternan had been everything in the world to her – husband, lover, father figure, teacher, friend and confidant.

Be glad for me, Edgar, be happy, my darling, she now whispered, talking to him as she so often did. *David is a good man, loving and kind and innately decent like you. I'll be happy with him, as I was happy with you. It won't be the same. Nothing is ever quite the same. But we do have a lot to offer each other. Thank you, Edgar, for everything . . . for helping me to become what I am today. If I had not had you, I would not be sitting here tonight.*

343

Goodbye, Edgar, my dearest darling. The time had come to finally let him go. She was about to embark on a different life, with a man who needed her as much as she needed him, and there could be no shadows from the past. She leaned back against the cushions, sighing lightly, but it was a peaceful sigh.

A clock chiming the half hour brought Doris fully out of her reveries. She crushed the cigarette in the crystal ashtray and stood up, smoothing the silken folds of her caftan. No more introspection, she told herself, walking slowly along the terrace and into the main salon.

Doris paused for a moment beside the ebony and ormolu *directoire* desk, straightening the magazines, her mind revolving around her problems again. If only it had not surfaced *now*, she thought dismally. It would have been so much easier to handle later. This is the worst possible time. There will be nothing but upset and embarrassment. Everyone is going to be affected, and it will cast a dreadful pall over the rest of the summer. Oh God, I don't know what to do for the best. *David must be told.* There was no alternative.

'Then so be it,' Doris said aloud, and simultaneously experienced a surge of relief, as she invariably did when she made a decision. Indecisiveness and procrastination were anathema to Doris. As were liars.

Intent on her purpose, she crossed the circular marble hall and climbed the grand sweeping staircase to David's suite of rooms, formulating sentences in her head. The situation was both delicate and explosive, and therefore every ounce of her diplomacy was required.

Victor opened his eyes and blinked in the filtered light leaking in through the shutters. He reached for his watch on the bedside table and glanced at it, realizing, as he did, that he had a vague headache. Too much burgundy at lunch, he thought, putting the watch down.

He stretched his body and turned on his side, reaching for Francesca. He wrapped his arms around her and kissed her hair. She murmured something to him, sleepy, unintelligible words, and opened her eyes. He bent his head, kissing her on the mouth gently, then pulled back, looking down into her face.

'You've got to get up, baby. You're going to be late. And anyway, if you stay here we'll only get into trouble again.'

Francesca smiled languorously. 'Then let's get into trouble.' She nestled closer to him, trailing her fingers across his shoulder. 'I'm all for it.'

Laughter caught in his throat. 'So am I,' he said, sitting up. 'But it's a fair drive to Cap Martin, and I don't want you – '

'Speeding on the roads again,' she finished for him. With a sudden movement she left the bed.

'You got it, kid. Right on the button. Now do as I say. Scoot. Get dressed at once. I'm going to call Nicky.'

She lingered. The smile on her face was secretive and knowing and just a shade tantalizing.

There were moments, such as this, when she was so irresistible it took all his self-control to contain himself. He wanted to crush her in his arms and make love with her over and over again, and never let her go. But she had to leave. Her father and Doris were expecting her and he did not want their suspicious aroused. Nor

344

did he want her pressing her foot down on the pedal, as she was predisposed to do. He said, in a domineering tone, 'I'll give you fifteen minutes to get your show on the road, lady. And listen, you'd better let Diana drive. Jeez, the way you race anybody would think you're practising for the *Grand Prix de Monte Carlo*.'

'Do you know, Vittorio Massonetti, you're beginning to sound like a cross between Napoleon Bonaparte and the Duke of Wellington. Always marshalling your troops, giving directives. Go there. Come here. Eat this. Sit down. Stand up. Get dressed. Get *undressed*.'

'Come on, Ches, shake a leg,' he broke in, swallowing a chuckle.

'Yes, *sir*! Right away, *sir*!' she retorted, blew him a kiss and glided across the floor. Her voice rang out gaily, 'Rule Britannia, Britannia rules the waves, and Britain's women never shall be slaves!'

His mouth twitched. She rarely failed to entertain him. He loved her sense of humour, her blitheness of spirit, her outspoken manner, and her feisty independence. He wondered what she would be like when she had a few more years on her shoulders. Probably one hell of a woman, he hazarded. His eyes followed her retreating figure, tenderness and admiration mingled in them. Her lithesome young body had acquired a smooth golden tan and her hair was bleached to the colour of ripe corn. In the last ten days in the South of France she had blossomed under the sun – and his loving.

She swung her head as she went into the bathroom, blew him another kiss. He stared at the closed door, half smiling to himself, thinking how well everything had worked out after all. He and Francesca had been able to spend a great deal of time together, openly and quite naturally, and also without awkwardness. This was due, in no small measure, to Doris Asternan, who had thrown them into each other's arms on a continuing basis, albeit inadvertently, unaware of their true relationship. Doris, who more than lived up to Francesca's glowing description, was gregarious, warm, and a generous hostess who loved to entertain. She had issued an open invitation to Nick and him, expressing the opinion that she was sure he, in particular, would appreciate the privacy the secluded villa afforded.

And so invariably he and Nick drifted up to the beautiful house on the promontory at Cap Martin almost every day, to play tennis, swim from the private beach, laze around the pool, enjoy a game of poker or gin, sometimes croquet on the lawn. There had been casual drawn-out lunches on the terrace, charming candlelight suppers in the garden, as well as trips to the casinos in Monte Carlo and Beaulieu. He had reciprocated her open-handed hospitality with several elegant dinners at La Réserve and the Château Madrid; Nick had taken them to the Chèvre d'Or in Eze, the picturesque village high in the hills, and to Le Pirate, the amusing outdoor restaurant near the villa. Jake, who had arrived three days ago, had immediately been included and made to feel welcome, part of the family. Yesterday Jake had hired a speedboat at the tiny port of Beaulieu, and they had cruised up the coastline, picnicking on the way, stopping off at Cannes, on the trip back, to have champagne on the Carlton terrace and browse in the boutiques.

From the first day he and Nick had been corralled by Doris, Victor had recognized the necessity for a certain posture. Discarding the avuncular role, since he had come to understand it infuriated Francesca, he had opted to play the part of a big brother. His behaviour could only be construed as fraternal, and he had kept everything light

345

and on a jocular level, yet without appearing stilted. Francesca did not seem to object. In point of fact, she reciprocated in kind, and with a vengeance, obviously relishing the chance to be preposterous, sassy and irreverent, much to his secret amusement. All in all, the atmosphere Doris generated was so light-hearted and casual, Victor had relaxed from the first day, and he had quickly discovered he was enjoying himself, having the best of times.

Being alone with Francesca did not present insurmountable problems either, in that Nick had elected to play a role himself. Genuinely interested in her talent, he had cast himself as writing professor to the budding author, and was advising her on the book. In consequence, she commuted between the villa and La Réserve with comparative ease, dragging the manuscript with her, and no one seemed to consider this coming and going remiss, particularly since Diana usually accompanied her. Also, there was a great deal of activity at the villa, and Doris and the Earl were so preoccupied with each other, the plans for the supper dance and their impending marriage, they were extremely *laisser-faire* in their attitudes towards the girls. Victor truly believed they were quite oblivious to the faint undercurrents, the innuendos and backchat, and most patently ignorant of Diana's growing romantic involvement with Nicholas.

Suddenly remembering the time, Victor jumped out of bed, slipped into his white silk robe, and went through into the sitting room. He poured himself a tall glass of Vichy water, took a long quenching swallow and sat down at the desk. He lifted the telephone and asked for Nick's suite.

'Hi, kid. About ten. Your neck. Okay?' he said, using their particular brand of shorthand.

'Deal, sport. Chow on?'

'Yep. Usual hour.'

'Good show,' Nick laughed, adopting an English accent.

'*Arrivederci.*' With a faint smile Victor replaced the receiver, put on his tortoise-shell glasses, absently searched for the list of guests he had invited to the big party he was giving at Le Pirate on Saturday.

Francesca said, 'Here I am, General. All ready for inspection. Do I look decent?'

He spun around in the chair. 'Positively indecent. Very sexy, I'd say. Your father ought to keep you under lock and key, kid.' This was said joshingly, but then he realized that he was not far off the mark. His eyes swept over her appraisingly, objectively, viewing her as another man might. She was wearing a white cotton shirt, the sleeves rolled up, the tails of the shirt knotted under her breasts to reveal bare midriff above very short white shorts. The marine-blue silk kerchief tied around her neck was the identical colour of her high, wedge-sole espadrilles, laced across the insteps with the strings finishing around her slender ankles. The outfit, simple though it was, flattered her in the most alluring way, emphasized her lovely figure, drew attention to her long, shapely legs. But apart from the clothes, he saw something else in her that made him catch his breath. There was a new voluptuousness implicit in her face, a certain kind of knowledge in her golden-topaz eyes, neither of which he had noticed before. She looked like a woman who had been well and truly loved and who had loved in return.

Her brows drew together and her head went to one side. 'What's wrong, Vic?' she asked, coming towards him.

He thought: Even her walk is different – looser, more rhythmic. Clearing his throat, he said, 'Just admiring you, that's all.'

'You're not half bad yourself, General,' she replied, laughing. Looping a strand of blonde hair over one ear, she continued, 'But will I get past Doris's eagle eye? I don't look as if I just fell out of bed, do I?'

She did. He was about to say so, but realizing this comment would make her jittery, he refrained. 'No, of course you don't,' he lied. 'And Doris doesn't scrutinize you all that closely, from what I've observed. It seems to me she only has eyes for your father.' He rose, placed his arm around her shoulder, and walked her to the door. When they reached it, he turned her bodily to face him. 'Please let Diana drive, baby. The *corniche* is murderous, and you're inclined to be reckless when you're hightailing it, pressed for time.'

'I promise.' She stood on tiptoe, kissed him on the cheek. 'I love you, Vic,' she whispered, clinging to him.

He tightened his hold. 'I love you too, darling,' he said, and released her with reluctance.

Stepping away from him, Francesca scooped up her handbag from the chair, hooked it over her shoulder. 'Are you coming to Zamir tomorrow?'

Victor grinned. 'Sure, we'll mosey on over in the late morning.'

He opened the door, peered up and down the corridor. 'All clear. Not a soul in sight. And don't forget, let Diana take the wheel.'

'Yes, I will. Don't worry so much, General.'

He stood in the doorway, watching her walk along the corridor in the direction of Nick's suite, so graceful, so carefree, so young, and her happiness was so palpable a thing it touched his heart. He wondered what would become of them both, for, with a rush of clarity and understanding, he suddenly realized how far their relationship had gone. His face sobered, and he frowned. He had said too much, taught her too much, loved her too much. It struck him, and with some force, that Francesca Cunningham would never be the same again. But then, would he?

Fifteen minutes later there was a sharp rapping on the door, and Nick called, 'It's me, Victor. Can I come in?'

'Sure. The door's open, kid.'

'Jake's been trying to call you from Monte Carlo,' Nick informed him, strolling across the floor, collapsing on the sofa. 'Your line was busy, so he spoke to me. He's still over there with the Bolding group. Jerry Massingham has invited him to stay for dinner, so he won't be back until eleven or so.'

'I've been on the 'phone to Le Pirate, checking the final details for Saturday. And talking of the party, we're short of women. I was looking at the guest list earlier, and we're top heavy with guys. I'm not sure how we're going to do it, but we'll have to lasso some females from somewhere. Incidentally, do you happen to know whether Jake dug up a date or not?'

'Yeah. Didn't he tell you? He's bringing Hilary . . . Hilary Pierce.'

Victor shot him a surprised look. 'I didn't even know she was down here. That's odd!'

'What is?'

347

'Hilary being alone. Mark's very possessive about her. I wouldn't have thought he'd let her out of his sight, never mind take a vacation without him. And I'm sure he's not coming. He's stuck in London editing the film. You know he overshot like crazy, so he's got some solid hours of editing ahead of him. Know where Hilary's staying?'

'She has one of the few rooms at the Chèvre d'Or in Eze, until tomorrow, so Jake told me. Then she's moving into a house in the village. Renting from a friend, I believe. It was Hilly Street's idea. I mean for Jake to bring Hilary. And Hillard is going to escort one of Beau Stanton's house guests. An Hon, no less.'

'What the hell's that?'

Nick burst out laughing. 'An Honourable. You know, the daughter of a something or other – a lord, I think. She's the Honourable Miss Pandora Tremaine, and beautiful, according to Hilly, who is so impressed that he's squiring a young debutante he actually stutters when he mentions her name.'

'Nancy's going to be impressed too, when she finds out he's running around with young girls. Jesus, I wouldn't like to be in Hilly's shoes, an Hon or not,' Victor said sardonically. His eyes flashed with merriment as he sat contemplating Hilly's domineering and shrewish wife, currently in California house-hunting. 'Well, at least we've got two extra women, more than I'd hoped for, and if Beau brings his own date that'll help even – '

'I heard he's planning to bring the mother of the Hon who's also staying at the Cap d'Antibes villa. Her name's Alicia, and she's just recently divorced from Pandora's father.'

'Jesus, Nicky, you're a regular Louella-Hedda rolled into one,' Victor said, shaking his head. 'I'd like to know where the hell you dig up all your information.'

'I have the kind of face that makes everyone confide in me,' Nick said. 'And while we're on the subject of female journalists, I bumped into Estelle Morgan earlier in the lobby. She told me she's staying at the Hôtel de Paris in Monte. I thought you'd like to know, in case you're still planning to invite her to the wing-ding.'

'I guess I have to, Nick,' Victor responded swiftly. 'I know you're not crazy about her, and she is a strange bird, I'll grant you that. But she has written a helluva lot of stories about the film, and she did some fabulous pieces on Katharine and Terry Ogden. I'd look like a real louse if I left her out. It's no secret I've invited practically everybody we know who's currently in this neck of the woods, so she's bound to hear about the bash.' He pursed his lips, nodded thoughtfully. 'Yes, I'm going to invite her, it would be unkind, even cruel, not to.'

'You're absolutely right, Vic,' Nick agreed. 'You can't ignore her. Anyway, Estelle's not so bad, and basically she's harmless.'

This comment took Victor aback, and he said slowly, wonderingly, 'My God, you're sounding mellow all of a sudden. To what do we owe this curious change of heart? Don't tell me, I know. *Diana*. It's her gentle influence on you, I've no doubt.' Victor smiled, glanced across at Nick with affection, studied him closely. He was delighted he was in such good spirits, a happy frame of mind, and top physical form. The lean boyish face was tanned, rested, the tension wiped off it, and the blue eyes sparkled, were no longer shadowed by sadness. Nick had also put on weight. Not a lot, but enough to give his tall, spare frame more solidity. Victor exclaimed, 'You're looking *great*, kid! The best I've seen you since you came back from New York. No, let me correct myself. In years.'

'Yes, I know.' Before he could prevent himself, Nick confessed. 'Diana is a terrific girl. I'm hooked, Vic. Really and truly hooked.'

Victor merely nodded, said nothing. Nick saw a hint of amusement in his black eyes, a perceptive smile surfacing. He cried, with unusual fervency, 'This isn't a passing fancy, Victor. I'm really serious about Diana.'

'*Serious* serious, Nicholas?' Victor asked, his attention centred on his friend.

'Yes. I'll tell you this too, she's the first woman I've ever wanted to marry . . . how do you like them apples, old buddy?' Nick waited, his eyes pinned on Victor, who was now staring at him in stupefaction. 'Well, say something, maestro.'

'Have you asked her?' Victor replied at last, his voice curiously quiet, his eyes subdued.

'No, not yet. And I don't plan to for a while, so this conversation is strictly *entre nous. Capisce?*'

Victor stood up. 'How about a drink? It's that hour of the day, and we've plenty of time before we dress for dinner.'

'Sure, why not,' Nick assented. 'Make mine a vodka and tonic, please.'

'It'll have to be a warm one, I've just remembered there's no ice,' Victor told him and poured the drinks at the small bar.

'I don't care. But call room service and order a bucket now, so we have it for later.'

Victor lifted the telephone and did as Nick suggested, then returned to his chair, handed Nick the drink. He said, 'Down the hatch, kid.'

'Cheers.' Nick took one swallow and then put the glass down on the table slowly. He had suddenly noticed the change in Vic's demeanour. 'Okay, let's have it,' Nick demanded softly. 'I know from the peculiar expression on your face that you've got something important on your mind. I also have a lousy feeling it's something I'm not going to like when I hear it.'

'No, no, you're wrong, Nicky!' Victor exclaimed, but his sharp denial held no conviction, and try as he might he could not erase the sombreness Nick had detected in him. He too leaned closer, and clearing his throat, he finished quietly, 'You and I had better have a serious talk. Man to man.'

'Shoot.' Nick felt his body stiffening, and he realized he was filled with alarm.

CHAPTER THIRTY-THREE

David Cunningham stood on the threshold of the french doors opening onto the terrace regarding Doris, the look on his face one that truly signified his adoration.

She sat at the circular table, shaded from the intense mid-morning sun by a large blue umbrella, her head bent in concentration on the papers spread out before her. She wore a strapless sundress of light cotton, its white ground patterned with tiny primroses, and her striking auburn hair was covered by a wide-brimmed picture hat of pale yellow leghorn. As he watched her, unobserved, he thought how girlish and lovely she looked, a charming portrait indeed, and his heart expanded with love for her.

Stepping forward, David said, 'You're very industrious, my darling, and so absorbed I hate to disturb you.'

Doris lifted her head swiftly, her face lighting up when she saw him approaching, and her voice vibrated with happiness as she said, 'I'm just finishing a few last-minute invitations to the dance. Then I'm going to take a deep breath and start on the place cards.'

He sat down next to her and took her hand in his, smiling into her welcoming face. 'I thought the girls were going to help you with this task. I do hope they haven't reneged on their promise. Where are they?'

'Taking a swim, darling, and no, they haven't broken their word. They'll be up shortly to give me a hand. And I don't mind doing some of the work myself for the time being. It's almost too hot for anything else, except floating in the pool perhaps.'

'So it is. I see you're taking more than adequate protection from the sun this morning,' he teased gently, loving her, his eyes roving over her appreciatively.

'It's imperative that I do. I'm turning into one huge freckle! If I'm not careful I'm going to look blotchy and ugly for the dance.'

'Hardly possible, my dear,' he laughed, reaching out and squeezing her hand.

'You've been gone for ages. What have you been doing since breakfast?'

'Reading the English newspapers and the *Herald Tribune*.' He grimaced, his face growing serious. 'The Suez situation is really rather grave, you know. It's a pity Nasser boycotted the London Conference on Suez last week, and rejected the American proposals for future international use of the Canal. Nationalizing it is one thing, but restricting world shipping traffic is quite another. *Inflammatory* is the only word for that action.'

'Yes, I see what you mean.' Doris responded, sitting back in the chair. 'What do you think is going to happen, David?'

He shook his head. 'I honestly can't hazard a guess. But I sincerely hope it doesn't mean war.'

'My God, *could* it go that far?' she asked, staring at him askance.

'Very easily, I'm afraid, Doris. Anthony Eden might well decide to invade Egypt. I wouldn't put it past him. And right now he does have the backing of the French and the Americans.'

'A *war*. Oh David!'

'Yes, it is a frightening prospect, but you mustn't worry your head about it, my darling. There's very little we can do. We simply have to leave it to the politicians, and pray it doesn't come to pass. A bit of adroit diplomacy has been known to work wonders. I hope the crisis will blow over without any skirmishes.' He gave her a reassuring smile, said firmly, 'Come along, Doris, don't look so gloomy. We can't let the political situation ruin our summer. I'm beginning to wish I hadn't brought it up.'

Doris summoned a more cheerful demeanour at once and said lightly, 'Don't be silly, and I would have seen the newspapers later anyway. But you're right, of course, we mustn't let problems beyond our control intrude. What are your plans today, darling?'

'I've decided to take Kim and Christian into Monte Carlo after all. We have a little shopping to do. Afterwards, we're going to Bunky Ampher's for lunch.'

'*Bunky Ampher's*. Is that a restaurant or a person?'

'A person,' David chuckled. 'He's the tall, heavyset fellow I introduced to you at the Sporting Club in Monte Carlo on Saturday evening. We were chatting to him for a while, don't you remember?'

'Oh yes, now I recall him. Perhaps I didn't catch his name, or I misheard it. *Bunky*.' She pursed her lips. 'That just has to be a nickname.'

'But of course. From our school days. We were at Harrow together. Splendid chap. In any event, Bunky rang up a short while ago and extended a most cordial invitation. He wants us to join him and an American friend by the name of Nelson Avery, a banker, I believe. I accepted, darling, since you said earlier you wanted to spend a restful day here. You don't mind, do you?'

'No, David. You'll enjoy it. So will the boys, and it'll be nice for me to spend a few hours with Frankie and Diana. I hardly seem to see them, they're so frenetic, rushing all over the place.'

'The mere *thought* of their social life exhausts me,' David said. 'I'm beginning to think those two never sleep. Anyway, we shan't be late. Lunch is at one-thirty, so we ought to be back around three-thirty, four at the latest. Bunky's villa is quite close by, on the shoulder of the mountainside above Roquebrune, a lovely place. He asked us all to go up for drinks with them on Sunday, late afternoon, and I accepted.' The Earl leaned forward, eagerness filling his eyes, and went on, 'In September Bunky plans to give a very special luncheon for our greatest and most illustrious Harrovian. He would like us to attend, if we're here.'

Sensing his sudden excitement, Doris asked curiously, 'Who is the lunch for, darling?'

'Why Sir Winston, of course. He sometimes stays with friends of Bunky's in Roquebrune, and he's rather partial to Bunky's gardens. Likes to paint them, you know.'

'Oh how marvellous. I'd love to meet him, David. But I think I shall be scared stiff. Heavens to Betsy, Winston Churchill!'

351

'I know what you mean,' David acknowledged with an understanding smile. 'I'm a little intimidated myself. And it's quite an honour to be included, my dear.' He rose, touched her shoulder lightly. 'In the meantime, I think I'd better go and chivvy Kim and Christian.'

'David, perhaps we should ask your friend Bunky to the dance.'

'Oh but we did, Doodles,' he exclaimed. He moved closer, leaned over her shoulder, rustled through the papers on the table, searching for the guest list. He found it, ran a finger down the names. 'Ah yes, here it is . . . Earl Winterton, and the Countess.'

Doris cocked her head around to look at him, her vivid green eyes crinkling with merriment. 'No wonder I didn't recognize the name Bunky Ampher. Sometimes I wonder about you, Your Lordship. I swear to God you do certain things just to confuse me!'

'I wouldn't do that to my lady love.' He bent forward and kissed her on the lips, stroking her face. 'You're very very special to me, my lovely Doris. I do adore you so,' he murmured against her cheek.

'The feeling is mutual, my darling.' She gazed at him with the same entrancement he was levelling at her. As always, he looked elegant and distinguished, but also undeniably boyish at this moment. It's his suntan, the casual summer clothes, Doris thought, taking in the white gabardine slacks, the crisp blue and white checked cotton shirt, open at the neck and worn with a pale-blue silk cravat. 'You do look handsome this morning, David. Quite the most marvellous thing I've seen on two legs lately. *Ever*, to be exact.'

His laughter reverberated around the terrace. 'You do say the nicest things to a chap, Doris. I'm getting a swollen head with all your compliments. Never had so many in my life – from anyone. Perhaps that's the *real* reason I love you,' he joked.

'It has been said of me that I'm the flatterer incarnate,' Doris rejoined, her tone soft. She regarded him carefully.

'Ah, but compliments are usually greatly appreciated by the recipient, and don't forget, flattery is supposed to get you everywhere.'

'That's what my friend meant, I suppose, when she pinned the label on me. Obviously she was being disparaging, suggesting my flattery was self-serving and fraudulent,' Doris responded with a tiny wry smile. 'But it isn't.'

A sober look settled on David's face, and he lowered his voice. 'One should never pay attention to the things people say about one, Doris. I have schooled myself to ignore that brand of backbiting, and so must you.'

Doris picked up something in his tone, and she pondered momentarily, frowning. 'So you've heard it too – the comment about me marrying you for your title?' Her eyes held his.

'Naturally. That sort of offensive statement always gets back to one.' He shrugged with nonchalance, but a sardonic expression tugged at his fine mouth. 'And there are those who say I'm marrying *you* for your great fortune.' He put his arm around her lovingly and asserted with some feeling, 'I am marrying you for *you*, my darling, because I love you, and I know, without a shadow of a doubt, that you are marrying me for the same reason. Friends who make derisive remarks behind our backs are most definitely not our friends. Furthermore, they are to be treated with the disdain they deserve. We must always rise above that sort of nastiness, Doris. Never forget, much of this kind of talk is engendered by envy and jealousy. Gossip! I *loathe* it. Thoughtless, malicious chatter is so destructive, has ruined more people's lives than I care to think about. But we're not going to let it affect us, are we, my sweet?'

'You bet we're not,' she cried with a jaunty laugh. 'And you are the dearest, sweetest man in the whole world. We are going to be happy, aren't we, David?'

He made no response, but his smile, the love in his eyes were confirmation enough. David kissed her, lingering over his kiss. 'By the way, did you get a chance to say anything to Francesca after breakfast?' His voice had dropped to a blurred monotone, and the tense way he held his body denoted his anxiousness.

'No.' Doris's face tightened with concern, and she explained slowly, 'I guess I lost my nerve. But apart from that, Diana was present, and I didn't want to broach it in front of her. Actually, that's been the main problem since *our* discussion on Tuesday evening. I can never get Frankie alone. There's always someone around, Kim, Christian or guests. It's such an awkward subject, and I don't want to create an untenable situation. I've been thinking . . . perhaps it might be wiser to wait until after the –' Doris gave David a warning look, raised her hand in greeting.

Christian said, 'Am I interrupting?'

David half turned to face his nephew. 'No, no, old chap, not at all.'

Wheeling himself over to join them, Christian came to a stop next to Doris's chair. He lifted her hand to his lips, kissed it graciously, sat beaming at her, his dark eyes glowing and alert, his expression uncommonly sunny. 'My Lord, Doris darling, you *are* true to your word, and most diligent. I really didn't take you seriously when you said you were going to tackle paperwork today. It's awfully brave of you to toil in this heat.'

'Oh it's not so bad, Christian. You should try Oklahoma City at the height of the summer. It's twice as hot. A furnace,' Doris laughed, giving him the benefit of the warmest and tenderest of looks. He touched her in so many ways, and on so many levels, with his old-fashioned gallantry, his charming manners and, not the least, his immense courage. He also had a tremendous sense of humour and the most positive approach to life she had ever come across in a human being. She marvelled constantly at this young man's total lack of self-pity, his determination to lead as normal a life as possible, this despite his disablement. No, not despite it, but *because* of his condition, Doris now thought, sudden comprehension telling her that this stoicism was generated by an immense will to overcome physical handicap.

Kim bounded onto the terrace, a wide grin spreading across his face. 'I see the clan has gathered!' he cried. 'And sorry to have kept you waiting, Dad, Christian.' He eyed Doris, went on, 'I say, you do look fetching, old thing. Absolutely scrumptious, Doodles.' He stepped back, his eyes running over her admiringly, and pronounced, 'A Renoir painting.'

'Why thank you, Kim.'

David remarked, with a dry chuckle. 'Flattery does seem to be in the air this morning, doesn't it. Bushels of it. Well, you two young bucks, let's get off. We've rather a lot to do and I don't want to be late for Bunky's lunch.'

'Enjoy yourselves.' Her eyes followed them as they left the terrace. How attractive they were, and warm and generous natured, and so caring in their individual ways. Doris had long since recognized that she was fortunate, indeed blessed, to be marrying into this family, and as the only child of an only child she revelled in

353

the sense of belonging they imparted, in being one of them. She considered their nickname for her, and a faint smile touched her eyes. She had never had a nickname before. Kim had started it, at first calling her Dodo, and then Doodles. The latter had stuck, and the name meant a lot to her, for it was a symbol of their complete acceptance and their deepest affection.

After a few seconds Doris got up and walked to the end of the terrace, which commanded a sensational view of the swimming pool, the tennis court, and the Mediterranean shimmering like a glassy and placid sapphire lake in the distance. Shading her eyes with her hand, she scanned the pool area immediately below her, saw that it was deserted. She returned to the chair, picked up her pen, finished the last of the last-minute invitations.

Suddenly Francesca appeared at the top of the steps leading up from the gardens, instantly followed by Diana. 'Coo-ee!' Francesca cried, waving.

Doris waved in return, thinking how enchanting the cousins looked in their colourful bikinis, their sun-browned bodies glistening with drops of water, their damp tresses pulled back into pony tails tied with bright ribbons: summer sprites, golden and glorious in their youthful beauty, full of joyousness and lighthearted gaiety, hands linked, laughter on their lips, faces wreathed in smiles as they tripped towards her.

Francesca kissed Doris on the cheek, slipped into a chair and said, 'Have the Three Musketeers gone adventuring then?'

'Yes, darling, you just missed them,' Doris replied. 'I'm afraid you'll have to settle for my company for the rest of the day. They've been invited out to lunch, and won't be back until late this afternoon.'

'Oh how lovely to be alone, just the three of us,' Diana declared, also sitting down. 'It's a welcome change not to have the men under our feet. We can have a jolly nice chat about all those feminine things they seem to think are inconsequential and frivolous ... such as what we're going to wear to Victor's party tomorrow night, and to the dance next week. Maybe you'll even tell us about your wedding outfit, Doris.'

Doris nodded, and smiled, and before she could respond, Francesca broke in curiously. 'Who's asked them to lunch, Doodles?'

'Bunky Ampher,' said Doris.

'Gosh, I didn't know *they* were on the Riviera. Did Daddy say if Belinda, their daughter, is with them?'

'No, he didn't, and we'd better make a point of asking him later. If she is with her parents, she should be invited to the dance, since Earl and Countess Winterton are coming.'

'Oh yes, you must ask Bel, Doris, she's a really super girl. Very special actually. A frightfully good sport too. She had to take an awful lot of ragging at Madame Rosokovsky's dancing classes. Poor thing, she was horrendously fat then. A lot of the girls used to call her Belly Bunter, after Billy Bunter. I thought it –'

'How unkind,' Doris cried.

'Yes, it was. Children *can* be very cruel. Belinda took it in her stride; still, *I* knew she was miserable. I befriended her, and they stopped. But then they started to call us Tweedle Dum and Tweedle Dee.' Francesca wrinkled her nose, giggled. 'Old Bel had the last laugh on those nasty little wretches. She turned into a raving beauty with a model girl's figure. She'll be an asset at the dance, Doodles, since you have such a lot of spare bods.'

Doris nodded absently, thinking how typical it was of the tender-hearted Francesca to defend and protect the underdog. She said, 'Speaking of the dance, we ought to make a start on the place cards. We've about a hundred and seventy-five to do. Here's a list of names each, and there are pens somewhere here.' Doris found them under the papers scattered on the table and lifted an empty shoe box from one of the chairs. 'We can put the finished cards in this.'

Diana, pen poised, cried, 'I bet I can do fifty cards in an hour, Cheska! I'll race you!'

'I'll top you with sixty, Dibs!' Francesca threatened, her head already bent.

As the hour progressed, Doris had to admire their industry and speed and concentration. Their pens flew, neither girl spoke, and the only sound was the rattle of the little cards as they were dropped into the Delman shoe box. Doris was much slower, mostly because her mind kept straying to other more pressing matters, and when, at one moment, she paused to peek at her watch, she saw they had been working for almost an hour and a half. She called a halt and said, 'I think we've had it for today, don't you?'

'Yes, I'm getting cramp.' Diana put down the pen, counted the names she had ticked off on her list, announced gleefully. 'Aha, I've done fifty-five!'

Francesca, who had followed suit, cried with a triumphant laugh, 'I win, Dibsido! I've done sixty-five!'

'To my puny forty,' Doris groaned. She stretched and remarked, 'We have accomplished a lot though. I noticed Yves bring out the drinks cart earlier. In my opinion we've earned a glass of bubbly before lunch.' She rose and went to open the bottle of champagne. Francesca and Diana drifted after her, giggling between themselves.

The three of them talked about a variety of things whilst they sipped their glasses of Dom Pérignon, relaxing, enjoying the glorious sunshine, the magnificent panoramic view from the terrace. It was Diana who finally brought the conversation around to the impending wedding. She leaned towards Doris and said, 'Don't be secretive any longer, darling. Do tell us what you're going to wear at your marriage. We're dying to know.'

'I'm not sure yet,' Doris said quite truthfully. 'But it will be by Balmain. I'm planning to go to Paris at the end of the summer to talk to my friend Ginette Spanier, his *directrice*. She always advises me on my clothes, and I know Pierre will come up with something really special. I thought a suit would be elegant, or perhaps a dress with a matching cape, possibly trimmed with fur. I'd like your bridesmaid's outfits to be designed by Pierre too, and they will be my gifts to you both.'

'Gosh, Doris, how generous of you! Do you really mean it?' Francesca was flabbergasted, but delightedly so, and she gazed at Doris through shining eyes.

'Yes, of course I mean it. I think my beautiful attendants should have the very best.'

Diana said. 'What a lovely gesture, Doris. I've always dreamed of owning a Balmain. Thank you.'

'Yes, thanks, Doodles. And shall we be coming to Paris with you? I mean, we'll have to, won't we?' Francesca stated.

Doris smiled warmly. Their youthful enthusiasm was infectious and she went on to exclaim, 'What else! We'll make it a fun trip, spend a few days, see the sights. And naturally you'll both be my guests.'

Both girls thanked her again, and most profusely. Francesca made a small moue and said, 'It's such a pity Katharine can't be a bridesmaid as well, isn't it?'

'Yes,' Doris murmured in her quietest tone and, averting her face, she poured more champagne into their flutes.

Diana, glancing across at Francesca with interest, asked, 'When is she arriving at Zamir, by the way? I can't remember what Kim said.'

'Tomorrow afternoon, and about time too,' Francesca cried, her voice bright with happiness. She then volunteered, 'I've missed her, and I'm delighted she'll be here for the party at Le Pirate. It wouldn't be the same without darling Kath. I expect she's thoroughly exhausted and I'm going to make sure she has a rest whilst she's here. That girl works like a little Trojan, and I certainly don't envy her . . . having to deal with those film moguls. They're so demanding.'

Neither of the women commented, and Francesca rushed on blithely, 'Getting back to the wedding, Doodles, I do hope Daddy will invite Mrs Moggs. When I asked him if he would he gave me the oddest of looks. But after all, she does fall into the category of family retainers. Well, sort of . . . and he is having *everyone* from the estate and the village. It will be mean if he doesn't include her, and I shall tell him so.'

Doris and Diana exchanged amused looks, and both started to laugh. Diana gasped, 'I hope you're going to make a new hat for her, Cheska.'

'That's a super idea. I must come up with a really chic bit of nonsense. She adores my concoctions.'

'Ah, but does Uncle David?'

'Oh, Daddy! What does he know about women's clothes,' Francesca pooh-poohed airily, but she had the good grace to laugh.

'Quite a lot,' replied Doris, smiling at her fondly. 'And since it's so important to you, I shall insist that Mrs Moggs receives an invitation.'

'Why didn't you let me know you were coming a day early, Katharine?' Kim asked, hovering uncertainly in the middle of the sun room.

'Then it wouldn't have been a surprise, would it, darling?'

'I suppose not,' he agreed quietly, nonetheless wishing she *had* seen fit to telephone him first. She had been waiting at the villa when he had returned with his father and Christian from lunch with the Amphers, and her unexpected presence had thrown him off balance.

Katharine studied him closely, trying to determine his mood, asking herself if she had made a *faux pas*. Did the English consider it bad form for a person to arrive sooner than planned, and unannounced? No, that was absurd. Francesca had welcomed her excitedly and with enthusiasm an hour before.

'Well, aren't you glad I managed to get away today?' she queried, her magnificent turquoise eyes suddenly flirtatious and teasing.

'Yes.' His eyes rested on her. She was sitting on a small wicker sofa, her face partially shadowed by the giant-sized green leaves of an exotic plant positioned next to it. He thought how delicate she appeared, even frail, in the navy blue linen dress which was tailored and severe, its plainness unrelieved by any adornment. She leaned forward with suddenness, and her face, struck by the sunshine pouring through the windows, was unbelievable in this golden late-afternoon light.

Her beauty, so sublime, so splendiferous, knocked the breath out of him, and he could not take his eyes off her, was held in fascination and beguilement. Eventually he did look away, staring into the space immediately above her dark head, blinking, trying to rid himself of her enchanting – and disturbing – image. After a moment's reflection, Kim roused himself and stepped up to the seating arrangement. He sat down opposite Katharine and his scrutiny became fixed again, and unwavering.

'Why did you lie to me?' he asked in an oddly flat, unemotional voice.

Katharine gaped at him, astounded, and she shook her head, seemed not to comprehend his accusation.

He repeated. 'Why did you lie to me . . . *Katie Mary O'Rourke?*'

She sucked in her breath with a small shocked gasp, fell against the sofa jerkily as if she had been pushed. Her radiance diminished and the animation fled her eyes. She was paralysed, unable to speak.

'That is your *real* name, isn't it?' Kim challenged, his voice soft, but dangerously so.

Still she did not respond, and he went on rapidly, 'Your silence confirms it. I want to know why you lied to me.' He leaned forward and his eyes revealed his cold anger. He was being relentless and this sickened him, yet he could not help himself. He had to know the truth.

'I am waiting for an answer. I demand an answer!'

Katharine clasped her hands together to control their trembling. 'I didn't actually lie to you, Kim,' she whispered finally. 'I simply didn't tell you my real name. I haven't told anybody my –'

'I'm not *anybody*,' he snapped, furious. 'I am your fiancé, albeit unofficially. I proposed to you, and you accepted me. You agreed to become my *wife*. Or had you forgotten that? It would have behoved you to confide in me at that time. Why didn't you?'

She said nervously, 'I didn't think it was very important.'

Kim stared at her incredulously. 'Not *important*. Good God, what strange concepts you do have. We have established your real name –' He shook his head in perplexity, peered at her. 'People who change their names usually have something to hide. What prompted *you*, what do *you* wish to conceal?'

'Nothing!' she protested fiercely. 'I simply dropped O'Rourke and started to use Tempest when I enrolled at RADA. I thought Tempest sounded more glamorous, that it had a lovely theatrical ring to it.' Katharine was managing to regain a measure of her self-possession; a suggestion of a smile flickered. She brought a lightness to her tone. 'It's not unusual for an actress to use a stage name, Kim. In fact, that's a common practice in Hollywood. Lots of stars adopt new names.'

'So I believe. Nevertheless, you seem to be missing the real point. You are going to be my wife . . . Viscountess Ingleton. One day you will be the 12th Countess of Langley, and that in itself is quite a responsibility. It seems to have escaped you that there can be no mystery, or suggestion of impropriety, surrounding the woman I marry. I therefore consider it irresponsible, and unforgivable, that you saw no reason to be direct, honest with *me*. I wonder, did you intend ever to apprise me of the truth? Or were you going to hide it from me for ever, gambling I might never find out?'

'Oh come on, Kim,' Katharine exclaimed, staring at him. Aware that she could twist him around her little finger, she felt she could thus slither out of the corner she was backed into – if she was adroit. 'Anyone would think I'm a murderer, concealing my crime, the way you're carrying on. And of course I would have told you. I had every int –'

'Were you also going to tell me you're not an orphan?' he countered, his eyes blazing. 'As you have pretended to me since we've known each other.' The look he now gave her was full of condemnation and, not waiting for an answer, he cried irately, 'However you excuse your deceitfulness about your name, you cannot, I repeat *cannot*, deny that you lied to me about your family circumstances, and in the most deliberate way. Tell me, Katharine, how is it possible for you to be an orphan when you have a father?' His voice simmered with rage. 'You really have behaved in the most deplorable manner towards me, and frankly I'm appalled. But apart from being shaken and shocked by your duplicity, I'm terribly, terribly hurt. *My* feelings aside, you've also abused my sister's loving friendship and my father's many kindnesses. I don't mind telling you, *he* is horrified. In our lexicon, liars are despicable, Katharine,' he concluded. He lit a cigarette, his hands shaking.

Katharine was ice cold, her stomach muscles taut and knotted. *She had lost her advantage.* However, she was nothing if not shrewd and quick witted and she recognized at once that to be cringing, apologetic and defensive would only weaken her position further, would compound her guilt. And so she went on the attack.

She drew herself up on the sofa, stiffly, and with a degree of regality. She said, with a cool superiority, 'I think I detect Doris's hand in this. Spying on a person! Prying into her private affairs! How contemptible! I'm surprised your father doesn't find that kind of . . . of . . . *questionable* activity perfectly reprehensible. I do. *Doris* is the one to be censured, not *I*.'

Kim felt the heat flooding into his face and he cried excitedly, 'Doris most certainly did not make inquiries about you. She's far too sweet and decent to engage in something so lowdown as spying. The information fell into her lap quite by accident –'

'So I am right! I *knew* it.' This was said with a flash of triumph, a show of bravado, both false in that Katharine was still somewhat unnerved and groping her way. 'Let me tell you something else, Kim. I believe you're wrong. I am convinced Doris went out of her way to investigate my life in Chicago. She was trying to dig up dirt on me. Well, I don't care, because there isn't any dirt to dig up. I don't have anything to hide, as I just told you. There are no skeletons in *my* closet.'

'I'm not sure what that last crack is supposed to mean, and I'm not going to dignify it with a response.' Kim glared at her again, his brow furrowing. 'Do you deny that you have a father who is living in Chicago?'

'No. It's true. I had my reasons for doing what I did, and I was going to explain everything to you this weekend, although I concede you may doubt that now.' Katharine shrugged and a derisive smile rippled across her pretty mouth, making it ugly. 'I don't have to tell you anything, it seems. Doris, the master spy, has saved me the trouble. Let her do some more of her filthy digging, and give you another report.'

Kim intensified his stare, indignant, his blood boiling. He curbed the impulse to reach out and shake her. His mouth tightened in aggravation, and he fumbled in his trouser pocket, pulled out a crumpled envelope. 'I will not permit you to place the blame on Doris when she is guiltless. It just so happens that some weeks ago, when she was in Monte Carlo shopping, she ran into an old acquaintance from Chicago. In passing, Doris mentioned your name, said you were seeing me. It was an innocuous comment, made along with a number of other remarks about her own life at the moment. The other day, Doris received this letter from the woman, with a clipping from a local newspaper. It's a story about you, with photographs of you taken at Langley Castle. When you were filming there. Here's the letter. Please read it.'

Katharine sat back on the sofa, her hands clenched in her lap, her face obstinate, her eyes defiant. 'I don't want to read it.'

'Then I shall read it for you,' Kim snapped, enraged by her cavalier attitude, her seeming indifference. He took the letter out of the envelope. He knew the whole epistle by heart, had no trouble finding the relevant paragraph.

'This is what the friend of Doris writes:

"I saw the enclosed interview with Katharine Tempest in the magazine section of Sunday's *Chicago Tribune*. I recognized her at once. We knew her as Katie Mary O'Rourke. Janet and she attended the same convent. Small world, isn't it? We've often wondered what happened to her. She disappeared from Chicago so suddenly and abruptly it's been quite a mystery for years. All very strange! We don't know her father, who is apparently unapproachable on the subject of his daughter. Of course we're delighted to know she is all right after all, and so successful. Do remember us to her."'

'The rest of the letter is of no interest to us, Katharine, merely chit-chat about social activities in Chicago.' Kim stuffed the letter back into the envelope and shoved it in his pocket. He placed the clipping on the table in front of her. 'You might like to read this later. Estelle Morgan has done you proud, written a glowing account of your talent.'

Katharine was silent, filled with embarrassment and mortification because her deception had been unmasked before she could reveal it herself. How foolish she had been. She *should* have confided in Kim weeks ago. At that time she had planned to tell her story in a way that would have gained his sympathy, understanding and support; by waiting she had brought his wrath down on her.

Kim expected a statement, some kind of response, and when none was offered he rose and walked to the window. He stared out at the sea blindly. Since his return from Grasse earlier in the week, and his talk with Doris and his father, he had been suppressing his anger and so many other emotions. The letter from Chicago had knocked the wind out of his sails. Not only that, he had been forced to dissemble, to keep up a lighthearted front for Francesca, his cousins, their innumerable guests. Dissimulation, not a natural Cunningham characteristic, had depleted him and he felt drained. Curiously though, now that he had confronted Katharine his rage had lessened. A calm was settling over him.

He returned to the chair, sat brooding for a while, his shoulders hunched, his refined face without expression. At last he directed his gaze on her. 'I'd like to ask you something, Katharine.'

She nodded, bracing herself.

'You're intelligent. How on earth did you think you could conceal your true identity in view of your burgeoning career in films? Surely you knew you'd be recognized by someone, that the truth would inevitably come out?'

'Yes, I did,' she admitted. 'I've been wanting to tell you for the longest time.'

'Then why didn't you?'

'I was waiting for the right opportunity. I've been so preoccupied with my work . . .' Her voice had dropped to a whisper and it ceased entirely. She twisted her hands, cleared her throat, added in a stronger tone, 'Don't forget, I was under a lot of pressure when we were shooting in Yorkshire, and when I went back to London you had to stay at Langley because your father was here with Doris. We've hardly seen each other lately. It seemed better to wait until we were on vacation . . .'

'If only you *had* told me before,' he sighed. For a moment Kim was introspective and then he murmured, 'There's so much more to love than love itself, Katharine. There must be trust and friendship, especially between two people who are going to marry, who plan to spend the rest of their lives together. By not confiding in me you have violated that trust, Katharine.'

Softly spoken though these words were, and gently couched, the reproach cut through her like a knife. She looked at him forlornly, her defences down, her huge eyes aquamarine pools in her ashen face and glistening with incipient tears.

He said urgently, 'Don't cry, for God's sake don't cry. I can't stand your tears.'

'No,' she said, swallowing hard. She reached for a cigarette in the white onyx box, lighting it before he could do it for her. She smoked in silence, avoiding his eyes, her misery running deep.

'Like my father, I believe that liars are basically untrustworthy, and on so many different levels,' Kim began and leaned in closer to her. 'Look at me, Katharine,' he commanded. She did as he asked, and he continued, 'Generally speaking, one lie begets another lie, and another, and so on. Inevitably lying becomes a way of life. There is no place in our family for someone who cannot speak the truth, no matter what the consequences of absolute candour might be. Lying is cheating, you see, and cheating is dishonourable. When you were at Langley you spent a long time looking at our armorial bearings in the stone hall, asked a great deal about our family crest. Do you remember our family motto?'

'Yes,' Katharine gulped. Kim said no more, sat watching her, and she knew instinctively that he wished her to say the few brief words that composed their ancient motto. Taking a deep breath, she said softly, '*Au dessus tout: Honneur.*'

Kim nodded, his light eyes compelling in their intensity. 'And I told you what those words meant . . . *Honour above all*. Since the days of the great warrior knights of Langley every Cunningham has lived by that motto. It is our code of behaviour.' His face became softer, gentler now. 'There's a poem by Richard Lovelace to which I'm rather partial, and my favourite lines are these: "I could not love thee, dear, so much, loved I not honour more." I think that simple sentence articulates what I am all about as a man.' Kim fell into silence and then he shook his head slowly, sadly, adding at last, 'Oh Katharine, Katharine, why didn't you trust in our love, have faith enough in me to tell me the truth about yourself? Don't you realize what you've done?'

She stared at him speechlessly.

'You've placed us both in the most precarious position with my father.'

She heard the desperation in his voice. 'Yes,' she whispered. 'I suppose I have. Kim, I want to tell you everything. Perhaps then you'll understand, and not judge me so harshly. Please, please let me explain.' Her face, so young and tender and earnest, beseeched him. He nodded, and Katharine went on, 'You see, the whole situation developed because –' She said no more, turned to look at the glass door.

Voices penetrated from the terrace. The door flew open. Francesca dashed into the room as though propelled by a whirlwind, followed, in a more sedate fashion, by the Earl and Doris, who each had a glass of champagne in their hands.

'There you are, Kim. Oh good, you've found Kath,' Francesca called gaily. She was halfway across the floor when she came to a sudden halt, staring at them both with a worried frown. 'My God, whatever's the matter? You both look so upset.'

Startled by this abrupt intrusion, neither Kim nor Katharine spoke. Francesca hurried forward anxiously, peering at the two of them more closely. Her concentration was on Katharine, sitting so still in the chair, white-faced and obviously distressed, her hands fidgeting nervously in her lap. Francesca perceived controlled agitation, felt a sudden uneasiness engendered by her manner. Pivoting on her bare feet to face Kim, his sister cried heatedly. 'What's happened? Tell me!'

Kim was mute. The Earl cleared his throat, walked rapidly to Francesca's side. 'Hello, Katharine,' he said in a voice curiously devoid of expression.

She inclined her head without meeting his eyes, said nothing.

David continued. 'My apologies for bursting in on you so unceremoniously. We weren't aware you and Kim were in the sun room. We'll leave you to finish your discussion.' He took hold of Francesca's arm firmly. 'Come along, my dear.'

Francesca resisted his pressure. 'But what's wrong?' she persisted, her voice rising. 'I want to –'

'No! Please don't go!' Katharine exclaimed, also adopting a fervent tone as she found her voice at last. 'I would like you to hear what I have to say to Kim, what I was about to tell him when you walked in, David. I want Francesca to hear it as well.' She cast a swift look in Doris's direction. 'And you too, Doris. This concerns you, as much as everyone else.'

'If you wish it, Katharine,' Doris turned to close the terrace door, came to join them.

Francesca threw Katharine a questioning look, took the chair adjacent to Kim's, sat facing her friend. Katharine did not seem prepared to enlighten her further, and so she eyed her brother keenly. He was equally uncommunicative, his face closed and unreadable.

Once Doris and David had seated themselves together on the other small sofa within the spacious seating arrangement, Katharine addressed Francesca in a low voice tight with emotion: 'I did something terrible, Frankie, really terrible, perhaps even truly unforgivable. I lied to Kim. And to you, too. To everyone. It was wrong of me, and I see that now –' She paused dramatically, bit her lip, blinked, bravely fighting back her tears.

She lowered her head, looked at her hands and exhaled softly. Finally, her head came up. 'Doris found out about my lies. Quite by accident, of course, and in a way I'm glad she did,' said Katharine, deeming diplomacy the smartest stratagem.

'Naturally Doris felt compelled to inform your father and Kim, and I do understand why. She had no choice. Kim has just confronted me, and I was about to give him a full explanation when you walked in.'

Consternation flashed across Francesca's face. 'What did you lie about, Kath?' she asked with the utmost gentleness, comprehending the other girl's discomfort and unhappiness, hoping to make Katharine feel more relaxed. But despite her tone, Francesca was exceedingly alarmed by this disturbing disclosure, for lying was tantamount to a crime in her family, whose standards of integrity and rectitude were stringent. No wonder the atmosphere was deadly, charged and reeking with tension.

Swiftly, in a sudden rush of words, Katharine recounted how she had adopted the name Tempest and gave her reasons for doing so, continuing to direct her words at Francesca, but all the while levelling glances at the Earl and Doris.

At the end of this short recital, as always springing to Katharine's defence, and wishing to smooth things over, Francesca endeavoured to make light of the situation. 'There's nothing really very odd about Katharine taking a new name, Daddy, a stage name.' She smiled winningly. 'I mean, Victor's real name is Vittorio Massonetti, and Nick's great-grandfather changed his name when he emigrated to America. He was a German Jew . . . with some kind of unpronounceable surname.'

'And how do you know these facts, Frankie?' the Earl inquired.

'Nicky and Victor told me.'

'Precisely,' the Earl murmured.

Katharine winced at his implication. Wanting to be done with all this now, she cried, 'And I'm not an orphan, Frankie. My father is alive. His name is Patrick Michael Sean O'Rourke. He's first generation Irish-American, and he lives in Chicago. I also have a brother, Ryan, who is nineteen.' She leaned back against the sofa. The blue-green eyes were startling in their vividness and depth of colour as they darted to Doris. 'I'm sure *you* know of my father. He is chairman of the Taramar Land Development Corporation, the biggest construction company in the Mid-west. He also has vast real-estate holdings . . . I guess he owns half of Chicago, and he's heavily involved in politics, a power in the Chicago Democratic Machine. *Have* you heard of him, Doris?'

'Yes, indeed I have.' Doris was unable to keep the surprise out of her voice. 'But I've not actually had the pleasure of meeting him,' she said as an afterthought, experiencing genuine puzzlement. She could not apprehend the reason for Katharine's prevarication in view of her father's wealth and standing.

Neither could Kim. He said slowly, 'But your father sounds like a prosperous and commendable man, one who is an upstanding member of the community. You obviously don't have anything to be ashamed of, to hide. Whyever did you tell that . . . that . . . silly story about being an orphan? It just doesn't make sense.'

'The reason I said I was an orphan is because I feel like an orphan. In fact, I consider myself to *be* one.' Katharine let the words hang there, paused a beat, then shook her head from side to side with vehemence. 'You're all looking doubtful, but it's true.'

No one uttered a word. They stared at her, the mingled incredulity and perplexity growing more pronounced on their faces. Despite the four pairs of questioning eyes zeroing in on her, she did not flinch, was unperturbed as they carefully measured her. She was accustomed to close scrutiny in her profession. Actresses were always in the spotlight . . . in the centre of the stage . . .

Sadness crept onto Katharine's face, and her eyes grew excessively wistful. She looked beyond these four, her captive audience now, gazing intently at the wall ahead. She had a vision of something extraordinarily lovely, surrounded by a halo of perfect light – her mother's beloved face. Katharine's voice rang out with clarity and purity in the hushed room, was pensive yet underscored by the matchless musicality she had made her very own.

'My mother was a great beauty and a great lady and she loved me very much. No child was ever loved more than I, and we were closer than I can possibly explain. She wanted me to be an actress, just as I wanted it, and she believed in me with all her heart and soul. And I . . . I worshipped her. When I was ten years old she became desperately ill. She died when I was thirteen.' A sob vibrated in Katharine's throat and tears welled. She brushed her hand across her eyes, and went on: 'I was heartbroken, and so terribly alone. My father *hated* me . . . it was because of my brother. Ryan wanted to be a painter, and I encouraged this, as Momma had fostered my creative talent. My father was furious with me. He had decided Ryan was going to become a politician. He drove a wedge between us, believing I had too much influence over my little brother. He separated us, deprived us of each other when we had the greatest need to be together. Ryan was sent away to school in the East, I became a boarder at the convent. When I was sixteen, through my aunt's intervention, my father agreed to send me to boarding school in England. I wanted to get away from Chicago; there was nothing there for me, with my mother in the grave and Ryan beyond my reach. I also knew my father wanted to get rid of me. *For ever.* So I left, and I've never been back. I do not have a family any more.' The flow of words ceased; she waited.

A deeper silence seemed to drift through the room and settle there. None had moved whilst she had been speaking, and still they did not stir. Kim and Francesca had been touched and saddened by her revelations and their quickly exchanged glances conveyed their feelings. But neither had the nerve to volunteer a single word for the time being. Both looked at their father expectantly.

The Earl's face was impassive, told them nothing. When he did speak his patrician voice was soft, kind. 'Hatred is a most harsh and powerful word to use, Katharine. Perhaps it's an exaggeration of your father's feeling for you. Being so young at the time, a child, I'm certain you misunderstood, believed hatred existed when, in all truth, it did not. I cannot comprehend any father harbouring *hatred* for his daughter –'

'He did! He did,' she broke in, her face whiter than ever. 'He still hates me. Hates me, do you hear,' she cried excitedly. She had been the recipient of *his* loathing far too often to doubt it, and the recollection of it sent a tremor through her and her dark lashes glistened with tears.

'Now, now, my dear, don't upset yourself like this.' The Earl was appalled at her passionate outburst, and also concerned for her state of well being. Her agitation was only too apparent, and it struck him how much more highly strung she was than he had previously realized. He stole a surreptitious look at Doris, signalling his distress with his eyes. Doris moved closer to him, placed her hand over his lovingly.

The Earl peered hard at Katharine. 'Are you all right, my dear?'

'I'm fine,' Katharine replied in a more even voice, striving for composure.

Since she did seem visibly calmer, David continued, 'I'm afraid I'm still somewhat baffled, despite the things you have told us about your early life. As Kim pointed out, it's hard to conceive why you would pass yourself off as an orphan. Such unnecessary complications, my dear. How much easier, and more truthful, it would have been if you had simply said you had broken off relations with your father because of a quarrel, and left it at that. None of your friends would have probed too deeply under the circumstances. The English are notoriously uncurious in certain areas and not inclined to be presumptuous. And certainly *we* would have accepted your story completely, indeed been most sympathetic.'

'Perhaps you're right, David,' Katharine acknowledged in a slightly grudging tone. 'But I was very upset and miserable when I started classes at RADA. I had suffered the most terrible shame and embarrassment at boarding school in Sussex – you can't imagine how unhappy I was.' Her lip quivered and the tears brimmed, slid down her cheeks unchecked. 'I was the odd girl out. I was the only one who had to spend holidays at school alone with Matron. I had nowhere else to go,' she whispered, her voice choked. '*He* didn't want me in Chicago, and my Aunt Lucy was not strong, so she couldn't have me either. Nobody ever came to visit me at school, or attended parents' day, or showed up for the school plays and other annual functions. Can't you understand how humiliated I was . . . I didn't have a family who loved me. Not one person who cared. I was unwanted. And very very lonely. It was sheer hell, and I was determined never to go through that painful experience again. So when I enrolled at the Royal Academy I invented a new name, said I was an orphan because I didn't want to have to make excuses, explain why my father and brother stayed away, were not interested in me. I had to do it. I had to protect myself.' The tears were falling profusely and she began to sob heart-brokenly, lifting her slender tapering fingers to her streaming face.

Kim jumped up and joined her on the sofa. He put his arms around her and held her to him. 'Hush, darling,' he said tenderly, rocking her, pressing her face to his chest, one hand stroking her hair. He did not care if his father disapproved of this show of concern on his part; his only thought was for Katharine. His anger had dissipated entirely, the last vestiges of his hurt were swept away. He still loved her. He could not give her up.

Francesca blinked back her own tears. Loving of heart as she was, and sensitive to other people's feelings, she was bereft for her friend. She had always believed Katharine had been exposed to a terrible sadness, and finally this had been confirmed. It occurred to her that Katharine needed their love and understanding, not criticism. After all, her lies had not been that serious. Francesca stiffened in the chair. She, of all people, was in no position to condemn Katharine Tempest. The dismaying thought which had been sparked at the outset of Katharine's story now nudged itself up to the surface of Francesca's mind: *She was as guilty as Katharine.* She had not actually lied about Victor and herself, but only because she had not been questioned. Yet she had been dishonest – she had lied by omission. Sudden remorse assailed her.

Nervously, Francesca leapt to her feet, announcing to no one in particular, 'Katharine's very upset, I'd better get her a drink.' Hurrying out onto the terrace, she resolved to talk to Vic in the next few days. The time for his ridiculous secretiveness was at an end. Her father must be told they were in love. Approve he might not, of that she was well aware; how much worse it would be if he discovered her underhandedness. Panic raced through her as she contemplated her father's disappointment in her.

Doris picked up her glass, asking herself what David's attitude would be. She was unable to formulate an answer. Katharine's pathetic little tale had not left Doris unmoved either, nonetheless she cautioned herself to be absolutely neutral, circumspect in what she said.

Katharine's sobs gradually abated, although she continued to cling to Kim, finding solace in his closeness. His arms so strongly holding her, his words of gentleness comforting her – these told her he was no longer enraged. Surely he has forgiven me, and Francesca will be supportive too . . .

'Here you are, Kath dear,' Francesca said. 'I've brought you a glass of champagne. It'll make you feel better.'

'Thank you, Frankie. How thoughtful.' Katharine took the glass, a smile bringing a look of ineffable sweetness to her face. 'I feel so terrible about deceiving you. I don't know how to make it up to everyone. You must think I'm the most awful person.'

'Don't be so silly, Katharine,' Francesca replied swiftly, returning the smile. 'I'm sure Daddy understands your reasons now, as we all do. In my opinion this is just a storm in a teacup.' Francesca flopped down onto a chair and began to fiddle abstractedly with the belt of her cotton sundress. Without realizing it, preoccupied as she was with her feelings of guilt, the worries flaring within her, Francesca had spoken sharply, a trifle dismissively.

Katharine, misinterpreting her friend's tone, felt unusually rebuffed and hurt. She stared at Francesca nonplussed, thinking, with a tinge of bitterness: She doesn't really understand what my life's been like. And how could she? All of her life *she's* been surrounded by people who adore her . . . Kim and her father, her cousins; the old Nanny, Melly, and the housekeeper, Val. And soon she'll have a stepmother. I have nobody. Nobody in this whole wide world. I've only ever had one person who loved me. Momma.

Abruptly, Katharine placed the champagne glass on the coffee table and stood up purposefully. She said softly, 'Now that I have told you everything, I guess there's nothing else for me to say. I'd better go up to my room and pack at once. I'll 'phone Victor at La Réserve, and ask him to get me a room there for a couple of nights. He'll be upset if I don't stay for his party. I'll go back to London on Monday.'

Kim cried, 'Don't be ridiculous, Katharine. I'm not going to let you stay in a hotel, much less permit you to return to London.' He sprang to his feet, took her arm possessively, stared at his father. 'Surely Katharine can be forgiven, Dad. The experiences of her childhood, her humiliation and unhappiness at school . . . all exonerate her as far as I'm concerned. Despite my initial anger and hurt, I do feel there have been mitigating circumstances. Granted she shouldn't have perpetuated the lie when she became involved with me, but earlier Katharine said she'd planned to confide in me this weekend, had been wanting to do so for a long time. I believe her. I also think she's been put through quite an ordeal this afternoon. My God, she's had to face us all, and explain her entire life, as though she were appearing before the Inquisition. Isn't a little compassion in order now?'

Pulling himself out of his troubled thoughts, David said, 'Of course, of course,

Kim.' He inclined his head in Katharine's direction. 'I think your frankness has cleared the air considerably, given us a better perspective about you and your background, a real understanding of your motivation. Yes.' He cleared his throat, looked at Doris. 'I'm sure I speak for you too, darling, when I say we wouldn't hear of Katharine going to a hotel, or curtailing her vacation. I am right, am I not?'

'Absolutely,' Doris said at once. 'We'll be very upset if you leave, Katharine.'

Francesca exclaimed fiercely, 'Oh Kath, don't be a silly goose! You can't go. We all love you, and we've been so looking forward to having you with us. I told you, this will all blow over, if you'll let it. Please *do* stay.'

'I don't know . . .' Katharine responded cautiously, and hesitated. Her eyes swept over them and came to rest on Kim, who was looking tense and nervous. She touched his arm lightly, and her face upturned to his was soft and appealing in its vulnerability. 'I'll stay then, if you're sure you want me.'

'Of course we want you!' he responded, squeezing her arm.

The Earl of Langley rose slowly from the sofa, smiling benignly despite his sinking heart. 'It's getting rather late, and our guests will be arriving shortly. I think we'd better dress for dinner.'

'My God, the dinner party. I'd forgotten.' Doris was on her feet and following him across the floor. She turned at the door. 'The Remsons and the Brooks are due around eight. Dinner's at nine, in the garden.'

Francesca exclaimed, 'Gosh, and I've got to wash my hair.' Rising, she blew a kiss to Katharine, then hurried out.

Half an hour later, after they had bathed and dressed in their evening clothes, Doris and the Earl met in the small sitting room which linked their suites, as they had previously arranged.

'It was a little difficult when we came upstairs,' he said, lighting a cigarette, positioning himself in the middle of the floor. 'I really didn't want to get involved in a long discussion in front of Francesca. Or with her, as she was hoping.' He peered at his watch. 'But we have a good fifteen minutes to chat before our guests get here.' He began to walk up and down, his head bent, thinking deeply.

Doris watched him, said nothing, knowing better than to start prodding him; nor did she have the desire to play devil's advocate, or say anything to influence him.

David stopped pacing, joined her on the long sofa in front of the windows. 'Well, Doris, what are *your* thoughts about the situation? About Katharine?'

'I have to admit I felt a bit sorry for her, and I'm sure she did have an unhappy time of it, after her mother died,' Doris replied, trying to be fair yet noncommittal.

'Quite so, my dear. I don't doubt the veracity of her story for one minute. Katharine's no fool, quite a clever little thing, really. She wouldn't be stupid enough to pile more lies on top of her original untruths . . .'

'But?'

'I didn't say *but*,' he smiled.

'You thought it though, darling.'

'Yes. How well you know me, Doris.' He chuckled to himself. 'Actually, when I was dressing, I couldn't help asking myself how much she had exaggerated, dramatized.'

'Don't you believe her father hates her then?' Doris asked, raising an eyebrow.

366

'Hard to say really. However, Katharine believes it. I'm absolutely convinced of that, so whatever anyone else thinks is immaterial.' David leaned back, crossed his legs, shot Doris a questioning glance. 'What do you know about O'Rourke?'

'Not a great deal, David. As I told Katharine, I've never met him. We mixed in different social circles in Chicago. He used to wield a lot of power in the city, because of his money and his political connections, chiefly his closeness to Richard Daley, who runs the city, Cook County and the Democratic Machine. I'm sure his power hasn't waned. Years ago I heard a rumour about him being something of a womanizer – he's a very handsome man. But there's no scandal attached to his name, to my knowledge anyway. Of course you never know about men like him . . . self-made, ambitious, driven, and a little ruthless.' Doris laughed dryly. 'A *lot* ruthless, I should say. I'm also sure he was strict with Katharine, even tyrannical as a father. I know the type, as I'm sure you do.'

'Mmmmm.' David contemplated, puffed on his cigarette. 'Kim is acting on emotion not intelligence right now, and I understand why. Katharine is a bewitching creature with an inordinate amount of charm.' A tiny smile surfaced wryly. 'She's persuasive, and yes, plausible. Let's face it, Doris, there's nothing more appealing than the little orphan girl story. That's probably the reason she invented it for herself. One would have to be frightfully hard boiled not to succumb to it . . . certainly it's guaranteed to evoke everyone's sympathy and compassion. I know there was a moment when she really had *me*. So naturally, the extraordinary reversal in Kim's attitude didn't surprise me at all, in spite of his initial anger, the things he said to us before she arrived. Kim's awfully softhearted, my dear, and so is Francesca. I realize they're both bending over backwards to make excuses for Katharine's behaviour, perhaps against their better judgment. Curious, isn't it, how they are equally mesmerized by her?'

'Yes.' Doris gave him a long look, asked quietly, 'What do you intend to do about Kim and Katharine?'

'Nothing.'

'But, David –'

'I've no intention of intervening,' he broke in peremptorily. 'By doing that I would push Kim into her arms, and the consequences could be dire. Forbidden fruit always tastes so much sweeter, you know.' David studied Doris, detecting her uncertainty, and he reached out and patted her hand. 'If I say anything critical about Katharine, or their relationship, I'll antagonize my son. He's in love and not thinking straight. Also, in some ways he's holding the whip hand. He knows there's no course of action I could take. I can't very well threaten to disinherit him, because the law of primogeniture protects him *absolutely*. No, all I *can* do is trust him to use his intelligence.'

Observing the troubled expression dulling the vivid greenness of her eyes, David moved closer, put his arms around Doris. 'Now listen to me, my darling, we mustn't go around with long faces, or behave strangely with Kim and Katharine. We must play this in a light key, a very light key indeed. You see, I believe that by giving him his head, not obstructing their relationship, Kim will eventually comprehend things more clearly, and see Katharine in a different light, the way I do now.'

'And how do you see her, David?' Doris asked, pulling away, looking into his face.

'As being unstable.'

'*Unstable?*'

'Yes, amongst other things. Katharine Tempest is a highly complex person, Doris. She's a raving beauty who can turn a man's head with the flutter of an eyelash, an incredibly gifted actress who can move an audience to tears, be it in a theatre or in that sun room downstairs. She is entirely fascinating. She's also a curiously disturbed young woman, unbalanced, in my opinion. Clever, as I said earlier, but dangerous.'

Doris sat mulling over his words, aware that he never made rash statements. 'My God, David, I feel alarmed all of a sudden – for Kim.'

'Yes, I know exactly what you mean. I experienced that same feeling earlier, but not any more.' He shook his head firmly, and although his face was serious his voice was suddenly shaded by confidence and lightness. 'I know what I raised. Kim has his feet on the ground. My instincts tell me that in the end he will fall back on the precepts of his upbringing. They may be slightly blurred in his mind right now, but they're so deeply ingrained he will never lose them. In a sense they protect him, and if he doesn't live by them he will be an extremely unhappy man. I know *he* knows this, deep down inside, and I have to gamble that my son will put duty and responsibility before this girl.'

'Yes,' Doris said quietly, hoping he was right. She squeezed his hand, gave him a reassuring smile.

'There's another thing. When all the fuss dies down, and Kim starts to think with his head instead of with his –' He broke off, coughed behind his hand. 'Er – er – with other parts of his anatomy, he'll begin to wonder if he can really trust her. I'm also quite certain he will understand that she is hardly cut out to be a farmer's wife, stuck away in the backwaters of Yorkshire.' A mischievous gleam entered his eyes. 'As you are,' he teased. David jumped up, offered Doris his hand. 'Now, let's close this book for tonight. We should go down, my dear. It's almost eight.'

As David opened the door, Doris said, 'You do have time on your side, darling. Don't forget, Katharine is leaving for California at the beginning of September. She'll be gone for three months.'

'Oh yes,' he said quietly. His eyes narrowed and he nodded his head slowly. 'Don't think I haven't taken that fact into consideration.'

CHAPTER THIRTY-FOUR

Nicholas Latimer burst into Victor's suite at La Réserve without knocking or announcing himself. He sprinted across the floor at breakneck speed, almost knocking over an occasional table in the process, and stumbled into the bedroom. He was flushed and out of breath.

'Jesus Christ! You're not even dressed!' he gasped, staring wild eyed at Victor.

Victor stared back at him, a brow lifting lazily. He was standing in the middle of the floor, wearing only his underpants, black knee-length socks, his dress shirt and black tie. 'What the hell's got into *you*?' he asked mildly, put down the cigarette he was smoking and reached for the Scotch and soda on the dressing table.

Nick leapt across the floor, snatched the drink out of his hand with little ceremony, and cried heatedly, 'You don't need this now, you can drink as much as you want when we get to the dance. Just get dressed. For God's sake get dressed. We gotta get outta here. *Pronto!*'

'What's the hurry all of a su – '

'You're not going to believe this, but Arlene's downstairs. In living Technicolor, standing in – '

'Aw shucks, Nicky, and she's catching me with my pants down again,' Victor cracked, the famous lopsided grin settling on his mouth. He lifted the cigarette out of the ashtray, drew on it, stubbed it out. 'Don't I have the lousiest luck.'

'You bet you do, old buddy. Please, Vic, get the rest of your clothes on. She's going to be up here in a couple of minutes, dragging her two-goddamn-dozen suitcases and six-goddamn-bellboys with her. Jesus, come *on*!' He banged the glass down on the dressing table, his eyes sweeping the room as he did. He spotted Victor's pants on the chair, grabbed them frantically, threw them at him.

As he caught his pants, Victor's face changed. He suddenly realized this was not one of Nick's usual jokes, that his friend was not playing the fool. He said slowly, 'Christ, you are serious, and I thought you were kidding.'

'Would I kid about *her* arrival on our goddamn doorstep. Where's your jacket, your shoes?'

'In the armoire.' Victor pulled on his pants, zipped them swiftly, took the black silk handkerchief from the chest of drawers, folded it with haste. 'When did you see her, Nicky?'

'A few minutes ago. Hurry up, for God's sake. Here's your shoes.' Nick dropped them at his feet, stood holding the white dinner jacket. 'What a rotten lousy break. Tonight of all nights. I was with Jake in the lobby. He was changing some large bills at the *caisse*. I happened to glance through the front door, saw her getting out of a car. With all this goddamn luggage. She looks as if she's moving in. I sent Jake to stall her. Somehow . . . God knows *how*, while I rushed up here. Vic, come on! Leave the cigarettes, the money. You don't need money, for Christ's sake.' Nick bundled Victor into his jacket, seized his arm, dragged him to the window. 'We gotta go out this way.'

'You crazy son of a bitch! I stopped doing my own stunts years ago!' Victor shouted, glowering at him. 'And let go of my arm. You're going to rip my dinner jacket.'

The window was open, and Nick pushed it farther back and peered down. 'It's not so bad. Come on, let's jump. You go first.'

Victor leaned over Nick's shoulder, also looking out. 'You *are* a crazy bastard,' he groaned. 'It's a twenty-foot drop. At least.'

'But it's *grass*!'

'Grass or no grass, I could break my back, my legs, at worst.'

'That's better than having your balls broken, isn't it, old sport? And I guarantee that's her intention. She's here to do her usual little number on – '

There was a loud knocking on the sitting room door, and they gazed at each other in dismay. The knocking increased. 'She's here, right enough,' Victor muttered. 'I guess she went through poor old Jake like a dose of salts.'

'Yep.' Nick grabbed Victor's arm again. 'You've still got a chance to elude her, if you go thatta way.' He indicated the window. 'I'll try to stall her.'

'Forget it, kid.'

'Then we'd better fasten our seat belts, maestro. We're in for a helluva rocky ride tonight.'

Victor was halfway across the floor. He swung his head, frowned, whispered, 'Not you, Nicky. I'll deal with Arlene. I want you to go on up to Zamir with Jake. And play it cool. For God's sake don't let Francesca know that Arlene's arrived. It'll throw her into a flat spin. Make some sort of excuse, explain I'll be a bit late. Delayed by – a business call from the Coast. Look, say anything – '

The door of the suite opened, and Arlene walked in self-confidently. 'Hello, Victor,' she said, waving at him. 'I would've called you, darling, but I decided to surprise you.'

'I'm too old to be surprised by anything,' he replied as evenly as possible, curbing his temper. He stepped into the sitting room and eyed, with some alarm, the luggage being carried in by two uniformed bellboys. He turned to Nick, hovering behind him in the doorway of the bedroom and said, 'There's money on the dressing table, kid. Can you get it for me, please?'

Nick ignored the request, reached into his trouser pocket, pulled out some francs, tipped the boys. When they had left, Nick studied Arlene with interest through blue eyes icy with hostility and remarked sarcastically, 'For someone who's only passing through, you certainly travel heavy.' He jabbed a finger at the suitcases surrounding her, his face sour with disgust. 'Who the hell do you think you are? The Queen of Sheba?'

'As charming as ever, dear Nicholas,' she replied with a cold smile. 'Written any good books lately? Or are you too busy with the ladies?' His only response was a disdainful glance. Arlene giggled fatuously and added, 'Well, how *is* the great genius of American literature?'

'I was feeling pretty good . . . until a few minutes ago.'

She simply smiled again and glided across the floor to the sofa. She sat down, crossed her long beautiful legs, smoothed the skirt of her cream shantung silk suit. Her eyes swung from Nick to Victor, 'My, my, don't you both look handsome. And white dinner jackets, no less. Where's the party?'

'That's none of your goddamn busi – '

Victor threw Nick a warning look, cut him off hurriedly. 'We're not going to a party, Arlene. Sorry to disappoint you. We were just about to leave for a business dinner, strictly stag.'

'I'll bet,' Arlene said.

Nicholas moved quickly to the bar, poured himself a vodka and took a swift swallow. He stole a glance at Victor, who was motionless in the centre of the floor. He marvelled at his self-containment, knowing his friend was seething inside and undoubtedly ready to do violence. Nick racked his brains, wondering how to ease him out of this unanticipated situation; ease him out of the room, out of the hotel and up to the Villa Zamir. But there was no escape hatch, at least not at the moment.

Familiar as he was with Arlene's tenacity and intransigence, not to mention her thick skin, he knew without question that she would insist on joining them if they made a move to leave. God forbid, he thought, envisioning Francesca's face if they arrived at the dance with Arlene. Nick shifted on his feet, his nervousness increasing as the minutes dragged by. The silence grew heavier, the atmosphere more taut.

'Fix me a drink, Nick, please,' Arlene said, breaking the silence.

'Fix your own,' Nick snapped back. He drained his glass.

'You never did know how to treat a lady,' Arlene sniffed.

'Oh yes I do. When they're around.'

'Why you bastard – '

'I think you'd best push off, old buddy,' Victor interjected before Arlene had a chance to castigate Nick further. 'Tell the boys I'll get there as soon as I can.' He stepped up to Nick, took his arm, led him to the door. In a lower key, he said, 'And tell Frank there's nothing to worry about, regarding the present deal, our deal.' He increased the pressure of his fingers on Nick's arm.

'You bet I will, Vic, don't worry about Frank.' Nick assured him in a positive voice. But he looked miserable as he left the suite.

Victor took a deep breath, steeled himself. Ignoring Arlene, he walked through the sitting room into the bedroom, found his cigarettes and lighter, and stood smoking by the window, meditating on the best course of action to take. He decided to be brisk, matter of fact, polite. Oh yes, very polite. Once he had ascertained her reasons for dropping in on him out of the blue, he would be fairly acquiescent. For tonight anyway, in order to duck out to the dance, using the pretext of the business dinner. With a stab of annoyance, it struck him he would have trouble ejecting her from the suite. She would be there, confronting him, when he returned. No problem about that, he assured himself. I'll bunk with Nicky or Jake for one night. And tomorrow I'll send her on her way.

Assuming a nonchalant air, Victor wandered back into the sitting room. He saw immediately that Arlene had poured herself a drink, and she sat on the sofa sipping it, looking unconcerned, cool and self-assured. He proceeded to the bar, mixed a Scotch and soda, sat down in a chair near the door. He said carefully, 'Well, why are you here, Arlene?'

'Isn't that obvious. I came to see you, Vic.'

'Don't call me Vic. You know I don't like it.'

'So sorry, *Victor*. I keep forgetting – only dear Nicholas is permitted to use the diminutive. Anyway, it's great to see you. How've you been, honey?'

'Let's cut the small talk, Arlene, and get to the point.' He bent forward, resting his arms on his knees, holding the drink between both hands. 'I think you've got a hell of a lot of nerve, landing on me like this when we're in the middle of a divorce,' he said, his mild tone belying the coldness of his eyes. 'But let's not belabour that point right now.'

'I'm still your wife, Victor, we're still legally married. Why, the proceedings haven't even begun yet. So what's so odd about me dropping in on you?'

He brushed her question aside with a wave of his hand and said impatiently, 'What *is* the purpose of this visit?'

'To see you, to talk to you, without the lawyers fencing us in, pitting us against each other.'

'What can you possibly hope to accomplish, Arlene?'

'I believe we can settle our problems and differences. I also figured we could make a better deal between ourselves, a more equitable deal for both of us, Victor. And it's so much cosier, honey, when we're on a one-to-one basis, just the two of us.'

Her sweet tone, the even sweeter smile, irritated him, but he endeavoured to remain pleasant. 'I doubt we can settle anything, make any kind of deal. Let's be honest, the situation is very acrimonious. You and your lawyers have gone too far lately. You're stretching your luck, Arlene.'

'So are you, honey bunny.'

He winced at this sickening term of endearment, but asked, 'What do you mean by that?'

She shook her head, leaned back, the perpetual smile in place. A sharp and knowing look entered her light blue eyes, and she lifted her hand to smooth her elaborately-coiffed strawberry-blonde hair.

He sat back himself, his eyes assessing her. Arlene was a beautiful woman, there was no denying that. Her features were perfect, her colouring exquisite. But over the years her beauty had become too polished, too carefully contrived by artifice and cosmetics, exquisite clothes and jewels, which gave her a veneer of sophisticated glamour whilst partially obscuring her natural loveliness. An eight-by-ten Hollywood glossy, he thought sardonically. Her lacquered appearance unequivocally shrieked: *Don't touch*. And how many times had *she* said that to *him*. He put the drink down on the occasional table and took his time lighting another cigarette before remarking casually, 'My luck's not stretched one inch, Arlene. I'm not the one making outrageous demands.'

'Oh, but you are doing outrageous things, honey,' She laughed lightly. 'I do marvel at you, Victor. Still playing Don Juan to the hilt.' Her eyes ran over him, lingered on him suggestively. 'It must be trying though, having to handle two baby dolls half your age. Rather demanding on you physically and emotionally, isn't it?'

Victor tensed in the chair. Trouble, he thought. She's here to make trouble. He held himself very still, kept his voice even as he said, 'I don't know what the hell you're talking about.'

'Of course you do, honey. Katharine and Francesca.'

The mask he could so easily don slipped onto his handsome face, hiding all expression. He disguised his rising apprehension behind a burst of dismissive laughter. 'Oh those two. Just kids . . . just members of Nick's small group of admirers. Pals, Arlene, merely pals.'

Suddenly coldness dislodged Arlene's smile. 'Come off it, Victor, you're talking to *me*, remember! I've had your number for years. Katharine Tempest is not merely a *pal*. She's under contract to Bellissima Productions and is your current protégée.'

Arlene held up a bejewelled hand to curtail the interruption on his lips. 'And don't start giving me the line about how she's *only* a fellow worker, starred in your last picture. I know all that. I also know she's starring in your bed right now. Along with Lady Francesca Cunningham, daughter of the Earl of Langley, presently tucked away in a villa in Cap Martin. Where, most conveniently for you, your little actress is also a house guest. Tell me, honey, how are you enjoying your delectable sandwich, continental style?' She cocked her head on one side, smirking. 'I guess it's thrilling for a man of your age to bed two young girls at the same time.

And best friends yet. How smart of you, Victor. Saves making introductions. Are they a couple of lesbians? Do they give hot shows for you, baby? Is that what gets you going these days?'

'You bitch!' he exploded, losing his control. He was enraged and horrified by her words, and he half rose from the chair as though to strike her. Then he fell back, his body trembling. He knew a display of temper would be ill advised, and he fought to get a grip on himself, knowing he could not permit her to goad him into saying or doing anything he would regret.

Choking on his disgust, he said with enormous iciness, 'What you're suggesting is preposterous. Where have you been playing since we split up? The gutter?'

'Recognize the territory, honey?'

'You've developed a filthy mind, Arlene. Most unbecoming. And I certainly don't owe you an explanation about my life. We've been separated for well over a year now. However, I'm not going to let two decent girls have their reputations besmirched by your revolting talk. Yes, Katharine Tempest is my protégée. It's no state secret I signed her up . . . but that's all there is to it. A business deal. As for Francesca Cunningham, it just so happens her father is a friend of mine. He permitted us to shoot some scenes at their family home. His daughter worked for my production manager when we were on location in Yorkshire, and – '

'I know all about Langley Castle, and what happened on location, Victor, so don't waste your breath. You ought to be more careful, incidentally, when you go a-courting, Romeo.' Her eyes mocked him. 'You're a world-famous movie star, highly visible at all times, but most especially in small places and in that new Bentley of yours. I'm surprised at you, meeting Lady Francesca at the *back* gates of the castle, then embracing her so passionately in the middle of Langley Lane, just like the common folk. My, my, Victor, you're slipping. Even her father's servants know better.'

'Garbage!' he bellowed, his black eyes flashing with anger, his face congested. 'Absolute goddamn garbage!' He took a deep breath, willed himself to say no more. Arlene had always had the ability to provoke him with her vicious tongue. He downed the rest of his drink, stubbed out his cigarette, rose, strode to the bar. He slopped Scotch into his glass hastily, and cautioned himself to resist any further response to her inflammatory pronouncements. His head cleared a little, and he returned to the chair, looking poker faced, even sanguine. But his mind raced. How much did she really know? Did she have facts or gossip? Was she bluffing? Of course she's not bluffing, he answered himself. His heart sank. He knew suddenly that he was on dangerous ground. Then he smiled inside. He was a much better poker player than she.

Arlene was watching him keenly, and through feline eyes. 'You're more acquainted with garbage than I am, *sport*,' she muttered softly, her voice dripping acid. '*I* make it a point of acquainting myself with facts. Cold hard facts. Say whatever you like, but I *know* you drove Francesca Cunningham to London that particular June afternoon. You arrived in the early evening. I can tell you the exact time.' She found a small travelling case, carried it back to the sofa. Opening it, she took out a folder of papers, studied them.

Lifting her head, she went on, 'Yes, you got to London at ten minutes past eight. The following afternoon you took her to London airport, and that night you and

Nick escorted her to dinner with a blonde woman.' Arlene handed him the folder. 'Here are the reports of your activities in general, and for the last eleven months.' She smiled at him, the sweet smile oozing poison. 'I'm not as dumb as I look, old buddy. I've had detectives on you since the day you walked out on me, the day you landed in London. There's nothing I don't know about you.'

Eaten up with curiosity though he was, and nervous, Victor remained, nonetheless, a cool customer. He tossed the folder onto the coffee table with indifference, without even opening it, knowing that to do so would be a fatal error. He glanced at her with amusement and then laughed uproariously – right in her face. 'Giving a girl a lift to London does not constitute adultery. Neither does signing an actress to a personal contract. Try and make such ridiculous and circumstantial evidence stick in a court of law. You'll sure have a hard time, *honey*.'

'Maybe I will, and maybe I won't. But in the process I'll ruin your aristocrat and your actress. Mud tends to stick, Victor. Your two little whores won't be able to lift their heads when I've finished with them.'

For a split second he was blinded by anger, wanted to smash his fist into her silly painted pretty face. Warning signals went off in his head. Keep calm, do nothing, and for God's sake don't react, he instructed himself. With a supreme effort he curbed his raging senses. His voice was steady when he said, 'You not only think dirty and talk dirty, but seemingly you play dirty as well.'

'I learned at the knee of a master,' she retaliated. 'Don't forget *I* used to be your protégée. I know all about cosy little lunches in your trailer, discussing script problems. Didn't you call it the happy hour? I recall, and with some pleasure I must admit, how *we* spent our lunch breaks on location.'

'That was different. We were engaged to be married.'

'Yes indeedy, so we were, and yet I don't believe you gave *me* a diamond bracelet, or a pearl choker with a diamond clasp.' She sat back, a look of smugness on her face. He, in turn, remained motionless. She continued, with a smirk, 'Don't tell me you've forgotten your recent gifts to your juvenile delinquents, the same way you seem to have forgotten scre – '

He held up his hand. 'Okay, that's enough, Arlene. I don't deny giving presents to the girls, as I gave presents to everybody who worked on the picture. As I always do, and as you well know.'

'I bet nothing else cost as much as the fancy jewellery . . . from Asprey's.' She shook her head. 'I can understand why you might have a yen for the actress – she's a looker. But the *debutante*! Hardly your style, Romeo.'

'Shut up!' he growled, glaring at her. 'You don't have any evidence on me regarding those girls, because there isn't any.'

A sudden complacency settled over her. 'You don't think all my cards are in that one folder, do you lover? I have much more detailed reports tucked away. Safely tucked away. Anyway, whatever additional evidence I have is, in a sense, beside the point. Once I hand copies of these reports to some of my journalist friends, you'll be in the mire along with your two beauties. The press will have a field day, Victor.'

Victor was silent, reflecting on everything she had said. He knew they were not idle threats. He cursed her under his breath. She had infuriated him with her lewd comments about Francesca and Katharine, her outlandish suggestions of sexual decadence on his part. However, he was not particularly surprised about the private detectives. He and Nick had discussed that possibility more than once. All those guys have managed to dig up is circumstantial, and therefore irrelevant, evidence, he told himself. And then he thought: But is it? He was not sure.

Victor said slowly, quietly, 'I assume, when you mention your journalist friends, that you're talking about that dandy little gang who write scurrilous filth for *Confidential?*'

'Among others?'

'I'll sue you and that damned magazine for millions!'

'No, you won't. No movie star has ever sued *Confidential* – and won. Besides, you wouldn't want all the additional publicity.'

'You know, Arlene, you're pretty stupid. We're separated. I can date other women if I want. There's nothing wrong – or newsworthy – in that.'

'But there *is* a lovely juicy story to be written about your love nest, the threesome you've got going – '

'Would you do that to me, Arlene?' he interrupted fiercely.

'Like to try me on for size, *sport?*'

Victor sighed. 'Why? In God's name *why*, Arlene?'

'Because you've caused me undue heartache and pain . . . and suffering. I guess I feel the need, the very urgent and pressing need, to hit back at you.' She reclined against the cushions, striking a pathetic pose.

'Wipe the Camille expression off your face, Arlene. It only makes you look ridiculous. You never were much of an actress,' he said, and laughed, knowing the thrust was cruel. That it was true did not make it less cruel, but he didn't care. She had asked for it. He scoffed mockingly, 'You can't damage *me*. I'm too big, too well established. You're only going to hurt two innocent girls.'

'So.'

Victor stood up and strolled to the small chest at the far side of the room. He took out a box of his favourite Monte Cristos and spent a few seconds clipping off the end of one and striking a match. His back was to her and he sneaked a look at his watch. It was almost nine o'clock. How the hell was he going to get out of here?

Deciding now to take a different tack, to bring this discussion to a close, he sat down, puffed on the cigar, said, 'I'm prepared to be very generous with you, Arlene. Make a good settlement. I originally offered you three million dollars, plus ten thousand alimony a month for five years, whether or not you remarry. Two weeks ago my lawyers offered your lawyers another five hundred thousand, as part of the settlement. I'll make it a round million, and I'll throw in the Bel-Air house. Surely that will help to ease your pain.'

She shook her head negatively.

'Isn't that enough for you?'

'No,' Arlene gave him a long searching stare then dropped her eyes. They rested on the folder. She picked it up, leafed through it, stared at him again, and thoughtfully so. She said, 'These reports are mild in comparison to the others in my possession. *They* are lethal. I know bad publicity doesn't worry you, Victor, but as you yourself said it would certainly create problems and embarrassment for those two . . . young ladies, particularly the Earl's daughter. Think about that, and most carefully.'

'This is blackmail.'

375

'No, honey, it's pragmatism,' she smiled.

Victor straightened up in the chair, his brows drawing together in concentration. 'Let me get this straight. Apart from what I've already offered you, I've also got to throw in my ranch and fifty per cent of the company, in return for these reports, in return for a peaceful divorce, free of any scandal, no names mentioned, no women cited. Am I right?'

'No, not really.'

Her voice was so soft, her face so unexpectedly gentle, Victor held his breath, wondering what she was about to spring on him next. He waited. She waited. Their eyes met. Finally Arlene blinked and looked away.

At last she brought her eyes back to his face, and said slowly, 'I don't want the settlement, the alimony or the Bel-Air house. Neither do I want Che Sarà Sarà or fifty per cent of Bellissima Productions.'

He said coolly, 'Then what do you want, Arlene?'

'You, darling,' she whispered.

His jaw dropped. Staggered, he sat back in the chair, staring at her speechlessly.

CHAPTER THIRTY-FIVE

For the first time in her life, Francesca knew with absolute certainty that she looked truly beautiful this night.

She gazed at herself in the cheval mirror, and a smile of unalloyed happiness illuminated her face. The girl who stared back from the glassy depths did not look like her at all, yet she loved this new image, one which was partially Katharine's creation.

Earlier in the evening, Katharine had come to her room and worked on her hair, parting it in the centre and brushing it into a pageboy. Burnished to a lighter, brighter hue by the sun, it fell in sleek golden swatches around her face. Simplicity itself, the pageboy, nevertheless, had a degree of elegance without being over sophisticated, and it was becoming to her. Her face looked different too, for Katharine had insisted on helping with her make-up as well. A brushing of rouge emphasized her high cheekbones; a trace of gold shadow brought out the topaz lights in her tawny eyes; mascara darkened her blonde lashes. These few expert and professional touches delicately underscored her natural attributes, gave additional depth to her features.

Stepping back, Francesca nodded to herself, delighted with her appearance, and most especially with her new evening gown. She had been captivated the moment she had seen it in the Model Room at Harte's in Knightsbridge. It was a cloud of gossamer peach organza, layers of it forming a bell-like crinoline below a strapless bodice moulded to her figure. Tiny crystal beads had been stitched in random clusters all over the skirt, and the long matching stole, and they introduced an iridescent gleam to the airy floating fabric.

It was a romantic dreamlike dress, one her father could barely afford. But he too had been entranced by it, had swept aside her protestations about the price, told her that every other dress she had tried on thereafter paled in comparison. 'And for once in your life, you're going to have something pretty to wear, which is not a compromise because of money, or homemade by you and Melly,' he had insisted with unusual gruffness. Francesca had not argued with him, understanding that the dress she wore to his engagement dance was as important to him as it was to her. It was a question of his love for her, his immense pride, and so much more besides. After the evening gown had been fitted for a few minor adjustments, he had whisked her off to lunch in the grill room of the Hyde Park Hotel as a special treat. A lovely day, she thought, remembering it with clarity and pleasure.

She touched the pearl choker at her neck. The diamond clasp, nestling in the centre of her throat, threw off prisms of sparkling light, and the creamy pearls looked even creamier against her sunburned skin. Victor's choker is perfect, the gown is exquisite, and I do look lovely, Francesca whispered to herself. She wanted to be especially beautiful for Vic tonight, and so fervently that she had been pent-up and breathless the entire time she was dressing. She could hardly wait for him to arrive, to witness his face when he saw her. She glanced at the clock on the bedside table. It was almost nine. He would be here soon, very soon now. He and Nicky and Jake had been invited early, to have drinks with the family, since Doris considered them to be part of the inner circle. The other guests would start arriving at ten, when the dance would officially begin, and supper would be served at midnight.

Adjusting the filmy stole around her bare shoulders, Francesca picked up the peach silk evening bag that exactly matched her high-heeled pumps and hurried out. As she moved with lightness and speed down the staircase she was a picture of loveliness and grace, the peach organza floating around her like a delicate hazy mist, her face shimmering with unrestrained joy, and not a little anticipation.

Gliding out onto the terrace, Francesca was surprised to find it entirely deserted, except for the bartender positioned behind the bar which had been set up at the far end. The terrace furniture had been removed, and small tables, covered with pink-muslin cloths and partnered with gold cane chairs, were scattered around. Every table held a bud vase with a pink or red rose, plus a votive candle in a ruby glass container, and these gleamed rosily, introducing a festive air along with huge pots of flowering plants banked in various corners.

Francesca edged her way through the tables, asked for a glass of champagne, wandered the length of the terrace, admiring the gardens, marvelling at the effect Doris's team of electricians and caterers had created. Always a source of aesthetic pleasure, with their lush greenery and glorious multicoloured flower beds, the grounds had acquired a fairytale quality that was magical, utterly breathtaking. Lights glowed everywhere, focused attention on the natural beauty of the setting, brought each flower, each leaf startlingly to life. Strings of tiny amber bulbs festooned the trees and bushes; colourful Chinese lanterns hung from branches, swaying gently in the breeze; small spots, strategically placed, washed the stately poplars bordering the walls with a shining radiance. It was the most spectacular scene imaginable.

Francesca scanned the main lawn. A portable dance floor rested in the centre, surrounded by pink-skirted tables set for ten and twenty, and, at the farthest edge, a small bandstand had been erected against the backdrop of the trees. On the adjoining lawn there were several bars, and long buffet tables from which the food would be served. The strumming of a guitar caught her attention and she glanced once more at the bandstand. A number of musicians in evening dress had begun to assemble, taking out their instruments and talking amongst themselves. Doris had engaged a group of mariachis, and they too had just arrived. It was one of the mariachis, resplendent in a colourful Mexican folk costume, who was playing. Francesca closed her eyes dreamily, thinking of Victor, of being in his arms, of swaying with him on the dance floor. The guitarist suddenly began to sing, his voice echoing across the lawn, rich and melodic, the familiar song stirring poignant memories of recent rapturous evenings spent with Victor.

> 'Yo se que soy una aventura más para ti
> Que después de esta noche
> Te olvidarás de mi.
> Yo se que soy una ilusion fugaz para ti
> Un capricho del alma
> Que hoy te une a mi.'

It was one of Victor's favourites, one of hers now, a Mexican ballad that was popular on the Riviera this year, and especially with the crowd who frequented La Chunga, a charming restaurant-club in Cannes. Victor loved to go there, to listen to the mariachis serenading, to watch the flamenco dancers. The music washed over her. Francesca's heart crested with euphoria. What a wonderful evening this was going to be. Romantic. Memorable. So very memorable. Blinking, she lifted her head and looked up. An indigo sky. Clear, cloudless, brilliant with stars and a shimmering crystal moon. A balmy breeze rustled through the trees, carrying the tangy salt smell of the sea to mingle with the spicey scent of the eucalyptus, the sweeter fragrance of honeysuckle and night-blooming jasmine. Francesca thought her heart would burst with love for him, and she knew then, deep within herself, that tonight he would ask her to marry him. She would accept, and when his divorce came through they would be joined in holy matrimony in the picturesque Norman church in the village of Langley, where her father would soon be marrying Doris.

'All alone, Frankie?'

She swung around, waved to Kim and Katharine who were walking out onto the terrace together. Katharine was dressed in white georgette, and she looked exquisitely dainty and fragile. The gown was an off-the-shoulder style, with a wide frill that fell from the gathered neckline to cover part of the bodice, and the billowing skirt was finished at the hemline with another deep frill. Her chestnut hair tumbled around her face in a mass of waves and curls, held back at each side with rhinestone combs. She wore no jewellery other than the diamond bracelet Victor had given her.

Kim looked his sister up and down when they came to a halt, and whistled. 'My God, you do look smashing, old thing. Whatever have you done to yourself?'

'Thanks for the backhanded compliment,' she retorted sharply.

'Oh you know what I mean, you silly girl,' he placated, smiling, his eyes fond and admiring.

'Don't pay any attention to this idiot farmer with me,' Katharine cried, hugging her. 'You always look lovely, but tonight you surpass yourself.'

'So do you, Kath.'

The two girls smiled at each other affectionately and Katharine, tucking her arm through Francesca's, walked her over to the bar, where she asked for a glass of red wine. Kim did the same, and once they had their drinks, Francesca said, 'Come and look at the gardens; they're out of this world.'

Kim whistled again, and several times said, 'Doris certainly knows how to do things, and she doesn't mind spending her lovely dollars. The grounds are enchanting.'

Katharine agreed, and she and Kim stood surveying the scene, discussing the overall effect, talking about the dance in general.

Francesca took little sips of her champagne, preoccupied with Victor. But although she was caught up in her internal world, she was a sensitive girl, attuned to others, and very soon began to realize that Katharine was unusually nervous tonight, puffing constantly on her cigarette, drinking the red wine a little too quickly, speaking in a tone that was singularly high-pitched for her. Francesca became aware of Katharine's extreme pallor, wondered if her friend was not feeling well. She dismissed this idea at once. Unlike everyone else at the villa, Katharine was avoiding the sun because of her impending film. In consequence, her paleness was unique, stood out markedly. Examining that extraordinarily beautiful face more closely, Francesca noticed the faint dark smudges under Katharine's eyes – tell-tale signs of sleepless nights. I hope everything is all right between her and Kim, Francesca thought, worrying about them. Of course it is, she told herself firmly. The past week had gone smoothly, without incident, and they had laughed a lot, enjoyed themselves. Except for yesterday. Now Francesca remembered Katharine's unexpected moodiness, the curious agitation which had taken hold of her around mid-morning. She had been morose and uncommunicative all through the rest of the day and well into the evening.

Katharine said, 'You're daydreaming, Frankie darling. I asked you what Doris is wearing.'

'Oh sorry. A gown by Madame Grès. Draped chiffon, with one shoulder. Sort of Grecian, Kath.'

'And the most incredible necklace you've ever seen,' Kim told them. 'I saw her a little earlier, and I was positively blinded.'

'As usual!' Katharine's laughter was shrill in the tranquil silence. She thought of Doris with some animosity. How that woman irritated her. Wisely, she went on in a softer voice, 'I've never seen such fabulous jewels. Every piece is unique.'

'Yes, that's true,' Francesca agreed. She looked at Katharine with keenness, immediately recalling her nickname for Doris. *Diamond Lil.* It had sounded rather mean when Victor had repeated it. But Katharine was never mean. Perhaps she thought the name was amusing, Francesca decided, for certainly it was not in this sweet and loving girl to ever be vindictive.

Kim exclaimed, 'Here come the engaged couple now, *avec* Christian, looking rather splendid in his togs.'

Doris and the Earl, flanking Christian in the wheelchair, strolled towards them. Doris was a vision in the pale turquoise gown, the collar of diamonds, sapphires and turquoises blazing around her neck. The three of them paused when they were a couple of feet away, their faces wreathed in smiles as they regarded Francesca, and they were so generous with their compliments that she found herself blushing furiously.

The Earl could not take his eyes off his daughter. He saw a new sophistication in her face and he thought: My little girl has grown up. His heart clenched with love for her. I'll be losing her soon, in the not too distant future. Some young buck is going to sweep her off her feet, carry her away.

Francesca walked up to her father, took his arm. 'Thank you, Daddy. For the dress. For everything.'

'Nothing I could ever do is quite enough for you, my darling,' he murmured, patting her hand resting on his arm. 'And Doris is right. You're simply breathtaking. You do me proud on this very special night of my life, Frankie.'

Katharine was on the sidelines, out of the limelight for once. She was silent, watching, drawing on her cigarette. Her mind strayed to the news she had received yesterday and worry gripped her again, quenching the brightness in her eyes.

David, turning to Katharine, said kindly, 'And you also look ravishing, my dear.'

'Thank you, David.' She smiled at all of them, then addressed Doris, 'If Francesca is the fairytale princess tonight, then you are the fairy godmother. You've certainly waved a magic wand and created a superb effect in the gardens.'

'How nice of you to say so,' Doris responded, summoning a smile. Try as she did, she could not warm to Katharine. Clearing her throat, Doris went on with briskness, 'However, I didn't do very much. I left most of it to the caterers and the staff. Now, David, shall we get a drink?'

'Immediately, my dear. We must toast my beautiful bride-to-be. What would you like, Christian?'

'I think champagne's in order, Uncle David, since we're going to drink to Doodles.'

The Earl and Doris headed for the bar, and Christian said to Francesca, 'Diana's a bit tardy.'

'Oh she'll be down in a few minutes, don't worry.' Bending her head to his, Francesca dropped her voice and asked gently, 'Was Aunt Arabella all right, when you spoke to her earlier?'

'Yes. In fact she sounded stronger, better than usual. Uncle David was with us when we 'phoned her, and she talked to him for a few minutes. He was disappointed she'd changed her mind, but glad she was in happier spirits.' Christian brought his cigarettes out, struck a match. 'Diana was right when she said Mother wouldn't leave West Berlin. But the trip would have done her good, and I know Grandmother was crushed when it was cancelled at the last minute.'

'Perhaps they'll attend the wedding. I know Daddy has high expectations that they will.'

The Earl and Doris returned with glasses of champagne. David proposed a toast to his beaming fiancée, and everyone drank her health, wishing them both the greatest of happiness. David led Doris to a table, and they sat down, holding hands, smiling into each other's faces, lost in their own world. Kim began a discussion with Christian about the speech he intended to make during supper, and Francesca slid away, her mind focusing, as always, on Victor. She wished he would arrive. She was taut and feverish with excitement. Hurry up, hurry up, her restless heart cried, and she drifted along the terrace, calming herself, aware the others would notice if her behaviour was at all unusual. She edged down the marble steps, regarding the gardens. But she saw only Victor's face, for her whole being was filled with him.

Eventually Francesca walked back up the steps. Katharine, who was at the bar getting another glass of wine, waved, then floated towards her. Francesca would never know exactly how it happened, but as Katharine drew level with her she seemed to stumble or trip, lurched forward, and then regained her balance awkwardly. Francesca stepped aside. Unfortunately her reflexes were slower than usual, and she was a fraction too late. The red wine streamed out of the glass wobbling dangerously in Katharine's unsteady hand, struck Francesca's evening gown on the bodice and splashed onto the skirt just below the waistline.

Horrified, Francesca stared down at the dripping peach organza, gasping, 'Oh no! My dress! My dress!' She was unable to move, could only gape at the disfiguring stains, the dripping fabric, through eyes wide with shock and disbelief and welling with tears. The evening gown was a disaster.

Katharine cried, 'Oh my God, Frankie! I'm sorry! It was an accident. I tripped.'

Doris, her face cold with anger, had leapt up and was hurrying over to the two girls. Without pausing, she shouted, 'Kim, get soda water from the bar. And salt. I *think* there's salt on the bar.'

Christian, wheeling himself furiously behind Doris, called over his shoulder to his cousin, 'And bring serviettes, Kim.'

Doris took hold of Francesca, who was trembling uncontrollably, and guided her back to the table, murmuring soothing words. David, also on his feet, stepped forward anxiously, his face etched with concern. He pressed Francesca into the chair gently, endeavoured to calm her. He felt completely helpless. He knew his daughter did not have another gown that was beautiful enough to wear to the dance, or even one that was remotely suitable. Dismay brought a shadow to his light eyes.

Doris said, 'Don't worry, my darling, we'll fix it somehow.'

Fresh tears sprang into Francesca's eyes, trickled down her cheeks, streaking them with mascara. 'We'll never fix it,' she sobbed. 'The dress is ruined before he . . . before the dance has even begun.'

Katharine hovered nervously, clutching the empty glass. Her white face had turned ashen, was stark. She was unable to speak. But Doris had not lost her voice. She pivoted to Katharine, hissing. 'You're not *usually* so clumsy. Quite the contrary, I'd say.' The look she gave the other girl expressed her distaste, her fulminating rage.

Spots of colour flamed on Katharine's cheeks. She drew in her breath, cried heatedly, 'It was an accident. I didn't do it on purpose. I'd never do anything to hurt Frankie.'

Oh no, Doris thought. I bet you wouldn't, you treacherous little monster. She grabbed the napkin and soda water from Kim, bent over Francesca, and started to clean the dress, dabbing it carefully. She sprinkled salt on the stains, watched the wine lift off, colouring the salt pink. She brushed the fabric quickly with a dry napkin, gave the salt cellar back to Kim. 'No more of this. It'll take the colour out.'

Kim turned to Katharine. 'What on earth happened?' he asked, his expression troubled.

'I'm not sure,' Katharine moaned, her distress evident. 'I must have slipped on the marble.'

Kim bit his lip, at a loss. Like his father he felt useless in this emergency. He also knew the situation, was aware his sister's wardrobe was meagre. Damn and blast, he said inwardly, annoyed with Katharine. A muscle worked in his temple.

Christian pulled out his handkerchief, passed it to Francesca. 'Mop your eyes, darling, your beautiful make-up is running.'

Diana arrived, glanced from one to the other, saw the gown. Astonishment and alarm registered at once. 'Oh Cheska, your beautiful dress!'

Christian explained what had transpired, and Diana cried, 'We must get the dress off immediately, iron out the dampness, and then cover the stains with something. But what? Let me think.'

Doris, her face brightening, exclaimed, 'Flowers, Diana! How about a long trailing corsage of fresh flowers? Pink roses, honeysuckle. There's lots to choose from in the gardens, and I have a vase of fresh pink rosebuds in my room.'

'That's it, Doris,' Diana said. 'Come on, I'll help you.'

At this moment Nicholas Latimer and Jake Watson sailed through the French doors, in a hurry, knowing they were late. Nick stopped short, clutched Jake's arm. His face stiffened and his heart missed a beat. Francesca was in his field of vision, slumped in the chair, her dress stained red. He leapt ahead of Jake. 'Is she injured?' he shouted, his fear running high.

The Earl came to greet him. His smile was wan as he said, 'No, no, Nick, a little accident I'm sorry to say. Red wine was spilled. I think Doris and Diana will be able to repair the damage, however, make the gown presentable.'

'No, they won't,' Francesca said dully, her voice tremulous, faltering. 'And it was such a beautiful gown. *Nobody*'s even seen it.' She stared at Nick pointedly, then beyond him to Jake, her eyes frantic, seeking that third, and most special, face.

Nick knew she was referring to Vic. He said, rather hurriedly, 'Oh, Doris, David, I'm afraid Victor's going to be slightly late. He had a 'phone call from the Coast. Just as we were leaving. Business. He'll be here shortly though.' His eyes remained on Francesca, signalling assurance.

'Of course. We do understand,' David said.

Doris, straightening up, inclined her head graciously. 'Excuse us, Nick, Jake, but Diana and I must get some garden tools.'

Diana half smiled at the two new arrivals and followed Doris at a rapid pace, her gown flaring out behind her.

Francesca fell back against the chair, nauseous and faint. She brushed her damp face with her hand, and then sudden relief trickled through her. She was glad Victor was late, that he was not seeing her like this. And quite unexpectedly her hopes soared. Perhaps Doris and Diana *would* be able to disguise the damage with the flowers. After all, her cousin was unusually creative, and imaginative with clothes. She looked down at the ugly splotches. Old blood, she thought. The stains look like old blood. She shivered.

Nick's expression revealed his love, his tenderness towards her, and he said, 'Come on, kid, dry your tears.' His laughter was lighthearted; he wished to diminish the importance of the problem, cheer her up. 'You're not meant to play the tragic heroine.' As he mouthed these words he pictured Victor wrangling with Arlene back at La Réserve, prayed his friend would manage to escape, otherwise Francesca would indeed be a tragic heroine. Oh Jesus, he muttered under his breath. Nevertheless, he kept his smile in place, and continued brightly, 'Let's get you to your room, so you can fix up that gorgeous face of yours.'

Jake, hovering solicitously, suggested, 'Perhaps we can do something with this stole, tie it around your waist, drape it down the front of the gown. I'm sure it would be easy to stitch in place.' Hs rested his hand on her shoulder comfortingly. 'We'll have you bandbox smart in no time, honey.'

Doris and Diana were back, armed with flower baskets, gardening gloves, garden scissors. Doris, in full command and bristling with efficiency, said, 'We're going to the gardens. We'll only be a few minutes. Yves is searching out some fine wire, so that we can bind the flowers into a corsage, maybe two. Marie has gone to my suite to heat the iron. Kim, please take your sister upstairs.'

'Righto,' Kim helped Francesca out of the chair.

Katharine stepped towards her, and said in a quivering voice, 'Frankie darling, I'm so terribly, terribly sorry. *You* know it was an accident, don't you?'

Francesca nodded. 'Yes, Kath, of course I do.' A tiny suggestion of a smile flicked into her hazel eyes, was gone. 'I'd better get a move on before the other guests start arriving.'

When his children had left, the Earl asked Jake and Nick what they would like to drink. 'I guess it's vodka on the rocks for both of us, please.' Jake looked at Nick, who nodded, and then accompanied David to the bar.

Nick stood alone with Katharine and Christian. Nick said incredulously, 'So this is *your* fault . . . *you* spilled the wine . . .' Anger bubbled inside him and he lit a cigarette, afraid to continue, afraid of what he might say.

Katharine looked up into his lean, bronzed face, gave him a direct, unwavering stare. He's wearing his flat blues, she thought, inspecting those eyes inspecting her, hating him. 'Yes,' she said at last. 'It was my fault. But it was an accident. I slipped.' The bleakness on his face, his cold reproachful look, so unnerved her that she started to tremble, and tears swamped her eyes.

Christian, witnessing this brief but icy exchange, was startled, for he had recognized the exceptional loathing they felt for each other. He broke the deathly silence when he said, 'Now, now, Katharine my dear, don't upset yourself further. Everyone knows it was an accident. Unfortunate, of course, but no one is blaming you. Come along, let's go and sit over there at one of the tables, until you feel more composed.'

'Yes,' she mumbled, wanting to escape Nicholas Latimer. Her *bête noire*.

Christian pushed himself ahead, then stopped. He swung his head, and said, 'I'm afraid I gave my handkerchief to Francesca, Nick. Do you have one please, old chap? For Katharine.'

Nick put his hand in his pocket, and gave her his white handkerchief without saying a word.

'Thank you,' she whispered with a small sniffle, choking back a sob, patting her eyes with it.

'Please excuse me, Christian.' Nick strode away as fast as possible. He joined Jake and the Earl at the bar, pressed down on his antipathy for Katharine, worried about Francesca.

*   *   *

383

'What do you think we ought to do?' Jake frowned, guided Nick away from the group of guests thronging one of the bars in the gardens.

Nick exhaled heavily. 'It beats me.' He glanced at his watch. 'Jesus, it's ten thirty already! I bet he can't shake free of Arlene.'

Nicky looked so depressed that Jake's own considerable worry intensified. 'You don't really mean that, do you?'

'Sure I do.'

Jake pondered briefly, then shook his head and asserted more positively, 'I have to disagree. If I know Victor, he'll extricate himself from that situation, and *pronto*. If he hasn't done so by now. Look, I bet he's on the road. Remember how long it took us to get here from Beaulieu tonight. Let's give him enough time. And we'd better play it cool, *bubeleh*. Nice and cool and easy. If we start showing our nervousness, Francesca's going to be alerted, and she'll be upset again.'

Startled though he was on hearing this, Nick kept a straight face. 'I don't get it . . . what do you mean?'

'I've had my suspicions about Victor and Francesca for some time. *He* sort of confirmed it, without really doing so, if you know what I mean. Their secret's safe with me. Victor knows I won't blab. I also get the picture. Arlene's a crafty dame, and as hard boiled as they come, as I've been telling him for the longest time. So I don't blame him for being cagey. Don't worry, Nicky, I've every intention of protecting him all the way in this. I love that guy, in much the same manner you do. I owe him everything. I think he deserves a bit of happiness in his life . . . Francesca's exactly right for him, and I told him so. In no uncertain terms.'

Nick realized there was no purpose to be served by dissembling any longer. Honesty was in order. 'Okay, so you know. And Vic knows you know. Let's just leave it at that for now. I think I'm going to call him, Jake, find out what's going – '

'Watch it,' Jake warned. 'Diana's heading this way. And look happy, for Christ's sake. Your face is funereal.'

Diana walked into Nicky's outstretched arms, her smile wide. 'There you are, darling,' she said, kissing his cheek. He hugged her fiercely, adoring her. After a second, she freed herself from his embrace, turned to Jake, who bent forward to kiss her.

She said, 'I'm sorry there was such an uproar when you first arrived. I didn't even get a chance to say hello to you both.'

'We understand,' Jake replied. 'How is Francesca? And where is she?'

Diana waved a hand in the direction of the terrace. 'Up there. We just came downstairs a few minutes ago, and she got caught up with some of her father's guests – from England. And she's marvellous, feeling happy again. We had the dress pressed, and Doris and I made several sprays of flowers. They cover the stains . . . well, just about. Cheska redid her make-up whilst we worked on the gown, and she's as beautiful as ever.'

'Thank God for that.' Nick stepped back, eyed Diana. A little silver odalisque, he thought, drinking in her beauty. She was dressed in a loose flowing gown of pearl-grey chiffon, the fabric shot through with silver threads. It was cut low at the front in a V neckline, and had long wide sleeves. A strand of diamonds gleamed at her throat, matching the delicate bracelets on each wrist, the single solitaires in each ear. Her silver-gilt hair was smoothed away from her face, and dropped down her back in a plait entwined with silver ribbons. 'And you never looked lovelier, Diana!' he exclaimed, and beamed approvingly.

'Why thank you, darling.' She dropped a small curtsy.

'I second that,' Jake said. 'Now, my fair one, what can I get you to drink?'

'I think I'll have a vodka and tonic, please. I need it after this rather fraught hour.'

'No sooner said than done.' Jake disappeared.

Putting his arm around her, pulling her to him possessively, Nick murmured. 'I haven't had a chance to tell you I love you today. And I do. More and more as the minutes tick by.'

'And I love you, my *dearest* Nicky,' she responded, her eyes glowing, confirming her words.

'Let's keep it that way, shall we?'

'For ever.' She smiled up at him. Their gaze held steady on each other. I hope it *will* be for ever, Nick thought. He considered Vic's cautionary words of a week ago, as he had been doing since they had had their man-to-man talk. Vic had warned him not to aim so high with Diana, not to expect his romance with her to become anything more than just that – a romance. Victor believed she was too devoted to her brother and her mother, too concerned about her father's fate, to make a serious commitment to any man. Vic had told him he would get hurt if he didn't watch his step. I'll take my chances with her, Nick decided for the hundredth time. He kissed the top of Diana's head, touched her face lightly.

'You looked so pensive for a moment, Nicholas Latimer. Are you all right?'

'I've got you in my arms, haven't I?'

'Yes. And for me that's the happiest, safest place to be.' Diana nestled closer. 'And you're the nicest, sweetest man I've ever known, and so very considerate. Thanks, darling, for bringing Christian to the gardens. Uncle David told me how solicitous you were, pushing him down the driveway and out here. Where is he, do you know?'

'Last seen in the clutches of pretty Belinda Ampher.' Nick glanced around. 'Look, they're down by the other bar. Want to join them?'

Diana's eyes found her brother. She smiled happily. 'No, he seems as if he's having a good time. I'm so glad Belinda's taken to him. Here comes the radiant Cheska!' She waved to her cousin.

'You're as good as new, kid,' Nick told Francesca enthusiastically when she joined them.

'Thanks to Doris, and this very talented girl,' she said, linking her arm through Diana's. 'Didn't she do an imaginative and skilful job with the flowers, Nicky?'

'And then some, kid. They look as if they belong to the gown. Nobody would guess they're camouflage.'

Jake meandered back with Diana's drink. He gave it to her, then took hold of Francesca's hand, twirled her around. 'You're perfection,' he announced.

The sweetest of smiles touched her lips. 'Thank you, Jake. Thanks also for being so nice earlier. You too, Nicky. You both made me feel so much better.' She craned her neck, her eyes sweeping the gardens, and remarked casually, 'There's quite a crowd here already I see. By the way, where's Victor?'

Nick had been dreading the question, and he swallowed. Jake, sensing he was discomfited, swiftly pronounced, 'Traffic! I mean he's undoubtedly stuck on the *corniche*. You know what it's like in this neck of the woods on Saturday nights. Particularly in August with all the tourists.'

'Yes, the roads are pretty gruesome. Well, I expect he'll get here some time.' Francesca hoped her dismay and disappointment were not showing, that she did not sound offhand. 'I'm afraid I was so distracted when you got here, I didn't actually hear what you said. About the reason for his delay.' She cast a sidelong look at Nick.

She heard all right, Nick thought. She's playing it cool because of Jake's presence. He said, 'Victor had a business call. From the Coast.' Improvising now, he went on, 'The studio called. Fox. About the Western he's going to make for them in November. Something to do with his co-stars. I'm not – ' The rest of Nick's sentence was smothered by a gasp. He frowned, his attention concentrated on the man approaching them from the main lawn. 'Holy Christ!' He grabbed Jake's arm. 'Do my eyes deceive me, old buddy, or is that really Mike Lazarus heading straight for us?'

'By God, it is!'

'What the hell is *he* doing here?' Nick asked Francesca.

'I believe he's staying with Beau Stanton, at the villa in Cap d'Antibes. I vaguely remember Doris saying something about Beau wanting to bring his house guests, the day we were writing the place cards. He has Pandora Tremaine and her mother in tow, as well as Mike Lazarus and Hilly Street. That's all I know.' Surprised at Nick's strong reaction, she asked anxiously, 'Why are you upset?'

Nick opened his mouth, shut it, as Lazarus drew to a stop in front of them. Mike Lazarus smiled, inclined his head courteously, his rapid glance encompassing them all. 'Hello, my friend. How are you?' He thrust his hand at Nick.

Knowing he had no option but to respond with cordiality, Nicky took the hand, shook it. 'I'm fine, Mike. And you?'

'Couldn't be better,' Lazarus replied.

Nick made the introductions, and Lazarus said to Francesca, 'Ah yes, you're the Earl of Langley's daughter. I just met your brother. Charming young man. We had a most enlightening talk about art, about Turner to be specific. I'm a collector, you know, and I've always hankered after a Turner. Your brother told me your father owns quite a number of incomparable watercolours by him. Apparently they're not for sale. A pity.'

Francesca nodded, answered several questions which Lazarus posed to her, and then stood listening politely as he continued his dissertation on art.

Nick had to admit that the man was extremely knowledgeable, knew his subject, spoke with authority. He was a connoisseur. He's also a son of a bitch, Nick said to himself. He studied Lazarus keenly, wary of him, responding to him with the same intense dislike and apprehension as he had the afternoon they met in the Ritz. Nick felt the man's enormous power, his controlled strength, caught the resonance of it in his voice. The smile on his dark face was benign, but the eyes, so palely blue, were cold, deadly. He's dangerous, Nick thought. Machiavellian. A throwback to those sinister Princes of the Blood. Scheming, plotting, manipulative. A killer.

Lazarus spoke.

'I'm sorry, Mike, I didn't quite catch that,' Nick apologized.

386

Irritation flicked into the pale eyes. 'I *said* Beau introduced me to Katharine Tempest.' His smile was almost a sneer. He went on, 'Seemingly I was wrong about the young lady. Beau says she is sublime. I must agree. Not that I have seen her on the screen, as Beau and Hillard have, but she is indeed sublime in the flesh. A perfect beauty. Flawless. She is like a delicate statue, cut from ivory. You know, she ought to be sculpted. But who could do her justice? Only a Michelangelo. I must apologize to Victor for being so dismissive of her. Incidentally, I hear from everyone that he pulled it off. From what Hillard says, *Wuthering Heights* is one hell of a picture after all.'

Nick and Jake immediately became embroiled with Lazarus on the subject of the film. Diana found this fascinating, gave her attention to the three men. But Francesca shut out their voices, dwelling on the things Lazarus had said about Katharine, reviewing his words. He talked about Kath as if she were an object, not a person. A beautiful inanimate thing to be acquired, another possession for his collection, to put in his gallery, she thought. Probably under glass and appropriately lighted. Francesca bit her inner lip. What a peculiar man. So cold and pompous and just a little frightening. She discovered she did not like him at all.

Lazarus said, 'Ah, excuse me, gentlemen, I see my fiancée.' He raised his right arm, beckoned with his index finger.

Nick's heart skipped. Hélène Vernaud, tall, splendid, outrageously glamorous in pale-green watered silk and a blaze of emeralds, was gliding across the grass, a smile fixed on her elegant, intelligent face. He almost fell over when she extended her hand to him.

'Hello, Nicholas. How nice to see you again.'

Her natural greeting, the warmth of her tone, the tranquil expression in her eyes told him that Lazarus was now acquainted with their past relationship, and that it did not matter. He took her hand, weighted by an impressive emerald that had to be all of thirty-five carats, and said, 'It's been a long time, Hélène. You're as beautiful as always.'

She smiled, dropped his hand, positioned herself next to Lazarus, and Nick introduced her to everyone. Hélène, looking at Francesca, said, 'How gracious Madame Asternan is, so *raffinée*, so *ravissante*. I am so happy to be here, to be part of the celebration of her engagement to your father. And to see many old friends. That is always a pleasure, *n'est-pas?*' she finished in her curiously stilted English.

'Oh yes, I couldn't agree more,' Francesca replied graciously, smiling inwardly at Nick's expression, fully aware that Hélène Vernaud was a former girlfriend. She wondered if Diana knew this.

Nick said, 'I understand you're staying with Beau Stanton, Hélène. Will you be on the Riviera long?'

'I do not know, Nicholas. That is up to Michel. The yacht sails into Monte Carlo tomorrow. We may cruise to the Greek Islands.' She smiled at Lazarus, as though asking him their plans. He looked enigmatic, made no comment, and Hélène added, 'I do not see Victor anywhere.'

Not giving Nick a chance to reply, Lazarus exclaimed, 'Yes, where are the Masons? I was looking for them, expected to find them here with you.'

Nick froze. He heard the faint rustle of Francesca's gown, was conscious that she had stiffened. He felt Diana's eyes on him, wide, questioning. He wished the ground would open up and swallow him.

'He's not arrived yet,' Nick muttered, hardly recognizing his own voice. He prayed Lazarus would probe no farther, would let the subject rest there.

Hélène laughed lightly, said with gaiety, 'I ran into Arlene Mason at the *aéroport* in Nice earlier this evening. I had arrived from Paris in Michel's plane. She had flown in from London. She did not have the car. I could not permit her to take the taxi. She came with me. Michel's chaffeur drove her to La Réserve.' She laughed again. 'So many reminiscences. We spent the entire drive from the *aéroport* to Beau's villa talking about the week we all spent in Rome together a few years ago. Do you remember it, Nicholas?'

'Yes,' he gulped, aghast at her words. She had spoken innocently – and she had flipped up the lid on Pandora's box.

There was a scathing note in Lazarus's voice as he remarked, 'Movie stars are persistently late. They like to make a grand entrance. Children, for the most part.'

No one said a word, and Diana, coughing loudly, threw Lazarus a disapproving look.

Lazarus, smiling with his usual superciliousness, went on, 'When Victor *does* get here, please tell him I'd like a chat for a moment, also that I intend to claim at least one dance with his glamorous wife. Come, Hélène, we'd better be moving along.' He nodded, Hélène smiled, and they walked away, chatting to each other.

Jake, as appalled as Nicky and aware of the stunned expressions on the girls' faces, had already planned his strategy. He sprang into the breach. 'How about fresh drinks for everybody?' He whisked the glasses away from Francesca and Nick before they could reply, then went on, 'Would you mind helping me to carry the refills, Diana?'

'Of course not,' Diana said, her eyes swinging from Nick's face to Francesca's and back to Nick's. Her stare was disbelieving. Nick attempted to reassure her with his eyes, as though saying everything would be all right. He hoped to God it would be.

Jake led Diana to the nearest bar, and with considerable speed, before she could say a word to Nicholas or Francesca. He knew it was wisest to leave these two alone for a few minutes.

Nicky could not bring himself to look at Francesca. He had no words. His mind floundered. How the hell was he going to explain?

She said, in a voice so low he could hardly hear it, 'I thought it sounded funny, a business call on Saturday night. Why did you lie to me, Nick?'

He turned to face her slowly, his expression pained. He reached out, pulled her closer to him, gazed down into her face. It was glazed with shock. 'What else could I do? Anyway, it was Vic's idea . . . the story about the 'phone call. And I elected to go along with it, because I thought it was the wisest thing, under the circumstances. Arlene landed on him unexpectedly, just as we were leaving. He had to stay and talk to her. But he'll be here in a minute.'

'*Will he?*'

'Sure he will! I'm expecting to see that ugly mug of his any second. You'll – '

'And will he have his *glamorous wife* on his arm?' Her voice was still virtually inaudible but now it held a hint of acerbity.

'Of course she won't be with him. He's coming alone.'

'We'll see, won't we?' Her lip trembled. She glanced away, then said in an accusatory tone, 'You could have told me the truth, Nick. It was ridiculous of Vic to make you fib. I'm not a child.'

'But sweetheart, he didn't want you to be unnecessarily upset, and for no real reason. Listen, he's – ' He paused as Jake and Diana hove in sight, carrying their drinks.

After these had been handed over, Jake stepped backwards, saying, 'Diana and I are going to find Christian and Belinda. If we can in this mob. Excuse us for a while?'

'Sure, see ya later, old buddy.' Nick was suddenly grateful for Jake's presence, his wonderful tact, and his ability to think fast.

Alone again, Francesca whispered miserably, 'I don't understand, Nicky. Why is *she* here?'

'I honestly don't know, kid, and that's the God's truth. Vic was baffled as well. But there's nothing to worry about. He asked me to assure you of that. Leave it to Vic. He'll – '

'Everything's going wrong,' Francesca wailed. 'First the accident with the dress, now this. The dress – that was a bad omen, and I have a terrible presentiment it's going to turn into a horrid evening.'

He saw the tears sparkling in her eyes, heard the unhappiness and disappointment in her young voice. He gripped her arm so tightly she winced. Nick bent closer, peered into her glum face. 'Now listen to me, kid. Stop being so negative!' he cried firmly. 'The dress is fabulous, you're gorgeous, and Vic is pretty damned smart. He'll get here. This unexpected development has merely delayed him. Remember one thing – Victor loves you. Hold that thought, sweetheart.'

When she made no response, Nick said in the softest of voices and with the utmost gentleness. 'That's all that counts, Francesca darling.'

Distressed though she was, and reeling from innumerable emotions, Francesca knew Nicholas Latimer spoke the truth. She took a deep breath and brushed her eyes with her hand. A tentative and watery smile appeared, and her voice was brighter as she said, 'Yes, you're right, Nick dear. I'd better pull myself together and behave like a big girl. I must also put up a gay front. I can see Daddy coming down the steps with Doris. I mustn't spoil their special evening, not for anything. That would be so unfair of me.' She touched his arm and appealed, 'Can you give Vic a ring to find out if he's left yet? Please, Nicky?'

'Sure thing, angel. I'll go and do it right away.'

He left her standing with her father and Doris, loped the length of the lawn and up the steps onto the terrace. He dodged between the guests milling around, went through the main salon and out into the entrance hall. He found the telephone, dialled La Réserve.

When the hotel operator answered, he said, 'Good evening. This is Monsieur Latimer. May I speak to Monsieur Mason, please.'

'*Ah, bon soir, Monsieur Latimer*. Monsieur Mason is in the restaurant. *Ne quittez pas!*'

What the hell's he doing in the restaurant? Nick asked himself, gripping the receiver tighter, his nerves jangling. There was only one answer to that. Victor was well and truly stuck with Arlene. Nick took a long swallow of his drink, placed it on the table, pulled out his cigarettes, lit one anxiously.

'Jesus Christ, Nicky, why didn't you call me before?' Victor hissed down the 'phone when he came on the line a minute later. 'You must have *known* I couldn't call *you*. I'm crazed with worry. How's Ches?'

'Okay, but the situation's not the greatest. I hate to tell you this, but the cat's out of the bag. About Arlene. Accidentally released by Hélène Vernaud.' Nick repeated Hélène's conversation to the accompaniment of muffled groans at the other end of the wire. When he had finished, Nick asked quietly, 'What are you going to do, Vic? Francesca knows I'm calling you. I'll have to tell her something.'

'Listen, Nicky, I've got real problems with Arlene. Goddamn serious problems. Can't go into them now. We're just finishing dinner. I've already told her I'm going to bunk with you or Jake tonight. This is my plan. After dinner, in about ten minutes, I'll take her back upstairs, say goodnight and leave, ostensibly for your suite. But I'll slip out, hightail it to the dance. Whose car did you take? Mine or Jake's?'

'Jake's, and the Citroën is parked where we left it after lunch.'

'Good. Arlene's poured a lot of booze down herself, before dinner and during. She won't be a problem. Hold the beachhead for me, kid. I'll be there.'

'All right, Vic. It sounds like a reasonable enough plan. But for God's sake get rolling as soon as you can.'

'Tell Ches I'm about to leave. Okay?'

'Okay, maestro.' Nick replaced the receiver with relief. He picked up his drink, turned, saw Jake Watson hurrying through the main salon.

'Been calling Victor? Is he still at the hotel? Is he going to make it?' Jake shot the questions at Nick with staccato delivery.

Nick nodded.

'Well, what's the scoop, kid?'

'He's about to leave.'

'Thank God for that.' Jake took out his handkerchief and patted his forehead. 'Phew! I feel as if I've been on a roller coaster for the last hour.'

'I know exactly what you mean. Is Francesca still with her father and Doris?'

'No. She's talking to Hilary Pierce and Terry Ogden.'

Surprise streaked across Nick's face. 'They're here together!'

'And how they're together. I guess they finally decided to go public, picked tonight to do it. Hilary told me she's divorcing Mark to marry Terry. Made no bones about it.' Jake grinned. 'Some evening, eh, *bubeleh*?'

'It's getting a bit too rich and heady for my blood, Jake.'

'But you can't say it's not interesting. Quite a cast of characters here and present when you make the roll call.'

'Yeah. And half of 'em stepped right out of the pages of a second-rate screenplay!'

Jake chuckled. 'Too true. But some of them are pretty nifty. Classy types, and it's a distinctive mix. High society, show business, big business. Incidentally, Doris informed me we're sitting at table three. It's near the bandstand. Numbered. You'll find it. I'll meet you back there.'

'Where are you going?'

'To the car. Forgot my cigars earlier.'

Nick saluted and hurried across the terrace and down into the gardens. He soon found Hilary, glowing and glorious in shocking-pink taffeta, flanked by a doting Terry and Jerry Massingham. Greetings were exchanged and Nick told them he was looking for Francesca.

Terry said, 'She's over there. On the dance floor. With Beau Stanton.'

Nick scanned the dancers, currently performing a cha-cha-cha to a Latin American beat, his eyes lighting on Francesca. She appeared to be in good hands with the elegant, debonair Stanton and looked as though she was enjoying herself. He relaxed.

'I've fallen madly in love,' Terry announced, placing his hand on Nick's shoulder, beaming at him delightedly.

Nick smiled. 'My congratulations. She's a lovely lady.' He winked at Hilary.

'Oh, I wasn't referring to Hilary,' Terry exclaimed. 'Although I do love and adore *her*, have for years. Actually, I was talking about Beau Stanton. I just met him for the first time. What a marvellous gent he is, and his easy charm is as irresistible off screen as it is on. I've always admired his talent as an actor – his style and grace, and his real flair for sophisticated comedy. He's a lot like Cary Grant actually. Anyway, he's going to give a dinner party for us when we get to Hollywood, sort of show us the ropes. Damned sweet of him.'

'Yes it is,' Nick agreed. 'And I'll tell you this, Terry, you'll meet only the very best with him. He's old guard Hollywood, the Establishment, and heads the English contingent. Has for years, since the thirties.' The music stopped, and Nick, who was facing the floor, saw Francesca and Beau pause to speak to Katharine Tempest. His eyes narrowed. *She* was draped on the arm of Mike Lazarus, had obviously been dancing with him. A well-matched pair. Birds of a feather, he thought sardonically.

Beau Stanton escorted Francesca over to them, shook Nick's hand, stood chatting for a few moments. He's got to be fifty, yet he *is* ageless, looks ten years younger, Nick noted, examining Stanton discreetly. Beau held the stage, the famous voice ringing out, its upper class English tones enlivened by the faintest undertone of cockney.

'What the deuce has happened to my mate Victor?' Beau suddenly demanded, focusing on Nick. 'Everybody's looking for him, misses his shining presence. Why, this little shindig won't be the same without him. I, for one, was counting on his company tonight.'

'He'll be here shortly, Beau,' Nick replied.

'Jolly good.' Beau lifted Francesca's hand and kissed it, making the old-world gesture seem perfectly natural. 'Don't forget, I've reserved several more dances, my dear. Not that you'll escape me so easily, since we're at the same table.'

Beau made a graceful exit, and Nick said, 'Can I have a word with you, sweetheart?'

'Of course, Nicky.' She grabbed his hand, and they excused themselves, drifted out of earshot. Francesca's face was radiant. 'I can tell from your expression that everything's all right, Nicky. Vic's on his way! He's left, hasn't he?'

'Just about, kid. I caught him as he was leaving the hotel,' Nick fibbed, adding quickly, 'The roads should be clearer at this hour. He'll shoot up here with no problems, be with us in no time at all.'

'Oh that's wonderful, Nicky!' She flung her arms around him, hugged him tightly, then pulled away from him. 'You are sure he's coming, aren't you?'

'I'm sure I'm sure, sweetheart. Now let's get ourselves a drink and start enjoying this bash. It's long overdue.' He took her arm, and they strolled up to one of the bars, where Nick ordered a glass of champagne for Francesca, a vodka on the rocks for himself. His eyes roamed about, seeking Diana.

Francesca stood next to him, the radiance unmarred on her lovely face. The feeling of heaviness and the black depression that had weighed her down for the past hour were lifting. The tension was slipping out of her, was being replaced by the high expectancy and feverish excitement of earlier. The evening had started badly, but everything was going to be all right now. Victor would soon be here, and it would be a romantic and memorable night, just the way she had planned.

But Victor Mason did not come.

CHAPTER THIRTY-SIX

The *Artemis* was a 2,000-ton ocean-going yacht that began her life as a British frigate originally christened the *Curlew*. Mike Lazarus bought the vessel for thirty-five thousand pounds from the Royal Navy, then spent over three million dollars transforming her into one of the most luxurious yachts in the world. Sleek of line, she was exquisitely furnished, and embellished with incomparable art treasures culled from all corners of the globe.

Once the frigate was in Lazarus's possession he had engaged Britain's most distinguished architect to redesign her, and the ship was converted by a team of the best naval architects at one of the prestigious shipyards in Newcastle-upon-Tyne. The *Artemis* was the only thing Lazarus had been known to show any emotion for, and if his conglomerate, Global-Centurion, was the crown that sat atop his greying head, then the *Artemis* was the rare diadem in its centre. She meant more to him than any woman ever had, was his real true love, and none of his mistresses had been able to dislodge or replace her in his affections.

This gleaming jewel had sailed from Marseilles into Monte Carlo harbour early on the Sunday morning following the dance at the Villa Zamir, and she had been moored in the prime berth for the past two days. Now, for the first time since she had dropped anchor, she was about to take on guests, invited to a luncheon in honour of Beau Stanton. Her captain and crew had been informed by Lazarus that he was expecting thirty people and, once they were aboard, the yacht was to sail down the French coastline to San Remo, returning to home port later in the afternoon.

Three of those guests had already arrived at the harbour and were regarding the yacht with considerable interest – Diana and Christian von Wittingen and Nicholas Latimer.

Diana shaded her eyes with her hand, her excitement growing as she studied the

Artemis, so brilliantly white and glittering in the intense mid-morning sunlight. 'You might not like Lazarus, Nicky darling, but you have to admit he has great taste when it comes to yachts!' she exclaimed.

'He's probably got great taste in a lot of things,' Nick retorted, grinning. 'Certainly he has enough dough to indulge himself in *taste*.'

Diana laughed. 'Oh, but she's so lovely. Look at her marvellous rakish lines and that high streamlined bow. Why she's perfectly beautiful. I wonder how many knots she can do per hour?'

'You sound as if you know a lot about boats,' Nick said, throwing her a surprised look.

'Ships,' she corrected. 'And I know a bit.'

'Don't let her fool you, Nicholas old chap,' Christian laughed. 'She has an enormous fund of knowledge, passed on from Grandmother, whose family have yards in Kiel and have been builders of ships for several generations.'

'You are a dark lady,' Nick teased. 'Every day I keep finding out new things about you.'

'I might say the same,' Diana rejoined with swiftness. 'You're pretty foxy yourself. Hélène Vernaud indeed!'

The puckish grin struck Nick's mouth again. 'I too have great taste – in ladies. Never more visible than at this precise moment, I might add.'

'Why thank you.' She smiled.

Christian said, 'I, for one, like Hélène immensely. We had quite an interesting chat on Saturday night. She's got a fine grasp of international big business, or so it seemed to me.'

'She does,' Nick said. 'There's a pretty shrewd brain behind that elegant face.'

'Yes, that's the *perfect* word to describe her,' Diana stated. 'Elegant of face and figure, and in the way she dresses. Very chic. She's also rather charming. She was telling me about the yacht the other evening. Apparently there is a crew of fifty-five and everything's very luxuriously done. She also told me Lazarus has a superb collection of art on board. Utrillos, a Sisley, a Pissarro, a Braque and a Degas or two, not to mention three Renoirs. I can't wait to see them.'

'I would have thought the salt air would be damaging to the canvases,' Nick murmured.

'I understand they are taken off the yacht in the winter months and stored,' Diana explained. 'It seems Lazarus only lives on her in the summer. From the things Hélène was saying, he's never in one place for very long anyway, always – '

Christian interrupted. 'I say, do excuse me, you two. I see Belinda Ampher and her parents arriving. I'll go and meet them.' He straightened his cravat, turned the wheelchair and rolled off.

'Uncle David, Doris and Kim should also be here soon and then we can go aboard,' Diana said, taking hold of Nick's hand. 'Let's go and stand over there by the wall, where it's cooler, until they come.'

'I wish *we* hadn't come,' Nick grumbled and pulled a face. 'I'm not looking forward to this jaunt.'

'Oh darling, why didn't you say so before? Perhaps we can get out of it, make our excuses – '

Nick put a finger on her lips, 'Sssh! I know you want to go, and I wouldn't disappoint you for anything, darling. Besides it would look strange if we ducked out now. There'll be plenty of other people to dilute his presence.' Nick edged closer to Diana in the cool shadow of the harbour wall, put his arm around her. 'And I'm always content when I'm with you, my love.'

She smiled up at him. 'Yes. Yes, I know. Isn't it wonderful to feel completely relaxed and happy with each other, whatever we're doing?'

He nodded, smiling back, and then his face tightened perceptibly. 'How's Francesca?'

'Even better today, and you saw how glowing she was yesterday, *after* she'd spoken to Victor. I never did get an opportunity to thank you, darling. That was such a sweet gesture on your part, getting us down to La Réserve and putting a call through to him.'

'That was Vic's idea, Diana. He was miserable about everything. Still is, if I know Vic.' Nick gave Diana a keen look, then continued, 'I know Francesca thinks it's strange. I mean the way he left for London so abruptly on Sunday. But it was the best thing under the circumstances. After all – '

'I think it's a bit odd myself,' Diana interjected quietly. 'I didn't want to bring it up in front of Cheska last night, but I really don't understand why he had to fly off with Arlene. Surely she can sit down alone with his solicitors in London, to work out the details of the settlement. Victor could have stayed here until they finished, and then gone to London later to finalize things.' Nick did not reply, and she pressed, 'Well, he could, couldn't he?'

'No, that wouldn't have worked,' Nick said, keeping his voice as even as possible, not wanting her to detect his concern. He had been apprised of the manifold complications by Victor, who had concocted the story about resolving his financial differences with Arlene to appease Francesca, explain his sudden departure. Whilst there was an element of truth in this, Nick knew the situation was a hundredfold more complex than it appeared, and explosive. He did not envy his friend's current predicament.

On an impulse Nick decided to tell Diana a few of the facts. 'I think Victor ought to have been a bit more direct with Francesca than he has.' He squeezed her hand. 'No, no, don't look like *that*. He *has* been honest, but only up to a point. He didn't want to worry her, alarm her. But there's a hell of a lot more money involved than either you or she realize, darling, and a number of annoying complications. That's why Vic felt it was necessary to be there, believed it would be easier to work things out if he was present at the meetings.' He paused to light a cigarette, went on, 'He'd been extremely generous to Arlene and she had more or less agreed to the terms, then she started to demand a lot more. For instance, fifty per cent of his production company and his ranch. That's hitting below the belt, as far as he's concerned.'

'Yes,' Diana said. 'I see what you mean.'

'Those are the chief stumbling blocks right now. He just couldn't leave these points to be settled by lawyers.'

'I suppose he couldn't,' Diana stared at Nick. 'He will be able to work it out, though, won't he?' she asked, looking troubled all of a sudden.

'You bet he will.' Nick spoke with firmness, whilst privately hoping he was right in this assumption.

'That's a relief,' Diana sighed. 'I'd hate to see Francesca hurt in any way. She's very much in love with him.' Diana pursed her lips, hesitated, then hurried on, 'I know this might sound like an unfair question to ask *you*, Nicky darling, but do you think Victor wants to marry Cheska?'

'He's a close-mouthed guy, and he hasn't actually come out and said so to me, but I do know he's heavily involved with her.' Nick shook his head slowly. 'However, I honestly don't think he'd ask Francesca to marry him until he's free to do so, to go to her father. He's aware of her age, and he wants to do everything correctly. I also know he wants his freedom, wants this divorce, and has for a long time, well before he met the little one.'

'I trust your judgment, darling.' Diana was positive Nick was speaking the truth, she also trusted Victor Mason. On the other hand, he was still married, and the difficulties about money and property were more serious and involved than she had realized. Sometimes, in this kind of complex situation, it was simpler for a man to remain married. She knew all about married men. Poor bets. No future. Nothing but heartache.

'You're looking thoughtful. A franc for them,' Nick said.

A quicksilver smile gleamed on Diana's face, and she began to laugh lightly. 'You just called Cheska *little one*. I know you meant it affectionately, but I don't think it's quite appropriate. Actually, she's pretty mature for her age. She behaved impeccably on Saturday. I'm not sure I'd have done so well, under the circumstances. She was crushed. Yet only you and I knew that. She presented a marvellous front, didn't she?'

'Breeding will out, Diana. She handled herself beautifully. I wish she'd agreed to come today. I don't like to think of her being by herself at the villa.'

'But she's not. Katharine's with her.'

'Yes.'

Diana frowned. 'Katharine's been behaving rather strangely since Saturday, wouldn't you say?' Her eyes were quizzical.

'Par for the course with her,' Nick muttered. 'Skittishness seems to be one of her characteristics.'

'I think the poor girl is still upset about the accident with the dress,' Diana said softly. 'She believes we all think she did it on purpose. Well, except for Cheska. She insists Katharine did slip, and she's been awfully sweet to her, trying to make her feel better.'

'That's your cousin for you. She always sees the best in everyone. But she'll learn.'

'Nicky, what a cynic you are!'

He shrugged. 'I guess I am. You'll have to love my faults as well as my virtues, and the prior far outweigh the latter.'

'I wouldn't say that, darling.' She hugged him, stepped away and gazed into his face, then smiled her slow grave smile. 'You know, Nicky, to tell you the truth, I'm inclined to agree with Cheska. I don't think Katharine would be so mean . . . spilling red wine all over her best friend's new evening gown. It's a pretty ghastly thing to do, if it was intentional. I suppose I want to give her the benefit of the doubt. Why don't you?'

The arrival of David Cunningham, Doris and Kim, along with Belinda Ampher, her parents and Christian, saved Nick the necessity of responding to this question.

Stewards in crisp white uniforms carrying silver trays glinting in sunshine. Champagne bubbling in the finest crystal. Mounds of Beluga caviar glistening darkly in huge bowls packed with ice. Guests strolling or chatting on the main deck. Familiar faces all. And Mike Lazarus presiding over the proceedings like a benevolent Roman emperor. Except he was not benevolent, so far as Nicholas Latimer was concerned. More like Caligula, Nick thought, eyeing Lazarus from a distance.

Nick looked down into the glass of champagne in his hand. He did not want to partake of this man's wine nor his food nor his hospitality – all stuck in his throat. He had not forgotten the parting shot Lazarus had made that afternoon at the Ritz. 'You'll live to regret this, Victor. Truly, truly regret it. I'll make damned sure of that, my friend.' Nick shivered at the memory, his intuition telling him his friend had not heard the last of the tyrannical megalomaniac. Nick detested him, was infuriated by his supercilious and condescending manner; nor had he forgotten the man's rudeness to him personally. He wondered about Lazarus, about his sudden cordiality. Nick did not trust the tycoon.

Diana waved. She was being propelled by Lazarus to the lower decks, along with David, Doris, Kim and the Wintertons. They were about to be shown the art collection. Nick had just declined the invitation to go with them. The paintings, like the food and drink, would choke him. He hovered next to Christian and Belinda, who were discussing music, for a few seconds longer, then excused himself and sauntered down the main deck, nodding to a few of the other guests, not stopping to chat. He wanted to be alone, to think. His mind was in a jumble. Momentarily he was preoccupied with Christian and his relationship with Belinda Ampher. They had been together constantly, appeared to be interested in each other. Nick hoped they were serious, not only because it would serve his purpose with Diana, but because he genuinely liked Christian, hoped he would find happiness with a woman.

Out of the corner of his eye Nick saw Hélène Vernaud talking to Beau Stanton. She was exquisitely dressed as always, in white linen pants, a canary-yellow silk shirt and masses of gold jewellery: a woman of taste, discernment and intelligence. So why is she involved with an odious man like Lazarus? To Nick they were poles apart. And yet she was now engaged to him, sporting the large emerald, acting as his hostess. She must have changed a lot, he muttered under his breath. But then, who hasn't? Nick smiled ironically as he swung his glance over the numerous guests. It is getting very inbred, incestuous, he thought. Jake is right: some cast of characters. He would miss Jake, did already. Jake had flown off to London earlier that morning, making the excuse he was bored with the sun, the sea and parties. But Nick knew Jake felt he should be on hand in London, in case Victor needed him in this crisis. He too had volunteered to go along, but Victor had wanted him to stay here, to keep an eye on Francesca.

Nick thought of Arlene Mason and her schemes. He moved closer to the rail, leaned against it, looking out to sea, replaying the events of Saturday.

At about one o'clock in the morning, alarmed by Victor's continuing absence, he had headed into the villa to call the hotel. He had run into Yves, who was coming to look for him. The butler had informed him, and apologetically, that Mr Mason had telephoned several times, asking for him. It seemed that one of the maids, hired for the evening, had only just relayed this information to Yves. Flying up the steps into the hall, he had dialled La Réserve and been put through to his own suite by the operator.

Victor had been encamped there, obviously boiling with rage and frustration, and trapped. He had said obliquely that Arlene was sick, that he had to stay with her. Victor had then asked him to apologize to David and Doris, had not mentioned Francesca at all. He had received the message loud and clear. His friend was not alone. He and Jake had returned to the hotel around four, riddled with curiosity, wondering what had really happened earlier.

And we soon found out, Nick now thought gloomily.

He had expected to find Victor in his suite, but not Arlene. Not at that hour. But she *had* been there, wearing a silver lamé evening gown, half a ton of diamonds, and a grim expression. Victor, tieless, in his shirtsleeves, his hornrimmed glasses perched on the end of his nose, was stretched out on the sofa, smoking a cigar, sipping a Scotch and studying his script for the Western. It had struck him at the time that she might not have been there. Vic had appeared totally oblivious of her.

Flabbergasted, he and Jake had strode into the suite, to be greeted by a snotty comment from Arlene.

'Your lonely vigil comes to an end,' Victor had drawled in a cutting tone, finally glancing at her with disdain. 'Nicholas will escort you to your suite. The revels are apparently over. You don't have to play watchdog any longer. I'm going to hit the sack.' Vic had jumped up, hurried into the bedroom, slammed the door.

In a boiling temper himself, Nick had rushed Arlene to Victor's suite without uttering a word to her, then made a hasty retreat.

'I saved the explanation until you were here, kid,' Victor had said when he walked back into the rooms to find the actor and Jake in a huddle on the sofa. 'I'm afraid I underestimated Arlene.' Vic had grimaced, gone on, 'I was signing the bill after dinner when she excused herself, went to the powder room. I sat there blithely planning an adroit escape, when I suddenly realized a good fifteen minutes had elapsed. I went looking for her. The concierge told me she had asked for the spare key and gone upstairs.'

Victor had paused then, had shaken his head dourly. 'And that's when I made my fatal error. I was about to slip out, beat it to the dance, when I remembered my briefcase. It was in my suite and unlocked. I didn't want Arlene rifling through it, so I came up to get it. I found her clothes strewn all over, and Arlene herself already gowned and piling on the loot. You see, she knew about the dance – from Hélène, who had mentioned it in passing on the drive from the airport. Arlene insisted on coming with me. We quarrelled, had a knock-down-drag-out fight. I gave up, said I was going to bed. She followed me to your suite, Nick, parked herself here.'

'But why didn't you simply blow?' Jake had asked wonderingly, at this point in the story.

'Oh, I thought about it,' Vic had told them with a pained and weary smile. 'But I knew she was hell bent on going, determined to make a stink, a scene, and I figured she'd get a cab, high-tail it after me if I left. So I settled in for the night. With the script. More or less ignored her. Refused to discuss anything with her.' He had leaned forward anxiously then and asked with apprehension, 'Now, tell me about Ches. Is she all right?'

Jake had said, 'Nick here can fill you in better than I.'

And he had done so, not missing one thing, and when he had finished Victor had nodded slowly. 'Yes, I knew she'd be hurt, disappointed. But I was trying to avert a disaster by staying away.' Slowly, and in sentences liberally interspersed with colourful expletives, Victor had gone on to reveal the details of Arlene's threats. He and Jake had listened carefully and with growing worry, but neither had been able to offer a possible solution to Victor's dilemma.

Victor, however, had made his own plans. 'I've decided to get her out of this neck of the woods, and *pronto*, before she can do any serious damage. Once we're in London I think I can neutralize her, reason with her, negotiate.'

Jake had agreed this was probably the best course, then retired to his own suite. Nick and Vic had talked for a while, then Vic had written a note of apology to Doris and the Earl, plus a longer letter to Francesca. Nick had delivered both on Sunday afternoon, when Victor and Arlene were already on their way to the airport in Nice.

It's a goddamn mess, Nick thought. In his anxiety to protect Francesca was Victor perhaps not underestimating the girl? He treats her like a child, when really she's pretty savvy. Nick wished he was on shore, not on this goddamned boat. Ship rather. On *terra firma* he could use a telephone, talk to Victor in London, advise him to confide his problems to Francesca.

'Pip pip! Hi there Nicholas, my darling!'

He swung around, saw Estelle, smiled, waved. Her company was infinitely less trying to him than that of some of the other imbeciles on board.

'You look smart, News Lady,' he said, his voice friendly. And she really did. For once her clothes were simple and tailored, less flamboyant than usual. She wore white slacks, a navy-blue sailor top, and a white cotton hat with a floppy brim perched on her bright red curls.

Estelle planted a kiss on his cheek and said, 'I've been looking all over for Katharine. Isn't she here?'

'No. She decided to stay at the Villa Zamir. So did Francesca. I think they've had enough parties. Haven't you? Aren't they getting you down too?'

'A bit,' she admitted, then laughed breezily. 'Still, socializing is my bread and butter, Nick. I pick up a lot of ideas for features and stories, getting around the way I do. And talking of stories, have you seen Hillard Steed?'

'No, I haven't. Didn't know he was coming. But then I guess he would be here. He's pretty close to Beau.'

'I'm hoping he's going to confirm it. Do you think he will?'

'Confirm what? I don't follow you.'

Estelle looked at him in surprise, leaned closer, dropped her tone to a confidential whisper. 'You mean you've not heard the rumours . . . about Mike Lazarus taking over Monarch Pictures? Or rather, Global-Centurion doing so?'

Nick gaped at her. 'No, I hadn't heard them,' he replied at last, and thought: Nor has Victor. Oh Jesus! If that's true, we're up a creek. Victor had a whole series of pictures planned with Monarch. Not only that, the treatment of the screenplay he planned to write for Victor and Katharine Tempest was already in Hilly Steed's hot little hands. Oh Jesus!

Estelle was saying, 'Hey Nicholas, you're looking green around the gills. Are you ill?' She peered at him.

'No, of course not. I was just analysing the possibilities of the takeover, that's all. Now, my sweet, let's get you a glass of bubbly and go over there where it's quiet and have a chat.' He took her arm firmly, propelled her towards a remote corner of the deck, whisking a glass of champagne off a tray as a waiter passed them.

'What about Hillard?' Estelle protested.

'You'll find him later. He can't very well get off and walk. We're already halfway out of the harbour, or hadn't you noticed?'

'Yes,' she giggled and snuggled closer. Giving him a look that left nothing to the imagination, she whispered huskily, 'And what do you want to talk to me about, Nicholas, my darling?'

Nick merely smiled enigmatically.

CHAPTER THIRTY-SEVEN

As the *Artemis* lifted anchor and sailed out of Monte Carlo harbour, its passengers gaily embarking on a day of merry-making, Francesca Cunningham sat on the terrace of the Villa Zamir.

She was not unhappy to be alone. In all truth, she was relieved that everyone had left, was delighted to have a few hours to herself. She was in an introspective mood this morning, and thus content to retreat into her myriad thoughts, without being disturbed by the continual comings and goings of the family, their constant chatter, the incessant round of activities.

An ineffable tranquillity hovered over the villa, broken only occasionally by the sounds of the staff going about their duties: the whir of the vacuum cleaner, the faint bird-like chirpings of the maids as they dusted adjacent rooms, the echo of the butler's brisk tones issuing orders, the click of a door closing, the patter of distant busy feet. Gradually these individual noises were beginning to merge, flowed together to create a vague and muffled hum that hardly intruded at all.

Francesca lay back on the *chaise longue*, her body relaxed and languorous. She closed her eyes, shutting out the brilliant sunshine, the azure sky so sharp and penetrating. Instantly, an image of Victor's face, that familiar and much-loved face, formed in minute detail and floated with tantalizing precision in her imagination, every feature clear and sharply defined. Where was he at this moment? What was he doing? Who was he with? She had no way of knowing, and she sighed inaudibly, longing for his presence, for his tenderness, the touch of his hand, the sound of his vibrant laughter. She earnestly wished he could be magically transported to this terrace, and to her. If only she could open her eyes and find him standing here, grinning irreverently, the black eyes teasing and full of humour. But that was not possible. He was enmeshed in problems in London. He was not returning to the Riviera.

He had told her that yesterday, when she had spoken to him from Nick's suite. Hearing his voice had stilled her troubled mind, her awful anxiety. Even so his decision to remain in England had plunged her into depression. *The summer was over for her.* She had announced this to him on the telephone, her misery so acute that she had been unable to conceal it. With his usual perception he had picked up her mood, had chided her quietly, told her not to be ridiculous. 'I'll be here when you get back. Stick to your plans. Go to Paris with Doris.' His words had held such a ring of finality that she had had little choice but to acquiesce. Even so, she had wanted to fly home without further delay. She was lonely without him, and lost. Part of her had gone with him. The best part really . . . her heart.

Before he had hung up, Victor had apologized yet again for spoiling her evening on Saturday. She had assured him it did not matter, wanting to alleviate his most transparent guilt, and she had meant those words. For with her intelligence, Francesca had come to terms with her crushing disappointment, reasoning that one dance gone awry was hardly meaningful in the span of a lifetime. There would obviously be many more special occasions to look beautiful for him, to enjoy with him. Years and years of occasions.

And yet it had mattered at the time . . . it had been the worst night of her life. She had smiled and danced and laughed and chatted, and entertained their guests with charm and vivacity. She had done her duty as she had been brought up to do it, with style and outward composure, hiding her feelings behind a mask of inscrutability. She had put up a front for her father's sake. But the effort had been enormous and inevitably draining. Only when she had retired to the blessed privacy of her room had she loosened her iron control, permitted herself to let go, to weep out her disappointment and frustration.

She had not left her room on Sunday, claiming a headache and a hangover. She did not want anyone to see her red eyes, her swollen face. She was also reluctant to be drawn into the usual gossipy post mortem of the preceding evening, which was an inevitability. In the late afternoon, Diana had come to her room to tell her that Nick had arrived with armfuls of flowers for Doris, and a note of apology from Victor. Plus a letter for her. Francesca had opened the envelope eagerly, and with trembling fingers. As love letters went, it was neither inspired nor romantic, being brief to the point of terseness. But she supposed he had been in a hurry, and excused him. Miraculously, her tears had ceased, her heart had lifted with renewed hope, her sadness had been transmuted into pure joy. But much later that night, in the quietness of her room, she had thought how curious it was that this particular man could affect her state of being so drastically. He had immense power over her. She had found this discomfiting, alarming even.

Francesca sat up on the *chaise*, sloughing off the residues of Saturday night. The dance was like a bad dream, therefore not worth pondering; wasting her precious time over. And so she relegated it to the back of her mind, buried the memory so carefully, so deeply and so thoroughly, that it would lie submerged, from this day on, for over two decades.

She considered the next two weeks. Today was Tuesday, and nothing special was happening until Friday, when Beau Stanton was giving a dinner party at his villa in Cap d'Antibes. The guests of honour were Katharine, Terry and Hilary, and from what Katharine had told her it was going to be a rather fancy affair. The following day Katharine was returning to London to prepare for her trip to Hollywood. Kim was leaving with her, since he was needed at Langley. Diana, Christian and Nicky would depart in the middle of the coming week, and she would remain at the villa with her father and Doris. They would be the last to leave, after her father and Doris attended the special luncheon for Winston Churchill at Bunky Ampher's house. The day after, the three of them were driving to Paris in Doris's Rolls-Royce, and her father would proceed to England, taking the car with him. She and Doris were staying in Paris, where Diana was to join them, and they would all choose their wedding outfits at Pierre Balmain's couture house.

Fourteen more days away from him. Not so long really, Francesca thought, a smile breaking through. I'll soon be back in London. With my dearest love. Her expression became beatific as she contemplated Victor. He was her reason for being.

Francesca began to daydream, planning their future life together. Once he had sorted out his problems, she knew he would ask her to marry him. Lady Francesca Mason. *Mason*. She repeated his surname several times, and lovingly so, liking the way it sounded. They would live at Che Sarà Sarà, she was certain of that. She didn't care where they lived really, so long as they were together. And she would have lots of babies. Well, two at least, and they would be beautiful, just like their father, and she and Vic would be so happy, so very very happy. Her mind ran on unchecked, fantasizing about the future.

Katharine Tempest was also in a reflective mood this morning as she sat at the small desk upstairs in her room. Like Francesca, she too felt the summer was over, was eager to leave for London, since she was exceedingly preoccupied with the months ahead and all that they entailed. *Hollywood. Her new film. Her career.* Priorities for some weeks, they had been uppermost in her mind for the past few days, more so than usual after the telephone call from London on the Friday before the dance. The call had momentarily stunned her, for it had put all she had worked for in certain jeopardy. As the dismal facts had sunk in she had been cast down into despair, and her desperation had manifested itself in a nervousness that was extreme. To her irritation she had found this difficult to control and camouflage.

Thankfully she was feeling better. After several sleepless nights, during which she had analysed the situation countless times, Katharine had made several crucial decisions, and she fully intended to execute them, no matter what the cost to herself. So, having made her plans, she was impatient to put them into operation, to plunge ahead, galvanized as always by her nervous energies and her intrinsic need for action. Naturally exigent, and for ever in a hurry, Katharine was, however, a pragmatist, and she recognized that in this instance her desire for speedy solutions was not merely a characteristic of her basic temperament but an absolute imperative. In two weeks she was leaving for California and everything must be properly resolved by the day of her departure.

At this moment there was no doubt in Katharine's mind that she could deal with matters in an orderly manner, and though some aspects of her solutions were a little unpalatable, the thrusting knowledge that she, and she alone, was in control of her own destiny had a calming effect on her. And so she was convinced she could cope with the few remaining days at the Villa Zamir with self-possession and equanimity.

Katharine brought her eyes back to the list of things she had to do before she left England and, satisfied that she had forgotten nothing, tucked the sheet of paper away in her current script. Rising from the desk, she walked over to the window. Opening the shutters, which she had closed to cool the room, she glanced down at the terrace. Her gaze rested on Francesca sunning herself, and a gentle expression flitted across her face. She thought, with a stab of sadness, I'm going to miss you, my dearest, dearest friend. Francesca was closer to her than anyone, and truly understood her; the loving relationship they enjoyed would be hard, if not indeed impossible, to duplicate. There would be a gap in her life when she was in Hollywood.

Sighing to herself, Katharine closed the shutters, realizing she was wasting time and neglecting Francesca. She had better go down and join her immediately. After all, she had stayed behind today to keep her friend company. No, that's not exactly true, Katharine now thought, remembering her apprehension when the invitation had arrived. She had understood at once that she was far too debilitated by her worries to face a day of hectic socializing, and had also blanched at the idea of being a captive on the yacht. She had decided she was definitely *not* going to be at the mercy of the two men who most made her feel ill at ease: Nicholas Latimer and Michael Lazarus. Nick with his disapproval and open hostility and bitchy one-line cracks; Mike with his obsessive attentiveness and penetrating scrutiny and probing questions. Her only regret about refusing to attend was Beau Stanton. He was the sweetest of men, kind, considerate and very chivalrous. He treated her like a person, not an *object*, a *thing* to be ogled and pawed and possessed, and so induced in her a feeling of femininity and self-worth. All her insecurities disappeared when she was with Beau, and he made her laugh a lot, brought out the best in her. She sincerely hoped he was not going to be offended by her absence. That was the last thing she wanted.

Katharine turned to the dressing table and picked up the brush, smoothing it over her flowing chestnut hair, contemplating Mike. There was no denying she found him fascinating. His personality compelled with its potency, and, being attracted to power, she could not help being impressed by the massive clout he wielded. It was like a narcotic to her. Yet withal, she was not sure she *liked* him, instinctively felt the need to be cautious with him. Self-protection, she murmured, and picked up a length of blue satin ribbon. She tied this around her head, fastening it in a bow on the crown, then sprayed herself with *Ma Griffe*, and lavishly so, liking its fresh green smell. Slipping out of her robe, she lifted the blue cotton shift off the chair and put it on, then stepped into white, low-heeled sandals. She found her sunglasses and left the room.

Halfway down the staircase, Katharine paused, struck by the realization that there was one other reason she had elected to stay behind today. She wanted to be alone with Francesca. To confide in her. Of course. This idea had been in her subconscious for days, and acknowledging it finally suddenly gave her a sense of the most profound relief. *Francesca Cunningham was the only person she really trusted.*

Apart from this, her friend was fair minded, compassionate and caring, would see the sense in everything she was doing, without passing judgment or thinking badly of her. That was not Francesca's way at all. Spurred on by these positive thoughts, which infected her with self-confidence and strengthened her resolve to be frank with her friend, Katharine continued down the stairs.

As she stepped out onto the terrace, the glaring light and the intense heat assaulted her in waves, and she knew that in minutes she would feel wilted and nauseated. But she pushed a smile onto her face, hurried forward and cried gaily, 'Good morning, Frankie darling!'

Francesca sat up on the *chaise longue* swiftly, shaded her eyes with her hand, squinting up at Katharine hovering in front of her. 'There you are, lazy bones! I was just about to come upstairs and drag you out of bed.'

'I've been up for hours,' Katharine retorted with a laugh. She pushed one of the chairs under the large yellow umbrella and sat down at the table, grateful for the shade. 'I've been writing letters. One of them was to Anna. My new dressmaker. I told her you would be going to see her when you get back to London. With the evening gown. I've asked her to copy it for you. And I've sent her a cheque to cover the cost of making it, and the price of the peach organza and the trimmings.'

'Oh Kath, you didn't have to do that! Honestly, you didn't –'

Katharine held up a hand, delighted to see the happy expression on Francesca's face. 'Hush, darling, I can't bear the thought that I ruined such a beautiful dress. Besides, whatever you say, I know you've been down in the dumps about it ever since Saturday. And let's face it, you can never wear it again, and I imagine it was expensive.'

'How sweet and dear of you, Kath, and very thoughtful. Thank you. And of course I'll visit Anna.' Francesca gave her the benefit of a loving smile, then said, 'There's nobody like you in this whole world, nobody at all. You're very special. I am going to miss you – so very much, Kath.'

'I feel the same way about you, darling.' A little smile played around Katharine's mouth, and thinking out loud, she exclaimed, 'I wish you could come with me. Why don't you? It wouldn't cost you anything. You could stay with me at the Bel-Air Hotel, in my suite, and I'd pay for your air ticket. And don't look at me like *that*! I know you're funny about accepting things, so let's just say it would be my way of repaying your father's hospitality at Langley, and this vacation.' Katharine's eagerness and excitement were infectious and were transmitted to Francesca, who smiled with pleasure, her head on one side as she thought it over.

'Gosh, that would be fun, Kath!' Immediately Francesca's face fell. 'But it's not possible. There's the wedding coming up, and Daddy will want me to be at home during the Christmas holidays. Tradition, you know, and I have to help with the Yule party at the church, all the activities at the castle for the estate workers and the villagers. But it was a lovely thought on your part. Anyway, you'll be busy with the picture, and I'm going to be working hard myself. I think the book on Chinese Gordon will go pretty smoothly now, thanks to Nicky. To be honest, I don't think I could have tackled it without him, I really don't.'

'Oh but you could!' Katharine cried with some fierceness, her face changing noticeably. 'You don't need *anyone* to babysit with you. You're as talented as Nicholas Latimer, and then some!'

Francesca merely smiled at these compliments, and made no further comment about Nick. In view of Katharine's antipathy towards him, she knew her words would fall on stony ground. She stood up, 'Yves brought out a jug of *citron pressé*. Would you like a glass? I'm going to have one.'

'Yes, thanks. It's very hot out here. This terrace is a real sun trap.' A copy of the latest *New York Herald Tribune* was lying on the table, and Katharine picked it up, fanned herself with it. 'I don't know how you can stand this heat.'

Francesca, busily pouring the lemonade, laughed merrily. 'I love the sun. I suppose that's because I come from a cold climate.' She returned to the table with the glasses and sat down with Katharine. 'What are you wearing to Beau's dinner on Friday? Do you know yet?'

'I was going through my clothes earlier and decided on the white silk tunic and matching pants.'

'Oh!'

Katharine took off her sunglasses, looked at Francesca quickly, noted her crestfallen face. 'What's wrong, darling? Does mine conflict with your outfit?'

'Well, sort of,' Francesca admitted with a rueful grin. 'Doris and I saw a lovely two-piece in Monte Carlo the other day. It's a bit similar to yours, narrow Capri pants and a loose top made of white silk. Doris loved me in it, and she's insisted on buying it for me. Today, after the boat trip. But I can wear my blue silk dress after all, if you've deci – '

'No, no, don't be silly. I'll choose something else.' Katharine did not want to deprive Francesca of the opportunity to wear the new outfit, conscious, as she was, of her paltry wardrobe. 'Come to think of it, I'm too pale to wear white, but it will look *super* on you with that fabulous tan. I'll probably go in the pink taffeta with the halter neck. It's settled. No arguments.'

'Are you sure, Kath?'

'Positive.' She picked up the glass of lemonade, took a sip, stole a glance at Francesca, over the rim. I can't put it off any longer, she thought. I must tell her. I need to tell her. She put the glass down carefully, cleared her throat. 'I'm glad we have this chance to be alone together, Frankie. I have something to say to you, explain to you . . .' She found she was unable to proceed, and her voice, slightly tremulous, faltered. She looked down at her hands, twined them nervously.

Francesca was immediately conscious of the grave tone, saw the deep frown furrowing Katharine's smooth brow. 'You sound upset, Kath dear. It occurred to me several times over the weekend that you're troubled. I have a broad shoulder, and I'm your best friend. If you can't confide in me, who *can* you confide in?' She waited expectantly.

Katharine was silent, gazing out towards the shimmering Mediterranean, and her extraordinary turquoise eyes were curiously empty and flat, her face was pensive in repose.

After a minute or two, Francesca asked softly, 'Is it something to do with Kim?'

Katharine swung her head, nodded, swallowed hard. 'Yes. I've – I've decided to break off with him.'

Francesca had not expected anything quite so drastic, and she was thunderstruck. 'You can't mean that, Katharine!' she cried, her eyes wide with surprise and disbelief.

'Yes, I do.' Katharine's voice was steadier as she continued. 'I've given a great deal of thought to our relationship, and come to the conclusion it will never work. The longer I know Kim, the more I understand how important his heritage is to him. He loves Langley with a passion, it's his life. And so are farming and your ancient lands. He wouldn't be happy for very long if he were far away from them. And I wouldn't be happy either, if I had to forgo my career in Hollywood. You see, Frankie darling, he's been hinting that I'd have to give up my acting eventually, and also grumbling about our being separated for months on end. Don't think I'm oblivious to what my long absences would mean to him, because I'm not. But by the same token I would only be half alive if I didn't act. Surely you of all people understand about my work.'

Francesca said, 'Yes, I do. But can't you work this out with Kim? Compromise perhaps?'

'I don't think so.' The love Katharine felt for Francesca flew to the surface, and she leaned forward, patted her hand affectionately. 'I'm aware you had great hopes for us, wanted Kim and me to marry, but it's just not in the cards. We lead such different lives, want different things, and we're *wrong* for each other in so many ways.'

'That's not true!' Francesca cried urgently. 'You're so *right* for each other. I *know* you are. Oh darling, I think you're being far too hasty.'

'I'm not, Frankie. I've mulled this over for a long time, and my decision is final. Please don't look so sad and unhappy.'

'I can't help it, Katharine. You'd make a wonderful wife for Kim, and be the best sister-in-law.' Francesca lifted her head, squinting in the sunlight, and dismay swamped her face. 'He's going to be crushed . . . my poor brother is going to be heartbroken.'

'Only for a little while. He'll get over me, and I'm sure he'll fall in love again. This morning I decided it would be kinder, and more considerate, to break the news to Kim later. After the vacation is over. It would be difficult for us both now, while we're here at the villa. And by *later* I mean when I'm in California. I thought I could call him in about six weeks and say I'd decided to stay on in Hollywood. I realize it won't be easy for him, whichever way I handle it. Still, it might be less painful for him to bear if I'm far away. What do you think?'

'I honestly don't know.' Francesca looked at her queerly.

'I'm not being a coward, if that's what you're thinking,' Katharine protested, her cheeks colouring. 'I'm considering Kim and his feelings – his pride, his ego. Nobody likes to be rejected, Frankie, and that's how he'll see it. He won't accept the fact that I'm being intelligent for both of us. Also, don't you think he'd be embarrassed and mortified if I tell him *now* – with all the family here?'

'Well, yes, I suppose he would be,' Francesca felt bound to agree, albeit with reluctance. She thought of the way Kim had defended Katharine, had been her champion. Yes, her brother would feel foolish, considering his staunch loyalty in the face of their father's disquiet and opposition. This had never been voiced, but intuitively Francesca knew it existed. Daddy and Doris are going to be delighted by this turn of events, she said to herself. They disapprove of Kath, think she's unworthy of Kim. They're so wrong. Another thought intruded, brought a bright smile to Francesca's glum face. 'You are right to wait, to tell Kim later,' she pronounced with sudden certainty. 'And not only to spare his feelings, but because you'll probably miss him so much, you won't *want* to break off with him after all. When you're in Hollywood you'll have a chance to truly evaluate your emotions, and maybe have second thoughts, Kath. Consider that for a moment.'

'I won't change my mind, darling,' Katharine spoke so quietly Francesca had trouble hearing her. 'Even if I thought there was a chance of the marriage working, I would not marry Kim. I *cannot* marry him. Not *now*. Not *ever.*'

Francesca was still straining to catch her friend's words, her attention concentrated on Katharine's face, which was paler and filling with distress. 'Why not?' demanded Francesca, her voice rising, reflecting her alarm.

'There's an impediment.'

'What on earth do you mean?' Her brows puckered. '*Impediment*. That's a peculiar word to use.'

Katharine turned her face away, closing her eyes. Despite her compelling desire to unburden herself to Francesca, to share her worries, the sentence stuck in her throat, and she bit her inner lip. At last she said in a small voice that was oddly firm and clear, 'I'm pregnant, Frankie. *That's* the impediment.'

Francesca's mouth opened, formed a perfectly round O, but not one sound came out. She sat staring at her friend in stupefaction.

'And obviously not by Kim,' Katharine added. She leaned back in the chair, experiencing a sense of relief, a lightness almost, glad this was finally out in the open.

'Oh Kath darling! Oh *Kath* – ' Francesca was unable to say anything more, and her heart went out to her friend with compassion and tenderness.

'I'm not going to insult you by asking you to promise not to repeat this,' said Katharine. 'I trust you, Frankie. With my life.'

'And you can, darling. *Always*. I would never tell anybody anything about you. I love you far too much to hurt you.' Francesca's eyes grew huge in her face, and she asked in a whisper, 'What are you going to do?'

'There's only one thing I can do. I'll have to have an abortion,' Katharine whispered back.

'Oh my God, no! You can't, Kath. You *mustn't*. That's so dangerous. *Risky*. It's illegal, and you'd be forced to go to a quack. I know a girl from school who went to one and she . . . almost bled to death.'

Katharine's mouth had gone dry, and she took a sip of the lemonade, found herself gagging on it. She put the glass down carefully, mumbled, 'I'm not going to a quack. When my doctor called me last Friday to tell me the tests were positive, he said he would arrange for me to go into a private nursing home where there are qualified doctors. It's expensive, but he assures me it's safe. I'll be all right,' she finished, adopting a positive tone, but her apprehension flared as she contemplated the ordeal facing her.

The mere idea of an abortion terrified Francesca, wherever it was being performed and by whom, for she vividly remembered the school friend who had so foolishly endangered her young life. She drew closer to Katharine, implored, 'Please, please don't go through with this, Kath darling. You're so delicate, and I'm worried about your health. What about the father? Won't he stand by you?' When these questions remained unanswered, Francesca discarded her usual reserve. 'Who is it, Kath? Who's the father?'

406

Katharine shook her head. 'I'd rather not mention his name.'

Francesca was surprised, but she did not say so. Instead, she intoned with firmness, 'Look here, Kath, I think you should have the baby, no matter what. An abortion is so dicey and – '

'I can't!' Katharine wailed, her voice breaking. 'Please don't try to dissuade me. I won't even begin to tell you the kind of hell I've been through, coming to the decision in the first place. I was brought up a Roman Catholic, and although I've been lapsed for years, I guess I'm still a Catholic in my heart. I'm committing a mortal sin. I'm killing my own child. Oh God, Frankie, don't make it worse – ' For the first time the tears brimmed, Katharine searched her pocket for a handkerchief, wiped her eyes, tried to recoup her self-control.

'Don't cry, Kath,' Francesca murmured, reaching for her hand, gentling her. 'I'm sorry. I didn't mean to upset you more than you are already. And you know I'll do anything I can to help you . . .' Francesca paused thoughtfully, plunged in again. 'About the man – '

'What about him?' Katharine interrupted fretfully.

'I'm not asking his name,' Francesca asserted. 'I was just wondering what he's said about your plans?'

'He doesn't know.'

'Why haven't you told him, for God's sake?' Francesca demanded.

'Because I'm not sure what he'd do, how he'd react.' Francesca bit her lip again and winced. It was raw from chewing nervously on it for days. She said, in a dim voice, 'He doesn't even know I'm pregnant.'

'Oh Kath!' Francesca straightened up, and a look of fierce determination flashed. 'My God, you must tell him! *Immediately*. This is a terrible burden for you to carry alone. Anyway, it's his responsibility too. You *have* to inform him, so that he can help you, comfort you, see you through this.'

'Thank you for saying *you'll* be there for me. I'm grateful for that.' Fresh tears sparkled and she brushed her eyes with her hand. 'I wish I'd told you about this before. I didn't because I wasn't sure how you'd take it. I thought you might despise me. I know how you feel about Kim . . . so protective of him. And while I'm not trying to excuse what I've done, I do want you to know I'm not promiscuous, and I – '

'I never thought you were!'

'I don't sleep around,' Katharine continued in a subdued manner. 'What I mean is, I wasn't having two affairs at once. I haven't ever slept with Kim, as long as I've known him.'

'I wasn't sure whether you had or not, and anyway, it's none of my business. Also, you should know I'd never moralize to you, nor do you have to justify yourself to me, Kath.'

'Thank you, darling. And thank you for being my friend.'

'As your friend I feel I must say something else to you,' began Francesca hesitantly. 'I can't fathom your attitude. I don't want to harp on about the man, but *why* won't you tell him about your predicament?'

'Because there's no point. Why worry him when I'm perfectly capable of dealing with this myself? It's bad enough *I've* been at my wits' end, without inflicting torment on him as well.'

Francesca was hard pressed to hide her irritation. 'That's typical of you. Thinking of others. But not very smart. Besides, he might not agree to this plan of yours. Hasn't it occurred to you he might want to marry you, want you to have the baby? And what about you? Wouldn't you marry him if he asked you?'

'He won't ask me. He's already married.'

'Oh no!'

Katharine dropped her eyes, her misery acute. She had not intended to go this far, to tell Francesca as much as she had. She had simply wanted to explain her reasons for breaking up with Kim, share her worries about the baby. She was wading in deep water unexpectedly, perhaps because she had not anticipated such persistent and pertinent questions from Francesca, who was normally so discreet.

'Couldn't he get a divorce, Kath?' Francesca suggested.

'I don't know. But to be honest, I don't want him to. I don't want to marry him and I'm sure he feels the same. We don't love each other, at least not in that way . . . we're very fond of each other of course.' Katharine shook her head vehemently, this gesture as negative as her expression. 'Marriage is a serious business, and if it's going to work, to be successful, it has to have a strong foundation, be based on much deeper emotions than those *we* share.' She exhaled wearily. 'So marriage is hardly a solution . . . it's out of the question.'

'I see.' Francesca did not know what to say or suggest. She had reached an impasse with Katharine, who was strong willed to the point of obduracy. Francesca was entirely convinced Katharine's judgment was seriously flawed, and that she must reveal her condition to the man with whom she was involved, to gain his emotional support, if nothing else. 'Are you afraid to tell him, Kath?'

Startled from her momentary abstraction, Katharine raised her dark head, shook it. 'No, of course I'm not. Why do you ask?'

'It struck me that this might be the reason you haven't explained the situation to him. I know I'm nagging, but he really ought to know. I'd certainly be willing to tell him for you if – '

'No!' Katharine almost shouted, alarmed at this proposal. 'Absolutely not.'

Francesca pulled back, startled and rebuffed.

Katharine, observing the hurt look, apologized swiftly. 'I'm sorry, darling. I didn't mean to snap at you. It was sweet of you to volunteer.' She instantly comprehended something else reflected in the tawny eyes, and scrutinized Francesca more closely. 'You're annoyed because I'm being mysterious about his identity, aren't you?'

'No, Kath, I'm not. I am a bit baffled though. You've confided so much in me, I can't imagine you don't trust me completely. Still . . .' Francesca shrugged, then added, 'I wasn't being nosey when I said I'd talk to him for you, I was merely trying to help.'

'Oh Frankie, I realize that.' Katharine pondered. She had vowed she would never disclose his name. To protect herself. She had to be in sole control of her future and her destiny, and who knew what emotions would be unleashed if he found out. She could not permit him to have that kind of power over her, to possibly dictate to her. Musing out loud, Katharine now remarked, 'He's an odd man, and difficult to read at times.' She leaned back, thinking. Innumerable images danced around in her head, and then a faraway expression washed over her delicately beautiful face and a faint smile touched her lips. 'But then I've told you that before . . .' The sentence remained unfinished.

Confused and bewildered, Francesca said, 'Mentioned what? I'm not following you.'

Katharine sighed, said with resignation, 'That Vic is a funny kind of man, so lonely really, and – '

'Vic! Why are you talking about Vic all of a sudden?'

Shaking her head, Katharine murmured softly, 'I hadn't meant to reveal his name, but as you said, you do know so much. I suppose it doesn't matter. I mean, I know I can count on your confidentiality, Frankie. Vic is the father of my child.'

Francesca recoiled. She stared at Katharine aghast, so stunned she was uncomprehending. What had Katharine just said? That Vic was the father of the baby? It wasn't possible. Not Vic. Katharine and *Vic*. For a fraction of a second Francesca convinced herself she had misheard, misunderstood. She blinked nervously. '*Victor Mason?*' As she mouthed his name horror swarmed over her, and her mind baulked at the shattering implications, refused to accept them.

'Why, yes.' Katharine's expression was suddenly rueful. 'You sound so surprised, yet *you* know better than anyone else how much we've been thrown together.'

A voice shrieked in Francesca's brain, denying, denying. Her eyes, wild with shock and disbelief, were fixed on Katharine. She opened her mouth. Nothing came out.

Katharine leaned across the table with urgency. 'You must promise me you won't tell him. He must never know about the baby. *Never*. Promise me, Frankie, please promise me. Give me your word of honour. Swear it on . . . the honour of the Cunninghams,' Katharine insisted with high-pitched intensity. Her eyes, more startlingly blue than ever, stretched wider, were pleading.

'Y-y-yes,' stammered Francesca, foundering, her shock spiralling. 'I promise. On my honour.' This was an automatic response; she hardly knew what she was saying. She thought she was choking. Her chest had tightened, and her heart, pounding at an accelerated rate, clattered against her ribcage. *It wasn't true! Katharine was lying. But why would she lie? She had no reason to name Victor if he was not the father of her child. To hurt me. Because she's jealous. No, she would never hurt me. She loves me. She doesn't know about us, so how could she be jealous? Victor had insisted on secrecy. Of course. He had had to do that. Because of Katharine. He had been sleeping with them both at the same time. Oh my God! Oh Vic! Oh Vic! How could you! Why? And why Katharine? Why my dearest friend? You betrayed me, Vic. No, they both betrayed me! And so treacherously. No, not Katharine. She never knew about us. I must tell her. No, don't tell her. Wait. First find out. About her and Vic. I don't want to know. Yes, you do. I couldn't stand it. Yes, you could. You have to know. For your own sanity.*

These chaotic thoughts, swirling in Francesca's brain, jostling violently against one another in the passage of a few minutes, were accompanied by a terrible silent scream. It was a scream of unbearable pain and anguish. She clasped her shaking hands together in her lap, digging her nails into her palms, striving for control, willing herself to continue this horrifying dialogue.

'I would have never guessed he was . . . that it was him.' Francesca heard her voice as if from a great distance. It was a hoarse and rasping whisper.

'I thought it was probably obvious, that you'd already put two and two together,' Katharine replied.

Now Francesca forced herself to ask the most difficult question of all. 'How long

. . . how long has it been going on?' She dreaded the answer. She wanted to run – and run fast. Away from this dark and dazzling beauty facing her, away from this terrace, away from this house. Run. Run anywhere. She looked at Katharine, waiting. She must know . . . know the worst, however much it pained her, destroyed her. And she knew in her heart of hearts, and with a sinking dread, that she *was* about to be destroyed. She asked, 'Has it been a long affair?'

'No, not long,' Katharine responded absently, again lost in her own ruminations, her eyes trained on the distant sea. Rousing herself, she went on, 'We've always been close, as you know, but not romantically entangled. Then in May, on location, it just happened, before either of us realized. In a sense, I believe it was an inevitability. We were so caught up with our work, the film, those passionate love scenes on the set. And there is something irresistible about Vic. He's so masculine, and very forceful.'

A sigh swept through Katharine and she shook her head, looked wistful. 'I couldn't help myself, in spite of Kim, and even though I knew deep down it probably wasn't a major involvement for Vic. He's accustomed to women swooning at his feet, you know what a lady-killer he is. As a matter of fact, it didn't take me long to realize our romance would fizzle out as swiftly as it had started. I was right. It was virtually meaningless to him.' Another tiny sigh. 'He's fond of me, cares about me, in his own way. Under the circumstances, I didn't have much alternative but to be philosophical about everything. Unfortunately, I hadn't bargained for this . . . the consequences.'

Francesca could not speak. *Meaningless to him. But not to me. Oh no, Vic, not to me. She calls him Vic! He doesn't let anyone call him Vic – only those closest to him. Me. Nicky. And obviously Katharine. Oh God! It happened on location. In Yorkshire. He must have slept with her that weekend they were staying at Langley Castle. He refused to come to my room. Because of Daddy. Because it was my home. He said it would be improper. Improper! Oh Vic! You lied. You cheated. You were unfaithful to me.* She saw the two of them then, in her mind's eye, the picture, sharp, vivid, detailed. Katharine in Victor's arms, kissing him, touching him, and Victor returning her kisses and caresses, possessing her. Did he make love to Katharine the same way he made love to me? Did he say the same things to her? Tender, passionate, intimate things? She could not bear to contemplate these probabilities, pushed aside the devastating thoughts, snapped her lids tightly shut. She was shaken by a sudden scorching jealousy and a fulminating rage mingled with enormous hatred. Hatred for Katharine Tempest. *It's her fault. She tempted him. Encouraged him. Inveigled him. Yes, that was the answer. Vic would never be unfaithful to me, to our love, of his own volition!*

Opening her eyes and without looking at Katharine, Francesca asked, in a small voice, 'When? When do you think you got pregnant?' The internal shaking intensified, held her completely in its grip, and she grasped the arm of the metal chair to steady herself.

'June. It had to be June.'

'Then you're three months . . .'

'Almost.'

'And you can still have the abortion? It's safe?'

'Oh yes, darling. The doctor told me I'm all right. Don't worry about me, Frankie. I'll be fine.' Katharine smiled warmly, touched by her friend's concern for her welfare. Meeting Katharine's direct gaze, Francesca instantly dropped her eyes, studied her bare feet in great concentration. *I hope she dies. She's going to kill his child. It should have been mine! My child! I want to die too. I've nothing to live for. He's lost to me. Oh Vic, why did you do this?*

Francesca stood up unsteadily, not sure that her trembling legs would hold her. All her strength was ebbing out of her. She moved forward. The sharp pain, somewhere in the region of her heart, was excruciating, a plunging, stabbing pain that came at her in long spasms, knocked the breath out of her. She was blinded by the scalding tears rushing out of her eyes, splashing onto her bare chest and down the front of her bathing suit, and she staggered as she reached the *chaise*.

Katharine was watching Francesca alertly. 'Are you all right, darling?' she called. 'You seemed a bit wobbly just then. Is something wrong? Don't you feel well?'

Without turning round, Francesca gasped disjointedly, 'No. Not well. Sick. Dizzy. The heat. The sun.' She bent over the *chaise longue*, hiding her contorted face, and groped for the towel, pressed it to her streaming eyes. Then after a minute or two she wiped her neck and her chest and shoulders. She was bathed in sweat. Yet she felt dreadfully cold inside. Icy. Numb. So very numb. She dropped the towel, searched around for her dark glasses, put them on very carefully, very slowly, fumbling like an old blind woman. With the same fumbling uncoordinated movements she lifted the large straw hat from the floor, placed it on her head.

Katharine had risen, was busily pushing the chair Francesca had vacated farther into the shade. 'I hope you don't have sunstroke,' she exclaimed with a quick glance, angling the umbrella. 'You were sitting in the blazing sun, you silly thing. No wonder you're suffering now. Shall I go in and get you some aspirins?'

'No. I'm okay. Thanks.' Francesca began to walk towards Katharine at a snail's pace, placing one foot carefully in front of the other, trying to balance herself properly. Unexpectedly, the white marble slabs under her feet tilted upwards to hit her in the face and she braced herself for the impact, not realizing it was she who was falling towards them.

Katharine ran forward, grasped Francesca's arm tightly, steadied her, kept her upright. 'Perhaps we'd better go inside,' she suggested with concern, her face ringed with worry. 'What do you think? It's cooler indoors and you could lie down.'

'I don't want to lie down, for God's sake!' Francesca pulled her arm free impatiently, and with unusual roughness, then seated herself on the chair. 'And I don't want any pills either. I'll drink a little of this lemonade. Don't fuss, I told you. I'm perfectly all right.'

'Yes, of course, Frankie dear. Anything you say.' Katharine also sat down, studying her friend, taken aback by her curt manner, her sudden and unfamiliar brusqueness. Then she thought: Francesca's furious with me because of Kim. It's understandable really. The facts are sinking in and now she is distressed for him, and, not unnaturally, put out with me. Katharine sighed under her breath, asking herself if her candidness had been a grave error.

Neither girl spoke for a while, and finally Francesca questioned in a muted tone, 'Why didn't you tell me you were involved with him before now?'

Astonishment whipped across Katharine's face. 'Oh, Frankie, how could I? I was also seeing Kim . . .' She pursed her lips. 'Perhaps I should have done, since we are very close and we don't have any secrets from each other. But I was self-conscious

411

and embarrassed because of my relationship with your brother. How could I possibly tell you about my affair with Vic.'

An unintelligible mumble was the only response, and it prompted Katharine to elucidate further. She exclaimed hurriedly, 'Besides, Victor was funny about our relationship, about it leaking out. You know he's terrified of scandal, and *paranoid* about *Confidential Magazine*. He insisted on absolute secrecy. You do understand my reasons, don't you, Frankie?' Katharine persisted, anxiety welling up in her.

'Yes.' Oh *how* I understand. You protected your flanks so shrewdly, Victor, Francesca thought with mounting bitterness.

'I can't help feeling you're mad at me, because of the way I've behaved towards Kim,' Katharine ventured hesitantly, praying she had not lost Francesca because of this convuluted mess with its ghastly ramifications. Being totally ignorant of Francesca's involvement with Victor, Katharine had no way of knowing that her confidence had created havoc in the other girl. Her frankness was about to trigger the most disastrous consequences imaginable. 'Why don't you answer me?' Katharine's tenseness took tighter hold, and she was on the verge of fresh tears induced by her friend's abnormal and unprecedented coolness.

'Oh sorry, what did you say?' Francesca asked abstractedly, fiercely trying to hang on to her sanity.

Repeating her questions, Katharine then insisted with great vehemence, 'I never meant to hurt Kim. You *must* believe that.'

'Yes . . . I do.' Francesca closed her eyes, thankful she was wearing the dark glasses. After a short pause, she began to speak in a faint and fading voice. 'Why don't you want . . . him to know you're pregnant?'

'For all the reasons I gave you earlier, and also because I don't want there to be any embarrassment between us, or any awkwardness. Don't forget, I have a professional relationship with Vic, and I mustn't damage that. My career is in *his* hands. Have you forgotten I'm tied to him contractually, or rather, to Bellissima?'

'No, I haven't.'

'There's another thing, too, I'll be working for him, and with him, for several years, and – '

'Won't you feel strange? Being with him constantly . . . after . . . after this?'

'I sincerely hope not.' Katharine shifted nervously in the chair, crossed her legs. 'But I would feel extremely uncomfortable if he knew about the baby and the – what I'm going to do. I can't guess what his attitude would be, so it's better he knows nothing. I am certain of one thing though, he won't pursue this romance. I told you, it's over. I suppose I was just a flash in the pan, as far as he's concerned. We're good friends, as we always were, but that's all, and I've every intention of keeping it that way. Strictly platonic.'

'Yes.' Francesca tightened her clasped hands and wished the pain would go away. She thought: He has destroyed our love for something which was apparently irrelevant, something *she* terms a flash in the pan! Oh my God! Her heart was splintering.

Desperately wanting to break through Francesca's reserve, Katharine reached out and rested her hand on the other girl's arm lovingly. She implored, 'Please tell me you don't hate me . . . because of Kim. *Please*, Frankie. I couldn't bear to lose *you.*' Francesca was unresponsive, and Katharine cried, 'I have to break off with him! It's the only honourable thing to do!'

There was a small sigh and Francesca nodded. 'Yes. Anything else would be wrong . . . unconscionable really. Kim will recover.' She swallowed. 'I'm not upset – about Kim.' She clamped her mouth shut, afraid to go on, afraid she would blurt everything out. She did not want to reveal her own affair with Victor. It would be too humiliating.

'Thank God! You're so important to me, Francesca. I couldn't stand it if you thought badly of me.' Katharine dropped her voice, whispered, 'I wish you were going to be with me in London next week, when I have this operation. The idea of it appals me, and it's going to be on my conscience for the rest of my life.' Her voice was choked as she finished, 'I don't know how I'll ever be able to live with myself.'

Francesca no longer had the strength to respond, nor did she care whether Katharine could live with herself or not. Then she swung her head at the sound of footsteps.

'Mademoiselle Tempest, there is a telephone call,' the butler announced.

'Oh. Thanks. Yes, *merci*, Yves.' She rose, said to Francesca, 'I won't be a minute, darling.'

Katharine had followed the butler into the main salon, and yet her presence lingered on the terrace. The scent of her perfume clung to the warm air, and her bell-like voice with its mellifluous intonations reverberated in Francesca's head. The devastating words she had uttered echoed with maddening clarity and unremitting persistence. *How will I ever be able to forget the things she told me? This is a nightmare, isn't it?*

Francesca knew deep down that this was not so. Her nightmare was the reality. She wanted, suddenly, to get up and walk into the garden and lie down in the grass and bury her aching face in its tender green coolness and sob away this pain and wretchedness and heartbreak. But she was immobilized by shock and despair, incapable of moving. Her body was leaden.

'Frankie! Frankie! Something terrible has happened!'

Yes, thought Francesca numbly, it has. My life is ruined.

'*Frankie!*' Katharine shrieked. 'Didn't you *hear* what I said?'

'Yes. What's wrong?' Francesca queried in an exhausted voice, not really caring. She blinked behind her glasses, regarding Katharine hovering in front of her, clutching a piece of paper, twisting it between nervous fingers. There was no mistaking the extreme agitation, the ashen face, the eyes flaring with shock.

'There's been an accident!' Katharine cried. 'A dreadful car crash. *Hilary and Terry*! They're in the hospital in Nice. That was Norman . . . Norman Rook on the 'phone. Terry's asking for me. I have to go to him at once. Try to help in any way I can.'

'Oh my *God*.' Francesca sat bolt upright, pulling herself out of her stupor, the import of Katharine's news penetrating her addled brain. 'How bad is it?'

'Pretty bad, from what Norman says. They're both seriously injured. Hilary is . . . Hilary is . . .' Katharine was unable to get the words out of her trembling mouth. 'She's been *gravely* hurt. Worse than Terry. Will you drive me to Nice, darling? I don't know the roads and I'm not a very good driver anyway.' Katharine ran to the *chaise*, picked up Francesca's sundress draped on its frame, brought it to her. 'Put this on. We don't have time to change. I know you're not feeling well, from the heat and the sun, but you'll just have to – '

'Of course I'll drive you!' Francesca exclaimed. She dragged her listless body out of the chair, took the cotton frock from Katharine, slipped it on. She began to fasten the buttons down the front, saw that her hands shook uncontrollably, and her heart was clattering again. In an unsteady voice she said, 'Don't you think they're going to . . . m-m-make it, Katharine?'

'I – I hope so. Oh God I hope so.'

CHAPTER THIRTY-EIGHT

They were on the *moyenne corniche*. This ran all the way from Menton to Nice, at the middle level between the coastal road bordering the Mediterranean and the higher mountain route. The butler had advised Francesca to take the *moyenne*, to save time and avoid the heavy traffic, after he had finished giving her directions to the hospital. Monte Carlo had been left behind some time ago. Far below, in the distance, the harbour in the old port of Villefranche was just visible: shimmering white sails fluttering like banners in the wind, flung against the azure backdrop of a cloudless sky . . . sleek white hulls reposing on a sea that was an aquamarine-tinted mirror . . . distant images glittering sharply, mirage-like in the relentless sunlight.

Doris had taken the Rolls that morning, and so Francesca was driving the small rented Renault. Although it lacked the immense thrust and power of the other car, she was managing to get the maximum out of it. She had her foot hard down on the accelerator, gunning the engine, concentrating on the road ahead. Neither she nor Katharine had said much to each other since they had left the villa, for both girls were trapped in their thoughts.

Katharine was frantic, her own troubles displaced by her concern for Terry and Hilary, lying in God knows what condition in the hospital. Norman, incoherent from hysteria, had told her so little. Her imagination kept running away with itself, and she could not help envisioning the worst. *Let them be all right, let them be all right*, she repeated over and over again to herself, and she desperately held on to the thought that Terry must be *conscious*, because he was asking for her and had told Norman to telephone her. This brought a measure of comfort at least. She hardly dared to think about poor Hilary, who, according to Norman, had been thrown out of the car and was the more seriously injured of the two. Katharine huddled farther in the corner of the seat, gazing out of the window, oblivious to the breathtaking scenic view.

By making a stupendous effort, Francesca was in control again, aware that she had to function as normally as possible in this tragic emergency. The accident, whilst not exactly diminishing or obscuring her distress and heartache about Victor, had taken precedence for the moment. True to form, and with uncommon backbone, Francesca had rallied remarkably well, drawing on her inner resources for strength.

In the past few weeks she had come to know Hilary and Terry better, and a gentle attachment had developed between her and the costume designer. On Saturday night Francesca had thought what a beautiful couple they made. Hilary's sweetness had been a balm to her at the dance, and now when she thought of their broken and battered bodies a lump came into her throat, made her heart clench with sadness.

Hunching over the wheel, Francesca pushed the Renault to its limits, wishing the car could fly. If only they had been in the Rolls they would have made Nice in half the time. There was a clear stretch of road ahead and she picked up speed, whizzing along for a while, then slowed with a screeching of brakes as she approached a blind corner. Although she was driving fast, she was less reckless than usual, conscious of the tortuous twists and turns on the *moyenne*, and mindful of the reason they were on their way to Nice in the first place.

A produce truck and a couple of cars were coming towards them from the opposite direction, and Francesca eased her foot off the accelerator and dropped down to a crawl. The road had narrowed considerably, and care and expertise were necessary with the oncoming vehicles only a few yards ahead. Once these vehicles had passed and the route was clear again, she sneaked a hurried glance at Katharine, morosely silent, encapsulated in worry, and unexpectedly she realized she had forgotten how unselfish and loyal the other girl was, particularly in a crisis. Nothing was ever too much trouble if her friends were in need. Francesca swung her eyes to the front, and as she peered ahead some of the hatred she had been harbouring for Katharine during the past two hours began to dissipate.

That analytical brain, which was to serve Francesca in such good stead as a writer in future years, began to work with great precision. Suddenly, with a clarity of perception, she saw the situation with Victor and Katharine in the harsh light of cold reality. Of course their affair had been an inevitability. And this had been staring her in the face all along. She had simply chosen not to see it. Making love on the screen had merely been a prelude to the real thing, was bound to have carried over into their private lives. He *was* irresistible; Katharine must have been mesmerized. Two and two now added up to ten in Francesca's active mind: his unavailability on location. Katharine's perpetual excuses, which had so infuriated Kim. Victor's attentiveness to Katharine during the filming; the lunches in his trailer; the care and coaching he had given her. Even Nick had remarked that Victor had *carried* her through the picture. Francesca pursed her lips thoughtfully, recalling the final party, the way *they* had been huddled together and intimately so, sharing things she was excluded from, and laughing and chatting. An echo came back: Nick's voice saying, 'You're on a fast track with a downhill racer, kid.' An oblique warning, no doubt. And there was the diamond bracelet. Dismissed casually by *him* – as a token of his appreciation. Appreciation for *what* exactly?

A small tremor ran through Francesca as another realization hit her, and most forcefully. Earlier she had tried to shift the burden of guilt on to Katharine. Yet it was transparent that Victor was the initiator of the affair, and therefore culpable, ultimately responsible. Katharine must be exonerated of all blame. She had been a victim really. They had both been his victims. He had used them for his own gratification, sexual and otherwise. An internal trembling took her, and her pain and hurt and rage and humiliation twisted together to form a tight steel band around her damaged heart. The heart she had so willingly and foolishly ransomed to *him*.

415

Katharine spoke, interrupting Francesca's thoughts. She said, 'Thanks for coming with me, Frankie. I know how rotten you were feeling from the sun. Are you still nauseous?'

'No, I'm much better, thanks. And I'm glad to drive you, to be with you, Kath. I'm as concerned as you are about Hilary and Terry.'

'Norman wasn't very articulate, or forthcoming. He gets so hysterical. I wish I'd asked him more questions. It's the *not knowing* that's so worrisome. If only we had a bit more information.'

'I agree. But try and relax, Katharine. We'll soon be there.'

'It's not easy. Shall I put the radio on?'

'Why not?'

Katharine twiddled with the knobs, settling on a station. The strumming of a guitar and the man's voice instantly filled the little car. *'Yo se que soy una ilusión fugaz para ti, un capricho del alma, que hoy te une a mi.'* Francesca gripped the steering wheel tighter, her knuckles sharp and white in her tanned hands, her breath strangled in her throat. *That* song again, evoking so many memories. At the dance on Saturday the mariachis had played it so incessantly it had become a litany to her misery. *'Una aventura más para ti,'* the unknown singer sang, the radio blaring in her face, and she thought of the meaning of the words, repeating them in English to herself: *I know that for you I am just another affair. That after tonight you will forget me. I know I am just a fleeting illusion for you, that just a whim of the soul joins me to you. Even though you kiss me with wild passion and I happily kiss you, when the hour comes my heart dies for you.*

Victor Mason's favourite song . . . and how prophetic the words turned out to be, thought Francesca. My heart *is* dead. And he was just an illusion for me. It's over. *I'll never see him again.* Tears sprang into her golden-topaz eyes and trickled down her face, splashed against her lips, and a sob broke free as all of the pent-up emotions of the morning finally spilled out.

Katharine whipped her head around swiftly. 'Darling, whatever is it?' She touched Francesca's arm lightly.

'I don't know,' Francesca gasped, blinking, trying to see through the mistiness in her eyes. 'But I think I'll have to stop for a minute.'

'There's a spot ahead where you can pull in, over there, the entrance to that house,' Katharine cried, pointing. She was riddled with alarm, wondering what had caused this rush of tears. She turned off the radio.

Francesca steered the car off the road and into a small gravelled area in front of tall iron gates. She braked jerkily, and bent forward, resting her head on the wheel, wracked with sobs. Katharine reached for her, held her close, stroking her hair. 'What is it, Frankie? What's upsetting you?'

'I'm not sure,' Francesca whispered through her tears, her shoulders heaving, her breath coming in gasps. She clung to Katharine, was about to confide in her, then changed her mind. She could never tell Katharine about Victor and herself. Never. Eventually the sobs subsided and she extricated herself from Katharine's embrace, wiped her damp face with her hand, tried to smile. 'I'm sorry,' she began falteringly, looking at Katharine, whose face was expectant and questioning.

Francesca went on slowly, in a tremulous voice, 'Everything's falling apart . . . the beautiful summer is disintegrating in tragedy . . .'

Katharine brought her hand to her mouth, her eyes apprehensive. 'Don't say that,' she exclaimed.

When they arrived at the hospital, Katharine got out and Francesca drove off to find a parking place. Katharine ran up the steps, and pushed through the doors. She found Norman Rook in the waiting room. He sat with his head in his hands, his shoulders hunched, shrivelled in the chair like an old man. At the sound of footsteps he lifted his head wearily. When he saw Katharine his dolorous face seemed to crumple and he shook his head slowly.

'Oh no!' Katharine cried, running to him. She sat down and took his hand in hers, holding it tightly, gazing at him, afraid to ask questions, her heart in her mouth.

He said, 'Hilary's still unconscious.'

'And Terry?' Katharine whispered.

'Sedated right now. He became a bit difficult when I was sitting with him. Violent almost. He got out of bed, wanted to go and find Hilary. I couldn't restrain him so I fetched the doctor. He gave him a shot.'

'Just how *bad* are their injuries, Norman dear?'

'Terry's are all superficial, thank God. Cuts, bruises, a gash on his face, plus a broken rib and a sprained shoulder. He'll be out of here in a few days . . .' Norman's eyes filled and he fumbled for his handkerchief, blew his nose loudly. 'But Hilary – I just don't know. It's the coma that's worrying the doctors. They're doing more tests.'

'Does she have other injuries?'

'Yes, but like Terry's they don't seem to be all that serious. A broken leg and arm, and one side of her face is smashed up. The doctor I spoke to didn't seem to think she'd need plastic surgery.' His hand tightened on Katharine's and he exclaimed fiercely, 'She mustn't die, Katharine. She *can't* die! I don't know what'll happen to Terry if she . . . if she doesn't make it. He won't make it either. Not without Hilary he won't.'

'She's going to be all right, Norman,' Katharine asserted gently, but nevertheless with firmness. 'We mustn't be negative at a time like this. We've got to hold good thoughts.'

'Yes,' Norman mumbled. He swung his head, stared out of the window for a few minutes, and then turned bodily, gave Katharine the most penetrating of looks. 'It's our fault,' he intoned dismally. 'We shouldn't have done what we did.'

Perplexed, Katharine asked, 'What did we do? I don't understand . . .'

Norman peered at Katharine curiously, and blinked. There was a small silence. He said in a low tone, 'We schemed and plotted, and talked them into doing the picture. It's because of us they got involved with each other again. We meddled in people's lives. It's wrong to meddle. Nobody has a right to play God, Katharine.'

She gazed at him thunderstruck. 'How can you say such things,' she admonished, her voice as low as his. 'We were trying to help Terry solve his problems, remember? Besides, we weren't driving the car today. You're being silly, Norman.'

Norman Rook seemed not to hear. The dresser sat gazing down at his sandals. 'I'll never forgive myself if Hilary dies,' he said at last. 'Meddling. That's not right. As sure as God made little apples it's not right. We'd both better *remember* that.'

He stood up, moved towards the door. 'I'm going to check on them both again. I'll be back in a jiffy.'

Katharine sat back in the chair, staring at the closed door. She was filled with distress and horrified at Norman's extraordinary pronouncement. It was unacceptable to her. How could *they* be blamed for the accident? Norman was in shock, rambling, she reasoned. He didn't know what he was saying. Rising, Katharine went to the window, stood looking out. Whilst she *had* counted on Hilary's emotional attachment to Terry to achieve her own ends, she had not anticipated a rekindling of their old love affair, nor that Hilary would leave Mark and run off with the actor. What I did, I did for *them*, she said inwardly, self-justifying. I had the best of intentions. Whatever Norman says, neither of us is responsible. Not for anything. And least of all for the car crash.

She closed her eyes, leaned her forehead against the window, recalled how beautiful Hilary had been on Saturday night at the dance. Her throat tightened. *Live*, Hilary, she cried inwardly. *Fight. You must fight. Don't give up. Fight for your life. For Terry. Oh Hilary, please, please live.* The phrases turned and turned in her mind, and she remained immobile in front of the window, concentrating on the injured girl, sending out waves of love with every ounce of her strength.

So immersed was Katharine in her inner thoughts, she did not hear the door opening.

Francesca came into the waiting room quietly, paused in the middle of the floor, intently regarding the motionless figure. There was a vulnerability about Katharine at this moment, and Francesca thought: She's such a tiny little thing, and so fragile. Like a child really. Her heart filled with tenderness and warmth, washing away the last vestiges of her anger. She took a step forward, 'Kath . . . Kath.'

Katharine swung around, and shook her head, conveying her misery. 'Things are bad, Frankie, and – '

Holding up her hand, Francesca also shook her head, but in a positive manner. 'It's *all right*, Kath. Everything's going to be all right. I just saw Norman talking to one of the doctors. Hilary's finally regained consciousness. We can see her in a few minutes.'

A smile of relief mingled with joy spread itself slowly across Katharine's face, which was as white as bleached linen and stark with anxiety. She flew across the room, almost fell into Francesca's arms, and the two girls stood holding each other tightly, laughter finally breaking through.

CHAPTER THIRTY-NINE

Mrs Moggs said, 'That's it then, Your Ladyship, the last of your suitcases.' The hat ablaze with poppies bobbed furiously, her head moving in rhythmic conjunction with her finger as she counted the pieces of luggage they had brought down to the hall. 'Seven cases,' she pronounced. 'I 'opes they'll all fit in Mrs Asternan's car.'

'Yes, there's ample room in the Rolls, Mrs Moggs,' Francesca replied. 'Thanks for helping me. Now, let's go into the kitchen to have that cup of tea and go over everything.'

'Right yer are, M'lady,' Mrs Moggs smiled. 'I've got the kettle on.' She stomped after Francesca, who was already swinging through the dining room. Seating herself at the kitchen table, Francesca proceeded to empty the contents of a manilla envelope on to the table.

Pouring hot water into the brown teapot, Mrs Moggs said, ''Ow about a nice Cadbury's chocolate finger with your cuppa char?'

'No, thank you,' Francesca murmured without looking up.

Mrs Moggs pursed her lips, her flinty eyes regarding Francesca with acuteness. 'You don't eat enough, if you don't mind me saying so, Your Ladyship,' Mrs Moggs clucked. 'You're all nice an' brown from yer 'olidays, and you looks well, but you're ever so thin, M'lady.'

'I'm really not hungry at the moment, Mrs Moggs. I'll have a snack for lunch before I leave for Yorkshire. Please, come and sit down.'

'Ta, ever so.' Mrs Moggs brought the tea tray to the table, shuffled into a chair opposite Francesca, commenced to pour the tea.

'These are Miss Tempest's door keys,' Francesca showed them to her. 'She wants you to go in once a week to dust and keep an eye on things.' Francesca slipped the keys in the envelope. 'Put everything in here, Mrs Moggs, so that nothing gets lost.'

'Yes, I will, Your Ladyship. An' is Miss Temple 'appy in 'Ollywood? 'Ow is things goin' with 'er now?'

'Very well. She likes it there.' Francesca did not bother to correct Mrs Moggs, who continued to mispronounce Katharine's name. 'Here's her cheque for the next three months. If she's delayed she'll send you another one. She has your address.'

'Thanks ever so.' Mrs Moggs folded the cheque, put it in her apron pocket.

Indicating the small white envelope on the table, Francesca explained, 'Your train ticket is in here, plus ten pounds for additional expenses. I've also included your wages for the next few months.'

Mrs Moggs instantly looked crestfallen, and she peered closely at Francesca. 'Won't you be comin' back 'ere then, before 'is Grace's weddin'?'

'I'm afraid not, Mrs Moggs. I'm staying in Yorkshire. I'll be writing my book. You can always give me a ring if there's a problem, and I'll let you know if Father is coming up to town.'

'Yes, M'lady. It won't be the same, with you gone, but I'll look after fings, don't you fret.'

'Yes, I know you will, Mrs Moggs.'

'Yer won't forget about me titfer, will you, Lady Francesca?'

Francesca smiled her first genuine smile in weeks. 'No, of course I won't. As a matter of fact, I've started working on it, and I made good progress when I was at Langley last weekend. It'll be ready for the wedding. A beautiful bonnet to match your blue coat and dress. You did say *blue*, didn't you?'

Mrs Moggs nodded and beamed. 'Yes, and thanks for making the 'at for me. I appreciates it ever so much.' Mrs Moggs hesitated. She cleared her throat. 'I'd like somefing like the Queen Mum always wears. You know, with feathers and a bit of veil and p'raps a rose. A red rose.'

'That's just what I had in mind,' Francesca assured her. 'And I – ' The telephone in the hall started to ring. 'Excuse me, Mrs Moggs.' Francesca hurried out, picked up the receiver. 'Hello?'

'Hi, Francesca,' Nick Latimer said. 'How are you?'

'Fine, Nick, and you?'

'Morose without Diana. I've decided to fly over and see her this weekend.'

'Again,' Francesca murmured, forcing a laugh.

Nick chuckled. 'Yep. Listen, kid, I think I've found an apartment. Just around the corner from you. On the corner of Grosvenor and North Audley. I wondered if you'd come and look at it, give me your opinion?'

'When, Nicky?' Francesca frowned. She had kept her departure for Langley a secret. She did not want Nick to know she was leaving that afternoon, or possibly delay her.

'I was hoping you could meet me there now – say in about half an hour. Is that an imposition?'

'No . . . no, that's all right. What's the address?'

Nicky gave it to her, then said, 'I'll be waiting in the apartment. It's on the first floor, I mean ground floor, to the left, after the entrance hall. See ya, kid, and thanks.'

'Goodbye, Nicky.' She replaced the receiver and returned to the kitchen. 'I think we've covered everything, Mrs Moggs.' She leaned over the table, returned all the items to the envelope, handed it to Mrs Moggs. 'I've got to pop out for a while. I'll be back in about an hour.'

The late-September morning was one of filtered sunlight and milky clouds adrift in a periwinkle sky. It was another lovely Indian summer day. And yet the streets of Mayfair were oddly alien to Francesca as she walked briskly in the direction of Grosvenor Square at eleven-thirty. The tall grey buildings were somehow forbidding and gloomy, and she could not wait to get back to Langley. She longed for the comforting familiarity of her home, the gentle peace of the ancient castle, the silence of her beloved moors. Up there on those remote and drifting hills, tinted purple now as the heather bloomed, where the air was cool and bracing and the light had a unique and shimmering clarity, she was able to find a degree of ease, a brief respite from the constant and inescapable pain of a love that was lost. She could walk for miles with her little dog Lada without encountering a single soul in that vast and awesome landscape, and the solitude was a benediction.

Ever since she had returned from Paris with Doris, Francesca had been retreating into herself, perpetually looking inward, living in her internal meanderings, shutting out the world. She felt isolated from everyone, found solace only in Lada and her work. Her research at the British Museum was finished, and the long and lonely days of real writing were about to begin. She welcomed them. Delving into the past, reliving history, were her means of escaping the present which had become so burdensome to her.

As she approached Grosvenor Square her thoughts swung to Nick, and the flat she was about to see. He had decided to stay in London until Christmas, when he was leaving for Wittingenhof to spend the holidays with Diana and Christian. From there he would return to New York in January, to visit his parents, and then go on to California. He was currently working on his screenplay, had explained he wanted the isolation London afforded to finish it as quickly as possible. But she knew Diana was the real reason he lingered on this side of the Atlantic. Francesca hoped things would work out for her cousin and Nicky, who were very much in love. But are there ever any happy endings? Very rarely, she answered herself dismally, contemplating her own misery, the unhappiness her brother would soon be confronting.

·Katharine had telephoned from California last night, full of excitement about the film and Hollywood and all the people she was meeting. She had then gone on to extol the virtues of Beau Stanton, seemingly her constant companion both on and off the set. Only at the end of the long conversation had Kim been mentioned, when Katharine had reiterated her intention of breaking off with him – but not until after their father's marriage to Doris, now scheduled for December. Francesca's heart sank. Her brother would be shattered.

Terrence Ogden was also in California, and Katharine had chatted about him for a few minutes. Hilary was not with him. She was still recuperating from the car crash, and had entered the London Clinic for new tests. There was something peculiar about her balance and coordination, and the doctors were baffled, would not let her fly to America until they had diagnosed the cause. When Francesca had visited her last week, Hilary had finally broken down and wept, had expressed her longing for Terry with such eloquence and emotion Francesca had been moved, fully understanding her feelings. So many tears lately, Francesca thought sadly. She increased her pace, blocking out the spectres that haunted her.

Before she realized it she was standing in front of the building where the flat was. It was rather imposing, with huge double doors made of wrought iron and heavy glass. She pushed them open, crossed the entrance hall, found the flat and rang the bell. Nick opened the door immediately, stood grinning down at her.

'Hello, Nicky,' she said warmly, always pleased to see him.

'Welcome, Beauty,' he replied, still grinning. He pulled her inside and into his arms. After hugging her affectionately, he held her away, examining her face, assessing her mood. 'Thanks for coming. I'm very grateful.'

'I'm glad to be of help, Nick.' She glanced around the large foyer, and nodded her head approvingly. 'Well, if this is anything to judge by, I think you've found the right place.' Her eyes took in the handsome antique pieces, the crystal chandelier, the Oriental rug on the white marble floor. 'Who does it belong to? It is rather *grand*.'

'A producer I know. Sam Legalle. He's going to L.A. for three months and wants a tenant while he's away. Since I don't want to rent for much longer than that, it suits me fine. Come on, let me show you the most important room of all – the library. And the place where I'd write.' He threw open the door, led her in, waited for her reaction.

'What a marvellous partner's desk, and all these books! Oh Nick, it's super. So conducive to work.' She tucked her arm in his.' How many other rooms are there?'

'A living room, a master bedroom, a couple of baths, and a guest room. Oh, and the kitchen. That's in here. Sam had it remodelled, and it's modern and more than adequate. No dining room though, I guess he always eats out.'

Francesca walked around the kitchen, which was a mixture of white and chrome, and far too sterile for her taste, but it was efficiently planned and suitable for Nick's requirements. 'So far I like the flat, and I'm sure Dibs will too,' she teased with a small smile. 'But aren't you going to finished your guided tour? What about the bedroom and the living room?'

'Oh sure, kid. The living room first.' They left the kitchen and Nick went on, 'It's at the other end of the foyer.' He ushered her towards the tall oak door, opened it, moved aside to let her enter first.

Francesca took two steps into the living room and stopped dead in her tracks. A sickening horror swamped her. Victor Mason, larger than life and staggeringly handsome in an elegant dark blue suit and an impeccable blue shirt and tie, was leaning against the mantelpiece, a drink in one hand, a cigarette in the other.

'Hello, Ches,' he said in a grave voice.

She did not respond, was unable to respond. She had not set eyes on him since he had left the South of France, and the sight of him now rendered her speechless, threw her off balance. Immediately, rage with Nick flared. He had trapped her in the most underhanded way. She swung her head to him, her eyes blazing, her expression one of fury mixed with disbelief. Finding her voice, she spluttered, 'I never expected this from you! How mean and unfair of you to take advantage of – '

Nick held up his hand, and not giving her the opportunity to berate him further, he exclaimed, 'The man wants to talk to you. If nothing else, you owe him that at least, Francesca.' He strode out, closed the door softly behind him.

Realizing she was alone with Victor, Francesca panicked. Oh God! Oh God! What was she going to *do*? She knew he would question her. How was she going to explain her behaviour towards him without revealing Katharine's confidences? She clutched her shoulder bag, wanted to bolt out after Nick. But she was rooted to the spot, afraid to move in case she stumbled. Her legs were wobbling and tremors were shooting through her. She could hardly keep a limb still.

'Why don't you sit down,' Victor suggested evenly, and strolled past her to an antique armoire which had been turned into an open bar.

Francesca sank into the nearest chair, not because she wished to stay and listen to his lies, but because she knew her legs were finally buckling. She closed her eyes for a minute, willing herself to keep cool, planning her strategy, formulating plausible reasons for ending their relationship weeks ago. And then she began to condemn Nicholas Latimer for his deviousness, cursed herself for her stupidity, for not anticipating this situation. It was typical of *them*. They were blood brothers, weren't they?

Dimly, through the pounding in her head, she heard Victor's voice asking her what she wanted to drink. 'Nothing, thank you,' she said and was startled by the steadiness of her tone.

He did not reply.

She heard the rattle of ice against glass, and various other small puttering noises. His shadow fell across her and she was acutely aware of his presence as he bent down and placed the drink on the coffee table without saying a word. He brushed so close she felt his breath, the familiar warmth of him, and her whole being was assaulted by that well-remembered smell which was so personally his. It was a pristine smell of soap and shampoo and recent barbering and the spicy scent of the cologne he used and just the faintest hint of tobacco. I'm going to faint, she thought, hardly daring to breathe until he had moved away.

He was leaning against the mantelpiece again, she saw out of the corner of her eye, looking nonchalant and perfectly at ease. This maddened her, and unexpectedly she wanted to fling abusive words and accusations at him, was on the brink of telling him she knew all about his affair with Katharine, informing him about the baby and the abortion. But she stopped herself in the nick of time. She could not betray Katharine to *their* betrayer. Furthermore, she had sworn on the honour of her family name never to divulge these secrets. She could not go back on her word.

Victor said, 'That's your favourite – vodka with lime juice and a splash of soda. Cheers.'

'Cheers,' she mumbled, and lifted the glass, not knowing what else to do. In a moment she would get up and leave, once her strength had returned. She was conscious of his eyes on her, but she resolutely kept her face averted, afraid to look at him, and suddenly she felt flustered and undone. A match flared and he lit another cigarette before walking slowly across the floor and seating himself opposite her.

Victor crossed his long legs, smoked in silence, observing her quietly, his gaze levelled on her, unwavering and intent. He was perfectly aware she was unnerved, and understandably so since she had been caught off guard. He wanted to give her a chance to settle down, to steady herself. She had lost weight. Too much, in his opinion, and yet her fresh young loveliness was undiminished. She wore a white silk shirt, a grey flannel skirt and a dark blue blazer. The plain understated clothes she usually favoured. Class, he thought, she's got the kind of class that comes out of a top drawer. She'll never lose it. It's bred in the bone. With a small shudder he considered the albatross around his neck, and his black eyes narrowed with loathing for Arlene.

Francesca unexpectedly shifted her position, swung her head to glance around, continuing to avoid his eyes. The bright sunlight trickled through her hair, turning it to burnished gold, and his heart clenched. He ached to pull her into his arms, to hold her close, to pour out his soul, to tell her he wanted to keep her safe with him for ever. An impulse came over him . . . a compulsion to take her by the hand and leave with her right now. Leave this room, leave England, catch the first flight back to L.A. Yes, run with her and suffer the consequences. Tell the whole world to go to hell. The world well lost. Get rid of the people who encumbered his life . . . Arlene . . . Hilly Steed . . . Katharine Tempest. Get rid of the *things* that were encumbrances. Sell Bellissima. Dump the Monarch stock and take the losses. Cancel the films. Retire. Go to the ranch. With her. Whatever happened they would make it together. They had everything going for them. Do it, a voice nudged. And then his extraordinary sense of responsibility, his fear of scandal, his awareness of her extreme youth plus her background came to the forefront of his mind, eroded his courage. He abandoned the idea of instant flight. And in so doing Victor Mason made the gravest mistake of his life, one he would live to regret most bitterly.

Wanting to get to the root of the trouble between them, he said, 'I don't usually play sneaky games, but I didn't know what else to do, how else to see you. I must talk to you, Ches.'

'What about?'

The question astonished him and his black brows drew together in perplexity. 'Surely that's obvious. Since you've been back in London you refuse to take my calls, to meet me, and finally, when I do manage to get you on the 'phone, you blithely announce everything is over between us and hang up. Jesus Christ, Ches, don't you think you owe me an explanation?'

Her head came up with swiftness. '*Explanation?*' She laughed hollowly. 'If anything is *obvious* it's your situation. Your marital situation to be precise. You are back with your wife. She is living with you at Claridge's,' Francesca snapped.

The iciness in her tone was so unprecedented he was astounded. He exclaimed heatedly, 'She's not living with me! Yes, she is staying at Claridge's, but not with *me*. She has her own suite.'

'I'm really quite uninterested in your family sleeping arrangements,' she retorted, her face stiff and closed.

He flinched, but chose to ignore both the crack and her derisive tone. 'The only reason Arlene is in London is to finalize the settlement, and you know that, Ches. It will be worked out. It's taking longer than I expected because of the many complexities. But look, I didn't ask Nicky to get you over here to talk about my . . . problems. I want to talk about *you*. Why are you acting so strangely? What's happened between us to cause this . . . this rift?'

She opened her mouth, and then closed it adamantly, terrified of saying the wrong thing, of telling him the truth. Suddenly, for the first time since entering the room, she really saw him, and his appearance appalled her. His eyes were bloodshot and red-rimmed and his handsome face was gaunt, even haggard. Exhaustion was written all over it, and despite the tan he looked ill. For a split second Francesca softened, wanted to reach out and touch him, to comfort him. *I love him so much. I will never stop loving him all the days of my life. There will only ever be him for me. He's my heart.* A lump wedged in her throat and she was afraid she would break down. And then she thought: He's not sick. He's been over indulging in the high life. His infidelity loomed larger than ever in her head, and the anguish of heart and mind he had caused her came rushing back, ran quick and virulent in her blood. Victor Mason had killed her soul. She could never trust him again. She did not dare. She hardened herself towards him.

Taking a deep breath, Francesca repeated softly, 'What happened?' Looking down at her hands, unable to meet the dark and penetrating gaze, she said, with enormous coldness, 'I came to my senses, Victor.'

'What do you mean by that *exactly*?' He leaned forward with such suddenness and urgency she shrank back in the chair and then her lovely amber eyes were raised to his. As he looked into them Victor saw something he could not quite define, and his heart twisted with dismay. He reached for his drink and, much to his annoyance, his hand shook. Putting the glass down unsteadily, he pressed, 'I asked you what you meant.' He waited, alarmed at the apprehension he was experiencing.

Francesca knew there was no going back now, that she must bring this meeting to a conclusion, and leave as rapidly and as gracefully as possible. She could not stand being near him any longer. She said, 'Arlene's arrival pointed up so much to me. I saw things clearly for the first time, as they really are. You are *married*, Victor, and your divorce could take years. I also began to realize that our relationship could never work. There are too many things against us.'

'Such as *what* precisely?' he asked in a strangled voice, his face tightening.

'Our age difference to begin with. You're too old for me.'

He stifled a small involuntary gasp, but he could not keep the hurt off his face. 'I don't believe that!' he cried with great vehemence.

'Oh but you did once. I haven't forgotten how ambivalent you were about me, because I'm twenty years younger than you. Then there are the differences in our backgrounds and the lives we lead. I know you're a sophisticated, well-travelled man, and perhaps you *do* understand my world. However, I don't understand yours at all, and I doubt I ever will. I would be like a fish out of water with you. And finally, there is my father. Quite frankly, although he might like you on a man-to-man basis, I hardly think he would approve of you as my . . . boyfriend.' She paused, looked away, then finished, 'All these things clarified for me. *That's what happened*. There's no point in making this a protracted dialogue. It's over, finished between us.'

Rarely had Victor been shaken as he was at this moment, and for once he was incapable of responding. In that politely insidious way, which was so typically English, she had adroitly insulted him on a number of levels. There had also been a hard, even cruel, note in her voice which he had trouble reconciling with the Francesca he knew. He was on the verge of sweeping aside her arguments, of asking her to marry him. But he was not free to do so. He lit a cigarette shakily and the strangest feeling came over him. He doubted her. Doubted the reasons she had given for ending their relationship.

Francesca stood up. 'I'd better go.'

He flung the cigarette in the ashtray, sprang to his feet, was by her side in two long strides, grasping her by the shoulders, swinging her to face him, staring into her face. His eyes were bleak with desperation, his mouth ringed in white. 'Ches, please, you can't leave like this. Please, baby. You must know how I feel, that I love you. I love you, darling.' He pulled her into his arms, gripping her to him.

No you don't love me, she thought angrily. You have a damaged ego because *I* walked out on *you*. She struggled free. 'Please, Victor, let us part in a civilized manner.'

He gaped at her, further shaken by her calculated cold control. 'Don't you love me any more, Ches?'

'No,' she lied, and turned away. 'Please don't come to the door. I'll find my own way out.'

'Yes,' he said numbly. He watched her leave. That's my life walking out of here, he thought. And there's absolutely nothing I can do about it.

The door clicked. He was alone. More alone than he had ever been in his entire forty years, except when Ellie died. He slumped into a chair, dazed by the abruptness with which their meeting had been terminated. He had planned it so differently. His plans had somehow gone awry, God knows why. He dropped his head into his hands, discovered, with a little spurt of surprise, that his face was wet. He pressed his fingers to his aching eyes. He heard the door opening and looked up eagerly, with renewed hope. But it was not her. It was Nicky.

'Are you okay?' Nicky walked across the room slowly, perturbed to see Victor's most obvious distress, his wet eyes.

'Sure, I'll live.' He cleared his throat. 'Sorry you're seeing me in this state.' He ran his hands over his face, shook his head. 'She just did me in, and in a way no woman ever has.'

'Christ, I'm sorry, Vic. I'd hoped it would turn out differently. But I knew it had blown when she left. I was on the steps, getting a breath of air. She flew straight past me, cut me dead. She looked awful. As upset as you are.'

'I guess it was an ordeal – for both of us.' He looked at Nick for the longest moment. 'I've only ever loved two women in my life . . . I mean *truly* loved. One died on me. The other just walked out on me.' He took a long swallow of his Scotch, then lit another cigarette, taking hold of himself. '*C'est la guerre*, old buddy,' he added with a laugh that had no laughter in it.

Nick went to the armoire, poured himself a vodka, added ice. He carried the drink back to the sofa, sat down, staring intently at Victor. 'What did she say?'

Victor told him everything. He finished slowly, thoughtfully, 'For a minute, though, I had the queerest feeling she was lying. But I guess I was wrong. It's not in Ches to lie. She told it to me *exactly* the way she sees it. Damn Arlene. She's the cause of this trouble. If she hadn't landed on me in the South of France none of this would have happened.'

'Did you tell Francesca about the detectives, the things Arlene has threatened to do?'

'No, I didn't get a chance, and – '

'Oh Jesus, Vic, you should have told her.'

'There was no point. It would have only frightened her, and it wouldn't have achieved one goddamn thing. Besides, Ches was pretty unbending. She made up her mind about us weeks ago, and she's not about to change it. Too stubborn, the little one.' He leaned back and closed his eyes. 'Ches is also very very young, Nicky, in a variety of ways. And the young are notoriously impatient. They want instant solutions, see everything in black and white. There are no greys for them, and yet the whole goddamn world is grey. To the young, compromise is a nonexistent word.' He exhaled, went on softly. 'I know Ches is intelligent, and abnormally perceptive about many things; even so, she simply doesn't have the maturity . . . to . . . understand my problems, nor the experience to grasp the countless complexities of my life. She hasn't lived long enough to learn how to cope.' His lids lifted and he straightened up in the chair. 'Perhaps it's for the best. I mean that she's ditched me.'

'You can't be serious! Aren't you going to do anything – '

'I'm not going to pursue her, Nicky, so don't try to persuade me. She said I was too old for her, and she's undoubtedly right. I certainly feel it today.'

'Come on, Vic, you're talking nonsense,' Nick exclaimed. Nonetheless, he had to admit that Victor did not look his usual robust self and had not for several weeks. He had been working long hours with Mark Pierce and the editor, preparing the answer print of *Wuthering Heights*, as well as attending to countless other details about the distribution. When he was not caught up with business, he was wrangling with Arlene, or conferring long-distance with his lawyers on the Coast, or with his brother Armando, who handled some of his other interests. No wonder he appeared to be worn out. Nick said, 'I wish you'd get a check-up. You look lousy, in my opinion.'

'I'm okay. It's just fatigue. I've spent the last few nights on the 'phone to L.A. so I've hardly had any sleep. None last night, as a matter of fact. Johnnie Seltzer and Perry Lukas saw to that. I must have talked to them both about half a dozen times. About the Monarch situation.'

Nick nodded. 'Is there about to be a débâcle?'

'Possibly. But I hope not. Johnnie is hell bent on helping Perry circumvent Mike Lazarus. I'm throwing in with them. Even if I didn't want to, which I do, I've no other choice really. Jesus, Nicky, I'm carrying so much Monarch stock I'm sinking under it.'

'How much?'

'About five million dollars worth.'

Nick whistled. 'Holy Christ!' Another thought struck him. 'Remember what I told you? That I believe Hilly Steed is hand-in-glove with Lazarus, even though he plays the innocent?' Victor nodded, and Nick continued, 'Well, the more I think about it, the more I'm convinced I'm right. It makes sense. He wants to head the studio, wrest control from Perry.'

'Sure, Perry's come around to believing that now, even though he didn't want to think his son-in-law was knifing him in the back. But that's Hollywood, old buddy. Or anywhere, for that matter, when big money is involved.' Victor laughed cynically. 'Johnnie Seltzer is the smartest lawyer that little old *ville* has ever seen. Tough. A brilliant negotiator and a shrewd manipulator. Fast talker, but sound. Perry's in good hands.'

'Do you think your team can win? Against Lazarus?'

'If anybody can outsmart Lazurus it's Johnnie Seltzer. Yes, with a bit of luck he might just pull it off. This time around.'

'What's that supposed to mean?'

'Lazarus has set his sights on the Monarch Picture Corporation of America. He wants it badly. So, although he might fail in his take-over bid this time, the bastard will keep trying. One day he may well succeed. But by then I will have unloaded my stock, and Perry will have protected his flanks in other ways.'

'What's the next move?'

'Perry's calling a special board meeting for next week, and Johnnie's collecting proxies from other stockholders. They've been urging me to fly back to L.A. and I think I will. There's nothing to keep me here now, and I have the picture to worry about, apart from my Monarch stock. Besides, I'll have Ben Challis in my backyard, and he might be able to talk some sense into Arlene. She's another reason I think I should beat it. I'll breathe easier when she's out of this town.'

'She's not going to be easy to handle, Vic.'

Victor laughed coldly. 'You're telling *me*.'

'What about Francesca?'

'There's nothing I can do about Ches until I've sorted out my problems, until I'm a free man.'

'By then it might be too late, maestro.'

Victor did not answer.

The winter came down hard in Yorkshire that year.

The autumn foliage that had brushstroked the landscape with glorious rafts of russet and gold seemed to fade and wither overnight, and the bright sunshine of those Indian summer days of late September and early October gave way to rain-filled clouds and biting winds that swept in across the fells from the North Sea. By the middle of the month, hoary frost coated the blackened fields with tracings of silver, and the remote etiolated skies presaged snow. This began to fall steadily before November was out, blanketing the wild and sombre moors with a soft white mantle that softened their bleak and daunting aspects, brought a shimmering beauty to the landscape surrounding Langley village.

Despite the snow and the blizzards, the roaring gales and the generally harsh weather, preparations for the marriage of Doris and the Earl continued without interruption, and the castle was a hive of feverish activity. Doris had virtually moved into the castle, and although she was shrewd enough not to interfere with the management of the household, she did begin to spruce up the family's private apartments, giving them a few touches of comfort. New slip covers were made for the faded, chintz-covered sofas and chairs; heated towel rails appeared in the bathrooms; radiators were installed in the draughty bedrooms. The latest Aga stove and a huge refrigerator-freezer were ordered for the old-fashioned kitchen.

For the most part, Francesca did not participate in any of Doris's projects, and everyone left her to her own devices. She spent her days working on the book. After returning home at the end of September, she had immediately transformed the old nursery into an office. This was a cosy room, comfortably shabby, with a great stone fireplace and immense windows overlooking the moors. Rummaging in the attics, she had discovered a serviceable Victorian desk, and Kim and the bailiff had hauled it down for her, positioning it in front of the windows. The old deal table, where she and Kim had eaten their childhood meals with Melly, was placed nearby. Still covered with a cloth patterned with nursery-rhyme characters, it now held reference books, dictionaries and the research material which had taken well over a year to assemble and coordinate.

The old nursery became her sanctuary, filled with memories and well-loved toys. Their old rocking horse, Dobbins, stood guard in a corner, her doll's house reposed in another; bookshelves with chipped white paint sagged with children's classics, their leaves much-thumbed; her baby doll, Clarissa, and her teddy bear, slightly mauled and missing an ear, presided over the scene with wise old eyes. No one dared to venture into this room uninvited. Francesca laboured from early morning until dusk, valiantly struggling to bring order and coherence to those first crucial chapters, which she was rewriting, following Nick Latimer's advice. Her constant and loving companion was the small Bichon Frise, Lada, who lay curled in a ball at her feet whilst she wrote, or trotted after her when she moved around the castle. She emerged only for meals, and to take Lada for walks on the estate, the moors being forbidden territory since they were treacherous. The huge drifting banks of snow obscured paths, hid dangerous gullies, and it was easy to get lost up there in that wild country.

If her father and Doris were at all concerned about this self-imposed isolation, or disturbed by her distracted air, they made no comment, attributing her reserve and her abstraction to preoccupation with her writing. This did consume her, it also became a refuge from her anguish. But there were days when she felt disconsolate and restless, and then she would bundle up and tramp over the fields with Lada. Sometimes, on those solitary long walks, she would find herself filling up with a curious yearning, a yearning for something just beyond her reach which she could not quite grasp, and she was baffled at herself.

But one November afternoon, when she and Lada were circling Capability Brown's ornamental lake, Francesca saw *his* face, and she knew it was Victor Mason for whom she endlessly yearned. For a fleeting moment, as she stood reflecting at the edge of the frozen water, she wondered if she had made a mistake in rejecting him. Perhaps he had really loved her. After all, Katharine had said *their* affair meant little to him. But it meant a lot to me, she thought, with a quick intake of breath. And it would always be there, nudging in between them, creating doubts about his trustworthiness in her mind. Because of his own selfish and careless action, Victor was lost to her, could never be hers again. With dim resignation she recognized she *must* accept this, and sighing, she turned away from the lake.

The sky had darkened and a wind had blown up, and Francesca bent down and lifted Lada into her arms; then she increased her pace. Wearily she climbed the hill to the castle on its crest, and as she climbed, innumerable memories came flooding back, bitter-sweet and unsettling. She steeled herself against them, and walked on blindly, unaware that she was crying and that Lada was licking away the tears steadily coursing down her cheeks.

And slowly the long, lonely days passed, turned into weeks, and Francesca withdrew farther, shutting out the world. Very deliberately, she began to build walls around herself, erecting them brick by brick until she was completely insulated from life. Sturdy and impenetrable was this towering fortress, engineered to keep her safe, to protect her from future hurt and suffering. No one was permitted to scale its ramparts, and it would be years before these came tumbling down.

However, for a few brief days in the middle of December, Francesca did venture outside her strong fortress, letting down her guard to become her old self, if only temporarily. It was the occasion of her father's marriage. Diana and Christian came, accompanied by their grandmother, Princess Hetti. She was old and frail, and had accepted the invitation out of deference to the Earl. Their mother was not with them. Once again Arabella von Wittingen had been unable to bring herself to leave Berlin, even for her brother's wedding. Nick drove them from London. Doris had asked him to give her away; Kim was to be the best man. A number of other guests were staying at the castle on the night before the wedding, and Francesca rose to the occasion. She was charming and gracious as she acted as her father's hostess for the last time.

There were snow flurries on the morning of the wedding, and it was icy, with a fierce wind. But miraculously the sun came out at the last minute, just as Doris and Nick arrived at the ancient Norman church in Langley village. Doris was a beautiful bride in a silver-grey wool dress and a matching cape trimmed with silver fox. Her auburn curls were covered by a silver-fox hat, and she carried a bouquet of white winter roses that reflected the milky pearls at her throat. Since it was a second marriage for both, Doris did not walk down the aisle, but entered the church from the vestry, accompanied by the groom and the other members of the wedding party. Francesca and Diana, in rose wool suits and carrying posies of pink rosebuds, followed behind the bride and groom. The church looked lovely, massed with flowers, and when they moved in a body towards the chancel the organ music swelled, the strains of the hymn *O Perfect Love* reverberating to the rafters. Francesca felt her heart squeezing as the poignant music washed over her in waves, and she almost stumbled. Diana steadied her, flashed her a worried look. Francesca's smile was faint but reassuring, and with immense resolution she put aside her own acute unhappiness, concentrated on the ceremony. But she barely heard a word the vicar said to the bridal couple, or their responses. Suddenly David was kissing Doris, the Mendelssohn march from *A Midsummer Night's Dream* was filling the church and they were following the bride and groom in the recessional.

Snowflakes and confetti, crystal and colour swirling together, caught in the sunshine, flying in the wind. Church bells ringing joyously. Outstretched hands offering congratulations. Vivid faces. Cheerful voices. Merry laughter floating on the cold December air. Everything seemed to blur before Francesca's eyes. She stood on the church steps with her father and Doris and Kim and Diana and Nick, and her sadness engulfed her. Then she remembered this was her father's wedding day, a day for rejoicing, and she smiled, and kept on smiling for the rest of the day.

After the reception and luncheon at Langley Castle, the Earl and his new Countess left for Paris where they were to spend their honeymoon, and most of the other guests took their leave in the late afternoon. Princess Hetti, Diana, Christian and Nicky remained behind. They were staying on for the weekend, returning to London on Monday, flying to Saltzburg on Tuesday. Nick was going with them to Königssee, since it was almost Christmas. The weekend sped by, but Francesca was glad to have Diana's company, even for this short time. Neither she nor Nick brought up Victor Mason's name. They did not dare to do so. Also, they had wearied of asking Francesca why she had changed her mind about him, for their probing questions had been met with hard stares and obstinate silences on her part. There *had* been a few quiet moments during the weekend when Francesca had wanted to take Diana into her confidence, tell her everything. But she had not done so. Her promise to Katharine stood in the way. Nor did she want to humiliate herself by discussing his unfaithfulness with her cousin.

Suddenly it was Monday morning, and Kim and Francesca were saying goodbye to their cousins, Princess Hetti and Nick, wishing them a safe journey. Feeling wistful because they were all departing, Francesca hugged each one of them warmly, and hurried up to the old nursery, leaving Kim and Nick to handle the luggage. A few minutes later there was a knock on the door, and Nick came in, carrying his portable typewriter. 'This is for you, kid,' he cried, striding across the room.

'For me?' Francesca's eyes widened. She stared first at him and then at the typewriter.

He placed it on the floor next to the desk. 'Yes. It's my parting gift. And it's brand new. Only the screenplay has been written on it.'

'I couldn't possibly take – '

Nick bent over, caught her to him, silencing her. 'Of course you can take it. You'll be doing me a favour. I sure as hell don't want to drag it half around the world.'

'Thank you, Nicky. It's very sweet of you, and so thoughtful.'

He said nothing, but continued to stand close to her, pressing her head to his chest, stroking the long fair hair. She broke his heart, but he had no words of comfort. Eventually he released her, walked over to the fire and stood with his back to the flames. He lit a cigarette, all the while watching her. He said, 'Diana's promised to visit me on the Coast in February. Want to come with her? You'd both be my guests.'

Her face changed ever so slightly. 'You know I can't, Nicky.'

'No, I guess not. It was just an idea,' he murmured softly.

'Thank you for the invitation, though.'

He stared at his shoes, and when he lifted his head his bright blue eyes pierced into her. 'You'll get over him, Francesca. Fall in love again. We do recover from our romantic tragedies.'

'Yes,' she agreed, doubting the accuracy of his words. She turned to look out of the window.

Nick exhaled heavily, and before he could stop himself, he cried fiercely, 'I wish to God you'd never got involved with *us*! We're a bunch of killers. Your life won't ever be the same, Francesca.'

'No, I don't suppose it will.' She was finding it too painful, so she said cheerily, 'Don't get cross with me, but I've changed the title of the book.'

Nick shook his head in mock exasperation and then he began to smile. 'Jesus, not again, kid! You've had *five* titles so far.'

Francesca had to laugh at his comical expression, which had brought the endearing puckish quality to his lean intelligent face. 'This one is the best though, and it will be the *last*, honestly.'

'So, come on, don't keep me in suspense,' he commanded. 'What the hell is it?'

'*The Sabres of Passion*. I think it's appropriate for a biography of a man like Chinese Gordon, who raised his sabre in passionate defence of his God, his Christian beliefs, etcetera, etcetera. Well, what do you think?'

'It's terrific. The best you've had, so keep it. Okay?' She nodded, and he came to the desk, tilted her chin. 'You'll be all right, Francesca. But I just want you to know that wherever I am in this world, I'm there for you. All you have to do is pick up a 'phone and call me. Promise me you'll do that.'

'I promise, Nick.'

'I'll see ya around, kid.' He kissed her quickly, and fled before he made a fool of himself, before she saw his brimming eyes.

For a long time after Nicky had left the nursery, Francesca sat gazing out of the window towards the snow-covered moors. She was finally alone. *Alone*. For the past year she had been involved with strangers from another world, strangers whom she had grown to love. Not one of them remained. It was as if they had never existed. But they had. Birds of passage, she thought pensively, and rose. She exchanged her ancient standard typewriter for Nick's sleek shiny portable, placing it carefully on the desk and removing the cover. He had left her a note in the typewriter. She turned the roller, pulled it out, read:

I'm sitting on your shoulder. Always. Write a good book, kid.

'Yes, Nicky, I will,' she said out loud, and sat down purposefully. She rolled in two pieces of paper and a carbon, and began to type.

As she sat working at the desk, Francesca Cunningham could not possibly know that the book would take her almost five years to write. Nor did she have the slightest notion that when it was published, in 1962, it would make her an instant celebrity and independently wealthy, bring her critical acclaim as an historical biographer of brilliance and perception, and garner two prestigious literary prizes. All she knew that Monday morning, as the year 1956 drew to its close, was that Nicholas Latimer had gone. The last link to Victor Mason had been severed.

In the Wings
1979

'And even then, I dare not let it languish,
Dare not indulge in Memory's rapturous pain;
Once drinking deep in that divinest anguish,
How could I seek the empty world again?'

Emily Brontë

CHAPTER FORTY

Nicholas Latimer lolled back on the sofa in his study, propped his feet on the onyx coffee table and concentrated his gaze on his companion. Even though he was angry, he could not suppress the disbelieving laughter in his throat, and finally he threw back his head and roared. But the sound was hollow, lacking in merriment, and as easily and as swiftly as it had bubbled up, the laughter fled.

Swinging his feet to the floor, he leaned forward, his blue eyes frosted with ice. 'I wonder if you ever listen to yourself, Carlotta? Hear the things you say? You're out of your mind sometimes. Stark raving bloody bonkers, as the English would say.'

'I am not!' she shot back with spirit, her face as furious as his.

'I beg to differ. *You're* going to leave me and take the baby back to Venezuela. *You're* going to sequester him in the bosom of your family. *You're* going to bring him up in the Catholic faith. *You're* going to do this and that and run and jump through hoops and scream and throw tantrums, and to hell with me. To hell with you, lady. I'll tell you what you're going to do – absolutely nothing!' His voice had risen, and he shouted, 'There's another thing. Stop all this muttering about your poor little baby. You sound as if he's still in swaddling clothes. He's four years old, for Christ's sake, and he's certainly not *poor*. Not by any stretch of the imagination. He's not only loved and adored, but surrounded by everything money can buy.'

Carlotta's dark eyes flashed dangerously and she waved a forefinger at Nick. 'You can't stop me doing anything I want. I *am* taking Victor back to Venezuela. He's *my* baby. We're not married. You have no rights – '

'Ah, but that's where you're wrong!' Nick pounced. '*I am his father*. And I acknowledged paternity, and I have the same rights as you. Exactly the same rights. Don't try anything foolish. You'll live to regret it. Furthermore, you might lose him altogether. There have been a number of court cases lately where the father of an illegitimate child has won custody over the natural mother. Remember what I'm saying, don't attempt to pull anything on me. I have the smartest and most prestigious lawyers this side of heaven.'

'What do I care about lawyers, yours or anyone else's, Nicholas,' she hissed, drawing herself up with imperious disdain. 'My father can buy and sell your lawyers.'

'Oh for God's sake, stop waving your father's goddamn money in front of my face.' Nick leapt to his feet, poured himself a vodka. 'No ice, as usual. Oh well, I suppose that's too much to expect with all the help we've got in this house. I'll drink it straight.'

'You drink too much these days.'

'I'll paddle my canoe. You paddle yours, Carlotta.'

'You sit up here drinking half the day. Instead of writing. The new novel won't be finished on the day you die.'

Nick laughed sardonically, swung to face her. 'You're a real bitch at times, *honey*, know that?'

Her shrug was one of indifference. 'Obviously you bring out that trait in me,' she snapped.

Exhaling wearily, Nick shook his head, continuing to regard her through frosty eyes, which had narrowed perceptibly. 'What happened to the demure and gentle young woman I first met? The girl Vic handpicked for me, because he thought she was the sweetest, prettiest thing he'd set eyes on.'

'I've been living with you for five years. Something rotten is bound to rub off.'

Nick decided to let the snotty remark slide past him and, adopting a more conciliatory manner, he said slowly, 'I can't imagine why you suddenly want to take a trip to Caracas. We've just returned from there. Wasn't the Christmas vacation enough?'

'It's too cold in New York,' she hedged carefully and in a quieter tone.

'Don't give me that, Carlotta. It's hardly a reason. You practically grew up on the East Coast, and have spent most of your life here. Now, all of a sudden, it's too *cold*. Come on!'

'You misunderstood,' Carlotta began, also wanting to be placatory, to get her own way. 'I didn't mean I want to go back permanently, only for a few months, until the spring. I was also thinking of you. It would give you a chance to concentrate on your work, you'd have peace and quiet.'

Nick was adamant. 'No way. Victor does not leave these United States without me. Ever, Carlotta, and that's final.' He smirked coldly. 'Of course, *you* can go if you wish. Victor stays here with me.'

'Leave my baby here with you! Never!' she shrieked. 'At the mercy of you and your women – ' She stopped and looked at him nervously, regretting the last remark.

'*Women*. Jesus, that's a laugh. You know damn well there aren't any other women in my life,' Nick exploded in irritation, glaring hard at her.

'So you say. I don't believe you. You're always disappearing for hours on end. And you must be sleeping with somebody. You're certainly not sleeping with me.' She crossed her legs, leaning back. 'Very few women would put up with the things I have to contend with,' she finished coldly, adopting the air of a martyr.

Nick winced at this reference to their arid sex life, a bone of contention between them, and sighed heavily. 'I am not sleeping with anyone else, Carlotta. Nor am I having any kind of relationship with another woman. I'm simply preoccupied with my novel. Haven't you learned *yet* that when I'm writing I'm not interested in most things, not only sex. My energy goes into my work.'

Deep down she recognized he probably spoke the truth, yet there was always a faint element of doubt about him in her mind. He had become so distant these last few months she could only attribute it to a romance. She could not resist needling him. 'That's just it . . . you're *not* working hard. So where *are* all your energies being directed?'

Into quarrels with you, Nick thought sourly. He said, 'I've hit a bad patch. This novel is highly complex, needs enormous thought. That's what I do when

I'm absent half the day. I walk and I think. I go to the Frick or the Metropolitan, and I sit and *think*. All I do when I go out of this house is visit museums or pound the pavements. I also have to think about plot, structure, dialogue, atmosphere, a sense of time and place. Oh hell, what's the use. You'll never understand, and perhaps I shouldn't expect you to.'

Carlotta gave him an odd look. 'When we first met you were in the middle of a book, and our sexual relationship wasn't affected. Anyway, you've always been writing a book, or a screenplay, as long as we've been together. It's only recently that you've changed towards me,' she whined petulantly, peering at him from under her silky lashes.

'Holy Christ, Carlotta! I'm *older* now. I'm fifty-one, not a young stud with a permanent erection.'

She threw him a look of condemnation. 'Excuses. That's *all* you ever *give* me – I happen to know you're seeing a woman, Nicholas. So you can stop denying it. She's been calling here today. All day. The nerve of her, intruding on my home!'

Nick gaped at Carlotta in honest astonishment. 'Calling *here*. Who's been calling? What woman? What the hell are you babbling about?'

'I'm not babbling . . . I'm simply telling you, and with a calmness that positively astounds me, that your lady friend has been pestering me the entire day. Calling up, asking for you. Naturally she didn't leave a name.' She held his attention completely, added, with a small sarcastic laugh, 'She'll probably call again – any minute now.'

Nick was mystified. He shook his head, said with vehemence, 'I have absolutely no idea who she is, honestly, I don't.' He rubbed his chin thoughtfully. 'I am telling you the truth, Carlotta.'

His bewilderment was so pronounced and genuine, Carlotta had no option but to believe him. Her anger began to subside. She said, with a new hint of softness, 'You can't blame me for being annoyed and upset. How would you feel if some strange man kept calling, asking for me, refusing to give his name?'

'I'd be bloody furious. And suspicious,' Nick admitted with a grin, understanding everything now. Her impossible jealousy, always unfounded, had flared yet again, had prompted the threats about leaving. His shoulders lifted in a shrug. 'Yes, she will call back, if it's anything important. Then the mystery will be neatly solved, won't it? In the meantime, let's pack this in. You know I hate fighting.' He rose, crossed the room, kissed the top of her head. 'Truce, darling?'

'For the moment, Nicholas,' she said sternly, but her velvety eyes were warmer, he noticed. Much warmer.

'And no more talk about flying off to Venezuela with little Victor. Okay?'

'Yes. Surely you knew I didn't mean for ever. And I would like to take a trip soon.' She felt him stiffen next to her, and hurried on, 'Even if I don't take the baby with me, I do think I'll have to go. My father's not been well. Mother is worried about him again.'

'He seemed fine at Christmas,' Nick answered, his brows drawing together. He squeezed her shoulder affectionately. 'He'll be all right. Don't worry so much about him. He's missing you, just as I'd miss you if you were gone.'

'Would you, Nicholas?'

Her face was upturned to his and he saw the doubt on it. 'Yes, of course,' he reassured, wondering if he really would. 'Incidentally, why are you all dressed up? I was about to ask you, when I first came in, but you launched your broadside before I had the chance.'

'Oh Nicholas!' She frowned at him in dismay. 'You haven't forgotten Dolores Orlando's party, have you?'

'Hell, I had.' He made a face. 'Do I have to go? You know I can't stand that jet-setty crowd she swings with. They're all such ... twerps. I have nothing in common with them. Dolores is okay,' he added immediately, aware of her disapproving glance. 'Look, she'll understand. I'll call and apologize. Now. So she has time to juggle her seating.'

Carlotta was about to present a variety of arguments, and then instantly decided against this. If she forced him to go, by throwing one of her scenes, he would be difficult and acerbic, and ruin their evening. 'Well, all right,' she agreed with just the right amount of hesitancy and reluctance. 'Would you mind very much if I went?'

'Of course not. I'd planned to do a little work tonight anyway, so I won't feel so guilty if you're out having a good time.' He loped over to his desk, flipped through his address book, made the call to Dolores. After apologizing profusely, he hung up, grinning jubilantly. 'It's a buffet supper. No problem about her seating. She was disappointed, so she said, but understanding. Now, how about a drink before you leave?'

Carlotta accepted a glass of Sauternes with soda, and they spent the next twenty minutes chatting in a more amiable vein, touching on their child, Nick's mother and her health, his niece Nicoletta's forthcoming engagement party. Putting down her half-finished drink, Carlotta stood up. 'Pearl thought we would be out tonight, so she hasn't made anything special. But she has prepared a pot roast for herself and Miss Jessica. You could have that. Or a steak perhaps?'

'I'd prefer the pot roast. But I'll tell Pearl, you don't have to bother.' He glanced at his watch; it was eight o'clock. 'I guess I've missed my bedtime story hour with Victor. I'll look in on him after you've left.'

'He's already asleep. Don't wake him up, otherwise he'll want to spend the evening with Daddy, who spoils him.' Her smile was friendly despite this mild chastisement, and she turned and swung out of the study with a swish of taffeta. Nick followed her downstairs, helped her into her mink coat, kissed her on the cheek.

After paying a visit to the kitchen and chatting with Pearl, their cook-housekeeper, Nick climbed the stairs to the third floor where his son's room was located. He opened the door carefully, crept inside on silent feet. In the dim glow from the rosy night-light he could see the child's fair head on the pillow, and a disreputable looking Snoopy lying alongside. Leaning over, he straightened the covers, touched the soft downy hair tenderly, bent lower to kiss the smooth round cheek. 'Sweet dreams, my darling,' he whispered. 'I love you.'

For the next forty minutes or so, Nicholas Latimer sat at his desk in his study on the second floor, scrupulously editing the pages he had written several days before. When he had finished, he stretched, took off his horn-rimmed glasses, rubbed his eyes wearily. The pages were good, and yet the chapter as a whole was not quite right. He was damned if he knew why. Running his hand through his blond hair,

438

tinged with grey now, he began to ruminate on those last pages. He had always had the ability to spot flaws in his writing. It was more important to be able to detect faults, and zero in on the reasons for them, than to recognize excellence. Lately he seemed to have lost that self-critical faculty, and this disturbed him. The book had started out fine, had rolled like a dream for a while. Over the last few months, quite unexpectedly, he had hit difficulties. He was not moving it well at all.

'*Why?* he demanded of himself out loud, and jumped up, irritated and filled with growing impatience.

After refreshing his drink, he flopped down on the sofa, lit a cigarette and stared into space. His eyes rested on the bookshelves facing him, and the long line of novels he had written. All had been international best sellers. All of them had been excruciating to write, had caused him much heartache and grief. He frowned. *Perhaps that was it.* Perhaps he was expecting it to be easier now. It was never easy. The day it was, and when he stopped worrying, he would hang up his pencil. Sighing, he stretched out on the sofa, thinking about his life.

Why was the book not going smoothly? Why was he so restless? Impatient? Irascible? And bored? He was one of the world's most successful novelists. He had more money than he knew what to do with. He had terrific health, touch wood. He looked pretty good for his age: not too may grey hairs or tired lines or flab. And most importantly, he had a small son whom he truly adored. A healthy, beautiful, intelligent little boy with an iridescent smile and a sweet and loving disposition. Certain critics did not love him any more, as they once had. But then, who cared about those particular critics? They were an elitist bunch of creeps who condemned him because they thought he had sold out, said he had gone commercial. He wasn't quite sure *why* they were angry with him because his novels *sold*. Wasn't *that* what it was all about? No writer worked his guts out for endless, back-breaking years, hoping his, or her, books would *not* sell. In any event, those critical critics were wrong. He had not copped out, tarnished his talents, as they suggested. He wrote what *he* wanted to write, the only way he *knew* how to write it. He gave of his best. More than his best. He gave every ounce of himself. His readers loved his words. Fortunately. They were the only ones who counted. His readers, God bless'em. *They* plonked down their hardearned cash for his books, wrote him generous, warming letters, encouraged him always with *their* touching words, made the frequently lonely life of a writer seem somehow less lonely. Those literary snobs who said he worshipped at the Altar of the Big Buck could take their literary prizes and shove'em up their *tochises*. He smiled broadly, wondering about the plural of *tochi*? He would have asked his father about that. Might it not be *tochi*? He laughed out loud.

Noticing that the unsmoked cigarette had smouldered down to the filter, he sat up and stubbed it out, hating the smell. He reached for another cigarette, withdrew his hand from the silver box. I am going to stop, he muttered. Soon. He took a sip of vodka, savouring it. Carlotta thought he was drinking a lot. Now his eyes strayed to the photograph of her on the antique table adjacent to the sofa. She was sitting astride a horse, on her father's four-thousand-acre ranch in Venezuela, looking proud, imperious and exotically beautiful. Carlotta Maria Caldicott Méndez Enright. The Caldicott came from her mother, the elegant and dignified Gillian, who was straight out of Philadelphia Main Line society; the

Méndez was from her father, Don Alejandro, scion of one of the richest and most powerful families in his country; the Enright was left over from that pip-squeak of a playboy husband, Jimmy. One of the California Enrights, as if anybody cared where *they* came from. She had married and divorced poor old sozzled dim-witted James by the time she was twenty-three. He had met her a year later, and they had been living together ever since.

Nick picked up the photograph, stared at the angelic face, the smouldering brown eyes, the cascading mane of blonde hair. Yes, she was a beauty, and yes, she could be sweet. She was also one helluva spitfire most of the time. A strange mixture, he mused, cool Yankee independence plus Puritan toughness and rigidity mingling with hot Latin blood and passionate emotions. A young woman of volatile mood swings. Then he thought: Admit it, Nicholas Latimer, you're unhappy with her. So goddamned rock-bottom unhappy everything is being tainted.

Replacing the picture, he pushed himself to his feet, went to the window, looked down into the backyard, his face dismal. The snow was days old and dirty, streaked with the city's grime, and the single tree, skeletal against the grey, illuminated Manhattan sky, seemed bereft. That makes two of us, Tree, he said inwardly. His shoulders drooped, indicating his dejection and spiralling misery. He tried to guide his thoughts in another direction, but they persisted in dwelling on Carlotta. He had wanted to marry her and she had wanted to marry him. Unfortunately, they had never been able to make their desire for wedded bliss coincide. They were always out of sync. And still unmarried. Because of Victor, lots of pressure was being exerted on them both these days. Two sets of doting, and enormously rich, grandparents were appalled at the way their grandson was being raised.

'It's your loose – to put it succinctly – life style, Nick, my boy,' his father had told him last week. 'Please, for the child's sake, your mother's sake, marry Carlotta. You must, Nicky, to protect yourself and the boy. Venezuela is a long way off. Who knows about their laws? A little child could disappear for ever behind walls constructed of that immense Méndez wealth and power. Don Alejandro would be a potent enemy. I'd never rest in my grave if this were still unresolved when I die.' He had told his father not to talk about dying, but his father was eighty-five, and although it was unspoken between them, they knew time was creeping up.

Nick grimaced. He had promised to give marriage serious thought; ask Carlotta to do the same. Yet he was not sure he could make their union legal. Her incessant social life, which she tried to foist on him, her constant demands on his time, her temperamental outbursts, and her irrational jealousy were terrible stumbling blocks in their relationship. And all invested the house with disharmony, a disharmony that was assuredly detrimental to the child, not to mention his own teering peace of mind.

He supposed he could not blame her entirely. Living with a writer like himself, who tended to be hermetic and dedicated to his craft and distracted half the time, could hardly be an exciting existence for a beautiful, fun-loving, vivacious young woman who was twenty-nine. With her natural attributes, plus the asset of being the only daughter of a multi-millionaire who worshipped her, there was no question in his mind that she would easily, and speedily, find another man. Possibly a husband.

If he had any balls at all he would exit smartly, without a backward glance. How could he? There was his beloved child. His son. Maybe he should take his father's advice and marry Carlotta without further procrastination. To protect himself and his son's future. he groaned. He had been skirting the issue for months, and with an unexpected glimmer of insight he now understood why. He was facing the truth finally. It was Carlotta who was affecting his writing. He was letting her do so. This sudden and unpalatable knowledge shook him. He ran his hand through his hair. How in God's name was he going to unravel this mess and ensure everyone involved came out of it unscathed?

The intercom buzzed, harsh and strident in the dim and silent room. He lifted the receiver. 'Sure, Pearl, I'll be right down.'

CHAPTER FORTY-ONE

Sudden perceptions, whilst illuminating the mind, can also cause depression when the intrinsic truths they reveal are troubling or unacceptable. And Nicholas Latimer was suffering from such a malaise of the spirits, when, after dinner, he sat in the living room drinking a second cup of coffee.

He did not like his realities. On the other hand, he was aware that his aversion to them would not make them go away. And they presented one dilemma which, at this moment, seemed to him to be insoluble: he had to bring order to his chaotic personal life whilst continuing to write. Yet it was not humanly possible to do both at once and succeed at either.

In a sense, the truth had crept up on Nick stealthily, had unexpectedly struck him harshly in the face when he had least expected it, and he was only just beginning to recover from the blow. Slowly, it was dawning on him that his work must take priority; therefore, he would have to put his personal problems on one side, in order to dedicate himself to finishing the novel. Past experience had taught him this was not always easy. The slightest disruption or pressure impinged on his concentration, cluttered his head when he needed absolute clarity of thought. Also, Nick's tendency to worry excessively had increased, rather than lessened, with the years, and worry was destructive to his creativity.

Turning all this over in his mind yet again, coldly and objectively assessing, he resolved to make a supreme effort to isolate himself from the household, Carlotta in particular, so that he could continue with the novel in an atmosphere of calmness. If necessary, he would acquiesce to the trip to Venezuela, providing she went alone, without their child; or perhaps he ought to go away himself. Where would he go? Che Sarà Sarà was one place he had always found conducive to work and he had written well there in the past. But Victor was coming to New York shortly, on one of his infrequent business trips, was planning to stay for a month at least. So there was hardly any point in going out to the ranch, or going anywhere for that matter. He had no intention of missing Vic's visit, or forgoing the time they had planned to spend together. Victor Mason was the one constant in his life, and after almost thirty years of friendship they were as close as they had ever been, if not closer.

I'll just have to stay put and cope, Nick decided. He rose, went to throw another log on the fire. As he straightened up he noticed that the Taurelle above the mantelpiece was crooked, and he moved the frame slightly to the right. Stepping back, his head on one side, he eyed it carefully, and, satisfied it was level, he returned to the chair.

Nick's gaze lingered on the painting, a modern Impressionist work by one of his favourite contemporary artists. It was of a lovely young girl standing in a sea of flowers in the middle of a sun-drenched garden, her nudity discreetly, and partially, hidden by the blossoms and foliage. With its subtle coloration, and its extraordinary play of trembling light on the girl and the pastoral scene, it was reminiscent of a latter-day Renoir. He had fallen in love with the Taurelle the minute he had seen it, and its airy pastel colours and the sunny mood it depicted were perfect in the living room.

Nick had decorated this in a *mélange* of cream, white and sandy tones, highlighted with touches of apricot and the palest of greens and blues. The ripe wood tones of the antiques, which he had purchased over the years on trips to England, added balance to the light colours and enhanced the traditional setting. It was very much *his* room, expressed his taste for quality, comfort and elegance, and everyone who entered it remarked on the beauty and tranquillity which prevailed.

Dragging his eyes away from the painting, he lifted the Georgian silver coffee pot but immediately put it down. Impatiently, he leapt up, filled with the restlessness which had become so paramount in him lately, and on the spur of the moment he decided to go out. A long walk would further clear his head, he reasoned, and he was certainly not in the right frame of mind to do any work at this hour.

Hurrying downstairs, he took his camel-coloured cashmere overcoat and scarf from the hall closet and stuck his head around the kitchen door. Pearl, and Miss Jessica, the marvellous Scottish woman who was his son's nanny, were engrossed in a pile of cook books, chatting about recipes. He told them he was going out for an hour and left the house.

Nick swung up Madison Avenue, and by the time he reached the Carlyle Hotel, only two blocks from his home, he was already regretting his decision. The weather had turned colder and there was a stinging icy wind. This buffeted him forward, tore at his hair, whipped his face and made his eyes water. He ducked under the awning of the hotel and peered at his watch. Flagging down the first cab he saw, he leapt in, gave the driver the address of Elaine's on Second Avenue, and sat back, shoving his hands in his pockets to keep them warm.

When he pushed through the door of Elaine's five minutes later, Nick was relieved to see the bar was not as jammed as usual, and after throwing his coat on a hook, he slid onto a stool. He ordered a Remy Martin and lit a cigarette. Elaine spotted him, waved, and sailed forward to greet him, welcoming him with her usual warmth and friendliness. He joked with her for a few minutes, until she was called away to deal with some restaurant problems. The cognac was smooth and it warmed him, tasted just fine with his cigarette. He was suddenly glad, after all, that he had ventured out, come here. He was beginning to relax, the tension easing out of him, and he was enjoying the noise and bustle of the place, the sense of life, of people, which it gave him.

He cupped his hands around the brandy balloon, stared down at it, musing. He had long ago ceased to crave happiness . . . who the hell was happy in this goddamn world? Anyway, as Colette had once written, happiness was a matter of changing troubles. Nonetheless, he had hoped that by now he might have snared contentment at the very least. Even this eluded him. Jesus, in a few months he would be celebrating his fifty-second birthday. What had happened to time? It had slid through his fingers, taking so much with it . . . the romantic idealism of his youth, so many dreams, so many hopes . . . leaving behind the ashes of shattered verities and disillusionment and despair and an intangible sorrow in his soul. Yes, the years had passed in the twinkling of a star, disappeared before he had had a chance to –

'Well, well, well, if it isn't Nicholas Latimer. The one and only Nicky.'

He swung his head swiftly, found himself staring into the bright and beaming face of Estelle Morgan. Slipping off the stool, he grasped the outstretched hand, leaned forward to kiss the proffered cheek. 'Hello, Estelle,' he said. 'How've you been? And where've you been hiding yourself?'

'I'm terrific, and I've been around and about, pushing the old pen, as usual,' she said, gazing up at him with her usual adoration, which had not waned with the years. 'You're certainly looking pretty good. As handsome and as charming as ever, dear Nicky.'

Nicky grinned. 'What's it been? Two years?'

'That's right. I haven't seen you since I did the interview with you for *Now*. I'm still with the magazine. I just adored your last book, and knowing you, I bet you're in the middle of a new one.'

'Sure I am. Coming into the home stretch. Say, Estelle, can I get you a drink?'

'No thanks. I can only chat for a minute. I'm having dinner with a bunch of chums over there.' She nodded in the direction of a table just beyond the bar.

Nick glanced at the group, saw a few familiar faces he could not name, plus a well-known actor, a controversial French film director and a Broadway press agent he vaguely knew. Nick inclined his head to the press agent, turned back to Estelle. 'Too bad. Not even a quick one?'

'No, thanks anyway.' She drew closer, touched his arm tentatively. 'It's funny I should run into you tonight. I've been trying to reach you all day.'

Nick pricked up his ears, threw her a sharp look. 'Have you been calling the house, by any chance?' he asked, realizing suddenly that she was probably the culprit, the mysterious female who had so riled Carlotta earlier.

'Yes. Several times.'

'You should have left your name,' he chastised, trying to keep his voice mild. He felt like throttling her for the trouble she had caused.

'I was running around all day, kept 'phoning you from the outside,' Estelle explained. 'So there was no point in leaving my name. You wouldn't have been able to reach me.'

'I see. Did you want to speak to me about something important?' he asked curiously, his expression quizzical.

'Sort of . . . I have a message for you . . . from an old friend.'

'And who might that be?'

'Katharine.'

The name floated between them, suspended in the air, and for a moment Nick was unable to reply. He had felt his body stiffen at the mention of that name, was fully aware of Estelle's beady eyes watching him closely. Finally, he echoed, '*Katharine.*'

'Yes. Tempest.'

'I know which Katharine you mean,' he snapped sharply and he laughed a little too loudly. Attempting to clamp down on the considerable agitation he was feeling, he forced more laughter, shook his head. 'You've got to be kidding, Estelle. A message from *her*. For *me!*'

'I don't know why you look and sound so surprised. You *were* the great love of her life, Nicky.'

He was silent. His heart skipped a couple of beats, and he thought: *After all these years*. He said quietly, 'What's the message, Estelle?'

'Katharine wants to see you, Nicky. She's going to be in New York in about ten days.'

Nicholas Latimer was struck dumb. This was the most staggering news he had heard in a long time, and he also found it hard to believe. His blondish brows lifted in amazement. 'Come off it, Estelle. If this is a joke, it's a bad one. She'd hardly want to see me. You know damn well we parted company in the worst possible circumstances. I haven't set eyes on her, or heard a peep out of her, since then. Jesus, it's at least ten, no, twelve years.'

'I wouldn't joke about a thing like this, knowing how you felt about her, how you felt about each other,' Estelle protested. Quickly she lowered her voice, 'She *does* want a meeting. Honestly. Whenever it's convenient.'

'*Why?* I wonder why she wants to see *me?*' Nick's enormous bafflement was evident as he lifted his drink, took a sip. He placed the glass on the bar, pinned his eyes on Estelle intently. 'Did she give you a reason?'

Estelle shook her head. 'I can guess though. I think she wants to be friends again. With you and several other people she asked me to contact as well.'

'Who for instance?' Nick asked.

'Her brother, for one.'

'Good God, the Senator from Illinois! The great white hope of the Democratic Party, the one they're whispering will seek the presidential nomination in 1984. I'll be damned! Now that *is* interesting. They were daggers drawn for years. Still must be if she's seeking to effect a reconciliation.' His look was questioning.

The journalist merely nodded in agreement.

Nick pursed his lips, his eyes thoughtful. 'You stayed pretty close to her, Estelle, when everything started to fall apart for her. And presumably the friendship has continued. Have you seen her?' Nick's curiosity was getting the better of him and he could not help wondering how *she* looked these days, now that she was in her forties.

'I haven't seen her for a while. She 'phones me from time to time, as she did the other day, to ask me to try and reach you.'

'Where did she call from? Is she still living in Europe?'

'Not exactly . . .' Estelle found herself hesitating, uncertain whether she should

444

divulge Katharine's whereabouts, tell him she was at the Bel-Air Hotel. Opting for a compromise, Estelle said cryptically, 'She's in the States, but that's all I can tell you at the moment.' Not wanting to hurt Nick's feelings, she felt bound to add, 'Katharine's sort of travelling around.'

Nick threw her a hard stare, decided not to press. 'Who else did she ask you to get in touch with, apart from Ryan and myself?'

'Francesca Cunningham, I mean Avery. I guess Katharine's trying to pick up the threads with her, and – '

'That'll be the day,' Nick cut in, and laughed hollowly.

'Yes, I agree.' Estelle's face stiffened. 'Her ladyship was snotty, very snotty. *She* hasn't changed, she's still cold and imperious. Anyway, she refused to meet Katharine, and practically threw me out of the apartment.'

Not surprising, Nick commented to himself. After a tiny silence, he said, 'I'm afraid I have to pass too, Estelle. Tell the lady thanks, but no thanks.'

Estelle had expected him to agree, to fix a firm date, and she blinked rapidly, appeared flustered. 'Are you sure?' she asked, touching his arm. 'What harm is there in – '

'No way, Estelle,' he interjected in a firm tone.

Not bothering to disguise her disappointment, Estelle remarked in a saddened and resigned voice, 'It's a pity really. You did love her so . . .' Her voice trailed off.

'A long time ago, Estelle. Things are different now.'

'Yes.' She knew it was useless to argue, knew this would only anger him. She did not want to risk that. She had always had a soft spot for Nicholas Latimer. Estelle began to edge away, a rueful smile playing around her mouth. 'I guess I'd better get back to my friends. You know where to reach me, Nicky. You might change your mind, you know.'

'No, I won't, Estelle.' Nick smiled faintly. 'Nice seeing you.' He turned abruptly and hunched over the bar, sipping his cognac. And he was shaken and alarmed by the fierce emotions which had seized him, and which he could neither quieten nor dispel.

He finished his drink and went home. He found Carlotta sitting up in bed, leafing through the current editions of French *Vogue* and *L'Officiel*. He told her about his encounter with Estelle Morgan, whom she had heard about but not met. Hugging the *Vogue* to her flimsily-covered breasts, Carlotta asked him the reason for the journalist's innumerable 'phone calls, her dark eyes riveted on him as he undressed.

Nick dropped one shoe, then the other, shook off his pants. Having anticipated the question, he was ready for her with the most plausible explanation. 'Estelle wants to do an interview with me,' he said, not daring to mention the name Katharine Tempest. 'I told her we'd arrange it when the novel's finished. I promised to have her over for drinks. And to meet you, darling,' he added diplomatically.

Appearing satisfied, Carlotta immediately launched into a glowing account of her evening, chattering on gaily about the other guests, what they had said and done and eaten, and what the women had worn. Nick listened with half an ear as he struggled into his pyjamas and robe. He went and sat on the edge of the bed, nodding and smiling and curbing his impatience to escape, to be alone, to think.

Eventually, Carlotta finished her convoluted recital and Nick said, 'You don't mind if I work for a while, do you, darling?' He held his breath. Expecting protestations, he was both surprised and relieved to hear her ready and friendly acquiescence. He kissed her on the cheek and left before she had a change of heart, or burst into a tirade about his perpetual sexual neglect.

Nick closed the door of his study and exhaled thankfully. He groped for the dimmer, turned it until the room was suffused in a soft warm glow. He stepped up to the small built-in bar, poured himself a cognac. He had reached for the bottle automatically, knew he did not really want the drink, nor did he need it since he was wide awake. He glanced at the snifter in his hand and thought: Oh what the hell, why *not*?

Sitting down on the sofa, he began to brood. Coming home in the taxi, a singular thought had sliced through Nick's brain, cutting away all his other troubling thoughts, rendering them insignificant. And he could not rid himself of that thought: *For the first time in over two decades the four of them were going to be in the same city and at exactly the same time. Francesca. Victor. Katharine. Nicholas.*

Is it merely one of those odd coincidences? Nick asked himself, frowning deeply. Or is it something beyond our control? A strange and terrible twist of fate? He shivered involuntarily and gooseflesh sprang onto his face. A very long time ago he had believed that their four destinies were so inextricably entwined, their lives so enmeshed that they would always be together. Somehow. Somewhere. It had not played that way. And yet − Perhaps he *had* been right after all. Perhaps the intervention of time had been quite meaningless, of no import in the overall scheme of things. Were the Fates working in some mysterious and incomprehensible way? Were the four of them being propelled inexorably towards each other? To fulfil their destinies finally?

Nick froze as he contemplated this possibility, shrinking away from it. Apprehension stabbed at him, and he instantly recalled something Victor had once said. 'What has to happen happens. Nothing can stop it, old buddy.' Vic had laughed and shrugged lightly, adding, '*Che sarà sarà* . . . what will be will be. Accept it, Nicky. I do. It's not only the name of my ranch, but my philosophy of life.'

What will be will be, Nick repeated softly, and fell back against the sofa with a peculiar sense of helplessness. Words of his own flew into his head: *The past is immutable.* He had written that in one of his books and seemingly this was one truth which had not been shattered. The past *was* inescapable. It kept coming back to swipe him in the face.

Unavoidably, his thoughts tumbled backwards in time, the years rushing by pell-mell until he was confronting 1956.

1956 . . . the fateful year. The year they had been drawn together, had become involved on innumerable emotional levels. And they had touched and affected and influenced each other so profoundly, so powerfully, so forcefully, none of their lives had been the same thereafter.

And they had separated in that year of 1956. They had each chosen their own path. The wrong paths, as it turned out. They had wandered down them boldly, stupidly, alone and lonely, isolated from one another. And not one of them had understood how blind they were being, had recognized that happiness was there for the taking, within easy reach. They had done what they believed they had to do, their emotions running high. They had acted out the scripts they had written for themselves, motivated by pride and hatred and anger and jealousy. Driven by ambition and self-interest, so self-involved, they had missed the best chance each one had ever had.

How different their lives would have been if they had not behaved so foolishly, if they had done things differently in 1956. It had been the most crucial year in all their lives. But they had not known that then. How could they have known it?

Nick shook his head sadly. Very simple to be wise now, after the fact. Past deeds, past actions always take on wholly new aspects, assume new proportions, when viewed from a great distance through mature and experienced eyes. And memories too are distorted and embellished and changed by time in its flight.

Memories, he repeated inwardly, then thought: Oh no, I'm not going to sift through *my* memories tonight, struggle with the demons buried deep in my soul. I don't trust them. I'm afraid of them. This admission startled him, but he knew it was true. Memories usually brought only anguish and yearning and discontent, and frequently anger, for him at least. Another truth gripped him, brought his head up sharply. He was shackled to his past. Shackled to his memories. Shackled to those who had once inhabited his life. Familiar faces flickered in the eye of his mind. Lovers. Friends. Enemies. It seemed he would never slough them off, or absolve them of all they had done to him. They lingered, pale ghosts in his subconscious.

What abominable things we do to each other in the name of love and friendship, Nick thought. To protect ourselves, no doubt, because love in particular has its own nameless terrors as well as its joys and ecstasies. He rubbed his aching face. Don't we ever do good to each other? Yes, sometimes, he answered. But, regretfully, far too rarely. We give so little, take so much. Every relationship has its small treacheries and betrayals, and we continually justify our ugly acts, see the manifold imperfections in others, disregard those in ourselves. Noble thoughts we may have, but nothing any one of us has ever done has been ennobling. No, none of them was without guilt, not even he himself.

Straightening up on the sofa, he lit a cigarette, tried to shake off this reflective and melancholic mood which had descended on him after his chance meeting with Estelle. Unwittingly, she had triggered all the switches, turned on the computer that was his brain. Lifting the snifter he rolled the cognac around on his tongue, enjoying the drink he had thought he did not want. Nick suddenly began to chuckle to himself as his eyes roamed around his study. How could he possibly expect to flee the past when so much of it was rooted in this room? The mementos it contained appeared more potent tonight, taunted him unexpectedly, reminded him of all which had gone before, all that might have been.

He put the glass down and, almost against his own volition, he walked over to the bookshelves. They housed years of his life as well as books. He touched the scripts he had written, bound in burgundy Morocco and tooled in gold. Below them stood his three Oscars, two of them rubbing shoulders. The Siamese twins, he called them. Both had been awarded to him for best screenplays adapted from another medium. One for *Wuthering Heights*, the other for his script based on Francesca's biography of Chinese Gordon. He trailed his hand along the shelf, let it rest on

The Sabres of Passion before lifting down the volume. He turned the pages, his eyes settling on the dedication, set in black type. *To Nicholas Latimer, my friend, my mentor, with love and gratitude.* He closed the book with a sharp slap, stared at her photograph on the jacket. He touched the imprint of her face, and lovingly so, remembering her as she had been then.

Involuntarily, Nick found himself focusing on the late fifties, that span of time after they had left England – he and Vic and Katharine. Hard years, he recollected, especially for Francesca. It seemed astonishing to him now that she had immured herself behind the grey walls of Langley, had lived like a cloistered nun, sustained only by her writing and her inner strength. He had gone to Yorkshire to see her whenever he was in Europe, and Katharine had been unwavering in her devotion to her friend. But they had been the only ones permitted to enter Francesca's private world. If they had not been wasted years exactly, they had been lost years for her . . . years spent mourning Victor Mason.

But Vic did his own penance, Nick reflected. He played Abelard to her Heloise. And he lived like a man on a rack, tortured and desperate in his loneliness and his longing for Francesca. But oh how he worked, Nick thought, remembering those specific years in Hollywood. Vic had made nothing but blockbusters in those days, and had consolidated his position as the biggest box-office star in the world. He had also been caught up in the maelstrom that rocked Monarch, and trapped in that grievous marriage with Arlene. There had been no respite, no resolution for Victor until 1960, when everything had levelled off and Arlene had finally divorced him.

Yes, emotionally troubled years for Vic, for all of us, Nick thought. Arid years in their personal lives, yet professionally they had not been able to put a foot wrong. Success and wealth and fame had showered down on them, but a price had been exacted. Even Katharine had not gone unscathed. She had won the Oscar she coveted, for her portrayal of Cathy Earnshaw, and had become an international star, as they had predicted she would. She had captured and enraptured the public, with her unique talent, her mesmeric magic, her startling looks. But turbulence and unhappiness had taken its toll on her too. She had married Beau Stanton in 1957, surprising everyone, himself included. He had attended that fairytale marriage, conducted by the side of the Swan Lake in the bucolic and picturesque gardens of the Bel-Air Hotel. But the fairy tale had not had a happy ending. The union had foundered on the rocks of Hollywood, and Katharine had divorced Beau several years later.

And what did I do in those disastrous years? Nick questioned himself, and then laughed ironically. He had run foul of emotional upsets too, had wasted his time and energy endeavouring to win Diana, to make her his wife, to no avail. He had been exceptionally prolific, despite his woes, had written two novels and two screenplays in between the countless transatlantic trips. Trips to see Diana.

Returning the book to the shelf, Nick swung his eyes to the antique porcelain clock on the right. Diana had given it to him for his thirty-second birthday, eight months before they had split up permanently in December 1960. He exhaled heavily, thinking how easy it was to be clever and perceptive about other people's lives. Victor had been absolutely right about the Princess. She *had* refused to marry him in the end, as Vic had predicted, because of her obligations to her family, who, she said, needed her desperately. At the time he had wondered: What about me?

I need her just as much. Poor Diana. She didn't waste five years, she wasted her entire life, threw it away, he thought as he went back to the sofa. He stretched out on it, clasped his hands behind his head, and closed his eyes.

He had run into Diana von Wittingen in Paris in 1971, for the first time since they had separated eleven years before. Even now he could recall, with clarity and vividness of detail, how she had looked that winter afternoon, how his heart had quickened at the sight of her. The spectacular silver hair had been coiled in a coronet on top of her head, and she had worn a violet-coloured wool dress and a sable jacket, with a bunch of real violets pinned to her lapel. And ever since that day, whenever he saw violets, or smelled them, he thought of her, and with gentleness.

They had met, quite by accident, in the lobby of the Ritz Hotel, where he had been waiting for Victor, and he had rushed her into the American Bar for a drink. For old times' sake, he had insisted. She had been beautiful and strong in spirit and as always very brave, and happy in her life, or so she had said. He had been sad when he had left her and that sadness had remained with him, unaccountably, for a whole week.

What had Diana done with her life in the past few years? Had she married since then? Somehow he doubted it. And what about Francesca? What a damned fool he had been, letting her leave his life after she had married Harrison Avery in 1970. She had begun to mix in different social circles, to spend her time in Virginia or travelling abroad, and he had allowed the friendship to gradually drift and drift until it had finally drifted away. No, he should not have given up Francesca so easily. She had a special place in his heart, was so very dear to him. It must be five years since he had seen her. Good God! Those five years had flown, and in that entire time he had never bumped into her once.

'I hope Francesca is happy,' Nick said out loud to the empty room. 'One of us has a right to be happy, haven't we?' Only the silence answered him, and then Diana's antique Bavarian timepiece chimed the hour. He glanced at the painted dial, saw that it was two o'clock. I'd better go to bed. I have work to do tomorrow. Besides, his head ached, and he'd had enough of memories for one night. Memories, whether good or bad, were cold comfort in the last analysis, quite apart from the distressing emotions they dredged up. Come on, finish your drink, old sport, he coaxed himself.

He reached for the cigarette box, but then, instead of taking a cigarette, he picked it up, rubbed the lid with the end of his robe to remove the finger marks. He studied the box carefully. Engraved in the centre of the lid was the American eagle, and the words inscribed above and below the spreading wings proclaimed the Inauguration of John Fitzgerald Kennedy as the Thirty-Fifth President of the United States. Nick clutched the box tightly, and the sixties engulfed him with a terrible suddenness.

The sixties . . . Katharine's years with him. Their time together. She might have been sitting in the room, so acutely did he feel her presence at this moment. He tried to push her away from him. Too much pain, he thought, and painful memories too quickly evoked, too slowly dispelled. Fever. She had been a fever in his blood. She had also been his grand passion. And his Nemesis.

Jack Kennedy. Katharine Tempest. They truly symbolize the sixties for me, Nick said inwardly, settling back against the cushions. Two bright stars in their unique and different ways. One snuffed out. The other dimmed. It was odd that he had come to know Katharine so much better, had gained new insight into her complex character because of the Kennedy campaign.

The antipathy they had previously had for each other had been overshadowed, and curiously lessened, by their shared belief in the Senator; in a sense it had created a bond between them. Vic had been working strenuously for the Kennedy group in Californian politics, after the Democratic Convention in 1960, and Nick had volunteered his services to Vic. So had Katharine. And after JFK had won the election, the three of them had been invited to the Inauguration in Washington, and they had gone together.

Nick placed the silver box on the coffee table, his eyes resting on its gleaming polished lid, and, as though looking into a crystal ball that told not the future but the past, he saw them in Washington in January of 1961, and he was hurtling into the past as time fell away again.

Icy weather. Blowing snow. Flaring bonfires down the Mall. Floodlights trained on the Washington Monument. The snowscape and the fires and the brilliant lights creating a setting that was eerily breathtaking and beautiful and impossible to forget. The Inaugural Gala that night. Victor, staggeringly handsome in evening dress, his eyes filled with pride and emotion. And Katharine poised between the two of them, exquisite in a ball gown of shimmering silver lace, diamonds sparkling at her throat and on her ears. The living embodiment of the word star. And the next day, huddling together, shivering in the cold in the Capital Plaza as Robert Frost had read the first lines of his commemorative poem. The poet unable to continue because he was blinded by the light from the sun bouncing off the snow. Vice President Lyndon Johnson shielding him with his hat, and then an apology from the frail old genius because still he could not read, and Frost finishing with another of his poems, recited from memory. Finally, the young President arriving, hatless and without a topcoat, standing before them to give his inaugural address. And hearing those first words in that distinctive Bostonian accent: 'Let the word go forth from this time and place, to friend and foe alike, that the torch has been passed to a new generation of Americans . . .'

Nick blinked. The voice faded away in his inner ear, was replaced by other voices . . . Victor's and Katharine's and his own, as they had talked excitedly and laughed joyously through those happy celebratory days in Washington and then afterwards in New York. There had been another shift in his relationship with Katharine that January, and the friendship slowly deepened. Whenever he went to California she always invited him to dinner, just the two of them at her house in Bel Air; and they saw movies and went to smart restaurants in Beverly Hills where she could show off her glamorous gowns and jewels and reign supreme like a young goddess. And all the while she giggled at the absurdity of it all and poked fun at herself with wit and humour and he had adored her for that characteristic. In 1963, two years after their trip to Washington for the inauguration ceremonies, she had come to New York to start rehearsing a Broadway play. It was a revival of her London hit, *Trojan Interlude*, which had never been performed in the States. Katharine was starring opposite Terry Ogden, by that time a popular movie star and a name to be reckoned with in his own right.

And it was during that autumn of sunlit days and gaiety and hard work and quiet evenings filled with intimate talks and gentle laughter that they had fallen in love. And so completely they had been dazed.

Nick brought his hands to his face, blocking out the image of her pale fragile face, her eyes the colour of the sea, her tumbling cloud of chestnut hair. Go away, go away, I don't want you in my head. I don't want you in my life. I will not see you, Katharine.

Lifting the brandy balloon, he drained it, shivering as he did so. And suddenly he thought of Francesca, wondered what her reactions had *really* been when she had first heard the news of Katharine's impending return. Whatever they had been, and were, he was certain they shared one emotion – fear.

Nick rose, turned off the lights and went to bed. But try as he might he could not sleep. He blamed his insomnia on the brandy, which he believed had over stimulated him. But as the grey dawn of morning trickled into the bedroom he recognized he was trapped in the net of his memories. Wearily he closed his eyes. Katharine. Ekaterina. Katya. Katinka. Kay. Cathy. Caitlin. Kit. Kate. Katie Mary O'Rourke. Her name in every variation came back to haunt him, and that face beguiled him, those turquoise eyes beckoned him. Go away, damn you, he told her in the silence of his heart. She would not.

Finally he dropped into a restless sleep.

451

Act Two
Downstage Left
1963–1967

'And the end and the beginning were always there
Before the beginning and after the end.'

T. S. Eliot

CHAPTER FORTY-TWO

'What's going on between Francesca and your brother?' Nick asked, eyeing Katharine carefully.

'Nothing,' she replied, but as she shifted her position in the garden chair her eyes held a mischievous sparkle as she added, 'At least not yet.'

'Aha! So they are about to fall into each other's arms. Is that what you're suggesting?' Nick leaned forward, staring at her expectantly, considerably intrigued.

'I didn't say that,' Katharine laughed, lifting her wine goblet. 'But they do seem to like each other quite a lot. And as you know, Ryan's taken her out constantly when he's been in New York over the past few months.'

'Yes, and that's why I asked the question in the first place.' Nick had witnessed the growing friendship between these two, and it troubled him. Francesca had not been involved with anyone since Victor, and it seemed incomprehensible to him that she could ally herself with O'Rourke, who he considered to be weak and ineffectual. He also knew Francesca was a deep, serious young woman, who did not love lightly. If she ended up with the wrong man she would undoubtedly suffer great misery. He wanted something better for her than a liaison with Katharine's brother. Momentarily Nick reflected on them both, and the disparities in their natures.

Katharine studied Nick for a second, and speculatively so, her brow knotted in a frown. Did he disapprove? Didn't he like Ryan? She was on the point of asking him, then changed her mind, glanced around the small garden Nick had created behind his new house on Seventy-Fourth Street. There was only one tree, but it was large, and its spreading leafy branches offered cool shade on this hot and sunny Sunday afternoon in early September. Clay troughs filled with pink geraniums and redwood boxes overflowing with white impatiens marched around the perimeter, and there was an old stone fountain gently splashing in one corner, an English Tudor sundial resting in the centre. With its white wrought-iron chairs and matching circular table, the area had acquired a charming rustic ambience, was a small oasis of calm green tranquillity in the middle of bustling Manhattan.

Katharine swung her head to Nick, smiled approvingly. 'Everything's looking so pretty out here, darling, and the house is coming along wonderfully. When do you think you'll be finished?'

Nick replied, 'Thanks, and it is nice out here, isn't it? And I guess I'll be through in a couple of months. Once the living room is done I'm going to stop all this remodelling for a while. The top floor can wait.' He grimaced. 'I'm sick of living with workmen. I feel as though they've moved in with me. Permanently.'

'A year *is* a long time, Nicky. Still, it's worth it, when you look at the results.' Her eyes drifted to the fountain, rested on the sparkling water jetting up into the bright sunlit air, and she went on, as though thinking aloud, '*If* the play's a hit, and *if* we're set for a long run, I'm seriously thinking of taking my own apartment in New York.'

This statement surprised him, and he said, 'But Francesca's place is large and luxurious. Don't you like sharing with her? I thought you were happy there.'

'Oh, yes, I am,' Katharine asserted quickly. 'And it is beautiful, but it's not really her apartment, is it? I mean it belongs to Doris, and I keep thinking *she'll* descend on us at any moment, along with the Earl and little Marigold.' With a light shrug, she added nonchalantly, as an afterthought, 'My decision has nothing to do with Francesca. You know we love each other dearly. But I think it would be nice to have my own apartment.'

'Sure, that's a good idea.' Nick hesitated, then, wanting to know more about Francesca's involvement with Ryan, he plunged in: 'What about Frankie and your brother? *Is* it developing into something serious?'

'Why? Are you perturbed? Don't you like Ryan?' A dark brow lifted and it was Katharine's turn to stare.

'My ethnic background must be rubbing off on you,' Nick laughed, looking amused.

'I don't understand . . .' Her perplexity showed in her eyes.

'Very Jewish, you know, answering a question with a string of questions. And of course I like him. He's charming and very good-looking. It's just, well . . . to be honest, I think he's too young for her.'

Katharine burst out laughing. 'Nicky, how can you say that! He's only a year younger. The age difference is negligible.'

'I know, but Frankie's twenty-seven going on ninety. And I wasn't talking about chronological age. I meant she is more mature than Ryan in an infinite number of ways. I don't see them connecting somehow. They're so different.'

'Perhaps that's the attraction. And obviously they do *connect*, otherwise they wouldn't continue the relationship.' Katharine looked at him curiously. 'In my opinion, it's about time Frankie had a flirtation, lived a little, enjoyed herself. That's why I'm glad she's taken to Ryan. He makes her laugh, and they do have fun. You don't begrudge her that, do you?'

'My darling girl, I don't begrudge Frankie anything. I just don't want her to get hurt again – ' Nick bit off the rest of his sentence sharply, and could have bitten off his tongue for qualifying his remark. Years ago, Francesca had tearfully begged him never to reveal her love affair with Vic to anyone, especially not to Katharine. And he had promised. Now he had left himself wide open to questions.

The turquoise eyes pinned so intently on his were stretched wide with surprise. 'What do you mean by *again*, Nicky?'

Her bewilderment registered with him at once, and he realized Katharine had most definitely been kept in the dark about Victor. His mind raced, and he improvised, 'Once, when I was visiting her in Yorkshire, I got the impression she had met someone, but that it hadn't worked out for her. Frankie seemed a bit hurt about it.'

'What year was that?' Katharine probed inquisitively.

'Oh, er, let me see, I guess around 1959 or thereabouts,' Nick lied, and lit a cigarette to gain time, to cover his own confusion.

'No, you're wrong,' Katharine pronounced firmly. 'I would have known, yes, I really would.' Nodding her head with great confidence, she proceeded, 'Frankie was too involved with *Sabres* to even lift her head up from the typewriter long enough to *see* any man, let alone become embroiled with one. Anyway, she would have told me, we don't have any secrets between us.'

Not strictly true. Nick thought, but said, 'Just like a man to make an assumption, isn't it? I guess I was mistaken.'

Nodding again, Katharine remarked softly, 'You know, Nicky, Ryan is a sweet person. He would never hurt Frankie, or anyone for that matter.'

'Spoken like a devoted and loving sister,' Nick teased.

'Perhaps, but nevertheless, I am right about him. And look, it's lovely of you to be protective of her, but don't overdo it, don't worry so much. You said yourself she was very mature. She'll be able to handle the relationship.' Katharine's incomparable smile flashed, and she exclaimed with vivacity, 'I hope they *do* have a romance. After all, Frankie's never been in love before. I think it's exciting, don't you?'

Nick could only nod, but he returned her smile, tried to look pleased, despite his misgivings about Ryan O'Rourke. He was also beginning to detect Katharine's manipulative little hand in this situation. Although he had shed his hatred of her completely, had grown to like her immensely in the past three years, he nevertheless disapproved of her tendency to meddle. And he was fully aware of her infinitely complex and brilliant mind with its many subtleties. He was never quite sure what she was up to, or what schemes she was concocting.

Impulsively, he said, 'I have a strong feeling you've been playing the matchmaker, my pet.'

Her lovely laughter tinkled around the yard. 'Not really, Nicky. But sometimes people do need a little shove. Don't you agree?'

'Most definitely,' he replied, and could not help thinking that a little shove, as she called it, was fine, providing it was in the right direction and *not* over the edge of a cliff. Then he made an effort to shake off his thoughts, admitted to himself that Francesca was capable of looking after herself. Another thought struck him and he began to chuckle.

'What's so amusing?' Katharine asked.

'Our group does have a penchant for getting involved in the most incestuous way! You were in love with Kim, now Frankie appears to have fallen for your baby brother, and – '

'You were crazy about Diana,' Katharine finished for him. 'Quite a merry-go-round.' She stood up, sauntered around the garden, touching the flowers lightly, and then she floated up to the sundial. After examining it for a few minutes, she lifted her dark head, asked, 'Does this really work, Nicky, my darling?'

He glanced at her swiftly. 'Yes,' he said, and his voice was so quiet it was practically a whisper. He found he could not take his eyes off her, was mesmerized. The sun was pouring down, bathing her in a shimmering light, and she looked glorious, her vividness of colouring more spectacular than ever. Unaccountably, his throat tightened and it struck him how young she seemed at this moment in the simple blue linen dress and low-heeled sandals. And she was so tiny and defenceless, and she seemed hardly to have aged a day in all the years he had known her. Unfamiliar emotions stirred within him, startled him with their intensity.

Katharine said, 'You're staring at me, Nicky. Is something wrong?'

'Er, no, nothing's wrong,' he muttered, deciding everything was very very right. 'I was only thinking how lovely you looked.'

'Why thank you,' she said sweetly, returning to the table.

Nick experienced a strange and sudden breathlessness: he leapt to his feet and loped over to the silver ice bucket, which he had placed under the tree to keep it cool. 'How about another glass of wine?'

'Yes, thanks, that would be nice.' Katharine peeked at her watch. 'I wonder what's keeping Frankie and Ryan?'

'I'm sure they'll be here any minute,' Nick replied, topping up their glasses. He sat down next to her, feeling light-headed, almost euphoric now, and he had to suppress the urge to take hold of her, to kiss her. He was conscious of her closeness, his nostrils filled with the perfume of her. Smiling hugely, he exclaimed, 'I'm glad you're in New York, Kathy. I know the play's going to be a sure-fire hit. We'll have some fun this fall.'

'I hope you're right . . . about the play I mean.' Her eyes lingered on him. 'And I'm happy to be here. You've been so sweet, and it's lovely to be with Frankie. She's a jewel, so loyal and devoted, and I adore her. I'm also thrilled she's decided to live in the States.'

Nick's forehead puckered. 'Do you really think she means it? That she's serious? After all, she's got an awful lot of ties in England.'

Katharine said emphatically, 'Oh yes, I know she has. She told me she finds it easier to write about English historical figures here, because distance gives her a better sense of perspective. And she has a marvellous contract with her American publishers, as well you know, for three more books. Besides, she's crazy about New York, much prefers it to London.' Katharine paused, took a sip of wine, dashed on gaily in a positive tone, 'Of course she'll be backwards and forwards to see her father, but she realizes he doesn't need her quite so much anymore, and hasn't since he married Doris. He's very engrossed in his new family, adores Marigold, and Doris has made him happy, has turned out to be a wonderful wife and mother.'

Nick's mouth twitched. 'I thought you didn't like Doris very much. You're being pretty generous about her,' he laughed. 'Why the sudden about-face?'

'Oh it's not so sudden,' Katharine remarked cryptically. 'Getting back to Frankie and her intentions. I don't think she would have brought Lada over here if she hadn't planned on staying. If she ever returned to England permanently she'd have to put her in quarantine for six months, and that would just about kill Frankie. She loves Lada like a child.'

Yes, Nick thought, because Vic gave her the dog. He nodded. 'Of course, I'd forgotten about Lada for a minute. What's Frankie going to do with our four-legged friend at Christmas? She mentioned she was going to Langley for two weeks in December – when we had lunch last week.'

'Like you, Frankie believes the play will be a big hit, and I've promised to look after Lada for her. If the show closes, I'll just stay on until she returns. I've no reason to hurry back to the Coast. Anyway, I rather fancy a Christmas in New York, and I'm hoping it snows so that it'll be a real old-fashioned holiday,' she finished, looking suddenly like a small excited child at the prospect of this.

Nick smiled at her. 'Hey, that's great news.'

Rising, Katharine strolled around the garden again, and paused near the fountain. 'It's so peaceful here, Nicky, and I am enjoying being with you, but I do wish Frankie and Ryan would arrive. I'm starving.'

'I'm glad to hear it. Usually you eat like a bird. I've made a terrific lunch. You're going to have a real feast,' he informed her jubilantly.

'You cooked lunch?' she giggled. '*You*. I can't believe it!'

'Of course I didn't, you silly girl,' he retorted. 'You know I'm no culinary genius. I ran over to Zabar's earlier and picked up lox, cream cheese and bagels, smoked white fish, herring in cream with sliced onions, plus kosher pickles, rye bread, chopped liver and a whole bunch of cold cuts. Enough to make your mouth water, isn't it?'

She smiled and her eyes danced, and then, adopting a rolling gait, she ambled over to the table, remarking in a deep, gruff voice, 'Sure does, old buddy, sounds like the whole enchilada to me.'

Nick cracked up. 'And you sound like Katharine Tempest doing an imitation of Victor Mason doing an imitation of Katharine Tempest. The walk's not bad though.'

'*Grazie*, kid.' She raised her glass to him, inclined her head, and asked, 'By the way, have you heard from Victor? Or Jake? When are they coming back to the States?'

'Vic called me last week from Morocco. They were about to wrap, so they should be in Paris by now, hitting L.A. in about ten days. From what he said, the shooting has been pretty gruelling. It's damned hot in Marrakesh right now. A hundred degrees in the shade. But he sounded great, and delighted with the footage.'

'I'm pleased it went well. *The Sabres of Passion* has been a pet project of his for the past year and it's totally absorbed him.' Katharine paused and peered at Nick, wrinkling her nose. 'I can't make Frankie out sometimes. She's not a bit enthusiastic about the film, or even remotely interested in it. Imagine, having your first book bought for the movies, and for such an enormous amount of money, and then not caring about how it's made, the finished product. Not only that, it's quite a compliment to have you write the screenplay and Victor star in it. That would thrill most authors, and yet she's been singularly cool, almost cavalier about the whole thing. If I didn't know her as well as I do, I'd say she was acting in a very blasé manner. I was flabbergasted when she didn't want to be special consultant on the picture, weren't you? Did she ever give you her reason for turning it down?'

Nick said nothing, merely shrugged, remembering the battles he had had with Francesca, who at first had refused to sell motion picture rights to Bellissima Productions. He had found himself doing a lot of fast talking, and Victor had kept raising the offer until it hit ceiling. Finally her exasperated, impatient and baffled literary agent had persuaded her to sell, pointing out that no other producer was battering down her door for the property and explaining that the price was the highest ever paid for a work of nonfiction. Perversity on her part, perseverance on Vic's, Nick thought. But he did pay too much for the book. Guilt, perhaps? Or only the desire to be near her again?

He became aware that Katharine was waiting for a response, cleared his throat, said off-handedly, 'She told me she wasn't prepared to break off, to leave the new book on Richard III hanging fire, just to go to Morocco with the unit.' And Victor Mason, he added to himself.

Katharine twiddled the stem of her glass. 'I had the distinct impression she didn't like the idea of Victor playing Chinese Gordon. I can't imagine why, unless she felt he wasn't good enough to portray her great British general, who became something of a hero to her. She had such an obsession about Gordon when she was writing.' Katharine shrugged lightly. 'Maybe she wanted an English actor for the part.'

Oh God, Katharine, if only you knew what you were saying, Nick thought. He drank a little of his wine, shook his head negatively. 'I don't know about that,' he began, then broke off when the doorbell shrilled. 'That's Frankie and Ryan now. Don't let's stay on this subject, love, it only makes her huffy,' Nick cautioned, striding towards the house.

'Yes, I know,' Katharine murmured and stared into her glass, wondering why this was so.

A second later, Francesca came into the garden, looking lovely in a white-and-pink cotton dress, and breathless and laughing, 'Sorry we're late, Kath,' she apologized, going over to kiss her friend.

Katharine returned the embrace, smiled affectionately. She was overjoyed to see Francesca's most transparent happiness, her glowing and radiant face. 'That's all right, my darling. Nick and I had a leisurely hour together chatting. Where's Ryan?'

'In the kitchen with Nicky, who's making him a rum and coke of all things,' Francesca replied and flopped into a chair.

'Ugh!' Katharine made a face. 'My brother's taste leaves a lot to be desired.'

'I wouldn't say that, Katie Mary,' Ryan remarked from the doorway, his eyes automatically flying to Francesca. 'I think I have terrific taste.'

'Yes, you do,' Katharine agreed with a little laugh. 'When it comes to women. However, not when it comes to drinks. Why don't you have a glass of wine like us civilized folk?'

'This suits me just fine right now.' Ryan, boyishly handsome in corduroys and a green checked cotton shirt, stepped outside. Bending over Katharine, he kissed her and said, 'Sorry we were delayed. My fault. I had a call from Da.'

'Oh.' Katharine took one of Nick's cigarettes, wishing Ryan would not persist in using his childish name for their father. 'What did *he* want?' she asked, after Ryan had given her a light. Her cold tone reflected her continuing and unalloyed antipathy for Patrick O'Rourke.

Ryan sat next to Francesca, placed his drink on the table and regarded his sister carefully. He said in a more subdued voice, 'Nothing in particular, other than to check the time my plane gets into O'Hare tonight.'

Naturally. He can't bear to have you out of his sight for one minute, Katharine thought to herself. Aloud, she said, 'It's a six o'clock flight, if I remember correctly. You'd better take my limousine to the airport.'

'Thanks, Katie, I'd sure appreciate it.' He gazed at Francesca. 'You'll come with me, won't you, honey?'

'Of course, Ryan darling.' Francesca returned his adoring look. 'I'll bring Lada too, if that's all right.'

'Sure, honey. Anything you say.' He reached for her hand, took it in his, began to stroke it.

Nick hurried out with a bottle of white wine. 'Sorry to keep you waiting, Beauty,' he said to Francesca. Filling her glass, he handed it to her.

'Thanks, Nicky,' she said.

Dropping into a chair between Katharine and Francesca, Nick asked, 'How's the new book coming along, kid?'

'Very well. I should be finished in about six months.'

'Jesus, you've been quick!'

'Not really, Nicky. Don't you remember, I started it in March 1961, immediately after handing in *Sabres*? I've been working on it for well over two years. Besides, Richard III is an old friend, figuratively speaking. It's proving to be a little easier than the first. How's your novel progressing?'

'Slowly but surely,' Nick answered, then addressed Ryan: 'Have you enjoyed your week in New York?'

'It's been splendid, thanks to Francesca.' Ryan glanced at Katharine. 'I feel terrible, Sis, we've hardly seen each other. How are rehearsals going?'

'Pretty good, thanks. I was a bit nervous at first. I mean, about doing a play after so long. It's been seven years since I walked the boards, you know. But it's all coming back very naturally, and Terry's as marvellous as he always was.' Katharine talked on animatedly, answering Ryan's questions about the play with enthusiasm. She kept them entertained with anecdotes about the cast and the director, and titillating backstage gossip.

Nick lolled in the chair, enjoying Katharine, happy to see her so relaxed, less jittery than usual. As he sipped his wine he could not help studying her brother surreptitiously. And through critically appraising eyes. Ryan was more expansive than he had been in the past, and Nick found himself laughing along, caught up in his gay and effervescent mood. Ryan was an engaging young man, there was no doubt about that, articulate and smooth of tongue, and he had a dry humour, a knack for telling a good yarn. The gift of the gab, Nick thought, with a flash of cynicism. Typically Irish. But then so are his looks. Ryan O'Rourke had a broad, open and guileless face, a wide Celtic mouth, sparkling green eyes and reddish-blond hair. With his tan, and the sprinkling of freckles across his nose, he gave an impression of college-boy wholesomeness, and his strong muscular body and height evoked images of the All-American athlete. He bore hardly any physical resemblance to Katharine, except for his mouth. His white and sparkling teeth were slightly prominent like hers. It suddenly occurred to Nick that this was not the only thing they had in common. There was also something of the actor in Ryan, and he had the ability to hold an audience, as he was so adroitly displaying. I suspect that's a trait that will be honed to perfection, Nick said under his breath. A professional charmer, Ryan O'Rourke.

Turning his head slightly, Nick stole a look at Francesca. Cool, contained and slightly removed though she seemed on the surface, her eyes gave her away. They not only expressed her amorous feelings for Ryan, but they never once left his face. So much for that, Nick decided. She's fallen for him all right, and very heavily.

461

He was not sure why this dismayed him. O'Rourke appeared to be nice enough, harmless really, and unlike his sister, he was ingenuous, as transparent as water. He totally lacked her guile, her subtleties of mind; obviously he was neither as clever nor as complex a person as Katharine. On the other hand, he did not seem to possess her devious and manipulative characteristics, which was a plus for him. Yes, a nice kid, but weak and indecisive somehow. Nick knew he was judging again, hated himself for making a sweeping assessment. It was hardly fair, in view of his short acquaintanceship with Ryan. Oh what the hell, Katharine's right, he thought. Francesca is entitled to a little fun, and she should get into the mainstream of life.

Shutting off his ruminations on the merits and flaws of Ryan O'Rourke's character. Nick stood up purposefully. 'How about lunch everybody? And where do you want to eat? Inside, or out here?'

Katharine rose, tucked her arm in Nick's and said, 'It's getting too hot in the yard. I'd prefer to eat in the dining room, if no one else objects.'

They all trooped indoors.

Ryan said, 'By the way, Katie, I start my new job tomorrow.'

Katharine had the coffee cup halfway to her mouth. She put it down with a clatter and stared at Ryan, her face filling with surprise. 'I thought you liked the job on the newspaper,' she exclaimed.

'Yes, I did, but it was only a stop-gap, Katie.'

'And what are you going to do? What's the new job?' she demanded.

'I'm going to work for the mayor . . . Mayor Daley,' Ryan said, looking at her nervously.

Katharine's heart sank. So all her persuasive words had fallen on stony ground. Her father had won this round. 'That can only mean one thing,' Katharine said in a voice of dismay. 'You're going into politics after all.'

Ryan cleared his voice, 'Well, er, yes, I guess I am. Eventually.'

'I can't believe it!' She sat back with a jerk, scrutinizing him through chilly eyes. 'You've said, and constantly, that you loathed the idea, that you didn't savour the prospect of a political career. Now, suddenly, you've changed your mind.' She laughed with enormous coldness, added scathingly, 'This is not *your* decision, Ryan, it's Father's.'

He coloured slightly and, unable to meet her piercing stare, he glanced away. 'It *is* my decision, Katharine,' he declared after a moment. 'I've given a lot of thought to my future in the past couple of years, and I've come to the conclusion Dad is right, has always been right. Men like me, with a vast family fortune behind them, *should* go into public office . . . it's their duty, their responsibility, Dad says. I agree. And Dad has always wanted me to be a politician. He brought me up with that in mind, as you well know. It's been the great dream of his life.'

'*He* doesn't always get what he wants, nor do all of *his* dreams come true. Fortunately,' Katharine snapped, and a triumphant gleam flickered in her eyes briefly.

Ignoring the comment, Ryan hurried on, 'Dad makes a lot of sense, Katie, and I've come around to realizing this lately. He's mapped out a whole programme for me, a total plan, in a sense. In a couple of years he wants me to run for the House of Representatives, and after several terms he says I'll be ready to stand for the Senate.'

462

'And one day you'll be President of these good old United States! Is that what he promised you?' Katharine's laughter was disdainful. 'One thing's for sure. *You* won't be the First Irish Catholic President of this country, as he boasted you would be when we were children. Someone else got there before you.'

'So perhaps I'll be the second,' Ryan retorted, and then flushed again, shifted in the chair, and, attempting to assume indifference, he lifted his cup.

Nick, who had listened to this exchange with considerable interest, glanced at Ryan quickly, saw that he seemed more nervous and uncomfortable than ever. Leaning forward, Nick took a cigarette, lit it, sneaked a look at Katharine, detected a cold but controlled anger in her. A number of things fell into place. Francesca caught his eye. Her own were pleading and signalled her acute embarrassment, told him to intercede.

Straightening up in the chair, Nick said, 'How about another cup of coffee and a cognac, Ryan? Katharine? Francesca?'

Ryan said, 'Thanks, Nick, but I'm afraid I'm running late. I've got to get back to the Carlyle to pick up my luggage.' He peered at his watch. 'It's turned four already.'

Recognizing an opportunity to escape, to bring this to an end, Francesca stood up. 'I *do* think we ought to be going, Nick. Thank you for a lovely lunch.' She kissed Katharine. 'I'll see you later, darling, at home,' she murmured, and began to edge away.

Katharine nodded her goodbye, then said to Nick, 'I think I will have a cognac, please.'

'No sooner said than done, my fair one,' Nick cried and, taking Francesca's arm, he diplomatically led her out.

Ryan had risen, hovered next to Katharine. He put his arm around her shoulder, kissed the top of her head. 'Please, don't be like this, Katie darling. It's what I want, really it is.' She made no response, and he hurried on, 'It's been a marvellous week, and I'll be here for your first night, standing in the aisle, cheering my beautiful, brilliant sister.'

Katharine pushed aside her disappointment and her dismay. He had been lost to her for too long. She could not risk losing him again. Why antagonize him? The closer she was to Ryan the more influence she could exercise over him. Her smile flashed and she stood up, hugged her brother. 'You'd better be at my opening, darling! Take care, have a good flight.'

Ryan beamed at her. 'I knew you'd understand, Katie. And *you* take care, and don't work so hard,' he admonished and hurried out.

After a few minutes Nick joined Katharine in the garden, carrying two brandy balloons. 'Here you are, love,' he said, placing them on the table. 'I've got another pot of coffee brewing. Incidentally, I didn't know what you wanted to do later, so I told Ryan to send the limousine back here from La Guardia. Okay?'

'Yes, thanks.' She sniffed the brandy, took a small tentative sip, settled back in the garden chair.

Noting the remote expression in her eyes, Nick said, 'Want to talk about it?'

She exhaled heavily. 'Oh, I don't know.' She shook her head. 'He's power hungry.'

Frowning, Nick exclaimed, 'Ryan? Surely not. He seems far too – '

'No, no,' she interrupted. 'My father. He's a terrible man. And he's always manipulated Ryan, turned him into a puppet.'

'Did your father really say that? I mean promised Ryan he was going to make him the First Irish Catholic President?'

'Yes,' she said softly.

'And Ryan believed it?'

'I don't know whether he did or not at the time. He was only ten years old. Mostly he was frightened. But *I* believed it then, and I still believe it now . . . my father boasted that with his money, his powerful friends and his clout he was going to propel Ryan into the Oval Office. It was never an idle boast. I'm sure he's brainwashed Ryan over the years, convinced him he can hold the highest political position in the country. I feel sorry for my brother. Deep down he doesn't want any of this, and ever since I returned to the States, and we became close again, I've been encouraging him to break away from my father, to get out on his own. I thought I'd succeeded.' Another small weary sigh, and then, 'If only Ryan had accepted my offer, and gone to Paris when he was twenty. To study art. He's tremendously talented . . . I offered to pay for everything, support him, and Ryan agreed to go, was thrilled. Until *he* talked him out of it.'

'I vaguely remember you being upset, troubled in your early days in Hollywood. Around 1957, I think. Vic told me it was something to do with your brother. I hadn't realized he had an artistic bent.'

She told him the story then, recounting slowly, and carefully, the details of the scene that had taken place in the old nursery in the house in Chicago, almost reliving it as she spoke. 'I don't think I'll ever forget the look on our father's face when he made that final announcement, boasted of what he was going to do, how he was going to manipulate Ryan's political career. That was the day I knew my father really hated me. It was also the day I vowed I would save Ryan, no matter what the cost to myself.'

Nick was silent, staring into the distance. He said eventually, 'Misplaced ambition is frightening. Your father is trying to live through Ryan, and I don't envy your brother. His life isn't his own.'

'I know that, Nicky.'

He gave her a sidelong glance, said carefully. 'Is that why you worked so hard for Jack Kennedy, campaigned so strenuously for him? Simply to thwart your father?'

'No, of course not,' she cried heatedly. 'I believe in Kennedy. I thought he was just what this country needed, and needs. He's unique. He fired my imagination, as he did yours and so many other people's.'

'And getting . . . *revenge* . . . on your father didn't enter your head, or influence your action at all?' Nick's expression was sceptical, and his eyes narrowed as they held hers.

Surprised at his use of so strong a word, Katharine was about to mouth denials, but suddenly she smiled instead. It was a long slow smile that held a hint of self-satisfaction. 'Let's just say that the opportunity to twist the knife was an added incentive,' she admitted, her mouth twitching with silent laughter. 'Especially since I knew *he* knew how hard I was campaigning for JFK. I envisioned him having apoplexy at the thought of old Joe Kennedy stealing his thunder, getting his son there first. Later, Ryan told me that my father had been enraged by my activities, had called me a traitor, among other rather choice nouns. It helped even the score, and I paid him back for some of the things he had done to me.'

Nick elected not to ask what these were. He said, 'I can well imagine he was furious.' Thoughtfully he swirled the brandy balloon, pursed his lips. Looking at her closely, he adopted a gentle tone and said, 'People have to lead their own lives, Katharine. I think Ryan has enough to contend with right now, and coping with your father must be difficult. I know what such men are like. So step away a little, give your brother breathing space. Please don't meddle. Please don't play God, as your father is doing.'

'No, I won't!' Katharine agreed with alacrity. 'You're absolutely right, Nicky.' Privately she thought: Patrick Michael Sean O'Rourke is not going to be the winner. I am going to be triumphant in the end. I *am* going to save Ryan's soul. He *will* be mine. And that will be sufficient to destroy my father.

Conscious of Nick's appraising gaze resting on her, Katharine shrugged, and her laughter echoed in the little garden. 'Oh enough of all this seriousness on such a gorgeous afternoon. Let's talk of more pleasant things.' Leaning her elbows on the table, she propped her chin in her hands, and her turquoise eyes became dreamy and soft. 'I'll tell you one thing, Nicky, I'm glad Ryan is getting so involved with Frankie, and it is pretty obvious how they feel. Yes, she's a good influence on Ryan, and I think he'll listen to her.'

'Perhaps,' Nick answered laconically. And then he asked himself if Katharine was encouraging the relationship in order to control her brother through Francesca. The idea troubled him, but he could not shake it off, and it nudged at the back of his mind for the rest of the day.

CHAPTER FORTY-THREE

She was an enchantress, and he was enchanted.

As the weeks passed, Nick and Katharine began to spend more and more time together, and although they did not mention it, neither was out of the other's thoughts for very long. Both were obsessive workers, wholly dedicated to their careers, and they found a measure of comfort and security in this shared characteristic, which others in the past had found distressing. It became a special bond between them.

Nicholas Latimer was nearing the completion of his current novel, and as September turned into October the words seemed to surge out of him, the pages flying off his typewriter at a record speed. For her part Katharine was rediscovering her tremendous love of the theatre, and every day, after rehearsals, she was excited and exhilarated.

Their evenings were spent quietly, usually at Nick's house. He was aware that acting took its toll on her, for she poured a great deal of emotion into her role and he did not want to tax her strength socializing. Occasionally Katharine joined them, sometimes Terry and Hilary Ogden, and then they would venture out to small restaurants off the beaten track. Nick recognized that his feelings for Katharine ran deep, and he accepted the fact that he was in love with her, suspected she felt the same about him. He had only once made a tentative move towards her, but she had slithered out of his arms, laughing nervously and looking distressed and embarrassed. After this gentle rebuff he had not pressed his attentions on her again, although he had continued to be warm and affectionate. He had decided to bide his time, waiting for the propitious moment, one he was convinced would present itself. He had sufficient insight to understand that Katharine Tempest could not be rushed, that she had to come to him of her own free will.

Her brother was rarely mentioned, except by Francesca Cunningham, who appeared to be more enamoured of him than ever. Nick was wisely silent, never referred to Ryan after the Sunday in September when they had lunched. Even when Katharine brought up his name, Nick was noncommittal, vague in his responses. Ryan had not visited New York, except for a flying one-day trip early in October, when neither Nick nor Katharine had seen him. But he had left a message with Francesca, renewing his promise to attend the opening of the play. Katharine told Nick she was confident her brother would not disappoint her, whatever arguments Patrick O'Rourke might present to keep him away.

In the middle of October, on a cool Wednesday evening, *Trojan Interlude* opened at the Morosco. It was a glittering first night, the likes of which Broadway had not seen in many a year. Katharine was a movie star of the first magnitude now, adored by the public, and they flocked to see her in her first stage appearance in America. Those who were unable to get tickets jammed the street, and mounted police had to be brought in to control the crowds outside the theatre.

Francesca, looking lovely in a daffodil-yellow brocade gown and matching evening coat, sat next to Hilary, elegantly turned-out in black velvet and diamonds. They were flanked by Ryan and Nick respectively. And they all knew, after the first fifteen minutes, that the play was going to be a big hit. Katharine was superb as Helen, a role she had made entirely her own, and Terry was equally electric as Paris, Prince of Troy. They were magnetic together, and unmatched as an acting team. The audience screamed the house down at the finale, gave them a standing ovation. Later Katharine made the traditional entrance at Sardi's, once more to thunderous acclaim. She walked in slowly, somewhat shyly, looking spectacular in a white wool-crêpe evening gown, the emerald necklace and teardrop earrings Beau Stanton had given her as a wedding present flashing like green fire around her face. Nick was waiting for her, seated at a table with Francesca, Ryan, Hilary, the producers and their wives. And as she walked towards them, bowing to the right and left, and smiling radiantly, Nick thought his heart would burst with love and pride. Terry followed quickly in her wake, and he also received a wild reception. Champagne toast followed champagne toast, and they stayed for an hour before leaving for the Rainbow Room where a supper dance was already in progress for the rest of the cast and honoured guests.

Katharine clung to Nick throughout the entire evening, and although she presented a vivacious and self-confident front, he was conscious of her inner tension and anxiety. This was not alleviated until the first editions of the newspapers were delivered by the excited press agent for the play. Waving them over his head, he rushed into the room, shouting, 'It's a smash!! We've got a smash on our hands!' Nobody could hear him above the noise and the band, but his beaming ecstatic face was more explicit than any words he could say. Every review was a rave, and even the jaundiced critic of the *New York Times*, who could make or break a play and was hard to please, had nothing to offer but accolades and superlatives.

Visibly relaxing immediately, Katharine was endearing in her unsuppressed joy. It was a memorable night, and a week later, one evening after the theatre, Nick took her to Pavillion for a quiet supper. It was another special occasion, in this instance to celebrate the delivery of his novel to his publishers. Sipping champagne and holding her hand, he told her that he had dedicated his new book to her. Katharine was so touched her eyes filled with tears.

'And to think how much you used to hate me,' she murmured, blinking, brushing her eyes with her hand.

'You used to hate me too,' Nick said softly, searching her face.

Katharine half smiled. 'I've come to the conclusion that I was simply responding to *your* enormous dislike of *me*.'

'Perhaps,' Nick replied. He clasped her hand tightly, pressed it to his face. 'Hasn't it occurred to you that there are two sides to a coin, that the reverse side of hatred is love, you silly adorable divine girl.'

Colour crept onto her pale face, and she dropped her eyes, said nothing. But after a moment she looked at him through the tangle of dark lashes. 'Yes,' she whispered. 'It has.'

Nick remembered this particular evening a month later, as he sat at his desk, doodling on a pad, drawing small hearts and scribbling her name in many variations. He was talking to his mother on the telephone. 'Yes, Ma, of course I'm coming to Thanksgiving dinner. Would I miss it?'

'You have sometimes, Nicholas,' Mrs Latimer chided softly. 'But I do realize those lapses on your part were unavoidable, only happened when you were off gallivanting abroad.' She cleared her throat, hesitated, and then announced, 'We're expecting Katharine too, you know.'

'That's sweet of you, Mother, but I'm not sure that she can make it. She's been out of the play for a couple of days, with a sore throat and – '

'I'm sorry to hear it. I hope it's not serious.'

'No, it's not. She'll probably go back to work tomorrow night. However, as far as Thanksgiving's concerned, I have a feeling the theatre's open that evening.'

'Oh dear, what a shame. Your father will be disappointed, as I am. You'll still come?'

'Yes, darling, I will.'

'That's wonderful. I must rush now. I have a dental appointment. Oh, Nick dear . . .'

'Yes, Mother?' he asked patiently, glancing at his watch, wanting to get to work on his new screenplay for Victor.

'Is there any truth in all the rumours? Your father and I have been wondering – ' Her voice trailed off lamely.

'What rumours are you referring to specifically, Mother?' he asked, knowing exactly what she meant.

'Er, er, all those items in the press. About your romance with Katharine, that you're seen here, there, and everywhere together. Are we about to get a daughter-in-law at last?'

'Don't rush me, Ma,' he laughed.

'You're forty, Nicky.'

'*Thirty-six*, Ma. So long. See you next week.'

'Goodbye, Nicky,' his long-suffering mother sighed and hung up.

He was still chuckling as he rolled paper into his typewriter, numbered the page and then sat back, staring at the wall facing him, letting the scene he was about to write roll past his eyes like a segment of film. The telephone rang again, and he cursed under his breath as he swung in the chair and answered it. His literary agent apologized for disturbing him, talking briefly about a possible motion picture sale of the new novel, and hung up. In rapid succession he received three more calls, from his editor, his part-time secretary Phyllis, and a sales assistant at Tiffany's, who told him his order was ready.

Lighting a cigarette, attempting to clear his head of all this extraneous matter, Nick put both of his telephones on the floor, removed the receivers and threw two large cushions over them. He finished his cigarette and slowly began to type, filling the blank page with words. After two hours of solid uninterrupted work he went to the kitchen, returned to his study with a mug of coffee, launched himself into the screenplay once more.

His concentration and his absorption in his writing were so complete it was a few minutes before he heard the strident pealing of the front door bell. He glanced at his watch, saw that it was almost three o'clock. Wondering who his unexpected caller was, he ran downstairs.

Flinging open the door, Nick was surprised to find Katharine standing on the steps, muffled up in a thick woollen headscarf and a sable coat, huge dark glasses masking her face. 'Hi, darling,' he said delightedly, drawing her inside out of the cold, glancing down the steps to the kerb, his eyes seeking the limousine. He frowned. 'Where's the car? You didn't walk di – '

'Nick, you don't know, do you?' Katharine gasped, seizing his arm fiercely, taking off her dark glasses, staring at him. Naturally pale, she was now chalk white and obviously dreadfully shaken. Before he could respond, she stammered, 'The P-P-P-President. He's been shot . . . assassinated. I've been trying to call you for ages. Your 'phones – '

'Oh my God!' Nick's eyes widened, filled with incredulity. As though he had been slammed hard in the stomach, he staggered back against the wall. Stunned and shocked, he said, again. 'Oh my *God*. Are you sure? Where? When? Oh Jesus, no!'

'Dallas. Around twelve-thirty,' Katharine replied shakily. She stepped towards him, her face crumpling. Nick took her in his arms, held her to him. His face was suddenly as deathly pale as hers, his eyes swamped with horror. He saw nothing in the small dim hall, only an image in his head of the handsome young President, so full of vitality and zest and hope for the future. How could he be dead? No, not *Jack Kennedy*. It wasn't possible. It couldn't *be*. It was a mistake. He cried, in a rasping tone, 'Kath, are you sure? How did you find out?'

She pulled away from him, looked up into his face, the words spilling out of her in a rush. 'It's *true*, Nick! I happened to have the television on. Reading, not really watching. It was a soap. *As the World Turns*, I think. Suddenly CBS interrupted the show with a news flash, and there was Walter Cronkite looking terribly serious and worried, saying three shots had been fired at the President's motorcade in Dallas, that he was seriously wounded. I remember glancing at the clock. It was just one-forty. I dialled you, but your lines were busy. I kept calling you, then realized you'd taken your – '

'Let's get to a TV set,' Nick cried and bounded up the stairs. He turned on the television in his study, stood staring at it, his disbelief rapidly dissipating. Cronkite had all the facts now, was delivering them in a grave and shaken voice, a muscle in his face twitching. He was repeating what he had apparently said a few minutes before, for viewers who had just turned on, confirming the horror. President Kennedy was dead. Lying in Parkland Memorial Hospital in Dallas. Nick could not accept it. The facts would not sink in, and he flipped stations repeatedly, catching additional bits of information from each stunned newscaster. He swung to Katharine. She had disappeared. He had not even noticed her leave. She was back a moment later, had shed her coat, was carrying two mugs of coffee. Silently she put them on the table, sat down on the sofa. Nick joined her and she placed her hand on his arm, and her voice quavered as she said, 'Nick, this is *America*, not a banana republic. We don't have assassins *here*. Oh Nick, I'm frightened . . . what's happening to the country?'

'I don't know,' he mumbled. 'And the crucial question is what's going to happen to it from now on?' He rubbed his hand over his forehead distractedly, took a cigarette, lit it, the flame from the lighter fluttering in his shaking hands.

They kept their vigil by the television set for hours, hardly speaking, straining to catch all the horrendous details of the ghastly and senseless murder of their President. Several times Katharine broke down and cried bitter tears, and Nick's own tears fell as he gentled her. 'I can't believe it. I keep thinking of his wit and humour, and his graciousness to us when we were campaigning. Oh God, Nicky, think of what his poor wife must be suffering. And those little children, they're so very young.' She shook her head mournfully. 'Why *Jack*? Why him, Nick?'

All he could say, sounding dazed, was, 'I don't know, Kath. I just don't know.' And he thought: What have they done to us? Why did they kill him?

When she was more composed, Katharine went down to the kitchen and made tuna-salad sandwiches, brought them back to the study. But neither of them could eat and the sandwiches remained untouched on their plates. A little later Nick remembered his telephones were off their hooks and he replaced them. The calls started coming in then, fast and furious: his literary agent, his brother-in-law Hunt, and his father, all of them in shock, grown men weeping unashamedly. Francesca rang from Connecticut, where she had gone for the weekend, and she too was stricken and numb, asking the same questions as Katharine. How could it happen here? What was happening in the country? Was it a conspiracy? He had no answers for her either, and he was filled with dread and rage and bitterness. Later in the afternoon, Victor called from California, his voice broken and charged with emotion, and as they talked Nick heard a twin echo of his own anger flowing back to him over the wire, and sorrow and bafflement dwelt in Victor's voice as well.

At six-fifteen that evening, Lyndon Baines Johnson appeared on television and made his first statement as President to a stunned and grieving nation. And it was only then that Nicholas Latimer accepted the fact that John Fitzgerald Kennedy was really dead, slain by an assassin's bullet. He felt so great a personal loss that he was as profoundly affected as he had been when his sister Marcia had been killed in the accident seven years before.

Nick lay on the sofa in his study, smoking a cigarette in the darkness, unable to sleep, his mind turning endlessly. Nick knew something dangerous and evil was loose in his country, that dark forces were at work, and this alarmed and terrified him. He was a voracious reader of newspapers and magazines, and a student of history, the past and in the making, and so he had long understood that the Radical Right was on the march, that hatred and bigotry flourished. His country had just been savaged by an insane and incomprehensible act of violence, but had it not been savaged for a long time and from within? *Fascism*? He shuddered. As a Jew he could not help thinking of Nazi Germany. He remembered, suddenly, how he had once had a conversation with Christian von Wittingen about the rise of Hitler, had asked him how in God's name Hitler had persuaded so cultured a nation as the Germans to espouse his anti-Semitism, his racist policies. Christian had looked at him in surprise, had answered with a question of his own: 'What has culture to do with anything?' Nick recalled now that he had shaken his head silently. And Christian had gone on to say, in a gloomy voice, 'You're a Rhodes Scholar, look to the history you read at Oxford. You will soon understand that hate and bigotry and prejudice are emotions all too easily engendered in people, in a nation as a whole, when evil and sinister men are at their diabolical work. Those maniacal fanatics play on weakness and fear and ignorance. Look into the history books, Nicholas. You will find atrocities jumping out from every page. Tomás de Torquemada and the Spanish Inquisition, the Turks slaughtering innocent Armenians, and what about the pogroms which started in Russia after the assassination of Csar Alexander II?' Christian had exhaled heavily, sorrowfully. 'Regrettably, lamentably, atrocity is a human crime, one that has been perpetrated for centuries, by *people*, Nick. Shocking, is it not, when one thinks that the most heinous acts imaginable have been committed by supposedly civilized men against other men? And we'd better watch ourselves, watch the whole world, be on our guard against that kind of blind and terrible wickedness, otherwise we may find ourselves facing new unholy terrors in the not too distant future. History is cyclic.'

Nick shuddered again, recollecting Christian's warning, recollecting how he had stared helplessly at Christian's stern and suffering face, and then at the young man's crippled and useless legs. And he remembered thinking at the time: He knows. He's been there. To hell and back.

Stubbing out his cigarette, Nick pulled the blanket up over himself. He wondered if Katharine was asleep in the other room. She had asked if she could stay the night, telling him she could not bear to go back to the empty apartment. Just after midnight she had donned a pair of his pyjamas and crept into his bed, looking as drained as he had been feeling.

Towards dawn, Nick heard the door creaking open and Katharine whispering, 'Are you awake, Nicky?'

'Yes, darling.' He sat up as she came into the room. 'I haven't closed my eyes all night,' she said, hovering near the sofa. He moved, made a place for her next to him, and she came into his arms gratefully, willingly, clinging to him.

After a while, she said, 'I'm so scared, Nicky.' He felt her breath near his cheek as she continued, 'Afraid for all of us, and especially for Ryan. I wish he weren't going into politics. If this kind of thing can happen once, it can happen again.' When he made no reply, she whispered, 'Well, it can, can't it?'

'Yes,' he admitted reluctantly, thinking of Christian's words, and praying that it never would.

They continued to talk, holding each other tightly, trying to console each other as best they could. And Nick, growing increasingly conscious of her warmth and sweetness and closeness, moved her hair away from her face at one moment, kissed her deeply. 'I love you, Katharine,' he told her, unable to contain himself a second longer.

'And I love you, Nicky,' she responded at once. Her arms crept around his neck and she kissed him in return.

And much later they made love for the first time, baring their feelings at last. And their act of love was an affirmation of life.

CHAPTER FORTY-FOUR

One morning, about four months later, Katherine awakened to find herself filled with a curious and unfamiliar sense of lightness. It was as if a terrible burden had been lifted from her, and for a few seconds she was baffled. Then it began to dawn on her that the feeling of lightness was compounded of two things: relief and joy. For the first time in years, the gnawing anxiety she lived with had evaporated, no longer existed; and she was euphoric with happiness because of Nicholas Latimer.

Jumping out of bed energetically, she pulled on her dressing gown and went into the kitchen of her new apartment, which Nick had found for her and which she had recently purchased. She made herself a pot of tea, toasted an English muffin and carried her simple breakfast back to bed on a small tray. Sipping the tea, she glanced at the framed photograph of Nick on her bedside table. She loved him so much, more than she had ever loved any other man, and so wholeheartedly she was continually dazed by the depth and strength of her emotions. Her gaze lingered on the lean and handsome face, the light, amused eyes, the puckish smile. He was everything she could ever want in another human being. Loving, thoughtful, intelligent, wise, tender and also very very funny at times. She wondered suddenly how she could have ever thought his one-line cracks were acerbic. She smiled to herself. They *were* a little sardonic, but now she understood that there was never any cruelty behind his words. They sprang, quite simply, from his wry view of the world, his penchant for poking fun at it, and at himself most of all.

Her thoughts swung to Beau Stanton. Like Nick, Beau had always made her feel safe and secure and at ease, and she *had* loved him, although not to the degree she loved Nick, and they had been happy. In the beginning at least. And then their relationship had started to deteriorate, why she had never been sure, and Beau had become withdrawn and moody. One day she had admitted to herself that he had changed towards her, was more of a friend and mentor than a husband. She had not minded this gentle shift, but apparently Beau had been bothered about it. In the end their marriage had collapsed, perhaps because Beau had totally misunderstood her and had attributed her placid acceptance of the situation to indifference on her part. No one had been more surprised than she when he had insisted on a divorce. Yet she knew Beau still cared for her, loved her even, in his own way, and they were now the dearest of friends. And instinctively Katherine was certain Beau would always be there for her, if ever she needed him.

Katherine laughed out loud, remembering how jealous Nick had been two weeks ago, when Beau had flown in from the Coast specially to see her in the play. Although it had opened as a limited engagement, it had been held over twice because of its enormous success, and was still playing to packed houses. Beau had been thrilled about this, crediting her with the long box office queues, and awed by her performance. He had insisted on taking them to dinner after the show, and he had so doted on her through the meal Nick had grown suspicious and wary of Beau. For days afterwards he had pestered her about her marriage, bombarding her with probing questions about its failure, but without eliciting any real responses from her. It was not that she was reluctant to confide in Nick. There was nothing to confide really, since she herself was uncertain why the marriage had gone on the rocks in the first place. Nick's jealousy had amused her. She and Beau had separated in 1959. It was now March 1964. There was hardly anything to be jealous about. Not any more.

The small Tiffany carriage clock shrilled, the alarm announcing it was ten o'clock, reminding Katherine it was Saturday and that she had a matinée as well as an evening performance to give. Hurrying into the bathroom, she turned on the taps, poured perfumed oil into the tub and pinned up her hair. Her fetish about cleanliness had not waned over the years; if anything, it was even more pronounced. Consequently, her toilet, grown increasingly ritualistic and lengthier than ever, always took well over an hour. After working through an assortment of toothpaste, mouthwash, deodorants and perfumes, she brushed her hair, secured it in a pony tail and went into the bedroom. The large chest of drawers held an incredible amount of exquisite and expensive underwear, stacked in meticulous piles, and she selected lace-trimmed white satin items to wear under her white silk shirt and an azure-blue trouser suit of tailored wool. Stepping into low-heeled black suede shoes, she tied a blue ribbon on her pony tail and added her watch, as well as the aquamarine-and-diamond pendant and matching ring Nick had given her for Christmas.

She put on her dark glasses, picked up her suede bag and a small overnight case and left the bedroom. Since it was Saturday she would spend the weekend with

Nick at his house, as she always did. She locked the apartment door behind her, glided to the elevator and, as she rode down to the lobby, realized how much she was looking forward to the next couple of days. Nick had been at Che Sarà Sarà for the entire week, conferring with Victor Mason on the new script, but was due back from California in the early evening. She could hardly wait to see him, to tell him how much she had missed him.

When she reached the lobby of the apartment building she saw Howard, her driver, chatting to the doorman. He came forward, greeted her pleasantly, took the case from her. 'Hello, Howard,' she said, smiling. She glanced out at the street. 'It looks like a lovely day. I wish I could walk to the theatre.'

Howard shook his head. 'No way, Miss T. Mr Latimer would kill me. You know you'd be mobbed in two minutes.'

'Yes,' she sighed, thinking the price of fame was a high one sometimes, especially when it came to small things such as taking a walk.

As the car rolled away from the kerb and proceeded down Seventy-Second Street towards Park Avenue, Katharine sat back, mentally ticking off the things she had to do the following week. There were the final decisions to be made on the last purchases for the apartment, which she had been decorating herself with Francesca's help. They must have it ready by the middle of the month, when she was throwing a party for Hilary Ogden. She also had to talk to the caterers about the menu for the buffet supper, send out invitations, buy a gift for Hilary, and go shopping for a new summer wardrobe. The play was closing at the end of March, and in April she and Nick were taking a vacation in Mexico, at a place Nick knew called Las Brisas, in Acapulco. It would be a marvellous, much-needed rest for them both, before he went to work on his next novel and she started her new picture.

She frowned, concentrating her thoughts on this. She liked the script and her co-star, and the director was one of her favourites. The only aspect of the deal which induced nervousness in her was the studio producing the film: Monarch. It belonged to Mike Lazarus now, or rather his conglomerate, Global-Centurion, had controlling interest. In an odd sort of way, Lazarus still fascinated her, and apparently he felt the same about her. Nick could not stand him, and had been vociferous in his condemnation of Mike, warning her repeatedly about becoming too friendly with him. But Nick had eventually agreed she should do the picture, particularly since it was a quality production and they were meeting her very high price. She now wondered what to do about her house in Bel Air, whether to sell it or not. She planned to reside in New York on a permanent basis. She loved the city and also wanted to be as close to Nick as possible; he had made it abundantly clear he would never live in California, because he found the atmosphere in Hollywood stultifying. Perhaps at the end of the summer she would put the house up for sale. They planned to live in it whilst she was filming, but after that she really had no use for it. In November they were all going to Africa, she and Nick and Victor, to start shooting the screenplay Nick had just finished for Bellissima Productions. Quite a year ahead of me, she thought, pursing her lips and looking out of the window. She was surprised to see they were heading into Times Square and Broadway.

*   *   *

473

Nick pressed Katherine back against the pillows and, leaning over her, he stared into her face, 'No, I'm not going to let you get up,' he said quietly.

Katharine laughed. 'Nicky, you're impossible, and quite insatiable.' She tried to slither out of bed, but he increased his pressure, securing her under him with the weight of his body. He gripped her arms a little too tightly, and she winced, 'Please, Nicky, let me –'

'No, not yet, Kath. And you're mistaken if you think I'm trying to make love again. I'm not. I want to talk to you.'

'We can talk as much as you wish, darling, if you'll just let me go to the bathroom first.'

He shook his head slowly. 'That's what I want to talk to you about – the way you rush out of my arms the minute we stop making love.' His voice became a shade quieter as he added, 'I don't like it, Katie darling. It bothers me.' He cleared his throat, and his blue eys, so steady and honest, pierced through her. 'To be truthful, I find it a bit insulting.'

Katherine gaped at him, her eyes wide with incredulity. 'I don't understand,' she began falteringly, and stopped.

'I know you have a desperate need to be pristine every minute of the day and night, but is it really necessary to leap out of bed so abruptly? It's as though you want to wash every trace of *me* off *you*.'

His words startled her, hurt her, and she bit her lip, blinked nervously. She touched his face with one finger, tracing a line down his cheek. 'Don't be silly, Nicky, you know how much I love you.' She laughed tensely, feeling inexplicably embarrassed. 'I can't help the way I'm made. I like to feel fresh, clean . . .'

Nick sighed. 'But you're always impeccable.' His voice trailed off and he eased away from her so that she was free of his weight. She slipped out of bed, as he had known she would, and disappeared without saying another word. Nick found a cigarette and lay back, smoking and thinking. He had spoken the truth when he had said this inevitable dash for the shower distressed him. Although it had been on his mind for weeks, he had procrastinated about discussing it, not wanting to upset her. But he had thought about his curious habit of hers all afternoon on the plane, had concluded it must be broached now. it had to be brought out in the open before it started to grow like a canker inside him. He suspected that her preoccupation with personal hygiene was rooted in something much more serious and significant than a mere desire for absolute cleanliness, and with any other woman he would have said so bluntly. But Katharine was shy, continually avoided any discussions about sex, and was selfconscious to a point of prudishness when it came to intimate matters. He loved her with a desperation that staggered him at times, and he wanted everything to be free and open between them.

A few minutes later the bathroom door opened and she came out, wearing a towel tied around her like a sarong, floating towards him on a cloud of mingled perfumes.

'I could have sworn I brought that bottle of wine upstairs with us,' he said, smiling at her genially, reminding himself to be both gentle and tactful. 'But I'm damned if I can remember where I put it. After being away for a week, I guess I was over anxious about getting you into bed.'

Katherine laughed, glanced around, spotted the bottle on the chest near the window. She brought it to him, filled the glasses on the bedside table, handed him one. Then she climbed onto the bed and sat in the middle of it, facing him, her legs crossed Indian style. 'I'm so glad you're back. I missed you, Nicky.'

'I missed you too, darling.' He reached for her hand, kissed her fingertips. He hesitated for only a fraction of a second, then said, 'There mustn't be any barriers between us, Katinka.'

Looking puzzled, she cried, 'But there aren't any!' He said nothing, simply held her eyes with his, and she ventured, softly, 'Are there? You must think –'

He held up his hand, shook his head. 'I want to talk to you about something, and I don't want you to get annoyed or distressed. You're twenty-nine, a grown woman, so you should be able to discuss intimate things in an intelligent, sensible way, without becoming embarrassed.'

Panic swept over her. She knew from the serious tone, the expression on his face, that he was going to embroil her in a conversation about sex and she was flustered. She swallowed, dropped her eyes, became mute.

Perceiving her discomfort, Nick remarked with great gentleness, 'I said, a few minutes ago, that you are always impeccable. So why do you continually think you're not?'

'I don't know,' she muttered, speaking the truth.

Deciding now to go right to the heart of the matter, Nick asked, 'Don't I make you happy, Kath?'

'You know you do!'

'I mean in bed. *Sexually*.'

'Yes,' she whispered. She lifted her head, searched his face. 'Don't . . . don't *I* please *you*?' As she spoke colour flamed in her cheeks and she felt herself tensing.

'Yes, most of the time. However, there are occasions –' He paused, thought: Far too many occasions, and proceeded carefully. 'Sometimes, I don't get the right responses from you, and I feel you're not as relaxed as you should be with me. Very often you're removed and distant, and just a little inhibited, as a matter of fact.' There, he had said it. Finally it was out in the open. He watched her closely, waiting for her reactions.

Katherine's face was scarlet. 'A-a-a-always? Am I always inhibited?'

'No,' he fibbed, wanting to spare her feelings as much as he could. 'When you've had a few drinks you're less uptight,' he added, since there was actually a degree of truth in this.

'Oh! Oh!' Her hands flew to her face.

'Look, darling, don't get so upset. We must talk this out tonight. It's very important for our future relationship.'

'Do . . . do . . . you think . . .' She dropped her hands, stared down at them. 'Do you think I'm f-f-f-frigid?' She stuttered over that hated word, and gulped, discovered she was afraid to look at him, more afraid of his answer.

'Being frigid is not a crime, Kath darling,' he murmured kindly, loving her more than ever. 'Usually there's a good reason for it.'

There was a long silence, and then she questioned in a tiny voice, 'What reason?'

Nick stubbed out his cigarette, took hold of her hand. It trembled in his. He stroked it, said in a warm and reassuring voice, '*I love you*, Katherine. I want to help you. Relax, angel. I'm on your side, you know.'

475

'Yes, I'll try to relax, Nicky. But please tell me . . . what reason?'

'A fear of intimacy and closeness can create frigidity in some women,' he explained. 'Then again, it might be caused by an unconscious desire to punish all men because of a subliminal hatred of the male species in general. Sometimes frigidness grows out of a bad sexual experience that happened in the past and which has caused trauma. Then, of course, there are women who are completely uninterested in sex because they are cold by nature.'

'Which one applies to me?' she whispered fearfully.

'Darling, how can I possibly hazard a guess?'

'Do you think I should see a psychiatrist, Nicky?'

He chuckled. 'No, not when you have me.' He reached for her, pulled her to him. 'Come, lie next to me, darling, sip your wine, have a cigarette and calm down. And let's talk about this some more.'

'Yes,' she murmured against his chest, and did as he suggested. She drank half the glass of wine in one long swallow, and then took a cigarette.

Nick lit it for her, said, 'I think the best thing to do is examine the reasons I gave, Kath.'

After a moment's thought, she exclaimed, 'I don't want to punish you. I love you. And I don't hate men –' She broke off, thinking this was not strictly correct: *Her father*. She did loathe him. But not Nick. 'No, I definitely do not hate men, subliminally or consciously,' she asserted in a strong and positive tone, sounding more like herself. She gave him a sidelong look. 'Do you think I'm one of those women who's cold by nature?'

Nick shook his head. 'No, not at all. That leaves one last reason, Kath, a bad sexual experience. Have you had one, darling? Is that it perhaps?'

'No! It's not!'

Her sudden vehement denial aroused his suspicions, and he asked, 'Not with Beau Stanton?' No reply was forthcoming, and he told her quietly, 'The other week when he was here, when I was questioning you about your marriage, I wasn't doing it out of jealousy. I was simply trying to understand why it went wrong, hoping you would throw some light on your attitude. Your attitude to sex, I mean.'

'Oh,' she said, taken aback. And she thought instantly: My God, did Beau think I was frigid too? Is that why he changed towards me? She blurted this thought out before she could stop herself, and waited, looking up at Nick.

He nodded, reflected, said, 'Yes, perhaps Beau *was* turned off because of your reserve, Kath. But I'm surprised he didn't deal with it, if that was the case. After all, he'd been married several times before you came along, and he's much older than you, sophisticated. Well, so much for that. If you didn't have a bad scene with Beau, what about Kim Cunningham?'

'I never slept with Kim,' she confessed.

'I see,' Nick responded evenly, sheathing his surprise. 'Then perhaps some other man gave you a bad time. Yes?'

Katharine leaned back against his shoulder, closed her eyes, forcing herself to remember that day, every ghastly detail of it, filled with a sudden and terrible revulsion. She had blocked it out for years, as best she could. Blocked out the memory of George Gregson, of the way he had molested her. She knew she owed it to Nick to tell him, and also to gain his understanding and his help. And yet she was afraid to do so. Branded a liar by her father, who had not believed her, she was rendered speechless now, terrified Nick Latimer would not believe her story either.

Intuitively understanding that he had triggered an unpleasant recollection, Nick stroked her hair, said in the tenderest of voices, 'Tell me all about it, Kathy.'

'I'm scared to,' she said with a shiver.

'No, you're not. I've always thought you one of the most fearless people I've ever met. Don't forget, I want to help you.'

Taking a deep breath, she said, 'There was this man, George Gregson. He was my father's partner. He came to the house one day. It was Sunday. He . . . he'd always tried to make advances, and I'd repulsed him. That day . . . well, he forced me.'

He held her closer, said in a low voice, 'You mean he raped you?'

'N-n-not really,' Katharine managed. Tears welled. 'He molested me . . . you know . . . touched me. All over. My breasts. My . . . put his hand up my dress. He made me touch his . . . p-p-penis. I was horrified and revolted. I tried to fight him off, but he was big, a big man, Nick, and he had me in a stranglehold. He p-p-pushed my face down onto it . . . into his lap . . . made me . . . put it in my mouth. Oh, Nick, it was vile. I thought it was going to choke me . . .' She began to sob, her shoulders shaking convulsively.

Nick soothed her, dried her tears with gentle, sensitive hands. 'How old were you?' he asked at last, appalled by her story.

'T-t-twelve,' she gasped through her sobs.

'Oh Jesus! Oh my God, Kath! You were only a child! The filthy depraved son of a bitch. I'd like to go out and find him. If I could get my hands on him I'd beat the goddamn life out of him.' Nick's harsh tone reflected his immense rage, his utter disgust. And he understood her then, understood so much about her. He cradled her for a long time, and as soon as she was calm, he asked. 'What did your father do about it?'

'Nothing. He didn't believe me. He said I was a liar.'

Nick was astounded. 'The stupid bastard!' He squeezed his eyes shut, and his arms tightened on her fragile body. Her abhorrence of Patrick O'Rourke was well founded. The man should have been horsewhipped for doubting his daughter. He was as responsible for her traumatization as the fiend who had molested her. Sweet Jesus, no wonder she was inhibited. And we're supposed to live in a civilized world. Animals. Animals, he thought, filled with contempt.

Katherine, misunderstanding his silence, whispered, 'You do believe me, don't you, Nicky?'

'Yes, of course I believe you, my darling.'

She told him then how she had gone to the bathroom and scrubbed herself raw, and cleaned her teeth half a dozen times, and gargled repeatedly; how she had covered her entire body with talcum powder and doused herself in a whole bottle of perfume, and that she had done all this because she felt dirty. And ashamed. Because of her shame she had purposely ruined the new dress she had been wearing that afternoon by spilling red ink on it, so that she would never have to wear it again and be reminded of her shattering experience. And later that night, she explained, when everyone was asleep, she had crept down to he basement and secretly burned her underwear and her white ankle socks in the furnace.

And she has been cleansing herself ever since, he said silently, and her pain was his own. Nick filled up with compassion and love for her, and his insight into Katharine Tempest was complete.

By unburdening herself to Nick, Katharine too had gained new insight into herself. In the ensuing days she began to realize how much that horrifying childhood experience had scarred her, what a devastating effect it had had on her adult life. Because her father had not given credence to her story, she had kept quiet thereafter, intimidated into silence and riddled with all manner of guilts. Yet by not ventilating her feelings, and so purging herself through catharsis, the incident had steadily been magnified out of all proportion in her mind. It had spiralled into a shameful secret that weighed her down and destroyed a great number of her natural feminine instincts, her very sexuality. One day it struck her that she had not been at fault, nor guilty of any wrongdoing, that she had simply been a victim of Gregson's depravity. This knowledge brought a measure of welcome inner peace. Nick had carefully explained to her that she would not instantly shed her frigidity just because she had faced, revealed and discussed a painful experience. 'Diagnosing complaints doesn't automatically cure them,' he had laughed. But she did find herself relaxing more often, and under Nick's gentle and sensitive tutelage her approach to sex and intimacy became more normal and healthy. Also, having always thought of men as untrustworthy, seeing them as extensions of her father and Gregson, she was startled to discover that she trusted Nicholas Latimer implicitly.

For his part, Nick quickly acknowledged to himself that he had assumed too much, too soon on the night of her confessional. It was true that he did have a better understanding of her, a fresh psychological insight into her personality and character, but there were many sides to this complex woman which he did not fully comprehend. As they became more involved he began to realize that Katharine was a mass of contradictions. Vivacious, joyous, gay and loving though she was, there were dark aspects to her nature which did not fail to trouble him. She had sudden mood swings, could become withdrawn, cold, argumentative, imperious or depressed in the batting of an eyelid. She was generous and openhanded, devoted and loyal to those she held dear; conversely, and just as easily, she was manipulative, calculating, scheming and secretive, and she constantly meddled in people's lives. This maddened Nick, especially since she tended to cloak her meddling in a mantle of do-goodery. He saw this as a self-serving device and told her as much one night, after she had involved herself in Terry's business, his future plans. He had gone on to voice the opinion that she was misguided in believing she knew best, knew better than anybody how people should run their lives, because she did not. He had also angrily pointed out that she had a need to control, was bossy and power mad. Airily, she pooh-poohed his accusations and had explained, nonchalantly, that there were a lot of different Katharines and that he had better get used to each and every one of them.

A minute later she had been sweet, endearing and beguiling, and he had found himself succumbing to her incomparable charm, that most dangerous of all her natural assets. He had grown increasingly remorseful during the night, convinced that his judgment of her was too harsh, and he had risen early and rushed out to Cartier's to buy her a gift. A week later he gave this to her and she had adored it. He had selected a large silver cigarette box, the lid inscribed with the words: *For the many Katharines, all of whom I love.* Surrounding these neatly engraved letters were the diminutives and variations of her name in facsimiles of his hand-writing.

After this somewhat one-sided quarrel they had settled down to a peaceful existence and did not exchange angry words again for many months. Three days after the play closed they flew to Mexico City. They spent the night there, and then travelled to Acapulco the next morning. Their four weeks at Las Brisas were quiet, idyllic and romantic. During this time Katharine opened up to Nick even more than ever, and told him much about her childhood. She spoke eloquently and lovingly of her mother and the deep feelings they had held for each other. And he was moved by the sentiments she expressed, and recognized then that her mother's death was at the root of the profound sadness he was aware lurked in Katharine's heart.

But their vacation in Mexico was also filled with laughter and light-hearted gaiety, and they had a great deal of fun together. Nick introduced her to deep-sea fishing, one of his passions, and although she did not fish herself, he saw that she enjoyed accompanying him on the boat. They swam and sunbathed, read books and lazed away the days, content to be alone with each other and isolated from the rest of the world.

In the evenings they ventured into the town, patronizing the quaint restaurants, sampling the local dishes; they sat listening to the mariachis, sipping wine and holding hands; they danced under the stars, locked in each other's arms, bewitched and entranced and in love.

And on one of these balmy evenings, when they lay together in the great bed in the cool darkness of their room, Katharine came to Nick with a new eagerness, begging him to make love to her. Entwining her body around his, she told him, in a breathless whisper, what she wanted, and for a moment he was startled by the unexpectedness of this intimacy. Inflamed by her words, he began to kiss and caress her, his hands and his mouth roaming over her body, bringing her to unparelleled heights of excitement. She responded in a manner he had not thought possible, with wildness and abandonment, and her inhibitions began to drop like veils. And she gave herself up to him, crying out her desire to be possessed and to possess, and that night Katharine experienced her first real passion, her first ecstasy.

As the days and nights passed they drew closer, became as one. Nothing marred this special time, and they knew they had never been happier in their lives. What they did not understand was that this drifting dreamlike month would never be recaptured, and that it heralded the beginning of the end for them.

CHAPTER FORTY-FIVE

Francesca sat staring at the telephone, hesitating, uncertain whether to call Nicholas Latimer or not. Looping a strand of her blonde hair over one ear, she groaned impatiently, irritated with herself. Decisive by nature, she had found herself incapable of making the smallest decision in the last eight hours.

She supposed she was wavering about making the call because she knew that if she spoke to Nicky she would say too much. The last thing she wanted to do was to make trouble, and her revelations might conceivably do just that. Old habits die hard, she muttered to herself, tightening the belt of her robe. I've always tended to protect Katharine, and I'm still doing it after ten years. Oh God, she thought, how can I confide in Nicky? But there is no one else to talk to.

With a weary gesture, Francesca rubbed her eyes. She had not slept, and a vague but debilitating fatigue hung over her. Wanting to shake off this feeling, she stood up, pushed back the chair and crossed the long spacious library to the window. The sky on this June day was a faultless blue and mild, and the verdant trees were a sea of green in Central Park, rippling under the light summer breeze. She pressed her head against the pane and closed her eyes, squeezing back the tears. Years ago, when she had been recovering from her heartbreak over Victor Mason, she had vowed no man would ever make her weep again. And least of all Ryan O'Rourke, she said under her breath. But *were* the incipient tears caused by him? Or by Katharine? Which one had hurt her the most?

With a sigh, she turned away from the window, saw Lada sitting in the middle of the floor, regarding her through soulful diamond-bright eyes as black as coal. 'This isn't getting us anywhere, is it, Lada?' Francesca said out loud, and bending down, she picked her up, hugged her tightly. The little white dog nuzzled her, licked her face, nestled closer. 'What shall we do, Lada?' she murmured, continuing to voice her thoughts as she went back to the Regency ebony desk. The dog wriggled out of her arms, jumped down, flopped under the desk, and Francesca drew her engagement book towards her. Flipping through the pages for the rest of June and early July, she noted they were mostly blank, except for a few social engagements pencilled in tentatively. A dinner at Nelson Avery's house; several luncheons; a weekend in Virginia, as a house guest of Nelson's brother, Harrison. After contemplating her social commitments for a moment, Francesca closed the book. Her inertia fell away, was replaced by her old incisiveness. Plans started to evolve in her head. After fifteen minutes of rapid but clear thinking, she glanced at the clock. It was almost nine. She began telephoning, and at the end of an hour and a half she had set everything in motion. There was no going back now. Her last call was to Nick.

After the usual greetings had been exchanged Francesca had said, 'I realize you're probably up to your neck, darling, but I wondered if I could possibly see you today? I suppose lunch would kill your concentration.'

'I finished the final draft of the new script last night, Frankie, so I'm all yours. As a matter of fact, I was about to call you, to invite you to lunch. You just beat me to it. Where would you like to go, Beauty?'

'Oh anywhere you like, Nicky. But could I come there for a drink first? There's something I'd like to talk to you about.'

Catching the odd inflection in her voice, Nick said swiftly, 'What's wrong, Francesca?'

'Nothing. *Truly*. What time shall I come over? About twelve-thirty?'

'Sure, that's great. See ya later, kid.'

'Yes, thanks so much, Nicky. 'Bye.' Dropping the receiver in the cradle, Francesca thought: *Kid*. I'm thirty years old.

Half an hour later, looking coolly elegant in a navy blue linen dress and pearls, her shining blonde hair swept back in a smooth chignon, Francesca sat in the sitting room drinking a cup of tea with Val, the former housekeeper of Langley Castle. Some seven years earlier, in 1959, Val had met an American, Bill Perry, at a trade fair for carpet manufacturers in Harrogate. Mutual friends had introduced them, and Bill, widowed like Val, had pursued the relationship. In 1961, they had been married, and Val and her daughter Rosemary had moved to the States. Now, in 1966, they were living in Forest Hills.

Francesca said, 'Thank you for coming into Manhattan on such short notice, Val, it's awfully nice of you.'

'Goodness, M'lady, it's no trouble I'm sure. I'm glad to be of help. To tell you the truth, I get a bit bored these days. I'm not used to having time on my hands, and I do seem to have a lot of that, what with Rosemary away at college and Bill travelling so much.'

Francesca leaned forward urgently. 'Did you speak to Bill? Is he agreeable?'

Val smiled, 'Yes, M'lady. I 'phoned him at the showroom before I left. He has no objections. In fact, he agrees with you that this place shouldn't be left empty while you're away. The Countess has such a lot of valuables, paintings and things.' Val glanced around, nodding to herself. 'Not that Agnes isn't responsible and efficient, as I've noticed in the past few years, but still, the flat ought to be occupied at night and at weekends. You never know. So many robberies these days.'

Francesca concurred; she said, 'Agnes will be coming in every day as usual, so there's no work for you to do, and as I told you, I'm taking Lada with me. But I will be gone about two months, Val, is that all right?'

'Yes, Lady Francesca. Now don't you worry about a thing. And while you're out to lunch I can start packing for you.'

'I think that will have to wait until I get back later this afternoon. But you could start putting all the light summer clothes, shoes, bags and swimwear on the bed. We can sort through them later.' Francesca rose. 'I'm running a bit late, so I'd better get off. Agnes will make lunch for you, Val.'

'Thank you, M'lady. By the way, what time's your plane tomorrow night?'

'Eight o'clock.' Francesca grimaced. 'Oh dear. I haven't given you much time to arrange things, have I?'

'I'll be installed by the time you leave, Lady Francesca, don't you fret. Bill can always move in a few days later. I also spoke to his sister after you rang this morning, and she's going to keep an eye on our flat for us. She lives in the same building. Now, you run along and have a nice lunch, and give my best to Mr Latimer. Such a gentleman.'

'Yes, I will. And thank you again, Val. I'm very grateful. 'Bye.'

A few minutes later, as she walked briskly down Seventy-Ninth Street from Fifth Avenue and turned onto Madison, Francesca concentrated on the things she had to say to Nick, wondering how much to tell him. The matter was still unresolved in her mind she climbed the flight of steps in front of his townhouse and rang the bell. I'll have to play this by ear, she decided, and arranged a smile on her face.

Nick opened the door, grinning hugely, delighted to see her. He ushered her into the small front hall, pecked her on the cheek, said, 'Let's go up to the living room. I have a bottle of white wine on ice.'

'That's lovely,' she replied.

Francesca started to chat about inconsequential things whilst Nick filled two crystal glasses, but after only a few seconds he cut her short. 'What did you want to talk to me about, Frankie?' he asked crisply, bringing the wine, sitting down opposite.

His alert shrewd blue eyes probed her face, and Francesca decided there was no point in procrastinating. She said, 'Ryan.'

'Oh.' Nick straightened up, and his eyes narrowed. 'What about him?'

'We've broken up,' Francesca said flatly.

Nick frowned, looked slightly taken aback. 'When? And *why?*'

'Last night. Around midnight to be precise.' She reached for the glass, marvelled at her steady hand, her contained tone.

'But why?' Nick repeated, his frown intensifying.

Francesca shook her head, unable to speak for a moment. Then she said. 'It was his idea, not mine.'

This astonished Nick, and he muttered, 'But he must have given you a reason . . .'

'For someone with a silver tongue and an abundance of Irish blarney he was somewhat reticent, I must admit.'

Nick sat back thoughtfully. Having always considered them an ill-matched pair, he was experiencing a sense of relief that their affair was finally over. In fact, privately he was delighted. He had observed the two of them for the past three years and with growing alarm, aware that Ryan was not good enough for Francesca, wanting someone more suitable for her. He studied her closely, trying to assess her present emotions, wondering how distressed she really was. This was hard to determine; self-possession and extraordinary self-control were natural traits in her. As he continued to study her, he was suddenly struck by her grace and style. She had become the loveliest of women, and he was proud of her growth as a person, her development as a writer of undeniable talent and professionalism. Yes, she had turned out well, and he was glad about this, glad she was his friend.

Francesca said, 'What are you thinking about, darling?'

'You. Ryan. What did you mean when you said he was reticent? He's usually very glib.'

'I shouldn't have characterized him that way, Nicky; obviously I misled you.

Although he wasn't his usual ebullient self, he wasn't actually reticent either, especially at the end of our discussion. But mind you, I did put a lot of pressure on him, insisted he explain himself. He finally opened up.'

'That sounds more like him. He's never been short of words. Shall we talk about it, love?' Nick, perplexed by the turn of events, was also anxious to pinpoint her state of mind and heart.

Francesca took a deep breath. 'Ryan was in New York yesterday, on family business. We'd made a date. He came up to the apartment for a drink and then we went to Caravelle for dinner. Ryan seemed normal, if quieter than usual. After dinner we went back to the apartment, and we –' She stopped herself abruptly, flushing slightly. 'Well, anyway, Ryan was very loving, and when he was dressing later he said he wanted to talk to me, asked me to get up and join him in the living room. I was baffled, surprised, I suppose, by his serious tone. I realized something was terribly wrong, Nicky, his face was so set . . . more determined than I'd ever seen it. He came straight to the point. He said he thought it would be wise if we didn't see each other again.'

The son of a bitch, Nick thought angrily. He had to get her into bed one last time. Pressing back his disgust, Nick said sarcastically, 'And he calls himself a gentleman!'

Francesca glanced at him, merely shrugged. 'I know what you're implying. I was furious about the way he handled the situation myself. I think it would have been more appropriate to tell me over drinks. Anyway, later it occurred to me that he might not have meant to tell me last night, that it was a sudden decision, made after dinner. You know, on the spur of the moment.'

Nick doubted this. He said, 'Possibly. But go on.'

'Naturally I was floored by his announcement, stunned really. It was the last thing I'd expected.' Francesca smiled faintly. 'To tell you the truth, I found it hard to absorb for a few minutes. I poured myself a brandy, smoked a cigarette, tried to compose myself. I remember thinking Ryan seemed nervous, even embarrassed. He wouldn't have a drink, was anxious to leave. But I demanded an explanation.'

Nick leaned over the table. 'And what reason *did* he give?'

'Ryan said he felt he wasn't being fair to me, that he was wasting my time . . . because there was no future for us.' Her face changed, became still and cold. 'He pointed out that I was thirty, not getting any younger, that I ought to be thinking about getting married, having children. Therefore, since he could not marry me, he was giving me my freedom, a chance to make a good life for myself with someone else.'

Nick pursed his lips. 'Did he say *could* not, or didn't *want*, to marry you?'

'Could not.' Francesca blinked. 'I asked him why. It was then that he started to hedge. I badgered him. Finally Ryan told me he was too young to saddle himself with a wife at this crucial period in his political career, that he had no time to devote to a wife, or to start a family right now. I said this was a silly attitude, and he retorted that he didn't want those heavy responsibilities, could not cope with them. He then gave me a long speech about his political aspirations, explained that these came first, were his priorities. He did not neglect to point out that he was overburdened with work as a Congressman. You know what Ryan's like, Nicky. So ambitious for himself.'

'You mean his father's ambitious for him,' Nick cut in sharply. 'The old man's behind this, Frankie. He pulls the strings of the puppet.'

Shaking her head violently, Francesca disagreed. 'No, no, you're wrong. I don't think Mr O'Rourke had anything to do with Ryan's decision. I even asked him if his father objected.'

'And?'

'Ryan said not really. He remarked that his father rather liked me.' A rueful smile flicked into her amber-hazel eyes. 'Ryan had to qualify this, of course, by saying that although his father detested the English, and especially the ruling class because of the things they'd done to Ireland, he nevertheless found me to be the exception to the rule.'

Nick snorted. 'I don't buy this story, Frankie. It's goddamn phony. Ryan is twenty-nine, exactly the age when he should be marrying and starting a family. As for saying he's too busy to devote himself to the domestic scene, that is absolute nonsense. For a junior Congressman he's certainly got plenty of aides and sidekicks, more help than most Senators. Which brings me to another point. The O'Rourke money. They have millions, probably billions. A man of Ryan's enormous wealth doesn't have to cope with the normal hassle and responsibilities of a family. He can afford dozens of servants, nannies, what have you.' Nick took a cigarette, went on. 'You would be a tremendous asset to him in Washington, not to mention campaigning. And he's bound to run for the Senate in a few years. That's written in cement.' Nick shook his head as vehemently as Francesca had. 'No, none of this gels with me, Frankie. Poor reasons – all of them.'

'Despite what *you* might think, Ryan doesn't believe I'd be an asset to him,' Francesca said softly. 'Just the opposite in fact.'

'What the hell do you mean?' Nick cried, his blond brows lifting, his expression incredulous.

'He listed all the things about me which he considers would be detrimental to him, to his career, and with his constituents.' She lifted a hand, began ticking them off on her fingers. 'I'm English. I'm the daughter of an earl. I have a title in my own right. I'm a career woman, dedicated to my writing. Obviously of no use as a political wife.' She laughed coldly. 'And get this, I'm a socialite. I'm just not acceptable, apparently, and then there's the –'

'You have got to be kidding!' Nick exploded.

'And then there's the question of religion,' she proceeded firmly. 'That's really at the root of it.'

Nick stared at her. 'Religion?' he echoed.

'Yes. Ryan felt it necessary to remind me he is a Catholic, pointed out he could not risk offending other Catholics – presumably the voters – by marrying a non-Catholic. Especially one who would not convert, would not agree to raise his children in the faith, and one who was known to be prejudiced.'

'I'm sorry, I'm not following you.' Nick seemed genuinely puzzled.

'Ryan thinks I'm anti-Catholic and that my family is anti-Catholic.'

Nick guffawed. 'Come on, Frankie, you can't be serious. No one is more tolerant than you.' He peered at her and his scepticism changed to sudden comprehension. 'This *is* his father talking!'

'No, Nicky, it's not Mr O'Rourke.' Francesca bit her lip and her mouth began to tremble. 'It's Katharine talking, I'm afraid,' she blurted out in an inaudible voice, and her eyes filled with tears for the first time.

Nick thought he had misheard her for a second, and his forehead puckered. 'Are you implying that Ryan puts the blame on Katharine for his decision? That he attributes this religious stuff to his *sister*? I can't believe it! I really can't!'

'You had better believe it, Nick, because it's the truth.' There was a moment's hesitation before she said carefully, 'Look, I was nervous about telling you because I knew you'd be upset with Katharine. But you really should know.' Her look was direct and unwavering. 'When Ryan made those statements about me, my religious persuasions, and my family, I was dumbfounded. They're simply not true and he knows it. Last year, when we contemplated getting married, we discussed these things in depth. At that time I told him I was willing to convert, go along with anything he wanted. Naturally he had to admit he remembered our talk, but he muttered something about doubting the veracity of my words, my promises. He was reluctant to continue the conversation, tried to leave. I wouldn't let him. I begged him to be honest, to tell me why he'd had a change of heart. He explained, rather nervously, that he'd been terribly worried about us and the religious aspects, and had gone seeking advice from Katharine. I couldn't believe my ears when he said she had told him not to marry me, had warned him he was asking for trouble if he did.'

Nick's jaw dropped and he could only gape at Francesca. He was speechless. At last he said, 'This is *incredible*. Ridiculous. I think –'

'You can think what you like, Nicky, but Ryan convinced *me*,' Francesca interjected fiercely. 'There's more. Apparently Katherine informed Ryan she broke up with Kim because of religious differences. And I gathered it was *she* who planted the idea that the Cunninghams are anti-Catholic. Both of her statements are without foundation. She broke up with Kim because of her career. And none of us is bigoted, or *anti* anything.' Nick was about to interrupt, but Francesca waved her hand at him. 'No, just a minute, let me finish. I started to quiz Ryan harder, and he murmured something about Katharine suggesting the marriage would never work, that I would make him miserable. She also reminded him that once he married me he was stuck with me, since he could never get a divorce. In a nutshell, she was saying: Don't do it, little brother, quote unquote.' Francesca sat back, flushed and angry, regarding Nick closely.

This all sounded preposterous to Nick, and he spluttered, 'Now, Frankie, listen to *me*. Ryan's a weak sister, I've always told you that. He's making Katharine the scapegoat, because he doesn't have the guts to accept the burden of his own decision. You know Kath – and intimately. She's not especially religious; furthermore, she's been divorced.'

'You're giving me the arguments I gave Ryan. His answer was simple. Katharine is a lapsed Catholic and has been for years. *He* is not. *He* is very devout. He also seems to think Katharine regrets her divorce, regrets leaving the Church, and wants to be taken back into the faith.'

'That's a lot of poppycock, wishful thinking on Ryan's part!' Nick cried.

'In my opinion, he might be right.' Francesca fidgeted with the lid of the cigarette box, and ventured, 'Don't you think Ryan was telling me the truth then?'

'No, I don't.' Although this was said with firmness, Nick suddenly wondered f Katharine *was* innocent. Or had she been busy at her mischievous work again? The idea appalled him. He rubbed his hand over his chin, his suspicions growing. He glanced at Francesca, saw she was hunched over and instantly joined her on the sofa.

Nick put his arms around her. 'Darling, don't cry. He's not worth it.'

'My tears are not solely because of Ryan,' Francesca gasped. 'I'm also crying about Katharine. How could she do such a thing, Nicky? Be so disloyal. Betray me in such a way? I'm her dearest friend, and have been for ten years. We've never had a cross word, well, hardly ever, and I've been devoted to her.'

'I know you have.' Until now Nick had always believed Frankie was safe from Katharine and her meddling. There had been times when Katharine had attempted to manipulate her friend and run her life, but Francesca had never permitted it. Had Katharine finally succeeded?

Nick said gently, 'Perhaps it's not quite the way it seems, perhaps Katharine was merely pointing out certain drawbacks to Ryan, playing devil's advocate, in a sense. *He* may have repeated things to you in such a way that he shifted the blame, whether intentionally or not.'

Francesca nodded, groped in her bag for a handkerchief. She dried her eyes. 'Sorry, Nick darling, I didn't mean to break down. I know you have no answers for me, just as I have no answers for myself. If she were here I would tackle her, have it out with her. But since she's in the Far East there's nothing I can do.'

'No, there isn't, not until she gets back,' Nick agreed, trying to still his rage with Katharine. He took hold of Francesca's hand. 'What about Ryan? How do you feel about him, darling?'

'I love him,' she whispered. 'You don't stop loving someone overnight. But I imagine I am in a state of shock. Not only because he dumped me, and rather unceremoniously, but by the abruptness of his action. And also because he took Katharine's word for gospel, made up his mind without talking it out with me first. And as for his sister, well, she's overstepped the mark this time.'

Francesca saw the denial in Nick's eyes, knew he was about to defend Katharine, and she continued rapidly, 'Look, even if I do give her the benefit of the doubt, accept that she only meant well, she should not have stuck her nose into my business. It was not her right to do so, brother or no brother. I don't like it, and I won't tolerate it, Nicky.'

He nodded, recognizing that she was right and that she meant every word. He could not help thinking Katharine had met her match, had made the biggest mistake in her life by interfering in Francesca's life. He continued to ponder for a moment, then said in the kindest and most loving tone, 'I'm not being cruel or unsympathetic, Frankie, but I must ask you something.' He paused, then said slowly, 'How deeply are you affected? I mean, are your present emotions about Ryan genuine? Is your hurt based on real love for him, or are you reacting in this way because he rejected you?'

Francesca thought for a long moment. 'My feelings are genuine, Nicky. I was very involved with Ryan, and on many levels.' She bit her lip. 'I do think I'm very confused though. That's why I'm going away.'

'Where are you going? When?' he demanded.

'To Paris. Tomorrow night. I have a reservation on the last Air France flight, leaving around eight o'clock. I'll be in Paris for a couple of days, and then I'm taking the Blue Train to Monte Carlo, where I'll stay at Doris's new villa. I promised Daddy and Doris I'd join them in late July or early August. I decided I might as well go a little earlier. I'm not running away, Nicky, but I've nothing to stay in New York for now, so I might as well have a pleasant and peaceful summer. I'm planning to be away about two months. It'll be lovely to see them all, I've missed my family. And I want to be in their midst, to have the comfort of them. It will also give me time to think, clear my head, decide what I'm going to do next.'

'And Ryan? And the future? Once this muddle is straightened out with Katharine, would you consider a reconciliation?'

'Oh no, Nicky! It's over. How can it not be?' she cried, aghast at his last question. 'He doesn't want the relationship, and even if he changed his mind, *I* couldn't possibly consider it now. No, I've made my decision and it's final. Maybe you were always right about Ryan – about him being weak and ineffectual.'

'Yes,' Nick said laconically. He drank his wine, eventually remarked, 'He certainly didn't handle the situation very nicely –'

'Oh, but he did, Nick,' Francesca interjected, wanting to be fair. 'Please don't get the wrong idea. I have a feeling I've recounted our emotional little scene of last night rather poorly. Ryan *was* sweet, concerned for me, and he *was* reluctant to spell things out, to involve Katharine. Truly, I did force the issue, did have to drag every word out of him.' She studied Nick, then concluded, 'Well, he's awfully young in some ways.'

'The understatement of the year, kid,' Nick said more snappishly than he had intended.

Francesca leaned her blonde head against the sofa; the smile she gave Nick was grave and there was a sudden wisdom in her lovely eyes. 'Years ago, in the old nursery at Langley, you told me we all recover from our romantic tragedies. I did get over Vic. And I expect I will also get over Ryan.'

'Yes, I'm sure you will, darling,' Nick assented, thinking this time it would not take her quite so long to recover. His intuition told him Francesca had never loved Ryan O'Rourke as deeply and as passionately as she had loved Victor Mason.

He took her to La Grenouille for lunch. Nick had chosen this restaurant because it had always been one of their favourite haunts, and they had enjoyed some happy times there in the past. It was elegant, the ambience was gay and the food perfection. But now, as they sat next to each other on the banquette, he felt as if he was attending a wake. Admittedly the restaurant was as festive as always, but Francesca was more pensive and quiet than ever and her dismal mood had intensified. His heart went out to her. Nick was not unsympathetic to her suffering, yet he did not know how to alleviate it. To tell her she was better off without Ryan would only be gratuitous and unkind. He wished he could cheer her up, help to dispel her sadness.

As though she had read his thoughts, Francesca turned to him suddenly, touched his arm. 'I'm sorry I'm so morose. I'm not much of a compa –'

'Don't apologize, darling,' he exclaimed, cutting her off. His smile was loving, as he added, 'You're entitled. I know you must be feeling lousy.'

She said, 'I'll be all right. I'm going to press on with my book about the

Plantagenets. I have to write – to save myself, to keep my sanity. If I don't, they'll cart me away in a straitjacket. I've got all this stuff rumbling around in my head . . .' She gave him a slight smile.

Nick glanced at her quickly. 'Yes, I understand. I feel the same way myself . . . and the pain of love is incomprehensible at times. Still, that pain does lessen, eventually pass. Oh hell, Frankie, I seem to be offering you nothing but cold comfort today.'

The faint smile flickered fleetingly again. 'I don't have much luck with men, do I? I'm beginning to think there's something wrong with me.'

'But there isn't, Francesca,' he exclaimed emphatically, reaching out, squeezing her arm. 'You've had a couple of bad experiences, that's all. Everyone does. And you haven't met the right man yet. But you will.' Her look was so sceptical, he added, with the utmost sincerity, 'You're the loveliest, most gentle, warm-hearted woman I know. As well as being charming and intelligent. You've got everything going for you, and then some. Please, don't put yourself down. There are always plenty of people willing to do that.'

'Well, yes, that's true I suppose.' She was silent, playing with the fish on her plate. She put her fork down. 'You and I do seem to have our trials and tribulations with the O'Rourkes, don't we? I'm beginning to wish I'd never met Ryan.' Her eyes swivelled, came up to meet his. 'Don't you feel that way occasionally? Wish that you'd never met Katharine?'

Her question startled him and his eyes clouded over; then he smiled. 'No. We've had our ups and downs, and Katharine can be difficult, but she's worth it. I do love her, you know,' he said, thinking he loved her far too much, if the truth be known. The worry and distress she had caused him, particularly in the last six months, had been unbearable. He was glad she was in the Far East. The respite had given him a chance to recoup; yet he missed her, longed for her, ached for her return.

Misunderstanding Nick's brooding silence, Francesca remarked hurriedly, 'Oh God, Nick, that did sound awful, didn't it?' She leaned closer. 'I didn't mean it quite the way it came out. I know you love her. So do I. Of course, I'm annoyed with her just now, I'm not going to pretend I'm not. However, that doesn't change the way I feel about her deep down.'

'Yes,' said Nick, nodding his head slowly. 'And that's the measure of the woman. She can be the most irritating and infuriating hellion, and yet conversely, so beguiling one instantly capitulates to her charm. Off-balance – that's how I feel most of the time.' He had been on the point of talking to Francesca about Katharine on several occasions in the last few months, but always changed his mind at the last minute.

Now he found himself saying, 'I've been concerned about Kath lately, her behaviour has been erratic. Haven't you noticed her strangeness?'

Francesca took hold of Nick's hand resting on the table, and her voice was low and gentle as she said, 'Yes, I have. So has Hilary. We . . . we talked about it only last week. Kath flew at Terry for no good reason, just before she went off to do the current film, and he was baffled and hurt. Hilary – I – well, to be honest, Nick, we both think Kath ought to see a doctor. Couldn't you persuade her to go to one when she gets back to New York?'

Nick swung his head, his eyes meeting Francesca's, and he saw the candour and compassion in them. 'So everyone's noticed it,' he muttered, and gripped her hand that much tighter. 'And you're right, of course. I think Kath *does* need medical help. I suggested it. *Once*. At the mention of the word psychiatrist she went into a kind of panic, then pulled herself up short, and overnight she was as normal and as sane as we are.' Pushing his plate away, he reached for a cigarette. 'She was marvellous after that, and for several weeks before she left in May.'

Observing his grave face, the distress in his eyes, Francesca bit back the words on the tip of her tongue. She rearranged them in her head and after a small silence, volunteered, 'About four years ago, just after I'd moved to New York, Doris told me that as far back as 1956 my father had detected certain things in Katharine.' She stopped, wondering whether she dare continue.

Nick said, 'What things?' His eyes were glued to hers. 'Please tell me.'

'Daddy apparently felt Kath was emotionally unstable and –' Francesca cleared her throat nervously, finished in a low tone, 'and mentally unbalanced. I'm sorry, Nick.'

He shook his head. 'That's all right, don't worry. And Doris? Did she agree? And what about you?'

Swallowing hard, Francesca murmured, 'Doris was ambivalent, didn't know whether to concur with Daddy or not. Katharine has never been her favourite person, but Doris is very fair, and she was prepared to give Kath the benefit of the doubt. As for me, at the time I laughed, pooh-poohed it. And then lately, well, I have wondered, Nick. In fact, when I got back from England in January I thought Katharine was on the edge . . .'

'Edge?' He frowned.

'The edge of a nervous breakdown.'

He sucked in his breath. 'Oh Frankie, don't say that,' he began, and clamped his mouth shut, acknowledging that Francesca spoke the truth. He had been blocking out the facts because he had not wanted to face them. He said reflectively, 'Her mood swings are like the curve of a parabola. One minute she's gay and happy, the dazzling Katharine we all adore, the next she is plunged into the deepest depression. I believe she's schizophrenic. Occasionally I've even thought she was paranoid as well.' He exhaled heavily. 'Then the curve rises, hits the middle, and she is imperious, demanding, intolerant.' His face changed imperceptibly. 'In March she even became abusive with me, verbally and physically.'

'Oh Nick, no!'

'I'm afraid so, and it happened because I mentioned the skiing at Königssee. She exploded, accused me of wanting to go there to see Diana. Insisted that I didn't love *her*, that I was hankering after Diana. I put it down to some kind of misplaced jealousy, and then, a week later, the abuse started again, for no real reason. I've no idea what triggered her off. After these two outbursts she was remorseful, begging my forgiveness.'

'Irrational. Erratic,' Francesca pointed out. 'And we both know Kath has a rather obsessive personality.'

Nick nodded, changed the subject as the waiter hovered, removed their plates. Nick ordered coffee, and once they were alone again, he confided, 'I remember thinking, when I first met Kath in 1956, that she was a troubled young woman. Do you recall the screen test for *Wuthering Heights*? The day we went to see it?'

'Yes, very well,' she replied. 'How could anyone forget it? She was spectacular.'

'I thought so too. When we were leaving the screening room I had this terrible sense of foreboding, felt everything was going too fast for her, and that she wouldn't be able to handle it well. I thought disaster loomed on the horizon. Years later I laughed at myself. I had been proved totally wrong. Katharine's handled her success and fame with the most remarkable aplomb. Don't you agree with me, darling?'

'Absolutely, Nicky. In fact, she's constantly amazed me. In certain ways she's remained quite unchanged. She's been a big star since the release of *Wuthering Heights* in 1957 – almost ten years ago. That's why it's so perplexing. I mean this sudden change in her now, in recent months.'

'It's not so sudden, when I pause to think about it,' Nick said. 'I guess I started to notice certain peculiarities several years ago, in 1964 to be exact, when she and I went to Africa with Victor to make the film I'd written for them. It was in November. She was extremely edgy on that trip, curt and snappy with Vic, and dictatorial with both of us. She was also impossibly energetic, almost manic, filling every spare moment between filming with unrelenting activity, and she didn't seem to need much sleep. The second unit went off to shoot background footage, and Vic and Kath had a week off. She insisted we go on safari, dragged us into the African bush with some weirdo big game hunter who was slightly crazed, in my opinion. And she also had to visit the kraals and talk to the natives, explore the jungle, do God knows what else. You name it, we did it. And the weather was so goddamn hot, Vic and I were dragging our feet, ready to expire, sweating like pigs, and Kath was as cool as a cucumber, revelling in every minute. That was the strange part . . . you know how she hates the heat, finds it enervating, has such a fetish about being pristine morning, noon and night. Believe me, her endless bathing took place in some very primitive surroundings.' Nick shrugged. 'I couldn't get over it, she was so unlike herself. The change in her was doubly noticeable because earlier in the year, when we were in Mexico, she was just the opposite. Wonderfully calm and relaxed, the nearest I've ever seen her to being placid. I'd never known her to be so happy and content before, nor since, if you want the truth.'

'Yes, she told me about both trips, as a matter of fact. She liked Mexico, but Africa captured her heart. She kept saying she wanted to go back there, spent hours talking to me about the beauty of the landscape, the vastness, the skies at night, the simplicity of the people, the animals. She was almost poetic about pink flamingos hovering over some extraordinary sapphire lake. And –' Francesca frowned, glanced at Nick as another thought intruded. 'Wasn't Kath on the Coast that summer?'

'Yes. She made a picture for Monarch, after we returned from Mexico. I was with her, at her house in Bel Air, just before she sold it. Why? What are you getting at, Frankie?'

'This may sound very odd to you, darling, but it suddenly struck me that Kath has always been a bit funny when she's returned from California. At least in the last four years I've been around to witness it.'

'How? In what way?'

'Certain traits seemed more pronounced, as if they had accelerated. You know, she was more moody, jittery and tense than usual, and vague. No, distracted is a much better word. And she was frequently quite snippy with me.' Francesca stared into the distance, her face thoughtful, concentrating on her memories of those periods. 'It's funny how one is inclined to push troubling things out of one's mind, and I realize I've been doing that for ages. Nick, I recollect something else very clearly now – my own behaviour towards Kath when she came back from the Coast. She always made *me* nervous, and it took me weeks to relax with her, to be my normal self. It was as if she transmitted something very intense and disturbing to *me*. And there was the strangest look in her eyes. Katharine's eyes are very beautiful – that unique turquoise colour – and they're very expressive. But they were different then, I don't know how to describe them. They held a burning light, no, a gleam, better still, a febrile glitter, a sort of wildness.' Francesca bit her lip. 'You're looking doubtful, but it's true. You can't possibly think I'm imagining all this.'

'No, I don't,' Nick said in a faint voice. 'I've seen that look in her eyes myself.' I wish to God I hadn't, he added inwardly.

There was a silence. Francesca took a sip of her coffee and reached for a cigarette.

Lighting it for her, Nick murmured, 'The many complexities of the human mind . . .' He shook his head wearily. 'Katharine is quite a study, I've got to admit.'

'I don't know how you'll ever persuade Kath to see a psychiatrist, Nicky darling, but I think you must try.'

'Oh yes, I agree. And if she listens to anybody, it's me.' He grimaced. 'It's going to be rough though.'

Francesca peered at him, mused out loud, 'I wonder if she *would* have interfered between Ryan and me if she weren't so disturbed?'

'Yes, I wonder. Still, she is meddlesome by nature, Frankie.' He gave her a wry little smile. 'You know, we've spent the entire lunch talking about Kath, not touched on your problems at all.'

Francesca thought: But *I* don't have any problems, not when I really think about it. And her heart tightened as she contemplated the difficulties ahead of Nick. She said, 'Don't worry about *me*, I'll be fine. I've acquired some resilience over the years.' She leaned into him, kissed his cheek. 'As well as a very special man for my dear dear friend. I don't know what I'd do without you, Nicky.'

'You don't have to, Beauty. I'm always here for you, as I once promised you at Langley. Now, I'd better get you home. You've got to pack.' He motioned to the head waiter for the bill, remarking, 'Incidentally, I'm taking you to the airport tomorrow night.' She started to protest, and he exclaimed, 'No, no, don't give me any arguments, Frankie.'

The discussion about Katharine remained foremost in Nicholas Latimer's mind for the next couple of weeks, long after Francesca had flown to France. He was pleased he had broached the subject that day at La Grenouille. Airing his concern had brought a measure of relief, especially since Francesca had voiced her own worries, opinions which paralleled his private assessment of Katharine's present mental state.

There had been times, of late, when Katharine had so rattled Nick he had begun to doubt his own sanity. The fact that Francesca and Hilary had also observed her debilitation, and considered her to be in need of professional help, confirmed his judgment, diminished his confusion and reinforced his resolve to take proper action when Katharine returned from the Far East. Since he was neither in the middle of a novel nor a screen-play, he had plenty of time on his hands, and this complex and patently disturbed woman, whom he dearly loved, wholly absorbed him, dominated his thoughts. He would sit for hours reflecting about her, endeavouring to understand her, to pinpoint the cause of her current problems.

The comedy she had made with Beau Stanton in the autumn of 1956 was shown on television late one night, and Nick found himself watching it totally engrossed. When it was over, his thoughts settled on Hollywood, and the ambience that prevailed in that glittering, power-ridden, crazy town of fantasy and flim-flam. He had never been fond of it, regarded it as *the* company town if there ever was one, insular and boring, and so inbred it fed upon itself. To Nick it was a place of twisted values and false perceptions, where money, sex and status, fame and power abundantly flourished, were the tyrannical masters that dictated and controlled so many lives. He saw it as the one spot on this earth where the gaudy and the vulgar, the flamboyant and the sleazy rubbed shoulders with, and sometimes overshadowed, the talented and the dedicated, the sincere and the honest. Many a performer had come to grief in its *shallow* shallows. Victor, who had never been a permanent resident, preferring the quieter regions of Santa Barbara, had once said: 'Hollywood is a great big back lot. All façade. So don't take it seriously, old buddy. It's only skin deep.'

Later scrutinizing its inhabitants, he himself had come to realize that Hollywood was actually a state of mind. Had Katharine not understood that? Had she been deluded into thinking it was the real world and not sham? Had she been affected by the Hollywood syndrome? Nick ran the years through the computer in his head. In the beginning she had been under contract to Bellissima Productions, and Victor had protected her. She had therefore been insulated, and also isolated from the monsters that roamed the jungles of Hollywood and Vine and Sunset Boulevard; and Beau Stanton, as her husband, had flung an impenetrable fence around her, a fence called the Hollywood Establishment, that highest echelon of movie society which was reserved, snobbish and cliquish. And eminently proper. Between 1959 and 1962 Katharine had been constantly abroad, either on location or with Francesca in England and Europe. On her return to Bel-Air she had always kept herself aloof, apart from the riff-raff, whether by calculation or happen-stance he was not sure. Most likely by choice, now that he thought about it. There was a conservative streak in Katharine's nature, Nick was well aware, and this had been apparent in her mode of living during her years in California. He had noted it many times. She had led a relatively quiet existence, kept a low profile, resisted the local pressures, elected not to fly high and fast. And she had never recklessly spent money for the sake of spending it. In a town where flash was the norm she had been understated to the point of drabness, at least by Rodeo Drive standards. She *had* bought jewels and furs and couture clothes, but never foolishly, nor to excess. He knew too that her money had been well invested and that she watched over it diligently, with an eagle eye, her mind quite clear and sane when it came to finances. Victor had taken her to a staid old-fashioned accounting firm in 1956, and they still handled her business. Through their good advice, and her own shrewdness, she was a millionairess many times over.

Yes, he decided, she did avoid the Hollywood pitfalls, came out of there with a minimum of scars. Then why does Francesca think she behaves strangely every time she returns from the Coast? This was an enigma to him, and he wished he had questioned Frankie more thoroughly. And yet the more he thought about her remark the more he was convinced she was wrong. Something else had wrought the changes in Katharine. But what exactly?

This question haunted Nick for one whole night as he prowled around the house, too preoccupied and overwrought to sleep. At one moment it occurred to him that disorders of the mind did not develop *suddenly*, *overnight*. They grew gradually. He pondered Katharine's childhood, her relationship with her father, the loss of her mother, her preoccupation with Ryan. His mind swung to her vile experience with Gregson, her father's condemnation of her, her obsessive nature. His thoughts ran on and on and he weighed everything he knew about her, and he came to the conclusion that her trouble *was* rooted in her early years. Surely this was the answer.

The following morning, seeking the proper enlightenment, Nick went out and bought a stack of books on mental illness, concentrating particularly on dementia praecox. For the next few days he read them avidly and with care, all the while asking himself if Katharine really *was* suffering from schizophrenia. Finally he had to acknowledge that he was out of his depth, and eventually he started to make discreet inquiries about reputable psychiatrists, knowing that he must formulate some sort of plan to prevent himself from going mad with worry about her. Being a well-informed man, Nick had heard of R. D. Laing's revolutionary work in psychiatry and he began to amass a wealth of material on the specialist's method of treatment, which he held in reserve for a future date.

As the weeks passed, Nick often found himself dwelling also on certain other aspects of Katharine's character as demonstrated by her behaviour in recent months, trying to fathom why she did incomprehensible things. He had withheld several facts from Francesca, had carefully edited himself over lunch at La Grenouille, not simply because of an intrinsic sense of privacy, but also from loyalty and devotion to Katharine. How could he tell Frankie that Kath really was an inveterate liar? And there was no denying that she was. The saddest part, to Nick, was that Katharine lied about the most inconsequential things. It occurred to him one morning that perhaps she could not help herself, and he wondered if lying was simply a nasty habit dating back to her youth, and not a manifestation or symptom of mental derangement.

Even more worrying to Nick, however, was another habit Katharine had acquired prior to her departure for Ceylon. She had taken to disappearing for long periods. On these occasions her transparently bogus explanations had astounded him, and they would have been laughable had the situation not been serious. When he questioned her about her lengthy absences, she either said she had been to church or to return a book to the library, at times when churches and libraries were closed. Furthermore, he was well aware she did not borrow books from any library anywhere, and had told her she was being preposterous in spinning such yarns and expecting him to believe her. Not in the least fazed, she had resolutely stuck to her story. Finally he had thrown up his hands in despair and frustration. Not long afterwards, she had truly frightened him when she had not arrived for dinner at his townhouse one evening, as arranged. After telephoning her every fifteen minutes for two hours without getting a reply, he had grown alarmed and had rushed up to her apartment on Seventy-Second Street. They had keys to each other's homes, and he had let himself in, filled with anxiety, wondering what he would find. But the apartment was empty. Katharine had wandered in around midnight, looking exhausted and distracted. Taken aback to find him waiting for her, she had vehemently denied that they had had a dinner date, had flown into a tantrum of no mean proportions, and had accused him of spying on her and reading her private papers. Realizing there was nothing to be gained by fighting with her, Nick had gone home, pressing back his own anger, and not a little fear, asking himself if she *was* spinning down into total madness. The following morning, Katharine had been her usual remorseful self, had apologized profusely, begged him to forgive her, promised it would not happen again. And she had behaved impeccably until she had left to make the film.

Now, as he contemplated these two new habits, it unexpectedly crossed his mind that she might be lying and disappearing for a valid reason: *another man.* He gave it serious consideration and dismissed the idea as ridiculous. Apart from the fact that she was not promiscuous by nature, she had retained a degree of frigidity, and Nick was aware sex was not a driving force in her life.

The possibility that she was indeed having an affair did not enter his head again for another year.

By the middle of July, as Katharine's return to the States grew closer, Nicholas Latimer's apprehension intensified. At the end of the month, she flew, with the rest of the cast and crew, from Ceylon to Hong Kong and then on to California. After post-production dubbing at the studio, she finally travelled back to New York.

The minute he met her at the airport he knew she had changed yet again. She was like her old self, not at all disturbed, and calmer than she had been for months. She had obviously enjoyed her stay in the Far East, and the film had gone extremely well, without a hitch. There was a lovely bloom on her, a freshness and vitality about her which staggered Nick. Dubious about it lasting, he nonetheless camouflaged his anxiety and his surprise, and treated her as if nothing had happened prior to her leaving. Once more, he soon found himself enchanted by her, held in her thrall. Very slowly he began to relax, but he did not let down his guard entirely. He watched her. And he waited.

Nick also wisely bided his time before telling Katharine about Ryan and Francesca, explaining only that Francesca had left earlier than planned for her vacation in the South of France. Only when Katharine was completely rested and settled in her apartment did he finally mention the break-up.

Genuinely astonished and upset, Katharine had telephoned the villa in Monte Carlo immediately. As he listened to her speaking to Francesca, Nick was convinced she was being forthright. Although he could only hear one side of this conversation, it was not difficult to piece together the facts. Within minutes Nick decided Ryan had undoubtedly shifted the blame, just as he had originally suspected. From the things Katharine was saying to Francesca, she had merely pointed out the drawbacks in the relationship, the religious difference, and had asked Ryan to think most carefully before making any decisions which would be irrevocable.

'And there's something else, Frankie darling,' Katharine exclaimed into the 'phone, 'I told Ryan that if he ever did anything to hurt you he would have to answer to *me*! I'm really going to let him have it when I see him. He's behaved abominably towards you. I can't begin to tell you how furious I am.'

Smoking on the sofa, Nick looked out of the window, nodded to himself, thinking Ryan had been a coward, and an underhanded one at that. He was relieved Francesca was free of him finally. Another more suitable man would soon come along.

A few days after this telephone call, Nick arrived at Katharine's apartment to find her engaged in a violent verbal battle with her brother, who had stopped off to see her during a quick visit to Manhattan. Grimacing, Nick retreated rapidly into the privacy of Katharine's bedroom and did not emerge until Ryan had left, when he was positive the family feathers had stopped flying.

Controlling her anger, and looking grave and thoughtful, Katharine informed Nick that she had finished with her brother, had washed her hands of him. 'I'm leaving him to God – and Patrick O'Rourke. If he can handle *both*,' she had said quietly, shaking her lovely head. 'I can't cope with him any more, darling. He's impossible. He *is* weak. I told him not to bother coming around here any more.'

Nick nodded, said nothing, not giving this statement much credibility. She had had altercations with Ryan many times, and had always been the first to seek reconciliation. But as the weeks passed and she made no move to contact her brother, Nick began to believe she had spoken the truth. He chided himself for thinking the worst, for suspecting her of deviousness and lying. In fact, Katharine had not displayed these dismaying traits at all since her return. Her disposition continued to be tranquil; she was considerate and affectionate. If she was sometimes strangely quiet and unusually subdued, even abstracted on occasion, she gave him no real cause for concern. This pleased Nick. However, he was not foolish enough to think her present behaviour signified a sudden recovery from all that ailed her. He was fully aware that at best Katharine was still a troubled woman.

At the end of September, Francesca came back, and it was like old times that particular fall. The friendship between the two women had not been damaged in any way whatsoever, and they were as close as they had ever been. Ryan O'Rourke might have never existed, or so it seemed to Nicholas. Francesca was delighted with the change in Katharine, and as October drew to a close she told Nick she thought they had probably exaggerated Katharine's mental problems, blown them out of proportion. They were standing in her living room, where a party for Doris and her father was in progress. 'Kath seems awfully normal to me, Nicky, and very well balanced, wouldn't you say?'

Nick nodded his agreement as he followed Francesca's gaze. Katharine was talking to Hilary Ogden and the Earl. This night she had never looked more beautiful, in a simple black velvet dress and a diamond pin and earrings he had never seen before. Her chestnut hair was drawn back from her face and knotted in a low chignon in the nape of her neck. The warmth of the room had brought a light pink blush to her pale complexion and her turquoise eyes were gay and sparkling. He dragged his eyes away and said, 'I thank God every day, Frankie. I don't know what happened when she was in the Far East, but she came back much more peaceful.' He laughed lightly. 'I can't say why I feel this, but I think something affected her there.'

Francesca glanced at him curiously. 'She's never said anything to me. In fact she's hardly mentioned the trip, or filming there, at all. Let's just be glad. I can't bear to think of her being tortured the way she was earlier in the year.'

'Neither can I. Oh, hello, Terry. How are you?'

Terrence Ogden, as debonair and handsome as ever, shook Nick's hand. 'I'm great. And you look pretty terrific yourself. Lovely party, Francesca. And I say, Nicky, your old lady is pretty nifty tonight. I've never seen Puss so relaxed. I don't know what your secret is, old chap, but it's worked wonders.'

Nick grinned. 'Thanks, Terry. Francesca and I were just agreeing Kath is very healthy these days.'

'Thank Christ! It took me a long time to recover from her verbal assault on me this spring. Hilary and I still don't know what set her off. Pressure of work perhaps, tension, strain. Who knows? Hell, the main thing is that she's her old self.'

Terry chatted for a few minutes about the film he had recently finished in Hollywood, and then he drifted off. Francesca went to the kitchen to speak to the caterers about supper, and Nick joined Katharine, cheered by Francesca's remarks and Terry's comments also.

Nick realized Terry had planted a germ of a thought in his mind, and for several days after the party he ruminated on the actor's words. Perhaps the strain and exhaustion of work had indeed induced Katharine's irritability, irrationality and explosive moods. It was a possibility worth considering, particularly since it was not so uncommon. Other performers had been known to collapse, and she had gone from one picture to the next, and at breakneck speed, starring in *Trojan Interlude* on Broadway in between. Terry's points were well taken, and Nick made up his mind to veto her next project, whatever it was.

As it turned out, he did not. He welcomed it. Katharine's new venture was the search for a country house which they could use as a weekend home. Nick encouraged her in this, recognizing it would be a distraction, and therapeutic. Once she became involved in its decoration and furnishing she would be reluctant to stop in order to make a film. Enlisting Francesca's help, the three of them spent November weekends scouring New Jersey, Long Island, Connecticut and the Berkshires, looking for a suitable place. It was Katharine herself who finally found her perfect 'retreat', one weekday when she had gone off to Connecticut alone. Nick was dismayed to discover he did not like the house when she took him to see it. Ever since he had been a child, he had thought that houses had atmospheres, retained memories of their past, and this one was redolent of unhappiness. It seemed to reek of grief and gloom, but he kept his mouth shut, acutely conscious of her excitement and enthusiasm. As he had guessed, she threw herself into remodelling with energy and fervour, turning down a film and a play. Five months after Katharine had purchased the property in New Canaan, in March of the following year, it was finally finished. He and Francesca spent the first weekend there with her.

The Friday afternoon he and Frankie arrived, Katharine dragged them into the sunny spacious living room and immediately broke open a bottle of Dom Pérignon. Hovering in front of the great log fire in the stone hearth, she cried excitedly, 'Nick, you must propose a toast to the house.'

He grinned. 'To the house,' he declared, lifting his flute high. 'May all who dwell in her be safe and well and happy.'

Francesca exclaimed, 'You sound as if you're launching a ship! Why that's exactly what we should do. I mean *christen* the house. What's its name, Kath?'

Wrinkling her nose, Katharine faked a thoughtful moment. 'How about Bide-A-Wee?'

'That's ghastly,' Francesca shrieked. 'Ugh! It's so twee. Positively revolting, darling.'

'Goddamned awful,' added Nick, pulling a face. 'Can't you come up with something more imaginative, Katinka?'

'I was kidding! And you know it. As for imagination, you and Frankie are the writers. Come on, think of a name, geniuses.'

Their hilarity increased over the next hour as Francesca and Nick gave her a string of preposterous suggestions, but they never did find one which was suitable and the house remained nameless.

By the early summer of 1967, Nick discovered he was totally relaxed with Katharine, and content in a quiet way. He had long known they would never be as deliriously happy with each other as they had been in Mexico in 1964, but he loved her and he thought there was a strong chance they could lead a good life together. By now he had managed to brainwash himself into believing Terry had accurately pinpointed the reason for Katharine's mental collapse. *Work*. She had not been in front of a camera for a whole year, nor put a foot on a stage, and she was in good health, mentally as well as physically. In all truth, and to Nick's surprise, she did not seem to miss acting. Encouraged by this attitude, he decided Katharine ought to go into semi-retirement.

He suggested it to her one Sunday afternoon, when they were sitting on the terrace of the New Canaan house. 'Do a film a year, or every eighteen months, and an occasional Broadway play for a limited engagement. Pace yourself better than you have in the past.'

Katharine began to laugh. 'I can't go into retirement, Nicky. I'm only thirty-two. People retire when they're *old*! Besides, I'd die of boredom.'

'No you wouldn't. It's about time you enjoyed the fruits of your hard labours. And you certainly don't need money.'

'But what would I do with my time?'

'Devote it to me.' He leaned forward with eager boyishness. 'We've talked about getting married in the past. Let's do it, Kath.'

She stared at him in amazement, her turquoise eyes widening, and then she went and knelt in front of him, resting her arms on his knees. 'Oh do you really mean it, my darling Mr Latimer?'

'I do, I do, my divine Miss Tempest.' He kissed her deeply on the mouth. 'I love you, Kath.'

'I love you too, Nicky.'

'So, what's your answer, lady?'

'Why it's *yes*, you fool!'

His heart leapt. 'Thank God for that. When? When shall we get married?'

'Soon darling.'

'Soon is not *soon* enough, my sweet girl. Nor is it very specific.' He touched her cheek. 'I'm not getting any younger, you know. I'm forty. Isn't it about time we settled down, and had a couple of kids?'

Her lips parted, but she said nothing, simply stared at him for the longest moment. The trace of a smile slipped away entirely. 'I'll give you a date next week, darling,' she promised.

But she never did, and suddenly everything started to fall apart again.

CHAPTER FORTY-SIX

Lights blazed everywhere, but the nameless house in Connecticut was deathly quiet. Francesca had come to think of it in this way, since it never had been christened as she had suggested. Now, as she stood in the middle of the entrance hall, she muttered under her breath: We should have called it The Loony Bin.

She shivered, sudden apprehension clutching at her, and instinctively she tightened her hold on Lada's leash. Nick came in with their luggage, and she swung around quickly. 'There's something wrong! I just know it!' she exclaimed.

Nick was instantly aware of the eerie silence himself. It was abnormal. He dumped the bags on the floor, glanced around, cocking his head on one side, listening. Usually the house reverberated with the sound of the radio or records, distant bustle in the kitchen, echoes of Mrs Jennings' motherly tones, Katharine's tinkling actressy voice issuing orders, talking on the telephone. And it was unlike her not to greet him when he arrived from Manhattan. But then she hadn't been like herself lately. He groaned inside. Maybe she had, maybe the strange abstracted disturbed creature who inhabited this place was the *real* Katharine Tempest.

Returning Francesca's worried stare, he strode towards the living room, called over his shoulder, 'Check the kitchen and the back of the house, Frankie, see if you can find Mrs Jennings or the maid. Perhaps Kath had to go out unexpectedly.'

'Yes, Nicky. Meet you back here in a couple of minutes.' Francesca hurried down the short corridor to the kitchen, taking the dog with her.

From the doorway of the living room everything looked in order to Nick. Several lamps had been turned on, cushions were plumped up on the sofas and chairs, and not one item was out of place. The only oddity was the fire. It had almost burned out, the last few dying embers visible through the guard surrounding it. Katharine had a penchant for huge fires and they blazed constantly even on summer evenings. It was now November and there was a chill in the air tonight. His eyes fell on the clock. It was seven-forty. Wherever she was, she had been gone a long time if the fire was anything to judge by. Unless . . . unless she had not left the house. Had she hurt herself? But where were the staff? Had they all been hurt? Foul play? He thought of her jewellery. Oh God, intruders would kill for that collection.

Nick raced into the hall, saw no sign of Francesca, took the stairs three at a time, ran across the upstairs landing and burst into Katharine's bedroom. He leaned against the doorjamb, panting and out of breath. The room was still, tranquil and undisturbed. Lamps glowed. The bed was unrumpled. Furniture was upright. And her fetish for meticulous order was very much in evidence. But here too the fire was low, crumbling to ashes. His eyes did a piercing second sweep of the room, and it was then that he noticed the empty jewellery cases lying open on the dressing table. He leapt across the floor, picked up the largest, which he had not seen before. It looked brand new, the leather pristine. He squinted at the inside lid, saw the name Van Cleef & Arpels stamped on the white satin, and underneath, in smaller letters: Beverly Hills. There were three cases in all, and of varying sizes. Was she wearing their contents? Or had they been stolen?

With a sinking heart he dropped the case, flung open the bathroom door and turned on the light. No sign of disarray here either. Gritting his teeth, Nick reached for the shower curtain, drew it back, looked down into the tub. A damp loofah was its sole occupant.

After checking every room on the two top floors, and finding nothing suspicious, Nick ran downstairs. Francesca was crossing the hall, still holding on to Lada's leash tightly. 'There's nothing unusual up there,' he said, pausing on the bottom step, his hand on the bannister. 'And no sign of anyone.'

'The house is empty, Nicky, completely deserted. I've been to the maid's room, the den, the dining room and the library. It's mystifying.'

'You didn't find *anything* untoward?'

'Not really. Except in the kitchen.'

'What about the kitchen?' he demanded sharply.

'Mrs Jennings must have been in the middle of preparing food, a meal, when she was interrupted. Come and look for yourself.' She led the way into the kitchen.

'See, over there, on the counter top,' Francesca said, inclining her head. 'All those unfinished vegetables, even the peelings. They seem to have been there for hours. And that apron was on the floor. I picked it up, put it on the stool.'

Nick examined the apron, prowled around the kitchen, poked into the pantry and several broom closets. He said, 'Stay here, Frankie. This is beginning to look mighty fishy to me. I'm going down into the basement.'

Francesca's hand flew to her mouth. 'Oh God, Nick, you don't think –'

'I don't know what to think. Just stay put, okay?'

She nodded, automatically bent down and lifted the dog into her arms. Francesca's heart accelerated, innumerable dire possibilities running through her mind. She also thought of the jewellery, and then of Katharine's fame. Everyone in the area knew she lived in this house. Such a prominent movie star was a prime target. Francesca closed her eyes, wishing Nick would hurry.

'It's all right, kid,' Nick said a few minutes later, emerging from the basement, banging the door behind him. 'We've covered the house. I'd better scout around outside.'

Francesca could only nod, her eyes huge in her troubled face as she followed him out. She watched him searching for a flashlight in the hall closet, and then he

499

opened the front door, flipped a switch on the porch wall. Instantly the driveway and the lawn were washed with pale lights from the spots hidden in the foliage.

'Do you want me to go with you?' she volunteered.

Nick pivoted. 'No, absolutely not,' he snapped. Stepping onto the lawn, he headed in the direction of the tangled mass of shrubs and bushes near the high stone wall surrounding the grounds. This area was dark and he beamed the flashlight on it.

The apprehension Francesca had experienced when first entering the house had turned into a nameless dread. She could not shake it off. She stood in the middle of the hall, rooted to the spot, staring out into the garden, her eyes seeking Nick. He had disappeared. She shivered, feeling terribly alone all of a sudden. And exposed. Exposed to this house. Although she had never said so, she shared Nick's dislike for it, had always found it alien, unwelcoming and oppressive. Unexpectedly, Lada's head lifted alertly, as if she had heard something, and then she barked, strained in Francesca's arms, tried to jump down.

Calming the dog, Francesca glanced about, listening. What had alarmed Lada? Nothing stirred. She swallowed nervously and stepped out onto the porch, took a few deep breaths of the crisp night air. And she began to chastise herself for being over imaginative. There was nothing wrong with this place. It was perfectly beautiful. And anyway, if she thought about it intelligently, her fear was for Katharine and the staff and their safety. To be afraid of a house was irrational, and she was hardly that. She glanced up at the old stone structure, its windows spilling reassuring light, but she could not help asking herself why she still felt that stealth and pain dwelt within its walls. Oh stop it, she muttered, walking across the gravel to Nick's car.

Francesca leaned against the wing, huddled farther into her thick sweater, shivering slightly in the wind. She looked up. Dark clouds in a moonless sky, she recited inwardly. That's by Rupert Brooke, isn't it? *Love in you went passing by . . .* As the next line of the poem filtered through her mind, she held herself perfectly still. With a rush of perception she understood then. *There was no love in this house.* Only Katharine's sickness. Why do Nicky and I constantly excuse her ghastly behaviour? Why do we continue to put up with it? Because we care for her. Oh poor dear Kath, she does need us both so much. We must try to help her . . .

'You can relax, Frankie,' Nick shouted, his voice carrying to her on the wind. He was sprinting across the lawn, waving the torch in the air. 'The garden's as deserted as the *maison*. Still, I'd better look in the garages just to be sure.'

'Right you are, darling,' she called back, some of the tension easing.

A couple of seconds later Nick was ushering her inside, shaking his head. He slammed the front door behind them, smoothed his wind-blown hair. 'That's the damnedest thing! Katharine's car is in the garage. Come on, kid, into the living room with you. Jesus, you're blue with cold. I think we both need a drink.'

'Thank God nothing's happened to Kath or the others. I'm sure she went out, that someone came to collect her. There's no other explanation, Nicky.'

'I guess so,' he said. 'But where is Mrs Jennings? She generally stays until ten. What interrupted her in the middle of her chores? And where in the hell is Renata?'

'Nick, I've just thought of something else –' Francesca grasped his arm. 'Could Katharine have been *kidnapped*, and the others?'

His eyes locked on hers, and then he shook his head. 'That's a tough job, taking three women, and there are no signs of a struggle. No, I honestly don't think any violence has taken place here today.'

'Mrs Jennings might have had some sort of emergency at home, and it could be Renata's day off. When is it?'

'Wednesday,' he answered, kneeling in front of the fire, attempting to rekindle it. 'Today's Thursday. Do you mind getting the ice, Frankie, while I struggle with this?'

'Of course not.' She turned, edged towards the hall.

Nick started to laugh. 'You're clutching poor Lada as if her life's in danger! Leave her here, darling, and for God's sake take the leash off.'

Francesca laughed with him, looking embarrassed. She unfastened the leash, took it off, and said, 'It's silly, I know, but I always feel . . . well, I feel as if there's something, some presence, lurking in this house. I can't explain it . . . perhaps it's the atmosphere.' She shrugged. 'You probably think I'm as batty as Kathar –' Her voice faltered, and she stared at him aghast, shook her head slowly, apologized, 'Oh Nick, I'm sorry, I didn't mean to imply that Katharine is crazy.'

His smile was faint. 'She *is* teetering on the edge again though, and you know it. Sometimes I think she's really flipped out. As for the house, I know what you mean about this pile of rubble. I've always hated the place. It *does* have an unpleasant atmosphere, an air of gloom and doom. Now, scoot, go and get the ice and I'll pour us two stiff drinks. Vodka as usual?'

'Please. With tonic. Why don't you give Mrs Jennings a call?'

'I thought of that in the garden. I'll get on to her now. And listen, kid, while you're in the kitchen see if there's some cheese and crackers. I'm starved.'

'That's a good idea. I'm a bit hungry myself.'

Nick stood up and went to the desk. Sitting down, he found Mrs Jennings' number and dialled it quickly. The line was busy. Damn, he mumbled impatiently, picked up a pencil and began his usual doodling on a scratch pad, making interlocking triangles. He kept trying the number, his exasperation increasing. Finally the line was clear and he experienced enormous relief when he heard the housekeeper's voice. Nick spoke to her for over ten minutes, listening carefully, nodding to himself, asking pertinent questions. He rubbed his eyes wearily when he at last hung up.

Francesca was mixing their drinks. She said, 'From what you were saying, I gather Katharine fired Mrs Jennings today.'

'Yes. And she's terribly upset about it. Apparently Katharine flew into a screaming rage early this evening and for no good reason. She became abusive and dismissed Mrs Jennings, as of tomorrow. Mrs J. wasn't about to spend another minute in the house, so she told me. She downed tools, flung off her apron and marched out. And she won't be coming back. Renata *is* off today; she asked to go into Manhattan to see her cousin who's visiting from Italy. *She'll* be back tomorrow.'

'And Kath? Did Mrs Jennings know anything?'

'She said Kath was dressed up when they had the row, was ready to go out to a dinner, or a party, the housekeeper wasn't sure which. Seemingly Kath had words with Renata as well, yesterday that is. She had her pressing dress after dress all day, uncertain what she would wear tonight.' He sighed. Same pattern, he thought and stared down at the pad.

'How *odd* that Kath should go out! She knew we were arriving. Oh hell, it's par for the course, I suppose. And at least we've accounted for the household.'

'Not quite. We don't know where Kath is.'

'Come and have this drink, darling,' Francesca urged, observing his worried expression. 'I'm sure she'll be back soon.'

'Yes,' Nick responded absently. His eyes were glued to the pad. Just below his doodlings were deep indentations of writing which had penetrated through onto the sheet of paper from the previous page. This had been torn off, and he noticed the ragged uneven edge at the top of the pad. He peered at the indentations under the light and read: *Michael. Thursday. Seven. Greenwich.* There were several numbers under these words, but they were so indistinct that he could not make them out.

'Nick, what *are* you doing over there?'

'Just a minute, Frankie. I think I've found a clue. Does Katharine know a man called Michael who lives in Greenwich?'

'I don't think so. *Why?*'

'Look at this.' He held out the pad to her. 'She wrote something down and the impressions are here on the new page.'

Francesca agreed it was Katharine's handwriting, and said, 'The numbers aren't very clear. Shade over them with a pencil. The lead should make them stand out.'

'Hey, good girl, now they *are* very legible,' Nick exclaimed, tossing the pencil aside. 'I bet you it's a 'phone number.' He grabbed the receiver, pausing to say, 'We shall now find out who the mysterious Michael is, and whether Katharine is with him in Greenwich.'

Clutching his arm, Francesca cried, 'Wait a minute, Nicky. Look, I know you're angry with Kath, and understandably so. It's irresponsible of her, going out without leaving a note, worrying us like this. But you'll only blow up at her, if she is at this number, create additional problems. She's been so paranoid lately, thinking people spy on her. Especially you. It'll look much better if *I* call, ask to speak to her. *Please.*'

He hesitated, then shrugged. 'Be my guest, kid.' Rising, he handed her the telephone and strode over to the fireplace.

Francesca dialled, waited. A hint of surprise flashed in her eyes briefly. 'Sorry, wrong number,' she murmured and replaced the receiver carefully, averting her face, unable to look at Nick.

'Why in the hell did you hang up so quickly?' he demanded furiously, frowning at her. 'How do you know it was a wrong number?' When she was unresponsive, Nick said quickly, 'And why did you look so surprised?'

Francesca walked back to the sofa slowly, endeavouring to hide her shock, wondering whether to tell him a white lie. But if she said she had reached a restaurant or a bar in Greenwich he would not believe her. And knowing him, he would dial the number himself. She could not permit him to do that under any circumstances. Clearing her throat, she said softly, 'I think it was a butler who answered.'

'*And?*'

Francesca sank onto the sofa, her misery acute. 'He said —' The words choked

502

in her throat, and she cleared it again, more nervously. 'He said . . . The butler said . . . "Lazarus residence".'

For a split second Nick seemed not to understand. He gaped at Francesca. His eyes held a startled expression. And then he exploded. 'Goddamn it to hell! I might have known! That son of a bitch has been sniffing around her for years.' He clenched his right hand, smashed his fist into the open palm of his left, and hard. 'Goddamn it, I'm going to call that bastard right now and let him have it. As for Katharine,' he shouted, 'I'm going to wring her neck. I've warned her about him. *Warned her repeatedly.*' He moved with swift agility, racing to the desk in a fulminating rage. Reaching for the telephone, he yelled, 'She knows how I feel about that monster. How could she do this to me?'

Francesca flew after him, grabbed his arm, tried to drag him away from the desk. He held his ground, but was unable to shake free of her tenacious grip. He clutched at the 'phone as Francesca, in turn, clung to him desperately, her eyes wide and pleading. 'For God's sake don't do this, Nick! Please, please, don't call there! You're jumping to conclusions. The wrong conclusions!'

Nick continued to wrestle with her, his face flushed and blazing with anger. 'Let go, Frankie. I know what I'm doing!' The telephone crashed to the floor, the chair tipped over, the desk lamp wobbled precariously. Unexpectedly, Nick let his arms fall limply to his sides and ceased his struggling. He stared at Francesca and shook his head slowly. 'You're right, kid,' he muttered and bent down, picked up the 'phone, righted the chair.

Francesca, breathing heavily, took his hand. 'Let's talk this over quietly,' she gasped, and drew him back to the fireside. After pressing him down onto the sofa, she brought their drinks and seated herself opposite. 'Don't judge her, Nicky, not without having all the facts. Her presence in Mike Lazarus's house means absolutely nothing, and you know it. This could be a perfectly innocent evening. After all, he does own Monarch, and he's in the picture business in a big way these days. Katharine is a superstar. And she has been edgy about not working lately, has indicated to me that she's ready for a project. Perhaps he wants her to do a film for Monarch.'

Nick peered at Francesca through the haze of their cigarette smoke. 'Do you really believe that?' he asked with a sarcastic laugh.

'It's a strong possibility,' she hedged, not certain what to think, aware that she had been dismayed when she had heard that particular name a moment ago. In a firmer tone, she added, 'Yes, yes, I'm sure that's why she's over there.'

'Don't be naïve, kid.'

She ignored his disdainful tone and said, 'What did you mean, when you said he's been sniffing around her for years?'

'Exactly that. As chairman of the board of the conglomerate that owns Monarch, he doesn't normally get involved with the movies they make. He leaves that to the head of production. He's only interested in balance sheets, the bottom line, profits. But he was parked in his office at the studio – and never off the set incidentally – when she made that film for Monarch in 1964. Look, Frankie, I was out there with her. I know he was ogling her, sucking up to her the entire time. I turned a blind eye. I'd no choice. And I –'

'Katharine couldn't possibly be interested in *him*! She was most likely being polite because of his position, tolerating him –'

'Tolerating him my goddamned foot!' Nick bellowed, and then fell back against the sofa, looking shamefaced. 'Sorry, Frankie, I shouldn't be taking it out on you. Let me calm down for a minute, get a hold of myself.'

She nodded, and he finished his cigarette, staring into the fire morosely. A number of things were clicking into place in his shrewd and agile mind: A comment Victor had made years ago was suddenly very meaningful; and a recent chance remark of Jake Watson's likewise assumed new significance. He sighed under his breath, looked across at Francesca. 'I'm sure she saw a lot of Lazarus last summer, you know, when she was dubbing the Far East picture at Twentieth after she got back from Ceylon. I read a story in the *Hollywood Reporter* . . . about a lavish party Lazarus had given at his new house in Bel-Air Estates. It said Katharine was the guest of honour. I was dumbfounded. After all, she knows how much I hate that slimy bastard. I remember thinking it was disloyal of her to socialize with him, when she didn't have to do so for business reasons.'

'Didn't you ask her about it?'

'Sure. When she got home I mentioned it in passing, in an off-handed way, as usual treading on eggs around her, not wanting to upset her. She denied she'd been at the party, said she *had* accepted, not wishing to offend him, but then cancelled at the last minute.'

'But you didn't believe her, did you?'

'Not really, Frankie. Still, I didn't want to make a big deal out of it, since she was so stable. I let it go.' He leaned forward. 'You've been concerned about her lying and the way she's been disappearing at the oddest times over the last few months. What you don't know is that none of it is new to me. She was behaving like that immediately before she went to Ceylon.'

'Oh Nicky, why didn't you tell me?'

'I guess I was being protective.' After enumerating some of these baffling incidents, he remarked, 'I'm beginning to think she was involved with Lazarus then, perhaps even as far back as 1964, when she made the film for Monarch. Just as I'm sure she's involved with him now.'

Francesca said swiftly, 'I think that's a hasty assumption. You have no real evidence.'

'I'm not shooting from the hip, kid!' Nick smoked for a moment, his eyes narrowed. 'When I ran upstairs to check the bedroom earlier, I saw a number of empty jewel cases on the dressing table. I've never seen them before. They're brand new. I'm putting two and two together, and coming up with Lazarus.'

Francesca stared at him, her brow creasing, her expression puzzled. 'She could have bought –'

'But I *know* she didn't,' he asserted. 'Besides, the stuff was purchased at Van Cleef's in Beverly Hills. She's not been out there for a year. And she always shows me everything, asks my opinion before making a final decision. And it's the Lazarus style. That joker has always decked his women out in expensive baubles. Don't you remember Hélène Vernaud and her emeralds?'

'Yes. Whatever happened to Hélène? Did he ever marry her?'

'Are you kidding!' Nick laughed derisively. 'Lazarus never marries his women, he simply discards them when he gets tired of their charms. Thank God for Hélène's built-in survival kit. She married an English duke and is sitting pretty. I thought you knew.'

'Yes, I do remember, now that you mention it.' Francesca grimaced. 'I can't picture Kath with Lazarus. Ugh! Beauty and the Beast. Why would she be interested in him?'

'*Money.*'

'But Katharine's a millionairess.'

'Yeah. But Lazarus is one of the richest men in the world, in the same category as Ludwig and Getty. Katharine's millions are pin money in comparison to his billions. And I didn't mean money *per se*. Perhaps I should have said his *power*, his clout. And what about the studio? She would love to have that as a little plaything.'

Francesca was silent, pondering, scrutinizing Nick. He sounded calm enough and certainly his initial fury had died down, and yet she saw the strain on his face, the pain in his eyes. He was chain smoking, occasionally tapping his foot, which he only did when he was excessively agitated. Wanting to alleviate his worry, she now said, 'Neither of us should jump to conclusions, as I said earlier. Let's wait to hear what Kath has to say. There's a good explanation, I'm positive.'

'She's been spending a lot of time out here lately. This is supposed to be a weekend retreat not a permanent residence,' Nick said, as though musing out loud. 'And don't forget, she is alone here, free as a bird, and *I'm* out of the way. She can do anything she wants. And Lazarus has a house in Greenwich. Convenient, eh?'

Passing over the question, Francesca bent forward, smiled reassuringly. '*You* seem to have forgotten one thing, Nicky. Katharine adores you. You're her dearest love.'

'Want to bet?' Not waiting for an answer, he took their glasses to the refectory table near the window, refreshed their drinks, returned to his seat. He tried to relax, slumping down on the sofa. He wished he could put Katharine out of his mind, knew this was an impossibility. Suddenly he sat bolt upright and fixed his vivid blue eyes on Francesca, his expression alert. 'I wonder . . . I wonder . . .' he began softly, and paused, reflecting.

'What is it?' she asked, watching him closely.

'Is it possible that she is *not* deranged at all? Is this an *act*? And a very clever one at that?'

Taken aback, Francesca exclaimed, 'Don't be ridiculous! She's positively batty at times. Flipped out.'

'She acts as if she is, and perhaps that's what she wants *us* to believe. But remember, Katharine is an actress. A consummate actress. Know what, Frankie, she might just be putting it on.'

Francesca's hazel-amber eyes stretched wider in her face, and she paled. 'If that's the case then she's behaving in the most disgusting manner. We've both been out of our minds with worry. And why would she want us to think she's crazy?'

Nick rose, paced the floor, stopped abruptly. 'Not guilty by reason of insanity,' he intoned. 'Murderers *have* got away with murder by using that plea. It *excuses* everything they've done. They hide behind their so-called insanity. Could she be doing that? In order to behave any way she wishes, and without having to take responsibility for her actions.'

'Nicky!' Appalled, Francesca drew back on the sofa, regarded him apprehensively. 'Oh God, Nicky, that's a horrendous idea, and frightening.'

'Isn't it just . . .'

He could not decide whether to call Victor Mason or not.

It had struck Nick earlier that Victor was the one person who could enlighten him on two points, and he had been on the verge of picking up the telephone an hour ago. But Francesca had come back into the living room at that precise moment, carrying a tray of smoked salmon sandwiches and a bowl of fresh fruit and had insisted they both eat.

Nick eyed the clock on the oak mantelpiece above the huge open stone fireplace. It was eleven-twenty, therefore eighttwenty in Santa Barbara. He was hesitating for a couple of reasons. Katharine might return at any minute; Victor had his own problems to contend with at the present, so that Nick was reluctant to disturb him. Lynn Mason, Victor's wife of a year, had been taken ill, and two days ago Vic had told him the prognosis was not good. The specialists had diagnosed leukaemia. Poor bastard, Nick thought, he has such lousy luck in his private life.

Francesca came in briskly, wearing a camel-coloured cape over her cream sweater and matching pants. 'I'm going to take Lada for a walk, Nick. We can have coffee when I get back. It's brewing.'

'Okay. Stay in the grounds.'

'Naturally. Come on, Lada.'

The dog was curled up in a ball next to Nick on the sofa. She jumped down obediently and trotted across the room. Nick watched Francesca leave, his eyes thoughtful. Victor frequently asked about her. She never mentioned his name. She must think about him sometimes though, Nick thought, and stood up. If he was going to call the ranch he had better do so immediately, while he was still alone. He hurried to the desk, lifted the receiver.

Victor himself answered a few seconds later, after several brief rings. 'Rancho Che Sarà Sarà.'

'Hello, Vic, it's Nicky.'

'Hi, old buddy. Jesus, this is mental telepathy. I was just about to call you.'

'Oh! Everything okay out there?' Nick cut in worriedly. 'How's Lynn?'

'She's a bit better than she was yesterday.' Vic sounded subdued but calm. 'The medication is helping, and we're seeing a big improvement. The doctors are very hopeful, think they've checked this, got it under control.'

'That's wonderful news. Give her my best love.'

'I will, Nicky. As I was about to say, I had my hand on the 'phone to call you, when Jake arrived. He drove down from L.A. to spend a few days with us. He's a sight for sore eyes.'

'I know what you mean. There's nobody like Jake, and it'll do you both good to have some company. I'll come out myself as soon as I can. Listen, Vic, Jake is one of the reasons I called tonight.'

'Oh really. Why?'

'I wanted to check something out with you – a chance remark he made in front

506

of us both recently. I felt he'd clam up if I called him, tackled him head on. But look, I'm jumping the gun. I have a question first. Have you got a few minutes?'

'Sure, kid. Shoot.'

'Do you remember when Katharine and Beau Stanton separated?'

There was a small silence at the other end of the line, where, three thousand miles away, Victor Mason was instantly filling with dismay. 'Sure I do, Nicky,' he said.

'*Okay*. I don't know whether you recall this, but around then you told me Beau Stanton blamed Mike Lazarus for some of their problems, that he thought Lazarus was a bad influence on Katharine. Remember?'

Oh Jesus, he's found out before I could tell him, Victor thought. He said slowly, 'Yes, I do. But Beau didn't say anything to me about Lazarus. That was *my* opinion. Beau and Lazarus were still very pally in those days. Lazarus was a constant visitor, always hanging around with them. I got the feeling that he idolized Katharine, had put her on a pedestal. Before Katharine and Beau split up I used to needle Beau a bit, you know, about the megalomaniac coming between them. But I must say Beau never took the bait.'

'I want to clarify another thing. When I was out on the Coast three months ago, for the Bellissima board meeting, Jake started to tell me something about seeing Kath and Lazarus at La Scala. They were having a cosy tête-à-tête one evening last year when she was dubbing at Twentieth. You cut him off, changed the subject. I decided not to press then, and I let it drop. Now I want to know more about that night. I thought you might fill me in, but listen, since Jake's at the ranch I might as well speak to him one to one. Put him on, Vic, please.'

Victor said regretfully, 'You don't have to talk to Jake, Nicky. I was there with Lynn that evening. The three of us saw them. I could have killed Jake when he mentioned it to you in September. I thought it wiser you didn't know. I didn't want him to open a can of worms, particularly since it might have been an innocuous date. I've been kicking myself for the last hour. I wish I'd told you myself, alerted you three months ago. It might have prevented the situation devel –'

'What situation?' Nick demanded shakily. He gripped the receiver tighter. 'What are you talking about, Vic?'

'Isn't that the reason for your call? I thought you wanted to discuss Katharine's association with Lazarus,' the actor answered, sounding confused.

'*What association*?' Nick asked, his voice rising.

'Jesus, Nicky, don't tell me you don't *know*. I thought you'd found out about them –'

'I only started to suspect something tonight,' Nick cut in sharply. 'Tell me what you've heard, Vic.' Nick's hand shook as he groped for a cigarette.

Vic said: 'Charlie Roberts came over to see Lynn earlier this evening. You know they've always been close friends. He's holed up down here, writing furiously. Lynn was teasing him about his secret, hush-hush project, asking him why he was being so mysterious. Charlie said he guessed it wouldn't matter if he told us, since it was going to be announced to the press on Monday anyway, and there had already been a few leaks in Hollywood in the last twenty-four hours. Apparently Charlie is writing a screenplay for Monarch. He's on the last few pages of the final draft. Plans to deliver it early next week. Lazarus is very much involved with this picture, and *he* insisted it be kept under wraps until *he* gave the okay to announce it to the trades. And Charlie told us –'

'Katharine's going to star in it, is that it?' Nick interjected swiftly, in an uneven tone.

Victor sucked in his breath. 'Yes. But there's more, Nicky. Jesus, this is the lousy part ... the screenplay Charlie's been writing ... it's an adaptation of *Florabelle*, kid.'

'*Florabelle*! My novel?'

'Yes, Nicky.'

Nick closed his eyes convulsively. 'It's not possible,' he began, the words strangling in his throat. '*It's just not possible.*'

'Yes, it is, Nicky. I reacted like you when Charlie told us. I was speechless. I couldn't believe you'd agreed to the sale, not to Monarch, knowing how we both feel about Lazarus, after all the things he did to me back in the 'fifties. That's why I was about to call you. Jake's arrival delayed me for a few minutes. Then *you* rang *me*. When I heard your voice I was sure you'd got a whiff of it. Obviously, you neither approved the deal, nor knew about it. So, how in the hell did it happen?'

Nick groaned into the receiver. 'When I sold the novel to Kort Productions I didn't make the usual option deal, with the property reverting to me if Kort didn't pick up the option and go ahead with the film. Kort bought the novel *outright*. Motion picture, television and all dramatic right – the whole enchilada. Kort, therefore, has total and absolute control, can do what they want with it. Make it, shelve it, resell it to anyone, or any company, they wish. *They*, of course, being Katharine O'Rourke Tempest, since she *is* Kort Productions,' he finished with mounting bitterness and anger.

'I don't know how she could do this to you, Nicky, go behind your back, make a deal with that bastard, a man she knows you detest, not to mention my feelings about him. It's inconceivable, goddamn it!' Victor exclaimed heatedly.

'But we know she's done it. And she and Lazarus are a team, working the angles together. I've reason to believe she's over at his house this very minute, concocting God knows what else.'

'Jesus, Nicky, I'm sorry about this development. Not only with the book but for you personally. It goes without saying you've got some serious problems there. Trouble, I'm afraid. Big, big trouble. *Capisce?*'

'Yes.' Nick drew on his cigarette nervously, then said, 'I can handle *them*. Listen, did Charlie tell you who's going to direct?'

'Alexander Vagasy's been signed. No casting, other than the lead.'

'Try to find out as much as you can. That's the front door closing. I'd better hang up. Thanks, Vic, thanks for everything. I'll get back to you tomorrow.'

'Hang in there, be alert. And look to yourself, kid.'

'I read you loud and clear, old buddy.' Nick replaced the receiver as Francesca flew through the doorway looking agitated.

'Nicky, a black Rolls is pulling in through the gates. She's back.'

He nodded, his hand resting on the telephone. He blinked, trying to marshal his swimming senses. He was unable to speak.

Francesca flung her cape on a chair and hurried into the living room. 'My God, what's wrong? You're as white as a sheet. You've had some sort of shock

'. . .' She stopped in mid-sentence, moved closer to the desk, her eyes searching his face.

'I have,' he said grimly. 'The biggest shock of my life.' He rose, went to the tray of drinks on the refectory table, poured himself a large cognac and turned to Francesca. 'Want one?' His voice was tight and bleak and she noticed that his hand holding the bottle trembled.

'Yes, please,' Francesca replied, unable to take her eyes off Nick. He looked ghastly, even ill. 'Nicky, what's happened?' she whispered, filled with sudden alarm. 'Who have you been talking to? You've obviously been on the 'phone whilst I've been walking Lada. Not Lazarus?'

'No. I wouldn't waste my breath. I'll tell you later.' Nick headed for the hearth and Francesca joined him, accepting the drink mutely. Then she said, 'I –'

The door slammed, startling her. They heard the sound of high heels clicking against the bare wood floor in the hall, and they glanced at each other quickly. Francesca noticed a muscle twitching in Nick's cheek and his eyes were icy. She remembered an expression of Katharine's from long ago: *He's wearing his flat blues.* She shivered involuntarily and she knew something terrible had occurred when she was out and her heart sank.

Katharine stood there, staring at them from the doorway, registering surprise. 'My darlings!' she exclaimed, her rippling laughter floating to them on the warm air. 'What are you two kiddikins doing here? I didn't expect you until tomorrow.' She slipped out of her sable coat and floated into the room, dramatically beautiful in wine-red velvet and a blaze of diamonds. As though somehow alerted to the brewing trouble, or perhaps aware of the tension in the atmosphere, Katharine lingered near the refectory table. 'I think I'll join you in a nightcap, my darlings,' she cried, the lilting laughter in her voice undiminished. Lifting the bottle, she poured herself a brandy, called over her shoulder, 'How could I have mixed the days up? I really *did* expect you on Friday.'

Francesca felt the controlled and deadly anger in Nick, was conscious of his heavy brooding expression and said, with a small nervous laugh, 'But you said *Thursday*, Katharine. And I confirmed it with you on Tuesday.'

'Did you, darling? Oh yes, I remember.' Katharine swung around, edged closer to the fireplace, yet nonetheless kept her distance. 'You poor things, what did you do about dinner? I fired Mrs Jennings today. Did you manage to rustle something up, Frankie dear?'

'Yes, I –'

Nick silenced her with a warning look. He stared at Katharine. 'Where . . . have . . . you . . . been?' he asked coldly, drawing the words out slowly for added emphasis.

'I guess I forgot to mention it, when we spoke yesterday, Nicky, but I was invited to a dinner party tonight.'

'*Where?*'

'At the Longleys'. You know, in Ridgefield.'

'*You are a liar.*'

Katharine blinked, recoiled slightly, and then those unique turquoise eyes opened wider, indicated surprise. 'Nicky, darling, whatever's got into you? That's a nasty thing to say.' She perched on the edge of the sofa, adopting a nonchalant

509

air. 'I told you, I've been to the Longleys. If you don't believe me, call them up and ask them.' She smiled her sweetest smile, her eyes loving, her manner insouciant. 'Shall I dial the number for you, my darling?' She half rose, the smile still playing around her mouth. She was fully aware he would stop her, would not lower himself by checking up on her.

'Don't bother,' he snapped. 'I wouldn't embarrass either one of us.' He threw her a scathing look and placed the brandy balloon on an end table. And then he moved with such suddenness, with such swiftness that he took both women by surprise.

Nick stepped forward, rushed at Katharine, gripped her by the shoulders and lifted her bodily off the arm of the sofa, swinging her out and down onto the floor. She gasped. The brandy balloon slipped out of her hands, crashed at their feet. Nick planted her firmly in front of him, stared down into her face, tightening his vice-like grip on her bare arms, his fingers biting into her flesh.

'You bitch!' he hissed. 'You rotten conniving scheming double-dealing little bitch! You come strolling in here with your smiles and your pretty talk and your wiles and your charm, behaving as if nothing's wrong. And all the while you know what you've done. What you've done to me. *You betrayed me!* And in the most contemptible way!'

'Nicky, Nicky, let go of me! You're hurting me!' she cried, squirming, endeavouring to wriggle free. 'I don't know what you're talking about. You're bruising my arm. Let go of –'

'You sold my novel!' he thundered, his face contorted with a mixture of anger and frustration. He began to shake her furiously, so that her head flew back and forth. 'The novel I sweated years to write, poured my guts into, dredged through my soul to create. The novel I loved the most of all my books, and which meant the most to me. You took it and sold it to that creep, Mike Lazarus. The man who has been my enemy for years. And Victor's enemy. What you did is unconscionable. You might as well have taken a knife and stuck it in my heart and held a cup to catch the drops of blood. I'll never forgive you for this . . . this act of treachery. I – I . . .' He was wild with the hurt and the pain of her betrayal, and unable to continue. His eyes pricked with unexpected tears and for one awful moment he thought he was going to do her bodily harm. He took a deep breath, gained control of himself, and then he flung her onto the sofa with great force, where she crumpled like a rag doll.

'Get away from me! I don't want to soil myself by touching you, you two-faced bitch.' He stepped over the broken glass and went to the window, stood gazing out, shaking from head to foot, his heart clamouring, the blood pounding in his head. Slowly an immense sorrow swamped him, and he knew the love he felt for her was draining, draining away, leaving him empty, and there was nothing in his damaged heart but the sorrow and the pain. And, as he had once hated her years ago, so he hated her again. And he knew there was no going back for them. It was over . . . the end.

Katharine lay against the sofa, gasping, fighting back her tears, her limbs trembling, her beautiful face ashen and pinched. She tried to think, but her thoughts were confused, running rampant through her befuddled brain. Why was he so angry with her? She stared at Nick's hunched shoulders, his broad back, wanting to explain, but she could not find the right words. She glanced across at Francesca helplessly and shook her head, as though denying everything.

Francesca was appalled at what she had heard and witnessed. She was terrified to speak, or move, even though she longed to flee. She did not move a muscle, sat paralysed in the chair. And she was afraid for Nick, afraid for Katharine, afraid of what he might do to her. She could not leave them alone. She groped for some understanding of his terrible accusations, wondering how he had found out.

Katharine was thinking the identical thing. Regaining her strength and her breath, she sat up, straightened the fabulous diamond necklace, and voiced this thought. 'Who told you about *Florabelle*, Nick?' She made her voice tiny, childlike, fawning.

He did not respond initially. He turned slowly, looked at her through eyes of ice. 'Victor.'

'Oh! Oh well, I might have guessed,' she murmured and looked down at her hands. 'I suppose he heard some gossip, and naturally he couldn't wait to tell you. That's typical. Now he's ruined everything, spoiled my pl –'

'You are preposterous!' Nick yelled, glaring at her, his mouth shaking. 'Suddenly, Victor's at fault, and you cleverly slide your wrongdoing under the rug. Oh God, you – you –' he spluttered and angrily balled his fists. He took a deep breath, yelled at her, 'Victor didn't hear any gossip! Charlie Roberts told him all about the deal. He's on the final draft, Alexander Vagasy's been signed as director, and Monarch are making a press announcement on Monday. *Victor got it from the horse's mouth*. You must have sold the book months ago for everything to be this far along. How could you look me in the face every day, knowing what you'd done? And why did you go behind my back? Don't answer that last question, I know why. The reason's obvious!'

Katharine stared at him, her extraordinary eyes bluer than ever and full of tender pleas. Brushing her tumbling chestnut hair away from her face, she said in a clear, bell-like voice, 'Please, darling, calm down. I started to explain – when I said Victor had spoiled my plans. I was going to tell you about the Monarch deal tomorrow. It was meant to be a wonderful surprise. I know how much you love *Florabelle*, want to get it on the screen, see it made into a film. That's why *I* bought it in the first place. I thought I could put it together. No one wanted to finance it, Nicky. You've been aware of this fact for a number of years. When I went to Michael it was solely for *you*, my darling. Don't you understand, it was for *you*, for *us*. He'd been after me to do a film, and I said the only thing I would star in was *Florabelle*. He finally agreed. He put Charlie Roberts to work. I *was* going to tell you tomorrow night. I even have Dom Pérignon – for the celebration I'd planned. And next week I was going to present you with the finished script. Charlie's final draft. I'll have it by then. But my beautiful, wonderful surprise has gone awry, because Victor told you first, and you've taken it the wrong way, and now you suddenly hate me. I haven't done anything terrible – except think of you, as I always do.' Tears brimmed, trickled down her cheeks, and her top lip quivered like a hurt child's as she lowered her head demurely.

Nick gaped at her in fascination. He thought: Oh she's good. She's very very good. He had just seen a superlative actress at work, watched a performance, and a brilliant one at that. He walked over to the sofa and stood looking down at her. A

511

faintly ironic smile played around his mouth and his voice was dangerously soft as he said, 'You did it for me, Katharine? As a wonderful surprise for me? And Victor spoiled your fun?'

Her head lifted and she proffered him a radiant smile through her misty tears. She nodded. 'Yes, darling, of course.' Believing she had convinced him, missing the underlying threat in his tone and manner, she reached out, touched his arm.

He flung her hand off him angrily and stepped away from her.

'You're a liar!' he hissed. 'A goddamned liar, and a cheat! Whatever your true motivations were I'll probably never know, but I do know one thing. You didn't do anything for me. As always, it was for yourself, your own selfish ends. I also know something else –' He paused a beat, came back to the sofa.

Nick brought his face down close to hers. 'You're having an affair with Mike Lazarus. And you've been having one for years!' In a lightning move, he yanked at the diamond necklace, clutching it in his hand before letting it fall back against her bare neck. 'Some badge of honour!' he intoned with immense disdain. 'So you've joined the long line of his whores, have you?'

Katharine was horrified and she shrank back into the cushions, brought both of her hands to her throat, covering the necklace. For the first time he noticed the diamond bracelets glittering on her arms.

As if she had been pulled upright on a tight string, she now sat rigid and straight and assumed an air of imperious dignity. 'I am not having an affair with Michael. We are business associates, that's all.'

Nick snorted with derision and strode to the fireplace. He had regained a degree of his self-possession, and unexpectedly he began to laugh. It was hard sardonic laughter that echoed the expression on his bleak face. 'Don't start playing the grand lady with me, Katie Mary O'Rourke. I know where you're coming from. And I know you're screwing around with Lazarus. But what the hell, you're well matched, I'll concede that!'

'You're insane!' Her voice was as cold and as hard as his, her face suddenly inscrutable.

'Come on, Katharine, stop lying in your teeth. I've put the many intricate pieces together. There's been talk, items in the trade gossip columns. Why, even Victor saw you having dinner with him at La Scala last year. Very intimate little tête-à-tête, from what I hear. And there's your own behaviour, which has been mighty suspicious –'

'Victor Mason again!' she screeched, flinging her head back, her eyes blazing. Something snapped in Katharine and she lost control. 'I'm sick and tired of hearing that name. Victor Mason would say anything about me as long as it discredits me. He's jealous. He's always been jealous!'

Nick's face underwent a vast change, and he peered at her intently. '*Jealous*. Vic's jealous? You've got to be out of your tiny mind. And if anybody present is insane, it's you. We're well acquainted with *your* insanity. *Jealous!*' He laughed hollowly, shaking his head.

'Of course he's jealous. I dumped him and he's never recovered from the shock. Women don't leave Victor Mason's bed voluntarily. They wait unt –'

'Are you trying to tell me you slept with Victor?' Nick interjected, his face now a picture of incredulity. 'Well, well, well, this is one for the books.'

'Yes, I did sleep with him.'

'I don't believe you. I would have known.'

'How could you have possibly known? You're not omnipotent. You were here, in the States. It happened when your sister was killed, when we were making *Wuthering Heights*.'

He felt the hackles rising on his neck and a horrifying thought twisted, snake-like, in the back of his racing mind. He glanced at Francesca, who sat pale and shrinking and huddled down in the chair. She returned his penetrating look stonily. He swung back to Katharine, poised on the edge of the sofa, erect and combative. His eyes were narrow slits in his keen intelligent face. 'You're making it up . . . to hurt me. I can –'

'No, I'm not! I slept with him. He got there first, Nicky.' She spat the words out with a feline hiss. 'I not only had a raging affair with him, I was pregnant by him. Carrying his child. His child, do you hear? And I had an abortion. It's true, Frankie knows all about it. Tell him it's true, Frankie darling. *Tell him it's true!*'

Oh my God, Nick thought. No. No. No. His chest tightened and his blood turned to icy water in his veins. Very slowly he pivoted, gazed at Francesca speechlessly. She too could not speak, merely inclined her head, then averted her drawn face.

Nick studied Katharine, perceived the triumphant glitter in her febrile eyes, the ugly, cold little smile on her face which had become a mask of deceit to him. 'You told Frankie you had an affair with Victor? That you were pregnant by him?'

'Yes. I tell her everything. She's my best friend.'

'And when did you make this announcement to her, Katharine?'

'The summer of 1956. That's when I was pregnant. We were staying at the villa. Frankie was the only person I could tell. After all, Victor was back with Arlene.'

A numbing coldness crept through him. He said to Francesca, 'And you believed her?'

'Yes,' Francesca whispered.

'You shouldn't have. She lied to you.'

Francesca gasped, her eyes flaring with shock.

Katharine screamed, 'I did *not* lie. I was pregnant by him. Almost three months pregnant.'

'You may have been pregnant,' Nick retorted in a sorrowing tone, 'but it was not *Victor's* child.' He leaned forward, impaling her eyes, and slowly his mouth lifted in a sneer. '*Victor Mason is sterile*. He has always been sterile. He can't make any woman pregnant.'

Francesca cried, 'Oh my God,' and fell back against the chair, clenching her hands.

Katharine laughed. 'Oh Nick, why do you want to absolve him always? *Sterile*? That's a joke. He has two sons.'

'Ellie's sons,' he shot back, his voice a whiplash. 'Ellie's husband ran off, a month after they were married. Deserted her. Her brother introduced her to Vic. They were construction workers together. Vic and Ellie fell in love; she started divorce proceedings. Then her husband was blown to bits in an explosion in the Texas oil fields. It happened about a month before the twins were born. Vic married Ellie immediately. He brought up Jamie and Steve as his sons, and he has been a wonderful father to them, but they were never his flesh and blood.'

Francesca had risen and was clutching the mantelpiece. She swayed slightly, and Nick steadied her, put his arm around her. 'Are you speaking the truth, Nick?' she managed, her voice cracked. 'Swear to me on your honour that you are?'

'Yes, darling, I am,' he said sadly. 'If only you'd told me then, Frankie. If only you'd told Vic. Things would have turned out so differently.'

Watching them closely, Katharine realized Francesca was unusually upset, and that her anguish had nothing to do with the quarrel which had just taken place. She said falteringly, 'Is something the matter, Frankie? What does Nick mean? What's he talking about?'

Francesca did not answer, and Nick said in a dim voice, 'Francesca and Victor were very much in love eleven years ago, and Vic was planning to marry Frankie when his divorce came through. She split with him that summer, giving a number of reasons. Apparently phony reasons, as I now understand it. And she did it because of you. It just about broke her heart, and that's one of the reasons she hid herself away at Langley all those years.'

'Oh darling, I didn't know! I didn't know!' Katharine cried, leaping to her feet, taking hold of Francesca's arm. '*I didn't know*. Honestly, I didn't. I would have kept my problems with Victor to myself if I had been aware of the facts. I would never have hurt you.'

'But you did hurt me.' Francesca lifted Katharine's bejewelled hand off her arm and dropped it quickly. She glided slowly to the refectory table, leaned against it. 'Did you lie about Victor, Kath?'

'No, I certainly did not.' Katharine ran to her, embraced her, clung to her. 'I'm telling the truth. It's Nick who is lying.' She began to weep hysterically. 'Frankie, Frankie, you're my dearest friend.'

A great revulsion for Katharine swept through Francesca, stunning her with its force and virulence. She pushed her away. 'It's Nicky I believe, not you.'

Katharine looked at her aghast, her face streaming. 'No, no, you mustn't believe him. I love you, I need you,' she sobbed brokenly. 'Please don't look at me like that, with such hatred in your eyes. I can't bear it. Oh Frankie, darling! Darling, I love you.'

'Stop saying that!' Francesca snapped. 'You don't love anyone. Only yourself. You're a monster.'

'Oh Frankie, please don't be cruel. And don't stare at me as if you think I'm something foul.' Katharine teetered, grabbed the chair back to steady herself. 'Don't turn against me. Not you, I couldn't bear it.'

'I'm afraid you'll have to,' Francesca said in a cool monotone, picking up her cape. 'I will never speak to you again as long as I live. I never want to set eyes on you again as long as I live. *You ruined my life*.' She threw the cape over her shoulders, glanced at Nick. 'I cannot stay in this dreadful house a moment longer, Nicky. Can I borrow your car to drive back to Manhattan? I'll get it back to you tomorrow. Somehow.'

'You don't think *I'm* staying here, do you?' He pocketed his cigarettes and matches and strode across the floor, brushing past Katharine indifferently, and without uttering one word to her. Katharine snatched at the back of his jacket, held on to it, pulling him back. He wrenched himself free.

'Nick! Nick!' she screamed, running after him. 'I love you. I love you. Don't go. Oh darling, I'll make everything all right. I promise you. I didn't mean to hurt you. I did it for you. I had only the best of intentions.'

He swung around so fast, so forcefully, he almost knocked her over, and she staggered back, fell against the wall. 'I second everything Francesca just said,' he told her unemotionally. 'And, as you once told your brother, I'm leaving you to God. And Michael Lazarus. He's welcome to you.'

Trembling and frightened, the tears gushing out of her eyes, Katharine moved to the doorway, braced herself against the jamb. Her gaze was riveted on Nicky and Francesca. The dog had trotted out, and Francesca was fastening the collar and leash around her neck. Nick opened the front door and carried out their bags, which had remained in the hall since their arrival. Francesca followed on Nick's heels. Neither looked back.

Katharine stood there for a long time as rigid as if she had been turned into a statue sculpted from marble.

They drove back to Manhattan, enshrouded in misery. Nick talked intermittently, but for the most part Francesca was silent. From time to time the tears would start, and she wept and dried her eyes and wept again. And they tried to console each other, tried to ease their mutual pain.

At one moment, Nick said, 'I don't know about you, kid, but I'm thinking of beating it out of New York. I have a feeling she's going to be banging on my door in a few days. And on yours. We've not seen or heard the last of her. Look, why don't we go somewhere together? Take a winter vacation?'

'I'm sure she *will* attempt to patch things up, Nick, and it's sweet of you to ask me. However, I've decided to go to Langley. It's almost the end of November, and I'd planned to leave on the tenth of December anyway, for my usual Christmas holiday with the family.'

'What about the fluffball? Want to leave her with my mother?' he volunteered, taking a hand off the wheel to pat the dog.

'Thanks, Nick, but Val will take her out to Forest Hills. I'd already arranged it.'

Once more, a silence fell between them as they burrowed down into their distressing thoughts, endeavoured to come to grips with their agony. As the car slid into Manhattan, Francesca lit another cigarette and touched Nick's arm lightly. 'I wish I had known the truth years ago, even last year. I might have been able to put things right with Victor, clear up the misunderstanding. And who knows –' Her sentence was left unfinished, and she exhaled wearily. 'But he's married now. It's too late.'

'Yes, kid, it is. And it's too late for me.'

One morning, at the beginning of December, Nick came down to breakfast at Rancho Che Sarà Sarà, feeling better than he had in weeks. He found Victor on the sun porch, his dark head buried in the *Los Angeles Times*.

Hearing Nick's swift steps, Victor glanced up, quickly folded the newspaper

515

in half, placed it next to his plate. ''Morning, old buddy. You're looking great. Sleep well?'

'Yes, I did, thanks,' Nick replied, sitting down at the table. 'I guess I was more exhausted than I realized when I first arrived. And the air's marvellous here and the pace so relaxed, it would be pretty strange if the tension hadn't left me.' He grinned. 'And you and Lynn have been wonderful.'

Victor nodded, then stared out of the window, his expression reflective. Eventually he brought his black eyes back to Nick. 'Brace yourself, kid. I don't know how to break this to you, so I'm going to give it to you straight. Katharine Tempest married Mike Lazarus yesterday. At his house in Bel Air.'

The laughter in Nick's eyes faded, and he stiffened in the chair. 'That's what you were reading so carefully in the paper, isn't it?'

Victor handed him the *Los Angeles Times*.

Nick read the story with rapidity, gave the photograph of the newlywedded couple a cursory glance. Then he folded the paper, passed it back to Victor without any comment.

'Che sarà sarà,' said Victor.

Act Three
Centre Stage
1979

''Tis time this heart should be unmoved,
Since others it hath ceased to move;
Yet though I cannot be beloved,
    Still let me love!'

George Gordon, Lord Byron

CHAPTER FORTY-SEVEN

She had come back to Ravenswood.

Once, a long time ago, for a brief and shining year, she had been happy here. The memory of that year had remained untarnished in her mind, undiluted by the passing of the years, and the memory had beckoned, had proved too compelling and irresistible to ignore.

Almost three weeks ago, on a chilly day in December, on that lonely pier in Santa Monica, she had suddenly understood that here she would find a measure of peace, the strength to begin her life again. She had never doubted for one moment that she would be welcomed; nevertheless, she had recognized that by returning to Ravenswood she was taking her first step into the unknown, into the future. She had stepped out boldly and intrepidly. She did not regret having done so.

Beau Stanton had been overjoyed to see her, touched that she had chosen to seek sanctuary with him, and gratified by her need for him and his loving friendship. And she herself had been overcome when she had first arrived, and most especially when he had led her into her bedroom. It was the room she had decorated as a young girl, as his bride, and to her amazement he had not changed one thing. It was exactly the same as it had been on the day she had left this house. Oh yes, he had redone it a number of times, Beau had told her, but he had always repeated her original scheme right down to the minutest detail.

It was an airy room of mingled whites and pale pastel tints, delicate fabrics and French country antiques. The four-poster bed was hung with a drifting cloud of white muslin, which matched the curtains at the many tall windows, and the walls were graced with exquisite watercolours. That afternoon she had moved slowly around the room, touching so many well-remembered, well-loved things . . . The pieces of blue Bristol glass on the étagère, favourite books on shelves flanking the white marble fireplace, old porcelain plates in an illuminated niche in one corner. And on the long mirrored dressing table there were her Baccarat crystal perfume bottles, the silver-framed photograph of Beau and herself, the antique vinaigrettes she had collected, each item as precisely placed as she had once positioned it herself.

Katharine sat at the dressing table on this Sunday morning, carefully applying make-up. She concealed the faint mauve smudges under her lower lashes with foundation and powder, dispelled her pallor with a touch of rouge, highlighted the unique eyes with turquoise liner and a few strokes of brown mascara. Deciding to leave her abundant chestnut hair loose, she ran a brush through it several times, stood up and dressed rapidly. She selected a tailored rose silk shirt with long sleeves, cream trousers and high wedged cream espadrilles, then added minimal jewellery. As an afterthought she sprayed herself with Diorissima scent, and left the bedroom.

Halfway down the circular staircase she heard Beau's voice echoing up to her as he talked on the telephone. She paused when she reached the bottom of the stairs, her hand resting on the newel post. From this angle she had a glimpse of him whilst remaining invisible. For a moment she studied him unobserved, thinking yet again how truly marvellous he looked for his age. He was seventy-three, appeared a good fifteen years younger, and certainly behaved as if he was in his prime, had none of the infirmities of the aged. He held his body erect, and his physique was strong, solid, trim, his handsome face firm and tanned, the healthy nutbrown complexion in striking contrast to his silvered hair. Beau Stanton had taken care of himself over the years and so he was physically fit and agile of mind. And young in heart, Katharine added to herself.

Beau shifted in the chair unexpectedly, lolled back, lifted his legs and stuck his feet on the desk, crossing them at the ankles. He saw her then. His face lit up and he waved.

She went and leaned against the entrance to the den, her vivid smile filling her face with incandescence. Automatically, her gaze drifted to the full-length portrait of herself, which Beau had commissioned twenty-two years ago. He had first seen her in the screen test for *Wuthering Heights* and had fallen in love with her instantly, before he ever met her. At Beau's request, the artist, Pietro Annigoni, had depicted her as Cathy Earnshaw. He had painted her against a background of heather-covered moors, and a fading sky filled with thunder clouds which was unearthly and eerie introduced a brooding aspect to the portrait. The dark implacable landscape threw the girl into bold relief, and Cathy-Katharine seemed to leap out, exuding life and energy and fire. The long white dress billowed around her legs and her chestnut hair streamed out behind her, as if blowing in a northern wind, and there was a wild ecstasy in the beautiful, compelling face that stared back at her now. It startled her, and she asked herself wonderingly if she had really been so lovely, so radiant. She was not sure. Perhaps the artist had exaggerated. With an imperceptible shrug she discarded these thoughts, brought her eyes back to Beau.

Silently she mouthed, 'I'm going outside.'

He nodded, smiled his understanding, and continued talking to Scott Raphael, his business manager in Beverly Hills.

As she walked down the broad white steps to the gardens, Katharine thought how strange it was that Beau had kept her portrait all these years. But then he had also kept her room intact, had not discarded even the smallest of the possessions she had left behind. And he had never remarried. She knew he still loved her. She loved him, as a dear and treasured friend and a wonderful companion. And, as in past years, she felt safe with him, unthreatened and completely at ease. These were the other reasons which had propelled her back to his house near San Diego.

When she reached the middle of the gently sloping lawn, Katharine hovered near a giant silk floss tree whose pinkblossomed branches dipped down to touch the ground. She swung around, gazed up at Ravenswood. It was a double-galleried house, with six soaring columns punctuating the façade, and its architecture was reminiscent of the great plantation homes of the pre-Civil-War South. Gleaming white, it shimmered in the January sunshine, under a stainless sky of the brightest blue. Beyond the rooftop, the rolling dusky hills of Rancho Sante Fe formed a semicircular collar around it like a Tudor ruff, and to the left there were wide, green arcadian pastures, the long grass rippling under the warm breeze. Katharine blinked, and shaded her eyes against the light, drinking in the loveliness of the landscape.

A long sigh escaped her lips. Of all the places she had lived, Ravenswood was the one she had loved the most, from the moment she had set eyes on it to this very day. It had not only afforded her peace and tranquillity but had enriched her soul as well. She wished, and fervently so, that she could stay at Ravenswood for ever. But that was not possible. Soon, very soon, she would have to leave.

Katharine meandered across the lawn and down another flight of stone steps, bypassed the swimming pool and followed a narrow winding path to the end of the gardens. Here, a bosky glade was ringed with whispering palms and exotic species and eucalyptus trees that tinged the air with a pungent smell faintly reminiscent of camphor. This semitropical glade was cool and sequestered even on the hottest days, and it was a favourite corner. Seating herself at the rustic wood table at the edge of the glade, she relaxed, retreated into her myriad thoughts, her eyes fixed on the great house glimmering in the distance. A smile of remembrance glanced across her face. Beau had brought her here for a weekend, just after she had arrived in Hollywood to make the film with him. And he had been amused and delighted by her astonishment. 'Unexpected, ain't it, ducks?' he had asked, the faint Cockney twang more pronounced. 'Who'd expect to find the son of an East End docker, born within the sound of Bow Bells, living in a mansion that smacks of Southern gentility?' She had told him the house suited him perfectly, that she could not picture anyone else living in it, and he had been pleased and flattered. And he had made love to her for the first time that weekend. A very romantic and special weekend, one she had never forgotten. He had asked her to marry him on that Saturday night. She had agreed, bowled over by this sophisticated, suave, elegant man of immense style and humour and gentleness.

Suddenly her plans for the coming weeks loomed. She reviewed everything Estelle had told her on the telephone ten days ago. None of them wanted to see her – not Ryan nor Nicky nor Francesca. There was a question mark next to Victor's name. He was in Mexico at the moment. She understood their reluctance, their reasoning. She had caused them grief and hurt and pain. They did not trust her. But they were wrong. She was different now. She had changed, and so radically she was almost unrecognizable to herself. It's over a decade, she mused. No, longer than that. It's at least twelve years since I've seen them. She pondered, fixing her thoughts on each one of them, and asked herself how *they* had weathered the years, wondering what life's hardships had wrought in *them*.

She saw Beau running lightly down the steps from the terrace, watched him striding the length of the lawn, until finally he drew to a standstill in front of her.

'How's Scott? Is everything all right?' she asked him as he sat down opposite her, lifted her hand, kissed her fingertips.

'Hello, Monkey Face. You look ravishing this morning. And Scott's in the pink. He sends you his love. I have to toddle off to Beverly Hills next week. He needs me to sign some papers, discuss a few important business matters at length. Won't you come along, my darling?'

521

'I can't, Beau.' She smiled wistfully.

'Yes, that place always did give you the willies, didn't it?'

'Sometimes. But you know very well that's not the reason I can't go with you.'

'Mmm.' Beau sat back, his eyes grew thoughtful. 'I wish you wouldn't insist on going back to New York.'

'I have to go.'

Beau shook his head. 'No, you don't.' He leaned forward, clasped her hand in his. 'Even if you only lift the lid of that box of magic the tiniest fraction, something horrid is bound to fly out and hit you in that beautiful kisser of yours, Monkey Face. I can't imagine why you should want to see those people. If I recall correctly, only Estelle and I have been around in the last ten years. Where were they when you needed them?'

She dropped her eyes, said nothing.

He waited expectantly, and held his breath. The last thing he wanted was for her to leave Ravenswood. She had finally come back, with no pressure on his part, and he hoped that she would stay. Indefinitely.

Finally she answered, 'They weren't around because they were furious with me.'

'So why in God's name do you want to see them?' he demanded, looking at her in puzzlement.

Her gaze was level, unflickering. Without hesitation she said, 'To ask their forgiveness.'

Amazement sprang onto his face. 'What could *you* have possibly done to *them?*'

'Oh, it's a long story. I don't think I'll bore you with it on this lovely day.' She laughed lightly, her sea-blue eyes dancing.

Her laughter, like her appearance, was still girlish and sweet. And it seemed to Beau, at this particular moment, that she had hardly aged at all. But of course she had. They had celebrated her forty-fourth birthday a few days ago. With resignation, he remarked quietly, 'You just got here and now you're running off again. So much for *my* famous persuasive and irresistible charm.' He chuckled softly. 'Don't look so chagrined, Monkey Face. I know you have this compulsion to see your old friends. I understand. Are you still planning to take a plane on Tuesday?'

'Yes.'

'And then what, my darling? What will you do after you've talked to them?'

'I don't know.' Her brow wrinkled. 'Maybe I'll look for an apartment in New York. Now that I've put my flat in London up for sale I don't have a home.'

'Oh but you do, Katharine!' Beau exclaimed, seizing on this point. 'Ravenswood is your home. It has been for the last twenty-two years – you simply didn't realize it. Go to New York, do what you must, and come back here. To me. Say yes quickly. Don't think so hard.'

'Perhaps.'

He pursed his lips, chuckled again. 'If I thought you'd accept, I'd ask you to marry me. But since you've said no twice in the past four years, I'm not so sure I could stand a third rejection.' He grinned and winked at her. 'Let me put it this way – I won't refuse you, should *you* decide to ask *me* to tie the knot.'

'You're a brave man, Beau Stanton. What's that saying? Once bitten, twice shy.'

He made no comment for a moment, and then he asked, 'Out of curiosity, why have you continued to say no to me?'

'I wasn't ready when you asked me. I'm not quite sure I'm ready now. I mean, to handle a one-to-one relationship on an intimate level, as someone's wife. Those relapses I've had, having to go back into the mental home –'

'Nursing home,' he corrected.

'*Mental* home, Beau,' she countered, and squeezed his hand. 'I have to face the truth, and so must *you*. I have been an awfully sick woman. Accepting this is part of my cure. But to return to your question, I must be absolutely certain I'm stable and rational, before I make a commitment to you, Beau. Or any other man.'

Leaning across the table, he kissed her cheek. 'Patience is one of my strong suits, Monkey Face. And I'm awfully proud of you, the strides you've made. You've come a long way.'

'Thank you, and I agree. I think I've done pretty well, under the circumstances.'

A worrying thought intruded into Beau's mind and, regarding her closely, he said slowly, in a sombre tone, 'You're not going to see Mike Lazarus, are you?'

Katharine straightened up and the light in her eyes faded. 'I must, if I want to get to Vanessa. And I want that more than I could ever tell you, Beau,' she said in a grave voice.

'I know, I know, my darling. But he'll never let you near the child. He's as obsessive and possessive about *her* as he was about *you*. He worships her, keeps her by his side night and day. And practically under lock and key.'

Katharine frowned. 'You've never mentioned this before, it doesn't sound too healthy to me. And how do you know? You've not spoken to him for years.'

'No I haven't, because of his treatment of you, amongst other things. And there was no point in my telling you. Not when you were ill and living in London. Now that you're back in the States and intend to stay, I believe you should understand exactly what you're facing. And how do I know about his attitude towards Vanessa? It's common knowledge in the industry that he idolizes his daughter.'

'She's also my daughter.'

'He won custody.'

'Yes . . . I was furious when he did. However . . . this past year I've come to accept the facts. I wasn't capable of looking after myself, never mind a child.'

Beau sighed heavily. 'He's an abysmal man, and what he did to you is unforgivable.' Beau gave her a pointed look. 'I've always felt *that* divorce pushed you over the edge.'

'Maybe it did, maybe it didn't. I've had to confront a lot of truths lately, and I understand Mike's behaviour now. You see, Beau, I let him down.'

'You! That's a load of codswallop, my darling. Why I –'

Katharine reached out, lightly pressed a forefinger on his lips. 'Listen to me, Beau. I *did* let him down, or perhaps I should say I disappointed him. For years and years before we married he had an image of me in his head. I was the beautiful work of art he could not buy, but which he wanted desperately, longed to add to his collection. To Mike I was priceless, flawless, beautiful, divine. Eventually he married me. Vanessa was born. I started to become – you know, weird. To Mike's shock and horror his piece of art was not perfect at all. For him it was like finding a fissure in the bronze, a crack in the marble, or a rip in the canvas . . . whatever. In other words he owned something that was actually *flawed*. Even worse, the piece of art had *always* been flawed, and despite his connoisseur's eye, he had never spotted it. Because I was not the perfect object he had envisioned me to be, he no longer wanted me. I offended him. Offended his eyes.'

'The bloody fool! Flaw or no flaw, you were, and are, one of the world's great beauties. But you *are* a woman, flesh and blood, not marble. And like the rest of us humans, you have your imperfections. He must have been unbalanced to . . . to punish you the way he did.' Beau rose, suppressing his sudden anger, an uncommon emotion for him, yet easily induced when he contemplated Mike Lazarus. He walked up and down, his hands pushed into his trouser pockets, his head bent, thinking. He sought a way to persuade her to abandon the idea of tangling with her former second husband but reluctantly acknowledged he was powerless to do anything. Because of her child.

He stopped, rested his hands on the table, bent towards her. 'Let me come to New York with you. I'll feel better if I'm there.'

She shook her head emphatically. 'No, Beau. I appreciate it, but I have to do this alone.'

'All right. I suppose there's no alternative, you'll have to approach him. But couldn't you do it on the 'phone, rather than in person?' he suggested.

'Perhaps. I'll certainly try,' she promised, glancing away. Much as she herself loathed the idea of confronting Mike Lazarus she did not have much option. *My child*, her heart said. *I must see my child*. Turning to Beau, she murmured softly, 'Vanessa will be eleven this coming June. I haven't seen her in nine years.'

'Yes,' he said. 'I know.' Beau sat down, and added, 'You're looking suddenly very pensive. Worrying about Vanessa? About seeing her?'

'No, not really. I'm very hopeful, in fact. I was thinking of something else . . . something I've been wanting to ask you for years. I never had the nerve until today.'

'Is it that bad?' A brow lifted, and an amused smile touched his humorous mouth.

'No, it's not. I was afraid of hearing the answer. I'm not any more. I wanted to know what happened to us? Why you pulled away from me after two years of marriage? Why you suggested, be it ever so sweetly and gently, that we divorce?'

'Because I was an idiot,' he laughed. Gravity entered his face. 'No, seriously, I mean it. I should have talked to you, tried to understand you, Katharine, not bowed out. I was cowardly, I believe, on reflection. And I've had years to reflect, you know. My ego came between us. You were oddly distant and removed, sexually I mean. I began to think I didn't have any appeal for you as a man, as a lover, and probably turned you off. I was fifty-one and going through some sort of male crisis, I think. You were only twenty-two, and the age difference really worried me. I persuaded myself I was too old for you.'

Katharine shook her head, said mildly, 'You should have helped me, Beau, that's true. After all, you'd had four wives before me, were much more experienced than I. On the other hand, I can't blame you . . . I was frigid, and nervous of sex and intimacy.' She looked down, twisted her hands together tightly, and then it struck her how greatly she *had* progressed to be able to pronounce these things to him.

Beau lifted her chin, looked into her face, gave her a warm smile. 'You had such an air of sexuality about you, it never occurred to me you had problems.' His eyes crinkled at the corners, gleamed wryly. 'I have a confession. After we called it quits, *I* went into analysis, trying to understand myself and you, and I soon realized your coolness had had nothing to do with me. But by then we were long divorced.'

'Weren't we foolish.'

'Oh yes, indeed.'

'I'm glad we've had this discussion. It's made me feel better.' Katharine smiled her incomparable smile. 'I've enjoyed being here with you, Beau. Ravenswood is so restful. It nourishes my spirit. So do you. You're a wonderful man. I don't know what I would have done without you through all my troubles. Knowing you were there, so strong and compassionate and caring, gave me courage.' She leaned her head on one side, and her eyes swept his face, searching. 'We were happy here once, weren't we, darling?'

'So very happy, Monkey Face.' Beau Stanton wanted to add: And we could be again. But he refrained.

CHAPTER FORTY-EIGHT

Francesca put down her coffee cup and regarded her husband through startled eyes. She said slowly, 'It would be awfully difficult for me to cancel the lunch with Nicholas Latimer. It's *today*, Harry.'

Harrison Avery appeared to be as surprised as she, when he replied, 'I didn't suggest you should cancel it, my dear. I simply said I hoped it would not lead to a meeting with Katharine Tempest. I should have thought that you and Nicholas, of all people, would want to steer clear of her. From what you've both told me, at different times, I gather she behaved abominably to you and Nicholas.'

'Well, yes, that's true of course. But what makes you think either of us would see her?' A blonde brow rose.

The kind and infinitely wise grey eyes behind the horn-rimmed glasses sharpened slightly. 'Isn't Katharine Tempest the reason for this luncheon? Aren't you going to discuss her impending return?'

'I'm sure we'll touch on it – briefly,' Francesca admitted. 'And on her too. But she's really not the reason for the lunch, Harry, although, in a sense, she was the catalyst that brought us together again after almost five years. On the spur of the moment, Nick asked me to meet him, to catch up on our lives, what we've been doing, and I accepted. Do you object, darling? I always thought you liked Nicky.'

'I do, and I don't object. I'm merely being protective of you, Francesca. I remember how hurt you were in 1968, when we started seeing each other on a more serious basis. I hate to think you're exposing yourself, that she might hurt you again, darling girl.'

'Apart from the fact that I am much much wiser, Nicky and I have a pact. We're going to support each other in our decision. If either of us begins to weaken in any way, we're going to 'phone each other instantly.' She laughed lightly. 'You know, like Alcoholics Anonymous.'

A trickle of dismay ran through Harrison Avery. Was the Tempest woman so seductive and compelling and persuasive that these two intelligent people needed to *support* each other in order to resist her request? The idea was unacceptable to him, and yet Francesca *had* implied that with her words. He thought of Katharine Tempest's brother, the Senator, and the dismay intensified. The Ambassador equated Ryan O'Rourke with pain: the pain he had caused Francesca. But as one of the world's greatest diplomats, Harrison was nothing if not tactful and he resisted the temptation to caution his wife about Senator O'Rourke, her former lover. It would be tasteless, since Francesca was impeccable. Nor did he think she would fall prey to the Senator's not inconsiderable charms; also, he trusted her absolutely. On the other hand, if she became entangled with Katharine Tempest again she might brush up against the brother, and this possibility appalled the Ambassador. He did not have much time for O'Rourke, whatever some of his Democratic Party cronies thought of the Senator. Nor did he relish his wife mixing with the Hollywood crowd who had been her friends in her younger days. Altogether too racy, particularly these days. You're worrying over nothing, he rationalized. Francesca is level-headed, sound of judgment, and mature. She will know how to handle . . .

'You're looking terribly reflective, Harry,' Francesca said. 'Please don't be concerned about Katharine Tempest, or the luncheon –'

'Oh I'm not, Frankie dear.' He was reassuring as he handed her his cup. 'May I have a little coffee please? And where is Nick taking you?' he asked, his voice full of warmth, his smile loving.

'The Carlyle . . . which is convenient for us both, and the weather is so awful we decided it was wiser to stay up town.' Adding milk to the cup of coffee she carried it to him, kissed him on the cheek. 'I wish you didn't have to go back to Washington today. Lately it has seemed as if you're never away from there.'

'I'm afraid I must.' He patted her hand. 'The President's expecting me. He has a lot on his plate. I don't envy the man, the problems facing him at the moment –'

'It's Iran, isn't it?' Francesca interjected as she returned to her chair. 'That's why he's asked you to go down there today.'

'Yes. The situation *is* explosive. I don't know how long the Shah can hold on. His grasp is tenuous, and the Ayatollah is sitting there in France, gearing up.' Harrison shook his head sadly. 'Personally I can't help thinking the Shah's days on the Peacock Throne are numbered.' He lifted his coffee cup, took a sip, went on, 'Let's not get into a discussion about the crisis in the Middle East, darling girl. I'll have nothing but Iran as a steady diet for the next few days. What's the decision from Kim? Is he coming to New York or not?'

'I promised I would give him a ring today, Harry. I think he'll want to wriggle out of it, if he can. Now that he's finally agreed to give Pandora the divorce I have the feeling he has some pressing problems to deal with.'

'Try to talk him into it, if you can. I thought he could go to Barbados with you, spend a few –'

'Have you changed your mind, Harry?' she shot back, not allowing him to finish.

He smiled. 'No, I haven't. However, I might not be able to get away. The present situation is not likely to clear up in a couple of weeks.'

'You work far too hard, darling. Remember what Dr Wallsingham said about taking it easy after your last heart attack.'

'If ever my country's needed me, it's at this very moment, Francesca,' he said. 'No one knows the meaning of duty better than you.'

She glanced away, accepting his words, realizing it was foolish to argue, and yet he did overtax himself constantly. She made up her mind to speak to his brother today. She hoped Nelson would be able to bully Harry into slowing down. She said, 'Yes, I do understand, but you must regulate yourself to shorter hours. Far better the President has you part of the time than not at all. Promise me you'll go home early every afternoon.'

'I promise.' A mischievous glint entered his eyes. 'I want a promise from you in return, though.'

'Anything, Harry.' She drew closer to him at the small table in the morning room, rested her hand on his arm. 'What is it?'

'I want you to go back to the gallery, either today or tomorrow, and look at the Marie Laurencin again. I do want you to have it, Frankie. Now promise.'

'All right, I promise, and I will go . . . after lunch perhaps. It's not that I don't like it. You know I love Laurencin's paintings, but you spoil me, always giving me presents. Christmas is hardly over, and here you are on another shopping spree.'

'And you spoil me. I don't know what my life would have been like without you, darling.' His tender smile became pensive. 'Have you been happy with me, Frankie?'

'Oh Harry *yes*, of course I have! And I am.' She studied him for a moment, her tawny eyes focused on him intently. 'I hope you've been happy with me. That you're still happy.'

'That goes without saying.' He pushed back his chair, stood up. 'I'll collect my papers from the library, have a quick word with Nelson, and then I'd better leave for the airport. I don't want to miss the next shuttle.'

'All right, darling. I'll be with you in a minute.' She watched him walk out briskly, his face grave, his mind already on affairs of state. Harrison was a tall, distinguished-looking man, with iron-grey hair and a lean somewhat severe face that belied his inherent kindness and humour. It was an attractive face, nonetheless, clean-lined, keen and intelligent. Proud of bearing, he radiated strength and determination, inspired confidence in everyone. She thought of this now, and decided it was one of the chief characteristics that had made him such a great diplomat. When she had first met him in the middle 'sixties, through his brother Nelson who was a friend of Bunky Ampher's, he had been grief-stricken and shattered. A widower for ten years or so, his only child, Simon, had just been killed in a plane crash, along with his young wife. Simon Avery had been piloting the plane, *en route* to his father's estate in Virginia, and it was only by a fluke that his two small daughters had not been in the plane. Harrison had clung unreasonably to his grand-daughters, Alison and Melanie, for the first few years after the tragic accident, had made them his entire life. One day he had realized he was being unfair to them, and had found the strength to adopt a more relaxed attitude, get on with the business of living. Francesca sighed. Poor Harrison had

had his share of misery too. But then, who on this earth hasn't? she thought, and hurried out of the morning room, across the hall and into the library.

Harrison was standing behind the desk. He glanced up, smiled, snapped his briefcase shut, said, 'I caught Nelson before he left for the bank. He's coming to Virginia this weekend after all, darling. He wants you to fly down with him on Friday.'

'That'll be lovely.' She perched on the edge of a chair. 'It has been nice having a weekend in Manhattan for once, hasn't it? Have you enjoyed it, Harry?'

'Indeed I have. We'll have to do it more often.' He joined her, put his arm around her shoulders and walked her out to the foyer. 'Now, don't forget, do go to the gallery, give some thought to the Laurencin.'

'Yes, I will, and thank you, Harry.' She embraced him, and he held her close, kissed her cheek. Francesca murmured against his shoulder, 'Have a good flight, and don't let the Chief crack the whip too hard.'

He chuckled. 'No, I won't. I'll call you tonight, darling girl.'

Francesca went back to the library, wrote several letters, perused the notes she had made about the charity concert, then picked up the telephone. She dialled the international code for England, the area digits for Yorkshire and finally the number of the office on the estate at Langley Castle.

The new bailiff answered and, after exchanging a few brief words with her, he put Kim on the line. 'Hello, Frankie,' Kim said, sounding happy to hear her voice. 'How is Harrison? How are you?'

'Fine, Kim, we're both fine. And you?'

'Not too bad. Rather snowed under with work here though, and about to leave for London. Tomorrow. The solicitors, you know.'

'How is the divorce coming along?'

'Relatively amicably, but there are some snags to iron out. Mainly financial. I'll cope. And Pandora has agreed to let me have custody of the children, so –'

'That's wonderful news,' Francesca exclaimed. 'She's getting visitation rights, I presume.'

'Correct. She didn't believe they wanted to stay with me, so I suggested she talk to them herself. I think she was pretty damned stunned when Giles, Melissa and even little Rolly, her darling angel, were quite definite about where they wanted to live. With Daddy. At Langley. Giles told me that Rolly piped up with, "We don't lub Oliber, Mummy," as usual having trouble pronouncing his Vs.'

Francesca laughed at Kim's squeaky imitation of his younger son's voice. Rolly was only three and precocious, but endearingly so. 'I second Rolly's statement. I've never liked Oliver Remmington myself. But that's secondary, of course. What about the trip to New York, Kim?'

'Well, it's a bit difficult at this particular time, Frankie, to be perfectly truthful. Now I've agreed to the divorce I really want to get it over with. And although Melissa and Giles will be back at boarding school, there's Rolly. I don't want to leave him with Nanny, not when he's given me such a vote of confidence.'

'Bring him with you.'

'In the spring perhaps. Not now. You do understand, don't you, old thing?'

'Yes, I suppose so, but I'm disappointed. On the other hand, I'm pleased to hear you sounding so cheerful, full of beans. It's a long time since I've noticed laughter in your voice, Kim.'

'I am feeling better, lovey. Actually, I think making the decision *finally*, letting her go in my head *finally* has worked wonders. And as Doris has said many times, if Pandora hadn't done a bolt with Remmington, she would have done so with someone else. I believe that too now.'

'Oh Kim I am happy for you, darling, happy to know you're not letting this cripple you. How is Doris by the way? I haven't had my usual weekly letter as yet, unless it's in today's mail.'

'Marvellous, as always. She's in the South of France for a few weeks.'

'Well, give her my love, and love to you and your little brood, Kim. Let me know what happens with the solicitors later this week.'

'I will, darling, and apologize to Harry for me. Tell him I'll be there in April, or thereabouts. 'Bye.'

''Bye, darling.'

Nicholas Latimer sat on the sofa holding both of Francesca's hands in his, his face full of smiles, his bright blue eyes sparkling. 'God, you look great, Frankie!' he exclaimed for the third time. 'And it's wonderful to see you.'

'Thank you, Nicky,' she laughed, her face registering as much delight as his. 'And we shouldn't have lost touch, should we? So silly of us. I've no intention of letting that happen again.'

'Me neither,' Nick released her hands and sat back, his head on one side, saying softly, 'I've missed you, Beauty. I've really missed you, kid.'

'And I've missed you, Nicky. Old friends, the friends we make in our youth, are always the best, aren't they?'

'Yes,' he began and halted, was momentarily thoughtful. 'It did occur to me the other day that perhaps you and I drifted apart because we reminded each other of the hurt and pain we'd suffered over the years.'

'Maybe you're right,' Francesca acknowledged.

'Sometimes, one has to start afresh in life, make a whole new set of friends, in order to forget, to begin the healing process.' He shrugged. 'Anyway, whatever prompted us to go our separate ways is really immaterial. I've continued to love you, held you in my heart, and very dearly so, Frankie.'

'Oh Nicky darling, what a lovely thing to say. And I have too. I only have the best and the brightest memories of *you*.'

He smiled, and then his face sobered. He leaned closer, took her hand in his again. 'When I first heard she was coming back, wanted to see us both, I experienced a number of emotions, ran a computer bank of memories through my head. And then, late that same night, I had to admit I was filled with sudden fear, and I wondered if you had felt that too, when *you* first heard. Did you, Frankie?'

'Oh yes indeed. I soon realized however that I wasn't afraid of Katharine, but of myself. Afraid I would permit myself to get sucked into her life once more. You must admit she *is* awfully seductive, and I've never met anyone with *her* brand of charm. I'm pretty sure your fear was identical to mine ... a very natural apprehension about being roped in by her, of becoming part of her again, and against your better judgment.'

Nick said quickly, 'You took the words right out of my mouth, Frankie. I was about to explain how I eventually analysed and rationalized my own fear – came up with the same conclusions as you.' Nick pulled a face. 'That's all I'm going to say about Katharine Tempest. The one thing we're not going to do is talk about *her* all through lunch. We've done that too many times in the past. I want to hear about you, your life, what you've been doing.'

'Me too, Nicky. First, let me get you a drink. Would you like wine or vodka?'

'Wine, please.' Nick rose and said, 'Mind if I look at the paintings?' He stood back, his eyes lingering on the Renoir above the sofa.

'Of course not.' Francesca joined him. They touched glasses and Nick said, 'To the beautiful unchangeable Francesca.'

'And to you, my darling Nicky, my dear dear friend,' she smiled.

His gaze focused once more on the painting. He took in the fresh bright colours, the delicate touch of the hazy bucolic river scene, with old boats on the bank and a man and woman standing by a broken-down shed. It was perfectly beautiful. But then he thought anything Renoir had painted was incomparable. He nodded his head in appreciation.

'I sometimes think of you when I look at this,' Francesca told him. 'It's one of my favourites, and it's called *La Grenouillère* – place full of frogs or marshy place – and Renoir painted it around 1869. The name evokes memories of your favourite New York restaurant!'

Nick grinned. 'I thought of taking you there today, but decided it would evoke too many memories of you know who, and the past. Unhappy memories too, perhaps.'

She shook her head. 'No, it really doesn't bother me, Nicky, and Harrison and I go to La Grenouille quite frequently.'

'How is Harrison?'

'Marvellous . . . well, perhaps I shouldn't say that. He's tired, Nicky, and worried to death about the situation in Iran. He went off to Washington this morning, and I know what his week is going to be like. Strenuous. He's had a couple of heart attacks, you know, and I wish he'd retire from public life, but he won't, and I'm wasting my breath.'

'No, I didn't know Harry's health was shaky. I'm sorry, darling. But he's an active man, used to being in the mainstream, and sometimes it's worse if you try to curtail a man of his type. It goes against the grain. He'll be all right. Don't worry so much.'

'Listen who's talking,' Francesca retorted with a light laugh.

Nick also laughed, then ambled around the room, stopping in front of *The Seine at Argenteuil* by Manet, and a splendid Degas called *At the Races*. Nodding to himself, he murmured, 'I'll say this for Harry, he certainly has superb taste in art.' As he turned away and went to rejoin Francesca, he passed a bow-fronted antique chest, and his eye fell on a silver-framed colour snapshot which had been enlarged. He picked it up, studied it, filled with a rush of nostalgic memories as the front lawn at Wittingenhof and the Schloss in the background sprang vividly to life. 'When was this taken?' he asked.

'Last summer, when Harry and I were staying there.'

'How is she, Frankie?' he asked softly. 'Did she ever marry?' He placed the picture on the chest, lowered himself into a chair.

'She's pretty good really. And no, Dibs never did get married.'

Before he could stop himself, he exclaimed, 'What a goddamned waste! The waste of a life.'

'Diana doesn't think so, although I'm inclined to agree with you. In her own way, she's happy, Nick.'

He pursed his lips, eased himself back in the chair, stared into the distance for a moment. Then he said slowly, 'It's Raoul Wallenberg in Lubyanka, not her father, isn't it?'

'Yes, I think so. So does Harry, and Diana and Christian are convinced of it too. But Dieter Mueller has his own ideas, insists that if Wallenberg has been there since the end of the Second World War, then there could easily be other prisoners within Lubyanka's walls, including Prince Kurt von Wittingen. He just won't give up, that man.' She shook her head.

'I almost wrote to her when the stories about Wallenberg started to break in the newspapers, but I felt it might be an intrusion, so I never did. How did she take it?'

Francesca pondered for a moment. 'Stoically, and perhaps relieved as well. But she wept for Wallenberg and his family, knowing what they had suffered, and were suffering. Of course, finding out about that poor man, realizing he was the mysterious prisoner in the Moscow jail, didn't solve the enigma of Uncle Kurt's fate. We still don't know what actually happened to him. But, as you know, Diana had always harboured the belief that her father was killed in the fighting, when Berlin fell to the Allies in 1945. And she's more than ever convinced of that now. So is Christian. Mind you, I think they desperately *want* to think their father *is* dead, buried in some unmarked grave somewhere, and not in Lubyanka with that poor Swedish martyr. They've both lived with the thought that their father might be alive all these years, and it's been sheer bloody torture for them. And it's wrecked their lives, particularly Diana's, who sacrificed her own personal happiness to look after Christian and their mother.'

'You're damned right on that score, kid! What about their mother?'

'Aunt Arabella is a very old lady, in her late seventies, and a bit senile. I don't think she's aware of what's going on any more, lives in her memories, I suppose. A few years ago, when she started to deteriorate, Diana took charge, insisted she came to live with them at Wittingenhof.'

'Diana ought to have married me – married someone!' Nick saw Diana in his mind's eye, and as always the terrible sadness enveloped him. After a moment, he turned to Francesca. 'She really is all right, isn't she, Frankie? I cared deeply for her once, and I can't bear to think she might be unhappy.'

'Oh, she's not unhappy, Nicky darling.' Francesca hesitated, then continued, 'Years ago, at Langley, Diana told me she believes there is a grand design to life, and incomprehensible as that design might be, it's meaning *would* be made clear to us all one day.' Her gaze intensified, and she held Nick's eyes. 'Didn't she ever mention this to you, darling?'

'Yes,' he said. 'Several times, and I felt she was talking about a kind of predestination. At least, that's the way I see it.'

'Yes . . . Diana truly believes that everything that happens is God's will. Her religion is an enormous comfort to her. More than ever these days, from what I've observed. Last summer, when we were in Bavaria, she told me she has a faith so monumental it leaves no room for doubt. Obviously it is her inner conviction which sustains her, gives her the strength to continue.'

Nick did not speak, and Francesca saw the hint of sorrow on his face. She reached out and touched his hand lovingly. 'Don't be sad, not for Diana. In some ways she's luckier than most people, having her religion to fall back on. And she *is* content, leads a full life. Please believe that, Nicky.'

'I do, and I'm glad she has peace. That's rare.'

'Yes . . . let me refill your glass.' Francesca took it from him, went to the ice bucket. Glancing over her shoulder, she said, 'I've read every one of your books in the last few years and loved them all. I'm still your greatest and most devoted fan, my darling. I assume you're working on a new one?'

'Naturally. It's almost finished.'

'What else is happening in your life, Nicky?'

'Not much. But I do have a son,' he said proudly, taking the wine goblet from her. 'He's four years old, and a beautiful little boy. Enchanting.'

'Then he obviously takes after his Daddy,' she teased. 'What's his name?'

'Victor.'

She blinked, then said softly, 'Oh yes, of course, that would be his name. I'd love to see him, Nicky. Perhaps you would bring him to lunch or tea one day.'

'Hey, that's a terrific idea, kid! By the way, I'm not married. I just live with Carlotta, his mother.'

'Yes, so I'd vaguely heard. She's Venezuelan, isn't she?'

'Yep. She's down there at the moment. In Caracas. Her father hasn't been well, so she flew off last week for a short stay. It's giving me a chance to move the novel along. I hope to be finished by the end of February or early March. Why haven't you continued writing? I was hoping to see another of your marvellous historical biographies published –' He broke off, smiled engagingly. 'So come on, I want an explanation. I'm your mentor, remember.'

Francesca shifted on the sofa, smoothed the skirt of her amber-coloured wool dress, and said, 'To tell you the truth, I haven't found a subject. I must be running out of historical figures, at least ones who appeal to me. I've been toying with the idea of one of the Tudors.' She laughed. 'But my books take so long, involve so much research. Oh dear, that does sound like a lame excuse, doesn't it?'

'No, not really.' He decided not to probe any further about the work and instead exclaimed, 'Say, how's that brother of yours? What's *he* up to?'

'To be precise, a divorce at the moment. His wife left him. For another man.'

'You mean Pandora Tremaine turned out to be a dud? I'll be damned. And I always thought she was something special. So did Hilly Street – that summer on the Côte d'Azur. He sure as hell was proud to be escorting an Hon. Don't you remember?'

'I certainly do. And I always found Pandora sweet and loving as well. But apparently she was miserable with Kim. Although she had me fooled for a number of years. And Kim, it seems. He was terribly distressed when Pandora did a bolt. Much more than he was when Katharine dumped him. As a matter of fact, a couple of years ago he finally confessed to me that he was genuinely relieved when Katharine decided to stay in Hollywood in 1956. As you and I always suspected, her career troubled him. He knew it would disturb their life. Doris had pointed that out. She also knew Pandora was unhappy, saw characteristics we didn't, considered her to be flighty.'

'And how is the delectable Doris? And your father?'

'Oh Nicky dear, you don't know. How could you? Daddy died two years ago. He had a stroke. Died almost immediately. Thank God. He would have hated to live out the rest of his life as a vegetable.'

Nick's eyes clouded and he went and sat next to her, took her hand. 'I'm so terribly sorry, Frankie. I know you were close to him. How old was he?'

'Sixty-eight. I'm just thankful he found Doris and married her, that they had twenty years together. Twenty years of sheer bliss. They were happy, Nicky, truly happy, those two.'

'How did Doris take it? She must have been heartbroken. She did adore him so.'

'Yes, she did. And she took it rather badly. But their daughter, Marigold, was a source of great comfort to her, as was Kim. And Doris is almost like her old self.' Francesca stood up, moved to the chest, reached out for a framed photograph. She handed it to Nick. 'This is Marigold, with Doris and Daddy at the villa in Monte Carlo, taken about four years ago.'

'What a lovely girl! Her name suits her . . . all that lovely auburn hair, like her mother. She must be twenty, or thereabouts.'

Francesca took the photograph from him, put it back on the chest. 'Yes, as a matter of fact she'll be twenty-one this summer. God, Nick, doesn't that make you feel old? I can hardly recollect what I was like at twenty-one.'

'Oh but I can, kid. You were gorgeous.' Nick looked her over appraisingly, and winked. 'And you still are. You don't look your age, not one bit, Beauty.'

'Neither do you! Now, what about lunch? I'm starving.'

CHAPTER FORTY-NINE

It was like old times for Francesca and Nicholas. They laughed a lot during lunch at the Carlyle and talked about their lives, and it was as if they had seen each other only yesterday. They were relaxed, and the old camaraderie was fully intact. The years had been bridged without one hint of awkwardness.

Frequently sentences began with, 'Do you remember when . . .' But for the most part they concentrated on the present, avoided deep discussions about the past, were careful not to evoke remembrances of old disappointments, of all the things which might have been.

Nonetheless, at one moment Francesca did become introspective and she turned to Nicky and said, 'It's funny, but I always thought I'd have a very different life from the one I've had. I imagined I would marry young, have babies, live in a nice country house, perhaps have a pied-à-terre in London, and grow old comfortably with the same man. You know, lead a staid life, become a matronly lady and eventually a grandmother. As it is, everything turned out quite the opposite.'

He had caught a certain wistfulness in her tone, and examined her face closely. 'Any regrets, Frankie?'

'Regrets are a waste of time, Nicky.' She laughed, and the laughter came easily, then added, 'Oh a few, I suppose. But then again, too few to mention, to quote that popular Sinatra song.'

Nick's smile reflected hers. 'You certainly did it your way, kid. Just as I did. And that particular film's been shot. It's in the can. There's no way we can shoot it again, is there?'

'Not really, darling. Unless you believe in reincarnation.' She played with the stem of her wine glass, said in a sudden rush, 'You were once very angry with me, Nicky, and I would like to –'

'I angry with you? Never!' he exclaimed, his surprise apparent. 'You've imagined it, Beauty.'

'No, I haven't. It was in the early sixties, when I refused to go with you to see *The Sabres of Passion*, when I vowed I would *never* see it. I'd like to confess something. I saw it twice.'

'*Twice.*' He flashed her a mildly reproving look which hinted at amusement, and laughed, 'And you never let on, you secretive little minx.'

'I suppose I was a bit shame-faced, embarrassed to admit it. Anyway, the first time I cried all the way through, hardly saw one scene clearly. So I went back.' She gave him a sidelong glance, her eyes filling with merriment. 'You could say I'm a glutton for punishment. Anyway, I thought it was –' She paused, finished with a sly grin, 'I thought it was the whole enchilada.'

Nick chuckled. 'Oh Frankie, you're too much. Whyever didn't you tell me?'

She shrugged, asked in the softest of voices, 'How is he, Nicky?'

Her question so startled him, Nick's jaw almost dropped. She had never mentioned Victor in previous years. But, he supposed, her wounds had healed by now. As his own wounds had healed. It would be strange if they had not, he thought, then said, 'Vic's the same. He hasn't changed much. In fact, hardly at all. He's been a widower a number of years, you know.'

'Yes, I'd heard. I'm sorry,' Francesca murmured. 'And he's never remarried, has he?'

'Nope.'

'Does he still live at the ranch?'

'Sure he does. He loves that place. He spends most of his time at Che Sarà Sarà. Jake Watson's with him a great deal. Jake runs Bellissima for Vic, which has become a big successful company. They're producing pictures for theatrical release, and for television as well. Vic doesn't make too many movies himself any more, as I guess you know. Although he did finish one last year.' Nick's face lit up. 'My screenplay. It's damned good, even if I do say so myself. It should be out soon. You ought to go and see it, kid.'

534

Her pretty mouth lifted in a smile. 'Maybe I will, and give you a critique,' she teased. 'And what about the boys?'

'Both married,' Nick answered and grinned. 'Vic's a grandfather, if you can believe that! And he relishes the role. Jamie has two daughters, Steve a son. Vic's very proud of his family, is devoted to them, gets tremendous pleasure from the grandchildren. And —' Nick stopped, took the menus the waiter was proffering, handed one to Francesca, and said, 'How about a nice fattening dessert, Beauty?'

'I don't think so! Oh well, I'll look anyway.' After a moment she placed the *carte* on the table, glanced around. The restaurant in the Carlyle had been jammed when they arrived, but it was much less crowded now. As she turned to the right, her eyes widened and she swung her head, picked up the menu and held it in front of her face. Squeezing Nick's knee, she whispered, 'We should have gone to La Grenouille after all. Estelle Morgan's sitting at the other side of the room. *With Katharine.*'

'Oh Christ!' Nick's mouth tightened in aggravation. 'So she's finally arrived in New York, and wouldn't you know we'd be the first to run into her. What goddamned luck we have. The worst.' He cursed under his breath, then said, 'Hell, kid, we can't very well sit here hiding behind these.' He took the menu away from Francesca, laid it down with his, and asked, 'Where are they sitting?'

'To my right. Diagonally across from you.'

Focusing on Francesca, he said, 'How does she look?'

'Nicky! You're impossible. Here we are, trapped, and you want to know how she *looks*. My priority is to get out of here, before Estelle sees us. You know what she's like. She'll be over in a flash. I'm surprised she hasn't landed on us already. Unless they haven't seen us yet. This place was awfully crowded until a few minutes ago.'

'We're going to finish lunch,' Nick pronounced decisively. His tone was even firmer as he continued, 'We are not going to run away. She's not going to drive us into the street. We'll just brazen it out. Besides, what the hell can *she* do to *us*? She's hardly going to sit down at our table. The worst that can happen is that she'll say hello. We're civilized people, we'll say hello in return, and she'll be on her merry way.'

He motioned to the waiter, ordered coffee, lit a cigarette. As he did so he glanced to the right of the restaurant, spotted Estelle and Katharine, glanced away quickly, but not before his eyes had registered an image of *her*. Chestnut hair pulled back. Face as pale as ivory. Eyes of a unique incomparable turquoise hue. And they had been staring directly at him. He felt himself tensing and a sudden chill swept through him, despite the warmth in the restaurant.

'You'd better fasten your seat belt,' he muttered, touching Francesca's hand. 'Estelle is bound to materialize any second. Katharine's seen us.'

'Oh *God*. Let's leave, Nicky.' Francesca smiled faintly at the waiter, thanked him as he placed the demitasse before her.

'Okay. I guess you're right. When the waiter comes back I'll get the check.'

'Too late, I'm afraid,' Francesca whispered, stiffening next to him.

'Francesca, Nicholas darling! Fancy running into you two!' Estelle planted herself solidly at the other side of their table, smiling hugely.

Francesca merely nodded, and Nick said, 'Hi, Estelle', made a motion to rise.

Estelle waved him back into his seat. 'Please, darling, don't disturb yourself. I just popped over to ask you to join us for a drink. You will, won't you? Katharine's longing to say hello. When you've finished your coffee, of course.'

Nick felt Francesca's fingers biting into his knee.

'Thanks Estelle, but I'm afraid we can't. Please give our regrets to . . . Katharine,' he said.

The journalist was about to attempt persuasion, but she instantly saw the unfamiliar coldness creeping on to Nick's face, and was aware of the hostility in Francesca. Stuck up snob, Estelle said to herself. Cold bitch. She beamed her attention on Nick. 'Oh dear, Kath will be so disappointed. She was very excited when she saw *you*, Nicholas.' Estelle hovered, her expression pleading.

'Sorry, Estelle, we can't,' he repeated. 'Nice seeing you.'

It was a dismissal and she knew it, and she flushed, backed away. 'Nice seeing you too,' she parroted. Giving Francesca a peremptory nod, Estelle bounced across the room to the table in the rear, bridling and filled with mortification.

'I really can't bear her,' Francesca said. 'I'm still irritated by her behaviour ten days ago, when she came to do that blatantly bogus interview.'

'I couldn't believe it when you told me. But that's Estelle; she's always had *chutzpah*. Where in the hell is the waiter? They're never around when you need them. Might as well finish the coffee.' Nick poured for them both, and added, 'I'm not going to scurry out of here like a scared rabbit.'

The words had barely left his mouth when he caught his breath, glancing up. Katharine was standing before them, looking cool, poised and elegantly beautiful in a white woolcrêpe dress and turquoise jewellery that reflected her spectacular eyes.

'Hello, Frankie, Nicky.'

They murmured their greetings, and Nick attempted to get up.

'No, please don't stand. This won't take a minute,' Katharine said, speaking rapidly, in a low voice. 'I understand why you have refused to see me and I don't blame you at all. You must hate me. What I did to the two of you has been on my conscience for a long time. I owe you both an explanation. I'm staying here in the hotel. Suite 2203. Will you come up for ten minutes? Please?'

Neither of them could speak. Finally Francesca found her voice, said, 'I'm afraid . . . that's quite impossible.'

Nick remained mute.

Katharine smiled diffidently, aware of their discomfiture, their awkwardness. She inclined her head slowly, graciously. 'Think about it for a few minutes, discuss it. One rarely gets an opportunity in life – to clear up unfinished business. And the three of us do have a lot of that.'

She smiled again, and returned to her table. Within seconds she left the restaurant, gliding out with her head held high, and without looking at them. Estelle hurried after her.

Nick's eyes followed Katharine. He was surprised at his reaction to her. For years he had experienced a variety of intense and explosive emotions when he dwelt on this complex and baffling woman, a woman whom he had loved more than any other. Anger, hurt, hatred and bitterness had smouldered in him, and yet, at certain times, these feelings had been counterbalanced by a terrible yearning, a longing for her that ate like acid into his very soul. Now, finally, after twelve years, he had

536

gazed upon her again – and he had felt only a strange calmness. Perhaps he was invulnerable to her after all. His fears of recent days were unexpectedly allayed.

Swinging his head, he gave Francesca his attention, said, 'Well, she's right, you know, we do have a great deal of unfinished business.'

Francesca gaped at him. Her mouth curved down into a grim line. 'My God, you capitulate pretty easily!' she gasped, clenching her hands in her lap.

Nick frowned in puzzlement at himself, for he was still sifting through his present emotions. He said thoughtfully, 'It's amazing, Frankie. *I felt nothing.* No, that's not exactly true. I did experience a twinge of curiosity about her life, what she had to say to us.'

'Curiosity killed the cat.'

'Not always. I must admit, I *would* like to know why she sold *Florabelle* ... amongst other things. Don't you want to know why she lied in her teeth about Victor?'

'It's not important any more. What difference does it make now? And what makes you think she'll tell us the truth, Nicky?' She knew he wanted to go up to that suite and confront Katharine, and she was afraid she would be coerced into accompanying him.

'It would resolve everything in our minds, wouldn't it, Frankie? I'll tell you something else, darling, she's haunted me for years. I think I'd like to expunge her ghostly presence from my mind and my heart once and for all. Yes, I honestly think I have to follow up on my unfinished business with . . . my dark lady of the sonnets.'

Francesca nodded, and her genuine love and friendship for Nicholas Latimer rose to the surface. She remembered all the good he had done her in the past, his loyalty and devotion and moral support. Her attitude softened, and she told him, 'I can understand the way you feel, Nicky. You loved her so much, and had a long and complicated relationship with her. It must have been sheer torture for you over the years, when you contemplated her betrayals, asked yourself why she treated you the way she did.' She took his hand, held it tightly. 'But I'm not letting you go up there alone. You see, Nicky, I don't trust her.'

'I'm not sure that I do either, Beauty.' He laughed. 'But we're old hands at the Tempest game. She can't fool us any more. And thanks for agreeing to come with me. Now, I'll pay and then we'll take the elevator up to the twenty-second floor to hear what the lady has to say for herself.'

They sat, the three of them, in front of the huge plate glass window overlooking Madison Avenue. Nick and Francesca had positioned themselves on the sofa together; Katharine was perched on the edge of an armchair facing them. There was a hint of expectancy and tension in the air, but to the naked eye all three appeared to be self-contained and surprisingly at ease. In all truth, it was Francesca who was the most nervous. She smoothed her skirt several times, crossed and uncrossed her legs, and then sat back. She looked at Katharine through wary eyes and her face was guarded.

Katharine's well-remembered voice broke the silence which had settled over them after the initial greetings. 'Thank you for coming up to the suite. I wasn't sure you would. This is not easy for me ... for any of us, I know ... quite painful really. So, I'm not going to waste time with small talk. I'll get straight to the point.'

'Yes,' Nick said. 'Why don't you.'

Katharine smiled ever so faintly, looked past him into the distance, her expression reflective. She said, 'When I decided in December that I wanted to come home, get back to my roots, to live in the States permanently, I knew I couldn't be in the same city as you, under the same bit of sky as you, without approaching you both. I cannot put the clock back, change what I did, but I would like to tell you the truth now, after so long. I'm not asking you to exonerate me. After all, I did hurt you both. But I hope you might find it in your hearts to forgive me.'

When neither of her former friends uttered a word, Katharine continued quietly, 'Frankie, I must address myself to you first.' Her eyes were levelled on Francesca's, and they were as steady as her voice. 'I was not pregnant by Victor Mason. In fact, I never had an affair with him. Victor was patently uninterested in me as a woman. He was only intrigued by Katharine the actress.' She sat back in the chair, and the relief she was experiencing was like a balm to her. Part of the slate had been wiped clean.

Francesca's face was impassive, betrayed none of the thoughts and feelings clamouring inside her. She glanced at Nick, whose expression was grim, then brought her eyes back to Katharine. She said, in an infinitely cold little voice, 'Then why in God's name did you tell such a rotten lie?'

'I never intended to lie, or place the blame for my pregnancy on Victor, honestly I didn't. His name just popped into my head, and I'd said it before I could stop myself, and then it was too late. I couldn't retract it. I was stuck with that lie.'

'Were you really pregnant by someone, or was that a lie too?' Francesca demanded.

'No, I *was* pregnant. That morning at the Villa Zamir, when I confided in you, I did so because I was sick with worry. I had to unburden myself. As we talked I began to feel as if I had betrayed your trust in me as well as Kim's. I hadn't ever intended to name the father, Frankie, but you pushed so hard, asked so many questions, I was hoist by my own petard. And I saw everything in a different light, through your eyes, as you would view it. I knew, suddenly, that I couldn't tell you who the real father was. I was embarrassed and ashamed about what I'd done. I looked at you, at one moment, and you were so *young*, so untouched, so unspoiled by life, and so very innocent and I thought you'd despise me. Not only because I'd slept with someone else, but also thrown away my relationship with *your brother* for another man. I decided you wouldn't understand, that you would take Kim's side.' Katharine halted, intensified her gaze. 'You see, Frankie, approval was always vital to me, and particularly *your* approval. I couldn't stand the idea of your condemnation.'

'How little you really knew me,' Francesca intoned. 'I never passed judgment on anyone, then or now. I certainly wouldn't have criticized you, whatever my feelings for Kim. I'm afraid you underestimated me.'

Katharine nodded. 'Yes, I did. But getting back to that morning – I was also worrying about the father of my child. He loved me, but he was very much married, had been married for years. I didn't think he would get a divorce, and I didn't want to marry him. On the other hand, he was a man of genuine feeling, and I didn't

538

know how he would react if he knew about the baby. I was sure he would try to prevent the abortion. I was confused. I began to say all this to you, if you remember, Frankie. Do you?'

'Oh yes, I remember. I haven't forgotten one thing about that particular morning.'

Katharine caught the sarcastic and biting edge to Francesca's tone, but she had no intention of reacting. Her purpose was to make a clean breast of this, without emotion. It was the only way she could deal with it. 'I was appalled at my unanticipated predicament. I'd made my mind up that you would be disgusted with me. I didn't know how to explain the reasons for my involvement with the man in question. I must emphasize again, *I thought you would not understand.* It struck me, all of a sudden, that you *would* understand, perhaps even be sympathetic, if the man were so special no woman could resist him, and therefore could not be blamed for succumbing to his charms. I had an instant mental picture of Victor Mason, and so I said his name.'

I don't believe I'm hearing this, Nick thought. His concentration had been riveted on Katharine, and now he said, 'Who was the father? Who were you pregnant by?'

'Ossie Edwards.'

'I'll be a son of a bitch!' Nick cried involuntarily. He had often wondered about her pregnancy over the years, asked himself who the father *could* have been if it *was* true. He was staggered.

Puzzled, Francesca asked, 'Who's Ossie Edwards?'

'The cameraman. On *Wuthering Heights*,' Nick informed her. He took his cigarettes out of his pocket, struck a match.

'Of course,' Francesca said. 'I remember him. He was a lovely man.'

'And talented,' Nick added. He pinned his penetrating blue gaze on Katharine. 'He certainly photographed *you* like a dream.'

'Look, that's not why I became involved with him,' Katharine exclaimed quickly, her voice sharpening for the first time. 'I wasn't using Ossie, if that's what you think.'

Nick made no comment, but his eyes held a cynical glint.

Katharine said, 'I hadn't intended to digress, get off the main points, but I think I have to explain about Ossie. May I?'

'Sure,' Nick said laconically.

'To understand my relationship with Ossie you must both cast your minds back to 1956, to *me* as I was at that time. I was twenty-one, making my first movie, in a starring role opposite one of the great superstars of all time. I may not have seemed it to either of you, but I was riddled with insecurities, about myself, my talent, my looks, my ability to pull it off. I was a novice amongst a lot of hard-boiled professionals. And that set!' She shook her head, turned to Nick. 'You weren't around much, you were back here, but later you heard what it had been like. On the set, on location, the situation was explosive. Emotions were running high, intrigue was rife, everybody was vying for position. Believe it or not, I felt out of my depth.'

Katharine shifted in the chair, stared out of the window, a faraway look in her eyes, 'Victor and Mark Pierce were staunchly behind me, but they were mainly concerned with the picture, the final product, and not with me as a person. They were tyrannical at times.' Her eyes flew to Francesca. 'You *know* that's true.'

'Yes,' Francesca admitted.

'There was a lot at stake for Victor and Mark. And as sweet as Victor can be, he's forever scanning the bottom line, and the budget, and the shooting schedule. He's very tough. Yes, he helped me, Mark helped me. With my performance, and that's all. I was often floundering, and I felt so *alone*. My one true friend on that movie was Ossie Edwards.'

'I've followed everything, and I get the general idea. But why did you become personally involved with him?' Nick probed, fascinated.

'He was a father figure to me perhaps. The father I'd never really had. He was so kind, Nick, and concerned for *me*, concerned for the woman as well as for the actress. He was loving and gentle. He boosted my self-confidence about my work in a way no one else ever had, or could, not even Mark and Victor. He also made me see myself as I really was then. Through the eye of the camera, he called it. I was never particularly vain. Ossie didn't promote vanity in me, but he did clarify my beauty for me. He taught me how to *react* to the camera, to play to it, to use it, to give it my innermost thoughts and feelings. With all due respect to Victor and Mark, if anyone made me a star it was Ossie Edwards, although they might think otherwise. All this aside, that sweet man offered me shelter, protection, refuge, call it what you will, on that difficult set. As I said, I was insecure, emotionally unstable, and I had many doubts about myself, and about my sexuality –' She stopped unexpectedly, dropped her eyes, played with the large diamond ring on her finger.

'You know my problems in that area, Nick. They were more pronounced in those days. I was a virgin.' She hesitated, went on. 'I had repulsed Kim continually, and I began to think there really was something wrong with me. Ossie led me into sex rather sweetly, gently. Perhaps because he was an older man he succeeded where Kim had not. He didn't frighten me off as Kim had. Mind you, Ossie didn't clear up my problems with . . . intimacy either.' She gave Nick a direct unblinking stare. 'Only you were able to accomplish that feat.'

For the first time, and against his will, Nick felt a flicker of compassion for Katharine. I always thought I knew her completely, understood her totally. But there are so many facets to this curious woman, he thought. Grudgingly, he said, 'I can't say I blame you for Ossie. It's a tough business. Goddamned rough.' He thought of Mike Lazarus then, and said no more. And his heart hardened towards her again.

Francesca, who had been listening as closely as Nick, said, 'But how could you pull a name from thin air? It was so – irresponsible.'

'Yes, I suppose it was. But I've just explained my motivation, Frankie. I thought you would be more sympathetic if the man involved was someone special, irresistible.'

'Why didn't you tell me the truth . . . tell me about Ossie? I would have understood.'

'Would you?' Katharine rose, walked to the sideboard, poured herself a glass of Perrier, added ice and a slice of lemon. 'Oh excuse me, would either of you like anything?' she asked, turning to them.

They both declined, and she came back to her chair. Looking at Francesca over the rim of the glass, her eyes flared brightly. 'Why didn't *you* tell me about Victor, Francesca? If I'd known about him none of it would have happened in the first place.' She leaned forward, her stare more intense. 'I wasn't trying to hurt you. I wasn't being malicious. I didn't *know* you and Victor were having a love affair. Surely, if nothing else, you must believe that.'

Francesca flushed slightly. 'Yes, I do.' She dropped her eyes, studied the tip of her boot. 'Only Nicky and Diana were acquainted with that fact.'

'You accused me of ruining your life on that horrendous night in Connecticut when we last saw each other. But hasn't it ever occurred to you that your own negligence and secretiveness were contributory factors in the situation that finally developed?' Katharine murmured gently. 'Not that I'm trying to shift the blame. What I did was bad enough.'

Francesca passed over this mild chastisement. 'I've always wondered . . . My peach dress. Did you spill the red wine on purpose?'

'No. It was an accident. I was nervous about the baby, overwrought, in fact. I did slip.'

'And Ryan? Did you interfere in our relationship?'

'I did talk to Ryan. I listened to him. Agreed with some of the things which worried him. So, if you call that interfering, then yes, I did. However, I never told him not to marry you, nor did I say he would be miserable with you. Those things were in his own head, planted by my father, although Ryan wouldn't admit it at the time. If you don't believe me, you can speak to Ryan right now. He's in New York. In his apartment in this hotel. We had dinner last night, cleared up our own misunderstandings and grievances. You see, Frankie, one of the reasons I have been estranged from Ryan for a number of years is because of his treatment of you. Please, let's settle this. Pick up the 'phone and ask for his apartment. It's 1208.'

'That's not necessary.' Francesca bit her lip. 'Are you saying it was your father who was opposed to me?'

'Yes. Ryan wouldn't tell you when he broke off with you. He was afraid of my father, and in a strange sort of way, protective of his relationship with him. I will say this, I am glad you never married him, Frankie. He wasn't good enough for you. Not then, at least. He's different now. He booted my father out of his life a number of years ago, along with all those aides and sidekicks my father had foisted on him. Patrick O'Rourke's spies. Ryan came to understand all this, perhaps because of me, the things I had said to him. We had a *rapprochement* in 1969, short-lived as it was, and I told him the way things really were. Gave it to him straight. He never spoke to me again. Until a couple of days ago. It was then I learned he had repudiated our father, become his own man.'

'I see.' Francesca sighed, closed her eyes wearily, her mind in a turmoil as she relived part of her past.

Nick stood up impatiently, walked over to the window, looked down at Madison Avenue, finally pivoted to Katharine. He was bursting with questions, and he exclaimed, 'Why did you sell *Florabelle* to Lazarus?'

'I never intended to, not at first,' Katharine began, and took a sip of the Perrier. 'The picture I'd made for Monarch in 1964 had been a big box-office hit. But you know that. Mike was after me to do another movie for them, badgered me constantly about it. I saw him from time to time, after all we were old friends, and he never let up. In 1967 he approached me once more. Almost as a joke, and, in a way, to make him stop pestering me, I said I would only make *Florabelle*. No one was more surprised than I when he agreed.' Katharine smiled sadly. 'My God, you think I'm manipulative, Nicky. He's the master of that technique. Before I could turn around he'd bought a copy of the book, read it, made an offer to my agent for the whole package. That is, the dramatic rights which Kort owned, and my services as an actress. Suddenly he was drawing contracts, hiring Charlie Roberts, signing a director, setting the wheels in motion. I suppose you could say I was railroaded.'

'*You*. Come on!' Nick threw her a disbelieving look.

'I realize you find that hard to accept, but it is the truth. Naturally I was worried,' Katharine told him, exhaling. 'However, I managed to convince myself you would be pleased in the end. Thrilled. You'd longed to see the novel filmed, were aware no other producer had shown interest. Suddenly I felt I'd done you a great favour. Wishful thinking on my part perhaps. In any event, I decided to keep it a secret until I could show you Charlie's finished script. I knew it would be great. He's one of the best in the business. In my mind I somehow turned it into a lovely surprise for you. But everything blew up. You found out before I could tell you.'

Nick frowned, uncertain about her explanation. Was she still an inveterate liar? He exclaimed quickly, 'But you're only telling me the same story you told me in 1967.'

'I'm not going to invent reasons just to satisfy you, confirm your suspicions of me. That's really the way it was. I admit I was preposterous in those days, that I could convince myself of anything, justify any action as a good deed. I've come to understand that now.'

'That's nice to know,' Nick snapped sardonically. He flung himself into a chair. 'You used to spin incredible yarns about where you'd been when you disappeared. Where did you go?'

'I wandered around like a lost soul sometimes, filled with the strangest of feelings, fighting a terrible pain in my head. Not really a headache, but a kind of pounding that never ceased.' She met his piercing eyes. His flat blues, she thought, and nodded as if to herself. 'It may sound weird, but then I was weird in those days. Often I *did* go to church, or I sat through three and four shows of the same movie. There were other evenings when I went up to Michael's, talked to him endlessly about art and movies, listened to him expound about his business. We were old friends, Nicky. Don't forget, I'd known him since 1956.'

'So you *were* having an affair with him!' Nick asserted.

'You're wrong. I was not!' Katharine cried, her voice rising. 'Of course, Mike had courted me for years, pursued me like a mad man, even when I was married to Beau,' she added in a softer tone. 'He fascinated me, I admit that. I suppose it was his power, his strength of personality, that great domain he ruled over. You once called it his fiefdom. It was, and is. Mike had idolized me for as long as he'd known me. Even before that. He had seen me in Les Ambassadeurs with Victor, and according to him he had been immediately bewitched. He had placed me on a pedestal. I was a priceless piece of art to him. He adored my beauty, worshipped me. I was all the more desirable because I was unattainable, don't you see?' Nick nodded, and she explained, 'His library at the apartment . . . it was like a shrine to Katharine Tempest. Filled with over a dozen photographs of me, framed in gold.'

542

Her dark brows lifted expressively. 'Nutty, I suppose. But then Beau Stanton used to say Mike was unbalanced. I was mixed up, Nick, unstable, and, not unnaturally, I was enormously flattered. Here he was, one of the richest and most powerful men in the world, literally grovelling at my feet. That's heady stuff, a narcotic to any woman, but especially to one who is unbalanced herself, as I was then.'

'When did you become involved with him on a more intimate basis? When you were still with me?' Nick asked in a tight voice.

'Yes,' she answered gently. 'I had always flirted with him, tantalized him, if you will. But I had never slept with him. Never. I swear I hadn't . . . not until 1967, just after I bought the house in Connecticut.'

Nick held himself still. His chest tightened, and he took sharp rein on himself. 'Why? Why? When you loved me.'

'I really couldn't handle you any longer, Nick. You see –'

'Was I so difficult?' he interjected, his eyes opening widely.

'No. It was *me*. You see, Nick, you knew me too well, knew too much about me . . . my problems . . . my faults . . . my craziness. I thought I was going to lose you. That's the only way I can explain it. I don't know if it makes sense.'

He shook his head, sorrow ringing his face. 'Genuine love is being able to look at a person and see their faults and their problems and still love them, Katharine.'

'I realize that now. I didn't then. And I also understand now that at that time in my life I was not able to face the thought of another loss. I'd lost my mother in death, my father and Ryan were alienated. I was unable to cope with the possibility, no the probability, of losing *you*.'

Unable to take his eyes off her, Nick plunged in deeper. 'Why did you marry Lazarus?'

'I was pregnant by him.' Katharine's face tightened, and her eyes were huge and full of pain, and reflected the emotions she had been concealing.

An unacceptable thought entered Nick's brain, and he asked slowly, in an inaudible voice, 'Were you pregnant by him when you were still with me?'

'Yes. I'm sorry, Nick.'

'How could you be so sure it was his baby?'

'I was. If you remember, *we* hadn't slept together for a number of weeks, almost two months. I was only *just* pregnant when I married Michael.'

'You could have had an abortion,' he began and clamped his mouth shut, hating himself for saying such a thing, thinking of his own child.

'Not a second time,' she whispered.

'No,' he said miserably, 'I don't suppose you could.'

'I'm so very sorry that I've had to hurt you again, Nicky. But I was determined to tell you the truth today, and to tell you the truth, Francesca. I know I've caused you grief in the past. But I have paid, believe me I have. And I still pay every day of my life.'

Francesca lifted her head and searched Katharine's face and she thought: I don't know why I believe she has suffered, and yet I do. She said, 'Yes, I'm sure you have had your share of pain, Katharine.' Francesca turned to Nick, observed his strained white face, was conscious of his inner torment. She went to him, put her arm around his shoulders. 'Katharine is at least right in one thing, Nicky darling.

It's better we know all the facts, painful as they may be. Now perhaps we can finally resolve everything in our minds.'

'Yes,' he mumbled.

Katharine's eyes swivelled from one to the other. She took a deep breath, and sat back, relaxing her tense muscles. After the longest moment, she said, 'From the bottom of my heart I ask you to forgive me . . . Nicky, Frankie. *I beg you.*'

There was a silence. Francesca spoke first. 'I forgave you a long time ago, Katharine. I just never forgot, that's all.'

'Please, could you say the actual words to me?' Katharine asked softly.

'I forgive you,' Francesca replied, her tone an echo of Katharine's.

'Thank you, Frankie. That means a lot to me. More than you will ever know.' Katharine looked at Nick, waiting.

His eyes met hers, blue impaled blue. He said, 'Unlike Francesca, *I* had never forgiven you, Katharine. But I do forgive you now. How could I not? You have shown immense courage today, facing us the way you have.'

'Thank you, Nicky. Thank you so very, very much.' Katharine went to the window, blinking, feeling the prick of tears. She composed herself, swung round to them. 'Is there any possibility that we might all be friends again?' Something in their faces warned her not to press this point, and she murmured, 'Well, perhaps it's too soon for that, too much to expect at this moment.

CHAPTER FIFTY

Katharine came out of the Seventy-Sixth Street entrance of the Carlyle, nodded to the doorman and walked briskly down the street. She crossed Madison Avenue and made her way towards Fifth, sauntering in the direction of the Frick a few blocks away. During lunch at the hotel she had asked Estelle to go with her to view one of her favourite art collections, but the journalist had a deadline and had had to return to her office.

It was a sparkling afternoon, cold but sunny and crisp and the sky was an unblemished blue and there was an electricity in the air. Manhattan electricity, Katharine thought. There really is no other city like it in the whole world. I am glad I came back. It has revitalized me. To her, London was masculine, comforting, smacked of leather and tweeds and log fires, whilst Paris was feminine, beguiling, evoked silks and satins and fragrant scents and candlelight. Ah, but Manhattan, she mused, it's androgynous, neither male nor female. She raised her head, looked up and then around her. Canyons of steel and shimmering glass and yellow cabs and Cadillacs. New York . . . it was the glitter of diamonds, the bubbles in champagne, the sleekness of mink and sable. It had a pulse, a beat, a special tempo, was challenging, exciting and utterly unique. My favourite city of all the cities I've known, she added under her breath.

She continued to observe as she strolled along, thinking how vibrant and alive everything seemed. But then the entire world looked different to her these days, for she saw it now through clearer, more perceptive eyes. Her mind strayed to Nick and Francesca, and she wondered if she would ever hear from them again. She hoped she would. If she did not she would be sad, but the decision about renewing their friendship was out of her hands, and she refused to speculate. She had recently taught herself to concentrate on the business at hand and of the moment, not to look to the future. The future was an imponderable.

She smiled to herself as she went into the building where the Frick Collection was housed. Beau worried about the future, her future anyway. He had called on Monday evening, anxious to know about her progress in New York, her immediate plans. She had told him of her chance encounter with Nick and Frankie at lunch that day, and he had sounded pleased they had met with her. However, she knew he was worrying excessively about her meeting with Mike Lazarus at five o'clock today, which she had mentioned in passing.

Katharine herself was no longer concerned. She felt calm, in control, and purposeful. And she was not going to dwell on Michael Lazarus. Before she left London, Dr Moss had reminded her she must not endeavour to solve problems before they presented themselves. Anticipatory despair, he had called it. And that, according to the renowned psychiatrist, was one of the chief causes of the debilitating anxiety she had lived with most of her life. How wonderful Edward Moss had been to her over the years. She owed her recovery, her very sanity, to him.

Well, I've come to look at paintings, to enjoy a little beauty, not contemplate illness, Katharine told herself firmly, and went through into the room where the Fragonards hung. For the next thirty minutes she moved around slowly, gazing at the art, entranced by the breathtaking portraiture and landscapes, which seemed to her to have a vitality and sensuousness that was unrivalled. No wonder Fragonard is considered to be one of the greatest painters of the eighteenth century, she thought, standing back, her head on one side.

'Fragonard originally intended those panels for Madame du Barry, you know.'

'Nick!' Startled to hear his voice, Katharine spun around swiftly. He stood a few feet away, a trenchcoat slung over his arm. He was smiling at her and she saw at once that his eyes were mild and friendly, the hostility of two days ago washed away. She returned his smile, and he stepped forward, took her hand, leaned over and kissed her cheek in the most natural manner.

'What are *you* doing here?' she asked.

'The same as you . . . looking at paintings. Aren't they extraordinary?'

She turned to regard the panels. 'Yes. Now that kind of talent truly fills me with awe.'

'Yes,' he said, positioning himself next to her. 'Our contributions to the arts do seem puny in comparison.'

'Tell me about Madame du Barry.' Her eyes turned to his face.

'Oh yes. Fragonard had intended them for her, when she was the mistress of King Louis XV of France. But the King died, Louis XVI ascended to the throne, and she retired to the country. The Revolution came and ruined Fragonard, who was essentially a court painter. He went to live in Grasse, where he decorated the

545

house of a friend with these panels. They're called "Progress of Love," and as you can see they depict love and gallantry of the period most beautifully. I can look at them for hours, endlessly fascinated by the exquisite detail.'

'I can too. And Madame du Barry? I can't remember my French history – whatever happened to her?'

'She was eventually arrested by the Revolutionary Tribunal on charges of treason, trumped up, of course. She died on the guillotine at the age of fifty. Not an enviable way for such a beauty to die. Gruesome really.'

'Yes.' A faint shadow struck Katharine's face fleetingly, and then she laughed. 'You know so much about history.'

'I studied it at Oxford, remember? And I'm blessed with a photographic memory. Come on, let's stroll around,' he said, taking her arm.

He told her more about Fragonard, and Madame du Barry and Louis XV, and he answered her questions with cordiality, warmth even, and she was astonished at the absence of awkwardness between them. Suddenly he changed the impersonal to the personal.

Nick said, 'It's not a coincidence . . . running into you like this. I was just talking about you a little while ago. With Estelle. I called her. Looking for you. She said you were coming here.'

'Oh.'

'Frankie also tried to 'phone you earlier today but your line was busy, and she had to rush out. She's buying a Laurencin painting and then going to Virginia. She plans to call you when she gets back early next week.'

'I'd like that.' There was a slight hesitation, and then Katharine murmured, 'I've carried a terrible burden of guilt about Frankie for years. She accused me of ruining her life, and that has weighed heavy. She is all right, isn't she? She is happy?'

He smiled wryly. 'I don't like that word much. It's so meaningless. What's happiness?' His shoulders lifted in a shrug. 'But I'm sure she's happier than most people. She has a nice life, Harrison's a good guy. But she feels badly about the other day. Frankie thinks she didn't finish your unfinished business.'

'I'm not sure I understand . . .'

'She believes you've suffered a lot, considers her accusation to have been unwarranted in a sense, made in anger, in the heat of the moment all those years ago. Frankie said to me today that no one ruins another person's life, that we are ultimately responsible for our own destinies. She said if anyone is to blame, it is she herself, for not trusting the man she loved, for condemning him without a hearing, repudiating him out of hand. Frankie takes full responsibility for her life, and I think she wants you to know that, Katharine. She's been worrying because she didn't say enough to you, or explain this, from what I gather. She asked me if I thought you truly understood that she's not harbouring a grudge. You do, don't you?'

'Yes.' There was a hesitation again, before Katharine stated, 'You are though, aren't you?' Harbouring grudges, I mean.'

'Maybe.' The furrow deepened on his brow. 'But I realized last night that I don't hate you any more.' He exhaled heavily. 'Hatred is such a wasted emotion, like the desire for revenge. It ravages the soul, eats away at a person's core. And there's always collusion, complicity in a relationship. One party is never solely to blame.'

He added quietly, 'Sadly, we all have flaws . . . flaws which we carry with us all of our lives.'

'Yes, and we have our frailties as well. And to be imperfect is to be human. I was thinking about *you* last night, asking myself if you had really forgiven me, truly, deep in your heart, or whether you just said you had . . .' Her voice faded away.

'Have you ever known me to say anything I don't mean?'

They were not looking at the paintings now. They were looking at each other. As he stared down into the pale and delicate face upturned to his, he saw that it had hardly been touched by time at all. Yet it *had* changed. An ethereal quality reposed there, and a serenity. And the eyes held a clarity and a deep wisdom that was wholly new. They really are turquoise, he thought, neither green nor blue, but a curious mingling of those shades. They were dazzling. And to his utter amazement he felt a familiar stirring in his blood, and then that same old breathlessness, a sense of expectation, of anticipation clutched at him. His gaze lingered on her.

For her part, she was noting the finely-drawn lines around the eyes and in the lean and clever face, detected the tiredness in those bright cornflower depths. The puckish irreverent mouth had a sterner curve to it, and the blond hair was speckled with grey. The boyishness had fled, had been replaced by a certain austerity, and there was authority in his face, though there was nothing unyielding about him, she could tell that. And despite the differences the years had wrought, he did not look fifty-one years old.

Katharine's gaze was as unwavering as Nick's. She continued to scrutinize him, endeavouring to understand his attitude towards her, and unexpectedly she felt a warmth pervading her and her heart reached out to him.

He did not miss the imperceptible flicker in her shining eyes, nor did the plea on her face escape his notice. Instinctive knowledge of her, his old understanding of her psyche, filled his heart to overflowing, and he stepped forward, took her hand in his, was vaguely conscious of its iciness.

'You need to hear me say it again, don't you, Kath?' he murmured, using the diminutive for the first time.

She nodded.

'I forgive you, I truly do, and from the bottom of my heart.'

'Thank you, Nicky.'

As if spellbound, they stood in the centre of the room, isolated by their varied emotions, oblivious to the people now drifting around them. It was only a brief moment; it seemed like eternity to Katharine. He released her hand, drew her with him to the door. 'Let's get out of here,' he said, and they left the Frick without exchanging a word.

He guided her down Fifth Avenue, still without speaking, and they walked seven blocks in total silence. Abruptly Nick stopped, looked down at her and grinned. 'Where are we going?'

'I don't know. I thought *you* did!'

They were standing on the corner of Sixty-Third and Fifth. He glanced ahead, saw the green-tinted tower of the Plaza Hotel in the distance. 'You always used to like tea at that little hole-in-the-wall yonder,' he joked. 'Shall we?'

'Of course, Nicky.'

He questioned himself why he was doing this as they ambled towards Fifty-Ninth

547

Street. It was asking for trouble, wasn't it? And he had enough troubles to contend with at the moment. His personal life was already one unholy mess, without Katharine Tempest in the wings, cued to take her one-man audience by storm. On the other hand, like Francesca, he felt there was unfinished business between Katharine and himself. He had so many questions, the answers to which had eluded him for years. Only she could supply them. And something about her *had* touched him in the Frick, had moved him even. When he and Frankie had left her at the Carlyle on Monday afternoon, they had both commented on Katharine's apparent rationality, her unusual calmness. *Was* she stable? And if so, why? What happened to her to bring about the changes? He had a compulsion to unearth the reasons if he could, and in so doing perhaps find some answers about himself.

Within a few minutes they were pushing through the revolving doors of the hotel, and being shown to a table in a corner of the Palm Court. Nick helped her off with her black mink coat, threw his trenchcoat on top of it in the vacant chair. 'Listen, I've got to make a 'phone call. To Nanny,' he explained. 'I told her I'd only be gone for an hour, that I'd be back to take the boy for his afternoon walk. I've got a son, you kn – '

'Yes, I do,' she interjected. 'Estelle told me. But I feel awful, depriving him of you. Please, let's go. We can have tea another day.' She started to rise.

He pressed her back into the chair, shook his head adamantly. 'No, it's all right. Sit down, and order me a vodka martini. I don't usually drink at this hour, but what the hell.' He smiled at her, and the puckish quality she thought had vanished for ever leapt out at her. 'Do you want a glass of wine or a glass of champagne?' Nick asked, searching his pockets for a dime.

'No, thanks. You know I've never been a big drinker. I'll order tea.'

'Okay. Back in a minute,' he said brightly, swinging away from the table, and there was a jaunty spring to his walk as he hurried out. He looks better than he did on Monday, she thought, and frowned, trying to pinpoint this change. It struck her he was suddenly exuding the infectious gaiety which had been so appealing in the Nick she had once known and loved. Did she still love him? Do not think of such things, she cautioned herself. You cannot revive the old feelings, the old yearnings. It is too late.

The waiter came and she ordered and took out a packet of cigarettes, lit one, sat back, waiting for Nick to return. She peeked at her watch. It was just turning three-thirty. She had plenty of time before her date with Michael Lazarus.

In no time at all Nick was back. 'I promised him two bedtime stories tonight. I believe it's called bribery.'

'Oh Nicky, really, I do think you – '

'Hey, be quiet, lady. Now, what else did Estelle tell you about my private life? She's bound to have exaggerated, added a few colourful details to introduce a bit of spice. Very imaginative, our Estelle.'

'I know Frankie never liked her, and Estelle *is* a strange person, but she's been very loyal to me, Nicky,' Katharine said, sounding softly reproving.

'Yes, you're right to defend her. She's *okay*. I was only kidding.'

Katharine smiled, half shrugged. 'Anyway, she didn't tell me very much, merely mentioned your son, said you live with a Venezuelan beauty. Your public life I know all about . . . your books and your screenplays, I mean.' She tapped her cigarette in the ashtray, leaned across the table, her smile widening, 'What's your little boy's name?'

'Victor.'

'Oh.' She pulled back, said quickly, 'I tried to speak to his namesake when I was staying at the Bel-Air Hotel, but his housekeeper said he was in Mexico.'

Nick eyed her speculatively, his face sobering. 'Do you also want to explain everything to Vic?'

'Yes. I think I owe it to him.'

'He won't be back for another week, Kath.'

'Then I shall call him then. Would that be all right, do you think?'

'Sure. Oh good, here's your tea and my martini.'

A quietness fell between them. Katharine poured tea, added lemon and sugar; Nick stirred his martini, lit a cigarette. Finally he raised his glass to her. 'Down the hatch,' he said.

She lifted her cup, repeated the toast.

'You always did look good in blue, Kath,' said Nick, his eyes roaming over her appreciatively.

'Thank you, so did you,' she quipped, focusing on his pale blue Turnbull and Asser shirt, darker blue tie, navy blue cashmere blazer.

'We do it to play up our eyes, don't you know?'

Merriment spilled out of Katharine. 'I'll never forget going to a party in London a couple of years ago, and hearing one guest tell another that I always wore sapphires because they matched my eyes, but that all my blue gems were actually artificial. And the second old biddy said, "Oh really, my deah, how extraordinary. And are her eyes artificial too?" Katharine mimicked in an exaggerated English accent. 'It made my day, Nicky.'

He said, 'There's never been anything artificial about your beauty, my darl –' He cut himself off abruptly.

Katharine looked away, and when she turned back to him she said, 'Could I ask you a question, Nick?'

'I'll trade you one for two.'

'It's a deal. I've been wondering for years why you never ever told me about Victor and Frankie.'

'Very simple. She made me promise not to say a word to anyone, including you.'

'I see.'

'*My* first question is: What have you been doing all this time? While you've lived in London. You've certainly not made any pictures.'

Without hesitation, she said, 'Getting my head straight. I've had almost nine solid years of deep psychiatric care and treatment for schizophrenia. Dr Edward Moss, who's been likened to R. D. Laing, pronounced me cured over a year ago, and I'm really quite proud of myself.'

Nick was silent, chilled to the bone at the thought of what she had been through. Eventually he said, 'It must have been sheer hell, but I'm glad you took care of your problems, Kath.' He was reflective momentarily, then added, 'I've never seen you quite like this. So serene.'

'Yes, I do feel good. You have a second question?'

549

Nick took a swallow of his drink, playing for time. He had wanted to ask her about her relationship with Lazarus, but had now lost his nerve. And so he said, 'You told me Ryan had dumped your father. What about you? Have you had any contact with him over the years? Or since you've been back?'

She shook her head, and her eyes darkened. 'No. When I arrived in the States, a few weeks ago, I did 'phone him in Chicago. I was thinking of going to see him.' She grimaced. 'My father didn't want to see me, and I decided to let it go. It suddenly occurred to me that I'd been wasting my time and my energy on my father and Ryan. When you've coped with the problems I've had to cope with – and alone – you gain new insights, formulate new priorities. But Ryan was always special to me, so I did finally write to him, and he agreed to meet me whenever I planned to be in New York.' She took a sip of tea, went on, 'When we did get together, Ryan told me he had broken with my father, and I almost laughed out loud. I'd wanted revenge, had sought to get back at my father for everything he had done to me, and to Ryan, and just like that – ' She snapped her fingers and finished, 'It was no longer necessary. Ryan had done the one thing I'd been after him to do since he was a boy. He had become his own man. Strong. Independent. Incorruptible.'

'I'm glad Ryan had the guts to strike out on his own, Kath. I'm even more delighted that you have walked away from your father . . . that's one of the sanest moves you've ever made.'

Katharine's smile was warm. 'I think so.' She looked at her watch. 'I'll have to go in a few minutes. I have a date . . . with Michael.'

His face tightened. 'Oh, you hadn't said. I'll get the check. Can I take you wherever you're going?'

'You can walk with me if you like. His office isn't far from here. On Park.'

'I know the building. Global-Centurion nobody can miss.'

The heavy sarcasm floated over her head. Gently she said, 'I'm hoping he's going to let me visit my daughter, Vanessa. It's been nine years since I've seen her, Nicky.'

Oh Jesus, he thought, filled with a rush of compassion. He said, with a small frown, 'Surely he will. No one could be that cruel.'

'I have good vibrations, Nicky. I think he'll consent.'

As they walked to Park Avenue, Katharine told Nicholas about the acrimonious custody fight for the child, the reasons for her divorce from Lazarus, her pain and anguish about the child, as she herself had striven to regain her mental health. Nick was appalled at Lazarus's callousness, as Beau Stanton had been; he was also impressed with Katharine's determination to recover, for her daughter's sake as well as her own. From what she was saying, it was Vanessa who had given her the motivation, the will to come to grips with her life. Nor could he help noticing her self-possession, her calm demeanour, as she recounted the details, and this pleased him enormously.

'I'd like to know how things turn out – with Vanessa,' Nick said when they reached the Global-Centurion skyscraper. 'Will you call me?'

'I don't have your number.'

'It's the same. But perhaps you've forgotten it. Or lost it.'

'Oh no, Nicky, I still have it in my book.'

'Until later then.' He kissed her cheek. 'Break a leg.'

She smiled and was gone.

Mike Lazarus received her with cordiality, ushering her into his gargantuan office handsomely furnished with French antique furniture of the Empire period and priceless works of art.

'Come and sit over here, Katharine my dear,' Lazarus intoned, leading her to a seating arrangement composed of sofas and chairs covered in fir-green cut velvet. Hanging on the wall above these rather overblown pieces was a Rubens of incalculable worth. Katharine eyed the painting surreptitiously, instantly hated it, chose to sit on the sofa where it was out of her line of vision.

'Thank you for seeing me, Michael,' she said.

'My pleasure.' He poured champagne, carried the flutes over to the coffee table on a small silver tray. 'Especially since you are looking so fit, my dear.'

He took a seat opposite her, his eyes rapidly appraising her from head to toe. He could not conceal his astonishment, nor did he attempt to do so. 'You are very beautiful, Katharine. Quite remarkable under the circumstances.'

'Thank you. I must say, you look well yourself, Michael.' She spoke the truth. Lazarus, who was sixty-eight, had retained his muscular, sturdy appearance, seemed to be in robust health. Yet he had visibly aged. She regarded him with impassivity, struck by the immense hardness in the man, which had only been magnified by time, and conscious of the controlled power, the dark stealth that surrounded him.

The pale cold eyes, sharp with calculation, watched her. Most people trembled in his presence. He did not frighten her one iota. 'Did you receive the letter and the reports from Dr Moss?' she asked, deciding to waste no time.

'Indeed I did, my dear. And I'm delighted to know you have made such a miraculous recovery.'

She smiled sweetly. 'I'm not sure one could call it miraculous, Mike. It's taken a number of years.'

'Yes, yes.' He lifted his glass. 'To your continued health, my dear.'

'And yours.' She took only a tiny sip, placed the flute on the onyx table. 'I'd like to see Vanessa. You always said I could when I was really better. I am.'

Lazarus nodded, steepled his fingers, looked excessively ponderous. 'I don't know . . . I think perhaps you ought to get settled first, find an apartment, establish yourself. I hate to think that we might start a relationship between the two of you, only to find it crumbling. It would be very upsetting to the child if she became fond of you and then you had – '

'A relapse, Mike?' Katharine interrupted softly, raising one perfectly shaped dark eyebrow. 'Is that what you're getting at?'

'No, of course not.'

Katharine sat back, almost complacently, crossed her legs and clasped her hands in her lap. She met his cold visage unflinchingly and with an icy implacability that matched his. She said, 'I am going to tell you a story, Michael. And when I have finished I hope you will not keep Vanessa from me any longer. If you do so, I'm afraid I will have no alternative but to start proceedings against you, resort to the law for visitation privileges. I realize you could keep me tied up legally for a great length of time. However, whether I win the suit or not is of no real consequence. Once

551

those legal documents are processed by the courts they become public record, as you are well aware. They are available to anyone . . . I am thinking, in particular, of the press.' A slow smile spread across her face and she paused to light a cigarette.

He said curtly, 'What of it?'

Her smile intensified. 'I don't think I would have any trouble getting an enormous turn-out if I called a press conference. I have become a bigger superstar than I ever was, since I disappeared so mysteriously from the public eye. It always happens that way, doesn't it? James Dean, Bogart, Marilyn Monroe, not to mention Garbo. My unavailability, my desire for total privacy has made me into a legend. My films are constantly replayed on television, and the Carnegie, here in New York, is about to have a week of Katharine Tempest classics.'

'Get to the point,' Lazarus snapped impatiently.

'Imagine the coverage I would get if I told those sympathetic reporters of my yearning to see my only child . . . kept from me by *you*. It would – '

'Don't be so ridiculous. I won custody of Vanessa in a *court of law*. I did the only thing any father would do. I was thinking of the child. You were incapable of looking after her, or of even visiting her. Don't you realize you would have to explain yourself, reveal where you have been these last few years. You would have to tell the press about your mental breakdown.'

'Oh yes, I know I would,' she said, not in the least ruffled. 'I would also recount to them the story you are about to hear. When I finish that story your image will not only be irreparably damaged, the general public will detest you. I wonder how that would affect Global-Centurion stock?'

'Threats are not going to get you anywhere!' he exclaimed angrily. 'I receive you in the most pleasant manner, and you abuse – '

'May I tell you the story?'

His mouth tightened. 'If you so wish.'

'I do.'

Twenty-five minutes later Michael Lazarus rose and went to his desk. He asked his secretary to telephone his apartment and replaced the receiver. He regarded Katharine through stunned eyes. In spite of the rosy glow from the lamps, his face looked grey and his whole body had visibly sagged. He was mesmerized by this beautiful composed woman sitting on his sofa, and when the telephone jangled he took a moment to answer it.

'Hello, Brooks. Is Miss Vanessa there? Please let me speak to her. Thank you.' He covered the mouthpiece, hissed, 'If this is a – Hello, Vanessa. No, I'm not working late. I'll be home for dinner. I called because I have a lovely surprise for you. Do you remember I told you last week that I'd heard from your mother's doctor, and that she was much better?' He listened, nodded, continued, 'Well, my love, she's so much better, she's been able to travel to New York. She's right here with me now in the office. She's coming to see you.' He listened again, smiled, said, 'No, now. Immediately. Simpson will bring her over to visit with you for a short while.' Another pause on his part. 'Good. Yes, do. I'll see you for dinner, Vanessa.' He hung up. His hand rested on the receiver. 'She wishes to change her dress. We have to give her a few minutes.'

'Of course, Michael,' Katharine smiled.

He said, 'If this is one of your tricks – '

552

She held up her hand, and her expression reflected her disgust. 'Do you honestly think I would lie about a thing like *this*?'

He paled. 'No, no. I'm sorry I made that remark. Excuse me.'

Katharine was so startled to hear an apology from him she blinked. Mike Lazarus never apologized to anyone. She was even more taken aback when he came to the sofa, sat down, took her hand in his. 'As a matter of fact, I am very sorry for so many things which have to do with you and me, Katharine.'

She gently removed her hand after a moment, and said, 'I hope you realize I won't repeat what I've told you to a soul. I presume you wouldn't want me to. After all, we don't wish to hurt . . . anyone, do we? Cause them undue misery. Particularly a child.'

'Vanessa? You can't possibly tell *her*!'

'I have no intention of doing so.' Katharine stood up. 'I shall go to see her now though.'

Katharine was greeted at the door of the Lazarus triplex on Fifth Avenue by Brooks, the English butler, who had been the mainstay of the household for twenty years.

'Hello, Madame, it's lovely to see you,' Brooks said, taking her coat.

'It's nice to see you too, Brooks.'

'Thank you, Madame. Miss Vanessa's waiting for you in the drawing room. Do you wish me to take you in to her, Mrs Lazarus?'

'No, thank you, Brooks. I think I can find my way.'

'Yes, Mrs Lazarus. Would you like any refreshments?'

Katharine shook her head. 'No, not right now. Thank you, Brooks.' He nodded, and she walked slowly across the entrance foyer. For the first time since she had come to New York, Katharine felt a stab of nervousness. Her legs trembled and her heart felt squeezed. She had almost reached the drawing room's large double doors when they opened and an elfin child peeped out inquisitively. Large green eyes widened and the pretty mouth formed a perfectly round O, but the child made no sound.

Katharine increased her pace, her face wreathed in smiles. 'Hello, Vanessa,' she said drawing to a standstill.

'Hello,' Vanessa's eyes grew even bigger, and she opened the door wider. 'Won't you come in, please,' she added solemnly.

Katharine did so, and stood looking down at her daughter, her heart clattering, her eyes bright with happiness.

Vanessa dropped a small curtsy and held out her hand. 'I'm very pleased to meet you . . . Mother.'

'Yes,' Katharine answered softly. 'But we've met before you know, when you were a very little girl.' She clasped the small hand tightly in her own.

'I remember . . . I've been waiting for you.'

'Your father thought I should give you time to change your dress.'

'Oh I don't mean *now*! I mean I've been waiting for you to come back, ever since *then*, when I was a very little girl. It's taken you a long time.'

The tears rushed to Katharine's eyes and she had to look away quickly. She choked them back, immediately swung her gaze to Vanessa. 'And I've been waiting to come back to you too, darling. Shall we go and sit down?'

'Oh, yes.' Vanessa, who was still clinging to Katharine's hand, led her across the room. 'You sit there, and I'll sit here, and we can look at each other for a long time, Mother. That's much better than looking at a photograph, isn't it?'

'Absolutely,' Katharine agreed, striving to keep her composure. She met the unabashed bright green gaze head-on, relaxed against the cushions and allowed herself to be minutely and painstakingly scrutinized. Her daughter was small and delicately made, as she herself was, and the face staring at Katharine was a childlike miniature version of her own, except for the dusting of freckles across the nose and the cheeks. But unlike Katharine, Vanessa had her maternal grandmother's vivid colouring. Her curly hair was the same burnished red-gold as Rosalie O'Rourke's had been, her eyes an identical tourmaline hue. Katharine had always been struck by this resemblance when Vanessa had been a baby, but it was even more pronounced in the eleven-year-old girl. She has a look of Ryan also, Katharine commented silently. She's an O'Rourke through and through.

After a great deal of assessing, Vanessa confided, 'Daddy has always said you are beautiful, and I knew you were, because I've seen all your movies. But you're much more beautiful in person.'

'Thank you for your lovely compliment, darling. I think you're beautiful too.'

'Do you really?' Vanessa sounded doubtful, eyed Katharine carefully, her head cocked to one side. 'If only I could get rid of these freckles I'd feel much better. I've tried all kinds of lotions but they're just stuck. Do you think they'll ever go away?'

Katharine could not resist smiling at Vanessa's mournful tone. 'They might, but I doubt it. Anyway, I like them. They're very distinctive, you know.' Katharine nodded, adopted an appropriately solemn air. 'If I were you, I'd try to keep them, Vanessa. Freckles are a mark of great beauty. Helen of Troy had freckles,' Katharine improvised, then went on, 'and *she* had such a gorgeous face, it launched a thousand ships.'

Vanessa looked both impressed and delighted. 'Oooh! I didn't know! Perhaps I'd better not use any more of those icky lotions and creams. I'm glad you're not a big tall person. The girls at school call me shrimplet, that's smaller than a shrimp, and I hate it. But now I can tell them *you're* a shrimplet too, can't I?'

'Yes,' Katharine laughed. 'Well, it's the first time I've ever been called that, but I rather like it.'

'So do I then.' Vanessa's smile slipped away and gravity settled in its place. 'Why did you wait so *long* to come back?' she asked with unnerving forthrightness.

'I was very sick, darling. I had to get better first.'

'What was wrong with you?'

'Hasn't your father told you?' Katharine hedged.

'Yes, he said you were in a nursing home because you were tired. But that didn't sound right to me. I mean, how can you have been tired for nine years. Don't you sleep well?'

'I didn't, but I do now. I had a nervous breakdown actually, darling.'

'Did it hurt?'

'Yes, a little bit. In my head. But the pains have gone. I'm cured.'

'I'm glad.' Vanessa thought hard, then said, 'Did you have to see a shrink?'

'Yes, Vanessa. Do you . . . do you know about shrinks . . . psychiatrists?'

'Oh sure,' she said off-handedly, looked unconcerned again. 'Now that you've come back, how long are you going to stay?'

'I'm going to live in New York. Permanently.'

'Hey, that's neat! Then I'll be able to see you all the time, won't I?' she cried, her elfin face lighting up with happiness. It instantly fell. 'You're sure you're not going away again?'

'No, I'm not. I'm staying in America,' Katharine reassured her. She added gently, 'Of course how often I see you depends on your father.'

'Oh don't worry about Mike. He's no problem.' She looked at her mother, wrinkled her nose. 'You haven't said you like my dress. I put it on for you. Specially for you. It's my favourite.'

'It's beautiful, darling, and green is the loveliest colour on you. It echoes your eyes. Stand up, turn around, let me look at you,' Katharine smiled. She was enjoying this effervescent, completely natural and confident little girl. It was a small miracle she was so unspoiled.

Vanessa was parading up and down, doing small pirouettes. 'I love velvet . . . Mother. Do you?'

'Yes. Particularly wine velvet.'

Vanessa stopped modelling, ran to the sofa and flopped down next to Katharine. She looked up at her, the gravity in place again. 'I used to be mad at you sometimes. You know, for leaving me. But I think I understand now. You couldn't help it, could you?'

'Oh my darling, no, of course I couldn't. I wouldn't have left you, not for anything in the whole world. You're my baby.' Katharine reached out and touched Vanessa's cheek lovingly. 'You're the very best part of me, my darling.' Katharine felt the tears stinging the back of her eyes and she opened her arms to her daughter. Vanessa came into them swiftly, clung to her with a child's tenacity. Katharine stroked her bright and shining hair. 'I've loved you more than you'll ever know,' Katharine told her. 'Since the very first minute you were born.' As she raised her eyes, blinking, Katharine saw Mike Lazarus in the doorway, watching them. She released Vanessa, said, 'Here's your father.'

Vanessa straightened up, jumped off the sofa, raced across the floor. 'Hi, Daddy!' she cried flinging herself at him. 'Everything's neat neat neat! Mom's going to stay in New York and we're going to see each other all the time and it's going to be great great great! And Mom's staying to dinner.' The girl swung around. 'You are, aren't you, Mommy?'

Katharine smiled, looked at Mike, not knowing how to respond. Vanessa pivoted to her father, grabbed him round the waist unceremoniously. 'Hey, Pops-Pops, Mom's waiting for you to invite her!'

Hugging his daughter to him, Mike said, 'Will you stay, Katharine, my dear?' His voice was pleasant and he was smiling lightly, but his eyes were frigid and unsettling.

'Thank you, Michael. I'd like that very much,' Katharine responded, thinking she had never seen a more unlikely pair than Michael and Vanessa Lazarus.

CHAPTER FIFTY-ONE

Katharine sat at the desk in the living room of her suite at the Carlyle. She picked up the felt-tipped pen and began to write in her neat meticulous script. After marking the page with the date and the time, she filled the sheet of thick smooth paper with her impressions of the day, her thoughts and her feelings about all that had happened in the last few hours.

Thirty minutes later, she put down the pen and closed the book, turned the key in the small brass lock. The book was ten inches by ten inches, bound in soft kid, the colour of the leather resembling the deep deep blue of lapis lazuli. On the front, gold embossed letters read: *To V.L. from K.T.* Early in December of 1978, when Katharine had decided to return to the States, she had gone to Smythson's in Bond Street and had the book custom-made to her specifications. It was not a diary as such, but rather a notebook of memoirs and intimate, wandering thoughts, often simple everyday happenings, and each entry truly revealed the woman. It was intended for Vanessa, at some time in the future when she was a little older, and Katharine hoped the notebook would be illuminating, would help her daughter to understand her on a variety of levels, to know her better. When she had been undergoing psychiatric treatment, and at a stage when she was recovering, Edward Moss had suggested to Katharine that she write in this manner, using the exercise as a kind of catharsis. She had quickly acquired the habit, enjoyed expressing herself through words. And later she had hit on the idea of producing her 'hours of the day', as she called the notebook, for her child.

Returning the book to the drawer of the desk, Katharine stood up, stretched and walked over to the sideboard. After filling a tall glass with Perrier and ice she went into the bedroom, made herself comfortable on the bed and picked up the telephone. Her first call was to her brother at his house in Georgetown. They chatted about generalities for a while, and Ryan reiterated his invitation, tried to cajole her into coming to Washington at the end of the coming week. He was anxious for her to meet his wife Anne, and his two small children, Toby and Patricia. Katharine declined graciously, made a tentative date for the middle of February, and they hung up. She spoke to Estelle Morgan, invited her for dinner that evening, then glanced at her watch. It was six-ten, three-ten in California, the ideal time to reach Beau.

Katharine had a great deal to report about her activities of the last three days and the time she had spent with Vanessa. 'She's very endearing,' she told Beau. 'In some ways not a bit like I expected. Singularly unspoilt, despite her father and all that money. Precocious, but not in a bratty way, you know, rather old-fashioned. I call her my little old lady. And she's very outspoken, sometimes unnervingly so, fast on the draw too.'

'Kids today are very sophisticated,' Beau laughed. 'They even make my jaw drop at times, and I've seen and heard more than most. And her father? How's he been behaving himself since he agreed to the visits?'

'So far so good, but remember I saw him on Wednesday ... today's only Saturday. Not much time to really judge. But he's been pleasant, in a removed sort of way, removed with me, I mean. He's perfectly marvellous with his daughter. They're pals, if you can believe such a thing. I think he just might have mellowed a little.'

Beau Stanton hooted at the other end of the line. 'Now that is hard for me to believe.'

'But it's true, darling. He took us to lunch today at Tavern on the Green, and actually cracked a few jokes. Vanessa says the most outrageous things to him, calls him Pops-Pops, teases him unmercifully. He takes it in his stride. They have a good relationship, Beau, which I'm pleased about. I also think he's been a good father. She's a gay little thing, fairy-like, and whimsical. And, most important, very natural. You'd think I'd been around continually and not absent for so long. She behaves as if we've never been apart, which has put me at ease. We're getting to know each other, and I adore her. She's pretty too, much prettier than those photographs I showed you – the snapshots Mike sent to England last year.'

'Any child of yours would be beautiful, Monkey Face,' Beau murmured. 'So it looks as if you'll be staying in New York for a while. Yes?'

'I think so, Beau.'

'I'm pleased things have been working out so well for you,' Beau said, genuinely delighted for her, if somewhat disappointed for himself.

'So am I!'

They continued to speak for another half hour. Beau reported his news, gossiped about old acquaintances whom he had seen on his recent trip to Beverly Hills, and regaled her with a few amusing anecdotes, as always loving the sound of her lilting ageless laughter. He promised to call her in a few days, and Katharine replaced the receiver, rested her head on the pillow, her thoughts instantly turning to Vanessa. My little sprite, she mused, golden and bright like a shiny new penny. Vanessa had admired the tiny diamond heart she had been wearing on Friday. I must get one for her. I'll go to Tiffany's ...

She jumped, startled from her reverie by the shrilling telephone, reached out for it. 'Hello?'

'Hi. It's me. Nicholas.'

'I know it's you, Nicky,' she laughed. 'Don't you think I know your voice after twenty-three years.'

There was a moment's silence, then he said in a rush, 'I've been trying to get through to you for ages. And I – '

'What's wrong, Nicky?' Katharine broke in, well acquainted with the particular inflection now echoing in his voice.

He chose to brush over the question, asked, 'Would it be an intrusion if I came up? I'm in the lobby. Or if there's someone with you, could you come down for a minute? It's important.'

'I'm alone. Please do come up.'

The telephone went dead. She stared at it worriedly, wondering what was

557

troubling Nick, then ran to the dressing table, smoothed her hair with the brush, straightened her shirt and put on her jacket. Hurrying into the living room, she found her shoes under the desk and stepped into them as Nick rapped on the door.

She let him in, took the overcoat slung over his arm, placed it on a chair, looked at him questioningly. Nick pecked her cheek, said, 'Sorry to burst in on you like this, Kath, but when I couldn't get through I decided to run up here.' He paced into the middle of the floor, swung to face her. 'I thought you might be going out to dinner, and I wanted to catch you before you left.' He shook his head. 'I've just had some rotten news.'

'What's happened?' she asked, sinking into a chair.

'I had a 'phone call about half an hour ago. From Nelson Avery, Frankie's brother-in-law. He's spending the weekend in Virginia with Harry and Frankie and –'

'Not *Frankie*! Has something hap – '

'No, no,' Nick exclaimed quickly. 'It's Harrison. He had a heart attack this afternoon. He's in Bethesda. Frankie's with him. She asked Nelson to call me.'

'Oh Nick, this is terrible. How bad is it?'

'Bad. He's had two seizures in the last couple of years, and he's no youngster. I keep forgetting that. He looks so damned good for his age. But he's got to be in his middle seventies.'

'Poor Frankie. This is awful for her, just awful.'

'Yes,' Nick said, sitting down, searching for his cigarettes. 'I'm afraid this means we have to cancel the dinner on Monday. Obviously Frankie's not going to be back in New York by then. I'm sorry. I could tell from your voice, when we spoke yesterday, that you were excited she wanted me to arrange it. But . . .' He lifted his hands in a helpless gesture.

'We'll do it the following week, whenever, as soon as things settle down.' She proffered him a faint smile. 'Her gesture was enough, in a sense, just knowing she feels we can be friends again makes me terribly happy.'

'Francesca has always been blessed with great generosity of spirit. There's not an ounce of meanness in that woman's body. I hope you don't mind, but I repeated a few of the things you'd told me about the last nine years, and she was heartsick for you, Kath. So filled with sympathy.'

'Yes, she would be. She's a very special person. I wish there was something we could do for her right now, but I suppose there isn't, except send her good thoughts and our prayers. And to her husband too.' Katharine had moved to the edge of the chair, and she said, 'Would you like a drink, Nicky?'

'Am I keeping you?'

'No, of course not,' she smiled, glancing over her shoulder at the sideboard. 'There's vodka, Scotch, sherry, various things over there. Or I could order a bottle of wine.' She rose purposefully. 'I think I will. I'd like a glass myself.'

'That's a good idea.' He watched her as she went to the 'phone, thinking how good she looked. Goddamned glorious, he said under his breath, his eyes taking in the stylish Adolfo suit of bright red wool trimmed with navy, the navy silk shirt, the gleam of gold chains and milky pearls against the soft fabric. The chestnut hair was shorter than he had ever seen it, deftly curled around her face, but it suited her. Her composure and tranquillity seemed to reach out to him, and he felt himself relaxing.

'Room service is pretty good here,' she informed him, returning to the chair. 'The wine will be up in a few minutes.' Lolling back and crossing her legs, she asked, 'And how are things with you otherwise, Nicky?'

'Pretty good. Carlotta's still in Venezuela, my son is fantastic, and the work has been going great.' He leaned forward, eagerness streaking across his face. 'I don't know what's happened to me in the last few days. It's as if the floodgates have opened. I've been turning out ten pages a day on an average. Good pages too. If I can keep it up the novel's going to be finished sooner than I expected.'

'That's wonderful to hear. I've read all of them you know.'

'And?' His brows lifted and he stared at her intently.

'I loved each and every one. You've never been better, Nick.'

'Thanks.' He beamed, looked pleased as he sat back.

There was a knock on the door and Nick jumped up. 'I'll get it.' When they were alone again and sipping their wine a few minutes later, he picked up the conversation where he had left off. 'Have dinner with me, Kath.'

'Oh Nicky, I'd like to, but I can't.' His face dropped, and she said, 'I invited Estelle, and not too long ago either. I can't very well cancel it now. Why don't you join us? I thought we'd eat in the Café Carlyle.'

'Terrific suggestion – about joining you. But I'll take you both out. I'm not wearing a tie, and I don't feel like a fancy-schmansy joint. We'll go to Elaine's. What time is Estelle due?'

'Eight o'clock.'

'Oh good, we can catch up on our lives some more.' He started to laugh.

Said Katharine, 'What's so funny?'

'Estelle's going to drop in her tracks when she sees *me* sitting here. She's very romantic. I think she secretly hopes we're going to get back together again – ' He thought: Oh Jesus, why did I say that? He stared at Katharine and she stared back, and there was an awkward silence.

Then Katharine laughed. 'No, she won't. She knows you're spoken for, Nicky.'

I'm not, he said inwardly, and was momentarily shaken by his thoughts. He grinned to hide his sudden confusion. 'That won't stop Estelle conjecturing. Anyway, if we're going to Elaine's I think you should change. It's not that you don't look beautiful, you do. Something more casual would be more in order though.'

'I'll change now. It won't take a minute. Excuse me.'

'Sure. And I'll make a reservation, nine-fifteen, nine-thirty okay with you? There's not much point going before then.'

'Fine, darling.' She disappeared into the bedroom. After calling the restaurant, he glanced at a number of framed photographs on the desk, picked up one of a child with reddish-gold hair and Katharine's exquisite, fragile face. Vanessa, he thought, and smiled as he put it down. There was a colour shot of Ryan, another of Francesca and Katharine taken in the South of France. They stood, arms entwined, on the terrace of the Villa Zamir. He peered at their tender faces. How young, how vulnerable they looked. A lot of water's sluiced over the old waterfall since then, he sighed, and wondered why he had not noticed the pictures the other day.

Either he had been too preoccupied or they had not been here. He sauntered around the room familiarizing himself with it. Katharine had always had a knack of making any place her own, filling it with small personal things. Apart from the photographs there were lots of fresh flowers, a bowl of fruit, smaller dishes of mixed nuts, magazines, books and several Rigaud perfumed candles. On an impulse he lit them all, poured himself another glass of white wine, returned to the sofa.

He reached for a cigarette but the packet was empty. Rising he strolled to the bedroom door, which was half open. He tapped lightly. 'Kath, do you have any cigarettes in there? I've run out.'

'Oh yes, Nicky. Come in, I'm dressed.'

'You've been fast,' he said, almost added, faster than you used to be, but stopped himself in time. He nodded approvingly. She was wearing a tailored white silk shirt and a pair of powder-blue wool trousers.

'Oh yes, I'm a quick-change artist these days,' she laughed, turned back to the mirror, remarked, 'There are some cigarettes in the box on the bedside table. Your box.'

Instantly he knew what she was referring to, and he was surprised. He was even more flabbergasted when he saw his own face staring up at him from a framed photograph next to the lamp. I'll be damned, he thought, but made no comment. He lifted the silver box, gazed at the many variations of her name engraved across its lid, and muttered, 'So you kept this.'

'Yes,' she answered lightly and swung to face him. 'I have everything you ever gave me. Including this, which I wear all the time.' She dangled the pendant in front of her, the large square-cut aquamarine and the diamonds glittering in the light. Putting it around her neck, she struggled with the clasp.

He placed the box on the bedside table. 'Here, let me do that.'

'Oh thanks.'

The clasp was small and it took him a moment, and he was a moment longer securing the safety catch. As he hovered over her, he was filled with the perfume of her, unexpectedly moved by the close proximity of her. His hands brushed against the soft downy skin on the back of her neck and he was shocked at the effect this had on him. An urgent forgotten desire flooded through him, brought the heat to his face, and as he stepped away, reached for the cigarette box, his hand trembled slightly.

'I'll be out in a minute, Nicky,' she said, running a comb through her hair.

'Take your time.' He almost ran back into the living room clutching the box.

He stood smoking by the window, the wine glass in his hand, staring out across the rooftops of Manhattan, his mind on Katharine. What was it about her that created this raging excitement in him? And after all these years, all the heartbreak and anguish she had caused him. It was some elusive quality he could not put his finger on, and yet it was a powerful and compelling force. His reaction to her a second ago had been intensely emotional, and surprisingly physical. Katharine had the ability to turn him on without even trying. She made him feel like a twenty-five-year-old stud, whilst Carlotta turned him off. Very off, he thought. Just before she had left for Venezuela she had told him he was impotent. Oh you're so wrong, lady. And then he realized he had not felt this good for years. Not since he had left Katharine's life. Twelve years. And you're back where you started, Latimer. His heart sank. And then it lifted. He didn't care. In fact, he was glad. Our destinies *are* entwined, he mused. We *have* been propelled towards each other again – inexorably. I cannot fight that, nor can I fight my emotions. What has to happen happens.

'By the way, Nicky, I feel awful. I never asked about your parents. How are they?' Katharine asked, walking in from the bedroom, sitting down.

He pivoted at the sound of her voice, joined her. 'My mother's wonderful; so is my father really. He hasn't been well this past week, but I don't think it's anything serious. Old age basically. I've got to face the fact that he's going to die soon. Nobody lives for ever.'

'No, they don't.' She smiled. 'But he could go on for a number of years yet. Ninety-year-olds are not unheard of, you know.'

'That's true.' His eyes rested on her, roved over her, and he nodded slowly, 'You really are the most beautiful woman I've ever known.'

She blushed and laughed. 'Thank you. But you're changing the subject. We were talking about – '

'My parents, I know. Hey, listen, I want you to come and visit them. They'd love to see you, Kath. They were always so fond of you.'

'I'd like that. Next week?'

'I'll arrange it. Perhaps we'll all have dinner.'

The 'phone rang, and Katharine jumped up. 'Yes, let's,' she agreed. 'That's probably Estelle.' She answered on the third ring, said, 'Hello? Oh yes, send her up. Thank you.'

Nicky began to laugh. 'Shall we play a joke on Estelle?'

'What kind of joke?' Katharine frowned.

'I'll go into the bedroom, take off my jacket and shirt and stroll out bare-chested. That should give her – '

'Nicky, no!'

'Better still, I'll climb into bed.' He rose, headed for the bedroom, struggling out of his coat, laughing uproariously.

'Please, don't!' Katharine cried, running to him, grabbing his arm. 'It'll be all over town tomorrow. Even if we tell her it's a joke, she'll never believe it.'

'She can print it in her magazine for all I care.'

Katharine stared at him aghast. 'But – what about Carlotta? You're in love with her . . .'

'Negative.' He shrugged himself into his sports jacket, gazed down at her, saw the puzzlement and confusion in her eyes. He pulled her into his arms, pressed her head close to his chest. 'How could I possibly be in love with anyone else when you're alive and well somewhere in this world. It's only you. It's only ever been you, my darling Caitlin, my sweet sweet Cait,' he murmured, using his old pet name for her.

'Oh Nicky, no! We mustn't, we can't.'

He noticed that despite her strenuous protestations, she clung to him. 'Why not?' he demanded. 'Give me one good reason?'

There was knocking on the door. 'That's Estelle,' Katharine laughed nervously. 'Now promise to behave yourself.'

'I'll consider it.'

Minutes later Estelle Morgan was still bouncing up and down like a rubber ball in front of him. Her strident laughter filled the room, and she kept saying, 'Nicholas! Nicholas! This is great, just great! It's wonderful to see you. Oh my, are you two – ?'

'No,' Katharine interjected. 'We're *not*. Now, come and have a glass of wine.' She linked her arm through Estelle's, drew her into the seating arrangement, explained softly, 'We've had some bad news.' Katharine told Estelle about Francesca's husband, and the journalist sobered at once, adopted a more decorous demeanour.

Estelle said, 'That's dreadful. I'm sorry. As you know, Francesca Avery's not my favourite person, but I don't wish her any harm. Too bad. Really too bad. Thanks,' she said to Nick, taking the glass from him.

As usual, Estelle was full of news and chit-chat about the rich and the famous, and she kept Nick and Katharine well entertained for the next half hour. At nine o'clock, Nick suggested they should leave for the restaurant.

'Of course. I'll get my bag and a jacket.' Katharine moved towards the bedroom.

'I'll call the house,' Nick announced, also rising. 'There might be a message from Nelson Avery.'

To Katharine's consternation he followed her into the bedroom. Once they were inside and out of Estelle's earshot, she hissed, 'Honestly, Nick, what's Estelle going to think.'

'Stop worrying. Besides, I do want to call Nanny privately, from this 'phone.' He took her hands in his, bent down, kissed her gently on the lips. 'Can I tell Nanny I'll be home late? Very very very late?'

'I – I – Oh Nicky, I don't know what to say.'

He laughed and let go of her hands.

Katharine picked up her bag and a mink jacket lying on the bed and fled without another word.

He lifted the telephone, dialled, stretched out on the bed and eyed his photograph on the bedside table. She'll have me in person tonight, he thought, and then said, 'Oh hello, Miss Jessica. Have you heard from Mr Avery?' His child's Nanny informed him there had been no telephone calls at all. 'Fine. I'll check in with you later. I'm going out to dinner now with friends. I'll be home late tonight, very late.'

CHAPTER FIFTY-TWO

Obelisks of brilliant light pierced the dark sky. An opaque moon dodged in and out between the wind-blown clouds. April rain skittered against the window. Katharine stood in the darkened bedroom, her face pressed against the cool glass, staring out at the magical skyline of Manhattan, listening to the metallic pinging of the rain, the sound of Nick's quiet breathing as he dozed.

I never wanted this to happen. For his sake, not mine. For me it has been so truly wonderful. Happiness . . . happiness I never thought possible again. It will last me all the days of my life. But he will be devastated, and there is no way I can ease his pain. Oh God, help me. Tell me what to do. Guide me. Give me the strength and the wisdom to help him.

Tears ran down her cheeks and she brushed them away quickly with her fingertips, swallowing the sob rising in her throat, not wanting to awaken him. My darling, my most beloved Nicky, how am I ever going to tell you?

She thought then of a line by the French poet Lamartine: *That voice of the heart which alone reaches the heart*. She closed her eyes. My heart speaks to your heart, my dearest darling. It cries out my love for you. My eternal and everlasting love. Listen with your heart, and you will hear mine speaking to you from wherever I am, for the rest of your life. You will always be by my side, Nicky, for you are a part of me, as Vanessa is a part of me . . .

'Kath, what are you doing standing there in the dark? You're going to catch your death of cold. Come back to bed, sweetheart,' Nick commanded. 'Immediately.'

'Yes,' Katharine answered, making her voice strong, gliding to the bed.

He pulled her down next to him, wrapped his arms around her and then his legs. 'My God, you're frozen.' He bent over her and kissed her face and he tasted the salt of her tears on her cheeks. He smoothed his hand over her wet face, gently and with tenderness. 'Why have you been weeping, my darling?'

'Oh Nicky . . . because I am so very happy. The last two months with you have been the most wonderful enchanted months of my life.'

He kissed her mouth lovingly, softly, the passion in him spent. 'It's just the beginning,' he murmured against her hair. 'I've made my mind up, you know. You can argue with me until you're purple, but I am going to set the wheels in motion as soon as Carlotta gets back in two weeks.' He chuckled. 'You and I are going to grow old together. As man and wife.'

A deep sigh rippled through her and she reached up and smoothed back his hair. 'You know that's just a dream, Nicky.'

'Don't say that! Anyway, dreams can come true, can't they? Secretly, in my innermost heart, I think I always dreamed you would come back to me, my sweet Kathy. And you did.'

'It's not possible, Nicky. Carlotta – '

He placed a finger on her lips. 'Sssh. Listen to me. Carlotta's not going to make any problems. Since January she's spent more time in Venezuela than she has in New York. I have a feeling she's met someone. She's not interested in me any more.'

'Perhaps. But there's little Victor. She's not going to let you keep him, if you split up. And even if she had met someone else, she's going to take the child with her, especially if she's going to live in Venezuela. Her family is there.'

'There's a bit of truth in what you say, darling, but I've already talked to my lawyers. It won't be quite so easy for her to trip off with the little one. Proper arrangements will have to be made, legal papers drawn, joint custody agreed upon.'

'I don't think it'll work. I think you're playing a dangerous game.'

'Let me do my own thinking, Kath. Please, don't try to think for me. Once I've settled everything with Carlotta and the lawyers, we can get married. When shall we get married?'

'I don't know,' she said softly.

'Don't you want to marry me?' he asked in a low worried tone.

'Don't be ridiculous! How can you ask such a silly question. But I am nervous, Nicky. About myself. About making a commitment to you. I do want to be sure of my mental state –'

'You're better,' he interrupted fiercely. 'My God, I've been with you night and day, every day for over eight weeks. Do you think *I* don't know your mental state. You are rational, composed, stable, and absolutely and completely sane.'

'If you say so,' she murmured, nestling closer. Afraid to continue this conversation, she faked a yawn.

Nick loosened his grip on her, rolled over and picked up his watch from the bedside table. Unable to see it clearly, he flicked on the lamp. 'Mmm. It's late. Shall we go to sleep?'

'Are you staying?' Katharine asked with surprise. 'Won't Nanny be –'

'I told her I wouldn't be home tonight. That I had a meeting out of town. Philadelphia. I'm not in the hit and run business, you know,' he said, snapping off the light.

'I'm glad you're here, darling. I always like it when you stay.'

He kissed her. 'Sleep well. I love you, Kath.'

'I love you too, my darling.'

The following morning Nicholas Latimer was in an ebullient mood, his spirits high. Katharine laughed at his one-line cracks and his quips and jokes, and she thought to herself that he had not been so amusing for a long time.

When he was showered, shaved and dressed, they had a leisurely breakfast. Nick scanned the *New York Times*, and Katharine gazed at him adoringly and drank her tea and her heart was full to overflowing with him.

But at ten-fifteen, she said firmly, 'I've got to kick you out, love. I have a lot to do today, and some shopping. I'm running late.'

'Yes, I have a few appointments myself.' He finished his coffee, stubbed out the cigarette smouldering in the ashtray. 'Where do you want to have dinner tonight?'

'Nick, did you forget? I'm having dinner with Vanessa.'

'Yes, I did, I'm afraid.' He hid his disappointment, knowing how important her daughter was to her. 'I'll tell you what though, why don't I stop off later this afternoon? Around four-thirty. Have tea with you.' He grinned. '*You* can have tea, I'll sit and watch you.'

'Yes, that'll be fine, darling.' She walked him to the door, hugged him tightly, then kissed his cheek.

Once she was alone, Katharine went through her usual morning chores. She made a few telephone calls, wrote several letters before taking a bath and dressing. Around noon she took a cab to Tiffany's, picked up the various gifts she had ordered and went back uptown, to the Carlyle. She ate a light lunch in her suite, made a call to Mike Lazarus to confirm the dinner with Vanessa, then picked up one of Nick's novels she was rereading. But inevitably her thoughts intruded, and she spent the rest of the afternoon pondering. Finally at four o'clock she changed into a delphinium blue silk dress, brushed her hair, and redid her make-up, then ordered ice from room service.

Katharine heard Nick's sharp rap as she was slipping the string of pearls around her neck, and she walked rapidly to the door, greeting him warmly. He picked her up in his arms, swung her around, deposited her on the floor. 'I've been to the lawyers, Kath! They think I'm right, that I can get a proper watertight legal agreement – one which will protect the child.' He held her away from him, grinning broadly. 'How do you like them apples?'

She smiled, walked over to the bar, poured two vodkas, plopped in ice. 'Here, darling,' she said, handing him the drink. 'Come and sit down.'

He took the glass and followed her. He was frowning. 'You sound serious. What's up?' He stood in the middle of the floor, staring at her.

'Aren't you going to sit down? I want to talk to you.'

'I've been sitting all day. I'll hop around on my legs for a few minutes.' He laughed nervously. 'What's wrong, Katinka? Come on, let's have it.'

'I can't marry you, Nicky.'

'Don't kid around with me, darling. I'm not in the mood. If I've ever been serious about anything in my life it's marrying you. Now – '

She held up her hand. 'I can't marry you, Nick. I am serious too.'

He peered at her, squinting in the sunlight. 'But why? Because of the boy? Look, I told you, we'll settle that in no time at all.'

'The minute you tell Carlotta to move out, or if you move out, she'll take that child to Venezuela. And you'll have one hell of a task trying to get him back. I can't let you risk such a thing, Nicky.' She shook her head. 'I know what it's like to be separated from one's own child. I've lived through it, remember.'

'It won't be like that!' he protested, pacing up and down, scowling hard.

'I'm not prepared to risk it. I don't want it on my conscience. I've carried too many burdens these past nine years to go borrowing new ones, darling.'

'I *want* to marry you. I'm *going* to marry you. Goddamn it, Kath, don't be so stubborn. I'm prepared to take my chances. I can't give you up because of Carlotta and my son. I love him desperately. But I need *you*.'

'Let me pose a hypothetical question, Nicky. Let's just say I do everything you wish, and Carlotta takes the boy away from you completely, never allows you to see him again. How would you feel?'

'I'd be heartbroken of course. But that's not going to happen. Anyway, I don't like hypothetical questions.'

Katharine took a swallow of the vodka, steeled herself and said, 'I have nothing to offer you, Nicky, so I'm certainly not going to jeopardize your relationship with your child.'

'Nothing to offer me! That's a laugh. I love you. You love me, and we've always been compatible, even more so, now that you're well.'

'I'm *not* well, Nicky, that's the whole point.'

'But Kath, you are. Your behaviour speaks for itself.'

'I don't have any *time* to offer you, Nicky.'

He looked at her, struck by the strangest note in her voice. 'Time? I'm not following you, Kath.'

'I'm dying, Nicky.'

Stunned, his jaw dropped, and he gripped the back of the chair. He opened his mouth but no words came out. He felt every ounce of his strength draining out of him.

Katharine said, 'I don't have very long. That's what I meant about time. Six to seven months, at the most.'

Nick thought he was going to collapse. He staggered to the sofa, unable to tear his eyes away from her. 'Kath, Kath,' he whispered. 'Please, say it's not true. It can't be true.'

'Yes, it is, my darling. I'm so sorry.'

'S-s-s-sorry?' he gasped, and the tears spurted. He shook his head vehemently. 'No! No!' he shouted. 'I won't accept this!'

'Darling, hush, hush.' She went and knelt at his feet, resting her hands on his knees, looking up into his face. 'I wanted to spare you this, Nicky. When I came back, all I wanted was to seek your forgiveness, so that I could die in peace. I didn't know we would fall in love again. Estelle had told me you lived with Carlotta. I thought you were settled, especially since you had a son.'

Nick's hands were shaking so violently vodka was spilling everywhere. Katharine took the glass from him, put it on the table, took his hands in hers. 'I'm afraid I have to ask you to forgive me again, for causing you more pain.'

'Oh Kath, Kath, my darling, I love you so much – ' His voice broke and tears coursed down his cheeks, and he put his arms around her, clung to her with desperation. 'You can't be dying, not *you*! I won't let you die!'

She held on to him for a long time, until his choked sobs lessened and he was calmer. Then she rose, found a box of tissues, wiped his damp hands and then his streaming face. She gave him his drink, lit two cigarettes, put one in his mouth, seated herself on the sofa next to him.

It took him several moments to regain a little of his self-possession, and he smoked the cigarette, took a long swallow of the vodka, all the while staring at her. Finally, he asked softly, and with apprehension, 'What's wrong with you, Kath?'

She cleared her throat, and her voice was as low as his had been. She told him: 'I have something called a nodular melanoma. It's a variant of the malignant melanoma, but the death rate is higher.'

'I'm not sure what that is . . . cancer?'

'Yes. A melanoma manifests itself on the skin. It starts as a tiny mole or a freckle-like spot.'

'But can't it be removed or treated?' he asked, filling with fear for her, his heart tight in his chest.

'Yes, it can be removed, but removing it doesn't mean I'm cured. You see, my nodular melanoma is at level four. That means it's three millimetres deep. When the melanoma gets into the bloodstream, one cell will get caught in an organ, such as the lungs or the liver, and it starts growing. That's called distant metastasis . . . Latin for spreading. That's already happened to me. It's spreading.'

Nick clenched his hand, squeezed his eyes tightly shut, unable to say a word.

After a moment he lifted his lids, focused on her lovely face, and the tears sprang to his eyes once more. He shook his head, choked.

She touched his hand. 'Shall I go on? Knowing you as well as I do, I realize you'll want all the facts.'

He nodded. His throat ached.

'The nodular melanoma is on my back,' Katharine explained. 'It's centred between the left shoulder-blade and the spine, about four inches above my waist. It has spread to my lymph nodes, my liver and lungs. Those organs are now diseased.'

'B-b-b-but you look so well, Kath . . .'

'Yes. The fact that it's spread to my lungs and my liver is immaterial because this does not affect general health. At least not in the beginning.'

'When *will* it begin to affect *you*?'

'As I understand from my doctors, a person who has a nodular melanoma usually has about a year. For the first nine months or so there's little deterioration of physical health or appearance. But once the person begins to deteriorate, death can take place within as short a time as one week.'

'Oh God! Oh Christ! Kath!'

'I'll have the ability to function normally for about another six, maybe even seven, months, and there shouldn't be any visible signs of deterioration.'

'Treatment. There must be some sort of treatment. Look, we'll find new doctors. We'll go to Sloan Kettering, the Skin and Cancer Pavilion of NYU. Surely there's a way to –'

'No, Nick,' Katharine interjected gently. 'I've been through all that in London. You see, treatment is extremely difficult when the melanoma is in the spinal area, as mine is. Radiation is useless, because the tumour is not sensitive to it. Chemotherapy is terribly disfiguring, loss of hair, among other things. It also causes nausea and vomiting. There are new drugs, but they only prolong life a short while, and it's not a very pleasant life at that. I elected not to take drugs. I'm going to die within a short space of time anyway, so I want to live these last few months graciously, looking the way I look, enjoying the days left to me.'

'When did you find out?' he whispered, terror rampant in him.

'Last November. That little pinprick of a mole I've had all my life turned black, grew slightly larger. My dressmaker noticed it. But it was already too far gone.'

'Will you – will you have any pain? I couldn't bear you to be in pain, Kath,' he gasped in a strangled voice.

'No, not really, Nick. When the deterioration starts there is a slow weight loss, severe debilitation, loss of appetite. I'll tire easily.'

He closed his eyes convulsively, his imagination running wild. He cut off the unacceptable and agonizing thoughts of her suffering, said, 'Are you sure about the prognosis?'

'Absolutely. My doctor in London called in every specialist there is. I've even seen specialists here. There is no remedy, Nicky.' She took his hand. 'My doctor in London told me I had some good time left, meaning about nine months at that point. That's why I came to New York. To see you, in particular, and Frankie, Ryan, and of course my darling child.'

'Is that why . . . *he* let you see her?' he asked sorrowfully.

567

'Yes. I sort of threatened him in a way. I told him if he didn't, I'd start a lawsuit, have a press conference, give reporters all the facts about my illness. Mike capitulated.' She smiled. 'But I wouldn't have done it. I wouldn't have subjected Vanessa to that kind of circus.'

'Does Ryan know?'

'No, Nick. You and Mike Lazarus are the only ones who do. I want to keep it that way. Promise. I don't want sympathy – or pity.'

He looked at her carefully. 'Is that why you didn't tell me, or Frankie, when you first arrived?'

'Yes. I wanted you to forgive me because you wanted to do so, not out of compassion or charity. Promise me you'll keep this to yourself.'

'I promise. What about Frankie and Victor?'

'I'll tell them myself, darling. Soon.'

Unexpectedly, suddenly, something snapped in Nick, and he leapt up, began to pace the floor, a raging anger temporarily subduing his sorrow. He kept smashing his clenched fist into his open palm, and he cursed under his breath. After a few minutes he swung to her.

'There must be a way out of this! There has to be. I won't accept it. Goddamn it, I won't accept it. Just because you have, I won't. You sit there, so calm, so contained, and my heart is breaking into infinitesimal pieces and you – ' He stopped, shocked at his words, the way he had spoken to her, his behaviour.

He ran to her, knelt at her feet. 'Forgive me, forgive me, my darling. Oh Kath, I'm sorry. I – I – love you so much. I'm crazy. I shouldn't have – ' He began to sob and buried his face against her body.

'It's all right, my dearest love. I understand. Your reaction is natural. When the shock recedes a little, the anger does take over, then the frustration sets in. Next comes fear. Then the anger returns. And finally one is left, very simply, with acceptance, resignation. Because there is nothing else to feel, nothing one can do.' She began to murmur gently to him, stroking his head, soothing him. 'Don't, darling, don't. Hush, my love.'

Eventually, he pulled himself upright, sat on the sofa with her, cradling her in his arms. 'I'll be with you, my darling Kath. The next few months are going to be happy for you . . . as happy as I can make them. We'll do anything you want, go anywhere you want. You can have your heart's desire.'

'No, Nicky, you can't be with me.'

'Why? In God's name, why not?'

'I'm not going to let you risk losing your child. And if you go away with me, you surely will.'

'Then we'll stay in New York. The way we are. Maintain separate establishments, keep up a pretence. Carlotta will never know.' He loathed the mere idea of this, had no intention of doing anything of the kind. He had said it to placate Katharine. Carlotta would do as she was told. He would arrange everything somehow. Nothing, no one, was going to keep him from his Kath.

She said, 'No, it's better I just go away now – '

'I won't let you!'

'It would kill me to witness your grief, Nicky,' she whispered, and then realized, with a stab of dismay, what she had said.

Nick ignored the unfortunate remark, shook his head. His eyes brimmed again. 'Please don't send me away. Let me have these last few months with you. I'm going to have to spend the rest of my life without you. Don't be cruel, Kath, please, please. I'll get down on my knees and beg you, if you want, but for God's sake don't send me away from you, my love.' He gazed at her with red-rimmed eyes. 'Don't be cruel. Let me be with you, *please* Kath.'

She nodded. Her eyes were bright and moist and the tears glistened on her lashes. 'All right, my darling. But you'll have to promise me you're going to be cheerful, as gay as possible. I couldn't bear to witness your grief and pain.'

'I promise.' A wavering smile touched his lips.

Katharine stood up. 'I'll have to change my dress, it's sopping wet. You cried all over it, my darling.' She touched his face with one finger. 'Are you going to walk me to my dinner date with my daughter?'

'Of course. But I'd better wash my face whilst you're changing. I told Victor I'd go over to the Pierre and have a drink with him, maybe a light supper.'

'Oh, I'm glad, Nicky. I'd hate you to be alone this evening. Has he decided when he's going back to the Coast?'

'No. But he had his final meeting today. I think he might stay through the week. He's enjoyed being with us, seeing Frankie again,' Nick said, as they walked into the bedroom together, forcing the words, making a stupendous effort to control himself.

Katharine smiled. 'Yes, it was nice.'

Later, as they strolled across to Fifth Avenue and then up towards Seventy-Ninth Street, where the Lazarus apartment was located, Nick said, 'About Frankie and Victor . . . when do you plan to tell them?'

'I'm not sure. But the right moment will present itself. I certainly don't want to tell them tomorrow, when we go to lunch at Frankie's. It would spoil everything.'

'Yes.'

Katharine squeezed his hand. 'I'm glad we forced Frankie to come to dinner with us and Victor last week. I think she was rather pleased at the end of the evening. And Victor was beaming.'

'Has she said anything to you? About Victor, I mean?'

'Nicky, are you playing matchmaker? And you call *me* manipulative!'

'What you mean is that I *used* to call you manipulative. But *did* she say anything?' he probed.

'Not really. Just that he was as charismatic and as sweet as he always was. I think she was startled by the white streaks in his hair. She told me she had always remembered him as he was in 1956. Even though she's noticed photographs of him from time to time, in the magazines, the old image had stuck in her head.'

'At sixty-two he's still the most handsome guy I've ever seen. And she's right. His presence is still as potent as ever,' Nick remarked, tucking her arm in his. 'I told her yesterday that she must get out more. I know Harrison's only been dead three months, but she can't sit around moping in that great big apartment. She's a young woman.'

'You won't sit around moping, will you, darling?' she asked quietly.

'*Don't.*' He turned his head, blinking hard, blinded by his tears. 'Please don't allude to your death again. I simply can't stand it.'

'I won't. But you must accept it, Nicky, otherwise the next few months are going to be terrible for me. We must try and be as normal as possible.'

Her immense courage staggered him, and he cursed himself inwardly. 'Okay. It's a deal.'

She reached up and kissed him when they arrived at the apartment building. 'See ya later, kid,' she growled, mi-micking him.

'You're damn right you will,' he shot back, forcing a gaiety he did not feel. 'What time shall I pick you up?'

'Oh, I guess around nine-thirty.' She stood on tiptoe to kiss him again, and her eyes filled. 'I love you, Nicholas Latimer. So very very much.'

CHAPTER FIFTY-THREE

Francesca said, 'Val, the dining room table looks really lovely. You've outdone yourself.'

'Thank you, M'lady. When you said you wanted to use the Royal Worcester china I thought how pretty spring flowers would look with the deep blue. I was lucky the florist had such a good selection. I bought a pot of hyacinths for the living room too, and some imported mimosa as well. It won't last long, but I couldn't resist it.'

Nodding, Francesca walked out to the hall. She noticed the large square package on one of the French chairs. She frowned, went to look at it. 'What's this, Val?'

'Oh, I'm sorry, M'lady, I forgot to mention it. You were out at the lawyers when it arrived earlier this morning. It's addressed to Mr Latimer, care of you.'

'Mmmm. So I see. I'll take it into the living room. Is the wine on ice?'

'Everything's ready, Lady Francesca, and Cook has prepared a very nice menu. Shrimp cocktail, roast veal with peas and carrots, a mixed green salad with Brie, and fresh fruit.'

'God, I hope everyone has a good appetite,' Francesca laughed. 'She's gone to town.'

Val smiled, followed her into the living room. 'Don't the flowers give the room a springlike air, M'lady?'

'Yes, they certainly do,' Francesca murmured, a vagrant memory stirring. It came to her then. *He* had sent her similar flowers long, long ago, when she had been a young and foolish girl, not a widow in widow's weeds as she was now.

She spun around to Val. 'Do you think the black dress looks a bit, well, you know, depressing?'

Val nodded. 'Yes, it does, M'lady, if you don't mind my saying so. It's awfully draining, and your face is very pale. What about that dark green silk shirtwaister you bought just before Mr Avery passed away? It's pretty on you, and subdued without being too drab.'

'Yes, I'd forgotten that dress. I think I *will* change. I just have time before Miss Tempest and the other guests arrive.'

'Yes, M'lady. I'll be in the kitchen if you need me.'

Upstairs in the bedroom, Francesca hurriedly unzipped the black wool dress, pulled the fir-green silk out of her wardrobe and stepped into it. She was wearing black pumps and they were suitable with the dress, as were the pearls. She glanced at herself as she passed the dressing table. She did look drawn and peaked. A touch of rouge rectified this, and she smoothed her hair with the brush, ran downstairs.

After straightening a cushion on one of the chairs, she went to the window. She stared out at Central Park, smiled to herself. It was a sunny April day. Spring. Renewal. Everything bursting out, green and fragrant after the harsh winter. She thought of the luncheon she was about to give for Victor. It had been Katharine's idea, and Nick had seconded it, and she had agreed because they were so enthusiastic. Had it been a mistake? The last thing she wanted was for Vic to get the wrong idea. But why should he? They were older now, wiser, and their love affair had been two decades ago. As Nick had said, what were old friends for, if not to comfort each other in times of trouble? And yet . . . There *had* been a faint undercurrent the other evening at Le Cirque, and memories had come rushing back to her ever since, unnerving in their clarity. The intercom buzzed. A moment later the doorbell rang, and she heard Val greeting Victor in the entrance hall.

She moved forward as he strode into the living room, found herself momentarily startled by his dark good looks, his vitality and his magnetism. He was impeccably groomed, elegant in a grey pin-striped suit, the kind he had always favoured.

'Hello, Ches,' he said, stretching out his hand.

Francesca took it, returned his greeting with a smile, said, 'You're the first. Shall we have a glass of wine whilst we're waiting for Nick and Kath? Or would you prefer something else?'

'Wine will be great. Thanks.' He glanced around the room appreciatively, then leaned closer to the bow-fronted chest where the large collection of photographs was arranged.

When Francesca brought him the drink Victor grinned, showed her the photograph he was holding, and said, 'Our little dog really was the whole enchilada, wasn't she?'

Francesca said, 'Yes, she was indeed. Come with me. I want to introduce you to someone very special. No, do bring your drink with you.' She guided him to the library, opened the door, showed him in. He had taken only a few steps when a small white dog leapt off a chair and bounded towards him. Victor looked at Francesca and shook his head. 'Well, I know it's not Lada. A grand-daughter?'

'No, not of Lada's, but of Tutzi's, Diana's dog. I brought this adorable little thing back with me from Bavaria a few years ago. She's four years old and very smart. Her name's Fluff-puff. Not my name. Diana's invention. I call her Fluff.'

Victor picked up the dog and scratched her head. 'I was surprised when you told me the other night that Lada had lived to be almost eighteen. That's a ripe old age for a dog, Ches.' He put Fluff on the floor and asked, 'And how are Diana and Christian?'

'Let's go back to the living room and I'll tell you all about them. We have to leave Fluff here. She wants to play when I have guests, and she gets very excited.'

They settled themselves in the living room, and Francesca gave him news of her cousins. 'Neither Diana nor Christian ever married. But they seem content, happy really, living together at Wittingenhof, and Diana still has her boutiques.'

'I thought of their father when I saw the stories about Raoul Wallenberg,' Victor said. 'All very tragic.'

'Yes, it was.' Francesca changed the subject, told him about Kim and his children, Doris and her daughter, Marigold. Several times she jumped up, brought him photographs to look at, and everything was easy and relaxed between them. Victor observed Francesca surreptitiously from time to time, noting her elegance, her intrinsic beauty. She turned out to be exactly the woman I thought she would become, he commented to himself. And he was proud of her. He was also immensely attracted to her, wanted her in the very same way he had when they were younger. His only regret was that he was meeting her again when she had been so recently widowed. Good taste prevented him from making any overt moves, and yet he longed to do so. There's plenty of time, old buddy, he told himself. Don't rush her. Take it nice an' easy. He began to make plans, decided to return to New York next month. Instinctively, he felt she was not entirely impervious to him, and they had had so much in the past, he was certain it could be recaptured. She was not going to escape from him a second time, if he could help it.

Francesca said, 'I'm so glad you met with Katharine, Vic, and that you're friends again. She really had some awful years in London, when she was undergoing psychiatric treatment.'

'Yes, Nick told me a few things. Anyway, I'm not one to hold a grudge. We all did some very foolish things in those days. Youth! Not that I was so young. I should have known better. I was forty, after all.'

She glanced at him, smiled. 'You don't look very different really. Your face is craggier, but you still have the most marvellous tan I've ever seen on anyone.'

'Thanks for the kind words. But I've also got a lotta white hair, kid.'

'Very distinguished, those white wings at the sides. Oh, that's the door-bell. Nick and Katharine.' She pushed herself up and was walking across the floor when Nick hurtled into the room as white as a sheet, his eyes wide and red-rimmed. He closed the door behind him swiftly, and stood staring at her.

'Nicky, whatever's the matter?' she cried, filling with alarm.

'Oh Frankie, Frankie, she's gone! Goddamn it, she's gone! Checked out. No message. Nothing. How will I ever *find* her?'

Victor had risen. Concern registered on his face. He strode over to them, took hold of Nick's arm and led him to a chair. 'Calm down, old sport. Ches, get Nicky a drink please. Vodka or wine?'

'Better make it vodka,' Nick mumbled.

Francesca hovered over him, squeezing his shoulder several times. 'Rest a moment, Nick dear. You seem out of breath.'

'I ran all the way here. I thought perhaps she'd told you everything. On the 'phone maybe, that she had moved in here.'

Victor caught Francesca's eye, raised a dark brow, looking as baffled as she did. He gave Nick the vodka, took hold of Francesca's hand, led her with him to the sofa. 'Now, Nicky, I think you'd better start at the beginning,' Victor said.

Nick took a deep breath and told them both the shocking news Katharine had broken to him last night. They were as stunned and as distressed as he was. Several times his voice broke during the recounting of the details, and he had to blow his nose constantly as he fought the tears. Victor interrupted several times, asking medical questions, nodding his head, following carefully. Halfway through the trying and heartbreaking recital Francesca began to weep quietly, brushing her eyes with her hands. Victor put his arm around her, fished in his pocket for his handkerchief, handed it to her.

At last Nick stopped, lit a cigarette and drank some of the vodka. He went on, 'That brings me up to the point when I left her at the Lazarus apartment. I came to see you, Vic, then picked her up there at nine-thirty, went back with her to the Carlyle. I left this morning at six, because I had to finish reading galleys of the new novel. I wanted them out of the way, so I could concentrate on Kath for the next few months. She was awake when I left. I told her I'd pick her up at ten minutes to one to come here for lunch. When I got to the Carlyle at that time she'd checked out. Around ten o'clock, the desk told me. No forwarding address, no message. I can't understand it. I must find her. Don't you see, she needs me. *Why? Why did she do this?*' He sprang up, walked to the window, stood staring out, his shoulders hunched.

'Oh my God, the package!' Francesca exclaimed, also leaping to her feet. Earlier she had placed it on a chair near the door, and now she ran for it, took it to Nick. 'This came for you when I was out this morning.'

He took it, ripped at the paper with shaking hands. 'It's Kath's hand writing,' he gasped. The paper was finally removed and he was holding an orange-coloured Hermes box. He recognized it immediately. The box had contained her favourite style of handbag, the Kelly she always carried, and he himself had bought it for her only a few weeks ago. He snatched at the lid. Inside were three small Tiffany boxes, three envelopes and, in the bottom, resting on a layer of tissue, a blue leather-bound book. He looked at the embossing on the front: *To V.L. from K.T.* He replaced the book, grabbed the letter addressed to himself, tore the envelope, searched for his glasses, stood reading, the tears welling, slowly trickling down his cheeks. 'There are letters here for you,' he mumbled, his voice cracked with emotion, and he moved to the far end of the living room, hiding his face from them, pain ripping through him. He was swamped by a sorrow he could not endure.

Victor collected the Hermes box and returned with it to the sofa, filled with sadness for Nick, and compassion and grief for Katharine, who had deserved a far better fate, whatever she had done to them all so long ago. He and Francesca read their letters, sat holding them, their faces vacant, not speaking, as benumbed as Nick, remembering so much.

The door opened and Val appeared. Francesca looked at her, shook her head, and the housekeeper quickly retreated. The sound of the door opening had roused Nicky, and he rejoined them near the fireplace. He said to Francesca, 'Read the letter she wrote to you . . . I mean read it aloud. I want to know what she said. Please, Frankie.'

'Yes, of course.' She blew her nose, began shakily, in a quavering voice:

573

'My dearest Frankie:

'Nick will explain everything. Excuse me for not telling you myself, but I thought it would be easier on everyone concerned if I handled it this way. The blue leather book at the bottom of the box is for my daughter Vanessa. It's filled with gentle thoughts, and impressions and internal meanderings of mine over the past four months. I would like you to give it to her when she is ready for it, perhaps in a year, or maybe two. I will leave that to your discretion. I hope she will come to know me better through my "hours of the day" and understand more about me.

'Michael has been, and is, a good father, and for that I am so very grateful, having never really had a father of my own. At least who loved me. However, I do feel that Vanessa needs a woman's influence and Michael has agreed that you can see her, be with her whenever you wish. Please be my daughter's friend as you were mine, my darling.'

Francesca halted, her voice trembling uncontrollably. She wiped her eyes with Vic's handkerchief, and went on:

'And now, Frankie, I must address myself to you. Facing imminent death as I am now doing, I see life with the most blinding clarity, all sham ripped away, truths revealed to me as never before. And I see all of those whom I love with the same vividness, through the clearest eyes, see their priorities and needs perhaps more acutely than they do themselves. I see you, my darling, so loving and tenderhearted, filled with the kind of inner purity and goodness that is, sadly, very rare. And you are terribly alone now. Don't be alone, Frankie. Loneliness is another form of death. I know that only too well. Nick and I thought we had another chance to right all wrongs. A second chance at life. We did not. But you do. Take it, Frankie, while you are still young. I say these things to you from my heart, with my heart so full of love for you.

'Impending death gives me the licence to say these things to you, and so I know you will understand, and will excuse my bluntness.

'Be well and happy, my darling friend. I shall think of you always, and you have my dearest love.

Kath'

Francesca wept unashamedly, and Victor's eyes were full as he took her hand, held it tightly in his. 'Can you light me a cigarette, please,' Francesca whispered, turning a tear-streaked face to him.

He did so, and glanced worriedly at Nick, who was huddled in the chair. It seemed to Victor that his friend had atrophied before his eyes. He said, 'Take a drink, Nicky.'

'Yes. Read your letter to me, Vic, please. I must know . . .'

Victor picked up the letter Katharine Tempest had written and scanned it again, almost afraid to begin. He took his horn-rimmed glasses from the end table, put them on, cleared his throat:

'My very dear Victor:

'First of all I want to thank you again for absolving me of the terrible wrong I did you so long ago. Your generosity of spirit last week was remarkable, and your understanding and forgiveness touched me deeply. As I told Nick after our meeting, I can now die with a peaceful heart, knowing I have made my peace with you and with Francesca.

'I know you love Nicky as much as I do, in a different way, of course. And so I ask you to look after him for me. He is going to need you and Frankie, and your loving friendship. The two of you will give him some of your strength, and so will help to pull him through these difficult months ahead. I do not want Nicky to be alone, Victor. Please take him back with you to Che Sarà Sarà this week, with little Victor and Frankie. My heart will be at ease if I know he is with his child and the two of you.

'Finally, do not let Nicky try to find me. I am going to a place where I will find tranquillity and repose, and where I will be safe and cared for at all times. It must be this way. I could not bear to see Nick suffering. And if he is with me I know he will suffer. That became so very clear to me last night. Only the three of you and Michael Lazarus know of my condition. I want it to remain confidential.

'Good-bye, my special friend, with my love always.

Katharine'

Victor placed the letter on the table, took off his wet glasses and went to Nick. He put his arm around him, held him close. 'I trust her, Nicky. Wherever she has gone she will be safe. Please don't try to find her. Let it be the way she wants it.'

Nick nodded. His throat ached with suppressed tears and the tearing pain inside him was monumental. He began to pace the floor, oblivious to Francesca and Victor, trying to think, his mind reeling with shock and despair. He could not conceive that he would never see her again, never hear her laughter, or gaze into her glorious turquoise eyes, or hold her in his arms. So absorbed was he in his inner conflict he was not aware that Francesca and Victor had left the room.

When they returned some fifteen minutes later he was still roaming around the room, looking lost and stricken.

Victor said, 'I think we should do as she wishes, Nicky. So does Ches.'

Nicky stared at them, drawn at last out of his benumbed state. 'Yes,' he said. 'Yes.' He went to the Hermes box, took out the blue Tiffany boxes, each one marked with a name. He handed them to Francesca and Victor. 'She wants me to give you these. She asked me in her letter.' He swallowed. 'Thank you for reading yours. I cannot read mine to you . . . it's very personal.'

'Oh Nicky, we don't expect you to,' Francesca exclaimed softly. She opened her box. There was a tiny diamond heart on a chain, similar to the one Katharine often wore. Last week, she and Kath had gone to Tiffany's to buy an identical heart for Vanessa, and she had admired it. Francesca held it in her hand tightly, incapable of speech, and she wept again for her friend.

For Victor, Katharine had found old Roman coins which had been dipped in gold and made into cufflinks. He stared at them blindly, his black eyes awash with sorrow. What a tragedy, he thought. Poor sweet Kath. Only forty-four.

Nick said dimly, 'She was always after me to get a pair of lapis lazuli cufflinks. To match my eyes, she used to say.' He opened his hand, displayed his gift, and turned away, remembering suddenly the story she had told him about the two old biddies in London.

Victor lifted Francesca's hand, and patted it tenderly, folded his own around it. 'We must have strong and happy memories of Katharine, and I say again, we *must* do all she wishes. Nick, you'll come to the ranch, won't you?'

'Yes, I will. And I'll bring my son. Just as my beloved Kath wanted it.'

'Will you come with us too, Ches?' Victor asked.

'Of course, Vic. Nicky needs me.'

Victor inclined his head, and he smiled at Francesca. His eyes held hers for the longest moment. He thought: I was her first love. Perhaps, with a little luck, I will be her last. Later, when all this is behind us. And then, under his breath he said: Che sarà sarà . . . what will be will be.

Finale
April 1979

'But when the days of golden dreams had perished,
And even despair was powerless to destroy,
Then did I learn how existence could be cherished,
Strengthened and fed without the aid of joy.'

Emily Brontë

The gardens at Ravenswood were so vibrant with colour and life, and fragrant with the mingled scents of the varied flowers, Katharine caught her breath as she walked down the lawn towards the bosky glade. She passed the giant pink floss tree and paused to admire its beauty, touching a rosy blossom gently. How tender it was, and perfectly made.

She drifted on, down the sloping lawn and past the swimming pool, until she came at last to her favourite spot. She settled on a rustic wooden chair, took a new packet of cigarettes from her pocket and lit one. Her doctor in London had asked her to cut down on her smoking. But she had wondered, for the last few months, what difference it made now.

She closed her eyes, but for only a moment, wanting to drink in the loveliness surrounding her. The house gleamed white and shining in the distance, and somewhere birds lifted their voices in warbling song and there was a rush of wings as the flock swept upwards into the lucent air, soared towards the incandescent azure sky. She sighed. It was peaceful here, so far away from the noise and clatter of the turbulent world.

Soon Beau would return. She had not let him know she was coming. And Beau had gone to play golf, so Tabella, his housekeeper, had told her when she had arrived a short while ago from New York. Her decision to come here had finally been made last night, as Nick had lain in an exhausted sleep in her arms. She thought of her most beloved Nicky and her heart stirred softly within her. She prayed he would go with Victor and Frankie to the ranch. He, too, would perhaps find a kind of peace there with them and his son. And her own child would join her next week, to stay as long as it was appropriate. Mike had promised. A smile flashed across her exquisite face. For weeks she had hidden her secret from Nick, from everyone. It had been the best acting of her life. And now it must continue for a while, this, her last performance. For Beau. He must not know. Not yet. Her gaze settled on the house. She had come to Ravenswood as a young bride. She had come back now to die.

Katharine squinted in the brilliant sunlight and shaded her eyes with her hand. Beau was running down the terrace steps, moving with speed across the lawn, hurrying, hurrying. To her. And then he was standing in front of her, a joyous expression flooding his face.

'Hello, Monkey Face,' he said. 'What are you doing here?'

Standing up, Katharine took hold of his hand, and laughed her tinkling girlish laugh. 'I've come home at last, Beau.'

He hugged her to him, overcome with happiness, his own laughter bubbling in his throat. And then he held her away, his face sobering, a frown knotting his brow. 'Yes, Monkey Face, but for how long?'

For half a second Katharine did not answer. She looked up at him, and her wondrous eyes, not blue, not green, but a curious unique turquoise, filled with sudden radiant light.

Her smile was sure. 'For the rest of my life,' she said.

Remember

This book is for my husband Robert,
who fights the good fight, with my
love and admiration.

Contents

Remember me when I am gone away,
Gone far away into the silent land;
When you can no more hold me by the hand,
Nor I half turn to go yet turning stay.
Remember me when no more day by day
You tell me of our future that you plann'd:
Only remember me; you understand
It will be late to counsel then or pray.
Yet if you should forget me for a while
And afterwards remember, do not grieve:
For if the darkness and corruption leave
A vestige of the thoughts that once I had,
Better by far you should forget and smile
Than that you should remember and be sad.

Christina Rossetti

PART ONE

Comrades-in-Arms

A friend may well be reckoned
the masterpiece of Nature.

Ralph Waldo Emerson

CHAPTER ONE

Sleep eluded her.

She lay in the darkness, trying to empty her head of every thought, troubling or otherwise, but this seemed to be an impossibility. Bone-tired though she had been earlier, when she had stripped off her clothes and fallen into bed, she was now wide-awake. All of her senses were alerted; she strained to catch any untoward sounds from outside. At this moment, though, very little noise penetrated the walls of the plush hotel suite. It was curious, ominous, the silence outside.

That's where I should be, she thought. Outside.

Certainly that was where she belonged, where her heart and mind were. Outside . . . with her crew: Jimmy Trainer, her cameraman, Luke Michaels, her sound engineer, and Arch Leverson, her producer. They usually hung together most of the time, like any good news team on foreign assignment.

It was rare for her not to be with them, but tonight, over an early dinner, she had been so weary, her eyelids dropping after several nights with little or no sleep, that Arch had insisted she grab a few hours in bed. He had promised to wake her in plenty of time for her to prepare for her nightly broadcast to the States. Common sense plus fatigue had prevailed; she had agreed, only to find herself unable to relax and drop off the moment she was between the cool sheets.

She was tense, expectant, and she knew the reason why. Her intelligence, judgement and instinct, combined with her experience as a war correspondent, were all telling her the same thing. It was going to happen tonight. The crackdown that had been in the wind for days would be tonight.

Involuntarily, she shivered at this foreknowledge, turned cold. Blessed with a prescience that was unusual, she knew better than to doubt herself, and she shivered again at the thought of bloodshed. Blood would be spilled if the People's Army moved against the people.

Pushing herself up against the pillows, she switched on the bedside lamp, glanced at her watch. It was a few minutes before ten. Throwing back the covers decisively, she got out of bed and hurried across the floor to the window. Opening it wide, she stepped out onto the balcony, anxious to see what, if anything, was happening in the streets of Beijing.

Her suite was on the fourteenth floor of the Beijing Hotel, overlooking Changan Avenue, also known as the Avenue of Eternal Peace, which led into Tiananmen Square. Below her on this wide boulevard, illuminated by cluster lights shaded in green, people were moving along steadily in a continuous flow, like trout heading upstream. As they passed through the pools of light cast by the lamps, she saw that they were mostly wearing white shirts or tops; they moved so quietly, so silently, she found this to be quite amazing.

587

They were making for Tiananmen Square, that vast rectangle of stone dating back to 1651 in the early Qing Dynasty, built to hold a million people in its one-hundred-acre expanse. She had come to understand that it was the symbolic heart of political power in China, and over the centuries the square had been the site of some momentous events in the country's turbulent history.

She sniffed the air. It was clear, held no hint of tear gas, or the smell of the yellow dust that perpetually blew in from the Gobi Desert and was normally all-pervasive in the congested capital. Perhaps the light wind was carrying both smells away from the hotel, or perhaps tear gas had not been used tonight. Glancing up and down the long avenue quickly, her eyes shifted back to the crowded pavement below her balcony and the people walking towards the square in such an orderly fashion. Everything appeared to be peaceful, and certainly the military were nowhere to be seen. At the moment.

The calm before the storm, she thought dismally, turned, and went back into the suite.

After switching on the rest of the lights in the bedroom, she hurried into the adjoining bathroom, where she splashed cold water on her face, patted it dry with a towel, and began to brush her hair in swift, even strokes.

The face surrounded by the soft blonde hair was somewhat wide with a strong jawline, but its individual features were classical, clean cut, well defined – high cheekbones, straight nose, pretty mouth, chin that was firm and resolute without being pugnacious. The eyes, set wide apart under arched blonde brows, were large and clear, their colour a light sea-blue that was almost but not quite turquoise. The features came together to create a face that was unusually attractive, lively with vivid intelligence and humour, highly photogenic. In her bare feet, as she was now, she stood five feet six inches tall; slender of frame yet surprisingly strong, she had long legs and possessed a willowy grace.

The young woman's name was Nicole Wells, known as Nicky to the world at large. But her family, crew and closest friends affectionately called her Nick most of the time.

At thirty-six she was at the height of her profession, war correspondent for the American Television Network, headquartered in New York. Renowned as a brilliant investigative reporter as well as a chronicler of war, and respected for her spectacular coverage of world events, she had a reputation for being courageous and intrepid. On camera she was charismatic: she had become a genuine superstar in the media.

Nicky put down the brush, pulled her hair straight back into a pony tail and anchored it firmly, before reaching into her makeup kit for a lipstick. Once she had outlined her mouth in pink, she leaned closer, grimacing at herself. She looked washed out, pallid, without makeup, but she was in too much of a hurry to start applying it. Besides, she was certain she would not be on camera tonight. When martial law had been declared on 20 May, almost two weeks ago now, the Chinese government had turned off the satellite; furthermore, television cameras had been banned in the square. No more live-spot location shots without that satellite feed or Jimmy behind his camera. At least not in Tiananmen Square, and that's where the story was – at the centre of the action. Once again, she would have to make do with a phoned-in report.

Swinging away from the mirror, Nicky returned to the bedroom, where she dressed rapidly in the clothes she had shed only a brief while ago: loose, beige cotton trousers, a blue cotton T-shirt, and a short-sleeved safari-style jacket which matched the pants. This was her standard uniform when she was abroad on assignment in the summer; she always packed three identical safari suits, plus a selection of T-shirts and man-tailored cotton shirts to add contrast colour to the suits, and for the benefit of the camera.

After she had slipped her feet into soft brown leather loafers, she went to the closet and took out her big shoulder bag, brought it back to the table. This was a commodious carryall made of some sort of sage-green waterproofed fabric; it contained what she laughingly referred to as 'my entire life,' and she rarely went anywhere without it when she was on foreign assignment. Now, as she always did before going out, she unlocked it, double-checked that her 'life' was indeed safely inside the bag. Passport, press credentials, plastic money, real money including US dollars, Hong Kong dollars, English pounds and the local yuan, door keys for her Manhattan apartment, world address book, a small cosmetic bag containing toothpaste, toothbrush, soap, makeup, eye drops, makeup mirror, hairspray, hair brush and a packet of tissues. All were neatly stashed in several separate compartments within the interior section of the bag; in the two large outside pockets were her cellular phone, tape recorder, notebook, pens, reading glasses, sun glasses and a packet of gauze surgical masks to protect against tear gas.

As long as she had the bag with her Nicky knew she could survive anywhere in the world without any other luggage and, just as importantly, do her job efficiently and effectively. But she did not need the bag with her tonight, only a few of its contents. These she now took out and locked the carryall. Her passport and press credentials, the cellular phone, reading glasses, notebook and pens, gauze masks, some of the US dollars and local yuan were the essential items, and she popped them into a much smaller shoulder bag made of brown leather.

Slinging the small bag over her shoulder, she pocketed the door key, picked up the carryall and returned it to the closet. She then left the suite, glancing at her watch as she did. It was just ten twenty.

Despite her sense of urgency, and her need to be outside in the square, Nicky nevertheless headed for the ATN suite a few doors away from her own, just in case Arch Leverson had returned to call New York. The time difference between China and the United States was exactly thirteen hours: it was nine twenty on Friday morning back home. This was about the time Arch generally checked in with Larry Anderson, the President of News at the ATN network.

The suite served as a makeshift newsroom-office for them, and when she got there it was her cameraman's voice she heard faintly echoing at the other side of the door. She knocked lightly.

A second later the door was wrenched open and Jimmy flashed her a huge grin when he saw it was she. 'Hi, honey,' he exclaimed, then walked back towards the desk, adding over his shoulder, 'I won't be a minute . . . just finishing a call to the States.'

Closing the door behind her, Nicky followed him into the room, placed her bag on a chair, and stood with her hand on the chair back, waiting.

At fifty-two Jimmy Trainer was in his prime. He was of medium height, slim

589

and spry, with greying dark hair, rosy cheeks in a merry face, and a twinkle in his pale-blue eyes. An ace cameraman who had won an endless number of awards, he loved his work and being part of Nick's team; his job was his life, even though he had a wonderful wife, a happy marriage and two children. And, like Luke and Arch, he was totally devoted to Nicky Wells. To Jimmy she was a dream to work with, and he would have put his life on the line for her.

Jimmy picked up the phone, resumed his conversation, talking in a low, fast tone, bringing the call to his wife to an end. 'Nicky just came in, Jo honey. I gotta go. Duty calls.' After listening a moment or two longer, he finally said an affectionate goodbye to her and broke the connection. Turning to Nicky, he remarked, 'This is the best damned phone system. Got to hand it to the Chinese, they certainly installed the most up-to-date equipment. Joanna sounded as if she was in the next room, instead of on Eighty-Third and Park, and she – '

'It's French,' Nicky interrupted. 'The phone system, I mean.'

'Yep, I guess I knew that. Jo sends her love.'

Nicky smiled at him. 'How is she?'

'Sounds fine. But she's watching the news on television, listening to the same news on the radio and worrying about the four of us. She seems to be handling it well, though, as she usually does.' His brow furrowed. 'But hey, kiddo, you're supposed to be grabbing a few hours' shut-eye, not hovering around here obviously anxious to start planning tonight's newscast.'

'I know, I know, but I couldn't sleep. I have a premonition something . . . no, *everything*, is going to blow tonight. My gut instinct tells me there's going to be a crackdown. Probably around midnight, or thereabouts.'

Catching the tension in her voice, noting her worried expression and the seriousness of her words, Jimmy looked at her alertly. After five and a half years of working with her in the trouble spots of the world, he trusted her intuition implicitly. Her judgement had rarely been flawed.

'If you say so, Nick, and you know I'm with you all the way. But look, I gotta tell you this, it *is* pretty quiet out there. At least it was twenty minutes ago.'

Nicky focused her eyes on him, the look in them quizzical. 'Nothing's happening in the square?'

'Not really. The kids in the tent encampment were starting to come out of their tents, mingling with each other and chatting, sort of sharing experiences, I suppose, as they appear to do every night.' For a moment he was thoughtful, before he went on, 'To tell you the truth, I was reminded of Woodstock tonight, without the drugs, of course. Or, if you prefer, one of those summer street festivals we have in New York. Everything was very relaxed, friendly, easygoing I'd say.'

'It won't be for much longer,' Nicky announced with quiet vehemence, and sat down heavily in a chair. 'I've been doing a lot of thinking, analysing, and I believe that Deng Xiaoping is at the end of his tether. He's been provoked and frustrated by the students for some time, and I'm sure he's about to make his move. It'll be a bungled move, just as he and the government have bungled the whole Tiananmen Square affair ever since it began. He'll have no compunction, you know. He'll order the troops to move on the students.' She sighed, finishing in a low, saddened voice, 'There's going to be a bloodbath, Jimmy.'

He stared at her. 'Not that, Nick, surely not! Deng wouldn't go so far.

590

He wouldn't *dare*. He'd hardly risk condemnation from the world and its leaders.'

She shook her head. 'You're wrong, James. He'll do it all right. And I'll tell you something else, I don't think Deng gives a damn about the rest of the world, its leaders, or what they think of him.'

The magnitude of her words struck him forcibly, and Jimmy exclaimed, 'Oh God! Those kids are so young, so idealistic!' His voice rose as he rushed on, 'And they're so peaceful. All they want is to be listened to . . . they just want to be *heard*.'

'That's never going to happen,' Nicky replied. 'You know as well as I do what the students call Deng and his cohorts . . . the Gang of the Old, and they're absolutely right. Deng is eighty-five and far, far *too* old to understand the way it is today. He's completely out of touch with this generation, all he's interested in is clinging to power. We know the students are not making unreasonable demands, and anyway, wanting freedom and democracy is a pretty normal thing, wouldn't you say?'

Jimmy nodded. He took a deep breath. 'Okay, so what do you want to do, Nick?'

'I want to be out there, right in the middle of it when it happens. That's why we're here, isn't it? To report the news, to bring the news to the people, to tell the outside world the way it is in China on this Friday night, the second day of June, in the year 1989.'

'We've still got one big problem, honey, we can't film out there,' Jimmy reminded her. 'The minute we appear, the police will smash the cameras and the sound equipment. What's more, we could get hauled in for questioning, like some of the other foreign correspondents have been. We could be detained, flung into jail – '

Jimmy broke off, glancing at the door as it opened to admit Arch.

Nicky's producer did not seem surprised to see her as he entered the room. 'And why might we be flung into jail?' he asked, focusing his attention on the cameraman.

'If we try to film in the square,' Jimmy answered.

'Only too true. Nothing's changed since yesterday,' Arch Leverson declared, and came to a standstill next to Nicky. He put a hand on her shoulder, squeezed it, gave her a warm smile, which she returned.

Always elegantly attired wherever he was, Arch was tall and thin, had a saturnine face, prematurely silver hair, and light-grey eyes behind steel-rimmed glasses. Forty-one years old and a veteran of the television news business, he had been lured away from another network by ATN three years ago. Quite aside from the hike in salary they offered, the most exciting inducement they dangled in front of him was Nicky Wells. The man who had produced her shows for several years had retired, and the job was open. There wasn't a producer in the television news business who didn't want to take over her newscasts, not to mention the documentaries she was famous for, and for which she had won several Emmys. His agent had negotiated a good contract for him and he had changed networks, had never once regretted doing so. He and Nicky had hit it off immediately; she was a real professional who had his utmost respect, not to mention his affection.

Nicky looked up at Arch, and said, 'There's going to be a crackdown . . . most probably tonight.'

Arch returned her quiet gaze with one equally steady, but he did not immediately respond. After a moment, he said slowly, 'You're not often wrong, Nicky, and I'm inclined to agree with you, military intervention is inevitable.'

'According to Jimmy, it was peaceful in the square earlier this evening. Has the atmosphere changed?' she asked Arch.

'Not really. In fact, I'd go as far as to say it's positively festive out there. Nevertheless, rumours are rife, mostly about troop movements seen in different parts of Beijing again. I just ran into one of the guys from CNN in the hotel lobby, and he told me he'd heard the same rumours.'

Arch moved across the room and sat down behind the desk, glanced from Nicky to Jimmy, looking considerably worried. 'We'd better prepare ourselves. I think it's going to be a rough weekend. Tough in every possible way.'

'I'm sure of it,' Nicky muttered.

Jimmy made no comment, nor did he react to the producer's dire prediction. Instead he paced up and down the room, looking preoccupied, fingering his chin. Finally he stopped, addressed Arch. 'Since we can't manage any live-shot locations in the square, I'm going to have to film Nick doing her standups in another part of town, the way we did at the beginning of the week.'

'I don't think we dare risk that again,' Arch exclaimed swiftly, shaking his head. 'The city's teeming with police, and we wouldn't get two steps before we were in deep trouble.'

'I was thinking of one of the districts on the edge of the city,' Jimmy explained, 'not anywhere remotely near Tiananmen. It'll be quieter out there.'

Arch shook his head again. '*No*. It won't be safe, Jimmy. It's putting Nick at risk, and needlessly so. I'm not going to take that chance – '

'Oh come on, Arch!' Nicky cut in peremptorily. 'I'm a war correspondent, remember. I've been in harm's way for years. I think we ought to do what Jimmy suggests – '

'But I don't!' Arch shot back, rather sharply for him. 'I just told you, I'm not putting you at risk. I'm not going to put any of us at risk, for that matter. Not here in China for this story.'

'Listen, Arch, I'm sick and tired of doing these phone narrations with my cellular from the square!' Nicky exclaimed. 'And I'm just as sure New York's sick of running stills of me to go with the narrations. Please, Arch, let's attempt to do at least one newscast live on camera tonight, no matter where we actually film it. I realize we can't feed it to New York via the satellite, that it'll have to be shipped, but even so the network would have it on time to run it Sunday or Monday.' Turning to her cameraman, she asked, 'There's no problem getting the moving film out by courier, via Hong Kong and Tokyo, is there?'

'The couriers are still operating,' Jimmy assured her. 'I suppose we could film you in your suite, even though you've been dead set against that, Nicky . . . ' Jimmy broke off, hurried over to the window. Pulling it open, he went out onto the balcony, stepped back inside, and stood gazing at the balcony from the room for a moment. He swung to Arch and said, 'I think there's a way to film Nick out there, with Changan and Tiananmen in the background. It'll be a tight squeeze, but it's worth a try.'

Arch sat up in the chair, looking suddenly more cheerful. 'Sure, Jimmy, why not! We've talked about it before, but always dismissed it. Now we don't have any choices left. In any case, out there on the balcony we'll be able to convey a sense of on-the-spot reporting. I hope. Which is what we're about, after all.'

'I'll start planning it,' Jimmy said.

Nicky went to the open window and surveyed the balcony, then, turning, she said to Jimmy, 'I'm sure it'll work, and I'm all for it.'

Arch said, 'Listen, Nick, I'm afraid you *will* have to do a phone narration for tonight's newscast, we've just no alternative. We'll do that first, then shoot out there, so that America can see you live, and in living colour, on Monday at the latest.'

'Okay. In the meantime, if you don't need me, I think I'll go to the square for a while.' Glancing over at Arch, she asked, 'Where's Clee? And Luke? At the Martyrs' Monument?'

'That's where I left them.'

'Then let's make that our rendezvous, shall we? Right now I want to walk around, nose about a bit, get a proper sense of what's really happening, talk to Yoyo and a few of the other students.'

'Jimmy and I will join you in about an hour,' Arch told her. 'After I've called the network.'

'See you later, guys.' Nicky picked up her bag, shrugged it onto her shoulder and hurried out of the suite, her manner efficient and breezy.

Arch Leverson sat staring at the door for a few minutes after she had left, his thoughts focused on Nicole Wells.

Whenever she went off on her own in a hazardous zone he automatically wanted to caution her to be careful, but he had schooled himself to resist the temptation. He had learned his lesson long ago, having had his head bitten off far too often in the early days of their association. He frequently wished he did not feel so protective about her, but he did, and there was little he could do to change his feelings. In any case, Jimmy and Luke were in the same boat as he was, constantly worrying about her well-being. And she was forever scaring the hell out of the three of them with the chances she took.

There was no question in his mind about her courage. She was fearless. Danger did not bother her; she thumbed her nose at it, seemed to relish it. More than once it had struck him that she behaved as though her life was of little consequence to her. But he knew this was a far-fetched idea, therefore it was always easy for him to dismiss it at once, which he now did. Naturally Nicky cared about her life, even if she *was* sometimes mighty casual about her personal safety.

Reaching into his pocket, Arch pulled out a packet of cigarettes, took one and lit it. Of course it was the story that mattered, that's what it was all about, what *she* was all about. The story came first, took precedence over everything else, and he understood why, being a newsman himself. Nicky Wells was like most other war correspondents, whatever their gender; she simply wanted to be at the centre of the action, where the excitement was. Both were potent

593

aphrodisiacs, as he well knew. And once tasted, those particular aphrodisiacs were hard to forgo.

She's a chip off the old block, he mused, thinking of her father as he drew on his cigarette. Andrew Wells had also been a renowned war correspondent in his earlier days. He continued to ply his trade, as a highly-respected columnist for the *New York Times*. Then there was her mother, who could hardly be overlooked: Elise Elliot Wells, Pulitzer Prize winner, former distinguished foreign correspondent, writer of important books.

Arch had often wondered what it must have been like, growing up with that formidable duo. Some childhood she must have had, being dragged around the world by two hot-shot journalists in search of headlines for their respective newspapers, who nonetheless had adored their only child, by all accounts. Still adored, in fact.

Once, in a confiding mood, she had told him that her father called her Nick because he had always wanted a son. That had explained a lot to him, and it had been a definitive clue to her personality, her devil-may-care attitude to danger. She wanted to be the brave 'son' whilst emulating daddy to the fullest, always seeking his approval.

Kind of a heavy load to dump on a kid, Arch thought, stubbing out his cigarette. Never once had he wished that his daughter Rachel had been a boy. He loved her exactly the way she was, didn't want to change her one iota. And not only was she his pride and joy, she had been a great comfort to him after he and her mother had been divorced.

As for Nicky, well, she was certainly very different from most people, undoubtedly because she had been exposed to so much at such a tender age, quite aside from having an extraordinary couple for parents. Also, she was well travelled, well educated, intelligent, cool-headed, determined, and very ambitious. Some combination in a young woman. Awesome, he had decided long ago.

Sadly her private life was a disaster, or so it seemed to him. There were no men around these days. At least, he had not heard her mention anyone special since the last relationship had gone bust in such an unfortunate way. Tragic really, when he thought about it, and it had certainly done Nicky in for a while. He wondered if she continued to be hurt, if she was still suffering because of the terrible way it had ended. It was hard for him to ascertain how she felt, because she never discussed her personal problems, and always kept up such a good front. Anyway, he did not dare pry. Nicky guarded her privacy fiercely. And so she should, Arch added to himself. What she does when she's not working is none of my business. Except that I care so damned much about her welfare.

Nicky Wells was one of the most decent human beings he had ever met. She was fair, thoughtful, kind, extraordinarily loyal, and she had immense integrity. He wanted only the best for her, the very best. He wanted her to be happy. What the hell, he thought, who's happy in this crazy world we live in today? He sighed and roused himself from these ruminations, reached for the telephone.

As he picked it up, Jimmy called out, 'Arch, before you get involved with New York, could you come over here for a minute, please? I'd like you to stand in for Nicky.'

'It'll be my pleasure,' Arch replied, putting the receiver down, pushing his chair back, and walking over to the window. 'But what exactly do you have in mind?'

'I'd like you to go outside on the balcony, so that I can get my camera angles set properly. It'll save time later. Shooting from this angle, I can get some good close-ups of her,' Jimmy explained. 'And with my long-range lens, if I position myself here among these plants, I can pick up the end of Changan Avenue and Tiananmen Square. We'll have to film when it's fairly light, unless I can rig up some sort of lighting out there. But it'll work, Arch, don't worry.'

'I'm not at all worried, James. Not when you're behind the camera.'

CHAPTER TWO

It was a balmy night, almost sultry.

Nicky walked along Changan Avenue at a steady pace, dodging in and out between the other pedestrians who were heading in the same direction.

When she first arrived in Beijing, Clee had told her that the Chinese always made their way to the square in the evenings and at weekends, whether to demonstrate or celebrate, mark a memorable occasion or simply while away the time. He had gone on to explain that they went there to think, to mourn, to stroll, and that it was also a place for Sunday outings.

Lately it had become a place for protests.

Since April students from every province in China had been peacefully demonstrating for democracy and freedom. It had actually begun at a memorial in the square for Hu Yaobang, a liberal and enlightened member of the government. A special favourite of the young, he had died earlier that month, and they had come to mourn his passing and celebrate everything he had stood for. Unexpectedly, the memorial had turned into a kind of sit-in, and then the hunger strikes and non-violent demonstrations had started.

This had happened over six weeks ago, and the students were still occupying the square – hundreds of thousands of them. What's more they were being fully supported by the citizens of Beijing, who brought them food and drinks, quilts and tents and umbrellas. And they sat with the students, commiserating and agreeing and airing their own grievances.

At exactly the same time these demonstrations were starting in Beijing in April, Nicky and her crew were in Israel, where they were doing a special on Mossad, the Israeli intelligence service. But by the end of the month, as they were finishing the special, Nicky had decided they must go to China. Mikhail Gorbachev was due to arrive in the Chinese capital in the middle of May for a state visit and, being fully aware of what the students were doing, Nicky smelled a story developing. A big story. She had phoned the President of News at the ATN network. 'Listen, Larry, the students aren't simply going to fold their tents and quietly steal away when Gorbachev comes to town,' she had pointed out. 'And it's my belief real trouble is brewing over there.'

Larry Anderson had hesitated momentarily, and she had pushed harder. 'Just think of it, Larry. Think of the scenario! How will the kids behave during Gorbachev's visit? Will they continue to demonstrate? Will they embarrass the government? How will Gorbachev react to them? And just as importantly, how will the Chinese government react to the situation? And what will they do?'

These were only a few of the questions she had posed that morning on the phone from Tel Aviv, and she had obviously been persuasive. After talking to Arch, Larry had agreed they should go. He had immediately pulled them out of the Middle East, brought them back to New York for a week's rest, then sent them jetting off to Mainland China with his blessing.

She and the crew had arrived on 9 May. Ostensibly they had come to cover the state visit of Mikhail Gorbachev, which was due to commence on 15 May. But they were really there because of the students – and Nicky's anticipation of trouble.

By the time the Russian leader, his wife, and entourage had descended, Nicky, Arch, Jimmy, and Luke were well ensconced in the Beijing Hotel, along with over one thousand foreign correspondents from every country in the world.

Just as Nicky had suspected, Gorbachev received something of a hero's welcome from the students, but there was a great deal of turmoil during his three-day visit, and the demonstrations continued unabated. As far as Nicky was concerned, the students had totally upstaged the summit meeting between the Russian and Chinese politicians, just as she had predicted they would. And she had made a point of focusing on the students and their predicament in her news reports.

At one point during Gorbachev's stay, one million demonstrators had converged on Tiananmen, demanding democratic rights, freedom of speech and a government free of corruption and graft. The students had hunkered down in the square, determined to remain there despite the heat of a scorching sun, sudden, violent thunderstorms and heavy rain.

Arch had made sure that Jimmy got everything on film, and Nicky's brilliant daily newscasts had been transmitted back to the States via the satellite. And for the short time that Gorbachev and the hordes of foreign reporters remained in Beijing, the government had turned a blind eye, assumed an air of tolerance about the students – and the foreign press as well.

But the authorities were quick to make their move two days after the Russians and much of the press had departed. They enforced martial law. Nicky and the crew had stayed on, as had several hundred other journalists. Something extraordinary was happening in China and the newsgatherers wanted to be there to do their job, to report unfolding events, history in the making.

Now, as she walked toward the square on this warm June night, Nicky's mind raced. She knew the end was imminent. The children were going to die. Thousands of them. With this terrible thought her step faltered, but only for a moment. She recovered herself at once, and walked on as steadily as before, even though her heart suddenly felt like a lead weight in her chest.

As a chronicler of war, revolution, famine, flood and earthquake, she was a constant witness to death and destruction, pain and anguish . . . on every level, in many countries. And she never grew accustomed to it, was forever pained and sickened by these catastrophic events.

Over the years she had come to know the world as a most terrifying and horrendous place to live. Unfortunately, there was nowhere else to go.

What she saw and reported on bit like corrosive acid into her. Yet she had learned a rigid self-control, had found a way to conceal her true emotions, not only for that all-seeing eye of the television camera, but for her crew and friends as well. Not even Clee knew her real feelings about such things, and he was the one person to whom she was the closest these days.

Nicky's pace quickened as her thoughts settled on Clee. He was in Tiananmen, and she needed to talk to him, to get his input. His instincts were excellent, and he had an emotional, visceral and intuitive response to events, just as she herself did. Moreover, she trusted his judgement. She always had, ever since they had first met in Lebanon, when they were both covering the long-running war there. They had been introduced on 3 June, the day after Premier Rashid Karami was assassinated, when a bomb had exploded in his helicopter. That was in 1987. Tomorrow she would have known Clee for exactly two years.

It was Arch Leverson who had made the introduction. Clee was an old friend of his, and they had accidentally bumped into each other in the lobby of the Commodore in West Beirut, the hotel favoured by the foreign press corps. Arch and Clee had made a date for drinks in the hotel bar that evening, and Arch had insisted on dragging her along.

Cleeland Donovan's fame had preceded him well in advance of this chance meeting, since he was something of a celebrity and a legend in his own time. He was considered to be the greatest war photographer and photojournalist since Robert Capa, and like Capa he had a reputation for being very courageous and daring. It was a well-known fact that Clee Donovan always flung himself into the middle of the action on a battlefield in order to get the most powerful images on film, his bravery and daring only serving to add to his legend. An expatriate American living in Paris, he had founded *Image*, his own photo news agency, at the age of twenty-five, and had seemingly never looked back. His pictures appeared in every leading magazine and newspaper in the world, he had published several books of his work, all of which had been best sellers, and he was the recipient of many awards for his photojournalism. Also, according to Arch, he was glamorous, worldly, loaded with sex appeal and highly attractive to women.

A faint smile touched Nicky's mouth as she remembered the night they had met. As she had changed into a fresh safari suit in her room at the Commodore, she had added up every single thing she had ever heard about Clee Donovan, and instantly she had known what to expect. Obviously he was going to be insufferable – a man who was more than likely far too handsome for his own good, extremely conceited, full of himself and certainly egocentric.

She had been wrong. He was none of these things.

When he had walked into the bar of the Commodore, glanced around and headed in their direction, she had believed he was someone else. She had at first surmised he was another friend of Arch's, who had also been invited to join them.

Clee did not have the glamorous movie-star looks she had expected him to have,

597

although he was quite good looking in a clean cut, all-American way. He had a *nice* face, that was the best way of describing it, and it was one that was open and honest. His hair was dark, his eyes brown, their expression gentle, and his sensitive mouth was quick to smile. He was about five feet ten inches in height, but appeared to be taller since his body was lean and athletic.

A pleasant, ordinary sort of guy, despite all that fame, all that success, she had decided, as he had seated himself at the table, ordered a drink and begun to chat amiably to them. Within twenty minutes or so she had changed her mind. *Ordinary* was certainly the wrong word to apply to Clee. He was highly intelligent, amusing, and blessed with a natural charm that was irresistible. It quickly became apparent to her that he was well informed and he had held them spellbound with his stories, fully living up to his reputation.

That evening she had believed him to be her age, maybe even a bit younger, but later Arch told her Clee was three years older than she was. This had surprised her, since he was so boyish in appearance.

The other thing Nicky had discovered at their first meeting was that he was a man with little or no conceit, contrary to what she had previously believed. He *was* sure of himself, but it was a self-assurance about his work, and it sprang from his ability and talent as a photojournalist. Eventually she had come to understand that his work was his lifeblood.

In any case, that night in Beirut they had taken a great liking to each other, and their friendship had grown over the weeks and months that followed. Frequently, they found themselves in the same trouble spots, covering the same stories. When they did they always joined forces.

Sometimes they went in different directions, and were on opposite sides of the world, but they always managed to stay in touch by phone, and through their respective offices.

A strong fraternal feeling had developed between them, and she had come to think of Clee as the brother she had never had; certainly he was her very good friend, her comrade-in-arms.

CHAPTER THREE

Cleeland Donovan sat on one of the ledges encircling the Monument to the People's Heroes, also known as the Martyrs' Monument, staring at the Goddess of Democracy.

This thirty-three-foot statue had been erected in the middle of the square by the students so that it was facing down a giant portrait of Mao Zedong which hung above Tiananmen Gate. The defiant white statue, composed of plaster and styrofoam, had been made by the students and faculty of the Central Academy of Fine Arts, who had then brought it to the square in a somewhat ceremonious fashion.

It reminded Clee of the Statue of Liberty. It was not so much the face that was familiar, but rather the posture, plus the toga-like robe draped around the body, with the raised arms holding high a torch of freedom. Clee found the statue ugly, but that did not matter. It was the symbolism that counted.

He had been present in Tiananmen when the students had erected the goddess and unveiled it three days ago. They had sung the 'Internationale' amidst much cheering, and shouts of 'Long live democracy!' had rung out across the square; the ceremony had been emotional, had touched him deeply.

Clee had managed to shoot several rolls of film surreptitiously, even though cameras were forbidden in the square; three of his had already been smashed by the police. Fortunately, he had several in reserve, including the Nikon F4 which was strapped to his shoulder underneath the loose cotton jacket he was wearing.

The night the statue had been brought to the square the weather had changed in the early hours. There had been strong winds and rain, but, remarkably, the goddess was undamaged the following morning; there wasn't even a scratch on her. How long she would remain so was another matter.

Clee knew the goddess had irritated and outraged the government more than anything else the students had done, and government officials had denounced it as a 'humiliation' in such a historically important and solemn place as Tiananmen Square.

On the other hand, it had been the shot in the arm the kids had needed, and just seeing the statue in such a strategic spot had really lifted their flagging spirits. To protect the goddess they had erected tents around her base, and groups of students were always present, always ready to defend her.

But the government *will* tear it down, Clee thought, and sighed heavily at this prospect.

Luke Michaels, seated next to Clee, looked at him swiftly. 'Something wrong?'

'I was just wondering how long *that's* going to be standing there?' he murmured softly, gesturing to the statue.

'I dunno.' Luke shrugged, ran a hand through his dark-red hair, turned his earnest, freckled face to Clee. 'Forever, perhaps?'

'You've got to be kidding!' Clee laughed hollowly. 'I give it a couple of days, that's all, before it's totally destroyed. I can guarantee you this, Luke, it definitely won't be standing there a week from today.'

'Yeah, I guess you're right, it's a thorn in Deng's side. Correction, it's a thorn in all of their sides. The Gang of the Old can't stand the sight of it, and they consider the making of it an act of pure defiance. It was wishful thinking on my part, hoping the statue would stand forever as a sort of tribute to the kids.'

'Nobody around here is going to pay *them* a tribute, except for us – the press. And our tribute is to keep telling the world about them and their struggle, whatever it takes to do that on our part.'

Luke nodded, made no comment. He shifted his position slightly, leaned back against the stone, closed his eyes. It was photojournalists like Clee and correspondents like Nicky who often risked their lives to bring the truth to the public, and he found the two of them inspiring. They were his heroes. He especially admired Nicky Wells. She was what his mother called a real trouper. *He* thought she was pretty neat. He wasn't married yet, or seriously dating anybody special, but when the time came for him to settle down, he hoped he would find a woman like Nicky. There was something warm and reassuring about her, and she didn't put men down.

He had been part of Nicky's crew for just over a year, and he had seen a lot, learned a lot, working with her and the guys. He was twenty-seven and had been in the television business for only five years, and he knew he was green in some respects. But Nicky had been helpful and very nice to him right from the beginning, had treated him like a seasoned veteran. She was a stickler about punctuality and many other things as well, and a perfectionist, and sometimes she could blow her stack. But she was a real pro, and he'd do just about anything for her. He wished she could find a good guy. There were times when she looked sad, and her eyes held a strange, distant expression as if she were remembering something awful or painful. And there *was* some sort of mystery in her past. It was about a man she'd been going with before he had joined her team. Arch and Jimmy were pretty close-mouthed about it, though, and he didn't like to ask too many questions. Still, it was a shame she was alone. What a waste of a lovely woman –

'Luke! Luke!'

The sound engineer opened his eyes, sat up with a jolt on hearing his name being called. He looked down. At the base of the monument people were milling about, as they usually were, since this spot was command headquarters for the student movement. The foreign press corps tended to congregate in the area and there was always a great deal of activity.

Luke spotted his buddy Tony Marsden immediately. Tony was beckoning to him.

Luke waved back, and stood up. 'I'll go and see what Tony wants,' he said to Clee. 'Maybe he knows something we don't, has some new information. I won't be long.'

'Take your time, Luke, I ain't going nowhere.' Not for a day or two at least, Clee added under his breath. He knew he would be leaving China soon, though. The end was in sight. He sat gazing down into the square, his elbows on his knees, his head propped in his hands. His face settled into morose lines; he felt sad for the kids – so idealistic, so innocent, so very brave. When he had first come to Beijing almost six weeks ago they had been full of excitement. And hope. They had spoken stirring words about liberty and democracy, and had sung their songs, played their guitars. Their guitars were still tonight. Soon their voices would be still. He shuddered slightly and goose flesh sprang up on his skin. He hated to think of their fate. He realized they were in grave danger, although he had not voiced this to Nicky or anyone else. He did not have to; they all knew that time was running out for the students.

Suddenly, Clee saw Nicky walking through the square towards the monument. Like Changan Avenue, Tiananmen was extremely well illuminated with numerous tall street lamps, each one topped with branches of lights, about nine altogether and shaded in white opaque glass. The square was so bright it was almost like daylight and everyone was visible; it was even possible to read a book quite comfortably.

A smile touched his eyes at the sight of Nicky, and he clambered down off the ledge and dodged through the crowd, hurrying forward to meet her.

600

Nicky spotted him and waved.

He raised his hand in greeting, and a moment later he was drawing to a standstill in front of her, smiling broadly. 'I knew you'd be out here before long,' he said.

She nodded. 'I had to be here, Clee. My instinct tells me the situation is about to blow.'

'Wide open,' he confirmed, then took her arm, guided her away from the monument. 'Do you mind if we walk around for a bit? I need to stretch my legs, I've been sitting on that ledge for about an hour.'

'No, of course I don't mind, that's what I'd like to do, and perhaps we'll see Yoyo. He's usually with Chai Ling and some of the other student leaders. He might know something new.'

'And he's constantly in touch with the Flying Tigers. I've noticed several of them whizzing around on their bikes in the last hour,' Clee remarked, referring to a motorcycle brigade of young entrepreneurs who had also been dubbed 'Paul Reveres' by the American press. They roared all over Beijing, carrying messages, monitoring troop movements and the actions of the police, and in general acting as look-outs for the students.

'Yoyo's probably in the tent encampment. Shall we head over there?' she suggested.

'You got it.'

'Where's Luke? Arch said he was with you.'

'He was, but he just went off with that guy from the BBC, Tony Marsden. They're somewhere around. Do you need him?'

'No, I just wondered, that's all. And talking of the BBC, have you seen Kate Adie this evening?'

'She's probably somewhere in the crowd. There are a helluva lot of foreign press out tonight – trouble in the wind.'

Nicky looked at him swiftly. 'I think the crackdown's almost upon us, don't you?'

'Yes. The students and the government have reached an impasse, something's got to give. It'll have to be the students, I'm afraid, and we're going to see a lot of force thrown against them.'

Nicky shivered despite the warmth of the evening. 'That's an awful prospect, but I have to agree. Where's your camera?'

'Strapped to my shoulder under my jacket. My buddies from Magnum and the Associated Press are doing exactly the same thing. As are most of the photographers. It's the only way to fly.'

'Clee . . . '

'Yes, Nick?' He glanced at her questioningly.

'It's going to get very dangerous out here . . . real soon.'

'I'm damned sure of it. And before you say it, yes, I'll be careful.' A faint smile played around his mouth. 'As careful as you are.'

'*I* don't take unnecessary chances, even though Arch seems to think I do. I try to minimize the odds against me.'

'That's another thing we have in common,' Clee said.

'What's the other?'

'We both have nerves of steel.'

'I suppose we do,' she agreed, laughing. 'We have to have in this business. Just as we have to have a sixth sense for danger.'

Clee nodded but did not say anything else, and they walked on in companionable silence for a few minutes. As they came to the tent encampment, Nicky turned to him. 'You know this place has really taken on a life of its own, what with the tents and the buses. It's like a small town, and – '

'A shanty town,' Clee cut in.

'You're right, and I hope to God it doesn't smell tonight.'

'I'm sure it won't, they've probably removed the garbage by now. In any case, there's a nice breeze blowing up.'

'The other day when I came looking for Yoyo it was very . . . malodorous. That's the only word for it. The stench was disgusting, awful, rotting food, unwashed bodies, heaven knows what else, and I felt nauseous the entire time I was in here.'

Nicky sniffed as they entered the encampment and walked past several buses where some of the students lived. The air was fresh, and the area looked as if it had been recently swept and cleaned up. It was perfectly clean; there was no trash in sight.

Nicky was constantly surprised when she saw the neat lines of olive-green tents, waterproof and commodious, which had been sent from Hong Kong. They were very orderly, arranged in horizontal patterns with almost military precision, and lettered signs hung over each group, the signs identifying where the different contingents had come from. There were delegations of students from almost every university in every province of China.

Weeks ago she had discovered that most of the students slept during the day, mainly because the action was at night. Now the majority of the tents were empty, although a few late stragglers were only just emerging, getting ready for the rest of the evening and the early hours of the morning which lay ahead.

Vendors hung around on the pavement, selling sodas, bottled water, ices, popsicles, and other small snacks.

Clee glanced at her. 'Would you like a popsicle?'

She made a face, shook her head.

The young Chinese student, Chin Yong Yu, nicknamed Yoyo, was standing with a young woman in the centre of the encampment near his own tent. They both wore blue jeans and white cotton shirts. She was attractive and looked to be about the same age as Yoyo, who was twenty-two. Nicky wondered if this was his girlfriend, whom he had mentioned to her and who had been visiting relatives in Shanghai for the past few weeks. He was deep in conversation with the girl, but when he saw them he broke off and waved enthusiastically. Turning to her, he said something, and then hurried over to greet them.

Yoyo was an art student, and Nicky had met him quite by accident in Tiananmen Square when she had first arrived in Beijing. She had been trying to speak to some of the students that day, actually seeking someone who understood English. Yoyo had approached her with a smile, and told her, in fairly understandable English, that he would be happy to help her if he could. He had been useful in all sorts of ways; he had passed on information, introduced her to other student leaders, such as Chai Ling and Wuer Kaixi, and kept her abreast of developments amongst the students and the leaders of the movement. He was bright, friendly, and she had grown quite fond of him, as had the crew, and Clee. They worried about Yoyo, and what would happen to him, especially when all this was over.

'Nicky!' Yoyo cried, coming towards her, smiling widely, his hand outstretched.

'Hello, Yoyo,' she said, shaking his hand. 'Clee and I were looking for you.'

'Good evening, Clee,' Yoyo said.

'Hi, Yoyo! What's going on?' Clee asked as he took the student's hand.

Yoyo's expression changed, and he looked grim as he confided quietly, 'Bad things coming. Army drop canisters of tear gas from helicopters. On square. Tonight. You see. You have masks? Also, troops coming.'

'*Tonight?* The troops are coming *tonight?*' Nicky probed.

Yoyo nodded. 'I hear troops hidden in buildings near square. They come. Very sure. Bad things happen. You tell world, yes?'

'We'll certainly keep telling the world, Yoyo,' Nicky assured him. 'But do you believe the People's Liberation Army will open fire on the people?'

'Oh yes. *Yes.*' He nodded emphatically. 'Some students say no, not possible. The People's Liberation Army our army, they say. Won't kill us. They foolish. Army very disciplined. Army follows orders. I know this.'

Nicky stared at him, her clear, intelligent eyes riveted on his face. 'You should leave the square. *Now.* While it's still possible, still safe.'

'That wise, yes,' Yoyo agreed. 'But not everyone go, Nicky. Hard get everyone go. Blood spilled tonight.'

Nicky shivered involuntarily and looked pointedly at Clee.

Clee said, 'What about Chai Ling and some of the other leaders? Can't they get the students to leave?'

Yoyo shrugged. 'Don't know.'

'Where are they?' Clee asked.

'Don't see tonight. You like water? Soda?'

'No thanks,' Clee answered.

Nicky shook her head, smiling at Yoyo.

The young Chinese was thoughtful, then he remarked, 'Movement lost spirit after martial law declared. Students very depressed. True, they should leave. They won't. End will be bad thing.'

'Come with us,' Nicky said urgently. 'Come with us to the Martyrs' Monument, find one of the bullhorns you've been using, and relay a message to the students. They'll listen to you, you're one of their leaders. Ask them to leave, beg them, if necessary. And you must leave with them. If you and the other students get out of Tiananmen while there's still time, you'll save your lives. Please, Yoyo, do this. It will be an act of bravery if you lead the students away from the square. It will be a good thing to do.'

She reached out impulsively, took hold of his arm, stared deeply into his eyes. 'Please, Yoyo, don't stay here. You could be killed.'

Her words appeared to reach him. 'I come monument. Soon. Bring Mai, my girlfriend. Go, Nicky. I come soon. I promise.'

'We'll be waiting for you. Don't be too long, Yoyo. There's not much time left.'

Nicky and Clee returned to the Martyrs' Monument.

They found Luke waiting for them, and Nicky told him what had transpired with Yoyo, repeating what the student leader had said to them about the troops coming that night or in the early hours of the morning.

'Oh Jesus!' Luke exclaimed. 'Those kids don't stand a chance if that happens.'

'They're sitting ducks,' Nicky pointed out. 'They're centred in a relatively small area, in relation to the overall size of the square, which is three-quarters empty right now. If the army comes in from the other side, it'll have a clear run straight across the square.'

'That's right,' Luke muttered, sounding troubled.

'Let's hope Yoyo can persuade the students to leave before that happens,' Clee said, wanting to be positive.

Nicky was silent, her expression anxious, but within seconds she brightened. 'Here he is now, thank goodness. Perhaps we can get him up on the monument with a bullhorn at once. He can at least *warn* the kids.'

Yoyo and his girlfriend Mai joined them. They were holding hands, and Yoyo said, 'This my friend, Mai. *Her* English not very excellent. Sorry.'

'No need to apologize,' Nicky replied with genuine warmth. She looked at Mai, and was startled by her. When she had seen the girl a little earlier, she had not realized how lovely Mai was. Her features were beautiful, and her black, almond-shaped eyes were enormous in her sweet, innocent young face. She had long glossy black hair, was a small and slender creature, and everything about her was delicate, almost dainty. Nicky thought she was enchanting, like a little doll.

Thrusting out her hand, Nicky said with a welcoming smile, 'I'm pleased to know you, Mai.'

The girl smiled back, although rather shyly, showing perfect white teeth. She took Nicky's hand in hers, and Nicky was surprised at the firmness of her hold; her grip was surprisingly strong. 'Hi,' she said softly.

Next, Mai shook hands with Clee and Luke, who murmured their greetings and smiled, obviously appreciating the girl's inherent loveliness as much as Nicky.

Nicky swung her eyes to Yoyo. 'Did you find a bullhorn?'

'Not necessary. *I* don't speak. Chai Ling speak. Later.'

'You've seen her?' Nicky asked, her voice suddenly sharp.

'Yes, near goddess. Chai Ling will take bullhorn, tell students to go home. She promise.'

'Let's hope she keeps that promise,' Clee murmured. 'In the meantime, let's take the weight off our feet.'

The five of them found places on the ledges that ran around the base and lower part of the monument, and sat down to wait for Arch and Jimmy. And hopefully Chai Ling, the respected leader of the student movement, commander-in-chief of the Tiananmen demonstrators, and a graduate student in psychology at Beijing Normal University.

*   *   *

604

It was almost one o'clock in the morning of 3 June when Arch and Jimmy finally appeared. They came running into the square at a rapid jog. As they drew to a stop in front of the small group clustered together on the monument, Nicky immediately noticed their troubled expressions.

'What is it?' she cried, glancing at Arch and then at Jimmy, a blonde brow raised speculatively. She sat forward tensely.

Between short gasps, trying to catch his breath, Arch blurted out, 'The troops are coming down Changan Avenue from the east. We just saw them as we were heading towards the square and – '

Jimmy interjected, 'They're being stopped by the people.'

'What do you mean?' Nicky cried, looking puzzled.

'The citizens of Beijing have formed a blockade . . . with their bodies. A human blockade. To stop the army getting to the students in the square. They're keeping the army out of the square,' Jimmy explained.

'I'll be damned,' Luke said.

Clee did not wait to hear another word, and neither did Nicky. They wanted to see everything for themselves, as always the observers, the reporters.

Simultaneously they both jumped off the ledge where they were sitting together and began to run towards Tiananmen Gate which led into Changan Avenue. They were closely followed by Yoyo, who was clutching Mai's hand, and behind them came Luke, sprinting forward at such a speed he soon caught up with Clee and Nicky. Arch and Jimmy took a few seconds to catch their breath, and then they also took off at a fast pace, making for the entrance onto the avenue.

Nicky and Clee were the first to reach the crowds of people flooding Changan. And almost instantly they were separated from each other by the swirling masses.

She had never seen anything like this in her life. It was formidable. What Jimmy had said was true. The citizens *were* blocking the army, preventing the soldiers from moving forward, literally holding them back with their bodies. They truly were a human shield. She saw that they were actually *pushing* the soldiers back. And what an army it was. Kids, she thought in astonishment, as she stared at the troops. They were just kids; they looked even younger than the students.

Nicky lost no time. Without considering her own safety, she moved closer to the crowds, needing to be nearer the action. Within seconds she was surrounded by people, caught in the middle of them against her own volition, and swept forward by the force and movement of their bodies. There was a lot of pushing and shoving. Several times she swayed, almost went down. At one moment, as people pressed into her from behind, she reached out, desperately clutched at a man's arm. He swung around angrily, then quickly helped her to regain her balance. Almost immediately, and unexpectedly, a young woman grabbed at her jacket, as the crowd surged forward yet again, carrying everyone closer to the troops. Nicky almost fell because the Chinese woman was clinging to her with such tenacity, but somehow she stayed upright, and they bolstered each other, gave each other physical support. The mass of people swept on and on, and Nicky thought she would stumble or be knocked over, or that she would be trampled. She was conscious of people jostling her, pressing into her from all sides. And so hemmed in was she that she had trouble keeping her balance, staying on her feet.

Exactly at the precise moment she experienced her first flicker of panic, wondered if she was going to be crushed to death, she felt a hand grasp her elbow roughly. Half turning her head, looking over her shoulder, she saw Arch standing immediately behind her.

'Thanks,' she gasped with relief, then shouted above the noise, 'The troops seem to be unarmed.'

'They also look frightened to death.'

'Bewildered.'

There was a great deal more pushing and shoving and jostling, as well as angry shouting on the part of the Beijingers before they surged onward en masse. They were like a huge tidal wave of immense force and power, as they propelled Nicky and Arch along with them.

Immediately ahead were the young soldiers, none of whom looked to be a day older than eighteen. They were being mauled and bruised and scratched as the people pushed at them, ranted at them. Nicky began to realize that the inflamed citizens of the capital were lecturing the soldiers, scolding them as if they were their children. Most of the troops were milling around in total confusion, and many of them had broken down and were starting to cry.

Clinging to Arch tightly, Nicky exclaimed, 'These kids don't know what the hell this is all about!'

'I'm convinced of it,' Arch answered, putting his arm around her waist, grabbing her to him, determined to keep her safe in this melee.

Unexpectedly, she saw Jimmy pushing his way closer to them.

How he had found them in the crowds Nicky would never know. He had sprung up as if from nowhere, and swiftly he took hold of her arm. 'Come on, we're getting out of this mob!' he cried.

By using great force and being ruthlessly aggressive, Jimmy and Arch managed to push Nicky and themselves through the seething mass of people until they were finally staggering out onto the extreme edge of Changan Avenue. They were sweating and panting, and the three of them stood huddled together under the trees at the side of the wide boulevard, breathing sighs of relief as they straightened their clothes.

Arch said, 'By the looks of those kids, we weren't in danger of being shot at, but we *were* in danger of being trampled to death by that mob.'

'Our best bet is to stand here and watch what's happening from the sidelines,' Nicky announced.

Arch and Jimmy were startled by her words.

Jimmy said, 'Hey, that's a new one for you, kiddo! When have *you* ever been on the sidelines?' Not waiting for an answer, he rushed on, 'But you're right, it *is* safer here. Being in the middle of that lot was like being in the centre of . . . a stampede. And what an army it is . . . just look at 'em. They're burdened down with camp gear, canteens and knapsacks, yet they don't have any weapons.' He shook his head wonderingly.

'I *told* you they weren't armed, Arch,' Nicky said.

Clee hurried to join them a few minutes later. His hair was rumpled, his jacket ripped, but otherwise he looked totally unscathed. His Nikon was slung around his neck and there was a triumphant glint in his dark eyes. 'I got some great shots,' he told them.

'Isn't that a bit dangerous, showing your camera, Clee?' Jimmy asked, eyeing the Nikon nervously. 'It's liable to get pulled off your neck and smashed.'

'Not by this bunch, James,' Clee shot back confidently. 'They're on my side, on *our* side. They *want* their pictures taken . . . they're chanting the usual thing . . . tell the world, tell the world.'

'But the riot police – ' Arch began and abruptly stopped. 'I guess there are no police around.'

'It's doubtful,' Clee responded. 'At this moment, anyhow.'

'Maybe I should go and get our cameras, try something live with Nicky,' Jimmy suggested, looking at Arch. 'We might just get away with it.'

'*No*,' Arch said.

'I'll do a phone narration, and we can film on the balcony later, Jimmy, as we planned,' Nicky soothed, knowing it was hopeless to argue with Arch when he was in this overly-cautious mood. She had frequently been in the line of fire on battlefields and he hadn't batted an eyelash or said anything about danger. But ever since they had been in Beijing he had been mouthing words of warning constantly, and she couldn't help wondering why. She would ask him later. Now was not the time. She glanced around, her eyes seeking Luke. He was nowhere to be seen; neither were Yoyo and little Mai. They had been swallowed up by that mass of swaying, shouting people.

But eventually, much to her relief, Luke hove in view, and Yoyo and Mai were with him. She was limping, had obviously hurt her leg or her foot, and Yoyo was helping her.

'Has Mai been injured?' Nicky cried in concern, running to them.

'Not serious,' Yoyo said. 'Man stand on Mai's foot. She okay.'

Nicky put her arm around the Chinese girl's shoulders in a rather motherly fashion, and the four of them walked over to the spot where the others were gathered.

Luke said to Nicky, 'It's surprising the rest of us weren't hurt. You *are* okay, aren't you, Nicky?'

'I'm fine, thanks, Luke. And presumably you are?'

'Not a scratch.'

They sat down under the trees on the side of Changan Avenue, wanting to collect themselves and cool off. In spite of the breeze, the air was warm, almost heavy, and both Nicky and Clee took their jackets off. Arch passed around a packet of cigarettes but everyone declined, except for Yoyo. Mai sat next to him, examining her foot, and said something to him in Chinese. He smiled, nodded, quickly turned to Nicky. 'Mai say foot not broken. Bruised.'

Nicky nodded. 'Good.' She leaned forward to Yoyo with enormous urgency. 'Did you find anything out? Where are those troops from? And what's happening?'

Yoyo puffed on his cigarette for a second, and then he told her, 'Troops from far away. From outside Beijing. They march many hours. They told go on manoeuvres. They told go stop troublemakers. They no understand. They afraid. They young boys. People lecture them. Tell them don't hurt students.

607

Soldiers don't know this Beijing. Don't know where this is. They no fight, Nicky. They too scared.'

'Thank God for that, but what an anticlimax!' Nicky exclaimed.

'Where are the helicopters?' Clee asked, looking up at the night sky, then at Yoyo.

'No come now,' Yoyo said, sounding as though he knew what he was talking about. 'No tear gas.'

There was a small silence.

It was Nicky who broke it. 'The People's Liberation Army came to Beijing to quell the student demonstrators, and were conquered by the citizens. Not a single shot was fired.'

And several hours later that was how she began her nightly newscast to the United States.

Saturday dawned bright and sunny.

The young soldiers, still bewildered and now very dispirited, finally retreated down Changan Avenue in the middle of the morning.

The Beijingers went home and stayed there, or continued on to their places of work. The students went to sleep in their tents and buses, and a certain air of calmness descended over Changan Avenue and Tiananmen Square. There was a semblance of order and normality.

Nicky was convinced the tranquillity was phony and that the situation had been contained for only a short while – a dozen or so hours at the most. The way she saw it, the Chinese government would take a hard line because they would perceive the army's retreat as a humiliation. They would automatically blame the students, even though it had been the ordinary citizens who had stood up to the troops, and prevented them from entering the square. And they would act accordingly, with great force and violence.

After snatching a few hours' sleep, once her broadcast was finished, she had been in and out of the square all day. Instinctively, she knew that the atmosphere of calmness was underscored by tension and fear, and she voiced this thought to Clee.

They sat having a snack in the Western Dining Room of the Beijing Hotel on Saturday afternoon. Leaning across the table, she added, 'The crackdown's still coming. I'm just off by a few hours, that's all.'

'I know,' Clee said, and took a sip of his coffee. Putting the cup down, he went on in a low tone, 'The government wants those kids out of the square in the worst way now. They're losing face in the West, and they can't stand that. I'll tell you something else, Nick, when it does happen it'll be fast.'

'And bloody. And short. It won't last very long, Clee.'

He nodded. 'By Monday it'll be all over bar the shouting, and the aftermath's going to be pretty goddamn lousy. There'll be arrests, trials, repression, and Christ knows what else.'

'I'm concerned about Yoyo,' Nicky confided, sudden worry flicking into her eyes. 'He's been in the thick of it, and he is one of the leaders. He's going to be in grave danger. I wish we could get him out of Beijing.'

'We can,' Clee said. Bringing his head closer to hers across the table, he continued, 'And incidentally, you just took the words right out of my mouth. I was about to tell you that I've been thinking about giving him money for an airline ticket. For Hong Kong. We'll take him along with us when we leave. He can stay there for a few days and decide what he wants to do.'

'I'll split the price of the ticket with you.'

'You don't have to,' he began, then seeing the determined look on her face, he finished, 'Okay, you've got a deal.'

'There's another problem.'

'What's that?'

'*Mai*. Yoyo won't leave Beijing without her.'

'So we'll give him enough for two plane tickets. I couldn't live with myself if we left those two kids behind, and I know for sure you couldn't, Nicky. Arch and the guys'll feel the same way, and it's the least we can do. Yoyo's been terrific, very helpful to all of us.' He grinned. 'So what the hell, Mai comes along as well. The more the merrier.'

Nicky smiled at him. 'You're a good guy, Clee Donovan.'

'So are you, Nicky Wells.' There was a little silence, and then Clee asked, 'Where are you heading when we leave here?'

'You mean after Hong Kong?'

'Yeah.'

'New York. Where are you going?'

'Back to gay Paree. But I may be in New York at the end of this month. When I spoke to the office last night, or rather, in the early hours of this morning, Jean-Claude told me there's an assignment in from *Life* Magazine for me. If I want it. And I'm thinking of taking it . . . I wouldn't mind a few weeks back in the good old US of A.'

'Oh God, finally I'm stuck!' Nicky exclaimed, rolling her eyes to the ceiling.

'What do you mean?'

'If you come to New York at long last, I'm going to have to cook you that fancy dinner I've been promising you for the last year and a half.'

'Hey, Nick, that'll be great!' he cried, his face lighting up. 'I'm holding you to it, and I'll bring the wine.' He motioned to one of the waitresses, and as she came gliding over to the table he asked her for the check. Turning to Nicky, he said, 'Let's mosey on back to the square, see what's going on. I get a bit nervous if I'm away for very long.'

'I know what you mean,' she said, pushing her chair away and standing up. 'Ready when you are.'

CHAPTER FOUR

The killing began just after ten o'clock on Saturday night.

At that time Nicky and Clee were standing with Yoyo and Mai near the Martyrs' Monument. Arch, Jimmy and Luke were mingling with the other broadcast journalists, mostly American and British, who were assembled nearby. All were comparing notes, trying to predict what would happen next, whilst knowing the worst was coming.

Nicky was speaking to Yoyo quietly, earnestly, trying to be as persuasive as possible. 'Please take the money, Yoyo. I know how proud you are, but this is not the moment for pride. You must be practical. Listen to me . . . we *insist* you take the three thousand dollars, it will get you and Mai out of Beijing. Clee and the guys and I think you should leave tomorrow, no matter what the situation is here. And the money is from the five of us. We want to help you . . . after all, you've helped us. And we care about you.'

'Too much money,' Yoyo said. 'Thank you. No.' He kept shaking his head. 'You, Clee, guys very nice. Kind. Very excellent people. But can't take money.'

'Come on, Yoyo, don't be so stubborn,' Nicky exclaimed. 'Please accept it, if not for yourself, for Mai. Think of her – of protecting her.'

The young Chinese student shook his head again.

Wanting to make it easier for Yoyo, Clee now took charge, and with a degree of firmness. 'I'll tell you what we'll do . . . I'll go and buy the airline tickets for you and Mai. I'll do it tomorrow – '

'Too much money, Clee,' Yoyo said, cutting him off. He paused and there was an unexpected change in his voice when he added slowly, 'Okay, I think about it – ' Yoyo broke off, cocked his head, listening intently before he threw Nicky a worried glance. '*Gunfire?*'

'No mistaking it,' she cried and glanced at Clee. They exchanged knowing looks. He nodded, and instantly took off without saying a word.

Nicky sprinted forward, catching up with Clee, everything else forgotten in her dash toward the action. The story was uppermost in her mind.

Everyone in the vicinity of the monument heard the sound of shots being fired, and there was a sudden mad rush as the correspondents, photographers and television crews raced after Clee and Nicky. They ran across the square at breakneck speed, heading for Changan Avenue.

Once Nicky was on Changan she lost Clee in the chaos. Immediately, she saw that armoured vehicles and trucks were moving down the wide boulevard, noted that the troops were armed with AK-47 assault rifles. It was obvious to her they were making for Tiananmen, and she knew they had every intention of entering it by force. There had been a rumour earlier that Deng had reportedly told the military commanders, 'Recover the square at all cost.' And there was no doubt in her mind that they would do exactly that; they had already demonstrated their deadly intentions that very afternoon.

She and Clee had been witness to their brutal actions when they had returned to the square after their rather late lunch at the Beijing Hotel. At the western end of the square, close to the Great Hall of the People, thousands of soldiers had beaten up demonstrators who had tried to block their entry into Tiananmen.

As far as she and Clee had been able to determine, no shots had been fired, but there had been much violence, and apparently the troops had used tear gas at one point. Enraged, the masses had hit back, throwing bricks and rocks at the soldiers; in turn, the troops had used truncheons and belts in an effort to quell the protestors.

Seemingly, this pitched battle had merely been the prelude to what was happening at this very moment. That was why she and Clee had just tried to persuade Yoyo to leave Beijing as soon as possible. Experienced as they were, and understanding the politics involved, they were aware that the situation could only worsen in the next twenty-four hours.

Now, suddenly, the troops who had been firing shots into the air were viciously turning their guns on the citizens and students crowding the sidewalks flanking the avenue.

Nicky stood watching in horror, unable to believe her eyes.

Howling like wounded animals, the people rushed forward, hurling bricks, rocks, pieces of iron pipes, and primitive gasoline bombs at the troops and trucks. Their anger spiralled up into greater rage, and they began to scream and shout furiously at the soldiers, who replied by firing rapid, lethal bursts at them.

People fell as they were hit by bullets, crying out in terror.

The carnage had begun.

Appalled by what she was seeing, Nicky found herself unable to move for a few seconds. She was paralysed, stood staring blankly, and chills swept through her. It was a Chinese woman next to her who roused her, when she grabbed her arm, peered into her face, and said in English, 'The People's Army are killing *us* – civilians. They are murderers! Bastards!'

'Don't stay here, go home!' Nicky said to the woman urgently. 'It's dangerous here. *Go home.*' The woman simply shook her head, remained standing exactly where she was.

The drone of helicopters circling made Nicky lift her head, and she gazed up into the night sky. She remembered what Yoyo had said about tear gas being dropped by the choppers. Opening the shoulder bag slung across her body, she groped for one of the surgical masks, stuffed it into her jacket pocket where it was handy, if she needed it.

When she pulled her hand out of her pocket she saw that it was shaking. She was hardly surprised. *The troops were mowing down innocent people.* It was the most unconscionable thing she had seen in the longest time; she was shocked, revolted. Changan Avenue had become a battleground. Tanks and truckloads of soldiers armed with machine guns were rolling inexorably down the avenue, one after the other.

God help the students, she thought, moving away from the road, trying to get to the safety of the trees on the sidewalk, which many people were hiding behind.

Fires were beginning to break out everywhere. Overturned buses, which had been used as barricades by the people, blazed at various intersections, and a number of military vehicles burned on the avenue. They had been set alight by the infuriated Beijing residents, and orange and red flames shot up into the dark sky, an inferno in the making.

Much to Nicky's amazement, people were continuing to emerge from the apartment buildings and houses that lined Changan. They were on a rampage, intent on fighting back, using any makeshift weapons they could find: brooms and sticks and bricks. Some of them were better armed with Molotov cocktails, and these they pelted at the tanks and armoured personnel carriers. Gunfire increased and the stench of cordite and blood hung heavy on the warm night air. She felt suddenly quite nauseous. Bullets were whizzing over her head and she ducked, deciding she had better get away from here as fast as she could.

A cart trundled through the crowd, carrying a man and a woman with gunshot wounds. When the people saw it they began to rant at the soldiers and shake their fists, and, in response, the soldiers pulled their triggers and gunfire spurted over and over again. Nicky dropped to the ground to protect herself. Several tear gas canisters exploded quite close to her, and she pulled out the gauze mask, swiftly tied it around her face, covering her mouth and nose. Nevertheless, she began to cough and splutter almost immediately. Pushing herself up onto her feet, she inched her way over to the far side of the pavement, where she sought refuge under a clump of trees.

Leaning against a tree trunk, Nicky continued to cough and gasp for breath for a few more minutes, and her eyes watered. She found a tissue in her pocket and wiped her streaming eyes; although she continued to heave for a short while, she soon began to breathe easier, felt a bit better.

The smoke was clearing, and she swung her head, looked about. Some sixty or so soldiers were advancing with fixed bayonets down Changan. She closed her eyes convulsively. Pessimistic though she had been, she had not anticipated anything quite like this. When she opened her eyes a second later she spotted Arch a few yards away. He was glancing from side to side worriedly, and she knew that he was seeking her.

Running forward, she cried, 'Arch! Arch! I'm here!'

He swung around just as she reached him, and grabbed hold of her, pulled her to him. 'Nicky! You're all right!'

'And you, Arch,' she said.

'Have you ever seen anything like this carnage?' he cried, his face as grim as hers. 'It's horrible, the way they are killing innocent civilians, and the avenue is so jammed with tanks and trucks, the ambulances can't get through to help the wounded.'

'They're inhuman,' she said, and began to shiver uncontrollably.

'The monstrous ways of man,' Arch muttered. Tightening his grip on her, he added, 'Let's get the hell out of here.'

612

Crouching low, they ran down the pavement under the shelter of the trees, returning to Tiananmen Square.

The moment they hit the square Nicky was struck by the curious calm which lay over it. The atmosphere was peaceful, weirdly so.

She and Arch slackened their pace, and continued up to the Martyrs' Monument at a steady, easy jog. Some of the press corps had returned, were gathered there once more, chatting amongst themselves. From the expressions on their faces, she could see they were as distressed as she and Arch by what they had just witnessed on Changan.

Yoyo and Mai were standing nearby talking with a small group of students, and Nicky headed over to them, drew them away from their friends.

'There's so much bloodshed out there, I don't know how to describe it to you. Or to anyone else, for that matter,' Nicky said tersely. Fishing around in her bag, she found the envelope of money and pressed it into Yoyo's hands. 'You must take this. *Please.*'

Yoyo stared at her. 'But Clee say he buy tickets – '

'Don't argue, Yoyo, take it,' Nicky responded sharply. 'Tomorrow's going to be worse than tonight, and I'll feel better, knowing you have the money on you. If anything happens and we get separated, or if we leave Beijing without you, just get yourselves to Hong Kong. We'll be at the Mandarin Hotel. You'll find us there.'

Realizing there was nothing else to do but take the money, Yoyo nodded, putting the envelope in his trouser pocket. 'Thank you,' he said. 'I understand. I have passport. Mai have passport. Everything be okay, Nicky.'

'I hope so.' Nicky swung her head, glanced around, then brought her gaze back to Yoyo. 'What's been happening in the square?'

'Not much. Very quiet. Wuer Kaixi speak. Say this government oppose the people. Say Chinese must sacrifice themselves. For beautiful tomorrow.'

Nicky expelled a deep breath, shook her head. 'It's going to be bad, Yoyo, especially if the students show resistance to the soldiers. If you stay, you must be peaceful. That's imperative.'

He nodded. 'I understand. Chai Ling say this.'

'Did she speak also?'

'Yes. She say this peaceful sit-in. Tell students stay seated. No resist army.'

Nicky stared hard at Yoyo. 'Listen to me, these troops are not wet behind the ears like the others were yesterday. They are hardened veterans. And dangerous.'

'Maybe 27th Army. They tough. Bad. We be okay, Nicky. Don't worry.'

But I do worry, she said under her breath.

'People from Workers' Federation here. They come protect students,' Yoyo explained.

'I can't help wishing you'd protect yourselves by leaving,' Nicky murmured for the umpteenth time, but she knew she was wasting her breath. Yoyo and Mai would stay until the end, even though *he* fully understood they were in peril, if Mai didn't. She hoped they would be safe, prayed they would be. They were so sweet and innocent, but naive in many ways. Most of the kids in the square were exactly the same.

Not long after this conversation Clee came hurrying up to them looking dishevelled but unhurt. 'Pretty rough back there, Nick. The worst bloodletting I've witnessed in years.'

'It's horrendous ... there are no words really ...' She touched the camera hanging round his neck. 'Still undamaged, I see.'

'They're too damned busy shooting unarmed people to be bothered with me and my camera!'

Arch walked over, accompanied by Jimmy and Luke. All three of them looked as miserable and concerned as she felt.

Putting his arm around Nicky's shoulders, Arch said, 'Jimmy and Luke are going back to the hotel for a while. Why don't you go with them? You've been out here for hours. It'll give you a chance to freshen up, rest for a while.'

'I think I will,' she answered. 'I want to make some notes for my broadcast anyway, and prepare my opening. I'll be back in an hour or so.'

'Take your time,' Arch replied. 'I can guarantee you this little shindig is going to last all night.'

CHAPTER FIVE

Nicky was in and out of Tiananmen for the next few hours, as were most of the foreign press corps.

The areas surrounding the square were a mess. Soldiers were everywhere and the crowds had not diminished. In fact, it seemed to Nicky that they had increased. Overturned vehicles and abandoned bicycles littered Changan Avenue, and an even bigger number of fires were flaring as residents continued to torch tanks and armoured personnel carriers, their grief and anger unassuaged.

In the immediate vicinity of the Beijing Hotel the scenes were chaotic. The wounded, the dying, and the dead were piling up, and distraught and weeping Beijingers, many of them covered in blood, were desperately trying to move the victims. Their aim was to get them to the hospitals and morgues as quickly as possible, and they were valiant in their efforts. They were using all kinds of makeshift stretchers; Nicky even saw one made out of a door ripped from a telephone booth and tied to two long pieces of iron pipe. Several Number 38 buses had been pressed into service as ambulances, and so had pedicabs and carts. Most of the injured were being taken to Xiehe Hospital. It was fairly close to Changan, since it was located in one of the streets immediately behind the Beijing Hotel.

Conversely, the square appeared to be peaceful enough when Nicky went back there for the fourth time, at three forty-five on the morning of 4 June. Yet after only a few minutes in the square she felt the tension in the air. It was a most palpable thing, and underlying the tension was the smell of fear.

The troops had moved in, were positioned at the far end.

Near the Goddess of Democracy she saw lines of soldiers drawn up. They stood staring at the square, their faces cold, cruel, brutal, rifles in their hands, ready to charge on their own people when the order was given.

As soon as she reached Clee, hovering near the monument, he told her there were machine guns positioned on the roof of the Museum of Chinese History on the eastern side of the square.

'They're well prepared, aren't they?' she said, her tone sarcastic. Contempt settled on her face. And then she noticed that some of the students on the monument were busy writing, and she tugged Clee's sleeve. 'What are they doing?' she asked, puzzled.

Clee sighed, shook his head. 'Yoyo told me they're writing their wills.'

'Oh God.' Nicky turned away, swallowing, and unexpectedly she felt the prick of tears behind her eyes. Immediately, she took control of herself. The more emotional the situation and the story, the cooler she must be.

Try though she had to conceal her feelings, Clee had noticed her reaction, and he put an arm around her. 'It's a lousy world we live in, Nick, and you know that better than anybody.'

'I do. Still, some things are really hard to take.'

'I should say.'

She gave him a half-hearted smile. 'You mentioned Yoyo. Where is he?'

'Somewhere around. I gave him hell a short while ago, told him to split. Then I saw him talking to Arch.'

'Where's Arch?'

'He went back to the hotel. To call New York, and have a pow-wow with Jimmy about your film segment.'

'We must have missed each other on Changan. It's a foul mess out there.' Again she glanced at the students on the monument. 'They must *know* how dangerous it is now.'

'That singer, Hou Dejian, and a couple of other leaders have been on the loudspeakers, asking the kids to leave in an orderly fashion, and – ' Clee stopped short as every light in Tiananmen went out.

'I wonder what this means?' Nicky peered at him in the gloom.

'The worst, I suspect,' he answered grimly. 'The lights didn't fail, they were turned off by the authorities.'

'Bastards,' Nicky muttered.

Within the space of only a few minutes the loudspeakers on the monument began to crackle. A disembodied voice said half a dozen words, and then the volume increased and music began to play.

'It's the "Internationale"!' Clee exclaimed. 'Christ, I wonder what the kids will do now?'

'*Leave*. Hopefully,' Nicky replied.

But as the words of the famous song rang out across the square, Nicky knew they would not do so. She could see, even in the dim light, that the students simply sat there listening to the record, motionless, unshakeable, proud in their resoluteness. The minute the record ended it was played again, and repeated several more times during the course of the next twenty minutes.

Nicky and Clee stayed together, conferring quietly from time to time, and talking to other journalists. Everyone expected the military attack to begin at any moment. Nicky and Clee steeled themselves for the confrontation between the students and the troops. But another half hour passed and nothing untoward occurred until, unexpectedly, an array of lights in front of the Great Hall of the People was turned on dramatically. They flooded that side of the square with the most powerful and brilliant illumination.

At the same time, the loudspeakers came alive once again, and several people spoke. Neither Nicky nor Clee could understand what was being said, but a British journalist standing next to them told them the gist of it. 'The leaders were urging the students to quit the square. They're all saying the same thing – get out before you're killed.'

'Ah, but will they? I doubt it,' Clee said, swiftly answering his own question.

'I agree with you,' the British journalist murmured. Then he shrugged, wandered off.

Clee said, 'Nicky, I gotta go. I want to get some shots of these guys on the loudspeakers, and of Chai Ling. This is one helluva moment.'

'Go ahead, Clee. I must look for Yoyo and Mai. They have to be somewhere around here,' she said as he hurried away.

Nicky spent the next ten minutes or so strolling in the area of the monument, her eyes scanning the crowds and the ledges hopefully. But there was no sign of Yoyo and Mai, and she began to wonder if they had finally heeded her earlier warnings and left the square. She fervently hoped that they had.

Someone else spoke to the students over the loudspeakers. There was a short silence, and then a second voice was heard echoing out, filling the warm air with words.

Nicky did not have the slightest idea what was being said, and she walked on, circling the monument one last time. Much to her surprise, a number of the kids were beginning to stand up. Slowly they climbed down off the ledges and walked away. She stood watching them go.

Many had tears streaming down their faces, and her heart went out to them. They had lost their peaceful fight for freedom and democracy. Military power had prevailed and many innocent people had been brutally slaughtered. But at least *some* lives will be saved now, she thought, and glanced around anxiously. Where the hell were Yoyo and Mai?

Dawn was breaking, streaking the sky with light, filling it with an eerie, incandescent glow. She peered at her watch. It was after five already, and she could not stay in the square much longer. Sighing under her breath, she left the monument and started to walk to Changan. It was time to return to the hotel to prepare her newscast and the film segment, shower, put on her makeup and change her clothes. Earlier, she and Arch had decided that she would do the filmed piece on the balcony of the hotel first, to be sent out by courier later that morning. At eight fifteen she would do her live phone narration for the seven o'clock nightly news.

Nicky had not walked very far when she suddenly remembered the small canvas travel bag Yoyo kept in his tent. He had once told her his most important possessions were in it. Was his passport in the bag? Had he gone back for it?

Making a swift decision, she spun around, dodged through the students who were now leaving, and sped towards the tent encampment. As she ran she saw to her dismay that an increasing number of soldiers were entering the square. It seemed to her that they were everywhere, and in the distance she heard the clatter and rumble of tanks and armoured personnel carriers moving forward across that vast rectangle of stone.

She paid no heed, but plunged ahead through the deserted encampment, shouting, 'Yoyo! Mai!'

One or two faces peered out of tents, and she cried, 'Leave! Tanks are coming!' Realizing that they did not understand English, she made wild and urgent gestures with her arms, and cried, 'Go! Go!', hoping they would somehow get the message. Then she ran on, making for the centre of the encampment, still calling at the top of her voice, 'Yoyo! Mai!'

They saw each other at exactly the same moment.

Yoyo and Mai were rounding the side of one tent when Nicky came out from behind another, and was instantly in their direct line of vision.

They had both put on jackets, and Yoyo was carrying the small canvas bag.

'I've been looking for you all over!' Nicky cried.

'Forgot bag,' Yoyo explained, holding it up. 'Bag important. Passport in it.'

I'll say it's important, Nicky thought, but said, 'Come on. Troops are here. Everyone's leaving.' She swung away from them, ready to return through the encampment.

'This way! It quicker!' Yoyo exclaimed.

He took the lead. The three of them ran down a narrow opening between the rows of tents, and came out into an open area of the square, just to the north of the Martyrs' Monument.

Lines of troops were rapidly advancing in their direction, and behind them came the APCs and tanks intent on destroying everything that stood in their path.

Nicky swung to her right, called, 'Follow me!' and ran the opposite way, aiming for the monument and the entrance to Changan just beyond it.

Her heart sank as she heard the sound of rifle fire behind her. Glancing over her shoulder, she saw that Yoyo and Mai were keeping up, were close on her heels. And so she continued to race across the square, putting distance between herself and the encroaching army as fast as she could. The sound of the oncoming armoured vehicles and the blazing guns were ominous to her ears.

Drawing closer to the monument, she saw, out of the corner of her eye, that the last few students were retreating, trying to escape as they were.

'Nicky! Nicky!'

Without slackening her pace she looked back. To her shock she saw that Mai was down. Yoyo was bending over her.

Nicky spun around and ran back to them. 'What happened?'

Yoyo's face was stricken. 'Mai shot.'

Nicky dropped to her knees, examined the girl's bleeding shoulder, touched her face gently. Mai opened her eyes, blinked, closed them. Nicky stood up, then, bending forward, she slipped her arms under Mai, trying to lift her.

The girl moaned and, afraid to move her, Nicky swiftly laid her on the ground again.

Her hands felt wet and she looked down at them, saw they were covered with blood. Her heart tightened. Mai must have been shot in more than one place. She wiped her hands on her pants, straightened, and raised her eyes, looking straight ahead of her.

The tanks had increased their speed, were almost upon them. There was no time left. She said to Yoyo, 'Quickly, take Mai's legs, I'll lift her under her arms. We'll carry her behind the monument.'

These words were barely out of her mouth when she was bodily pulled away from Mai and pushed, almost flung, to one side. As she rolled over, she heard Clee shouting, 'Move it, Nick! Move it, Yoyo! The tanks are closing in!'

People were scattering in panic around her, and screaming.

Struggling to her feet, she spotted Clee running out of the line of fire, carrying Mai in his arms. Yoyo was right behind him. Nicky half ran, half stumbled after them and they made it to safety just in time.

Tanks and APCs, their guns blazing, rolled over the spot where, a split second before, she and Yoyo had been crouching next to Mai. Several students had been less lucky. They lay dead or injured, crushed by the tanks. One boy had had his head smashed in, and there was a pool of his blood and brain on the stones.

With a convulsive shudder, Nicky averted her eyes, and went to take cover behind the Martyrs' Monument, where Clee was placing Mai on the ground. This area seemed to be relatively safe, at least for the moment, and there were no troops in sight. She sank onto the steps and discovered she was shaking all over.

Clee came and sat on the steps with her, put his arms around her, held her.

She clung to him tightly. 'That was a close call, Clee,' she muttered. After a small pause, she said against his bloodstained jacket, 'And you just saved my life. Thanks.'

He put his hand under her chin and lifted her face, stared at her without speaking.

Nicky stared back. He had the most peculiar expression on his face, one she had never seen there before. It puzzled her.

Finally, he said, 'Let's get Mai to a hospital.' He took his camera off, hung it around Nicky's neck. 'Look after this for me,' he said, bent down, and lifted Mai up into his arms.

Yoyo, who had been hovering over his girlfriend, let go of her hand, grabbed his canvas bag, and together he and Nicky followed Clee.

When they reached Tiananmen Gate, Nicky paused and turned to look back at the square.

The Goddess of Democracy was no more. It had been toppled by a tank and demolished – smashed to smithereens. The tent encampment had been flattened to the ground. She prayed that the few remaining students had managed to escape before this had happened.

And she felt an immense sadness flowing through her as she hurried after Yoyo and Clee.

*　　*　　*

618

Changan Avenue was congested with tanks and troops. The dead and the dying lay in pools of their own blood, and the anguished residents of the city were trying to do what they could to help those less fortunate than they.

Nicky and Yoyo walked ahead of Clee, pushing through the chaos and the crowds, clearing the way for him as he carried Mai.

They had almost reached the Beijing Hotel when Yoyo caught hold of Nicky's arm. 'Look!' he cried excitedly, pointing. 'Red Cross flag on Number 38 bus. *Ambulance*. Take Mai to Xiehe Hospital.'

Nicky turned around to Clee. 'Let's get her to that ambulance. The medics can take over.'

Clee merely nodded, ploughed forward with the injured girl. He hoped to God the doctors could save her.

Nicky stood in the middle of the ATN suite at the Beijing Hotel, concentrating hard, focusing on what she had to say. It was fifteen minutes past eight on Sunday morning in China. In New York it was thirteen hours earlier, exactly fifteen minutes past seven on Saturday night.

She held her cellular phone, talking into it clearly, steadily, and without pause, using what she termed her television speed. She was coming to the end of her hardhitting newscast about the events she had just witnessed in Tiananmen, and her final words were dramatic:

'The late Mao Zedong once said political power grows out of the barrel of a gun. The People's Liberation Army turned their guns on ordinary citizens and students today. Innocent people. Unarmed people. It was a massacre. And they did it at the command of ageing leaders desperate to hang onto their political power. Seemingly Mao Zedong spoke the truth. At least, as far as China is concerned.' There was a small beat, before she finished, 'This is Nicky Wells saying goodnight from Beijing.'

At the other end of the line she heard Mike Fowler, the ATN anchorman, saying, 'Thank you, Nicky, for that extraordinary and tragic report from Beijing. And now to the news from Eastern Europe . . . '

Nicky clicked off the cellular, looked over at Arch who was sitting at the desk, the phone to his ear.

He smiled, nodded several times, held up a bunched fist, his thumb jerking to the ceiling, indicating that she had done a good job.

He was on the wire to the network, talking to the News Editor, Joe Speight, who was in the control room at ATN Headquarters in New York. 'Thanks, Joe,' Arch said, beaming. 'We'll ship the film out in an hour. You should have it tomorrow night. Okay. *Ciao*.' He hung up, rose, walked across the floor to her. 'Great, Nick! They loved it. You were just great!'

Jimmy said, 'That's one of the best pieces you've done from here . . . but the moving film we just shot is even better.'

'I second that,' Luke said, grinning at her.

'Thanks, guys.' She smiled at them. Their praise mattered, meant a lot to her. They always spoke the truth, did not hesitate to tell her when she had not been as good as she usually was.

There was a knock on the door and Luke went to open it. Clee walked in. He looked awful, drained, even haggard, and Nicky knew what he was going to say before he said it. She could tell from the empty expression in his dark eyes.

She stared at him.

'Mai died,' he said in a flat tone. 'They just couldn't save her. They tried. But she'd lost too much blood.'

'That's tragic,' Jimmy said. 'Poor kid.'

Luke sat down heavily on a chair without uttering a word; Arch looked bereft, and was also rendered silent by the sad news.

Nicky walked over to Clee, feeling a little unsteady on her legs. 'I had a horrible feeling she wasn't going to make it,' she said, biting her lip. She paused, overcome by emotion, but swiftly regaining her equilibrium, she continued, 'You look terrible, Clee. Come and sit down, let's get you some coffee.'

Clee took a step closer to her. He lifted his hand and with his fingertips wiped away the tears on her cheeks, which she did not even know were there. 'It's all right to cry, you know,' he said.

'Yes.' She took a deep breath. 'How's Yoyo?'

'Devastated.'

She nodded. 'I can imagine. Where is he?'

'At Xiehe Hospital, making arrangements to take Mai's body home to her parents. They live on the outskirts of Beijing.'

Suddenly all words failed her and she was unable to speak.

Clee put his arm around her and walked her over to the sofa. They both sat down, and he said, very quietly, 'We journalists deal with war and death and tragedy on a daily basis, and because we're tough we think we're invincible. But none of us are, not really, Nicky. Not even you.'

PART TWO

Lovers

Come live with me, and be my love;
And we will all the pleasures prove . . .

Christopher Marlowe

CHAPTER SIX

It was Cézanne country, Van Gogh country, so Clee had told her, and he had been correct.

Colours from the artists' palettes were the colours of the day, the colours of the Provençal earth and sky: rich russet browns and burnt sienna, terracotta bleeding into orange and apricot, pink and peach tints balanced by acid yellow and vibrant marigold, and a gamut of brilliant blues and greens so sharp and shiny they resembled glazed enamel. And all were enhanced by a soft golden glow as if they had been liberally soaked in the hot Provençal sunshine.

From the moment she had arrived in Provence, Nicky had been entranced by the beauty of the countryside which surrounded the old *mas*, or farmhouse, which Clee owned. A day did not pass without her catching her breath in surprise and delight at one thing or another. In an infinite number of small and grand ways, nature in all its glory was constantly revealing itself to her in this fabled southeastern corner of France.

On this sun-filled afternoon, as she sat near the white stone-flagged swimming pool under the shade of a plane tree, sipping a *citron pressé* and day-dreaming, she almost laughed out loud at herself. She had been so reluctant to come here, but now she realized she would not have missed this brief respite from the business of reporting catastrophes for anything in the world.

And she was grateful to Clee for so generously giving her the use of his home, his very private retreat into which few were ever admitted. But then that was Clee. He was always thinking of her well-being, and this latest gesture was only one of his many kindnesses. He was such a good friend, and very dear to her.

The idea of her coming to Provence had begun in Hong Kong almost three weeks ago, when she and Clee were finishing dinner at the Mandarin Hotel. Out of the blue, Clee had suddenly said to her, 'Go to my farm, Nick. It'll do you good to be there. It'll take your mind off things, be restorative for you.'

She had shaken her head vehemently, balking at the mere idea of it. At this moment in time, France did not particularly appeal to her, even though she had always loved it and felt at home there in the past. Unfortunately, it was now associated with pain and hurt in her mind.

Almost three years ago she had gone there with her fiancé, Charles Devereaux, a man with whom she had been very much in love, and whom she had been about to marry. Unexpectedly, without any kind of forewarning, or hint of trouble between them, he had terminated their relationship in the most brutal of ways. No explanations or reasons were given, and it had happened only a couple of months after the idyllic trip to the Côte d'Azur.

She had not set eyes on Charles Devereaux ever again.

623

Naturally she did not want to upset herself further by visiting a place where they had spent their last few days together. There were moments when she still felt savaged by him, was filled with a fulminating anger, and this was enough for her to cope with, without having additional, unwelcome memories thrust upon her.

Of course Clee had no way of knowing any of this, and so he had been extremely persistent, using every argument he could. She had remained adamant.

Just before leaving Hong Kong for Paris, he had offered her the farm once again. 'I'm afraid I can't be there, Nicky, but my housekeeper will be, and she'll look after you very well.' A smile had flashed on his boyish face, and he had added, 'She'll spoil you to death, and I guarantee *you'll* fall in love with *her*. Amelia's a doll. Listen, babe, the farm's in beautiful country, artists' country – Cézanne and Van Gogh both painted in the area, and I know you'll enjoy it. Please go. You need to do something special for yourself, to have a few weeks of peace after the horror of Beijing. Be good to yourself, Nick.'

Touched by his thoughtfulness, she had thanked him profusely, and, relenting slightly, she had told him she would think about it. And back in New York she had done exactly that. Much to her continuing astonishment, thoughts of Clee's farmhouse in France and a summer vacation *had* flitted in and out of her head, with surprising frequency.

In the few spare moments she had between filming and editing a special on Tiananmen Square and its aftermath, she had pondered whether to take the trip or not. She had continued to be oddly ambivalent, could not make up her mind to buy an airline ticket, pack her bags and go.

Unknowingly, it was Arch who had finally helped her come to a decision. Once the special was in the can he had told her she looked more exhausted than he had ever seen her. 'Done in,' was the way he had put it. 'We have no other specials coming up until later in the year, and a bit of R and R wouldn't do you any harm,' he had pointed out. 'Take a break while you can – you really need it, Nick.'

When she had muttered that she did not want to have a vacation at this time, in case something world shaking occurred, Arch had laughed, had said he would fly her back from wherever she was if a war broke out somewhere.

She had laughed with him, had then protested, 'But I know I don't look quite as bad as you say I do, Arch. You're exaggerating, as usual!'

His answer had been pithy and to the point. '*Lousy*, that's the way you look, kiddo, take my word for it.'

Later, she had looked at herself in a mirror, and had had to admit that Arch had spoken the truth. She had examined her face minutely, with objectivity, and had decided that he had actually understated the facts. She looked positively ill; her face was unusually pale, even haggard, she had dark rings, and her hair was lifeless. Much to her alarm, her eyes, always so clear and vividly blue, had seemed dull, faded almost, as if they were losing their colour, if such a thing were possible.

Nicky was well aware that cosmetics could camouflage a number of flaws for the benefit of the camera, and that she could continue to hide the tell-tale signs of fatigue with a few clever makeup tricks. But she had also recognized that afternoon that it would be foolish not to take a rest, especially since the network owed her so much time off. She *had* been feeling debilitated and emotionally drained, and apparently the signs were now all too evident to others.

And so she had put her mirror away and made a snap decision. The same day she had phoned Clee at his Paris office, and told him she would like to accept his offer of the farmhouse, if it was still open. He had been thrilled that she wanted to go to Provence.

'Hey, babe, that's great,' he had said, his excitement echoing down the wire. 'I'm leaving for Moscow tomorrow, to photograph Gorbachev for *Paris Match*, but Jean-Claude will make arrangements for you to be met in Marseille, and then driven up to the farm. All you have to do is get yourself to Marseille, either via Paris or Nice. Just let Jean-Claude know the day you'll be arriving, and the time. I'll call you from Moscow, to find out how you're doing, how you've settled in.'

Within forty-eight hours she was zooming across the Atlantic faster than the speed of sound, a passenger on board the French Concorde, landing in Paris a short three hours and forty-five minutes later. After spending the night at the Plaza Athénée, her favourite hotel, she had taken a plane from Orly Airport to Marseille the following morning.

Jean-Claude, Clee's office manager, had explained to her that a chauffeur from the car company they used would be waiting for her at the airport. 'You won't be able to miss him. He'll be holding up a card with your name written on it in bold letters,' Jean-Claude had said on the telephone.

True to Jean-Claude's promise, the chauffeur had been there when she had alighted from the plane and gone to the baggage area. He had introduced himself as Etienne, and he was a pleasant, chatty and informative Provençal, who throughout the drive inland had kept her highly entertained with rather fantastic folkloric tales of the region. He had also recited more facts about Aix and Arles than she could possibly absorb at one time.

Although she spoke French well, having spent part of her youth in Paris with her globe-trotting parents, Nicky had nonetheless found the Provençal accent a bit difficult to understand at first. But relatively quickly she had realized that Etienne was adding the letter *g* to many words, so that *bien* became *bieng*, and so forth. Once she had got the hang of this adjustment of the French language, had attuned her ear to the rich and throaty cadence of his speech, and his rapid delivery, she had discovered she had no problems grasping everything he said.

On the way to Aix-en-Provence from Marseille, Nicky had begun to notice that the landscape was completely different from the Côte d'Azur, which was the part of southern France she knew so intimately. Her parents were Francophiles, and as a child she had been taken to many of the renowned coastal resorts by them, for annual holidays and shorter stays. In particular, her mother and father had favoured Beaulieu-sur-Mer, Cannes and Monte Carlo. And then in October of 1986 she had spent those two extraordinary weeks in Cap d'Antibes with Charles Devereaux, before he had disappeared from her life altogether. And forever.

But this area of Provence was entirely new to her and, as such, it did not hold any kind of memories, neither good nor bad.

This sudden knowledge had made her feel more at ease, and finally she had begun to relax in the air-conditioned comfort of the Mercedes, continuing to glance out of the window from time to time.

They had passed through a land of flat plains interspersed with hills and mountains. There were quaint little towns set in bucolic surroundings, and picturesque hilltop villages that looked as if they were propping up the vast unblemished blue sky. Many fields and hillsides were luxuriant with purple lavender, and dark vineyards and an abundance of cherry and fruit orchards stretched for miles. And dotting this fertile landscape intermittently were lines of crooked olive trees and stately black cypresses which stood like sentinels against the far horizon.

Clee's farmhouse was in the department of Provence called the Bouches-du-Rhône, situated between the ancient university town of Aix-en-Provence and St Rémy. It was on the outskirts of a tiny village close to the lush green foothills of Lubéron, one of the great mountain ranges of Provence.

The farmhouse was larger than Nicky had expected it to be. It was sprawling yet had a certain gracefulness and was obviously quite old. It had looked beautiful in the late afternoon sunshine which glanced across its red-tiled roof and cast a warm honey-coloured glaze over the pale stone walls. Standing at the end of a long straight driveway lined with cypress trees, it was visible for the entire approach to the white front door.

When the car had finally been brought to a halt by Etienne, he had exclaimed, 'Eh, voilà!' and had waved one hand at the farm with a grand flourish. Then he had swung his head and smiled at her triumphantly, looking as though getting her here had been a major achievement on his part.

Clee's housekeeper Amelia and her husband Guillaume had been waiting for her on the doorstep, and they had welcomed her enthusiastically, their smiles warm, their manner friendly.

Guillaume had then promptly whisked away her luggage – along with Etienne. The latter had apparently not needed a second invitation from Guillaume to 'come inside the kitchen for a pastis.'

With billowing laughter and perpetual smiles, Amelia had ushered Nicky inside the farmhouse, and had insisted on showing her around before taking her upstairs to her quarters.

They had started out in the kitchen, obviously Amelia's favourite spot in the entire house, and she was apparently proud of it.

The room was large, painted white, and had dark wood beams on the ceiling, terracotta tiles on the floor. A massive stone fireplace took up an end wall; to the side of this stood a big oven, and several marble-topped counters for baking and food preparation were set under the three windows. Placed on these were flat woven baskets brimming with local produce. One held a selection of fruit – apples, oranges, pears, plums, peaches, apricots, cherries and grapes; the other overflowed with vegetables – carrots, cabbage, potatoes, beans, artichokes and peas. Ropes of onions and garlic, and bunches of the herbs of Provence swung from a ceiling beam, and the lovely aroma of marjoram, rosemary and thyme wafted to her on the air.

A round table stood in the centre of the kitchen, covered with a red-and-white gingham cloth to match the neat little tied-back curtains at the windows, and taking pride of place on the far wall was an antique baker's rack made of black wrought-iron trimmed with brass. It had been stacked with a variety of copper pots and pans that glittered and winked in the sunlight, while on the wall opposite

626

a series of built-in shelves displayed colourful pottery platters, plates, soup bowls and double-sized *café-au-lait* cups and saucers.

The dining room opened off the kitchen, and these two rooms flowed into each other, were visually linked through the use of the same terracotta floor tiles, white-painted walls and ceiling beams.

Here there was a big, old-fashioned fireplace and hearth made of the local cream-coloured stone and stacked with logs for the winter, and a window at each end of the room filled it with light. A country feeling had been created by the long oak dining table, high-backed chairs and carved sideboard. Floating over the table was a rustic black-iron chandelier, and running down the centre of the table was a collection of brass candlesticks holding thick white candles. Huge bowls of flowers in the centre of the table and on the sideboard brought touches of vivid colour to the rather simply furnished room.

Hurrying forward, Amelia had next shown her out into the main hall, and had opened a door into a small downstairs sitting room. Highly polished cream flagstones gleamed on the floor, the walls were painted a soft butter yellow, and two sofas covered in cream linen faced each other in front of a small fireplace. Wood occasional tables were scattered around, and two tall pottery lamps with cream shades stood on antique chests on either side of the chimney. A table under the window held all the latest magazines from around the world, copies of *Life* and *Paris Match* being much in evidence, as well as *Time* and *Newsweek*.

'Now we shall go upstairs?' Amelia had said to her, swinging around and guiding her back to the front hall. Nicky had dutifully followed her up a white stone staircase, broad and curved, which stopped on a square landing.

On either side of this were the library and the main living room. Both were painted white, had soaring fireplaces, pale wood floors and flat woven rugs from Morocco.

The living room was decorated with French country furniture in the Provençal style, and the sofas and chairs were upholstered in cream, *café-au-lait* and caramel-coloured fabrics. Again, masses of flowers introduced vivid colour everywhere, and Nicky had an instant impression of air and light and spaciousness, and the most marvellous sense of tranquillity.

Across the landing, the library was lined with books and furnished with two overstuffed sofas covered in melon-coloured cotton. Clee had created an audio-visual centre in one corner, using the most up-to-date equipment: a large-screen television, video player, tape deck, compact disc player. Stereo speakers were positioned high on the bookshelves.

'This is Monsieur Clee's room, he likes it the best, I think,' Amelia had informed her, nodding her head. She had then pointed her finger at the ceiling, and announced, 'One more flight, Mademoiselle. *Allons!*'

The two of them had gone out onto the large landing and climbed up a narrower flight of white stone steps to the bedroom floor.

Nicky had discovered that she had her own suite under the eaves: a bathroom, a bedroom and a sitting room. The latter were quaint, and charmingly decorated, again with lots of white, cream and caramel. Several good wooden pieces were set against the walls of the sitting room and an antique armoire and a chest graced the bedroom; with only a cursory glance, she had noticed that a great deal of care had been taken, and every comfort had been provided.

'I will bring up your cases,' Amelia had said, after showing her around, opening the armoire doors, sliding out drawers in the chest. 'And please, Mademoiselle Nicky, you must tell me if there is anything else you need. Monsieur Clee will be angry if I do not look after you properly.'

'Thank you very much, Amelia,' Nicky had answered, smiling. 'I'm sure I have everything. And thank you for the grand tour.'

'Ah, it is a pleasure, Mademoiselle,' Amelia had answered with a smile, before disappearing down the stairs.

This conversation had taken place only four days ago, but already Nicky was beginning to feel rested. The farmhouse and the surrounding grounds had had a soothing effect on her, and she was more tranquil than she had been for a long time. She had slept better than she usually did, and had relaxed completely in this peaceful environment.

Her days were slow, lazy, without pressure, and she had done nothing more complicated than walk around the grounds and the woods close by, and swum in the pool. The fresh air and exercise, and Amelia's delicious cooking had done her good; in the evenings she had read, listened to music or watched French television in the library, although mostly she had found herself tuning into CNN, being such a news addict.

According to Guillaume, Clee had recently installed cable to pick up the American news network. 'For his work, you know, Mademoiselle,' Guillaume had found it necessary to add, and she had turned away to hide the small, amused smile that had touched her lips.

Nicky shifted slightly on the chaise, reached for the *citron pressé*, took a long swallow, enjoying the tart taste of the lemonade.

It was the last week of June and already hot, although not yet unbearable. Amelia had told her only this morning that July and August were the worst of the summer months in this part of Provence. *Blistering* was the word she had used. Then Amelia had suddenly launched into a little *histoire* about the Mistral, the dry north wind that could blow so furiously even in the summer, bringing with it havoc. It came whistling down to the south from the Rhône Valley, and it was often the first real warning of mean weather brewing. Amelia, like most Provençaux, blamed a variety of problems and ailments on the Mistral.

'Animals can go mad. And people,' she had confided somewhat dolorously as she had poured Nicky a second cup of *café-au-lait*. 'It causes migraine. And *la grippe*. And toothache. And earache. And sometimes in winter it can blow for as long as three weeks. It destroys property! Uproots trees and flings tiles off the roofs! *Quel vent!*' And then with a typical Gallic shrug she had hurried off to the kitchen to refill the coffee pot and warm up more milk for Nicky.

Just as Clee had suggested she would, Nicky had fallen in love with Amelia. The housekeeper was small, stocky, and obviously a very strong woman physically, undeniably Mediterranean with blue-black hair pulled back in a bun, eyes like black olives and a nutbrown complexion. Forever laughing and smiling, and always in a high good humour, she went through the farmhouse doing her vast number of chores like a whirlwind. Or the Mistral perhaps. She cleaned and polished, washed and ironed, baked bread and cakes and tarts, prepared the most wonderful meals, and arranged the beautiful vases of flowers and the decorative baskets of fruit that were all around the house.

Like Amelia, Guillaume was a typical Provençal. He was as brown as a berry with a weatherbeaten face from being outdoors, jet-black hair spreckled with grey, and kindly, humorous brown eyes. Medium in height, and very muscular, he tackled every job with the same vigour and enthusiasm as his wife.

He swept the yard, the outdoor dining terrace and the barbecue patio, cleaned the pool, kept the garden and the orchard spruce, and attended to the little vineyard. This stretched out behind the farmhouse, and covered about four or five acres. Guillaume did the spraying, the cropping and the pruning, and he and Amelia, with some local hired help, picked the grapes, kegged the wine and bottled it.

'Some of it is sold. Some we keep for ourselves. And for Monsieur Clee, *naturellement*,' he had explained to her when he had taken her around the property yesterday, pointing out many of its distinctive features.

Amelia and Guillaume had a son, François, who was studying at the Sorbonne in Paris, of whom they were very proud; Nicky had already heard rave notices about him from his doting mother. Their two daughters, Paulette and Marie, were married and lived in the village, and were frequently pressed into service at the farm whenever Clee had more than one guest.

When Clee had called from Moscow, on the night of her arrival, he had described Amelia and Guillaume as the salt of the earth. Now she knew exactly what he meant. They were devoted to him, took care of the farmhouse and the land as if they themselves were the owners. The house they lived in adjoined the main farmhouse and was entered through a door opening off the kitchen. It was built of the same local stone, pale beige in colour and weathered by the years, and had an identical red-tiled roof, heavy wooden shutters and doors painted gleaming white.

Both houses were visible to her from the pool area where she was sitting, and it seemed to her that they appeared to grow up out of the earth, as if they were part of the land itself. And in a sense, they were. The farm and its out-buildings were a hundred and fifty years old, so Guillaume had told her, and they did look as if they had been there forever.

Everything about the farm fascinated Nicky; she was beginning to realize how much she enjoyed being in the country, close to the land. It was easy to see why Clee loved the farm, although he was not able to come here as often as he would like. During the two years she had known him, he had talked about this place occasionally, and she understood why his voice changed slightly whenever he discussed his home in Provence. It was a very special corner of peace and beauty in the troubled and turbulent world.

Nicky stayed outside until almost six o'clock, enjoying the changing light as the sun slowly began to sink down behind the rim of the distant dark hills. Then she took her book and glasses and walked slowly up the flagged garden path to the house.

Climbing the two staircases to her rooms under the eaves, she thought of Yoyo, as she did at some moment during every day. His whereabouts were unknown, and this was the only thing marring her stay here. She and Clee had looked hard for him in Beijing before they had left for Hong Kong. He had disappeared. But then so had most of the other student leaders. 'Gone underground,' Clee had said to her, and she had hoped this was really the case, that he had not been arrested.

She and the crew and Clee had hung around Hong Kong for several days, hoping he would show up, but he had not and in the end they had had no alternative but to leave.

Nicky's only consolation was that Yoyo knew where to find them. She had given him her business card in the first week she had met him, as had Arch and Clee. She could only hope that he would be able to get himself out of China, using the money they had given him.

At one moment she had thought about writing to him at the Central Academy of Arts, but had resisted, knowing that a letter from a Western journalist could easily create untold problems for him. Who knew whether the mail was censored or not? In her opinion, it most probably was these days. And a letter from her might cost him his freedom. Or his life.

Sighing under her breath, Nicky pushed open the door to her rooms and went in, trying to set aside her worries about Yoyo. She was helpless. There was nothing she could do except pray he was still safe, and that he would find a way to escape to the West.

CHAPTER SEVEN

The scream shattered her nightmare.

It echoed around the bedroom and seemed to pierce her brain, almost as if she herself were screaming. Nicky sat up with a jerk, instantly wide awake, her face and arms bathed in sweat. She tilted her head and listened, blinking as she adjusted her eyes to the dimness of the room.

There was no sound except for the faint ticking of the clock on the bedside table, the rustle of the leaves on the tree outside the window as they brushed against the panes of glass.

Had she herself screamed out loud during her frightening dream? Or had it been someone else? Someone outside? She was not sure, and just to make certain she climbed out of bed and went to the window. She looked out. The sky was dark, cloudless. A full moon was slung high above the old stables, and it cast a silvery sheen over everything in the yard, throwing into focus the cypress tree, the old wheelbarrow planted with flowers, the garden seat, the flight of steps leading down into the orchard. But there was no one out there, so it was not possible that anyone had screamed. Except for her, of course.

A small shiver passed through Nicky even though it was an exceptionally warm night. Turning away from the window, she went back to bed, troubled by the nightmare that had so frightened her it had brought that scream to her lips. And woken her up. Slithering down, she pulled the sheet around her bare shoulders, and tried to go back to sleep.

But she had little success, and when she was still wide awake after half an hour she slid out of bed, slipped into her cotton robe and went down to the library. After turning on a lamp and the television set, she curled up on one of the sofas, deciding that since she could not sleep she might as well watch CNN.

Once the round-up of international news was finished, and the programming changed to a local American story about farmers in the midwest, her mind began to wander. Not unnaturally, she discovered she was focusing on the nightmare she had just had. It had been awful, and try as she did to shake it off, it remained so vivid it was still dominating her mind. The nightmare had been about Clee, and she could remember every detail of it clearly.

She was in a vast, empty desert. It was warm, pleasant, and even though she was alone she was not afraid. She felt content. She was walking up a sand dune, and when she was on top of it and looked down she saw an oasis below. Feeling thirsty, she ran down the slope of the dune and began to drink the water, scooping it up in her hands, until she saw that it was streaked with blood. She pulled back, filled with horror, and as she crouched on her heels she noticed a crumpled magazine splattered with mud and blood. It was Life. *She picked it up, leafed through it, and came across a picture of Clee. The caption said he was dead, killed in action while he was on assignment for the magazine. But it did not say where he had died, or when. And there was no date on the magazine. She was frightened, and turned icy even though it was so hot under the desert sun. She got up and began to run, looking for Clee. She had this feeling that he was somewhere nearby. And alive.*

She walked for hours and eventually she was no longer in the desert. She was wearing thick winter clothes and it was dawn on a frosty day. All around her were dead men and the bloody signs of war and destruction. Clee walked towards her through the mist and took hold of her hand. He helped her to climb over the dead bodies. Suddenly they saw a jeep in the distance. Clee said, 'Look, Nick! We can get a lift back with the retreat!' He leapt forward, running. She ran, too, but stumbled. When she stood up he was not there. For a split second she was afraid, and then she went searching for him amongst the dead soldiers. But she could not find him. There were miles and miles of dead bodies, and everything was so silent she wondered if it was the end of the world. She saw two bodies lying close to each other side by side. She hurried to them, turned their cold, dead faces to see if either one was Clee. She drew back in shock. One of the bodies was Yoyo. The other was Charles Devereaux. She turned and ran away, stumbling and falling against the dead soldiers in her haste to escape the carnage. At one moment she looked down at her hands and clothes. They were covered in warm, sticky blood from the dead. A wave of horror and nausea swept over her, and just as she began to despair at not finding Clee she reached the end of the battlefield. Now she was walking along a white, sandy beach, and parked under a palm tree was the jeep she had seen earlier with Clee. It was abandoned. She looked towards the dark-blue sea. Not far out she saw a body floating. It was Clee. He beckoned to her. He was alive! She rushed into the water. It was icy but curiously thick like oil, so that swimming was tedious. And then she realized that the sea was not blue but red. It was made of blood.

Clee smiled and held out his hand to her. She reached for it. Their fingers were inches apart. She struggled to grasp his hand. And then his body sank into the sea.

At this moment the dream had ended and she had awakened because someone had screamed. It had been her, she *knew* that. Nicky shuddered. Goose flesh sprang up on her face and arms, and she pulled the robe around her, feeling suddenly so cold. Rising, she went over to the small bar next to the bookcase and looked at the bottles, reached for the *Marc de Bourgogne*. The label rang a bell. Of course, it was one of the brandies Charles had imported from France. With a small grimace she put the bottle down on the silver tray, then immediately picked it up again, poured herself a small glass and, taking a sip of it, she slowly walked back to the sofa.

Nicky did not know a lot about dreams, but she was well enough informed to realize that her recent nightmare was simply a manifestation of things jostling around in her subconscious. Once, several years ago, her mother had told her that one dreamed one's terrors, and that whatever truly frightened a person came to the fore in sleep, when the subconscious rises. And so it did not take her long to analyse her dream. She knew very well what it meant: firstly she was afraid that Yoyo was dead. Secondly, she was worried that Clee, a war photographer and in constant danger, might one day be killed.

It's all very understandable, she told herself, taking another little sip of the *marc*. Both men had been on her mind lately, and were therefore at the forefront of her thoughts.

But why had *Charles Devereaux* been part of the nightmare? She had no answer for herself . . . but, yes, of course she did. Several times in the last few days he had insinuated himself into her thoughts, for the simple reason that she was in France, where he had travelled often, buying wine for his importing company. And where they had spent those two weeks together before he had chosen to vacate her life.

The more she thought about it, there was no denying the fact that she had dreamed about those three men because each one of them, in his own way, troubled her enormously.

CHAPTER EIGHT

Clee stood staring at the dozen or so transparencies arranged on the large light box in his Paris office, an expression of deep concentration on his face.

After a couple of minutes studying the pictures, he turned to Jean-Claude Roche, who ran his photo agency, Image, and nodded. 'I think you're onto a winner, and the pictures *are* good, Jean-Claude. Damned good, as a matter of fact. So let's get the guy to come in and see me, and the sooner the better. We can certainly use another world-class photographer around here, there's more work than we can handle right now.'

Jean-Claude looked pleased. 'Marc Villier is really terrific, Clee. Very bright, aggressive, yet sensitive. And he possesses the unflinching eye, as you do. You are going to like him, he is . . . how shall I say . . . very personable.'

'Good. And if these photographs are anything to go by, his work is more than excellent. It's brilliant. Let's move on. Do you have anything else to go over with me?'

Jean-Claude shook his head. 'No. Everything is under control. The assignment sheet is on your desk. Everyone is booked out for the next few weeks. Except for you. I've kept you free.'

'That's *great*. I could use a few days respite after Beijing and Moscow,' Clee exclaimed, his face brightening at the prospect of some time off. Turning around, he collected the transparencies which lay on the light box and handed them to Jean-Claude.

'Thanks,' Jean-Claude said as he slipped them into a large envelope. 'I shall go and call Marc, ask him to come in tomorrow morning. Is that all right with you?'

'Sure. By the way, where do we stand with my assignment for *Life*?'

'They need you for about three weeks, late July and early August. They want you to go to Washington first to photograph the President and Mrs Bush, this is their priority.'

'Yeah, that figures. Congress is still in session through July, and Bush is probably going to be gone in August, either to Camp David or Kennebunkport. And who am I doing after the President and Mrs B?'

'They have not said, Clee. But they want you for a few specials. I told them I would give them the date of your arrival as soon as possible. They need to confirm with the White House. So, when *will* you go?'

'About the fourteenth, I guess.' Clee walked over to his cluttered desk and sat down. 'Ask Marc Villier if he can come in early tomorrow, around seven thirty, eight.'

'I will.' Jean-Claude crossed the floor to the door, paused before leaving and looked back at Clee. 'There will not be any problem, he will come whenever you wish. He wants nothing more than to work with you, Clee. You are his . . . idol.'

Clee merely smiled, made no comment. He knew all about idols and what having one could mean.

Jean-Claude nodded and left.

Clee's eyes automatically strayed to the photograph of Robert Capa, which hung on the side wall along with a collection of other pictures, and he felt a little stab of familiar sadness, as he often did when he looked at it. His one and only regret in his life was that he had not known Capa. He had been born too late and Capa's tragic death had been so untimely, far too soon.

After a moment, he swung his gaze and dropped his eyes to the papers littering his desk, shuffled through them without paying much attention, which was quite normal for him. Paperwork was not his strong suit; in fact, it bored him. He clipped the letters together, scrawled across the top one: *Louise, please deal with this stuff any way you see fit*, and dropped the pile into the tray in readiness for his secretary the following day.

Glancing at the clock he saw that it was almost six. If he was going to cancel the dinner with his close friends Henry and Florence Devon he had better do it immediately. Henry was a writer and worked at the Paris bureau of *Time*, and Clee dialled his direct line. It rang and rang then was finally picked up and Henry's gravelly Boston-accented voice was saying, '*Allo, oui?*'

'Hank, it's Clee. How're you, old buddy?'

'Jaysus, Clee, don't tell me you're cancelling!'

'I have to, Hank. Business, I'm afraid. Look, I'm sorry, but it can't be helped.'

'Oh hell, Flo has invited this Lacroix model, whatever-her-name-is. Stunning girl. You wouldn't want to miss meeting *her*, would you?'

'I wish you two would stop trying to fix me up!' Clee exclaimed a bit impatiently, then he laughed and continued swiftly, 'There's really no way I can make it tonight. This meeting just came up and it's important.'

'I'll bet it is. Knowing you, I suspect you've suddenly got a hot and heavy date with a beautiful blonde. Or redhead. Or brunette.'

'If only. From your mouth to God's ear,' Clee retorted and chuckled. In a more serious voice he said, 'Look, I wouldn't pass up Flo and you and what's-her-name for some hit-and-run date with a dame. *Never*. Come on, Hank, surely you know me better than that.'

'Don't I just,' Henry shot back and cackled wickedly down the phone.

Ignoring this, Clee said soberly, 'Flo usually hedges her bets and invites a couple of single guys as well as me, so I'm sure the Lacroix lady won't be short of flattering male attention this evening.'

'That's quite true. On the other hand, Flo really wanted *you* to meet her, Clee.'

'I will. Another time. Tonight I'm stuck. How about lunch tomorrow?'

'No can do. I'm flying to Nice. I'm working on a piece about the Grimaldis of Monaco, and I have to do some interviews in Monte Carlo.'

'Then call me when you're back and we'll catch up.'

'It's a deal. And Clee?'

'Yes, Hank?'

'We'll miss you tonight.'

'I'll miss being there. Give my apologies to Flo, and kiss her for me.' As he hung up Clee made a mental note to send flowers to Florence tomorrow morning. Flowers from Lachaume, no less. That ought to do the trick in the apology department.

Picking up the phone he dialled again. A female voice answered immediately. 'Is that you, Mel?'

'Hello, Clee. What's wrong?'

'Nothing's wrong . . . Mel, I –'

'You're cancelling our date tonight.'

'Listen, honey, I'm sorry, but I have an American picture editor in town, and he –'

'Must see you tonight, because he's leaving first thing tomorrow, and it's vitally important for the agency,' she finished for him, sounding as if she knew the words by heart.

'You got it.'

'Why don't you come over later, Clee?'

'It'll be too late.'

'I don't mind.'

There was a small pause. He said finally, 'I would prefer to see you at the weekend, Mel. If you're free. We could drive out to the country for dinner on Saturday night. How about it?'

He heard her sigh at the other end of the phone.

She said, after a moment, 'Oh all right then. But I don't know why I let you do this to me, Cleeland Donovan. Most other guys couldn't get away with it.'

'Get away with what?'

'Being so elusive.'

'Ah, but that's what makes me so very irresistible,' he retorted flippantly.

'Sadly, I think that happens to be the truth,' she answered him in the softest of tones.

'Okay, so do we have a date for Saturday night?'

'You know we do, Clee.'

'I'll call you tomorrow, honey, and I'm sorry about tonight.'

They murmured their goodbyes and he dropped the phone back in its cradle. Another order of flowers from Lachaume tomorrow, he thought, putting his feet up on the desk, leaning back in the chair and closing his eyes.

Clee felt a sudden and most marvellous surge of relief that he had so easily managed to cancel Flo and Hank, and the conflicting date with Mel as well, by telling a couple of harmless white lies. The truth was he did not have a business date, nor any kind of date, for that matter. On the other hand, he did not have the head for a fancy dinner party at the Devons'; nor was he in the mood to dine alone with Melanie Lowe, bright and lovely as she was, and of whom he was quite fond. He simply wanted to be alone; he had a lot on his mind and a great deal of thinking to do. This was the other reason why he had been so pleased when Jean-Claude had told him he was free, that he had no other assignments before he left for the States to do the work for *Life*. He was not only going to take it easy for the next week and have a much-needed rest, but he would concentrate on a few personal problems which needed sorting out. One in particular had been at the back of his mind for several weeks.

Opening his eyes, Clee stood up, lifted his jacket off the chair back and shrugged himself into it, then walked towards the door.

He paused halfway across the room and stood for the longest moment looking at the portrait of Capa. Of all the photographs that had been taken of him, whether in combat fatigues or civilian clothes, this was Clee's favourite. It was of Capa and David 'Chim' Seymour, and it had been taken in a leafy Paris square in the early 1950s. The two friends were sitting on metal garden chairs, and Capa was wearing a raincoat over his suit, had a cigarette dangling from his lips. There was a quizzical expression in his eyes and he appeared to be faintly smiling. One hand was resting on his knee, and Clee had always been struck by that hand –

the long, sensitive fingers which looked so capable. And how darkly handsome Capa was in this picture: the strong masculine features, the thick black brows and hair, the smouldering dark eyes, the seductive mouth all added up to one helluva knock-out guy.

Seemingly Capa had been the possessor of a legendary charm and a debonair personality as well as good looks, and it was not difficult for Clee to imagine why Ingrid Bergman and so many other women had fallen head over heels in love with him.

Everything Clee had ever read about Capa had underscored his intrinsic courage and daring as a photographer, his compassion and humanity as a man. Once, the British magazine *Picture Post*, now defunct, had run a photograph of Capa, and the headline above the caption had read: *the greatest war-photographer in the world*. And that was what he had been and it had cost him his life in the end.

Capa had been killed on 25 May 1954, when he had stepped on a Vietminh anti-personnel mine on a small, grassy slope above a dyke, five kilometres outside Dongquithon in Indochina, during the French–Indochina war. He had been forty-one years old. Two years older than I am now, Clee reminded himself, thinking of his own mortality and how fragile life truly was in the long run.

In 1955, *Life* Magazine and the Overseas Press Club of America had established the Robert Capa Award 'for the best photographic reporting from abroad requiring exceptional courage and enterprise'. Clee had won the award for his coverage of the war in Lebanon, and it was his most treasured and proudest possession. It was in a box lined with blue velvet and stood on a shelf next to the Capa photograph, set slightly apart from the other international awards he had won for the excellence of his work.

Lifting the lid, Clee stared at the award for a second, and he wondered, as he often had in the past, why he felt so close to a man he had never known and yet whom he missed as if he had been his dearest friend. It constantly baffled him. Yet there was no denying that Capa, a dead man, had been the single most important influence in his life.

Jean-Claude's voice was reverberating outside in the corridor and Clee threw off his thoughts about Capa and went to see what was wrong, if anything.

'Hey, guys, what's going on?' he asked, striding out, closing the door behind him. He headed toward Jean-Claude, who was talking excitedly, and Michel Bellond, a partner in the agency and a photographer of some talent and courage.

'*Rien*,' Michel said, and winked at Clee.

'He is right, it is nothing, really,' Jean-Claude said and grinned. 'We were just discussing the merits of various restaurants, trying to decide where to have the dinner for Steve,' he explained, referring to another partner in Image.

'Let's hear the choices,' Clee said. 'Perhaps I'll cast the deciding vote.'

CHAPTER NINE

It was drawing close to dusk when Clee finally left the Image offices on the rue de Berri, that time of day when the sky has changed to twilight colours but has not yet turned to black.

He lifted his head as he walked towards the Champs-Élysées and looked up at the sky. Tonight it was a deep pavonine blue, almost peacock in tone, and it had a soft incandescent glow to it, as if it was softly illuminated from behind.

Magic hour, he said to himself, using the movie term which best described this time of day, and which movie directors and cinematographers loved with such enormous passion. It was especially effective on film.

When he reached the Champs-Élysées he drew to a standstill and gazed up that long, wide boulevard, his eyes focusing on the Arc de Triomphe in the distance. The *Tricolore* was suspended inside the arch from the top, and inventively illuminated with spots so that it was bathed in light. It was blowing through the arch in the wind and looked unusually dramatic at this moment. Clee thought the arch was the most moving and magnificent sight he had seen in a very long time. But then the whole of Paris was particularly glorious right now. This was because a large number of the impressive, ancient buildings had recently been thoroughly washed, carefully cleaned up for the bi-centennial celebrations taking place this year.

Turning left, Clee strolled down the Champs-Élysées, enjoying the walk after being cooped up in the office all day; he generally felt slightly constrained when he was inside and not out on assignment. But, in any case, he enjoyed walking in Paris more than any other place in the world.

This was his city. He had first come here when he was eighteen, and had fallen in love with it. At first sight. He had wanted to come to Paris because of Capa, who had lived in the French capital for so many years, and had founded Magnum, his photo agency, there in 1947, with 'Chim' Seymour and Henri Cartier-Bresson. Capa had been his hero since he was fifteen and growing up in New York. That year, 1965, he had read an article about the late photographer in a photographic magazine, and ever after this he had searched for anything and everything that had been written about Capa.

Clee had first started taking pictures when he was nine years old, using an inexpensive camera his parents had given him for his birthday. Even as a child his pictures had been so extraordinary everyone had been taken aback and amazed at his talent. His mother and father, and sisters Joan and Kelly, were his willing victims, and had allowed themselves to be photographed day and night doing every conceivable thing, and were his models on special family occasions.

Naturally gifted, sensitive, intelligent, and with an exacting eye, he was completely self-taught, and had never had a lesson. Photography had been his great passion and his whole life when he was a teenager; nothing had changed much in the intervening years.

It was in 1968 that Clee had discovered Paris for himself, and instantly fallen under its exciting and seductive spell. That summer he had made up his mind that he was going to live here one day, and he had returned to New York determined to become a great photographer. He wanted to be another Robert Capa if that was humanly possible.

At the time, Clee had been working in the darkroom of a portrait photographer in Manhattan, and he had stayed on for only another year. Through a connection of his father's, he had managed to get a job on the *New York Post* as a junior photographer. Very rapidly he had made a name for himself on the paper, and he had never looked back.

During this period he had taken himself off to night school several evenings a week to study French, which he knew was an absolute necessity if he was ever to achieve his ambition and live in Paris. By the time he was twenty-one he was fluent in the language. He was also a far better photographer than some of the most seasoned veterans in the news business.

A staff job on the *New York Times* followed in 1971, but when he was twenty-three Clee left the paper. He had decided to become a roving photojournalist covering Europe, and worked as a freelancer for a number of American and English magazines.

Naturally, he had chosen to base himself in Paris, and two years later, when he was twenty-five, he had started Image. Banding together with two other photographers, he had hired three darkroom assistants, a secretary, and Jean-Claude, who managed the agency.

Michel Bellond, a Frenchman, and Steve Carvelli, an American of Italian descent, were his partners. Less than a year after Image had been founded, Peter Naylor from London became the fourth and last photographer to join the co-operative as a partner.

Right from the outset, Image had been successful, quickly garnering big international assignments, commanding high fees for the star photographers, and soon winning a clutch of awards. After fourteen years it was still going strong with the four original partners, several staff photographers, and additional darkroom assistants and secretarial help. And it had become one of the most prestigious photo agencies in the world.

Clee was well aware that his family had been dismayed, even distressed, when he had become an expatriate and settled in Paris. At the time, he was regretful of this, but he had never had any intention of changing his life. It was his own to live the way he saw fit. In the early years, his parents and sisters had come to visit him frequently, and whenever he had gone back to New York he had spent as much time with them as he could. And he still did, whenever he was there.

Despite the fact that he had defied his father and had not gone to college, choosing instead to plunge into the world of the working photographer, they had, nevertheless, remained truly good friends. Second-generation Irish, with an analytical mind, a golden tongue and the gift of the gab, his father, Edward

Donovan, had been a successful, well-known attorney in Manhattan, and highly respected in the field of criminal law.

His father had died unexpectedly of a heart attack in 1981, and Clee had felt the loss most acutely. As indeed had his mother and his sisters, for Ted Donovan had been very much a family man, a devoted husband and a loving father.

To Clee's considerable relief, his mother had managed to cope with her grief rather well, and quite bravely, he thought, thanks in no small measure to his sisters' offspring. Both Joan and Kelly were married, and between them they had three daughters and one son. Martha Donovan's grandchildren had become her life, and she appeared to be at peace with herself these days.

Clee's thoughts stayed with his mother as he hailed a passing cab, got in and gave the driver his address. He must call her this weekend to let her know he would be in New York in late July, tell her that they would be seeing each other soon. This would please her as much as it pleased him.

They had remained close over the years, and he knew she worried about him a great deal, especially when he was in a combat zone. This was only one of the many reasons he stayed in constant touch with her wherever he was.

Within a short time the cab was turning into the rue Jacob in the sixth *arrondissement*, that charming part of Paris known as the Quartier Latin. It was here that Clee lived in a fourth floor apartment of a handsome old building.

Clee sat on the sofa in the living room, the lights dim, the Mozart disc on the player turned low. He nursed a beer, lost to the world as he pondered his personal life.

Nicole Wells. He repeated her name to himself in the silence of his head. She had become a problem. A nagging problem, as it so happened.

For two years they had been *copains* – best buddies in the truest sense. In Beijing he had saved her life and everything had changed.

She was no longer simply his best buddy. She was a woman he cared about as a *woman*.

He had realized this when he had put his arms around her on the steps of the Martyrs' Monument in Tiananmen, after flinging her away from the approaching tanks. In fact, he was so filled with relief she was safe, for a moment all of his strength had seemed to ebb out of him. Momentarily undone by this surge of unexpected and unprecedented emotion about her, he had been incapable of saying a word.

Nicky had thanked him for saving her life, and he had turned her face to his and looked into those cool, appraising blue eyes. Suddenly he was brimming with feelings he did not fully understand.

Ever since leaving Hong Kong he had tried hard to shake off these feelings without much success. Off and on, they had continued to both confuse and trouble him, but he was aware of the reasons to some extent.

He and Nicky had drawn closer and closer, had grown to love each other like brother and sister. Now his emotions were engaged on a different level, and he was not sure what to do about it. To begin with, he did not want to get seriously involved with any woman because he did not want to care so much for someone that he would feel bound to make a commitment, get married and eventually have children. For most of his adult life he had believed that this would be unfair, in view of the dangerous life he led as a war photographer. And certainly he was not prepared to give up that life of travel and excitement. Besides, he enjoyed his freedom. He had no desire to be pinned down by marital obligations. If he was honest, he was a bachelor at heart.

And then there was Nicky herself. She was perfect as a friend, but hardly the most suitable candidate for a lover. She was too complicated, too complex by far. She was a woman with myriad problems, though carefully concealed they may well be. And then there were the very obvious, glaring problems . . . she lived an ocean away and she had one of the biggest careers in American television. Hardly the right ingredients for a harmonious love affair with him.

Also, for a long time Clee had been convinced that she lived out her life on various battlegrounds . . . the battlegrounds of the wars she covered, the battleground of network politics, the battleground of her damaged heart.

Furthermore, he could not help thinking that she was still in love with Charles Devereaux, as futile as that was, even though she had never made a single reference to the guy in the entire time he had known her. This omission had always struck him as odd, in as much as they *were* best friends.

Arch Leverson had partially filled him in, and therefore he had a fairly good picture of what had happened. In his considered opinion, and Arch's, the guy had behaved like a louse. But then brilliant and successful women such as Nicky were not necessarily discriminating when it came to men. Very frequently they picked the wrong ones, the bastards.

The clock on the white marble mantelpiece chimed nine and Clee sat up with a jolt, realizing that he had been thinking about Nicky ever since returning from the office.

What the hell am I going to do about her?

The question hung there for a while, and then all of a sudden it occurred to him that he did not have to *do* anything. She had absolutely no idea that he was harbouring these strange new feelings for her. If he was smart and did not reveal them she would be none the wiser. Very simply, he would go on treating her as a pal. This was the ideal solution, the *only* solution to his predicament. When he was with her he must behave *exactly* as he had in the past and everything would be all right.

Considerably relieved that he had finally solved a problem that had hovered over his head since Beijing, Clee got up and went to the kitchen, took another bottle of beer out of the refrigerator and opened it.

As he was crossing the foyer the phone began to ring and he hurried through the living room to answer it.

'Hello?'

'Hi, Clee, it's me.'

'Nicky!' he exclaimed, so happy to hear her voice he felt the smile of pleasure sliding onto his mouth. This sudden rush of euphoria so startled him he sat down heavily in the nearest chair.

'So what's happening down there?' he asked a bit lamely, and fell silent. He was amazed at his reaction to her tonight, and glad that she was hundreds of miles away.

'It's very quiet here, but it's been wonderful for me these last few days,' she said. 'Sunny and peaceful. And you were right, I did need the rest. By the way, I love the farm. It's just beautiful, and so comfortable. You made a wonderful job of it, Clee.'

When he did not immediately respond, she said quickly, 'I hope I'm not calling at an inconvenient time.'

'No, no,' he assured her, finding his voice at last. After clearing his throat, he said, 'And I'm glad you like it there, Nick. My sister Joan will be delighted, she's the one responsible for the farm. She restored and decorated it for me.'

'And here I've been thinking you've got hidden talents,' she said, and laughed her throaty laugh which suddenly sounded very sexual to him.

He muttered, 'How long are you planning to stay in Provence?'

'I don't know. Originally I thought a week, but maybe I'll stay on for a while. Clee?'

'Yes, Nick?'

'I was wondering if you might come down for a few days? Keep me company, if you don't have anything better to do?'

'I'd love to, Nick, but I'm jammed. The agency's flooded with jobs.'

'Oh.'

'Sorry, babe.'

'Never mind.'

'Look, I'm just in the middle of something I have to finish. Let me call you back later,' he said. 'Or will you be going to bed early?'

'No, that's fine. Talk to you later. Bye.'

She hung up on him before he could say another word, and he felt rotten for being so abrupt with her. Then he laughed. He had been having the occasional erotic thought about Nicky lately, and he had begun to feel self-conscious, ill at ease on the phone with her just now.

Nicky was a baffling woman in a variety of ways. When he had first met her in Beirut two years ago he had thought she was the classiest looking blonde he had ever seen. Beautiful, elegant even in her battered safari suit, and very photogenic. At that time he had categorized her in his mind as a Grace Kelly for the eighties and nineties. She had that very poised, cool exterior which could be so off-putting to some men, but which he was sure concealed great warmth. Eventually he had come to believe that deep down she was romantic and passionate by nature, but that she had been so badly hurt by Devereaux she was frozen cold when it came to men.

None of this had mattered to him before, because they were platonic friends and nothing more. In any case, when he had first met her he had been heavily involved with another woman and had not been interested in Nicky as a lover.

But it mattered now. Everything about her mattered now. But it mustn't. I have to care about her as a friend, and that's all, he cautioned himself.

Jumping up, Clee went back to the kitchen where he tore a piece off the fresh baguette on the table, and made himself a salami sandwich. Then he wandered around the kitchen, pacing restlessly, munching on the sandwich and taking an occasional swig from the bottle of beer.

And try though he did to put her out of his mind, his thoughts continued to turn on Nicky Wells.

At ten o'clock he called her back, and he went out of his way to be warm and friendly.

They chatted for about twenty minutes; he told her about Marc Villier and the interview planned for the following morning; they discussed his trip to the States for *Life* Magazine. And, as they usually did, they touched on the subject of Yoyo, of whom there was still no news.

Just before he said goodbye, Clee murmured, 'I'm sorry I can't come down to the farm, babe. There's nothing I'd like better than a few days in the sun, a chance to relax with you. But duty calls, I've just got too much work.'

'Please don't worry about it, Clee,' she said pleasantly. 'Honestly, I do understand.'

As he hung up he was not so sure that *he* did.

Clee sat for a moment with his hand resting on the phone, his face reflective. He had nothing planned for the next few days, other than the meeting with Villier tomorrow and the date with Mel on Saturday night. He could easily cancel Saturday and go down to Provence for a long weekend.

A small sigh escaped him as he thought of Mel. He was forever cancelling dates with her for one reason or another, and that was damned unfair of him. Still, if nothing else, he supposed this told him something important about the status of his relationship with her. She was lovely but his feelings for her were not particularly intense. If he was truthful, he was only mildly fond of Melanie Lowe, and this would never change.

His thoughts veered back to Provence. There was no reason why he could not go down there. *Not true.* There was an excellent reason. *Nicky Wells.*

He was also forgetting his decision of a short while ago ... to keep his relationship with Nicky exactly the way it had been from their first meeting. *Platonic.* He had absolutely no intention of changing that. Nor did he have any intention of going to the farm this weekend. Why expose himself when he felt vulnerable to her at present? Surely it was better to get a grip on his feelings, wait for them to change, to settle down and normalize before he saw her again.

He would be with Mel for the weekend, and for as long as they both wished to continue their pleasant liaison. Mel suited him fine. She was sweet and loving and undemanding. Furthermore, he liked being with her, enjoyed her wry sense of humour, her easy-going ways, and her brightness.

And Nicky would remain his comrade-in-arms with whom he shared so much on an entirely different level. She was ideal to have as his best buddy, and he knew he must never do anything to jeopardize their friendship, which he cherished.

CHAPTER TEN

'What Guillaume told you is true, Mademoiselle Nicky,' Amelia said, nodding her head several times for emphasis. 'Soon it will be scorching hot. Unbearable. This is not the day to go to Arles.' As she finished speaking, Amelia threw back her head and squinted up at the sky, then repeated, 'Scorching, *oui*.'

Nicky tilted her head, following Amelia's gaze.

The sky was so vividly blue it almost hurt her eyes and she blinked, took her sun glasses out of her pocket and put them on.

'If you think I shouldn't go, then I won't,' she murmured, deeming it best to trust the couple's judgement. Amelia and Guillaume were wise to the ways of the Provençal land and the weather, and in the week she had been staying here they had not been wrong in anything they had told her about the area.

'Too hot to go tramping the streets of the city,' Amelia went on, waving her hand in a dismissive manner. 'Better to be here. Sit under the trees in the shade. Swim in the pool. Stay cool. That is the best thing on a day like this, Mademoiselle Nicky.'

'Then that's what I'll do, Amelia.' Nicky smiled at her and added, 'Thanks for your good advice. I appreciate it.'

'*De rien, Mademoiselle.*'

It was eight o'clock on Friday morning. The two women were standing in the middle of the lawn that stretched from the edge of the outdoor dining terrace on one side of the house to the pool area at the bottom of the garden. The sun was shining brilliantly in that azurine sky of dazzling clarity, and the air was already vibrating with intense heat. Nothing moved, not a blade of grass nor a single leaf stirred, and even the birds were curiously silent this morning, as if they were taking refuge in the dark green branches of the trees.

Amelia straightened her crisp white apron, peered at Nicky and asked, 'What would you like for lunch?'

Nicky burst out laughing. 'Amelia! I've only just had *breakfast*! You're going to have to stop feeding me in this way. I'm beginning to feel like a duck being force fed . . . fattened up for *foie gras*.'

Shaking her head, Amelia exclaimed, 'But Mademoiselle Nicky, you are too thin!' Opening her arms wide, Amelia threw them around her solid Provençal body and hugged herself. Then she winked and announced, 'A man likes something to hold onto, *n'est-ce pas*? That is my opinion.'

'Perhaps you're right,' Nicky said, the laughter echoing in her voice. 'But please don't make anything too heavy for lunch. It's much too hot to eat.'

'I will prepare the perfect lunch for the weather,' Amelia reassured her. 'Yesterday Guillaume bought wonderful melons in the village, from Cavaillon.

They are the best in the whole of France, Mademoiselle. So sweet, like honey. *Mmmm.*' Amelia kissed her fingertips eloquently, and went on, 'So you will commence with the chilled melon. Then you will have a simple salad Niçoise, and for dessert, vanilla ice cream.'

'Thank you, it sounds delicious. But no ice cream, Amelia, iced tea instead.'

'As you say, Mademoiselle Nicky.' Amelia flashed her a warm smile. 'Excuse me, I must go to my kitchen. So much to do. And I must also think about your dinner for tonight. Nothing fattening, no.' And so saying she hurried up the steps leading to the terrace, bustled through into the farmhouse, intent on her purpose.

Nicky looked after her, shaking her head in bemusement. Amelia was determined to put some flesh on her bones whatever it took, at least so it seemed to her. Turning, she strolled over to the narrow flagged path cutting through the long stretch of sloping green lawn, and headed down to the pool area located at the very tip of the garden.

This had been skilfully designed to flow into the landscape and it had a lovely natural look to it. The pool was set in a rectangle of lawn, its edges surrounded by local white flagstones. Only a few yards away, a cluster of trees formed a small copse where flowers had been randomly planted here and there to give the effect of growing wild.

Under these trees Guillaume had arranged several chaises, old-fashioned deck chairs and low occasional tables, as he did every morning. Nicky had discovered that this was the coolest spot in the garden; frequently, a light breeze rustled through the trees, and it was her favourite place for reading.

She smiled inwardly as she walked towards the copse. Amelia had been fussing and mothering her all week long, and nothing was too much trouble for her or Guillaume. In consequence, she felt rested and spoiled, but she was also beginning to grow just a little bored after a week here alone.

Nicky had said this to her mother last night, when she had called her in New York. Her mother had exclaimed, 'Good Lord, darling, how can you be bored in Provence! There's so much to see and do. Besides, it's about time you stayed put for a moment or two. If only to catch your breath. You're never still ... forever rushing around the world in search of stories.'

Flabbergasted, Nicky had retorted, 'Mother, how can *you* of all people say such a thing! You were doing exactly the same as me when you were my age. Not only that, you had *me* in tow.'

Her mother had had the good grace to laugh. '*Touché*,' she had responded. 'But to tell you the truth, darling, your father and I do wish you *would* slow down a bit. For the past ten years you've been covering wars and uprisings and revolutions, been in the thick of all kinds of catastrophic events, in every corner of the globe. And when I look back, I can't help but shudder to think what you've been through, the risks you've taken ...' Her mother had stopped at this juncture in the conversation, and there had been a little pause before Nicky had asked softly, 'Mom, are you trying to say that you and Dad want me to stop being a war correspondent?'

Her mother had been quick to deny this. 'Of course not, your father and I would never interfere in your life, or your career, but *I* know it must get wearying for you. And it *is* dangerous.'

Nicky had laughed dismissively. 'Don't forget, Mother, I have a guardian angel.'

Elise Wells had chosen to ignore this remark, and she had gone on to suggest that Nicky return home to New York for the remainder of her vacation if she was tired of France. 'You can always join us in Connecticut, if you wish. Your father and I are going to stay at the house for the rest of the summer, and you know how much we adore to have you with us, Nick.'

They had chatted about this idea for several minutes, and Nicky had agreed to spend a few days in the country with her parents when she got back to the States.

They were closely knit, the three of them, and they had been for as long as Nicky could remember. She was an only child, and as such she sometimes felt the responsibility of this. Only children were expected to excel, to bring home the bacon, so to speak, since parents generally centred their hopes and dreams in that one child.

Her parents were no different from any others with a single offspring. And yet they were eminently fair, had never made unreasonable demands on her. She loved them as much as they loved her; they were her champions, her chief supporters in everything she did, had been wonderful to her all of her life. And spectacular through the entire Charles Devereaux debacle.

Immediately, she pushed the thought of him away. She had no wish to remember someone who had caused her pain, however long ago that was.

Reaching the pool area, Nicky put her book down on one of the tables, took off the loose cotton shirt she was wearing over her black bikini and settled on a chaise.

Diffused sunlight trickled through the cool green canopy of leafy branches above her head, and she stretched out her long legs, closed her eyes and drifted with her thoughts for a while, which were still focused on her parents. She knew her mother and father wondered why she had not had a serious involvement with a man since Devereaux, and that at one moment they had even believed her to be hung up on him. But she had explained that she was not. She had spoken the truth. The reason why there was no special man in her life was very simple really. She hadn't met anyone who had genuinely interested her in the past two and a half years, at least not for a long-term relationship.

One day, she thought. One day my prince will come. When I'm least expecting it. And no doubt he'll knock me for a loop. That was the way it was supposed to be, wasn't it? Wobbly knees, palpitating heart, and all that stuff. She laughed to herself.

In the meantime, she wasn't unhappy with her life. She had a successful career and she loved her work; whenever she wanted it, there was a family life with her parents, and she had several close girl friends with whom she shared a great deal. And then there was her best buddy, Cleeland Donovan. He was caring and loving and protective, and she treasured his friendship.

Suddenly Nicky realized how disappointed she was that he had not been able to come down for the weekend. It would have been nice to see him, enjoy his company in these peaceful surroundings.

She sighed. Usually when they were together they were in a combat zone, or some other trouble spot in the world. At these times they were under immense pressure, intensely involved in what they were doing, scrambling to do their work properly, to get the story, and, more often than not, under the most adverse circumstances. They were also fighting the horror of what they were witnessing, plus the fear, which never failed to surface at some point, generally at night for her, when she was trying to fall asleep.

What a lovely change it would have been if they could have relaxed together, and had some fun this weekend. But seemingly he could not get away, or did not want to, or was otherwise engaged, and that was that.

Now that she thought about it, spending a few days with her mother and father in New Milford was a rather appealing idea. If she left the farm on Monday morning, went to Marseille and then directly on to Paris, she could easily take the Concorde to New York on Tuesday morning, and drive up to Connecticut on Wednesday afternoon. She would speak to Guillaume later about ordering a car and have the driver Etienne come and get her.

Having made this decision, Nicky pulled her reading glasses out of the pocket of her shirt and picked up her book. It was Richard Whelan's biography of Robert Capa, which she had found in the library upstairs, and it made fascinating reading. From the moment she had started it, she had understood why Clee had always been so intrigued and fascinated by Capa. He had been a cool guy.

Opening the book, Nicky found her page, began to read, and was soon completely absorbed in Capa's life story. An hour slipped by, and then another.

In the middle of the morning, Amelia appeared, and came sailing down the garden path carrying a tray.

'Eh voilà!' she cried, drawing to a standstill next to Nicky's chaise. 'I have made fresh lemonade for you, I know how much you enjoy it, Mademoiselle.' She poured a glass from the jug.

'Thank you, Amelia,' Nicky said, taking it from her. 'This is just what I need. It's getting hotter by the minute out here.'

'Oui. The sun can be dangerous, faites attention,' the housekeeper cautioned, smiled, and hurried back to the farmhouse.

Nicky looked up from the biography of Capa at the exact moment Clee reached the middle of the garden path leading down to the pool.

He stood perfectly still, waiting for her reaction, grinning at her.

Nicky's face broke into delighted smiles. She threw her book down and leaped to her feet.

'Clee! How did you suddenly get here?' she cried.

'On a plane.'

Nicky ran across the grass and threw her arms around him, hugged him to her.

He hugged her back, then swiftly let go of her, and the two of them walked back to the pool area together.

'And how did you manage to get away?' she asked, looking up at him, her smile radiant, her eyes filled with sudden merriment.

'Jean-Claude reshuffled the assignments, gave my jobs to the other guys,' Clee lied. 'He thought I looked tired, decided I needed a rest. So I took the last flight

646

from Paris to Marseille yesterday. When I arrived it was far too late to start driving here, and anyway I didn't want to disturb the household at that late hour, so I stayed at a hotel in Marseille. Etienne drove me up this morning.'

'I'm glad you're here! It's wonderful to see you!' Nicky said, her enthusiasm bubbling up as she glanced at him out of the corner of her eye. Then she confided, 'I was getting a bit lonely.'

He looked at her, nodded, but did not say a word.

Nicky continued, 'I almost drove to Arles today, but Amelia persuaded me to stay here because of the heat – .' Abruptly she broke off and shook her head as the truth suddenly dawned on her. 'She *knew* you were coming. That's the reason why she went on and on *ad infinitum* about the weather . . . said it was far too hot to go into the city.'

'As a matter of fact, she was right about the weather, it *is* murderous in the cities at this time of year, much worse than out here,' Clee said. 'But yes, she did know I was coming. I told her not to tell you, when I spoke to her yesterday, Nicky. I wanted to surprise you.'

'You succeeded!' She laughed as she flopped down on the chaise and stared up at Clee, eyeing his cream linen pants and cotton shirt. 'Why don't you take your clothes off?'

Startled, he gaped at her. '*What?*'

'You look so hot, Clee. Don't you think you'd be more comfortable in swimming trunks?'

'*Oh*. Yes. Yes, of course, you're right, I'll go and change. What I need after that long drive is a dip in the pool and a glass of ice-cold champagne. I'll be back in a minute, suitably attired and bearing a bottle of Dom Pérignon.'

CHAPTER ELEVEN

'Think of it, Nicky, I was only four years old when Capa bought it in Vietnam during the French–Indochina war in 1954,' Clee said and paused, staring at her for a long moment. Then he added quietly, 'He's the only person I've ever really missed.'

Nicky stared back at him, frowning slightly, but she made no comment.

Clee went on in the same quiet voice, 'I just wish I'd met him, been a friend of his. I miss not having known him. Do you understand what I mean?'

She nodded.

He laughed a bit self-consciously and muttered, 'I bet you think I'm nuts.'

'No, I don't, you've explained it very well. It's a kind of sadness inside, a feeling of regret that you were born too late to meet someone whom you consider very special, a person who is somehow extremely meaningful to you, even though your lives never crossed. Isn't that it?'

'Yes, it is, Nicky.'

'Quite aside from being a remarkable photographer, Capa was obviously a fascinating man, by all accounts,' Nicky continued. 'In the biography I've been reading, the photographer Eve Arnold is quoted as saying he had charm and grace and a lightness, that when he came into a room it was as if a light had been turned on. She said you wanted to be near him, that you wanted to be part of that effervescence, part of that zest. He had enormous . . . charisma. I think that's the word for it, Clee.'

'I remember reading that myself, as well as a wonderful description of Capa by Irwin Shaw which was also quoted in Whelan's biography.'

'Yes, I read it, too.' Nicky half smiled at him. 'Capa must have seemed so glamorous to you when you were growing up, and his life must have seemed very adventurous and exciting.'

'He did, it did,' Clee admitted. 'But actually, I'd wanted to get into combat to take war photographs even when I was a kid, long before I'd ever heard of Robert Capa. Still, he was my inspiration in so many different ways.' Clee shifted in the chair, crossed his legs, and after a moment asked, 'When did you decide you wanted to be a war correspondent, Nick?'

'When I was little, like you. I was emulating my father, I suppose.'

'Do you think that's really why you do it? I mean *now*, *today*, after all these years?'

'Oh no, not any more, definitely not. I do what I do because I want to report history in the making. I find that challenging, Clee. I want to watch, to witness events, to report on them as accurately, and as truthfully, as I can. I want to bring the news to the people . . . and with as much integrity as possible.'

'I think our reasons are much the same. I just hope my pictures have as much integrity as your newscasts.'

'They do.' The look Nicky now gave him was curious, probing as she asked, 'Do you think you'll ever give it up?'

'I doubt it, babe.' Clee shrugged, then grinned at her good-naturedly. 'Well, maybe one day. When I'm too old to dodge the bullets. And what about you?'

'I feel the same.'

'Unless you get married and have babies!'

'Fat chance of that!' she retorted, and began to laugh.

Clee chuckled with her, then lifted his glass, took a swallow of his vodka martini, sat back, amusement reflected in his dark eyes.

Nicky suddenly said, 'It's funny about the fear, isn't it? And how alike we are in that respect. You and I never seem to experience it until after the action is over. Do you think all journalists are the same as we are?'

'No, I don't. Some feel the fear at the time they're working. Others are like us, get knocked out by it afterwards. Joe Glass of the London *Sunday Times* once told me when we were in Lebanon together that he suffers immense fatigue *immediately* after he's had a very frightening experience in a war zone. You and I are lucky in a sense, Nick, because our emotions don't close in on us until much, much later.'

'You take too many risks on the battlefield, Clee.'

'Calculated risks. Anyway, you're exactly the same.'

648

'No, not really. I'm much more cautious than you, despite what you and Arch think.'

'I should hope you are.'

A thoughtful expression settled on Nicky's face, and after a moment, she said slowly, 'We broke the golden rule in Beijing, didn't we, Clee?'

'What do you mean?' His brows puckered; he seemed slightly mystified.

'We became *involved* with Yoyo. That has such inherent dangers . . . and you know it, Clee. We should never let our emotions become engaged with a subject when we're covering a story. We really have to remain a little aloof, a bit removed, to do our job. We have to have a proper perspective.'

'Sometimes it's pretty tough not to get involved,' he responded quickly. 'None of us are *that* hardboiled, are we? And listen, Arch and the guys felt exactly the same as we did about Yoyo. How could you not get involved with the kid, he's something else, really special, wouldn't you say?'

'Yes, that's true.'

Nicky leaned against the sofa, and looked across at Clee. There was a small silence before she asked softly, 'What do you think happened to him? You don't think he's . . . dead, do you, Clee?'

'No, I don't. I have a feeling Yoyo is hiding out, that he went underground. I've always said that to you, and I can only reiterate it now. You'll see, he'll turn up, and probably sooner than we think.'

'You're not just saying that to make me feel better are you?' She sounded worried; her eyes were focused steadily on his.

Clee shook his head. His expression was serious. 'No, I'm not,' he said, in an adamant tone. He leaned forward, intent on what he had to say to her. 'Yoyo is bright, enterprising, resourceful. He'll make it out of China, I feel very strongly about this . . . I really do have a lot of faith in him.'

As he finished speaking, Clee rose, crossed the library where they were sitting, and swung around when he reached the doorway. 'I want to show you something. I won't be a minute.'

Whilst Clee was gone, Nicky relaxed, closed her eyes, thinking briefly of Yoyo.

Clee had spoken with such conviction about his fate, she had to believe that he was correct in his assessment of what had happened to Yoyo. She had no alternative, and she must go on hoping that he would surface eventually. Either in New York or Paris or Hong Kong. Practically the last thing she had said to him was that if he arrived in the British Crown Colony and needed help, he was to telephone one of them immediately, person to person collect. She had promised Yoyo that she or Clee or Arch would take it from there, would get him out of Hong Kong no matter what it took.

Opening her eyes, Nicky sat up, leaned forward and reached for her glass, took a sip of the vodka martini Clee had made earlier. Knowing it was futile to worry, she put thoughts of Yoyo at the back of her mind.

She glanced around approvingly, enjoying the peacefulness of this room, understanding why it was Clee's favourite. It was also hers. Its tranquillity was like a balm to her troubled spirit.

Washed throughout in pale colours, primarily white and cream with touches of melon and terracotta, it was filled with numerous bowls of flowers and tall pots of leafy branches. Hundreds of books spilled out of the shelves soaring to the ceiling, and there were magazines and big art books arranged on various tables. Some of Clee's photographs, obviously those he liked the most, were framed on the walls, and hanging above the gargantuan stone fireplace was a collection of ethereal watercolours of the area by a local artist. It was a casual room, full of great comfort, and designed for relaxing, reading, listening to music, and watching television and films.

Today the weather had been extremely hot again, oppressively so. Fortunately, the two large fans on the ceiling – Casablanca fans she called them – circulated the air, and now that the sun had slunk off to the west the atmosphere was pleasant. Outside the windows the summer light was rapidly fading, the sky turning a deeper blue as night fell. It was almost eight thirty on Sunday evening; earlier, Clee had suggested that they could have a picnic in the library and watch a video of an old movie later, and she had agreed.

It seemed to Nicky that the weekend had passed in the blink of an eye. She and Clee had pottered around the farm on Friday, after his unexpected arrival, chatting endlessly, laughing, reminiscing and catching up with each other's news. As Clee had pointed out to her on Friday evening, in the two years they had known each other this was the first time they had ever had a chance to relax together, to talk in the way they had that day – and about so many diverse things.

On Saturday, because it was so much cooler, Clee had driven her to Arles. 'But don't expect to see many of Van Gogh's old haunts,' he had warned her on the way there. 'There's not much left that's associated with the time he spent in Provence. Even the house he shared with Gauguin has been torn down. But there is the Allée des Sarcophages, which he painted so wonderfully and with such vibrancy. We can go and see that. And of course there are the fields and fields of sunflowers where he used to go and pick bunches for his still lifes. They should be in full bloom now.'

Arles, as Nicky had discovered, was a captivating place, charming, very ancient, almost otherworldly in a certain sense. Clee had taken her sightseeing through the old city and she had been fascinated. Her father had always said she made a good tourist, with her curious mind and investigative nature, her desire to know about everything.

The old city was filled with crumbling Roman ruins juxtaposed against strong medieval stonework; there were numerous monuments and museums, and a lot of other quaint things to see. She had been in her element, and Clee had seemed pleased she was enjoying herself so much.

After strolling for several hours through the old city, with its ramparts and air of antiquity, they had gone for a late lunch at a charming bistro Clee obviously knew well. He was greeted with affection and enthusiasm by Madame Yvonne and Monsieur Louis, the owners, who had given them the best table in the house, according to Clee.

He had ordered for them both, selecting various local dishes, telling her she would love them, and explaining each one to her. He had also insisted she join him in a *pastis*, the popular local drink, an *apéritif* tasting of aniseed which turned milky in colour when mixed with the mandatory splash of water.

After lunch they had wandered around the newer part of Arles, window shopping mostly, although Nicky had bought a handful of postcards to send off to Arch, her crew and girlfriends in New York. As she had pored over the cards in the book store, Clee had selected a dozen or so magazines and a stack of newspapers, then they had meandered back to the car.

It was late afternoon when they had set off for the farm, driving along at a leisurely pace, arriving in time for icy champagne on the terrace, and, a little later, a light supper. This had been lovingly prepared by Amelia, and she and Guillaume had served it to them in the garden.

The couple had departed early this morning to go to the wedding of a niece in Marseille, and they would not return until Monday afternoon. As much as she liked and appreciated Amelia, Nicky was glad to have a respite from all the meals, delicious and tempting though they were.

Much to her relief, Clee had not made any comment when she had refused the cold chicken, cold fish, stuffed vegetables and various other dishes Amelia had prepared in advance for their lunch. Instead, she had made herself a small tomato salad, which she had eaten with a chunk of bread torn from a fresh baguette.

Taking another sip of her drink, Nicky reflected on the day. It really had been lovely. She and Clee had done absolutely nothing, mostly because of the intense heat. In the morning they had taken it easy under the trees near the pool, reading magazines and newspapers; in the afternoon they had come up here to the library to listen to Kiri Te Kanawa's extraordinary rendition of *Tosca*, performed with the National Philharmonic Orchestra and conducted by Sir Georg Solti.

Nicky had curled up on one of the big, squashy sofas, closed her eyes and drifted off into another world, transported by Puccini's music and Dame Kiri's wonderfully melodious voice. Yes, she reflected, it has been a special day, and in so many ways . . .

The door opened and Clee returned carrying two large portfolios.

He strode over to the long library table, and said, 'I haven't told you . . . but I'm planning a photographic book on Beijing, on Tiananmen. I'd like to show you some of the pictures, Nicky.'

'I'd love to see them,' she exclaimed, jumping up to join him at the table.

Clee pushed aside a pile of magazines, took the photographs out of the first portfolio and spread them out on the table. The collection was a mixture of colour and black and white.

The pictures were so powerful, had such an amazing sense of immediacy, Nicky caught her breath and instantly she was carried back to Tiananmen Square. Those tense and turbulent days leading up to the bloody massacre at the beginning of the month were suddenly vividly alive in her mind.

Yet again she recognized how accurate Clee's eye was, and it was unflinching. He had taken very direct and candid photographs of people and events. Each shot had a feeling of intimacy, and the people looked so vibrant, she thought.

'They're extraordinary, Clee,' Nicky said, her admiration clearly written across her face. 'They're powerful, extremely moving.'

Her words brought a quick, pleased smile to his face, and he took another batch

651

out of the second portfolio. 'These are more personal,' he explained, lining them up, watching her, waiting for her reaction.

Nicky found herself looking down at pictures Clee had taken of *her* ... alone in Tiananmen Square and in other parts of Beijing. Some were with Arch and her crew, with Yoyo, and also with Yoyo and Mai. There were additional shots of Yoyo with the other student leaders, and with Mai, and all of the backgrounds were so familiar to her they brought a lump to her throat: the Martyrs' Monument, the tent encampment, the Goddess of Democracy, Changan Avenue.

'Oh Clee, they're stunning! That old cliché about one photograph saying more than a thousand words is true, isn't it?'

'I guess so,' he agreed with a shrug of his broad shoulders, and brought out the last set of photographs.

Nicky's eyes were riveted to them. A sudden rush of memories flooded her. She stood staring at them speechlessly.

Across the vast rectangle of stone that was Tiananmen Square came the inexorable flow of tanks and armoured personnel carriers. Down Changan Avenue marched the implacable, cold-faced soldiers, toting machine guns and death for their own people. Standing at the barricades, defiant and angry, were the ordinary citizens of Beijing, shaking their fists at the People's Liberation Army, and desperately trying to save the lives of the students – the children of China. And blowing in the wind were the giant banners of white bearing the students' slogans of democracy and freedom, written out boldly in bright red paint the colour of blood.

Finally Nicky's eyes settled on the pictures of the fallen students, those who had been shot, or crushed by the tanks, who lay dead or dying in pools of their own blood in the streets. All at once she could smell the cordite again, hear the sharp crack of rifles and the ominous rumble of tanks rolling across cold stone, the screams of terror, and a tremor ran through her. She snapped her eyes shut, opened them after a split second, and stared once more at the children of the massacre, innocent victims of a power struggle mounted by decrepit old men.

Nicky was so moved by the breathtaking images Clee had captured on film, tears sprang into her eyes and she brought her hand up to her mouth. She blinked several times, turned to him, but discovered she was unable to speak.

He saw the tears glistening, and he reached out for her, pulled her to him. 'Don't be upset,' he began, and his voice faltered. He had been conscious of her the entire weekend, and never more than today, and he knew now that it was a mistake to take her in his arms in this way. Her perfume was fragrant in his nostrils, her body warm and vibrantly alive next to his.

He let go of her, smiled faintly. Nicky had never looked so lovely to him, so glowing and youthful. She wore no makeup, but then he had always thought she looked wonderful without it. Her skin was a golden brown, her blonde hair sunstreaked after the week in Provence, and her eyes seemed bluer than ever in her bronzed face. It took all of his self-control not to reach out for her again and kiss her.

She said, 'That's what you want, isn't it?'

'What?' he asked, startled, and wondered if she had just read his mind.

'For me to be upset ... for everyone who looks at these pictures to be upset.

And to be touched and moved and appalled and horrified and angered.'

'I suppose so, yes,' he admitted.

'They will be. The photographs are so stunning they literally take my breath away. I feel as if I've been kicked in the stomach. They pack one hell of a punch, that's for sure. The book is going to be sensational.'

'I hope so, darling.' He held his breath. The word darling had popped out by accident, but if she had noticed this careless slip of the tongue she certainly did not show it. In fact, she was displaying no reaction whatsoever.

Clee began to put the pictures away and Nicky helped him. At one moment he stopped, and said, 'You know, Nick, I can do the captions okay, I'm used to doing that, but what this book needs is some really great text up front. An introduction. I've been thinking . . . well, you're one of the best writers I know. Would you be interested in doing it, in collaborating with me?'

His suggestion took her aback and she swung to face him, her surprise apparent. 'I don't know,' she said hesitantly.

'Who better than *you*, Nick? *You* were there, were witness to it all, and you *felt* it as acutely as I did. You'd bring the right emotions to the writing. The text must back up the pictures, must also pack a punch, as you call it. Say yes.'

'Yes.'

'Hey, that's great, babe!' He wanted to hug her but he refrained. He exclaimed, with a huge smile, 'We'll make a terrific team!'

Nicky laughed and walked over to the coffee table, picked up her glass and raised it. 'I think we ought to drink to that.'

'Agreed.' Clee found his glass, clinked it to hers. 'So . . . here's to our collaboration!'

'To our collaboration!' she repeated, and they both took a sip of their drinks.

'These are lukewarm, they need topping up,' Clee announced, walked over to the chest where he had deposited the pitcher of martinis and bucket of ice earlier. He threw a handful of ice cubes into the jug, added more vodka and a splash of vermouth, then carefully stirred the contents.

As he walked back to her, carrying the jug, he said, 'Shall we have a swim before dinner?'

'Why not?' Nicky began to chuckle. 'You said *picnic*, earlier, which meant a *snack*, as far as I'm concerned. Now, suddenly, it's *dinner*. What is it about *me* that makes everyone want to feed me? First Amelia, now you.'

'That's Amelia's calling in life . . . getting slender girls plump.'

'Oh, she does it all the time, does she?'

'She's never had the opportunity with any girls of mine,' he swiftly shot back. 'I was sort of . . . well, I was kidding you, Nicky. Anyway, Amelia's forever wanting to stuff me too, so join the club.'

'I think I'd like something very American for our *picnic*,' she said, holding her glass out to be filled.

'That's tough in this house,' he answered, pouring the martini. 'Amelia has left us all sorts of delicious goodies, and naturally they're all Provençal. But I'll see what I can rustle up. In the meantime, let's take our drinks down to the pool and have that swim, shall we?'

'What a great idea, Clee.'

CHAPTER TWELVE

She floated towards him in the water.

'It's lovely, Clee, so refreshing,' she called out. 'I thought it would be warm like a bath tub, but it isn't, it's perfect.'

'The breeze is cooling everything off,' he called back.

Nicky made no response, and floated closer to the end of the pool where Clee was catching his breath after several fast laps. Suddenly, she flipped over onto her stomach and swam forward, coming to a stop next to him.

Clinging to the side of the pool with one hand, she pushed her wet hair back with the other, and laughed softly, as if to herself, shaking her head at the same time.

'What is it?'

'I was just thinking how odd it is that we sometimes forget that the simplest things in life can be so wonderful . . . the best things of all.'

'I know exactly what you mean,' he replied, and swung his head, glanced around the garden. Just before they had left the house and come outside to swim, he had turned on the small spots hidden in the foliage, and the shrubs and trees and flowers were now highlighted by circles of pale silver light. Thanks to his sister's remarkable talent, the spots had been strategically placed, and there was nothing artificial about the effect she had created. The garden looked as natural as it did during the day, and, to Clee, infinitely more beautiful after sunset.

He lifted his eyes and looked up. Overhead the sky had changed colour yet again; the mauves and amethysts had deepened to marine blue and a dim and heavy twilight was descending. A peaceful hush had settled over everything, and the only sounds were the rustling of the trees in the copse, the faint slap of the water as it lapped against the sides of the pool. The air was clear, much cooler, and sweet with the fragrance of honeysuckle and frangipani which grew close to the old stone wall running down one side of the garden.

Clee took several deep breaths, exhaled, and brought his eyes back to Nicky. 'What could be better than being in this glorious spot . . . the two of us here together, enjoying each other's company.'

'Nothing could, it's pure heaven,' Nicky said, 'and it's been such a wonderful weekend, Clee. I've enjoyed every minute of it. And this is a perfect end to an especially lovely day.'

'It's not the end yet,' he said, looking at her carefully, 'we still have the evening ahead of us – ' He glanced at his watch. 'It's only nine thirty.'

'Ah yes, the night is young,' she answered, smiling, her affection for him filling her face.

'But it *is*, Nicky,' he asserted. 'We can stay up as late as we wish, since we don't have to be awake early in the morning. Neither of us has a deadline to meet, you know.'

'Thank God,' she replied with a light laugh. 'I must admit, it has been nice to have a vacation. My first in two and a half years, I might add.'

'I know . . . and this place has done you good, Nick.'

'Thanks for inviting me, and thank you for coming down for the weekend. It's been . . . well, wonderful, Clee. You're so good to me, such a wonderful friend.'

She reached out, touched his arm resting along the edge of the pool.

He caught hold of her hand, held it tightly. Then before he could stop himself he pulled her to him, put his arms around her and kissed her on the mouth.

At first he met resistance, then she partially responded, letting her body slacken, her mouth go soft under his. But abruptly she pulled away, looked up into his face, and stared long and hard at him.

He could not read her expression; it baffled him.

He said rapidly, catching hold of her hand again, 'Don't pull away from me, Nicky. This isn't a cheap shot, and surely after knowing me for two years, you must realize that.'

She was silent.

'I mean this,' he said.

'What do you mean?' she asked in a voice that was barely audible.

'I'm not sure,' he replied, as always being honest with her. 'Except that since Beijing you've become very special to me. Look, you were always special, but now it's different. And you've been on my mind a great deal.'

She made no comment to this, extracted her hand from his and swam away, heading for the far end of the pool.

Clee followed her, doing a fast crawl. Pushing himself up and over the edge, he scrambled out of the water, hurried over to where she stood near the chaises under the trees.

Her head was turned away from him and she was shivering under the light breeze.

Clee reached for one of the large beach towels on a chaise, went to her, wrapped her in it, then quickly took a step back. 'You're cold,' he said.

She swung her head finally and looked directly at him, but still she did not speak.

They were motionless, staring at each other.

Neither one was able to break the intense gaze that stretched between them and which held them in its thrall.

It seemed to Clee that her bright blue eyes were impaling his, and inwardly he flinched. Yet he discovered he could not look away. And oh God, how he wanted her, wanted to take her in his arms, to make love to her. He understood something else: he wanted to possess her completely, and be possessed by her. And yet he was unable to make a move in her direction, was momentarily paralysed, his breath strangled in his throat.

She spoke first. At last breaking the silence between them, she said, 'Clee . . .

oh *Clee* . . . ' and then paused as though she were afraid to finish what she had to say.

Long afterward he would remember the inflection in her voice quite precisely, would recall the way she had said his name at that exact moment, for it was the inflection that had told him everything. Longing had been implicit in her tone.

'Nicky darling,' he said in a voice thickened by desire, and moved swiftly towards her.

She rushed forward into his arms.

He wrapped them around her, held her tightly, keeping her close to him. He could feel her heart hammering against his chest, keeping time with his own. He kissed her deeply, passionately, almost roughly, the way he wanted to kiss her, and she responded with ardour, her lips pliable, yielding, as he moved his tongue against them. Instantly, they parted slightly so that he could slide his tongue inside her mouth, and their tongues touched, lay still, touched again. It was a moment of the greatest intimacy.

Her hands were on the nape of his neck and in his hair, then moved onto his shoulders and his back, and he loved the feel of her fingers, so strong and supple, on his skin. Pulling her even closer, he slid his hands down her back, pushing her buttocks against him, moulding her body to his body, fitting her into him.

Nicky pressed herself closer, as filled with desire for Clee as he was for her. She was slightly dizzy, her legs were weak, and her whole body trembled as she leaned against him, clinging to him. He was tremendously aroused. She could feel him through the thin fabric of her bikini.

Clee brought his mouth to the hollow in her neck, kissed it tenderly, slipped the beach towel off her shoulder, let his mouth linger there, covering her with his tender kisses.

Eventually he relaxed his hold on her, took her face between his hands and looked down into her eyes. In the dusky light he saw a look of intense yearning reflected on her face. It was for him. He knew then that she felt the same as he did, and this inflamed him further.

Taking her by the hand, he led her over to the chaise. Gently, he pushed her down onto it and then sat on the edge. Leaning over her, he covered her mouth with his, all the while fumbling with the towel and then the top of her black bikini. Suddenly the fastening on the back came loose and he pulled the top away so that her breasts broke free. Cupping them between his hands, he kissed first one and then the other.

'Clee.'

Immediately he stopped what he was doing and looked at her. 'Yes?'

'I'm afraid,' she told him in a voice so low he could hardly hear it.

'Of me?'

'No.'

'Of yourself? Is that it, Nicky?' he asked, speaking as softly as she had, and reaching out he gently touched her cheek with his fingertips, wanting to reassure her.

'I'm afraid of . . . of . . . of making love . . . it's been so long,' she whispered.

'It'll be all right.' As he spoke he took her in his arms. 'Trust me,' he said against her hair. 'Trust me.'

656

Releasing her, Clee stood up, offered her both his hands.

Taking hold of them, she looked up at him questioningly as he pulled her to her feet.

He said, 'Let's go over there,' and nodded toward the copse.

Clee spread the towels on the grass and they slipped out of their swimsuits and lay down together under the trees.

Nicky was shaking inside, filled with desire for him. But it was a desire tinged with fear – a fear of disappointing him, of failing him, she realized that now. She wished she were not so tense, and she tried to relax her taut body, then turned her head to look at him, touching his face with one hand, her eyes focused on his.

Clee smiled slightly, again hoping to put her at ease.

It was the same lopsided boyish smile he had smiled at her the first time they had met in the bar of the Commodore in West Beirut, and one she knew so well by now, but tonight it seemed to tug at her heart. A rush of feeling for him rose up in her. A curious thought struck her. Had she been emotionally involved with Clee for the past two years without knowing it? Was *he* the reason no other man had interested her in all that time?

This thought was stopped in its tracks as Clee pushed himself up on one elbow, bent over her body and began to fondle her breasts. He brought his mouth to one of them, kissing the nipple. Instantly, it came erect under his lips, and he moved his mouth to the other one, kissing it in exactly the same way.

A small moan trickled out of Nicky's throat, and she put her arms loosely around him, her fingers slowly trailing down over his shoulder blades until they came to rest in the small of his back.

After a few seconds, Clee raised his head, kissed her passionately on the lips, devouring her with his mouth and his tongue, and all the while he continued to caress her breasts. Eventually his hands wandered down onto her flat stomach and her thighs, touching and stroking her silky skin until the tension in her dissipated.

Soon her body was limp, pliable to his touch. He moved his own body so that his head rested on her stomach, and he kissed it as his hands fluttered down onto her inner thighs. Lightly, gently, his fingers caressed, explored, probed, until she opened herself up to his hands and his mouth as a flower opens under warming sunlight. As he savoured the velvet texture of her he was consumed by a raging desire. It took all of his self-control not to take possession of her immediately.

Nicky lifted her lids, looked down at Clee, brought her hands to his shoulders, closed her eyes again, luxuriating in the feel of his strong yet sensitive hands on her body. Her senses were reeling. They had tumbled into each other's arms so unexpectedly, so suddenly she was still slightly shaken. And yet she knew their coming together was right; she felt this deep within herself. He was arousing her fully now, bringing her to the edge of ecstasy, his tongue and his fingers centred on the core of her. Overwhelmed by their mutual sensuality, the erotic feelings he engendered in her, she gave herself up to him completely. She was transported, floating, as he continued to touch and kiss her. He did so with such sureness and expertise, he might have been making love to her in this way for aeons of time.

He stopped for a moment and moved her legs, pushed her knees into a bent

657

position, and then he slipped his hands under her buttocks, brought his mouth to her again, touching her so lightly she could scarcely feel it. An exquisite sensation shot through her and she began to quiver. 'Oh Clee, don't stop, please don't stop,' she whispered.

'I won't,' he said, looking up, then he bent over her again and his mouth and hands went on loving her with sensitivity and delicacy, and consummate skill.

Clee was so inflamed by Nicky's mounting excitement he thought he would explode, and he ached to be inside her with every fibre of his being. But she had made it clear to him that she had been celibate for a long time, and he wanted to give her pleasure, to ensure she was totally relaxed and ready for him by bringing her to fulfilment first.

She cried his name again; her quivering increased, and she gripped his shoulders harder. The desire she had for him was acting as an extraordinary aphrodisiac, and he had to bring her to a climax quickly now, so that he could take her to him, possess her finally and give himself to her.

The very moment her quivering evolved into a deep, racking spasm he lifted himself onto her and went into her with a power and force that made both of them gasp.

Nicky clung to him, wrapped her legs around his back, and cried out, 'Clee, oh Clee, oh my God,' and he brought his mouth down hard on hers and they began to move in unison, instantly finding their own rhythm.

Their passion mounted. He moved against her harder, more urgently, thrust himself deeper inside her, and Nicky was as unrestrained as he, her body arching up to his. She cleaved to him.

Suddenly Clee stopped abruptly, pushed himself up on his hands and gazed down at her.

Nicky opened her eyes, and returned his gaze. Her look was questioning.

'You're beautiful, Nicky.'

'Oh Clee . . . '

He held her with his eyes, staring deeply into hers, and just as they had been mesmerized by each other a short while earlier so they were again. Their eyes locked, held fast; they looked deeper and deeper, as if peering into each other's hearts and minds and souls.

Clee thought: this isn't only sexual desire, though God knows it's stronger with her than I've ever known it to be with anyone else. I love her. That's what this is all about. I *love* Nicky. I've loved her since Beijing.

As she looked up into Clee's dark and brilliant eyes, her scrutiny fixed, intense and probing, Nicky began to understand something: she had been waiting for him to come to her as a lover for months, even though she had not realized it until this moment in time. With a little spurt of surprise, she thought, I'm free of Charles at last. Perhaps I'll be able to love again . . . perhaps I'll fall in love with Cleeland Donovan.

Clee began to move again, slowly at first, loving her with his eyes. She opened her arms to him, and he devoured her mouth and tongue with his own once more, and she moved against him, picked up his rhythm. He increased his speed, and so did she, matching him all the way.

Nicky was filled with a sudden intense heat. It flooded up from her thighs to suffuse her whole being, and she clung to him tighter, her hands biting into his shoulders, his name on her lips. Clee felt her warmth enveloping him, and he plunged deeper into her, moving faster and faster. He murmured, 'Come to me, my love, become part of me.' And she did, and so did he, and as he flowed into her they were truly joined, became one.

He called her name, heard her shouting his, and they soared upward together, higher and higher, until he was weightless and floating in a bright blue sky the colour of her eyes. Floating into infinity, holding her in his arms as if to never let her go. He never would. She was his love. His only love. There never had been anyone like her before; there never would be again. She was meant for him, just as he was meant for her, just as this was meant to be.

He opened his eyes at last and looked down at her.

In this bosky corner of the garden the light was dim. But several small spots were hidden in the leafy bower above their heads, so he could see her face. It was flushed, and he saw that it was filled with pleasure and happiness. Her eyes were wide, and very, very blue as they looked back at him unblinkingly, and he noticed they held an expression he had never seen in them before. Was it adoration? Did she feel the same way he did? She had to . . . this joining had not been one-sided.

'Nicky,' he began, but before he could say another word she reached up and put her fingertips on his mouth.

'Don't say anything, Clee.'

'But Nicky, I – '

'Sssh,' she said and put her hands around his neck, pulled his face down to hers. She kissed him softly, wrapped her arms around him and held him close to her. And she felt a little more at peace with herself – for the first time since Charles Devereaux had vacated her life.

CHAPTER THIRTEEN

'*Eh voilà, Mademoiselle!* Your American picnic,' Clee said, placing the large wooden tray on the coffee table in the middle of the library. With a wry little smile he added, 'I'm afraid this was the best I could do, babe.'

Nicky jumped up off the sofa, went over to the low table and sat down on the large cushions Clee had arranged on the floor earlier. She scanned the food he had prepared and immediately began to laugh.

'Oh Clee, how marvellous! You've managed to find some of my real favourites. Chunky peanut butter, *Skippy*, no less. I love that brand. Oh, and grape jelly to go with it. Tuna-salad sandwiches, and bacon, lettuce and tomato on rye. Pickled cucumbers. Hellmann's mayonnaise. Where did you get all this? Especially the rye bread?' Her surprise was apparent.

Clee's mouth twitched with laughter. 'The rye came out of the freezer earlier this evening. My sisters bring it when they come to stay. They also bring loads of other American things for me, stuff I can't always find in France. Amelia puts some of it in the freezer, such as the rye bread and the bags of bagels, and the rest goes in the pantry. Now – ' He picked up a can of diet coke, pulled the tab, and went on, ' – how about one of these to wash it all down?'

'I'd love it, and come and sit over here with me,' she said, patting the cushion next to her.

'I will in a minute. Let me put the video in first.' Stepping over to the bookcase, he continued, 'Which movie did you choose in the end?'

'It's called *Somewhere I'll Find You*, with Clark Gable and Lana Turner playing foreign correspondents who ... get involved with each other on a foreign assignment.'

'Aha!' he exclaimed. A wide grin spread across his face. 'How appropriate. I couldn't have chosen better myself.'

The minute the film was rolling, Clee went and sat down on the cushions, leaned over and kissed the tip of her nose, then picked up a tuna-salad sandwich and settled back to watch.

They laughed a lot during the film. It had been made in 1942 and was somewhat unrealistic. It had a sweetness, an innocence about it, and this made it seem dated to the two of them – both tough news veterans accustomed to difficult, often harrowing foreign assignments.

'Hey, Nick, this is really sappy stuff,' Clee muttered at one moment, looking at her through the corner of his eye.

'I know. But a lot of old movies are.'

'Not *Casablanca*, now that's held up pretty well.'

'You're right, but occasionally this one does have a ring of truth to it, especially when Gable's on the screen.' The legendary star was Nicky's favourite, and a few seconds later, when Gable said, 'I don't print anything until I've heard it twice and seen it three times,' Nicky punched Clee on the arm and cried, 'That's going to be *my* motto from now on!'

He rolled his eyes to the ceiling, a look of mock horror crossing his face.

'Wait a minute,' Nicky said swiftly, 'you've got to admit Gable plays a terrific newspaperman, with just the right amount of dash and panache. And he *is* gorgeous.'

'True, true.' Clee turned her face to his and kissed her lightly on the mouth. 'And so are you,' he said softly.

When the movie was over, Clee began stacking the plates and glasses on the tray. 'Do you want to watch another film, or shall we go downstairs and have coffee on the terrace?'

'Coffee on the terrace sounds great,' Nicky answered, and followed him out.

They sat at the kitchen table waiting for the coffee to brew, and as Clee peeled an apple and offered pieces to her, he said, 'I'm coming to New York around the tenth of July. I have to go to Washington to photograph the President and Mrs Bush for *Life*. After that I'll be in New York for them until the end of the month. Is there any chance of working on the book together then, do you think?'

'Yes, of course, I'd love to, and I know I'll be there, providing a war doesn't break out somewhere – '

'In which case,' Clee interjected, 'we'll be covering it together.'

Nicky nodded. 'I guess so. Anyway, Arch and I will be working on another special during July and August, so I'll probably be writing the script and doing the preparation. But that doesn't prevent me from starting on the book. Do you have a title yet?'

'No, I don't and any and all suggestions will be gratefully accepted. That coffee smells great, let's get some and go outside.'

They sat on the terrace together, not talking, enjoying the peacefulness and beauty of their surroundings. It was well past midnight and glorious. The great arch of the sky was like inky black velvet scattered with tiny crystal beads, and there was a full moon. The breeze ruffled the trees and wafted the scent of honeysuckle towards them.

Clee and Nicky had long understood that conversation was not always necessary, and the silence between them tonight was as companionable as it usually was. Though their relationship had changed radically – and irrevocably – in the space of only a few hours they were completely at ease with each other. Perhaps more than ever, in fact.

Taking hold of her hand at one moment, Clee said in the quietest voice, 'We're good together, Nicky, and good for each other. You know that, don't you?'

'Yes, I do,' she responded and leaned her head against his shoulder, feeling comfortable, protected with him.

Clee put his arm around her, held her close, and he could not help wondering what would happen to them, where tonight would lead. He had no idea. All he knew for certain was that he had saved her life in Beijing and in so doing had fallen in love with her. Or perhaps he had loved her for a long time before that, but had only realized it when he had almost lost her. But no matter . . . tonight he had become her lover and that was good enough for him right now.

For her part, Nicky was marvelling at the way they had come together so naturally . . . and marvelling at herself as well. She had not made love to a man since Charles Devereaux had ended their relationship. During the past two years she had built up so many barriers; Clee had made them all come tumbling down. She was glad she had been with Clee. He had made everything seem so easy and simple, and he had aroused such passion in her she had been momentarily startled. She smiled to herself in the darkness. Clee had made her feel like a woman again.

Much later, when they were in the kitchen stacking the dishwasher, Clee said, 'How long are you staying here with me, Nicky?'

She shrugged lightly, and said, 'As long as you'll have me.'

'All this week then,' he replied, looking well pleased.

'Oh Clee, I forgot for a minute . . . I've got to be back in Manhattan a week from tonight, in order to go to work at the network on Monday morning.'

'*Oh.*' He looked suddenly crushed, then instantly his face brightened and he said, 'Tell you what, we'll fly to Paris on Thursday night. You can stay with me at my apartment, and I'll put you on the Concorde on Sunday morning. Does that idea appeal to you?'

661

'Yes, it does.'

'And *you* certainly appeal to *me*, lady.' Putting down the plate he was holding, walking over to her, he took her in his arms. 'I don't know whether it's occurred to you yet, but you and I have wasted a helluva lot of time.'

'Two years, if you want me to be exact.'

'I aim to make up for it.'

'You do?'

'You bet.' Clee covered her mouth with his for a long voluptuous kiss, and then he took her hand in his and led her upstairs to his bedroom.

CHAPTER FOURTEEN

Holding hands, they walked slowly down the Cours Mirabeau, the main avenue in the ancient university town of Aix-en-Provence.

Nicky glanced around, and she could not help thinking that this was one of the most beautiful boulevards she had ever seen. Long and wide, it had four rows of tall, stately plane trees running down the middle of it, the branches of which intertwined overhead to form an immense, elongated arch.

Nicky felt as though she and Clee were walking down a pale green tunnel made entirely of leaves. It seemed endless, since it stretched a good five hundred yards or so, and placed at intervals down the centre between the trees were three nineteenth-century fountains which sprayed arcs of crystal-clear water up into the diffused morning sunlight. One side of the Cours, the sunny side, was lined with sprawling cafés; standing in the shade on the other were handsome and ancient buildings, many of them private residences.

'Clee, it's extraordinary, and so lovely,' Nicky exclaimed, turning to him, her face a picture of delight.

'Isn't it just. I knew you'd be impressed, everyone is when they see it. And in my opinion this is the most beautiful main street in any city anywhere in the world. There's a certain elegance about it – the interplay of the architecture, the trees, the fountains, and the way the space has been so brilliantly arranged, and it's always at its best in the spring and summer.' He paused, gave her a smile, and finished, 'Now, let's pick a café and have coffee, before we plunge into the old town behind the Cours so that you can visit some of the local *ateliers*.'

'You don't really have to come shopping with me,' she said quickly. 'Perhaps you'd prefer to browse around a bookstore while I pick up a few gifts.'

'Nope, I'm coming with you.' He tightened his grip on her hand, glanced down at her, the boyish smile playing around his mouth. 'I'm not letting you out of my sight for the next three days. I've got to make the most of you, honeybunch.'

Nicky laughed. 'I haven't heard that term of endearment for years. My mother used to call me honeybunch when I was little.'

'Isn't that odd, so did mine,' Clee said, and led her towards a lively-looking café close to the Fontaine de la Rotonde, the huge fountain which dominated the western entrance to the boulevard.

Although the café terrace was busy with attractive young people, pretty girls and handsome young men who were obviously university students, there were several empty tables. A couple of these were close to the windows in the shade of an awning and slightly removed from the busy sidewalk.

Swiftly scanning the area, Clee chose one of the tables near the café's windows, and as they sat down he said, 'We can cool off here and watch the world go by at the same time. I love French cafés, they're so convivial, yet they can also be quite private in a certain way.' Taking off his sun glasses, he drew close to her and kissed her lightly on the lips. 'See what I mean?'

'Yes.' She smiled, looking into his eyes.

A waiter was with them almost immediately and Clee ordered *café-au-lait* for them both; once they were alone again he relaxed in his chair, and turned to face her. 'I like most of the titles you wrote down for me last night, but my favourite is *Children of the Beijing Spring*. I'd love to use that for our book, Nick.'

'I'm flattered!' Her pleasure was self-evident, and she added, 'It happens to be my favourite, too.'

He leaned across the table and kissed her on the lips again. 'Now that we have a title, we're in business, babe.'

'With those superb photographs you took, you were always in business, Clee. No question about that, and my text is of secondary importance. After all, it *is* a picture book.'

'True. On the other hand, the introduction is pretty damned important . . . not only to underscore my pictures but to explain China, the politics, the events leading up to the Tiananmen demonstrations, and the massacre. Few people understand how it all came about.'

'Yes, I'm well aware of that, and on the plane on Sunday I'll make some notes. I think I'll have a bit of reading to do, before I start writing the introduction. Incidentally, I've been thinking – ' She broke off as the waiter arrived with the coffee.

'*Merci,*' she and Clee said, almost in unison, then she went on, 'What I started to say is that I've been thinking about our working arrangements, and it occurred to me that you might like to spend a couple of weekends in New Milford, at my parents' place, when you're in New York later this month. A few years ago, my father built a studio across the lawn from the main house, and I think it's a terrific place to work. We could really spread out there . . . you know, arrange the pictures consecutively, and in an orderly fashion, even do a pagination. We could leave everything laid out there on card tables, no one would touch it during the week.'

'It sounds great, but what about your parents? Don't they use the studio to write in?'

Nicky shook her head and began to laugh. 'When Dad built the studio it was actually for my mother, his gift to her. He thought she would enjoy working there. It's airy, spacious, quiet, and very peaceful.'

'And didn't she?'

'No. I think perhaps it was *too* peaceful, if you want to know the truth. She only loved it for about a month. Then she moved back into the house, into the small room which opens off their bedroom. She told Dad she felt more comfortable writing in a room she'd been using for years. That's true I'm sure, but knowing my mother, she also likes being in the house, in the centre of all of that swirling activity. I suppose it is very lonely writing long, complicated books, without being isolated across the garden, away from my father, the housekeeper, screaming telephones and a busy household.'

'Doesn't your father use the studio?'

'Not very often.' Nicky made a small *moue* with her mouth. 'I suspect he likes being close to my mother, and also in the middle of all that activity just as much as she does. So he pushes his pen, or rather his word processor, in the library, which is where he has always written his column . . . that way, he's close to the kitchen, can pop in for a cup of tea or coffee and chat to Annie, the housekeeper, or Bert, the gardener. Anyway, the point is we could easily set up shop there, if you want to, Clee.'

'Will your parents mind?'

'Of course not! Anyway, since meeting you in Paris last year they've been rather taken with you.'

'Is their daughter?'

Nicky took off her sun glasses, gave him a long look through penetrating blue eyes. Although she was well aware of what he meant, she asked, somewhat coyly, 'Is their daughter *what?*'

'Taken with me?'

'Oh yes.'

'She'd better be.'

'She is . . . definitely . . . absolutely . . . taken with Cleeland Donovan.'

Clee bent closer to her across the zinc-topped table and took her hand in his. 'These last few days have been so wonderful, Nick. It's never been quite like this before, for me. There's something I want to say . . . about you and me . . . the way I feel about you, darling, and – '

'Please don't say anything, Clee,' she interrupted, her voice as low as his had been. 'Please, not now, not yet.' She gently extracted her hand, sat back in her chair looking solemn.

'But why not?' he asked, his expression perplexed.

Nicky was silent for a moment, then said, remembering the fiasco of her engagement, 'I want this, want *us*, to go slowly . . . I don't want you – . No, I don't want *either* of us to say anything now that we might regret . . . that we might change our minds about later. I want you to be really sure before you say anything at all to me. And *I* want to be sure, too. Sure about what *I* really feel for you.'

'But I am sure,' he began and stopped, immediately understanding that she was afraid of commitments. 'I see what you mean, Nicky, and you're right, of course you are. I know how much Charles Devereaux hurt you.' The words slipped out before he could stop them. He could have bitten off his tongue, and he stared at her in confusion, appalled at himself.

She gaped at him, her face draining of its vivacity. Instantly it became terribly still, and closed. She did not say a word, merely bit her lip, and then she glanced away.

Clee reached for her hand again, held her fingers tightly in his, wondering how to make amends. He was a clumsy fool and he had obviously upset her. She did not have to utter one word for him to recognize that. He had read it on her face the very second he had spoken.

'Look at me, Nick.'

Gradually she turned her head, brought her gaze to meet his.

'I'm sorry,' he apologized. 'Really sorry, babe. I shouldn't have mentioned his name.'

'It's all right,' Nicky replied after a few seconds and she forced a smile onto her face. 'Honestly it is. I just don't like to talk about him. Whenever I do, unpleasant memories inevitably get stirred up. Anyway, talking about him serves no purpose. He was the past. I prefer to think of the future.'

'I couldn't agree more.' He took a deep breath, wanting this awkward moment to pass as quickly as possible.

'Clee, you look upset. Please don't be. It was only natural for you to mention Charles. After all, we *were* engaged.'

'I'm pretty dumb though, at times.'

'*I* don't think you are.' The dark expression which had been clouding her lovely blue eyes disappeared, and she smiled at him, then picked up her cup, took a sip. 'The coffee's gone cold,' she remarked evenly, 'shall we order two more *hot* ones?'

Clee nodded, motioned to the waiter and gave the order. Then he said to her, 'You told me you wanted to get your mother some Provençal fabric. I know just the right shop in the old town. They'll even send it back to the States for you.'

'Hey, that's great.'

Nicky began to chat to him about the gifts she wanted to buy, and for whom. Much to his relief her voice sounded normal again, and he relaxed.

A short while later Clee paid and they left the café, wandered off into the old town situated behind the Cours Mirabeau. They walked through the tiny, narrow streets, stopping to look in the windows of the smart new boutiques as well as the much older establishments selling liqueurs, cheeses, local produce, crafts and fanciful Provençal creations.

Clee took her into the *atelier* Fouque, where *santons* were made. These little figures of local peasants, created from clay or dough, and beautifully painted in bright colours, were amazingly life-like, and Nicky purchased a whole collection of them for her father. After Clee had introduced her to Paul Fouque, one of the great masters of *santon* making, they stood and watched him at work for fifteen minutes before heading to the confectionary to buy *calissons*. This local-made almond-paste sweet was Amelia's favourite, according to Clee, and Nicky wanted to give her a box of it, along with the silk scarf she had bought for her the day before, when Clee had taken her to St Rémy.

A short while later they walked down to the Souleiado shop. Here Nicky selected several bolts of beautiful fabrics in the colourful traditional patterns of Provence, and arranged for these to be shipped to her mother in New York. Then she picked out several address books covered in similar fabrics

665

for girl friends, and these she took with her, as well as various aprons and other small items.

They continued to meander through the cobbled streets, stepping into all kinds of little shops, sometimes merely to look around and savour the atmosphere. In one shop, Nicky made a few purchases of lavender essence, bags of lavender, and bags of *herbes de Provence*.

When the latter were being wrapped, she turned to Clee and grinned. 'You do know I can buy all of this stuff in New York, don't you? At Bloomingdale's, actually. And exactly the same products, too. But it's not quite the same as bringing it from here.'

'No, it isn't,' he agreed, accepting the shopping bag from the proprietor and guiding her out of the shop. 'Come on, I want to show you the place d'Albertas, it's very quaint, and then we'd better be getting back to the farm for lunch.'

'Oh God, not another meal,' she groaned, and grimaced through her laughter.

Holding her arm Clee led her towards the ancient square, saying as he did, 'Speaking of meals, I told Amelia to make a very light lunch, just a green salad, cold chicken and fruit. I'm taking you somewhere very special for dinner tonight.'

'You are? Where?' She looked at him quickly, her expression curious.

'It's quite a famous restaurant, people go there from all over the world, and it's elegant. So if you didn't bring a dress, Nicky, we'd better go and buy one now. There are several chic boutiques around here.'

'It's all right, Clee, I came well prepared. I packed a couple of silk dresses. And my pearls, just in case. So you can take me anywhere.'

'Oh I know that,' he murmured, and leered at her wickedly.

Clee's bedroom was shady and pleasant, the bright afternoon sunlight outside blocked by the wooden shutters, the warm air cooled by the ceiling fan.

They were lying close together on the bed, bodies touching, resting now after their frantic lovemaking of earlier. Clee had brought her up here after lunch, to rest, he had said, but within minutes the inevitable had happened. Clee had started to kiss her and touch her, and she had responded ardently, as always instantly on fire for him whenever she felt his hands on her in that particular way. They had undressed each other, and once they were naked he had taken her to him swiftly, without preamble, and once more their wild ecstasy had begun.

It now struck Nicky how odd it was that they had known each other for two years and had never ever thought of making love. In the last few days they hadn't been able to get enough of each other, were unable to keep their hands off each other when they were alone.

Nicky moved her head slightly on the pillow, in order to look at him.

Clee was stretched out on his back, as she was. His eyes were closed, his thick dark lashes resting lightly on his bronzed cheeks. He took the sun well, had acquired a tan since he had been at the farm. His whole body was a golden brown, except for the white triangle across his stomach where his swimming trunks had been.

In repose his face had a gentleness to it, and his mouth, so wide and generous, was vulnerable. She had a sudden impulse to reach out and touch his mouth, but refrained, not wishing to awaken him.

Cleeland Donovan. She said his name to herself, thinking about him intently. He was a lovely man, a decent man, who did not have one bad bone in his body. He was honest and just and kind and fair. And so very trustworthy. Her mother had a phrase for people who were genuinely admirable. True blue, she called them. Cleeland Donovan was definitely true blue.

He was her closest, dearest friend and she had loved him like a brother right from the beginning of their friendship. But now he was her lover. They were sexually involved with each other, and obviously well on the way to becoming emotionally entangled. Perhaps they already were. She wasn't sure what would happen, what would become of them, how long they would be together in this way. But she did know she could trust him implicitly. With her life, as he had proved in Beijing. He was that type of man, courageous and dependable and strong. She felt safe with Clee. She always had, right from the beginning. He gave her a sense of being cared for, of being completely protected.

Clee opened his eyes quite suddenly and caught her studying him. He reached for her, pulled her into his arms, nuzzled his face in her neck, kissing her tenderly.

Then he whispered against her ear, 'You had such a pensive look on your face when I opened my eyes . . . what were you thinking about?'

'You, actually.'

'Ah, I see. And what were you thinking about me?'

'I decided you were . . . true blue. That's what my mother calls people she admires.'

She felt him smile against her neck.

He said, 'Is that a roundabout way of telling me you admire me?' Not waiting for her answer, he added, 'I wish you felt *more* than admiration.'

'I do,' she protested, 'I feel a lot of things – ' She broke off, pulled away, looked into his dark brown eyes which were dancing with mischief. 'Oh you! You!' she cried, putting her hand against his chest, making a weak attempt to push him away. 'You were trying to trap me into saying something I may later regret.'

'Who, little old me? *Never.*' He grinned at her, looking highly amused, and brought her back into the circle of his arms. Stroking her hair gently, he then began to smooth his hands down over her back, and found her mouth with his, devoured it, and ever so slowly he began to make love to her.

Instantly Nicky was aflame, hungry for him even though they had made love only a couple of hours ago. She ached to feel the hardness of him inside her, ached to be joined to him, to be part of him.

As if he could read her mind, he was suddenly on top of her, bracing his hands on either side of her body, pushing himself up above her, looking down into her face.

She reached up to touch him, let her fingers trace a delicate line across his mouth, her eyes focused on his intently.

He returned her gaze unblinkingly, and entered her with that same force he had used the first night they had made love in the garden, and it brought a cry of surprise and pain to her lips. He paid no attention, was working against her harder and harder, and the pain eased and she was opening up to him, flowing to him. She wrapped her arms and legs around his body, binding him to her, her skin against his skin, her breath mingling with his breath.

Clee kissed her hard, almost with violence, and then unexpectedly he arched back and away from her, groaned as if in anguish. 'I love you, Nicky,' he cried. 'I love you.' She felt him flowing into her as she had flowed into him only a split second before, and at this moment she thought: and I am falling in love with you. But she was unable to say this, and so remained silent, holding him close when he collapsed against her and buried his face in her hair.

CHAPTER FIFTEEN

Clee paused in the doorway of the library and leaned against the door jamb, staring at Nicky.

'Hi,' she said when she saw him and, smiling, she walked towards him.

The dress she wore had a round neck and no sleeves, was cut loose and full, and it fell in folds from ruching on the shoulders. Its colour was a delphinium blue that exactly matched her marvellous eyes, and as she moved forward the light silk swirled around her like a cloud. The pearls encircling her throat in a choker and the matching studs on her ears looked unusually luminous against her tan, and with her golden skin, golden hair and brilliant eyes Clee thought there was a special kind of sheen about her tonight.

When she drew to a standstill in front of him he saw, on closer inspection, that she had the inner glow of a woman who has recently been well and truly loved, and who has loved in return. There was a subtle sexuality about her – a rosy bloom on her skin, a ripeness around her mouth, and a wise expression in her eyes. It was an unmistakable look, and one which a man always recognizes.

'You look gorgeous, Nicky,' he said, straightening up, taking hold of her bare arm possessively, kissing her lightly on the cheek.

'You don't look so bad yourself,' she responded, eyeing him appraisingly, noting the excellent cut of his cream sports jacket, the fineness of the cream voile shirt that set off his tan and dark colouring, the expensive wine-silk tie, the well-tailored black linen slacks and highly-polished black loafers. After giving him another admiring glance, she added, 'Good enough to eat, in fact.'

'We'll leave that for later,' he quipped, breaking into a chuckle. Moving her forward towards the landing, he went on, 'We'd better be on our way. I had a tough time getting a table, and I don't want to lose it.'

A few minutes later Clee was pulling out of the courtyard and rolling down the driveway.

Nicky asked him, 'Where are we going? You've been so mysterious.'

'Have I? I didn't mean to be.' He glanced at her out of the corner of his eye, brought his gaze back to the road, concentrating on his driving. Then he

668

explained, 'We're going to Les Baux, a town not far from here, just beyond St Rémy. The restaurant is called L'Oustau de Baumanière. It's a charming place and the food is excellent. And I *know*, before you say it again for the umpteenth time, you've had enough meals to last you a lifetime. But you don't have to eat very much, Nick, just a taste. In any case, I really wanted to take you there because it's a unique spot, and besides, tonight's a celebration.'

'What are we celebrating?' She turned to look at him, wedging herself in the corner of the seat, resting her shoulder against the car window.

'We're celebrating our book – which we now have a title for. And a few other things.'

'Such as what?'

'I'll tell you later.'

Clee turned on the disc player and the car was instantly flooded with George Gershwin's 'Rhapsody in Blue', and they drove in silence for a long while, listening to the music; as usual they were at ease with each other whether they spoke or not.

But at one moment, as they were passing through St Rémy, Nicky said, 'Les Baux rings a bell in my mind . . . I think my mother had several references to it in one of her books. But I can't remember *exactly* why, or which book, for that matter.'

'Les Baux is very old,' Clee told her. 'It's a feudal city that's been around for thousands of years, and it sits on soaring rocky outcroppings high above some of the deep valleys in this region. It's mostly ruins now, a sort of ghost town in a sense. Still, it's quite imposing on its airy perch, and it was very famous in the Middle Ages, from the eleventh to the fifteenth centuries, when the Lords of Baux ruled the area. They were rather bloody and violent, ferocious men, rough, and yet they gave their patronage to the troubadours – '

'Of course!' Nicky exclaimed. 'That's it! *Troubadours*. Now I *remember*. My mother wrote about Les Baux in her book on Eleanor of Aquitaine, when she touched on Eleanor's patronage of Bernard de Ventadour, one of the most famous troubadours of all. It was at Les Baux that respect for the lady and the ritual of worshipping her beauty began. The first troubadours started writing, singing, and playing their lutes there.'

'Exactly,' Clee responded, 'and the Baux fortress when it was in its heyday and at the height of its great splendour was renowned for its "Court of Love", and chivalry towards women.'

'I'm so glad we're going there, Clee. My mother will be fascinated to hear all about it when I get back to New York.'

'I'm not planning to take you up to the fortress and the ruins tonight,' Clee said quickly, glancing at her askance. 'It's far too complicated, not to mention a strenuous climb. You'd never make it in those high heels you're wearing, babe.'

Nicky laughed. 'That's all right, I don't feel much like sightseeing or climbing to great heights this evening.'

*　　*　　*

Not long after this conversation, Clee was pulling up outside L'Oustau de Baumanière, which was set under the white stone cliffs below the ancient town of Les Baux.

After parking the car, he ushered Nicky into the famous restaurant, where they were greeted pleasantly by the *maître d'*, who obviously knew Clee, and who suggested they have an *apéritif* outside on the terrace.

Ten minutes later Clee lifted his flute of champagne, touched it to hers and said, 'Here's to you, Nicky darling.'

'And to you, Clee.' She smiled at him over the rim of her glass and, after taking a sip of the cold sparkling wine, she said, 'Now, tell me what else we're celebrating, as well as the book.'

He reached for her hand resting on the table, and placed his over it. 'We're celebrating being alive, being together, being lucky enough to have lived our lives the way we've wanted to live them – at least so far in the game. And most importantly, we're celebrating being lovers as well as friends.'

'Oh Clee, those are lovely things to say and to celebrate, and we *are* lucky, aren't we. Most people have so little, really.'

'Sadly, that's true.'

'And thank you for bringing me here tonight.' She looked around her again . . . the terrace was ablaze with flowers . . . the gardens were lushly green . . . the varied species of trees growing under the white stone cliffs were in full bloom. The setting was one she truly appreciated and she said, 'This is such a beautiful place, Clee . . . ' Sitting back in her chair, she eyed him carefully. 'And what with all its ancient symbolism to do with the troubadours and their songs of love, I'm beginning to think you're a romantic at heart, however much you might want to disguise that fact.'

'I don't, at least not with you, and I think you're right, I am a bit of a romantic,' he admitted, giving her a half smile. Almost immediately, his expression changed, became more serious and he glanced down into his drink, looking unexpectedly reflective.

This sudden change in him was almost imperceptible, but Nicky noticed it and leaning forward she asked, 'What is it? Is something wrong?'

'No, no, of course not,' he answered, looking up and shaking his head. He gazed at her for a long moment, his eyes riveted on hers. 'I said something to you this afternoon, and because it was said at the height of passion, you probably think that I didn't really mean it. But I did, and I do, and I'm going to say it again, even if you don't wish to hear it . . . ' There was a small pause. 'I love you, Nicky.'

She stared at him. Her eyes were huge in her face and glittering brilliantly. There was no question in her mind that Clee was speaking the truth, being sincere; he didn't know any other way to be. 'Clee,' she began, and stopped.

'You don't have to say you love me, Nicky. Maybe you do, maybe you don't. We have plenty of time, you and I, to find out about that. One day you'll tell me how you feel about me – when you know yourself. In the meantime, I just wanted to tell *you*, here and now when we're not in bed, that I love you. I have for a long time, without realizing it.'

Her lips parted and she looked as if she was about to speak.

Clee shook his head. 'Not a word, Nicky, not now. It's not necessary,' he said, his smile warm and loving.

'But I want to say something.' She hesitated fractionally, before murmuring, 'I have all kinds of feelings for you, Clee, and not the least of which is my . . . my physical passion for you.' She was on the verge of telling him that she thought she was falling in love with him, and then changed her mind. Instead, she said, 'And I do love you, as my dearest friend . . .' Her sentence trailed off.

'I know you do.' He squeezed her hand. 'Don't look so worried.'

Nicky laughed. 'I didn't realize I did.' She sighed lightly. 'These past few days have been just . . . *glorious*, Clee, there's no other way of describing them.' A wistful expression flitted onto her face. 'I'm so sorry they're coming to an end.'

'But they're not. You'll be with me tomorrow night in Paris, and on Friday and Saturday, before you leave for the States on Sunday.' He stroked her arm lightly, traced little lines up and down with his fingertips. 'Three whole days and nights, not counting this evening.' Bending into her, he kissed the tip of her nose. 'And I'm going to make love to you the entire time – circumstances and surroundings permitting.'

'Clee Donovan, you're incorrigible!'

'If I am, it's because of you.'

'I'm sorry.'

'Don't be, I'm not complaining. Now, let's look at the menu.' He swung his head, spotted a waiter hovering, and gestured to him. The man hurried over and Clee asked for more champagne to be poured, adding that they would like to see the menu.

'*Oui, Monsieur*,' the waiter answered as he filled their flutes.

CHAPTER SIXTEEN

The interior of the restaurant was equally as eye-catching as the exterior.

An arched ceiling, stone walls and matching floor gave it a medieval feeling, as did the high-backed chairs covered in blue-and-gold brocade velvet, the Provençal antiques made of dark wood, and the lantern-style ceiling lamps. Pretty floral cloths covered the tables, each of which had its own three-branch silver candelabra and bowl of flowers, and there were other huge bowls of colourful blooms scattered throughout.

Because Clee had ordered the dinner whilst they were sitting outside on the terrace drinking champagne, they were served their first course almost immediately. Nicky had selected melon, Clee one of the specialities of the house. This was ravioli with truffles and leeks, which he insisted she try.

'Just one piece,' he cajoled, 'it's delicious. It'll melt in your mouth.' Spearing a square of ravioli with his fork, he leaned over the table and fed it to her. He watched her eat it, his warm, dark eyes full of love for her.

'It *is* wonderful, but that's enough, thanks, Clee.' Dropping her voice, she whispered, 'If I get fat, I won't turn you on anymore. How would you like them apples?'

'You'll always turn me on. That is the one thing I'm certain of in this uncertain world.'

Nicky merely smiled, and dug her spoon into the sweet and succulent Cavaillon melon, which Amelia kept insisting was the best in the whole of *la belle France*. She decided Amelia was correct.

Whilst they waited for their main course, Clee spoke about the book, and the various sequences for the photographs, which he had been planning since his return from Beijing. When he had explained everything to her, he leaned back and said, 'Well, what do you think?'

'It sounds great, and anyway, you know best, Clee, you really do. You've done these books before, whereas I'm just a novice, besides which I'm only writing the introduction.'

'Hey, don't say *only* in that way, the words are just as important as the pictures.'

'Not really. But it's nice of you to say so.'

'I was thinking of dedicating the book to Yoyo, and to the memory of Mai. How do you feel about that, Nick?'

'Oh Clee, what a good idea. By the way, I've been wanting to tell you, I feel very positive about Yoyo and I have for the past few days. I'm pretty sure he's going to make it.'

'We've got to keep on believing that.'

The wine waiter was suddenly at their table, pouring more of the white wine with which they had started their meal. 'It is an excellent wine, is it not, Monsieur Donovan?' he said.

'Marvellous. And I've had this particular Puligny-Montrachet before. In fact, you recommended it to me the last time I was here.'

'I believe I did,' the wine waiter responded with a deferential smile. He nodded politely to Nicky, then stepped away, moving in the direction of another table.

'I hope you like this wine, Nicky,' Clee said. 'I ordered it because it has enough power to hold its own with the richest-flavoured food, and the *daurade* we both chose has a rich orange sauce. Also, the fish itself is flavoured with herbs. Anyway, I think this fruity Chardonnay goes well with it.' Clee shifted in his chair, turned the bottle around and studied it for a second. 'This is a great label – Clos du Vieux Château, Laboure-Roi, and it comes from the world's capital of Chardonnay, the village in the Côte d'Or where no other type of grape is grown.'

Nicky sat gaping at Clee, taken aback by this unexpected display of knowledge about wine. Finding her voice, she said, 'I didn't know you were an oenologist.'

'Good God, I'm not, *I'm* hardly an expert!' He looked across at her and explained. 'I just happen to like good wine, and since I live in France I've made a point of knowing a bit about some of the best vineyards. After all, I can't always drink that plonk we make at the farm.' He frowned. 'What is it, Nick? You've got the queerest look on your face.'

'Nothing, honestly.' Nicky shivered slightly and a small nervous laugh escaped. 'I had a funny sense of *déjà vu*, as if I'd heard those exact words before, but of course I haven't.'

'That's right, I've never discussed wine with you.'

No, but Charles always did, she thought, picked up her glass and took a sip of the Puligny-Montrachet. 'Mmmm, it *is* good, Clee. Delicious.'

At this moment the main course arrived, accompanied by several waiters. It was served to them with quite a few fancy flourishes. Nicky caught Clee's eye and winked at him, and he had to swallow the sudden laughter rising in his throat.

When they were finally left alone to eat the fish, he grinned at her. 'That wink and the expression on your face said more to me than a thousand words ever could.'

'Isn't that what I keep telling you?'

'And I don't recall disagreeing with you. How's the *daurade*, do you like it?'

'Yes, thank you, it's one of my favourites. I often had it as a child when my parents brought me down to the south of France. And fish isn't fattening.'

Clee burst out laughing. 'Honestly, Nicky, I wish you'd stop this. You don't have to worry, you're as thin as a rail.'

'I won't be, if I stick around you and Amelia.'

'Will you stick around me if I promise to serve you only bread and water?' he said teasingly, but his eyes were serious.

Nicky noticed the expression in them and nodded. 'I'll stick around, Clee . . .'

Putting down his fork, he said, 'What are you doing in September?'

'Why?'

'You told me the network owes you a lot of time off, and I thought that you might like to come back here in September. To the farm . . . to be with me. I plan to take a break then, and it's lovely here at that time of year. The July and August tourists have split, and it's peaceful.'

'I'd love to come, *if* I've finished the script for my fall special.'

'*Try*,' he said.

'I will. I'll work like a mad woman through the rest of July and August.'

'Promise?'

'I do.'

'Don't think I won't hold you to that, because I will.' Clee brought his head closer to hers, and said, *sotto voce*, 'I don't want you to turn around, but there's a woman over there who hasn't been able to take her eyes off you since she sat down. I have a feeling she knows you, Nick.'

'*Oh*. What makes you think that?'

'Because she looked at you several times, spoke to the man she is with, who eventually turned and glanced at you. Very discreetly. And in between her conversation with him and bites of food, she keeps sneaking looks at you.'

'Perhaps she's seen me on the television . . . perhaps she's a fan. Is she an American?'

'I don't think so. She looks English to me. Very English, and so does the guy she's with. Okay, she's talking to a waiter, you can look now.'

Nicky twisted in her chair and turned her head slightly. She saw the woman immediately. Her breath caught in her throat; she felt a tightening in her chest. She was about to turn back to Clee, when the woman looked across the room.

Nicky was in her direct line of vision.

Two pairs of blue eyes met and held.

The woman smiled at Nicky, her whole face lighting up with obvious pleasure.

Nicky smiled in return, lifted her hand in a small gesture of acknowledgement.

The woman spoke to her companion. Instantly, he swung his head, then swivelled around in his chair, and beamed at Nicky.

Nicky glanced at Clee, and explained, 'They're old friends. I must go and have a quick word with them. Excuse me a minute.'

She got up and walked across the room, and Clee could not help wondering who they were. Nicky's voice had sounded odd, breathless, even strained. She's uptight all of a sudden, he decided, and lolled back against the chair, watching. He was filled with curiosity.

'Anne, it's lovely to see you,' Nicky said when she came to a stop at the other table. .

'And you, my darling,' Anne responded, immediately rising, embracing her, holding her close for a moment.

The man also got to his feet, and a second later he was hugging Nicky to him. 'You look wonderful, my dear, more beautiful than ever, if I may say so.'

'Thank you, Philip, you look pretty terrific yourself, and so do you, Anne. Please sit down both of you, *please*.'

They did so, and Nicky leaned against the back of Anne's chair, bending slightly forward in order to speak to them. 'You must think I'm very rude, Anne, I haven't been in touch for ages. I have no excuse, except that I've been travelling the world for my work.'

'Darling, don't apologize, I understand perfectly. You lead a frightfully busy life. But I must admit, I have missed your phone calls . . . quite a lot, actually, Nicky. However, I do realize you have another life to lead now.' Anne gazed up into her face, smiling faintly. They exchanged a long look, full of understanding, then Anne said, 'Who is that awfully attractive man you're with, Nicky?'

'An old friend . . . a colleague. Cleeland Donovan.'

'The famous war photographer?' Philip asked.

'Yes,' Nicky said.

'Brilliant chap. I have several of his books, and I recently saw some of the most remarkable pictures which he took in Beijing. Can't remember the magazine.'

'*Paris Match*, perhaps,' Nicky said. 'We were there together, covering the crackdown.'

'Nasty business that. Very tragic outcome,' Philip said.

'The bloodshed was unbelievable,' Nicky told him, and turned to look at Anne. 'Are you here on vacation?'

'Yes. We're staying with friends of Philip's at Tarascon, not far from St Rémy. Are you on holiday, too?'

Nicky nodded. 'Clee has a farm between St Rémy and Aix, a lovely old *mas*, and I've just spent a week there. Resting. Clee came down for the weekend. We were both pretty done in after China.'

'I can well imagine,' Anne said. 'I do wish you would come over to Tarascon with your friend, for lunch or dinner one day. Will you?'

'It's kind of you to invite us, Anne, but I'm afraid I have to be back in New York on Monday. I'm leaving for Paris tomorrow morning.'

'What a pity, it would have been so nice to catch up . . .' Anne reached out, put her hand on Nicky's arm. 'I've missed you.'

'Oh Anne, I know, I've missed you too, and it's all my fault. I've been so neglectful.'

Anne smiled, but made no comment.

Philip volunteered, 'Perhaps we can have coffee later?'

'We've almost finished dinner, Philip, and you and Anne are just starting.' Her smile was rueful as she explained, 'I have to be up at the crack of dawn tomorrow, to drive to Marseille. I have an early plane to Paris.'

'*C'est dommage*,' he said, sounding as disappointed as Anne had only a moment ago.

Nicky took her leave of them graciously, and returned to the table. Immediately, she apologized to Clee. 'I'm sorry. That took longer than I expected.'

'Who are they?'

'English friends.'

'Is she related to you?'

'No. Why do you ask that?' Nicky's brows drew together in puzzlement.

'You look alike. Same blonde hair, blue eyes, and there's even a facial resemblance.'

'Oh, do you think so?'

'Are they here on vacation?'

Nicky nodded. 'They're staying with friends in Tarascon.'

'A lot of English people have homes down here these days, and smart Parisians as well. Provence has become very popular. I hope it's not going to get taken over by the rich and the chic.'

'I know what you mean,' Nicky said. 'That would really spoil it.'

Clee expected Nicky to say more about her friends, but she made no further comment about them, merely sipped her wine in silence. Eventually he said, 'Would you like dessert? That's the one thing I didn't order when we were out on the terrace. *Crêpes* are one of their specialties.'

'No, thanks. Just coffee, Clee, please.'

'I guess I'll have the same.' Clee ordered for them both, and then sat studying Nicky for a few minutes. Without understanding what exactly it was, he knew there was something different about her. On the surface her demeanour was the same as it had been all evening. Yet there had been a subtle change in her, indefinable though this was.

Convinced that it had something to do with the English couple, he said, 'The woman was very affectionate with you, Nicky. Obviously she's extremely fond of you.'

'Yes, she is.'

'Who are they? I mean, what are their names?'

'Philip and Anne.'

'What does he do?'

'He's in Whitehall. You know, with the British Foreign Office. He has some important job, but I don't know exactly what it is.'

'How do you know them?' he probed.

'Through my parents, I met them through my parents. My father's known Philip for a number of years. But why are you so interested in them, Clee?'

He shrugged. 'I'm not sure, except that you and she have a look of each other, and she was very loving with you. And when you were talking to her I noticed that you appeared to care, and quite deeply, for her.'

'I do, in my own way.'

The coffee was served and the wine waiter came back and asked if they wished to have cognac, or any other after-dinner drink. Nicky shook her head.

'No, thank you,' Clee said.

Once they were alone, Nicky leaned into Clee. 'I haven't told you about my fall special,' she said. 'I decided to call it *Decade of Destruction*, a title Arch wasn't completely sold on, to tell you the truth. But I'm going to fight like hell for it. It's perfect for my show.'

'What's the subject?' Clee asked, intrigued. 'As if I didn't know. The last few years of wars and uprisings and revolutions, right?'

'More or less. That's how I'm starting it, but I'm leading right into the nineties, and, in a way, sort of forecasting what's to come . . . that's the decade I'm referring to – 1990 to the year 2000. The decade of destruction.'

'Why doesn't Arch like the title?'

'He does, actually. However, he thinks the network will balk, that they'll say it's too depressing.'

'That figures. On the other hand, you're a big number, and surely your opinion carries some weight.'

'Only *some*,' she said, measuring a tiny space between her thumb and forefinger. 'About this much. You don't know networks.'

'I thought you were going to do a special about the child soldiers, the kids we've seen fighting in Cambodia, Ireland, Iran, and all over the world,' Clee said. 'The little kids toting guns for their governments.'

'I am, but that's for next spring.'

They talked for a while about the two programmes she was planning, and Clee decided that perhaps after all he had imagined the change in her. She looked and sounded perfectly normal to him now.

A short while later, when they were leaving, Nicky had no alternative but to stop at the English couple's table. She introduced him. 'Anne, I'd like you to meet Clee, and Clee, this is Anne.'

He shook hands with the Englishwoman. She smiled up into his face and he thought she was one of the loveliest-looking women he had ever seen. He also realized that she did not resemble Nicky facially; they simply had the same blonde colouring.

'And Philip, this is Clee,' Nicky went on, and he was forced to let go of Anne's hand in order to greet the other man.

'We're so sorry you can't come over to see us in Tarascon,' Anne said. 'But perhaps we'll meet again one day.'

'I hope so,' he replied.

'Keep up the good work,' Philip said to him. 'I'm a great admirer of yours – of your extraordinary photography.'

'Thank you,' Clee said. He was about to suggest they meet up on the terrace a little later for an after-dinner drink, when Nicky took hold of his arm, gripped it tightly, and edged away.

'It's been lovely to see you both, but we really must go,' she said to Anne and Philip. 'I'm afraid I still have to pack.'

'Of course,' Anne said. 'And *bon voyage*, darling.'

As they walked to the car, Clee remarked, 'She's a really beautiful woman. But her resemblance to you is negligible. By the way, you didn't tell me their name, I mean their surname.'

There was a silence.

Finally Nicky said, 'They're not married. He's called Philip Rawlings.'

'And Anne?'

Nicky cleared her throat. 'She's Anne Devereaux . . . Lady Anne Devereaux.'

Clee stopped in his tracks, and swung to face her. 'Is she related to Charles?' he asked, surprise reverberating in his voice.

'Yes.'

'His sister?'

'No. His mother.'

'But she's so young looking!'

'She's fifty-eight. She had Charles when she was only eighteen.'

'Her husband, where's he?'

'He's dead. He has been for years.'

'So Philip is her boyfriend?'

'Yes.'

'She cares for you a lot, Nick, but then I've already said that.'

'Yes,' Nicky responded softly. 'She thought of me as the daughter she'd never had.'

Clee said nothing. They had arrived at the car, and he unlocked the door, helped her to get in. As they drove off in the direction of St Rémy he decided not to ask any more questions about Anne Devereaux. He knew that Nicky was touchy about Charles, and he did not want to create any problems.

Nicky hardly spoke on the drive back to the farm. She appeared to be far away.

Clee stole surreptitious glances at her from time to time, and he noticed how rigidly set her face had become. Even in profile this was quite apparent. Eventually, he put a tape in the player in the dashboard and concentrated on his driving. He sank down into himself and was soon lost in his thoughts.

After a while, Nicky leaned her head against the car window and closed her eyes.

Clee was not sure whether she was dozing or merely feigning sleep. His heart sank. The evening which had begun so wonderfully, so auspiciously, had suddenly fizzled out. He realized that he was vaguely angry, even a bit distressed, and he was aware that this was because of the change in Nicky, or rather what had wrought it. She had been reminded of the past tonight, and in the strongest possible way. He cursed Charles Devereaux under his breath. That man seemed to have an uncanny way of coming back to haunt Nicky – and now, indirectly, him.

CHAPTER SEVENTEEN

'This is one of the best scripts you've ever written, Nick,' Arch said, handing it to her across his desk.

'I'm glad you like it,' Nicky replied, looking pleased as she took it from him. 'But let's not forget that I had some help from Ellen, Sam and Wilma, not to mention you. It was a team effort.'

Arch shook his head. 'No, it wasn't. Basically, it's all yours. It's definitely got your inimitable stamp on it, and you were in cracking form when you wrote this.'

'Thanks,' she said, smiling at him.

'Incidentally, we're coming up with some great footage to go with the script,' Arch volunteered. 'Stuff we found in the archives, as you said we would. The show's going to be a humdinger, Nick, very powerful.' He leaned forward intently, pinning her with his eyes. 'Listen, I've made a couple of changes, only minor ones, if you wouldn't mind looking 'em over now. They're on pages six, twenty, and forty-one.'

Nicky nodded, did as he said, and read the changes he had made, as well as his explanatory notes in the margin of each page. Then she looked up and nodded quickly. 'You've really strengthened some of my points. Thanks, Arch. And the changes are fine, I think this does it – let's go with this script. There's nothing else to add.'

'You're right, and since you obviously approve, I'll get the script out to retype immediately.'

Handing it back to him, Nicky remarked casually, 'I suppose you've spoken to our venerable President of News again . . . about the title?'

'I sure have, and Larry's with us, kid. He agrees *Decade of Destruction* is a great title, and appropriate, and he's pushing it through, so don't worry. In any case, you know Larry's never been one to shy away from doom and gloom. In fact, he thinks viewers are fascinated by catastrophes, and I'm inclined to agree with him.'

'So we're all set to go?' Nicky asked. 'Is that what you're saying?'

'You betcha! I also got an okay from Larry for your other special – the one about the gun-toting kids. Have you had any thoughts about titles yet?'

'My working title is *Innocents with Guns*. What do you think?'

'Not bad, Nicky, not bad at all.' Arch leaned back in his chair, his expression thoughtful. After a moment, he glanced at her, gave her a long, steady look.

Nicky said, 'What's wrong? What is it?'

'Nothing's wrong, on the contrary, everything's right. Larry wants to move you in another direction next year, Nick, and he's going to talk to you about it.'

'What kind of direction?' she asked sharply, her eyes suddenly wary.

'He wants you to do some different stuff, maybe just a fraction lighter than – '

'Hey, wait a minute,' she cut in peremptorily, intensifying her stare. 'I've always covered hard news, politics and wars! What are you trying to tell me? That he wants to pull me off my assignment as chief war correspondent for the network?'

'No, no, I'm not saying that at all. Just hold your horses and listen. Don't get so excited, okay?'

'Okay. Shoot. I'm *all* ears.'

'Larry's talking about your specials, that's all. He thought that after *Decade*, which he plans to air in November, and the special on the kids with guns, which he's programming for next year, that you yourself might want a bit of a change. He was thinking of a series of interviews with world leaders – the President, Mrs Thatcher, Gorbachev. So, how do you feel about it?'

'Not sure, and I'll tell Larry that when we have our meeting.' She shrugged. 'But it could be interesting, I suppose.'

'You don't sound very enthusiastic.'

'Don't be misled by my tone, Arch, I'm interested. Very interested, as a matter of fact. But you know me well enough to realize that I've got to have an angle, come up with a strong point of view, for my specials. They can't be wishy-washy. And I'm not averse to change, on the contrary. Actually, I like new innovations.'

'I know that, and so does Larry, and in any case he's looking to you, and to me, to come up with some suggestions.' He flashed her a wide grin. 'You can even interview movie stars, if you want.'

Nicky shook her head vehemently, though she was also grinning. 'No, thanks. I ain't even going to try to compete with Barbara Walters. She's the best at that, and we all know it.'

'Barbara also interviews political leaders, Nick, and she does a really good mix of celebrities at times. It might be worth thinking about that type of show. Let's not forget that her specials get very big ratings. And I mean *big*.'

'I told you, she's the best. And I certainly don't want to be second best. I'll stick to my formula. Anyway, I prefer to come up with some ideas of my own.' She sat back in the chair, and sighed lightly. 'To tell you the honest truth, Arch, a change might be what I need. I felt a bit exhausted after Beijing. Sort of burnt out.'

'I know you did, and you looked it, Nicky. But I guess it was burn out time for all of us in June.' There was a little pause before he said, 'You're looking great now. I guess Provence did you the world of good . . . *and* being with Clee, of course.'

'It was great,' Nicky replied, her voice lighter, happier. 'And he's great.'

'Do I hear the sound of wedding bells?'

'Don't be so ridiculous!'

'It's not ridiculous. Hey, Nick, it's *me* you're talking to. Arch Leverson. I've known Cleeland Donovan a long time, and I can assure you that he's crazy about you. Hell, honey, it's written all over his face. When we had dinner at "21" last week I knew he had it bad for you.' He gave her a penetrating look. 'I guess I find it hard to believe that you don't feel the same way he does.'

There was a moment's hesitation on her part. 'I do care for Clee,' she admitted finally, sounding suddenly quiet, even slightly shy. 'But that doesn't necessarily mean there's going to be a wedding.' She got up, walked across the floor to the window, stood staring out, a far away look settling on her face.

It was a beautiful Wednesday morning in the middle of August. Nicky gazed at a sky that was an intense, vivid blue, without a single cloud. The impressive skyscrapers of Manhattan shimmered in the brilliant sunlight, and she could not help thinking how extraordinary the city looked from up here on the forty-ninth floor of the American Television Network building.

There's no city like it in the whole world, she thought, and she knew that wherever she lived she would always be a New Yorker at heart. She had been born here, had lived here for the biggest part of her life. It was her city. Just as Paris was her city in its own special way; she had such happy memories of her years spent there as a child. It would be no hardship for her to live there again . . .

Eventually turning around, Nicky leaned against the wide window ledge and gazed across at Arch. Taking a deep breath, she said in a cool and careful voice, 'Are you worried about me marrying Clee and moving to Paris, Arch?'

'Hell, no, Nicky, how could you possibly think a thing like that?' he asked, his voice rising several octaves, hinting at indignation.

Instead of answering his question, she said, 'Because if you are, don't forget that I have a binding contract with this network, and I would never attempt to break it. *Never*. Nor would my agent let me.' Without pausing, she plunged on, 'And in any case, whatever happens in my personal life, I have every intention of continuing my career. I love my work. It's a very big part of my life, and it always has been. I've been a broadcast journalist since I left college, as you well know, and it's in my blood. I wouldn't be myself without it.'

Arch pushed back his chair and rose; his expression was serious. Slowly he walked over to her and took hold of her by the shoulders, peered deeply into her face and said, 'I don't care about this network or your contract. I only care about *you*, and about what happens to *you*. I want you to be happy, Nicky, and if Clee's the right guy for you, if you think you can make a decent life with him, then I say go for it, grab it. Listen, honey, life's all too brief and difficult and painful, so if you have a chance of making it work with a good guy, then for God's sake do it. Don't think about anything, or anybody, only yourself.'

Nicky leaned forward, hugged Arch to her, touched by his words. Then, pulling away from him, she smiled up into his face. 'Thanks for that, Arch. Your affection for me means such a lot, and I appreciate the moral support you've always given me, that you're giving me now.' Clearing her throat, she added, 'And he *is* a good guy, isn't he?'

'And then some, Nicky, there's no man I know who is a better man than Cleeland Donovan. As my mother would say, he's a real *mensch*.'

Taking hold of his arm, she led him over to the sofa, where they sat down together.

Nicky said, after a moment, 'I must admit, I have been worrying a bit. I mean worrying about how I would work it out – my career and Clee and living in Paris, if we ever did decide to get married. Mind you, let me hasten to add, he hasn't proposed to me.'

'Give him half a chance and he will.'

'I'm not as certain as you are about that, Arch. Clee has always been reluctant about settling down, and for several good reasons. He – '

'I know the reasons,' Arch interjected a trifle impatiently, 'he's told me often enough. He doesn't want to expose a wife and a family to grief and pain, should he get himself killed in the line of duty, and he doesn't want to give up the challenge, excitement and danger of being a war photographer. Isn't that what you were going to say?'

'Yes.'

Arch began to laugh. 'That was all very easy for Clee to say before you came into his life, at least, before you became his lover. Because, in my opinion, he's never really been head over heels in love. But he is with you, Nick,' Arch pointed out. 'Take my word for it. He loves you very *deeply*. I know this because I know the man so well. And I'll tell you something else . . . Clee would turn his life upside down for you.'

Nicky had listened carefully and now she bit her lip, appeared momentarily worried. 'Oh, I don't know . . . ' She let her sentence trail off uncertainly. A split second later, she exclaimed, 'In any case, Clee thinks of himself as a bachelor at heart! You know, in the same way Robert Capa was.'

'It's often struck me in the past that Clee has patterned his life on Bob Capa's, but I'm not so certain of that anymore,' Arch answered. 'Oh sure, Capa's been his idol since he was a kid, and he's always striven to be as great a photographer as Capa, especially on a battlefield. But I think that's where the identification stops, deep down inside himself.'

'Maybe.'

'Listen, Nick, Clee's coming from a different place than Capa was, this is a different time, a different world we live in today, and we're talking about a different man. I truly believe Clee will marry, but only someone he considers to be the right woman for him, the *only* woman, and in my opinion, that's you.'

Nicky remained silent.

Arch said, 'Tell me something, honey, what would you say and do, if he did ask you to marry him?'

'I'm not sure, and I'm being absolutely honest with you, Arch, I'm just not sure.'

'If you're worrying about the network, *don't*. We can work it out. You're contracted to make between two and four specials a year, and those you could easily plan from Paris, or anywhere else in the world for that matter. If you think about it, that's what you've been doing all along – coming up with ideas for specials while covering the news. So, all you would have to do, once the planning stage was over, would be to fly in here for two or three weeks, a month at the most, to do the taping, or the live broadcast, depending on the type of special it was.'

'I know, Arch, I've already realized that. But I'm also this network's war correspondent. How could I possibly be based in Paris?'

'I'm not sure, I'd have to give some thought to that, work something out with you, your agent, Larry Anderson and Joe Speight. The network doesn't want to lose you, Nicky, I can assure you of that, so they'd be willing to be . . . well, accommodating, to say the least. Also, don't lose sight of the fact that ATN has a big Paris bureau, and I don't see why you couldn't work out of that bureau, operate from there, if you had to, Nicky.'

'I guess it might be a viable proposition,' she agreed.

'You and Clee could cover wars together, you know. You certainly have an advantage over most women in that respect . . . Clee wouldn't have to give up that side of his career for you.'

'That's true, yes. But do you know something, Arch? There are days when I wonder if I want to go on being a war correspondent for the rest of my life.'

If Arch Leverson was startled by this statement, he did not show it. He merely nodded, and said, 'It gets to everybody one day. You've certainly had *your* bellyful of wars and revolutions these past eight years or so. I also know that one day Clee will be turned off, too, even though he thinks otherwise right now. Burn out is not uncommon when you've seen as much killing and death as we have. It's deadly. But – ' He stopped, eyed her carefully, and finished, ' – keep your options open for the moment, and don't make any hasty decisions about your career.'

'No, I won't . . . about anything.'

'I'd like to ask you something.' He raised a brow quizzically.

'Go ahead.'

'I know you don't like to talk about Charles Devereaux, but if I remember correctly, you weren't planning to give up your career after you'd married him. Nor were you going to move to London. So, how were you intending to swing it?'

'Charles was eventually going to open a branch of his wine-importing company here in New York, and he was going to live here most of the time, except when he had to travel to Europe to buy wines. And, of course, he planned to keep his office and the flat in London. We were going to straddle the Atlantic, so to speak.'

'I see. I guess it's a bit different with Clee, because of his photo news agency. Although, come to think of it, he could start an Image office here in New York, couldn't he? Base himself here, perhaps?'

'Everything's possible,' Nicky admitted, and then shrugged lightly. 'Maybe Clee doesn't want to do that.'

Arch nodded. Several other questions were on the tip of his tongue, but he decided not to ask them at this moment in time. They could wait.

Settling back in the corner of the sofa, he remarked, 'Clee told me before he left for Paris that you're going to be spending September with him at the farm. I'm glad about that, honey. You've not taken enough time off in the past few years.'

Nicky reached for his hand, and squeezed it. 'Thanks for caring.'

'I worry about you,' he admitted with a wry smile. 'A *lot*.' Then he glanced at his watch, and exclaimed, 'It's time for lunch! I've booked a table at your favourite spot – the Four Seasons. So come on, let's get going. And on my way out I'll give the script to Hildy to be sent out for a retype.'

They both rose.

Nicky said, 'I'll give it to her, Arch. I've got to go back to my office to get my bag and some other stuff.' As she finished speaking, she crossed the floor to his desk, picked up the script, and swung to face him. 'If you don't need me this afternoon for further discussions on the special, I'm going to take the rest of the day off.'

'I'm glad to hear it, you work far too hard.'

'So my parents keep telling me,' she responded and grinned at him. 'Very conveniently, they forget that they set an example for me years ago, and are still setting it, in fact.'

'Talking of your parents, I hear on the grapevine that they're as crazy about Clee as he is about you.'

'*Grapevine!* What grapevine? Surely you mean Clee told you.'

Arch laughed.

Nicky said, 'But yes, it's true, they all got on very well when we were up in Connecticut working on the picture book. They think he's . . . the bee's knees.'

Arch laughed again, and said, 'I told you once, and I'll say it again, Clee is everybody's favourite, folks just love him.'

'You don't have to tell *me*. My parents haven't stopped raving about him.' Nicky hurried over to the door, paused before going out. 'I'll pick up my things, and alert Annette that I'm not coming back after lunch, then I'll meet you at the elevators. Okay?'

'Okay, kid, see you in five.'

CHAPTER EIGHTEEN

After lunch at the Four Seasons, Nicky went shopping at Bergdorf Goodman. Here she bought several pairs of cotton pants, a selection of cotton shirts, and three summer dresses, items she needed for her vacation in Provence in September.

Then she walked across town slowly, heading back to her apartment which was located on Sutton Place, overlooking the East River and part of downtown Manhattan.

It was a stifling hot afternoon, somewhere around a hundred degrees, and even though she was wearing a lightweight cotton suit she soon felt damp and sticky from the overpowering heat. She was glad when she finally arrived at her building and stepped inside the cool, dim lobby.

After picking up her mail, she took the elevator to the top floor where she had a large and airy penthouse. Gertrude, her maid, who came every day whether Nicky was in town or not, had closed all of the sun blinds at the windows, and turned up the air conditioning before leaving for the day. In consequence, the apartment was beautifully cool and shady, and it was a relief to Nicky to be inside, after tramping through the boiling hot streets of Manhattan.

Nicky dumped the Bergdorf shopping bags on the floor of her bedroom with its sea-green walls, matching carpet and French country furnishings, and went back through the hall to the kitchen. Opening the refrigerator, she took out a bottle of carbonated water, poured a glass, drank some of it thirstily, then carried it back to the bedroom. Shedding her smart little summer Trigère, she hung the black and white suit in the large walk-in closet, then slipped on one of the loose cotton caftans she had bought on a trip to Morocco some years before.

Several minutes later, Nicky was seated behind her desk in her booklined library-den. This had a magnificent view of the river, the Empire State and Chrysler buildings, and the other soaring skyscrapers that stretched from midtown down to the Twin Towers on the tip of Manhattan Island.

Taking another long swallow of the water, she glanced at the carriage clock on the English Victorian desk, and was surprised to see that it was almost six o'clock. The folder in front of her was marked *Children of the Beijing Spring*, and she opened it, glanced at the first few pages of her introduction to Clee's book. Annette, her secretary, had sent it to him by courier several days ago, and he had phoned her very early this morning from Paris to tell her that it was perfect, that he loved it. Nicky was delighted he had been so pleased, and that he had not minded the length. It was only fifty pages of typescript, but Clee had said she had told everything succinctly – but movingly so. 'I'd rather have it short and brilliant, than long and boring,' he had said before hanging up.

Nicky now put the folder away in one of the deep drawers of the desk, and began to sort through her mail, which she had brought in with her from the bedroom. There was nothing of consequence – a few bills, postcards from several girl friends away on summer vacations, and a letter from her lawyer about Nickwell, her own production company. But not even this was of any great importance, and she put the mail in the black lacquer Japanese tray on her desk to be dealt with another day.

Standing up, Nicky went back to the kitchen, carrying the empty glass. On her way, she paused in the doorway of the living room, looking at it appraisingly with a keen and critical eye. There was no question that it was beautiful; nobody could deny that. It was large, with a huge picture window which also looked downtown, and was furnished with English antique pieces and washed throughout in light colours. Primarily, she had used varying shades of peach and apricot, pale greens and blues; it was a room that was especially effective at night, warm and mellow and inviting.

Nicky loved her apartment floating high in the sky. Light-filled, airy and cheerful, she found it a joy to be in, whatever the time of day or night, and whatever the weather was like outside. It was sunny and lighthearted when the weather was good; equally, it was highly dramatic in a thunderstorm or blizzard. After dark it became part of the fairyland that was Manhattan when the lights went on and glittered brilliantly outside its many windows.

Her parents had persuaded her to buy the apartment four years ago, and she was glad that she had. It was a real home, attractively decorated, comfortable, reassuring, and something of a refuge for her between her travels and foreign assignments.

In the kitchen, which was white and blue, sleek and modern and convenient, Nicky poured herself another glass of water and returned to the library.

Flopping down on the sofa, she propped her feet on the coffee table and focused her thoughts on Clee and their affair, ruminating on everything that Arch had said in the office, and later, over lunch.

Of course, he had made it sound easy; but in her opinion he had over-simplified the situation. She still wasn't so sure she could handle Clee, marriage, living in Paris, *and* her career in American television, which necessitated that she be here in New York, part of the time, at least.

Oh, yes, you can, a small voice inside her head told her.

Maybe I can at that, she thought, and laughed out loud. Like most other modern young women, she wanted it all. And then some. Was that possible?

Also, if she and Clee did marry, he might want to have a child. Did she? Some days, the answer was yes. Others, it was no, and most especially when she reflected about the horrors she reported on, and on a daily basis. Who would want to bring a child into a terrible world like this? Only a mad woman, surely?

Her mother, the historian, kept saying that the world had always been a pretty lousy place – since time immemorial, in fact.

'You mustn't, indeed you *can't* have these attitudes,' her mother had recently said to her. 'If everyone had thought as you do over the centuries, and decided not to procreate because of the evil and horror in the world, then the human race today would be extinct.' Well, there was no denying her mother was a wise woman, and smart. Still . . .

Nicky let these thoughts go, sighing heavily. Leaning her head against the chintz cushions on the sofa, she closed her eyes, drifted with her complex reflections about her life.

In a sense, what it finally boiled down to was her feelings for Clee. She *was* emotionally involved with him, there was no denying that, and her physical passion for him knew no bounds. But was she really in love with him? And sufficiently enough to make a life with him? Forever? Might she not be merely infatuated? She wasn't sure. Anyway, although he had told her he loved her *twice* in Provence, once in bed and once at the restaurant at Les Baux, he had not said those words to her again. Furthermore, he had never ever mentioned marriage. And did *she* want to marry *Clee*? Damn, I just don't know, she answered herself.

Nicky sat up and opened her eyes, feeling suddenly quite irritated. Why was she so ambivalent? She had no answer, at least not *exactly*. However, she *was* fully aware of the importance of her career. It was her lifeblood, in all truth. Was that at the root of it? Was that the stumbling block? The fact was, Clee lived in Paris and liked living there, and obviously did not want to return to the States to take up residence. She lived in New York and needed to, because the network was here and she was a big number in American television.

Maybe that *is* the reason I'm so uncertain, she finally admitted, and grimaced wryly to herself. She obviously wasn't prepared to jeopardize her brilliant career.

A few minutes later Nicky automatically glanced at her watch. It was ten minutes to seven and time to put ATN on, to catch the evening news on her own network with anchorman Mike Fowler, to whom she was close.

Rising, she stepped over to the bookshelves where the large television set was housed, turned it on, and went back to the sofa.

The current coverage was the local New York news, and Nicky paid scant attention to this, picked up *Time* magazine from the coffee table, flipped the pages to the section on the press, and began to read, listening with only half an ear.

A short while later, at the sound of the familiar music, the splendid, rather grand theme that heralded ATN's nightly national and international news, Nicky lifted her head.

There sat Mike in all his glory, looking as wonderful and as reassuring as he always did. Like Peter Jennings of ABC, Mike was extremely good looking and glamorous, but also a superb journalist. Peter and Mike were two of the best in the business as far as she was concerned – first-rate reporters who got the point, were informative and reasonable, and for those reasons they took all the ratings.

Only vaguely listening to Mike giving the headlines of the world news, she continued to read the *Time* piece, and went on reading it as he gave more in-depth details of the national news.

But when she heard the voice of her channel's Rome correspondent, Tony Johnson, Nicky looked up, suddenly more attentive.

She listened carefully as he told of a shooting incident at a political rally outside Rome. Several people had been hit when a gunman had gone berserk and fired a machine gun into the crowd. Tony said there was speculation that the incident had really been an assassination attempt by the opposition party.

As the camera moved away from Tony, and slowly panned around, it lingered for a moment on a group to the left of the speaker's platform, then settled briefly on a face in the crowd.

Suddenly Nicky sat bolt upright, and stared in shock at a face on the screen. 'Charles!' she said. 'It's Charles!' But how could it be? Charles was dead.

Charles Devereaux had killed himself two and a half years ago, just a few weeks before their wedding. How could he be in Rome, larger than life? No, it can't be him, Nicky thought. Charles had drowned off the English coast.

It was true, however, that his body had never been found.

Suddenly Nicky knew; yes, it *was* him. Charles Devereaux was alive. But how could that be? Why had he disappeared from her life? And what was she going to do about it?

PART THREE

Conspirators

False face must hide
what the false heart doth know.

William Shakespeare

CHAPTER NINETEEN

The house where Anne Devereaux lived was old, very old: a place of historical significance and singular beauty.

Pullenbrook was its name, and it stood on a low plateau of parkland in a dell beneath the rolling hills of the South Downs. Cradled as it was deep in the heart of the Sussex countryside, it was unusually well-secluded for a great house of its kind.

It was hidden in the folds of the soft pastoral land, and the tips of its chimneys only became visible at the very last moment of its approach. Then, unexpectedly, the manor could be seen through the lush green foliage of the high trees that fringed the edge of the park, and it never failed to take the breath away.

Built in 1565 by an ancestor of Anne's, it was a Tudor house of exceptional distinction, typical of the Elizabethan period, with its grey-stone walls, half-timbered gables, soaring leaded windows, square-cut bays and many tall chimneys.

Clustered around the main house were the out-buildings, the stables, a small church and two walled gardens; flaring out on either side and running along the front facade was the lovely park where fallow deer grazed as they had for centuries.

A house of unchanging appearance, it had remained much the same since it was built by one Sir Edmund Clifford, a magnate and warrior knight in service to Elizabeth Tudor, the Queen of England. The lands of Pullen were granted to Sir Edmund by the Queen, in gratitude for services rendered to the Crown; later she showered him with more royal favours when she elevated him to the peerage by creating him Earl Clifford of Allendale, and giving him Castle Allendale and additional lands in Sussex.

Edmund, his eldest son Thomas, who became the second earl, and *his* subsequent descendants, divided their time between the manor and the castle. But by the end of the seventeenth century the Cliffords were residing permanently at the castle, which had grown in size and magnificence over the years, and in consequence the manor house was used only part of the year. However, it had always been kept in good repair and its outer structure and interiors were unimpaired over the centuries.

Fortunately, because the Clifford family lived mostly at Castle Allendale for the next few hundred years, Pullenbrook had been saved from certain and perhaps excessive modernization, so it had retained its purity of architecture and Tudor character.

It was Anne's grandfather, the ninth earl named for the first, who preferred to live at the manor rather than at the great castle, and thus, in 1910, Pullenbrook once again became the main residence of the Cliffords. His son, Julian, the tenth earl and Anne's father, followed this tradition and resided at the manor house until his death.

Anne Clifford Devereaux's entire life had been spent at Pullenbrook. She was born there on 26 April 1931. As the daughter of an earl she had the honorary title of Lady, a title which was retained even after marriage.

She was raised in the ancient house, married from it in 1948, and three years later she had returned to live there as a young widow with a small son. At this time in her life she had needed to be in the bosom of her family, rather than alone in the grand London town house her late husband, Henry Devereaux, had left her.

When her brother Geoffrey had inherited the Clifford earldom, estates and lands, after their father's death in 1955, he had chosen to make Castle Allendale his home. And understanding how much his sister cared for the manor in West Sussex, he had suggested she continue to live there for as long as she wished, whether or not she remarried.

Thirty-four years later she was still in residence, *châtelaine* of the house for her brother. To say that Anne loved Pullenbrook was something of an understatement. In a sense, she revered it, and much of her life revolved around it; it gave her constant succour and comfort. She felt safe and protected within its familiar walls, deriving much pleasure from its ancient and stately beauty, its timelessness, the continuity of family line and history which it represented.

There were times when she often wondered what she would have done without the house, for it had seen her through many hours of unhappiness – sadness, loneliness and heartache, grief, sorrow and illness. Its very existence over so many centuries seemed to reassure her that she too could, indeed *would*, survive, and that she would go on – somehow.

Now on this Saturday morning in August Anne came into the Great Hall, her step light, her high heels clicking sharply against the stone floor. She stood poised in the doorway, regarding the hall, marvelling at its peaceful beauty, as she so frequently did. It never failed to hold her in its spell.

Thousands of dust motes rose up in the shafts of trembling light that slanted in through the leaded windows, but otherwise there was no motion whatsoever in the room. It was all stillness and quiescence, filled with bright sunlight that burnished the ancient wood pieces, gave them a mellow glow, and brought into focus the old paintings of her ancestors by such master portraitists as Peter Lely, Thomas Gainsborough and George Romney.

A fleeting smile crossed her face. Every aspect of this house gave her immense pleasure, but this room in particular was a special favourite. Moving forward to the long refectory table, Anne placed the bowl of roses she was carrying in the centre of it, stepped back, eyeing them for a moment.

The head gardener had picked the flowers earlier that morning and they were beautiful. They were in variated shades of pink, and looked perfect in the crested silver bowl set against the ripe old wood of the table. The roses were full blown, and several petals suddenly fell. She was about to pick them up, then changed her mind, left them lying where they were, thinking how natural they looked next to the silver bowl.

Turning on her heels, Anne went back through the heavy carved-wood door leading into the private quarters of the house, which were not open to the public.

690

The flower room where she had been working was off to one side, across a small stone-flagged foyer; Anne went in, lifted the last vase of flowers from the old deal work table and took it down the corridor to the drawing room.

This was a wonderfully spacious room with a series of soaring, leaded windows set in a square-cut bay, a huge stone fireplace and a high, coffered ceiling. The room had been decorated mostly in various shades of celadon green, and these washed across the walls, were repeated in various upholstery fabrics and in the Aubusson carpet on the floor; some of the celadons were so pale they were almost a silvery grey. Fine Georgian antiques and paintings graced the room, which, like the Great Hall, had an air of timelessness and tranquillity about it.

After placing the tall crystal vase of white roses on an antique fruitwood table in the centre of the room, Anne hurried out. Several seconds later she was sitting down behind her desk in the small parlour she used as an office. Cosy, comfortable, this seemed full of sunshine because of its yellow walls; a raspberry-coloured carpet stretched across the floor, and a loveseat covered in a raspberry-and-white striped fabric was placed in front of the fireplace.

The most important piece of furniture in the room was the Georgian walnut desk where Anne now sat going through the morning post. After reading it all, she picked up the menus she had written out the night before for Pilar, the cook, and glanced at them again. Then she looked over the list of things to do, which she had scribbled yesterday and systematically began to check off those chores she had already accomplished.

At this moment a shadow fell across the doorway, and she lifted her head, smiled warmly when she saw Philip Rawlings standing there looking slightly hesitant.

'Am I disturbing you, Anne?'

'No, darling, not at all. I've just been checking my list, and I'm happy to tell you that I've done everything I had to do. I'm now as free as a bird – and all yours.'

'Well, I'm certainly glad to hear that,' he answered and sauntered into the room. A slender man of medium height, with intelligent grey eyes in a pleasantly attractive, somewhat boyish face, Philip looked much younger than his fifty-six years, despite the silver wings in his dark hair. This morning he wore a wine-coloured paisley-patterned cravat with an open-necked pale blue shirt, dark grey slacks and a grey-checked sports jacket; his appearance was more like that of a country squire than an important member of the British Foreign Office.

'I thought we might have a stroll before lunch,' Philip went on, smiling as he came to a stop in front of her desk.

'And why not? Actually, I'd rather like it,' Anne said. 'I was going to come looking for you, to suggest the very same thing. So, come along, let's go to the coat room where I'll change these shoes, put on a pair of flats, and then we can stroll up Sweetheart Hill. That's a pleasant walk, and not too long, either.'

'Splendid,' Philip said.

Anne glanced at her watch as she rose, and went on, 'We have about an hour. Plenty of time for the walk *and* a drink before lunch. Inez is going to serve Pilar's cheese soufflé promptly at one. She's making it specially for you, you know.'

Philip put his arm around Anne's shoulders as they walked out into the corridor together. 'The problem in this house is that you all spoil me,' he murmured genially, spontaneously kissing her cheek.

Anne looked at him and began to laugh. 'You're worth spoiling, my darling,' she said, her pretty eyes mirroring the love and affection reflected in his.

Sweetheart Hill rose up behind the house, an extraordinary vantage point with spectacular views for miles around.

Several hundred years before, in 1644, during the ill-fated reign of Charles I, one of Anne's female ancestors had climbed the hill every day for months. The Lady Rosemary Clifford had hoped and prayed to see her sweetheart returning from the Battle of Marston Moor, during the bloody Civil War which had racked England at that time – and this was how it had acquired its romantic and charming name.

A stone bench had been built on top of the hill for the Lady Rosemary, so that she could sit and watch and wait in comfort. She had waited in vain, as it turned out. Her Royalist sweetheart, Lord Colin Greville, had been killed by the Roundheads – Cromwell's men – and had never returned to claim her as his bride. Eventually, she had recovered from her sorrow and had married some other young nobleman, but the place where she had so devotedly waited had been known as Sweetheart Hill ever after.

Anne and Philip now sat on that bench, enjoying the mild air, and the serene and splendid views of the great Tudor house and the surrounding bucolic countryside on this glittering summer's day.

'You're glad Nicky is coming for the weekend, aren't you?' Philip said, breaking the silence that had settled between them after their climb up the hill.

Anne turned her face to his, and nodded quickly, her blue eyes lighting up. 'Oh yes, very happy, Philip. I've missed her terribly . . . but then you know that. I can't wait to spend these few days with her. Nicky has always been unusually special to me.'

'I know, and I'm delighted she phoned from London, and that she more or less invited herself down here.' He smiled at Anne, and remarked, 'Actually, I have to admit I'm looking forward to seeing her myself. There's no one quite like Nicky Wells.'

'Wasn't it lucky we went to Tarascon?' Anne did not wait for an answer, but hurried on, 'And to think that we almost didn't go to stay with the Norells.'

'Not only that, if we'd listened to them we wouldn't have gone to Les Baux for dinner that evening. Remember how they kept telling us it was a tourist trap in the summer months?'

'Yes. But it was meant to be . . . that we ran into Nicky the way we did.'

Philip did not say anything. He put his arm around her and brought her closer to him, and after a moment he said softly, against her hair, 'There is something else that is meant to be, Anne.'

She swung her head to look at him, her eyes questioning.

'Marry me, Anne. *Please.*'

'Oh Philip,' she began, and was about to reject him, but her voice faltered as she looked into his face. There was such a silent plea in his eyes, and his expression was so loving, so full of sincerity, she felt her breath catching in her throat. As far as she was concerned, there was no one who could hold a candle to Philip Rawlings. He was a man of great kindness and generosity, and he had been inordinately loyal

692

and a source of great strength to her over many years. He had asked her several times to marry him during the past six or seven years, and always she had refused. Now, suddenly, she realized how cruel she had been, and was being, to this truly good man who cared so much about her, and her well-being.

She took a deep breath. 'You simply want to make an honest woman of me, that's what this is all about, isn't it?' she said, adopting a light tone, one echoing with gaiety, and she laughed.

He shook his head very slowly and emphatically. 'No, that's not it at all, Anne. I don't care what the world thinks of me, or of you, or of *us*, or of the fact that we've been living together for years. I want to marry you because I love you very much indeed . . . and I thought you loved me in the same way.'

'But I do! Oh darling, you know I do! But marriage seems so . . . well, to be honest, *irrelevant* at our age. As far as I'm concerned, we *are* married. What difference does a little bit of paper make in the long run?'

'It makes a lot of difference to me. You see, I want you to be my *wife*, and it's important to me that you bear my name, that we are . . . *married*.' He began to laugh as lightly as she had a split second before, even a bit self-deprecatingiy, and added, 'Having just said I don't care about the world, perhaps I really do, after all. Maybe I want the world to know that I belong to you, and that you belong to me. I believe I *need* us to be married, Anne. We've been together an awfully long time, darling, and marriage seems to me to be the natural, logical and most wonderful conclusion to our relationship.'

Anne nodded, but found she was quite unable to say anything for a moment. She averted her head, sat gazing out across the landscape, her eyes reflective, her face full of sudden contemplation.

Everything Philip said was true, of course. They had known each other for fifteen years, and had been deeply involved with each other for fourteen of those years. They had met in 1974, just after Philip had left his wife, and what had begun as a friendship had eventually developed into a full-blown affair of the heart. She had dropped the man she had been seeing at the time, Philip had become her lover, and for them both it had been a relationship made in heaven. They were ideally suited to each other, temperamentally and sexually, and they had quickly bonded. Philip's divorce had taken four years, and by then they had settled into a perfectly happy, congenial, and contented routine, seeing each other every weekend when Philip came down to Pullenbrook, and during the week whenever she was up in London.

Philip's children, Vanessa and Timothy, had been quite young in the seventies, and he had not wanted to marry until they were older. She had not minded this; marriage always had been somewhat irrelevant to her, in the sense that her love for Philip existed without it, and would always exist, no matter what. The kind of deep and abiding love she felt for him did not need a marriage licence to give it validity, make it stronger or more real. Besides which, her first marriage had been such a mockery she had been quite cold about the idea of it ever since.

Obviously, though, Philip needed them to be married at this time in their lives. Hadn't he just said as much? If she truly loved him, and of course she did, then his happiness had to be of some importance to her. And it was. Thinking about it, she realized there was no truly good reason why she should not marry him.

Quite unexpectedly, she discovered she rather liked the prospect of being his wife, especially since it would give him such enormous pleasure.

Bringing her gaze to meet his, she said quietly, 'Yes.'

'Yes what?'

'Yes, I'll marry you, Philip. I will be happy and honoured to marry you. As you said a moment ago, it's only right and proper that we get married at this particular time.'

'Oh darling, that makes me so very, very happy.' He leaned into her, kissed her gently on the mouth, took her in his arms, held her very tightly. He had never loved a woman the way he loved Anne Devereaux – and there had been plenty of women in his life before he had met her. Anne had known such hurt and pain, and the only thing he wanted was to love and cherish her, protect and safeguard her all the days of his life – and hers.

Finally releasing her, Philip said, 'Let's set a date for our marriage here and now, before you change your mind. That way I can have my secretary send an announcement to *The Times* first thing on Monday morning.'

'Never fear, I'm not going to change my mind,' she responded, her face radiant, her eyes shining. 'And I'll be glad to work on the announcement with you over the weekend. But let me think for a moment about the date . . . I believe we should get married in December, Philip.'

'But that's months away,' he protested.

'After all these *years* of living in sin, surely a few more *months* don't matter!' Anne exclaimed, her ready laughter surfacing. 'And I'm suggesting December for a very good reason . . . *Geoffrey*. I would like my brother to give me away, and I know he's going to be abroad quite a lot between now and the end of November.'

'Very well, darling, December it is.'

'A Christmas wedding in the little church here at Pullenbrook will be very pretty, rather picturesque, don't you think?'

'Indeed it will. Anne?'

'Yes, darling?'

'I do hope you're going to allow me to give you an engagement ring.'

'What a lovely idea! And of course I am. Every girl likes to have a ring, Philip, expects it, actually.'

A huge smile spread across his face, and he reached into his pocket and brought out a small leather box. 'I went to Asprey's earlier in the week, looking for a ring for you. You see, I was determined to propose this weekend, and equally, I was absolutely determined you would accept me this time. Anyway, I found this, and I hope you like it.' As he finished speaking he handed her the box.

Anne was flabbergasted and her astonishment showed on her face. She lifted the lid and gasped when she saw the deep blue sapphire set within a circle of diamonds nestling in the velvet. 'Oh Philip, it's simply beautiful.'

'I selected this particular ring because I know how much you like antique jewellery,' he explained. 'Anyway, the colour matches your lovely eyes, my darling.'

'Thank you, Philip, for the ring . . . and for everything.'

'Here, let me do that,' he said, as she fumbled with the box, and took it away from her. As he slipped the sapphire on her finger, he added softly, 'There, we are now properly engaged, and what more appropriate place to pledge our troth to each other than here on Sweetheart Hill?'

CHAPTER TWENTY

Nicky had not been in this house for almost three years, and two days ago in New York, when she had made the decision to come to see Anne Devereaux, she had dreaded the thought of being within its walls once again.

But now that she was here at Pullenbrook most of her fears were evaporating. This was due in no small measure to Anne's warmth, her loving demeanour, and Philip's avuncular kindness and his special brand of geniality.

When she had arrived from London an hour ago the two of them had greeted her with much affection; she knew this to be very genuine on their part, and it was an affection she fully reciprocated. Instantly she had begun to relax because they made her feel so welcome and had put her completely at ease.

And then there was the house itself. The minute she had stepped over the threshold into the Great Hall she had felt its peacefulness most forcibly. This was something she had never quite forgotten, but which she had resolutely pushed to the back of her mind in recent years, and for the most obvious of reasons. But there was no denying that there was a special kind of tranquillity within the boundaries of Pullenbrook, a truly palpable thing which enfolded itself around her, seemed literally to envelop her like a cloak. In fact, she now recalled what a soothing effect the old manor had had on her in the past, and she understood why Anne thought of it as her safe haven, why she never wanted to leave it, at least not for very long.

Suddenly it struck Nicky that this ancient Tudor house had seen so much, witnessed so much over the centuries, that if only its walls could talk they would reveal some incredible secrets.

Goose flesh sprang up on her arms and she shivered involuntarily. What dark secrets about Charles Devereaux did this house hold? *Was* he alive, as she believed? And if so, *why* had he faked his own death?

She shivered again and pushed these disturbing thoughts away – for the moment, at any rate. She had come here to tell Anne that she had seen Charles on American television four days ago, and that she had good reason to think he was living in Rome. But now she realized this was not the right time to broach it. She would have to wait for a more opportune moment later this evening.

Nicky sat up straighter in her chair and glanced around.

She and Anne were sitting in the drawing room; Anne was busy pouring tea, and she could not help thinking how exquisite this room was with its interplay of celadons. They made a perfect backdrop for the mellow antiques and the fine paintings, most of them English landscapes, several of them priceless masterpieces by Constable and Turner. She had always marvelled at Anne's extraordinary taste, her skill at creating decorative beauty, and the way she kept up this house, undoubtedly a gargantuan task for anyone.

Surreptitiously Nicky looked across at the fruitwood table in the centre of the room. A vase of white roses stood in the middle of it and was surrounded by a collection of family photographs in silver frames. There were several of her – alone, with her parents, with Anne and Philip in the gardens here at Pullenbrook, and of course with Charles. She swung her head to look at an end table next to the sofa near the fireplace. On this stood their engagement picture, taken by Patrick Lichfield, which was framed in gold. Her gaze was riveted on it for several seconds and then she swiftly averted her eyes, biting her inner lip nervously. But within seconds she was totally in control of herself again, and calm, a look of neutrality settling on her face, masking her real feelings.

'You're awfully quiet, Nicky darling,' Anne remarked, glancing at her as she rose and walked across the floor, bringing the cup of tea.

'Thanks,' Nicky said, accepting it from her. 'I didn't mean to be rude, sitting here like an idiot and gaping so avidly at everything, as if I'd never been here before. I was savouring the room, admiring it . . . I'd forgotten how beautiful it is . . . how beautiful the whole of Pullenbrook is, Anne.'

'You always did love this house,' Anne murmured, looking down at her, a faint smile touching her mouth. 'And in the same way I love it. At least, that is what I've believed for years now. You have a true *feeling* for Pullenbrook, and I realized this the first time you came here. I couldn't help noticing that you were . . . well, emotionally drawn to it. That's the best way for me to describe what I thought your reaction was to my home. And the house *accepted* you, *welcomed* you, Nicky.'

Anne went back to the sofa, continuing, 'It doesn't always do that, you know. It *can* reject people.' Quite suddenly she started to laugh a bit self-consciously. 'Good Lord, that does sound bizarre, doesn't it? You must think I've turned into a dotty old woman, talking in this strange way about a house.'

'No, I don't. You're making perfect sense to me. And *you*, of all people, a dotty old lady! Never. Why, Anne, you're looking fantastic.'

'Thank you for saying so.' Anne leaned over the silver tea service on the table in front of her, and confided, 'I was fifty-eight in April, but I must admit I don't feel it, not one little bit. Anyway, getting back to what I was saying, I know *you know* what I mean about the house, the way it made you feel as though you belonged in it from the very first moment.'

'And that feeling came rushing back today,' Nicky told her quietly. 'And you know something else, I happen to think of houses as *living* things. They do have atmospheres and vibrations, some good, some very bad. This place has good vibes to me.'

Anne nodded. 'We're an odd couple, you and I, Nicky. But then we've always understood each other extremely well.' Anne took a sip of tea, and a second later exclaimed, 'Oh dear, I've been so busy chattering to you about the house, I forgot to offer you a sandwich, or would you prefer sponge cake?'

'Nothing, thanks, Anne. I'm trying to watch my weight, especially after that fattening trip to France.'

'Oh gosh, yes, I know exactly what you mean,' Anne laughed.

At this moment Philip came back into the room, having been summoned to the phone a few minutes before. He said to them both, 'Sorry I took so long,' and then glanced at Anne. 'It was Timothy, darling. He's just arrived in London. He sends his love, by the way.'

Anne nodded and smiled up at him. 'I'm glad he's safely back home.'

Philip took the cup of tea Anne had just poured for him, and went and sat down on the chair next to Nicky. Turning to her, he explained, 'My son's just started working as a journalist on the *Sunday Times*, and he's been in Leipzig. There's a lot going on there, all sorts of political situations on the bubble, as I'm sure you're aware, Nicky.'

'Yes, my friend Cleeland Donovan, who you met in Les Baux, leaves for Germany tomorrow. He wants to photograph the Berlin Wall . . . while it's still standing, he says.'

Philip looked at her alertly. 'Does he think it's about to come down?'

'He's been saying it would for the past two years, but, of course, he was never certain exactly when, who *could* be certain of that? At one point he thought it would take another twenty or thirty years, perhaps even longer. But recently he's been muttering that the Wall will be dismantled imminently.'

'Has he now?' Philip put his cup and saucer on a nearby occasional table, and sat back in his chair, his attention still focused on Nicky. 'That's very interesting to know, especially since I happen to agree . . . as do a number of my colleagues, actually.' Philip shook his head, and went on with a hint of acerbity, 'However, only six months ago, East Germany's President Erich Honecker vowed that the Berlin Wall would remain standing for another hundred years. But I'm inclined to believe that that was an idle boast on his part.'

'Or merely wishful thinking,' Nicky volunteered. 'And in any case, let's hope Honecker is wrong and Clee is right.'

'I couldn't agree more,' Philip murmured, and asked, 'And is Cleeland going anywhere else in the Eastern bloc?'

'Yes, after Berlin he intends to roam around for a few days, and he wants to go to Leipzig, too. He plans to cover the demonstrations that keep erupting all over the place.'

Philip nodded. 'Those demonstrations are going to be on the increase, I think. And I have a strong suspicion we're going to see any number of Communist regimes come tumbling down this year.'

Nicky was thoughtful for a few seconds, and then she said slowly, with some deliberation, 'Only the other day I told Arch Leverson that we're going to see the tectonic plates of history shifting under our feet in the not too distant future. There's going to be a lot of movement, a lot of changes, especially in the Iron Curtain countries.'

'Very astute of you to say so, Nicky. You're right on the button,' Philip exclaimed with a hint of admiration.

Nicky smiled at him; she was pleased to get his confirmation of her opinions about world affairs. After all, Philip Rawlings was an important man with the Foreign Office.

When they had spent time together in the past, Philip and Nicky had inevitably become embroiled in political discussions, and this afternoon was no exception.

They went on chatting about the state of the world for the next ten minutes or so, until Philip finally curtailed their conversation.

Shaking his head, he said, 'Here we go again, Nicky, boring poor Anne with all this dry stuff about politics and politicians, which she couldn't care less about. Sorry, darling,' he apologized, and looked at Anne affectionately.

'But that's not true!' Anne spluttered. 'I'm not bored. You seem to have forgotten that I grew up with politics, and that my father was quite a statesman in his day.'

'I hadn't forgotten, but I do know that's not where your interests lie, not really.' Philip pushed himself up out of the chair and went to sit with Anne on the sofa. Taking hold of her hand, he said, 'And now, onto more important things . . . have you told Nicky our happy news?'

Anne said, 'I haven't had a chance yet, and in any case I thought it would be much nicer if we told her together.'

'Told me what?' Nicky looked from one to the other, filled with curiosity.

'Philip asked me to marry him today – '

'For about the twentieth time,' Philip cut in.

'And I accepted him,' Anne added, her face suddenly full of radiance.

'*Finally*,' Philip said. 'Anne has finally agreed to become my wife and she's even set the date. We're going to have a Christmas wedding here in the little church at Pullenbrook.'

'Oh Anne, Philip, this is wonderful news!' Nicky exclaimed, meaning these words, and, jumping up, she walked across the room to congratulate them.

CHAPTER TWENTY-ONE

Nicky sat in the window seat in her room, staring out across the formal gardens of Pullenbrook. But she was not really looking at them. Her gaze was turned inward.

How she wished now that she had not come down here today, that she had delayed her visit until Monday, as she had originally intended when she had set out from New York yesterday.

When she had arrived in London last night, the first thing she had done, after she had checked into her hotel, was telephone Pullenbrook. Anne had been overjoyed to hear from her, and so soon after their chance meeting in France. They had chatted for a few minutes, and then she had more or less invited herself down for the weekend, telling Anne that she was only in England for a few days and would love to see her.

Anxiety had prompted her expediency; she had a desperate need to talk to Anne. Who else was there in whom to confide her terrible suspicions about Charles?

But to her dismay she had walked into this house on a very special day in Anne

Devereaux's life. How awful it would be if she ruined it by revealing to her that her only child, the son whom she had adored, had not drowned after all, as they believed, but that he had faked his own death.

In doing so she would be branding Charles dishonourable, duplicitous, a liar and a cheat. And a savagely cruel man who had caused his mother untold suffering and grief, as well as herself, Philip, his Uncle Geoffrey, and everyone else who was close to him. Of course, he *was* all of those things, if he were alive and living under a new identity. But she couldn't drop that bombshell tonight, as she had planned.

Nicky leaned her head against the window pane, turning things over in her mind. She might not even be able to tell Anne tomorrow either; she may well have to stay over until Monday and talk to her then. It was not that she was afraid to speak out; she simply didn't want to spoil Anne's weekend. It was going to be very difficult, keeping up a relaxed front, putting on a good face for the next few days. Still, she must conceal her anxiety and impatience for Anne's sake. She was such a nice woman, so straightforward and honest, and she deserved a little happiness at this stage in her life. No, she couldn't dump this on her at the moment; she had to let her have this chance to celebrate with Philip.

For another half hour Nicky sat on the window seat, mulling everything over in her mind. But eventually she got to her feet and walked into the middle of the vast room, her eyes scanning it quickly. It was full of pale lavender tints, soft pinks and dove greys; it was a gentle, rather feminine room with pretty watercolours on the walls and painted-wood pieces that were elegant and graceful.

With her usual tact and thoughtfulness, Anne had chosen a bedroom for her which she had never occupied before, in an effort perhaps to ease the burden of unhappy memories. But every corner of Pullenbrook held memories for her . . . yet not all of them were bad. In fact, some of them were positive and happy.

The fourposter bed with its lavender silk hangings and matching eiderdown looked inviting all of a sudden, and Nicky took off her shoes and went and lay down on it. She pulled the eiderdown over her, hoping to have a nap before getting ready for dinner, but her mind continued to turn.

Not unnaturally, Nicky was thinking of the last time she had been in this house – *that* particular visit had been heartbreaking, one of the saddest times in her life, and the memories of it were very bad indeed.

October 1986. A Saturday in the middle of the month. She had arrived at Pullenbrook in the morning. She and Anne had talked for hours, and they had hardly noticed when Inez had brought the tea into the drawing room promptly at four o'clock, automatically observing that traditional British ritual. They had been far too devastated to care about the tea and it had gone untouched.

Her own pain had begun the day before when Philip had shown up in New York unexpectedly, ringing her doorbell just after ten o'clock. He had stepped off the early morning British Concorde into a waiting limousine, and had ridden into Manhattan to break the bad news to her in person, at Anne's request, rather than doing so on the telephone from London.

Philip had not wasted any time. He had told her as gently as he could that Charles was believed to be dead, that he had apparently drowned off Beachy

Head on the Sussex coast several days earlier. His pale-blue Jaguar had been found parked nearby, late on Wednesday afternoon. In it were his raincoat and a locked briefcase bearing his initials with a leather luggage tag on the handle. The name on the tag read Charles A.C. Devereaux, and, of course, the local police had known at once who to contact: his mother, Lady Anne Devereaux of Pullenbrook Manor.

When the locks of the briefcase had been prised open by the police, in front of Anne, the only item they found inside had been a letter addressed to his mother. And that letter had told them everything they needed to know – Charles Devereaux had taken his own life. There were no *ifs* or *buts* about it; everything had been spelled out quite precisely and explicitly, and he had made his intentions very clear. But there would have to be a police investigation; that was the law. However, the police had agreed to keep the matter under wraps until Charles Devereaux's fiancée in New York had been informed. Again, this had been one of Anne's requests, which the local police chief, Superintendent Willis, had said they would be willing to accede to, out of deference to her ladyship and her standing in the county.

Philip had recounted all this to her on that horrendous Friday, when her whole world had fallen apart with such abruptness and finality. She had been shattered, in shock, when she had phoned Arch at the network, and told him in a shaky voice that she had to fly to England immediately because Charles had committed suicide. By then she had been trembling so excessively, as the facts had truly begun to sink in, she had been unable to continue, had handed the phone to Philip. Carefully he had given the pertinent details to Arch, and had promised to be in touch with more news as soon as possible.

Not long after this she had thrown a few clothes into a bag, and packed her toilet articles and makeup, with the help of Gertrude, who had arrived to clean the apartment in the middle of it all. And then, just before they had set off for Kennedy Airport, Philip had attempted to reach her parents, who were staying at the Cipriani in Venice, but they had been out. Philip had left his name and the number at Pullenbrook, along with an urgent message for them to telephone Anne as soon as they could.

By one thirty she and Philip were on board the French Concorde, taking off for Paris. Philip had pointed out that this was the simplest, easiest and fastest route to London. They would be flying for just under four hours, would spend the night in Paris, and be on the first plane to London on Saturday.

She had wept for almost the entire journey across the Atlantic. Philip had done his level best to console her, although with little success. Yet, from time to time, she had had her moments of sudden calm, and during those moments they had asked each other the same question. *Why?* Why had Charles done this terrible thing? There seemed to be no valid reason to either of them, and therefore no explanation.

Upon arrival at Charles de Gaulle Airport they had taken rooms at one of the hotels, and on Saturday they had been on the seven o'clock flight to Heathrow. From there they had driven directly to Pullenbrook where Anne, still suffering from shock, and grief stricken, was waiting for them.

Later that day she had asked Anne if there had been any mention of her in

Charles's letter. Anne had shaken her head sadly. She had been stunned to hear this. *Charles had killed himself without one last word to her.* And she couldn't quite get over that.

Her parents had arrived from Venice via London on Sunday. They were full of compassion and concern for her, kind and loving, and they had both done their best to help her. But in the end it was she and Anne who had helped each other the most, had given each other the most sustenance and support.

She had stayed with Anne for several weeks, the two of them inseparable and moving between Pullenbrook and Anne's flat in Eaton Square. During this difficult and painful time for them both, things had become crystal clear. Charles had been quite deliberate in everything he had done before his suicide. Very diligently he had put all his affairs in order. His flat in Knightsbridge had been sold; the shares he held in his privately-owned wine importing company in London had been sold to his partner; his shares in the European end of the business had been bought by his Spanish partner. And, finally, he had made a new will a few weeks before his death. In it he had left everything to his mother.

Ever since then, for almost three years now, she had asked herself why he had killed himself, and she had never been able to come up with an answer. At least, not one that was acceptable.

At one point, anger had replaced her initial grief, and this had troubled her. On several occasions, when she had been in New York and not on foreign assignment, she had gone to see a psychiatrist, one who had been recommended by Arch. Her aim had been to understand the anger fulminating inside her and to come to grips with it. The psychiatrist, Dr Alvin Foxgrove, had patiently explained that most people who had been close to, or emotionally involved with, suicides inevitably experienced great anger, and that it was a perfectly normal reaction. This knowledge had helped her somewhat, especially since Dr Foxgrove had told her that the anger would go away eventually. But in her case it had not. The awful truth was that she was still angry deep down inside.

After a while, Nicky managed to pull her thoughts away from the past, and concentrated on the present. It had always bothered her that there was no body . . . but then Charles had slipped into the English Channel and been washed away to sea. Or had he?

Her plan now was to find out exactly what had happened. After she had spoken to Anne she would return to London, and from there she intended to fly to the Continent. She was going to use her skills as a journalist to solve the mystery of Charles Devereaux's death, to find out the truth about him.

701

An hour later, at about seven o'clock, having changed from her tailored safari suit into a navy silk dress, high-heeled shoes and pearls, Nicky went downstairs for drinks before dinner.

Neither Anne nor Philip were anywhere in sight when she looked inside the drawing room, but as she glanced toward the windows she spotted Anne outside. Nicky crossed the small foyer and went through the side door which led to the terrace. This ran along the back facade of the house, facing Sweetheart Hill and the South Downs.

Anne half turned, and looked over her shoulder at the sound of Nicky's step, and her face instantly lit up with pleasure. 'Ah, there you are, darling, I was just thinking about you, thinking how glad I am that you're here with us this weekend.'

'It's wonderful to see you, Anne,' Nicky responded, truly meaning what she said. Ever since running into Anne in France, she had felt guilty about the way she had neglected her, and she had planned to stop off to see her en route to Paris and Provence in September. Then when Charles Devereaux had suddenly stared out at her from the television set the other night, she had suddenly had more reason than ever to come to Pullenbrook to talk to Anne. And so she had revised her plans, moved them up by two weeks.

Clearing her throat, Nicky said slowly, and with genuine sincerity, 'I realize I've been unkind to you for the past year and a half, by not being in touch, and I'm sorry for that, Anne. I've no excuse. Of course, it's true that I've been away on foreign assignments consistently, covering some pretty lousy wars and other disasters, but I'm not going to hide behind my work. I often do that, but I won't now, not with you. The truth is, it was easier not to see you. Easier for me.'

'I know that,' Anne replied softly. 'And I understand perfectly. Seeing me, whether here or in London, or even in New York, would have only prolonged your agony about Charles. Under the circumstances, I think it was wise of you to cut me off the way you did. It enabled you to start afresh.'

'Yes, that's true. But still, it *was* selfish of me.' There was a little pause before Nicky ventured cautiously, 'How ... how did you manage to cope these past couple of years?'

'I had a great deal of support from Philip, and from my brother and his family. And the house helped me – ' Anne broke off, shook her head. 'Oh dear, here I am, talking about the house in a strange way again. What I meant, actually, is that I got involved with a project to do with the house, and that has kept me very busy. It's been quite absorbing, and I'm still working on it.'

'What kind of project?' Nicky asked curiously.

'The library. I decided to make order out of chaos, and to have the thousands of books catalogued. There are some very rare ones, including some special first editions, and naturally I had to engage a professional to help me. Anyway, in the first few months I fell upon the diaries of the Cliffords, which had been kept by the women of the family over the centuries. I'd vaguely heard about them from my grandfather, but I'd never read them. Needless to say, I became fascinated with the diaries. And at my worst moments I would suddenly pull myself up short and remind myself about those generations of Clifford women who had gone before me, who had been through so much themselves, lost so much, and so many loved ones: husbands, sons, fathers, brothers . . . daughters and mothers and sisters. Just think about it – my ancestors lived through the invasion of the Spanish Armada, the Civil War, the Great Plague, and so much else . . . ensuing wars, extraordinary changes in England, and family tragedies as well. Yet they went on stoically, and they survived. I suppose I simply refused to give in to my grief, or feel sorry for myself, out of pride. You see, the Clifford women of the past set a great example for me.'

Nicky nodded, and was about to ask her more about the diaries when Anne sighed heavily, and glanced away. A look of such intense pain crossed her face, Nicky wanted to reach out to her, put her arms around her, but she refrained.

After a moment, Anne said, 'Losing a child is a terrible thing . . . one never expects that, you know, Nicky. You always believe that you'll die first, for that really is the correct order of things . . . ' Her voice floated away on the heavy evening air, her sentence remaining unfinished. Again, she stared off into the distance, and then, almost to herself, she finally murmured, 'I have always believed that a child, that children, are the justification of life . . . that they make life worthwhile, worth living.'

Nicky found she could not speak. She felt the other woman's sudden, overwhelming sadness most acutely, and her eyes filled with tears. Swallowing hard, taking a grip on herself, she impulsively took hold of Anne's hand, held it tightly in hers, wanting to give her comfort of some sort.

Eventually, Anne turned her head and looked into Nicky's face intently. A slight smile quavered on her lips, and then was gone. She said, in the same quiet voice as before, 'I was so pleased when I saw you with another man in Les Baux, Nicky. It lifted my heart, to tell you the truth. It meant you had recovered from Charles. I hope you won't think I'm prying too much when I ask whether it's serious or not?'

Nicky hesitated only momentarily before saying, 'I'm not sure. I think it could be. Clee *has* told me he's in love with me.'

'And what about you? How do you feel?'

'I've known Clee for two years; he's my best friend, and very dear to me. But it's only in these past few weeks that we've become romantically involved, and nobody was more surprised than me when it happened. And yes, to answer your question, I think I'm falling in love with him.'

'I'm so happy to hear that. There was certainly no doubt in my mind how Clee felt about you. It was patently obvious just from the way he looked at you.' Anne squeezed her hand and then extracted it. She finished, 'Nicky, he adores you.'

'But love isn't always enough to make a relationship work as a marriage, though.

A lot of other things are tremendously important . . . if you're going to spend the rest of your life with someone.'

'That's very true,' Anne agreed. 'But you appeared to be comfortable with each other, obviously compatible, and, of course, you do share the same kind of work, so that must be quite a plus, surely.' A blonde brow was raised, and she looked at Nicky questioningly.

'It is. On the other hand, my career might present a few problems in the long run, and I – '

'There's nothing in the world that can take the place of a good man,' Anne interjected, and then she laughed quietly, as if to herself. 'Who am I to talk? I've certainly kept a good man dangling on a string for years.'

Leaning closer to Nicky, she added, 'Take my advice, don't do what I did. Instead, take the plunge. I only began to realize today that I should have married Philip years ago.' She gave Nicky a most piercing stare, and in a much stronger voice, she said, 'You must reach out for life, Nicky. Grab it with both hands. Live it to its fullest. Because before you know it, years will have slipped away, and you'll be middle-aged, and then old, and it will be too late. Far, far too late.'

'After the age of thirty time does seem to pass very quickly. I've begun to notice that recently.'

'And there's another thing,' Anne continued. 'Don't sacrifice a good relationship, one that works well, because of your career. You might end up being alone, if you do. And believe me, Nicky, loneliness is the most terrifying thing. It's another kind of death.'

Anne leaned her elbow on the balustrade and stared at the South Downs, as though ruminating.

Watching her, Nicky thought she had never seen her looking lovelier than she did this evening. She wore a deep rose-coloured silk dress that enhanced her fine English complexion, a double strand of pearls and pearl earrings. In Nicky's opinion, Anne Devereaux could easily pass for a woman in her mid-forties; aside from her beautiful blonde hair, incomparable skin, and lack of wrinkles, she had a slender figure and beautiful legs with finely-turned ankles.

Suddenly Anne straightened up and glanced at Nicky, and said a little sadly, with a rueful smile, 'Oh Nicky, I was such a stupid fool years ago. Fairly early on in my widowhood there was a man I loved, and I should have married him. He wanted me to do so, but there were certain obstacles. And so I rejected him, and, in some ways, I lived to regret it. And then about twenty years ago, when I was thirty-eight, another man came into my life. I cared for him deeply, as he did for me, but I rejected him as well, because of – . Well, never mind *why*, that's not really important. In both instances I chose to be by myself, and as a result I had some pretty dreadful years of loneliness until I met Philip.'

'Do I hear my name being taken in vain?' Philip demanded in a jocular manner as he strolled out onto the terrace.

The two women turned around to face him, and Anne said, 'Not at all, my darling. I was simply telling Nicky what a lot of lonely and unhappy years I spent before you came into my life.'

Philip seemed touched by her words, although he did not make any comment. He simply nodded, and put his arm around her waist, held her close to him.

Anne's expression was affectionate as she glanced at him and explained, 'I was talking to Nicky about Cleeland Donovan, telling her how happy I am that she's involved with him. How happy we both are.'

'And relieved,' Philip said, offering Nicky a warm smile. 'We've been worried about you, my dear.' Turning back to Anne, he went on, 'I have champagne waiting in the drawing room. Shall we go inside?'

Anne smiled, and nodded, and took hold of his arm. 'Yes, let's do that.'

Much later, after the champagne had been consumed, the three of them sat down around the circular table in the small family dining room, which Anne used for more intimate dinners.

Inez served the light supper Pilar had prepared, and between the vichyssoise, the grilled sole and the summer pudding, Philip and Anne plied Nicky with questions about her work.

Nicky talked about her sojourn in Beijing, and recounted some of the things which had happened there. They seemed particularly moved when she told them about Yoyo and Mai, Mai's death, and Yoyo's subsequent disappearance.

'Clee and I, and Arch and the crew, just hope and pray he's going to show up, and that he used the money we gave him to advantage,' Nicky confided. 'Clee thinks he'll make it to Hong Kong, and so do I.'

'That's the most likely place,' Philip remarked, nodding thoughtfully. 'And there *is* an underground operating between Beijing and Hong Kong, so I've been told. If Yoyo has *guanxi*, in other words connections, he might slip through.'

'As my father would say, from your mouth to God's ears, Philip. Yoyo's pretty smart, if anyone can get out, then he can.'

'How terribly tragic that the young woman was killed,' Anne murmured. 'From the way you tell it, Nicky, the Chinese army sounds very harsh.'

'They are brutal, murderous, cruel beyond belief. Clee has much proof of that on film. He was able to take hundreds of photographs, because they were so busy killing their own people, innocent people, they didn't have time to grab his camera. Mind you, the authorities smashed three of his other cameras in the days before the crackdown. In any case, he's created an amazing book about Tiananmen with those photographs, and I've written the introduction. It's called *Children of the Beijing Spring*, and it'll make your hair stand on end when you see it. I'll be sending you a copy when it's published next year.'

'Thank you,' Anne said.

'We watched a lot of the Kate Adie coverage of the student demonstrations on the BBC,' Philip said. 'And at the time Anne and I were utterly appalled by the brutality, the bloodbath. China has a very large black mark against it, and the world is already making its disapproval and abhorrence known. The PRC has been pretty short-sighted.'

'Yes, its violation of human rights has been, and still is, horrendous,' Nicky pointed out.

Philip nodded, and took a sip of the Pouilly Fumé. Giving Nicky a probing look, he changed the subject when he asked, 'And why are you in England, Nicky? Holiday or business?'

'A bit of both,' Nicky answered quickly, and she had to exercise the most enormous control not to blurt something out about Charles. 'I'm hoping to do an in-depth interview with the Prime Minister,' she improvised, and rushed on, 'Next year, not now. And Arch wanted me to start talking to a few people in advance. You know, sort of get the lay of the land.'

'So how can I be of assistance?' Philip asked.

'I'm not sure yet. I'll let you know later. Right now I want to formulate my ideas for the special, think about it in visual terms as well as content.' Nicky sat back, filling with relief that she had not said the wrong thing.

'Well, just give me a shout if you need my help,' Philip said. 'You know I'll do anything I can.'

'Thanks, Philip, I appreciate it. You're very kind.'

'Shall we have coffee in the drawing room?' Anne said, pushing back her chair and rising.

'Yes, of course,' Philip agreed.

Anne slipped her arm through Nicky's as they left the dining room and walked across the foyer. 'Your work is very dangerous, Nicky, and yet you're quite intrepid. At least, so it seems to me. Aren't you ever afraid, darling?'

'Not when I'm actually reporting, only afterwards,' Nicky admitted. 'That's the way it is for Clee, and a lot of other journalists as well, Anne. I guess we're so concentrated, so busy doing our jobs during the action, we don't have time for fear.'

CHAPTER TWENTY-THREE

'Anne, I'd like to talk to you about something,' Nicky said, hovering in the doorway of the library on Sunday morning. She had changed her mind after a sleepless night and wanted to talk to Anne now. She couldn't wait until Monday.

Anne stood next to a long mahogany table, picking up fallen rose petals; she lifted her head, looked across at Nicky, and with a little frown she said, 'You sound awfully serious. Is something wrong?'

'Yes, I think so,' Nicky murmured as she came into the room. 'Where's Philip? I'd like him to hear what I have to say.'

'Here I am,' Philip said from the depths of a leather wing chair positioned at the other end of the room.

Nicky heard the rustle of newspaper before his head appeared around the side of the chair. He pushed himself to his feet, folded the paper, and dropped it on the floor with the others piled up near the fender.

Anne deposited the handful of rose petals in an ashtray and walked over to join Philip, who stood in front of the fireplace. The two of them exchanged glances, then sat down together on a Chesterfield sofa; Nicky seated herself on the identical one facing them.

Anne and Philip both focused their attention on her, their expressions expectant, and Anne said, 'You look strange, Nicky. What is it?'

'Before I tell you, I'd like to explain something,' Nicky began. 'After we ran into each other in Provence, I decided I wanted to come and see you – to make amends really – and I'd planned to do so at the end of August, on my way to join Clee in Paris. Then the other night, in New York, something happened that caused me to change my plans. I decided to come a couple of weeks earlier, because I needed to talk to you urgently, Anne. And to you, Philip.'

'Please tell us what this is all about,' Anne said.

Nicky took a deep breath, and plunged in. 'Four days ago, on Wednesday night, I was at home in my apartment watching the world nightly news on television. Our Rome correspondent was reporting a shooting incident at a political rally outside Rome – '

'I read about that in Thursday's *Daily Telegraph*,' Philip cut in. 'There was a suggestion that it might have been an assassination attempt . . . by a member of the opposition party. Isn't that so?'

'Yes, that's correct,' Nicky answered. 'But to continue, as Tony Johnson, our man in Rome, was finishing his report, the camera moved away from him, and panned around the immediate area. It picked up a face in the crowd.' Nicky leaned forward, clasping her hands together, and finished quietly but intensely, '*It was Charles. The face in the crowd was Charles's face.*'

Startled, Anne drew back, gaping at Nicky. She was aghast, so stunned she was unable to speak.

Philip exclaimed, 'How could it possibly be Charles, Nicky? Charles will have been dead for three years in October. We know he drowned off Beachy Head.'

'But did he?' Nicky gave Philip a probing stare. 'There never was a body, and that has always troubled me, frankly.' To her surprise, her voice had sounded perfectly steady, and she continued calmly, 'I don't blame you for being disbelieving, I was myself when I saw his face staring out at me from the television set. Nevertheless, I know it – '

'If you believe Charles is alive, then you must think he faked his own death,' Anne interrupted, her voice rising, her sudden agitation showing. 'Why would my son do such a thing?'

Nicky said, 'I don't know, Anne.'

'And how would he have done it?' Anne demanded with a penetrating look.

'I've kind of figured that out . . . it would have been quite easy for him.'

'It would?' Philip said, eyeing her with some curiosity. 'Tell us how.'

'Charles could have had an accomplice,' Nicky said, returning Philip's direct gaze. 'Someone who helped him to rig his death, then disappear afterward. That person, whether a man or a woman, could have done one of two things: either he or she followed Charles to Beachy Head; Charles parked the Jaguar where it would be easy to find, and then his accomplice drove him back to London. From there, Charles would have had no problem leaving immediately for Europe, whether by plane or train, using a forged passport,' Nicky pointed out. 'Alternatively, the accomplice could have been waiting in a boat just off the coast, near Beachy Head. Charles could quite easily have swum out to the boat, been picked up and ferried across the English Channel to a French port.'

'This sounds a bit far-fetched to me!' Philip exclaimed. 'As Anne just said, why on earth would Charles do such a thing?'

Nicky shook her head, then lifted her shoulders in a small shrug. 'I've racked my brains, and I can't really come up with a good reason.' She hesitated fractionally, and volunteered, 'Well, that's not strictly true. I have thought of one.'

'What is it?' Anne leaned forward alertly, her eyes riveted on Nicky.

'That he wanted to start a new life,' Nicky said.

'That's ridiculous!' Anne cried heatedly. 'He was in love with you, about to marry you, and to all intents and purposes Charles was a happy man, with everything to look forward to.'

'What you say is true,' Nicky acknowledged, 'but only on the surface.' It was her turn to give Anne a long, knowing look, then she said pointedly, after the briefest pause, 'Because whether Charles killed himself, *or* did a disappearing act, he wasn't happy with his life. If he had been, he wouldn't have done *either* thing. Therefore, we must assume that he was discontented with everything in his life, including me.'

Anne looked as if she was about to say something, and then obviously had second thoughts. She pursed her lips, sat staring at Nicky in silence, twisting her hands in her lap nervously.

'Nicky does have a point there, darling.' Philip turned to Anne, took her hands in his. 'In fact, we agreed three years ago that Charles must have been excessively troubled and unhappy, even temporarily deranged perhaps, for him to take his own life.' Now Philip glanced across at Nicky, and announced, in a very firm voice, '*Which is what I believe he did*. You know, my dear, it's often been said that we each have a double, someone who looks exactly like us, living somewhere in the world. Isn't it just possible you saw a man on television who resembled Charles very closely, but that's all?'

'Philip is right,' Anne interjected. 'He really is, Nicky darling. My son committed suicide whilst the balance of his mind was disturbed . . . about something.'

'I wish I could truly believe that.'

'You really *must*, for your own good,' Anne told her, and leaned forward again. Choosing her words carefully, she went on, 'It's a well known fact that young women who are widowed frequently feel guilty when they become involved with another man. Even though you weren't married to Charles, you were about to be. Perhaps you feel guilty about Clee, and in believing Charles is now alive you're giving yourself a reason to break off with Clee. Isn't that a –'

'No, Anne! It's nothing like that!' Nicky shot back fiercely. 'First of all, I don't feel guilty about my relationship with Clee. Not at all. Secondly, it is *not* wishful thinking on my part – believing that I've seen Charles alive on television. I know what I saw. Or rather, who I saw.'

'People who do disappearing acts, and assume new identities, have to be awfully devious by nature,' Anne retorted. 'My son wasn't like that. Nor would Charles be cruel to me, or to you . . . why, he loved us both.'

Nicky fumbled with the flap of her handbag and brought out an envelope. 'On Wednesday night I was as stunned as you and Philip are now, Anne. But once I'd recovered my equilibrium, I raced down to my network, where I had one of the studio technicians rerun the Rome segment of the nightly world news.

He froze the frame with Charles in it. In other words, he stopped the film at that juncture, so that I could study the man's face for a few minutes. Which I did, and very intently, I might add. And I took a photograph with my Polaroid. Then the technician also took a picture for me with his own camera, which he developed that night and gave to me the following morning. In the meantime, I went back home to my apartment, and I compared my Polaroid shot of the man in the network's film with a photograph of Charles.' Nicky opened the envelope and took out several photographs.

Handing one of them to Anne, she explained, 'This is my Polaroid of the man who was on television. As you can see, he has darker hair than Charles, and a moustache.' She immediately passed a second photograph to Anne, continuing, 'And this is Charles in the south of France the year of his ... death, or disappearance. What I did was darken his hair and give him a moustache, like the man on television. Look at the two pictures closely, Anne. I'm convinced they are one and the same man.'

'Oh, I don't know,' Philip said somewhat dismissively, glancing up at Nicky, after looking at the photographs Anne was holding in her hands. 'Rather flimsy evidence, wouldn't you say?'

Anne was silent. She sat studying the pictures, her face thoughtful.

Nicky said, 'Here is the other photograph, which the studio technician took for me. It's much larger than my Polaroid, and a bit clearer. Surely the man in Rome is Charles – Charles with a slightly altered appearance. Look at it closely. There's no denying it, Anne.'

'There *is* a resemblance,' Anne admitted quietly, 'but I'm still not convinced it's Charles. How could it be?'

'Why are you telling us this, Nicky? What do you want us to do about it?' Philip asked, sounding slightly put out, even irritated, all of a sudden.

'I'm not sure,' Nicky confessed. 'But I had nobody else to talk to except you and Anne. And after all, the two of you knew Charles best.'

'I'm very concerned for you, my dear,' Philip murmured, shaking his head sadly. 'And I'm sure Anne is, too.'

'I am,' Anne agreed.

Philip went on, 'It's obvious to me that this whole incident has truly upset you. Certainly you still seem to think that Charles is alive. I wish you wouldn't persist in this belief, Nicky, you're only going to make yourself ill if you do. Once and for all, let me say that *I* do not believe that Charles Devereaux is alive. And *you* don't, do you, Anne darling?'

'Absolutely not. Look here, Nicky,' Anne said, adopting a loving tone, 'Charles cannot be anything else but dead. Please take my word for it. I'm his mother ... I'd know instinctively, deep down within myself, if he were alive. You mustn't let Charles haunt you in this way, darling. Please put him to rest again, for your own sake. And for Clee's. You have a new life to lead with him. Charles is the past. Let him *be* the past.'

Nicky looked from Anne to Philip, and she saw their sympathetic expressions, the anxiety reflected in their eyes. It suddenly dawned on her that they thought she was off-the-wall. Therefore, there was nothing else she could say to them about Charles.

A long sigh trickled out of her. 'I brought the photographs to you because I thought you would see what I see . . . I suppose I was looking for corroboration, and neither of you can give me that. I guess I understand . . . sort of . . . '

Anne rose and went and sat next to Nicky on the sofa. She took hold of Nicky's hand, and her expression was a mixture of love and genuine concern. After a little while, Anne said slowly, in a very gentle voice, 'Let's examine the character of the man for a minute. Charles was the kindest, most thoughtful person, and very loving. You know this from your own experience of him, without me having to tell you. And he had such immense integrity. Good Lord, honour was his by-word. Everyone who knew Charles said his word was his bond. He was a true gentleman in the best and most noble sense of that word, and he never did a shoddy thing in his life. That would have been quite alien to his nature.'

Anne paused, and her light-blue eyes filled with tears as she remembered her son, the qualities he had had, and all the things he had stood for. 'Charles was such a good man, Nicky, a decent man, and he didn't have a bad bone in his body. He certainly wasn't duplicitous, and he couldn't have dissembled if his life had depended on it. I bore him, brought him up, and I knew my son exceedingly well, especially as a single parent.' Her voice began to tremble with emotion, as she went on, '*Nothing, no one*, will ever be able to persuade me that Charles contrived his disappearance. Very simply, I *know* he didn't. He couldn't have, not the Charles Devereaux who was my son.' Anne swallowed hard, blinked back her incipient tears, and took a hold of herself.

'Oh Anne, the last thing I wanted was to cause you pain, please believe that,' Nicky said with dismay, aware of Anne's increasing distress. 'But I *had* to come and tell you. I suppose you think I'm crazy . . . '

'No, I don't,' Anne replied in a shaky voice. 'And I know Philip doesn't.'

'Of course I don't!' Philip exclaimed, smiling at Nicky. 'But I don't think Charles is alive either. The whole idea is quite far-fetched, Nicky, as I said before. Preposterous, in fact.'

'But people have disappeared, and they have often done so most successfully,' Nicky pointed out, still unable to let go. 'There was Lord Lucan for instance, whose body has never been found. For all we know, Lucan could be alive and well and living *somewhere* in the world. South America. Bora Bora. Darkest Africa. Under a new identity, of course.'

'I doubt it.' Philip shook his head vehemently. 'I'm positive Lucan is dead – that he drowned, as was generally believed at the time of his disappearance.'

'What about that British Member of Parliament – John Stonehouse? *He* did a very clever disappearing act in the seventies,' Nicky was quick to add.

'Ah, but he was eventually found,' Philip countered swiftly.

Anne said in a voice reverberating with sorrow, 'Nicky, it is *not* Charles in these photographs. Truly, it isn't. My son is dead.'

CHAPTER TWENTY-FOUR

Nicky went for a walk through the grounds of Pullenbrook on Sunday afternoon.

Earlier, she and Anne and Philip had struggled through lunch, the three of them carefully avoiding the subject of Charles. Only Philip had seemed interested in eating. She and Anne had picked at their food, and she had been glad to escape after the pudding, politely refusing coffee and then excusing herself.

She had felt the need to be alone. Now that she was outside in the sunlight she breathed a little easier, and she tried to shake off the tension that had held her in its grip for the past few hours.

Unexpectedly, the past tugged at her, enticed her, drew her toward the rose garden, and she swung around and began to walk in that direction. When she arrived at the ancient wooden door set between the mellow stone walls, she reached for the wrought-iron handle, turned it, and pushed open the door. Six stone steps led down into the garden, and when she got to the bottom she stood marvelling at the loveliness of the scene spread out before her.

There were a number of gardens at Pullenbrook, but to Nicky this was the most beautiful of them all. Enclosed by high, grey stone walls, the sunken rose garden was large but most effectively laid out, with different sections devoted to individual species of roses and plants and flowers.

Nicky knew from Anne that its intricate design dated back to the eighteenth century, including the parterres, those ornamental areas where flower beds and paths formed a distinctive pattern. There was a small green lawn in the centre of the garden, and this was bordered by shrub roses; the parterres were laid out on all four sides of the lawn, beyond the shrubs.

Rambling and climbing roses clad the ancient walls with a melange of pinks, bleeding from palest blush to brightest crimson. Under the walls grew hybrid tea roses and floribunda, including cool white Iceberg roses which Anne had surrounded with lavender. Beds of other old-fashioned plants were set in the parterres, as well as such herbs as hyssop, savory, thyme and rosemary, mingling with pinks, pansies, violas and cistus. The idea of combining herbs in amongst the roses and other flowers was very much in the manner of the Tudor and Stuart gardens of the past, at least this was what Anne had told her once.

But quite aside from its beauty and fragrance, the rose garden held a very special meaning for Nicky. She had first met Charles here, and later it was in the garden that she had realized she was in love with him. Also, he had chosen to propose to her as they had strolled along its paths one evening.

Now Nicky moved forward, breathing in the sweet and heady scent of the roses, and she was almost overcome by it today. Automatically she headed for the old wooden garden seat which stood in a bosky corner under the walls, shaded by a sycamore tree. Sitting down and leaning back, she closed her eyes, and allowed herself to drift with her thoughts. But after only a short while she opened her eyes and looked up.

The sky was blameless, without a cloud, that perfect blue Charles had always called the colour of speedwells, and which he had said exactly matched her eyes. The scent of the roses was more intoxicating than ever, and somewhere nearby a bee buzzed and hummed as it danced on the balmy air. It had been on such a day as this that she had first encountered Charles Devereaux.

Innumerable memories assailed her. Four years fell away. It was suddenly that Friday afternoon in June of 1985 when Charles had entered her life. She closed her eyes once more, reliving that day all over again, remembering . . . remembering . . .

A perfect rose, Nicky thought. The most perfect rose I've seen in a long time. It was large, a pale pearly yellow, and it had opened fully, but was not yet overblown and fragile, ready to fall. She leaned forward, touched a velvet petal of the rose lightly with a fingertip, and breathed in its lovely scent.

It was then that she heard the crunch of footsteps on the path and swung her head. A man was strolling toward her, a youngish man, obviously in his thirties. As he drew closer, she saw that he was not much taller than she, about five foot eight in height, and slender and compact of build. He was fair of colouring, although when he came to a stop she noticed how tanned he was, and his light brown hair had been streaked blond by the sun. He was good looking in a lean and hungry way, with high cheekbones, sharply chiselled, somewhat gaunt features and a thin, aristocratic nose.

'You're Andrew's daughter,' he said, staring at her with intensity, not even bothering to conceal his immense curiosity and interest in her.

Thrusting out her hand, she nodded. 'Nicky Wells.'

'Charles Devereaux,' he responded as he grasped her hand in a firm grip.

Nicky found herself looking into a pair of appraising green eyes, the clearest green eyes she had ever seen. The two of them continued to stare at each other, their hands still clasped. Nicky was experiencing an overwhelming and spontaneous attraction to him. His sensitive face and his looks in general were very appealing to her, and at once she wanted to know him better.

His scrutiny was intense, the way he looked at her even a bit suggestive, and she knew that he was as taken with her as she was with him. Her face grew warm at the thought of him, and she felt the colour rising from her neck to suffuse her face.

'You're blushing, Miss Wells. Are you not accustomed to having a man look at you with undisguised admiration?'

Nicky gaped at him, feeling suddenly tongue-tied and at a loss. He was certainly direct, and not in the least impeded by social conventions. He got straight to the point. Very brash, especially for an Englishman, and an aristocrat at that, she thought and smiled inwardly. She rather liked his directness; it was refreshing, if a little unnerving. And she found his upper-class English voice a joy to listen to. It was beautiful, mellifluous, the voice of a Shakespearean actor, full of colour and cadences and rhythms. Richard Burton, she thought. He sounds like Richard Burton.

Charles said, 'You're very silent . . . oh dear, I'm afraid I've embarrassed you, Miss Wells.'

712

'No you haven't and call me Nicky.'

'I will. And please, do excuse my bad manners. But you are very beautiful, you know. Undoubtedly the most beautiful woman I've ever met.'

'Beware of a suave Englishman paying lavish compliments.' Leaning back, she eyed him carefully, with a certain amusement.

'I meant what I said. Look here, will you have dinner with me on Monday evening? In London. Just the two of us. I want to be alone with you, Nicky, get to know you better.'

'Yes, I'll have dinner with you, I'd love it,' Nicky found herself saying.

'Excellent. We'll have an intimate dinner in a quiet little restaurant. Leave it to me, I know the ideal spot. Are you staying at Claridge's with your parents?'

'Yes.'

'I'll pick you up at seven o'clock. Please be prompt. I can't bear to be kept waiting by women. And dress casually. The place where we'll be dining is not very fancy.'

'Are you always this dictatorial, Mr Devereaux?'

'Call me Charles and no, I'm not. I do apologize. I didn't intend to sound so insufferable.'

'You didn't, not really.'

'I have a confession to make.'

'Oh. So soon in our relationship?' Nicky quipped, and raised her blonde brows.

Charles chuckled. 'Ah, a sense of humour, I see, as well as a perfect face. Almost too good to be true.' He chuckled again, and told her in that mellifluous voice of his, 'A week ago today I went to fetch your parents from the hotel, to drive them down here for the weekend. In their suite I saw a photograph of you.' He took a deep breath, and finished with some deliberation, 'I was utterly bowled over by you.'

Nicky made no comment.

Charles went on, 'Your mother caught me studying your photograph, and she told me all about you.' He paused and there was a very direct look in his green eyes when he added, 'I'm afraid I haven't been able to get you out of my mind since then. You've haunted me.'

'This is the best line I've heard in a long time,' Nicky said, her tone teasing.

Charles had the good grace to laugh. 'But I really mean what I say. When I arrived at the house fifteen minutes ago, the first thing I did was ask my mother where you were. And when she told me, I came straight out here to find you.'

'Charles,' Nicky began and stopped abruptly. It struck her that he was in earnest, that he was being quite serious, and she murmured, 'I honestly don't know what to say, how to respond to you. You're so outspoken, so blunt, even a bit aggressive. You knock the breath right out of me.'

'And you take my breath away.'

Very gently, Nicky extricated her hand and glanced down at it. He had held it so tightly there were red marks on her skin and it felt sore.

Charles followed her gaze, and apologized. 'I'm so sorry! Sometimes I don't know my own strength. My grip can be far too strong.' As he finished speaking, he gently caught her hand in his, brought it to his mouth, brushed his lips across it.

Nicky thought she was going to jump out of her skin. His touch was like an electric shock. Swiftly, she pulled her hand out of his and glanced away, conscious of those cool green eyes watching her so intently, so alertly.

713

There was a silence.

Then Charles asked, 'And tell me, what on earth were you doing, lingering out here?'

'Looking at the roses.' Nicky turned to him, and striving to sound normal, said, 'In particular, I was studying this one. It's the most perfect rose of all.' She touched the yellow bloom, looked at him, and said, 'Isn't it?'

Charles glanced at the rose, and then at her and exclaimed, 'Your eyes are the exact colour of speedwells.'

'What are they?'

'Little flowers of the brightest blue.'

Suddenly taking firm hold of her elbow, Charles steered Nicky towards the wooden door at the other end of the garden. 'I think we'd better go in for tea. That's the safest thing for us to do right now.'

Charles stayed close by her side for the next hour or so, only disappearing for about ten minutes towards the end of tea, which was being served in the drawing room. Nicky was acutely conscious of his eyes on her for most of this time. So were her mother and Anne, who kept exchanging knowing and delighted glances. Her father was too busy talking to Philip about Margaret Thatcher and the British political scene to notice anything. The two older men sat off to one side of the room by themselves, and were so deeply engrossed in each other and their conversation they were oblivious.

Later, when she went upstairs to dress for dinner, the first thing Nicky noticed when she entered her room was the yellow rose she had admired in the garden. It was in a crystal bud vase on her bedside table. Propped next to it was an envelope with her name on it. The note inside was written in a neat precise hand. It said, very simply: I didn't mean to embarrass or offend you. Think kindly of me. C.D.

She dropped the note on the bed, picked up the vase and pressed her face into the centre of the rose breathing deeply of its scent. She felt overwhelmed by Charles Devereaux. He's going to be my undoing, she thought and sighed, knowing she was incapable of doing anything about that now. It was already too late. She had fallen for him in the space of a few hours, captivated by his looks, his voice, his charisma and even his somewhat domineering manner. He had charm and panache and the most extraordinary nerve. He is unique, she decided, as she dressed for the evening. I've never met anyone like him.

A little while later, when she ran into him in the foyer outside the drawing room, she thanked him for the rose. He said, with a slight smile, 'Perfection deserves perfection,' and for the rest of the evening he hovered over her so solicitously, so constantly, that even her father became aware of his attentions to her. He even remarked about it to her privately, when they went up to bed. As her mother hurried along the corridor to their bedroom, her father lingered outside hers, and finally followed her inside. 'I don't want you to think I'm interfering, Nicky,' he said quietly, putting his hand on her shoulder affectionately. 'But I've known Charles for several years, and he's quite the man about town. And used to getting his own way with women.'

'I can well imagine that, Daddy,' Nicky said, looking into a pair of eyes as blue as her own, noticing immediately their worried expression. 'Hey, Dad, relax! I can take care of myself!' She laughed, and kissed him lightly on the cheek. 'I'm a pretty tough journalist, remember, and the independent, feisty, capable woman you brought me up to be.'

Andrew Wells nodded. 'I know that your mother and I instilled the best and bravest instincts in you, angel face. And I know you can look after yourself. You've been facing danger for years in your work. But this is not your work, and Charles Devereaux is a special breed of man. He's Eton, Oxford, and the British Establishment, very much the aristocrat with an august lineage and an impeccable background. Don't forget, his grandfather was a peer of the realm, his uncle is the present earl, and his mother has a title in her own right.'

'I'm not quite sure I know what you're getting at, Dad.'

'The British aristocracy is a world unto itself, very snobbish, and inbred. And closed to most.'

Nicky burst out laughing. 'I can't believe I'm hearing you say this, Andrew Wells! Are you suggesting that I may be viewed as "not suitable", quote unquote for Charles Devereaux, because I'm an American?'

Andrew laughed with her. 'Not really. As far as I'm concerned, you're good enough for anyone, my dearest girl. And probably far too good for most men.'

'Spoken like a true, devoted, adoring dad.'

'I'm simply trying to say that he comes from a different world than you. And I merely want to caution you, and to explain that Philip once told me Charles was a bit of a playboy, that's all.'

'I can handle myself, Pops, honestly I can.'

'I know. Just watch your step.'

'And keep my eyes peeled. That's what you used to say when I was little. Watch your step and keep your eyes peeled, Nick. And that's what I always did, and I've never forgotten any of your instructions, Daddy,' she finished with a small grin.

Andrew hugged her to him. 'You're the best, Nick. The very best there is, and the apple of my eye. I just don't want you to get hurt unnecessarily. Now, good night, darling.'

Nicky and Charles spent the entire day together on Saturday; they got to know each other better as he drove her around Pullenbrook estate in his Land Rover. She soon discovered he was well-read, knowledgeable, informed about world politics, extremely intelligent and erudite. And she found herself liking him as a person, quite aside from being attracted to him as a man.

Anne gave a dinner party on Saturday night, and invited several local couples, and it was a pleasant evening. Once again, Charles was assiduous in his attentions to her, and scarcely seemed to notice his mother's guests or anyone else except her. And she was equally engrossed in him, although she played it a little cooler than he, conscious of her father's beady eyes on her for a good part of the evening.

By the time she went to bed she was euphoric, floating, and, after she had undressed, she sat on the window seat dreamily gazing out at the moonlit grounds. Her thoughts were only of Charles. There was a sudden, light tapping on the door, and she went to open it, not in the least surprised to see Charles standing there. Without a word he came into the room quickly, closed the door behind him and leaned against it.

'Forgive the intrusion at this late hour,' he said. 'But I couldn't sleep. I had to come and see you, if only for a moment.'

He took a step forward, reached for her hand, and pulled her towards him. 'I had the most pressing and desperate need to . . . kiss you goodnight.' He gazed at her closely, and smiled a quiet little smile. Without another word he leaned into her, kissed her fully on the mouth. Her arms went around his neck, and immediately he drew her even closer, held her tightly. After a moment he loosened his hold, and said against her hair, 'I want to make love to you, Nicky. Let me stay with you tonight . . . don't send me away.'

She was silent.

He kissed her again, more passionately than before; she could not help responding, and swayed against him, clung to him.

'Oh, my darling,' he said, and brushed his mouth against her cheek. 'Please let me stay.'

'But I hardly know you,' she began, and then let her voice trail off uncertainly. She was unnerved by him, and afraid. Charles Devereaux was having a potent effect on her. He was lethal, and she suddenly understood that she could quite easily be devastated by him.

Charles took her face in his hands and looked deeply into her eyes. His voice was tender when he murmured, 'Oh Nicky, Nicky, don't let's play games with each other. We're both adults, we're mature, intelligent people.' Again the faint smile played around his mouth, and he added, 'And do you honestly think you'll know me any better on Monday? What difference does it make whether we make love tonight or wait until then?' He brought his mouth to hers, kissed her long and hard and then released her, left her standing in the middle of the floor.

He went to the door and locked it. As he walked back to her, he took off his silk dressing gown and threw it on a chair, and began to unbutton his pyjama top. When he came to a stop in front of her, he said in his low-pitched, seductive voice, 'You know you want me as much as I want you, Nicky. It's written all over your face.' Very sure of himself and entirely in command, he took hold of her hand and led her towards the fourposter bed.

Nicky sat up on the garden seat, blinked in the bright sunlight, and reached into her pocket for her sun glasses. As she put them on she felt dampness on her cheeks, and she realized, with a little jolt, that she had been crying. But she was not going to cry any more tears for Charles Devereaux. She had used them up years ago.

Pushing herself to her feet, she walked down the path between the parterres, trying to shake off the past, to quench the memories. Climbing the steps, she turned the wrought-iron handle of the old door and went out, leaving the sunken rose garden behind.

Pullenbrook soon hove into view. She could not help thinking how extraordinary it looked, bathed as it was in the late afternoon light. The sunshine brought a warmth to its old grey stone, and the many windows glittered and winked; it was like a living thing to her. Anne had spoken the truth when they had discussed the house the other day; she *had* loved Pullenbrook from the moment she had first set eyes on it.

On that fateful Friday I've just been remembering, she thought, gazing up at the great Tudor edifice so steeped in English history, and the history of the Cliffords. That was the day I was snared by a man, by a woman, and by a stately family home. Yes, she had fallen in love with them all. Instantly. She still loved Anne and the house. As for Charles, her love for him had died three years ago.

Inside the house, the Great Hall was eerily quiet and filled with pale sunshine when she entered a few minutes later. The family portraits that hung on the fireplace wall caught her eye, and she walked over to them, stood staring up at them thoughtfully. Then she moved on, scrutinizing the others as she traversed the length of the huge room.

Suddenly, she thought: Charles Adrian Clifford Devereaux was descended from a great line of noblemen, magnates and warrior knights in service to the Crown of England. He *was* a true aristocrat, and in the *best* sense of that word. Honour and nobility were bred in the bone; justice and fair play were inculcated from birth. He *was* a good man, a decent man. I could not have loved him the way I did, had he been otherwise. Certainly I could not have loved a man capable of shoddy behaviour, a man who could cold-bloodedly fake his own death for reasons of his own, a man who could callously bring pain and heartache to me, the woman he loved, and to his mother. I would never have planned to marry a man like that. Never. Never.

The sound of footsteps caused Nicky to swing around.

Anne was walking towards her, and there was a look of concern on her face. She took hold of Nicky's arm. 'Are you all right, darling?'

Nicky nodded and gave her a half smile.

'You rushed off, you were in such a hurry to escape, I've been worried about you. I hope you're not angry with me, or with Philip?'

'Of course not, just the opposite.' Nicky cleared her throat, before continuing, 'I've been thinking about Charles, remembering things this afternoon, and I've come to a conclusion. You're right, Anne, I don't think he faked his death. Very simply, he wasn't capable of being devious. I recognize that now. I agree with you and Philip that the man my network filmed in Rome merely bears a likeness to Charles.'

Anne appeared startled, but quickly recovering herself she said, 'This is quite a *volte-face* . . . you're not just agreeing with us to make *me* feel better, are you?'

'No, I'm not. Surely you know me better than that. I'm my parents' daughter and a stickler for the truth, just as they are. Not only in my work but in my private life. In all things, in fact.'

Anne began to walk towards the door leading to the private quarters of the house without answering. Nicky caught up with her, and slipped her arm through Anne's. She said, 'I'm sorry if I've upset you, truly, truly sorry. It was never my intention to cause you pain by coming here . . . with my story and the photographs.'

'I know that, and you did the only thing you could, under the circumstances.'

'I hadn't meant to blurt it out today,' Nicky explained, shaking her head. 'I really hadn't. I was going to tell you tomorrow, because I didn't want to spoil your engagement. But I was so terribly worried this morning, and unfortunately the words came out before I could stop them.'

'No harm has been done, and I'm glad you had the confidence to come to me . . . ' Anne smiled. Her face was full of love and warmth. 'At least it's brought you back into my life, Nicky.'

'Yes, that's true.'

Now Anne said softly, 'I feel absolutely certain Charles committed suicide. *Why* he did we will never know. He had everything to live for. Over these past few years

I've come to believe that he must have been ill. Physically ill, I mean, with some sort of fatal disease – cancer, a brain tumour, leukaemia, something dreadful like that, which he never told us about, of course. I think he took his life in order to save us the pain of his eventual suffering and death from that fatal disease. To me, this is the only possible explanation.'

'Charles's death will always be a mystery,' Nicky murmured, almost to herself.

After Nicky had gone upstairs to rest before supper, Anne returned to the Great Hall, where she locked and bolted the front door. Retracing her steps across the hall, she hurried through into her own wing of the house.

Earlier, she and Philip had had tea in the drawing room, and she had left him there when she had gone in search of Nicky. Glancing through the open door she now saw that he was no longer sitting there.

Perhaps he's also gone to his room to rest, she thought, and headed down the corridor. She was making for the library, wanting to rescue the magazine sections of the Sunday newspapers before Inez scooped them up and threw them out.

The door was ajar, and faintly she heard Philip's voice. He was obviously speaking on the telephone, and she increased her pace, anxious to tell him about Nicky's unexpected about-face.

Pushing open the door, she saw that Philip sat on the edge of the desk with his back to her. Before she could announce herself, she heard him say, ' . . . and won't let go. Like a dog with a bone . . . ' There was a short pause as he listened, and then he exclaimed, 'No, no! *Rome.*'

Anne went into the room, exclaiming, as she did, 'Philip, I've something to tell you.'

Startled, he swung around, and she knew from the expression on his face that she had caught him unawares.

He gave her a little nod of acknowledgement, and said into the receiver, 'Look I've got to go now. I'll talk to you tomorrow; better still, I'll see you tomorrow,' then he hastily hung up.

Anne walked over to the desk, her clear blue eyes full of questions. She frowned slightly. 'You were obviously talking about Nicky, Philip. Who were you speaking to?'

'My son. I was speaking to Timothy, my dear,' Philip said with a smile, without missing a beat.

'About Nicky?' Anne sounded incredulous.

'Yes. When I was on the phone with Tim the other evening, just after he'd returned from Leipzig, I sort of half promised I'd go back to town tonight. To have supper with him. I just begged off. He wanted to know why I wasn't coming up, and I was simply explaining about Nicky, and her weird story about the man in Rome.'

'Why did you beg off? You didn't have to, you know. You could have gone up, I wouldn't have minded.'

'Darling, don't you see? I didn't want to leave you alone this evening,' Philip said. 'You've been somewhat upset by all this . . . fuss. I felt I ought to be here with you, *wanted* to be with you. I can see Tim tomorrow.'

'I see,' she murmured, and gave him an odd look.

CHAPTER TWENTY-FIVE

On Monday night Nicky caught the last flight to Rome.

Once the plane was airborne and she was well settled in her seat, she took out her notebook and scanned the notes she had made in her suite at Claridge's Hotel, earlier in the day.

After a couple of seconds of studying them, she slipped the notebook back into her handbag, then reached for the glass of white wine which the flight attendant had brought to her a short while before. She took a few sips, trying to relax, but her mind continued to turn as rapidly as it had for the last few days.

Despite her discussion with Anne and Philip at Pullenbrook this past weekend, and their opinions, her gut instinct told her that the man accidentally captured on the ATN news footage was no one else but Charles Devereaux. And because her father had always said she should rely on her gut instinct, this was exactly what she was doing now.

Putting her wine glass down on the flat section of the armrest, she reached into her bag again. This time she pulled out the photograph taken from the news footage by Dave, the studio technician. She gazed at it intently, as she had done quite frequently since last Wednesday, frowning to herself. However many times she tried to convince herself she was wrong, she always came back to her first conclusion: the man *was* Charles Devereaux.

Yesterday, at Pullenbrook, she had begun to waver in this belief, no doubt influenced by the house and the history it represented, by the prestige of the family and, not unnaturally, by Anne Devereaux herself. If Anne said that the man in the picture was definitely not her son, then who was to argue otherwise with her? And so on Sunday afternoon she had done that sudden and unexpected *volte-face*, had agreed with Anne, somewhat to her own surprise, as well as the other woman's.

But then this morning, when she had arrived back at Claridge's, she had come back to her original opinion.

I suppose there's nothing quite like the cold light of a drizzly Monday morning in London to bring one to one's senses, Nicky now thought, putting the picture away. Anne and Philip had said that the man in Rome merely had a *look* of Charles. She could not agree; the resemblance was much stronger than that. If the man in the picture was not Charles after all, then he was his identical twin.

This morning at the hotel in London, as she had sat ruminating on everything that had happened, she had asked herself how his partner would react if she showed *him* the photograph. Christopher Neald and Charles had been friends for years, as well as being in business together, and they had always been exceptionally close — since their twenties, in fact.

On the spur of the moment, she had picked up the phone and called Chris at Vintage Wines, only to be informed by his new secretary, Michael Cronin, that he was away on holiday. She had pressed for more information, had been told that Mr Neald was 'island hopping in Polynesia,' and was therefore quite unreachable, and would not be back in England until the middle of September. Disappointed, she had said she would phone again next month before hanging up.

It was then that she had decided to go to the source of the film footage – the ATN Bureau in Rome. Maybe Tony Johnson, the Rome bureau chief, could help her in some way; perhaps there was additional footage, which had not been transmitted by satellite to New York, footage which might give her some leads.

In any case, here she was on a plane en route to Rome, and she could not help wondering if she was on a wild goose chase. How did you go about finding a man who had so cleverly and effectively disappeared three years ago? A man who obviously did not want to be found, and whose presence in Rome was only known to her *now* because of a fluke, an accident, chance, fate, call it what you will. If the ATN cameraman covering the story with Tony that night hadn't picked up a face in the crowd on film, and if she hadn't been watching the news intently at that *precise* moment, she would have been none the wiser. A million to one chance, she thought, remembering how that face was on and off the screen in a flash, in a matter of seconds. How easily she could have missed it if she had gone to the kitchen for a glass of water, or if she had been on the phone and not paying strict attention. But then life was like that . . . full of flukes and coincidences. It was meant to be, she said under her breath, and shivered involuntarily. But looking for Charles Devereaux would be like looking for a needle in a haystack.

Nicky shifted in her seat, glanced out of the window at the dark night sky, and wondered why she was continuing to pursue this matter, why she was persisting with it? Naturally, she came up with the answer immediately: given who and what she was as a person, as well as a journalist, she simply *had* to know the *truth*, needed to know it. That trait had been nurtured in her since childhood. Also, there was another thing . . . she wanted finally to *close* that chapter of her life which had once been centred around Charles Devereaux. It was not that she harboured any emotional feelings for him; those had been well and truly killed off long ago. But she certainly had no desire whatsoever to be haunted by the spectre of him.

After all there was Cleeland Donovan now, a very special man, one who had grown more and more important to her in the last couple of months. Clee represented a new beginning for her. There was the most wonderful chance to make a life with him, if they could work it out, given all the logistics involved. Lately she had come to believe that they probably could, with a little give and take on both sides.

Clee was the future. Her future. Therefore, she must not permit any shadows from the past to hang over her or them. The fact was, she wanted and needed to be truly free in her heart and mind and soul . . . to be free for Clee, with no encumbrances from the past.

As often happened these days, her thoughts now settled on him, and as always she felt a lovely warmth spreading through her. Having Clee in her life, knowing he loved her, made her feel good, even when he wasn't with her. Fortunately, she had managed to reach him at the Kempinski in West Berlin late this afternoon, before setting out for the airport. She had wanted to tell him she was off to Rome on business for a few days.

Because of the nature of their work, he had not been unduly surprised, nor had he found it unusual that she was suddenly flying off somewhere.

'What's cooking, Cookie?' he had asked, laughing, and had then added, 'I guess you've just had a brainstorm, Nick, dreamed up some sort of exotic special.'

Quickly, concisely, she had explained that it was not one bit exotic, that she was considering doing a piece on the European Common Market, and the changes which would take place when all the frontiers came down. 'Later I'll have to interview politicians in every country, but right now I want to poke around, get a feeling for things in Rome, since I've done that in London,' she had said.

He had understood; they had gone on to chat about his impending trip to Leipzig, and arranged to stay in touch by phone, or through the Image office in Paris, if necessary. And they had agreed they would still meet in Paris in a week's time, as they had originally planned to do.

'*Ciao*, babe,' Clee had said. 'I can't wait to see you on the twenty-eighth.' And she had answered, 'Neither can I, darling,' before breaking the connection.

I wish Clee were here with me, Nicky thought, closing her eyes, feeling unexpectedly drowsy and blaming the wine. She missed him very much, more than she had ever missed anybody. It suddenly struck her that he might be rather annoyed with her, if he knew the reason why she was *really* going to Rome, and she sat up with a start at the prospect of incurring his anger. Then she asked herself whether she *would* tell him when she saw him. She wasn't sure. But by next Monday she was bound to have all the answers about Charles Devereaux. Or none at all, perhaps. The decision about confiding in Clee would be made then, and not before. And she would only tell him in person, not on the telephone.

Two and a half hours after the flight had left Heathrow it was landing at Rome's Fiumicino Airport exactly on time. When Nicky had cleared customs, she went through into the terminal, and within the space of a few minutes she spotted the limousine driver holding up a card with her name printed on it.

Forty-five minutes later the car was pulling up outside the Hassler Hotel on the Trinita dei Monti atop the famous and very beautiful Spanish Steps. Her parents had first brought her here as a child, and whenever she came to Rome she invariably stayed at the Hassler. The night manager recognized both her name and her face, and, after she had registered, he escorted her to her suite, chatting amiably and being as helpful as he could.

Once she was alone, Nicky went to the windows, parted the curtains and looked out. The view of Rome was spectacular, a sea of flickering lights under a star-strewn inky sky. Was Charles Devereaux living somewhere out there in the Eternal City? And if so, what were her chances of finding him? With a little stab of dismay, she had to admit that the odds were against her.

The following morning, as soon as she had had her simple breakfast of tea and toast, Nicky telephoned the ATN Bureau. After asking for Tony she sat back, waiting.

The woman who had answered had not bothered to ask her name, and she had

721

not given it. When the bureau chief came in he said, 'Tony Johnson here. Who is this?'

'It's Nick, Tony. How're you doing?'

There was a startled silence, and then he exclaimed, 'Nicky Wells? Is this *that* Nick?'

'Of course it is! What other woman do you know called Nick?'

Tony chuckled, obviously delighted to hear her voice. 'Hey, Nicky, how are you? And more importantly, *where* are you?'

'Around the corner.'

'You mean *here*? In *Rome*?'

'I most certainly do.'

'Good God! The entire network seems to be descending on me today.'

'What do you mean?'

'A friend of yours just arrived, Nicky. Now he's trying to grab the phone from me, itching to talk to you, it seems. But before I pass it over, let's make a date. For lunch. *Today*. Is that okay?'

'More than okay, it's wonderful, Tony. But who wants to speak to me?'

Again Tony's deep chuckle echoed down the wire. He said, '*Ciao*, Nick.'

'Hi, Nicky, what the hell are you doing in Rome?' Arch Leverson asked, his tone jocular but curious.

'I could ask the same of you, Arch,' she said, completely taken aback, but keeping a cool head as usual.

'You're slipping, honey. Or rather, your memory is. I told you last week that I was going on vacation to Capri. I just stopped off here for a couple of days, to break the journey and see my old buddy Tony.'

It was true, Arch *had* told her, but somehow she had not associated Capri with Rome. Anyway, she had been so preoccupied last week. Now she said swiftly, 'Yes, you're right, I did forget.'

'Last I heard from you, Nicky, you were off to London to investigate the possibilities of doing a special on Margaret Thatcher. So why *are* you in Rome?'

'To buy shoes,' she said, improvising, not knowing how to answer him at this moment.

Arch guffawed. 'Hey, come on, it's me you're talking to, kid! You're about as much into shopping as I'm into fly fishing. Come on, Nicky, what gives?'

'I can't go into it now,' she answered, wanting to buy time. She would come up with a suitable story later.

Her answer seemed to satisfy Arch, who now said, 'Fine, fine. Is Clee with you?'

'No, he's not. He's in Berlin today, Leipzig tomorrow, Paris on Sunday night. I'm meeting him there on Monday, and we're going down to Provence some time next week.'

'That's great, Nick, and I guess I'll be seeing you for lunch with Tony. Right?'

'It's the best offer I've had all day. Where shall we meet? At the bureau?'

'Good idea. Where are you staying, by the way?'

'At the Hassler, as usual. And you?'

'The Eden. Listen, Nicky, I've got another offer for you. Dinner tonight. I'm

722

leaving for Capri very early tomorrow morning, to join Patricia and the Grants at the villa they've rented for the season. Hey, wait a minute, here's a thought. Come with me. You don't really have anything better to do, do you? And they'd love to have you for a couple of days.'

'Thanks, but I can't, honestly. However, I will have dinner with you tonight.'

'It's a date. Now, why don't you plan on picking us up at the bureau around one thirty?'

'You've got a deal.'

CHAPTER TWENTY-SIX

After she had hung up, Nicky sat staring at the telephone for a few minutes, a frown lingering on her face.

Arch Leverson was the last person she had expected to find at the Rome bureau, and she had been taken aback to say the least, although she had quickly recouped. Well aware that Arch did not believe her story, she nonetheless had no idea what she *would* say to him when she saw him later. She would have to think of something, since she did not want to tell him the truth. He worried and fussed about her far too much at times, and instinctively she knew he would try to dissuade her from her purpose. When she had left for London, she had been able to fob him off with a few words about the Margaret Thatcher special; she doubted he would buy the story she had told Clee about being in Rome to do research for a possible Common Market piece.

She sighed under her breath. Unfortunately, because Arch was at the ATN bureau with Tony, she could not go over there this morning and start asking leading questions about the news footage transmitted last Wednesday. The questions would have to wait until Arch left for Capri; there was no alternative but to talk to Tony tomorrow.

In the meantime, she now had nothing to do until she met Arch and Tony for lunch, and she felt a sudden surge of frustration, loathing the thought of having to kill time until then.

Rome was a most familiar place to her; she had visited it so many times in the past, and, in any case, she was hardly in the mood to go sightseeing. Besides which, she had done that years ago, and had had the best guide there was – Andrew Wells.

Her father loved Rome in much the same way she loved Paris – he felt a spiritual affinity for it – and so as a child she had seen the Eternal City through his eyes. 'Rome is the cradle of civilization,' he had told her when she was twelve, old enough to understand one of his history lessons as they had tramped around the city. He had taken her down the Spanish Steps below their hotel, to the Trevi Fountain, the catacombs, the Borghese Gardens, St Peter's Church, Vatican City and the Sistine Chapel. There was not much she had been allowed to miss as a child; her father had seen to that on their different visits over the years.

Sometimes, when she returned to places she knew well, she enjoyed visiting old haunts that held a special meaning for her, but not today, not on this trip. The mystery surrounding Charles Devereaux filled her mind, as it had for the past five days, and she recognized this was the way it would be until she arrived at the truth.

Once again letting out a sigh of frustration, Nicky went through into the bathroom to take a shower, deciding as she did that she would buy some shoes after all. Why not turn the white lie into a verity? Her mother had a favourite boutique on the Via Veneto, and she would stop by there before heading over to the ATN bureau.

As it turned out, Arch did not ask any questions when she arrived at the bureau at one thirty, carrying a shopping bag of shoes. He merely glanced at it and winked at her.

Tony was as tanned and handsome as ever, and his usual exuberant, affectionate self. After hugging and kissing her, he introduced her to his new secretary, Jennifer Allen, and other members of the staff she had not met before. Then she, Arch and Tony retreated to the latter's private office to chat and catch up.

Nicky and Tony were old friends from the early days, when she had started at the network and he had been based in New York. Tony and Arch dated back even further than that, to the time they had both been in their first jobs at another network.

'It's like old home week,' Tony said as the three of them trooped out of the office and went around the corner to lunch at Tony's favourite trattoria. 'The best in Rome,' he explained as he ushered them inside. Over drinks they continued to catch up with each other's news, and lunch was a wonderful, breezy affair, full of warmth and camaraderie, plenty of laughter, joking around, shop talk, and industry gossip.

Much to her relief, Nicky found herself relaxing completely with Tony and Arch. She felt at home with the two men; they were colleagues, and were all on the same wave length, and she enjoyed every minute of being with them. So much so, she actually forgot about the Devereaux problem for a short while. For the first time in several days she was like her old self.

But thoughts of Charles came rushing back to trouble her soon enough. The minute she was alone in her suite at the Hassler, in fact. And that evening, as she was getting ready for dinner, she made a decision. She was going to confide in Arch after all. She needed a sounding board, someone to whom she could unburden herself, and someone who would bring both an open and an analytical mind to the discussion.

'Well, aren't you the beauty,' Arch said as he strolled into her suite in the Hassler at a few minutes past eight.

'Thank you,' she said and gave him a faint smile.

After kissing her on the cheek, Arch stepped back and nodded approvingly as he regarded the cream silk suit she was wearing. 'Now *that* little number is the epitome of elegance,' he said, and nodded again.

'Pauline Trigère made it for me.'

Arch glanced down at her feet, appeared to be studying her high-heeled cream silk pumps, before saying, in an amused tone, 'And tell me, Nicky, did Miss Trigère also make your shoes?'

Nicky had to laugh. 'No, she didn't. I bought them this morning. On the Via Veneto.'

'Pretty expensive shoes, I guess, when you take into consideration the price of the air ticket from London to Rome.'

'You know very well I didn't come to buy shoes,' she shot back. 'Although shoes I did indeed buy. I'll tell you why I came here in a minute. Now, would you like a glass of white wine? I ordered a bottle, just in case. But if you don't, I can easily order something else from room service.'

'Thanks, the wine'll be great.'

'Why don't you sit down over there, and I'll bring you a glass,' Nicky said, walking over to the console near the window. She poured wine into two crystal goblets and carried them back.

Arch, who had remained standing, touched his glass to hers silently, took a sip, and finally seated himself on the sofa.

Nicky took the chair opposite him, and after a quick swallow of wine, she put the goblet on the table and leaned against the cream brocade of the chair back.

Arch said, 'So, why *are* you in Rome, Nick?' His eyes held a probing expression.

Nicky did not at first respond. After taking a deep breath, she said, 'I think Charles Devereaux is alive and well and living in Rome. That's why.'

Arch sat up on the sofa with a jerk, almost spilling his wine as he did. He was so thunderstruck his jaw dropped. He was speechless. Eventually, he said, 'I know you wouldn't say that unless you had some real evidence. What is it? What've you got? *Shoot*.'

'Last Wednesday night I saw Charles Devereaux on television,' Nicky began, and then slowly, precisely, leaving nothing out, she told him everything that had happened since then.

When she had finished, Arch muttered, 'I tend to agree with Philip Rawlings. It's just not enough for me, Nick, I'd – '

'Let me show you the pictures,' she interrupted, getting to her feet, hurrying into the bedroom, and returning with the photographs. Seating herself next to Arch, she leaned forward and spread them out on the coffee table.

Pointing to one of them, she said, 'This is my Polaroid of the man in the news footage.' Moving on to the next, she continued, 'And this is the larger photograph which Dave took. The third is the one of Charles, which I doctored up. I darkened the hair and added the moustache.'

Arch studied all three photographs very carefully. 'There's a strong likeness, a very strong likeness, in fact. Yes, I think you're right, Nicky. These three pictures could be of one and the same man.' He turned to her and finished, 'The guy on our news footage could very easily be Charles Devereaux, no doubt about it.'

Relieved to hear him say this, Nicky exclaimed, 'Thank God you agree with me, that you don't think I should be in a padded cell!'

Arch said, 'Who, *you*? Never, honey, you're one of the sanest people I know.'

'Thanks, Arch.' She touched his arm lightly, affectionately. 'I appreciate you saying that. I began to feel a bit peculiar at Pullenbrook this weekend.'

Bringing his hand up to his face, Arch rubbed his chin, looking thoughtful. 'Answer me this, Nicky. Why would Charles want to fake his own death, and disappear?'

'I've no idea.'

'Usually people only do that if they're in some kind of trouble. You know, financial trouble, for instance.'

'Charles didn't have money problems. I know that from his will. Anyway, people do disappear for other reasons.'

'Such as?'

'If they've done something criminal, if they are criminals.'

Arch exclaimed, 'Jesus Christ! You're not suggesting Charles was a crook, are you?'

She shrugged. 'I don't know whether I am or not . . . but I am giving you reasons why people melt into thin air and start a new life . . . such as murderers, drug traffickers, arms smugglers, big-time swindlers . . . and the like.' Nicky rose, and walked over to the window, where she stood looking out. Eventually she turned around and gave Arch a long stare, and said, 'How well does anyone know another person? Truly *know*, I mean. There are secret parts to all of us, parts we don't always know well ourselves.'

'Yes,' Arch murmured and lifted his glass to his mouth, at a loss for words.

Nicky said, 'Maybe he was homosexual. Maybe he wanted to escape me and our marriage.'

Arch gaped at her. 'Only you have the answer to that!' he exclaimed, and asked, 'Was he?'

'No.'

'That was a very weak *no*, honey.'

She was silent as she slowly walked back to the chair, where she sat down. 'It *was* a weak no, that's true, but it didn't mean anything, I wasn't implying anything. You know as well as I do that there are men who have often hidden their homosexuality even from *themselves* for years, and then they suddenly come out . . . that's all I meant, when I brought up homosexuality. And if you're asking me if Charles showed any homosexual tendencies in our sex life, the answer to that is a categoric *no*.'

'Still, he could have been . . . in the closet?' Arch lifted a brow questioningly.

'Anybody can be anything, I suppose, but I'm absolutely certain Charles was straight.'

'I have to agree with you. I didn't know Charles well, but he struck me as being a pretty tough sort of guy. Maybe a bit ruthless. He wasn't the sort to vanish without a trace just because he was afraid to break off his engagement. He'd have done that no matter what the reason, Nicky, if he'd wanted to do it. If he did disappear, it was for a reason that had nothing to do with you.'

'I came to that conclusion myself. *Finally*.'

'I'm stumped,' Arch muttered.

'What do you mean?'

'*Why?* Why would a man like Charles drop off the face of the earth?'

'Don't you think I've asked myself a thousand times since last Wednesday?' She shrugged wearily. 'I just don't know.'

'Perhaps it *wasn't* him on our news footage.'

'Arch!'

'Well, what do you want me to say, for God's sake! It seems to me Charles Devereaux had no possible reason to walk away from his life. Therefore, he must have committed suicide.'

'I don't believe he's dead,' Nicky said quietly but with vehemence, focusing on Arch intently. 'Not here, not inside.' She paused, pressed her hand against her stomach. 'My gut instinct tells me that he's alive, and that he dropped out of sight for a very, very serious reason. A reason so *bizarre* that you and I couldn't possibly imagine what it is. And that's why I haven't been able to come up with an answer. Why no one else has.'

Arch looked at her alertly but made no comment.

Nicky now spoke slowly, to give even greater emphasis to her words. 'We're lacking some *information*, Arch. There's something about Charles that we don't know, and that's why we're at a loss. He vanished for a reason that's not *apparent*, that's not in the least obvious. Not to us, anyway. And believe me, it's no ordinary, everyday reason.'

'Do you mean he had, *has*, some sort of secret?'

'Yes, maybe. But whatever it is, neither his mother nor Philip have an inkling of it, and I certainly don't.'

'Hell, Nick, I don't know what to say . . . ' Arch shook his head, and lifted his shoulders helplessly.

Bending forward, her eyes levelled on him earnestly, Nicky said, 'Listen, Arch, Charles came to Rome, to Continental Europe. He didn't go to Australia or Africa or . . . Polynesia. So obviously he wanted, or needed, to be in Europe, had to stay here.'

'There's another point. If he *is* alive, what's this dude using for money? How's he living?'

'He could have been stashing money away in Europe for years. He did a lot of business in France and Spain – wine business – and even here in Italy from time to time,' Nicky explained. 'He probably had a Swiss bank account. In fact, that's more than likely. Yes, I'm certain he did. You never knew this, but Charles was always something of a financial genius, even when very young. Of course he inherited money, but aside from that he made his own fortune, and in a variety of different ways. Stocks and bonds, real estate, to mention only a few things. And he turned his wine importing company into a real gold mine. Money and its management and manipulation were never problems to him.'

'He left everything to his mother, didn't he?'

'Everything that was visible, and in England. How do I know what he got out over the years? Or the deals he made in Europe?' She nodded, as if confirming something to herself. 'Charles would have no problem living, and living pretty damned well, Arch.'

'I guess you're right. Do you think Charles had, and still has, a secret life?'

'Again, I don't know ... but the indications are there, aren't they? A man doesn't do what he did without a truly compelling motive.'

Taking another tack, Arch asked, 'When you came to Rome what was your plan, Nicky? I mean how did you aim to find him?'

'I didn't really have a plan, Arch. I just decided to come to the source of the film. I was going to talk to Tony about the footage, show him those pictures.' She gestured to the photographs on the coffee table. 'I intended to ask Tony if he'd ever seen that man knocking around Rome, and if he had, and knew his haunts, I was going to go and look for him. If Charles *is* living here, he's obviously doing so quite openly, quite freely. The reason he was captured on film is because he was *outside* in the square with the crowds that night ... not hiding away somewhere.'

'Yes, that's true. On the other hand, you've so little to go on, honey. It'd be like looking for a needle in a haystack.'

'I said that to myself only the other day.'

'Does Clee know that you're here?'

'Yes, of course.'

'Did you tell him *why*?'

'No. When I spoke to him on the phone, I said I was here on business.'

'I don't think Clee would be too happy if he knew you were roaming around looking for Charles Devereaux. I think he'd be pretty damned mad. After all, you two seem to be very heavily involved.'

'Yes, we are. But that doesn't mean he runs my life, or that I have to ask his permission about anything,' Nicky said in a firm voice. 'I'm a very independent woman. Nobody tells me what to do, or when or how to do it. I'm my own person. That's the way I was brought up, as you well know. So Clee doesn't come into play. What I'm doing in Rome is my business, Arch, and only mine.'

'All I meant is that Clee wouldn't relish the thought of you investigating Charles's disappearance.' Arch gave her a long, very direct look. 'Hasn't it ever occurred to you that it might be dangerous? Charles Devereaux doesn't *want* to be found, honey. I'll bet my bottom dollar on that. You could be opening a real can of worms.'

She nodded. 'Maybe.'

'Tell me something. What are you going to do if you do find him, Nick? Take him to task for running out on you? Chastise him and walk away? Or turn him in to the authorities?'

Nicky's mouth tightened but she said nothing.

'Are you still in love with Charles Devereaux?' he asked, deciding to confront her with this possibility. 'Is that why you're hellbent on tracking him down?'

'No, it isn't. I'm not in love with him. I haven't been for a long time.'

'Then why *are* you doing this?'

'Because I have to get to the truth, Arch, to know what really happened. And why. I'm a reporter, remember, and training will out, as they say. Besides, I want to close the chapter on Charles Devereaux, and get on with my life ... with Clee.'

'Close it now, Nick. Stop this. It's a waste of time, in my opinion.'

Nicky stared across at Arch. There had been anxiety in his voice and she saw at once how serious he was. He was worrying about her again, as she had guessed

728

he would. 'Perhaps I should do as you say,' she murmured, wanting to pacify him, to put his mind at rest. 'I suppose it would be wise to let it drop. There's only the remotest chance that I might find Charles. And as you said, even if I did, what then?' She sighed lightly. 'You're right, Arch, as you so often are.'

He smiled at her, and a look of immense relief flooded his face. 'Go to Paris, Nick. Promise me you'll go to Paris tomorrow.'

'Yes, I will,' Nicky said, and reached for her glass of wine. What did one more white lie matter in the scheme of things?

'Let's go and sit in Tony's office, it's more comfortable there,' Jennifer Allen said, ushering Nicky into her boss's inner sanctum. 'Can I get you anything, Miss Wells? A cup of coffee, perhaps?'

'Nothing, thanks, Jennifer, and please call me Nicky.'

The young woman smiled at her. 'Thanks, I will.'

'So Tony won't be back until late this afternoon?' Nicky said, lowering herself onto the low-slung Italian leather sofa.

'He said about five or six o'clock,' Jennifer answered, taking a chair next to Nicky. 'He went to Vatican City, and after the meeting there he has a lunch. And after that he's got to go to the dentist.'

Nicky pursed her lips and nodded, wishing now that she had spoken to Tony on the phone earlier.

'Can I be of help in any way?' Jennifer asked, impressed by Nicky and wanting to please one of the superstars of the network.

'No, not really. I'd hoped to speak to Tony about a piece of news footage that was transmitted from here last Wednesday, a week ago today, in fact.'

'Oh, the segment on the shooting incident at the political rally,' Jennifer exclaimed. 'That's the footage you're referring to, isn't it?'

'Yes, I was wondering if all of it was sent, or whether there might be some spare footage left over?'

Jennifer shook her head. 'No, there isn't, Nicky. We passed everything to New York.'

'I see.'

'Are you sure I can't be of help? You look worried.'

Nicky forced a laugh. 'I'm not. Only curious, actually. And maybe you can help after all.' As she spoke, Nicky opened her handbag and took out the three photographs; she handed only two of them to Jennifer. 'The man in these pictures was caught on that news footage, just a face in the crowd. I had the frame frozen at the network and these pictures taken of him, because – '

'Why? Is he important or something?' Jennifer cut in.

'In a way, but only to me, Jennifer. About a year ago, in New York, I was working on a piece. This man was one of the key figures involved,' Nicky said in a cool voice, having worked out a suitable story in advance. 'Then he disappeared, and I've not been able to pull the special together without him. I've been wanting to contact him ever since. To interview him. Seemingly he's living in Rome. I thought Tony might know him, that he might be a local character, one who mixes with the international crowd. I was hoping Tony might suggest a few places I could look for him. Bars, restaurants.'

Jennifer had listened carefully, and now she glanced down at the photographs she was holding. She shook her head after a few seconds, and handed them back. 'No, I don't think I've ever seen him around. But – ' She paused, looking thoughtful, then shook her head. 'No, I don't know him.'

'But *what*?' Nicky pressed. 'You were about to say something.'

'I thought, for a minute, that he looked slightly familiar, but no . . . No, I can't place him.'

Putting the photographs back in her handbag, Nicky smiled at her and said, 'A pity. Well, never mind.'

The two of them walked through into the outer office, and Nicky headed for the door, realizing there was no point hanging around the Rome bureau. 'Tell Tony I'll call him later, and thanks, Jennifer.'

'Sorry I couldn't be of more help. Bye, Nicky.'

Nicky went down the corridor to the elevator, pressed the button and stood waiting. The elevator arrived, and she was about to step inside when she heard her name being called. Turning, she saw Jennifer rushing down the corridor towards her.

'I'm glad I caught you!' Tony's secretary cried as she came to a halt. 'I've just realized why that man's face seemed a bit familiar to me. Could I look at the photographs once again please, Nicky?'

'Yes, of course,' Nicky said, her heart skipping a beat as she opened her purse and took out the pictures.

Jennifer peered at the larger one which Dave had taken, and nodded her head. 'I'm pretty sure this guy was on the same plane as me last Thursday.'

'A plane to where?' Nicky asked.

'Athens. I went there for the weekend. This guy was standing next to me at the carousel, waiting for the baggage. He helped me get my bag off.' She passed the pictures back to Nicky.

'Are you sure it was the same man?' Nicky's voice was suddenly lower, very quiet.

'Yes. He was very polite. Gentlemanly. And he had a beautiful voice.'

Nicky looked at her swiftly and, hardly daring to breathe, asked, 'What nationality was he, Jennifer?'

'English. He was an Englishman.'

CHAPTER TWENTY-SEVEN

That afternoon Nicky flew from Rome to Athens.

The flight time was only an hour and a half, and around five o'clock the plane landed at Ellinikon Airport. As soon as she had cleared customs, Nicky found a porter to help her with her luggage, and within minutes they were standing outside in the suffocating heat, waiting in line for a taxi.

The drive into Athens did not take long, just half an hour, but by the time she arrived at the Hotel Grande Bretagne in Syntagma Square Nicky felt like a wet rag. The cab had not been very well air-conditioned, and August was the hottest month in Greece.

Her suite overlooked the Acropolis, and it was large and roomy. To her immense relief, the air-conditioning was turned on at full blast when she walked in, and she soon felt cooler. After taking a few clothes out of her hanging bag, Nicky showered, redid her makeup, brushed her hair and then dressed in a pair of white cotton pants, a pale-blue cotton shirt and flat white sandals. Her aim was to be as cool and comfortable as possible. Slinging her white leather handbag over her shoulder, she left the suite and took the elevator down to the lobby.

Walking over to the reception desk, she leaned against the polished wood and smiled at the two dark-suited young men standing behind it. They both returned her smile, flashing two sets of perfect teeth which looked very white in their tanned Mediterranean faces.

'I'm Nicky Wells of the American Television Network in New York,' she said, focusing on the smaller of the two young men, who was closest to her.

'Yes, miss, I know. I am Costa Theopopoulos, and this is my colleague, Aristotle Gavros. How may we be of assistance?' he asked politely.

Nicky gave a little nod of acknowledgement, and said, 'I'm trying to locate someone, a friend, and I'm not sure whether he's staying here or not.' Opening her bag she took out the photograph of Charles which had been taken by the studio technician, since this was the best one. She showed it to the young man.

After studying it for a few seconds, Costa looked her right in the eye and shook his head. 'I've never seen this gentleman before.' Glancing at his colleague, he asked, 'Have you, Aristotle?' and handed him the photograph.

Whilst the other desk clerk eyed the picture, Costa said, 'What is this man's name, miss?'

'Charles Devereaux,' Nicky replied. However, knowing full well that Charles would not be using his own name, she added, 'But Mr Devereaux frequently travels incognito, and so he may well be registered under a different name ... that's the reason I showed you the photograph of him.'

'Oh,' Costa said and stared at her in the oddest way. 'Why would he do such a thing?'

Nicky had her story ready, and she said pleasantly, 'Mr Devereaux is a famous writer. Very, very famous, actually, and he seeks anonymity much of the time. Hence the various names he hides behind.'

'And what would *they* be?' Costa asked.

'*Smith* is one of them. *Charles Smith*,' Nicky invented. 'Another one is *Charles Dixon.*'

Costa had been writing the names down on a pad as she spoke, and lifting his head he said, 'I will look at the register,' and then he stepped away.

731

The other desk clerk, Aristotle, came to her and handed her the photograph. 'I have seen this man,' he said quietly, 'or someone like him.'

Nicky gave him a swift glance, and exclaimed, 'So I was right! I *was* fairly certain my friend would be staying here.'

Aristotle shook his head. 'I bumped into a man who looked like this when he was entering GB Corner last Saturday. I do not believe he was a guest in the hotel.'

'What's GB Corner?' Nicky asked.

'It is a restaurant for light meals and snacks to the right, off the hotel lobby,' he explained.

At this moment Costa walked over to them. He said, 'None of the names you gave me are listed in our hotel register, miss. I am sorry.'

'Thanks anyway. Aristotle says he saw my friend going into GB Corner last Saturday. They bumped into each other. Did *you* happen to see him, by any chance?'

Costa said, 'I was not here. It was my day off.'

Nicky shrugged her shoulders lightly. 'I see. Well, anyway, I do have another question – regarding hotels. Aside from this one and the Hilton, what are the names of the other big hotels in Athens?'

'There aren't any,' Aristotle said, suddenly taking charge as Costa sidled away. 'There are many small hotels of course, but – ' It was his turn to give a shrug. 'I doubt this gentleman would stay in any of them. But there are some beautiful hotels out at Vouliagmeni. You could try those.'

'Where is Vouliagmeni?'

'Oh, not so far away. Only about forty-five minutes by car,' Aristotle told her.

'Perhaps you could arrange a car and driver for me, for tomorrow,' Nicky said. 'I think I'd better go out there.'

'What time would you like to leave?'

'Mid morning, I think.'

'That is wise, miss. It will not be too hot then.' Aristotle smiled, pulled a note pad towards him and began writing.

Nicky leaned against the desk and plied him with questions about Vouliagmeni.

So engrossed was she in her discussion with Aristotle she did not notice Costa. He had retreated to the small office behind the front desk, and was busy dialling a number, looking almost furtive as he did. After a brief moment of waiting, he muttered rapidly into the receiver. His expression was anxious, and as he spoke he did not take his eyes off Nicky.

Aristotle handed her the piece of paper. 'This is the name of my brother-in-law, miss. He is a good driver. Careful. He speaks English. I will arrange for him to be here at ten o'clock tomorrow.'

'Thank you very much, you've been most helpful.'

He leaned closer and murmured, 'His price is fair, and much less than some of the other drivers would charge.'

She smiled at Aristotle, then looked around for Costa, spotted him on the phone in the office and raised her hand in a half wave. 'Thank Costa for me,' she said to Aristotle.

'I will, miss.'

Next, Nicky found her way to GB Corner opening off the lobby, and went inside. She spoke to one of the waiters before showing him the picture. The waiter shook his head, but went off with the photograph, quite obviously trying to be of help. This he passed around amongst the other waiters. When he returned to Nicky a few minutes later he said in a most regretful voice, 'Cannot help, miss. We have not seen this man. If he was here on Saturday no one noticed him. No one. Sorry.'

She took a cab to the Hilton Hotel and went through the same routine all over again, asking questions of the three clerks at the reception desk, and the cashier, and showing them the picture of Charles.

It was exactly the same story once more. No one had seen this man, and none of the names she mentioned showed up on the hotel register. Of course not. She had not expected them to be there. Asking the desk clerks to check was just a ploy, one she hoped would help to give her story the absolute ring of truth. It would seem odd, to say the least, to be looking for a friend if you didn't know his name. And the men on desk duty always asked his name.

As she left the Athens Hilton, Nicky's sense of frustration was now so enormous she almost went back to her hotel in disgust, and then she suddenly changed her mind and took a cab to Plaka.

This was the oldest part of Athens, full of quaint little streets, shops, bars, restaurants and cafés. She strolled through the narrow streets for an hour or so, alertly looking around, keeping her eyes peeled as her father had taught her to do when she was a child. She knew only too well that life was full of strange coincidences and flukes; there was always the odd chance she might just spot Charles sitting outside at one of the open-air cafés or restaurants.

Plaka was crowded, jammed with tourists, as it usually was in August, and Nicky soon grew weary of being pushed and jostled; also, it was unbearably hot tonight. And so in the end she gave up her search. Deep down, she was beginning to admit to herself that it was futile, a waste of time, looking for Charles in the streets like this. Finally, she took a cab back to the Hotel Grande Bretagne, deciding she might as well be in comfort, if nothing else.

Once she had cooled off in her air-conditioned suite, she went to the phone, dialled room service and ordered grilled fish, fresh fruit and a bottle of carbonated water for dinner. Then she strolled over to the window, where she parted the curtains and stood looking out at the Acropolis on the hill.

This evening the Parthenon was dramatically illuminated, as it usually was in summer, and the ancient ruins looked extremely impressive, even heartstopping, incredibly beautiful thrown into relief as they were against the darkening night sky.

She suddenly realized that a performance of Light and Sound was in progress right at this very moment. The lights were constantly changing as a story of ancient Greece was being narrated to the audience seated on the hill opposite the Acropolis. For a moment Nicky was transported back in time; she remembered attending such a performance with her mother and father years ago, and it was something she had found very moving and touching. It had held her in its grip, so that she had never really forgotten it.

Her knowledge of Greece was limited to what her father, that inveterate traveller, had told her. These were mostly things about Greek mythology; she had also garnered some knowledge from the wonderfully vivid novels of Mary Renault. She had read her last book, *Fire from Heaven*, in 1969, at the age of sixteen, and had been unable to put it down. This had been another of the writer's classical novels about ancient Greece, and she wished, all of a sudden, that she had one of the Renault books with her right now. She suspected it was more than likely that she would have another sleepless night.

The driver's name was Panayotis. He was a cheerful young man with a deferential manner, a fairly decent command of English, and a brilliant smile that seemed to be permanently pasted on his face.

He picked her up at the hotel promptly at ten o'clock the following morning, and she was delighted to see the relatively new-looking Mercedes, even more delighted to discover it had an efficient air-conditioning system. It was already steaming hot in the streets, and the cool interior of the car was welcome.

'Aristotle tell me you want to go out to Vouliagmeni, to see the Astir Palace Hotels,' Panayotis said as he pulled out of Syntagma Square.

'Yes, I do. He said there were three altogether.'

'It is . . . how do you say . . . a complex. Yes. There are the hotels, bungalows. Very nice place. Very beautiful. Forty-five minutes we get there. Okay? You comfortable, miss?'

'I'm fine, thank you.' Nicky leaned back against the soft leather and placed her handbag on the seat next to her.

'You like music, miss?' Panayotis asked, half glancing over his shoulder. 'You like I put on radio?'

'Why not,' she said, not really caring either way. Turning her head, she looked out of the window, and asked herself if she had been foolish to come to Athens. Yesterday had been a genuine waste of her time, and although Aristotle had said he had recognized Charles, had seen him going into the snack restaurant, what did that mean in the long run? Athens was a big city, just as Rome was, and, if she were honest with herself, she had to acknowledge that she really had very little chance of finding Charles, even if he *were* here.

Perhaps she should have done what Arch had suggested and gone to Paris. Instead, she had been determinedly stubborn, hellbent on doing her own thing, following her own instincts. So she had rushed here just because of Jennifer Allen's story. But for what? And what was her ultimate goal if she found Charles? She wasn't too sure about anything anymore, and she sighed heavily. Seemingly she was unable to let go of the idea that Charles Devereaux was alive. At least, she wasn't ready to just yet. I'm like a terrier with a bone, worrying it to death, she thought, and sighed again.

As they approached Vouliagmeni, Nicky realized that it was a resort area. There was a marina with yachts; a long, curving road led up to the top of high cliffs where the hotels were located at intervals. The area was actually a large and rather beautifully laid-out compound, with the three hotels built at varying levels on the sides of the cliffs. The bungalows were situated to one side of the hotel

734

which stood on the lowest level; there were various restaurants, a tennis court, swimming pools and beaches.

The setting was quite extraordinary, breathtaking really, perched high above the Mediterranean. Homer's wine-dark sea, Nicky thought, glancing out of the car window. This morning it was intensely, brilliantly blue, glittering like a sheet of glass under the golden sun, and the reflection it threw off was almost blinding. She blinked rapidly and averted her eyes.

Panayotis finally brought the Mercedes to a standstill in front of the hotel which was located on the highest point of the cliffs.

'I wait over there,' he said through his huge smile, and took a piece of paper out of his trouser pocket. 'From my brother-in-law, Aristotle. Ask for this man.'

'Thank you,' Nicky said, looking down at the piece of paper she was holding. It was a short note from Aristotle. He had written: *Demosthenes Zoulakis is Assistant Manager. He is friend of my father. He will help if he can. A.G.*

Within moments of asking for him at the reception desk in the hotel, Mr Zoulakis was grasping her hand in his, smiling broadly, and telling her in impeccable English that Aristotle had telephoned to explain everything.

'Would you please show me the photograph of the friend you are seeking, Miss Wells,' he said, taking out a pair of horn-rimmed glasses and slipping them on.

'Yes, of course, right away,' Nicky said, and reached into her bag for the famous picture.

Mr Zoulakis took it from her, studied it intently, frowned slightly, looked at it more closely, then shook his head. 'This man was never a guest at any of the hotels. I always make a point of knowing everyone, and I have a good memory for faces.'

'But you were frowning, and you looked as though you *did* know him,' Nicky pointed out, having carefully observed the man's initial reaction.

'Yes, that is so, Miss Wells. For a split second he *seemed* familiar, but that is all. It is possible that I saw him briefly in one of the restaurants or in one of the other hotels. Perhaps I got a glimpse of him at the pool, or on the beach. However, if I did see him, it *was* fleeting.' He smiled at her, and ushered her across the lobby. 'But come along, Miss Wells, we will visit the hotels on the lower levels, and talk to the staff. Maybe they will have some information.'

'Thanks, Mr Zoulakis, you're being so very kind. I appreciate it.'

'It is nothing, Miss Wells, truly it is nothing,' Demosthenes Zoulakis said, wishing he could help this beautiful American woman who was apparently so important.

Two hours later Nicky was being led to the Mercedes by the affable assistant manager, who had genuinely put himself out for her, but to no avail. 'I am so sorry we have not been able to help you, Miss Wells,' he said. 'Perhaps your friend merely passed through Athens, en route to another destination.'

'That is a possibility,' Nicky agreed, and thanked him again.

Nicky was halfway across the lobby of the Hotel Grande Bretagne when she stopped dead in her tracks. A second before, she had passed the newspaper and magazine kiosk, and now she realized that Clee's photograph had been on the cover of one of the magazines being prominently displayed.

Clee was the most famous war photographer in the world today, and the only reason he would be on the cover of a magazine was if something had happened to him. He was in Leipzig, and that wasn't a battlefront, but there were demonstrations going on in East Germany, and there *were* other places to die as well as in a war zone. But she knew he was all right. She had spoken to him only last night. Perhaps he was on the magazine cover because he had won an award for his coverage of the demonstrations in Beijing. That was a possibility. But if so, why hadn't he mentioned it? *Modesty?* Clee was one of the most modest people she had ever met.

Nicky swung around and walked back to the kiosk. She opened her purse, took out some money and handed it to the vendor. Then she lifted the magazine off the rack and held it up for the vendor to see what she was buying.

The man nodded his head, counted out the change, and dropped it into her outstretched hand.

Turning away from the kiosk, Nicky took a few steps, and looked down at the magazine. It was called *Tachydromos*; it was a news magazine similar to *Life* or *Paris Match*, and there was Clee on the cover, smiling faintly and wearing an open-necked shirt and his worn, brown-leather bomber jacket. Except that it wasn't Clee. It was Kevin Costner, the actor, she was looking at. It was true that they did bear a striking resemblance to each other, and it had been an easy mistake to make.

Once she was inside her suite, Nicky threw the magazine down on the coffee table and went to the mini-bar. Taking out a bottle of coke, she opened it and poured herself a glass. After a long swallow, she carried the drink over to the sofa and sat down.

My God, Kevin Costner really does look like Clee in this shot, Nicky thought, eyeing the magazine cover facing her. He's the spitting image of him. He could be his twin. In the back of her mind a voice suddenly echoed. It was Philip's, and she heard his words again. '*They say we all have a double living somewhere in the world.*'

Nicky sat bolt upright with a start. It had just dawned on her that if she could mistake Kevin Costner for Clee Donovan, then perhaps she was mistaking some other man for Charles Devereaux.

Damnation, she muttered to herself, I *am* on a wild goose chase. She leaped to her feet, impatient, irritated with herself, and walked over to the window, stood looking out, her mind racing.

It was quite possible that the man filmed in the news segment emanating from Rome was a total stranger. Certainly that's what Anne and Philip believed. Who was to argue with them, really. She had no one who could endorse her opinion that the man was Charles. What a pity Christopher Neald was on vacation. Charles's English partner would have agreed with her, she was certain of that. A small sigh escaped, and she leaned her head against the pane of glass. Admit it, there's no point continuing with this search, she muttered, then she straightened as a thought suddenly struck her. There *was* one person who might back her up, if he was shown the photographs: Don Pedro Alejandro Perez, Charles's Spanish partner.

One last shot. I'm going to give this one last shot, Nicky thought as she hurried across the room to the desk and her address book. Within the space of ten minutes she had found Don Pedro's number, telephoned Madrid and spoken to a receptionist at Don Pedro's sherry and wine exporting company. The woman had told her that Don Pedro was out of town until Monday, that she should ring again after lunch, at five o'clock, in order to speak to Don Pedro's secretary, Señorita Lopez.

Nicky sat at the desk for a short while, hesitating, wondering what to do next. She could stay in Athens until Sunday and fly to Madrid that morning, but it was unbearably hot in Athens; also, she didn't know a soul here, whereas ATN had a decent-sized bureau in Madrid, and although Peter Collis, the bureau chief, was not a close friend, he was at least an acquaintance of long standing. Madrid it is, she thought, making a snap decision to leave immediately. She would go today, if that was possible.

Years of travelling with her parents as a child had taught her one thing: if you wanted to get something done, and especially in a hurry, ask a concierge to help you. They knew everything; they also had a network that stretched from hotel to hotel across Europe. And so now she dialled the desk downstairs to enlist the head concierge's help. The line was busy, so she left the suite and went down to the lobby, feeling more impatient than ever to move on.

Yannis, the head concierge, greeted her pleasantly and asked how he could be of assistance.

'I need to get on a flight to Madrid today. Any airline, it doesn't matter which, and I need a suite booked at the Ritz. Can you do that for me please, Yannis?'

'Yes, immediately, leave it to me, Miss Wells. I will telephone your suite as soon as I have news.' He glanced at his watch. 'Are you packed, miss?'

'More or less.'

'It is almost three. I think you should be prepared to leave for the airport soon. I know there is a late afternoon flight to Madrid. I will try to get a seat on it for you.'

'Thank you, Yannis,' she said, smiled at him and walked across to the reception desk. Aristotle was nowhere in sight, but Costa was on duty. She had felt his eyes on her all the time she had been talking to the concierge.

Nicky said, 'Hello, Costa. Thanks for trying to help me yesterday.'

He inclined his head with his usual politeness, and asked, 'Did you have any luck at Vouliagmeni?'

'No, unfortunately, I didn't. Would you please arrange for my bill, Costa?'

'You are leaving, miss?'

Nicky nodded.

'Back to America?' he asked.

'No, I'm going to Madrid, as a matter of fact.'

'*Madrid*,' he repeated, sounding slightly startled.

Nicky stared at him curiously. He had such a look of consternation on his face she could not help wondering why. She said, 'What's wrong with Madrid?'

The young desk clerk seemed baffled for a split second. Then he murmured, 'Excuse me, I don't understand.'

'You sounded so surprised when I said I was going to Madrid.'

'Not at all,' he responded, sudden denial on his face. He offered her a faint smile, and added, 'I will have your bill prepared, miss. Immediately.'

She reached into her bag, pulled out a handful of drachmas, and pressed them on Costa. 'Thank you,' she said.

'Thank *you*, miss,' he answered, pocketing the money.

Costa watched her walk across the lobby to the elevators. When she had entered one and disappeared from sight, he left the reception desk and went over to speak to the head concierge.

'Do you think you can get Miss Wells a seat on a plane to Madrid?'

'I am sure I can,' Yannis said somewhat sharply, frowning at Costa, obviously puzzled by his interest.

'And the hotel? Did you get her a hotel?'

'The head concierge of the Ritz is an old friend. I will have no problem when I speak to him,' Yannis boasted. 'And what's it to you?'

Costa grinned, and winked. 'She's nice. She tips well. I want to be sure everything goes smoothly for her.'

Yannis nodded, and turned away to answer one of the shrilling telephones.

Costa walked back to the reception desk where another colleague was speaking with a guest. He hurried into the back office, which was empty, and made a quick phone call.

'She's leaving,' he muttered into the receiver. 'She's going to Madrid. What could she have found out at Vouliagmeni? She must know *something*. She'll be at the Ritz. Tell him.'

CHAPTER TWENTY-EIGHT

It only occurred to Nicky that she really was being followed when she came out of the Prado Museum early on Friday evening, and stood for a moment under its shady portico.

She was debating whether or not to go directly back to the Ritz Hotel when she noticed the man with the black cigarillo again.

He had first sprung to life that morning, had suddenly appeared by her side whilst she was speaking to the concierge. The man had been puffing hard on his little black cigar, and the smoke billowing around her had caused her to splutter and cough. The concierge had said something politely but firmly in rapid Spanish, and the man had immediately moved away from her, stepping to one side. Once she had finished her business she had hurried across the lobby, glad to be away from the man with the cigar, who was deep in conversation with the concierge. On her way up to the suite in the elevator she had silently cursed him, since she was still coughing behind her hand.

Then later, on her way to lunch with Peter Collis of the ATN Madrid bureau, she had stopped to wander along the Galeria del Prado, a shopping arcade under the Palace Hotel. As she had left a boutique she had seen the man with the cigar gazing in its window. Immediately, he had glanced away, looking somewhat self-conscious, had swung around and darted into a shop on the opposite side of the arcade.

Now, here he was once again, only a few yards from her. He stood near the statue located between the steps and the small park just beyond, and he was with another man. In his mouth was the usual black cigarillo.

The man had not seen her. Not yet, anyway. The only reason she had spotted him so quickly and so easily was because of the screaming children. They were toddlers and flanked a young woman, were clinging to her hands, and they were bawling at the tops of their lungs. Their harassed mother had stopped to speak to the two men near the statue, and the man with the cigar was saying something, apparently in response to a question. He was pointing and gesticulating, obviously giving her directions.

Suddenly a group of young German students came out of the museum, surrounding her and laughing and chattering, and Nicky fell in with them. She stayed close as they trooped through the little park and into the Paseo del Prado.

Within a few minutes Nicky was entering the Plaza de la Lealtad where the Ritz stood in its own lovely gardens. The man with the cigar was nowhere in sight. Not that it mattered, since he clearly knew where she was staying anyway.

After collecting her door key and several messages, Nicky went up to her suite, preoccupied with thoughts of the strange man, and the possibility that someone was having her movements monitored. *Someone?* If it was anybody, it was Charles Devereaux.

The minute she walked into her suite Nicky was conscious of the smell of an unfamiliar perfume. She stood in the small foyer, frowning and glancing about, the door key clutched in her hand. She sniffed several times. There was no mistaking it – a pungent odour clung to the air. It struck her then that it smelled more like a man's cologne than a woman's perfume, so this eliminated the maid. Had the valet been here? But for what reason? She had not sent any clothes out for pressing. Had the strange man gained entry to her suite? If so, how? That's stupid, she muttered. He could very easily have bribed a member of the staff. As her father always said, money talked. And certainly he would have had the opportunity. She had seen him in the shopping arcade around eleven o'clock that morning, before going to the ATN bureau to pick up Peter. They had gone to lunch at the Gran Café de Gijón around one thirty and from lunch she had strolled off to the Prado. Once there she had spent several hours gazing in wonder at the paintings by Goya and Velázquez, and she had been out of her suite for most of the day.

A worried crease wrinkled her brow as she went into the sitting room and put her key, the messages and her handbag on the coffee table. Her suspicions now fully aroused, Nicky walked through into the bedroom, went immediately to the wardrobe and pulled open the door. Her big carryall bag, which she never travelled without, looked oddly askew, yet she knew that she had placed it neatly in the corner before leaving to meet Peter.

Reaching for the carryall, she dragged it out and carried it over to the bed. Inspecting the lock on the front, she noticed at once that it had been tampered with; when she touched it with her finger she realized that it was very loose. Seemingly someone had picked the lock, then had been unable to close it properly afterward because it was badly damaged. Certainly the carryall had been secure when she had left earlier, so someone had definitely been in her suite, poking around.

Nicky inspected the carryall. Nothing was missing. Her notebook, tape recorder and all of the other items were intact. She had her passport, press credentials, credit cards and Spanish money in her white leather shoulder bag, but she had left a wallet containing foreign currency in the carryall. Pulling this out and examining it, she saw that none of the money had been taken. But she was positive the bag had been searched, and very thoroughly at that. Quite aside from the broken lock, her things were not as neatly placed inside as they usually were. And her tape recorder was not in the corner of the carryall, where she invariably put it for easy access.

Closing the bag and returning it to the wardrobe, Nicky hurried over to the chest on the other side of the bedroom, and began to open the drawers one after the other. Again she knew that someone had rifled through her things, for the simple reason she always stacked everything carefully. They were now rumpled, and, like the carryall, slightly askew. There was no doubt that someone had handled them.

She shook her head, a concerned expression settling on her face as she closed the drawers and walked back into the sitting room. Flopping down onto a chair, she closed her eyes, trying to concentrate on the problems at hand. Was it just a coincidence that the man with the black cigarillo had been under her feet several times today? Or was he actually following her? If he was, then it certainly proved one thing: *Charles Devereaux was really alive.* There was no question in her mind that her rooms had been searched and her carryall tampered with; the evidence was there. Obviously this also reinforced her theory that her former fiancé was flourishing here on the Continent.

Suddenly Nicky snapped her eyes open and sat up jerkily. *If* Charles was having her followed in order to know what she was doing, who she was seeing, and *if* he had had her room searched, then he must be aware that she was in Madrid. But how did he know that? Did he have a contact here in the Ritz? Or one in the Hotel Grande Bretagne in Athens, perhaps? More importantly, why was he doing it?

There was only one answer to that: he wanted to know what she was up to, and very badly.

It struck her then that he might possibly think she was doing an investigation on him for a story. After all, he knew full well that she had been an investigative journalist before she had become a war correspondent, and still was one, in fact. But if he believed this, then he must be involved in something that merited an investigation. Something illicit. Something immense, maybe. What was illicit and immense and made big money? Arms smuggling. Drug trafficking. But why would Charles want to make more big bucks? He was already a rich man. Still, she kept coming back to the idea that whatever he was doing involved money.

Unless it was something else, something quite bizarre, as she had suggested to Arch in Rome. But what could that be . . .

The telephone rang, interrupted her thoughts, and she rose, went to the desk to answer it. 'Hello?'

'Nicky, Peter here. I called before and left a message. Did you get it?'

'Oh Peter, I'm sorry, I just came in and I haven't opened any of my messages yet.'

'No problem. Amy and I want you to have dinner with us tonight. Are you free?'

'Yes, and I'd love to meet your wife. But look, Peter, you don't have to feel obliged to look after me, really – '

'We want you to join us,' he interrupted. 'We've invited a few friends. We're going to the Jockey Club, it's quite famous.'

'I've heard of it.'

'I'll pick you up around eight thirty, and take you home for drinks. Dinner won't be until ten, even ten thirty, I'm afraid. When in Madrid do as the *madrileños*. See you later, Nicky.'

'I'm looking forward to it, Peter. Bye for now.'

Immediately after she had hung up the phone rang again. 'Hello?'

'Hi, babe, it's me,' Clee said.

'Darling, hello. How are you? Where are you calling from?'

'I'm terrific, and I'm in Berlin . . . at the Intercontinental. Didn't you get my message?'

'Yes, but I only just got back. I haven't had a chance to look at it.'

'Nicky, I've got great news! The greatest!' he exclaimed.

She could almost feel his excitement flowing down the wire. 'What is it? Tell me!'

'Yoyo! I've had a message from Yoyo, Nick.'

'Oh Clee, thank God. He is all right, isn't he? And where is he? Is he in Paris?'

Clee laughed. 'Whoa, I can only answer one question at a time. He's fine. He's in Hong Kong, but he'll be in Paris soon. Hopefully in a few days, another week at the most.'

'That's wonderful,' she said, and unexpectedly her eyes filled with tears of relief and gratitude that he was alive and well. She was unable to speak for a couple of seconds.

Clee said, 'Are you there, babe?'

Swallowing hard, Nicky replied, 'Yes . . . I felt very emotional for a moment or two, that's all.'

'I know what you mean. I had the same reaction when I heard the news from Jean-Claude.'

'Oh, so you didn't actually speak to Yoyo yourself?'

'No, he called the office from Hong Kong, and said he'd be in touch the moment he arrived in Paris.'

'Clee, it's just wonderful. Perhaps we'll be able to have a reunion on Monday.'

'Maybe. And, yes, it's the best news we could have. What time will you be arriving in Paris, Nick?'

'Late afternoon, I think.'

'Then it's dinner that night. Just the three of us. You, me and Yoyo. Providing that Yoyo has arrived, of course, and is feeling up to it.'

'I can't wait to see him,' Nicky said.

'And I can't wait to see you, darling.'

Nicky laughed. 'It goes without saying that that's mutual.'

They talked for a few more minutes and then they said goodbye and hung up. Nicky stood with her hand resting on the receiver for a moment. Clee had been so excited about Yoyo, he had not asked her why she had moved on to Madrid. He had simply assumed she was there on business, much to her profound relief. She had not had to lie to him again, thank goodness.

Later that evening, when she was putting finishing touches to her makeup, the phone began to shrill. Going into the bedroom, she picked it up, and said, 'Hello?'

No one answered.

For a second time, Nicky said, 'Hello?' and did so somewhat sharply. There was a click and the phone went dead. Immediately, she dialled the operator. 'This is Nicky Wells in suite 705. My phone just rang. I answered, but no one spoke. *Did* you have a call for me?'

'Yes, Miss Wells. I put it through myself,' the operator answered.

'Who was calling? Do you know?'

'I'm sorry, no, I don't. But it was a man who asked for you.'

'Thank you.' Nicky put the receiver down and returned to the bathroom to do her hair. Quite suddenly she stopped brushing it, and stood for a moment staring into the mirror, but without seeing herself. Her mind was elsewhere. She could not help wondering if someone was checking on her movements again. And then she remembered something Arch had said to her in Rome. He had pointed out that a man who does a disappearing act does not want to be found. Not ever. He had also said she could be putting herself in danger. Was she?

Her fertile brain focused on Charles Devereaux. Arch had remarked that Charles was tough, hard, and ruthless. All of these things were true. She had spotted those characteristics in him herself.

A look of comprehension flashed in her bright blue eyes. Yes, she could be in danger.

CHAPTER TWENTY-NINE

The news about Yoyo had lifted Nicky's spirits; it had completely overshadowed the Devereaux problem and her search for Charles.

Last night she had felt a great sense of buoyancy and lightness when she had gone out to dinner with Peter and Amy Collis, and their friends. Even the troublesome thought that Arch might be correct, that she could be in danger, had been considerably diminished. Now, on this lovely, warm Saturday morning, all of the bogeymen had fled. They had been chased away by her happy mood, and by the bright sunlight, the incredible turquoise sky and the thin, dry Castilian air which gave that sky its extraordinary clarity. Not only that, the briskness and bustle of this elegant and imposing hotel was reassuring, as was the atmosphere of normality which pervaded it.

Ever since the phone call from Clee, Nicky had been caught up with thoughts of Yoyo. The fact that he had escaped from China to Hong Kong, and was safe in the British Crown Colony, did much to ease the anxiety she had lived with lately; she felt as though her burdens had been lifted. Well, one of them, anyway. She could not wait to see Yoyo, to find out what had happened to him since they had last seen each other three months ago.

Just as importantly, she wanted and needed to see Clee, to be with him. They had not been together for several weeks, and this separation had only made her appreciate him that much more. She longed for his warmth and intelligence, his love and affection and understanding.

Nicky picked up her cup and finished her coffee. Then she sat back in the chair and glanced around, absorbing her surroundings. She was having a late breakfast in the restaurant set in the midst of the trees in the hotel gardens; in some ways, it was these gardens which helped to make the Ritz so special. The hotel was situated in the very heart of Madrid, and they surrounded it with tranquillity and loveliness, were like an oasis of calm in this busy, noisy and hectic metropolis.

Lifting her head, she looked up at the sky. It really was a phenomenal colour, like none she had ever seen anywhere, and it was cloudless. The sun was high, and by noon it would be unbearably hot, as torrid as it had been yesterday. But it was shady here under the trees, and pleasant; nonetheless, she was glad she was wearing a loose cotton trapeze-shaped dress and flat sandals. Keeping cool was a major consideration in this city.

'Señorita Wells.'

Nicky looked around and found herself staring into the scrubbed young face of a bellboy. 'Yes?'

'For you.' He was holding a small silver tray on which lay an envelope, and he thrust this at her, smiling.

Nicky pulled some pesetas out of her handbag, dropped them on the tray and picked up the white envelope. 'Thank you,' she said.

The bellboy eyed the money, smiled at her and pocketed it. '*Gracias, señorita.*'

Nicky examined the letter with curiosity, wondering who it was from. Peter? The *madrileños* she had met last night? They were a lovely young couple who had wanted to take her out over the weekend. Her name was neatly printed across the front, along with the hotel's name and address, but the sender's name was missing.

Tearing it open, she took out the note, and the moment she saw the handwriting she froze in the chair. That beautiful script was unmistakable . . . the note was from Charles Devereaux.

He had written: *Dear Nicky: Since you are looking so hard for me I believe it has now become imperative that we meet. The man who delivers this note will wait in the lobby for you. I have sent him to fetch you to me. C.*

Nicky stared out at the gardens, a remote expression settling on her face. She clutched the note in her hand, and swallowed several times. Her throat had gone very dry. Then she looked down at the note and re-read it again. There was no question in her mind that it was from Charles. Quite aside from the recognizable handwriting, only Charles would use the word *fetch*. He had done so frequently in the past, and it was very English.

So, I was right all along, she thought, sitting up straighter in the chair. *I just knew I was.* From the very moment I saw Tony's newscast from Rome. And yet she realized she derived no satisfaction from this knowledge, only a sense of immense dismay and a terrible feeling of sadness. But the sadness was more for Anne Devereaux than herself.

As she sat holding the note, her mind focusing on the man waiting to take her to Charles, a thought struck her. Last night, remembering Arch's words, she had wondered if she was in danger. If she truly believed she was, how could she possibly go off with Charles's messenger? For most of her working life as a war correspondent she had been in harm's way, and she had never flinched. And long ago she had accepted the fact that she was fearless by nature. On the other hand, she was not going to let her overriding curiosity and her quest for the truth be her undoing now. Certainly she was not going to do something foolhardy and put herself at risk.

But I won't be at risk. Whatever Charles Devereaux is, he is not a killer. Deep down in her heart she knew that Charles would never hurt her. Not one hair of her head, she was absolutely convinced of that. Still, it would be prudent to be a bit cautious.

She wished Peter Collis were available to accompany her. They could have taken his car, and he could have waited outside for her while she had her meeting with Charles. Unfortunately, Peter and Amy were away for the day, visiting friends who lived outside Madrid.

She was on her own. So be it.

Nicky walked across the lobby to speak to Enrique, the head concierge.

'Good morning, Señorita Wells. Can I be of some help?' he asked with his usual geniality.

She nodded. 'I need a car and a driver. Immediately. And I'd like a driver who speaks English, please.'

'No problem, señorita, I'll arrange it right away. How long will you need the car?'

'I'm not sure. Several hours, at least, maybe the whole day. How soon can it be here?'

'It is already here, Señorita Wells. We have cars and drivers standing outside, in readiness for the hotel guests.'

'How convenient. A short while ago someone delivered a letter to me. I believe he's waiting.'

'Yes, he's over there,' Enrique told her.

Nicky followed his gaze. She saw a youngish man, well-dressed, hovering at the other end of the lobby. 'Thank you,' she murmured to the head concierge, and hurried away from the desk.

Coming to a stop next to the young man, she said, 'I'm Nicky Wells. Do you speak English?'

The young man nodded. 'Yes.'

'What's your name?'

There was a slight hesitation, and then he said, 'Javier.'

'All right, Javier.' She showed him the envelope. 'You brought this letter to me. Correct?'

'Yes.'

'And you're supposed to take me to the man who sent it, aren't you?'

'Yes. He waits for you.'

'Very well, I'm coming with you now. But I'm using my own car and driver.'

'I don't understand. I have car. I take you, Señorita Wells.'

Nicky shook her head. 'No, absolutely not! I prefer to come with my own car, or I don't come at all,' she said firmly, and her expression was suddenly tough, determined.

Javier could not fail to notice her attitude, but again he hesitated, looking uncertain and at a loss. Then he said, 'Okay. Wait please. I make phone call.'

'Oh, I'll wait,' Nicky answered coolly, understanding that he was now going to put through a call to Charles. Her eyes followed him as he crossed the lobby in search of a telephone.

Within minutes he returned. 'Okay. We go now. Your car follow mine.'

Her driver's name was José, and once she was settled comfortably in the car he went to speak to Javier.

Nicky sat watching them through the car window. It was open and she could hear their voices. However, since she spoke no Spanish she did not understand a word they were saying.

A second or two later, José got into the driver's seat, released the brake and turned on the ignition.

As they slid smoothly away from the hotel and into the street, Nicky said, 'Did Javier explain where we are going?'

'Yes, señorita. We are going out to the area near the ring.'

'The ring?'

'*Si, si*. The bullring of Madrid, the famous Plaza de Toros de Las Ventas. It is not too far, twenty minutes, maybe half an hour, depending on the traffic.'

'Oh yes, that's right.'

'Do you know the ring, señorita? Have you been to a *corrida*?'

'Yes, I have, some years ago,' she said, remembering the time she had met Charles in Madrid, just a few weeks before they had become engaged. Don Pedro had taken them to a bullfight on the Sunday afternoon.

'Did you enjoy it?' José asked, half glancing over his shoulder, smiling at her.

'Yes, I did, thank you.'

Leaning back against the car seat, Nicky cast her mind back to that long weekend. She and Charles had stayed in Madrid for four days, and now she recalled how taken with it Charles had seemed to be. Well, it *was* affluent, fashionable and vibrant. Life was lived to the hilt here, and he had appeared to enjoy that – and the night life – as well as everything else. She wondered if he lived here permanently. Perhaps he did, maybe he had only been visiting Rome. *Drugs*, she thought, seizing on the South American connection, the common bond

745

of language and heritage. And for all its glossy facade, she knew that Madrid had its problems like anywhere else. Recently she had read that heroin was responsible for a death every two days in Madrid.

Was Charles somehow involved in drug smuggling? Was that what it was all about? Was that the reason he had faked his death and fled abroad to start a new life? Soon she would know the answers to everything, she presumed.

Half an hour later, José was pulling up behind Javier on a side street, and parking in front of a brownish-coloured brick apartment building. He helped her to alight, and she said, 'Please wait for me here, José, however long I am.'

'*Si, si*, yes, I understand. I will not go away. I will stay here all day if necessary.'

Nicky nodded. 'But I probably won't be much longer than a couple of hours,' she added, and walked over to join Javier, who was already standing near the front door.

'This is the place, is it?' she asked, staring into his face.

'He waits here,' Javier said, pushed open the door and stood back to let her enter the building first.

As she strode across the small foyer, following Javier to the lift, Nicky steeled herself. She had no idea what to expect, and her mouth had gone dry again.

CHAPTER THIRTY

Javier opened the door of the apartment with his own key, and ushered her inside.

Nicky found herself standing in a small, dark foyer that was rather nondescript. It had an Oriental rug on the floor, a console table holding a vase of bedraggled artificial flowers, and framed posters of bullfighters on the walls. She glanced from side to side, riddled with curiosity, and saw several closed doors, as well as a long corridor leading off the foyer. The sitting room was straight ahead, through an arched entranceway.

Everything was quiet. There was no sign of life, and Nicky could not help wondering where Charles was. She glanced about again, straining to catch the slightest noise.

'Please, go in there,' Javier said, indicating the living room, and as she walked forward he hurried down the corridor.

Her eyes swiftly scanned the room she had just entered. It was as ordinary and unprepossessing as the foyer, with more Oriental rugs on the wood floor, another, larger collection of bullfight posters on the white walls, and several dark wood pieces. A sofa and two chairs were covered in drab olive velvet, and arranged around a cheap metal coffee table with a top made of decorative tiles.

Half expecting to find Charles waiting for her, Nicky was disappointed when she realized the room was empty. Stepping over to the window and looking out, she saw that the bullring, the famous Plaza de Toros de Las Ventas, was only a stone's throw away. Whoever it was that lived here, and she knew it was not Charles, was undoubtedly an *aficionado*. Charles must have borrowed this apartment for our meeting, she thought, he wouldn't live in a place like this. It would offend not only his sensibilities but his sense of taste.

'Hello, Nicky.'

She almost jumped out of her skin on hearing his voice, and swung around, stared at Charles, who had entered the room through another door at the far end. And it really was Charles Devereaux she was regarding, although he looked very different. His hair and the moustache he had grown had been dyed black, and his deep tan only served to underscore an unexpected look of swarthiness about him, one which was quite alien to her. He was naturally fair, like his mother, and had always been extremely Anglo-Saxon in appearance. He was wearing a pair of navy blue cotton pants and white shirt, open at the neck; she had never seen him dressed quite as casually as this.

Nicky discovered she could not speak. She had not anticipated the shock of coming face to face with him, and the impact was enormous. It packed the most tremendous wallop, and she felt as though she had been punched in the stomach. Actually seeing him alive and well and obviously in good health, after believing him to be dead until very recently, was overwhelming. She was shaking inside, and her heart was beating at an uncommonly rapid rate.

'You look very well, Nicky,' Charles said at last, breaking the silence between them, walking towards her. 'And thank you for coming.' He stopped about a foot away from her, and offered her a faint smile.

She did not return it, merely stared at him. Her face was cold, her eyes blue ice. Finally, she said in a voice that was positively glacial, 'Let's cut the small talk shall we? That's not why I came here.'

'I was merely attempting to put you at ease, my dear,' he answered, and once more the faint smile flickered.

On hearing these words, and observing that superior little smile again, something in Nicky snapped. Grief, anguish and pain had long ago coalesced and become a simmering anger. And now that anger spiralled into unmitigated rage.

The dam burst and she exploded. 'You rotten son-of-a-bitch! Why did you do it? Why did you do such a terrible thing? To me, to Anne. How could you hurt your mother, and me, be so horribly cruel? You caused us both so much heartache and suffering. We *grieved* for you, you callous bastard! I'll never understand how I could have ever loved you! I hate you for what you did!'

Charles visibly flinched at this torrent of angry words, her venomous tone, and a small muscle twitched in his clenched jaw. But he said nothing to defend himself, merely stood watching her, his eyes unblinking, his gaze perfectly steady.

Tears of outrage spurted in Nicky's eyes and ran down her face, and unexpectedly she leaped forward, her anger propelling her towards him. She began to pummel his chest and face fiercely with her clenched hands, showing unusual and surprising strength as she beat him.

Charles was taken by surprise at her sudden and violent behaviour, and he staggered under her incessant blows, but swiftly regained his balance. He began to struggle with her. At last he managed to catch her hands in his, and held them tightly at the wrist.

'Stop it, Nicky! Do you hear me, stop this at once!' he exclaimed vehemently, although with immense control. 'This ridiculous display will not get us anywhere. I had you fetched here to tell you something, to explain – '

'You had me followed!' she shouted.

'I certainly did not!' he shot back.

'You had my suite searched, you bastard!'

He hesitated only fractionally, then obviously decided to admit to this. 'Yes, that is perfectly true, I did. But followed?' He shook his head. 'No, no. Most decidedly not. I did not have you followed, Nicky.'

She ignored this denial. 'You faked your death and ran away to start a new life,' she cried in an accusatory tone. 'That was despicable and cowardly. *Unconscionable.* I don't know what your reason was, but nothing you could tell me now will ever explain that to – '

'I had no choice,' he cut in peremptorily, in a voice that was icily calm and controlled. 'I did what I did because I had no choice.'

'Everybody has a choice!'

'In this instance, *I* did not. It was a question of duty.'

'*Duty!*' she exclaimed shrilly. 'That's hard to believe!'

'I want to explain why I did what I did, then perhaps you'll understand and go away and leave me alone.'

When she did not respond, Charles added, 'You're putting me in jeopardy, Nicky.'

'What do you mean by jeopardy?'

'You're putting me at risk, putting my life at risk, running around the world asking questions about me, showing my photograph to all and sundry,' he said, his voice suddenly low, almost conspiratorial. 'No one must know I'm alive. Not even my mother.'

Although she was extremely startled by this statement, and thrown off-balance, Nicky made no comment. She simply gave him a curious look. Her eyes were full of speculation as she weighed his words.

Charles said, 'Come and sit down, and try not to be so angry.'

'It'll take me a long time to get over *my* anger!'

'Just so,' he murmured, nodding. 'But won't you endeavour to calm yourself sufficiently, in order to listen to me quietly, and in a reasonable fashion? Your anger is only getting in the way, blocking you.'

'Reasonable fashion!' she repeated, sounding incredulous. 'Good God, you expect too much!'

Unexpectedly, he released her, let go of her wrists, and her arms fell to her sides.

Nicky lifted them immediately, looked at her wrists, and began to rub first one, then the other. They were red and sore. 'Look what you've done.'

He said, apologetically, 'I'm so sorry. I never did know my own strength, did I? Would you excuse me for a moment, Nicky, I'll be right back.' He went out through the side door.

Nicky leaned against the wall, feeling weak in the legs. She was still shaking, and the anger fulminated inside her. But that was the only emotion she experienced; there was nothing left but anger, and perhaps a degree of hatred for Charles Devereaux. Otherwise she felt absolutely nothing for him.

When Charles returned a few seconds later, he was followed by another young man, not Javier. The man carried a tray with a bottle of water and two glasses on it, and as he walked past Nicky, and placed it on the coffee table, she caught a whiff of a pungent cologne. It was one she recognized instantly, and she stiffened, drew back slightly, staring hard at him.

Immediately, Charles noticed this, and when they were alone again he said, 'Why did you react to Pierre like that?'

'Because he's the one who searched my suite,' she replied in a hard voice.

Charles was silent.

'Don't even try to deny it!' she exclaimed, her anger surfacing again.

'How do you know that? Did you see him leave your suite?'

'No, but I smelled him.' She glared at Charles.

Charles frowned. 'What do you mean?'

'*His cologne.* My suite smelled of his cologne!'

Charles frowned once more. 'He's too young,' he muttered, almost to himself. 'Too inexperienced yet. He was very careless.' Charles did not say anything else for a split second, looked thoughtful, then murmured quietly, 'Pierre didn't find anything.'

'That's because there wasn't anything to find,' Nicky said. 'Except the photographs, and I had them on me.'

Charles made no comment about the pictures, but said, 'Now come, sit down, Nicky. Your temper hasn't helped us thus far. Please, do try to be calmer so that we can talk in a sensible, civilized manner.'

Nicky remained standing where she was, her bright blue eyes focused on Charles. She knew her anger was justified; it was an anger that had bubbled in her for three years now. And she did not regret her outburst, or anything she had said. But he did have a point. She would not find anything out if she did not control herself and let him speak, tell his tale.

'Come, Nicky,' he said again, waving his hand at the chair nearest to her. 'Please, do sit down, won't you?' As he spoke he lowered himself into the other chair, reached for the bottle and poured himself a glass of water. He glanced up at her. 'Would you care for a glass of this?'

She nodded. 'Thanks, it's very hot in here.'

He jumped up at once, went to turn on a fan standing on a table in a corner, and returned to the chair. After sitting down, he poured water for her, picked up his own glass and drank.

Nicky still continued to watch him intently. This was a man she had loved and adored, whom she had been intending to marry, and to whom she had been wholly committed. She had slept with him, been intimate with him on every level, shared so much with him, but at this moment he seemed like a total stranger to her.

Finally walking forward, she sat down, took a drink of water and said, 'I'm calmer now, Charles. So talk.'

'What I'm about to tell you is extremely confidential. You cannot tell anyone. Not ever. And not even my mother.'

When Nicky remained completely silent, he said, 'Promise me that you won't reveal that I am alive, or repeat what I'm about to tell you to anyone, least of all my mother.'

'I don't know that I can do that.'

'Then I'm afraid I cannot tell you.'

'Why mustn't Anne know anything?'

'Because she would want to see me, if she knew I were alive, and that's impossible. It could be dangerous . . . for her,' he said.

'*Why?*'

He did not answer this question. Instead, he told her, 'If you give me your promise, swear on your honour that what I say will remain absolutely confidential, then I will tell you everything. Well, at least I will tell you why I faked my own death and disappeared.'

'Okay, I promise. I won't tell Anne, or anyone else, that you're alive. Nor will I disclose what you now say to me in confidence.'

'No other living soul, Nicky. Say it.'

'I won't tell another living soul. I promise.'

'I sincerely hope you mean that. I think you do.' He gave her a hard stare. 'It's not in your nature to break your word. So I trust you. But let me just add this . . . what I'm involved in has to do with national security. British national security.'

Nicky leaned forward, returning his stare, her eyes narrowing. 'I told you I wouldn't say a word, and I won't.'

'All right.' He sank back in the chair, and after a moment said in a low voice, 'I'm a British agent.'

This was the last thing she had expected to hear, but thunderstruck though she was she kept her expression neutral. Why ever didn't I think of the intelligence business, she wondered, but said in a cool, very steady voice, 'You're with MI6, is that it?'

'The Secret Intelligence Service, which is the same as MI6, more or less. And I faked my suicide and disappeared because it became necessary for me to assume a new identity.'

'Why?' Nicky asked, leaning forward ever so slightly again.

'I needed a new identity in order to infiltrate a foreign intelligence service.'

'Are you telling me that you're a mole?'

'That is correct, I am.'

'Which foreign intelligence service have you infiltrated?'

'Now you know damn well I can't reveal that to you, Nicky. Come on, use that intelligent head of yours,' he said in that mellifluous voice of his.

She nodded. 'I understand. How long have you been an agent?'

'For years. Fifteen years to be exact. Since I was twenty-five.'

'So you were working for British Intelligence when you met me,' she said, twisting her hands together, suddenly understanding there was a part of him she had never known.

'I was indeed,' he confirmed.

'But we were going to be married. How did you ever hope to keep that a secret from me?'

'Very easily. First of all, you were heavily involved with your career, to the

750

exclusion of all else, except for our relationship, of course. And you travelled a lot as a war correspondent. My secret had been safe from everyone for years. I had the perfect cover, you see. My wine importing company.'

'But it was so successful,' she exclaimed, sounding surprised. 'Most cover operations are just that, *a cover*. They don't necessarily make money.'

He smiled. 'That was always one of my problems, Nicky. Whatever business I became involved with instantly prospered. My immediate boss, my spymaster, said I had the golden touch. That's why I dropped my other businesses in the early years. I then started the wine company, and although this too flourished, at least it was a splendid cover.'

'I can see that it worked very well for you.'

'It truly was ideal. I could travel anywhere I wanted, any time,' Charles said. 'But you know that. Once I'd brought Chris Neald in as my partner, I wasn't tied to a desk at all. Chris ran the business, and I wandered around the world, doing what I had to do whilst purchasing a bit of wine for the company.'

'It always seemed so legitimate to me,' Nicky murmured with a small frown.

'Oh, but it was. In the end, of course, it was really Chris's company, in as much as he was doing most of the real work. Naturally, that suited me very well. I gained more and more freedom.'

'Did Chris know you were an agent?'

'Good God, no!'

'But you did have an accomplice, didn't you? I mean someone who helped you to fake your death and get out of England.'

'Yes, I did.'

'Who was it?'

'You know very well I can't tell you that.'

'Another agent?'

He nodded.

'Why did you have to do a vanishing act at all? You just said you had the perfect business cover. Why couldn't you have married me and then just continued as before, Charles?'

'That's what I had always intended to do. But a few months before our marriage I found out I had to go away for a long time. You see, it had become imperative for an SIS agent to infiltrate a particular foreign intelligence agency and to go under deep cover in order to do so,' he explained. 'And we all understood that the deep cover would last for years . . . many years, perhaps, if it was to be effective. And so it seemed kinder to disappear before we were married than afterward.'

'I see. But why *you*, Charles? Why not another British agent?'

'Because of my expertise in certain areas, the foreign languages I speak perfectly. I was the best candidate. And it was vital for British national security that I infiltrate as soon as possible. You don't do that overnight, you know. It takes time to gain people's confidence and trust, to be accepted.' He took a sip of the water, and continued, 'As I said, we all knew that I would be working undercover for many, many years. That's the gist of it really.'

'And so you sacrificed our life together,' Nicky murmured softly, looking at him closely.

'I had to . . . for my country,' he replied, gazing back at her, his eyes suddenly very soft. There was a regretful look on his face.

She was quiet, sat extremely still in the chair.

He said gently, 'If it's any consolation, I did love you very much.' He wanted to add that he still loved her, but he did not dare, and, anyway, it would be inappropriate.

She said slowly, 'You caused me a lot of pain, Charles.'

'I know I did. Can you ever forgive me?'

'Under the circumstances, I suppose I can. I do already.' Now she gave him a penetrating look. 'Your mother was as devastated as I was, inconsolable.'

'Yes . . . '

'She's much better now. She's become engaged to Philip Rawlings.'

'I know. I saw the announcement in *The Times*. He's wanted to marry her for years. He must be very happy.'

'They both are.'

'I'd like to ask *you* something now, Nicky. How did you discover that I was actually alive? And how on earth did you get that photograph of me, I mean the photograph of me as I look today?'

'It was a fluke,' she said, and proceeded to explain everything to him.

When she had finished, he shook his head. 'And I never knew that that damnable television camera was even focused on me. I'd been dining with a friend in a restaurant near the square where the rally was being held, when we heard the hullabaloo. It was the shooting. My friend and I dashed out to see what was happening. I saw the television camera, of course, and I should have followed my instinct and left the scene at once. I'm usually much more careful.'

Nicky nodded. Then she remarked, 'You changed your appearance by growing a moustache and dyeing your hair. But you didn't change your eyes; they're still green.'

'I have brown contact lenses, which I usually wear,' he confided. 'But I didn't think it was necessary to do so for you. But not to digress. Tell me what led you to Athens, Nicky.'

'After I'd spent the weekend at Pullenbrook, two weeks ago, I decided to go to Rome, which was the source of the film. I was hoping I would come across something that would lead me to you. By a curious coincidence, our bureau chief's secretary recognized your photograph. She'd seen you at the airport in Athens.'

'Ah, yes, the lovely American girl I assisted with her luggage, I've no doubt.'

'That's right.'

'And so from Rome you went to Athens,' he asserted. 'And started asking questions at the various big hotels.'

'You *had* been there, hadn't you? I mean, you weren't merely passing through, were you?'

'No, I wasn't. I spent two days in Athens, as it happens.'

'You stayed out at Vouliagmeni, didn't you?' Nicky said, leaning back in the chair, studying him again.

'Actually, I didn't. But I did spend some time there with one of my contacts. I had several luncheons there and dinner. But I was living in a safehouse in the city.'

752

'Is this a safehouse?'

'It is.'

'But you don't live in this apartment, do you?'

He shook his head. 'No.'

'Did you find out I was in Madrid when I got here, or did you know I was coming before I arrived?'

'Before. I knew of your presence in Athens the moment you started inquiring about me, and I knew when you left for Madrid. I was always one step ahead of you, Nicky.'

'Someone at the Grande Bretagne told you, didn't they? Was it Costa? Aristotle? Or Mr Zoulakis out at Vouliagmeni?'

'I can't tell you that. And incidentally, *why* did you suddenly come here? What led you to me?'

'Nothing led me to you, Charles. I didn't even know you were here. I wanted to see your former Spanish partner. I hoped Don Pedro would agree with me that it *was* you in the photograph. Or tell me I was wrong.'

'But you said my mother didn't believe it was me!' he exclaimed. 'Wasn't that enough for you?'

'Not really. In any case, deep inside myself I felt you were still alive. Call it gut instinct.'

'Yes, you always were very strong on that. I'm curious about another thing . . . once you decided I was alive, what did you think my motive had been for slipping off the face of the earth?'

'To be very honest, I wasn't sure. After your so-called suicide, there'd been no scandal in England, so I knew you couldn't have been involved in a big financial swindle. Therefore, I thought it must be some kind of illicit operation, and that you'd decided it was wiser to disappear and start a new life.'

'What kind of illicit operation did you think I was caught up in?' Charles asked, his brows coming together in puzzlement.

'Arms dealing or drug smuggling,' she said in a low voice.

'Good heavens, Nicky, you didn't think very highly of me, did you?'

'How could I?'

He rose, walked over to the window, paced up and down for a second or two, and then came back to his chair. After a moment, he said, 'It perturbs me that you believe someone followed you in Madrid. Are you sure of this?'

She shrugged. 'Not absolutely certain, no.'

'Tell me what leads you to think this?'

'There was a man who was hovering around me, when I was speaking to the concierge yesterday morning. I almost stumbled over him again in the shopping arcade underneath the Plaza Hotel a short while later. Then when I came out of the Prado, early last evening, he was there too, but he was preoccupied momentarily, and I slipped past him.'

'I see. Can you describe him to me?'

'Of course. He was definitely Spanish, of that I'm quite sure. Medium height. Well dressed, dark hair slicked back. About forty years old, or thereabouts, and always smoking a black cigarillo.'

'What makes you think he's Spanish?'

'He looks it. Also, he spoke Spanish to the concierge. I heard him as I was walking away from the desk.'

'Do you think he might have been a guest in the hotel?'

'I don't know.'

'He may not have been following you. He could have been a local lothario who likes beautiful blondes,' Charles pointed out. 'A man who was simply trying to pick you up. That's not so unusual.'

'Are you worried that I might have led him to you?'

'No, I'm sure you didn't do that,' he reassured her confidently.

'There's one other thing. My phone rang last night, but when I went to answer it, no one spoke. However, I checked with the operator and I did get a phone call. Someone did ask for me.'

He nodded. 'That was me.'

'Why didn't you say something?'

'I was going to ask you to meet me last night, and then I changed my mind. I thought I might frighten you off, and I decided it was better to wait until this morning.'

'Do you live in Madrid?'

'No.'

'Where do you live?'

'Everywhere. Nowhere. I sort of . . . float around. I'm never in one place for very long.'

'For security reasons?'

'That's about it.'

'I'm sorry that I might have put you in danger, Charles, showing your photograph and asking questions about you. That foreign intelligence agency would have you killed, if they knew you were a mole, wouldn't they?'

He laughed lightly. 'Oh yes, they'd have no compunction. But that's the intelligence business. No one ever said it was safe.'

Nicky opened her handbag and took out the photographs of him. 'I want you to have these,' she said and handed them to him.

'Thanks, Nicky.' He tore them into shreds and dropped the pieces on the tray.

'You *do* know I won't tell a soul that you're alive, or discuss what you've told me, don't you?'

'Yes. I know you'll be my conspirator, keep my secret.'

'I could have blown your entire operation,' she began, and stopped, biting her lip.

'You could have, that's true,' he agreed. 'And that could have been quite horrendous, because it's taken several years to set up. However, don't look so worried, I'm positive you haven't. If you had, I'd know by now. I probably wouldn't even be around to have this conversation with you. I would have been taken out.'

This thought chilled her to the bone, and she fell silent. But after a short while, she said, 'About the man I thought was following me . . . Shall I ask if he's a guest in the hotel? You could call me later, to find out what the concierge said.'

'Oh no, Nicky, I don't want you to be involved in anything I do. It's far too dangerous. Please don't worry, I'll find out who the man is. I have my ways, my contacts. Just leave everything to me. Please leave everything alone. *Do you understand me?*'

'Yes.'

'Nothing is ever as it seems in the world of intelligence and counter intelligence. You might say that everything is upside down in the clandestine world that I live in.' He let out a small breath. 'You never really know who anyone is.' He straightened in the chair, and added, 'I want you to leave Madrid as soon as possible.'

'I will. I intend to go tomorrow.'

'That's good, Nicky. I'll feel better knowing that you're nowhere near me.'

Nicky understood there was nothing more to say, and she pushed herself to her feet. 'I think I'd better be going.' She began walking towards the archway that led into the foyer.

Charles also rose and followed her.

She turned, waited for him to draw closer, and then she said, 'I'm glad we met, that we had this meeting, Charles. So much has been clarified for me.'

'Yes, I'm glad we saw each other too, Nicky.' He studied her for a moment, his head on one side, and then the small smile touched his mouth, and he said, 'You're as beautiful as ever.'

She nodded, but discovered she could not speak.

He went on, 'You're obviously still flying around the world, covering disasters and the like. But you're not married, I see. Or rather, I should say you're not wearing a ring. Are you married, by any chance?'

'No, I'm not married.'

'There's no special man in your life?'

'Yes, there is, as a matter of fact, but only recently.'

'Are you in love with him?'

'I think so . . . I'm not sure.'

'Are you going to marry him?'

'He hasn't asked me.'

'He's a fool if he doesn't. And if he does ask? Will you?'

'I don't know.'

'I wouldn't have done you any physical harm, you know,' Charles remarked, changing the subject. 'However, I can't say that I blame you for wanting your own car and driver to come out here to see me.'

'I was being cautious.'

'And independent. That was one of the many things I always loved about you.'

She turned to walk into the foyer and he caught hold of her arm, pulled her to him, took her in his arms and held her tightly, held her very close to him.

Nicky was taken by surprise, but she did not resist him, let him hold her, understanding that he needed to do this, needed to be close to her. She could feel his heart hammering under his thin shirt, and with a sudden flash of insight, she thought: oh God, he still loves me. Swallowing hard, she gently pushed him away.

'It's better that I leave now,' she murmured softly, and then against her own volition she reached up and touched his cheek. 'Please don't worry. I will never betray you, Charles.'

'I believe you, Nicky,' he said, taking her arm, walking with her to the front door. 'I trust you. With my life.'

Once she was back at the Ritz Hotel, and in the privacy of her suite, Nicky broke down.

She lay on the bed and cried bitterly, sobbing as if her heart would break. Her tears were for Charles and the dangerous and lonely life he had chosen to lead, for herself and what they had once had together, and for what might have been.

But eventually she calmed down, and she took control of herself. The tears ceased, and she lay for a long time propped up against the pillows, thinking of everything that had happened in the past few weeks. And not unnaturally, she felt a sharp stab of guilt when she considered some of the dreadful things she had ascribed to Charles. How could she have ever thought that he was some sort of criminal . . . an arms smuggler, a drug trafficker? She should have known better.

Yes, he had sacrificed her, their love, their future, the future of the children they might have had together. But he had done it for a noble cause. He had done it for his country. And yes, she ought to have known it was something like this, not some grubby deal. After all, his mother's family, the famous Cliffords of Pullenbrook, had always been in service to the Crown of England since time immemorial. Honour and duty and loyalty to country had been inculcated in him since birth. He was simply following in the footsteps of his illustrious ancestors.

PART FOUR

Enemies and Friends

In thy face I see
The map of honour, truth
and loyalty.

William Shakespeare

For I have sworn thee fair,
and thought thee bright,
Who art as black as hell, as
dark as night.

William Shakespeare

CHAPTER THIRTY-ONE

It was that time of the year when Parisians have fled to summer resorts for their annual vacations, and the tourists have invaded, and Paris was awash with foreigners. But Nicky did not care; she was both relieved and glad to be here.

Madrid was not a city she knew well, and she had only visited it once before this last trip, but she had no desire to return. The past forty-eight hours had left their mark on her, particularly the confrontation with Charles yesterday, and she knew that thereafter Madrid was always going to hold unpleasant memories for her.

She had managed to get a flight out of Madrid late on Saturday afternoon, and had checked into the Plaza Athénée when she had arrived last night. Clee was not returning until Sunday evening, and was not expecting to see her until Monday. In any case, she needed some time alone, time to sort out her turbulent thoughts, to come to terms with all that had happened since she had last seen him in New York at the beginning of August.

Though she had been on a quest for Charles Devereaux, the unexpectedness of his note, of suddenly coming face to face with him, had been an enormous shock, as indeed was the news that he had a secret life as an agent with British Intelligence. She had not slept well last night, even though she had been bone tired, and after restlessly tossing and turning for hours she had finally fallen asleep as dawn broke.

When she had awakened around ten, she had felt out of sorts with herself, and by noon a heavy sadness had settled over her. It was a sadness so acute it verged on melancholy, and in an effort to throw this off she had dressed and left the hotel.

Optimistic by nature, positive, and generally upbeat, Nicky was not accustomed to feeling down in the dumps, nor was she prone to depression, and she loathed the feelings enveloping her now. And so she hoped that being outside in the sunshine, walking the familiar streets and visiting favourite haunts, would help to diminish the sadness, if not make it evaporate entirely.

For as long as Nicky could remember she had felt a spiritual affinity for Paris. It was her city in so many different ways, and the childhood years she had spent here in the sixties had been extraordinarily happy. And so it was that she tried to recapture some of that youthful joy as she walked in the direction of the Left Bank; perhaps the happy memories of the past would help to chase away the demons of the present.

Nicky was not actually sad for herself, but for Charles. Long ago, long before he had known her, he had set himself upon a deadly course that was irrevocable. He had made a choice, one that had ultimately led him to that safehouse in Madrid, where they had met yesterday. In deciding to serve his country, he had elected to live in the covert world of espionage, a dangerous, nether world of secrets and spying, duplicity and double-dealing . . . and, more often than not, death.

A chill ran through her, despite the warmth of the day and the radiant sunlight. Such a life had little to commend it, or to offer a man, really; she knew Charles could never marry now, never have children, never lead a normal existence. The loneliness and fear he had to contend with must be excruciating, and the spectre of betrayal or discovery unnerving. That kind of terror must strike close to the bone, she thought, and shivered involuntarily.

Nicky walked on at a steady pace, but her mind raced.

Charles had admitted to being a British agent since the age of twenty-five, and since he was so obviously deeply committed, then why on earth had he ever become involved with her in the first place? She wished she had asked him this; she also wished she had asked him why he had not left one last word for her, as he had his mother. Maybe he had not known what to say to her, or had had nothing to say, perhaps; certainly the letter to Anne had been brief and to the point, a bleak little epistle. Well, she would never find out now. It was too late, the chance had gone.

Having come down the Avenue Montaigne from the hotel and turned onto the Champs-Élysées, Nicky now struck out across the vast Place de la Concorde, and was soon entering the Jardin des Tuileries. She slowed her steps as she did, and glanced around. It was years since she had been here in the gardens, but there were so many good things to remember, so many lovely memories of her childhood associated with this spot.

Quite unexpectedly, she thought of Marie Thérèse Bouret, the *au pair* who had looked after her. She had been seven years old, Marie Thérèse seventeen, when she had come to live with them, and the young French girl had been more like a big sister than a nanny. Vivacious, loving and joyful of spirit, Marie Thérèse had brought her to the gardens to play almost every day in summer. And she had taken her to so many other places as well, during the six years her parents had been based in Paris for their respective newspapers. It was with Marie Thérèse that she had gone to the Louvre for the first time to see the *Mona Lisa* and the other great paintings; together they had gone up the Eiffel Tower to view Paris from on high, and, as the young nanny had explained, for her to see how the Arc de Triomphe resembled the hub of a giant wheel, with the great avenues and boulevards designed by Georges Haussmann stretching out from it like long spokes.

And when her mother had taken her to Fontainebleau, Versailles and Malmaison, on her 'historical outings' as she called them, Marie Thérèse had always accompanied them. She, too, had been treated to her mother's unique lessons in French history, which were never dull and boring, but intriguing and fascinating. And it was Marie Thérèse to whom she had clung when her parents were away, plying their trade as journalists, and to whom she had said her first halting words in French. Yes, she had been indispensable to her when she was little, had loved her dearly, taught her so much about the language, about Paris and the French way of life.

They had stayed in close touch over the years, and saw each other from time to time, whenever Nicky was in Paris. Marie Thérèse had married at twenty-three, and had had a son a year later. Sadly, her husband Jean-Pierre had been killed ten years ago in a car crash in Mozambique, where he was working on an engineering job. Her son Paul, now twenty-two and an engineer like his father, had recently married. I must call her, Nicky thought. I'll do it later when I get back to the hotel, and take her to lunch tomorrow. I hope she can make it. The thought of seeing the woman she held in such affection, and who had played such an important role in her life when she was a child, cheered Nicky; a little of the sadness evaporated.

After dawdling in the gardens for a while, Nicky finally went on her way, passed the Jardin du Carrousel and strolled across the Pont des Arts. This was the only metal bridge in Paris, and one she knew well, since her father had a very good painting of it by Jacques Bouyssou, the official painter of the French navy.

When she arrived at the Quai Malaquais, Nicky hesitated, looked up and down, wondering whether to wander along the Seine to Notre Dame, or to plunge into the streets behind the quais. The apartment she, her parents and Marie Thérèse had lived in had been on the two top floors of an eighteenth-century house on the Île St Louis. It stood in the shadow of the ancient cathedral, and she loved that particular part of the city. She decided to wander up there later.

Striking out down the rue Bonaparte, she headed for the Place St-Germain-des-Prés. Napoleon Bonaparte, she murmured under her breath, recalling how that name had been a common one in their home for years. She had learned it young, and at once it evoked another rush of memories. Her mother had been fascinated by Bonaparte, and after years of scholarly research had finally written a masterful biography of the great general and France's first emperor.

To Nicky the book had been extraordinary, and she still believed it to be her mother's best. It was a portrait that was extremely fair and well-balanced; her mother had made the man accessible in modern terms. He had been all too human, and so had Josephine, his grand passion, the only woman he had ever really loved. But their love had foundered on the sharp rocks of his overweening ambition; he had had their marriage annulled in order to beget an heir to his empire with a younger woman.

According to her mother, this heartbreaking decision had ruined their lives. Without Josephine at his side, Napoleon's luck turned bad, and Josephine died of a broken heart just after his first abdication and exile to Elba in 1814. 'They never stopped loving each other,' her mother had said to her time and time again when she was writing the book. 'And that was the tragedy of it all.'

Nicky sighed. The anguish men and women caused each other, the terrible things they did to each other in the name of love never failed to amaze her. Nothing has changed and it never will, she thought, because human beings are exactly the same as they were thousands of years ago. And we've learnt nothing over the centuries. What Charles had done to her was cruel, unconscionable, however important his cause might be. It had been wrong of him to even contemplate marrying her under the circumstances. He had been selfish. But then who isn't? she asked herself.

By the time she reached the Place St-Germain, Nicky was damp with perspiration, tired from the heat and footsore. Heading in the direction of a café on the shady side of the square, she took a table, and a few minutes later was ordering *café-au-lait*, bread, a tomato salad, sliced chicken and a bottle of water. She had not really eaten much in the last few days and she discovered she was starving.

The waiter brought the bottle of water immediately, and she thirstily drank a glass straight down, and then leaned back in the chair. The long walk had done her good, and she felt certain she would sleep tonight, and tomorrow she would be with Clee. This prospect filled her with warmth and pleasure. She could hardly wait.

Taking off her sun glasses, Nicky blinked and looked around. The area was busy. People were strolling around or sitting at cafés as she was, whiling away the time, enjoying the nice weather on this pleasant Sunday afternoon. The noise of people talking and laughing surrounded her, and as her eyes scanned the Place St-Germain she could not help thinking how ordinary and normal everybody looked and sounded. This was reassuring, and she pulled her thoughts away from Charles Devereaux and the treacherous and cynical world he occupied. Suddenly it struck her that he had done her a favour in vanishing when he did. How terrible her life might have turned out to be if she *had* married him.

Marie Thérèse lived on the opposite side of Paris, just off the Boulevard de Belleville. Since this was quite a distance from the Plaza Athénée, almost as far as the Porte des Lilas, Nicky allowed herself a good half hour to get there by taxi on Monday. Even so, she was a bit late when she finally arrived, because of the distance and the heavy traffic congesting the streets at this busy time of day.

As she climbed the long flight of stairs to the apartment, she could not help wondering why her friend now lived in this section of the city. Belleville certainly did not live up to its name – pretty town. It was an odd area, not at all salubrious, totally lacking in elegance, and even a bit scruffy. It struck her that it was rather off the beaten track for a woman like Marie Thérèse, who was used to so much better.

But after she had hugged and kissed the Frenchwoman in the small foyer of the apartment, Nicky quickly glanced around and saw that the living room ahead was large, and nicely appointed. Also, there was a happy feeling about the place; it had a pleasant atmosphere.

As for Marie Thérèse, she was as pretty and vivacious as she had always been, her large, dark eyes dancing, her generous mouth twitching with hidden laughter, just as it had years ago.

'Now you can see why it is difficult for me to get around,' she said and pointed to her left leg encased up to the knee in a plaster cast. 'The stairs are hard for me – with this.'

Nicky nodded sympathetically. 'I was sorry to hear about your accident, and sorry that I couldn't take you to lunch at the Relais Plaza. But it's great to see you, and you do look wonderful, Marie Thérèse.'

'I feel it, *ma chérie*, except for this silly thing.' She tapped the cast with her cane and grimaced.

'This is for you,' Nicky said, giving her the black shopping bag she was carrying.

'Nicky, you shouldn't have! But how wonderful . . . something from Chanel.'

Nicky told her: 'I hope you like it. I popped across the street this morning, to their boutique. They said you can change it, if you wish.'

'I am sure that I will adore it, thank you. But come, let us not stand here, let us go and sit down so that I can open your *cadeaux*. You are so generous, *ma petite*.'

They sat in wide *bergère* chairs opposite each other, and within a few seconds Marie Thérèse had opened the Chanel box and pulled out a beautiful red-and-white silk scarf. It was obvious from her expression that she loved it, and Nicky was delighted to see this.

'Thank you, Nicky, you are such a darling.' Pushing herself up, she went to kiss her, and then added, 'I have a bottle of white wine ready for us, and a little of the country pâté you always liked.'

With a chuckle, Nicky said, 'I hope you've got cornichons to go with it.'

'*Bien sûr!* I wouldn't dare to serve pâté to *you* without them. I have not forgotten how much you love them. Why, you and your little friend Natalie used to eat them like the candy!'

Nicky burst out laughing. 'And I've never lost the taste for them. Neither has Natalie.'

'And where is the beautiful Natalie these days?'

'Living in Los Angeles, and being very successful in films.'

'She was certainly beautiful enough to be a movie star when she was a child.'

'And she's still a beauty, but she works in production, behind the scenes, not in front of the camera.'

'But you are in front of it, my Nicky, and you are fantastic. One of the French networks recently showed a documentary you had done for ATN on the women of Beirut, and their point of view about the war. It was very touching. I was so proud of you.'

'Thank you,' Nicky murmured, and gave her a fond little smile. 'As I recall, they dubbed me in French.'

Hobbling across the floor of the living room, Marie Thérèse said, 'Yes, they did. I will get the wine from the refrigerator, so that we can have a drink.'

'Let me help you!' Nicky cried, jumping up.

'*Merci, chérie.*'

Nicky followed her through the foyer and down a short corridor to the kitchen, where she opened the wine and put it on the tray along with the loaf of pâté, the plate of toast, and the crystal dish of cornichons. Marie Thérèse placed several paper napkins on the plastic tray, and then Nicky carried it back to the living room.

Once they were settled in their chairs and had clinked glasses, Nicky let her eyes roam around the cheerful room. 'Your things look beautiful here, and the apartment seems to be large, but why did you move? You were comfortable on the Left Bank, weren't you?'

'I was, Nicky, this is true. But my apartment only had one bedroom. It was too small for three people.'

'*Three?* Are Paul and his wife living with you then?'

The Frenchwoman shook her head. '*Non, non, chérie*, they have their own apartment. I live here because of Marcel, my friend. He is a widower, with a son, and he already had this place. It was so much easier to move in here with them. Marcel and I did it up a little, and brought my things . . . ' She shrugged. 'We are content here.'

'I'm glad,' Nicky replied, and eyed her former nanny. Marie Thérèse looked younger than her forty-six years. The short curly hair was still dark, untouched by grey, the rosy complexion youthful, and those warm brown eyes she remembered so well from her childhood shone with happiness. 'Why, Marie Thérèse, I do believe you've fallen madly in love with your friend Marcel! I can see it in your eyes!'

Marie Thérèse blushed slightly and nodded, suddenly looking shy and girlish.

Nicky said, 'I think Marcel must be very good for you.'

'Oh he is, Nicky. I have not been so happy in years. Marcel is a nice man, very kind, and we are happy together.'

'Are you going to marry him?'

'Yes, perhaps. There is no hurry.' She lifted her shoulders, gave a Gallic shrug. 'When we feel like it, we will.' Marie Thérèse leaned forward slightly, and asked, 'But what of you, Nicky? Last night, on the telephone, you said you had a boyfriend in Paris. Is that why you are here? To be with him?'

'Yes, it is. He's a photographer, and we met in Beirut two years ago. And then just after we came out of China, where we'd been covering the demonstrations in Tiananmen Square, we sort of got involved. That was at the end of June.'

'I never thought you'd be interested in a Frenchman. You were such an all-American girl when you were small.'

'I guess I still am,' Nicky laughed. 'And my friend is an American, even though he lives here. His name's Cleeland Donovan, Clee for short, maybe you've seen his photographs in *Paris Match*.'

'*Oui, oui!*' Marie Thérèse exclaimed. 'I have! And are you going to marry him?'

'Maybe,' Nicky answered noncommittally.

'That would be wonderful for me, if you came to live in Paris . . . perhaps we could see each other more often than once every couple of years,' Marie Thérèse said, sounding wistful.

'Of course we could see each other if I lived here.'

At this moment the doorbell rang, and Marie Thérèse said, 'Ah, Nicky, can you go to the door, please? It is the lunch arriving, I ordered it from the restaurant next door.'

Nicky rose and hurried into the foyer, and as Marie Thérèse struggled to her feet, she called after her, 'It is paid for. All you have to do is put the dishes in the oven for me. It is already turned on.'

'Okay,' Nicky said over her shoulder, and opened the front door, took the large tray from the waiter standing there. '*Merci beaucoup*,' she said, and again glanced over her shoulder at Marie Thérèse, who was hobbling toward her. 'What about a – '

'It's already taken care of,' her friend cut in, and then she looked at the waiter, and murmured, '*Merci*, Olivier, *merci*.'

The waiter inclined his head. '*De rien, Madame Bouret*,' he said before he disappeared down the stairs.

Once they were in the kitchen, Marie Thérèse leaned against the door jamb whilst Nicky put each of the dishes in the oven. 'I ordered couscous from downstairs, they make it with chicken, and it's delicious,' she explained.

'It certainly smells it,' Nicky replied as she straightened, and pushed her hair out of her face.

Marie Thérèse continued, 'Now, let us go back to the salon and have another glass of wine before lunch. And you can tell me all about your friend Clee.'

'I'd be delighted to do that.' Nicky flashed her a wide smile, and added, 'I'll begin now if you like by telling you that he's absolutely wonderful.'

'Aha, my Nicky, I think you too are in love!'

'I just might be at that,' Nicky found herself agreeing.

CHAPTER THIRTY-TWO

Nicky felt her mood changing the minute she opened the door to Clee on Monday evening. The last vestiges of her sadness, that awful feeling of melancholy, dissipated instantly, and her spirits lifted. All of the things which had troubled her for the last few days were pushed to the back of her mind. The only thing that mattered was Clee.

He stood there, saying nothing, a huge smile spreading across his face, his love spilling from his dark eyes.

She smiled back, her face filling with radiance, opened the door wider, and stepped to one side so he could enter.

'I've missed you, Nick,' he said, striding into the suite, grabbing hold of her, wrapping his arms around her, pushing the door closed with his foot. 'It's been too long, babe,' he went on, brushing her cheek with his lips. 'Far too long for me.'

'And me,' she said, holding on to him tightly. 'I've missed you too, you know.'

'I'm glad,' Clee said, and bent his face to hers, kissed her lightly on the mouth, and then releasing her, he put his arm around her shoulders, walked her into the small sitting room.

Pausing in the centre he held her away from him, exclaimed, 'God, it's so good to see you! You've lost weight . . . pining for me, I've no doubt.' He gave her a cheeky grin and added, 'Well I hope that's the reason.'

'It's true, I have longed for you,' Nicky responded, taking herself by surprise with this unexpected admission. She was usually so cautious in what she said to him.

'That makes two of us. But hey, I'm going to have to fatten you up a bit, otherwise Amelia will be after me when we get to the farm. You know what she's like.'

'Sure I do, she wants to turn me into a butterball,' Nicky declared, laughing. 'But nevertheless, I'm counting the minutes . . . I can't wait to get there. It's going to be wonderful!' She meant this; she ached to escape to Provence, wanting to obliterate everything that had happened since she had arrived in Europe, and most of all to forget about Charles Devereaux entirely.

'Well, I guess I'd better dump my problems on you now, before we do anything else,' he announced, and made a grimace.

Nicky stared at him, raised a blonde brow, looking concerned. 'What kind of problems, Clee?'

He didn't immediately answer this question. Instead, he asked, 'Is that a bottle of champagne I spy in the ice bucket over there?'

'Dom Pérignon. Your favourite.'

'Let's have a glass, darling, and then I'll explain.'

'Fine,' Nicky said, and sat down on the sofa, experiencing a little pang of anxiety, hoping the problems he had mentioned were not insurmountable. She couldn't bear it if he had to go away on another assignment. All she wanted was to be with him. She needed him, needed his gentleness and affection.

Clee went over to the coffee table, fiddled with the cork, opened the bottle of champagne with efficiency and filled the two crystal flutes on the tray. After clinking his glass against hers, he took a long swallow. 'Mmmm, that's good,' he murmured, and walked over to the fireplace. 'It's been a helluva rough day at the office.'

'The problems, Clee, what are they?' she pressed, sounding anxious.

He put his glass down on the mantelpiece, and said, 'Okay, here goes. Firstly, I've got a leak in the bathroom. I came back last night to find a flood. Bathroom *and* bedroom under water – well, almost. I called several plumbers today but, in typical French fashion, not one was available until tomorrow. I could float away in the meantime. Anyway, my housekeeper has done her best to contain the deluge, but there's no way I can move you into my apartment tonight. So – '

Reaching into his jacket pocket, he pulled out a toothbrush and banged it down on the mantel. 'I've got to sleep here tonight, babe. I can camp out in the suite with you, can't I?'

'Of course you can, you fool!' she cried, the laughter rising in her as she filled with relief. 'I'd love it, and I'd hardly call *that* a problem. I mean, staying here isn't, but I am sorry about your apartment.'

He grinned at her. 'It needed redecorating anyway.' His face sobered as he went on. 'Second one coming up . . . we can't leave for the farm on Wednesday as we'd planned, Nick. I've got *beaucoup* problems at the office – '

'Such as what?' she cut in, her brow puckering as worry took hold of her again.

'Two of my partners are kaput, so to speak. Steve's mother died yesterday, very suddenly and unexpectedly. She wasn't even sick, just dropped dead in her kitchen of a heart attack. He took off for the States this morning, and he'll be gone a week at least. That wouldn't be too hard for the office to handle normally, except that unfortunately Michel put his back out ten days ago. A slipped disc. And he's still not well enough to come in, is laid up in agony, in fact. Pete Naylor and I will have to split their assignments between us, which are mostly in Paris, thank God.'

'I'm sorry to hear about Steve's mother, and I feel for Michel with his back. And of course I understand.'

'Do you mind being in Paris another week?'

'You know I love Paris. Besides which, I don't really care where I am, as long as I'm with you.'

'That's the best news I've had today,' he said, smiling broadly, his manner nonchalant. But his eyes were fastened on hers very intently all of a sudden.

Clee was no fool, and he realized the progress he had made with her since the had been together in Provence and later in New York. Maybe his absence from her life had been effective, had helped his case.

Taking a sip of champagne, he continued, 'There's another thing, although it's not really a problem, more of a disappointment. Yoyo won't be arriving in Paris until the end of the week. So I'm afraid there's no celebration tonight.'

'Oh yes there is,' she said, giving him a pointed look.

'That's right!' he exclaimed.

'I'm sorry we won't be seeing Yoyo,' Nicky remarked between sips of champagne. 'But the main thing is that he's on his way here, not rotting in a Beijing jail. Have you actually spoken to him yet?'

'No. He phoned the office again. On Saturday. Jean-Claude says Yoyo knew you would be in Paris today. Apparently he'd spoken to your secretary in New York at some point.'

'Last week. He phoned me at the network. Annette told me today, when I checked in with her.'

Clee nodded, finished his champagne, and stepped over to the coffee table, poured himself another one. 'Are you ready for a refill, Nicky?'

She shook her head. 'No more for me just now, thanks.'

Propping himself against the mantel, Clee asked, 'How did your research go in Rome, Athens and Madrid?'

'Okay . . . Fine, thanks. And how did you get on in Berlin and Leipzig?'

'Not bad, Nick, not bad at all. And I have a feeling I might go back there in the not too distant future. A lot's happening – we've seen nothing yet.' He began to speak about the political situations now existing in East and West Berlin, Leipzig, the Eastern European bloc in general, most especially Russia.

Nicky sat back on the sofa, listening attentively, interested in everything he had to say, respecting his judgement, as she always had. But at the same time, part of her mind was focused on him. She could not help thinking how marvellous he looked this evening. His face was lightly tanned, as it usually was from being outdoors so much, and his brown hair had been lightened by the sun. He wore a dark-blue silk suit, a pale-blue shirt and a navy tie; she had never seen him looking smarter. But although he had long ago acquired that inimitable stylishness of the French, and looked European in a certain sense, his face was wholly American. It was boyish and open, a nice face. The brown eyes were full of candour and sincerity, his wide Irish mouth was generous, also very gentle. Yes, Cleeland Donovan was a quietly handsome man, and very appealing.

Unexpectedly, her feelings for him seemed to engulf her, overwhelm her. For the first time she *truly* understood how much this man really meant to her. There was no one in the world who was more important than he was, and momentarily she was startled by this sudden self-knowledge.

Lost for a few seconds in her contemplation of him and of her feelings for him, she wasn't aware that he had stopped speaking until he let out a low whistle. He startled her. With a jolt she sat up straighter, and blinked.

'Hey, Nicky, where are you drifting off to?' he asked and broke into laughter. 'Hell, I guess I'm boring you!'

'No, no, Clee, you're not, honestly,' she protested, staring at him.

767

'What's wrong?' he demanded. 'You've got a peculiar expression on your face.'

'I love you.'

He gaped at her. 'What?'

'You heard what I said.'

He crossed the floor in three strides and sat down on the sofa next to her, reached for her hands, held them tightly in his, peered into her face. 'Yes, it's true, I did hear. But would you mind repeating that phrase one more time?'

'I love you, Clee.'

'Oh Nicky.' He took her face between his hands and kissed her, then, leaning against her, he pushed her down onto the cushions. Moving a strand of blonde hair away from her face, he said, 'I love you too. And it's been hellish not having you with me.'

Nicky lifted her hand, touched his mouth, traced its shape with a fingertip. 'I know, it was the same for me, darling.'

Once more he lowered his mouth to hers and kissed her more passionately than before, his tongue finding hers, grazing it, lingering against it. Abruptly he stopped, and whispered against her hair, 'Let's find a bed. I want you.'

Clee stood up, offered her his hand, and together they walked into the bedroom. He flung off his clothes, and so did she; they met in the middle of the floor, wrapped their arms around each other. They stood for a long moment, without saying a word, without moving, just glad to be close and intimate and together again.

At last Clee said, 'It's never been like this before for me, it really hasn't.'

'It hasn't for me either,' she answered, and she knew now that this was the truth. She had not loved Charles in quite the same way that she loved Clee, because each man had brought out something different in her.

There was another moment of silence as he nuzzled his face in her hair, stroked his hands down over her back, slid them onto her buttocks, pulled her closer so that their pelvic bones touched.

Nicky trembled slightly, becoming aroused as he already was. Now it was she who took the lead, pushed him gently away from her and led him over to the bed.

They lay on their sides, facing each other, gazing into each other's eyes, saying nothing. But neither of them needed words. They could read each other's faces, etched as they were with love and desire.

'Ah Nicky, my lovely Nicky,' he whispered, and reached out for her, brought her closer, his right hand settling on the nape of her neck. 'I want to possess you completely, take all of you to me . . .'

'I know . . . I want that too.'

Their mouths came together again, and immediately he slipped on top of her, pushed his hands under her back and pulled her against him. His mouth became insistent, demanding; ardently she responded to him, her passion mounting as his did. He entered her unexpectedly, without any preamble, as he had several times in Provence, and she gasped in astonishment. And then as he eased deeper into her, her legs went around his back and she cleaved to him, became part of him. At once they found their own rhythm, as they always did, moving faster and faster.

'Oh God, Nicky, oh God,' Clee cried as he lifted his mouth from hers at one moment. His breathing was laboured; he gasped as she was gasping.

She stiffened under him, began to quiver. 'Clee! I love you!' She opened her eyes and looked up into his face. 'I love you,' she moaned softly. Her quivering intensified and she gave herself up to him, came to him swiftly.

As always her passion for him brought Clee to the height of excitement, and he began to lose control. Before he could stop himself, he was flowing into her, calling her name as she had his, telling her that he loved her as he had not loved any woman ever in his life.

He fell against her, breathing heavily, then lifted his head, bent over her and kissed her face. Her cheeks were damp; he tasted the salt of her tears.

'You're crying,' he said in surprise, wiping the tears away with one hand. 'Why, Nicky? What is it? Why are you weeping?'

'I don't know,' she murmured, looking up at him. Half laughing, she added, 'Because I'm so happy, I guess.'

He merely smiled that lopsided smile of his, which she knew so well, and said nothing. He simply took her in his arms and held her close.

'This is a much better picnic than the one we had that night at the farm,' Clee said, between bites on a chicken leg.

'I don't agree!' Nicky looked at him swiftly and shook her head. 'That was the best picnic I've ever had in my entire life. You made some wonderful things, including the greatest peanut butter and jelly sandwiches I've ever eaten.'

Clee threw back his head and guffawed. 'If that's all it takes to please you, I can see I'm going to have an easy time with you, honeybunch.'

Nicky laughed with him, reached for her glass of white wine on the bedside table. 'I can be very tough about some things, kiddo.'

'Oh, I know that,' he shot back.

The two of them sat cross-legged in the middle of the large bed, wrapped in the hotel's white towelling bathrobes. There was a plate of chicken and the bread basket between them; on the room-service table nearby, which Clee had wheeled in from the living room, there was a bowl of green salad, a basket of fresh fruit and a bottle of Montrachet in an ice bucket.

'I bet all the girls mistake you for Kevin Costner,' Nicky suddenly said, eyeing him appraisingly.

'Fat chance of that!'

'You know he's your look-alike, Clee.'

He grinned at her but made no comment and drank his wine.

'*I* mistook you for him.'

'What does that mean?'

Nicky told him about the mistake she had made in Athens, how she had bought a magazine because she thought it was he on the cover.

'It must be wishful thinking on your part,' Clee said dismissively, chuckling. 'Is that what you really want? A movie star?'

'No, I want you.'

'You've got me, in case you hadn't realized it.'

Nicky offered him a smug little smile, and said, 'I'm glad.'

'What about you? Do I have you?'

'You know you do, Clee.'

He grinned and blew her a kiss.

Reaching for her wine, Nicky took a sip, then sat nursing it in both hands, looking thoughtful. After a moment or two she said slowly, 'Clee, when I was in London and called you in Berlin, just before I left for Rome, I told you I'd been to see Anne Devereaux at Pullenbrook – '

'You went to make amends, right?'

'Yes, that's true, but I also had another reason to go and see her.'

'Oh, what reason?' he asked casually, picking up the chicken leg again.

Nicky cleared her throat, plunged in. 'I thought that Charles might be alive, that he might very well have faked his own death, then vanished for his own reasons.'

Clee was dumbfounded for a split second, and put the chicken leg back on the plate, then exclaimed, 'You've got to be kidding! You can't be serious!' He shook his head, began to laugh, incredulity echoing. 'Come on, Nick, it's me you're talking to . . . stop kidding around.'

'But I'm not. I'm serious, deadly serious, Clee.'

Her sober tone registered with him, and he stared at her alertly, carefully weighing what she had said. Finally, he asked, 'What happened to make you think *that* after all these years?'

Nicky told him the story, reciting most of the pertinent details, but stopping short once she had filled him in about the events in Rome and Athens. She said nothing at all about Madrid.

When she had finished, Clee said in an oddly subdued voice, 'Why the hell would you want to traipse all over Europe looking for a dead man? Well, a supposedly dead man. Hadn't he caused you enough pain? Or do you still have feelings for him, Nick? Is that it?'

'No, I don't! Absolutely not! I don't, Clee!' she protested fiercely. 'I'm emotionally free of Charles Devereaux, and I have been for a long time. Long before I fell in love with you, in fact. Please believe that, darling. You do, don't you?'

He simply nodded and looked at her more closely, his eyes pinning hers. Then he said quietly, 'If you say so . . . Yes, I believe you, Nick. Just tell me why you went looking for him.'

'I wanted to get to the truth. Wouldn't you?'

'I guess so . . . '

'Listen, Clee, I was stunned, shocked, disbelieving, when I saw that face on our newscast from Rome. But the guy did look so much like Charles I felt I had to go and talk to Anne. I just couldn't get that face out of my mind. And I'd always been a bit dismayed, sort of troubled because Charles's body was never found.' Nicky paused, bit her lip. 'I suppose it's human nature to want to have a funeral, bury the dead . . . I think I wanted to get to the truth so that I could close that chapter of my life.'

'Is it closed? Really and truly closed? Or is he going to haunt you?'

'No, I've just told you, it's closed.'

'So tell me something else, Nick. Why are you now so sure he committed suicide, that he's really dead? What made you change your mind?'

'Because I kept coming up against brick walls wherever I went. There was no trace of him in Rome or in Athens.'

'Why did you go to Madrid?' Clee frowned slightly before reaching for his drink and taking a long swallow. 'What did you hope to find there?'

'I wasn't sure what I'd find, actually. I wanted to show the pictures to his former Spanish partner. I guess I was seeking a confirmation or a denial from Don Pedro.'

'And what did the Spanish guy say?'

'I didn't see Don Pedro. He was away until today, and I decided not to wait around. As I told you on the phone this morning, I took a flight out of Madrid late on Saturday afternoon and checked in here.'

'Why the sudden change of heart?'

'It hit me that if I could so easily mistake Kevin Costner for you on the cover of a magazine, then I could also mistake another man for Charles Devereaux . . . with a slightly altered appearance, of course.'

'Photographs can be very deceptive and misleading. Let me see them, Nicky, I'd like to take a look at them.'

'I got rid of them . . . what was the point of keeping them?'

'There wasn't one, I guess.'

'You're angry with me, aren't you, Clee?'

'No, I'm not, just startled, troubled.'

'Because I lied to you, because I said I was in those different cities doing research for a special, when I wasn't?'

He shook his head. 'No, they were only white lies.'

'Why then?' she pressed anxiously, wanting to make things right with him.

'Because you didn't tell me immediately, the day after you'd seen the newscast. I'd have understood, Nick, once I'd got used to the idea that the guy might be alive – and giving me competition.'

'You have no competition. I love *you*.'

'I'd also like you to trust me . . . I'm a pretty intelligent guy, and I respect you and your mind, your professionalism. And your independence. I would never interfere with anything you wanted to do, unless I thought you might get hurt in some way. For God's sake, you're a mature woman, a tough, seasoned broadcast journalist, a war correspondent that I've worked side-by-side with for two years. Do you think I don't know you and trust you? Anyway, I'd never treat you like a little girl.'

'Thanks for those words, Clee, and yes, you *do* know me, perhaps better than anyone else. I'm pleased you trust me, and *I* do trust you, you know. I really do. Please say you're not angry with me.'

'I'm not, honestly, Nicky.' He gave her a small, reassuring smile.

There was a sudden silence.

After a couple of minutes, Clee said, 'So his mother didn't think the photographs resembled him?'

'No, she didn't. She was adamant, in fact. And so was Philip Rawlings, her boyfriend. You know, the man she was with in Les Baux.'

He nodded. 'I remember. What's the legal situation in England? I mean about Charles Devereaux.'

'He was listed as a missing person, because there was no body. A suicide note doesn't make any difference when there's no body. I'm not sure whether the police have closed their files on him yet. I never thought to ask Anne.'

'You've never ever discussed Charles Devereaux with me. You've always balked. What little I know came from Arch Leverson. But he was pretty closed-mouthed about the whole thing, Nick, didn't say very much, out of loyalty to you. I didn't even know Devereaux had left a suicide note. Was it addressed to you?'

'No, to his mother.'

'What did it say . . . do you know?'

'Yes, she showed it to me when I flew to England a few days after the suicide. It was only a couple of lines, very brief, almost cold. He said in the note that he didn't want to live any longer, that he was doing the only thing he possibly could – taking his own life, and that he hoped she would forgive him.'

'Has she?'

'I don't really know . . . she still grieves for him, I'm certain of that, although she keeps up a good front.'

'Was there a letter for you?'

'No.'

'Didn't you find that strange?'

'Yes, I did. But maybe he didn't have any last words for me.'

'Why do you say that?'

'Because in the months before he killed himself he did everything very deliberately. He sold his shares in the wine importing company to his British and Spanish partners, he also sold his flat, made a will, and put all of his affairs in order. It was all done very, very methodically, Clee, so if he *had* had anything he wanted to say to me, he would have written me a letter, don't you think?'

'I suppose he would,' Clee murmured. 'Who got his money?'

'Anne is the beneficiary under his will, but of course she hasn't inherited it yet, because Charles is not considered to be legally dead. Under British law, Anne can only go to court for a legal declaration of death after seven years, not before. She's got four more years to wait.'

'I see.' Clee leaned forward slightly, a frown furrowing his brow, his eyes thoughtful. He said slowly, 'When a man melts into thin air to start a new life with a new identity, he usually does so for a hell of a good reason. When you thought Devereaux might be alive, why did you think he'd faked his own death? For what reason, Nick?'

'I wasn't sure. I told Arch when I saw him in Rome that it might be a reason so bizarre no one could even imagine it. But actually I thought Charles was involved in something illegal.'

'Such as?'

'Arms smuggling or drug trafficking.'

'Yeah, I guess I'd have come to the same conclusion,' Clee agreed. 'Especially in view of the world we live in today.'

'I brought all this up tonight because I wanted you to know what I'd been doing, Clee,' Nicky said, gazing at him earnestly. 'I didn't want there to be anything between us.'

'I'm glad you told me, and I'm not angry, babe.' Clee's boyish, lopsided smile flashed, and he went on, 'I just feel a bit protective of you, that's all . . . I love you.'

'And I love you.'

'Let's not discuss this guy Devereaux any more. Let's bury him once and for all, shall we?'

'He's already buried,' Nicky said, and slipped off the bed. She went around to Clee's side and hugged him hard. 'Thanks for being such a good guy, and for understanding,' she murmured. 'I'll be back in a minute. Don't go away.'

'I'm *never* leaving,' Clee said, laughing.

Nicky went into the bathroom, locked the door and leaned against it, exhaling with relief. She had genuinely wanted to tell Clee as much of the truth as she possibly could, but she had known all along that she must edit her story. Thankfully she had done so adroitly, had managed to tell it without a hitch. No one must ever know that Charles Devereaux was alive. She had given her promise and she would not betray him; his life was in her hands. And her secret did no harm to Clee. Besides, she would never see Charles Devereaux again. That chapter was finally closed.

CHAPTER THIRTY-THREE

'After Mai die in Xiehe Hospital I take her body to parents,' Yoyo said, looking from Clee to Nicky. 'Friends help me. We find two pedicabs. They take us. We go to Mai's house. Her parents weep. Weep a lot. They very sad. I very sad.' Yoyo shook his head, and his tone was mournful when he added, 'Mai such young girl – ' His voice quavered, and he stopped speaking.

Nicky reached out and touched his arm sympathetically, with great affection. It was hard to believe that he was with them in Paris at last, and looking so well, almost prosperous, she thought. He wore a neat, dark suit, a white shirt and a red tie, seemed totally in command of himself and the situation.

Clearing her throat, she said, 'Clee and I know how terrible it was for you, how grief-stricken you must have been, and still are. It is so tragic. We were all upset and so very sorry when Mai died of her wounds in Beijing.'

Yoyo tried to smile without much success. 'I know, Nicky.' He turned to Clee. 'Thank you, Clee, for carrying Mai so far. Trying to save Mai. Taking her to Xiehe. You a good man, Clee. You a good friend. And you a good friend, Nicky.'

'I just wish we could have saved her,' Clee said, his heart going out to the young Chinese student who sat with them in his apartment on the rue Jacob. It was early on Friday evening, on the first day of September. Yoyo had come over to the sixth *arrondissement* on the Left Bank to visit them, tell them how he had escaped from Beijing, and share his news. Later they were going out to have the long-awaited celebration dinner with Yoyo, as the guests of his benefactor, a Mr Loong.

Yoyo suddenly said, 'Mai's death bad joss.'

'Yes, it *was* bad luck,' Clee agreed. He and Nicky glanced at each other, and in an attempt to change the subject, Clee went on, 'Nicky and I have been terribly worried about you all these weeks, Yoyo. So have Arch and the guys. We didn't know what had happened to you after we left Beijing. We waited in Hong Kong for you, as we promised we would, and for several days, you know.'

'Sorry I did not come. It was hard for me, Clee.'

Nicky said, 'Don't apologize, Yoyo, we understand. It's just that we were so concerned for your safety. We hoped nothing bad had happened, that you weren't locked up in a Beijing jail.' She squeezed his arm again, gave him a warm smile. 'Thank God you're all right.'

'Many things happened to me. But I lucky. Really.'

'Tell us everything. How you got out of Beijing, how you came to Paris,' Clee said.

'I begin at beginning. Yes?'

'Okay, Yoyo, shoot,' Clee replied, smiling at him.

Yoyo nodded, took a deep breath. 'After you leave police everywhere in Beijing. I go Mai's house. Mai's parents hide me. Police asking many questions about students. Many arrests. Many students go to jail. At Qinghua University very bad things happen. It dangerous. I stay Mai's house one week. Mai's parents worry police find me. Arrest me. Mai's father take me house of friends. They hide me for ten days. It difficult. Dangerous. Necessary I leave Beijing.'

'Is that when you left the city? In the middle of June?' Nicky asked.

'No. No. I stayed in Beijing. I move many times. I go to friends of Mai's parents. They hide me. Mai's mother say she help me escape. She have *guanxi* – '

'That means connections,' Nicky interrupted, looking across at Clee. 'Philip Rawlings told me when I was at Pullenbrook.'

'How would he know a thing like that?' Clee asked, frowning.

'I told you before, he's got an important job at the British Foreign Office. Hong Kong is a British Crown Colony and under British protection and government until 30 June 1997.' Nicky shrugged. 'Who knows, maybe he's on the China Desk or the Hong Kong Desk at the Foreign Office. He's always been very cagey about what he actually does there.'

'I understand,' Clee said, then addressed Yoyo. 'Sorry for the interruption. Keep going, Yoyo.'

'Mai's mother have many connections. She sent me to southern China. Mai's father give me money. I have your money. I keep it safe. Mai's mother say I need much money. For bribes. They very important.'

'How did you get to Hong Kong?' Nicky asked, her curiosity now getting the better of her.

'Many people help me. Ordinary people. They hate government. They hate what government did to students. They sorry for students. They like democracy movement. Many different people help me. Mai's mother help me go to Shenzhen – '

'That's adjacent to Hong Kong,' Clee cut in, looking at Nicky and explaining, 'It's an economic zone, something like Hong Kong, and it became a sort of boom town overnight. Correct, Yoyo?'

Yoyo nodded. 'You know Shenzhen, Clee?'

'Yes. I did a story there about a year ago.' Once again he glanced at Nicky. 'It's kind of honky-tonk, full of criminals and low life, as well as legit businessmen and entrepreneurs. But continue with your story, Yoyo.'

'I needed papers to go to Shenzhen. All Chinese citizens need special certificate. Mai's father have friend. This friend have *guanxi* – connections. This man buy certificate for me.'

'But how did you get to Shenzhen from Beijing? It's a long way,' Nicky asserted.

'Mai's father take me to Shanghai. In car. His brother help. He pass me along. To many friends. It is network, Nicky. They help students. I cannot say more. Okay? You understand?'

'Yes, of course I do,' she said. 'You don't want to divulge too much about the network, because other students may have to use it as an escape route.'

'That is correct, Nicky. I arrive Shenzhen beginning of August. I have special connection. Friend of friend. I stay two weeks. Friend in Shenzhen take me to Zhong-Ying Street one day. It busy shopping street. One side China. Other side Hong Kong. Many tourists. We bribe police. They look other way. I go over border.'

'But there are Hong Kong police stationed on the other side of Zhong-Ying Street,' Clee said. 'On the Hong Kong side. I know that area because of the story I did on Shenzhen. How did you manage once you'd crossed over?'

'I run. I slip through back streets. Alleyways. I hide. I get to water. Hong Kong on other side of bay. Mr Loong have boat waiting. Every day boat wait for me. Until I come. I go to Hong Kong on Mr Loong's boat. Mr Loong look after me in Hong Kong. He good man.'

'Who exactly is Mr Loong, Yoyo?'

'Oh Nicky, he brother Mai's mother. He very important man in Hong Kong. Big businessman. He leave Shanghai in 1948 before Communists come in 1949. He start export-import business in Hong Kong. Now he very rich man. He help me. He bring me to Paris.'

'You were an illegal immigrant in Hong Kong with no papers. How did you manage? And how did you get out?' Clee asked. 'You have a Chinese passport, I know, but what about visas and all that?'

'Mr Loong fix everything. He has many friends. Important friends. He buy me *real* Hong Kong passport. It is in my name.'

Nicky said, 'May we see it, Yoyo? You don't mind showing it to us, do you?'

'No, Nicky.' He reached into his jacket and pulled out the passport, handed it to her.

Clee rose and walked over to join her on the sofa. Together they examined it, and then looked at each other. They had expected to see a forgery. But it appeared to be an authentic and valid Hong Kong passport in Yoyo's full name: Chin Yong Yu.

Handing it back to him, Clee said, 'Very good, Yoyo. Your friend Mr Loong obviously has big *guanxi*.'

Yoyo laughed and nodded.

'And what are your plans?' Clee now asked. 'Are you going to stay here in France, or what?'

'Mr Loong has Paris office for import-export company. He brought me here as secretary. Maybe I stay. Maybe I go New York.' As he said this he looked at Nicky questioningly.

'We'll talk that over tomorrow, decide later, shall we, Yoyo?' she said, and eyed the clock on the mantelpiece. 'I think we ought to be going. Isn't Mr Loong expecting us at eight o'clock?'

'Yes.' Yoyo got up, and continued, 'He and Mrs Loong expect us then. At Ritz Hotel. Place Vendôme. Ernest Hemingway suite.'

Clee caught Nicky's eye and they stared at each other in astonishment, and then before she could stop herself Nicky burst out laughing. Clee stood next to her, grinning.

'What is it?' Yoyo looked puzzled.

'I can't help thinking that your luck has changed, Yoyo. Mr Loong is definitely good joss.'

'Oh yes, Mr Loong very good joss,' Yoyo agreed.

CHAPTER THIRTY-FOUR

Anne Devereaux had been on Nicky's mind ever since Madrid, and on Sunday morning she decided to phone her at Pullenbrook.

'It's lovely to hear your voice, Nicky,' Anne said.

'And yours, Anne. I'm here in Paris with Clee, and I thought I'd call to say hello. How've you been?'

'Oh, all right, I suppose. I'm so glad you phoned . . . I didn't know where to find you . . . I've been wanting to talk to you.'

Nicky caught something odd in Anne's tone, and she shifted in the chair, sat up straighter. 'What about?' she asked carefully.

'Charles. Nicky, I – '

'Oh Anne, I'm so very sorry I came to see you at Pullenbrook two weeks ago. I know how much I upset you. It was wrong of me. I acted impulsively, without really thinking things through. Charles *did* commit suicide three years ago. I know he did. It wasn't him in the news segment. I was wrong about that.'

'I'm not so sure anymore,' Anne said.

Nicky stiffened, gripped the phone tighter. 'What do you mean?'

'I've been thinking . . . mostly about the two photographs you had. When you first showed them to me I *did* see the resemblance. In fact, I thought it was quite striking. But then I immediately convinced myself that they couldn't possibly be of Charles. For the simple reason that my son would never do anything shoddy, like fake his own death. But in the last two weeks those photographs have haunted me, Nicky.'

'Forget them, Anne! It wasn't Charles! Honestly, it wasn't.'

'I'd like to see the pictures again,' Anne said quietly. 'Would you be kind enough to send them to me please?'

'I don't have them. I destroyed them.'

'*Oh.*'

'There was no point in keeping them, Anne.'

'You really don't have them?'

'I told you, I got rid of them, they were torn up and thrown away.'

There was a silence at the other end of the phone. Nicky waited for a moment, and then she said, 'Anne, are you there?'

'Yes, I'm here, Nicky.'

To Nicky her voice sounded very faint, and she exclaimed, 'Aren't you feeling well?'

'I haven't been sleeping much lately, to tell you the truth. I suppose my mind has been on Charles. So many memories coming back . . . '

'Oh, Anne darling, don't do this to yourself,' Nicky said very softly, filling with compassion for the other woman. 'This is all my fault. I don't know what to do to help you, to put your mind at rest, to make you feel better.' When there was no response at the other end of the line, Nicky said, 'Is there anything at all that I can do?'

'Could you come to England, Nicky? I would like to talk to you . . . need to talk to you . . . there's no one else. Perhaps if I saw you I'd feel less alone . . . '

Nicky's heart dropped, and she was about to refuse, but knowing she was responsible for this woman's present pain and heartache she changed her mind. Instead, she said, 'I could come over tomorrow, Anne, but only for the day, I'm afraid. I wouldn't be able to come to Pullenbrook. Could you meet me in London? Maybe we could get together for lunch?'

'Of course I can come up! That would be marvellous, Nicky!' Anne's voice sounded suddenly stronger, more cheerful and she hurried on, 'Why don't we meet at the flat? It's quiet and private, and so much more comfortable than a restaurant.'

'Yes, that'll be fine, Anne. I'll see you tomorrow – let's say between noon and twelve thirty.'

'I'm so looking forward to it.'

'Give my best to Philip.'

'I will. He's out taking a walk at the moment, otherwise I would have put him on. I know he would have wanted to say hello. Well, I'll see you tomorrow, darling, goodbye.'

'Bye, Anne.'

After Nicky had hung up she sat in the chair at Clee's desk in his small den, pondering her conversation with Anne for a few minutes. Anne had sounded wan and low-spirited at the beginning of their conversation, and she knew it was her fault. She was the one who had ripped open a wound that had partially healed during the past three years, and in so doing had created new suffering.

The past had come rushing back to torment this lovely woman, who deserved so much better. Nicky experienced a flash of sudden anger, thinking of Charles and what he had done to his mother when he had vanished, and then she instantly pushed this to one side. He no longer played a part in any of this, and certainly not in Anne's life. She was going to find a way to stop the bleeding, to help Anne's wound to heal again. In order to do this she had to go to London, and so she would fly over in the morning. It was only an hour's flight, after all. And when she got there she was going to convince Anne Devereaux that her son was dead. He was – to all intents and purposes.

The front door banged and startled her, and she jumped up and went into the small entrance foyer. Clee was standing there, his arms laden with shopping bags. Two baguettes poked out of one, vegetables out of another, and flowers were balanced on top of a third.

'Hi, babe,' he said, grinning at her over the top of them. 'Come on and talk to me while I unpack this stuff.'

She followed him into the kitchen. 'It looks as if you bought enough food to feed an army!' she exclaimed. 'What are you intending to make for lunch?'

'Donovan's famous farm omelette, for one thing,' he replied, dumping the armful of bags on the kitchen table.

'And what's that, may I ask?'

'You'll have to wait and see. It's my speciality, and it's delicious. You'll love it.' Whipping the bunch of flowers out of the bag, he spun around and handed it to her.

'For my best girl,' he said, leaning forward, kissing her on the cheek. 'And the top of the mornin' to you, mavourneen,' he added in a strong Irish brogue.

'Oh Clee, how sweet of you, thank you,' she said, taking them, pressing her face into the blooms. Then impulsively she went to him, threw her arms around him and hugged him close. Her face was next to his, and she whispered, 'I love you.'

'I love you too, Nick.' He lifted her face with one hand, looked into her eyes, and added, 'And you'll never know how much . . . I'll just have to try and show you. In the meantime, I've got to get started and make brunch, otherwise we'll be eating at four o'clock this afternoon.'

'What can I do to help?'

'Once I've moved the groceries over to the counter top, you can set the table. Then you can open the bottle of champagne and pour us two glasses, and add a dash of orange juice to them. After that, you can sit here and watch me make the omelettes. Okay by you?'

'Okay by me, chief,' she said, laughing, and helped him to carry the grocery bags to the other side of the room before putting the flowers in a vase of water. Once she had spread the cloth on the table, and added the plates and knives and forks, she busied herself with the bottle of champagne. Her father liked Bucks Fizz, the mixture of champagne and orange juice, and now she made it with great expertise.

'Here's to the girl I adore,' Clee said, clinking his glass against hers. '*Santé.*'

'*Santé*, darling,' she murmured and smiled at him.

Clee strode to the long counter top under the window, began emptying the bags, and then started to prepare the food.

Nicky sat watching him, thinking how fast and efficient he was as he handled the vegetables, all of which were obviously intended as ingredients in the omelette.

Looks as if he's making a Spanish omelette to me, she thought, and bit back a smile.

'Are you still going to Brussels tomorrow, Clee?' Nicky asked after a moment.

'Yep, sure am, honey. Why?'

'I called Anne Devereaux while you were out buying the groceries, and I was a bit upset when I heard how depressed she sounded. That's a bad word; I thought she was troubled, Clee.'

He turned around and looked at Nicky thoughtfully. 'I guess you think you've opened a can of worms. Or, perhaps more appropriately, Pandora's Box. Is that it, babe?'

'Yes. And it really is my fault, Clee. I was very stupid, rushing to see her the way I did. It was far too impulsive on my part. I should have waited, thought things over, and spoken to you.'

'You most certainly should have done that, and I would have told you to forget it. But never mind. No use crying over milk on the floor.' He turned back to the counter, and began to peel the three large potatoes lying on the chopping board. 'What do you want to do about her, Nicky? Is there a way to help her?' he asked as he worked.

'She wanted me to come and see her. Asked me to, in fact. She says she has no one else to talk to but me.'

'What about Philip? Isn't he sympathetic to her needs?'

'I'm sure he is, but she and I have always been extremely close, and anyway, I was . . . ' She let her sentence trail off.

'And anyway, you were engaged to Charles,' he finished for her, glancing over his shoulder. He smiled at her. 'You don't have to tiptoe around me, about Charles Devereaux, I mean. You *were* engaged to him, and you did have a relationship with him, and none of us are without a past, a history, at our age. We all carry a certain amount of baggage with us.'

'Thanks for understanding. Anyway, I did agree to go to London tomorrow, to have lunch with her at the flat in Eaton Square. Since you'd said you were going to be in Brussels for two or three days I thought you wouldn't mind.'

'I don't, and I wouldn't have minded even if I were going to be here. You have to do what you have to do, and I'm never going to put a leash on you. Hey, Nicky, I'm not that kinda guy.' He turned to face her, and leaning against the counter top, he added, 'And I hope you're not going to put a leash on me either.'

Nicky shook her head. 'Never! That's *verboten*, for sure. Besides, you're a bachelor at heart, remember? You cast yourself in the same mould as Robert Capa years ago, when you were still a boy. And I know that you want to take your camera and roam the world as he did, footloose and fancy free. I understand, and it's acceptable to me, Clee.'

He put the knife he was holding on the counter top, walked across the kitchen, and stood looking at her. Then he took the glass out of her hand and placed it on the table, pulled her to her feet.

'Listen, honeybunch, I might want to roam the world taking photographs, and I might want to be footloose, but I certainly don't want to be fancy free. I want you at my side.' He brought her into his arms and kissed her hard on the mouth, then he held her away from him, and the lopsided smile flickered.

779

He touched her face lightly with one finger, and said, 'Shall we get married?'

Nicky was totally caught off guard, and she stared at him. 'You've taken me by surprise . . . do I have to decide today?'

'No, you don't have to decide today.' He grinned and kissed the tip of her nose. 'You can decide tomorrow or next week, or whenever you want, just as long as you say yes.'

CHAPTER THIRTY-FIVE

Like Pullenbrook, Anne's flat in Eaton Square was beautiful, and impressive in its own way. It had been decorated years before by the great English interior designer John Fowler, one of his last assignments before his death.

The living room was spacious, high-ceilinged, its walls painted a peculiar faded pink, which the late interior decorator had named Ointment Pink. The taffeta draperies at the two tall windows were slightly deeper, and this soft shade, used throughout, helped to give the room its rosy glow. Georgian antiques, an Aubusson rug on the floor, and several large horse paintings by Stubbs added to the room's quiet elegance. As she always did, Anne had put her inimitable stamp on it; there were skirted tables laden with family photographs in silver frames, pots of tall white orchids, vases of flowers everywhere, and slow-burning scented candles.

On this sunny Monday morning, Anne and Nicky sat on a small sofa in front of one of the windows overlooking Eaton Square and the leafy green bower of trees in its central gardens.

Anne was more at ease with herself than she had been since Nicky's last visit, and this showed in her face. The tight lines around her mouth had all but disappeared, and her body was less taut. In fact, most of the tension had fled, and she was relaxed and smiling.

Nicky, relieved that she had succeeded in putting Anne's mind at rest, was also feeling more comfortable, and she was pleased she had come to London. The trip had been worth it just to know that the wounds she had opened would quickly heal now. Anne was already looking and sounding more like herself.

These two women had always been compatible, and after their intense, hour-long talk this morning there seemed to be an even deeper bond between them.

'You don't know what it means to me that you came,' Anne said, reaching out for Nicky's hand, taking it in hers. 'You made me see sense, helped to put me back together again, and for that I'm very grateful, darling. I had become rather depressed, and sad.' She paused, and shook her head. 'I think I was even beginning to feel sorry for myself, which is not like me at all. I can't abide self-pity, it's such a sign of weakness, and I'm intolerant of it in others. Anyway, thank you, Nicky, you've worked wonders.'

'You don't have to thank me, Anne, I was glad to come,' Nicky said, squeezing her hand. 'Quite aside from loving you, and caring about your well-being, I feel very responsible. It was I who opened Pandora's Box and let all the horrors out. I wanted to put things right, make you feel better, if I could.'

'Well, you did, so don't fret anymore, and the lid is firmly closed.' Anne looked deeply into Nicky's eyes, and added in a loving voice, 'You always were very special to me, Nicky, like the daughter I never had ... and you've brought me such enormous comfort today, helped me to draw on my inner strength again.' A smile touched her mouth. 'You've put me back on the track, so to speak.'

Nicky smiled back at her. 'That makes me feel good, Anne, it really does. I was so worried about you yesterday, and I could feel your pain. I knew what you were going through.' There was a slight hesitation on Nicky's part, and then she said slowly, 'Two weeks ago at Pullenbrook, you begged me to put Charles to rest again ... I have, and I hope you can do the same.'

'I think so ... now. Yes, I'm sure I can, darling.'

Nicky said, 'Anne, I have some great news. Yoyo, the young Chinese student we met in Beijing, has managed to escape. He showed up in Paris last Thursday, and Clee and I had dinner with him on Friday. He's in terrific spirits, looks wonderful.'

'I'm thrilled he escaped, that he's safe,' Anne exclaimed, her face lighting up, growing animated for the first time in days. 'Do tell me about him.'

Nicky did so, and she was just finishing recounting the details about Yoyo's journey to Hong Kong, their celebration dinner at the Ritz with him and Mr and Mrs Loong, when the doorbell rang.

'Oh, that must be Philip,' Anne said, rising, crossing the floor. She paused half way, and turned her head. 'I was rather surprised when he called at eleven and asked if he could join us. He usually lunches at his club. Then I realized he wanted to see you. He's so very fond of you, Nicky.'

'I'm glad he's having lunch with us. I'm fond of him, too,' Nicky said, genuinely meaning this. 'He's a lovely man.' As she spoke she put down her glass of white wine and stood up, wandered over to the fireplace, hovered in front of it.

A moment later Philip Rawlings was striding into the room, embracing first Anne, then Nicky. 'I thought you were supposed to be in Provence,' he said, eyeing Nicky curiously.

'We were,' she answered. 'But Clee has problems at the office. Two of his partners are out, one because of a death in the family, the other with a slipped disc. So he had to pitch in for a few days. But we hope to leave sometime next week.'

'Nice time of year, down there,' Philip murmured, and went to a tray of drinks on a chest. He proceeded to mix himself one. He usually did not drink at lunch during the week, and today was an exception. In fact, this was not his first scotch and soda. On his way here he had done something he had not done in years – stopped off at a pub. He had gone to the Grenadier, which was the only pub he remembered in the Belgravia area, and downed a quick one, before walking over to Eaton Square.

False courage, he thought, as he dropped a piece of ice into his crystal tumbler, and turned around to face Anne and Nicky. The latter was lowering herself into a chair next to the sofa where Anne was already seated.

He lifted his glass to his mouth, said, 'Down the hatch,' and took a long swallow.

No use putting it off, he thought, and taking a deep breath, bracing himself, he went over to the window area, sat down next to Anne.

'I'm afraid it's not a very fancy lunch, Philip,' Anne remarked. 'I left Pilar and Inez in the country when I came up to town this morning. So I stopped off at Harrod's and picked up a few cold meats, and I made a salad.'

'Don't worry about it, I'm not very hungry,' he said.

'I'm feeling so much better, darling,' Anne continued, smiling at him. 'Being with Nicky, talking to her, has been a wonderful tonic.'

'I can see that.'

'I'm really all right now, Philip. *Truly.*'

'Yes,' he said.

'I was just telling Anne about Yoyo,' Nicky volunteered. 'You know, the Chinese student who was so helpful in Beijing. He managed to get to Hong Kong, and finally to Paris, and we saw him this past week.'

'One of the lucky ones.' Philip shook his head. 'Sadly, quite a few of the students who were involved in the democracy movement, and who escaped, were sent back to China by the Hong Kong Government. God knows what their fate has been.'

'How terrible!' Anne exclaimed. 'How could we do a thing like that!'

Philip did not answer. He took another long swallow of his drink, almost gulping it down, and then he put the glass on the antique lacquered table in front of him. Again steeling himself, he said, 'Anne, I have something to tell you, and I'm glad Nicky is with us. She has a right to hear this too.'

Both women looked at him swiftly, noting his serious tone, the grim expression settling on his face.

'It's about Charles – '

'What about him?' Anne interrupted, her voice rising.

Nicky stiffened in the chair, and apprehension unexpectedly stabbed at her.

'This morning some information came across my desk at the Foreign Office. It's restricted, classified information, but I felt, under the circumstances, that I was morally obliged to take both of you into my confidence. However, because it is a privileged communication, is top secret, actually, I must warn you that what I tell you must never be repeated. It cannot go beyond these walls. I count on your confidentiality. I must have your word on this, Anne. And yours, Nicky.'

'You know I would never discuss anything you told me about the office, confidential or otherwise,' Anne said, looking at him slightly askance.

'I give you my word,' Nicky murmured. She was worried, wondering what this was about, what Philip was going to tell them.

Philip nodded, and then he reached for Anne's hand. 'When Nicky came to see us at Pullenbrook in August, she was correct in everything she said, Anne. It *was* Charles on that ATN newscast from Rome. He *had* faked his death three years ago.'

Anne gasped. Her eyes were wide with shock. She was speechless for a moment, and then she exclaimed, 'Are you saying he's alive? Is my son alive?'

Philip did not immediately answer.

Nicky held herself perfectly still, clasping her hands together in her lap. She knew she must be careful in her reactions, that she must not betray anything.

Anne repeated, 'Is he alive? Philip, please answer me! Is Charles alive?'

Philip took a deep breath, and very gently he said, 'No, Anne, he's not. Charles is dead.'

'I don't understand!' she cried, her agitation increasing. 'You just said Nicky was right, that Charles did fake his own death, and was alive. Now you're saying that he's dead. How can that be? Are you sure?'

'I'm positive.'

Nicky, who was as shocked as Anne, was doing her level best to control herself. Now she said in the steadiest voice she could muster, 'But how do you know Charles is dead, Philip?'

'My friend Frank Littleton told me this morning. Frank and I were at Harrow together, and Cambridge, and we've been close friends since those days, for donkey's years. Frank's with the Secret Intelligence Service – MI6 – but he's not an agent out in the field. He has a desk job. He sent me a note this morning, asking me to come and see him. I did, and he told me that Anne's son had been killed.'

'Oh God, what are you saying?' Anne looked at him frantically. 'MI6. Agents. Intelligence. Was Charles involved in something dangerous?'

'Frank didn't go into too many details,' Philip responded quietly, wondering how he was going to help her get through this new ordeal.

'You just said *killed*.' Nicky stared at Philip. 'So he didn't die of natural causes. Nor in an accident, presumably. Are you saying he was murdered?'

Philip nodded. He put his arm around Anne as she let out a strangled cry. She began to tremble.

'When was Charles killed?' Nicky demanded.

'Late last week,' Philip said.

'*Where?*' Nicky clasped her hands tighter, hardly breathing.

'In Madrid. He was in a plane that blew up at Madrid airport, a small private plane, a Falcon.'

'Oh my God!' Anne pressed her hands to her mouth. 'My son! Charles!' She turned to Philip, pleaded, 'Please tell me what this is all about, Philip. *Please tell me*. I don't understand.'

Nicky cut in, 'Was his body recovered?'

'No, it wasn't.' Philip paused, then added in a low voice, 'It was a very bad explosion.'

Anne was sobbing quietly, leaning against Philip's shoulder. He held her closer, tried to comfort her without much success.

'You said the information came to you through your old friend with MI6,' Nicky continued. 'That implies Charles was an operative, working in the covert world of intelligence. And if he was, then he was probably killed by foreign agents. Is that the case?'

'I think so, Nicky.'

'You're not sure?'

'Frank gave me the barest details. He's not supposed to tell me anything. But he knows Anne, is aware we're going to be married, and he wanted me to have the information. He stuck his neck out for me. But he certainly wasn't going to breach security. That's more than his job's worth.'

Leaning forward, Nicky said, 'But didn't he give you any clue at all about the killer, or killers?'

Philip hesitated. 'I got the impression they might have been Israeli agents.'

'*Mossad!*' Nicky was startled. 'Why would Mossad want to kill Charles Devereaux? From what you've just told us, it sounds as if he was a British agent. The British and the Israelis don't bump each other off. They're on the same side.'

Philip said nothing.

'He *was* working for British Intelligence, wasn't he?' Nicky probed, all of her journalistic training coming out.

Philip shook his head. 'Perhaps not. Frank told me – ' He broke off and, changing his mind, he finished, 'I think that perhaps I ought not to say anything else. Not that I know much more than I've already told you.'

'Just one thing,' Nicky pressed. 'If Charles wasn't working for the British, he must have been working for someone else. *Who?*'

'Frank didn't actually say, Nicky. However, he implied Charles was involved with an organization based in the Middle East.'

Nicky gaped at him. 'A terrorist organization? Is that what you're saying?'

Philip nodded.

'Do you mean he was a terrorist?'

'It's possible,' Philip said.

'Did he work for the PLO? Abu Nidal? The PFLP-GC? *Who?*'

'Frank didn't mention any of those groups. But he did indicate that Charles was working for the Palestinians.'

'I don't believe it!' Nicky exclaimed incredulously. 'I don't!'

'The Palestinians,' Anne repeated, suddenly pulling away from Philip, sitting up straighter on the sofa. She looked from Philip to Nicky and back to Philip, as if bewildered. 'Did you say Charles was working for the Palestinians?'

'That is what Frank implied, yes.'

Anne's face went as white as chalk. Her eyes glazed over, were suddenly devoid of all expression. She sat staring ahead, appeared to be gazing into some far distant place; it was as if she saw something Nicky and Philip could not see. There was an extraordinary remoteness about her; she was utterly still, silent, as if she had fallen into a trance.

Philip glanced at Nicky worriedly.

Nicky nodded, then looked across at Anne. Drawing on the information she had been given by Charles in Madrid, she said slowly, 'Perhaps Charles wasn't a traitor to the British. Maybe he was a *mole*. A British agent who had assumed a new identity and gone undercover.'

'I don't know,' Philip replied. 'But it's possible, of course. Sometimes these things are done at a very high level. Often others in an agency don't even know, for security reasons. Maybe Frank doesn't have all the information.'

'Exactly,' Nicky exclaimed. 'And if Charles was a mole, that would make him a *counterfeit* traitor, wouldn't it?'

'Yes,' Philip agreed, and glanced at Anne, hoping she had heard what Nicky had just said. It was a possibility. A very strong possibility. Certainly Nicky's theory made more sense.

Nicky sat back in the chair, rapidly turning over all the facts. Charles is not dead, she suddenly thought. He has faked his own death for a second time. He just didn't trust me not to betray him. He thought I would put him in jeopardy. Yes, that's got to be it. Somehow he faked his death in order to continue working as a mole for the British. Then her heart tightened. Or is he really dead this time? If he is, then Mossad killed the wrong man. They assassinated a British agent.

There was no noise in Clee's apartment. Everything was perfectly still. Not even the ticking of a clock disturbed the silence. It was late, almost midnight. Nicky was alone; Clee was still in Brussels on assignment for *Paris Match*. She had spoken to him on the phone earlier, and had managed to avoid too much discussion about her day in London, and he had not seemed to think that odd at all.

Now she sat in the living room, finishing a bowl of canned tomato soup and crackers, reflecting on the events of the day.

Philip's extraordinary revelations had not startled her as much as they had Anne – for obvious reasons. After all, she had seen Charles ten days ago, had heard his story, and it was a story she fully believed. She also believed he was alive. The Charles Devereaux she had known, been engaged to, had always been excessively clever, a brilliant man. And so it was reasonable to assume that he was a superlative agent, and the best mole in the business. Therefore, he had not been sitting in that plane at the airport in Madrid. Yet somehow he had managed to make it look as though he had, because he wanted her, and everyone else, to think he *was* dead. But another man had been in the Falcon in his place, she was certain.

And whether he was alive, or dead, she was positive that he had not worked for the Palestinian cause; he had simply infiltrated a terrorist organization as a mole.

Deep within herself she wished she could have told Anne what she knew, if only to make her feel better about her son. But she had not dared to do this for Charles's sake, just in case he *was* alive, as she believed.

Eventually Anne had roused herself from her trance-like state, and Nicky had had the opportunity to repeat her theory that Charles was a counterfeit traitor, a double agent, a mole. And she had expounded on the idea that Frank Littleton, Philip's friend, did not have all of the facts at his disposal.

All of this had seemed to give Anne a measure of comfort, and after a while she had excused herself and retired to her bedroom, explaining that she needed to be alone.

She and Philip had talked for another hour, before she had left for Heathrow and her plane back to Paris. At one moment he had started to worry out loud that he had made a terrible mistake. 'Perhaps I shouldn't have told Anne anything at all, Nicky,' he had said. 'I ought to have kept it to myself, don't you think?'

Nicky had reassured him that he had done the right thing, and he had appeared to be heartened when he heard this. Then he had confided, 'I love her very much, Nicky, I've loved her for years. I couldn't believe my good fortune when she finally agreed to marry me. And I told her about Charles because I respect her, and because there's never been anything but honesty and truth between us. She and I have never dealt in lies. Anne's a mature, intelligent woman, and I thought she was entitled to know absolutely everything that I knew about her son, to know what Frank had told me out of friendship. And I thought you should know the truth, too, Nicky.'

If it's really the truth, Nicky had thought at the time, but she had said: 'Yes, you're right, Philip, and you really did do the best thing. No woman wants to be treated as a second-class citizen by a man.'

Marie Thérèse said, 'Ah, Nicky, *ma petite*, you are being evasive. How can you say you don't know if you are going to marry this Clee of yours . . . you must have some idea what you intend to do.'

'But I don't,' Nicky protested. 'He only asked me on Sunday morning – '

'But it's *Thursday* today!' Marie Thérèse exclaimed, laughing. 'You should know how you feel by now. Anyway, I think he will expect an answer when he returns to Paris tomorrow. *N'est-ce pas?* In my opinion, you must say yes, *chérie*. What else is there to say?'

Nicky smiled at the Frenchwoman, her dear old friend from childhood. 'Ah, Marie Thérèse, you are an incurable romantic. I could say no, you know.'

'Mmmm, that's true. On the other hand, why would you want to do that when you are so very much in love with your Clee?'

'And what makes you say that?'

'I see it in your eyes, *ma petite*, and when you speak about him your face glows with love.'

Nicky sighed. 'We'll see. I guess I'll make up my mind in Provence . . . I haven't had time to think straight in the last few days.' Glancing at her watch, Nicky exclaimed, 'I've got to go! I promised Yoyo I would have dinner with him tonight, and I've so much to do this afternoon. Thanks for another delicious lunch. Hopefully, you'll have your cast off by the time I get back from Provence, and then I'll take you for that fancy lunch at the Relais Plaza.'

'With Clee, I hope.'

Nicky nodded. 'With Clee.'

'And if we can't have lunch, you will phone me before you go back to the States at the end of September, won't you, Nicky?'

'Of course I will . . . but don't worry, we'll be having our lunch, I promise.' Bending forward, Nicky kissed Marie Thérèse on the cheek. 'Don't get up, I can let myself out.'

'*Au revoir, chérie.*'

'*Au revoir*, and take care.'

Nicky closed the door of the apartment behind her and ran down the steep flight of stairs. Dashing out of the front door and into the street, she turned right, hoping she would not have trouble finding a taxi. As she did so she ran into a group of men leaving the restaurant next door to Marie Thérèse's apartment building.

'*Oh, pardon!*' she exclaimed as she bumped into one of them.

'*De rien, mademoiselle*,' the man said, and swung around, smiling.

Nicky's jaw dropped. She was staring at Charles Devereaux.

'Oh my God!'

Stepping forward, Charles took hold of her arm, and moving her forward quickly, he propelled her into the car waiting on the kerb. '*Au revoir*, Bernard, Haji,' Charles said, as he got in behind her.

786

'What's happening, where are you taking me, Cha – '

'Be quiet,' he hissed, cutting her off. 'Don't say another word until we're alone.'

CHAPTER THIRTY-SIX

Charles and Nicky stood facing each other in the living room of the drab apartment to which he had just brought her.

'What in God's name were you doing in a disreputable district like Belleville?' Charles asked. 'I could hardly believe my eyes when I saw you. So, what were you doing there?'

'Hold it!' Nicky cried, giving him an irate look. 'Before *I* answer any questions, I'd like to pose a couple myself.'

He nodded. 'Ask. I'll answer, if I can.'

'Okay. First of all, where are we? You bundle me into a car, which shoots across Paris and turns into a side street, the name of which I don't see, then you drag me out and into this building, and I haven't the slightest idea where I am. I'd like to know!'

'This apartment is in the rue Georges Berger.'

'And where's that?'

'On the far side of the Arc de Triomphe, behind the Parc Monceau, just off the Boulevard de Courcelles.'

'I see. Secondly, why did you push me into the car the way you did? So unceremoniously, so roughly?'

'I'm sorry, Nicky, if I hurt you. You know I forget how strong I am.'

'So you keep telling me. And you didn't hurt me, I've only got a few bruises. I just didn't like the way you did it. Answer me this, Charles. Why *did* you drag me off in that way? We could have spoken in the street, or gone into the restaurant.'

'I didn't know what you were going to say, what you would blurt out. As for going into the restaurant, there were other . . . friends in there. It would have become complicated. It was much easier to come here.'

'For you, yes. Not necessarily for me,' she pointed out angrily.

'Just so, Nicky, just so. Now, tell me why you were in that area. Belleville is not a pretty place. Are you on to some sort of story there? Interviewing people in Belleville?'

'No, I'm not. But what do you mean? Is there a story in Belleville?'

He shrugged. 'How should I know?'

'But *you* just brought it up!'

'I can't imagine why you would be there, that's all I'm saying. It's the Arab area . . . a lot of North African immigrants live there. But surely you knew that.'

'I didn't. I was visiting Marie Thérèse Bouret, the Frenchwoman who was

787

ur *au pair*, a sort of nanny to me when I was little. I'm sure I told you about her, once.'

'I think you did, yes.'

'She moved to Belleville because her boyfriend lives there. She's moved in with him.'

'Is he Moroccan, Tunisian or Algerian?'

'I don't know ... I've never met him.' Immediately Nicky remembered the couscous Marie Thérèse had ordered for lunch the previous week, and the name of the restaurant: Café Tangier. She exclaimed, 'That restaurant you were leaving ... I guess it's North African, isn't it?'

'Moroccan.'

Nicky went on, 'Why did you bring me here?'

'I didn't want to talk to you in the middle of the street.'

'Do we have anything to say to each other? I don't think so, Charles.' She paused, looked at him closely, and added softly, almost accusingly, 'You could've trusted me. I wouldn't have betrayed you. I gave you my word of honour in Madrid. So you see there was no need for you to fake your death a second time.'

'I didn't! And I did trust you – do trust you – Nicky.'

'You were thought to be in that private jet, that Falcon, that blew up in Madrid late last week. I was told you'd been killed in the explosion.'

He was startled by this statement, and threw her a keen look. 'Who told you about the plane?'

'Philip Rawlings.'

'*Oh.*' His eyes fastened on hers intently. 'So you saw Philip?'

'Yes. I went to London earlier this week, on Monday. I went to visit your mother. She was depressed, upset. And she was wavering in her belief that you had committed suicide three years ago. I met her at her apartment for lunch. I wanted to convince her that you were dead – '

'Why did she have a change of heart?'

'The photographs ... of the man in the newscast. *You.*'

'Yes, I understand. Go on.'

'I talked to your mother for about an hour, and I succeeded, I brought her back to believing you were dead. Then Philip arrived. He had invited himself to lunch apparently. He broke the news of your death, and explained to your mother that I had been right all along.' Nicky now repeated everything Philip had told them, although she omitted Frank Littleton's name.

When she had finished, Charles nodded, touched his mouth, his eyes reflective. 'I suppose Philip learned about the plane in Madrid from an old friend in intelligence. I know all about the British Establishment and the old-school-tie network.' Now he motioned to a group of chairs, and said, 'Let's sit, shall we? I think we will be more comfortable.'

Once they were settled, Charles continued, 'Contrary to what you believe, I didn't fake my death by having that plane blown up. In fact, I would have been on it, if not for a last minute change in my plans. I had to stay on in Madrid unexpectedly – an assignment. Because there was an extra seat available, my seat, Javier took it. The destination of the plane was Gibraltar, where his sister lives. He was going for a weekend visit.'

788

'Are you implying the plane was sabotaged? That someone was trying to assassinate you?'

'I'm not implying it, I'm telling you.'

'Who?'

'I'm not exactly sure . . . although I do have a few suspects, and a few theories.'

'Mossad?'

Charles frowned at her. 'Why do you mention Israeli Intelligence?'

'Philip suggested that the Falcon might have been blown up by them . . . that *they* could have been after you.'

He was silent.

'I didn't say anything to your mother or Philip, Charles. I never mentioned our meeting in Madrid. I was also extremely careful in my reaction to Philip's news.' She took a deep breath. 'You see, I thought you were alive all along. No, *believed* you were. I just knew you weren't dead, and so there was no way I would have put you in jeopardy. Put your life at risk.'

Still he said nothing.

Nicky hurried on, 'Philip told me something very odd, Charles.'

'Oh, and what was that?' he asked, raising a brow.

'He said the person who gave him the information on Monday morning – about your death in Madrid – also implied that you were a terrorist.'

Charles sat perfectly still in the chair, a reflective expression settling on his face again. Finally, he gave her a very direct look, and said, 'One man's terrorist is another man's freedom fighter.'

Nicky shook her head. 'Sorry, but I'm not sure I understand what you're getting at.'

'It depends on your point of view, doesn't it?'

'That's what I thought you meant.' She stared at him for the longest moment, and then said, 'Are you telling me you *are* a terrorist?'

'Of course I'm not a terrorist!'

With a smile of relief she exclaimed, 'No, you're a British agent who has gone undercover. You're a British mole who has *infiltrated* a terrorist organization based in the Middle East. Right?'

'No, I'm not.'

'You're not a British agent?'

'No, and I never have been. Nor am I a mole.'

'You lied to me in Madrid?'

'I did.'

'Why?'

'Because I didn't want to tell you the truth.'

'What is the truth?'

'I *am* involved with a Middle East organization, actually, Nicky.'

'What's it called?'

'Al Awad . . . it means The Return.'

'I know what it means,' she cried, shifting in the chair, staring at him aghast. 'It means the return to the homeland . . . Palestine.' She leaned forward, and added with intensity, 'And it is a terrorist organization. A Palestinian terrorist

789

organization, to be exact. I'm a journalist, remember. I've heard of it, even though it's not quite as high profile as Abu Nidal and some of the other groups.'

'It's not a terrorist organization,' he snapped.

'Oh come off it! And what do you do for them?' she demanded, her voice rising. 'Kill little children and women, innocent people, I've no doubt.'

Charles said, 'I told you, I'm not a terrorist, Nicky! I handle the money, the financial matters.'

She glared at him, and cried, 'Don't split hairs with me. You may not tote a Kalashnikov or a Beretta, but you're still a terrorist. The money you handle finances those goddamned barbaric acts of terrorism!'

'Nicky, Nicky, it's you who are splitting hairs! Do you think the British Secret Intelligence Service, the CIA, Mossad, or the French DST are any different? They're all the same the world over. Everyone lies, cheats, kills, dies, and for what? *Patriotism*, they say. The Palestine freedom fighters are also patriotic.'

'Oh boy do you have your rhetoric down pat!' she exploded angrily, scarcely believing what she was hearing. Charles Devereaux involved with Palestinians was the most unlikely thing she had ever heard. Now she took total control of herself, realizing that she must not let her past relationship with Charles or her feelings of anger and outrage get in the way. Emotion must not cloud judgement. Think with your head, she cautioned herself, and ask a few more leading questions, get to the bottom of this. Solve the enigma of Charles Devereaux once and for all.

She said, 'And why are you doing this? For money? Or what?'

He recoiled. A look of contempt touched his face, and he said in an indignant tone, 'How little you know me, Nicky, if you think I can be *bought*. I work for the group because I believe in it, and in its aims.'

'You believe in its aims!' Nicky's bright blue eyes narrowed dangerously. 'Are you saying that you believe in its ideology? Is that it?'

'Yes, I am saying that.'

'*Why?* Why *you*? An Englishman, an aristocrat. I just don't get it.'

'Do you really want to know?'

'That's a pretty stupid question . . . of course I do.'

Charles leaned back in the chair, crossed his legs, and stared at her.

Nicky suddenly realized he was wearing the brown contact lenses. They did make a difference, added to the change in his appearance. He suddenly seemed less than ever like the Charles she had once loved.

After a few seconds of contemplation, he said, 'It was a man I loved – '

'A man!'

'Ah, no, Nicky, it's not what you think.' That faint superior smile struck his mouth, and he murmured, 'To continue, it was a man I loved, and the love that that man felt for me which brought me to Al Awad, and the Palestinian cause. His love, his influence over me, his greatness as a man, all of those things induced me to adopt his beliefs, follow in his footsteps.'

'He's a Palestinian, correct?'

'He was.'

'He's dead?'

'Sadly, yes.'

'Who was he?'

There was only the merest hesitation on his part before he said, 'My father. He was my father.'

Nicky was thunderstruck. After a second, she managed to say, 'Are you telling me that Henry Devereaux was not your father?'

'I am.'

'So Anne adopted you.'

'No, she didn't. Anne is my mother.'

'Your *biological* mother?'

'Yes. Just as Nayef Al Kabil was my biological father.'

'Anne Devereaux had an affair with a Palestinian?' Nicky's voice echoed with incredulity.

'Yes, she did. But that's my mother's story, not mine, and I'm not going to tell it. If you want to know more, you must ask her.'

'But you were born and brought up in England, educated in England, at Eton and Oxford. How did all this come about? How did you become involved . . . become involved with your father?'

'My mother thought I should know him.'

'When did you meet him?'

'When I was a little boy . . . six years old.'

'And is that when your indoctrination started?'

'No, later, when I was older, when I could understand everything properly. But *I* wouldn't call it indoctrination. It was his legacy to me. I have his blood in my veins! I am his son!'

'Your father's bloodline is more important to you than your mother's? Is that what you're telling me?'

'I am more of an Al Kabil than a Clifford, I suppose. That's what it comes down to in the end. I am my father's son.'

'When did your father die?'

'He was killed in 1981. In southern Lebanon, during the hostilities there.'

'Is that when you became involved with his cause?'

'No, about two years before that, in 1979. That was when he asked me to help with the group's finances. He had started Al Awad in 1958, and, for what it's worth, he was a moderate. He believed in moderation. Violence was not his way, Nicky. He believed in the conference table.'

Nicky ignored these comments. She said, 'So you were part of the group when we met?'

'Yes.'

'Then why did you ever get involved with me in the first place?' she demanded, staring hard at him.

There was a hesitation, and then he said quietly, 'It was a sexual attraction at first. I wanted you . . . wanted to have an affair with you. But I made the same mistake as my father.'

'What does that mean?'

'He fell in love with a beautiful blonde Englishwoman. I fell in love with a beautiful blonde American. I hadn't intended our relationship to go that far, Nicky. Then when I did get emotionally entangled with you, I thought I could handle it, handle you, and my involvement with my father's group, and our marriage as well.'

'And you changed your mind?'

'No, not really.'

'Then why did you decide to vanish into thin air three years ago?'

'Not actually because of you, although you were starting to become something of a problem. I faked my death because I thought certain foreign intelligence agencies were on my trail, were about to take me out.'

'Which ones?'

'The CIA and Mossad, to be precise.'

'Why was I becoming a problem?'

'As I told you, my father was killed in 1981. His second in command, who took over after his death, relied on me rather heavily, more than my father had, in some ways. I was getting really sucked in, and more so than I had intended, although I did believe in my father's cause. Nevertheless – '

'You wanted to lead your life in London as well, isn't that so?'

He nodded. 'Yes. By 1986, just after we became engaged, I realized that it wasn't going to work. That you were a problem after all. I also realized that I wasn't being fair to you, I didn't want to put you in any kind of danger. And that, combined with my worry that agents *were* tracking me, convinced me I should disappear. So I did.'

'And your mother never knew anything?'

'*Never*. My father didn't want her to know, and neither did I.'

'Why are you telling me all this?'

'Because there's no reason you shouldn't know.'

'Are you going to have me killed?'

'Don't be so damned ridiculous, Nicky!'

'I could expose you.'

'It wouldn't matter if you did. Not anymore.'

'Why not?'

'I'm leaving today for the Middle East. I won't be returning to Europe. I shall live there for the rest of my life.'

'Why?'

'It's too dangerous for me here now. And there are other reasons, which I can't go into.'

'Are you going to Lebanon?'

'I can't tell you where I'm going, surely you know that.'

There was a sudden knock on the door. Charles looked towards it, and said, 'Come in.'

Pierre, the man who had searched her suite in Madrid, was standing there. 'The car is downstairs,' he said.

Charles nodded, and stood up. Turning to Nicky, he said, 'I have to go. I have a plane waiting at Bourget.'

Nicky also stood. 'I won't tell your mother anything, or mention our meeting today, you know.'

He nodded. 'No, it would only hurt her even more.'

Nicky glared at him, the anger so close to the surface flaring for a split second, and then she bit it back, took hold of herself. 'She wept bitter tears for you the other day,' she said.

'I love her . . . but . . . ' He left his sentence unfinished, picked up his briefcase and went out into the hallway.

Nicky followed him.

Pierre opened the front door, lifted the two suitcases standing next to it, hurried down the short flight of stairs and out into the street.

When Nicky and Charles reached the bottom of the staircase, he turned to her in the little vestibule and said, 'This is finally goodbye, Nicky.'

She nodded. 'In case you think I was doing a story on you, I wasn't.'

'I know. You love my mother far too much. You'd never hurt her in that way.'

They were outside on the pavement. 'Small world, isn't it?' Charles said suddenly. 'The way you ran into me today in Belleville.'

'Yes.'

'Can I give you a lift?'

'No thanks, I'd prefer to walk,' she said.

He smiled at her faintly. 'Goodbye, Nicky.'

'Goodbye, Charles.'

Pierre had stowed the luggage, and after Charles got into the back seat he went to sit next to the driver. The car slid smoothly down the narrow street.

Nicky turned away and began to walk in the direction of the Boulevard de Courcelles, so many thoughts whirling around in her mind.

The blast from the explosion was so forceful it threw her forward onto the pavement. For a split second she was dazed and then a strangled cry escaped her throat as she struggled to her knees, and swung her head. The car Charles had been travelling in had exploded about eighty feet away. She gaped at it in horror, and pushed herself up onto her feet. Suddenly the air was filled with smoke and the smell of burning. From the Parc Monceau across the street a policeman who had been on duty and several passers-by were rushing towards her.

Nicky leaned against the wall of the building and closed her eyes convulsively. There was no chance that he was alive. Not in that inferno. And it was his car that had exploded. There was no other vehicle on the rue Georges Berger.

CHAPTER THIRTY-SEVEN

The two women sat on the old stone bench at the top of Sweetheart Hill.

It was Sunday afternoon, sunny and warm, and a light breeze rustled through the trees, sent the white clouds scudding across the arch of the shining blue sky. It was a perfect September day.

Neither woman noticed the weather. They sat with their arms around each other, their blonde heads close together, sharing a moment of quiet after a long and frequently painful conversation, one which had lasted well over an hour.

It was Nicky who now pulled slightly away, looked into Anne's eyes, and said, hat's it. I've told you the whole truth, and I've left nothing out. Now you know .verything, Anne.'

Anne nodded and squeezed her hand, then she reached into her jacket pocket and pulled out a handkerchief, wiped her eyes, blew her nose.

'So, my son is dead.' She shook her head sorrowfully. 'It's funny, you know, I just don't think I can weep any more tears after today. There are none left. I've grieved for Charles for three years, I don't think I can grieve all over again, Nicky.'

'No, you can't. You must go forward, Anne. You must get on with your life . . . your life with Philip.'

'Yes, darling, you're absolutely right.' She smiled and continued, 'A moment ago you said that I knew everything, and thanks to you, I do. But *you* don't know everything, Nicky. You don't know my side of the story. I think I should tell you about Nayef Al Kabil, and what happened forty-one years ago.'

'Only if you really want to tell me, Anne.'

'I'd like to, yes. And I shall tell Philip later. He has every right to know as well.'

Anne stared into the distance, her face still, her eyes pensive, and it was a few minutes before she began to speak.

At last, she said, 'I remember every moment as if it were only yesterday, each nuance as clear to me now as it was then. My father Julian Clifford was a renowned statesman in his day, Nicky. He was frequently associated with that very great man Winston Churchill, especially during the Second World War and at the end of it. They were political allies. They were also both Zionists, and my father became involved with the creation of the State of Israel in 1948. He and I were rather close at this time; he was a widower – my mother had died during the war. Anyway, my father took me with him to Palestine, as it still was then, in 1947. He liked to have me with him when he travelled abroad or stayed away for long periods. In January of 1948 I met Nayef. He was from an old, very good Palestinian family, a prominent family, who came from Gaza. They owned land, orange groves, and were well-established in the area, respected. Nayef was only a few years older than I was, and naturally we fell in love.'

Unexpectedly Anne fell silent.

Nicky looked at her, squeezed her hand, but said nothing, and she noticed then that the other woman was trying to compose herself.

Within seconds Anne picked up her story again. 'We were very much in love, Nicky. It was the first time for us both, and you know what first love is like. We were blind to everything except ourselves. He was so handsome, a slender young man, not all that tall, but very fair, with the most beautiful light-green eyes, so clear and innocent. He was kind to me, very loving and devoted, and we became inseparable. In May of 1948, just after my seventeenth birthday, I discovered I was pregnant.'

Anne paused once more, and looked at Nicky pointedly. 'Things were very different in those days. There was nothing I could do, even if I'd wanted to, which I didn't. Naturally, I was distressed and frightened. Nayef and I told my father together, and then Nayef explained how much he loved me, said that he wanted to marry me. And I told my father that I felt the same way about Nayef. My father reacted badly. He was horrified, furious. He took me home to England immediately. I was heartbroken. And it was seven years before I sa Nayef again.'

'Oh Anne darling, how sad. I feel for you. You were so young, just a child.'

'Yes, we both were. And inexperienced in so many ways. As it happened my father's oldest and dearest friend was Henry Devereaux, the British industrialist. Henry had known me all my life, and loved me. Since he was a widower and childless, he agreed to marry me at my father's request. Our marriage was in September of 1948. Imagine my horror, being torn from Nayef, carrying his child, and marrying a man I hardly knew, except as my father's friend. I was in agony of mind and spirit, but there was nothing I could do except obey my father. Actually, Henry knew he had Hodgkin's Disease, cancer of the lymph glands, by that time, was aware that he did not have long to live. Since he had no family, other than a distant cousin, and because he had always cared for me, he was excited about our marriage. It pleased him to have someone to care for, and also to have a young companion for the last few years of his life. I must say, he was good to me, and he did love Charles. But I was not happy with him. How could I be? Our marriage was a mockery. But I suppose, looking back, that I didn't make much of an effort. He seemed like an old man to me. He was, being a contemporary of my father.'

'And naturally you yearned for Nayef,' Nicky murmured, reaching out, taking hold of her hand again.

'Oh yes, Nicky, how I yearned for him! But there was nothing I could do. Also, I did have my beautiful child . . . Charles. Nayef's child. I loved my son to distraction, and he did help to heal the hole in my heart. And eventually I adjusted – one always does, you know. Charles had been born in February of 1949, but it wasn't until he was six years old that I decided he ought to meet Nayef, his real father. Things were much easier for me by then, in as much as Henry and my father had both died. So in 1955 I took Charles to the south of France, to Nice, to meet Nayef.'

'And from that time on he saw his father on a regular basis over the years. Charles explained that to me in Paris.'

Anne nodded. 'Very regularly. I'd told him it was a secret, that no one must know about Nayef . . . I was worried about my brother Geoffrey, you see. I must say, Charles was very good. He kept the secret. He loved Nayef, and Nayef loved him. Little did I know he was brainwashing our child.' She paused, took a deep breath, then added, 'But I couldn't have stopped that. Once Charles was eighteen, he came and went as he pleased, and he was always strong-willed, independent. But to tell you the truth, Nicky, I had no idea how strong the bond was between them, the extent the relationship had grown, until you told me today. Charles was very secretive about that . . . I suppose he had to be.'

'Did *you* continue your relationship with Nayef?'

'No, I didn't. Well, that's not strictly true. I did for a couple of years, between 1955 and 1957. We picked up where we had left off. But it was never quite the same . . . it never is . . . and then it ended by mutual consent. It wasn't feasible, darling. He was living in Lebanon, and I was here at Pullenbrook, and by then he was starting to become involved in politics, was consumed by them. I think he was already deeply committed to the cause.'

'Charles told me his father was a moderate. Do you believe that?'

'*Absolutely*. Nayef wasn't a man who would ever condone violence, or resort to it. He always believed that peace could be achieved by other means.'

'Did he ever marry? Have other children?'

'No, he didn't marry. Nor did he have children . . . not to my knowledge, anyway. Perhaps that's one of the reasons why Charles was so important to him. He was his only son, and he claimed him for himself, didn't he?'

Nicky said softly, 'Yes, he did. And Charles allowed himself to be claimed. He did have a choice.'

Anne sighed heavily and looked at her. She said slowly, 'It's all my fault, Nicky . . . if I had not become involved with Nayef when I was a young girl, none of this would have happened . . . '

'But you wouldn't have had Charles either.'

'That's true.' Anne forced a small smile and murmured, 'Well, darling, perhaps we'd better go inside for a while. You and Clee will have to leave for the airport soon. Also, Philip and I have something to tell you. And I have something to show you.'

The two women stood. In the distance, the great Tudor house gleamed under the brilliant sky, ancient, unchanging, everlasting. Together they walked down the hill towards it, their arms linked.

Philip and Clee were in the library talking when Anne and Nicky came in a few minutes later.

Philip exclaimed, 'There you are! I was about to come looking for you. Inez will be bringing tea shortly. I'm sure you'd both like a cup.'

'Thanks, I would,' Nicky said.

Anne merely nodded, walked over to the desk and opened a drawer, took an envelope out of it.

Nicky looked across at Clee and smiled. It was such a comfort to have him here, and over lunch he had seemed to make everyone feel more relaxed. He was not only warm and understanding, but sane and down-to-earth: you knew where you stood with him. It pleased Nicky that Anne had responded so well to him, was comfortable around him. She had been so uptight when they had arrived from Paris late last night.

Clee walked over to Nicky, took her arm, and led her to one of the Chesterfield sofas near the fireplace. They sat down together.

Anne came to Nicky, and handed her the envelope she had taken out of the desk. 'I think you should read this, Nicky. It arrived last Thursday morning.'

Nicky took it from her and when she saw Charles's handwriting she flinched. His letter had arrived at Pullenbrook the day he had died. Goose flesh spreckled her arms, and then shaking off the sudden chilly feeling, she looked more carefully at the envelope. It was postmarked Tuesday, September 5th, and it had been mailed in Paris. Slipping the letter out of the envelope, she read it slowly.

Paris, Monday evening, 4 September 1989

Dear Mother:

Three years ago I faked my own death but allowed you to believe I had committed suicide. I could not take you into my confidence, because if my suicide was to be effective

you above all had to believe it. This was a cruel thing to do to you, I know, but I w
certain my life was in danger. I had to slip off the face of the earth, become someon
else if I was going to live. I was being sought by intelligence agents from various foreign
countries. You see, unbeknown to you, I had adopted my father's cause long ago and
I had been active in his organization since 1979.

My father, whom I loved very much, was a moderate man, as you well know. And
so am I. Sadly, there are those in the group he founded, The Return, who have not
held to those principles. There is a faction within it now which is embracing violence.
I cannot and will not condone that. I have spoken up many times in the past year,
made my feelings clear. In consequence of this I know that once again my life is in
danger – this time from within my own organization. They tried to eliminate me last
week by blowing up my plane at Madrid airport.

There has been too much killing in the Middle East over the years. It must come to
an end. Palestinians and Israelis must learn to live together. And in peace. Terrorism
is foul. It must be outlawed, once and for all.

I know my time is limited now, a few weeks, a couple of months at the most. And
before I die there is something I must do to help the innocents in the Middle East. Arab
and Jew alike. For the past ten years I have managed the financial affairs of my father's
organization, I've done it well, even if I say so myself. Today the funds belonging to the
group total three hundred million US dollars. That money is deposited in a numbered
account in a bank in Zurich. I want that money used for the good of the Middle East,
not for killing and mayhem. Only I know the number of the account and which bank
it is in. This is the International Bank of Zurich. You will also know the number of
my account if you think of my favourite childhood toy. The name of that toy is the
number. I want you and Philip to go to Zurich the day you receive this letter. Take
the money out of the International Bank of Zurich and deposit it in another Swiss
bank, using a numbered account again. Invent your own number.

I want you and Philip to use that money to help the children of the Middle East,
to help ease their suffering. And it must be used for all children, no matter their race,
creed or colour.

I know you can never forgive me, Mother, but I do hope you will think more kindly
of me one day. I have always loved you.

Charles

Nicky held the letter in her hand, and looked across at Anne. 'May Clee read it?'

'Of course, I would like him to.'

Clee did so, and then silently handed the letter back to Nicky, who sat holding it, her face reflective. Finally, she said, 'Did you remember the favourite childhood toy, Anne?'

'Of course I did. His rocking horse. It's still upstairs in the old nursery. Charles called the horse Foxy. If you take the letters that make up the name and give each one a number, working on the principle that the letter A is number one, then you have 6152425.'

'Did you go to Zurich?' Nicky asked.

'Oh yes, that very day. I drove up to London immediately. Philip and I took an afternoon flight, and we visited the bank on Friday morning.'

'Was the number correct?' Nicky knew the answer from the look on Anne's face.

'Yes,' Anne said.

Philip now explained, 'We withdrew the money from the account, received a cashier's cheque for the three hundred million US dollars and went to another bank, where we opened an account and deposited the cheque. We want to create a fund with it. We plan to build hospitals, canteens and schools for the children of the Middle East, just as Charles wanted. Yes, you can be damned sure it's going to be done.'

Nicky turned to Anne. 'It was an act of redemption on Charles's part, wasn't it?'

'Yes, it was, Nicky.'

'Can you ever forgive him?'

'I don't know . . . perhaps . . . in time.'

Later, after tea, Nicky and Clee went upstairs to the lavender-and-grey bedroom where they had slept last night.

As she packed the few items of clothing they had brought with them, she said to Clee, 'Thanks for coming with me. You've been wonderful.'

'You *are* glad you came now, aren't you, Nick?'

She zipped the bag, lifted it off the bed, and took it to the door. Then she came back and stood looking down at him in the chair where he sat. 'Yes, I am,' she said. 'And I'm grateful to you for making me. I almost lost my nerve at the last minute.'

He stood up, and placed his hands on her shoulders. 'Nicky Wells lose her nerve. Never!'

She smiled. 'But I did. You gave me the courage to face Anne, to tell her that Charles was dead.'

'You owed her that, Nicky, in view of the relationship you have with her, all she had meant to you, still means, and the kind of woman she is . . . a wonderful woman.'

'Isn't she just!'

He inclined his head in agreement, and then made a little grimace. 'God knows if we'll ever get to Provence at this rate . . . there's always something preventing us going down there. Problems at my office, Yoyo arriving, and now all this.'

'Oh don't let's worry about Provence,' she murmured, looking into his eyes. 'We've got the rest of our lives to go to the farm.'

A huge smile spread across his face. 'Does that mean you're saying yes?'

'Yes, I'm saying yes.'

He hugged her to him, then held her away. His smile grew bigger, and he exclaimed, 'But if you marry me you'll be living in Paris. What about your big career in American television?'

She laughed, and shrugged her shoulders lightly. 'I'm going to let Arch worry about that. He'll find a way to work it all out.'

Clee bent forward and kissed her. 'I promise you I'll be the best husband.'

'That means a lot, coming from a man who's a bachelor at heart, like you.'

'Not anymore I'm not. No siree! Come on, let's go!'

Downstairs, Anne and Philip were waiting for them in the small entrance hall, and Anne said, 'Your car just arrived, but you've plenty of time to get to Heathrow, so don't worry, you won't miss your plane.'

'Thanks for everything, Anne,' Nicky said, stepping forward, embracing her. Against her hair, she murmured, 'I'm going to marry Clee.'

Anne gently extracted herself from Nicky's arms and looked deeply into her bright blue eyes. Her own, so similar in colour, filled with sudden tears. She smiled through them and said, 'I'm so happy for you, Nicky darling. And it's I who should be thanking you for being such a good friend . . . '

Philip said, 'I couldn't help but hear what you said, Nicky. Congratulations to both of you.' He shook Clee's hand, and then opened his arms to Nicky.

She stepped into them, and they hugged. 'Thank you for caring enough to come and tell us everything, Nicky.'

'It was the only thing I could do.'

The four of them went outside and said their goodbyes, and Nicky and Clee got into the car. The driver turned on the ignition and they rolled slowly down the gravel driveway, heading for the huge front gates.

When they came to the bend in the corner, Nicky looked back through the window. Anne and Philip were still standing on the steps, waving farewell. Behind them, in the fading afternoon light, Pullenbrook glimmered. The first time ever I came here I fell in love with a fascinating man, an extraordinary woman and a great house that might have been my home one day. I thought my life was going to be here with them. It was not meant to be, and I'll probably never come back. But I'm leaving a little bit of my heart with Anne Devereaux; I'll always remember . . . Everything.

ACKNOWLEDGEMENT

My very special thanks to my friend Barbara Victor of Paris, for making available some special research and for giving so generously of her time.